HARRIET BEECHER STOWE

HARRIET BEECHER STOWE

THREE NOVELS

UNCLE TOM'S CABIN
or, Life among the Lowly

THE MINISTER'S WOOING

OLDTOWN FOLKS

THE LIBRARY OF AMERICA

Volume arrangement, notes, and chronology Copyright © 1982 by
Literary Classics of the United States, Inc., New York, N.Y.
All rights reserved.
No part of this book may be reproduced commercially
by offset-lithographic or equivalent copying devices without
the permission of the publisher.

Distributed to the trade by the Viking Press

Library of Congress Catalog Card Number 81-18629
For Cataloging in Publication Data, see end of *Notes* section.
ISBN 0—940450—01—1

Fourth Printing

Manufactured in the United States of America

KATHRYN KISH SKLAR
WROTE THE NOTES AND CHRONOLOGY
AND SELECTED THE TEXTS
FOR THIS VOLUME

The publishers wish to thank the Stowe-Day Foundation and the Library of Congress for their assistance.

Grateful acknowledgement is made to the National Endowment for the Humanities and the Ford Foundation for their generous financial support of this series.

Contents

Uncle Tom's Cabin; or, Life among the Lowly 1

The Minister's Wooing 521

Oldtown Folks 877

Chronology 1469

Note on the Texts 1474

Notes 1476

UNCLE TOM'S CABIN;

or,

Life among the Lowly

Contents

VOLUME I

Preface 9

CHAPTER I.
In Which the Reader Is Introduced to a Man of Humanity . . 11

CHAPTER II.
The Mother 22

CHAPTER III.
The Husband and Father 26

CHAPTER IV.
An Evening in Uncle Tom's Cabin 32

CHAPTER V.
Showing the Feelings of Living Property on Changing Owners . 45

CHAPTER VI.
Discovery 57

CHAPTER VII.
The Mother's Struggle 67

CHAPTER VIII.
Eliza's Escape 81

CHAPTER IX.
In Which It Appears that a Senator Is but a Man 98

CHAPTER X.
The Property Is Carried Off 116

CHAPTER XI.
In Which Property Gets into an Improper State of Mind . . . 127

CHAPTER XII.
Select Incident of Lawful Trade 142

CHAPTER XIII.
The Quaker Settlement 162

CHAPTER XIV.
Evangeline 172

CHAPTER XV.
Of Tom's New Master, and Various Other Matters 183

CHAPTER XVI.
Tom's Mistress and Her Opinions 200

CHAPTER XVII.
The Freeman's Defence 220

CHAPTER XVIII.
Miss Ophelia's Experiences and Opinions 240

VOLUME II

CHAPTER XIX.
Miss Ophelia's Experiences and Opinions, Continued 257

CHAPTER XX.
Topsy 278

CHAPTER XXI.
Kentuck 295

CHAPTER XXII.
"The Grass Withereth—The Flower Fadeth" 301

CHAPTER XXIII.
Henrique 311

CHAPTER XXIV.
Foreshadowings 320

CHAPTER XXV.
The Little Evangelist 327

CHAPTER XXVI.
Death 333

CHAPTER XXVII.
"This Is the Last of Earth" 347

CHAPTER XXVIII.
Reunion 355

CHAPTER XXIX.
The Unprotected 371

CHAPTER XXX.
The Slave Warehouse 379

CHAPTER XXXI.
The Middle Passage 391

CHAPTER XXXII.
Dark Places 398

CHAPTER XXXIII.
Cassy 408

CHAPTER XXXIV.
The Quadroon's Story 416

CHAPTER XXXV.
The Tokens 430

CHAPTER XXXVI.
Emmeline and Cassy 437

CHAPTER XXXVII.
Liberty 446

CHAPTER XXXVIII.
The Victory 453

CHAPTER XXXIX.
The Stratagem 464

CHAPTER XL.
The Martyr 475

CHAPTER XLI.
The Young Master 483

CHAPTER XLII.
An Authentic Ghost Story 490

CHAPTER XLIII.
Results 497

CHAPTER XLIV.
The Liberator 506

CHAPTER XLV.
Concluding Remarks 510

List of Illustrations

Illustrations courtesy of the Library of Congress and John Fleming.

Eliza comes to tell Uncle Tom that he is sold and that she is running away to save her child 53

The Auction Sale 147

The freeman's defence 233

Little Eva reading the Bible to Uncle Tom in the arbor . . 305

Cassy ministering to Uncle Tom after his whipping . . . 417

The fugitives are safe in a free land 443

Preface

THE scenes of this story, as its title indicates, lie among a race hitherto ignored by the associations of polite and refined society; an exotic race, whose ancestors, born beneath a tropic sun, brought with them, and perpetuated to their descendants, a character so essentially unlike the hard and dominant Anglo-Saxon race, as for many years to have won from it only misunderstanding and contempt.

But, another and better day is dawning; every influence of literature, of poetry and of art, in our times, is becoming more and more in unison with the great master chord of Christianity, "good will to man."

The poet, the painter, and the artist, now seek out and embellish the common and gentler humanities of life, and, under the allurements of fiction, breathe a humanizing and subduing influence, favorable to the development of the great principles of Christian brotherhood.

The hand of benevolence is everywhere stretched out, searching into abuses, righting wrongs, alleviating distresses, and bringing to the knowledge and sympathies of the world the lowly, the oppressed, and the forgotten.

In this general movement, unhappy Africa at last is remembered; Africa, who began the race of civilization and human progress in the dim, gray dawn of early time, but who, for centuries, has lain bound and bleeding at the foot of civilized and Christianized humanity, imploring compassion in vain.

But the heart of the dominant race, who have been her conquerors, her hard masters, has at length been turned towards her in mercy; and it has been seen how far nobler it is in nations to protect the feeble than to oppress them. Thanks be to God, the world has at last outlived the slave-trade!

The object of these sketches is to awaken sympathy and feeling for the African race, as they exist among us; to show their wrongs and sorrows, under a system so necessarily cruel and unjust as to defeat and do away the good effects of all that can be attempted for them, by their best friends, under it.

In doing this, the author can sincerely disclaim any invidious feeling towards those individuals who, often without any fault of their own, are involved in the trials and embarrassments of the legal relations of slavery.

Experience has shown her that some of the noblest of minds and hearts are often thus involved; and no one knows better than they do, that what may be gathered of the evils of slavery from sketches like these, is not the half that could be told, of the unspeakable whole.

In the northern states, these representations may, perhaps, be thought caricatures; in the southern states are witnesses who know their fidelity. What personal knowledge the author has had, of the truth of incidents such as here are related, will appear in its time.

It is a comfort to hope, as so many of the world's sorrows and wrongs have, from age to age, been lived down, so a time shall come when sketches similar to these shall be valuable only as memorials of what has long ceased to be.

When an enlightened and Christianized community shall have, on the shores of Africa, laws, language and literature, drawn from among us, may then the scenes of the house of bondage be to them like the remembrance of Egypt to the Israelite,—a motive of thankfulness to Him who hath redeemed them!

For, while politicians contend, and men are swerved this way and that by conflicting tides of interest and passion, the great cause of human liberty is in the hands of one, of whom it is said:

> "He shall not fail nor be discouraged
> Till He have set judgment in the earth."
> "He shall deliver the needy when he crieth,
> The poor, and him that hath no helper."
> "He shall redeem their soul from deceit and violence,
> And precious shall their blood be in His sight."

I.

In Which the Reader Is Introduced to a Man of Humanity

LATE in the afternoon of a chilly day in February, two gentlemen were sitting alone over their wine, in a well-furnished dining parlor, in the town of P——, in Kentucky. There were no servants present, and the gentlemen, with chairs closely approaching, seemed to be discussing some subject with great earnestness.

For convenience sake, we have said, hitherto, two *gentlemen*. One of the parties, however, when critically examined, did not seem, strictly speaking, to come under the species. He was a short, thick-set man, with coarse, commonplace features, and that swaggering air of pretension which marks a low man who is trying to elbow his way upward in the world. He was much over-dressed, in a gaudy vest of many colors, a blue neckerchief, bedropped gayly with yellow spots, and arranged with a flaunting tie, quite in keeping with the general air of the man. His hands, large and coarse, were plentifully bedecked with rings; and he wore a heavy gold watch-chain, with a bundle of seals of portentous size, and a great variety of colors, attached to it,—which, in the ardor of conversation, he was in the habit of flourishing and jingling with evident satisfaction. His conversation was in free and easy defiance of Murray's Grammar, and was garnished at convenient intervals with various profane expressions, which not even the desire to be graphic in our account shall induce us to transcribe.

His companion, Mr. Shelby, had the appearance of a gentleman; and the arrangements of the house, and the general air of the housekeeping, indicated easy, and even opulent circumstances. As we before stated, the two were in the midst of an earnest conversation.

"That is the way I should arrange the matter," said Mr. Shelby.

"I can't make trade that way—I positively can't, Mr. Shelby," said the other, holding up a glass of wine between his eye and the light.

"Why, the fact is, Haley, Tom is an uncommon fellow; he is certainly worth that sum anywhere,—steady, honest, capable, manages my whole farm like a clock."

"You mean honest, as niggers go," said Haley, helping himself to a glass of brandy.

"No; I mean, really, Tom is a good, steady, sensible, pious fellow. He got religion at a camp-meeting, four years ago; and I believe he really *did* get it. I 've trusted him, since then, with everything I have,—money, house, horses,—and let him come and go round the country; and I always found him true and square in everything."

"Some folks don't believe there is pious niggers, Shelby," said Haley, with a candid flourish of his hand, "but *I do*. I had a fellow, now, in this yer last lot I took to Orleans—'t was as good as a meetin, now, really; to hear that critter pray; and he was quite gentle and quiet like. He fetched me a good sum, too, for I bought him cheap of a man that was 'bliged to sell out; so I realized six hundred on him. Yes, I consider religion a valeyable thing in a nigger, when it 's the genuine article, and no mistake."

"Well, Tom 's got the real article, if ever a fellow had," rejoined the other. "Why, last fall, I let him go to Cincinnati alone, to do business for me, and bring home five hundred dollars. 'Tom,' says I to him, 'I trust you, because I think you 're a Christian—I know you would n't cheat.' Tom comes back, sure enough; I knew he would. Some low fellows, they say, said to him—'Tom, why don't you make tracks for Canada?' 'Ah, master trusted me, and I could n't,'— they told me about it. I am sorry to part with Tom, I must say. You ought to let him cover the whole balance of the debt; and you would, Haley, if you had any conscience."

"Well, I 've got just as much conscience as any man in business can afford to keep,—just a little, you know, to swear by, as 't were," said the trader, jocularly; "and, then, I 'm ready to do anything in reason to 'blige friends; but this yer, you see, is a leetle too hard on a fellow—a leetle too hard." The trader sighed contemplatively, and poured out some more brandy.

"Well, then, Haley, how will you trade?" said Mr. Shelby, after an uneasy interval of silence.

"Well, have n't you a boy or gal that you could throw in with Tom?"

"Hum!—none that I could well spare; to tell the truth, it 's only hard necessity makes me willing to sell at all. I don't like parting with any of my hands, that 's a fact."

Here the door opened, and a small quadroon boy, between four and five years of age, entered the room. There was something in his appearance remarkably beautiful and engaging. His black hair, fine as floss silk, hung in glossy curls about his round, dimpled face, while a pair of large dark eyes, full of fire and softness, looked out from beneath the rich, long lashes, as he peered curiously into the apartment. A gay robe of scarlet and yellow plaid, carefully made and neatly fitted, set off to advantage the dark and rich style of his beauty; and a certain comic air of assurance, blended with bashfulness, showed that he had been not unused to being petted and noticed by his master.

"Hulloa, Jim Crow!" said Mr. Shelby, whistling, and snapping a bunch of raisins towards him, "pick that up, now!"

The child scampered, with all his little strength, after the prize, while his master laughed.

"Come here, Jim Crow," said he. The child came up, and the master patted the curly head, and chucked him under the chin.

"Now, Jim, show this gentleman how you can dance and sing." The boy commenced one of those wild, grotesque songs common among the negroes, in a rich, clear voice, accompanying his singing with many comic evolutions of the hands, feet, and whole body, all in perfect time to the music.

"Bravo!" said Haley, throwing him a quarter of an orange.

"Now, Jim, walk like old Uncle Cudjoe, when he has the rheumatism," said his master.

Instantly the flexible limbs of the child assumed the appearance of deformity and distortion, as, with his back humped up, and his master's stick in his hand, he hobbled about the room, his childish face drawn into a doleful pucker, and spitting from right to left, in imitation of an old man.

Both gentlemen laughed uproariously.

"Now, Jim," said his master, "show us how old Elder Robbins leads the psalm." The boy drew his chubby face down to a formidable length, and commenced toning a psalm tune through his nose, with imperturbable gravity.

"Hurrah! bravo! what a young 'un!" said Haley; "that chap 's a case, I 'll promise. Tell you what," said he, suddenly clapping his hand on Mr. Shelby's shoulder, "fling in that chap, and I 'll settle the business—I will. Come, now, if that ain't doing the thing up about the rightest!"

At this moment, the door was pushed gently open, and a young quadroon woman, apparently about twenty-five, entered the room.

There needed only a glance from the child to her, to identify her as its mother. There was the same rich, full, dark eye, with its long lashes; the same ripples of silky black hair. The brown of her complexion gave way on the cheek to a perceptible flush, which deepened as she saw the gaze of the strange man fixed upon her in bold and undisguised admiration. Her dress was of the neatest possible fit, and set off to advantage her finely moulded shape;—a delicately formed hand and a trim foot and ankle were items of appearance that did not escape the quick eye of the trader, well used to run up at a glance the points of a fine female article.

"Well, Eliza?" said her master, as she stopped and looked hesitatingly at him.

"I was looking for Harry, please, sir;" and the boy bounded toward her, showing his spoils, which he had gathered in the skirt of his robe.

"Well, take him away, then," said Mr. Shelby; and hastily she withdrew, carrying the child on her arm.

"By Jupiter," said the trader, turning to him in admiration, "there 's an article, now! You might make your fortune on that ar gal in Orleans, any day. I 've seen over a thousand, in my day, paid down for gals not a bit handsomer."

"I don't want to make my fortune on her," said Mr. Shelby, dryly; and, seeking to turn the conversation, he uncorked a bottle of fresh wine, and asked his companion's opinion of it.

"Capital, sir,—first chop!" said the trader; then turning, and slapping his hand familiarly on Shelby's shoulder, he added—

"Come, how will you trade about the gal?—what shall I say for her—what 'll you take?"

"Mr. Haley, she is not to be sold," said Shelby. "My wife would not part with her for her weight in gold."

"Ay, ay! women always say such things, cause they ha'nt no sort of calculation. Just show 'em how many watches, feathers, and trinkets, one's weight in gold would buy, and that alters the case, *I* reckon."

"I tell you, Haley, this must not be spoken of; I say no, and I mean no," said Shelby, decidedly.

"Well, you 'll let me have the boy, though," said the trader; "you must own I 've come down pretty handsomely for him."

"What on earth can you want with the child?" said Shelby.

"Why, I 've got a friend that 's going into this yer branch of the business—wants to buy up handsome boys to raise for the market. Fancy articles entirely—sell for waiters, and so on, to rich 'uns, that can pay for handsome 'uns. It sets off one of yer great places—a real handsome boy to open door, wait, and tend. They fetch a good sum; and this little devil is such a comical, musical concern, he 's just the article."

"I would rather not sell him," said Mr. Shelby, thoughtfully; "the fact is, sir, I 'm a humane man, and I hate to take the boy from his mother, sir."

"O, you do?—La! yes—something of that ar natur. I understand, perfectly. It is mighty onpleasant getting on with women, sometimes. I al'ays hates these yer screachin', screamin' times. They are *mighty* onpleasant; but, as I manages business, I generally avoids 'em, sir. Now, what if you get the girl off for a day, or a week, or so; then the thing 's done quietly,—all over before she comes home. Your wife might get her some ear-rings, or a new gown, or some such truck, to make up with her."

"I 'm afraid not."

"Lor bless ye, yes! These critters an't like white folks, you know; they gets over things, only manage right. Now, they say," said Haley, assuming a candid and confidential air, "that this kind o' trade is hardening to the feelings; but I never found it so. Fact is, I never could do things up the way some fellers manage the business. I 've seen 'em as would pull a woman's child out of her arms, and set him up to sell, and she screechin' like mad all the time;—very bad policy—damages the article—makes 'em quite unfit for service sometimes. I knew a real handsome gal once, in Orleans, as was entirely ruined by this sort o' handling. The fellow that was trading for her did n't want her baby; and she was one of your real high sort, when her blood was up. I tell you, she·squeezed up her child in her arms, and talked, and went on real awful. It kinder makes my blood run cold to think on't; and when they carried off the child, and locked her up, she jest went ravin' mad, and died in a week. Clear waste, sir, of a thousand dollars, just for want of management,—there 's where 't is. It 's always best to do the humane thing, sir; that 's been *my* experience." And the trader leaned back in his chair, and folded his arm, with an air of virtuous decision, apparently considering himself a second Wilberforce.

The subject appeared to interest the gentleman deeply; for while Mr. Shelby was thoughtfully peeling an orange, Haley broke out afresh, with becoming diffidence, but as if actually driven by the force of truth to say a few words more.

"It don't look well, now, for a feller to be praisin' himself; but I say it jest because it 's the truth. I believe I 'm reckoned to bring in about the finest droves of niggers that is brought in,—at least, I 've been told so; if I have once, I reckon I have a hundred times,—all in good case,—fat and likely, and I lose as few as any man in the business. And I lays it all to my management, sir; and humanity, sir, I may say, is the great pillar of *my* management."

Mr. Shelby did not know what to say, and so he said, "Indeed!"

"Now, I 've been laughed at for my notions, sir, and I 've been talked to. They an't pop'lar, and they an't common; but I stuck to 'em, sir; I 've stuck to 'em, and realized well on 'em; yes, sir, they have paid their passage, I may say," and the trader laughed at his joke.

There was something so piquant and original in these elucidations of humanity, that Mr. Shelby could not help laughing in company. Perhaps you laugh too, dear reader; but you know humanity comes out in a variety of strange forms now-a-days, and there is no end to the odd things that humane people will say and do.

Mr. Shelby's laugh encouraged the trader to proceed.

"It's strange, now, but I never could beat this into people's heads. Now, there was Tom Loker, my old partner, down in Natchez; he was a clever fellow, Tom was, only the very devil with niggers,—on principle 't was, you see, for a better hearted feller never broke bread; 't was his *system*, sir. I used to talk to Tom. 'Why, Tom,' I used to say, 'when your gals takes on and cry, what's the use o' crackin on 'em over the head, and knockin' on 'em round? It's ridiculous,' says I, 'and don't do no sort o' good. Why, I don't see no harm in their cryin',' says I; 'it's natur,' says I, 'and if natur can't blow off one way, it will another. Besides, Tom,' says I, 'it jest spiles your gals; they get sickly, and down in the mouth; and sometimes they gets ugly,—particular yallow gals do,—and it's the devil and all gettin' on 'em broke in. Now,' says I, 'why can't you kinder coax 'em up, and speak 'em fair? Depend on it, Tom, a little humanity, thrown in along, goes a heap further than all your jawin' and crackin'; and it pays better,' says I, 'depend on 't.' But Tom could n't get the hang on 't; and he spiled so many for me, that I had to break off with him, though he was a good-hearted fellow, and as fair a business hand as is goin'."

"And do you find your ways of managing do the business better than Tom's?" said Mr. Shelby.

"Why, yes, sir, I may say so. You see, when I any ways can, I takes a leetle care about the onpleasant parts, like selling young uns and that,—get the gals out of the way—out of sight, out of mind, you know,—and when it's clean done, and can't be helped, they naturally gets used to it. 'Tan't, you know, as if it was white folks, that's brought up in the way of 'spectin' to keep their children and wives, and all that. Niggers, you know, that's fetched up properly, ha' n't no kind of 'spectations of no kind; so all these things comes easier."

"I 'm afraid mine are not properly brought up, then," said Mr. Shelby.

"S'pose not; you Kentucky folks spile your niggers. You mean well by 'em, but 'tan't no real kindness, arter all. Now, a nigger, you see, what's got to be hacked and tumbled round the world, and sold to Tom, and Dick, and the Lord knows who, 'tan't no kindness to be givin' on him notions and expectations, and bringin' on him up too well, for the rough and tumble comes all the harder on him arter. Now, I venture to say, your niggers would be quite chop-fallen in a place where some of your plantation niggers would be singing and whooping like all possessed. Every man, you know, Mr. Shelby, naturally thinks well of his own ways, and I think I treat niggers just about as well as it 's ever worth while to treat 'em."

"It 's a happy thing to be satisfied," said Mr. Shelby, with a slight shrug, and some perceptible feelings of a disagreeable nature.

"Well," said Haley, after they had both silently picked their nuts for a season, "what do you say?"

"I 'll think the matter over, and talk with my wife," said Mr. Shelby. "Meantime, Haley, if you want the matter carried on in the quiet way you speak of, you 'd best not let your business in this neighborhood be known. It will get out among my boys, and it will not be a particularly quiet business getting away any of my fellows, if they know it, I 'll promise you."

"O! certainly, by all means, mum! of course. But I 'll tell you, I 'm in a devil of a hurry, and shall want to know, as soon as possible, what I may depend on," said he, rising and putting on his overcoat.

"Well, call up this evening, between six and seven, and you shall have my answer," said Mr. Shelby, and the trader bowed himself out of the apartment.

"I 'd like to have been able to kick the fellow down the steps," said he to himself, as he saw the door fairly closed, "with his impudent assurance; but he knows how much he has me at advantage. If anybody had ever said to me that I should sell Tom down south to one of those rascally traders, I should have said, 'Is thy servant a dog, that he should do this thing?' And now it must come, for aught I see. And Eliza's child, too! I know that I shall have some fuss with wife about that; and, for that matter, about Tom, too. So much for being in debt,—heigho! The fellow sees his advantage, and means to push it."

Perhaps the mildest form of the system of slavery is to be seen in the State of Kentucky. The general prevalence of ag-

ricultural pursuits of a quiet and gradual nature, not requiring
those periodic seasons of hurry and pressure that are called
for in the business of more southern districts, makes the task
of the negro a more healthful and reasonable one; while the
master, content with a more gradual style of acquisition, has
not those temptations to hardheartedness which always overcome frail human nature when the prospect of sudden and
rapid gain is weighed in the balance, with no heavier coun-
terpoise than the interests of the helpless and unprotected.

Whoever visits some estates there, and witnesses the good-
humored indulgence of some masters and mistresses, and the
affectionate loyalty of some slaves, might be tempted to
dream the oft-fabled poetic legend of a patriarchal institution,
and all that; but over and above the scene there broods a
portentous shadow—the shadow of *law*. So long as the law
considers all these human beings, with beating hearts and living affections, only as so many *things* belonging to a
master,—so long as the failure, or misfortune, or imprudence, or death of the kindest owner, may cause them any
day to exchange a life of kind protection and indulgence for
one of hopeless misery and toil,—so long it is impossible to
make anything beautiful or desirable in the best regulated administration of slavery.

Mr. Shelby was a fair average kind of man, good-natured
and kindly, and disposed to easy indulgence of those around
him, and there had never been a lack of anything which might
contribute to the physical comfort of the negroes on his estate. He had, however, speculated largely and quite loosely;
had involved himself deeply, and his notes to a large amount
had come into the hands of Haley; and this small piece of
information is the key to the preceding conversation.

Now, it had so happened that, in approaching the door,
Eliza had caught enough of the conversation to know
that a trader was making offers to her master for somebody.

She would gladly have stopped at the door to listen, as she
came out; but her mistress just then calling, she was obliged
to hasten away.

Still she thought she heard the trader make an offer for her
boy;—could she be mistaken? Her heart swelled and

throbbed, and she involuntarily strained him so tight that the little fellow looked up into her face in astonishment.

"Eliza, girl, what ails you to-day?" said her mistress, when Eliza had upset the wash-pitcher, knocked down the work-stand, and finally was abstractedly offering her mistress a long night-gown in place of the silk dress she had ordered her to bring from the wardrobe.

Eliza started. "O, missis!" she said, raising her eyes; then, bursting into tears, she sat down in a chair, and began sobbing.

"Why, Eliza, child! what ails you?" said her mistress.

"O! missis, missis," said Eliza, "there 's been a trader talking with master in the parlor! I heard him."

"Well, silly child, suppose there has."

"O, missis, *do* you suppose mas'r would sell my Harry?" And the poor creature threw herself into a chair, and sobbed convulsively.

"Sell him! No, you foolish girl! You know your master never deals with those southern traders, and never means to sell any of his servants, as long as they behave well. Why, you silly child, who do you think would want to buy your Harry? Do you think all the world are set on him as you are, you goosie? Come, cheer up, and hook my dress. There now, put my back hair up in that pretty braid you learnt the other day, and don't go listening at doors any more."

"Well, but, missis, *you* never would give your consent—to—to—"

"Nonsense, child! to be sure, I should n't. What do you talk so for? I would as soon have one of my own children sold. But really, Eliza, you are getting altogether too proud of that little fellow. A man can't put his nose into the door, but you think he must be coming to buy him."

Reässured by her mistress' confident tone, Eliza proceeded nimbly and adroitly with her toilet, laughing at her own fears, as she proceeded.

Mrs. Shelby was a woman of a high class, both intellectually and morally. To that natural magnanimity and generosity of mind which one often marks as characteristic of the women of Kentucky, she added high moral and religious sensibility and principle, carried out with great energy and ability

into practical results. Her husband, who made no professions
to any particular religious character, nevertheless reverenced
and respected the consistency of hers, and stood, perhaps, a
little in awe of her opinion. Certain it was that he gave her
unlimited scope in all her benevolent efforts for the comfort,
instruction, and improvement of her servants, though he
never took any decided part in them himself. In fact, if not
exactly a believer in the doctrine of the efficiency of the extra
good works of saints, he really seemed somehow or other to
fancy that his wife had piety and benevolence enough for
two—to indulge a shadowy expectation of getting into
heaven through her superabundance of qualities to which he
made no particular pretension.

The heaviest load on his mind, after his conversation with
the trader, lay in the foreseen necessity of breaking to his wife
the arrangement contemplated,—meeting the importunities
and opposition which he knew he should have reason to encounter.

Mrs. Shelby, being entirely ignorant of her husband's embarrassments, and knowing only the general kindliness of his
temper, had been quite sincere in the entire incredulity with
which she had met Eliza's suspicions. In fact, she dismissed
the matter from her mind, without a second thought; and
being occupied in preparations for an evening visit, it passed
out of her thoughts entirely.

II.

The Mother

ELIZA had been brought up by her mistress, from girlhood, as a petted and indulged favorite.

The traveller in the south must often have remarked that peculiar air of refinement, that softness of voice and manner, which seems in many cases to be a particular gift to the quadroon and mulatto women. These natural graces in the quadroon are often united with beauty of the most dazzling kind, and in almost every case with a personal appearance prepossessing and agreeable. Eliza, such as we have described her, is not a fancy sketch, but taken from remembrance, as we saw her, years ago, in Kentucky. Safe under the protecting care of her mistress, Eliza had reached maturity without those temptations which make beauty so fatal an inheritance to a slave. She had been married to a bright and talented young mulatto man, who was a slave on a neighboring estate, and bore the name of George Harris.

This young man had been hired out by his master to work in a bagging factory, where his adroitness and ingenuity caused him to be considered the first hand in the place. He had invented a machine for the cleaning of the hemp, which, considering the education and circumstances of the inventor, displayed quite as much mechanical genius as Whitney's cotton-gin.*

He was possessed of a handsome person and pleasing manners, and was a general favorite in the factory. Nevertheless, as this young man was in the eye of the law not a man, but a thing, all these superior qualifications were subject to the control of a vulgar, narrow-minded, tyrannical master. This same gentleman, having heard of the fame of George's invention, took a ride over to the factory, to see what this intelligent chattel had been about. He was received with great

*A machine of this description was really the invention of a young colored man in Kentucky.

enthusiasm by the employer, who congratulated him on possessing so valuable a slave.

He was waited upon over the factory, shown the machinery by George, who, in high spirits, talked so fluently, held himself so erect, looked so handsome and manly, that his master began to feel an uneasy consciousness of inferiority. What business had his slave to be marching round the country, inventing machines, and holding up his head among gentlemen? He 'd soon put a stop to it. He 'd take him back, and put him to hoeing and digging, and "see if he 'd step about so smart." Accordingly, the manufacturer and all hands concerned were astounded when he suddenly demanded George's wages, and announced his intention of taking him home.

"But, Mr. Harris," remonstrated the manufacturer, "is n't this rather sudden?"

"What if it is?—is n't the man *mine*?"

"We would be willing, sir, to increase the rate of compensation."

"No object at all, sir. I don't need to hire any of my hands out, unless I 've a mind to."

"But, sir, he seems peculiarly adapted to this business."

"Dare say he may be; never was much adapted to anything that I set him about, I 'll be bound."

"But only think of his inventing this machine," interposed one of the workmen, rather unluckily.

"O yes!—a machine for saving work, is it? He 'd invent that, I 'll be bound; let a nigger alone for that, any time. They are all labor-saving machines themselves, every one of 'em. No, he shall tramp!"

George had stood like one transfixed, at hearing his doom thus suddenly pronounced by a power that he knew was irresistible. He folded his arms, tightly pressed in his lips, but a whole volcano of bitter feelings burned in his bosom, and sent streams of fire through his veins. He breathed short, and his large dark eyes flashed like live coals; and he might have broken out into some dangerous ebullition, had not the kindly manufacturer touched him on the arm, and said, in a low tone,

"Give way, George; go with him for the present. We 'll try to help you, yet."

The tyrant observed the whisper, and conjectured its import, though he could not hear what was said; and he inwardly strengthened himself in his determination to keep the power he possessed over his victim.

George was taken home, and put to the meanest drudgery of the farm. He had been able to repress every disrespectful word; but the flashing eye, the gloomy and troubled brow, were part of a natural language that could not be repressed,—indubitable signs, which showed too plainly that the man could not become a thing.

It was during the happy period of his employment in the factory that George had seen and married his wife. During that period,—being much trusted and favored by his employer,—he had free liberty to come and go at discretion. The marriage was highly approved of by Mrs. Shelby, who, with a little womanly complacency in match-making, felt pleased to unite her handsome favorite with one of her own class who seemed in every way suited to her; and so they were married in her mistress' great parlor, and her mistress herself adorned the bride's beautiful hair with orange-blossoms, and threw over it the bridal veil, which certainly could scarce have rested on a fairer head; and there was no lack of white gloves, and cake and wine,—of admiring guests to praise the bride's beauty, and her mistress' indulgence and liberality. For a year or two Eliza saw her husband frequently, and there was nothing to interrupt their happiness, except the loss of two infant children, to whom she was passionately attached, and whom she mourned with a grief so intense as to call for gentle remonstrance from her mistress, who sought, with maternal anxiety, to direct her naturally passionate feelings within the bounds of reason and religion.

After the birth of little Harry, however, she had gradually become tranquillized and settled; and every bleeding tie and throbbing nerve, once more entwined with that little life, seemed to become sound and healthful, and Eliza was a happy woman up to the time that her husband was rudely torn from his kind employer, and brought under the iron sway of his legal owner.

The manufacturer, true to his word, visited Mr. Harris a week or two after George had been taken away, when, as he hoped, the heat of the occasion had passed away, and tried every possible inducement to lead him to restore him to his former employment.

"You need n't trouble yourself to talk any longer," said he, doggedly; "I know my own business, sir."

"I did not presume to interfere with it, sir. I only thought that you might think it for your interest to let your man to us on the terms proposed."

"O, I understand the matter well enough. I saw your winking and whispering, the day I took him out of the factory; but you don't come it over me that way. It 's a free country, sir; the man 's *mine,* and I do what I please with him,— that 's it!"

And so fell George's last hope;—nothing before him but a life of toil and drudgery, rendered more bitter by every little smarting vexation and indignity which tyrannical ingenuity could devise.

A very humane jurist once said, The worst use you can put a man to is to hang him. No; there is another use that a man can be put to that is WORSE!

III.

The Husband and Father

M RS. SHELBY had gone on her visit, and Eliza stood in the verandah, rather dejectedly looking after the retreating carriage, when a hand was laid on her shoulder. She turned, and a bright smile lighted up her fine eyes.

"George, is it you? How you frightened me! Well; I am so glad you 's come! Missis is gone to spend the afternoon; so come into my little room, and we 'll have the time all to ourselves."

Saying this, she drew him into a neat little apartment opening on the verandah, where she generally sat at her sewing, within call of her mistress.

"How glad I am!—why don't you smile?—and look at Harry—how he grows." The boy stood shyly regarding his father through his curls, holding close to the skirts of his mother's dress. "Is n't he beautiful?" said Eliza, lifting his long curls and kissing him.

"I wish he 'd never been born!" said George, bitterly. "I wish I 'd never been born myself!"

Surprised and frightened, Eliza sat down, leaned her head on her husband's shoulder, and burst into tears.

"There now, Eliza, it 's too bad for me to make you feel so, poor girl!" said he, fondly; "it 's too bad. O, how I wish you never had seen me—you might have been happy!"

"George! George! how can you talk so? What dreadful thing has happened, or is going to happen? I 'm sure we 've been very happy, till lately."

"So we have, dear," said George. Then drawing his child on his knee, he gazed intently on his glorious dark eyes, and passed his hands through his long curls.

"Just like you, Eliza; and you are the handsomest woman I ever saw, and the best one I ever wish to see; but, oh, I wish I 'd never seen you, nor you me!"

"O, George, how can you!"

"Yes, Eliza, it's all misery, misery, misery! My life is bitter as wormwood; the very life is burning out of me. I'm a poor, miserable, forlorn drudge; I shall only drag you down with me, that's all. What's the use of our trying to do anything, trying to know anything, trying to be anything? What's the use of living? I wish I was dead!"

"O, now, dear George, that is really wicked! I know how you feel about losing your place in the factory, and you have a hard master; but pray be patient, and perhaps something—"

"Patient!" said he, interrupting her; "haven't I been patient? Did I say a word when he came and took me away, for no earthly reason, from the place where everybody was kind to me? I'd paid him truly every cent of my earnings,—and they all say I worked well."

"Well, it *is* dreadful," said Eliza; "but, after all, he is your master, you know."

"My master! and who made him my master? That's what I think of—what right has he to me? I'm a man as much as he is. I'm a better man than he is. I know more about business than he does; I am a better manager than he is; I can read better than he can; I can write a better hand,—and I've learned it all myself, and no thanks to him,—I've learned it in spite of him; and now what right has he to make a dray-horse of me?—to take me from things I can do, and do better than he can, and put me to work that any horse can do? He tries to do it; he says he'll bring me down and humble me, and he puts me to just the hardest, meanest and dirtiest work, on purpose!"

"O, George! George! you frighten me! Why, I never heard you talk so; I'm afraid you'll do something dreadful. I don't wonder at your feelings, at all; but oh, do be careful—do, do—for my sake—for Harry's!"

"I have been careful, and I have been patient, but it's growing worse and worse; flesh and blood can't bear it any longer;—every chance he can get to insult and torment me, he takes. I thought I could do my work well, and keep on quiet, and have some time to read and learn out of work hours; but the more he sees I can do, the more he loads on. He says that though I don't say anything, he sees I've got the devil in me, and he means to bring it out; and one of these days it will come out in a way that he won't like, or I 'm mistaken!"

"O dear! what shall we do?" said Eliza, mournfully.

"It was only yesterday," said George, "as I was busy loading stones into a cart, that young Mas'r Tom stood there, slashing his whip so near the horse that the creature was frightened. I asked him to stop, as pleasant as I could,—he just kept right on. I begged him again, and then he turned on me, and began striking me. I held his hand, and then he screamed and kicked and ran to his father, and told him that I was fighting him. He came in a rage, and said he 'd teach me who was my master; and he tied me to a tree, and cut switches for young master, and told him that he might whip me till he was tired;—and he did do it! If I don't make him remember it, some time!" and the brow of the young man grew dark, and his eyes burned with an expression that made his young wife tremble. "Who made this man my master? That 's what I want to know!" he said.

"Well," said Eliza, mournfully, "I always thought that I must obey my master and mistress, or I could n't be a Christian."

"There is some sense in it, in your case; they have brought you up like a child, fed you, clothed you, indulged you, and taught you, so that you have a good education; that is some reason why they should claim you. But I have been kicked and cuffed and sworn at, and at the best only let alone; and what do I owe? I 've paid for all my keeping a hundred times over. I *won't* bear it. No, I *won't*!" he said, clenching his hand with a fierce frown.

Eliza trembled, and was silent. She had never seen her husband in this mood before; and her gentle system of ethics seemed to bend like a reed in the surges of such passions.

"You know poor little Carlo, that you gave me," added George; "the creature has been about all the comfort that I 've had. He has slept with me nights, and followed me around days, and kind o' looked at me as if he understood how I felt. Well, the other day I was just feeding him with a few old scraps I picked up by the kitchen door, and Mas'r came along, and said I was feeding him up at his expense, and that he could n't afford to have every nigger keeping his dog, and ordered me to tie a stone to his neck and throw him in the pond."

"O, George, you did n't do it!"

"Do it? not I!—but he did. Mas'r and Tom pelted the poor drowning creature with stones. Poor thing! he looked at me so mournful, as if he wondered why I did n't save him. I had to take a flogging because I would n't do it myself. I don't care. Mas'r will find out that I 'm one that whipping won't tame. My day will come yet, if he don't look out."

"What are you going to do? O, George, don't do anything wicked; if you only trust in God, and try to do right, he 'll deliver you."

"I an't a Christian like you, Eliza; my heart 's full of bitterness; I can't trust in God. Why does he let things be so?"

"O, George, we must have faith. Mistress says that when all things go wrong to us, we must believe that God is doing the very best."

"That 's easy to say for people that are sitting on their sofas and riding in their carriages; but let 'em be where I am, I guess it would come some harder. I wish I could be good; but my heart burns, and can't be reconciled, anyhow. You could n't, in my place,—you can't now, if I tell you all I 've got to say. You don't know the whole yet."

"What can be coming now?"

"Well, lately Mas'r has been saying that he was a fool to let me marry off the place; that he hates Mr. Shelby and all his tribe, because they are proud, and hold their heads up above him, and that I 've got proud notions from you; and he says he won't let me come here any more, and that I shall take a wife and settle down on his place. At first he only scolded and grumbled these things; but yesterday he told me that I should take Mina for a wife, and settle down in a cabin with her, or he would sell me down river."

"Why—but you were married to *me*, by the minister, as much as if you 'd been a white man!" said Eliza, simply.

"Don't you know a slave can't be married? There is no law in this country for that; I can't hold you for my wife, if he chooses to part us. That 's why I wish I 'd never seen you,—

why I wish I 'd never been born; it would have been better for us both,—it would have been better for this poor child if he had never been born. All this may happen to him yet!"

"O, but master is so kind!"

"Yes, but who knows?—he may die—and then he may be sold to nobody knows who. What pleasure is it that he is handsome, and smart, and bright? I tell you, Eliza, that a sword will pierce through your soul for every good and pleasant thing your child is or has; it will make him worth too much for you to keep!"

The words smote heavily on Eliza's heart; the vision of the trader came before her eyes, and, as if some one had struck her a deadly blow, she turned pale and gasped for breath. She looked nervously out on the verandah, where the boy, tired of the grave conversation, had retired, and where he was riding triumphantly up and down on Mr. Shelby's walking-stick. She would have spoken to tell her husband her fears, but checked herself.

"No, no,—he has enough to bear, poor fellow!" she thought. "No, I won't tell him; besides, it an't true; Missis never deceives us."

"So, Eliza, my girl," said the husband, mournfully, "bear up, now; and good-by, for I 'm going."

"Going, George! Going where?"

"To Canada," said he, straightening himself up; "and when I 'm there, I 'll buy you; that 's all the hope that 's left us. You have a kind master, that won't refuse to sell you. I 'll buy you and the boy;—God helping me, I will!"

"O, dreadful! if you should be taken?"

"I won't be taken, Eliza; I 'll *die* first! I 'll be free, or I 'll die!"

"You won't kill yourself!"

"No need of that. They will kill me, fast enough; they never will get me down the river alive!"

"O, George, for my sake, do be careful! Don't do anything wicked; don't lay hands on yourself, or anybody else! You are tempted too much—too much; but don't—go you must—but go carefully, prudently; pray God to help you."

"Well, then, Eliza, hear my plan. Mas'r took it into his head to send me right by here, with a note to Mr. Symmes, that lives a mile past. I believe he expected I should come here to tell you what I have. It would please him, if he thought it would aggravate 'Shelby's folks,' as he calls 'em. I 'm going home quite resigned, you understand, as if all was over. I 've got some preparations made,—and there are those that will help me; and, in the course of a week or so, I shall be among the missing, some day. Pray for me, Eliza; perhaps the good Lord will hear *you*."

"O, pray yourself, George, and go trusting in him; then you won't do anything wicked."

"Well, now, *good-by*," said George, holding Eliza's hands, and gazing into her eyes, without moving. They stood silent; then there were last words, and sobs, and bitter weeping,— such parting as those may make whose hope to meet again is as the spider's web,—and the husband and wife were parted.

IV.

An Evening in Uncle Tom's Cabin

THE cabin of Uncle Tom was a small log building, close
adjoining to "the house," as the negro *par excellence* des-
ignates his master's dwelling. In front it had a neat garden-
patch, where, every summer, strawberries, raspberries, and a
variety of fruits and vegetables, flourished under careful tending. The whole front of it was covered by a large scarlet
bignonia and a native multiflora rose, which, entwisting and
interlacing, left scarce a vestige of the rough logs to be seen.
Here, also, in summer, various brilliant annuals, such as mar-
igolds, petunias, four-o'clocks, found an indulgent corner in
which to unfold their splendors, and were the delight and
pride of Aunt Chloe's heart.

Let us enter the dwelling. The evening meal at the house is
over, and Aunt Chloe, who presided over its preparation as
head cook, has left to inferior officers in the kitchen the business of clearing away and washing dishes, and come out into
her own snug territories, to "get her ole man's supper;" therefore, doubt not that it is her you see by the fire, presiding
with anxious interest over certain frizzling items in a stew-
pan, and anon with grave consideration lifting the cover of a
bake-kettle, from whence steam forth indubitable intimations
of "something good." A round, black, shining face is hers, so
glossy as to suggest the idea that she might have been washed
over with white of eggs, like one of her own tea rusks. Her
whole plump countenance beams with satisfaction and contentment from under her well-starched checked turban, bearing on it, however, if we must confess it, a little of that tinge
of self-consciousness which becomes the first cook of the
neighborhood, as Aunt Chloe was universally held and acknowledged to be.

A cook she certainly was, in the very bone and centre of
her soul. Not a chicken or turkey or duck in the barn-yard
but looked grave when they saw her approaching, and seemed

evidently to be reflecting on their latter end; and certain it was that she was always meditating on trussing, stuffing and roasting, to a degree that was calculated to inspire terror in any reflecting fowl living. Her corn-cake, in all its varieties of hoe-cake, dodgers, muffins, and other species too numerous to mention, was a sublime mystery to all less practised compounders; and she would shake her fat sides with honest pride and merriment, as she would narrate the fruitless efforts that one and another of her compeers had made to attain to her elevation.

The arrival of company at the house, the arranging of dinners and suppers "in style," awoke all the energies of her soul; and no sight was more welcome to her than a pile of travelling trunks launched on the verandah, for then she foresaw fresh efforts and fresh triumphs.

Just at present, however, Aunt Chloe is looking into the bake-pan; in which congenial operation we shall leave her till we finish our picture of the cottage.

In one corner of it stood a bed, covered neatly with a snowy spread; and by the side of it was a piece of carpeting, of some considerable size. On this piece of carpeting Aunt Chloe took her stand, as being decidedly in the upper walks of life; and it and the bed by which it lay, and the whole corner, in fact, were treated with distinguished consideration, and made, so far as possible, sacred from the marauding inroads and desecrations of little folks. In fact, that corner was the *drawing-room* of the establishment. In the other corner was a bed of much humbler pretensions, and evidently designed for *use*. The wall over the fireplace was adorned with some very brilliant scriptural prints, and a portrait of General Washington, drawn and colored in a manner which would certainly have astonished that hero, if ever he had happened to meet with its like.

On a rough bench in the corner, a couple of woolly-headed boys, with glistening black eyes and fat shining cheeks, were busy in superintending the first walking operations of the baby, which, as is usually the case, consisted in getting up on its feet, balancing a moment, and then tumbling down,— each successive failure being violently cheered, as something decidedly clever.

A table, somewhat rheumatic in its limbs, was drawn out in front of the fire, and covered with a cloth, displaying cups and saucers of a decidedly brilliant pattern, with other symptoms of an approaching meal. At this table was seated Uncle Tom, Mr. Shelby's best hand, who, as he is to be the hero of our story, we must daguerreotype for our readers. He was a large, broad-chested, powerfully-made man, of a full glossy black, and a face whose truly African features were characterized by an expression of grave and steady good sense, united with much kindliness and benevolence. There was something about his whole air self-respecting and dignified, yet united with a confiding and humble simplicity.

He was very busily intent at this moment on a slate lying before him, on which he was carefully and slowly endeavoring to accomplish a copy of some letters, in which operation he was overlooked by young Mas'r George, a smart, bright boy of thirteen, who appeared fully to realize the dignity of his position as instructor.

"Not that way, Uncle Tom,—not that way," said he, briskly, as Uncle Tom laboriously brought up the tail of his *g* the wrong side out; "that makes a *q*, you see."

"La sakes, now, does it?" said Uncle Tom, looking with a respectful, admiring air, as his young teacher flourishingly scrawled *q*'s and *g*'s innumerable for his edification; and then, taking the pencil in his big, heavy fingers, he patiently recommenced.

"How easy white folks al'us does things!" said Aunt Chloe, pausing while she was greasing a griddle with a scrap of bacon on her fork, and regarding young Master George with pride. "The way he can write, now! and read, too! and then to come out here evenings and read his lessons to us,—it 's mighty interestin'!"

"But, Aunt Chloe, I 'm getting mighty hungry," said George. "Is n't that cake in the skillet almost done?"

"Mose done, Mas'r George," said Aunt Chloe, lifting the lid and peeping in,—"browning beautiful—a real lovely brown. Ah! let me alone for dat. Missis let Sally try to make some cake, t'other day, jes to *larn* her, she said. 'O, go way, Missis,' says I; 'it really hurts my feelin's, now, to see good vittles spilt dat ar way! Cake ris all to one side—no shape at all; no more than my shoe;—go way!"

And with this final expression of contempt for Sally's greenness, Aunt Chloe whipped the cover off the bake-kettle, and disclosed to view a neatly-baked pound-cake, of which no city confectioner need to have been ashamed. This being evidently the central point of the entertainment, Aunt Chloe began now to bustle about earnestly in the supper department.

"Here you, Mose and Pete! get out de way, you niggers! Get away, Mericky, honey,—mammy 'll give her baby some fin, by and by. Now, Mas'r George, you jest take off dem books, and set down now with my old man, and I 'll take up de sausages, and have de first griddle full of cakes on your plates in less dan no time."

"They wanted me to come to supper in the house," said George; "but I knew what was what too well for that, Aunt Chloe."

"So you did—so you did, honey," said Aunt Chloe, heaping the smoking batter-cakes on his plate; "you know'd your old aunty 'd keep the best for you. O, let you alone for dat! Go way!" And, with that, aunty gave George a nudge with her finger, designed to be immensely facetious, and turned again to her griddle with great briskness.

"Now for the cake," said Mas'r George, when the activity of the griddle department had somewhat subsided; and, with that, the youngster flourished a large knife over the article in question.

"La bless you, Mas'r George!" said Aunt Chloe, with earnestness, catching his arm, "you wouldn't be for cuttin' it wid dat ar great heavy knife! Smash all down—spile all de pretty rise of it. Here, I 've got a thin old knife, I keeps sharp a purpose. Dar now, see! comes apart light as a feather! Now eat away—you won't get anything to beat dat ar."

"Tom Lincon says," said George, speaking with his mouth full, "that their Jinny is a better cook than you."

"Dem Lincons an't much count, no way!" said Aunt Chloe, contemptuously; "I mean, set along side *our* folks. They 's 'spectable folks enough in a kinder plain way; but, as to gettin' up anything in style, they don't begin to have a notion

on 't. Set Mas'r Lincon, now, alongside Mas'r Shelby! Good
Lor! and Missis Lincon,—can she kinder sweep it into a
room like my missis,—so kinder splendid, yer know! O, go
way! don't tell me nothin' of dem Lincons!"—and Aunt
Chloe tossed her head as one who hoped she did know something of the world.

"Well, though, I 've heard you say," said George, "that
Jinny was a pretty fair cook."

"So I did," said Aunt Chloe,—"I may say dat. Good, plain,
common cookin', Jinny 'll do;—make a good pone o'
bread,—bile her taters *far*,—her corn cakes is n't extra, not
extra now, Jinny's corn cakes is n't, but then they 's far,—
but, Lor, come to de higher branches, and what *can* she do?
Why, she makes pies—sartin she does; but what kinder crust?
Can she make your real flecky paste, as melts in your mouth,
and lies all up like a puff? Now, I went over thar when Miss
Mary was gwine to be married, and Jinny she jest showed me
de weddin' pies. Jinny and I is good friends, ye know. I never
said nothin'; but go long, Mas'r George! Why, I should n't
sleep a wink for a week, if I had a batch of pies like dem ar.
Why, dey wan't no 'count 't all."

"I suppose Jinny thought they were ever so nice," said
George.

"Thought so!—did n't she? Thar she was, showing 'em, as
innocent—ye see, it 's jest here, Jinny *don't know*. Lor, the
family an't nothing! She can't be spected to know! 'Ta'nt no
fault o' hern. Ah, Mas'r George, you does n't know half your
privileges in yer family and bringin' up!" Here Aunt Chloe
sighed, and rolled up her eyes with emotion.

"I 'm sure, Aunt Chloe, I understand all my pie and pudding privileges," said George. "Ask Tom Lincon if I don't
crow over him, every time I meet him."

Aunt Chloe sat back in her chair, and indulged in a hearty
guffaw of laughter, at this witticism of young Mas'r's, laughing till the tears rolled down her black, shining cheeks, and
varying the exercise with playfully slapping and poking Mas'r
Georgey, and telling him to go way, and that he was a case—
that he was fit to kill her, and that he sartin would kill her,
one of these days; and, between each of these sanguinary pre-
dictions, going off into a laugh, each longer and stronger

than the other, till George really began to think that he was
a very dangerously witty fellow, and that it became him to be
careful how he talked "as funny as he could."

"And so ye telled Tom, did ye? O, Lor! what young uns
will be up ter! Ye crowed over Tom? O, Lor! Mas'r George,
if ye would n't make a hornbug laugh!"

"Yes," said George, "I says to him, 'Tom, you ought to see
some of Aunt Chloe's pies; they 're the right sort,' says I."

"Pity, now, Tom could n't," said Aunt Chloe, on whose
benevolent heart the idea of Tom's benighted condition
seemed to make a strong impression. "Ye oughter just
ask him here to dinner, some o' these times, Mas'r George,"
she added; "it would look quite pretty of ye. Ye know,
Mas'r George, ye oughtenter feel 'bove nobody, on 'count
yer privileges, 'cause all our privileges is gi'n to us; we ought
al'ays to 'member that," said Aunt Chloe, looking quite serious.

"Well, I mean to ask Tom here, some day next week," said
George; "and you do your prettiest, Aunt Chloe, and we 'll
make him stare. Won't we make him eat so he won't get over
it for a fortnight?"

"Yes, yes — sartin," said Aunt Chloe, delighted; "you 'll see.
Lor! to think of some of our dinners! Yer mind dat ar great
chicken pie I made when we guv de dinner to General Knox?
I and Missis, we come pretty near quarrelling about dat ar
crust. What does get into ladies sometimes, I don't know;
but, sometimes, when a body has de heaviest kind o' 'sponsi-
bility on 'em, as ye may say, and is all kinder 'seris' and taken
up, dey takes dat ar time to be hangin' round and kinder in-
terferin'! Now, Missis, she wanted me to do dis way, and she
wanted me to do dat way; and, finally, I got kinder sarcy,
and, says I, 'Now, Missis, do jist look at dem beautiful white
hands o' yourn, with long fingers, and all a sparkling with
rings, like my white lilies when de dew 's on 'em; and look at
my great black stumpin hands. Now, don't ye think dat de
Lord must have meant *me* to make de pie-crust, and you to
stay in de parlor?' Dar! I was jist so sarcy, Mas'r George."

"And what did mother say?" said George.

"Say? — why, she kinder larfed in her eyes — dem great
handsome eyes o' hern; and, says she, 'Well, Aunt Chloe, I

think you are about in the right on 't,' says she; and she went
off in de parlor. She oughter cracked me over de head for
bein' so sarcy; but dar 's whar 't is—I can't do nothin' with
ladies in de kitchen!"

"Well, you made out well with that dinner,—I remember
everybody said so," said George.

"Did n't I? And wan't I behind de dinin'-room door dat
bery day? and did n't I see de General pass his plate three
times for some more dat bery pie?—and, says he, 'You must
have an uncommon cook, Mrs. Shelby.' Lor! I was fit to split
myself.

"And de Gineral, he knows what cookin' is," said Aunt
Chloe, drawing herself up with an air. "Bery nice man, de
Gineral! He comes of one of de bery *fustest* families in Old
Virginny! He knows what 's what, now, as well as I do—de
Gineral. Ye see, there 's *pints* in all pies, Mas'r George; but
tan't everybody knows what they is, or as orter be. But the
Gineral, he knows; I knew by his 'marks he made. Yes, he
knows what de pints is!"

By this time, Master George had arrived at that pass to
which even a boy can come (under uncommon circumstances,
when he really could not eat another morsel), and, therefore,
he was at leisure to notice the pile of woolly heads and glistening eyes which were regarding their operations hungrily
from the opposite corner.

"Here, you Mose, Pete," he said, breaking off liberal bits,
and throwing it at them; "you want some, don't you? Come,
Aunt Chloe, bake them some cakes."

And George and Tom moved to a comfortable seat in the
chimney-corner, while Aunt Chloe, after baking a goodly pile
of cakes, took her baby on her lap, and began alternately filling its mouth and her own, and distributing to Mose and
Pete, who seemed rather to prefer eating theirs as they rolled
about on the floor under the table, tickling each other, and
occasionally pulling the baby's toes.

"O! go long, will ye?" said the mother, giving now and
then a kick, in a kind of general way, under the table, when
the movement became too obstreperous. "Can't ye be decent
when white folks comes to see ye? Stop dat ar, now, will ye?

Better mind yerselves, or I 'll take ye down a button-hole lower, when Mas'r George is gone!"

What meaning was couched under this terrible threat, it is difficult to say; but certain it is that its awful indistinctness seemed to produce very little impression on the young sinners addressed.

"La, now!" said Uncle Tom, "they are so full of tickle all the while, they can't behave theirselves."

Here the boys emerged from under the table, and, with hands and faces well plastered with molasses, began a vigorous kissing of the baby.

"Get along wid ye!" said the mother, pushing away their woolly heads. "Ye 'll all stick together, and never get clar, if ye do dat fashion. Go long to de spring and wash yerselves!" she said, seconding her exhortations by a slap, which resounded very formidably, but which seemed only to knock out so much more laugh from the young ones, as they tumbled precipitately over each other out of doors, where they fairly screamed with merriment.

"Did ye ever see such aggravating young uns?" said Aunt Chloe, rather complacently, as, producing an old towel, kept for such emergencies, she poured a little water out of the cracked tea-pot on it, and began rubbing off the molasses from the baby's face and hands; and, having polished her till she shone, she set her down in Tom's lap, while she busied herself in clearing away supper. The baby employed the intervals in pulling Tom's nose, scratching his face, and burying her fat hands in his woolly hair, which last operation seemed to afford her special content.

"Aint she a peart young un?" said Tom, holding her from him to take a full-length view; then, getting up, he set her on his broad shoulder, and began capering and dancing with her, while Mas'r George snapped at her with his pocket-handkerchief, and Mose and Pete, now returned again, roared after her like bears, till Aunt Chloe declared that they "fairly took her head off" with their noise. As, according to her own statement, this surgical operation was a matter of daily occurrence in the cabin, the declaration no whit abated the merriment, till every one had roared and

tumbled and danced themselves down to a state of composure.

"Well, now, I hopes you 're done," said Aunt Chloe, who
had been busy in pulling out a rude box of a trundle-bed;
"and now, you Mose and you Pete, get into thar; for we 's
goin' to have the meetin'."

"O mother, we don't wanter. We wants to sit up to meetin',—meetin's is so curis. We likes 'em."

"La, Aunt Chloe, shove it under, and let 'em sit up," said
Mas'r George, decisively, giving a push to the rude machine.

Aunt Chloe, having thus saved appearances, seemed highly
delighted to push the thing under, saying, as she did so,
"Well, mebbe 't will do 'em some good."

The house now resolved itself into a committee of the
whole, to consider the accommodations and arrangements for
the meeting.

"What we 's to do for cheers, now, I declar I don't know,"
said Aunt Chloe. As the meeting had been held at Uncle
Tom's, weekly, for an indefinite length of time, without any
more "cheers," there seemed some encouragement to hope
that a way would be discovered at present.

"Old Uncle Peter sung both de legs out of dat oldest cheer,
last week," suggested Mose.

"You go long! I 'll boun' you pulled 'em out; some o' your
shines," said Aunt Chloe.

"Well, it 'll stand, if it only keeps jam up agin de wall!" said
Mose.

"Den Uncle Peter mus'n't sit in it, cause he al'ays hitches
when he gets a singing. He hitched pretty nigh across de
room, t' other night," said Pete.

"Good Lor! get him in it, then," said Mose, "and den he 'd
begin, 'Come saints and sinners, hear me tell,' and den down
he 'd go,"—and Mose imitated precisely the nasal tones of
the old man, tumbling on the floor, to illustrate the supposed
catastrophe.

"Come now, be decent, can't ye?" said Aunt Chloe; "an't
yer shamed?"

Mas'r George, however, joined the offender in the laugh,
and declared decidedly that Mose was a "buster." So the maternal admonition seemed rather to fail of effect.

"Well, ole man," said Aunt Chloe, "you 'll have to tote in them ar bar'ls."

"Mother's bar'ls is like dat ar widder's, Mas'r George was reading 'bout, in de good book,—dey never fails," said Mose, aside to Pete.

"I 'm sure one on 'em caved in last week," said Pete, "and let 'em all down in de middle of de singin'; dat ar was failin', warnt it?"

During this aside between Mose and Pete, two empty casks had been rolled into the cabin, and being secured from rolling, by stones on each side, boards were laid across them, which arrangement, together with the turning down of certain tubs and pails, and the disposing of the rickety chairs, at last completed the preparation.

"Mas'r George is such a beautiful reader, now, I know he 'll stay to read for us," said Aunt Chloe; " 'pears like 't will be so much more interestin'."

George very readily consented, for your boy is always ready for anything that makes him of importance.

The room was soon filled with a motley assemblage, from the old gray-headed patriarch of eighty, to the young girl and lad of fifteen. A little harmless gossip ensued on various themes, such as where old Aunt Sally got her new red head-kerchief, and how "Missis was a going to give Lizzy that spotted muslin gown, when she 'd got her new berage made up;" and how Mas'r Shelby was thinking of buying a new sorel colt, that was going to prove an addition to the glories of the place. A few of the worshippers belonged to families hard by, who had got permission to attend, and who brought in various choice scraps of information, about the sayings and doings at the house and on the place, which circulated as freely as the same sort of small change does in higher circles.

After a while the singing commenced, to the evident delight of all present. Not even all the disadvantage of nasal intonation could prevent the effect of the naturally fine voices, in airs at once wild and spirited. The words were sometimes the well-known and common hymns sung in the churches about, and sometimes of a wilder, more indefinite character, picked up at camp-meetings.

The chorus of one of them, which ran as follows, was sung with great energy and unction:

> "Die on the field of battle,
> Die on the field of battle,
> Glory in my soul."

Another special favorite had oft repeated the words—

> "O, I'm going to glory,—won't you come along with me?
> Don't you see the angels beck'ning, and a calling me away?
> Don't you see the golden city and the everlasting day?"

There were others, which made incessant mention of "Jordan's banks," and "Canaan's fields," and the "New Jerusalem;" for the negro mind, impassioned and imaginative, always attaches itself to hymns and expressions of a vivid and pictorial nature; and, as they sung, some laughed, and some cried, and some clapped hands, or shook hands rejoicingly with each other, as if they had fairly gained the other side of the river.

Various exhortations, or relations of experience, followed, and intermingled with the singing. One old gray-headed woman, long past work, but much revered as a sort of chronicle of the past, rose, and leaning on her staff, said—

"Well, chil'en! Well, I'm mighty glad to hear ye all and see ye all once more, 'cause I don't know when I'll be gone to glory; but I've done got ready, chil'en; 'pears like I'd got my little bundle all tied up, and my bonnet on, jest a waitin' for the stage to come along and take me home; sometimes, in the night, I think I hear the wheels a rattlin', and I'm lookin' out all the time; now, you jest be ready too, for I tell ye all, chil'en," she said, striking her staff hard on the floor, "dat ar *glory* is a mighty thing! It's a mighty thing, chil'en,—you don'no nothing about it,—it's *wonderful*." And the old creature sat down, with streaming tears, as wholly overcome, while the whole circle struck up—

> "O Canaan, bright Canaan,
> I'm bound for the land of Canaan."

Mas'r George, by request, read the last chapters of Revelation, often interrupted by such exclamations as "The *sakes* now!" "Only hear that!" "Jest think on 't!" "Is all that a comin' sure enough?"

George, who was a bright boy, and well trained in religious things by his mother, finding himself an object of general admiration, threw in expositions of his own, from time to time, with a commendable seriousness and gravity, for which he was admired by the young and blessed by the old; and it was agreed, on all hands, that "a minister could n't lay it off better than he did;" that " 't was reely 'mazin'!"

Uncle Tom was a sort of patriarch in religious matters, in the neighborhood. Having, naturally, an organization in which the *morale* was strongly predominant, together with a greater breadth and cultivation of mind than obtained among his companions, he was looked up to with great respect, as a sort of minister among them; and the simple, hearty, sincere style of his exhortations might have edified even better educated persons. But it was in prayer that he especially excelled. Nothing could exceed the touching simplicity, the child-like earnestness, of his prayer, enriched with the language of Scripture, which seemed so entirely to have wrought itself into his being, as to have become a part of himself, and to drop from his lips unconsciously; in the language of a pious old negro, he "prayed right up." And so much did his prayer always work on the devotional feelings of his audiences, that there seemed often a danger that it would be lost altogether in the abundance of the responses which broke out everywhere around him.

While this scene was passing in the cabin of the man, one quite otherwise passed in the halls of the master.

The trader and Mr. Shelby were seated together in the dining room afore-named, at a table covered with papers and writing utensils.

Mr. Shelby was busy in counting some bundles of bills, which, as they were counted, he pushed over to the trader, who counted them likewise.

"All fair," said the trader; "and now for signing these yer."

Mr. Shelby hastily drew the bills of sale towards him, and signed them, like a man that hurries over some disagreeable business, and then pushed them over with the money. Haley produced, from a well-worn valise, a parchment, which, after looking over it a moment, he handed to Mr. Shelby, who took it with a gesture of suppressed eagerness.

"Wal, now, the thing 's *done!*" said the trader, getting up.

"It 's *done!*" said Mr. Shelby, in a musing tone; and, fetching a long breath, he repeated, *"It 's done!"*

"Yer don't seem to feel much pleased with it, 'pears to me," said the trader.

"Haley," said Mr. Shelby, "I hope you 'll remember that you promised, on your honor, you would n't sell Tom, without knowing what sort of hands he 's going into."

"Why, you 've just done it, sir," said the trader.

"Circumstances, you well know, *obliged* me," said Shelby, haughtily.

"Wal, you know, they may 'blige *me*, too," said the trader. "Howsomever, I 'll do the very best I can in gettin' Tom a good berth; as to my treatin' on him bad, you need n't be a grain afeard. If there 's anything that I thank the Lord for, it is that I 'm never noways cruel."

After the expositions which the trader had previously given of his humane principles, Mr. Shelby did not feel particularly reässured by these declarations; but, as they were the best comfort the case admitted of, he allowed the trader to depart in silence, and betook himself to a solitary cigar.

V.

Showing the Feelings of Living Property on Changing Owners

M R. and Mrs. Shelby had retired to their apartment for the night. He was lounging in a large easy-chair, looking over some letters that had come in the afternoon mail, and she was standing before her mirror, brushing out the complicated braids and curls in which Eliza had arranged her hair; for, noticing her pale cheeks and haggard eyes, she had excused her attendance that night, and ordered her to bed. The employment, naturally enough, suggested her conversation with the girl in the morning; and, turning to her husband, she said, carelessly,

"By the by, Arthur, who was that low-bred fellow that you lugged in to our dinner-table to-day?"

"Haley is his name," said Shelby, turning himself rather uneasily in his chair, and continuing with his eyes fixed on a letter.

"Haley! Who is he, and what may be his business here, pray?"

"Well, he 's a man that I transacted some business with, last time I was at Natchez," said Mr. Shelby.

"And he presumed on it to make himself quite at home, and call and dine here, ay?"

"Why, I invited him; I had some accounts with him," said Shelby.

"Is he a negro-trader?" said Mrs. Shelby, noticing a certain embarrassment in her husband's manner.

"Why, my dear, what put that into your head?" said Shelby, looking up.

"Nothing,—only Eliza came in here, after dinner, in a great worry, crying and taking on, and said you were talking with a trader, and that she heard him make an offer for her boy—the ridiculous little goose!"

"She did, hey?" said Mr. Shelby, returning to his paper,

which he seemed for a few moments quite intent upon, not perceiving that he was holding it bottom upwards.

"It will have to come out," said he, mentally; "as well now as ever."

"I told Eliza," said Mrs. Shelby, as she continued brushing her hair, "that she was a little fool for her pains, and that you never had anything to do with that sort of persons. Of course, I knew you never meant to sell any of our people,—least of all, to such a fellow."

"Well, Emily," said her husband, "so I have always felt and said; but the fact is that my business lies so that I cannot get on without. I shall have to sell some of my hands."

"To that creature? Impossible! Mr. Shelby, you cannot be serious."

"I 'm sorry to say that I am," said Mr. Shelby. "I 've agreed to sell Tom."

"What! our Tom?—that good, faithful creature!—been your faithful servant from a boy! O, Mr. Shelby!—and you have promised him his freedom, too,—you and I have spoken to him a hundred times of it. Well, I can believe anything now,—I can believe *now* that you could sell little Harry, poor Eliza's only child!" said Mrs. Shelby, in a tone between grief and indignation.

"Well, since you must know all, it is so. I have agreed to sell Tom and Harry both; and I don't know why I am to be rated, as if I were a monster, for doing what every one does every day."

"But why, of all others, choose these?" said Mrs. Shelby. "Why sell them, of all on the place, if you must sell at all?"

"Because they will bring the highest sum of any,—that 's why. I could choose another, if you say so. The fellow made me a high bid on Eliza, if that would suit you any better," said Mr. Shelby.

"The wretch!" said Mrs. Shelby, vehemently.

"Well, I did n't listen to it, a moment,—out of regard to your feelings, I would n't;—so give me some credit."

"My dear," said Mrs. Shelby, recollecting herself, "forgive me. I have been hasty. I was surprised, and entirely unprepared for this;—but surely you will allow me to intercede for these poor creatures. Tom is a noble-hearted, faithful fellow, if he is black. I do believe, Mr. Shelby, that if he were put to it, he would lay down his life for you."

"I know it,—I dare say;—but what 's the use of all this?— I can't help myself."

"Why not make a pecuniary sacrifice? I 'm willing to bear my part of the inconvenience. O, Mr. Shelby, I have tried— tried most faithfully, as a Christian woman should—to do my duty to these poor, simple, dependent creatures. I have cared for them, instructed them, watched over them, and known all their little cares and joys, for years; and how can I ever hold up my head again among them, if, for the sake of a little paltry gain, we sell such a faithful, excellent, confiding creature as poor Tom, and tear from him in a moment all we have taught him to love and value? I have taught them the duties of the family, of parent and child, and husband and wife; and how can I bear to have this open acknowledgment that we care for no tie, no duty, no relation, however sacred, compared with money? I have talked with Eliza about her boy—her duty to him as a Christian mother, to watch over him, pray for him, and bring him up in a Christian way; and now what can I say, if you tear him away, and sell him, soul and body, to a profane, unprincipled man, just to save a little money? I have told her that one soul is worth more than all the money in the world; and how will she believe me when she sees us turn round and sell her child?—sell him, perhaps, to certain ruin of body and soul!"

"I 'm sorry you feel so about it, Emily,—indeed I am," said Mr. Shelby; "and I respect your feelings, too, though I don't pretend to share them to their full extent; but I tell you now, solemnly, it 's of no use—I can't help myself. I did n't mean to tell you this, Emily; but, in plain words, there is no choice between selling these two and selling everything. Either they must go, or *all* must. Haley has come into possession of a mortgage, which, if I don't clear off with him directly, will take everything before it. I 've raked, and scraped, and bor- rowed, and all but begged,—and the price of these two was needed to make up the balance, and I had to give them up. Haley fancied the child; he agreed to settle the matter that

way, and no other. I was in his power, and *had* to do it. If
you feel so to have them sold, would it be any better to have
all sold?"

Mrs. Shelby stood like one stricken. Finally, turning to her
toilet, she rested her face in her hands, and gave a sort of
groan.

"This is God's curse on slavery!—a bitter, bitter, most accursed thing!—a curse to the master and a curse to the slave!
I was a fool to think I could make anything good out of such
a deadly evil. It is a sin to hold a slave under laws like ours,—
I always felt it was,—I always thought so when I was a
girl,—I thought so still more after I joined the church; but I
thought I could gild it over,—I thought, by kindness, and
care, and instruction, I could make the condition of mine better than freedom—fool that I was!"

"Why, wife, you are getting to be an abolitionist, quite."

"Abolitionist! if they knew all I know about slavery, they
might talk! We don't need them to tell us; you know I never
thought that slavery was right—never felt willing to own
slaves."

"Well, therein you differ from many wise and pious men,"
said Mr. Shelby. "You remember Mr. B.'s sermon, the other
Sunday?"

"I don't want to hear such sermons; I never wish to hear
Mr. B. in our church again. Ministers can't help the evil, perhaps,—can't cure it, any more than we can,—but defend
it!—it always went against my common sense. And I think
you did n't think much of that sermon, either."

"Well," said Shelby, "I must say these ministers sometimes
carry matters further than we poor sinners would exactly dare
to do. We men of the world must wink pretty hard at various
things, and get used to a deal that is n't the exact thing. But
we don't quite fancy, when women and ministers come out
broad and square, and go beyond us in matters of either modesty or morals, that 's a fact. But now, my dear, I trust you
see the necessity of the thing, and you see that I have done
the very best that circumstances would allow."

"O yes, yes!" said Mrs. Shelby, hurriedly and abstractedly
fingering her gold watch,—"I have n't any jewelry of any
amount," she added, thoughtfully; "but would not this watch

do something?—it was an expensive one, when it was bought. If I could only at least save Eliza's child, I would sacrifice anything I have."

"I'm sorry, very sorry, Emily," said Mr. Shelby, "I'm sorry this takes hold of you so; but it will do no good. The fact is, Emily, the thing's done; the bills of sale are already signed, and in Haley's hands; and you must be thankful it is no worse. That man has had it in his power to ruin us all,—and now he is fairly off. If you knew the man as I do, you'd think that we had had a narrow escape."

"Is he so hard, then?"

"Why, not a cruel man, exactly, but a man of leather,—a man alive to nothing but trade and profit,—cool, and unhesitating, and unrelenting, as death and the grave. He'd sell his own mother at a good per centage—not wishing the old woman any harm, either."

"And this wretch owns that good, faithful Tom, and Eliza's child!"

"Well, my dear, the fact is that this goes rather hard with me; it's a thing I hate to think of. Haley wants to drive matters, and take possession to-morrow. I'm going to get out my horse bright and early, and be off. I can't see Tom, that's a fact; and you had better arrange a drive somewhere, and carry Eliza off. Let the thing be done when she is out of sight."

"No, no," said Mrs. Shelby; "I'll be in no sense accomplice or help in this cruel business. I'll go and see poor old Tom, God help him, in his distress! They shall see, at any rate, that their mistress can feel for and with them. As to Eliza, I dare not think about it. The Lord forgive us! What have we done, that this cruel necessity should come on us?"

There was one listener to this conversation whom Mr. and Mrs. Shelby little suspected.

Communicating with their apartment was a large closet, opening by a door into the outer passage. When Mrs. Shelby had dismissed Eliza for the night, her feverish and excited mind had suggested the idea of this closet; and she had hidden herself there, and, with her ear pressed close against the crack of the door, had lost not a word of the conversation.

When the voices died into silence, she rose and crept

stealthily away. Pale, shivering, with rigid features and compressed lips, she looked an entirely altered being from the soft
and timid creature she had been hitherto. She moved cautiously along the entry, paused one moment at her mistress'
door, and raised her hands in mute appeal to Heaven, and
then turned and glided into her own room. It was a quiet,
neat apartment, on the same floor with her mistress. There
was the pleasant sunny window, where she had often sat singing at her sewing; there a little case of books, and various
little fancy articles, ranged by them, the gifts of Christmas
holidays; there was her simple wardrobe in the closet and in
the drawers:—here was, in short, her home; and, on the
whole, a happy one it had been to her. But there, on the bed,
lay her slumbering boy, his long curls falling negligently
around his unconscious face, his rosy mouth half open, his
little fat hands thrown out over the bed-clothes, and a smile
spread like a sunbeam over his whole face.

"Poor boy! poor fellow!" said Eliza; "they have sold you!
but your mother will save you yet!"

No tear dropped over that pillow; in such straits as these,
the heart has no tears to give,—it drops only blood, bleeding
itself away in silence. She took a piece of paper and pencil,
and wrote, hastily,

"O, Missis! dear Missis! don't think me ungrateful,—don't
think hard of me, any way,—I heard all you and master said
to-night. I am going to try to save my boy—you will not
blame me! God bless and reward you for all your kindness!"

Hastily folding and directing this, she went to a drawer and
made up a little package of clothing for her boy, which she
tied with a handkerchief firmly round her waist; and, so fond
is a mother's remembrance, that, even in the terrors of that
hour, she did not forget to put in the little package one or
two of his favorite toys, reserving a gayly painted parrot to
amuse him, when she should be called on to awaken him. It
was some trouble to arouse the little sleeper; but, after some
effort, he sat up, and was playing with his bird, while his
mother was putting on her bonnet and shawl.

"Where are you going, mother?" said he, as she drew near
the bed, with his little coat and cap.

His mother drew near, and looked so earnestly into his

eyes, that he at once divined that something unusual was the matter.

"Hush, Harry," she said; "musn't speak loud, or they will hear us. A wicked man was coming to take little Harry away from his mother, and carry him 'way off in the dark; but mother won't let him—she 's going to put on her little boy's cap and coat, and run off with him, so the ugly man can't catch him."

Saying these words, she had tied and buttoned on the child's simple outfit, and, taking him in her arms, she whispered to him to be very still; and, opening a door in her room which led into the outer verandah, she glided noiselessly out.

It was a sparkling, frosty, star-light night, and the mother wrapped the shawl close round her child, as, perfectly quiet with vague terror, he clung round her neck.

Old Bruno, a great Newfoundland, who slept at the end of the porch, rose, with a low growl, as she came near. She gently spoke his name, and the animal, an old pet and playmate of hers, instantly, wagging his tail, prepared to follow her, though apparently revolving much, in his simple dog's head, what such an indiscreet midnight promenade might mean. Some dim ideas of imprudence or impropriety in the measure seemed to embarrass him considerably; for he often stopped, as Eliza glided forward, and looked wistfully, first at her and then at the house, and then, as if reässured by reflection, he pattered along after her again. A few minutes brought them to the window of Uncle Tom's cottage, and Eliza, stopping, tapped lightly on the window-pane.

The prayer-meeting at Uncle Tom's had, in the order of hymn-singing, been protracted to a very late hour; and, as Uncle Tom had indulged himself in a few lengthy solos afterwards, the consequence was, that, although it was now between twelve and one o'clock, he and his worthy helpmeet were not yet asleep.

"Good Lord! what 's that?" said Aunt Chloe, starting up and hastily drawing the curtain. "My sakes alive, if it an't Lizy! Get on your clothes, old man, quick!—there 's old Bruno, too, a pawin' round; what on airth! I 'm gwine to open the door."

And, suiting the action to the word, the door flew open,

and the light of the tallow candle, which Tom had hastily lighted, fell on the haggard face and dark, wild eyes of the fugitive.

"Lord bless you!—I 'm skeered to look at ye, Lizy! Are ye tuck sick, or what 's come over ye?"

"I 'm running away—Uncle Tom and Aunt Chloe—carrying off my child—Master sold him!"

"Sold him?" echoed both, lifting up their hands in dismay.

"Yes, sold him!" said Eliza, firmly; "I crept into the closet by Mistress' door to-night, and I heard Master tell Missis that he had sold my Harry, and you, Uncle Tom, both, to a trader; and that he was going off this morning on his horse, and that the man was to take possession to-day."

Tom had stood, during this speech, with his hands raised, and his eyes dilated, like a man in a dream. Slowly and gradually, as its meaning came over him, he collapsed, rather than seated himself, on his old chair, and sunk his head down upon his knees.

"The good Lord have pity on us!" said Aunt Chloe. "O! it don't seem as if it was true! What has he done, that Mas'r should sell *him?*"

"He has n't done anything,—it is n't for that. Master don't want to sell; and Missis—she 's always good. I heard her plead and beg for us; but he told her 't was no use; that he was in this man's debt, and that this man had got the power over him; and that if he did n't pay him off clear, it would end in his having to sell the place and all the people, and move off. Yes, I heard him say there was no choice between selling these two and selling all, the man was driving him so hard. Master said he was sorry; but oh, Missis—you ought to have heard her talk! If she an't a Christian and an angel, there never was one. I 'm a wicked girl to leave her so; but, then, I can't help it. She said, herself, one soul was worth more than the world; and this boy has a soul, and if I let him be carried off, who knows what 'll become of it? It must be right: but, if it an't right, the Lord forgive me, for I can't help doing it!"

"Well, old man!" said Aunt Chloe, "why don't you go, too?

Eliza comes to tell Uncle Tom that he is sold and that she is running away to save her child

Will you wait to be toted down river, where they kill niggers with hard work and starving? I 'd a heap rather die than go there, any day! There 's time for ye,—be off with Lizy,— you 've got a pass to come and go any time. Come, bustle up, and I 'll get your things together."

Tom slowly raised his head, and looked sorrowfully but quietly around, and said,

"No, no—I an't going. Let Eliza go—it 's her right! I would n't be the one to say no—'t an't in *natur* for her to stay; but you heard what she said! If I must be sold, or all the people on the place, and everything go to rack, why, let me be sold. I s'pose I can b'ar it as well as any on 'em," he added, while something like a sob and a sigh shook his broad, rough chest convulsively. "Mas'r always found me on the spot—he always will. I never have broke trust, nor used my pass no ways contrary to my word, and I never will. It 's better for me alone to go, than to break up the place and sell all. Mas'r an't to blame, Chloe, and he 'll take care of you and the poor—"

Here he turned to the rough trundle-bed full of little woolly heads, and broke fairly down. He leaned over the back of the chair, and covered his face with his large hands. Sobs, heavy, hoarse and loud, shook the chair, and great tears fell through his fingers on the floor: just such tears, sir, as you dropped into the coffin where lay your first-born son; such tears, woman, as you shed when you heard the cries of your dying babe. For, sir, he was a man,—and you are but another man. And, woman, though dressed in silk and jewels, you are but a woman, and, in life's great straits and mighty griefs, ye feel but one sorrow!

"And now," said Eliza, as she stood in the door, "I saw my husband only this afternoon, and I little knew then what was to come. They have pushed him to the very last standing-place, and he told me, to-day, that he was going to run away. Do try, if you can, to get word to him. Tell him how I went, and why I went; and tell him I 'm going to try and find Canada. You must give my love to him, and tell him, if I never see him again,"—she turned away, and stood with her back to them for a moment, and then added, in a husky voice, "tell him to be as good as he can, and try and meet me in the kingdom of heaven."

"Call Bruno in there," she added. "Shut the door on him, poor beast! He must n't go with me!"

A few last words and tears, a few simple adieus and blessings, and, clasping her wondering and affrighted child in her arms, she glided noiselessly away.

VI.

Discovery

Mr. and Mrs. Shelby, after their protracted discussion of the night before, did not readily sink to repose, and, in consequence, slept somewhat later than usual, the ensuing morning.

"I wonder what keeps Eliza," said Mrs. Shelby, after giving her bell repeated pulls, to no purpose.

Mr. Shelby was standing before his dressing-glass, sharpening his razor; and just then the door opened, and a colored boy entered, with his shaving-water.

"Andy," said his mistress, "step to Eliza's door, and tell her I have rung for her three times. Poor thing!" she added, to herself, with a sigh.

Andy soon returned, with eyes very wide in astonishment.

"Lor, Missis! Lizy's drawers is all open, and her things all lying every which way; and I believe she 's just done clared out!"

The truth flashed upon Mr. Shelby and his wife at the same moment. He exclaimed,

"Then she suspected it, and she 's off!"

"The Lord be thanked!" said Mrs. Shelby. "I trust she is."

"Wife, you talk like a fool! Really, it will be something pretty awkward for me, if she is. Haley saw that I hesitated about selling this child, and he 'll think I connived at it, to get him out of the way. It touches my honor!" And Mr. Shelby left the room hastily.

There was great running and ejaculating, and opening and shutting of doors, and appearance of faces in all shades of color in different places, for about a quarter of an hour. One person only, who might have shed some light on the matter, was entirely silent, and that was the head cook, Aunt Chloe. Silently, and with a heavy cloud settled down over her once joyous face, she proceeded making out her breakfast biscuits, as if she heard and saw nothing of the excitement around her.

Very soon, about a dozen young imps were roosting, like so many crows, on the verandah railings, each one determined to be the first one to apprize the strange Mas'r of his ill luck.

"He 'll be rael mad, I 'll be bound," said Andy.

"*Won't* he swar!" said little black Jake.

"Yes, for he *does* swar," said woolly-headed Mandy. "I hearn him yesterday, at dinner. I hearn all about it then, 'cause I got into the closet where Missis keeps the great jugs, and I hearn every word." And Mandy, who had never in her life thought of the meaning of a word she had heard, more than a black cat, now took airs of superior wisdom, and strutted about, forgetting to state that, though actually coiled up among the jugs at the time specified, she had been fast asleep all the time.

When, at last, Haley appeared, booted and spurred, he was saluted with the bad tidings on every hand. The young imps on the verandah were not disappointed in their hope of hearing him "swar," which he did with a fluency and fervency which delighted them all amazingly, as they ducked and dodged hither and thither, to be out of the reach of his riding-whip; and, all whooping off together, they tumbled, in a pile of immeasurable giggle, on the withered turf under the verandah, where they kicked up their heels and shouted to their full satisfaction.

"If I had the little devils!" muttered Haley, between his teeth.

"But you ha'nt got 'em, though!" said Andy, with a triumphant flourish, and making a string of indescribable mouths at the unfortunate trader's back, when he was fairly beyond hearing.

"I say now, Shelby, this yer 's a most extro'rnary business!" said Haley, as he abruptly entered the parlor. "It seems that gal 's off, with her young un."

"Mr. Haley, Mrs. Shelby is present," said Mr. Shelby.

"I beg pardon, ma'am," said Haley, bowing slightly, with a still lowering brow; "but still I say, as I said before, this yer 's a sing'lar report. Is it true, sir?"

"Sir," said Mr. Shelby, "if you wish to communicate with me, you must observe something of the decorum of a gentleman. Andy, take Mr. Haley's hat and riding-whip. Take a seat, sir. Yes, sir; I regret to say that the young woman, excited by overhearing, or having reported to her, something of this business, has taken her child in the night, and made off."

"I did expect fair dealing in this matter, I confess," said Haley.

"Well, sir," said Mr. Shelby, turning sharply round upon him, "what am I to understand by that remark? If any man calls my honor in question, I have but one answer for him."

The trader cowered at this, and in a somewhat lower tone said that "it was plaguy hard on a fellow, that had made a fair bargain, to be gulled that way."

"Mr. Haley," said Mr. Shelby, "if I did not think you had some cause for disappointment, I should not have borne from you the rude and unceremonious style of your entrance into my parlor this morning. I say thus much, however, since appearances call for it, that I shall allow of no insinuations cast upon me, as if I were at all partner to any unfairness in this matter. Moreover, I shall feel bound to give you every assistance, in the use of horses, servants, &c., in the recovery of your property. So, in short, Haley," said he, suddenly dropping from the tone of dignified coolness to his ordinary one of easy frankness, "the best way for you is to keep good-natured and eat some breakfast, and we will then see what is to be done."

Mrs. Shelby now rose, and said her engagements would prevent her being at the breakfast-table that morning; and, deputing a very respectable mulatto woman to attend to the gentlemen's coffee at the side-board, she left the room.

"Old lady don't like your humble servant, over and above," said Haley, with an uneasy effort to be very familiar.

"I am not accustomed to hear my wife spoken of with such freedom," said Mr. Shelby, dryly.

"Beg pardon; of course, only a joke, you know," said Haley, forcing a laugh.

"Some jokes are less agreeable than others," rejoined Shelby.

"Devilish free, now I've signed those papers, cuss him!" muttered Haley to himself; "quite grand, since yesterday!"

Never did fall of any prime minister at court occasion wider surges of sensation than the report of Tom's fate among his compeers on the place. It was the topic in every mouth, everywhere; and nothing was done in the house or in the field, but to discuss its probable results. Eliza's flight—an unprecedented event on the place—was also a great accessory in stimulating the general excitement.

Black Sam, as he was commonly called, from his being about three shades blacker than any other son of ebony on the place, was revolving the matter profoundly in all its phases and bearings, with a comprehensiveness of vision and a strict look-out to his own personal well-being, that would have done credit to any white patriot in Washington.

"It 's an ill wind dat blows nowhar,—dat ar a fact," said Sam, sententiously, giving an additional hoist to his pantaloons, and adroitly substituting a long nail in place of a missing suspender-button, with which effort of mechanical genius he seemed highly delighted.

"Yes, it 's an ill wind blows nowhar," he repeated. "Now, dar, Tom 's down—wal, course der 's room for some nigger to be up—and why not dis nigger?—dat 's de idee. Tom, a ridin' round de country—boots blacked—pass in his pocket—all grand as Cuffee—who but he? Now, why should n't Sam?—dat 's what I want to know."

"Halloo, Sam—O Sam! Mas'r wants you to cotch Bill and Jerry," said Andy, cutting short Sam's soliloquy.

"High! what 's afoot now, young un?"

"Why, you don't know, I s'pose, that Lizy 's cut stick, and clared out, with her young un?"

"You teach your granny!" said Sam, with infinite contempt; "knowed it a heap sight sooner than you did; this nigger an't so green, now!"

"Well, anyhow, Mas'r wants Bill and Jerry geared right up; and you and I 's to go with Mas'r Haley, to look arter her."

"Good, now! dat 's de time o' day!" said Sam. "It 's Sam dat 's called for in dese yer times. He 's de nigger. See if I don't cotch her, now; Mas'r 'll see what Sam can do!"

"Ah! but, Sam," said Andy, "you 'd better think twice; for Missis don't want her cotched, and she 'll be in yer wool."

"High!" said Sam, opening his eyes. "How you know dat?"

"Heard her say so, my own self, dis blessed mornin', when I bring in Mas'r's shaving-water. She sent me to see why Lizy did n't come to dress her; and when I told her she was off, she jest ris up, and ses she, 'The Lord be praised;' and Mas'r, he seemed rael mad, and ses he, 'Wife, you talk like a fool.' But Lor! she 'll bring him to! I knows well enough how that 'll be,—it 's allers best to stand Missis' side the fence, now I tell yer."

Black Sam, upon this, scratched his woolly pate, which, if it did not contain very profound wisdom, still contained a great deal of a particular species much in demand among politicians of all complexions and countries, and vulgarly denominated "knowing which side the bread is buttered;" so, stopping with grave consideration, he again gave a hitch to his pantaloons, which was his regularly organized method of assisting his mental perplexities.

"Der an't no sayin'—never—'bout no kind o' thing in *dis* yer world," he said, at last.

Sam spoke like a philosopher, emphasizing *this*—as if he had had a large experience in different sorts of worlds, and therefore had come to his conclusions advisedly.

"Now, sartin I 'd a said that Missis would a scoured the varsal world after Lizy," added Sam, thoughtfully.

"So she would," said Andy; "but can't ye see through a ladder, ye black nigger? Missis don't want dis yer Mas'r Haley to get Lizy's boy; dat 's de go!"

"High!" said Sam, with an indescribable intonation, known only to those who have heard it among the negroes.

"And I 'll tell yer more 'n all," said Andy; "I specs you 'd better be making tracks for dem hosses,—mighty sudden, too,—for I hearn Missis 'quirin' arter yer,—so you 've stood foolin' long enough."

Sam, upon this, began to bestir himself in real earnest, and after a-while appeared, bearing down gloriously towards the house, with Bill and Jerry in a full canter, and adroitly throwing himself off before they had any idea of stopping, he brought them up alongside of the horse-post like a tornado. Haley's horse, which was a skittish young colt, winced, and bounced, and pulled hard at his halter.

"Ho, ho!" said Sam, "skeery, ar ye?" and his black visage lighted up with a curious, mischievous gleam. "I 'll fix ye now!" said he.

There was a large beech-tree overshadowing the place, and the small, sharp, triangular beech-nuts lay scattered thickly on the ground. With one of these in his fingers, Sam approached the colt, stroked and patted, and seemed apparently busy in soothing his agitation. On pretence of adjusting the saddle, he adroitly slipped under it the sharp little nut, in such a manner that the least weight brought upon the saddle would annoy the nervous sensibilities of the animal, without leaving any perceptible graze or wound.

"Dar!" he said, rolling his eyes with an approving grin; "me fix 'em!"

At this moment Mrs. Shelby appeared on the balcony, beckoning to him. Sam approached with as good a determination to pay court as did ever suitor after a vacant place at St. James' or Washington.

"Why have you been loitering so, Sam? I sent Andy to tell you to hurry."

"Lord bless you, Missis!" said Sam, "horses won't be cotched all in a mimit; they 'd done clared out way down to the south pasture, and the Lord knows whar!"

"Sam, how often must I tell you not to say 'Lord bless you, and the Lord knows,' and such things? It 's wicked."

"O, Lord bless my soul! I done forgot, Missis! I won't say nothing of de sort no more."

"Why, Sam, you just *have* said it again."

"Did I? O, Lord! I mean—I did n't go fur to say it."

"You must be *careful*, Sam."

"Just let me get my breath, Missis, and I 'll start fair. I 'll be berry careful."

"Well, Sam, you are to go with Mr. Haley, to show him the road, and help him. Be careful of the horses, Sam; you know Jerry was a little lame last week; *don't ride them too fast.*"

Mrs. Shelby spoke the last words with a low voice, and strong emphasis.

"Let dis child alone for dat!" said Sam, rolling up his eyes with a volume of meaning. "Lord knows! High! Did n't say dat!" said he, suddenly catching his breath, with a ludicrous flourish of apprehension, which made his mistress laugh, spite of herself. "Yes, Missis, I'll look out for de hosses!"

"Now, Andy," said Sam, returning to his stand under the beech-trees, "you see I would n't be 't all surprised if dat ar gen'lman's crittur should gib a fling, by and by, when he comes to be a gettin' up. You know, Andy, critturs *will* do such things;" and therewith Sam poked Andy in the side, in a highly suggestive manner.

"High!" said Andy, with an air of instant appreciation.

"Yes, you see, Andy, Missis wants to make time,—dat ar 's clar to der most or'nary 'bserver. I jis make a little for her. Now, you see, get all dese yer hosses loose, caperin' permiscus round dis yer lot and down to de wood dar, and I spec Mas'r won't be off in a hurry."

Andy grinned.

"Yer see," said Sam, "yer see, Andy, if any such thing should happen as that Mas'r Haley's horse *should* begin to act contrary, and cut up, you and I jist lets go of our'n to help him, and *we 'll help him*—oh yes!" And Sam and Andy laid their heads back on their shoulders, and broke into a low, immoderate laugh, snapping their fingers and flourishing their heels with exquisite delight.

At this instant, Haley appeared on the verandah. Somewhat mollified by certain cups of very good coffee, he came out smiling and talking, in tolerably restored humor. Sam and Andy, clawing for certain fragmentary palm-leaves, which they were in the habit of considering as hats, flew to the horse-posts, to be ready to "help Mas'r."

Sam's palm-leaf had been ingeniously disentangled from all pretensions to braid, as respects its brim; and the slivers starting apart, and standing upright, gave it a blazing air of freedom and defiance, quite equal to that of any Fejee chief; while the whole brim of Andy's being departed bodily, he rapped the crown on his head with a dexterous thump, and looked about well pleased, as if to say, "Who says I have n't got a hat?"

"Well, boys," said Haley, "look alive now; we must lose no time."

"Not a bit of him, Mas'r!" said Sam, putting Haley's rein

in his hand, and holding his stirrup, while Andy was untying the other two horses.

The instant Haley touched the saddle, the mettlesome creature bounded from the earth with a sudden spring, that threw his master sprawling, some feet off, on the soft, dry turf. Sam, with frantic ejaculations, made a dive at the reins, but only succeeded in brushing the blazing palm-leaf afore-named into the horse's eyes, which by no means tended to allay the confusion of his nerves. So, with great vehemence, he overturned Sam, and, giving two or three contemptuous snorts, flourished his heels vigorously in the air, and was soon prancing away towards the lower end of the lawn, followed by Bill and Jerry, whom Andy had not failed to let loose, according to contract, speeding them off with various direful ejaculations. And now ensued a miscellaneous scene of confusion. Sam and Andy ran and shouted,—dogs barked here and there,—and Mike, Mose, Mandy, Fanny, and all the smaller specimens on the place, both male and female, raced, clapped hands, whooped, and shouted, with outrageous officiousness and untiring zeal.

Haley's horse, which was a white one, and very fleet and spirited, appeared to enter into the spirit of the scene with great gusto; and having for his coursing ground a lawn of nearly half a mile in extent, gently sloping down on every side into indefinite woodland, he appeared to take infinite delight in seeing how near he could allow his pursuers to approach him, and then, when within a hand's breadth, whisk off with a start and a snort, like a mischievous beast as he was, and career far down into some alley of the wood-lot. Nothing was further from Sam's mind than to have any one of the troop taken until such season as should seem to him most befitting,—and the exertions that he made were certainly most heroic. Like the sword of Cœur De Lion, which always blazed in the front and thickest of the battle, Sam's palm-leaf was to be seen everywhere when there was the least danger that a horse could be caught;—there he would bear down full tilt, shouting, "Now for it! cotch him! cotch him!" in a way that would set everything to indiscriminate rout in a moment.

Haley ran up and down, and cursed and swore and

stamped miscellaneously. Mr. Shelby in vain tried to shout directions from the balcony, and Mrs. Shelby from her chamber window alternately laughed and wondered,—not without some inkling of what lay at the bottom of all this confusion.

At last, about twelve o'clock, Sam appeared triumphant, mounted on Jerry, with Haley's horse by his side, reeking with sweat, but with flashing eyes and dilated nostrils, showing that the spirit of freedom had not yet entirely subsided.

"He's cotched!" he exclaimed, triumphantly. "If't hadn't been for me, they might a bust theirselves, all on 'em; but I cotched him!"

"You!" growled Haley, in no amiable mood. "If it hadn't been for you, this never would have happened."

"Lord bless us, Mas'r," said Sam, in a tone of the deepest concern, "and me that has been racin' and chasin' till the sweat jest pours off me!"

"Well, well!" said Haley, "you've lost me near three hours, with your cursed nonsense. Now let's be off, and have no more fooling."

"Why, Mas'r," said Sam, in a deprecating tone, "I believe you mean to kill us all clar, horses and all. Here we are all just ready to drop down, and the critters all in a reek of sweat. Why, Mas'r won't think of startin' on now till arter dinner. Mas'r's hoss wants rubben down; see how he splashed hisself; and Jerry limps too; don't think Missis would be willin' to have us start dis yer way, no how. Lord bless you, Mas'r, we can ketch up, if we do stop. Lizy never was no great of a walker."

Mrs. Shelby, who, greatly to her amusement, had overheard this conversation from the verandah, now resolved to do her part. She came forward, and, courteously expressing her concern for Haley's accident, pressed him to stay to dinner, saying that the cook should bring it on the table immediately.

Thus, all things considered, Haley, with rather an equivocal grace, proceeded to the parlor, while Sam, rolling his eyes after him with unutterable meaning, proceeded gravely with the horses to the stable-yard.

"Did yer see him, Andy? *did* yer see him?" said Sam, when he had got fairly beyond the shelter of the barn, and fastened the horse to a post. "O, Lor, if it warn't as good as a meetin', now, to see him a dancin' and kickin' and swarin' at us. Did n't I hear him? Swar away, ole fellow (says I to myself); will yer have yer hoss now, or wait till you cotch him? (says I). Lor, Andy, I think I can see him now." And Sam and Andy leaned up against the barn, and laughed to their hearts' content.

"Yer oughter seen how mad he looked, when I brought the hoss up. Lord, he 'd a killed me, if he durs' to; and there I was a standin' as innercent and as humble."

"Lor, I seed you," said Andy; "an't you an old hoss, Sam?"

"Rather specks I am," said Sam; "did yer see Missis up stars at the winder? I seed her laughin'."

"I 'm sure, I was racin' so, I did n't see nothing," said Andy.

"Well, yer see," said Sam, proceeding gravely to wash down Haley's pony, "I'se 'quired what yer may call a habit o' *bobservation,* Andy. It 's a very 'portant habit, Andy; and I 'commend yer to be cultivatin' it, now yer young. Hist up that hind foot, Andy. Yer see, Andy, it 's *bobservation* makes all de difference in niggers. Did n't I see which way the wind blew dis yer mornin'? Did n't I see what Missis wanted, though she never let on? Dat ar 's bobservation, Andy. I 'spects it 's what you may call a faculty. Faculties is different in different peoples, but cultivation of 'em goes a great way."

"I guess if I had n't helped your bobservation dis mornin', yer would n't have seen your way so smart," said Andy.

"Andy," said Sam, "you 's a promisin' child, der an't no manner o' doubt. I thinks lots of yer, Andy; and I don't feel no ways ashamed to take idees from you. We oughtenter overlook nobody, Andy, cause the smartest on us gets tripped up sometimes. And so, Andy, let 's go up to the house now. I 'll be boun' Missis 'll give us an uncommon good bite, dis yer time."

VII.

The Mother's Struggle

IT is impossible to conceive of a human creature more wholly desolate and forlorn than Eliza, when she turned her footsteps from Uncle Tom's cabin.

Her husband's suffering and dangers, and the danger of her child, all blended in her mind, with a confused and stunning sense of the risk she was running, in leaving the only home she had ever known, and cutting loose from the protection of a friend whom she loved and revered. Then there was the parting from every familiar object,—the place where she had grown up, the trees under which she had played, the groves where she had walked many an evening in happier days, by the side of her young husband,—everything, as it lay in the clear, frosty starlight, seemed to speak reproachfully to her, and ask her whither could she go from a home like that?

But stronger than all was maternal love, wrought into a paroxysm of frenzy by the near approach of a fearful danger. Her boy was old enough to have walked by her side, and, in an indifferent case, she would only have led him by the hand; but now the bare thought of putting him out of her arms made her shudder, and she strained him to her bosom with a convulsive grasp, as she went rapidly forward.

The frosty ground creaked beneath her feet, and she trembled at the sound; every quaking leaf and fluttering shadow sent the blood backward to her heart, and quickened her footsteps. She wondered within herself at the strength that seemed to be come upon her; for she felt the weight of her boy as if it had been a feather, and every flutter of fear seemed to increase the supernatural power that bore her on, while from her pale lips burst forth, in frequent ejaculations, the prayer to a Friend above—"Lord, help! Lord, save me!"

If it were *your* Harry, mother, or your Willie, that were going to be torn from you by a brutal trader, to-morrow morning,—if you had seen the man, and heard that the pa-

pers were signed and delivered, and you had only from twelve
o'clock till morning to make good your escape,—how fast
could *you* walk? How many miles could you make in those
few brief hours, with the darling at your bosom,—the little
sleepy head on your shoulder,—the small, soft arms trust-
ingly holding on to your neck?

For the child slept. At first, the novelty and alarm kept him
waking; but his mother so hurriedly repressed every breath or
sound, and so assured him that if he were only still she would
certainly save him, that he clung quietly round her neck, only
asking, as he found himself sinking to sleep,

"Mother, I don't need to keep awake, do I?"

"No, my darling; sleep, if you want to."

"But, mother, if I do get asleep, you won't let him get me?"

"No! so may God help me!" said his mother, with a paler
cheek, and a brighter light in her large dark eyes.

"You 're *sure*, an't you, mother?"

"Yes, *sure!*" said the mother, in a voice that startled herself;
for it seemed to her to come from a spirit within, that was no
part of her; and the boy dropped his little weary head on her
shoulder, and was soon asleep. How the touch of those warm
arms, the gentle breathings that came in her neck, seemed to
add fire and spirit to her movements! It seemed to her as if
strength poured into her in electric streams, from every gentle
touch and movement of the sleeping, confiding child. Sublime is the dominion of the mind over the body, that, for a
time, can make flesh and nerve impregnable, and string the
sinews like steel, so that the weak become so mighty.

The boundaries of the farm, the grove, the wood-lot,
passed by her dizzily, as she walked on; and still she went,
leaving one familiar object after another, slacking not, pausing not, till reddening daylight found her many a long mile
from all traces of any familiar objects upon the open highway.

She had often been, with her mistress, to visit some connections, in the little village of T——, not far from the Ohio
river, and knew the road well. To go thither, to escape across
the Ohio river, were the first hurried outlines of her plan of
escape; beyond that, she could only hope in God.

When horses and vehicles began to move along the highway, with that alert perception peculiar to a state of excite-

ment, and which seems to be a sort of inspiration, she became
aware that her headlong pace and distracted air might bring
on her remark and suspicion. She therefore put the boy on
the ground, and, adjusting her dress and bonnet, she walked
on at as rapid a pace as she thought consistent with the preservation of appearances. In her little bundle she had provided
a store of cakes and apples, which she used as expedients for
quickening the speed of the child, rolling the apple some
yards before them, when the boy would run with all his
might after it; and this ruse, often repeated, carried them over
many a half-mile.

After a while, they came to a thick patch of woodland,
through which murmured a clear brook. As the child complained of hunger and thirst, she climbed over the fence with
him; and, sitting down behind a large rock which concealed
them from the road, she gave him a breakfast out of her little
package. The boy wondered and grieved that she could not
eat; and when, putting his arms round her neck, he tried to
wedge some of his cake into her mouth, it seemed to her that
the rising in her throat would choke her.

"No, no, Harry darling! mother can't eat till you are safe!
We must go on—on—till we come to the river!" And she
hurried again into the road, and again constrained herself to
walk regularly and composedly forward.

She was many miles past any neighborhood where she was
personally known. If she should chance to meet any who
knew her, she reflected that the well-known kindness of the
family would be of itself a blind to suspicion, as making it an
unlikely supposition that she could be a fugitive. As she was
also so white as not to be known as of colored lineage, without a critical survey, and her child was white also, it was
much easier for her to pass on unsuspected.

On this presumption, she stopped at noon at a neat farm-
house, to rest herself, and buy some dinner for her child and
self; for, as the danger decreased with the distance, the supernatural tension of the nervous system lessened, and she found
herself both weary and hungry.

The good woman, kindly and gossipping, seemed rather
pleased than otherwise with having somebody come in to talk
with; and accepted, without examination, Eliza's statement,

that she "was going on a little piece, to spend a week with her friends,"—all which she hoped in her heart might prove strictly true.

An hour before sunset, she entered the village of T——, by the Ohio river, weary and foot-sore, but still strong in heart. Her first glance was at the river, which lay, like Jordan, between her and the Canaan of liberty on the other side.

It was now early spring, and the river was swollen and turbulent; great cakes of floating ice were swinging heavily to and fro in the turbid waters. Owing to the peculiar form of the shore on the Kentucky side, the land bending far out into the water, the ice had been lodged and detained in great quantities, and the narrow channel which swept round the bend was full of ice, piled one cake over another, thus forming a temporary barrier to the descending ice, which lodged, and formed a great, undulating raft, filling up the whole river, and extending almost to the Kentucky shore.

Eliza stood, for a moment, contemplating this unfavorable aspect of things, which she saw at once must prevent the usual ferry-boat from running, and then turned into a small public house on the bank, to make a few inquiries.

The hostess, who was busy in various fizzing and stewing operations over the fire, preparatory to the evening meal, stopped, with a fork in her hand, as Eliza's sweet and plaintive voice arrested her.

"What is it?" she said.

"Is n't there any ferry or boat, that takes people over to B——, now?" she said.

"No, indeed!" said the woman; "the boats has stopped running."

Eliza's look of dismay and disappointment struck the woman, and she said, inquiringly,

"May be you 're wanting to get over?—anybody sick? Ye seem mighty anxious?"

"I 've got a child that 's very dangerous," said Eliza. "I never heard of it till last night, and I 've walked quite a piece to-day, in hopes to get to the ferry."

"Well, now, that 's onlucky," said the woman, whose motherly sympathies were much aroused; "I 'm re'lly consarned for ye. Solomon!" she called, from the window, to-

wards a small back building. A man, in leather apron and very dirty hands, appeared at the door.

"I say, Sol," said the woman, "is that ar man going to tote them bar'ls over to-night?"

"He said he should try, if 't was any way prudent," said the man.

"There's a man a piece down here, that's going over with some truck this evening, if he durs' to; he'll be in here to supper to-night, so you'd better set down and wait. That's a sweet little fellow," added the woman, offering him a cake.

But the child, wholly exhausted, cried with weariness.

"Poor fellow! he isn't used to walking, and I've hurried him on so," said Eliza.

"Well, take him into this room," said the woman, opening into a small bed-room, where stood a comfortable bed. Eliza laid the weary boy upon it, and held his hands in hers till he was fast asleep. For her there was no rest. As a fire in her bones, the thought of the pursuer urged her on; and she gazed with longing eyes on the sullen, surging waters that lay between her and liberty.

Here we must take our leave of her for the present, to follow the course of her pursuers.

———

Though Mrs. Shelby had promised that the dinner should be hurried on table, yet it was soon seen, as the thing has often been seen before, that it required more than one to make a bargain. So, although the order was fairly given out in Haley's hearing, and carried to Aunt Chloe by at least half a dozen juvenile messengers, that dignitary only gave certain very gruff snorts, and tosses of her head, and went on with every operation in an unusually leisurely and circumstantial manner.

For some singular reason, an impression seemed to reign among the servants generally that Missis would not be particularly disobliged by delay; and it was wonderful what a number of counter accidents occurred constantly, to retard the course of things. One luckless wight contrived to upset the gravy; and then gravy had to be got up *de novo*, with due care and formality, Aunt Chloe watching and stirring with dogged precision, answering shortly, to all suggestions of haste, that she "warn't a going to have raw gravy on the table, to help nobody's catchings." One tumbled down with the water, and had to go to the spring for more; and another precipitated the butter into the path of events; and there was from time to time giggling news brought into the kitchen that "Mas'r Haley was mighty oneasy, and that he could n't sit in his cheer no ways, but was a walkin' and stalkin' to the winders and through the porch."

"Sarves him right!" said Aunt Chloe, indignantly. "He 'll get wus nor oneasy, one of these days, if he don't mend his ways. *His* master 'll be sending for him, and then see how he 'll look!"

"He 'll go to torment, and no mistake," said little Jake.

"He desarves it!" said Aunt Chloe, grimly; "he 's broke a many, many, many hearts,—I tell ye all!" she said, stopping, with a fork uplifted in her hands; "it 's like what Mas'r George reads in Ravelations,—souls a callin' under the altar! and a callin' on the Lord for vengeance on sich!—and by and by the Lord he 'll hear 'em—so he will!"

Aunt Chloe, who was much revered in the kitchen, was listened to with open mouth; and, the dinner being now fairly sent in, the whole kitchen was at leisure to gossip with her, and to listen to her remarks.

"Sich 'll be burnt up forever, and no mistake; won't ther?" said Andy.

"I 'd be glad to see it, I 'll be boun'," said little Jake.

"Chil'en!" said a voice, that made them all start. It was Uncle Tom, who had come in, and stood listening to the conversation at the door.

"Chil'en!" he said, "I 'm afeard you don't know what ye 're sayin'. Forever is a *dre'ful* word, chil'en; it 's awful to think on 't. You oughtenter wish that ar to any human crittur."

"We would n't to anybody but the soul-drivers," said Andy; "nobody can help wishing it to them, they 's so awful wicked."

"Don't natur herself kinder cry out on em?" said Aunt Chloe. "Don't dey tear der suckin' baby right off his mother's breast, and sell him, and der little children as is crying and holding on by her clothes,—don't dey pull 'em off and sells em? Don't dey tear wife and husband apart?" said Aunt Chloe, beginning to cry, "when it's jest takin' the very life on 'em?—and all the while does they feel one bit,—don't dey drink and smoke, and take it oncommon easy? Lor, if the devil don't get them, what's he good for?" And Aunt Chloe covered her face with her checked apron, and began to sob in good earnest.

"Pray for them that 'spitefully use you, the good book says," says Tom.

"Pray for 'em!" said Aunt Chloe; "Lor, it's too tough! I can't pray for 'em."

"It's natur, Chloe, and natur's strong," said Tom, "but the Lord's grace is stronger; besides, you oughter think what an awful state a poor crittur's soul's in that'll do them ar things,—you oughter thank God that you an't *like* him, Chloe. I'm sure I'd rather be sold, ten thousand times over, than to have all that ar poor crittur's got to answer for."

"So'd I, a heap," said Jake. "Lor, *shouldn't* we cotch it, Andy?"

Andy shrugged his shoulders, and gave an acquiescent whistle.

"I'm glad Mas'r didn't go off this morning, as he looked to," said Tom; "that ar hurt me more than sellin', it did. Mebbe it might have been natural for him, but 't would have come desp't hard on me, as has known him from a baby; but I've seen Mas'r, and I begin ter feel sort o' reconciled to the Lord's will now. Mas'r couldn't help hisself; he did right, but I'm feared things will be kinder goin' to rack, when I'm gone. Mas'r can't be spected to be a pryin' round everywhar, as I've done, a keepin' up all the ends. The boys all means well, but they's powerful car'less. That ar troubles me."

The bell here rang, and Tom was summoned to the parlor.

"Tom," said his master, kindly, "I want you to notice that I give this gentleman bonds to forfeit a thousand dollars if you are not on the spot when he wants you; he's going to-day to look after his other business, and you can have the day to yourself. Go anywhere you like, boy."

"Thank you, Mas'r," said Tom.

"And mind yerself," said the trader, "and don't come it over your master with any o' yer nigger tricks; for I'll take every cent out of him, if you an't thar. If he'd hear to me, he would n't trust any on ye—slippery as eels!"

"Mas'r," said Tom,—and he stood very straight,—"I was jist eight years old when ole Missis put you into my arms, and you was n't a year old. 'Thar,' says she, 'Tom, that's to be *your* young Mas'r; take good care on him,' says she. And now I jist ask you, Mas'r, have I ever broke word to you, or gone contrary to you, 'specially since I was a Christian?"

Mr. Shelby was fairly overcome, and the tears rose to his eyes.

"My good boy," said he, "the Lord knows you say but the truth; and if I was able to help it, all the world should n't buy you."

"And sure as I am a Christian woman," said Mrs. Shelby, "you shall be redeemed as soon as I can any way bring together means. Sir," she said to Haley, "take good account of who you sell him to, and let me know."

"Lor, yes, for that matter," said the trader, "I may bring him up in a year, not much the wuss for wear, and trade him back."

"I'll trade with you then, and make it for your advantage," said Mrs. Shelby.

"Of course," said the trader, "all's equal with me; li'ves trade 'em up as down, so I does a good business. All I want is a livin', you know, ma'am; that's all any on us wants, I s'pose."

Mr. and Mrs. Shelby both felt annoyed and degraded by the familiar impudence of the trader, and yet both saw the absolute necessity of putting a constraint on their feelings. The more hopelessly sordid and insensible he appeared, the greater became Mrs. Shelby's dread of his succeeding in re-capturing Eliza and her child, and of course the greater her motive for detaining him by every female artifice. She there-fore graciously smiled, assented, chatted familiarly, and did all she could to make time pass imperceptibly.

At two o'clock Sam and Andy brought the horses up to the posts, apparently greatly refreshed and invigorated by the scamper of the morning.

Sam was there new oiled from dinner, with an abundance

of zealous and ready officiousness. As Haley approached, he was boasting, in flourishing style, to Andy, of the evident and eminent success of the operation, now that he had "farly come to it."

"Your master, I s'pose, don't keep no dogs," said Haley, thoughtfully, as he prepared to mount.

"Heaps on 'em," said Sam, triumphantly; "thar 's Bruno — he 's a roarer! and, besides that, 'bout every nigger of us keeps a pup of some natur or uther."

"Poh!" said Haley, — and he said something else, too, with regard to the said dogs, at which Sam muttered,

"I don't see no use cussin' on 'em, no way."

"But your master don't keep no dogs (I pretty much know he don't) for trackin' out niggers."

Sam knew exactly what he meant, but he kept on a look of earnest and desperate simplicity.

"Our dogs all smells round considable sharp. I spect they 's the kind, though they han't never had no practice. They 's *far* dogs, though, at most anything, if you 'd get 'em started. Here, Bruno," he called, whistling to the lumbering Newfoundland, who came pitching tumultuously toward them.

"You go hang!" said Haley, getting up. "Come, tumble up now."

Sam tumbled up accordingly, dexterously contriving to tickle Andy as he did so, which occasioned Andy to split out into a laugh, greatly to Haley's indignation, who made a cut at him with his riding-whip.

"I 's 'stonished at yer, Andy," said Sam, with awful gravity. "This yer 's a seris bisness, Andy. Yer must n't be a makin' game. This yer an't no way to help Mas'r."

"I shall take the straight road to the river," said Haley, decidedly, after they had come to the boundaries of the estate. "I know the way of all of 'em, — they makes tracks for the underground."

"Sartin," said Sam, "dat 's de idee. Mas'r Haley hits de thing right in de middle. Now, der 's two roads to de river, — de dirt road and der pike, — which Mas'r mean to take?"

Andy looked up innocently at Sam, surprised at hearing this new geographical fact, but instantly confirmed what he said, by a vehement reiteration.

"Cause," said Sam, "I'd rather be 'clined to 'magine that Lizy'd take de dirt road, bein' it's the least travelled."

Haley, notwithstanding that he was a very old bird, and naturally inclined to be suspicious of chaff, was rather brought up by this view of the case.

"If yer warn't both on yer such cussed liars, now!" he said, contemplatively, as he pondered a moment.

The pensive, reflective tone in which this was spoken appeared to amuse Andy prodigiously, and he drew a little behind, and shook so as apparently to run a great risk of falling off his horse, while Sam's face was immovably composed into the most doleful gravity.

"Course," said Sam, "Mas'r can do as he'd ruther; go de straight road, if Mas'r thinks best,—it's all one to us. Now, when I study 'pon it, I think de straight road de best, *deridedly*."

"She would naturally go a lonesome way," said Haley, thinking aloud, and not minding Sam's remark.

"Dar an't no sayin'," said Sam; "gals is pecular; they never does nothin' ye thinks they will; mose gen'lly the contrar. Gals is nat'lly made contrary; and so, if you thinks they've gone one road, it is sartin you'd better go t' other, and then you'll be sure to find 'em. Now, my private 'pinion is, Lizy took der dirt road; so I think we'd better take de straight one."

This profound generic view of the female sex did not seem to dispose Haley particularly to the straight road; and he announced decidedly that he should go the other, and asked Sam when they should come to it.

"A little piece ahead," said Sam, giving a wink to Andy with the eye which was on Andy's side of the head; and he added, gravely, "but I've studded on de matter, and I'm quite clar we ought not to go dat ar way. I nebber been over it no way. It's despit lonesome, and we might lose our way,—whar we'd come to, de Lord only knows."

"Nevertheless," said Haley, "I shall go that way."

"Now I think on 't, I think I hearn 'em tell that dat ar road was all fenced up and down by der creek, and thar, an't it, Andy?"

Andy was n't certain; he 'd only "hearn tell" about that road, but never been over it. In short, he was strictly noncommittal.

Haley, accustomed to strike the balance of probabilities between lies of greater or lesser magnitude, thought that it lay in favor of the dirt road aforesaid. The mention of the thing he thought he perceived was involuntary on Sam's part at first, and his confused attempts to dissuade him he set down to a desperate lying on second thoughts, as being unwilling to implicate Eliza.

When, therefore, Sam indicated the road, Haley plunged briskly into it, followed by Sam and Andy.

Now, the road, in fact, was an old one, that had formerly been a thoroughfare to the river, but abandoned for many years after the laying of the new pike. It was open for about an hour's ride, and after that it was cut across by various farms and fences. Sam knew this fact perfectly well,—indeed, the road had been so long closed up, that Andy had never heard of it. He therefore rode along with an air of dutiful submission, only groaning and vociferating occasionally that 't was "desp't rough, and bad for Jerry's foot."

"Now, I jest give yer warning," said Haley, "I know yer; yer won't get me to turn off this yer road, with all yer fussin'—so you shet up!"

"Mas'r will go his own way!" said Sam, with rueful submission, at the same time winking most portentously to Andy, whose delight was now very near the explosive point.

Sam was in wonderful spirits,—professed to keep a very brisk look-out,—at one time exclaiming that he saw "a gal's bonnet" on the top of some distant eminence, or calling to Andy "if that thar was n't 'Lizy' down in the hollow;" always making these exclamations in some rough or craggy part of the road, where the sudden quickening of speed was a special inconvenience to all parties concerned, and thus keeping Haley in a state of constant commotion.

After riding about an hour in this way, the whole party made a precipitate and tumultuous descent into a barn-yard belonging to a large farming establishment. Not a soul was in sight, all the hands being employed in the fields; but, as the

barn stood conspicuously and plainly square across the road,
it was evident that their journey in that direction had reached
a decided finale.

"Wan't dat ar what I telled Mas'r?" said Sam, with an air
of injured innocence. "How does strange gentleman spect to
know more about a country dan de natives born and raised?"

"You rascal!" said Haley, "you knew all about this."

"Did n't I tell yer I *know'd*, and yer would n't believe me?
I telled Mas'r 't was all shet up, and fenced up, and I did n't
spect we could get through,—Andy heard me."

It was all too true to be disputed, and the unlucky man had
to pocket his wrath with the best grace he was able, and all
three faced to the right about, and took up their line of march
for the highway.

In consequence of all the various delays, it was about three-
quarters of an hour after Eliza had laid her child to sleep in
the village tavern that the party came riding into the same
place. Eliza was standing by the window, looking out in another direction, when Sam's quick eye caught a glimpse of
her. Haley and Andy were two yards behind. At this crisis,
Sam contrived to have his hat blown off, and uttered a loud
and characteristic ejaculation, which startled her at once; she
drew suddenly back; the whole train swept by the window,
round to the front door.

A thousand lives seemed to be concentrated in that one
moment to Eliza. Her room opened by a side door to the
river. She caught her child, and sprang down the steps towards it. The trader caught a full glimpse of her, just as she
was disappearing down the bank; and throwing himself from
his horse, and calling loudly on Sam and Andy, he was after
her like a hound after a deer. In that dizzy moment her feet
to her scarce seemed to touch the ground, and a moment
brought her to the water's edge. Right on behind they came;
and, nerved with strength such as God gives only to the desperate, with one wild cry and flying leap, she vaulted sheer
over the turbid current by the shore, on to the raft of ice
beyond. It was a desperate leap—impossible to anything but
madness and despair; and Haley, Sam, and Andy, instinctively
cried out, and lifted up their hands, as she did it.

The huge green fragment of ice on which she alighted

pitched and creaked as her weight came on it, but she staid there not a moment. With wild cries and desperate energy she leaped to another and still another cake;—stumbling—leaping—slipping—springing upwards again! Her shoes are gone—her stockings cut from her feet—while blood marked every step; but she saw nothing, felt nothing, till dimly, as in a dream, she saw the Ohio side, and a man helping her up the bank.

"Yer a brave gal, now, whoever ye ar!" said the man, with an oath.

Eliza recognized the voice and face of a man who owned a farm not far from her old home.

"O, Mr. Symmes!—save me—do save me—do hide me!" said Eliza.

"Why, what 's this?" said the man. "Why, if 'tan't Shelby's gal!"

"My child!—this boy!—he 'd sold him! There is his Mas'r," said she, pointing to the Kentucky shore. "O, Mr. Symmes, you 've got a little boy!"

"So I have," said the man, as he roughly, but kindly, drew her up the steep bank. "Besides, you 're a right brave gal. I like grit, wherever I see it."

When they had gained the top of the bank, the man paused.

"I 'd be glad to do something for ye," said he; "but then there 's nowhar I could take ye. The best I can do is to tell ye to go *thar*," said he, pointing to a large white house which stood by itself, off the main street of the village. "Go thar; they 're kind folks. Thar 's no kind o' danger but they 'll help you,—they 're up to all that sort o' thing."

"The Lord bless you!" said Eliza, earnestly.

"No 'casion, no 'casion in the world," said the man. "What I 've done 's of no 'count."

"And, oh, surely, sir, you won't tell any one!"

"Go to thunder, gal! What do you take a feller for? In course not," said the man. "Come, now, go along like a likely, sensible gal, as you are. You 've arnt your liberty, and you shall have it, for all me."

The woman folded her child to her bosom, and walked firmly and swiftly away. The man stood and looked after her.

"Shelby, now, mebbe won't think this yer the most neighborly thing in the world; but what 's a feller to do? If he catches one of my gals in the same fix, he 's welcome to pay back. Somehow I never could see no kind o' critter a strivin' and pantin', and trying to clar theirselves, with the dogs arter 'em, and go agin 'em. Besides, I don't see no kind of 'casion for me to be hunter and catcher for other folks, neither."

So spoke this poor, heathenish Kentuckian, who had not been instructed in his constitutional relations, and consequently was betrayed into acting in a sort of Christianized manner, which, if he had been better situated and more enlightened, he would not have been left to do.

Haley had stood a perfectly amazed spectator of the scene, till Eliza had disappeared up the bank, when he turned a blank, inquiring look on Sam and Andy.

"That ar was a tolable fair stroke of business," said Sam.

"The gal 's got seven devils in her, I believe!" said Haley. "How like a wildcat she jumped!"

"Wal, now," said Sam, scratching his head, "I hope Mas'r 'll 'scuse us tryin' dat ar road. Don't think I feel spry enough for dat ar, no way!" and Sam gave a hoarse chuckle.

"*You* laugh!" said the trader, with a growl.

"Lord bless you, Mas'r, I could n't help it, now," said Sam, giving way to the long pent-up delight of his soul. "She looked so curi's, a leapin' and springin'—ice a crackin'—and only to hear her,—plump! ker chunk! ker splash! Spring! Lord! how she goes it!" and Sam and Andy laughed till the tears rolled down their cheeks.

"I 'll make ye laugh t' other side yer mouths!" said the trader, laying about their heads with his riding-whip.

Both ducked, and ran shouting up the bank, and were on their horses before he was up.

"Good-evening, Mas'r!" said Sam, with much gravity. "I berry much spect Missis be anxious 'bout Jerry. Mas'r Haley won't want us no longer. Missis would n't hear of our ridin' the critters over Lizy's bridge to-night;" and, with a facetious poke into Andy's ribs, he started off, followed by the latter, at full speed,—their shouts of laughter coming faintly on the wind.

VIII.

Eliza's Escape

Eliza made her desperate retreat across the river just in the dusk of twilight. The gray mist of evening, rising slowly from the river, enveloped her as she disappeared up the bank, and the swollen current and floundering masses of ice presented a hopeless barrier between her and her pursuer. Haley therefore slowly and discontentedly returned to the little tavern, to ponder further what was to be done. The woman opened to him the door of a little parlor, covered with a rag carpet, where stood a table with a very shining black oil-cloth, sundry lank, high-backed wood chairs, with some plaster images in resplendent colors on the mantel-shelf, above a very dimly-smoking grate; a long hard-wood settle extended its uneasy length by the chimney, and here Haley sat him down to meditate on the instability of human hopes and happiness in general.

"What did I want with the little cuss, now," he said to himself, "that I should have got myself treed like a coon, as I am, this yer way?" and Haley relieved himself by repeating over a not very select litany of imprecations on himself, which, though there was the best possible reason to consider them as true, we shall, as a matter of taste, omit.

He was startled by the loud and dissonant voice of a man who was apparently dismounting at the door. He hurried to the window.

"By the land! if this yer an't the nearest, now, to what I 've heard folks call Providence," said Haley. "I do b'lieve that ar 's Tom Loker."

Haley hastened out. Standing by the bar, in the corner of the room, was a brawny, muscular man, full six feet in height, and broad in proportion. He was dressed in a coat of buffalo-skin, made with the hair outward, which gave him a shaggy and fierce appearance, perfectly in keeping with the whole air of his physiognomy. In the head and face every organ and lineament expressive of brutal and unhesitating violence was in a state of the highest possible development. Indeed, could our readers fancy a bull-dog come unto man's estate, and walking about in a hat and coat, they would have no unapt idea of the general style and effect of his physique. He was accompanied by a travelling companion, in many respects an exact contrast to himself. He was short and slender, lithe and cat-like in his motions, and had a peering, mousing expression about his keen black eyes, with which every feature of his face seemed sharpened into sympathy; his thin, long nose, ran out as if it was eager to bore into the nature of things in general; his sleek, thin, black hair was stuck eagerly forward, and all his motions and evolutions expressed a dry, cautious acuteness. The great big man poured out a big tumbler half full of raw spirits, and gulped it down without a word. The little man stood tip-toe, and putting his head first to one side and then to the other, and snuffing considerately in the directions of the various bottles, ordered at last a mint julep, in a thin and quivering voice, and with an air of great circumspection. When poured out, he took it and looked at it with a sharp, complacent air, like a man who thinks he has done about the right thing, and hit the nail on the head, and proceeded to dispose of it in short and well-advised sips.

"Wal, now, who 'd a thought this yer luck 'ad come to me? Why, Loker, how are ye?" said Haley, coming forward, and extending his hand to the big man.

"The devil!" was the civil reply. "What brought you here, Haley?"

The mousing man, who bore the name of Marks, instantly stopped his sipping, and, poking his head forward, looked shrewdly on the new acquaintance, as a cat sometimes looks at a moving dry leaf, or some other possible object of pursuit.

"I say, Tom, this yer 's the luckiest thing in the world. I 'm in a devil of a hobble, and you must help me out."

"Ugh? aw! like enough!" grunted his complacent acquaintance. "A body may be pretty sure of that, when *you 're* glad to see 'em; something to be made off of 'em. What 's the blow now?"

"You 've got a friend here?" said Haley, looking doubtfully at Marks; "partner, perhaps?"

"Yes, I have. Here, Marks! here 's that ar feller that I was in with in Natchez."

"Shall be pleased with his acquaintance," said Marks, thrusting out a long, thin hand, like a raven's claw. "Mr. Haley, I believe?"

"The same, sir," said Haley. "And now, gentlemen, seein' as we 've met so happily, I think I 'll stand up to a small matter of a treat in this here parlor. So, now, old coon," said he to the man at the bar, "get us hot water, and sugar, and cigars, and plenty of the *real stuff*, and we 'll have a blow-out."

Behold, then, the candles lighted, the fire stimulated to the burning point in the grate, and our three worthies seated round a table, well spread with all the accessories to good fellowship enumerated before.

Haley began a pathetic recital of his peculiar troubles. Loker shut up his mouth, and listened to him with gruff and surly attention. Marks, who was anxiously and with much fidgeting compounding a tumbler of punch to his own peculiar taste, occasionally looked up from his employment, and, poking his sharp nose and chin almost into Haley's face, gave the most earnest heed to the whole narrative. The conclusion of it appeared to amuse him extremely, for he shook his shoulders and sides in silence, and perked up his thin lips with an air of great internal enjoyment.

"So, then, ye 'r fairly sewed up, an't ye?" he said; "he! he! he! It 's neatly done, too."

"This yer young-un business makes lots of trouble in the trade," said Haley, dolefully.

"If we could get a breed of gals that did n't care, now, for their young uns," said Marks; "tell ye, I think 't would be 'bout the greatest mod'rn improvement I knows on,"—and Marks patronized his joke by a quiet introductory sniggle.

"Jes so," said Haley; "I never could n't see into it; young uns is heaps of trouble to 'em; one would think, now, they 'd be glad to get clar on 'em; but they arn't. And the more trouble a young un is, and the more good for nothing, as a gen'l thing, the tighter they sticks to 'em."

"Wal, Mr. Haley," said Marks, "jest pass the hot water. Yes, sir; you say jest what I feel and all'us have. Now, I bought a gal once, when I was in the trade,—a tight, likely wench she was, too, and quite considerable smart,—and she had a young un that was mis'able sickly; it had a crooked back, or something or other; and I jest gin 't away to a man that thought he 'd take his chance raising on 't, being it did n't cost nothin';—never thought, yer know, of the gal's takin' on about it,—but, Lord, yer oughter seen how she went on. Why, re'lly, she did seem to me to valley the child more 'cause *'t was* sickly and cross, and plagued her; and she warn't making b'lieve, neither,—cried about it, she did, and lopped round, as if she 'd lost every friend she had. It re'lly was droll to think on 't. Lord, there an't no end to women's notions."

"Wal, jest so with me," said Haley. "Last summer, down on Red river, I got a gal traded off on me, with a likely lookin' child enough, and his eyes looked as bright as yourn; but, come to look, I found him stone blind. Fact—he was stone blind. Wal, ye see, I thought there warn't no harm in my jest passing him along, and not sayin' nothin'; and I 'd got him nicely swapped off for a keg o' whiskey; but come to get him away from the gal, she was jest like a tiger. So 't was before we started, and I had n't got my gang chained up; so what should she do but ups on a cotton-bale, like a cat, ketches a knife from one of the deck hands, and, I tell ye, she made all fly for a minit, till she saw 'twan't no use; and she jest turns round, and pitches head first, young un and all, into the river,—went down plump, and never ris."

"Bah!" said Tom Loker, who had listened to these stories with ill-repressed disgust,—"shif'less, both on ye! *my* gals don't cut up no such shines, I tell ye!"

"Indeed! how do you help it?" said Marks, briskly.

"Help it? why, I buys a gal, and if she 's got a young un to be sold, I jest walks up and puts my fist to her face, and says, 'Look here, now, if you give me one word out of your head, I 'll smash yer face in. I won't hear one word—not the beginning of a word.' I says to 'em, 'This yer young un 's mine, and not yourn, and you 've no kind o' business with it. I 'm going to sell it, first chance; mind, you don't cut up none o' yer shines about it, or I 'll make ye wish ye 'd never been born.' I tell ye, they sees it an't no play, when I gets hold. I makes 'em as whist as fishes; and if one on 'em begins and gives a yelp, why,—" and Mr. Loker brought down his fist with a thump that fully explained the hiatus.

"That ar 's what ye may call *emphasis*," said Marks, poking Haley in the side, and going into another small giggle. "An't Tom peculiar? he! he! he! I say, Tom, I s'pect you make 'em *understand*, for all niggers' heads is woolly. They don't never have no doubt o' your meaning, Tom. If you an't the devil, Tom, you 's his twin brother, I 'll say that for ye!"

Tom received the compliment with becoming modesty, and began to look as affable as was consistent, as John Bunyan says, "with his doggish nature."

Haley, who had been imbibing very freely of the staple of the evening, began to feel a sensible elevation and enlargement of his moral faculties,—a phenomenon not unusual with gentlemen of a serious and reflective turn, under similar circumstances.

"Wal, now, Tom," he said, "ye re'lly is too bad, as I al'ays have told ye; ye know, Tom, you and I used to talk over these yer matters down in Natchez, and I used to prove to ye that we made full as much, and was as well off for this yer world, by treatin' on 'em well, besides keepin' a better chance for comin' in the kingdom at last, when wust comes to wust, and thar an't nothing else left to get, ye know."

"Boh!" said Tom, "*don't* I know?—don't make me too sick with any yer stuff,—my stomach is a leetle riled now;" and Tom drank half a glass of raw brandy.

"I say," said Haley, and leaning back in his chair and gesturing impressively, "I 'll say this now, I al'ays meant to drive my trade so as to make money on 't, *fust and foremost*, as much as any man; but, then, trade an't everything, and money an't everything, 'cause we 's all got souls. I don't care, now, who hears me say it,—and I think a cussed sight on it,—so I may as well come out with it. I b'lieve in religion, and one of these days, when I 've got matters tight and snug, I calculates to tend to my soul and them ar matters; and so what 's the use of doin' any more wickedness than 's re'lly necessary?—it don't seem to me it 's 't all prudent."

"Tend to yer soul!" repeated Tom, contemptuously; "take

a bright look-out to find a soul in you,—save yourself any care on that score. If the devil sifts you through a hair sieve, he won't find one."

"Why, Tom, you 're cross," said Haley; "why can 't ye take it pleasant, now, when a feller 's talking for your good?"

"Stop that ar jaw o' yourn, there," said Tom, gruffly. "I can stand most any talk o' yourn but your pious talk,—that kills me right up. After all, what 's the odds between me and you? 'Tan't that you care one bit more, or have a bit more feelin',—it 's clean, sheer, dog meanness, wanting to cheat the devil and save your own skin; don't I see through it? And your 'gettin' religion,' as you call it, arter all, is too p'isin mean for any crittur;—run up a bill with the devil all your life, and then sneak out when pay time comes! Boh!"

"Come, come, gentlemen, I say; this is n't business," said Marks. "There 's different ways, you know, of looking at all subjects. Mr. Haley is a very nice man, no doubt, and has his own conscience; and, Tom, you have your ways, and very good ones, too, Tom; but quarrelling, you know, won't answer no kind of purpose. Let 's go to business. Now, Mr. Haley, what is it?—you want us to undertake to catch this yer gal?"

"The gal 's no matter of mine,—she 's Shelby's; it 's only the boy. I was a fool for buying the monkey!"

"You 're generally a fool!" said Tom, gruffly.

"Come, now, Loker, none of your huffs," said Marks, licking his lips; "you see, Mr. Haley 's a puttin' us in a way of a good job, I reckon; just hold still,—these yer arrangements is my forte. This yer gal, Mr. Haley, how is she? what is she?"

"Wal! white and handsome—well brought up. I 'd a gin Shelby eight hundred or a thousand, and then made well on her."

"White and handsome—well brought up!" said Marks, his sharp eyes, nose and mouth, all alive with enterprise. "Look here, now, Loker, a beautiful opening. We 'll do a business here on our own account;—we does the catchin'; the boy, of course, goes to Mr. Haley,—we takes the gal to Orleans to speculate on. An't it beautiful?"

Tom, whose great heavy mouth had stood ajar during this communication, now suddenly snapped it together, as a big dog closes on a piece of meat, and seemed to be digesting the idea at his leisure.

"Ye see," said Marks to Haley, stirring his punch as he did so, "ye see, we has justices convenient at all p'ints along shore, that does up any little jobs in our line quite reasonable. Tom, he does the knockin' down and that ar; and I come in all dressed up—shining boots—everything first chop, when the swearin' 's to be done. You oughter see, now," said Marks, in a glow of professional pride, "how I can tone it off. One day, I 'm Mr. Twickem, from New Orleans; 'nother day, I 'm just come from my plantation on Pearl river, where I works seven hundred niggers; then, again, I come out a distant relation of Henry Clay, or some old cock in Kentuck. Talents is different, you know. Now, Tom 's a roarer when there 's any thumping or fighting to be done; but at lying he an't good, Tom an't,—ye see it don't come natural to him; but, Lord, if thar 's a feller in the country that can swear to anything and everything, and put in all the circumstances and flourishes with a longer face, and carry 't through better 'n I can, why, I 'd like to see him, that 's all! I b'lieve my heart, I could get along and snake through, even if justices were more particular than they is. Sometimes I rather wish they was more particular; 't would be a heap more relishin' if they was,—more fun, yer know."

Tom Loker, who, as we have made it appear, was a man of slow thoughts and movements, here interrupted Marks by bringing his heavy fist down on the table, so as to make all ring again. *"It 'll do!"* he said.

"Lord bless ye, Tom, ye need n't break all the glasses!" said Marks; "save your fist for time o' need."

"But, gentlemen, an't I to come in for a share of the profits?" said Haley.

"An't it enough we catch the boy for ye?" said Loker. "What do ye want?"

"Wal," said Haley, "if I gives you the job, it 's worth something,—say ten per cent. on the profits, expenses paid."

"Now," said Loker, with a tremendous oath, and striking the table with his heavy fist, "don't I know *you*, Dan Haley? Don't you think to come it over me! Suppose Marks and I have taken up the catchin' trade, jest to 'commodate gentle-

men like you, and get nothin' for ourselves?—Not by a long
chalk! we 'll have the gal out and out, and you keep quiet, or,
ye see, we 'll have both,—what 's to hinder? Han't you
show'd us the game? It 's as free to us as you, I hope. If you
or Shelby wants to chase us, look where the partridges was
last year; if you find them or us, you 're quite welcome."

"O, wal, certainly, jest let it go at that," said Haley,
alarmed; "you catch the boy for the job;—you allers did trade
far with me, Tom, and was up to yer word."

"Ye know that," said Tom; "I don't pretend none of your
snivelling ways, but I won't lie in my 'counts with the devil
himself. What I ses I 'll do, I will do,—you know *that,* Dan
Haley."

"Jes so, jes so,—I said so, Tom," said Haley; "and if you 'd
only promise to have the boy for me in a week, at any point
you 'll name, that 's all I want."

"But it an't all I want, by a long jump," said Tom. "Ye
don't think I did business with you, down in Natchez, for
nothing, Haley; I 've learned to hold an eel, when I catch
him. You 've got to fork over fifty dollars, flat down, or this
child don't start a peg. I know yer."

"Why, when you have a job in hand that may bring a clean
profit of somewhere about a thousand or sixteen hundred,
why, Tom, you 're onreasonable," said Haley.

"Yes, and has n't we business booked for five weeks to
come,—all we can do? And suppose we leaves all, and goes
to bushwhacking round arter yer young un, and finally
does n't catch the gal,—and gals allers is the devil *to* catch,—
what 's then? would you pay us a cent—would you? I think
I see you a doin' it—ugh! No, no; flap down your fifty. If
we get the job, and it pays, I 'll hand it back; if we don't, it 's
for our trouble,—that 's *far,* an't it, Marks?"

"Certainly, certainly," said Marks, with a conciliatory tone;
"it 's only a retaining fee, you see,—he! he! he!—we lawyers,
you know. Wal, we must all keep good-natured,—keep easy,
yer know. Tom 'll have the boy for yer, anywhere ye 'll name;
won't ye, Tom?"

"If I find the young un, I 'll bring him on to Cincinnati,
and leave him at Granny Belcher's, on the landing," said Loker.

Marks had got from his pocket a greasy pocket-book, and

taking a long paper from thence, he sat down, and fixing his keen black eyes on it, began mumbling over its contents: "Barnes—Shelby County—boy Jim, three hundred dollars for him, dead or alive.

"Edwards—Dick and Lucy—man and wife, six hundred dollars; wench Polly and two children—six hundred for her or her head.

"I 'm jest a runnin' over our business, to see if we can take up this yer handily. Loker," he said, after a pause, "we must set Adams and Springer on the track of these yer; they 've been booked some time."

"They 'll charge too much," said Tom.

"I 'll manage that ar; they 's young in the business, and must spect to work cheap," said Marks, as he continued to read. "Ther 's three on 'em easy cases, 'cause all you 've got to do is to shoot 'em, or swear they is shot; they could n't, of course, charge much for that. Them other cases," he said, folding the paper, "will bear puttin' off a spell. So now let 's come to the particulars. Now, Mr. Haley, you saw this yer gal when she landed?"

"To be sure,—plain as I see you."

"And a man helpin' on her up the bank?" said Loker.

"To be sure, I did."

"Most likely," said Marks, "she 's took in somewhere; but where, 's a question. Tom, what do you say?"

"We must cross the river to-night, no mistake," said Tom.

"But there 's no boat about," said Marks. "The ice is running awfully, Tom; an't it dangerous?"

"Don'no nothing 'bout that,—only it 's got to be done," said Tom, decidedly.

"Dear me," said Marks, fidgeting, "it 'll be—I say," he said, walking to the window, "it 's dark as a wolf's mouth, and, Tom—"

"The long and short is, you 're scared, Marks; but I can't help that,—you 've got to go. Suppose you want to lie by a day or two, till the gal 's been carried on the underground line up to Sandusky or so, before you start."

"O, no; I an't a grain afraid," said Marks, "only—"

"Only what?" said Tom.

"Well, about the boat. Yer see there an't any boat."

"I heard the woman say there was one coming along this evening, and that a man was going to cross over in it. Neck or nothing, we must go with him," said Tom.

"I s'pose you 've got good dogs," said Haley.

"First rate," said Marks. "But what 's the use? you han't got nothin' o' hers to smell on."

"Yes, I have," said Haley, triumphantly. "Here 's her shawl she left on the bed in her hurry; she left her bonnet, too."

"That ar 's lucky," said Loker; "fork over."

"Though the dogs might damage the gal, if they come on her unawars," said Haley.

"That ar 's a consideration," said Marks. "Our dogs tore a feller half to pieces, once, down in Mobile, 'fore we could get 'em off."

"Well, ye see, for this sort that 's to be sold for their looks, that ar won't answer, ye see," said Haley.

"I do see," said Marks. "Besides, if she 's got took in, 'tan't no go, neither. Dogs is no 'count in these yer up states where these critters gets carried; of course, ye can't get on their track. They only does down in plantations, where niggers, when they runs, has to do their own running, and don't get no help."

"Well," said Loker, who had just stepped out to the bar to make some inquiries, "they say the man 's come with the boat; so, Marks—"

That worthy cast a rueful look at the comfortable quarters he was leaving, but slowly rose to obey. After exchanging a few words of further arrangement, Haley, with visible reluctance, handed over the fifty dollars to Tom, and the worthy trio separated for the night.

If any of our refined and Christian readers object to the society into which this scene introduces them, let us beg them to begin and conquer their prejudices in time. The catching business, we beg to remind them, is rising to the dignity of a lawful and patriotic profession. If all the broad land between the Mississippi and the Pacific becomes one great market for bodies and souls, and human property retains the locomotive tendencies of this nineteenth century, the trader and catcher may yet be among our aristocracy.

While this scene was going on at the tavern, Sam and Andy, in a state of high felicitation, pursued their way home.

Sam was in the highest possible feather, and expressed his exultation by all sorts of supernatural howls and ejaculations, by divers odd motions and contortions of his whole system. Sometimes he would sit backward, with his face to the horse's tail and sides, and then, with a whoop and a somerset, come right side up in his place again, and, drawing on a grave face, begin to lecture Andy in high-sounding tones for laughing and playing the fool. Anon, slapping his sides with his arms, he would burst forth in peals of laughter, that made the old woods ring as they passed. With all these evolutions, he contrived to keep the horses up to the top of their speed, until, between ten and eleven, their heels resounded on the gravel at the end of the balcony. Mrs. Shelby flew to the railings.

"Is that you, Sam? Where are they?"

"Mas 'r Haley's a-restin' at the tavern; he 's drefful fatigued, Missis."

"And Eliza, Sam?"

"Wal, she 's clar 'cross Jordan. As a body may say, in the land o' Canaan."

"Why, Sam, what *do* you mean?" said Mrs. Shelby, breathless, and almost faint, as the possible meaning of these words came over her.

"Wal, Missis, de Lord he persarves his own. Lizy 's done gone over the river into 'Hio, as 'markably as if de Lord took her over in a charrit of fire and two hosses."

Sam's vein of piety was always uncommonly fervent in his mistress' presence; and he made great capital of scriptural figures and images.

"Come up here, Sam," said Mr. Shelby, who had followed on to the verandah, "and tell your mistress what she wants. Come, come, Emily," said he, passing his arm round her, "you are cold and all in a shiver; you allow yourself to feel too much."

"Feel too much! Am not I a woman,—a mother? Are we not both responsible to God for this poor girl? My God! lay not this sin to our charge."

"What sin, Emily? You see yourself that we have only done what we were obliged to."

"There's an awful feeling of guilt about it, though," said Mrs. Shelby. "I can't reason it away."

"Here, Andy, you nigger, be alive!" called Sam, under the verandah; "take these yer hosses to der barn; don't ye hear Mas'r a callin'?" and Sam soon appeared, palm-leaf in hand, at the parlor door.

"Now, Sam, tell us distinctly how the matter was," said Mr. Shelby. "Where is Eliza, if you know?"

"Wal, Mas'r, I saw her, with my own eyes, a crossin' on the floatin' ice. She crossed most 'markably; it was n't no less nor a miracle; and I saw a man help her up the 'Hio side, and then she was lost in the dusk."

"Sam, I think this rather apocryphal,—this miracle. Crossing on floating ice is n't so easily done," said Mr. Shelby.

"Easy! could n't nobody a done it, widout de Lord. Why, now," said Sam, " 't was jist dis yer way. Mas'r Haley, and me, and Andy, we comes up to de little tavern by the river, and I rides a leetle ahead,—(I 's so zealous to be a cotchin' Lizy, that I could n't hold in, no way),—and when I comes by the tavern winder, sure enough there she was, right in plain sight, and dey diggin' on behind. Wal, I loses off my hat, and sings out nuff to raise the dead. Course Lizy she hars, and she dodges back, when Mas'r Haley he goes past the door; and then, I tell ye, she clared out de side door; she went down de river bank;—Mas'r Haley he seed her, and yelled out, and him, and me, and Andy, we took arter. Down she come to the river, and thar was the current running ten feet wide by the shore, and over t' other side ice a sawin' and a jiggling up and down, kinder as 't were a great island. We come right behind her, and I thought my soul he 'd got her sure enough,—when she gin sich a screech as I never hearn, and thar she was, clar over t' other side the current, on the ice, and then on she went, a screeching and a jumpin',—the ice went crack! c'wallop! cracking! chunk! and she a boundin' like a buck! Lord, the spring that ar gal 's got in her an't common, I 'm o' 'pinion."

Mrs. Shelby sat perfectly silent, pale with excitement, while Sam told his story.

"God be praised, she is n't dead!" she said; "but where is the poor child now?"

"De Lord will pervide," said Sam, rolling up his eyes piously. "As I 've been a sayin', dis yer 's a providence and no mistake, as Missis has allers been a instructin' on us. Thar 's allers instruments ris up to do de Lord's will. Now, if 't had n't been for me to-day, she 'd a been took a dozen times. Warn't it I started off de hosses, dis yer mornin', and kept 'em chasin' till nigh dinner time? And did n't I car Mas'r Haley nigh five miles out of de road, dis evening, or else he 'd a come up with Lizy as easy as a dog arter a coon. These yer 's all providences."

"They are a kind of providences that you 'll have to be pretty sparing of, Master Sam. I allow no such practices with gentlemen on my place," said Mr. Shelby, with as much stern-ness as he could command, under the circumstances.

Now, there is no more use in making believe be angry with a negro than with a child; both instinctively see the true state of the case, through all attempts to affect the contrary; and Sam was in no wise disheartened by this rebuke, though he assumed an air of doleful gravity, and stood with the corners of his mouth lowered in most penitential style.

"Mas'r 's quite right,—quite; it was ugly on me,—there 's no disputin' that ar; and of course Mas'r and Missis would n't encourage no such works. I 'm sensible of dat ar; but a poor nigger like me 's 'mazin' tempted to act ugly sometimes, when fellers will cut up such shines as dat ar Mas'r Haley; he an't no gen'l'man no way; anybody 's been raised as I 've been can't help a seein' dat ar."

"Well, Sam," said Mrs. Shelby, "as you appear to have a proper sense of your errors, you may go now and tell Aunt Chloe she may get you some of that cold ham that was left of dinner to-day. You and Andy must be hungry."

"Missis is a heap too good for us," said Sam, making his bow with alacrity, and departing.

It will be perceived, as has been before intimated, that Mas-ter Sam had a native talent that might, undoubtedly, have raised him to eminence in political life,—a talent of making capital out of everything that turned up, to be invested for his own especial praise and glory; and having done up his piety and humility, as he trusted, to the satisfaction of the parlor, he clapped his palm-leaf on his head, with a sort of

rakish, free-and-easy air, and proceeded to the dominions of
Aunt Chloe, with the intention of flourishing largely in the
kitchen.

"I 'll speechify these yer niggers," said Sam to himself,
"now I 've got a chance. Lord, I 'll reel it off to make 'em
stare!"

It must be observed that one of Sam's especial delights had
been to ride in attendance on his master to all kinds of political gatherings, where, roosted on some rail fence, or perched
aloft in some tree, he would sit watching the orators, with
the greatest apparent gusto, and then, descending among the
various brethren of his own color, assembled on the same errand, he would edify and delight them with the most ludicrous burlesques and imitations, all delivered with the most
imperturbable earnestness and solemnity; and though the
auditors immediately about him were generally of his own
color, it not unfrequently happened that they were fringed
pretty deeply with those of a fairer complexion, who listened,
laughing and winking, to Sam's great self-congratulation. In
fact, Sam considered oratory as his vocation, and never let
slip an opportunity of magnifying his office.

Now, between Sam and Aunt Chloe there had existed,
from ancient times, a sort of chronic feud, or rather a decided
coolness; but, as Sam was meditating something in the provision department, as the necessary and obvious foundation
of his operations, he determined, on the present occasion, to
be eminently conciliatory; for he well knew that although
"Missis' orders" would undoubtedly be followed to the letter,
yet he should gain a considerable deal by enlisting the spirit
also. He therefore appeared before Aunt Chloe with a touch-
ingly subdued, resigned expression, like one who has suffered
immeasurable hardships in behalf of a persecuted fellow-
creature,—enlarged upon the fact that Missis had directed
him to come to Aunt Chloe for whatever might be wanting
to make up the balance in his solids and fluids,—and thus
unequivocally acknowledged her right and supremacy in
the cooking department, and all thereto pertaining.

The thing took accordingly. No poor, simple, virtuous
body was ever cajoled by the attentions of an electioneering
politician with more ease than Aunt Chloe was won over by

Master Sam's suavities; and if he had been the prodigal son himself, he could not have been overwhelmed with more maternal bountifulness; and he soon found himself seated, happy and glorious, over a large tin pan, containing a sort of *olla podrida* of all that had appeared on the table for two or three days past. Savory morsels of ham, golden blocks of corn-cake, fragments of pie of every conceivable mathematical figure, chicken wings, gizzards, and drumsticks, all appeared in picturesque confusion; and Sam, as monarch of all he surveyed, sat with his palm-leaf cocked rejoicingly to one side, and patronizing Andy at his right hand.

The kitchen was full of all his compeers, who had hurried and crowded in, from the various cabins, to hear the termination of the day's exploits. Now was Sam's hour of glory. The story of the day was rehearsed, with all kinds of ornament and varnishing which might be necessary to heighten its effect; for Sam, like some of our fashionable dilettanti, never allowed a story to lose any of its gilding by passing through his hands. Roars of laughter attended the narration, and were taken up and prolonged by all the smaller fry, who were lying, in any quantity, about on the floor, or perched in every corner. In the height of the uproar and laughter, Sam, however, preserved an immovable gravity, only from time to time rolling his eyes up, and giving his auditors divers inexpressibly droll glances, without departing from the sententious elevation of his oratory.

"Yer see, fellow-countrymen," said Sam, elevating a turkey's leg, with energy, "yer see, now, what dis yer chile 's up ter, for fendin' yer all,—yes, all on yer. For him as tries to get one o' our people, is as good as tryin' to get all; yer see the principle 's de same,—dat ar 's clar. And any one o' these yer drivers that comes smelling round arter any our people, why, he 's got *me* in his way; *I 'm* the feller he 's got to set in with,—I 'm the feller for yer all to come to, bredren,—I 'll stand up for yer rights,—I 'll fend 'em to the last breath!"

"Why, but Sam, yer telled me, only this mornin', that you 'd help this yer Mas'r to cotch Lizy; seems to me yer talk don't hang together," said Andy.

"I tell you now, Andy," said Sam, with awful superiority, "don't yer be a talkin' 'bout what yer don't know nothin' on;

boys like you, Andy, means well, but they can't be spected to collusitate the great principles of action."

Andy looked rebuked, particularly by the hard word collusitate, which most of the youngerly members of the company seemed to consider as a settler in the case, while Sam proceeded.

"Dat ar was *conscience*, Andy; when I thought of gwine arter Lizy, I railly spected Mas'r was sot dat way. When I found Missis was sot the contrar, dat ar was conscience *more yet*,—cause fellers allers gets more by stickin' to Missis' side,—so yer see I's persistent either way, and sticks up to conscience, and holds on to principles. Yes, *principles*," said Sam, giving an enthusiastic toss to a chicken's neck,— "what's principles good for, if we is n't persistent, I wanter know? Thar, Andy, you may have dat ar bone,—'tan't picked quite clean."

Sam's audience hanging on his words with open mouth, he could not but proceed.

"Dis yer matter 'bout persistence, feller-niggers," said Sam, with the air of one entering into an abstruse subject, "dis yer 'sistency's a thing what an't seed into very clar, by most anybody. Now, yer see, when a feller stands up for a thing one day and night, de contrar de next, folks ses (and nat'rally enough dey ses), why he an't persistent,—hand me dat ar bit o' corn-cake, Andy. But let's look inter it. I hope the gen'lmen and der fair sex will scuse my usin' an or'nary sort o' 'parison. Here! I'm a tryin' to get top o' der hay. Wal, I puts up my larder dis yer side; 'tan't no go;—den, cause I don't try dere no more, but puts my larder right de contrar side, an't I persistent? I'm persistent in wantin' to get up which ary side my larder is; don't you see, all on yer?"

"It's the only thing ye ever was persistent in, Lord knows!" muttered Aunt Chloe, who was getting rather restive; the merriment of the evening being to her somewhat after the Scripture comparison,—like "vinegar upon nitre."

"Yes, indeed!" said Sam, rising, full of supper and glory, for a closing effort. "Yes, my feller-citizens and ladies of de other sex in general, I has principles,—I'm proud to 'oon 'em,—they's perquisite to dese yer times, and ter *all* times. I has principles, and I sticks to 'em like forty,—jest anything that I thinks is principle, I goes in to 't; — I would n't mind if dey burnt me 'live, — I 'd walk right up to de stake, I would, and say, here I comes to shed my last blood fur my principles, fur my country, fur der gen'l interests of s'ciety."

"Well," said Aunt Chloe, "one o' yer principles will have to be to get to bed some time to-night, and not be a keepin' everybody up till mornin'; now, every one of you young uns that don't want to be cracked, had better be scase, mighty sudden."

"Niggers! all on yer," said Sam, waving his palm-leaf with benignity, "I give yer my blessin'; go to bed now, and be good boys."

And, with this pathetic benediction, the assembly dispersed.

IX.

In Which It Appears that a Senator Is but a Man

THE light of the cheerful fire shone on the rug and carpet of a cosey parlor, and glittered on the sides of the tea-cups and well-brightened tea-pot, as Senator Bird was drawing off his boots, preparatory to inserting his feet in a pair of new handsome slippers, which his wife had been working for him while away on his senatorial tour. Mrs. Bird, looking the very picture of delight, was superintending the arrangements of the table, ever and anon mingling admonitory remarks to a number of frolicsome juveniles, who were effervescing in all those modes of untold gambol and mischief that have astonished mothers ever since the flood.

"Tom, let the door-knob alone,—there 's a man! Mary! Mary! don't pull the cat's tail,—poor pussy! Jim, you must n't climb on that table,—no, no!—You don't know, my dear, what a surprise it is to us all, to see you here to-night!" said she, at last, when she found a space to say something to her husband.

"Yes, yes, I thought I 'd just make a run down, spend the night, and have a little comfort at home. I 'm tired to death, and my head aches!"

Mrs. Bird cast a glance at a camphor-bottle, which stood in the half-open closet, and appeared to meditate an approach to it, but her husband interposed.

"No, no, Mary, no doctoring! a cup of your good hot tea, and some of our good home living, is what I want. It 's a tiresome business, this legislating!"

And the senator smiled, as if he rather liked the idea of considering himself a sacrifice to his country.

"Well," said his wife, after the business of the tea-table was getting rather slack, "and what have they been doing in the Senate?"

Now, it was a very unusual thing for gentle little Mrs. Bird ever to trouble her head with what was going on in the house of the state, very wisely considering that she had enough to do to mind her own. Mr. Bird, therefore, opened his eyes in surprise, and said,

"Not very much of importance."

"Well; but is it true that they have been passing a law forbidding people to give meat and drink to those poor colored folks that come along? I heard they were talking of some such law, but I did n't think any Christian legislature would pass it!"

"Why, Mary, you are getting to be a politician, all at once."

"No, nonsense! I would n't give a fip for all your politics, generally, but I think this is something downright cruel and unchristian. I hope, my dear, no such law has been passed."

"There has been a law passed forbidding people to help off the slaves that come over from Kentucky, my dear; so much of that thing has been done by these reckless Abolitionists, that our brethren in Kentucky are very strongly excited, and it seems necessary, and no more than Christian and kind, that something should be done by our state to quiet the excitement."

"And what is the law? It don't forbid us to shelter these poor creatures a night, does it, and to give 'em something comfortable to eat, and a few old clothes, and send them quietly about their business?"

"Why, yes, my dear; that would be aiding and abetting, you know."

Mrs. Bird was a timid, blushing little woman, of about four feet in height, and with mild blue eyes, and a peach-blow complexion, and the gentlest, sweetest voice in the world;—as for courage, a moderate-sized cock-turkey had been known to put her to rout at the very first gobble, and a stout house-dog, of moderate capacity, would bring her into subjection merely by a show of his teeth. Her husband and children were her entire world, and in these she ruled more by entreaty and persuasion than by command or argument. There was only one thing that was capable of arousing her, and that provocation came in on the side of her unusually gentle and sympathetic nature;—anything in the shape of cruelty would throw her into a passion, which was the more alarming and inexplicable in proportion to the general softness of her nature. Generally the most indulgent and easy to be entreated of all mothers, still her boys had a very reverent remembrance of a most vehement chastisement she once bestowed on them, because she found them leagued with several graceless boys of the neighborhood, stoning a defenceless kitten.

"I'll tell you what," Master Bill used to say, "I was scared that time. Mother came at me so that I thought she was crazy, and I was whipped and tumbled off to bed, without any supper, before I could get over wondering what had come about; and, after that, I heard mother crying outside the door, which made me feel worse than all the rest. I'll tell you what," he'd say, "we boys never stoned another kitten!"

On the present occasion, Mrs. Bird rose quickly, with very red cheeks, which quite improved her general appearance, and walked up to her husband, with quite a resolute air, and said, in a determined tone,

"Now, John, I want to know if you think such a law as that is right and Christian?"

"You won't shoot me, now, Mary, if I say I do!"

"I never could have thought it of you, John; you did n't vote for it?"

"Even so, my fair politician."

"You ought to be ashamed, John! Poor, homeless, houseless creatures! It's a shameful, wicked, abominable law, and I'll break it, for one, the first time I get a chance; and I hope I *shall* have a chance, I do! Things have got to a pretty pass, if a woman can't give a warm supper and a bed to poor, starving creatures, just because they are slaves, and have been abused and oppressed all their lives, poor things!"

"But, Mary, just listen to me. Your feelings are all quite right, dear, and interesting, and I love you for them; but, then, dear, we must n't suffer our feelings to run away with our judgment; you must consider it 's not a matter of private feeling,—there are great public interests involved,—there is such a state of public agitation rising, that we must put aside our private feelings."

"Now, John, I don't know anything about politics, but I can read my Bible; and there I see that I must feed the hungry, clothe the naked, and comfort the desolate; and that Bible I mean to follow."

"But in cases where your doing so would involve a great public evil—"

"Obeying God never brings on public evils. I know it can't. It's always safest, all round, to *do as He* bids us."

"Now, listen to me, Mary, and I can state to you a very clear argument, to show—"

"O, nonsense, John! you can talk all night, but you would n't do it. I put it to you, John,—would *you* now turn away a poor, shivering, hungry creature from your door, because he was a runaway? *Would* you, now?"

Now, if the truth must be told, our senator had the misfortune to be a man who had a particularly humane and accessible nature, and turning away anybody that was in trouble never had been his forte; and what was worse for him in this particular pinch of the argument was, that his wife knew it, and, of course, was making an assault on rather an indefensible point. So he had recourse to the usual means of gaining time for such cases made and provided; he said "ahem," and coughed several times, took out his pocket-handkerchief, and began to wipe his glasses. Mrs. Bird, seeing the defenceless condition of the enemy's territory, had no more conscience than to push her advantage.

"I should like to see you doing that, John—I really should! Turning a woman out of doors in a snow-storm, for instance; or, may be you 'd take her up and put her in jail, would n't you? You would make a great hand at that!"

"Of course, it would be a very painful duty," began Mr. Bird, in a moderate tone.

"Duty, John! don't use that word! You know it is n't a duty—it can't be a duty! If folks want to keep their slaves from running away, let 'em treat 'em well,—that's my doctrine. If I had slaves (as I hope I never shall have), I 'd risk their wanting to run away from me, or you either, John. I tell you folks don't run away when they are happy; and when they do run, poor creatures! they suffer enough with cold and hunger and fear, without everybody's turning against them; and, law or no law, I never will, so help me God!"

"Mary! Mary! My dear, let me reason with you."

"I hate reasoning, John,—especially reasoning on such subjects. There's a way you political folks have of coming round and round a plain right thing; and you don't believe in it yourselves, when it comes to practice. I know *you* well enough, John. You don't believe it's right any more than I do; and you would n't do it any sooner than I."

At this critical juncture, old Cudjoe, the black man-of-all-work, put his head in at the door, and wished "Missis would come into the kitchen;" and our senator, tolerably relieved, looked after his little wife with a whimsical mixture of amusement and vexation, and, seating himself in the arm-chair, began to read the papers.

After a moment, his wife's voice was heard at the door, in a quick, earnest tone,—"John! John! I do wish you'd come here, a moment."

He laid down his paper, and went into the kitchen, and started, quite amazed at the sight that presented itself:—A young and slender woman, with garments torn and frozen, with one shoe gone, and the stocking torn away from the cut and bleeding foot, was laid back in a deadly swoon upon two chairs. There was the impress of the despised race on her face, yet none could help feeling its mournful and pathetic beauty, while its stony sharpness, its cold, fixed, deathly aspect, struck a solemn chill over him. He drew his breath short, and stood in silence. His wife, and their only colored domestic, old Aunt Dinah, were busily engaged in restorative measures; while old Cudjoe had got the boy on his knee, and was busy pulling off his shoes and stockings, and chafing his little cold feet.

"Sure, now, if she an't a sight to behold!" said old Dinah, compassionately; " 'pears like 't was the heat that made her faint. She was tol'able peart when she cum in, and asked if she could n't warm herself here a spell; and I was just a askin' her where she cum from, and she fainted right down. Never done much hard work, guess, by the looks of her hands."

"Poor creature!" said Mrs. Bird, compassionately, as the woman slowly unclosed her large, dark eyes, and looked vacantly at her. Suddenly an expression of agony crossed her face, and she sprang up, saying, "O, my Harry! Have they got him?"

The boy, at this, jumped from Cudjoe's knee, and, running to her side, put up his arms. "O, he's here! he's here!" she exclaimed.

"O, ma'am!" said she, wildly, to Mrs. Bird, "do protect us! don't let them get him!"

"Nobody shall hurt you here, poor woman," said Mrs. Bird, encouragingly. "You are safe; don't be afraid."

"God bless you!" said the woman, covering her face and sobbing; while the little boy, seeing her crying, tried to get into her lap.

With many gentle and womanly offices, which none knew better how to render than Mrs. Bird, the poor woman was, in time, rendered more calm. A temporary bed was provided for her on the settle, near the fire; and, after a short time, she fell into a heavy slumber, with the child, who seemed no less weary, soundly sleeping on her arm; for the mother resisted, with nervous anxiety, the kindest attempts to take him from her; and, even in sleep, her arm encircled him with an unrelaxing clasp, as if she could not even then be beguiled of her vigilant hold.

Mr. and Mrs. Bird had gone back to the parlor, where, strange as it may appear, no reference was made, on either side, to the preceding conversation; but Mrs. Bird busied herself with her knitting-work, and Mr. Bird pretended to be reading the paper.

"I wonder who and what she is!" said Mr. Bird, at last, as he laid it down.

"When she wakes up and feels a little rested, we will see," said Mrs. Bird.

"I say, wife!" said Mr. Bird, after musing in silence over his newspaper.

"Well, dear!"

"She could n't wear one of your gowns, could she, by any letting down, or such matter? She seems to be rather larger than you are."

A quite perceptible smile glimmered on Mrs. Bird's face, as she answered, "We 'll see."

Another pause, and Mr. Bird again broke out,

"I say, wife!"

"Well! What now?"

"Why, there's that old bombazin cloak, that you keep on purpose to put over me when I take my afternoon's nap; you might as well give her that,—she needs clothes."

At this instant, Dinah looked in to say that the woman was awake, and wanted to see Missis.

Mr. and Mrs. Bird went into the kitchen, followed by the two eldest boys, the smaller fry having, by this time, been safely disposed of in bed.

The woman was now sitting up on the settle, by the fire. She was looking steadily into the blaze, with a calm, heart-broken expression, very different from her former agitated wildness.

"Did you want me?" said Mrs. Bird, in gentle tones. "I hope you feel better now, poor woman!"

A long-drawn, shivering sigh was the only answer; but she lifted her dark eyes, and fixed them on her with such a forlorn and imploring expression, that the tears came into the little woman's eyes.

"You need n't be afraid of anything; we are friends here, poor woman! Tell me where you came from, and what you want," said she.

"I came from Kentucky," said the woman.

"When?" said Mr. Bird, taking up the interrogatory.

"To-night."

"How did you come?"

"I crossed on the ice."

"Crossed on the ice!" said every one present.

"Yes," said the woman, slowly, "I did. God helping me, I crossed on the ice; for they were behind me—right behind—and there was no other way!"

"Law, Missis," said Cudjoe, "the ice is all in broken-up blocks, a swinging and a tetering up and down in the water!"

"I know it was—I know it!" said she, wildly; "but I did it! I would n't have thought I could,—I did n't think I should get over, but I did n't care! I could but die, if I did n't. The Lord helped me; nobody knows how much the Lord can help 'em, till they try," said the woman, with a flashing eye.

"Were you a slave?" said Mr. Bird.

"Yes, sir; I belonged to a man in Kentucky."

"Was he unkind to you?"

"No, sir; he was a good master."

"And was your mistress unkind to you?"

"No, sir—no! my mistress was always good to me."

"What could induce you to leave a good home, then, and run away, and go through such dangers?"

The woman looked up at Mrs. Bird, with a keen, scrutinizing glance, and it did not escape her that she was dressed in deep mourning.

"Ma'am," she said, suddenly, "have you ever lost a child?"

The question was unexpected, and it was a thrust on a new wound; for it was only a month since a darling child of the family had been laid in the grave.

Mr. Bird turned around and walked to the window, and Mrs. Bird burst into tears; but, recovering her voice, she said,

"Why do you ask that? I have lost a little one."

"Then you will feel for me. I have lost two, one after another,—left 'em buried there when I came away; and I had only this one left. I never slept a night without him; he was all I had. He was my comfort and pride, day and night; and, ma'am, they were going to take him away from me,—to *sell* him,—sell him down south, ma'am, to go all alone,—a baby that had never been away from his mother in his life! I could n't stand it, ma'am. I knew I never should be good for anything, if they did; and when I knew the papers were signed, and he was sold, I took him and came off in the night; and they chased me,—the man that bought him, and some of Mas'r's folks,—and they were coming down right behind me, and I heard 'em. I jumped right on to the ice; and how I got across, I don't know,—but, first I knew, a man was helping me up the bank."

The woman did not sob nor weep. She had gone to a place where tears are dry; but every one around her was, in some way characteristic of themselves, showing signs of hearty sympathy.

The two little boys, after a desperate rummaging in their pockets, in search of those pocket-handkerchiefs which mothers know are never to be found there, had thrown themselves disconsolately into the skirts of their mother's gown, where they were sobbing, and wiping their eyes and noses, to their hearts' content;—Mrs. Bird had her face fairly hidden in her pocket-handkerchief; and old Dinah, with tears streaming down her black, honest face, was ejaculating, "Lord have mercy on us!" with all the fervor of a camp-meeting;—while old Cudjoe, rubbing his eyes very hard with his cuffs, and making a most uncommon variety of wry faces, occasionally responded in the same key, with great fervor. Our senator was a statesman, and of course could not be expected to cry, like other mortals; and so he turned his back to the company, and looked out of the window, and seemed particularly busy in clearing his throat and wiping his spectacle-glasses, occasionally blowing his nose in a manner that was calculated to excite suspicion, had any one been in a state to observe critically.

"How came you to tell me you had a kind master?" he suddenly exclaimed, gulping down very resolutely some kind of rising in his throat, and turning suddenly round upon the woman.

"Because he *was* a kind master; I 'll say that of him, any way;—and my mistress was kind; but they could n't help themselves. They were owing money; and there was some way, I can't tell how, that a man had a hold on them, and they were obliged to give him his will. I listened, and heard him telling mistress that, and she begging and pleading for me,—and he told her he could n't help himself, and that the papers were all drawn;—and then it was I took him and left my home, and came away. I knew 't was no use of my trying to live, if they did it; for 't 'pears like this child is all I have."

"Have you no husband?"

"Yes, but he belongs to another man. His master is real hard to him, and won't let him come to see me, hardly ever; and he 's grown harder and harder upon us, and he threatens to sell him down south;—it 's like I 'll never see *him* again!"

The quiet tone in which the woman pronounced these words might have led a superficial observer to think that she was entirely apathetic; but there was a calm, settled depth of anguish in her large, dark eye, that spoke of something far otherwise.

"And where do you mean to go, my poor woman?" said Mrs. Bird.

"To Canada, if I only knew where that was. Is it very far

off, is Canada?" said she, looking up, with a simple, confiding air, to Mrs. Bird's face.

"Poor thing!" said Mrs. Bird, involuntarily.

"Is 't a very great way off, think?" said the woman, earnestly.

"Much further than you think, poor child!" said Mrs. Bird; "but we will try to think what can be done for you. Here, Dinah, make her up a bed in your own room, close by the kitchen, and I 'll think what to do for her in the morning. Meanwhile, never fear, poor woman; put your trust in God; he will protect you."

Mrs. Bird and her husband reëntered the parlor. She sat down in her little rocking-chair before the fire, swaying thoughtfully to and fro. Mr. Bird strode up and down the room, grumbling to himself, "Pish! pshaw! confounded awkward business!" At length, striding up to his wife, he said,

"I say, wife, she 'll have to get away from here, this very night. That fellow will be down on the scent bright and early to-morrow morning; if 't was only the woman, she could lie quiet till it was over; but that little chap can't be kept still by a troop of horse and foot, I 'll warrant me; he 'll bring it all out, popping his head out of some window or door. A pretty kettle of fish it would be for me, too, to be caught with them both here, just now! No; they 'll have to be got off to-night."

"To-night! How is it possible?—where to?"

"Well, I know pretty well where to," said the senator, beginning to put on his boots, with a reflective air; and, stopping when his leg was half in, he embraced his knee with both hands, and seemed to go off in deep meditation.

"It 's a confounded awkward, ugly business," said he, at last, beginning to tug at his boot-straps again, "and that 's a fact!" After one boot was fairly on, the senator sat with the other in his hand, profoundly studying the figure of the carpet. "It will have to be done, though, for aught I see,—hang it all!" and he drew the other boot anxiously on, and looked out of the window.

Now, little Mrs. Bird was a discreet woman,—a woman who never in her life said, "I told you so!" and, on the present occasion, though pretty well aware of the shape her husband's meditations were taking, she very prudently forbore to meddle with them, only sat very quietly in her chair, and looked quite ready to hear her liege lord's intentions, when he should think proper to utter them.

"You see," he said, "there's my old client, Van Trompe, has come over from Kentucky, and set all his slaves free; and he has bought a place seven miles up the creek, here, back in the woods, where nobody goes, unless they go on purpose; and it's a place that isn't found in a hurry. There she'd be safe enough; but the plague of the thing is, nobody could drive a carriage there to-night, but *me*."

"Why not? Cudjoe is an excellent driver."

"Ay, ay, but here it is. The creek has to be crossed twice; and the second crossing is quite dangerous, unless one knows it as I do. I have crossed it a hundred times on horseback, and know exactly the turns to take. And so, you see, there's no help for it. Cudjoe must put in the horses, as quietly as may be, about twelve o'clock, and I'll take her over; and then, to give color to the matter, he must carry me on to the next tavern, to take the stage for Columbus, that comes by about three or four, and so it will look as if I had had the carriage only for that. I shall get into business bright and early in the morning. But I'm thinking I shall feel rather cheap there, after all that's been said and done; but, hang it, I can't help it!"

"Your heart is better than your head, in this case, John," said the wife, laying her little white hand on his. "Could I ever have loved you, had I not known you better than you know yourself?" And the little woman looked so handsome, with the tears sparkling in her eyes, that the senator thought he must be a decidedly clever fellow, to get such a pretty creature into such a passionate admiration of him; and so, what could he do but walk off soberly, to see about the carriage. At the door, however, he stopped a moment, and then coming back, he said, with some hesitation,

"Mary, I don't know how you'd feel about it, but there's that drawer full of things—of—of—poor little Henry's." So saying, he turned quickly on his heel, and shut the door after him.

His wife opened the little bed-room door adjoining her room, and, taking the candle, set it down on the top of a bureau there; then from a small recess she took a key, and put it thoughtfully in the lock of a drawer, and made a sudden pause, while two boys, who, boy like, had followed close on her heels, stood looking, with silent, significant glances, at their mother. And oh! mother that reads this, has there never been in your house a drawer, or a closet, the opening of which has been to you like the opening again of a little grave? Ah! happy mother that you are, if it has not been so.

Mrs. Bird slowly opened the drawer. There were little coats of many a form and pattern, piles of aprons, and rows of small stockings; and even a pair of little shoes, worn and rubbed at the toes, were peeping from the folds of a paper. There was a toy horse and wagon, a top, a ball,—memorials gathered with many a tear and many a heart-break! She sat down by the drawer, and, leaning her head on her hands over it, wept till the tears fell through her fingers into the drawer; then suddenly raising her head, she began, with nervous haste, selecting the plainest and most substantial articles, and gathering them into a bundle.

"Mamma," said one of the boys, gently touching her arm, "are you going to give away *those* things?"

"My dear boys," she said, softly and earnestly, "if our dear, loving little Henry looks down from heaven, he would be glad to have us do this. I could not find it in my heart to give them away to any common person—to anybody that was happy; but I give them to a mother more heart-broken and sorrowful than I am; and I hope God will send his blessings with them!"

There are in this world blessed souls, whose sorrows all spring up into joys for others; whose earthly hopes, laid in the grave with many tears, are the seed from which spring healing flowers and balm for the desolate and the distressed. Among such was the delicate woman who sits there by the lamp, dropping slow tears, while she prepares the memorials of her own lost one for the outcast wanderer.

After a while, Mrs. Bird opened a wardrobe, and, taking from thence a plain, serviceable dress or two, she sat down busily to her work-table, and, with needle, scissors, and thimble, at hand, quietly commenced the "letting down" process which her husband had recommended, and continued busily at it till the old clock in the corner struck twelve, and she heard the low rattling of wheels at the door.

"Mary," said her husband, coming in, with his overcoat in his hand, "you must wake her up now; we must be off."

Mrs. Bird hastily deposited the various articles she had collected in a small plain trunk, and locking it, desired her husband to see it in the carriage, and then proceeded to call the woman. Soon, arrayed in a cloak, bonnet, and shawl, that had belonged to her benefactress, she appeared at the door with her child in her arms. Mr. Bird hurried her into the carriage, and Mrs. Bird pressed on after her to the carriage steps. Eliza leaned out of the carriage, and put out her hand,—a hand as soft and beautiful as was given in return. She fixed her large, dark eyes, full of earnest meaning, on Mrs. Bird's face, and seemed going to speak. Her lips moved,—she tried once or twice, but there was no sound,—and pointing upward, with a look never to be forgotten, she fell back in the seat, and covered her face. The door was shut, and the carriage drove on.

What a situation, now, for a patriotic senator, that had been all the week before spurring up the legislature of his native state to pass more stringent resolutions against escaping fugitives, their harborers and abettors!

Our good senator in his native state had not been exceeded by any of his brethren at Washington, in the sort of eloquence which has won for them immortal renown! How sublimely he had sat with his hands in his pockets, and scouted all sentimental weakness of those who would put the welfare of a few miserable fugitives before great state interests!

He was as bold as a lion about it, and "mightily convinced" not only himself, but everybody that heard him;—but then his idea of a fugitive was only an idea of the letters that spell the word,—or, at the most, the image of a little newspaper picture of a man with a stick and bundle, with "Ran away from the subscriber" under it. The magic of the real presence of distress,—the imploring human eye, the frail, trembling human hand, the despairing appeal of helpless agony,—these he had never tried. He had never thought that a fugitive might be a hapless mother, a defenceless child,—like that one which was now wearing his lost boy's little well-known cap;

and so, as our poor senator was not stone or steel,—as he was a man, and a downright noble-hearted one, too,—he was, as everybody must see, in a sad case for his patriotism. And you need not exult over him, good brother of the Southern States; for we have some inklings that many of you, under similar circumstances, would not do much better. We have reason to know, in Kentucky, as in Mississippi, are noble and generous hearts, to whom never was tale of suffering told in vain. Ah, good brother! is it fair for you to expect of us services which your own brave, honorable heart would not allow you to render, were you in our place?

Be that as it may, if our good senator was a political sinner, he was in a fair way to expiate it by his night's penance. There had been a long continuous period of rainy weather, and the soft, rich earth of Ohio, as every one knows, is admirably suited to the manufacture of mud,—and the road was an Ohio railroad of the good old times.

"And pray, what sort of a road may that be?" says some eastern traveller, who has been accustomed to connect no ideas with a railroad, but those of smoothness or speed.

Know, then, innocent eastern friend, that in benighted regions of the west, where the mud is of unfathomable and sublime depth, roads are made of round rough logs, arranged transversely side by side, and coated over in their pristine freshness with earth, turf, and whatsoever may come to hand, and then the rejoicing native calleth it a road, and straightway essayeth to ride thereupon. In process of time, the rains wash off all the turf and grass aforesaid, move the logs hither and thither, in picturesque positions, up, down and crosswise, with divers chasms and ruts of black mud intervening.

Over such a road as this our senator went stumbling along, making moral reflections as continuously as under the circumstances could be expected,—the carriage proceeding along much as follows,—bump! bump! bump! slush! down in the mud!—the senator, woman and child, reversing their positions so suddenly as to come, without any very accurate adjustment, against the windows of the down-hill side. Carriage sticks fast, while Cudjoe on the outside is heard making a great muster among the horses. After various ineffectual pullings and twitchings, just as the senator is losing all patience, the carriage suddenly rights itself with a bounce,—two front wheels go down into another abyss, and senator, woman, and child, all tumble promiscuously on to the front seat,—senator's hat is jammed over his eyes and nose quite unceremoniously, and he considers himself fairly extinguished;—child cries, and Cudjoe on the outside delivers animated addresses to the horses, who are kicking, and floundering, and straining, under repeated cracks of the whip. Carriage springs up, with another bounce,—down go the hind wheels,—senator, woman, and child, fly over on to the back seat, his elbows encountering her bonnet, and both her feet being jammed into his hat, which flies off in the concussion. After a few moments the "slough" is passed, and the horses stop, panting;—the senator finds his hat, the woman straightens her bonnet and hushes her child, and they brace themselves firmly for what is yet to come.

For a while only the continuous bump! bump! intermingled, just by way of variety, with divers side plunges and compound shakes; and they begin to flatter themselves that they are not so badly off, after all. At last, with a square plunge, which puts all on to their feet and then down into their seats with incredible quickness, the carriage stops,—and, after much outside commotion, Cudjoe appears at the door.

"Please, sir, it 's powerful bad spot, this yer. I don't know how we 's to get clar out. I 'm a thinkin' we 'll have to be a gettin' rails."

The senator despairingly steps out, picking gingerly for some firm foothold; down goes one foot an immeasurable depth,—he tries to pull it up, loses his balance, and tumbles over into the mud, and is fished out, in a very despairing condition, by Cudjoe.

But we forbear, out of sympathy to our readers' bones. Western travellers, who have beguiled the midnight hour in the interesting process of pulling down rail fences, to pry their carriages out of mud holes, will have a respectful and mournful sympathy with our unfortunate hero. We beg them to drop a silent tear, and pass on.

It was full late in the night when the carriage emerged, dripping and bespattered, out of the creek, and stood at the door of a large farm-house.

It took no inconsiderable perseverance to arouse the inmates; but at last the respectable proprietor appeared, and undid the door. He was a great, tall, bristling Orson of a fellow, full six feet and some inches in his stockings, and arrayed in a red flannel hunting-shirt. A very heavy *mat* of sandy hair, in a decidedly tousled condition, and a beard of some days' growth, gave the worthy man an appearance, to say the least, not particularly prepossessing. He stood for a few minutes holding the candle aloft, and blinking on our travellers with a dismal and mystified expression that was truly ludicrous. It cost some effort of our senator to induce him to comprehend the case fully; and while he is doing his best at that, we shall give him a little introduction to our readers.

Honest old John Van Trompe was once quite a considerable land-holder and slave-owner in the State of Kentucky. Having "nothing of the bear about him but the skin," and being gifted by nature with a great, honest, just heart, quite equal to his gigantic frame, he had been for some years witnessing with repressed uneasiness the workings of a system equally bad for oppressor and oppressed. At last, one day, John's great heart had swelled altogether too big to wear his bonds any longer; so he just took his pocket-book out of his desk, and went over into Ohio, and bought a quarter of a township of good, rich land, made out free papers for all his people,—men, women, and children,—packed them up in wagons, and sent them off to settle down; and then honest John turned his face up the creek, and sat quietly down on a snug, retired farm, to enjoy his conscience and his reflections.

"Are you the man that will shelter a poor woman and child from slave-catchers?" said the senator, explicitly.

"I rather think I am," said honest John, with some considerable emphasis.

"I thought so," said the senator.

"If there's anybody comes," said the good man, stretching his tall, muscular form upward, "why here I'm ready for him: and I've got seven sons, each six foot high, and they'll be ready for 'em. Give our respects to 'em," said John; "tell 'em it's no matter how soon they call,—make no kinder difference to us," said John, running his fingers through the shock

of hair that thatched his head, and bursting out into a great
laugh.

Weary, jaded, and spiritless, Eliza dragged herself up to the
door, with her child lying in a heavy sleep on her arm. The
rough man held the candle to her face, and uttering a kind of
compassionate grunt, opened the door of a small bedroom
adjoining to the large kitchen where they were standing, and
motioned her to go in. He took down a candle, and lighting
it, set it upon the table, and then addressed himself to Eliza.

"Now, I say, gal, you need n't be a bit afeard, let who will
come here. I 'm up to all that sort o' thing," said he, pointing
to two or three goodly rifles over the mantel-piece; "and most
people that know me know that 't would n't be healthy to try
to get anybody out o' my house when I 'm agin it. So *now*
you jist go to sleep now, as quiet as if yer mother was a
rockin' ye," said he, as he shut the door.

"Why, this is an uncommon handsome un," he said to the
senator. "Ah, well; handsome uns has the greatest cause to
run, sometimes, if they has any kind o' feelin, such as decent
women should. I know all about that."

The senator, in a few words, briefly explained Eliza's history.

"O! ou! aw! now, I want to know?" said the good man,
pitifully; "sho! now sho! That 's natur now, poor crittur!
hunted down now like a deer,—hunted down, jest for havin'
natural feelin's, and doin' what no kind o' mother could help
a doin'! I tell ye what, these yer things make me come the
nighest to swearin', now, o' most anything," said honest
John, as he wiped his eyes with the back of a great, freckled,
yellow hand. "I tell yer what, stranger, it was years and years
before I 'd jine the church, 'cause the ministers round in our
parts used to preach that the Bible went in for these ere cut-
tings up,—and I could n't be up to 'em with their Greek and
Hebrew, and so I took up agin 'em, Bible and all. I never
jined the church till I found a minister that was up to 'em all
in Greek and all that, and he said right the contrary; and then
I took right hold, and jined the church,—I did now, fact,"
said John, who had been all this time uncorking some very
frisky bottled cider, which at this juncture he presented.

"Ye 'd better jest put up here, now, till daylight," said he, heartily, "and I 'll call up the old woman, and have a bed got ready for you in no time."

"Thank you, my good friend," said the senator, "I must be along, to take the night stage for Columbus."

"Ah! well, then, if you must, I 'll go a piece with you, and show you a cross road that will take you there better than the road you came on. That road 's mighty bad."

John equipped himself, and, with a lantern in hand, was soon seen guiding the senator's carriage towards a road that ran down in a hollow, back of his dwelling. When they parted, the senator put into his hand a ten-dollar bill.

"It 's for her," he said, briefly.

"Ay, ay," said John, with equal conciseness.

They shook hands, and parted.

X.

The Property Is Carried Off

THE February morning looked gray and drizzling through the window of Uncle Tom's cabin. It looked on downcast faces, the images of mournful hearts. The little table stood out before the fire, covered with an ironing-cloth; a coarse but clean shirt or two, fresh from the iron, hung on the back of a chair by the fire, and Aunt Chloe had another spread out before her on the table. Carefully she rubbed and ironed every fold and every hem, with the most scrupulous exactness, every now and then raising her hand to her face to wipe off the tears that were coursing down her cheeks.

Tom sat by, with his Testament open on his knee, and his head leaning upon his hand;—but neither spoke. It was yet early, and the children lay all asleep together in their little rude trundle-bed.

Tom, who had, to the full, the gentle, domestic heart, which, woe for them! has been a peculiar characteristic of his unhappy race, got up and walked silently to look at his children.

"It 's the last time," he said.

Aunt Chloe did not answer, only rubbed away over and over on the coarse shirt, already as smooth as hands could make it; and finally setting her iron suddenly down with a despairing plunge, she sat down to the table, and "lifted up her voice and wept."

"S'pose we must be resigned; but oh Lord! how ken I? If I know'd anything whar you 's goin', or how they 'd sarve you! Missis says she 'll try and 'deem ye, in a year or two; but Lor! nobody never comes up that goes down thar! They kills 'em! I 've hearn 'em tell how dey works 'em up on dem ar plantations."

"There 'll be the same God there, Chloe, that there is here."

"Well," said Aunt Chloe, "s'pose dere will; but de Lord lets drefful things happen, sometimes. I don't seem to get no comfort dat way."

"I 'm in the Lord's hands," said Tom; "nothin' can go no furder than he lets it;—and thar 's *one* thing I can thank him for. It 's *me* that 's sold and going down, and not you nur the chil'en. Here you 're safe;—what comes will come only on me; and the Lord, he 'll help me,—I know he will."

Ah, brave, manly heart,—smothering thine own sorrow, to comfort thy beloved ones! Tom spoke with a thick utterance, and with a bitter choking in his throat,—but he spoke brave and strong.

"Let 's think on our marcies!" he added, tremulously, as if he was quite sure he needed to think on them very hard indeed.

"Marcies!" said Aunt Chloe; "don't see no marcy in 't! 'tan't right! tan't right it should be so! Mas'r never ought ter left it so that ye *could* be took for his debts. Ye 've arnt him all he gets for ye, twice over. He owed ye yer freedom, and ought ter gin 't to yer years ago. Mebbe he can't help himself now, but I feel it 's wrong. Nothing can't beat that ar out o' me. Sich a faithful crittur as ye 've been,—and allers sot his business 'fore yer own every way,—and reckoned on him more than yer own wife and chil'en! Them as sells heart's love and heart's blood, to get out thar scrapes, de Lord 'll be up to 'em!"

"Chloe! now, if ye love me, ye won't talk so, when perhaps jest the last time we 'll ever have together! And I 'll tell ye, Chloe, it goes agin me to hear one word agin Mas'r. Wan't he put in my arms a baby?—it 's natur I should think a heap of him. And he could n't be spected to think so much of poor Tom. Mas'rs is used to havin' all these yer things done for 'em, and nat'lly they don't think so much on 't. They can't be spected to, no way. Set him 'longside of other Mas'rs—who 's had the treatment and the livin' I 've had? And he never would have let this yer come on me, if he could have seed it aforehand. I know he would n't."

"Wal, any way, thar 's wrong about it *somewhar*," said Aunt Chloe, in whom a stubborn sense of justice was a predominant trait; "I can't jest make out whar 't is, but thar 's wrong somewhar, I 'm *clar* o' that."

"Yer ought ter look up to the Lord above—he 's above all—thar don't a sparrow fall without him."

"It don't seem to comfort me, but I spect it orter," said Aunt Chloe. "But dar 's no use talkin'; I 'll jes wet up de corncake, and get ye one good breakfast, 'cause nobody knows when you 'll get another."

In order to appreciate the sufferings of the negroes sold south, it must be remembered that all the instinctive affections of that race are peculiarly strong. Their local attachments are very abiding. They are not naturally daring and enterprising, but home-loving and affectionate. Add to this all the terrors with which ignorance invests the unknown, and add to this, again, that selling to the south is set before the negro from childhood as the last severity of punishment. The threat that terrifies more than whipping or torture of any kind is the threat of being sent down river. We have ourselves heard this feeling expressed by them, and seen the unaffected horror with which they will sit in their gossiping hours, and tell frightful stories of that "down river," which to them is

> "That undiscovered country, from whose bourn
> No traveller returns."

A missionary among the fugitives in Canada told us that many of the fugitives confessed themselves to have escaped from comparatively kind masters, and that they were induced to brave the perils of escape, in almost every case, by the desperate horror with which they regarded being sold south,—a doom which was hanging either over themselves or their husbands, their wives or children. This nerves the African, naturally patient, timid and unenterprising, with heroic courage, and leads him to suffer hunger, cold, pain, the perils of the wilderness, and the more dread penalties of re-capture.

The simple morning meal now smoked on the table, for Mrs. Shelby had excused Aunt Chloe's attendance at the great house that morning. The poor soul had expended all her little energies on this farewell feast,—had killed and dressed her choicest chicken, and prepared her corn-cake with scrupulous exactness, just to her husband's taste, and brought out certain mysterious jars on the mantel-piece, some preserves that were never produced except on extreme occasions.

"Lor, Pete," said Mose, triumphantly, "han't we got a

buster of a breakfast!" at the same time catching at a fragment of the chicken.

Aunt Chloe gave him a sudden box on the ear. "Thar now! crowing over the last breakfast yer poor daddy 's gwine to have to home!"

"O, Chloe!" said Tom, gently.

"Wal, I can't help it," said Aunt Chloe, hiding her face in her apron; "I 's so tossed about, it makes me act ugly."

The boys stood quite still, looking first at their father and then at their mother, while the baby, climbing up her clothes, began an imperious, commanding cry.

"Thar!" said Aunt Chloe, wiping her eyes and taking up the baby; "now I 's done, I hope,—now do eat something. This yer 's my nicest chicken. Thar, boys, ye shall have some, poor critturs! Yer mammy 's been cross to yer."

The boys needed no second invitation, and went in with great zeal for the eatables; and it was well they did so, as otherwise there would have been very little performed to any purpose by the party.

"Now," said Aunt Chloe, bustling about after breakfast, "I must put up yer clothes. Jest like as not, he 'll take 'em all away. I know thar ways—mean as dirt, they is! Wal, now, yer flannels for rhumatis is in this corner; so be carful, 'cause there won't nobody make ye no more. Then here 's yer old shirts, and these yer is new ones. I toed off these yer stockings last night, and put de ball in 'em to mend with. But Lor! who 'll ever mend for ye?" and Aunt Chloe, again overcome, laid her head on the box side, and sobbed. "To think on 't! no crittur to do for ye, sick or well! I don't railly think I ought ter be good now!"

The boys, having eaten everything there was on the break-fast-table, began now to take some thought of the case; and, seeing their mother crying, and their father looking very sad, began to whimper and put their hands to their eyes. Uncle Tom had the baby on his knee, and was letting her enjoy herself to the utmost extent, scratching his face and pulling his hair, and occasionally breaking out into clamorous explo-sions of delight, evidently arising out of her own internal re-flections.

"Ay, crow away, poor crittur!" said Aunt Chloe; "ye 'll

have to come to it, too! ye 'll live to see yer husband sold, or
mebbe be sold yerself; and these yer boys, they 's to be sold,
I s'pose, too, jest like as not, when dey gets good for somethin'; an't no use in niggers havin' nothin'!"

Here one of the boys called out, "Thar 's Missis a-comin'
in!"

"She can't do no good; what 's she coming for?" said Aunt
Chloe.

Mrs. Shelby entered. Aunt Chloe set a chair for her in a
manner decidedly gruff and crusty. She did not seem to notice either the action or the manner. She looked pale and anxious.

"Tom," she said, "I come to—" and stopping suddenly,
and regarding the silent group, she sat down in the chair,
and, covering her face with her handkerchief, began to sob.

"Lor, now, Missis, don't—don't!" said Aunt Chloe, bursting out in her turn; and for a few moments they all wept in
company. And in those tears they all shed together, the high
and the lowly, melted away all the heart-burnings and anger
of the oppressed. O, ye who visit the distressed, do ye know
that everything your money can buy, given with a cold,
averted face, is not worth one honest tear shed in real sympathy?

"My good fellow," said Mrs. Shelby, "I can't give you anything to do you any good. If I give you money, it will only
be taken from you. But I tell you solemnly, and before God,
that I will keep trace of you, and bring you back as soon as I
can command the money;—and, till then, trust in God!"

Here the boys called out that Mas'r Haley was coming, and
then an unceremonious kick pushed open the door. Haley
stood there in very ill humor, having ridden hard the night
before, and being not at all pacified by his ill success in re-
capturing his prey.

"Come," said he, "ye nigger, ye 'r ready? Servant, ma'am!"
said he, taking off his hat, as he saw Mrs. Shelby.

Aunt Chloe shut and corded the box, and, getting up,
looked gruffly on the trader, her tears seeming suddenly
turned to sparks of fire.

Tom rose up meekly, to follow his new master, and raised
up his heavy box on his shoulder. His wife took the baby in

her arms to go with him to the wagon, and the children, still crying, trailed on behind.

Mrs. Shelby, walking up to the trader, detained him for a few moments, talking with him in an earnest manner; and while she was thus talking, the whole family party proceeded to a wagon, that stood ready harnessed at the door. A crowd of all the old and young hands on the place stood gathered around it, to bid farewell to their old associate. Tom had been looked up to, both as a head servant and a Christian teacher, by all the place, and there was much honest sympathy and grief about him, particularly among the women.

"Why, Chloe, you bar it better 'n we do!" said one of the women, who had been weeping freely, noticing the gloomy calmness with which Aunt Chloe stood by the wagon.

"I 's done *my* tears!" she said, looking grimly at the trader, who was coming up. "I does not feel to cry 'fore dat ar old limb, no how!"

"Get in!" said Haley to Tom, as he strode through the crowd of servants, who looked at him with lowering brows.

Tom got in, and Haley, drawing out from under the wagon seat a heavy pair of shackles, made them fast around each ankle.

A smothered groan of indignation ran through the whole circle, and Mrs. Shelby spoke from the verandah, —

"Mr. Haley, I assure you that precaution is entirely unnecessary."

"Do'n know, ma'am; I 've lost one five hundred dollars from this yer place, and I can't afford to run no more risks."

"What else could she spect on him?" said Aunt Chloe, indignantly, while the two boys, who now seemed to comprehend at once their father's destiny, clung to her gown, sobbing and groaning vehemently.

"I 'm sorry," said Tom, "that Mas'r George happened to be away."

George had gone to spend two or three days with a companion on a neighboring estate, and having departed early in the morning, before Tom's misfortune had been made public, had left without hearing of it.

"Give my love to Mas'r George," he said, earnestly.

Haley whipped up the horse, and, with a steady, mournful

look, fixed to the last on the old place, Tom was whirled away.

Mr. Shelby at this time was not at home. He had sold Tom under the spur of a driving necessity, to get out of the power of a man whom he dreaded,—and his first feeling, after the consummation of the bargain, had been that of relief. But his wife's expostulations awoke his half-slumbering regrets; and Tom's manly disinterestedness increased the unpleasantness of his feelings. It was in vain that he said to himself that he had a *right* to do it,—that everybody did it,—and that some did it without even the excuse of necessity;—he could not satisfy his own feelings; and that he might not witness the unpleasant scenes of the consummation, he had gone on a short business tour up the country, hoping that all would be over before he returned.

Tom and Haley rattled on along the dusty road, whirling past every old familiar spot, until the bounds of the estate were fairly passed, and they found themselves out on the open pike. After they had ridden about a mile, Haley suddenly drew up at the door of a blacksmith's shop, when, taking out with him a pair of handcuffs, he stepped into the shop, to have a little alteration in them.

"These yer's a little too small for his build," said Haley, showing the fetters, and pointing out to Tom.

"Lor! now, if thar an't Shelby's Tom. He han't sold him, now?" said the smith.

"Yes, he has," said Haley.

"Now, ye don't! well, reely," said the smith, "who'd a thought it! Why, ye need n't go to fetterin' him up this yer way. He's the faithfullest, best crittur—"

"Yes, yes," said Haley; "but your good fellers are just the critturs to want ter run off. Them stupid ones, as does n't care whar they go, and shifless, drunken ones, as don't care for nothin', they'll stick by, and like as not be rather pleased to be toted round; but these yer prime fellers, they hates it like sin. No way but to fetter 'em; got legs,—they'll use 'em,— no mistake."

"Well," said the smith, feeling among his tools, "them plantations down thar, stranger, an't jest the place a Kentuck nigger wants to go to; they dies thar tol'able fast, don't they?"

"Wal, yes, tol'able fast, ther dying is; what with the 'climating and one thing and another, they dies so as to keep the market up pretty brisk," said Haley.

"Wal, now, a feller can't help thinkin' it's a mighty pity to have a nice, quiet, likely feller, as good un as Tom is, go down to be fairly ground up on one of them ar sugar plantations."

"Wal, he's got a fa'r chance. I promised to do well by him. I'll get him in house-servant in some good old family, and then, if he stands the fever and 'climating, he'll have a berth good as any nigger ought ter ask for."

"He leaves his wife and chil'en up here, s'pose?"

"Yes; but he'll get another thar. Lord, thar's women enough everywhar," said Haley.

Tom was sitting very mournfully on the outside of the shop while this conversation was going on. Suddenly he heard the quick, short click of a horse's hoof behind him; and, before he could fairly awake from his surprise, young Master George sprang into the wagon, threw his arms tumultuously round his neck, and was sobbing and scolding with energy.

"I declare, it's real mean! I don't care what they say, any of 'em! It's a nasty, mean shame! If I was a man, they should n't do it,—they should not, *so!*" said George, with a kind of subdued howl.

"O! Mas'r George! this does me good!" said Tom. "I could n't bar to go off without seein' ye! It does me real good, ye can't tell!" Here Tom made some movement of his feet, and George's eye fell on the fetters.

"What a shame!" he exclaimed, lifting his hands. "I'll knock that old fellow down—I will!"

"No you won't, Mas'r George; and you must not talk so loud. It won't help me any, to anger him."

"Well, I won't, then, for your sake; but only to think of it— is n't it a shame? They never sent for me, nor sent me any word, and, if it had n't been for Tom Lincoln, I should n't have heard it. I tell you, I blew 'em up well, all of 'em, at home!"

"That ar was n't right, I 'm 'feard, Mas'r George."

"Can't help it! I say it's a shame! Look here, Uncle Tom," said he, turning his back to the shop, and speaking in a mysterious tone, *"I 've brought you my dollar!"*

"O! I could n't think o' takin' on 't, Mas'r George, no ways in the world!" said Tom, quite moved.

"But you *shall* take it!" said George; "look here—I told Aunt Chloe I 'd do it, and she advised me just to make a hole in it, and put a string through, so you could hang it round your neck, and keep it out of sight; else this mean scamp would take it away. I tell ye, Tom, I want to blow him up! it would do me good!"

"No, don't, Mas'r George, for it won't do *me* any good."

"Well, I won't, for your sake," said George, busily tying his dollar round Tom's neck; "but there, now, button your coat tight over it, and keep it, and remember, every time you see it, that I 'll come down after you, and bring you back. Aunt Chloe and I have been talking about it. I told her not to fear; I 'll see to it, and I 'll tease father's life out, if he don't do it."

"O! Mas'r George, ye must n't talk so 'bout yer father!"

"Lor, Uncle Tom, I don't mean anything bad."

"And now, Mas'r George," said Tom, "ye must be a good boy; 'member how many hearts is sot on ye. Al'ays keep close to yer mother. Don't be gettin' into any of them foolish ways boys has of gettin' too big to mind their mothers. Tell ye what, Mas'r George, the Lord gives good many things twice over; but he don't give ye a mother but once. Ye 'll never see sich another woman, Mas'r George, if ye live to be a hundred years old. So, now, you hold on to her, and grow up, and be a comfort to her, thar 's my own good boy,—you will now, won't ye?"

"Yes, I will, Uncle Tom," said George, seriously.

"And be careful of yer speaking, Mas'r George. Young boys, when they comes to your age, is wilful, sometimes— it 's natur they should be. But real gentlemen, such as I hopes you 'll be, never lets fall no words that is n't 'spectful to thar parents. Ye an't 'fended, Mas'r George?"

"No, indeed, Uncle Tom; you always did give me good advice."

"I 's older, ye know," said Tom, stroking the boy's fine, curly head with his large, strong hand, but speaking in a voice as tender as a woman's, "and I sees all that 's bound up in you. O, Mas'r George, you has everything,—l'arnin', privileges, readin', writin',—and you 'll grow up to be a great, learned, good man, and all the people on the place and your mother and father 'll be so proud on ye! Be a good Mas'r, like yer father; and be a Christian, like yer mother. 'Member yer Creator in the days o' yer youth, Mas'r George."

"I 'll be *real* good, Uncle Tom, I tell you," said George. "I 'm going to be a *first-rater*; and don't you be discouraged. I 'll have you back to the place, yet. As I told Aunt Chloe this morning, I 'll build your house all over, and you shall have a room for a parlor with a carpet on it, when I 'm a man. O, you 'll have good times yet!"

Haley now came to the door, with the handcuffs in his hands.

"Look here, now, Mister," said George, with an air of great superiority, as he got out, "I shall let father and mother know how you treat Uncle Tom!"

"You 're welcome," said the trader.

"I should think you 'd be ashamed to spend all your life buying men and women, and chaining them, like cattle! I should think you 'd feel mean!" said George.

"So long as your grand folks wants to buy men and women, I 'm as good as they is," said Haley; " 'tan't any meaner sellin' on 'em, than 't is buyin'!"

"I 'll never do either, when I 'm a man," said George; "I 'm ashamed, this day, that I 'm a Kentuckian. I always was proud of it before;" and George sat very straight on his horse, and looked round with an air, as if he expected the state would be impressed with his opinion.

"Well, good-by, Uncle Tom; keep a stiff upper lip," said George.

"Good-by, Mas'r George," said Tom, looking fondly and admiringly at him. "God Almighty bless you! Ah! Kentucky han't got many like you!" he said, in the fulness of his heart, as the frank, boyish face was lost to his view. Away he went, and Tom looked, till the clatter of his horse's heels died away, the last sound or sight of his home. But over his heart there seemed to be a warm spot, where those young hands had placed that precious dollar. Tom put up his hand, and held it close to his heart.

"Now, I tell ye what, Tom," said Haley, as he came up to

the wagon, and threw in the hand-cuffs, "I mean to start fa'r
with ye, as I gen'ally do with my niggers; and I 'll tell ye now,
to begin with, you treat me fa'r, and I 'll treat you fa'r; I an't
never hard on my niggers. Calculates to do the best for 'em I
can. Now, ye see, you 'd better jest settle down comfortable,
and not be tryin' no tricks; because nigger's tricks of all sorts
I 'm up to, and it 's no use. If niggers is quiet, and don't try
to get off, they has good times with me; and if they don't,
why, it 's thar fault, and not mine."

Tom assured Haley that he had no present intentions of
running off. In fact, the exhortation seemed rather a superfluous one to a man with a great pair of iron fetters on his feet.
But Mr. Haley had got in the habit of commencing his relations with his stock with little exhortations of this nature, calculated, as he deemed, to inspire cheerfulness and confidence,
and prevent the necessity of any unpleasant scenes.

And here, for the present, we take our leave of Tom, to
pursue the fortunes of other characters in our story.

XI.

In Which Property Gets into an Improper State of Mind

It was late in a drizzly afternoon that a traveller alighted at the door of a small country hotel, in the village of N——, in Kentucky. In the bar-room he found assembled quite a miscellaneous company, whom stress of weather had driven to harbor, and the place presented the usual scenery of such reunions. Great, tall, raw-boned Kentuckians, attired in hunting-shirts, and trailing their loose joints over a vast extent of territory, with the easy lounge peculiar to the race, —rifles stacked away in the corner, shot-pouches, game-bags, hunting-dogs, and little negroes, all rolled together in the corners,—were the characteristic features in the picture. At each end of the fireplace sat a long-legged gentleman, with his chair tipped back, his hat on his head, and the heels of his muddy boots reposing sublimely on the mantel-piece, —a position, we will inform our readers, decidedly favorable to the turn of reflection incident to western taverns, where travellers exhibit a decided preference for this particular mode of elevating their understandings.

Mine host, who stood behind the bar, like most of his countrymen, was great of stature, good-natured, and loose-jointed, with an enormous shock of hair on his head, and a great tall hat on the top of that.

In fact, everybody in the room bore on his head this characteristic emblem of man's sovereignty; whether it were felt hat, palm-leaf, greasy beaver, or fine new chapeau, there it reposed with true republican independence. In truth, it appeared to be the characteristic mark of every individual. Some wore them tipped rakishly to one side—these were your men of humor, jolly, free-and-easy dogs; some had them jammed independently down over their noses—these were your hard characters, thorough men, who, when they wore their hats, *wanted* to wear them, and to wear them just as they had a mind to; there were those who had them set far over back—wide-awake men, who wanted a clear prospect; while careless men, who did not know, or care, how their hats sat, had them shaking about in all directions. The various hats, in fact, were quite a Shakspearean study.

Divers negroes, in very free-and-easy pantaloons, and with no redundancy in the shirt line, were scuttling about, hither and thither, without bringing to pass any very particular results, except expressing a generic willingness to turn over everything in creation generally for the benefit of Mas'r and his guests. Add to this picture a jolly, crackling, rollicking fire, going rejoicingly up a great wide chimney,—the outer door and every window being set wide open, and the calico window-curtain flopping and snapping in a good stiff breeze of damp raw air,—and you have an idea of the jollities of a Kentucky tavern.

Your Kentuckian of the present day is a good illustration of the doctrine of transmitted instincts and peculiarities. His fathers were mighty hunters,—men who lived in the woods, and slept under the free, open heavens, with the stars to hold their candles; and their descendant to this day always acts as if the house were his camp,—wears his hat at all hours, tumbles himself about, and puts his heels on the tops of chairs or mantel-pieces, just as his father rolled on the green sward, and put his upon trees and logs,—keeps all the windows and doors open, winter and summer, that he may get air enough for his great lungs,—calls everybody "stranger," with nonchalant bonhommie, and is altogether the frankest, easiest, most jovial creature living.

Into such an assembly of the free and easy our traveller entered. He was a short, thick-set man, carefully dressed, with a round, good-natured countenance, and something rather fussy and particular in his appearance. He was very careful of his valise and umbrella, bringing them in with his own hands, and resisting, pertinaciously, all offers from the various servants to relieve him of them. He looked round the bar-room with rather an anxious air, and, retreating with his valuables to the warmest corner, disposed them under his chair, sat down, and looked rather apprehensively up at the worthy whose heels illustrated the end of the mantel-piece, who was spitting from right to left, with a courage and energy rather alarming to gentlemen of weak nerves and particular habits.

"I say, stranger, how are ye?" said the aforesaid gentleman, firing an honorary salute of tobacco-juice in the direction of the new arrival.

"Well, I reckon," was the reply of the other, as he dodged, with some alarm, the threatening honor.

"Any news?" said the respondent, taking out a strip of tobacco and a large hunting-knife from his pocket.

"Not that I know of," said the man.

"Chaw?" said the first speaker, handing the old gentleman a bit of his tobacco, with a decidedly brotherly air.

"No, thank ye—it don't agree with me," said the little man, edging off.

"Don't, eh?" said the other, easily, and stowing away the morsel in his own mouth, in order to keep up the supply of tobacco-juice, for the general benefit of society.

The old gentleman uniformly gave a little start whenever his long-sided brother fired in his direction; and this being observed by his companion, he very good-naturedly turned his artillery to another quarter, and proceeded to storm one of the fire-irons with a degree of military talent fully sufficient to take a city.

"What's that?" said the old gentleman, observing some of the company formed in a group around a large handbill.

"Nigger advertised!" said one of the company, briefly.

Mr. Wilson, for that was the old gentleman's name, rose up, and, after carefully adjusting his valise and umbrella, proceeded deliberately to take out his spectacles and fix them on his nose; and, this operation being performed, read as follows:

"Ran away from the subscriber, my mulatto boy, George. Said George six feet in height, a very light mulatto, brown curly hair; is very intelligent, speaks handsomely, can read and write; will probably try to pass for a white man; is deeply scarred on his back and shoulders; has been branded in his right hand with the letter H.

"I will give four hundred dollars for him alive, and the same sum for satisfactory proof that he has been killed."

The old gentleman read this advertisement from end to end, in a low voice, as if he were studying it.

The long-legged veteran, who had been besieging the fire-iron, as before related, now took down his cumbrous length, and rearing aloft his tall form, walked up to the advertisement, and very deliberately spit a full discharge of tobacco-juice on it.

"There's my mind upon that!" said he, briefly, and sat down again.

"Why, now, stranger, what's that for?" said mine host.

"I'd do it all the same to the writer of that ar paper, if he was here," said the long man, coolly resuming his old employment of cutting tobacco. "Any man that owns a boy like that, and can't find any better way o' treating on him, *deserves* to lose him. Such papers as these is a shame to Kentucky; that's my mind right out, if anybody wants to know!"

"Well, now, that's a fact," said mine host, as he made an entry in his book.

"I've got a gang of boys, sir," said the long man, resuming his attack on the fire-irons, "and I jest tells 'em—'Boys,' says I,—'*run* now! dig! put! jest when ye want to! I never shall come to look after you!' That's the way I keep mine. Let 'em know they are free to run any time, and it jest breaks up their wanting to. More 'n all, I've got free papers for 'em all recorded, in case I gets keeled up any o' these times, and they knows it; and I tell ye, stranger, there an't a fellow in our parts gets more out of his niggers than I do. Why, my boys have been to Cincinnati, with five hundred dollars' worth of colts, and brought me back the money, all straight, time and agin. It stands to reason they should. Treat 'em like dogs, and you'll have dogs' works and dogs' actions. Treat 'em like men, and you'll have men's works." And the honest drover, in his warmth, endorsed this moral sentiment by firing a perfect *feu de joie* at the fireplace.

"I think you're altogether right, friend," said Mr. Wilson; "and this boy described here *is* a fine fellow—no mistake about that. He worked for me some half-dozen years in my bagging factory, and he was my best hand, sir. He is an ingenious fellow, too: he invented a machine for the cleaning of hemp—a really valuable affair; it's gone into use in several factories. His master holds the patent of it."

"I'll warrant ye," said the drover, "holds it and makes money out of it, and then turns round and brands the boy in his right hand. If I had a fair chance, I'd mark him, I reckon, so that he'd carry it *one* while."

"These yer knowin' boys is allers aggravatin' and sarcy," said a coarse-looking fellow, from the other side of the room; "that's why they gets cut up and marked so. If they behaved themselves, they would n't."

"That is to say, the Lord made 'em men, and it's a hard squeeze getting 'em down into beasts," said the drover, dryly.

"Bright niggers is n't no kind of 'vantage to their masters," continued the other, well intrenched, in a coarse, unconscious obtuseness, from the contempt of his opponent; "what's the use o' talents and them things, if you can't get the use on 'em yourself? Why, all the use they make on't is to get round you. I've had one or two of these fellers, and I jest sold 'em down river. I knew I'd got to lose 'em, first or last, if I did n't."

"Better send orders up to the Lord, to make you a set, and leave out their souls entirely," said the drover.

Here the conversation was interrupted by the approach of a small one-horse buggy to the inn. It had a genteel appearance, and a well-dressed, gentlemanly man sat on the seat, with a colored servant driving.

The whole party examined the new comer with the interest with which a set of loafers in a rainy day usually examine every new comer. He was very tall, with a dark, Spanish complexion, fine, expressive black eyes, and close-curling hair, also of a glossy blackness. His well-formed aquiline nose, straight thin lips, and the admirable contour of his finely-formed limbs, impressed the whole company instantly with the idea of something uncommon. He walked easily in among the company, and with a nod indicated to his waiter where to place his trunk, bowed to the company, and, with his hat in his hand, walked up leisurely to the bar, and gave in his name as Henry Butler, Oaklands, Shelby County. Turning, with an indifferent air, he sauntered up to the advertisement, and read it over.

"Jim," he said to his man, "seems to me we met a boy something like this, up at Bernan's, did n't we?"

"Yes, Mas'r," said Jim, "only I an't sure about the hand."

"Well, I did n't look, of course," said the stranger, with a careless yawn. Then, walking up to the landlord, he desired him to furnish him with a private apartment, as he had some writing to do immediately.

The landlord was all obsequious, and a relay of about seven negroes, old and young, male and female, little and big, were soon whizzing about, like a covey of partridges, bustling, hurrying, treading on each other's toes, and tumbling over each other, in their zeal to get Mas'r's room ready, while he seated himself easily on a chair in the middle of the room, and entered into conversation with the man who sat next to him.

The manufacturer, Mr. Wilson, from the time of the entrance of the stranger, had regarded him with an air of disturbed and uneasy curiosity. He seemed to himself to have met and been acquainted with him somewhere, but he could not recollect. Every few moments, when the man spoke, or moved, or smiled, he would start and fix his eyes on him, and then suddenly withdraw them, as the bright, dark eyes met his with such unconcerned coolness. At last, a sudden recollection seemed to flash upon him, for he stared at the stranger with such an air of blank amazement and alarm, that he walked up to him.

"Mr. Wilson, I think," said he, in a tone of recognition, and extending his hand. "I beg your pardon, I did n't recollect you before. I see you remember me,—Mr. Butler, of Oaklands, Shelby County."

"Ye—yes—yes, sir," said Mr. Wilson, like one speaking in a dream.

Just then a negro boy entered, and announced that Mas'r's room was ready.

"Jim, see to the trunks," said the gentleman, negligently; then addressing himself to Mr. Wilson, he added—"I should like to have a few moments' conversation with you on business, in my room, if you please."

Mr. Wilson followed him, as one who walks in his sleep; and they proceeded to a large upper chamber, where a new-made fire was crackling, and various servants flying about, putting finishing touches to the arrangements.

When all was done, and the servants departed, the young man deliberately locked the door, and putting the key in his pocket, faced about, and folding his arms on his bosom, looked Mr. Wilson full in the face.

"George!" said Mr. Wilson.

"Yes, George," said the young man.

"I could n't have thought it!"

"I am pretty well disguised, I fancy," said the young man, with a smile. "A little walnut bark has made my yellow skin a genteel brown, and I 've dyed my hair black; so you see I don't answer to the advertisement at all."

"O, George! but this is a dangerous game you are playing. I could not have advised you to it."

"I can do it on my own responsibility," said George, with the same proud smile.

We remark, *en passant,* that George was, by his father's side, of white descent. His mother was one of those unfortunates of her race, marked out by personal beauty to be the slave of the passions of her possessor, and the mother of children who may never know a father. From one of the proudest families in Kentucky he had inherited a set of fine European features, and a high, indomitable spirit. From his mother he had received only a slight mulatto tinge, amply compensated by its accompanying rich, dark eye. A slight change in the tint of the skin and the color of his hair had metamorphosed him into the Spanish-looking fellow he then appeared; and as gracefulness of movement and gentlemanly manners had always been perfectly natural to him, he found no difficulty in playing the bold part he had adopted—that of a gentleman travelling with his domestic.

Mr. Wilson, a good-natured but extremely fidgety and cautious old gentleman, ambled up and down the room, appearing, as John Bunyan hath it, "much tumbled up and down in his mind," and divided between his wish to help George, and a certain confused notion of maintaining law and order: so, as he shambled about, he delivered himself as follows:

"Well, George, I s'pose you 're running away—leaving your lawful master, George—(I don't wonder at it)—at the same time, I'm sorry, George,—yes, decidedly—I think I must say that, George—it's my duty to tell you so."

"Why are you sorry, sir?" said George, calmly.

"Why, to see you, as it were, setting yourself in opposition to the laws of your country."

"*My* country!" said George, with a strong and bitter emphasis; "what country have I, but the grave,—and I wish to God that I was laid there!"

"Why, George, no—no—it won't do; this way of talking is wicked—unscriptural. George, you've got a hard master— in fact, he is—well he conducts himself reprehensibly—I can't pretend to defend him. But you know how the angel commanded Hagar to return to her mistress, and submit herself under her hand; and the apostle sent back Onesimus to his master."

"Don't quote Bible at me that way, Mr. Wilson," said George, with a flashing eye, "don't! for my wife is a Christian, and I mean to be, if ever I get to where I can; but to quote Bible to a fellow in my circumstances, is enough to make him give it up altogether. I appeal to God Almighty;— I'm willing to go with the case to Him, and ask Him if I do wrong to seek my freedom."

"These feelings are quite natural, George," said the good-natured man, blowing his nose. "Yes they're natural, but it is my duty not to encourage 'em in you. Yes, my boy, I'm sorry for you, now; it's a bad case—very bad; but the apostle says, 'Let every one abide in the condition in which he is called.' We must all submit to the indications of Providence, George,—don't you see?"

George stood with his head drawn back, his arms folded tightly over his broad breast, and a bitter smile curling his lips.

"I wonder, Mr. Wilson, if the Indians should come and take you a prisoner away from your wife and children, and want to keep you all your life hoeing corn for them, if you'd think it your duty to abide in the condition in which you were called. I rather think that you'd think the first stray horse you could find an indication of Providence—should n't you?"

The little old gentleman stared with both eyes at this illustration of the case; but, though not much of a reasoner, he had the sense in which some logicians on this particular subject do not excel,—that of saying nothing, where nothing could be said. So, as he stood carefully stroking his umbrella, and folding and patting down all the creases in it, he proceeded on with his exhortations in a general way.

"You see, George, you know, now, I always have stood your friend; and whatever I 've said, I 've said for your good. Now, here, it seems to me, you 're running an awful risk. You can't hope to carry it out. If you 're taken, it will be worse with you than ever; they 'll only abuse you, and half kill you, and sell you down river."

"Mr. Wilson, I know all this," said George. "I *do* run a risk, but—" he threw open his overcoat, and showed two pistols and a bowie-knife. "There!" he said, "I 'm ready for 'em! Down south I never *will* go. No! if it comes to that, I can earn myself at least six feet of free soil,—the first and last I shall ever own in Kentucky!"

"Why, George, this state of mind is awful; it 's getting really desperate, George. I 'm concerned. Going to break the laws of your country!"

"My country again! Mr. Wilson, *you* have a country; but what country have *I,* or any one like me, born of slave mothers? What laws are there for us? We don't make them,—we don't consent to them,—we have nothing to do with them; all they do for us is to crush us, and keep us down. Have n't I heard your Fourth-of-July speeches? Don't you tell us all, once a year, that governments derive their just power from the consent of the governed? Can't a fellow *think,* that hears such things? Can't he put this and that together, and see what it comes to?"

Mr. Wilson's mind was one of those that may not unaptly be represented by a bale of cotton,—downy, soft, benevolently fuzzy and confused. He really pitied George with all his heart, and had a sort of dim and cloudy perception of the style of feeling that agitated him; but he deemed it his duty to go on talking *good* to him, with infinite pertinacity.

"George, this is bad. I must tell you, you know, as a friend, you 'd better not be meddling with such notions; they are bad, George, very bad, for boys in your condition,—very;"

and Mr. Wilson sat down to a table, and began nervously
chewing the handle of his umbrella.

"See here, now, Mr. Wilson," said George, coming up and
sitting himself determinately down in front of him; "look at
me, now. Don't I sit before you, every way, just as much a
man as you are? Look at my face,—look at my hands,—look
at my body," and the young man drew himself up proudly;
"why am I *not* a man, as much as anybody? Well, Mr. Wilson,
hear what I can tell you. I had a father—one of your Kentucky gentlemen—who did n't think enough of me to keep
me from being sold with his dogs and horses, to satisfy the
estate, when he died. I saw my mother put up at sheriff's
sale, with her seven children. They were sold before her eyes,
one by one, all to different masters; and I was the youngest.
She came and kneeled down before old Mas'r, and begged
him to buy her with me, that she might have at least one
child with her; and he kicked her away with his heavy boot.
I saw him do it; and the last that I heard was her moans and
screams, when I was tied to his horse's neck, to be carried off
to his place."

"Well, then?"

"My master traded with one of the men, and bought my
oldest sister. She was a pious, good girl,—a member of the
Baptist church,—and as handsome as my poor mother had
been. She was well brought up, and had good manners. At
first, I was glad she was bought, for I had one friend near me.
I was soon sorry for it. Sir, I have stood at the door and
heard her whipped, when it seemed as if every blow cut into
my naked heart, and I could n't do anything to help her; and
she was whipped, sir, for wanting to live a decent Christian
life, such as your laws give no slave girl a right to live; and at
last I saw her chained with a trader's gang, to be sent to
market in Orleans,—sent there for nothing else but that,—
and that 's the last I know of her. Well, I grew up,—long
years and years,—no father, no mother, no sister, not a living
soul that cared for me more than a dog; nothing but whipping, scolding, starving. Why, sir, I 've been so hungry that
I have been glad to take the bones they threw to their dogs;
and yet, when I was a little fellow, and laid awake whole
nights and cried, it was n't the hunger, it was n't the whip-

ping, I cried for. No, sir; it was for *my mother* and *my sisters,*—it was because I had n't a friend to love me on earth. I never knew what peace or comfort was. I never had a kind word spoken to me till I came to work in your factory. Mr. Wilson, you treated me well; you encouraged me to do well, and to learn to read and write, and to try to make something of myself; and God knows how grateful I am for it. Then, sir, I found my wife; you 've seen her,—you know how beautiful she is. When I found she loved me, when I married her, I scarcely could believe I was alive, I was so happy; and, sir, she is as good as she is beautiful. But now what? Why, now comes my master, takes me right away from my work, and my friends, and all I like, and grinds me down into the very dirt! And why? Because, he says, I forgot who I was; he says, to teach me that I am only a nigger! After all, and last of all, he comes between me and my wife, and says I shall give her up, and live with another woman. And all this your laws give him power to do, in spite of God or man. Mr. Wilson, look at it! There is n't *one* of all these things, that have broken the hearts of my mother and my sister, and my wife and myself, but your laws allow, and give every man power to do, in Kentucky, and none can say to him nay! Do you call these the laws of *my* country? Sir, I have n't any country, any more than I have any father. But I 'm going to have one. I don't want anything of *your* country, except to be let alone,—to go peaceably out of it; and when I get to Canada, where the laws will own me and protect me, *that* shall be my country, and its laws I will obey. But if any man tries to stop me, let him take care, for I am desperate. I 'll fight for my liberty to the last breath I breathe. You say your fathers did it; if it was right for them, it is right for me!"

This speech, delivered partly while sitting at the table, and partly walking up and down the room,—delivered with tears, and flashing eyes, and despairing gestures,—was altogether too much for the good-natured old body to whom it was addressed, who had pulled out a great yellow silk pocket-handkerchief, and was mopping up his face with great energy.

"Blast 'em all!" he suddenly broke out. "Have n't I always said so—the infernal old cusses! I hope I an't swearing, now. Well! go ahead, George, go ahead; but be careful, my boy;

don't shoot anybody, George, unless—well—you'd *better* not shoot, I reckon; at least, I would n't *hit* anybody, you know. Where is your wife, George?" he added, as he nervously rose, and began walking the room.

"Gone, sir, gone, with her child in her arms, the Lord only knows where;—gone after the north star; and when we ever meet, or whether we meet at all in this world, no creature can tell."

"Is it possible! astonishing! from such a kind family?"

"Kind families get in debt, and the laws of *our* country allow them to sell the child out of its mother's bosom to pay its master's debts," said George, bitterly.

"Well, well," said the honest old man, fumbling in his pocket. "I s'pose, perhaps, I an't following my judgment,—hang it, I *won't* follow my judgment!" he added, suddenly; "so here, George," and, taking out a roll of bills from his pocket-book, he offered them to George.

"No, my kind, good sir!" said George, "you've done a great deal for me, and this might get you into trouble. I have money enough, I hope, to take me as far as I need it."

"No; but you must, George. Money is a great help everywhere;—can't have too much, if you get it honestly. Take it,—*do* take it, *now*,—do, my boy!"

"On condition, sir, that I may repay it at some future time, I will," said George, taking up the money.

"And now, George, how long are you going to travel in this way?—not long or far, I hope. It's well carried on, but too bold. And this black fellow,—who is he?"

"A true fellow, who went to Canada more than a year ago. He heard, after he got there, that his master was so angry at him for going off that he had whipped his poor old mother; and he has come all the way back to comfort her, and get a chance to get her away."

"Has he got her?"

"Not yet; he has been hanging about the place, and found no chance yet. Meanwhile, he is going with me as far as Ohio, to put me among friends that helped him, and then he will come back after her."

"Dangerous, very dangerous!" said the old man.

George drew himself up, and smiled disdainfully.

The old gentleman eyed him from head to foot, with a sort of innocent wonder.

"George, something has brought you out wonderfully. You hold up your head, and speak and move like another man," said Mr. Wilson.

"Because I 'm a *freeman*!" said George, proudly. "Yes, sir; I 've said Mas'r for the last time to any man. *I 'm free!*"

"Take care! You are not sure,—you may be taken."

"All men are free and equal *in the grave*, if it comes to that, Mr. Wilson," said George.

"I 'm perfectly dumb-foundered with your boldness!" said Mr. Wilson,—"to come right here to the nearest tavern!"

"Mr. Wilson, it is *so* bold, and this tavern is so near, that they will never think of it; they will look for me on ahead, and you yourself would n't know me. Jim's master don't live in this county; he is n't known in these parts. Besides, he is given up; nobody is looking after him, and nobody will take me up from the advertisement, I think."

"But the mark in your hand?"

George drew off his glove, and showed a newly-healed scar in his hand.

"That is a parting proof of Mr. Harris' regard," he said, scornfully. "A fortnight ago, he took it into his head to give it to me, because he said he believed I should try to get away one of these days. Looks interesting, does n't it?" he said, drawing his glove on again.

"I declare, my very blood runs cold when I think of it,— your condition and your risks!" said Mr. Wilson.

"Mine has run cold a good many years, Mr. Wilson; at present, it 's about up to the boiling point," said George.

"Well, my good sir," continued George, after a few moments' silence, "I saw you knew me; I thought I 'd just have this talk with you, lest your surprised looks should bring me out. I leave early to-morrow morning, before daylight; by to-morrow night I hope to sleep safe in Ohio. I shall travel by daylight, stop at the best hotels, go to the dinner-tables with the lords of the land. So, good-by, sir; if you hear that I 'm taken, you may know that I 'm dead!"

George stood up like a rock, and put out his hand with the air of a prince. The friendly little old man shook it heartily, and after a little shower of caution, he took his umbrella, and fumbled his way out of the room.

George stood thoughtfully looking at the door, as the old man closed it. A thought seemed to flash across his mind. He hastily stepped to it, and opening it, said,

"Mr. Wilson, one word more."

The old gentleman entered again, and George, as before, locked the door, and then stood for a few moments looking on the floor, irresolutely. At last, raising his head with a sudden effort—

"Mr. Wilson, you have shown yourself a Christian in your treatment of me,—I want to ask one last deed of Christian kindness of you."

"Well, George."

"Well, sir,—what you said was true. I *am* running a dreadful risk. There is n't, on earth, a living soul to care if I die," he added, drawing his breath hard, and speaking with a great effort,—"I shall be kicked out and buried like a dog, and nobody 'll think of it a day after,—*only my poor wife!* Poor soul! she 'll mourn and grieve; and if you 'd only contrive, Mr. Wilson, to send this little pin to her. She gave it to me for a Christmas present, poor child! Give it to her, and tell her I loved her to the last. Will you? *Will* you?" he added, earnestly.

"Yes, certainly—poor fellow!" said the old gentleman, taking the pin, with watery eyes, and a melancholy quiver in his voice.

"Tell her one thing," said George; "it 's my last wish, if she *can* get to Canada, to go there. No matter how kind her mistress is,—no matter how much she loves her home; beg her not to go back,—for slavery always ends in misery. Tell her to bring up our boy a free man, and then he won't suffer as I have. Tell her this, Mr. Wilson, will you?"

"Yes, George, I 'll tell her; but I trust you won't die; take heart,—you 're a brave fellow. Trust in the Lord, George. I wish in my heart you were safe through, though,—that 's what I do."

"*Is* there a God to trust in?" said George, in such a tone of utter despair as arrested the old gentleman's words. "O, I 've seen things all my life that have made me feel that there can't be a God. You Christians don't know how these things look to us. There 's a God for you, but is there any for us?"

"O, now, don't—don't, my boy!" said the old man, almost sobbing as he spoke; "don't feel so! There is—there is; clouds and darkness are around about him, but righteousness and judgment are the habitation of his throne. There 's a *God*, George,—believe it; trust in Him, and I 'm sure He 'll help you. Everything will be set right,—if not in this life, in another."

The real piety and benevolence of the simple old man invested him with a temporary dignity and authority, as he spoke. George stopped his distracted walk up and down the room, stood thoughtfully a moment, and then said, quietly,

"Thank you for saying that, my good friend; I 'll *think of that*."

XII.

Select Incident of Lawful Trade

"In Ramah there was a voice heard,—weeping, and lamentation, and great mourning; Rachel weeping for her children, and would not be comforted."

M R. Haley and Tom jogged onward in their wagon, each, for a time, absorbed in his own reflections. Now, the reflections of two men sitting side by side are a curious thing,—seated on the same seat, having the same eyes, ears, hands and organs of all sorts, and having pass before their eyes the same objects,—it is wonderful what a variety we shall find in these same reflections!

As, for example, Mr. Haley: he thought first of Tom's length, and breadth, and height, and what he would sell for, if he was kept fat and in good case till he got him into market. He thought of how he should make out his gang; he thought of the respective market value of certain supposititious men and women and children who were to compose it, and other kindred topics of the business; then he thought of himself, and how humane he was, that whereas other men chained their "niggers" hand and foot both, he only put fetters on the feet, and left Tom the use of his hands, as long as he behaved well; and he sighed to think how ungrateful human nature was, so that there was even room to doubt whether Tom appreciated his mercies. He had been taken in so by "niggers" whom he had favored; but still he was astonished to consider how good-natured he yet remained!

As to Tom, he was thinking over some words of an unfashionable old book, which kept running through his head, again and again, as follows: "We have here no continuing city, but we seek one to come; wherefore God himself is not ashamed to be called our God; for he hath prepared for us a city." These words of an ancient volume, got up principally by "ignorant and unlearned men," have, through all time, kept up, somehow, a strange sort of power over the minds of poor, simple fellows, like Tom. They stir up the soul from its depths, and rouse, as with trumpet call, courage, energy, and enthusiasm, where before was only the blackness of despair.

Mr. Haley pulled out of his pocket sundry newspapers, and began looking over their advertisements, with absorbed interest. He was not a remarkably fluent reader, and was in the habit of reading in a sort of recitative half-aloud, by way of calling in his ears to verify the deductions of his eyes. In this tone he slowly recited the following paragraph:

"EXECUTOR'S SALE,—NEGROES!—Agreeably to order of court, will be sold, on Tuesday, February 20, before the Court-house door, in the town of Washington, Kentucky, the following negroes: Hagar, aged 60; John, aged 30; Ben, aged 21; Saul, aged 25; Albert, aged 14. Sold for the benefit of the creditors and heirs of the estate of Jesse Blutchford, Esq.

SAMUEL MORRIS,
THOMAS FLINT,
Executors."

"This yer I must look at," said he to Tom, for want of somebody else to talk to.

"Ye see, I'm going to get up a prime gang to take down with ye, Tom; it'll make it sociable and pleasant like,—good company will, ye know. We must drive right to Washington first and foremost, and then I'll clap you into jail, while I does the business."

Tom received this agreeable intelligence quite meekly; simply wondering, in his own heart, how many of these doomed men had wives and children, and whether they would feel as he did about leaving them. It is to be confessed, too, that the naïve, off-hand information that he was to be thrown into jail by no means produced an agreeable impression on a poor fellow who had always prided himself on a strictly honest and upright course of life. Yes, Tom, we must confess it, was rather proud of his honesty, poor fellow,—not having very much else to be proud of;—if he had belonged to some of the higher walks of society, he, perhaps, would never have been reduced to such straits. However, the day wore on, and the evening saw Haley and Tom comfortably accommodated in Washington,—the one in a tavern, and the other in a jail.

About eleven o'clock the next day, a mixed throng was gathered around the court-house steps,—smoking, chewing, spitting, swearing, and conversing, according to their respective tastes and turns,—waiting for the auction to commence. The men and women to be sold sat in a group apart, talking in a low tone to each other. The woman who had been advertised by the name of Hagar was a regular African in feature and figure. She might have been sixty, but was older than that by hard work and disease, was partially blind, and somewhat crippled with rheumatism. By her side stood her only remaining son, Albert, a bright-looking little fellow of fourteen years. The boy was the only survivor of a large family, who had been successively sold away from her to a southern market. The mother held on to him with both her shaking hands, and eyed with intense trepidation every one who walked up to examine him.

"Don't be feard, Aunt Hagar," said the oldest of the men, "I spoke to Mas'r Thomas 'bout it, and he thought he might manage to sell you in a lot both together."

"Dey need n't call me worn out yet," said she, lifting her shaking hands. "I can cook yet, and scrub, and scour,—I 'm wuth a buying, if I do come cheap;—tell em dat ar,—you *tell* em," she added, earnestly.

Haley here forced his way into the group, walked up to the old man, pulled his mouth open and looked in, felt of his teeth, made him stand and straighten himself, bend his back, and perform various evolutions to show his muscles; and then passed on to the next, and put him through the same trial. Walking up last to the boy, he felt of his arms, straightened his hands, and looked at his fingers, and made him jump, to show his agility.

"He an't gwine to be sold widout me!" said the old woman, with passionate eagerness; "he and I goes in a lot together; I 's rail strong yet, Mas'r, and can do heaps o' work,—heaps on it, Mas'r."

"On plantation?" said Haley, with a contemptuous glance. "Likely story!" and, as if satisfied with his examination, he walked out and looked, and stood with his hands in his pocket, his cigar in his mouth, and his hat cocked on one side, ready for action.

"What think of 'em?" said a man who had been following Haley's examination, as if to make up his own mind from it.

"Wal," said Haley, spitting, "I shall put in, I think, for the youngerly ones and the boy."

"They want to sell the boy and the old woman together," said the man.

"Find it a tight pull;—why, she 's an old rack o' bones,—not worth her salt."

"You would n't, then?" said the man.

"Anybody 'd be a fool 't would. She 's half blind, crooked with rheumatis, and foolish to boot."

"Some buys up these yer old critturs, and ses there 's a sight more wear in 'em than a body 'd think," said the man, reflectively.

"No go, 't all," said Haley; "would n't take her for a present,—fact,—I 've *seen*, now."

"Wal, 't is kinder pity, now, not to buy her with her son,—her heart seems so sot on him,—s'pose they fling her in cheap."

"Them that 's got money to spend that ar way, it 's all well enough. I shall bid off on that ar boy for a plantation-hand;—would n't be bothered with her, no way,—not if they 'd give her to me," said Haley.

"She 'll take on desp't," said the man.

"Nat'lly, she will," said the trader, coolly.

The conversation was here interrupted by a busy hum in the audience; and the auctioneer, a short, bustling, important fellow, elbowed his way into the crowd. The old woman drew in her breath, and caught instinctively at her son.

"Keep close to yer mammy, Albert,—close,—dey 'll put us up togedder," she said.

"O, mammy, I 'm feard they won't," said the boy.

"Dey must, child; I can't live, no ways, if they don't," said the old creature, vehemently.

The stentorian tones of the auctioneer, calling out to clear the way, now announced that the sale was about to commence. A place was cleared, and the bidding began. The different men on the list were soon knocked off at prices which showed a pretty brisk demand in the market; two of them fell to Haley.

"Come, now, young un," said the auctioneer, giving the boy a touch with his hammer, "be up and show your springs, now."

"Put us two up togedder, togedder,—do please, Mas'r," said the old woman, holding fast to her boy.

"Be off," said the man, gruffly, pushing her hands away; "you come last. Now, darkey, spring;" and, with the word, he pushed the boy toward the block, while a deep, heavy groan rose behind him. The boy paused, and looked back; but there was no time to stay, and, dashing the tears from his large, bright eyes, he was up in a moment.

His fine figure, alert limbs, and bright face, raised an instant competition, and half a dozen bids simultaneously met the ear of the auctioneer. Anxious, half-frightened, he looked from side to side, as he heard the clatter of contending bids,—now here, now there,—till the hammer fell. Haley had got him. He was pushed from the block toward his new master, but stopped one moment, and looked back, when his poor old mother, trembling in every limb, held out her shaking hands toward him.

"Buy me too, Mas'r, for de dear Lord's sake!—buy me,— I shall die if you don't!"

"You 'll die if I do, that 's the kink of it," said Haley,— "no!" And he turned on his heel.

The bidding for the poor old creature was summary. The man who had addressed Haley, and who seemed not destitute of compassion, bought her for a trifle, and the spectators began to disperse.

The poor victims of the sale, who had been brought up in one place together for years, gathered round the despairing old mother, whose agony was pitiful to see.

"Could n't dey leave me one? Mas'r allers said I should have one,—he did," she repeated over and over, in heart-broken tones.

"Trust in the Lord, Aunt Hagar," said the oldest of the men, sorrowfully.

"What good will it do?" said she, sobbing passionately.

"Mother, mother,—don't! don't!" said the boy. "They say you 's got a good master."

"I don't care,—I don't care. O, Albert! oh, my boy! you 's my last baby. Lord, how ken I?"

The Auction Sale

"Come, take her off, can't some of ye?" said Haley, dryly; "don't do no good for her to go on that ar way."

The old men of the company, partly by persuasion and partly by force, loosed the poor creature's last despairing hold, and, as they led her off to her new master's wagon, strove to comfort her.

"Now!" said Haley, pushing his three purchases together, and producing a bundle of handcuffs, which he proceeded to put on their wrists; and fastening each handcuff to a long chain, he drove them before him to the jail.

A few days saw Haley, with his possessions, safely deposited on one of the Ohio boats. It was the commencement of his gang, to be augmented, as the boat moved on, by various other merchandise of the same kind, which he, or his agent, had stored for him in various points along shore.

The La Belle Rivière, as brave and beautiful a boat as ever walked the waters of her namesake river, was floating gayly down the stream, under a brilliant sky, the stripes and stars of free America waving and fluttering over head; the guards crowded with well-dressed ladies and gentlemen walking and enjoying the delightful day. All was full of life, buoyant and rejoicing; — all but Haley's gang, who were stored, with other freight, on the lower deck, and who, somehow, did not seem to appreciate their various privileges, as they sat in a knot, talking to each other in low tones.

"Boys," said Haley, coming up, briskly, "I hope you keep up good heart, and are cheerful. Now, no sulks, ye see; keep stiff upper lip, boys; do well by me, and I 'll do well by you."

The boys addressed responded the invariable "Yes, Mas'r," for ages the watchword of poor Africa; but it 's to be owned they did not look particularly cheerful; they had their various little prejudices in favor of wives, mothers, sisters, and children, seen for the last time, — and though "they that wasted them required of them mirth," it was not instantly forthcoming.

"I 've got a wife," spoke out the article enumerated as "John, aged thirty," and he laid his chained hand on Tom's knee, — "and she don't know a word about this, poor girl!"

"Where does she live?" said Tom.

"In a tavern a piece down here," said John; "I wish, now, I *could* see her once more in this world," he added.

Poor John! It *was* rather natural; and the tears that fell, as he spoke, came as naturally as if he had been a white man. Tom drew a long breath from a sore heart, and tried, in his poor way, to comfort him.

And over head, in the cabin, sat fathers and mothers, husbands and wives; and merry, dancing children moved round among them, like so many little butterflies, and everything was going on quite easy and comfortable.

"O, mamma," said a boy, who had just come up from below, "there 's a negro trader on board, and he 's brought four or five slaves down there."

"Poor creatures!" said the mother, in a tone between grief and indignation.

"What 's that?" said another lady.

"Some poor slaves below," said the mother.

"And they 've got chains on," said the boy.

"What a shame to our country that such sights are to be seen!" said another lady.

"O, there 's a great deal to be said on both sides of the subject," said a genteel woman, who sat at her state-room door sewing, while her little girl and boy were playing round her. "I 've been south, and I must say I think the negroes are better off than they would be to be free."

"In some respects, some of them are well off, I grant," said the lady to whose remark she had answered. "The most dreadful part of slavery, to my mind, is its outrages on the feelings and affections,—the separating of families, for example."

"That *is* a bad thing, certainly," said the other lady, holding up a baby's dress she had just completed, and looking intently on its trimmings; "but then, I fancy, it don't occur often."

"O, it does," said the first lady, eagerly; "I 've lived many years in Kentucky and Virginia both, and I 've seen enough to make any one's heart sick. Suppose, ma'am, your two children, there, should be taken from you, and sold?"

"We can't reason from our feelings to those of this class of persons," said the other lady, sorting out some worsteds on her lap.

"Indeed, ma'am, you can know nothing of them, if you say so," answered the first lady, warmly. "I was born and brought up among them. I know they *do* feel, just as keenly,—even more so, perhaps,—as we do."

The lady said "Indeed!" yawned, and looked out the cabin window, and finally repeated, for a finale, the remark with which she had begun,—"After all, I think they are better off than they would be to be free."

"It 's undoubtedly the intention of Providence that the African race should be servants,—kept in a low condition," said a grave-looking gentleman in black, a clergyman, seated by the cabin door. " 'Cursed be Canaan; a servant of servants shall he be,' the scripture says."

"I say, stranger, is that ar what that text means?" said a tall man, standing by.

"Undoubtedly. It pleased Providence, for some inscrutable reason, to doom the race to bondage, ages ago; and we must not set up our opinion against that."

"Well, then, we 'll all go ahead and buy up niggers," said the man, "if that 's the way of Providence,—won't we, Squire?" said he, turning to Haley, who had been standing, with his hands in his pockets, by the stove, and intently listening to the conversation.

"Yes," continued the tall man, "we must all be resigned to the decrees of Providence. Niggers must be sold, and trucked round, and kept under; it 's what they 's made for. 'Pears like this yer view 's quite refreshing, an't it, stranger?" said he to Haley.

"I never thought on 't," said Haley. "I could n't have said as much, myself; I ha'nt no larning. I took up the trade just to make a living; if 't an't right, I calculated to 'pent on 't in time, *ye* know."

"And now you 'll save yerself the trouble, won't ye?" said the tall man. "See what 't is, now, to know scripture. If ye 'd only studied yer Bible, like this yer good man, ye might have know'd it before, and saved ye a heap o' trouble. Ye could jist have said, 'Cussed be'—what 's his name? —'and 't would all have come right.' " And the stranger, who was no other than the honest drover whom we intro-

duced to our readers in the Kentucky tavern, sat down, and
began smoking, with a curious smile on his long, dry face.

A tall, slender young man, with a face expressive of great
feeling and intelligence, here broke in, and repeated the
words, " 'All things whatsoever ye would that men should do
unto you, do ye even so unto them.' I suppose," he added,
"*that* is scripture, as much as 'Cursed be Canaan.' "

"Wal, it seems quite *as* plain a text, stranger," said John the
drover, "to poor fellows like us, now;" and John smoked on
like a volcano.

The young man paused, looked as if he was going to say
more, when suddenly the boat stopped, and the company
made the usual steamboat rush, to see where they were landing.

"Both them ar chaps parsons?" said John to one of the
men, as they were going out.

The man nodded.

As the boat stopped, a black woman came running wildly
up the plank, darted into the crowd, flew up to where the
slave gang sat, and threw her arms round that unfortunate
piece of merchandise before enumerated—"John, aged
thirty," and with sobs and tears bemoaned him as her husband.

But what needs tell the story, told too oft,—every day
told,—of heart-strings rent and broken,—the weak broken
and torn for the profit and convenience of the strong! It
needs not to be told;—every day is telling it,—telling it, too,
in the ear of One who is not deaf, though he be long silent.

The young man who had spoken for the cause of humanity
and God before stood with folded arms, looking on this
scene. He turned, and Haley was standing at his side. "My
friend," he said, speaking with thick utterance, "how can you,
how dare you, carry on a trade like this? Look at those poor
creatures! Here I am, rejoicing in my heart that I am going
home to my wife and child; and the same bell which is a
signal to carry me onward towards them will part this poor
man and his wife forever. Depend upon it, God will bring
you into judgment for this."

The trader turned away in silence.

"I say, now," said the drover, touching his elbow, "there 's differences in parsons, an't there? 'Cussed be Canaan' don't seem to go down with this 'un, does it?"

Haley gave an uneasy growl.

"And that ar an't the worst on 't," said John; "mabbe it won't go down with the Lord, neither, when ye come to settle with Him, one o' these days, as all on us must, I reckon."

Haley walked reflectively to the other end of the boat.

"If I make pretty handsomely on one or two next gangs," he thought, "I reckon I 'll stop off this yer; it 's really getting dangerous." And he took out his pocket-book, and began adding over his accounts—a process which many gentlemen besides Mr. Haley have found a specific for an uneasy conscience.

The boat swept proudly away from the shore, and all went on merrily, as before. Men talked, and loafed, and read, and smoked. Women sewed, and children played, and the boat passed on her way.

One day, when she lay to for a while at a small town in Kentucky, Haley went up into the place on a little matter of business.

Tom, whose fetters did not prevent his taking a moderate circuit, had drawn near the side of the boat, and stood listlessly gazing over the railings. After a time, he saw the trader returning, with an alert step, in company with a colored woman, bearing in her arms a young child. She was dressed quite respectably, and a colored man followed her, bringing along a small trunk. The woman came cheerfully onward, talking, as she came, with the man who bore her trunk, and so passed up the plank into the boat. The bell rung, the steamer whizzed, the engine groaned and coughed, and away swept the boat down the river.

The woman walked forward among the boxes and bales of the lower deck, and sitting down, busied herself with chirruping to her baby.

Haley made a turn or two about the boat, and then, coming up, seated himself near her, and began saying something to her in an indifferent undertone.

Tom soon noticed a heavy cloud passing over the woman's brow; and that she answered rapidly, and with great vehemence.

"I don't believe it,—I won't believe it!" he heard her say. "You're jist a foolin with me."

"If you won't believe it, look here!" said the man, drawing out a paper; "this yer's the bill of sale, and there's your master's name to it; and I paid down good solid cash for it, too, I can tell you,—so, now!"

"I don't believe Mas'r would cheat me so; it can't be true!" said the woman, with increasing agitation.

"You can ask any of these men here, that can read writing. Here!" he said, to a man that was passing by, "jist read this yer, won't you! This yer gal won't believe me, when I tell her what 't is."

"Why, it's a bill of sale, signed by John Fosdick," said the man, "making over to you the girl Lucy and her child. It's all straight enough, for aught I see."

The woman's passionate exclamations collected a crowd around her, and the trader briefly explained to them the cause of the agitation.

"He told me that I was going down to Louisville, to hire out as cook to the same tavern where my husband works,— that's what Mas'r told me, his own self; and I can't believe he'd lie to me," said the woman.

"But he has sold you, my poor woman, there's no doubt about it," said a good-natured looking man, who had been examining the papers; "he has done it, and no mistake."

"Then it's no account talking," said the woman, suddenly growing quite calm; and, clasping her child tighter in her arms, she sat down on her box, turned her back round, and gazed listlessly into the river.

"Going to take it easy, after all!" said the trader. "Gal's got grit, I see."

The woman looked calm, as the boat went on; and a beautiful soft summer breeze passed like a compassionate spirit over her head,—the gentle breeze, that never inquires whether the brow is dusky or fair that it fans. And she saw sunshine sparkling on the water, in golden ripples, and heard gay voices, full of ease and pleasure, talking around her everywhere; but her heart lay as if a great stone had fallen on it. Her baby raised himself up against her, and stroked her cheeks with his little hands; and, springing up and down, crowing and chatting, seemed determined to arouse her. She strained him suddenly and tightly in her arms, and slowly one tear after another fell on his wondering, unconscious face; and gradually she seemed, and little by little, to grow calmer, and busied herself with tending and nursing him.

The child, a boy of ten months, was uncommonly large and strong of his age, and very vigorous in his limbs. Never, for a moment, still, he kept his mother constantly busy in holding him, and guarding his springing activity.

"That's a fine chap!" said a man, suddenly stopping opposite to him, with his hands in his pockets. "How old is he?"

"Ten months and a half," said the mother.

The man whistled to the boy, and offered him part of a stick of candy, which he eagerly grabbed at, and very soon had it in a baby's general depository, to wit, his mouth.

"Rum fellow!" said the man. "Knows what's what!" and he whistled, and walked on. When he had got to the other side of the boat, he came across Haley, who was smoking on top of a pile of boxes.

The stranger produced a match, and lighted a cigar, saying, as he did so,

"Decentish kind o' wench you've got round there, stranger."

"Why, I reckon she *is* tol'able fair," said Haley, blowing the smoke out of his mouth.

"Taking her down south?" said the man.

Haley nodded, and smoked on.

"Plantation hand?" said the man.

"Wal," said Haley, "I'm fillin' out an order for a plantation, and I think I shall put her in. They told me she was a good cook; and they can use her for that, or set her at the cotton-picking. She's got the right fingers for that; I looked at 'em. Sell well, either way;" and Haley resumed his cigar.

"They won't want the young 'un on a plantation," said the man.

"I shall sell him, first chance I find," said Haley, lighting another cigar.

"S'pose you'd be selling him tol'able cheap," said the stranger, mounting the pile of boxes, and sitting down comfortably.

"Don't know 'bout that," said Haley; "he's a pretty smart young 'un,—straight, fat, strong; flesh as hard as a brick!"

"Very true, but then there's all the bother and expense of raisin'."

"Nonsense!" said Haley; "they is raised as easy as any kind of critter there is going; they an't a bit more trouble than pups. This yer chap will be running all round, in a month."

"I've got a good place for raisin', and I thought of takin' in a little more stock," said the man. "One cook lost a young 'un last week,—got drownded in a wash-tub, while she was a hangin' out clothes,—and I reckon it would be well enough to set her to raisin' this yer."

Haley and the stranger smoked a while in silence, neither seeming willing to broach the test question of the interview. At last the man resumed:

"You would n't think of wantin' more than ten dollars for that ar chap, seeing you *must* get him off yer hand, any how?"

Haley shook his head, and spit impressively.

"That won't do, no ways," he said, and began his smoking again.

"Well, stranger, what will you take?"

"Well, now," said Haley, "I *could* raise that ar chap myself, or get him raised; he's oncommon likely and healthy, and he'd fetch a hundred dollars, six months hence; and, in a year or two, he'd bring two hundred, if I had him in the right spot;—so I shan't take a cent less nor fifty for him now."

"O, stranger! that's rediculous, altogether," said the man.

"Fact!" said Haley, with a decisive nod of his head.

"I'll give thirty for him," said the stranger, "but not a cent more."

"Now, I'll tell ye what I will do," said Haley, spitting again, with renewed decision. "I'll split the difference, and say forty-five; and that's the most I will do."

"Well, agreed!" said the man, after an interval.

"Done!" said Haley. "Where do you land?"

"At Louisville," said the man.

"Louisville," said Haley. "Very fair, we get there about dusk. Chap will be asleep,—all fair,—get him off quietly, and no screaming,—happens beautiful,—I like to do everything quietly,—I hates all kind of agitation and fluster." And so, after a transfer of certain bills had passed from the man's pocket-book to the trader's, he resumed his cigar.

It was a bright, tranquil evening when the boat stopped at the wharf at Louisville. The woman had been sitting with her baby in her arms, now wrapped in a heavy sleep. When she heard the name of the place called out, she hastily laid the child down in a little cradle formed by the hollow among the boxes, first carefully spreading under it her cloak; and then she sprung to the side of the boat, in hopes that, among the various hotel-waiters who thronged the wharf, she might see her husband. In this hope, she pressed forward to the front rails, and, stretching far over them, strained her eyes intently on the moving heads on the shore, and the crowd pressed in between her and the child.

"Now's your time," said Haley, taking the sleeping child up, and handing him to the stranger. "Don't wake him up, and set him to crying, now; it would make a devil of a fuss with the gal." The man took the bundle carefully, and was soon lost in the crowd that went up the wharf.

When the boat, creaking, and groaning, and puffing, had loosed from the wharf, and was beginning slowly to strain herself along, the woman returned to her old seat. The trader was sitting there,—the child was gone!

"Why, why,—where?" she began, in bewildered surprise.

"Lucy," said the trader, "your child's gone; you may as well know it first as last. You see, I know'd you could n't take him down south; and I got a chance to sell him to a first-rate family, that 'll raise him better than you can."

The trader had arrived at that stage of Christian and political perfection which has been recommended by some preachers and politicians of the north, lately, in which he had completely overcome every humane weakness and prejudice. His heart was exactly where yours, sir, and mine could be brought, with proper effort and cultivation. The wild look of anguish and utter despair that the woman cast on him might have disturbed one less practised; but he was used to it. He had seen that same look hundreds of times. You can get used to such things, too, my friend; and it is the great object of recent efforts to make our whole northern community used to them, for the glory of the Union. So the trader only re-

garded the mortal anguish which he saw working in those
dark features, those clenched hands, and suffocating breathings, as necessary incidents of the trade, and merely calculated
whether she was going to scream, and get up a commotion
on the boat; for, like other supporters of our peculiar institution, he decidedly disliked agitation.

But the woman did not scream. The shot had passed too
straight and direct through the heart, for cry or tear.

Dizzily she sat down. Her slack hands fell lifeless by her
side. Her eyes looked straight forward, but she saw nothing.
All the noise and hum of the boat, the groaning of the machinery, mingled dreamily to her bewildered ear; and the
poor, dumb-stricken heart had neither cry nor tear to show
for its utter misery. She was quite calm.

The trader, who, considering his advantages, was almost as
humane as some of our politicians, seemed to feel called on
to administer such consolation as the case admitted of.

"I know this yer comes kinder hard, at first, Lucy," said he;
"but such a smart, sensible gal as you are, won't give way to
it. You see it's *necessary,* and can't be helped!"

"O! don't, Mas'r, don't!" said the woman, with a voice like
one that is smothering.

"You're a smart wench, Lucy," he persisted; "I mean to do
well by ye, and get ye a nice place down river; and you'll
soon get another husband,—such a likely gal as you—"

"O! Mas'r, if you *only* won't talk to me now," said the
woman, in a voice of such quick and living anguish that the
trader felt that there was something at present in the case
beyond his style of operation. He got up, and the woman
turned away, and buried her head in her cloak.

The trader walked up and down for a time, and occasionally stopped and looked at her.

"Takes it hard, rather," he soliloquized, "but quiet, tho';—
let her sweat a while; she'll come right, by and by!"

Tom had watched the whole transaction from first to last,
and had a perfect understanding of its results. To him, it
looked like something unutterably horrible and cruel, because, poor, ignorant black soul! he had not learned to generalize, and to take enlarged views. If he had only been instructed by certain ministers of Christianity, he might have

thought better of it, and seen in it an every-day incident of a lawful trade; a trade which is the vital support of an institution which an American divine* tells us has *"no evils but such as are inseparable from any other relations in social and domestic life."* But Tom, as we see, being a poor, ignorant fellow, whose reading had been confined entirely to the New Testament, could not comfort and solace himself with views like these. His very soul bled within him for what seemed to him the *wrongs* of the poor suffering thing that lay like a crushed reed on the boxes; the feeling, living, bleeding, yet immortal *thing,* which American state law coolly classes with the bundles, and bales, and boxes, among which she is lying.

Tom drew near, and tried to say something; but she only groaned. Honestly, and with tears running down his own cheeks, he spoke of a heart of love in the skies, of a pitying Jesus, and an eternal home; but the ear was deaf with anguish, and the palsied heart could not feel.

Night came on,—night calm, unmoved, and glorious, shining down with her innumerable and solemn angel eyes, twinkling, beautiful, but silent. There was no speech nor language, no pitying voice or helping hand, from that distant sky. One after another, the voices of business or pleasure died away; all on the boat were sleeping, and the ripples at the prow were plainly heard. Tom stretched himself out on a box, and there, as he lay, he heard, ever and anon, a smothered sob or cry from the prostrate creature,—"O! what shall I do? O Lord! O good Lord, do help me!" and so, ever and anon, until the murmur died away in silence.

At midnight, Tom waked, with a sudden start. Something black passed quickly by him to the side of the boat, and he heard a splash in the water. No one else saw or heard anything. He raised his head,—the woman's place was vacant! He got up, and sought about him in vain. The poor bleeding heart was still, at last, and the river rippled and dimpled just as brightly as if it had not closed above it.

Patience! patience! ye whose hearts swell indignant at wrongs like these. Not one throb of anguish, not one tear of the oppressed, is forgotten by the Man of Sorrows, the Lord

*Dr. Joel Parker, of Philadelphia.

of Glory. In his patient, generous bosom he bears the anguish of a world. Bear thou, like him, in patience, and labor in love; for sure as he is God, "the year of his redeemed *shall* come."

The trader waked up bright and early, and came out to see to his live stock. It was now his turn to look about in perplexity.

"Where alive is that gal?" he said to Tom.

Tom, who had learned the wisdom of keeping counsel, did not feel called on to state his observations and suspicions, but said he did not know.

"She surely could n't have got off in the night at any of the landings, for I was awake, and on the look-out, whenever the boat stopped. I never trust these yer things to other folks."

This speech was addressed to Tom quite confidentially, as if it was something that would be specially interesting to him. Tom made no answer.

The trader searched the boat from stem to stern, among boxes, bales and barrels, around the machinery, by the chimneys, in vain.

"Now, I say, Tom, be fair about this yer," he said, when, after a fruitless search, he came where Tom was standing. "You know something about it, now. Don't tell me,—I know you do. I saw the gal stretched out here about ten o'clock, and ag'in at twelve, and ag'in between one and two; and then at four she was gone, and you was a sleeping right there all the time. Now, you know something,—you can't help it."

"Well, Mas'r," said Tom, "towards morning something brushed by me, and I kinder half woke; and then I hearn a great splash, and then I clare woke up, and the gal was gone. That 's all I know on 't."

The trader was not shocked nor amazed; because, as we said before, he was used to a great many things that you are not used to. Even the awful presence of Death struck no solemn chill upon him. He had seen Death many times,—met him in the way of trade, and got acquainted with him,—and he only thought of him as a hard customer, that embarrassed his property operations very unfairly; and so he only swore that the gal was a baggage, and that he was devilish unlucky, and that, if things went on in this way, he should not make a cent on the trip. In short, he seemed to consider himself an ill-used man, decidedly; but there was no help for it, as the woman had escaped into a state which *never will* give up a fugitive,—not even at the demand of the whole glorious Union. The trader, therefore, sat discontentedly down, with his little account-book, and put down the missing body and soul under the head of *losses!*

"He's a shocking creature, is n't he,—this trader? so un-feeling! It 's dreadful, really!"

"O, but nobody thinks anything of these traders! They are universally despised,—never received into any decent so-ciety."

But who, sir, makes the trader? Who is most to blame? The enlightened, cultivated, intelligent man, who supports the sys-tem of which the trader is the inevitable result, or the poor trader himself? You make the public sentiment that calls for his trade, that debauches and depraves him, till he feels no shame in it; and in what are you better than he?

Are you educated and he ignorant, you high and he low, you refined and he coarse, you talented and he simple?

In the day of a future Judgment, these very considerations may make it more tolerable for him than for you.

In concluding these little incidents of lawful trade, we must beg the world not to think that American legislators are en-tirely destitute of humanity, as might, perhaps, be unfairly inferred from the great efforts made in our national body to protect and perpetuate this species of traffic.

Who does not know how our great men are outdoing themselves, in declaiming against the *foreign* slave-trade. There are a perfect host of Clarksons and Wilberforces risen up among us on that subject, most edifying to hear and be-hold. Trading negroes from Africa, dear reader, is so horrid! It is not to be thought of! But trading them from Kentucky,—that 's quite another thing!

XIII.

The Quaker Settlement

A QUIET scene now rises before us. A large, roomy, neatly-painted kitchen, its yellow floor glossy and smooth, and without a particle of dust; a neat, well-blacked cooking-stove; rows of shining tin, suggestive of unmentionable good things to the appetite; glossy green wood chairs, old and firm; a small flag-bottomed rocking-chair, with a patch-work cushion in it, neatly contrived out of small pieces of different colored woollen goods, and a larger sized one, motherly and old, whose wide arms breathed hospitable invitation, seconded by the solicitation of its feather cushions,—a real comfortable, persuasive old chair, and worth, in the way of honest, homely enjoyment, a dozen of your plush or brochetelle drawing-room gentry; and in the chair, gently swaying back and forward, her eyes bent on some fine sewing, sat our old friend Eliza. Yes, there she is, paler and thinner than in her Kentucky home, with a world of quiet sorrow lying under the shadow of her long eyelashes, and marking the outline of her gentle mouth! It was plain to see how old and firm the girlish heart was grown under the discipline of heavy sorrow; and when, anon, her large dark eye was raised to follow the gambols of her little Harry, who was sporting, like some tropical butterfly, hither and thither over the floor, she showed a depth of firmness and steady resolve that was never there in her earlier and happier days.

By her side sat a woman with a bright tin pan in her lap, into which she was carefully sorting some dried peaches. She might be fifty-five or sixty; but hers was one of those faces that time seems to touch only to brighten and adorn. The snowy lisse crape cap, made after the strait Quaker pattern,— the plain white muslin handkerchief, lying in placid folds across her bosom,—the drab shawl and dress,—showed at once the community to which she belonged. Her face was round and rosy, with a healthful downy softness, suggestive of a ripe peach. Her hair, partially silvered by age, was parted smoothly back from a high placid forehead, on which time had written no inscription, except peace on earth, good will to men, and beneath shone a large pair of clear, honest, loving brown eyes; you only needed to look straight into them, to feel that you saw to the bottom of a heart as good and true as ever throbbed in woman's bosom. So much has been said and sung of beautiful young girls, why don't somebody wake up to the beauty of old women? If any want to get up an inspiration under this head, we refer them to our good friend Rachel Halliday, just as she sits there in her little rocking-chair. It had a turn for quacking and squeaking,—that chair had,—either from having taken cold in early life, or from some asthmatic affection, or perhaps from nervous derangement; but, as she gently swung backward and forward, the chair kept up a kind of subdued "creechy crawchy," that would have been intolerable in any other chair. But old Simeon Halliday often declared it was as good as any music to him, and the children all avowed that they would n't miss of hearing mother's chair for anything in the world. For why? for twenty years or more, nothing but loving words, and gentle moralities, and motherly loving kindness, had come from that chair;—head-aches and heart-aches innumerable had been cured there,—difficulties spiritual and temporal solved there,—all by one good, loving woman, God bless her!

"And so thee still thinks of going to Canada, Eliza?" she said, as she was quietly looking over her peaches.

"Yes, ma'am," said Eliza, firmly. "I must go onward. I dare not stop."

"And what 'll thee do, when thee gets there? Thee must think about that, my daughter."

"My daughter" came naturally from the lips of Rachel Halliday; for hers was just the face and form that made "mother" seem the most natural word in the world.

Eliza's hands trembled, and some tears fell on her fine work; but she answered, firmly,

"I shall do—anything I can find. I hope I can find something."

"Thee knows thee can stay here, as long as thee pleases," said Rachel.

"O, thank you," said Eliza, "but"—she pointed to Harry—
"I can't sleep nights; I can't rest. Last night I dreamed I saw
that man coming into the yard," she said, shuddering.

"Poor child!" said Rachel, wiping her eyes; "but thee
must n't feel so. The Lord hath ordered it so that never hath
a fugitive been stolen from our village. I trust thine will not
be the first."

The door here opened, and a little short, round, pincush-
iony woman stood at the door, with a cheery, blooming face,
like a ripe apple. She was dressed, like Rachel, in sober gray,
with the muslin folded neatly across her round, plump little
chest.

"Ruth Stedman," said Rachel, coming joyfully forward;
"how is thee, Ruth?" she said, heartily taking both her hands.

"Nicely," said Ruth, taking off her little drab bonnet, and
dusting it with her handkerchief, displaying, as she did so, a
round little head, on which the Quaker cap sat with a sort of
jaunty air, despite all the stroking and patting of the small fat
hands, which were busily applied to arranging it. Certain
stray locks of decidedly curly hair, too, had escaped here and
there, and had to be coaxed and cajoled into their place again;
and then the new comer, who might have been five-and-
twenty, turned from the small looking-glass, before which she
had been making these arrangements, and looked well
pleased,—as most people who looked at her might have
been,—for she was decidedly a wholesome, whole-hearted,
chirruping little woman, as ever gladdened man's heart
withal.

"Ruth, this friend is Eliza Harris; and this is the little boy
I told thee of."

"I am glad to see thee, Eliza,—very," said Ruth, shaking
hands, as if Eliza were an old friend she had long been expecting; "and this is thy dear boy,—I brought a cake for
him," she said, holding out a little heart to the boy, who came
up, gazing through his curls, and accepted it shyly.

"Where's thy baby, Ruth?" said Rachel.

"O, he's coming; but thy Mary caught him as I came in,
and ran off with him to the barn, to show him to the children."

At this moment, the door opened, and Mary, an honest,

rosy-looking girl, with large brown eyes, like her mother's, came in with the baby.

"Ah! ha!" said Rachel, coming up, and taking the great, white, fat fellow in her arms; "how good he looks, and how he does grow!"

"To be sure, he does," said little bustling Ruth, as she took the child, and began taking off a little blue silk hood, and various layers and wrappers of outer garments; and having given a twitch here, and a pull there, and variously adjusted and arranged him, and kissed him heartily, she set him on the floor to collect his thoughts. Baby seemed quite used to this mode of proceeding, for he put his thumb in his mouth (as if it were quite a thing of course), and seemed soon absorbed in his own reflections, while the mother seated herself, and taking out a long stocking of mixed blue and white yarn, began to knit with briskness.

"Mary, thee 'd better fill the kettle, had n't thee?" gently suggested the mother.

Mary took the kettle to the well, and soon reäppearing, placed it over the stove, where it was soon purring and steaming, a sort of censer of hospitality and good cheer. The peaches, moreover, in obedience to a few gentle whispers from Rachel, were soon deposited, by the same hand, in a stew-pan over the fire.

Rachel now took down a snowy moulding-board, and, tying on an apron, proceeded quietly to making up some biscuits, first saying to Mary,—"Mary, had n't thee better tell John to get a chicken ready?" and Mary disappeared accordingly.

"And how is Abigail Peters?" said Rachel, as she went on with her biscuits.

"O, she 's better," said Ruth; "I was in, this morning; made the bed, tidied up the house. Leah Hills went in, this afternoon, and baked bread and pies enough to last some days; and I engaged to go back to get her up, this evening."

"I will go in to-morrow, and do any cleaning there may be, and look over the mending," said Rachel.

"Ah! that is well," said Ruth. "I 've heard," she added, "that Hannah Stanwood is sick. John was up there, last night,—I must go there to-morrow."

"John can come in here to his meals, if thee needs to stay all day," suggested Rachel.

"Thank thee, Rachel; will see, to-morrow; but, here comes Simeon."

Simeon Halliday, a tall, straight, muscular man, in drab coat and pantaloons, and broad-brimmed hat, now entered.

"How is thee, Ruth?" he said, warmly, as he spread his broad open hand for her little fat palm; "and how is John?"

"O! John is well, and all the rest of our folks," said Ruth, cheerily.

"Any news, father?" said Rachel, as she was putting her biscuits into the oven.

"Peter Stebbins told me that they should be along to-night, with *friends*," said Simeon, significantly, as he was washing his hands at a neat sink, in a little back porch.

"Indeed!" said Rachel, looking thoughtfully, and glancing at Eliza.

"Did thee say thy name was Harris?" said Simeon to Eliza, as he reëntered.

Rachel glanced quickly at her husband, as Eliza tremulously answered "yes;" her fears, ever uppermost, suggesting that possibly there might be advertisements out for her.

"Mother!" said Simeon, standing in the porch, and calling Rachel out.

"What does thee want, father?" said Rachel, rubbing her floury hands, as she went into the porch.

"This child's husband is in the settlement, and will be here to-night," said Simeon.

"Now, thee does n't say that, father?" said Rachel, all her face radiant with joy.

"It's really true. Peter was down yesterday, with the wagon, to the other stand, and there he found an old woman and two men; and one said his name was George Harris; and, from what he told of his history, I am certain who he is. He is a bright, likely fellow, too."

"Shall we tell her now?" said Simeon.

"Let's tell Ruth," said Rachel. "Here, Ruth,—come here."

Ruth laid down her knitting-work, and was in the back porch in a moment.

"Ruth, what does thee think?" said Rachel. "Father says Eliza's husband is in the last company, and will be here to-night."

A burst of joy from the little Quakeress interrupted the speech. She gave such a bound from the floor, as she clapped her little hands, that two stray curls fell from under her Quaker cap, and lay brightly on her white neckerchief.

"Hush thee, dear!" said Rachel, gently; "hush, Ruth! Tell us, shall we tell her now?"

"Now! to be sure,—this very minute. Why, now, suppose 't was my John, how should I feel? Do tell her, right off."

"Thee uses thyself only to learn how to love thy neighbor, Ruth," said Simeon, looking, with a beaming face, on Ruth.

"To be sure. Is n't it what we are made for? If I did n't love John and the baby, I should not know how to feel for her. Come, now, do tell her,—do!" and she laid her hands persuasively on Rachel's arm. "Take her into thy bed-room, there, and let me fry the chicken while thee does it."

Rachel came out into the kitchen, where Eliza was sewing, and opening the door of a small bed-room, said, gently, "Come in here with me, my daughter; I have news to tell thee."

The blood flushed in Eliza's pale face; she rose, trembling with nervous anxiety, and looked towards her boy.

"No, no," said little Ruth, darting up, and seizing her hands. "Never thee fear; it 's good news, Eliza,—go in, go in!" And she gently pushed her to the door, which closed after her; and then, turning round, she caught little Harry in her arms, and began kissing him.

"Thee 'll see thy father, little one. Does thee know it? Thy father is coming," she said, over and over again, as the boy looked wonderingly at her.

Meanwhile, within the door, another scene was going on. Rachel Halliday drew Eliza toward her, and said, "The Lord hath had mercy on thee, daughter; thy husband hath escaped from the house of bondage."

The blood flushed to Eliza's cheek in a sudden glow, and went back to her heart with as sudden a rush. She sat down, pale and faint.

"Have courage, child," said Rachel, laying her hand on her head. "He is among friends, who will bring him here to-night."

"To-night!" Eliza repeated, "to-night!" The words lost all meaning to her; her head was dreamy and confused; all was mist for a moment.

When she awoke, she found herself snugly tucked up on the bed, with a blanket over her, and little Ruth rubbing her hands with camphor. She opened her eyes in a state of dreamy, delicious languor, such as one has who has long been bearing a heavy load, and now feels it gone, and would rest. The tension of the nerves, which had never ceased a moment since the first hour of her flight, had given way, and a strange feeling of security and rest came over her; and, as she lay, with her large, dark eyes open, she followed, as in a quiet dream, the motions of those about her. She saw the door open into the other room; saw the supper-table, with its snowy cloth; heard the dreamy murmur of the singing tea-kettle; saw Ruth tripping backward and forward, with plates of cake and saucers of preserves, and ever and anon stopping to put a cake into Harry's hand, or pat his head, or twine his long curls round her snowy fingers. She saw the ample, moth-erly form of Rachel, as she ever and anon came to the bed-side, and smoothed and arranged something about the bed-clothes, and gave a tuck here and there, by way of expressing her good-will; and was conscious of a kind of sunshine beam-ing down upon her from her large, clear, brown eyes. She saw Ruth's husband come in,—saw her fly up to him, and commence whispering very earnestly, ever and anon, with im-pressive gesture, pointing her little finger toward the room. She saw her, with the baby in her arms, sitting down to tea; she saw them all at table, and little Harry in a high chair, under the shadow of Rachel's ample wing; there were low murmurs of talk, gentle tinkling of tea-spoons, and musical clatter of cups and saucers, and all mingled in a delightful dream of rest; and Eliza slept, as she had not slept before, since the fearful midnight hour when she had taken her child and fled through the frosty star-light.

She dreamed of a beautiful country,—a land, it seemed to her, of rest,—green shores, pleasant islands, and beautifully glittering water; and there, in a house which kind voices told her was a home, she saw her boy playing, a free and happy child. She heard her husband's footsteps; she felt him coming nearer; his arms were around her, his tears falling on her face, and she awoke! It was no dream. The daylight had long faded; her child lay calmly sleeping by her side; a candle was burning dimly on the stand, and her husband was sobbing by her pillow.

The next morning was a cheerful one at the Quaker house. "Mother" was up betimes, and surrounded by busy girls and boys, whom we had scarce time to introduce to our readers yesterday, and who all moved obediently to Rachel's gentle "Thee had better," or more gentle "Had n't thee better?" in the work of getting breakfast; for a breakfast in the luxurious valleys of Indiana is a thing complicated and multiform, and, like picking up the rose-leaves and trimming the bushes in Paradise, asking other hands than those of the original mother. While, therefore, John ran to the spring for fresh water, and Simeon the second sifted meal for corn-cakes, and Mary ground coffee, Rachel moved gently and quietly about, making biscuits, cutting up chicken, and diffusing a sort of sunny radiance over the whole proceeding generally. If there was any danger of friction or collision from the ill-regulated zeal of so many young operators, her gentle "Come! come!" or "I would n't, now," was quite sufficient to allay the difficulty. Bards have written of the cestus of Venus, that turned the heads of all the world in successive generations. We had rather, for our part, have the cestus of Rachel Halliday, that kept heads from being turned, and made everything go on harmoniously. We think it is more suited to our modern days, decidedly.

While all other preparations were going on, Simeon the elder stood in his shirt-sleeves before a little looking-glass in the corner, engaged in the anti-patriarchal operation of shaving. Everything went on so sociably, so quietly, so harmoniously, in the great kitchen,—it seemed so pleasant to every one to do just what they were doing, there was such an atmosphere of mutual confidence and good fellowship everywhere,—even the knives and forks had a social clatter as they went on to the table; and the chicken and ham had a cheerful and joyous fizzle in the pan, as if they rather enjoyed being cooked than otherwise;—and when George and Eliza and little Harry came out, they met such a hearty, rejoicing welcome, no wonder it seemed to them like a dream.

At last, they were all seated at breakfast, while Mary stood at the stove, baking griddle-cakes, which, as they gained the true exact golden-brown tint of perfection, were transferred quite handily to the table.

Rachel never looked so truly and benignly happy as at the head of her table. There was so much motherliness and full-heartedness even in the way she passed a plate of cakes or poured a cup of coffee, that it seemed to put a spirit into the food and drink she offered.

It was the first time that ever George had sat down on equal terms at any white man's table; and he sat down, at first, with some constraint and awkwardness; but they all exhaled and went off like fog, in the genial morning rays of this simple, overflowing kindness.

This, indeed, was a home,—*home*,—a word that George had never yet known a meaning for; and a belief in God, and trust in his providence, began to encircle his heart, as, with a golden cloud of protection and confidence, dark, misanthropic, pining, atheistic doubts, and fierce despair, melted away before the light of a living Gospel, breathed in living faces, preached by a thousand unconscious acts of love and good will, which, like the cup of cold water given in the name of a disciple, shall never lose their reward.

"Father, what if thee should get found out again?" said Simeon second, as he buttered his cake.

"I should pay my fine," said Simeon, quietly.

"But what if they put thee in prison?"

"Could n't thee and mother manage the farm?" said Simeon, smiling.

"Mother can do almost everything," said the boy. "But is n't it a shame to make such laws?"

"Thee must n't speak evil of thy rulers, Simeon," said his

father, gravely. "The Lord only gives us our worldly goods that we may do justice and mercy; if our rulers require a price of us for it, we must deliver it up."

"Well, I hate those old slaveholders!" said the boy, who felt as unchristian as became any modern reformer.

"I am surprised at thee, son," said Simeon; "thy mother never taught thee so. I would do even the same for the slave-holder as for the slave, if the Lord brought him to my door in affliction."

Simeon second blushed scarlet; but his mother only smiled, and said, "Simeon is my good boy; he will grow older, by and by, and then he will be like his father."

"I hope, my good sir, that you are not exposed to any difficulty on our account," said George, anxiously.

"Fear nothing, George, for therefore are we sent into the world. If we would not meet trouble for a good cause, we were not worthy of our name."

"But, for *me*," said George, "I could not bear it."

"Fear not, then, friend George; it is not for thee, but for God and man, we do it," said Simeon. "And now thou must lie by quietly this day, and to-night, at ten o'clock, Phineas Fletcher will carry thee onward to the next stand,—thee and the rest of thy company. The pursuers are hard after thee; we must not delay."

"If that is the case, why wait till evening?" said George.

"Thou art safe here by daylight, for every one in the settlement is a Friend, and all are watching. It has been found safer to travel by night."

XIV.

Evangeline

"A young star! which shone
O'er life—too sweet an image for such glass!
A lovely being, scarcely formed or moulded;
A rose with all its sweetest leaves yet folded."

THE Mississippi! How, as by an enchanted wand, have its scenes been changed, since Chateaubriand wrote his prose-poetic description of it, as a river of mighty, unbroken solitudes, rolling amid undreamed wonders of vegetable and animal existence.

But, as in an hour, this river of dreams and wild romance has emerged to a reality scarcely less visionary and splendid. What other river of the world bears on its bosom to the ocean the wealth and enterprise of such another country?—a country whose products embrace all between the tropics and the poles! Those turbid waters, hurrying, foaming, tearing along, an apt resemblance of that headlong tide of business which is poured along its wave by a race more vehement and energetic than any the old world ever saw. Ah! would that they did not also bear along a more fearful freight,—the tears of the oppressed, the sighs of the helpless, the bitter prayers of poor, ignorant hearts to an unknown God—unknown, unseen and silent, but who will yet "come out of his place to save all the poor of the earth!"

The slanting light of the setting sun quivers on the sea-like expanse of the river; the shivery canes, and the tall, dark cypress, hung with wreaths of dark, funereal moss, glow in the golden ray, as the heavily-laden steamboat marches onward.

Piled with cotton-bales, from many a plantation, up over deck and sides, till she seems in the distance a square, massive block of gray, she moves heavily onward to the nearing mart. We must look some time among its crowded decks before we shall find again our humble friend Tom. High on the upper deck, in a little nook among the everywhere predominant cotton-bales, at last we may find him.

Partly from confidence inspired by Mr. Shelby's representations, and partly from the remarkably inoffensive and quiet character of the man, Tom had insensibly won his way far into the confidence even of such a man as Haley.

At first he had watched him narrowly through the day, and never allowed him to sleep at night unfettered; but the uncomplaining patience and apparent contentment of Tom's manner led him gradually to discontinue these restraints, and for some time Tom had enjoyed a sort of parole of honor, being permitted to come and go freely where he pleased on the boat.

Ever quiet and obliging, and more than ready to lend a hand in every emergency which occurred among the workmen below, he had won the good opinion of all the hands, and spent many hours in helping them with as hearty a good will as ever he worked on a Kentucky farm.

When there seemed to be nothing for him to do, he would climb to a nook among the cotton-bales of the upper deck, and busy himself in studying over his Bible,—and it is there we see him now.

For a hundred or more miles above New Orleans, the river is higher than the surrounding country, and rolls its tremendous volume between massive levees twenty feet in height. The traveller from the deck of the steamer, as from some floating castle top, overlooks the whole country for miles and miles around. Tom, therefore, had spread out full before him, in plantation after plantation, a map of the life to which he was approaching.

He saw the distant slaves at their toil; he saw afar their villages of huts gleaming out in long rows on many a plantation, distant from the stately mansions and pleasure-grounds of the master;—and as the moving picture passed on, his poor, foolish heart would be turning backward to the Kentucky farm, with its old shadowy beeches,—to the master's house, with its wide, cool halls, and, near by, the little cabin, overgrown with the multiflora and bignonia. There he seemed to see familiar faces of comrades, who had grown up with him from infancy; he saw his busy wife, bustling in her preparations for his evening meals; he heard the merry laugh of his boys at their play, and the chirrup of the baby at his knee; and then, with a start, all faded, and he saw again the cane-brakes and cypresses and gliding plantations, and heard again the creaking and groaning of the machinery, all telling him too plainly that all that phase of life had gone by forever.

In such a case, you write to your wife, and send messages to your children; but Tom could not write,—the mail for him had no existence, and the gulf of separation was un-bridged by even a friendly word or signal.

Is it strange, then, that some tears fall on the pages of his Bible, as he lays it on the cotton-bale, and, with patient finger, threading his slow way from word to word, traces out its promises? Having learned late in life, Tom was but a slow reader, and passed on laboriously from verse to verse. Fortunate for him was it that the book he was intent on was one which slow reading cannot injure,—nay, one whose words, like ingots of gold, seem often to need to be weighed separately, that the mind may take in their priceless value. Let us follow him a moment, as, pointing to each word, and pronouncing each half aloud, he reads,

"Let—not—your—heart—be—troubled. In—my—Father's—house—are—many—mansions. I—go—to—prepare—a—place—for—you."

Cicero, when he buried his darling and only daughter, had a heart as full of honest grief as poor Tom's,—perhaps no fuller, for both were only men;—but Cicero could pause over no such sublime words of hope, and look to no such future reünion; and if he *had* seen them, ten to one he would not have believed,—he must fill his head first with a thousand questions of authenticity of manuscript, and correctness of translation. But, to poor Tom, there it lay, just what he needed, so evidently true and divine that the possibility of a question never entered his simple head. It must be true; for, if not true, how could he live?

As for Tom's Bible, though it had no annotations and helps in margin from learned commentators, still it had been embellished with certain way-marks and guide-boards of Tom's own invention, and which helped him more than the most learned expositions could have done. It had been his custom to get the Bible read to him by his master's children, in particular by young Master George; and, as they read, he would designate, by bold, strong marks and dashes, with pen and ink, the passages which more particularly gratified his ear or affected his heart. His Bible was thus marked through, from one end to the other, with a variety of styles and designations; so he could in a moment seize upon his favorite passages, without the labor of spelling out what lay between them; — and while it lay there before him, every passage breathing of some old home scene, and recalling some past enjoyment, his Bible seemed to him all of this life that remained, as well as the promise of a future one.

Among the passengers on the boat was a young gentleman of fortune and family, resident in New Orleans, who bore the name of St. Clare. He had with him a daughter between five and six years of age, together with a lady who seemed to claim relationship to both, and to have the little one especially under her charge.

Tom had often caught glimpses of this little girl, — for she was one of those busy, tripping creatures, that can be no more contained in one place than a sunbeam or a summer breeze, — nor was she one that, once seen, could be easily forgotten.

Her form was the perfection of childish beauty, without its usual chubbiness and squareness of outline. There was about it an undulating and aërial grace, such as one might dream of for some mythic and allegorical being. Her face was remarkable less for its perfect beauty of feature than for a singular and dreamy earnestness of expression, which made the ideal start when they looked at her, and by which the dullest and most literal were impressed, without exactly knowing why. The shape of her head and the turn of her neck and bust was peculiarly noble, and the long golden-brown hair that floated like a cloud around it, the deep spiritual gravity of her violet blue eyes, shaded by heavy fringes of golden brown, — all marked her out from other children, and made every one turn and look after her, as she glided hither and thither on the boat. Nevertheless, the little one was not what you would have called either a grave child or a sad one. On the contrary, an airy and innocent playfulness seemed to flicker like the shadow of summer leaves over her childish face, and around her buoyant figure. She was always in motion, always with a half smile on her rosy mouth, flying hither and thither, with an undulating and cloud-like tread, singing to herself as she moved as in a happy dream. Her father and female guardian were incessantly busy in pursuit of her,—but, when caught, she melted from them again like a summer cloud; and as no word of chiding or reproof ever fell on her ear for whatever she chose to do, she pursued her own way all over the boat. Always dressed in white, she seemed to move like a shadow through all sorts of places, without contracting spot or stain; and there was not a corner or nook, above or below, where those fairy footsteps had not glided, and that visionary golden head, with its deep blue eyes, fleeted along.

The fireman, as he looked up from his sweaty toil, sometimes found those eyes looking wonderingly into the raging depths of the furnace, and fearfully and pityingly at him, as if she thought him in some dreadful danger. Anon the steersman at the wheel paused and smiled, as the picture-like head gleamed through the window of the round house, and in a moment was gone again. A thousand times a day rough voices blessed her, and smiles of unwonted softness stole over hard faces, as she passed; and when she tripped fearlessly over dangerous places, rough, sooty hands were stretched involuntarily out to save her, and smooth her path.

Tom, who had the soft, impressible nature of his kindly race, ever yearning toward the simple and childlike, watched the little creature with daily increasing interest. To him she seemed something almost divine; and whenever her golden head and deep blue eyes peered out upon him from behind some dusky cotton-bale, or looked down upon him over some ridge of packages, he half believed that he saw one of the angels stepped out of his New Testament.

Often and often she walked mournfully round the place where Haley's gang of men and women sat in their chains. She would glide in among them, and look at them with an air of perplexed and sorrowful earnestness; and sometimes she would lift their chains with her slender hands, and then sigh wofully, as she glided away. Several times she appeared sud-

denly among them, with her hands full of candy, nuts, and
oranges, which she would distribute joyfully to them, and
then be gone again.

Tom watched the little lady a great deal, before he ventured
on any overtures towards acquaintanceship. He knew an
abundance of simple acts to propitiate and invite the approaches of the little people, and he resolved to play his part
right skilfully. He could cut cunning little baskets out of
cherry-stones, could make grotesque faces on hickory-nuts, or
odd-jumping figures out of elder-pith, and he was a very Pan
in the manufacture of whistles of all sizes and sorts. His pockets were full of miscellaneous articles of attraction, which he
had hoarded in days of old for his master's children, and
which he now produced, with commendable prudence and
economy, one by one, as overtures for acquaintance and
friendship.

The little one was shy, for all her busy interest in everything going on, and it was not easy to tame her. For a while,
she would perch like a canary-bird on some box or package
near Tom, while busy in the little arts afore-named, and take
from him, with a kind of grave bashfulness, the little articles
he offered. But at last they got on quite confidential terms.

"What's little missy's name?" said Tom, at last, when he
thought matters were ripe to push such an inquiry.

"Evangeline St. Clare," said the little one, "though papa
and everybody else call me Eva. Now, what's your name?"

"My name's Tom; the little chil'en used to call me Uncle
Tom, way back thar in Kentuck."

"Then I mean to call you Uncle Tom, because, you see, I
like you," said Eva. "So, Uncle Tom, where are you going?"

"I don't know, Miss Eva."

"Don't know?" said Eva.

"No. I am going to be sold to somebody. I don't know
who."

"My papa can buy you," said Eva, quickly; "and if he buys
you, you will have good times. I mean to ask him to, this
very day."

"Thank you, my little lady," said Tom.

The boat here stopped at a small landing to take in wood,

and Eva, hearing her father's voice, bounded nimbly away. Tom rose up, and went forward to offer his service in wooding, and soon was busy among the hands.

Eva and her father were standing together by the railings to see the boat start from the landing-place, the wheel had made two or three revolutions in the water, when, by some sudden movement, the little one suddenly lost her balance, and fell sheer over the side of the boat into the water. Her father, scarce knowing what he did, was plunging in after her, but was held back by some behind him, who saw that more efficient aid had followed his child.

Tom was standing just under her on the lower deck, as she fell. He saw her strike the water, and sink, and was after her in a moment. A broad-chested, strong-armed fellow, it was nothing for him to keep afloat in the water, till, in a moment or two, the child rose to the surface, and he caught her in his arms, and, swimming with her to the boat-side, handed her up, all dripping, to the grasp of hundreds of hands, which, as if they had all belonged to one man, were stretched eagerly out to receive her. A few moments more, and her father bore her, dripping and senseless, to the ladies' cabin, where, as is usual in cases of the kind, there ensued a very well-meaning and kind-hearted strife among the female occupants generally, as to who should do the most things to make a disturbance, and to hinder her recovery in every way possible.

It was a sultry, close day, the next day, as the steamer drew near to New Orleans. A general bustle of expectation and preparation was spread through the boat; in the cabin, one and another were gathering their things together, and arranging them, preparatory to going ashore. The steward and chambermaid, and all, were busily engaged in cleaning, furbishing, and arranging the splendid boat, preparatory to a grand entree.

On the lower deck sat our friend Tom, with his arms folded, and anxiously, from time to time, turning his eyes towards a group on the other side of the boat.

There stood the fair Evangeline, a little paler than the day before, but otherwise exhibiting no traces of the accident which had befallen her. A graceful, elegantly-formed young man stood by her, carelessly leaning one elbow on a bale of cotton, while a large pocket-book lay open before him. It was quite evident, at a glance, that the gentleman was Eva's father. There was the same noble cast of head, the same large blue eyes, the same golden-brown hair; yet the expression was wholly different. In the large, clear blue eyes, though in form and color exactly similar, there was wanting that misty, dreamy depth of expression; all was clear, bold, and bright, but with a light wholly of this world: the beautifully cut mouth had a proud and somewhat sarcastic expression, while an air of free-and-easy superiority sat not ungracefully in every turn and movement of his fine form. He was listening, with a good-humored, negligent air, half comic, half contemptuous, to Haley, who was very volubly expatiating on the quality of the article for which they were bargaining.

"All the moral and Christian virtues bound in black morocco, complete!" he said, when Haley had finished. "Well, now, my good fellow, what 's the damage, as they say in Kentucky; in short, what 's to be paid out for this business? How much are you going to cheat me, now? Out with it!"

"Wal," said Haley, "if I should say thirteen hundred dollars for that ar fellow, I should n't but just save myself; I should n't, now, re'ly."

"Poor fellow!" said the young man, fixing his keen, mocking blue eye on him; "but I suppose you 'd let me have him for that, out of a particular regard for me."

"Well, the young lady here seems to be sot on him, and nat'lly enough."

"O! certainly, there 's a call on your benevolence, my friend. Now, as a matter of Christian charity, how cheap could you afford to let him go, to oblige a young lady that 's particular sot on him?"

"Wal, now, just think on 't," said the trader; "just look at them limbs,—broad-chested, strong as a horse. Look at his head; them high forrads allays shows calculatin niggers, that 'll do any kind o' thing. I 've marked that ar. Now, a nigger of that ar heft and build is worth considerable, just, as you may say, for his body, supposin he 's stupid; but come to put in his calculatin faculties, and them which I can show he has oncommon, why, of course, it makes him come higher. Why, that ar fellow managed his master's whole farm. He has a strornary talent for business."

"Bad, bad, very bad; knows altogether too much!" said the young man, with the same mocking smile playing about his mouth. "Never will do, in the world. Your smart fellows are always running off, stealing horses, and raising the devil generally. I think you'll have to take off a couple of hundred for his smartness."

"Wal, there might be something in that ar, if it warnt for his character; but I can show recommends from his master and others, to prove he is one of your real pious,—the most humble, prayin, pious crittur ye ever did see. Why, he's been called a preacher in them parts he came from."

"And I might use him for a family chaplain, possibly," added the young man, dryly. "That's quite an idea. Religion is a remarkably scarce article at our house."

"You're joking, now."

"How do you know I am? Did n't you just warrant him for a preacher? Has he been examined by any synod or council? Come, hand over your papers."

If the trader had not been sure, by a certain good-humored twinkle in the large blue eye, that all this banter was sure, in the long run, to turn out a cash concern, he might have been somewhat out of patience; as it was, he laid down a greasy pocket-book on the cotton-bales, and began anxiously studying over certain papers in it, the young man standing by, the while, looking down on him with an air of careless, easy drollery.

"Papa, do buy him! it's no matter what you pay," whispered Eva, softly, getting up on a package, and putting her arm around her father's neck. "You have money enough, I know. I want him."

"What for, pussy? Are you going to use him for a rattle-box, or a rocking-horse, or what?"

"I want to make him happy."

"An original reason, certainly."

Here the trader handed up a certificate, signed by Mr. Shelby, which the young man took with the tips of his long fingers, and glanced over carelessly.

"A gentlemanly hand," he said, "and well spelt, too. Well, now, but I 'm not sure, after all, about this religion," said he, the old wicked expression returning to his eye; "the country is almost ruined with pious white people: such pious politicians as we have just before elections,—such pious goings on in all departments of church and state, that a fellow does not know who 'll cheat him next. I don't know, either, about religion's being up in the market, just now. I have not looked in the papers lately, to see how it sells. How many hundred dollars, now, do you put on for this religion?"

"You like to be a jokin, now," said the trader; "but, then, there 's *sense* under all that ar. I know there 's differences in religion. Some kinds is mis'rable: there 's your meetin pious; there 's your singin, roarin pious; them ar an't no account, in black or white;—but these rayly is; and I 've seen it in niggers as often as any, your rail softly, quiet, stiddy, honest, pious, that the hull world could n't tempt 'em to do nothing that they thinks is wrong; and ye see in this letter what Tom's old master says about him."

"Now," said the young man, stooping gravely over his book of bills, "if you can assure me that I really can buy *this* kind of pious, and that it will be set down to my account in the book up above, as something belonging to me, I would n't care if I did go a little extra for it. How d' ye say?"

"Wal, raily, I can't do that," said the trader. "I 'm a thinkin that every man 'll have to hang on his own hook, in them ar quarters."

"Rather hard on a fellow that pays extra on religion, and can't trade with it in the state where he wants it most, an't it, now?" said the young man, who had been making out a roll of bills while he was speaking. "There, count your money, old boy!" he added, as he handed the roll to the trader.

"All right," said Haley, his face beaming with delight; and pulling out an old inkhorn, he proceeded to fill out a bill of sale, which, in a few moments, he handed to the young man.

"I wonder, now, if I was divided up and inventoried," said the latter, as he ran over the paper, "how much I might bring. Say so much for the shape of my head, so much for a high forehead, so much for arms, and hands, and legs, and then so much for education, learning, talent, honesty, religion! Bless me! there would be small charge on that last, I'm thinking. But come, Eva," he said; and taking the hand of his daughter, he stepped across the boat, and carelessly putting the tip of his finger under Tom's chin, said, good-humoredly, "Look up, Tom, and see how you like your new master."

Tom looked up. It was not in nature to look into that gay, young, handsome face, without a feeling of pleasure; and Tom felt the tears start in his eyes as he said, heartily, "God bless you, Mas'r!"

"Well, I hope he will. What's your name? Tom? Quite as likely to do it for your asking as mine, from all accounts. Can you drive horses, Tom?"

"I've been allays used to horses," said Tom. "Mas'r Shelby raised heaps on 'em."

"Well, I think I shall put you in coachy, on condition that you won't be drunk more than once a week, unless in cases of emergency, Tom."

Tom looked surprised, and rather hurt, and said, "I never drink, Mas'r."

"I've heard that story before, Tom; but then we'll see. It will be a special accommodation to all concerned, if you don't. Never mind, my boy," he added, good-humoredly, seeing Tom still looked grave; "I don't doubt you mean to do well."

"I sartin do, Mas'r," said Tom.

"And you shall have good times," said Eva. "Papa is very good to everybody, only he always will laugh at them."

"Papa is much obliged to you for his recommendation," said St. Clare, laughing, as he turned on his heel and walked away.

XV.

Of Tom's New Master, and Various Other Matters

S INCE the thread of our humble hero's life has now become interwoven with that of higher ones, it is necessary
to give some brief introduction to them.

Augustine St. Clare was the son of a wealthy planter of
Louisiana. The family had its origin in Canada. Of two brothers, very similar in temperament and character, one had settled on a flourishing farm in Vermont, and the other became
an opulent planter in Louisiana. The mother of Augustine
was a Huguenot French lady, whose family had emigrated to
Louisiana during the days of its early settlement. Augustine
and another brother were the only children of their parents.
Having inherited from his mother an exceeding delicacy of
constitution, he was, at the instance of physicians, during
many years of his boyhood, sent to the care of his uncle in
Vermont, in order that his constitution might be strengthened by the cold of a more bracing climate.

In childhood, he was remarkable for an extreme and
marked sensitiveness of character, more akin to the softness
of woman than the ordinary hardness of his own sex. Time,
however, overgrew this softness with the rough bark of manhood, and but few knew how living and fresh it still lay at
the core. His talents were of the very first order, although his
mind showed a preference always for the ideal and the
æsthetic, and there was about him that repugnance to the actual business of life which is the common result of this balance of the faculties. Soon after the completion of his college
course, his whole nature was kindled into one intense and
passionate effervescence of romantic passion. His hour
came,—the hour that comes only once; his star rose in the
horizon,—that star that rises so often in vain, to be remembered only as a thing of dreams; and it rose for him in vain.
To drop the figure,—he saw and won the love of a high-

minded and beautiful woman, in one of the northern states, and they were affianced. He returned south to make arrangements for their marriage, when, most unexpectedly, his letters were returned to him by mail, with a short note from her guardian, stating to him that ere this reached him the lady would be the wife of another. Stung to madness, he vainly hoped, as many another has done, to fling the whole thing from his heart by one desperate effort. Too proud to supplicate or seek explanation, he threw himself at once into a whirl of fashionable society, and in a fortnight from the time of the fatal letter was the accepted lover of the reigning belle of the season; and as soon as arrangements could be made, he became the husband of a fine figure, a pair of bright dark eyes, and a hundred thousand dollars; and, of course, everybody thought him a happy fellow.

The married couple were enjoying their honeymoon, and entertaining a brilliant circle of friends in their splendid villa, near Lake Pontchartrain, when, one day, a letter was brought to him in *that* well-remembered writing. It was handed to him while he was in full tide of gay and successful conversation, in a whole room-full of company. He turned deadly pale when he saw the writing, but still preserved his composure, and finished the playful warfare of badinage which he was at the moment carrying on with a lady opposite; and, a short time after, was missed from the circle. In his room, alone, he opened and read the letter, now worse than idle and useless to be read. It was from her, giving a long account of a persecution to which she had been exposed by her guardian's family, to lead her to unite herself with their son: and she related how, for a long time, his letters had ceased to arrive; how she had written time and again, till she became weary and doubtful; how her health had failed under her anxieties, and how, at last, she had discovered the whole fraud which had been practised on them both. The letter ended with expressions of hope and thankfulness, and professions of undying affection, which were more bitter than death to the unhappy young man. He wrote to her immediately:

"I have received yours,—but too late. I believed all I heard. I was desperate. *I am married*, and all is over. Only forget,— it is all that remains for either of us."

And thus ended the whole romance and ideal of life for Augustine St. Clare. But the *real* remained,—the *real*, like the flat, bare, oozy tide-mud, when the blue sparkling wave, with all its company of gliding boats and white-winged ships, its music of oars and chiming waters, has gone down, and there it lies, flat, slimy, bare,—exceedingly real.

Of course, in a novel, people's hearts break, and they die, and that is the end of it; and in a story this is very convenient. But in real life we do not die when all that makes life bright dies to us. There is a most busy and important round of eating, drinking, dressing, walking, visiting, buying, selling, talking, reading, and all that makes up what is commonly called *living*, yet to be gone through; and this yet remained to Augustine. Had his wife been a whole woman, she might yet have done something—as woman can—to mend the broken threads of life, and weave again into a tissue of brightness. But Marie St. Clare could not even see that they had been broken. As before stated, she consisted of a fine figure, a pair of splendid eyes, and a hundred thousand dollars; and none of these items were precisely the ones to minister to a mind diseased.

When Augustine, pale as death, was found lying on the sofa, and pleaded sudden sick-headache as the cause of his distress, she recommended to him to smell of hartshorn; and when the paleness and headache came on week after week, she only said that she never thought Mr. St. Clare was sickly; but it seems he was very liable to sick-headaches, and that it was a very unfortunate thing for her, because he did n't enjoy going into company with her, and it seemed odd to go so much alone, when they were just married. Augustine was glad in his heart that he had married so undiscerning a woman; but as the glosses and civilities of the honeymoon wore away, he discovered that a beautiful young woman, who has lived all her life to be caressed and waited on, might prove quite a hard mistress in domestic life. Marie never had possessed much capability of affection, or much sensibility, and the little that she had, had been merged into a most intense and unconscious selfishness; a selfishness the more hopeless, from its quiet obtuseness, its utter ignorance of any claims but her own. From her infancy, she had been surrounded with servants, who lived only to study her caprices; the idea that they had either feelings or rights had never dawned upon her, even in distant perspective. Her father, whose only child she had been, had never denied her anything that lay within the compass of human possibility; and when she entered life, beautiful, accomplished, and an heiress, she had, of course, all the eligibles and non-eligibles of the other sex sighing at her feet, and she had no doubt that Augustine was a most fortunate man in having obtained her. It is a great mistake to suppose that a woman with no heart will be an easy creditor in the exchange of affection. There is not on earth a more merciless exactor of love from others than a thoroughly selfish woman; and the more unlovely she grows, the more jealously and scrupulously she exacts love, to the uttermost farthing. When, therefore, St. Clare began to drop off those gallantries and small attentions which flowed at first through the habitude of courtship, he found his sultana no way ready to resign her slave; there were abundance of tears, poutings, and small tempests, there were discontents, pinings, upbraidings. St. Clare was good-natured and self-indulgent, and sought to buy off with presents and flatteries; and when Marie became mother to a beautiful daughter, he really felt awakened, for a time, to something like tenderness.

St. Clare's mother had been a woman of uncommon elevation and purity of character, and he gave to this child his mother's name, fondly fancying that she would prove a reproduction of her image. The thing had been remarked with petulant jealousy by his wife, and she regarded her husband's absorbing devotion to the child with suspicion and dislike; all that was given to her seemed so much taken from herself. From the time of the birth of this child, her health gradually sunk. A life of constant inaction, bodily and mental,—the friction of ceaseless ennui and discontent, united to the ordinary weakness which attended the period of maternity,—in course of a few years changed the blooming young belle into a yellow, faded, sickly woman, whose time was divided among a variety of fanciful diseases, and who considered herself, in every sense, the most ill-used and suffering person in existence.

There was no end of her various complaints; but her principal forte appeared to lie in sick-headache, which sometimes would confine her to her room three days out of six. As, of course, all family arrangements fell into the hands of servants, St. Clare found his menage anything but comfortable. His only daughter was exceedingly delicate, and he feared that, with no one to look after her and attend to her, her health and life might yet fall a sacrifice to her mother's inefficiency. He had taken her with him on a tour to Vermont, and had persuaded his cousin, Miss Ophelia St. Clare, to return with him to his southern residence; and they are now returning on this boat, where we have introduced them to our readers.

And now, while the distant domes and spires of New Orleans rise to our view, there is yet time for an introduction to Miss Ophelia.

Whoever has travelled in the New England States will remember, in some cool village, the large farm-house, with its clean-swept grassy yard, shaded by the dense and massive foliage of the sugar maple; and remember the air of order and stillness, of perpetuity and unchanging repose, that seemed to breathe over the whole place. Nothing lost, or out of order; not a picket loose in the fence, not a particle of litter in the turfy yard, with its clumps of lilac-bushes growing up under the windows. Within, he will remember wide, clean rooms, where nothing ever seems to be doing or going to be done, where everything is once and forever rigidly in place, and where all household arrangements move with the punctual exactness of the old clock in the corner. In the family "keeping-room," as it is termed, he will remember the staid, respectable old book-case, with its glass doors, where Rollin's History, Milton's Paradise Lost, Bunyan's Pilgrim's Progress, and Scott's Family Bible, stand side by side in decorous order, with multitudes of other books, equally solemn and respectable. There are no servants in the house, but the lady in the snowy cap, with the spectacles, who sits sewing every afternoon among her daughters, as if nothing ever had been done, or were to be done,—she and her girls, in some long-forgotten fore part of the day, *"did up the work*," and for the rest of the time, probably, at all hours when you would see them, it is *"done up*." The old kitchen floor never seems stained or spotted; the tables, the chairs, and the various

cooking utensils, never seem deranged or disordered; though
three and sometimes four meals a day are got there, though
the family washing and ironing is there performed, and
though pounds of butter and cheese are in some silent and
mysterious manner there brought into existence.

On such a farm, in such a house and family, Miss Ophelia
had spent a quiet existence of some forty-five years, when her
cousin invited her to visit his southern mansion. The eldest of
a large family, she was still considered by her father and
mother as one of "the children," and the proposal that she
should go to *Orleans* was a most momentous one to the family circle. The old gray-headed father took down Morse's At-
las out of the book-case, and looked out the exact latitude
and longitude; and read Flint's Travels in the South and
West, to make up his own mind as to the nature of the country.

The good mother inquired, anxiously, "if Orleans was n't
an awful wicked place," saying, "that it seemed to her most
equal to going to the Sandwich Islands, or anywhere among
the heathen."

It was known at the minister's, and at the doctor's, and at
Miss Peabody's milliner shop, that Ophelia St. Clare was
"talking about" going away down to Orleans with her
cousin; and of course the whole village could do no less than
help this very important process of *talking about* the matter.
The minister, who inclined strongly to abolitionist views, was
quite doubtful whether such a step might not tend somewhat
to encourage the southerners in holding on to their slaves;
while the doctor, who was a stanch colonizationist, inclined
to the opinion that Miss Ophelia ought to go, to show the
Orleans people that we don't think hardly of them, after all.
He was of opinion, in fact, that southern people needed encouraging. When, however, the fact that she had resolved to
go was fully before the public mind, she was solemnly invited
out to tea by all her friends and neighbors for the space of a
fortnight, and her prospects and plans duly canvassed and inquired into. Miss Moseley, who came into the house to help
to do the dress-making, acquired daily accessions of importance from the developments with regard to Miss Ophelia's
wardrobe which she had been enabled to make. It was credi-

bly ascertained that Squire Sinclare, as his name was commonly contracted in the neighborhood, had counted out fifty dollars, and given them to Miss Ophelia, and told her to buy any clothes she thought best; and that two new silk dresses, and a bonnet, had been sent for from Boston. As to the propriety of this extraordinary outlay, the public mind was divided,—some affirming that it was well enough, all things considered, for once in one's life, and others stoutly affirming that the money had better have been sent to the missionaries; but all parties agreed that there had been no such parasol seen in those parts as had been sent on from New York; and that she had one silk dress that might fairly be trusted to stand alone, whatever might be said of its mistress. There were credible rumors, also, of a hemstitched pocket-handkerchief; and report even went so far as to state that Miss Ophelia had one pocket-handkerchief with lace all around it,—it was even added that it was worked in the corners; but this latter point was never satisfactorily ascertained, and remains, in fact, unsettled to this day.

Miss Ophelia, as you now behold her, stands before you, in a very shining brown linen travelling-dress, tall, square-formed, and angular. Her face was thin, and rather sharp in its outlines; the lips compressed, like those of a person who is in the habit of making up her mind definitely on all subjects; while the keen, dark eyes had a peculiarly searching, advised movement, and travelled over everything, as if they were looking for something to take care of.

All her movements were sharp, decided, and energetic; and, though she was never much of a talker, her words were remarkably direct, and to the purpose, when she did speak.

In her habits, she was a living impersonation of order, method, and exactness. In punctuality, she was as inevitable as a clock, and as inexorable as a railroad engine; and she held in most decided contempt and abomination anything of a contrary character.

The great sin of sins, in her eyes,—the sum of all evils,—was expressed by one very common and important word in her vocabulary—"shiftlessness." Her finale and ultimatum of contempt consisted in a very emphatic pronunciation of the word "shiftless;" and by this she characterized all modes of procedure which had not a direct and inevitable relation to accomplishment of some purpose then definitely had in mind. People who did nothing, or who did not know exactly what they were going to do, or who did not take the most direct way to accomplish what they set their hands to, were objects of her entire contempt,—a contempt shown less frequently by anything she said, than by a kind of stony grimness, as if she scorned to say anything about the matter.

As to mental cultivation,—she had a clear, strong, active mind, was well and thoroughly read in history and the older English classics, and thought with great strength within certain narrow limits. Her theological tenets were all made up, labelled in most positive and distinct forms, and put by, like the bundles in her patch trunk; there were just so many of them, and there were never to be any more. So, also, were her ideas with regard to most matters of practical life,—such as housekeeping in all its branches, and the various political relations of her native village. And, underlaying all, deeper than anything else, higher and broader, lay the strongest principle of her being—conscientiousness. Nowhere is conscience so dominant and all-absorbing as with New England women. It is the granite formation, which lies deepest, and rises out, even to the tops of the highest mountains.

Miss Ophelia was the absolute bond-slave of the *"ought."* Once make her certain that the "path of duty," as she commonly phrased it, lay in any given direction, and fire and water could not keep her from it. She would walk straight down into a well, or up to a loaded cannon's mouth, if she were only quite sure that there the path lay. Her standard of right was so high, so all-embracing, so minute, and making so few concessions to human frailty, that, though she strove with heroic ardor to reach it, she never actually did so, and of course was burdened with a constant and often harassing sense of deficiency;—this gave a severe and somewhat gloomy cast to her religious character.

But, how in the world can Miss Ophelia get along with Augustine St. Clare,—gay, easy, unpunctual, unpractical, sceptical,—in short, walking with impudent and nonchalant freedom over every one of her most cherished habits and opinions?

To tell the truth, then, Miss Ophelia loved him. When a boy, it had been hers to teach him his catechism, mend his clothes, comb his hair, and bring him up generally in the way he should go; and her heart having a warm side to it, Augustine had, as he usually did with most people, monopolized a large share of it for himself, and therefore it was that he succeeded very easily in persuading her that the "path of duty" lay in the direction of New Orleans, and that she must go with him to take care of Eva, and keep everything from going to wreck and ruin during the frequent illnesses of his wife. The idea of a house without anybody to take care of it went to her heart; then she loved the lovely little girl, as few could help doing; and though she regarded Augustine as very much of a heathen, yet she loved him, laughed at his jokes, and forbore with his failings, to an extent which those who knew him thought perfectly incredible. But what more or other is to be known of Miss Ophelia our reader must discover by a personal acquaintance.

There she is, sitting now in her state-room, surrounded by a mixed multitude of little and big carpet-bags, boxes, baskets, each containing some separate responsibility which she is tying, binding up, packing, or fastening, with a face of great earnestness.

"Now, Eva, have you kept count of your things? Of course you have n't,—children never do: there 's the spotted carpet-bag and the little blue band-box with your best bonnet,—that 's two; then the India rubber satchel is three; and my tape and needle box is four; and my band-box, five; and my collar-box, six; and that little hair trunk, seven. What have you done with your sunshade? Give it to me, and let me put a paper round it, and tie it to my umbrella with my shade;—there, now."

"Why, aunty, we are only going up home;—what is the use?"

"To keep it nice, child; people must take care of their things, if they ever mean to have anything; and now, Eva, is your thimble put up?"

"Really, aunty, I don't know."

"Well, never mind; I 'll look your box over,—thimble, wax, two spools, scissors, knife, tape-needle; all right,—put it in here. What did you ever do, child, when you were coming on with only your papa. I should have thought you 'd a lost everything you had."

"Well, aunty, I did lose a great many; and then, when we stopped anywhere, papa would buy some more of whatever it was."

"Mercy on us, child,—what a way!"

"It was a very easy way, aunty," said Eva.

"It 's a dreadful shiftless one," said aunty.

"Why, aunty, what 'll you do now?" said Eva; "that trunk is too full to be shut down."

"It *must* shut down," said aunty, with the air of a general, as she squeezed the things in, and sprung upon the lid;—still a little gap remained about the mouth of the trunk.

"Get up here, Eva!" said Miss Ophelia, courageously; "what has been done can be done again. This trunk has *got to be* shut and locked—there are no two ways about it."

And the trunk, intimidated, doubtless, by this resolute statement, gave in. The hasp snapped sharply in its hole, and Miss Ophelia turned the key, and pocketed it in triumph.

"Now we 're ready. Where 's your papa? I think it time this baggage was set out. Do look out, Eva, and see if you see your papa."

"O, yes, he 's down the other end of the gentlemen's cabin, eating an orange."

"He can't know how near we are coming," said aunty; "had n't you better run and speak to him?"

"Papa never is in a hurry about anything," said Eva, "and we have n't come to the landing. Do step on the guards, aunty. Look! there 's our house, up that street!"

The boat now began, with heavy groans, like some vast, tired monster, to prepare to push up among the multiplied steamers at the levee. Eva joyously pointed out the various spires, domes, and way-marks, by which she recognized her native city.

"Yes, yes, dear; very fine," said Miss Ophelia. "But mercy on us! the boat has stopped! where is your father?"

And now ensued the usual turmoil of landing—waiters running twenty ways at once—men tugging trunks, carpet-bags, boxes—women anxiously calling to their children, and everybody crowding in a dense mass to the plank towards the landing.

Miss Ophelia seated herself resolutely on the lately vanquished trunk, and marshalling all her goods and chattels in fine military order, seemed resolved to defend them to the last.

"Shall I take your trunk, ma'am?" "Shall I take your baggage?" "Let me 'tend to your baggage, Missis?" "Shan't I carry out these yer, Missis?" rained down upon her unheeded. She sat with grim determination, upright as a darning-needle stuck in a board, holding on her bundle of umbrella and parasols, and replying with a determination that was enough to strike dismay even into a hackman, wondering to Eva, in each interval, "what upon earth her papa could be thinking of; he could n't have fallen over, now,—but something must have happened;"—and just as she had begun to work herself into a real distress, he came up, with his usually careless motion, and giving Eva a quarter of the orange he was eating, said,

"Well, Cousin Vermont, I suppose you are all ready."

"I 've been ready, waiting, nearly an hour," said Miss Ophelia; "I began to be really concerned about you."

"That 's a clever fellow, now," said he. "Well, the carriage is waiting, and the crowd are now off, so that one can walk out in a decent and Christian manner, and not be pushed and shoved. Here," he added to a driver who stood behind him, "take these things."

"I 'll go and see to his putting them in," said Miss Ophelia.

"O, pshaw, cousin, what 's the use?" said St. Clare.

"Well, at any rate, I 'll carry this, and this, and this," said Miss Ophelia, singling out three boxes and a small carpet-bag.

"My dear Miss Vermont, positively, you must n't come the Green Mountains over us that way. You must adopt at least a piece of a southern principle, and not walk out under all that load. They 'll take you for a waiting-maid; give them to this fellow; he 'll put them down as if they were eggs, now."

Miss Ophelia looked despairingly, as her cousin took all her treasures from her, and rejoiced to find herself once more in the carriage with them, in a state of preservation.

"Where 's Tom?" said Eva.

"O, he 's on the outside, Pussy. I 'm going to take Tom up

to mother for a peace-offering, to make up for that drunken fellow that upset the carriage."

"O, Tom will make a splendid driver, I know," said Eva; "he 'll never get drunk."

The carriage stopped in front of an ancient mansion, built in that odd mixture of Spanish and French style, of which there are specimens in some parts of New Orleans. It was built in the Moorish fashion,—a square building enclosing a court-yard, into which the carriage drove through an arched gateway. The court, in the inside, had evidently been arranged to gratify a picturesque and voluptuous ideality. Wide galleries ran all around the four sides, whose Moorish arches, slender pillars, and arabesque ornaments, carried the mind back, as in a dream, to the reign of oriental romance in Spain. In the middle of the court, a fountain threw high its silvery water, falling in a never-ceasing spray into a marble basin, fringed with a deep border of fragrant violets. The water in the fountain, pellucid as crystal, was alive with myriads of gold and silver fishes, twinkling and darting through it like so many living jewels. Around the fountain ran a walk, paved with a mosaic of pebbles, laid in various fanciful patterns; and this, again, was surrounded by turf, smooth as green velvet, while a carriage-drive enclosed the whole. Two large orange-trees, now fragrant with blossoms, threw a delicious shade; and, ranged in a circle round upon the turf, were marble vases of arabesque sculpture, containing the choicest flowering plants of the tropics. Huge pomegranate trees, with their glossy leaves and flame-colored flowers, dark-leaved Arabian jessamines, with their silvery stars, geraniums, luxuriant roses bending beneath their heavy abundance of flowers, golden jessamines, lemon-scented verbenum, all united their bloom and fragrance, while here and there a mystic old aloe, with its strange, massive leaves, sat looking like some hoary old enchanter, sitting in weird grandeur among the more perishable bloom and fragrance around it.

The galleries that surrounded the court were festooned with a curtain of some kind of Moorish stuff, and could be drawn down at pleasure, to exclude the beams of the sun. On the whole, the appearance of the place was luxurious and romantic.

As the carriage drove in, Eva seemed like a bird ready to burst from a cage, with the wild eagerness of her delight.

"O, is n't it beautiful, lovely! my own dear, darling home!" she said to Miss Ophelia. "Is n't it beautiful?"

" 'T is a pretty place," said Miss Ophelia, as she alighted; "though it looks rather old and heathenish to me."

Tom got down from the carriage, and looked about with an air of calm, still enjoyment. The negro, it must be remembered, is an exotic of the most gorgeous and superb countries of the world, and he has, deep in his heart, a passion for all that is splendid, rich, and fanciful; a passion which, rudely indulged by an untrained taste, draws on them the ridicule of the colder and more correct white race.

St. Clare, who was in his heart a poetical voluptuary, smiled as Miss Ophelia made her remark on his premises, and, turning to Tom, who was standing looking round, his beaming black face perfectly radiant with admiration, he said,

"Tom, my boy, this seems to suit you."

"Yes, Mas'r, it looks about the right thing," said Tom.

All this passed in a moment, while trunks were being hustled off, hackman paid, and while a crowd, of all ages and sizes,—men, women, and children,—came running through the galleries, both above and below, to see Mas'r come in. Foremost among them was a highly-dressed young mulatto man, evidently a very *distingue* personage, attired in the ultra extreme of the mode, and gracefully waving a scented cambric handkerchief in his hand.

This personage had been exerting himself, with great alacrity, in driving all the flock of domestics to the other end of the verandah.

"Back! all of you. I am ashamed of you," he said, in a tone of authority. "Would you intrude on Master's domestic relations, in the first hour of his return?"

All looked abashed at this elegant speech, delivered with quite an air, and stood huddled together at a respectful distance, except two stout porters, who came up and began conveying away the baggage.

Owing to Mr. Adolph's systematic arrangements, when St. Clare turned round from paying the hackman, there was nobody in view but Mr. Adolph himself, conspicuous in satin vest, gold guard-chain, and white pants, and bowing with inexpressible grace and suavity.

"Ah, Adolph, is it you?" said his master, offering his hand to him; "how are you, boy?" while Adolph poured forth, with great fluency, an extemporary speech, which he had been preparing, with great care, for a fortnight before.

"Well, well," said St. Clare, passing on, with his usual air of negligent drollery, "that's very well got up, Adolph. See that the baggage is well bestowed. I'll come to the people in a minute;" and, so saying, he led Miss Ophelia to a large parlor that opened on to the verandah.

While this had been passing, Eva had flown like a bird, through the porch and parlor, to a little boudoir opening likewise on the verandah.

A tall, dark-eyed, sallow woman, half rose from a couch on which she was reclining.

"Mamma!" said Eva, in a sort of a rapture, throwing herself on her neck, and embracing her over and over again.

"That'll do,—take care, child,—don't, you make my head ache," said the mother, after she had languidly kissed her.

St. Clare came in, embraced his wife in true, orthodox, husbandly fashion, and then presented to her his cousin. Marie lifted her large eyes on her cousin with an air of some curiosity, and received her with languid politeness. A crowd of servants now pressed to the entry door, and among them a middle-aged mulatto woman, of very respectable appearance, stood foremost, in a tremor of expectation and joy, at the door.

"O, there's Mammy!" said Eva, as she flew across the room; and, throwing herself into her arms, she kissed her repeatedly.

This woman did not tell her that she made her head ache, but, on the contrary, she hugged her, and laughed, and cried, till her sanity was a thing to be doubted of; and when released from her, Eva flew from one to another, shaking hands and kissing, in a way that Miss Ophelia afterwards declared fairly turned her stomach.

"Well!" said Miss Ophelia, "you southern children can do something that *I* could n't."

"What, now, pray?" said St. Clare.

"Well, I want to be kind to everybody, and I would n't have anything hurt; but as to kissing—"

"Niggers," said St. Clare, "that you 're not up to,—hey?"

"Yes, that 's it. How can she?"

St. Clare laughed, as he went into the passage. "Halloa, here, what 's to pay out here? Here, you all—Mammy, Jimmy, Polly, Sukey—glad to see Mas'r?" he said, as he went shaking hands from one to another. "Look out for the babies!" he added, as he stumbled over a sooty little urchin, who was crawling upon all fours. "If I step upon anybody, let 'em mention it."

There was an abundance of laughing and blessing Mas'r, as St. Clare distributed small pieces of change among them.

"Come, now, take yourselves off, like good boys and girls," he said; and the whole assemblage, dark and light, disappeared through a door into a large verandah, followed by Eva, who carried a large satchel, which she had been filling with apples, nuts, candy, ribbons, laces, and toys of every description, during her whole homeward journey.

As St. Clare turned to go back, his eye fell upon Tom, who was standing uneasily, shifting from one foot to the other, while Adolph stood negligently leaning against the banisters, examining Tom through an opera-glass, with an air that would have done credit to any dandy living.

"Puh! you puppy," said his master, striking down the opera glass; "is that the way you treat your company? Seems to me, Dolph," he added, laying his finger on the elegant figured satin vest that Adolph was sporting, "seems to me that 's *my* vest."

"O! Master, this vest all stained with wine; of course, a gentleman in Master's standing never wears a vest like this. I understood I was to take it. It does for a poor nigger-fellow, like me."

And Adolph tossed his head, and passed his fingers through his scented hair, with a grace.

"So, that 's it, is it?" said St. Clare, carelessly. "Well, here, I 'm going to show this Tom to his mistress, and then you take him to the kitchen; and mind you don't put on any of your airs to him. He 's worth two such puppies as you."

"Master always will have his joke," said Adolph, laughing. "I'm delighted to see Master in such spirits."

"Here, Tom," said St. Clare, beckoning.

Tom entered the room. He looked wistfully on the velvet carpets, and the before unimagined splendors of mirrors, pictures, statues, and curtains, and, like the Queen of Sheba before Solomon, there was no more spirit in him. He looked afraid even to set his feet down.

"See here, Marie," said St. Clare to his wife, "I've bought you a coachman, at last, to order. I tell you, he's a regular hearse for blackness and sobriety, and will drive you like a funeral, if you want. Open your eyes, now, and look at him. Now, don't say I never think about you when I'm gone."

Marie opened her eyes, and fixed them on Tom, without rising.

"I know he'll get drunk," she said.

"No, he's warranted a pious and sober article."

"Well, I hope he may turn out well," said the lady; "it's more than I expect, though."

"Dolph," said St. Clare, "show Tom down stairs; and, mind yourself," he added; "remember what I told you."

Adolph tripped gracefully forward, and Tom, with lumbering tread, went after.

"He's a perfect behemoth!" said Marie.

"Come, now, Marie," said St. Clare, seating himself on a stool beside her sofa, "be gracious, and say something pretty to a fellow."

"You've been gone a fortnight beyond the time," said the lady, pouting.

"Well, you know I wrote you the reason."

"Such a short, cold letter!" said the lady.

"Dear me! the mail was just going, and it had to be that or nothing."

"That's just the way, always," said the lady; "always something to make your journeys long, and letters short."

"See here, now," he added, drawing an elegant velvet case out of his pocket, and opening it, "here's a present I got for you in New York."

It was a daguerreotype, clear and soft as an engraving, representing Eva and her father sitting hand in hand.

Marie looked at it with a dissatisfied air.

"What made you sit in such an awkward position?" she said.

"Well, the position may be a matter of opinion; but what do you think of the likeness?"

"If you don't think anything of my opinion in one case, I suppose you would n't in another," said the lady, shutting the daguerreotype.

"Hang the woman!" said St. Clare, mentally; but aloud he added, "Come, now, Marie, what do you think of the likeness? Don't be nonsensical, now."

"It's very inconsiderate of you, St. Clare," said the lady, "to insist on my talking and looking at things. You know I've been lying all day with the sick-headache; and there's been such a tumult made ever since you came, I'm half dead."

"You're subject to the sick-headache, ma'am?" said Miss Ophelia, suddenly rising from the depths of the large arm-chair, where she had sat quietly, taking an inventory of the furniture, and calculating its expense.

"Yes, I'm a perfect martyr to it," said the lady.

"Juniper-berry tea is good for sick-headache," said Miss Ophelia; "at least, Auguste, Deacon Abraham Perry's wife, used to say so; and she was a great nurse."

"I'll have the first juniper-berries that get ripe in our garden by the lake brought in for that especial purpose," said St. Clare, gravely pulling the bell as he did so; "meanwhile, cousin, you must be wanting to retire to your apartment, and refresh yourself a little, after your journey. Dolph," he added, "tell Mammy to come here." The decent mulatto woman whom Eva had caressed so rapturously soon entered; she was dressed neatly, with a high red and yellow turban on her head, the recent gift of Eva, and which the child had been arranging on her head. "Mammy," said St. Clare, "I put this lady under your care; she is tired, and wants rest; take her to her chamber, and be sure she is made comfortable;" and Miss Ophelia disappeared in the rear of Mammy.

XVI.

Tom's Mistress and Her Opinions

"And now, Marie," said St. Clare, "your golden days are dawning. Here is our practical, business-like New England cousin, who will take the whole budget of cares off your shoulders, and give you time to refresh yourself, and grow young and handsome. The ceremony of delivering the keys had better come off forthwith."

This remark was made at the breakfast-table, a few mornings after Miss Ophelia had arrived.

"I'm sure she's welcome," said Marie, leaning her head languidly on her hand. "I think she'll find one thing, if she does, and that is, that it's we mistresses that are the slaves, down here."

"O, certainly, she will discover that, and a world of wholesome truths besides, no doubt," said St. Clare.

"Talk about our keeping slaves, as if we did it for our *convenience*," said Marie. "I'm sure, if we consulted *that*, we might let them all go at once."

Evangeline fixed her large, serious eyes on her mother's face, with an earnest and perplexed expression, and said, simply, "What do you keep them for, mamma?"

"I don't know, I'm sure, except for a plague; they are the plague of my life. I believe that more of my ill health is caused by them than by any one thing; and ours, I know, are the very worst that ever anybody was plagued with."

"O, come, Marie, you've got the blues, this morning," said St. Clare. "You know 't is n't so. There's Mammy, the best creature living,—what could you do without her?"

"Mammy is the best I ever knew," said Marie; "and yet Mammy, now, is selfish—dreadfully selfish; it's the fault of the whole race."

"Selfishness *is* a dreadful fault," said St. Clare, gravely.

"Well, now, there's Mammy," said Marie, "I think it's selfish of her to sleep so sound nights; she knows I need little attentions almost every hour, when my worst turns are on, and yet she's so hard to wake. I absolutely am worse, this very morning, for the efforts I had to make to wake her last night."

"Has n't she sat up with you a good many nights, lately, mamma?" said Eva.

"How should you know that?" said Marie, sharply; "she's been complaining, I suppose."

"She did n't complain; she only told me what bad nights you'd had,—so many in succession."

"Why don't you let Jane or Rosa take her place, a night or two," said St. Clare, "and let her rest?"

"How can you propose it?" said Marie. "St. Clare, you really are inconsiderate. So nervous as I am, the least breath disturbs me; and a strange hand about me would drive me absolutely frantic. If Mammy felt the interest in me she ought to, she'd wake easier,—of course, she would. I've heard of people who had such devoted servants, but it never was *my* luck;" and Marie sighed.

Miss Ophelia had listened to this conversation with an air of shrewd, observant gravity; and she still kept her lips tightly compressed, as if determined fully to ascertain her longitude and position, before she committed herself.

"Now, Mammy has a *sort* of goodness," said Marie; "she's smooth and respectful, but she's selfish at heart. Now, she never will be done fidgeting and worrying about that husband of hers. You see, when I was married and came to live here, of course, I had to bring her with me, and her husband my father could n't spare. He was a blacksmith, and, of course, very necessary; and I thought and said, at the time, that Mammy and he had better give each other up, as it was n't likely to be convenient for them ever to live together again. I wish, now, I'd insisted on it, and married Mammy to somebody else; but I was foolish and indulgent, and did n't want to insist. I told Mammy, at the time, that she must n't ever expect to see him more than once or twice in her life again, for the air of father's place does n't agree with my health, and I can't go there; and I advised her to take up with somebody else; but no—she would n't. Mammy has a kind of obstinacy about her, in spots, that everybody don't see as I do."

"Has she children?" said Miss Ophelia.

"Yes; she has two."

"I suppose she feels the separation from them?"

"Well, of course, I could n't bring them. They were little dirty things—I could n't have them about; and, besides, they took up too much of her time; but I believe that Mammy has always kept up a sort of sulkiness about this. She won't marry anybody else; and I do believe, now, though she knows how necessary she is to me, and how feeble my health is, she would go back to her husband to-morrow, if she only could. I *do,* indeed," said Marie; "they are just so selfish, now, the best of them."

"It 's distressing to reflect upon," said St. Clare, dryly.

Miss Ophelia looked keenly at him, and saw the flush of mortification and repressed vexation, and the sarcastic curl of the lip, as he spoke.

"Now, Mammy has always been a pet with me," said Marie. "I wish some of your northern servants could look at her closets of dresses,—silks and muslins, and one real linen cambric, she has hanging there. I 've worked sometimes whole afternoons, trimming her caps, and getting her ready to go to a party. As to abuse, she don't know what it is. She never was whipped more than once or twice in her whole life. She has her strong coffee or her tea every day, with white sugar in it. It 's abominable, to be sure; but St. Clare will have high life below-stairs, and they every one of them live just as they please. The fact is, our servants are over-indulged. I suppose it is partly our fault that they are selfish, and act like spoiled children; but I 've talked to St. Clare till I am tired."

"And I, too," said St. Clare, taking up the morning paper.

Eva, the beautiful Eva, had stood listening to her mother, with that expression of deep and mystic earnestness which was peculiar to her. She walked softly round to her mother's chair, and put her arms round her neck.

"Well, Eva, what now?" said Marie.

"Mamma, could n't I take care of you one night—just one? I know I should n't make you nervous, and I should n't sleep. I often lie awake nights, thinking—"

"O, nonsense, child—nonsense!" said Marie; "you are such a strange child!"

"But may I, mamma? I think," she said, timidly, "that Mammy is n't well. She told me her head ached all the time, lately."

"O, that 's just one of Mammy's fidgets! Mammy is just like all the rest of them—makes such a fuss about every little head-ache or finger-ache; it 'll never do to encourage it— never! I 'm principled about this matter," said she, turning to Miss Ophelia; "you 'll find the necessity of it. If you encourage servants in giving way to every little disagreeable feeling, and complaining of every little ailment, you 'll have your hands full. I never complain myself—nobody knows what I endure. I feel it a duty to bear it quietly, and I do."

Miss Ophelia's round eyes expressed an undisguised amazement at this peroration, which struck St. Clare as so supremely ludicrous, that he burst into a loud laugh.

"St. Clare always laughs when I make the least allusion to my ill health," said Marie, with the voice of a suffering martyr. "I only hope the day won't come when he 'll remember it!" and Marie put her handkerchief to her eyes.

Of course, there was rather a foolish silence. Finally, St. Clare got up, looked at his watch, and said he had an engagement down street. Eva tripped away after him, and Miss Ophelia and Marie remained at the table alone.

"Now, that 's just like St. Clare!" said the latter, withdrawing her handkerchief with somewhat of a spirited flourish when the criminal to be affected by it was no longer in sight. "He never realizes, never can, never will, what I suffer, and have, for years. If I was one of the complaining sort, or ever made any fuss about my ailments, there would be some reason for it. Men do get tired, naturally, of a complaining wife. But I 've kept things to myself, and borne, and borne, till St. Clare has got in the way of thinking I can bear anything."

Miss Ophelia did not exactly know what she was expected to answer to this.

While she was thinking what to say, Marie gradually wiped away her tears, and smoothed her plumage in a general sort of way, as a dove might be supposed to make toilet after a shower, and began a housewifely chat with Miss Ophelia, concerning cupboards, closets, linen-presses, store-rooms, and other matters, of which the latter was, by common under-standing, to assume the direction,—giving her so many cautious directions and charges, that a head less systematic and business-like than Miss Ophelia's would have been utterly dizzied and confounded.

"And now," said Marie, "I believe I've told you everything; so that, when my next sick turn comes on, you'll be able to go forward entirely, without consulting me;—only about Eva,—she requires watching."

"She seems to be a good child, very," said Miss Ophelia; "I never saw a better child."

"Eva's peculiar," said her mother, "very. There are things about her so singular; she isn't like me, now, a particle;" and Marie sighed, as if this was a truly melancholy consideration.

Miss Ophelia in her own heart said, "I hope she isn't," but had prudence enough to keep it down.

"Eva always was disposed to be with servants; and I think that well enough with some children. Now, I always played with father's little negroes—it never did me any harm. But Eva somehow always seems to put herself on an equality with every creature that comes near her. It's a strange thing about the child. I never have been able to break her of it. St. Clare, I believe, encourages her in it. The fact is, St. Clare indulges every creature under this roof but his own wife."

Again Miss Ophelia sat in blank silence.

"Now, there's no way with servants," said Marie, "but to *put them down*, and keep them down. It was always natural to me, from a child. Eva is enough to spoil a whole house-full. What she will do when she comes to keep house herself, I'm sure I don't know. I hold to being *kind* to servants—I always am; but you must make 'em *know their place*. Eva never does; there's no getting into the child's head the first beginning of an idea what a servant's place is! You heard her offering to take care of me nights, to let Mammy sleep! That's just a specimen of the way the child would be doing all the time, if she was left to herself."

"Why," said Miss Ophelia, bluntly, "I suppose you think your servants are human creatures, and ought to have some rest when they are tired."

"Certainly, of course. I 'm very particular in letting them have everything that comes convenient,—anything that does n't put one at all out of the way, you know. Mammy can make up her sleep, some time or other; there 's no difficulty about that. She 's the sleepiest concern that ever I saw; sewing, standing, or sitting, that creature will go to sleep, and sleep anywhere and everywhere. No danger but Mammy gets sleep enough. But this treating servants as if they were exotic flowers, or china vases, is really ridiculous," said Marie, as she plunged languidly into the depths of a voluminous and pillowy lounge, and drew towards her an elegant cut-glass vinaigrette.

"You see," she continued, in a faint and lady-like voice, like the last dying breath of an Arabian jessamine, or something equally ethereal, "you see, Cousin Ophelia, I don't often speak of myself. It is n't my *habit*; 't is n't agreeable to me. In fact, I have n't strength to do it. But there are points where St. Clare and I differ. St. Clare never understood me, never appreciated me. I think it lies at the root of all my ill health. St. Clare means well, I am bound to believe; but men are constitutionally selfish and inconsiderate to woman. That, at least, is my impression."

Miss Ophelia, who had not a small share of the genuine New England caution, and a very particular horror of being drawn into family difficulties, now began to foresee something of this kind impending; so, composing her face into a grim neutrality, and drawing out of her pocket about a yard and a quarter of stocking, which she kept as a specific against what Dr. Watts asserts to be a personal habit of Satan when people have idle hands, she proceeded to knit most energetically, shutting her lips together in a way that said, as plain as words could, "You need n't try to make me speak. I don't want anything to do with your affairs,"—in fact, she looked about as sympathizing as a stone lion. But Marie did n't care for that. She had got somebody to talk to, and she felt it her duty to talk, and that was enough; and reinforcing herself by smelling again at her vinaigrette, she went on.

"You see, I brought my own property and servants into the connection, when I married St. Clare, and I am legally entitled to manage them my own way. St. Clare had his fortune and his servants, and I'm well enough content he should manage them his way; but St. Clare will be interfering. He has wild, extravagant notions about things, particularly about the treatment of servants. He really does act as if he set his servants before me, and before himself, too; for he lets them make him all sorts of trouble, and never lifts a finger. Now, about some things, St. Clare is really frightful—he frightens me—good-natured as he looks, in general. Now, he has set down his foot that, come what will, there shall not be a blow struck in this house, except what he or I strike; and he does it in a way that I really dare not cross him. Well, you may see what that leads to; for St. Clare would n't raise his hand, if every one of them walked over him, and I—you see how cruel it would be to require me to make the exertion. Now, you know these servants are nothing but grown-up children."

"I don't know anything about it, and I thank the Lord that I don't!" said Miss Ophelia, shortly.

"Well, but you will have to know something, and know it to your cost, if you stay here. You don't know what a provoking, stupid, careless, unreasonable, childish, ungrateful set of wretches they are."

Marie seemed wonderfully supported, always, when she got upon this topic; and she now opened her eyes, and seemed quite to forget her languor.

"You don't know, and you can't, the daily, hourly trials that beset a housekeeper from them, everywhere and every way. But it's no use to complain to St. Clare. He talks the strangest stuff. He says we have made them what they are, and ought to bear with them. He says their faults are all owing to us, and that it would be cruel to make the fault and punish it too. He says we should n't do any better, in their place; just as if one could reason from them to us, you know."

"Don't you believe that the Lord made them of one blood with us?" said Miss Ophelia, shortly.

"No, indeed, not I! A pretty story, truly! They are a degraded race."

"Don't you think they've got immortal souls?" said Miss Ophelia, with increasing indignation.

"O, well," said Marie, yawning, "that, of course—nobody

doubts that. But as to putting them on any sort of equality with us, you know, as if we could be compared, why, it's impossible! Now, St. Clare really has talked to me as if keeping Mammy from her husband was like keeping me from mine. There's no comparing in this way. Mammy couldn't have the feelings that I should. It's a different thing altogether,—of course, it is,—and yet St. Clare pretends not to see it. And just as if Mammy could love her little dirty babies as I love Eva! Yet St. Clare once really and soberly tried to persuade me that it was my duty, with my weak health, and all I suffer, to let Mammy go back, and take somebody else in her place. That was a little too much even for *me* to bear. I don't often show my feelings. I make it a principle to endure everything in silence; it's a wife's hard lot, and I bear it. But I did break out, that time; so that he has never alluded to the subject since. But I know by his looks, and little things that he says, that he thinks so as much as ever; and it's so trying, so provoking!"

Miss Ophelia looked very much as if she was afraid she should say something; but she rattled away with her needles in a way that had volumes of meaning in it, if Marie could only have understood it.

"So, you just see," she continued, "what you've got to manage. A household without any rule; where servants have it all their own way, do what they please, and have what they please, except so far as I, with my feeble health, have kept up government. I keep my cowhide about, and sometimes I do lay it on; but the exertion is always too much for me. If St. Clare would only have this thing done as others do—"

"And how's that?"

"Why, send them to the calaboose, or some of the other places to be flogged. That's the only way. If I wasn't such a poor, feeble piece, I believe I should manage with twice the energy that St. Clare does."

"And how does St. Clare contrive to manage?" said Miss Ophelia. "You say he never strikes a blow."

"Well, men have a more commanding way, you know; it is easier for them; besides, if you ever looked full in his eye, it's peculiar,—that eye,—and if he speaks decidedly, there's a

kind of flash. I'm afraid of it, myself; and the servants know
they must mind. I could n't do as much by a regular storm
and scolding as St. Clare can by one turn of his eye, if once
he is in earnest. O, there's no trouble about St. Clare; that's
the reason he's no more feeling for me. But you'll find, when
you come to manage, that there's no getting along without
severity,—they are so bad, so deceitful, so lazy."

"The old tune," said St. Clare, sauntering in. "What an
awful account these wicked creatures will have to settle, at
last, especially for being lazy! You see, cousin," said he, as he
stretched himself at full length on a lounge opposite to Marie,
"it's wholly inexcusable in them, in the light of the example
that Marie and I set them,—this laziness."

"Come, now, St. Clare, you are too bad!" said Marie.

"Am I, now? Why, I thought I was talking good, quite
remarkably for me. I try to enforce your remarks, Marie, always."

"You know you meant no such thing, St. Clare," said
Marie.

"O, I must have been mistaken, then. Thank you, my dear,
for setting me right."

"You do really try to be provoking," said Marie.

"O, come, Marie, the day is growing warm, and I have just
had a long quarrel with Dolph, which has fatigued me excessively; so, pray be agreeable, now, and let a fellow repose in
the light of your smile."

"What's the matter about Dolph?" said Marie. "That fellow's impudence has been growing to a point that is perfectly
intolerable to me. I only wish I had the undisputed management of him a while. I'd bring him down!"

"What you say, my dear, is marked with your usual acuteness and good sense," said St. Clare. "As to Dolph, the case
is this: that he has so long been engaged in imitating my
graces and perfections, that he has, at last, really mistaken
himself for his master; and I have been obliged to give him a
little insight into his mistake."

"How?" said Marie.

"Why, I was obliged to let him understand explicitly that
I preferred to keep *some* of my clothes for my own personal
wearing; also, I put his magnificence upon an allowance of

cologne-water, and actually was so cruel as to restrict him to one dozen of my cambric handkerchiefs. Dolph was particularly huffy about it, and I had to talk to him like a father, to bring him round."

"O! St. Clare, when will you learn how to treat your servants? It's abominable, the way you indulge them!" said Marie.

"Why, after all, what's the harm of the poor dog's wanting to be like his master; and if I haven't brought him up any better than to find his chief good in cologne and cambric handkerchiefs, why shouldn't I give them to him?"

"And why haven't you brought him up better?" said Miss Ophelia, with blunt determination.

"Too much trouble,—laziness, cousin, laziness,—which ruins more souls than you can shake a stick at. If it weren't for laziness, I should have been a perfect angel, myself. I'm inclined to think that laziness is what your old Dr. Botherem, up in Vermont, used to call the 'essence of moral evil.' It's an awful consideration, certainly."

"I think you slaveholders have an awful responsibility upon you," said Miss Ophelia. "I wouldn't have it, for a thousand worlds. You ought to educate your slaves, and treat them like reasonable creatures,—like immortal creatures, that you've got to stand before the bar of God with. That's my mind," said the good lady, breaking suddenly out with a tide of zeal that had been gaining strength in her mind all the morning.

"O! come, come," said St. Clare, getting up quickly; "what do you know about us?" And he sat down to the piano, and rattled a lively piece of music. St. Clare had a decided genius for music. His touch was brilliant and firm, and his fingers flew over the keys with a rapid and bird-like motion, airy, and yet decided. He played piece after piece, like a man who is trying to play himself into a good humor. After pushing the music aside, he rose up, and said, gayly, "Well, now, cousin, you've given us a good talk, and done your duty; on the whole, I think the better of you for it. I make no manner of doubt that you threw a very diamond of truth at me, though you see it hit me so directly in the face that it wasn't exactly appreciated, at first."

"For my part, I don't see any use in such sort of talk," said

Marie. "I 'm sure, if anybody does more for servants than we do, I 'd like to know who; and it don't do 'em a bit good,— not a particle,—they get worse and worse. As to talking to them, or anything like that, I 'm sure I have talked till I was tired and hoarse, telling them their duty, and all that; and I 'm sure they can go to church when they like, though they don't understand a word of the sermon, more than so many pigs,—so it is n't of any great use for them to go, as I see; but they do go, and so they have every chance; but, as I said before, they are a degraded race, and always will be, and there is n't any help for them; you can't make anything of them, if you try. You see, Cousin Ophelia, I 've tried, and you have n't; I was born and bred among them, and I know."

Miss Ophelia thought she had said enough, and therefore sat silent. St. Clare whistled a tune.

"St. Clare, I wish you would n't whistle," said Marie; "it makes my head worse."

"I won't," said St. Clare. "Is there anything else you would n't wish me to do?"

"I wish you *would* have some kind of sympathy for my trials; you never have any feeling for me."

"My dear accusing angel!" said St. Clare.

"It 's provoking to be talked to in that way."

"Then, how will you be talked to? I 'll talk to order,—any way you 'll mention,—only to give satisfaction."

A gay laugh from the court rang through the silken curtains of the verandah. St. Clare stepped out, and lifting up the curtain, laughed too.

"What is it?" said Miss Ophelia, coming to the railing.

There sat Tom, on a little mossy seat in the court, every one of his button-holes stuck full of cape jessamines, and Eva, gayly laughing, was hanging a wreath of roses round his neck; and then she sat down on his knee, like a chip-sparrow, still laughing.

"O, Tom, you look so funny!"

Tom had a sober, benevolent smile, and seemed, in his quiet way, to be enjoying the fun quite as much as his little mistress. He lifted his eyes, when he saw his master, with a half-deprecating, apologetic air.

"How can you let her?" said Miss Ophelia.

"Why not?" said St. Clare.

"Why, I don't know, it seems so dreadful!"

"You would think no harm in a child's caressing a large dog, even if he was black; but a creature that can think, and reason, and feel, and is immortal, you shudder at; confess it, cousin. I know the feeling among some of you northerners well enough. Not that there is a particle of virtue in our not having it; but custom with us does what Christianity ought to do,—obliterates the feeling of personal prejudice. I have often noticed, in my travels north, how much stronger this was with you than with us. You loathe them as you would a snake or a toad, yet you are indignant at their wrongs. You would not have them abused; but you don't want to have anything to do with them yourselves. You would send them to Africa, out of your sight and smell, and then send a missionary or two to do up all the self-denial of elevating them compendiously. Is n't that it?"

"Well, cousin," said Miss Ophelia, thoughtfully, "there may be some truth in this."

"What would the poor and lowly do, without children?" said St. Clare, leaning on the railing, and watching Eva, as she tripped off, leading Tom with her. "Your little child is your only true democrat. Tom, now, is a hero to Eva; his stories are wonders in her eyes, his songs and Methodist hymns are better than an opera, and the traps and little bits of trash in his pocket a mine of jewels, and he the most wonderful Tom that ever wore a black skin. This is one of the roses of Eden that the Lord has dropped down expressly for the poor and lowly, who get few enough of any other kind."

"It 's strange, cousin," said Miss Ophelia; "one might almost think you were a *professor*, to hear you talk."

"A professor?" said St. Clare.

"Yes; a professor of religion."

"Not at all; not a professor, as your town-folks have it; and, what is worse, I 'm afraid, not a *practiser*, either."

"What makes you talk so, then?"

"Nothing is easier than talking," said St. Clare. "I believe Shakspeare makes somebody say, 'I could sooner show twenty what were good to be done, than be one of the twenty to follow my own showing.' Nothing like division of labor. My forte lies in talking, and yours, cousin, lies in doing."

––––––––––

In Tom's external situation, at this time, there was, as the world says, nothing to complain of. Little Eva's fancy for him—the instinctive gratitude and loveliness of a noble nature—had led her to petition her father that he might be her especial attendant, whenever she needed the escort of a servant, in her walks or rides; and Tom had general orders to let everything else go, and attend to Miss Eva whenever she wanted him,—orders which our readers may fancy were far from disagreeable to him. He was kept well dressed, for St. Clare was fastidiously particular on this point. His stable services were merely a sinecure, and consisted simply in a daily care and inspection, and directing an under-servant in his duties; for Marie St. Clare declared that she could not have any smell of the horses about him when he came near her, and that he must positively not be put to any service that would make him unpleasant to her, as her nervous system was entirely inadequate to any trial of that nature; one snuff of anything disagreeable being, according to her account, quite sufficient to close the scene, and put an end to all her earthly trials at once. Tom, therefore, in his well-brushed broadcloth suit, smooth beaver, glossy boots, faultless wristbands and collar, with his grave, good-natured black face, looked respectable enough to be a Bishop of Carthage, as men of his color were, in other ages.

Then, too, he was in a beautiful place, a consideration to which his sensitive race are never indifferent; and he did enjoy with a quiet joy the birds, the flowers, the fountains, the perfume, and light and beauty of the court, the silken hangings, and pictures, and lustres, and statuettes, and gilding, that made the parlors within a kind of Aladdin's palace to him.

If ever Africa shall show an elevated and cultivated race,— and come it must, some time, her turn to figure in the great drama of human improvement,—life will awake there with a gorgeousness and splendor of which our cold western tribes faintly have conceived. In that far-off mystic land of gold, and gems, and spices, and waving palms, and wondrous flowers, and miraculous fertility, will awake new forms of art, new styles of splendor; and the negro race, no longer despised and trodden down, will, perhaps, show forth some of the latest and most magnificent revelations of human life. Certainly they will, in their gentleness, their lowly docility of heart, their aptitude to repose on a superior mind and rest on a higher power, their childlike simplicity of affection, and facility of forgiveness. In all these they will exhibit the highest form of the peculiarly *Christian life*, and, perhaps, as God chasteneth whom he loveth, he hath chosen poor Africa in the furnace of affliction, to make her the highest and noblest in that kingdom which he will set up, when every other kingdom has been tried, and failed; for the first shall be last, and the last first.

Was this what Marie St. Clare was thinking of, as she stood, gorgeously dressed, on the verandah, on Sunday morning, clasping a diamond bracelet on her slender wrist? Most likely it was. Or, if it was n't that, it was something else, for Marie patronized good things, and she was going now, in full force,—diamonds, silk, and lace, and jewels, and all,—to a fashionable church, to be very religious. Marie always made a point to be very pious on Sundays. There she stood, so slender, so elegant, so airy and undulating in all her motions, her lace scarf enveloping her like a mist. She looked a graceful creature, and she felt very good and very elegant indeed. Miss Ophelia stood at her side, a perfect contrast. It was not that she had not as handsome a silk dress and shawl, and as fine a pocket-handkerchief; but stiffness and squareness, and bolt-uprightness, enveloped her with as indefinite yet appreciable a presence as did grace her elegant neighbor; not the grace of God, however,—that is quite another thing!

"Where 's Eva?" said Marie.

"The child stopped on the stairs, to say something to Mammy."

And what was Eva saying to Mammy on the stairs? Listen, reader, and you will hear, though Marie does not.

"Dear Mammy, I know your head is aching dreadfully."

"Lord bless you, Miss Eva! my head allers aches lately. You don't need to worry."

"Well, I 'm glad you 're going out; and here,"—and the

little girl threw her arms around her,—"Mammy, you shall take my vinaigrette."

"What! your beautiful gold thing, thar, with them diamonds! Lor, Miss, 't would n't be proper, no ways."

"Why not? You need it, and I don't. Mamma always uses it for headache, and it 'll make you feel better. No, you shall take it, to please me, now."

"Do hear the darlin talk!" said Mammy, as Eva thrust it into her bosom, and, kissing her, ran down stairs to her mother.

"What were you stopping for?"

"I was just stopping to give Mammy my vinaigrette, to take to church with her."

"Eva!" said Marie, stamping impatiently,—"your gold vinaigrette to *Mammy*! When will you learn what 's *proper*? Go right and take it back, this moment!"

Eva looked downcast and aggrieved, and turned slowly.

"I say, Marie, let the child alone; she shall do as she pleases," said St. Clare.

"St. Clare, how will she ever get along in the world?" said Marie.

"The Lord knows," said St. Clare; "but she 'll get along in heaven better than you or I."

"O, papa, don't," said Eva, softly touching his elbow; "it troubles mother."

"Well, cousin, are you ready to go to meeting?" said Miss Ophelia, turning square about on St. Clare.

"I 'm not going, thank you."

"I do wish St. Clare ever would go to church," said Marie; "but he has n't a particle of religion about him. It really is n't respectable."

"I know it," said St. Clare. "You ladies go to church to learn how to get along in the world, I suppose, and your piety sheds respectability on us. If I did go at all, I would go where Mammy goes; there 's something to keep a fellow awake there, at least."

"What! those shouting Methodists? Horrible!" said Marie.

"Anything but the dead sea of your respectable churches, Marie. Positively, it 's too much to ask of a man. Eva, do you like to go? Come, stay at home and play with me."

"Thank you, papa; but I'd rather go to church."

"Is n't it dreadful tiresome?" said St. Clare.

"I think it is tiresome, some," said Eva; "and I am sleepy, too, but I try to keep awake."

"What do you go for, then?"

"Why, you know, papa," she said, in a whisper, "cousin told me that God wants to have us; and he gives us everything, you know; and it is n't much to do it, if he wants us to. It is n't so very tiresome, after all."

"You sweet, little obliging soul!" said St. Clare, kissing her; "go along, that 's a good girl, and pray for me."

"Certainly, I always do," said the child, as she sprang after her mother into the carriage.

St. Clare stood on the steps and kissed his hand to her, as the carriage drove away; large tears were in his eyes.

"O, Evangeline! rightly named," he said; "hath not God made thee an evangel to me?"

So he felt a moment; and then he smoked a cigar, and read the Picayune, and forgot his little gospel. Was he much unlike other folks?

"You see, Evangeline," said her mother, "it 's always right and proper to be kind to servants, but it is n't proper to treat them *just* as we would our relations, or people in our own class of life. Now, if Mammy was sick, you would n't want to put her in your own bed."

"I should feel just like it, mamma," said Eva, "because then it would be handier to take care of her, and because, you know, my bed is better than hers."

Marie was in utter despair at the entire want of moral perception evinced in this reply.

"What can I do to make this child understand me?" she said.

"Nothing," said Miss Ophelia, significantly.

Eva looked sorry and disconcerted for a moment; but children, luckily, do not keep to one impression long, and in a few moments she was merrily laughing at various things which she saw from the coach-windows, as it rattled along.

———

"Well, ladies," said St. Clare, as they were comfortably

seated at the dinner-table, "and what was the bill of fare at church to-day?"

"O, Dr. G——preached a splendid sermon," said Marie. "It was just such a sermon as you ought to hear; it expressed all my views exactly."

"It must have been very improving," said St. Clare. "The subject must have been an extensive one."

"Well, I mean all my views about society, and such things," said Marie. "The text was, 'He hath made everything beautiful in its season;' and he showed how all the orders and distinctions in society came from God; and that it was so appropriate, you know, and beautiful, that some should be high and some low, and that some were born to rule and some to serve, and all that, you know; and he applied it so well to all this ridiculous fuss that is made about slavery, and he proved distinctly that the Bible was on our side, and supported all our institutions so convincingly. I only wish you 'd heard him."

"O, I did n't need it," said St. Clare. "I can learn what does me as much good as that from the Picayune, any time, and smoke a cigar besides; which I can't do, you know, in a church."

"Why," said Miss Ophelia, "don't you believe in these views?"

"Who,—I? You know I 'm such a graceless dog that these religious aspects of such subjects don't edify me much. If I was to say anything on this slavery matter, I would say out, fair and square, 'We 're in for it; we 've got 'em, and mean to keep 'em,—it 's for our convenience and our interest;' for that 's the long and short of it,—that 's just the whole of what all this sanctified stuff amounts to, after all; and I think that will be intelligible to everybody, everywhere."

"I do think, Augustine, you are so irreverent!" said Marie. "I think it 's shocking to hear you talk."

"Shocking! it 's the truth. This religious talk on such matters,—why don't they carry it a little further, and show the beauty, in its season, of a fellow's taking a glass too much, and sitting a little too late over his cards, and various providential arrangements of that sort, which are pretty frequent among us young men;—we 'd like to hear that those are right and godly, too."

"Well," said Miss Ophelia, "do you think slavery right or wrong?"

"I 'm not going to have any of your horrid New England directness, cousin," said St. Clare, gayly. "If I answer that question, I know you 'll be at me with half a dozen others, each one harder than the last; and I 'm not a going to define my position. I am one of the sort that lives by throwing stones at other people's glass houses, but I never mean to put up one for them to stone."

"That 's just the way he 's always talking," said Marie; "you can't get any satisfaction out of him. I believe it 's just because he don't like religion, that he 's always running out in this way he 's been doing."

"Religion!" said St. Clare, in a tone that made both ladies look at him. "Religion! Is what you hear at church religion? Is that which can bend and turn, and descend and ascend, to fit every crooked phase of selfish, worldly society, religion? Is that religion which is less scrupulous, less generous, less just, less considerate for man, than even my own ungodly, worldly, blinded nature? No! When I look for a religion, I must look for something above me, and not something beneath."

"Then you don't believe that the Bible justifies slavery," said Miss Ophelia.

"The Bible was my *mother's* book," said St. Clare. "By it she lived and died, and I would be very sorry to think it did. I 'd as soon desire to have it proved that my mother could drink brandy, chew tobacco, and swear, by way of satisfying me that I did right in doing the same. It would n't make me at all more satisfied with these things in myself, and it would take from me the comfort of respecting her; and it really is a comfort, in this world, to have anything one can respect. In short, you see," said he, suddenly resuming his gay tone, "all I want is that different things be kept in different boxes. The whole frame-work of society, both in Europe and America, is made up of various things which will not stand the scrutiny of any very ideal standard of morality. It 's pretty generally understood that men don't aspire after the absolute right, but only to do about as well as the rest of the world. Now, when any one speaks up, like a man, and says slavery is necessary to us, we can't get along without it, we should be beggared if we give it up, and, of course, we mean to hold on to it,—this is strong, clear, well-defined language; it has the respectability of truth to it; and, if we may judge by their practice, the majority of the world will bear us out in it. But when he begins to put on a long face, and snuffle, and quote Scripture, I incline to think he is n't much better than he should be."

"You are very uncharitable," said Marie.

"Well," said St. Clare, "suppose that something should bring down the price of cotton once and forever, and make the whole slave property a drug in the market, don't you think we should soon have another version of the Scripture doctrine? What a flood of light would pour into the church, all at once, and how immediately it would be discovered that everything in the Bible and reason went the other way!"

"Well, at any rate," said Marie, as she reclined herself on a lounge, "I 'm thankful I 'm born where slavery exists; and I believe it 's right,—indeed, I feel it must be; and, at any rate, I 'm sure I could n't get along without it."

"I say, what do you think, Pussy?" said her father to Eva, who came in at this moment, with a flower in her hand.

"What about, papa?"

"Why, which do you like the best,—to live as they do at your uncle's, up in Vermont, or to have a house-full of servants, as we do?"

"O, of course, our way is the pleasantest," said Eva.

"Why so?" said St. Clare, stroking her head.

"Why, it makes so many more round you to love, you know," said Eva, looking up earnestly.

"Now, that 's just like Eva," said Marie; "just one of her odd speeches."

"Is it an odd speech, papa?" said Eva, whisperingly, as she got upon his knee.

"Rather, as this world goes, Pussy," said St. Clare. "But where has my little Eva been, all dinner-time?"

"O, I 've been up in Tom's room, hearing him sing, and Aunt Dinah gave me my dinner."

"Hearing Tom sing, hey?"

"O, yes! he sings such beautiful things about the New Jerusalem, and bright angels, and the land of Canaan."

"I dare say; it 's better than the opera, is n't it?"

"Yes, and he's going to teach them to me."

"Singing lessons, hey?—you *are* coming on."

"Yes, he sings for me, and I read to him in my Bible; and he explains what it means, you know."

"On my word," said Marie, laughing, "that is the latest joke of the season."

"Tom is n't a bad hand, now, at explaining Scripture, I'll dare swear," said St. Clare. "Tom has a natural genius for religion. I wanted the horses out early, this morning, and I stole up to Tom's cubiculum there, over the stables, and there I heard him holding a meeting by himself; and, in fact, I have n't heard anything quite so savory as Tom's prayer, this some time. He put in for me, with a zeal that was quite apostolic."

"Perhaps he guessed you were listening. I've heard of that trick before."

"If he did, he was n't very politic; for he gave the Lord his opinion of me, pretty freely. Tom seemed to think there was decidedly room for improvement in me, and seemed very earnest that I should be converted."

"I hope you'll lay it to heart," said Miss Ophelia.

"I suppose you are much of the same opinion," said St. Clare. "Well, we shall see,—shan't we, Eva?"

XVII.

The Freeman's Defence

THERE was a gentle bustle at the Quaker house, as the afternoon drew to a close. Rachel Halliday moved quietly to and fro, collecting from her household stores such needments as could be arranged in the smallest compass, for the wanderers who were to go forth that night. The afternoon shadows stretched eastward, and the round red sun stood thoughtfully on the horizon, and his beams shone yellow and calm into the little bed-room where George and his wife were sitting. He was sitting with his child on his knee, and his wife's hand in his. Both looked thoughtful and serious, and traces of tears were on their cheeks.

"Yes, Eliza," said George, "I know all you say is true. You are a good child,—a great deal better than I am; and I will try to do as you say. I 'll try to act worthy of a free man. I 'll try to feel like a Christian. God Almighty knows that I 've meant to do well,—tried hard to do well,—when everything has been against me; and now I 'll forget all the past, and put away every hard and bitter feeling, and read my Bible, and learn to be a good man."

"And when we get to Canada," said Eliza, "I can help you. I can do dress-making very well; and I understand fine washing and ironing; and between us we can find something to live on."

"Yes, Eliza, so long as we have each other and our boy. O! Eliza, if these people only knew what a blessing it is for a man to feel that his wife and child belong to *him*! I 've often wondered to see men that could call their wives and children *their own* fretting and worrying about anything else. Why, I feel rich and strong, though we have nothing but our bare hands. I feel as if I could scarcely ask God for any more. Yes, though I 've worked hard every day, till I am twenty-five years old, and have not a cent of money, nor a roof to cover me, nor a spot of land to call my own, yet, if they will only let me alone now, I will be satisfied—thankful; I will work, and send back the money for you and my boy. As to my old master, he has been paid five times over for all he ever spent for me. I don't owe him anything."

"But yet we are not quite out of danger," said Eliza; "we are not yet in Canada."

"True," said George, "but it seems as if I smelt the free air, and it makes me strong."

At this moment, voices were heard in the outer apartment, in earnest conversation, and very soon a rap was heard on the door. Eliza started and opened it.

Simeon Halliday was there, and with him a Quaker brother, whom he introduced as Phineas Fletcher. Phineas was tall and lathy, red-haired, with an expression of great acuteness and shrewdness in his face. He had not the placid, quiet, unworldly air of Simeon Halliday; on the contrary, a particularly wide-awake and *au fait* appearance, like a man who rather prides himself on knowing what he is about, and keeping a bright look-out ahead; peculiarities which sorted rather oddly with his broad brim and formal phraseology.

"Our friend Phineas hath discovered something of importance to the interests of thee and thy party, George," said Simeon; "it were well for thee to hear it."

"That I have," said Phineas, "and it shows the use of a man's always sleeping with one ear open, in certain places, as I've always said. Last night I stopped at a little lone tavern, back on the road. Thee remembers the place, Simeon, where we sold some apples, last year, to that fat woman, with the great ear-rings. Well, I was tired with hard driving; and, after my supper, I stretched myself down on a pile of bags in the corner, and pulled a buffalo over me, to wait till my bed was ready; and what does I do, but get fast asleep."

"With one ear open, Phineas?" said Simeon, quietly.

"No; I slept, ears and all, for an hour or two, for I was pretty well tired; but when I came to myself a little, I found that there were some men in the room, sitting round a table, drinking and talking; and I thought, before I made much muster, I'd just see what they were up to, especially as I heard them say something about the Quakers. 'So,' says one, 'they are up in the Quaker settlement, no doubt,' says he.

Then I listened with both ears, and I found that they were talking about this very party. So I lay and heard them lay off all their plans. This young man, they said, was to be sent back to Kentucky, to his master, who was going to make an example of him, to keep all niggers from running away; and his wife two of them were going to run down to New Orleans to sell, on their own account, and they calculated to get sixteen or eighteen hundred dollars for her; and the child, they said, was going to a trader, who had bought him; and then there was the boy, Jim, and his mother, they were to go back to their masters in Kentucky. They said that there were two constables, in a town a little piece ahead, who would go in with 'em to get 'em taken up, and the young woman was to be taken before a judge; and one of the fellows, who is small and smooth-spoken, was to swear to her for his property, and get her delivered over to him to take south. They 've got a right notion of the track we are going to-night; and they 'll be down after us, six or eight strong. So, now, what 's to be done?"

The group that stood in various attitudes, after this communication, were worthy of a painter. Rachel Halliday, who had taken her hands out of a batch of biscuit, to hear the news, stood with them upraised and floury, and with a face of the deepest concern. Simeon looked profoundly thoughtful; Eliza had thrown her arms around her husband, and was looking up to him. George stood with clenched hands and glowing eyes, and looking as any other man might look, whose wife was to be sold at auction, and son sent to a trader, all under the shelter of a Christian nation's laws.

"What *shall* we do, George?" said Eliza, faintly.

"I know what *I* shall do," said George, as he stepped into the little room, and began examining his pistols.

"Ay, ay," said Phineas, nodding his head to Simeon; "thou seest, Simeon, how it will work."

"I see," said Simeon, sighing; "I pray it come not to that."

"I don't want to involve any one with or for me," said George. "If you will lend me your vehicle and direct me, I will drive alone to the next stand. Jim is a giant in strength, and brave as death and despair, and so am I."

"Ah, well, friend," said Phineas, "but thee 'll need a driver, for all that. Thee 's quite welcome to do all the fighting, thee knows; but I know a thing or two about the road, that thee does n't."

"But I don't want to involve you," said George.

"Involve," said Phineas, with a curious and keen expression of face. "When thee does involve me, please to let me know."

"Phineas is a wise and skilful man," said Simeon. "Thee does well, George, to abide by his judgment; and," he added, laying his hand kindly on George's shoulder, and pointing to the pistols, "be not over hasty with these,—young blood is hot."

"I will attack no man," said George. "All I ask of this country is to be let alone, and I will go out peaceably; but,"—he paused, and his brow darkened and his face worked,—"I 've had a sister sold in that New Orleans market. I know what they are sold for; and am I going to stand by and see them take my wife and sell her, when God has given me a pair of strong arms to defend her? No; God help me! I 'll fight to the last breath, before they shall take my wife and son. Can you blame me?"

"Mortal man cannot blame thee, George. Flesh and blood could not do otherwise," said Simeon. "Woe unto the world because of offences, but woe unto them through whom the offence cometh."

"Would not even you, sir, do the same, in my place?"

"I pray that I be not tried," said Simeon; "the flesh is weak."

"I think my flesh would be pretty tolerable strong, in such a case," said Phineas, stretching out a pair of arms like the sails of a windmill. "I an't sure, friend George, that I should n't hold a fellow for thee, if thee had any accounts to settle with him."

"If man should *ever* resist evil," said Simeon, "then George should feel free to do it now: but the leaders of our people taught a more excellent way; for the wrath of man worketh not the righteousness of God; but it goes sorely against the corrupt will of man, and none can receive it save they to whom it is given. Let us pray the Lord that we be not tempted."

"And so *I* do," said Phineas; "but if we are tempted too much—why, let them look out, that 's all."

"It 's quite plain thee was n't born a Friend," said Simeon, smiling. "The old nature hath its way in thee pretty strong as yet."

To tell the truth, Phineas had been a hearty, two-fisted backwoodsman, a vigorous hunter, and a dead shot at a buck; but, having wooed a pretty Quakeress, had been moved by the power of her charms to join the society in his neighborhood; and though he was an honest, sober, and efficient member, and nothing particular could be alleged against him, yet the more spiritual among them could not but discern an exceeding lack of savor in his developments.

"Friend Phineas will ever have ways of his own," said Rachel Halliday, smiling; "but we all think that his heart is in the right place, after all."

"Well," said George, "is n't it best that we hasten our flight?"

"I got up at four o'clock, and came on with all speed, full two or three hours ahead of them, if they start at the time they planned. It is n't safe to start till dark, at any rate; for there are some evil persons in the villages ahead, that might be disposed to meddle with us, if they saw our wagon, and that would delay us more than the waiting; but in two hours I think we may venture. I will go over to Michael Cross, and engage him to come behind on his swift nag, and keep a bright look-out on the road, and warn us if any company of men come on. Michael keeps a horse that can soon get ahead of most other horses; and he could shoot ahead and let us know, if there were any danger. I am going out now to warn Jim and the old woman to be in readiness, and to see about the horse. We have a pretty fair start, and stand a good chance to get to the stand before they can come up with us. So, have good courage, friend George; this is n't the first ugly scrape that I 've been in with thy people," said Phineas, as he closed the door.

"Phineas is pretty shrewd," said Simeon. "He will do the best that can be done for thee, George."

"All I am sorry for," said George, "is the risk to you."

"Thee 'll much oblige us, friend George, to say no more

about that. What we do we are conscience bound to do; we can do no other way. And now, mother," said he, turning to Rachel, "hurry thy preparations for these friends, for we must not send them away fasting."

And while Rachel and her children were busy making corn-cake, and cooking ham and chicken, and hurrying on the *et ceteras* of the evening meal, George and his wife sat in their little room, with their arms folded about each other, in such talk as husband and wife have when they know that a few hours may part them forever.

"Eliza," said George, "people that have friends, and houses, and lands, and money, and all those things, *can't* love as we do, who have nothing but each other. Till I knew you, Eliza, no creature ever had loved me, but my poor, heart-broken mother and sister. I saw poor Emily that morning the trader carried her off. She came to the corner where I was lying asleep, and said, 'Poor George, your last friend is going. What will become of you, poor boy?' And I got up and threw my arms round her, and cried and sobbed, and she cried too; and those were the last kind words I got for ten long years; and my heart all withered up, and felt as dry as ashes, till I met you. And your loving me,—why, it was almost like raising one from the dead! I 've been a new man ever since! And now, Eliza, I 'll give my last drop of blood, but they *shall not* take you from me. Whoever gets you must walk over my dead body."

"O, Lord, have mercy!" said Eliza, sobbing. "If he will only let us get out of this country together, that is all we ask."

"Is God on their side?" said George, speaking less to his wife than pouring out his own bitter thoughts. "Does he see all they do? Why does he let such things happen? And they tell us that the Bible is on their side; certainly all the power is. They are rich, and healthy, and happy; they are members of churches, expecting to go to heaven; and they get along so easy in the world, and have it all their own way; and poor, honest, faithful Christians,—Christians as good or better than they,—are lying in the very dust un-der their feet. They buy 'em and sell 'em, and make trade of their heart's blood, and groans and tears,—and God *lets* them."

"Friend George," said Simeon, from the kitchen, "listen to this Psalm; it may do thee good."

George drew his seat near the door, and Eliza, wiping her tears, came forward also to listen, while Simeon read as follows:

"But as for me, my feet were almost gone; my steps had well-nigh slipped. For I was envious of the foolish, when I saw the prosperity of the wicked. They are not in trouble like other men, neither are they plagued like other men. Therefore, pride compasseth them as a chain; violence covereth them as a garment. Their eyes stand out with fatness; they have more than heart could wish. They are corrupt, and speak wickedly concerning oppression; they speak loftily. Therefore his people return, and the waters of a full cup are wrung out to them, and they say, How doth God know? and is there knowledge in the Most High?"

"Is not that the way thee feels, George?"

"It is so, indeed," said George,—"as well as I could have written it myself."

"Then, hear," said Simeon: "When I thought to know this, it was too painful for me until I went unto the sanctuary of God. Then understood I their end. Surely thou didst set them in slippery places, thou castedst them down to destruction. As a dream when one awaketh, so, oh Lord, when thou awakest, thou shalt despise their image. Nevertheless, I am continually with thee; thou hast holden me by my right hand. Thou shalt guide me by thy counsel, and afterwards receive me to glory. It is good for me to draw near unto God. I have put my trust in the Lord God."

The words of holy trust, breathed by the friendly old man, stole like sacred music over the harassed and chafed spirit of George; and after he ceased, he sat with a gentle and subdued expression on his fine features.

"If this world were all, George," said Simeon, "thee might, indeed, ask, where is the Lord? But it is often those who have least of all in this life whom he chooseth for the kingdom. Put thy trust in him, and, no matter what befalls thee here, he will make all right hereafter."

If these words had been spoken by some easy, self-indulgent exhorter, from whose mouth they might have come

merely as pious and rhetorical flourish, proper to be used to
people in distress, perhaps they might not have had much
effect; but coming from one who daily and calmly risked fine
and imprisonment for the cause of God and man, they had a
weight that could not but be felt, and both the poor, desolate
fugitives found calmness and strength breathing into them
from it.

And now Rachel took Eliza's hand kindly, and led the way
to the supper-table. As they were sitting down, a light tap
sounded at the door, and Ruth entered.

"I just ran in," she said, "with these little stockings for
the boy,—three pair, nice, warm woollen ones. It will be
so cold, thee knows, in Canada. Does thee keep up good
courage, Eliza?" she added, tripping round to Eliza's side of
the table, and shaking her warmly by the hand, and slipping a seed-cake into Harry's hand. "I brought a little parcel of these for him," she said, tugging at her pocket to get
out the package. "Children, thee knows, will always be eating."

"O, thank you; you are too kind," said Eliza.

"Come, Ruth, sit down to supper," said Rachel.

"I could n't, any way. I left John with the baby, and some
biscuits in the oven; and I can't stay a moment, else John will
burn up all the biscuits, and give the baby all the sugar in the
bowl. That's the way he does," said the little Quakeress,
laughing. "So, good-by, Eliza; good-by, George; the Lord
grant thee a safe journey;" and, with a few tripping steps,
Ruth was out of the apartment.

A little while after supper, a large covered-wagon drew up
before the door; the night was clear starlight; and Phineas
jumped briskly down from his seat to arrange his passengers.
George walked out of the door, with his child on one arm
and his wife on the other. His step was firm, his face settled
and resolute. Rachel and Simeon came out after them.

"You get out, a moment," said Phineas to those inside,
"and let me fix the back of the wagon, there, for the women-
folks and the boy."

"Here are the two buffaloes," said Rachel. "Make the seats
as comfortable as may be; it's hard riding all night."

Jim came out first, and carefully assisted out his old

mother, who clung to his arm, and looked anxiously about, as if she expected the pursuer every moment.

"Jim, are your pistols all in order?" said George, in a low, firm voice.

"Yes, indeed," said Jim.

"And you 've no doubt what you shall do, if they come?"

"I rather think I have n't," said Jim, throwing open his broad chest, and taking a deep breath. "Do you think I 'll let them get mother again?"

During this brief colloquy, Eliza had been taking her leave of her kind friend, Rachel, and was handed into the carriage by Simeon, and, creeping into the back part with her boy, sat down among the buffalo-skins. The old woman was next handed in and seated, and George and Jim placed on a rough board seat front of them, and Phineas mounted in front.

"Farewell, my friends," said Simeon, from without.

"God bless you!" answered all from within.

And the wagon drove off, rattling and jolting over the frozen road.

There was no opportunity for conversation, on account of the roughness of the way and the noise of the wheels. The vehicle, therefore, rumbled on, through long, dark stretches of woodland,—over wide, dreary plains,—up hills, and down valleys,—and on, on, on they jogged, hour after hour. The child soon fell asleep, and lay heavily in his mother's lap. The poor, frightened old woman at last forgot her fears; and, even Eliza, as the night waned, found all her anxieties insufficient to keep her eyes from closing. Phineas seemed, on the whole, the briskest of the company, and beguiled his long drive with whistling certain very unquaker-like songs, as he went on.

But about three o'clock George's ear caught the hasty and decided click of a horse's hoof coming behind them at some distance, and jogged Phineas by the elbow. Phineas pulled up his horses, and listened.

"That must be Michael," he said; "I think I know the sound of his gallop;" and he rose up and stretched his head anxiously back over the road.

A man riding in hot haste was now dimly descried at the top of a distant hill.

"There he is, I do believe!" said Phineas. George and Jim

both sprang out of the wagon, before they knew what they were doing. All stood intensely silent, with their faces turned towards the expected messenger. On he came. Now he went down into a valley, where they could not see him; but they heard the sharp, hasty tramp, rising nearer and nearer; at last they saw him emerge on the top of an eminence, within hail.

"Yes, that's Michael!" said Phineas; and, raising his voice, "Halloa, there, Michael!"

"Phineas! is that thee?"

"Yes; what news—they coming?"

"Right on behind, eight or ten of them, hot with brandy, swearing and foaming like so many wolves."

And, just as he spoke, a breeze brought the faint sound of galloping horsemen towards them.

"In with you,—quick, boys, *in!*" said Phineas. "If you must fight, wait till I get you a piece ahead." And, with the word, both jumped in, and Phineas lashed the horses to a run, the horseman keeping close beside them. The wagon rattled, jumped, almost flew, over the frozen ground; but plainer, and still plainer, came the noise of pursuing horsemen behind. The women heard it, and, looking anxiously out, saw, far in the rear, on the brow of a distant hill, a party of men looming up against the red-streaked sky of early dawn. Another hill, and their pursuers had evidently caught sight of their wagon, whose white cloth-covered top made it conspicuous at some distance, and a loud yell of brutal triumph came forward on the wind. Eliza sickened, and strained her child closer to her bosom; the old woman prayed and groaned, and George and Jim clenched their pistols with the grasp of despair. The pursuers gained on them fast; the carriage made a sudden turn, and brought them near a ledge of a steep overhanging rock, that rose in an isolated ridge or clump in a large lot, which was, all around it, quite clear and smooth. This isolated pile, or range of rocks, rose up black and heavy against the brightening sky, and seemed to promise shelter and concealment. It was a place well known to Phineas, who had been familiar with the spot in his hunting days; and it was to gain this point he had been racing his horses.

"Now for it!" said he, suddenly checking his horses, and springing from his seat to the ground. "Out with you, in a twinkling, every one, and up into these rocks with me. Michael, thee tie thy horse to the wagon, and drive ahead to Amariah's, and get him and his boys to come back and talk to these fellows."

In a twinkling they were all out of the carriage.

"There," said Phineas, catching up Harry, "you, each of you, see to the women; and run, *now*, if you ever *did* run!"

There needed no exhortation. Quicker than we can say it, the whole party were over the fence, making with all speed for the rocks, while Michael, throwing himself from his horse, and fastening the bridle to the wagon, began driving it rapidly away.

"Come ahead," said Phineas, as they reached the rocks, and saw, in the mingled starlight and dawn, the traces of a rude but plainly marked foot-path leading up among them; "this is one of our old hunting-dens. Come up!"

Phineas went before, springing up the rocks like a goat, with the boy in his arms. Jim came second, bearing his trembling old mother over his shoulder, and George and Eliza brought up the rear. The party of horsemen came up to the fence, and, with mingled shouts and oaths, were dismounting, to prepare to follow them. A few moments' scrambling brought them to the top of the ledge; the path then passed between a narrow defile, where only one could walk at a time, till suddenly they came to a rift or chasm more than a yard in breadth, and beyond which lay a pile of rocks, separate from the rest of the ledge, standing full thirty feet high, with its sides steep and perpendicular as those of a castle. Phineas easily leaped the chasm, and sat down the boy on a smooth, flat platform of crisp white moss, that covered the top of the rock.

"Over with you!" he called; "spring, now, once, for your lives!" said he, as one after another sprang across. Several fragments of loose stone formed a kind of breast-work, which sheltered their position from the observation of those below.

"Well, here we all are," said Phineas, peeping over the stone breast-work to watch the assailants, who were coming tumultuously up under the rocks. "Let 'em get us, if they can. Whoever comes here has to walk single file between those two rocks, in fair range of your pistols, boys, d' ye see?"

"I do see," said George; "and now, as this matter is ours, let us take all the risk, and do all the fighting."

"Thee 's quite welcome to do the fighting, George," said Phineas, chewing some checkerberry-leaves as he spoke; "but I may have the fun of looking on, I suppose. But see, these fellows are kinder debating down there, and looking up, like hens when they are going to fly up on to the roost. Had n't thee better give 'em a word of advice, before they come up, just to tell 'em handsomely they 'll be shot if they do?"

The party beneath, now more apparent in the light of the dawn, consisted of our old acquaintances, Tom Loker and Marks, with two constables, and a posse consisting of such rowdies at the last tavern as could be engaged by a little brandy to go and help the fun of trapping a set of niggers.

"Well, Tom, yer coons are farly treed," said one.

"Yes, I see 'em go up right here," said Tom; "and here 's a path. I 'm for going right up. They can't jump down in a hurry, and it won't take long to ferret 'em out."

"But, Tom, they might fire at us from behind the rocks," said Marks. "That would be ugly, you know."

"Ugh!" said Tom, with a sneer. "Always for saving your skin, Marks! No danger! niggers are too plaguy scared!"

"I don't know why I *should n't* save my skin," said Marks. "It 's the best I 've got; and niggers *do* fight like the devil, sometimes."

At this moment, George appeared on the top of a rock above them, and, speaking in a calm, clear voice, said,

"Gentlemen, who are you, down there, and what do you want?"

"We want a party of runaway niggers," said Tom Loker. "One George Harris, and Eliza Harris, and their son, and Jim Selden, and an old woman. We 've got the officers, here, and a warrant to take 'em; and we 're going to have 'em, too. D 'ye hear? An't you George Harris, that belongs to Mr. Harris, of Shelby county, Kentucky?"

"I am George Harris. A Mr. Harris, of Kentucky, did call me his property. But now I 'm a free man, standing on God's free soil; and my wife and my child I claim as mine. Jim and his mother are here. We have arms to defend ourselves, and we mean to do it. You can come up, if you like; but the first one of you that comes within the range of our bullets is a dead man, and the next, and the next; and so on till the last."

"O, come! come!" said a short, puffy man, stepping forward, and blowing his nose as he did so. "Young man, this an't no kind of talk at all for you. You see, we 're officers of justice. We 've got the law on our side, and the power, and so forth; so you 'd better give up peaceably, you see; for you 'll certainly have to give up, at last."

"I know very well that you 've got the law on your side, and the power," said George, bitterly. "You mean to take my wife to sell in New Orleans, and put my boy like a calf in a trader's pen, and send Jim's old mother to the brute that whipped and abused her before, because he could n't abuse her son. You want to send Jim and me back to be whipped and tortured, and ground down under the heels of them that you call masters; and your laws *will* bear you out in it,—more shame for you and them! But you have n't got us. We don't own your laws; we don't own your country; we stand here as free, under God's sky, as you are; and, by the great God that made us, we 'll fight for our liberty till we die."

George stood out in fair sight, on the top of the rock, as he made his declaration of independence; the glow of dawn gave a flush to his swarthy cheek, and bitter indignation and despair gave fire to his dark eye; and, as if appealing from man to the justice of God, he raised his hand to heaven as he spoke.

If it had been only a Hungarian youth, now bravely defending in some mountain fastness the retreat of fugitives escaping from Austria into America, this would have been sublime heroism; but as it was a youth of African descent, defending the retreat of fugitives through America into Canada, of course we are too well instructed and patriotic to see any heroism in it; and if any of our readers do, they must do it on their own private responsibility. When despairing Hungarian fugitives make their way, against all the search-warrants and authorities of their lawful government, to America, press and political cabinet ring with applause and welcome. When despairing African fugitives do the same thing,—it is—what *is* it?

Be it as it may, it is certain that the attitude, eye, voice,

The freeman's defence

manner, of the speaker, for a moment struck the party below to silence. There is something in boldness and determination that for a time hushes even the rudest nature. Marks was the only one who remained wholly untouched. He was deliberately cocking his pistol, and, in the momentary silence that followed George's speech, he fired at him.

"Ye see ye get jist as much for him dead as alive in Kentucky," he said, coolly, as he wiped his pistol on his coat-sleeve.

George sprang backward,—Eliza uttered a shriek,—the ball had passed close to his hair, had nearly grazed the cheek of his wife, and struck in the tree above.

"It 's nothing, Eliza," said George, quickly.

"Thee 'd better keep out of sight, with thy speechifying," said Phineas; "they 're mean scamps."

"Now, Jim," said George, "look that your pistols are all right, and watch that pass with me. The first man that shows himself I fire at; you take the second, and so on. It won't do, you know, to waste two shots on one."

"But what if you don't hit?"

"I *shall* hit," said George, coolly.

"Good! now, there 's stuff in that fellow," muttered Phineas, between his teeth.

The party below, after Marks had fired, stood, for a moment, rather undecided.

"I think you must have hit some on 'em," said one of the men. "I heard a squeal!"

"I 'm going right up for one," said Tom. "I never was afraid of niggers, and I an't going to be now. Who goes after?" he said, springing up the rocks.

George heard the words distinctly. He drew up his pistol, examined it, pointed it towards that point in the defile where the first man would appear.

One of the most courageous of the party followed Tom, and, the way being thus made, the whole party began pushing up the rock,—the hindermost pushing the front ones faster than they would have gone of themselves. On they came, and in a moment the burly form of Tom appeared in sight, almost at the verge of the chasm.

George fired,—the shot entered his side,—but, though

wounded, he would not retreat, but, with a yell like that of a mad bull, he was leaping right across the chasm into the party.

"Friend," said Phineas, suddenly stepping to the front, and meeting him with a push from his long arms, "thee is n't wanted here."

Down he fell into the chasm, crackling down among trees, bushes, logs, loose stones, till he lay, bruised and groaning, thirty feet below. The fall might have killed him, had it not been broken and moderated by his clothes catching in the branches of a large tree; but he came down with some force, however,—more than was at all agreeable or convenient.

"Lord help us, they are perfect devils!" said Marks, heading the retreat down the rocks with much more of a will than he had joined the ascent, while all the party came tumbling precipitately after him,—the fat constable, in particular, blowing and puffing in a very energetic manner.

"I say, fellers," said Marks, "you jist go round and pick up Tom, there, while I run and get on to my horse, to go back for help,—that's you;" and, without minding the hootings and jeers of his company, Marks was as good as his word, and was soon seen galloping away.

"Was ever such a sneaking varmint?" said one of the men; "to come on his business, and he clear out and leave us this yer way!"

"Well, we must pick up that feller," said another. "Cuss me if I much care whether he is dead or alive."

The men, led by the groans of Tom, scrambled and crackled through stumps, logs and bushes, to where that hero lay groaning and swearing, with alternate vehemence.

"Ye keep it agoing pretty loud, Tom," said one. "Ye much hurt?"

"Don't know. Get me up, can't ye? Blast that infernal Quaker! If it had n't been for him, I'd a pitched some on 'em down here, to see how they liked it."

With much labor and groaning, the fallen hero was assisted to rise; and, with one holding him up under each shoulder, they got him as far as the horses.

"If you could only get me a mile back to that ar tavern.

Give me a handkerchief or something, to stuff into this place, and stop this infernal bleeding."

George looked over the rocks, and saw them trying to lift the burly form of Tom into the saddle. After two or three ineffectual attempts, he reeled, and fell heavily to the ground.

"O, I hope he is n't killed!" said Eliza, who, with all the party, stood watching the proceeding.

"Why not?" said Phineas; "serves him right."

"Because, after death comes the judgment," said Eliza.

"Yes," said the old woman, who had been groaning and praying, in her Methodist fashion, during all the encounter, "it 's an awful case for the poor crittur's soul."

"On my word, they 're leaving him, I do believe," said Phineas.

It was true; for after some appearance of irresolution and consultation, the whole party got on their horses and rode away. When they were quite out of sight, Phineas began to bestir himself.

"Well, we must go down and walk a piece," he said. "I told Michael to go forward and bring help, and be along back here with the wagon; but we shall have to walk a piece along the road, I reckon, to meet them. The Lord grant he be along soon! It 's early in the day; there won't be much travel afoot yet a while; we an't much more than two miles from our stopping-place. If the road had n't been so rough last night, we could have outrun 'em entirely."

As the party neared the fence, they discovered in the distance, along the road, their own wagon coming back, accompanied by some men on horseback.

"Well, now, there 's Michael, and Stephen, and Amariah," exclaimed Phineas, joyfully. "Now we *are* made,—as safe as if we 'd got there."

"Well, do stop, then," said Eliza, "and do something for that poor man; he 's groaning dreadfully."

"It would be no more than Christian," said George; "let 's take him up and carry him on."

"And doctor him up among the Quakers!" said Phineas; "pretty well, that! Well, I don't care if we do. Here, let 's have a look at him;" and Phineas, who, in the course of his hunting and backwoods life, had acquired some rude experience of surgery, kneeled down by the wounded man, and began a careful examination of his condition.

"Marks," said Tom, feebly, "is that you, Marks?"

"No; I reckon 't an't, friend," said Phineas. "Much Marks cares for thee, if his own skin 's safe. He 's off, long ago."

"I believe I 'm done for," said Tom. "The cussed sneaking dog, to leave me to die alone! My poor old mother always told me 't would be so."

"La sakes! jist hear the poor crittur. He 's got a mammy, now," said the old negress. "I can't help kinder pityin' on him."

"Softly, softly; don't thee snap and snarl, friend," said Phineas, as Tom winced and pushed his hand away. "Thee has no chance, unless I stop the bleeding." And Phineas busied himself with making some off-hand surgical arrangements with his own pocket-handkerchief, and such as could be mustered in the company.

"You pushed me down there," said Tom, faintly.

"Well, if I had n't, thee would have pushed us down, thee sees," said Phineas, as he stooped to apply his bandage. "There, there,—let me fix this bandage. We mean well to thee; we bear no malice. Thee shall be taken to a house where they 'll nurse thee first rate,—as well as thy own mother could."

Tom groaned, and shut his eyes. In men of his class, vigor and resolution are entirely a physical matter, and ooze out with the flowing of the blood; and the gigantic fellow really looked piteous in his helplessness.

The other party now came up. The seats were taken out of the wagon. The buffalo-skins, doubled in fours, were spread all along one side, and four men, with great difficulty, lifted the heavy form of Tom into it. Before he was gotten in, he fainted entirely. The old negress, in the abundance of her compassion, sat down on the bottom, and took his head in her lap. Eliza, George and Jim, bestowed themselves, as well as they could, in the remaining space, and the whole party set forward.

"What do you think of him?" said George, who sat by Phineas in front.

"Well, it's only a pretty deep flesh-wound; but, then, tumbling and scratching down that place did n't help him much. It has bled pretty freely,—pretty much dreaned him out, courage and all,—but he'll get over it, and may be learn a thing or two by it."

"I'm glad to hear you say so," said George. "It would always be a heavy thought to me, if I'd caused his death, even in a just cause."

"Yes," said Phineas, "killing is an ugly operation, any way they'll fix it,—man or beast. I've been a great hunter, in my day, and I tell thee I've seen a buck that was shot down, and a dying, look that way on a feller with his eye, that it reely most made a feller feel wicked for killing on him; and human creatures is a more serious consideration yet, bein', as thy wife says, that the judgment comes to 'em after death. So I don't know as our people's notions on these matters is too strict; and, considerin' how I was raised, I fell in with them pretty considerably."

"What shall you do with this poor fellow?" said George.

"O, carry him along to Amariah's. There's old Grandmam Stephens there,—Dorcas, they call her,—she's most an amazin' nurse. She takes to nursing real natural, and an't never better suited than when she gets a sick body to tend. We may reckon on turning him over to her for a fortnight or so."

A ride of about an hour more brought the party to a neat farm-house, where the weary travellers were received to an abundant breakfast. Tom Loker was soon carefully deposited in a much cleaner and softer bed than he had ever been in the habit of occupying. His wound was carefully dressed and bandaged, and he lay languidly opening and shutting his eyes on the white window-curtains and gently-gliding figures of his sick room, like a weary child. And here, for the present, we shall take our leave of one party.

XVIII.

Miss Ophelia's Experiences and Opinions

O UR friend Tom, in his own simple musings, often compared his more fortunate lot, in the bondage into which
he was cast, with that of Joseph in Egypt; and, in fact, as time
went on, and he developed more and more under the eye of
his master, the strength of the parallel increased.

St. Clare was indolent and careless of money. Hitherto
the providing and marketing had been principally done by
Adolph, who was, to the full, as careless and extravagant as
his master; and, between them both, they had carried on the
dispersing process with great alacrity. Accustomed, for many
years, to regard his master's property as his own care, Tom
saw, with an uneasiness he could scarcely repress, the wasteful
expenditure of the establishment; and, in the quiet, indirect
way which his class often acquire, would sometimes make his
own suggestions.

St. Clare at first employed him occasionally; but, struck
with his soundness of mind and good business capacity, he
confided in him more and more, till gradually all the marketing and providing for the family were intrusted to him.

"No, no, Adolph," he said, one day, as Adolph was deprecating the passing of power out of his hands; "let Tom alone.
You only understand what you want; Tom understands cost
and come to; and there may be some end to money, bye and
bye if we don't let somebody do that."

Trusted to an unlimited extent by a careless master, who
handed him a bill without looking at it, and pocketed the
change without counting it, Tom had every facility and temptation to dishonesty; and nothing but an impregnable simplicity of nature, strengthened by Christian faith, could have
kept him from it. But, to that nature, the very unbounded
trust reposed in him was bond and seal for the most scrupulous accuracy.

With Adolph the case had been different. Thoughtless and

self-indulgent, and unrestrained by a master who found it easier to indulge than to regulate, he had fallen into an absolute
confusion as to *meum tuum* with regard to himself and his
master, which sometimes troubled even St. Clare. His own
good sense taught him that such a training of his servants was
unjust and dangerous. A sort of chronic remorse went with
him everywhere, although not strong enough to make any
decided change in his course; and this very remorse reäcted
again into indulgence. He passed lightly over the most serious
faults, because he told himself that, if he had done his part,
his dependents had not fallen into them.

Tom regarded his gay, airy, handsome young master with
an odd mixture of fealty, reverence, and fatherly solicitude.
That he never read the Bible; never went to church; that he
jested and made free with any and every thing that came in
the way of his wit; that he spent his Sunday evenings at the
opera or theatre; that he went to wine parties, and clubs, and
suppers, oftener than was at all expedient,—were all things
that Tom could see as plainly as anybody, and on which he
based a conviction that "Mas'r was n't a Christian;"—a conviction, however, which he would have been very slow to express to any one else, but on which he founded many prayers,
in his own simple fashion, when he was by himself in his little
dormitory. Not that Tom had not his own way of speaking
his mind occasionally, with something of the tact often observable in his class; as, for example, the very day after the
Sabbath we have described, St. Clare was invited out to a
convivial party of choice spirits, and was helped home, between one and two o'clock at night, in a condition when the
physical had decidedly attained the upper hand of the intellectual. Tom and Adolph assisted to get him composed for the
night, the latter in high spirits, evidently regarding the matter
as a good joke, and laughing heartily at the rusticity of Tom's
horror, who really was simple enough to lie awake most of
the rest of the night, praying for his young master.

"Well, Tom, what are you waiting for?" said St. Clare, the
next day, as he sat in his library, in dressing-gown and slippers. St. Clare had just been intrusting Tom with some
money, and various commissions. "Is n't all right there,
Tom?" he added, as Tom still stood waiting.

"I 'm 'fraid not, Mas'r," said Tom, with a grave face.

St. Clare laid down his paper, and set down his coffee-cup, and looked at Tom.

"Why, Tom, what 's the case? You look as solemn as a coffin."

"I feel very bad, Mas'r. I allays have thought that Mas'r would be good to everybody."

"Well, Tom, have n't I been? Come, now, what do you want? There 's something you have n't got, I suppose, and this is the preface."

"Mas'r allays been good to me. I have n't nothing to complain of, on that head. But there is one that Mas'r is n't good to."

"Why, Tom, what 's got into you? Speak out; what do you mean?"

"Last night, between one and two, I thought so. I studied upon the matter then. Mas'r is n't good to *himself*."

Tom said this with his back to his master, and his hand on the door-knob. St. Clare felt his face flush crimson, but he laughed.

"O, that 's all, is it?" he said, gayly.

"All!" said Tom, turning suddenly round and falling on his knees. "O, my dear young Mas'r! I 'm 'fraid it will be *loss of all—all*—body and soul. The good Book says, 'it biteth like a serpent and stingeth like an adder!' my dear Mas'r!"

Tom's voice choked, and the tears ran down his cheeks.

"You poor, silly fool!" said St. Clare, with tears in his own eyes. "Get up, Tom. I 'm not worth crying over."

But Tom would n't rise, and looked imploring.

"Well, I won't go to any more of their cursed nonsense, Tom," said St. Clare; "on my honor, I won't. I don't know why I have n't stopped long ago. I 've always despised *it*, and myself for it,—so now, Tom, wipe up your eyes, and go about your errands. Come, come," he added, "no blessings. I 'm not so wonderfully good, now," he said, as he gently pushed Tom to the door. "There, I 'll pledge my honor to you, Tom, you don't see me so again," he said; and Tom went off, wiping his eyes, with great satisfaction.

"I 'll keep my faith with him, too," said St. Clare, as he closed the door.

And St. Clare did so,—for gross sensualism, in any form, was not the peculiar temptation of his nature.

But, all this time, who shall detail the tribulations manifold of our friend Miss Ophelia, who had begun the labors of a Southern housekeeper?

There is all the difference in the world in the servants of Southern establishments, according to the character and capacity of the mistresses who have brought them up.

South as well as north, there are women who have an extraordinary talent for command, and tact in educating. Such are enabled, with apparent ease, and without severity, to subject to their will, and bring into harmonious and systematic order, the various members of their small estate,—to regulate their peculiarities, and so balance and compensate the deficiencies of one by the excess of another, as to produce a harmonious and orderly system.

Such a housekeeper was Mrs. Shelby, whom we have already described; and such our readers may remember to have met with. If they are not common at the South, it is because they are not common in the world. They are to be found there as often as anywhere; and, when existing, find in that peculiar state of society a brilliant opportunity to exhibit their domestic talent.

Such a housekeeper Marie St. Clare was not, nor her mother before her. Indolent and childish, unsystematic and improvident, it was not to be expected that servants trained under her care should not be so likewise; and she had very justly described to Miss Ophelia the state of confusion she would find in the family, though she had not ascribed it to the proper cause.

The first morning of her regency, Miss Ophelia was up at four o'clock; and having attended to all the adjustments of her own chamber, as she had done ever since she came there, to the great amazement of the chamber-maid, she prepared for a vigorous onslaught on the cupboards and closets of the establishment of which she had the keys.

The store-room, the linen-presses, the china-closet, the kitchen and cellar, that day, all went under an awful review. Hidden things of darkness were brought to light to an extent that alarmed all the principalities and powers of kitchen and chamber, and caused many wonderings and murmurings about "dese yer northern ladies" from the domestic cabinet.

Old Dinah, the head cook, and principal of all rule and authority in the kitchen department, was filled with wrath at what she considered an invasion of privilege. No feudal baron in *Magna Charta* times could have more thoroughly resented some incursion of the crown.

Dinah was a character in her own way, and it would be injustice to her memory not to give the reader a little idea of her. She was a native and essential cook, as much as Aunt Chloe,—cooking being an indigenous talent of the African race; but Chloe was a trained and methodical one, who moved in an orderly domestic harness, while Dinah was a self-taught genius, and, like geniuses in general, was positive, opinionated and erratic, to the last degree.

Like a certain class of modern philosophers, Dinah perfectly scorned logic and reason in every shape, and always took refuge in intuitive certainty; and here she was perfectly impregnable. No possible amount of talent, or authority, or explanation, could ever make her believe that any other way was better than her own, or that the course she had pursued in the smallest matter could be in the least modified. This had been a conceded point with her old mistress, Marie's mother; and "Miss Marie," as Dinah always called her young mistress, even after her marriage, found it easier to submit than contend; and so Dinah had ruled supreme. This was the easier, in that she was perfect mistress of that diplomatic art which unites the utmost subservience of manner with the utmost inflexibility as to measure.

Dinah was mistress of the whole art and mystery of excuse-making, in all its branches. Indeed, it was an axiom with her that the cook can do no wrong; and a cook in a Southern kitchen finds abundance of heads and shoulders on which to lay off every sin and frailty, so as to maintain her own immaculateness entire. If any part of the dinner was a failure, there were fifty indisputably good reasons for it; and it was the fault undeniably of fifty other people, whom Dinah berated with unsparing zeal.

But it was very seldom that there was any failure in Dinah's last results. Though her mode of doing everything was peculiarly meandering and circuitous, and without any sort of calculation as to time and place,—though her kitchen generally looked as if it had been arranged by a hurricane blowing through it, and she had about as many places for each cooking utensil as there were days in the year,—yet, if one would have patience to wait her own good time, up would come her dinner in perfect order, and in a style of preparation with which an epicure could find no fault.

It was now the season of incipient preparation for dinner. Dinah, who required large intervals of reflection and repose, and was studious of ease in all her arrangements, was seated on the kitchen floor, smoking a short, stumpy pipe, to which she was much addicted, and which she always kindled up, as a sort of censer, whenever she felt the need of an inspiration in her arrangements. It was Dinah's mode of invoking the domestic Muses.

Seated around her were various members of that rising race with which a Southern household abounds, engaged in shelling peas, peeling potatoes, picking pin-feathers out of fowls, and other preparatory arrangements,—Dinah every once in a while interrupting her meditations to give a poke, or a rap on the head, to some of the young operators, with the pudding-stick that lay by her side. In fact, Dinah ruled over the woolly heads of the younger members with a rod of iron, and seemed to consider them born for no earthly purpose but to "save her steps," as she phrased it. It was the spirit of the system under which she had grown up, and she carried it out to its full extent.

Miss Ophelia, after passing on her reformatory tour through all the other parts of the establishment, now entered the kitchen. Dinah had heard, from various sources, what was going on, and resolved to stand on defensive and conservative ground,—mentally determined to oppose and ignore every new measure, without any actual and observable contest.

The kitchen was a large brick-floored apartment, with a great old-fashioned fireplace stretching along one side of it,—an arrangement which St. Clare had vainly tried to persuade Dinah to exchange for the convenience of a modern cook-stove. Not she. No Puseyite, or conservative of any school,

was ever more inflexibly attached to time-honored inconven-
iencies than Dinah.

When St. Clare had first returned from the north, impressed with the system and order of his uncle's kitchen arrangements, he had largely provided his own with an array of
cupboards, drawers, and various apparatus, to induce systematic regulation, under the sanguine illusion that it would be
of any possible assistance to Dinah in her arrangements. He
might as well have provided them for a squirrel or a magpie.
The more drawers and closets there were, the more hiding-
holes could Dinah make for the accommodation of old rags,
hair-combs, old shoes, ribbons, cast-off artificial flowers, and
other articles of *vertu,* wherein her soul delighted.

When Miss Ophelia entered the kitchen, Dinah did not
rise, but smoked on in sublime tranquillity, regarding her
movements obliquely out of the corner of her eye, but apparently intent only on the operations around her.

Miss Ophelia commenced opening a set of drawers.

"What is this drawer for, Dinah?" she said.

"It's handy for most anything, Missis," said Dinah. So it
appeared to be. From the variety it contained, Miss Ophelia
pulled out first a fine damask table-cloth stained with blood,
having evidently been used to envelop some raw meat.

"What's this, Dinah? You don't wrap up meat in your mistress' best table-cloths?"

"O Lor, Missis, no; the towels was all a missin',—so I jest
did it. I laid out to wash that ar,—that's why I put it thar."

"Shif'less!" said Miss Ophelia to herself, proceeding to
tumble over the drawer, where she found a nutmeg-grater
and two or three nutmegs, a Methodist hymn-book, a couple
of soiled Madras handkerchiefs, some yarn and knitting-work,
a paper of tobacco and a pipe, a few crackers, one or two
gilded china-saucers with some pomade in them, one or two
thin old shoes, a piece of flannel carefully pinned up enclosing
some small white onions, several damask table-napkins, some
coarse crash towels, some twine and darning-needles, and several broken papers, from which sundry sweet herbs were sifting into the drawer.

"Where do you keep your nutmegs, Dinah?" said Miss
Ophelia, with the air of one who prayed for patience.

"Most anywhar, Missis; there's some in that cracked tea-cup, up there, and there's some over in that ar cupboard."

"Here are some in the grater," said Miss Ophelia, holding them up.

"Laws, yes, I put 'em there this morning,—I likes to keep my things handy," said Dinah. "You, Jake! what are you stopping for! You'll cotch it! Be still, thar!" she added, with a dive of her stick at the criminal.

"What's this?" said Miss Ophelia, holding up the saucer of pomade.

"Laws, it's my har *grease;*—I put it thar to have it handy."

"Do you use your mistress' best saucers for that?"

"Law! it was cause I was driv, and in sich a hurry;—I was gwine to change it this very day."

"Here are two damask table-napkins."

"Them table-napkins I put thar, to get 'em washed out, some day."

"Don't you have some place here on purpose for things to be washed?"

"Well, Mas'r St. Clare got dat ar chest, he said, for dat; but I likes to mix up biscuit and hev my things on it some days, and then it an't handy a liftin' up the lid."

"Why don't you mix your biscuits on the pastry-table, there?"

"Law, Missis, it gets sot so full of dishes, and one thing and another, der an't no room, noways—"

"But you should *wash* your dishes, and clear them away."

"Wash my dishes!" said Dinah, in a high key, as her wrath began to rise over her habitual respect of manner; "what does ladies know 'bout work, I want to know? When'd Mas'r ever get his dinner, if I was to spend all my time a washin' and a puttin' up dishes? Miss Marie never told me so, nohow."

"Well, here are these onions."

"Laws, yes!" said Dinah; "thar *is* whar I put 'em, now. I could n't 'member. Them's particular onions I was a savin' for dis yer very stew. I'd forgot they was in dat ar old flan-nel."

Miss Ophelia lifted out the sifting papers of sweet herbs.

"I wish Missis would n't touch dem ar. I likes to keep my

things where I knows whar to go to 'em," said Dinah, rather decidedly.

"But you don't want these holes in the papers."

"Them 's handy for siftin' on 't out," said Dinah.

"But you see it spills all over the drawer."

"Laws, yes! if Missis will go a tumblin' things all up so, it will. Missis has spilt lots dat ar way," said Dinah, coming uneasily to the drawers. "If Missis only will go up stars till my clarin' up time comes, I 'll have everything right; but I can't do nothin' when ladies is round, a henderin'. You, Sam, don't you gib the baby dat ar sugar-bowl! I 'll crack ye over, if ye don't mind!"

"I 'm going through the kitchen, and going to put everything in order, *once,* Dinah; and then I 'll expect you to *keep* it so."

"Lor, now! Miss Phelia; dat ar an't no way for ladies to do. I never did see ladies doin' no sich; my old Missis nor Miss Marie never did, and I don't see no kinder need on 't;" and Dinah stalked indignantly about, while Miss Ophelia piled and sorted dishes, emptied dozens of scattering bowls of sugar into one receptacle, sorted napkins, table-cloths, and towels, for washing; washing, wiping, and arranging with her own hands, and with a speed and alacrity which perfectly amazed Dinah.

"Lor, now! if dat ar de way dem northern ladies do, dey an't ladies, nohow," she said to some of her satellites, when at a safe hearing distance. "I has things as straight as anybody, when my clarin' up time comes; but I don't want ladies round, a henderin', and getting my things all where I can't find 'em."

To do Dinah justice, she had, at irregular periods, paroxysms of reformation and arrangement, which she called "clarin' up times," when she would begin with great zeal, and turn every drawer and closet wrong side outward, on to the floor or tables, and make the ordinary confusion seven-fold more confounded. Then she would light her pipe, and leisurely go over her arrangements, looking things over, and discoursing upon them; making all the young fry scour most vigorously on the tin things, and keeping up for several hours a most energetic state of confusion, which she would explain to the satisfaction of all inquirers, by the remark that she was a "clarin' up." "She could n't hev things a gwine on so as they had been, and she was gwine to make these yer young ones keep better order;" for Dinah herself, somehow, indulged the illusion that she, herself, was the soul of order, and it was only the *young uns*, and the everybody else in the house, that were the cause of anything that fell short of perfection in this respect. When all the tins were scoured, and the tables scrubbed snowy white, and everything that could offend tucked out of sight in holes and corners, Dinah would dress herself up in a smart dress, clean apron, and high, brilliant Madras turban, and tell all marauding "young uns" to keep out of the kitchen, for she was gwine to have things kept nice. Indeed, these periodic seasons were often an inconvenience to the whole household; for Dinah would contract such an immoderate attachment to her scoured tin, as to insist upon it that it should n't be used again for any possible purpose, — at least, till the ardor of the "clarin' up" period abated.

Miss Ophelia, in a few days, thoroughly reformed every department of the house to a systematic pattern; but her labors in all departments that depended on the coöperation of servants were like those of Sisyphus or the Danaides. In despair, she one day appealed to St. Clare.

"There is no such thing as getting anything like system in this family!"

"To be sure, there is n't," said St. Clare.

"Such shiftless management, such waste, such confusion, I never saw!"

"I dare say you did n't."

"You would not take it so coolly, if you were housekeeper."

"My dear cousin, you may as well understand, once for all, that we masters are divided into two classes, oppressors and oppressed. We who are good-natured and hate severity make up our minds to a good deal of inconvenience. If we *will keep* a shambling, loose, untaught set in the community, for our convenience, why, we must take the consequence. Some rare cases I have seen, of persons, who, by a peculiar tact, can produce order and system without severity; but I 'm not one of them, — and so I made up my mind, long ago, to let things go just as they do. I will not have the poor devils thrashed and cut to pieces, and they know it,—and, of course, they know the staff is in their own hands."

"But to have no time, no place, no order,—all going on in this shiftless way!"

"My dear Vermont, you natives up by the North Pole set an extravagant value on time! What on earth is the use of time to a fellow who has twice as much of it as he knows what to do with? As to order and system, where there is nothing to be done but to lounge on the sofa and read, an hour sooner or later in breakfast or dinner is n't of much account. Now, there 's Dinah gets you a capital dinner,— soup, ragout, roast fowl, dessert, ice-creams and all,—and she creates it all out of chaos and old night down there, in that kitchen. I think it really sublime, the way she manages. But, Heaven bless us! if we are to go down there, and view all the smoking and squatting about, and hurryscur-ryation of the preparatory process, we should never eat more! My good cousin, absolve yourself from that! It 's more than a Catholic penance, and does no more good. You 'll only lose your own temper, and utterly confound Dinah. Let her go her own way."

"But, Augustine, you don't know how I found things."

"Don't I? Don't I know that the rolling-pin is under her bed, and the nutmeg-grater in her pocket with her tobacco,— that there are sixty-five different sugar-bowls, one in every hole in the house,—that she washes dishes with a dinner-napkin one day, and with a fragment of an old petticoat the next? But the upshot is, she gets up glorious dinners, makes superb coffee; and you must judge her as warriors and states-men are judged, by *her success*."

"But the waste,—the expense!"

"O, well! Lock everything you can, and keep the key. Give out by driblets, and never inquire for odds and ends,—it is n't best."

"That troubles me, Augustine. I can't help feeling as if these servants were not *strictly honest*. Are you sure they can be relied on?"

Augustine laughed immoderately at the grave and anxious face with which Miss Ophelia propounded the question.

"O, cousin, that's too good,—*honest!*—as if that's a thing to be expected! Honest!—why, of course, they arn't. Why should they be? What upon earth is to make them so?"

"Why don't you instruct?"

"Instruct! O, fiddlestick! What instructing do you think I should do? I look like it! As to Marie, she has spirit enough, to be sure, to kill off a whole plantation, if I'd let her manage; but she would n't get the cheatery out of them."

"Are there no honest ones?"

"Well, now and then one, whom Nature makes so impracticably simple, truthful and faithful, that the worst possible influence can't destroy it. But, you see, from the mother's breast the colored child feels and sees that there are none but underhand ways open to it. It can get along no other way with its parents, its mistress, its young master and missie playfellows. Cunning and deception become necessary, inevitable habits. It is n't fair to expect anything else of him. He ought not to be punished for it. As to honesty, the slave is kept in that dependent, semi-childish state, that there is no making him realize the rights of property, or feel that his master's goods are not his own, if he can get them. For my part, I don't see how they *can* be honest. Such a fellow as Tom, here, is—is a moral miracle!"

"And what becomes of their souls?" said Miss Ophelia.

"That is n't my affair, as I know of," said St. Clare; "I am only dealing in facts of the present life. The fact is, that the whole race are pretty generally understood to be turned over to the devil, for our benefit, in this world, however it may turn out in another!"

"This is perfectly horrible!" said Miss Ophelia; "you ought to be ashamed of yourselves!"

"I don't know as I am. We are in pretty good company, for all that," said St. Clare, "as people in the broad road generally are. Look at the high and the low, all the world over, and it's the same story,—the lower class used up, body, soul and spirit, for the good of the upper. It is so in England; it is so everywhere; and yet all Christendom stands aghast, with virtuous indignation, because we do the thing in a little different shape from what they do it."

"It is n't so in Vermont."

"Ah, well, in New England, and in the free States, you have the better of us, I grant. But there's the bell; so, Cousin, let us for a while lay aside our sectional prejudices, and come out to dinner."

As Miss Ophelia was in the kitchen in the latter part of the afternoon, some of the sable children called out, "La, sakes! thar's Prue a coming, grunting along like she allers does."

A tall, bony colored woman now entered the kitchen, bearing on her head a basket of rusks and hot rolls.

"Ho, Prue! you've come," said Dinah.

Prue had a peculiar scowling expression of countenance, and a sullen, grumbling voice. She set down her basket, squatted herself down, and resting her elbows on her knees, said,

"O Lord! I wish 't I's dead!"

"Why do you wish you were dead?" said Miss Ophelia.

"I'd be out o' my misery," said the woman, gruffly, without taking her eyes from the floor.

"What need you getting drunk, then, and cutting up, Prue?" said a spruce quadroon chambermaid, dangling, as she spoke, a pair of coral ear-drops.

The woman looked at her with a sour, surly glance.

"Maybe you'll come to it, one of these yer days. I'd be glad to see you, I would; then you'll be glad of a drop, like me, to forget your misery."

"Come, Prue," said Dinah, "let's look at your rusks. Here's Missis will pay for them."

Miss Ophelia took out a couple of dozen.

"Thar's some tickets in that ar old cracked jug on the top shelf," said Dinah. "You, Jake, climb up and get it down."

"Tickets,—what are they for?" said Miss Ophelia.

"We buys tickets of her Mas'r, and she gives us bread for 'em."

"And they counts my money and tickets, when I gets home, to see if I's got the change; and if I han't, they half kills me."

"And serves you right," said Jane, the pert chambermaid, "if you will take their money to get drunk on. That's what she does, Missis."

"And that's what I *will* do,—I can't live no other ways,—drink and forget my misery."

"You are very wicked and very foolish," said Miss Ophelia, "to steal your master's money to make yourself a brute with."

"It's mighty likely, Missis; but I will do it,—yes, I will. O Lord! I wish I's dead, I do,—I wish I's dead, and out of my misery!" and slowly and stiffly the old creature rose, and got her basket on her head again; but before she went out, she looked at the quadroon girl, who still stood playing with her ear-drops.

"Ye think ye're mighty fine with them ar, a frolickin' and a tossin' your head, and a lookin' down on everybody. Well, never mind,—you may live to be a poor, old, cut-up crittur, like me. Hope to the Lord ye will, I do; then see if ye won't drink,—drink,—drink,—yerself into torment; and sarve ye right, too—ugh!" and, with a malignant howl, the woman left the room.

"Disgusting old beast!" said Adolph, who was getting his master's shaving-water. "If I was her master, I'd cut her up worse than she is."

"Ye could n't do that ar, no ways," said Dinah. "Her back's a far sight now,—she can't never get a dress together over it."

"I think such low creatures ought not to be allowed to go round to genteel families," said Miss Jane. "What do you think, Mr. St. Clare?" she said, coquettishly tossing her head at Adolph.

It must be observed that, among other appropriations from his master's stock, Adolph was in the habit of adopting his name and address; and that the style under which he moved, among the colored circles of New Orleans, was that of *Mr. St. Clare*.

"I'm certainly of your opinion, Miss Benoir," said Adolph.

Benoir was the name of Marie St. Clare's family, and Jane was one of her servants.

"Pray, Miss Benoir, may I be allowed to ask if those drops are for the ball, to-morrow night? They are certainly bewitching!"

"I wonder, now, Mr. St. Clare, what the impudence of you men will come to!" said Jane, tossing her pretty head till the ear-drops twinkled again. "I shan't dance with you for a whole evening, if you go to asking me any more questions."

"O, you could n't be so cruel, now! I was just dying to know whether you would appear in your pink tarletane," said Adolph.

"What is it?" said Rosa, a bright, piquant little quadroon, who came skipping down stairs at this moment.

"Why, Mr. St. Clare 's so impudent!"

"On my honor," said Adolph, "I 'll leave it to Miss Rosa, now."

"I know he 's always a saucy creature," said Rosa, poising herself on one of her little feet, and looking maliciously at Adolph. "He 's always getting me so angry with him."

"O! ladies, ladies, you will certainly break my heart, between you," said Adolph. "I shall be found dead in my bed, some morning, and you 'll have it to answer for."

"Do hear the horrid creature talk!" said both ladies, laughing immoderately.

"Come,—clar out, you! I can't have you cluttering up the kitchen," said Dinah; "in my way, foolin' round here."

"Aunt Dinah 's glum, because she can't go to the ball," said Rosa.

"Don't want none o' your light-colored balls," said Dinah; "cuttin' round, makin' b'lieve you 's white folks. Arter all, you 's niggers, much as I am."

"Aunt Dinah greases her wool stiff, every day, to make it lie straight," said Jane.

"And it will be wool, after all," said Rosa, maliciously shaking down her long, silky curls.

"Well, in the Lord's sight, an't wool as good as har, any time?" said Dinah. "I 'd like to have Missis say which is worth the most,—a couple such as you, or one like me. Get out wid ye, ye trumpery,—I won't have ye round!"

Here the conversation was interrupted in a two-fold manner. St. Clare's voice was heard at the head of the stairs, asking Adolph if he meant to stay all night with his shaving-water; and Miss Ophelia, coming out of the dining-room, said,

"Jane and Rosa, what are you wasting your time for, here? Go in and attend to your muslins."

Our friend Tom, who had been in the kitchen during the conversation with the old rusk-woman, had followed her out into the street. He saw her go on, giving every once in a while a suppressed groan. At last she set her basket down on a door-step, and began arranging the old, faded shawl which covered her shoulders.

"I 'll carry your basket a piece," said Tom, compassionately.

"Why should ye?" said the woman. "I don't want no help."

"You seem to be sick, or in trouble, or somethin'," said Tom.

"I an't sick," said the woman, shortly.

"I wish," said Tom, looking at her earnestly,—"I wish I could persuade you to leave off drinking. Don't you know it will be the ruin of ye, body and soul?"

"I knows I 'm gwine to torment," said the woman, sullenly. "Ye don't need to tell me that ar. I 's ugly,—I 's wicked,— I 's gwine straight to torment. O, Lord! I wish I 's thar!"

Tom shuddered at these frightful words, spoken with a sullen, impassioned earnestness.

"O, Lord have mercy on ye! poor crittur. Han't ye never heard of Jesus Christ?"

"Jesus Christ,—who 's he?"

"Why, he 's *the Lord*," said Tom.

"I think I 've hearn tell o' the Lord, and the judgment and torment. I 've heard o' that."

"But did n't anybody ever tell you of the Lord Jesus, that loved us poor sinners, and died for us?"

"Don't know nothin' 'bout that," said the woman; "nobody han't never loved me, since my old man died."

"Where was you raised?" said Tom.

"Up in Kentuck. A man kept me to breed chil'en for market, and sold 'em as fast as they got big enough; last of all, he sold me to a speculator, and my Mas'r got me o' him."

"What set you into this bad way of drinkin'?"

"To get shet o' my misery. I had one child after I come here; and I thought then I 'd have one to raise, cause Mas'r was n't a speculator. It was de peartest little thing! and Missis she seemed to think a heap on 't, at first; it never cried,—it was likely and fat. But Missis tuck sick, and I tended her; and I tuck the fever, and my milk all left me, and the child it pined to skin and bone, and Missis would n't buy milk for it. She would n't hear to me, when I telled her I had n't milk. She said she knowed I could feed it on what other folks eat; and the child kinder pined, and cried, and cried, and cried, day and night, and got all gone to skin and bones, and Missis got sot agin it, and she said 't wan't nothin' but crossness. She wished it was dead, she said; and she would n't let me have it o' nights, cause, she said, it kept me awake, and made me good for nothing. She made me sleep in her room; and I had to put it away off in a little kind o' garret, and thar it cried itself to death, one night. It did; and I tuck to drinkin', to keep its crying out of my ears! I did,—and I will drink! I will, if I do go to torment for it! Mas'r says I shall go to torment, and I tell him I 've got thar now!"

"O, ye poor crittur!" said Tom, "han't nobody never telled ye how the Lord Jesus loved ye, and died for ye? Han't they telled ye that he 'll help ye, and ye can go to heaven, and have rest, at last?"

"I looks like gwine to heaven," said the woman; "an't thar where white folks is gwine? S'pose they 'd have me thar? I 'd rather go to torment, and get away from Mas'r and Missis. I had *so*," she said, as, with her usual groan, she got her basket on her head, and walked sullenly away.

Tom turned, and walked sorrowfully back to the house. In the court he met little Eva,—a crown of tuberoses on her head, and her eyes radiant with delight.

"O, Tom! here you are. I 'm glad I 've found you. Papa says you may get out the ponies, and take me in my little new carriage," she said, catching his hand. "But what 's the matter, Tom?—you look sober."

"I feel bad, Miss Eva," said Tom, sorrowfully. "But I 'll get the horses for you."

"But do tell me, Tom, what is the matter. I saw you talking to cross old Prue."

Tom, in simple, earnest phrase, told Eva the woman's history. She did not exclaim, or wonder, or weep, as other children do. Her cheeks grew pale, and a deep, earnest shadow passed over her eyes. She laid both hands on her bosom, and sighed heavily.

XIX.

Miss Ophelia's Experiences and Opinions, Continued

"Toм, you need n't get me the horses. I don't want to go," she said.

"Why not, Miss Eva?"

"These things sink into my heart, Tom," said Eva,—"they sink into my heart," she repeated, earnestly. "I don't want to go;" and she turned from Tom, and went into the house.

A few days after, another woman came, in old Prue's place, to bring the rusks; Miss Ophelia was in the kitchen.

"Lor!" said Dinah, "what's got Prue?"

"Prue is n't coming any more," said the woman, mysteriously.

"Why not?" said Dinah. "She an't dead, is she?"

"We does n't exactly know. She's down cellar," said the woman, glancing at Miss Ophelia.

After Miss Ophelia had taken the rusks, Dinah followed the woman to the door.

"What *has* got Prue, any how?" she said.

The woman seemed desirous, yet reluctant, to speak, and answered, in a low, mysterious tone.

"Well, you must n't tell nobody. Prue, she got drunk agin,—and they had her down cellar,—and thar they left her all day,—and I hearn 'em saying that the *flies had got to her*,—and *she's dead*!"

Dinah held up her hands, and, turning, saw close by her side the spirit-like form of Evangeline, her large, mystic eyes dilated with horror, and every drop of blood driven from her lips and cheeks.

"Lor bless us! Miss Eva's gwine to faint away! What got us all, to let her har such talk? Her pa'll be rail mad."

"I shan't faint, Dinah," said the child, firmly; "and why

should n't I hear it? It an't so much for me to hear it, as for poor Prue to suffer it."

"*Lor sakes!* it is n't for sweet, delicate young ladies like you,—these yer stories is n't; it 's enough to kill 'em!"

Eva sighed again, and walked up stairs with a slow and melancholy step.

Miss Ophelia anxiously inquired the woman's story. Dinah gave a very garrulous version of it, to which Tom added the particulars which he had drawn from her that morning.

"An abominable business,—perfectly horrible!" she exclaimed, as she entered the room where St. Clare lay reading his paper.

"Pray, what iniquity has turned up now?" said he.

"What now? why, those folks have whipped Prue to death!" said Miss Ophelia, going on, with great strength of detail, into the story, and enlarging on its most shocking particulars.

"I thought it would come to that, some time," said St. Clare, going on with his paper.

"Thought so!—an't you going to *do* anything about it?" said Miss Ophelia. "Have n't you got any *selectmen*, or anybody, to interfere and look after such matters?"

"It 's commonly supposed that the *property* interest is a sufficient guard in these cases. If people choose to ruin their own possessions, I don't know what 's to be done. It seems the poor creature was a thief and a drunkard; and so there won't be much hope to get up sympathy for her."

"It is perfectly outrageous,—it is horrid, Augustine! It will certainly bring down vengeance upon you."

"My dear cousin, I did n't do it, and I can't help it; I would, if I could. If low-minded, brutal people will act like themselves, what am I to do? They have absolute control; they are irresponsible despots. There would be no use in interfering; there is no law that amounts to anything practically, for such a case. The best we can do is to shut our eyes and ears, and let it alone. It 's the only resource left us."

"How can you shut your eyes and ears? How can you let such things alone?"

"My dear child, what do you expect? Here is a whole class,—debased, uneducated, indolent, provoking,—put, without any sort of terms or conditions, entirely into the hands of such people as the majority in our world are; people who have neither consideration nor self-control, who have n't even an enlightened regard to their own interest,—for that 's the case with the largest half of mankind. Of course, in a community so organized, what can a man of honorable and humane feelings do, but shut his eyes all he can, and harden his heart? I can't buy every poor wretch I see. I can't turn knight-errant, and undertake to redress every individual case of wrong in such a city as this. The most I can do is to try and keep out of the way of it."

St. Clare's fine countenance was for a moment overcast; he looked annoyed, but suddenly calling up a gay smile, he said,

"Come, cousin, don't stand there looking like one of the Fates; you 've only seen a peep through the curtain,—a specimen of what is going on, the world over, in some shape or other. If we are to be prying and spying into all the dismals of life, we should have no heart to anything. 'T is like looking too close into the details of Dinah's kitchen;" and St. Clare lay back on the sofa, and busied himself with his paper.

Miss Ophelia sat down, and pulled out her knitting-work, and sat there grim with indignation. She knit and knit, but while she mused the fire burned; at last she broke out—

"I tell you, Augustine, I can't get over things so, if you can. It 's a perfect abomination for you to defend such a system,—that 's *my* mind!"

"What now?" said St. Clare, looking up. "At it again, hey?"

"I say it 's perfectly abominable for you to defend such a system!" said Miss Ophelia, with increasing warmth.

"*I* defend it, my dear lady? Who ever said I did defend it?" said St. Clare.

"Of course, you defend it,—you all do,—all you Southern-ers. What do you have slaves for, if you don't?"

"Are you such a sweet innocent as to suppose nobody in this world ever does what they don't think is right? Don't you, or did n't you ever, do anything that you did not think quite right?"

"If I do, I repent of it, I hope," said Miss Ophelia, rattling her needles with energy.

"So do I," said St. Clare, peeling his orange; "I 'm repenting of it all the time."

"What do you keep on doing it for?"

"Did n't you ever keep on doing wrong, after you 'd repented, my good cousin?"

"Well, only when I 've been very much tempted," said Miss Ophelia.

"Well, I 'm very much tempted," said St. Clare; "that 's just my difficulty."

"But I always resolve I won't, and I try to break off."

"Well, I have been resolving I won't, off and on, these ten years," said St. Clare; "but I have n't, some how, got clear. Have you got clear of all your sins, cousin?"

"Cousin Augustine," said Miss Ophelia, seriously, and laying down her knitting-work, "I suppose I deserve that you should reprove my short-comings. I know all you say is true enough; nobody else feels them more than I do; but it does seem to me, after all, there is some difference between me and you. It seems to me I would cut off my right hand sooner than keep on, from day to day, doing what I thought was wrong. But, then, my conduct is so inconsistent with my profession, I don't wonder you reprove me."

"O, now, cousin," said Augustine, sitting down on the floor, and laying his head back in her lap, "don't take on so awfully serious! You know what a good-for-nothing, saucy boy I always was. I love to poke you up,—that 's all,—just to see you get earnest. I do think you are desperately, distressingly good; it tires me to death to think of it."

"But this is a serious subject, my boy, Auguste," said Miss Ophelia, laying her hand on his forehead.

"Dismally so," said he; "and I—well, I never want to talk seriously in hot weather. What with mosquitos and all, a fellow can't get himself up to any very sublime moral flights; and I believe," said St. Clare, suddenly rousing himself up, "there 's a theory, now! I understand now why northern nations are always more virtuous than southern ones,—I see into that whole subject."

"O, Auguste, you are a sad rattle-brain!"

"Am I? Well, so I am, I suppose; but for once I will be serious, now; but you must hand me that basket of oranges;—you see, you'll have to 'stay me with flagons and comfort me with apples,' if I'm going to make this effort. Now," said Augustine, drawing the basket up, "I'll begin: When, in the course of human events, it becomes necessary for a fellow to hold two or three dozen of his fellow-worms in captivity, a decent regard to the opinions of society requires—"

"I don't see that you are growing more serious," said Miss Ophelia.

"Wait,—I'm coming on,—you'll hear. The short of the matter is, cousin," said he, his handsome face suddenly settling into an earnest and serious expression, "on this abstract question of slavery there can, as I think, be but one opinion. Planters, who have money to make by it,—clergymen, who have planters to please,—politicians, who want to rule by it,—may warp and bend language and ethics to a degree that shall astonish the world at their ingenuity; they can press nature and the Bible, and nobody knows what else, into the service; but, after all, neither they nor the world believe in it one particle the more. It comes from the devil, that's the short of it;—and, to my mind, it's a pretty respectable specimen of what he can do in his own line."

Miss Ophelia stopped her knitting, and looked surprised; and St. Clare, apparently enjoying her astonishment, went on.

"You seem to wonder; but if you will get me fairly at it, I'll make a clean breast of it. This cursed business, accursed of God and man, what is it? Strip it of all its ornament, run it down to the root and nucleus of the whole, and what is it? Why, because my brother Quashy is ignorant and weak, and I am intelligent and strong,—because I know how, and *can* do it,—therefore, I may steal all he has, keep it, and give him only such and so much as suits my fancy. Whatever is too hard, too dirty, too disagreeable, for me, I may set Quashy to doing. Because I don't like work, Quashy shall work. Because the sun burns me, Quashy shall stay in the sun. Quashy shall earn the money, and I will spend it. Quashy shall lie down in every puddle, that I may walk over dry-shod. Quashy shall do my will, and not his, all the days of his mortal life, and have such chance of getting to heaven, at last, as I find convenient. This I take to be about what slavery *is*. I defy anybody on earth to read our slave-code, as it stands in our law-books, and make anything else of it. Talk of the *abuses* of slavery! Humbug! The *thing itself* is the essence of all abuse! And the only reason why the land don't sink under it, like Sodom and Gomorrah, is because it is *used* in a way infinitely better than it is. For pity's sake, for shame's sake, because we are men born of women, and not savage beasts, many of us do not, and dare not,—we would *scorn* to use the full power which our savage laws put into our hands. And he who goes the furthest, and does the worst, only uses within limits the power that the law gives him."

St. Clare had started up, and, as his manner was when excited, was walking, with hurried steps, up and down the floor. His fine face, classic as that of a Greek statue, seemed actually to burn with the fervor of his feelings. His large blue eyes flashed, and he gestured with an unconscious eagerness. Miss Ophelia had never seen him in this mood before, and she sat perfectly silent.

"I declare to you," said he, suddenly stopping before his cousin "(it 's no sort of use to talk or to feel on this subject), but I declare to you, there have been times when I have thought, if the whole country would sink, and hide all this injustice and misery from the light, I would willingly sink with it. When I have been travelling up and down on our boats, or about on my collecting tours, and reflected that every brutal, disgusting, mean, low-lived fellow I met, was allowed by our laws to become absolute despot of as many men, women and children, as he could cheat, steal, or gamble money enough to buy,—when I have seen such men in actual ownership of helpless children, of young girls and women,—I have been ready to curse my country, to curse the human race!"

"Augustine! Augustine!" said Miss Ophelia, "I 'm sure you 've said enough. I never, in my life, heard anything like this, even at the North."

"At the North!" said St. Clare, with a sudden change of expression, and resuming something of his habitual careless tone. "Pooh! your northern folks are cold-blooded; you are cool in everything! You can't begin to curse up hill and down as we can, when we get fairly at it."

"Well, but the question is," said Miss Ophelia.

"O, yes, to be sure, the *question is,*—and a deuce of a question it is! How came *you* in this state of sin and misery? Well, I shall answer in the good old words you used to teach me, Sundays. I came so by ordinary generation. My servants were my father's, and, what is more, my mother's; and now they are mine, they and their increase, which bids fair to be a pretty considerable item. My father, you know, came first from New England; and he was just such another man as your father,—a regular old Roman,—upright, energetic, noble-minded, with an iron will. Your father settled down in New England, to rule over rocks and stones, and to force an existence out of Nature; and mine settled in Louisiana, to rule over men and women, and force existence out of them. My mother," said St. Clare, getting up and walking to a picture at the end of the room, and gazing upward with a face fervent with veneration, "*she* was *divine!* Don't look at me so!—you know what I mean! She probably was of mortal birth; but, as far as ever I could observe, there was no trace of any human weakness or error about her; and everybody that lives to remember her, whether bond or free, servant, acquaintance, relation, all say the same. Why, cousin, that mother has been all that has stood between me and utter unbelief for years. She was a direct embodiment and personification of the New Testament,—a living fact, to be accounted for, and to be accounted for in no other way than by its truth. O, mother! mother!" said St. Clare, clasping his hands, in a sort of transport; and then suddenly checking himself, he came back, and seating himself on an ottoman, he went on:

"My brother and I were twins; and they say, you know, that twins ought to resemble each other; but we were in all points a contrast. He had black, fiery eyes, coal-black hair, a strong, fine Roman profile, and a rich brown complexion. I had blue eyes, golden hair, a Greek outline, and fair complexion. He was active and observing, I dreamy and inactive. He was generous to his friends and equals, but proud, dominant, overbearing, to inferiors, and utterly unmerciful to whatever set itself up against him. Truthful we both were; he from pride and courage, I from a sort of abstract ideality. We loved each other about as boys gener-

ally do,—off and on, and in general;—he was my father's
pet, and I my mother's.

"There was a morbid sensitiveness and acuteness of feeling
in me on all possible subjects, of which he and my father had
no kind of understanding, and with which they could have
no possible sympathy. But mother did; and so, when I had
quarrelled with Alfred, and father looked sternly on me, I
used to go off to mother's room, and sit by her. I remember
just how she used to look, with her pale cheeks, her deep,
soft, serious eyes, her white dress,—she always wore white;
and I used to think of her whenever I read in Revelations
about the saints that were arrayed in fine linen, clean and
white. She had a great deal of genius of one sort and another,
particularly in music; and she used to sit at her organ, playing
fine old majestic music of the Catholic church, and singing
with a voice more like an angel than a mortal woman; and I
would lay my head down on her lap, and cry, and dream, and
feel,—oh, immeasurably!—things that I had no language to
say!

"In those days, this matter of slavery had never been canvassed as it has now; nobody dreamed of any harm in it.

"My father was a born aristocrat. I think, in some
preëxistent state, he must have been in the higher circles of
spirits, and brought all his old court pride along with him;
for it was ingrain, bred in the bone, though he was originally
of poor and not in any way of noble family. My brother was
begotten in his image.

"Now, an aristocrat, you know, the world over, has no human sympathies, beyond a certain line in society. In England
the line is in one place, in Burmah in another, and in America
in another; but the aristocrat of all these countries never goes
over it. What would be hardship and distress and injustice in
his own class, is a cool matter of course in another one. My
father's dividing line was that of color. *Among his equals*,
never was a man more just and generous; but he considered
the negro, through all possible gradations of color, as an intermediate link between man and animals, and graded all his
ideas of justice or generosity on this hypothesis. I suppose, to
be sure, if anybody had asked him, plump and fair, whether
they had human immortal souls, he might have hemmed and

hawed, and said yes. But my father was not a man much troubled with spiritualism; religious sentiment he had none, beyond a veneration for God, as decidedly the head of the upper
classes.

"Well, my father worked some five hundred negroes; he
was an inflexible, driving, punctilious business man; everything was to move by system,—to be sustained with unfailing
accuracy and precision. Now, if you take into account that all
this was to be worked out by a set of lazy, twaddling, shiftless
laborers, who had grown up, all their lives, in the absence of
every possible motive to learn how to do anything but 'shirk,'
as you Vermonters say, and you 'll see that there might naturally be, on his plantation, a great many things that looked
horrible and distressing to a sensitive child, like me.

"Besides all, he had an overseer,—a great, tall, slab-sided,
two-fisted renegade son of Vermont—(begging your pardon),—who had gone through a regular apprenticeship in
hardness and brutality, and taken his degree to be admitted
to practice. My mother never could endure him, nor I; but
he obtained an entire ascendency over my father; and this
man was the absolute despot of the estate.

"I was a little fellow then, but I had the same love that I
have now for all kinds of human things,—a kind of passion
for the study of humanity, come in what shape it would. I
was found in the cabins and among the field-hands a great
deal, and, of course, was a great favorite; and all sorts of complaints and grievances were breathed in my ear; and I told
them to mother, and we, between us, formed a sort of committee for a redress of grievances. We hindered and repressed
a great deal of cruelty, and congratulated ourselves on doing
a vast deal of good, till, as often happens, my zeal overacted.
Stubbs complained to my father that he could n't manage the
hands, and must resign his position. Father was a fond, indulgent husband, but a man that never flinched from anything that he thought necessary; and so he put down his foot,
like a rock, between us and the field-hands. He told my
mother, in language perfectly respectful and deferential, but
quite explicit, that over the house-servants she should be entire mistress, but that with the field-hands he could allow no
interference. He revered and respected her above all living

beings; but he would have said it all the same to the virgin Mary herself, if she had come in the way of his system.

"I used sometimes to hear my mother reasoning cases with him,—endeavoring to excite his sympathies. He would listen to the most pathetic appeals with the most discouraging politeness and equanimity. 'It all resolves itself into this,' he would say; 'must I part with Stubbs, or keep him? Stubbs is the soul of punctuality, honesty, and efficiency,—a thorough business hand, and as humane as the general run. We can't have perfection; and if I keep him, I must sustain his administration as a *whole*, even if there are, now and then, things that are exceptionable. All government includes some necessary hardness. General rules will bear hard on particular cases.' This last maxim my father seemed to consider a settler in most alleged cases of cruelty. After he had said *that*, he commonly drew up his feet on the sofa, like a man that has disposed of a business, and betook himself to a nap, or the newspaper, as the case might be.

"The fact is, my father showed the exact sort of talent for a statesman. He could have divided Poland as easily as an orange, or trod on Ireland as quietly and systematically as any man living. At last my mother gave up, in despair. It never will be known, till the last account, what noble and sensitive natures like hers have felt, cast, utterly helpless, into what seems to them an abyss of injustice and cruelty, and which seems so to nobody about them. It has been an age of long sorrow of such natures, in such a hell-begotten sort of world as ours. What remained for her, but to train her children in her own views and sentiments? Well, after all you say about training, children will grow up substantially what they *are* by nature, and only that. From the cradle, Alfred was an aristocrat; and as he grew up, instinctively, all his sympathies and all his reasonings were in that line, and all mother's exhortations went to the winds. As to me, they sunk deep into me. She never contradicted, in form, anything that my father said, or seemed directly to differ from him; but she impressed, burnt into my very soul, with all the force of her deep, earnest nature, an idea of the dignity and worth of the meanest human soul. I have looked in her face with solemn awe, when she would point up to the stars in the evening, and say to me,

'See there, Auguste! the poorest, meanest soul on our place will be living, when all these stars are gone forever,—will live as long as God lives!'

"She had some fine old paintings; one, in particular, of Jesus healing a blind man. They were very fine, and used to impress me strongly. 'See there, Auguste, she would say; 'the blind man was a beggar, poor and loathsome; therefore, he would not heal him *afar off*! He called him to him, and put *his hands on him*! Remember this, my boy.' If I had lived to grow up under her care, she might have stimulated me to I know not what of enthusiasm. I might have been a saint, reformer, martyr,—but, alas! alas! I went from her when I was only thirteen, and I never saw her again!"

St. Clare rested his head on his hands, and did not speak for some minutes. After a while, he looked up, and went on:

"What poor, mean trash this whole business of human virtue is! A mere matter, for the most part, of latitude and longitude, and geographical position, acting with natural temperament. The greater part is nothing but an accident! Your father, for example, settles in Vermont, in a town where all are, in fact, free and equal; becomes a regular church member and deacon, and in due time joins an Abolition society, and thinks us all little better than heathens. Yet he is, for all the world, in constitution and habit, a duplicate of my father. I can see it leaking out in fifty different ways,—just that same strong, overbearing, dominant spirit. You know very well how impossible it is to persuade some of the folks in your village that Squire Sinclair does not feel above them. The fact is, though he has fallen on democratic times, and embraced a democratic theory, he is to the heart an aristocrat, as much as my father, who ruled over five or six hundred slaves."

Miss Ophelia felt rather disposed to cavil at this picture, and was laying down her knitting to begin, but St. Clare stopped her.

"Now, I know every word you are going to say. I do not say they *were* alike, in fact. One fell into a condition where everything acted against the natural tendency, and the other where everything acted for it; and so one turned out a pretty wilful, stout, overbearing old democrat, and the other a wilful, stout old despot. If both had owned plantations in Louisiana, they would have been as like as two old bullets cast in the same mould."

"What an undutiful boy you are!" said Miss Ophelia.

"I don't mean them any disrespect," said St. Clare. "You know reverence is not my forte. But, to go back to my history:

"When father died, he left the whole property to us twin boys, to be divided as we should agree. There does not breathe on God's earth a nobler-souled, more generous fellow, than Alfred, in all that concerns his equals; and we got on admirably with this property question, without a single unbrotherly word or feeling. We undertook to work the plantation together; and Alfred, whose outward life and capabilities had double the strength of mine, became an enthusiastic planter, and a wonderfully successful one.

"But two years' trial satisfied me that I could not be a partner in that matter. To have a great gang of seven hundred, whom I could not know personally, or feel any individual interest in, bought and driven, housed, fed, worked like so many horned cattle, strained up to military precision,—the question of how little of life's commonest enjoyments would keep them in working order being a constantly recurring problem,—the *necessity* of drivers and overseers,—the ever-necessary whip, first, last, and only argument,—the whole thing was insufferably disgusting and loathsome to me; and when I thought of my mother's estimate of one poor human soul, it became even frightful!

"It's all nonsense to talk to me about slaves *enjoying* all this! To this day, I have no patience with the unutterable trash that some of your patronizing Northerners have made up, as in their zeal to apologize for our sins. We all know better. Tell me that any man living wants to work all his days, from day-dawn till dark, under the constant eye of a master, without the power of putting forth one irresponsible volition, on the same dreary, monotonous, unchanging toil, and all for two pairs of pantaloons and a pair of shoes a year, with enough food and shelter to keep him in working order! Any man who thinks that human beings can, as a general thing, be made about as comfortable that way as any other, I wish he might try it. I 'd buy the dog, and work him, with a clear conscience!"

"I always have supposed," said Miss Ophelia, "that you, all of you, approved of these things, and thought them *right*,—according to Scripture."

"Humbug! We are not quite reduced to that yet. Alfred, who is as determined a despot as ever walked, does not pretend to this kind of defence;—no, he stands, high and haughty, on that good old respectable ground, *the right of the strongest*; and he says, and I think quite sensibly, that the American planter is 'only doing, in another form, what the English aristocracy and capitalists are doing by the lower classes;' that is, I take it, *appropriating* them, body and bone, soul and spirit, to their use and convenience. He defends both,—and I think, at least, *consistently*. He says that there can be no high civilization without enslavement of the masses, either nominal or real. There must, he says, be a lower class, given up to physical toil and confined to an animal nature; and a higher one thereby acquires leisure and wealth for a more expanded intelligence and improvement, and becomes the directing soul of the lower. So he reasons, because, as I said, he is born an aristocrat;—so I don't believe, because I was born a democrat."

"How in the world can the two things be compared?" said Miss Ophelia. "The English laborer is not sold, traded, parted from his family, whipped."

"He is as much at the will of his employer as if he were sold to him. The slave-owner can whip his refractory slave to death,—the capitalist can starve him to death. As to family security, it is hard to say which is the worst,—to have one's children sold, or see them starve to death at home."

"But it 's no kind of apology for slavery, to prove that it is n't worse than some other bad thing."

"I did n't give it for one,—nay, I 'll say, besides, that ours is the more bold and palpable infringement of human rights; actually buying a man up, like a horse,—looking at his teeth, cracking his joints, and trying his paces, and then paying down for him,—having speculators, breeders, traders, and brokers in human bodies and souls,—sets the thing before the eyes of the civilized world in a more tangible form, though the thing done be, after all, in its nature, the same; that is, appropriating one set of human beings to the use and improvement of another, without any regard to their own."

"I never thought of the matter in this light," said Miss Ophelia.

"Well, I 've travelled in England some, and I 've looked over a good many documents as to the state of their lower classes; and I really think there is no denying Alfred, when he says that his slaves are better off than a large class of the population of England. You see, you must not infer, from what I have told you, that Alfred is what is called a hard master; for he is n't. He is despotic, and unmerciful to insubordination; he would shoot a fellow down with as little remorse as he would shoot a buck, if he opposed him. But, in general, he takes a sort of pride in having his slaves comfortably fed and accommodated.

"When I was with him, I insisted that he should do something for their instruction; and, to please me, he did get a chaplain, and used to have them catechized Sunday, though, I believe, in his heart, that he thought it would do about as much good to set a chaplain over his dogs and horses. And the fact is, that a mind stupefied and animalized by every bad influence from the hour of birth, spending the whole of every week-day in unreflecting toil, cannot be done much with by a few hours on Sunday. The teachers of Sunday-schools among the manufacturing population of England, and among plantation-hands in our country, could perhaps testify to the same result, *there and here*. Yet some striking exceptions there are among us, from the fact that the negro is naturally more impressible to religious sentiment than the white."

"Well," said Miss Ophelia, "how came you to give up your plantation life?"

"Well, we jogged on together some time, till Alfred saw plainly that I was no planter. He thought it absurd, after he had reformed, and altered, and improved everywhere, to suit my notions, that I still remained unsatisfied. The fact was, it was, after all, the THING that I hated,—the using these men and women, the perpetuation of all this ignorance, brutality and vice,—just to make money for me!

"Besides, I was always interfering in the details. Being myself one of the laziest of mortals, I had altogether too much fellow-feeling for the lazy; and when poor, shiftless dogs put stones at the bottom of their cotton-baskets to make them weigh heavier, or filled their sacks with dirt, with cotton at the top, it seemed so exactly like what I should do if I were they, I could n't and would n't have them flogged for it. Well, of course, there was an end of plantation discipline; and Alf and I came to about the same point that I and my respected father did, years before. So he told me that I was a womanish sentimentalist, and would never do for business life; and advised me to take the bank-stock and the New Orleans family mansion, and go to writing poetry, and let him manage the plantation. So we parted, and I came here."

"But why did n't you free your slaves?"

"Well, I was n't up to that. To hold them as tools for money-making, I could not;—have them to help spend money, you know, did n't look quite so ugly to me. Some of them were old house-servants, to whom I was much attached; and the younger ones were children to the old. All were well satisfied to be as they were." He paused, and walked reflectively up and down the room.

"There was," said St. Clare, "a time in my life when I had plans and hopes of doing something in this world, more than to float and drift. I had vague, indistinct yearnings to be a sort of emancipator,—to free my native land from this spot and stain. All young men have had such fever-fits, I suppose, some time,—but then—"

"Why did n't you?" said Miss Ophelia;—"you ought not to put your hand to the plough, and look back."

"O, well, things did n't go with me as I expected, and I got the despair of living that Solomon did. I suppose it was a necessary incident to wisdom in us both; but, some how or other, instead of being actor and regenerator in society, I became a piece of drift-wood, and have been floating and eddying about, ever since. Alfred scolds me, every time we meet; and he has the better of me, I grant,—for he really does something; his life is a logical result of his opinions, and mine is a contemptible *non sequitur*."

"My dear cousin, can you be satisfied with such a way of spending your probation?"

"Satisfied! Was I not just telling you I despised it? But, then, to come back to this point,—we were on this liberation business. I don't think my feelings about slavery are peculiar. I find many men who, in their hearts, think of it just as I do. The land groans under it; and, bad as it is for the slave, it is worse, if anything, for the master. It takes no spectacles to see that a great class of vicious, improvident, degraded people, among us, are an evil to us, as well as to themselves. The capitalist and aristocrat of England cannot feel that as we do, because they do not mingle with the class they degrade as we do. They are in our houses; they are the associates of our children, and they form their minds faster than we can; for they are a race that children always will cling to and assimilate with. If Eva, now, was not more angel than ordinary, she would be ruined. We might as well allow the small-pox to run among them, and think our children would not take it, as to let them be uninstructed and vicious, and think our children will not be affected by that. Yet our laws positively and utterly forbid any efficient general educational system, and they do it wisely, too; for, just begin and thoroughly educate one generation, and the whole thing would be blown sky high. If we did not give them liberty, they would take it."

"And what do you think will be the end of this?" said Miss Ophelia.

"I don't know. One thing is certain,—that there is a mustering among the masses, the world over; and there is a *dies iræ* coming on, sooner or later. The same thing is working in Europe, in England, and in this country. My mother used to tell me of a millennium that was coming, when Christ should reign, and all men should be free and happy. And she taught me, when I was a boy, to pray, 'Thy kingdom come.' Sometimes I think all this sighing, and groaning, and stirring among the dry bones foretells what she used to tell me was coming. But who may abide the day of His appearing?"

"Augustine, sometimes I think you are not far from the kingdom," said Miss Ophelia, laying down her knitting, and looking anxiously at her cousin.

"Thank you for your good opinion; but it's up and down

with me,—up to heaven's gate in theory, down in earth's dust in practice. But there's the tea-bell,—do let's go,—and don't say, now, I have n't had one downright serious talk, for once in my life."

At table, Marie alluded to the incident of Prue. "I suppose you'll think, cousin," she said, "that we are all barbarians."

"I think that's a barbarous thing," said Miss Ophelia, "but I don't think you are all barbarians."

"Well, now," said Marie, "I know it's impossible to get along with some of these creatures. They are so bad they ought not to live. I don't feel a particle of sympathy for such cases. If they'd only behave themselves, it would not happen."

"But, mamma," said Eva, "the poor creature was unhappy; that's what made her drink."

"O, fiddlestick! as if that were any excuse! I'm unhappy, very often. I presume," she said, pensively, "that I've had greater trials than ever she had. It's just because they are so bad. There's some of them that you cannot break in by any kind of severity. I remember father had a man that was so lazy he would run away just to get rid of work, and lie round in the swamps, stealing and doing all sorts of horrid things. That man was caught and whipped, time and again, and it never did him any good; and the last time he crawled off, though he could n't but just go, and died in the swamp. There was no sort of reason for it, for father's hands were always treated kindly."

"I broke a fellow in, once," said St. Clare, "that all the overseers and masters had tried their hands on in vain."

"You!" said Marie; "well, I'd be glad to know when *you* ever did anything of the sort."

"Well, he was a powerful, gigantic fellow,—a native-born African; and he appeared to have the rude instinct of freedom in him to an uncommon degree. He was a regular African lion. They called him Scipio. Nobody could do anything with him; and he was sold round from overseer to overseer, till at last Alfred bought him, because he thought he could manage him. Well, one day he knocked down the overseer, and was fairly off into the swamps. I was on a visit to Alf's plantation, for it was after we had dissolved partnership. Alfred was greatly exasperated; but I told him that it was his own fault, and laid him any wager that I could break the man; and finally it was agreed that, if I caught him, I should have him to experiment on. So they mustered out a party of some six or seven, with guns and dogs, for the hunt. People, you know, can get up just as much enthusiasm in hunting a man as a deer, if it is only customary; in fact, I got a little excited myself, though I had only put in as a sort of mediator, in case he was caught.

"Well, the dogs bayed and howled, and we rode and scampered, and finally we started him. He ran and bounded like a buck, and kept us well in the rear for some time; but at last he got caught in an impenetrable thicket of cane; then he turned to bay, and I tell you he fought the dogs right gallantly. He dashed them to right and left, and actually killed three of them with only his naked fists, when a shot from a gun brought him down, and he fell, wounded and bleeding, almost at my feet. The poor fellow looked up at me with manhood and despair both in his eye. I kept back the dogs and the party, as they came pressing up, and claimed him as my prisoner. It was all I could do to keep them from shooting him, in the flush of success; but I persisted in my bargain, and Alfred sold him to me. Well, I took him in hand, and in one fortnight I had him tamed down as submissive and tractable as heart could desire."

"What in the world did you do to him?" said Marie.

"Well, it was quite a simple process. I took him to my own room, had a good bed made for him, dressed his wounds, and tended him myself, until he got fairly on his feet again. And, in process of time, I had free papers made out for him, and told him he might go where he liked."

"And did he go?" said Miss Ophelia.

"No. The foolish fellow tore the paper in two, and absolutely refused to leave me. I never had a braver, better fellow,—trusty and true as steel. He embraced Christianity afterwards, and became as gentle as a child. He used to oversee my place on the lake, and did it capitally, too. I lost him the first cholera season. In fact, he laid down his life for me. For I was sick, almost to death; and when, through the panic, everybody else fled, Scipio worked for me like a giant, and actually brought me back into life again. But, poor fellow! he was taken, right after, and there was no saving him. I never felt anybody's loss more."

Eva had come gradually nearer and nearer to her father, as he told the story,—her small lips apart, her eyes wide and earnest with absorbing interest.

As he finished, she suddenly threw her arms around his neck, burst into tears, and sobbed convulsively.

"Eva, dear child! what is the matter?" said St. Clare, as the child's small frame trembled and shook with the violence of her feelings. "This child," he added, "ought not to hear any of this kind of thing,—she's nervous."

"No, papa, I'm not nervous," said Eva, controlling herself, suddenly, with a strength of resolution singular in such a child. "I'm not nervous, but these things *sink into my heart*."

"What do you mean, Eva?"

"I can't tell you, papa. I think a great many thoughts. Perhaps some day I shall tell you."

"Well, think away, dear,—only don't cry and worry your papa," said St. Clare. "Look here,—see what a beautiful peach I have got for you!"

Eva took it, and smiled, though there was still a nervous twitching about the corners of her mouth.

"Come, look at the gold-fish," said St. Clare, taking her hand and stepping on to the verandah. A few moments, and merry laughs were heard through the silken curtains, as Eva and St. Clare were pelting each other with roses, and chasing each other among the alleys of the court.

———

There is danger that our humble friend Tom be neglected amid the adventures of the higher born; but, if our readers will accompany us up to a little loft over the stable, they may, perhaps, learn a little of his affairs. It was a decent room, containing a bed, a chair, and a small, rough stand, where lay Tom's Bible and hymn-book; and where he sits, at present, with his slate before him, intent on something that seems to cost him a great deal of anxious thought.

The fact was, that Tom's home-yearnings had become so strong, that he had begged a sheet of writing-paper of Eva, and, mustering up all his small stock of literary attainment acquired by Mas'r George's instructions, he conceived the bold idea of writing a letter; and he was busy now, on his slate, getting out his first draft. Tom was in a good deal of trouble, for the forms of some of the letters he had forgotten entirely; and of what he did remember, he did not know exactly which to use. And while he was working, and breathing very hard, in his earnestness, Eva alighted, like a bird, on the round of his chair behind him, and peeped over his shoulder.

"O, Uncle Tom! what funny things you *are* making, there!"

"I 'm trying to write to my poor old woman, Miss Eva, and my little chil'en," said Tom, drawing the back of his hand over his eyes; "but, some how, I 'm feard I shan't make it out."

"I wish I could help you, Tom! I 've learnt to write some. Last year I could make all the letters, but I 'm afraid I 've forgotten."

So Eva put her little golden head close to his, and the two commenced a grave and anxious discussion, each one equally earnest, and about equally ignorant; and, with a deal of consulting and advising over every word, the composition began, as they both felt very sanguine, to look quite like writing.

"Yes, Uncle Tom, it really begins to look beautiful," said Eva, gazing delightedly on it. "How pleased your wife 'll be, and the poor little children! O, it 's a shame you ever had to go away from them! I mean to ask papa to let you go back, some time."

"Missis said that she would send down money for me, as soon as they could get it together," said Tom. "I 'm 'spectin' she will. Young Mas'r George, he said he 'd come for me; and he gave me this yer dollar as a sign;" and Tom drew from under his clothes the precious dollar.

"O, he 'll certainly come, then!" said Eva. "I 'm so glad!"

"And I wanted to send a letter, you know, to let 'em know whar I was, and tell poor Chloe that I was well off, — cause she felt so drefful, poor soul!"

"I say, Tom!" said St. Clare's voice, coming in the door at this moment.

Tom and Eva both started.

"What's here?" said St. Clare, coming up and looking at the slate.

"O, it's Tom's letter. I'm helping him to write it," said Eva; "is n't it nice?"

"I would n't discourage either of you," said St. Clare, "but I rather think, Tom, you'd better get me to write your letter for you. I'll do it, when I come home from my ride."

"It's very important he should write," said Eva, "because his mistress is going to send down money to redeem him, you know, papa; he told me they told him so."

St. Clare thought, in his heart, that this was probably only one of those things which good-natured owners say to their servants, to alleviate their horror of being sold, without any intention of fulfilling the expectation thus excited. But he did not make any audible comment upon it,—only ordered Tom to get the horses out for a ride.

Tom's letter was written in due form for him that evening, and safely lodged in the post-office.

Miss Ophelia still persevered in her labors in the housekeeping line. It was universally agreed, among all the household, from Dinah down to the youngest urchin, that Miss Ophelia was decidedly "curis,"—a term by which a southern servant implies that his or her betters don't exactly suit them.

The higher circle in the family—to wit, Adolph, Jane and Rosa—agreed that she was no lady; ladies never kept working about as she did;—that she had no *air* at all; and they were surprised that she should be any relation of the St. Clares. Even Marie declared that it was absolutely fatiguing to see Cousin Ophelia always so busy. And, in fact, Miss Ophelia's industry was so incessant as to lay some foundation for the complaint. She sewed and stitched away, from daylight till dark, with the energy of one who is pressed on by some immediate urgency; and then, when the light faded, and the work was folded away, with one turn out came the everready knitting-work, and there she was again, going on as briskly as ever. It really was a labor to see her.

XX.

Topsy

ONE morning, while Miss Ophelia was busy in some of her domestic cares, St. Clare's voice was heard, calling her at the foot of the stairs.

"Come down here, Cousin; I 've something to show you."

"What is it?" said Miss Ophelia, coming down, with her sewing in her hand.

"I 've made a purchase for your department,—see here," said St. Clare; and, with the word, he pulled along a little negro girl, about eight or nine years of age.

She was one of the blackest of her race; and her round, shining eyes, glittering as glass beads, moved with quick and restless glances over everything in the room. Her mouth, half open with astonishment at the wonders of the new Mas'r's parlor, displayed a white and brilliant set of teeth. Her woolly hair was braided in sundry little tails, which stuck out in every direction. The expression of her face was an odd mixture of shrewdness and cunning, over which was oddly drawn, like a kind of veil, an expression of the most doleful gravity and solemnity. She was dressed in a single filthy, ragged garment, made of bagging; and stood with her hands demurely folded before her. Altogether, there was something odd and goblin-like about her appearance,—something, as Miss Ophelia afterwards said, "so heathenish," as to inspire that good lady with utter dismay; and, turning to St. Clare, she said,

"Augustine, what in the world have you brought that thing here for?"

"For you to educate, to be sure, and train in the way she should go. I thought she was rather a funny specimen in the Jim Crow line. Here, Topsy," he added, giving a whistle, as a man would to call the attention of a dog, "give us a song, now, and show us some of your dancing."

The black, glassy eyes glittered with a kind of wicked drollery, and the thing struck up, in a clear shrill voice, an odd

negro melody, to which she kept time with her hands and
feet, spinning round, clapping her hands, knocking her knees
together, in a wild, fantastic sort of time, and producing in
her throat all those odd guttural sounds which distinguish the
native music of her race; and finally, turning a summerset or
two, and giving a prolonged closing note, as odd and
unearthly as that of a steam-whistle, she came suddenly down
on the carpet, and stood with her hands folded, and a most
sanctimonious expression of meekness and solemnity over her
face, only broken by the cunning glances which she shot
askance from the corners of her eyes.

Miss Ophelia stood silent, perfectly paralyzed with amazement.

St. Clare, like a mischievous fellow as he was, appeared to
enjoy her astonishment; and, addressing the child again, said,

"Topsy, this is your new mistress. I 'm going to give you
up to her; see now that you behave yourself."

"Yes, Mas'r," said Topsy, with sanctimonious gravity, her
wicked eyes twinkling as she spoke.

"You 're going to be good, Topsy, you understand," said
St. Clare.

"O yes, Mas'r," said Topsy, with another twinkle, her
hands still devoutly folded.

"Now, Augustine, what upon earth is this for?" said Miss
Ophelia. "Your house is so full of these little plagues, now,
that a body can't set down their foot without treading on 'em.
I get up in the morning, and find one asleep behind the door,
and see one black head poking out from under the table, one
lying on the door-mat,—and they are mopping and mowing
and grinning between all the railings, and tumbling over the
kitchen floor! What on earth did you want to bring this one
for?"

"For you to educate—did n't I tell you? You 're always
preaching about educating. I thought I would make you a
present of a fresh-caught specimen, and let you try your hand
on her, and bring her up in the way she should go."

"*I* don't want her, I am sure;—I have more to do with 'em
now than I want to."

"That 's you Christians, all over!—you 'll get up a society,
and get some poor missionary to spend all his days among

just such heathen. But let me see one of you that would take one into your house with you, and take the labor of their conversion on yourselves! No; when it comes to that, they are dirty and disagreeable, and it 's too much care, and so on."

"Augustine, you know I did n't think of it in that light," said Miss Ophelia, evidently softening. "Well, it might be a real missionary work," said she, looking rather more favorably on the child.

St. Clare had touched the right string. Miss Ophelia's conscientiousness was ever on the alert. "But," she added, "I really did n't see the need of buying this one;—there are enough now, in your house, to take all my time and skill."

"Well, then, Cousin," said St. Clare, drawing her aside, "I ought to beg your pardon for my good-for-nothing speeches. You are so good, after all, that there 's no sense in them. Why, the fact is, this concern belonged to a couple of drunken creatures that keep a low restaurant that I have to pass by every day, and I was tired of hearing her screaming, and them beating and swearing at her. She looked bright and funny, too, as if something might be made of her;—so I bought her, and I 'll give her to you. Try, now, and give her a good orthodox New England bringing up, and see what it 'll make of her. You know I have n't any gift that way; but I 'd like you to try."

"Well, I 'll do what I can," said Miss Ophelia; and she approached her new subject very much as a person might be supposed to approach a black spider, supposing them to have benevolent designs toward it.

"She 's dreadfully dirty, and half naked," she said.

"Well, take her down stairs, and make some of them clean and clothe her up."

Miss Ophelia carried her to the kitchen regions.

"Don't see what Mas'r St. Clare wants of 'nother nigger!" said Dinah, surveying the new arrival with no friendly air. "Won't have her round under *my* feet, *I* know!"

"Pah!" said Rosa and Jane, with supreme disgust; "let her keep out of our way! What in the world Mas'r wanted another of these low niggers for, I can't see!"

"You go long! No more nigger dan you be, Miss Rosa,"

said Dinah, who felt this last remark a reflection on her-self. "You seem to tink yourself white folks. You an't nerry one, black *nor* white. I 'd like to be one or turrer."

Miss Ophelia saw that there was nobody in the camp that would undertake to oversee the cleansing and dressing of the new arrival; and so she was forced to do it herself, with some very ungracious and reluctant assistance from Jane.

It is not for ears polite to hear the particulars of the first toilet of a neglected, abused child. In fact, in this world, mul-titudes must live and die in a state that it would be too great a shock to the nerves of their fellow-mortals even to hear de-scribed. Miss Ophelia had a good, strong, practical deal of resolution; and she went through all the disgusting details with heroic thoroughness, though, it must be confessed, with no very gracious air,—for endurance was the utmost to which her principles could bring her. When she saw, on the back and shoulders of the child, great welts and calloused spots, ineffaceable marks of the system under which she had grown up thus far, her heart became pitiful within her.

"See there!" said Jane, pointing to the marks, "don't that show she 's a limb? We 'll have fine works with her, I reckon. I hate these nigger young uns! so disgusting! I wonder that Mas'r would buy her!"

The "young un" alluded to heard all these comments with the subdued and doleful air which seemed habitual to her, only scanning, with a keen and furtive glance of her flickering eyes, the ornaments which Jane wore in her ears. When ar-rayed at last in a suit of decent and whole clothing, her hair cropped short to her head, Miss Ophelia, with some satisfac-tion, said she looked more Christian-like than she did, and in her own mind began to mature some plans for her instruc-tion.

Sitting down before her, she began to question her.

"How old are you, Topsy?"

"Dun no, Missis," said the image, with a grin that showed all her teeth.

"Don't know how old you are? Did n't anybody ever tell you? Who was your mother?"

"Never had none!" said the child, with another grin.

"Never had any mother? What do you mean? Where were you born?"

"Never was born!" persisted Topsy, with another grin, that looked so goblin-like, that, if Miss Ophelia had been at all nervous, she might have fancied that she had got hold of some sooty gnome from the land of Diablerie; but Miss Ophelia was not nervous, but plain and business-like, and she said, with some sternness,

"You must n't answer me in that way, child; I 'm not playing with you. Tell me where you were born, and who your father and mother were."

"Never was born," reiterated the creature, more emphatically; "never had no father nor mother, nor nothin'. I was raised by a speculator, with lots of others. Old Aunt Sue used to take car on us."

The child was evidently sincere; and Jane, breaking into a short laugh, said,

"Laws, Missis, there 's heaps of 'em. Speculators buys 'em up cheap, when they 's little, and gets 'em raised for market."

"How long have you lived with your master and mistress?"

"Dun no, Missis."

"Is it a year, or more, or less?"

"Dun no, Missis."

"Laws, Missis, those low negroes,—they can't tell; they don't know anything about time," said Jane; "they don't know what a year is; they don't know their own ages."

"Have you ever heard anything about God, Topsy?"

The child looked bewildered, but grinned as usual.

"Do you know who made you?"

"Nobody, as I knows on," said the child, with a short laugh.

The idea appeared to amuse her considerably; for her eyes twinkled, and she added,

"I spect I grow'd. Don't think nobody never made me."

"Do you know how to sew?" said Miss Ophelia, who thought she would turn her inquiries to something more tangible.

"No, Missis."

"What can you do?—what did you do for your master and mistress?"

"Fetch water, and wash dishes, and rub knives, and wait on folks."

"Were they good to you?"

"Spect they was," said the child, scanning Miss Ophelia cunningly.

Miss Ophelia rose from this encouraging colloquy; St. Clare was leaning over the back of her chair.

"You find virgin soil there, Cousin; put in your own ideas,—you won't find many to pull up."

Miss Ophelia's ideas of education, like all her other ideas, were very set and definite; and of the kind that prevailed in New England a century ago, and which are still preserved in some very retired and unsophisticated parts, where there are no railroads. As nearly as could be expressed, they could be comprised in very few words: to teach them to mind when they were spoken to; to teach them the catechism, sewing, and reading; and to whip them if they told lies. And though, of course, in the flood of light that is now poured on education, these are left far away in the rear, yet it is an undisputed fact that our grandmothers raised some tolerably fair men and women under this régime, as many of us can remember and testify. At all events, Miss Ophelia knew of nothing else to do; and, therefore, applied her mind to her heathen with the best diligence she could command.

The child was announced and considered in the family as Miss Ophelia's girl; and, as she was looked upon with no gracious eye in the kitchen, Miss Ophelia resolved to confine her sphere of operation and instruction chiefly to her own chamber. With a self-sacrifice which some of our readers will appreciate, she resolved, instead of comfortably making her own bed, sweeping and dusting her own chamber,—which she had hitherto done, in utter scorn of all offers of help from the chambermaid of the establishment,—to condemn herself to the martyrdom of instructing Topsy to perform these operations,—ah, woe the day! Did any of our readers ever do the same, they will appreciate the amount of her self-sacrifice.

Miss Ophelia began with Topsy by taking her into her chamber, the first morning, and solemnly commencing a course of instruction in the art and mystery of bed-making.

Behold, then, Topsy, washed and shorn of all the little

braided tails wherein her heart had delighted, arrayed in a clean gown, with well-starched apron, standing reverently before Miss Ophelia, with an expression of solemnity well befitting a funeral.

"Now, Topsy, I'm going to show you just how my bed is to be made. I am very particular about my bed. You must learn exactly how to do it."

"Yes, ma'am," says Topsy, with a deep sigh, and a face of woful earnestness.

"Now, Topsy, look here;—this is the hem of the sheet,—this is the right side of the sheet, and this is the wrong;—will you remember?"

"Yes, ma'am," says Topsy, with another sigh.

"Well, now, the under sheet you must bring over the bolster,—so,—and tuck it clear down under the mattress nice and smooth,—so,—do you see?"

"Yes, ma'am," said Topsy, with profound attention.

"But the upper sheet," said Miss Ophelia, "must be brought down in this way, and tucked under firm and smooth at the foot,—so,—the narrow hem at the foot."

"Yes, ma'am," said Topsy, as before;—but we will add, what Miss Ophelia did not see, that, during the time when the good lady's back was turned, in the zeal of her manipulations, the young disciple had contrived to snatch a pair of gloves and a ribbon, which she had adroitly slipped into her sleeves, and stood with her hands dutifully folded, as before.

"Now, Topsy, let's see *you* do this," said Miss Ophelia, pulling off the clothes, and seating herself.

Topsy, with great gravity and adroitness, went through the exercise completely to Miss Ophelia's satisfaction; smoothing the sheets, patting out every wrinkle, and exhibiting, through the whole process, a gravity and seriousness with which her instructress was greatly edified. By an unlucky slip, however, a fluttering fragment of the ribbon hung out of one of her sleeves, just as she was finishing, and caught Miss Ophelia's attention. Instantly she pounced upon it. "What's this? You naughty, wicked child,—you've been stealing this!"

The ribbon was pulled out of Topsy's own sleeve, yet was she not in the least disconcerted; she only looked at it with an air of the most surprised and unconscious innocence.

"Laws! why, that ar 's Miss Feely's ribbon, an't it? How could it a got caught in my sleeve?"

"Topsy, you naughty girl, don't you tell me a lie,—you stole that ribbon!"

"Missis, I declar for 't, I did n't;—never seed it till dis yer blessed minnit."

"Topsy," said Miss Ophelia, "don't you know it 's wicked to tell lies?"

"I never tells no lies, Miss Feely," said Topsy, with virtuous gravity; "it 's jist the truth I 've been a tellin now, and an't nothin else."

"Topsy, I shall have to whip you, if you tell lies so."

"Laws, Missis, if you 's to whip all day, could n't say no other way," said Topsy, beginning to blubber. "I never seed dat ar,—it must a got caught in my sleeve. Miss Feely must have left it on the bed, and it got caught in the clothes, and so got in my sleeve."

Miss Ophelia was so indignant at the barefaced lie, that she caught the child and shook her.

"Don't you tell me that again!"

The shake brought the gloves on to the floor, from the other sleeve.

"There, you!" said Miss Ophelia, "will you tell me now, you did n't steal the ribbon?"

Topsy now confessed to the gloves, but still persisted in denying the ribbon.

"Now, Topsy," said Miss Ophelia, "if you 'll confess all about it, I won't whip you this time." Thus adjured, Topsy confessed to the ribbon and gloves, with woful protestations of penitence.

"Well, now, tell me. I know you must have taken other things since you have been in the house, for I let you run about all day yesterday. Now, tell me if you took anything, and I shan't whip you."

"Laws, Missis! I took Miss Eva's red thing she wars on her neck."

"You did, you naughty child!—Well, what else?"

"I took Rosa's yer-rings,—them red ones."

"Go bring them to me this minute, both of 'em."

"Laws, Missis! I can't,—they 's burnt up!"

286 UNCLE TOM'S CABIN

"Burnt up!—what a story! Go get 'em, or I'll whip you."

Topsy, with loud protestations, and tears, and groans, declared that she *could* not. "They's burnt up,—they was."

"What did you burn 'em up for?" said Miss Ophelia.

"Cause I's wicked,—I is. I's mighty wicked, any how. I can't help it."

Just at this moment, Eva came innocently into the room, with the identical coral necklace on her neck.

"Why, Eva, where did you get your necklace?" said Miss Ophelia.

"Get it? Why, I've had it on all day," said Eva.

"Did you have it on yesterday?"

"Yes; and what is funny, Aunty, I had it on all night. I forgot to take it off when I went to bed."

Miss Ophelia looked perfectly bewildered; the more so, as Rosa, at that instant, came into the room, with a basket of newly-ironed linen poised on her head, and the coral ear-drops shaking in her ears!

"I'm sure I can't tell anything what to do with such a child!" she said, in despair. "What in the world did you tell me you took those things for, Topsy?"

"Why, Missis said I must 'fess; and I couldn't think of nothin' else to 'fess," said Topsy, rubbing her eyes.

"But, of course, I didn't want you to confess things you didn't do," said Miss Ophelia; "that's telling a lie, just as much as the other."

"Laws, now, is it?" said Topsy, with an air of innocent wonder.

"La, there an't any such thing as truth in that limb," said Rosa, looking indignantly at Topsy. "If I was Mas'r St. Clare, I'd whip her till the blood run. I would,—I'd let her catch it!"

"No, no, Rosa," said Eva, with an air of command, which the child could assume at times; "you mustn't talk so, Rosa. I can't bear to hear it."

"La sakes! Miss Eva, you's so good, you don't know nothing how to get along with niggers. There's no way but to cut 'em well up, I tell ye."

"Rosa!" said Eva, "hush! Don't you say another word of

that sort!" and the eye of the child flashed, and her cheek deepened its color.

Rosa was cowed in a moment.

"Miss Eva has got the St. Clare blood in her, that 's plain. She can speak, for all the world, just like her papa," she said, as she passed out of the room.

Eva stood looking at Topsy.

There stood the two children, representatives of the two extremes of society. The fair, high-bred child, with her golden head, her deep eyes, her spiritual, noble brow, and prince-like movements; and her black, keen, subtle, cringing, yet acute neighbor. They stood the representatives of their races. The Saxon, born of ages of cultivation, command, education, physical and moral eminence; the Afric, born of ages of oppression, submission, ignorance, toil, and vice!

Something, perhaps, of such thoughts struggled through Eva's mind. But a child's thoughts are rather dim, undefined instincts; and in Eva's noble nature many such were yearning and working, for which she had no power of utterance. When Miss Ophelia expatiated on Topsy's naughty, wicked conduct, the child looked perplexed and sorrowful, but said, sweetly,

"Poor Topsy, why need you steal? You 're going to be taken good care of, now. I 'm sure I 'd rather give you anything of mine, than have you steal it."

It was the first word of kindness the child had ever heard in her life; and the sweet tone and manner struck strangely on the wild, rude heart, and a sparkle of something like a tear shone in the keen, round, glittering eye; but it was followed by the short laugh and habitual grin. No! the ear that has never heard anything but abuse is strangely incredulous of anything so heavenly as kindness; and Topsy only thought Eva's speech something funny and inexplicable,—she did not believe it.

But what was to be done with Topsy? Miss Ophelia found the case a puzzler; her rules for bringing up did n't seem to apply. She thought she would take time to think of it; and, by the way of gaining time, and in hopes of some indefinite moral virtues supposed to be inherent in dark closets, Miss

Ophelia shut Topsy up in one till she had arranged her ideas further on the subject.

"I don't see," said Miss Ophelia to St. Clare, "how I'm going to manage that child, without whipping her."

"Well, whip her, then, to your heart's content; I'll give you full power to do what you like."

"Children always have to be whipped," said Miss Ophelia; "I never heard of bringing them up without."

"O, well, certainly," said St. Clare; "do as you think best. Only I'll make one suggestion: I've seen this child whipped with a poker, knocked down with the shovel or tongs, whichever came handiest, &c.; and, seeing that she is used to that style of operation, I think your whippings will have to be pretty energetic, to make much impression."

"What is to be done with her, then?" said Miss Ophelia.

"You have started a serious question," said St. Clare; "I wish you'd answer it. What is to be done with a human being that can be governed only by the lash,—*that* fails,— it's a very common state of things down here!"

"I'm sure I don't know; I never saw such a child as this."

"Such children are very common among us, and such men and women, too. How are they to be governed?" said St. Clare.

"I'm sure it's more than I can say," said Miss Ophelia.

"Or I either," said St. Clare. "The horrid cruelties and outrages that once and a while find their way into the papers,— such cases as Prue's, for example,—what do they come from? In many cases, it is a gradual hardening process on both sides,—the owner growing more and more cruel, as the servant more and more callous. Whipping and abuse are like laudanum; you have to double the dose as the sensibilities decline. I saw this very early when I became an owner; and I resolved never to begin, because I did not know when I should stop,—and I resolved, at least, to protect my own moral nature. The consequence is, that my servants act like spoiled children; but I think that better than for us both to be brutalized together. You have talked a great deal about our responsibilities in educating, Cousin. I really wanted you to *try* with one child, who is a specimen of thousands among us."

"It is your system makes such children," said Miss Ophelia.

"I know it; but they are *made*,—they exist,—and what is to be done with them?"

"Well, I can't say I thank you for the experiment. But, then, as it appears to be a duty, I shall persevere and try, and do the best I can," said Miss Ophelia; and Miss Ophelia, after this, did labor, with a commendable degree of zeal and energy, on her new subject. She instituted regular hours and employments for her, and undertook to teach her to read and to sew.

In the former art, the child was quick enough. She learned her letters as if by magic, and was very soon able to read plain reading; but the sewing was a more difficult matter. The creature was as lithe as a cat, and as active as a monkey, and the confinement of sewing was her abomination; so she broke her needles, threw them slyly out of windows, or down in chinks of the walls; she tangled, broke, and dirtied her thread, or, with a sly movement, would throw a spool away altogether. Her motions were almost as quick as those of a practised conjurer, and her command of her face quite as great; and though Miss Ophelia could not help feeling that so many accidents could not possibly happen in succession, yet she could not, without a watchfulness which would leave her no time for anything else, detect her.

Topsy was soon a noted character in the establishment. Her talent for every species of drollery, grimace, and mimicry,— for dancing, tumbling, climbing, singing, whistling, imitating every sound that hit her fancy,—seemed inexhaustible. In her play-hours, she invariably had every child in the establishment at her heels, open-mouthed with admiration and wonder,— not excepting Miss Eva, who appeared to be fascinated by her wild diablerie, as a dove is sometimes charmed by a glittering serpent. Miss Ophelia was uneasy that Eva should fancy Topsy's society so much, and implored St. Clare to forbid it.

"Poh! let the child alone," said St. Clare. "Topsy will do her good."

"But so depraved a child,—are you not afraid she will teach her some mischief?"

"She can't teach her mischief; she might teach it to some children, but evil rolls off Eva's mind like dew off a cabbage-leaf,—not a drop sinks in."

"Don't be too sure," said Miss Ophelia. "I know I'd never let a child of mine play with Topsy."

"Well, your children need n't," said St. Clare, "but mine may; if Eva could have been spoiled, it would have been done years ago."

Topsy was at first despised and contemned by the upper servants. They soon found reason to alter their opinion. It was very soon discovered that whoever cast an indignity on Topsy was sure to meet with some inconvenient accident shortly after;—either a pair of ear-rings or some cherished trinket would be missing, or an article of dress would be suddenly found utterly ruined, or the person would stumble accidentally into a pail of hot water, or a libation of dirty slop would unaccountably deluge them from above when in full gala dress;—and on all these occasions, when investigation was made, there was nobody found to stand sponsor for the indignity. Topsy was cited, and had up before all the domestic judicatories, time and again; but always sustained her examinations with most edifying innocence and gravity of appearance. Nobody in the world ever doubted who did the things; but not a scrap of any direct evidence could be found to establish the suppositions, and Miss Ophelia was too just to feel at liberty to proceed to any lengths without it.

The mischiefs done were always so nicely timed, also, as further to shelter the aggressor. Thus, the times for revenge on Rosa and Jane, the two chamber-maids, were always chosen in those seasons when (as not unfrequently happened) they were in disgrace with their mistress, when any complaint from them would of course meet with no sympathy. In short, Topsy soon made the household understand the propriety of letting her alone; and she was let alone, accordingly.

Topsy was smart and energetic in all manual operations, learning everything that was taught her with surprising quickness. With a few lessons, she had learned to do the proprieties of Miss Ophelia's chamber in a way with which even that particular lady could find no fault. Mortal hands could not lay

spread smoother, adjust pillows more accurately, sweep and
dust and arrange more perfectly, than Topsy, when she
chose,—but she did n't very often choose. If Miss Ophelia,
after three or four days of careful and patient supervision, was
so sanguine as to suppose that Topsy had at last fallen into
her way, could do without overlooking, and so go off and
busy herself about something else, Topsy would hold a perfect carnival of confusion, for some one or two hours. Instead
of making the bed, she would amuse herself with pulling off
the pillow-cases, butting her woolly head among the pillows,
till it would sometimes be grotesquely ornamented with
feathers sticking out in various directions; she would climb
the posts, and hang head downward from the tops; flourish
the sheets and spreads all over the apartment; dress the bolster up in Miss Ophelia's night-clothes, and enact various scenic performances with that,—singing and whistling, and
making grimaces at herself in the looking-glass; in short,
as Miss Ophelia phrased it, "raising Cain" generally.
On one occasion, Miss Ophelia found Topsy with her very
best scarlet India Canton crape shawl wound round her head
for a turban, going on with her rehearsals before the glass in
great style,—Miss Ophelia having, with carelessness most unheard-of in her, left the key for once in her drawer.
"Topsy!" she would say, when at the end of all patience,
"what does make you act so?"
"Dunno, Missis,—I spects cause I 's so wicked!"
"I don't know anything what I shall do with you, Topsy."
"Law, Missis, you must whip me; my old Missis allers
whipped me. I an't used to workin' unless I gets whipped."
"Why, Topsy, I don't want to whip you. You can do well,
if you 've a mind to; what is the reason you won't?"
"Laws, Missis, I 's used to whippin'; I spects it 's good for
me."
Miss Ophelia tried the recipe, and Topsy invariably made
a terrible commotion, screaming, groaning and imploring,
though half an hour afterwards, when roosted on some projection of the balcony, and surrounded by a flock of admiring
"young uns," she would express the utmost contempt of the
whole affair.
"Law, Miss Feely whip!—would n't kill a skeeter, her

whippins. Oughter see how old Mas'r made the flesh fly; old Mas'r know'd how!"

Topsy always made great capital of her own sins and enormities, evidently considering them as something peculiarly distinguishing.

"Law, you niggers," she would say to some of her auditors, "does you know you 's all sinners? Well, you is—everybody is. White folks is sinners too,—Miss Feely says so; but I spects niggers is the biggest ones; but lor! ye an't any on ye up to me. I 's so awful wicked there can't nobody do nothin' with me. I used to keep old Missis a swarin' at me half de time. I spects I 's the wickedest critter in the world;" and Topsy would cut a summerset, and come up brisk and shining on to a higher perch, and evidently plume herself on the distinction.

Miss Ophelia busied herself very earnestly on Sundays, teaching Topsy the catechism. Topsy had an uncommon verbal memory, and committed with a fluency that greatly encouraged her instructress.

"What good do you expect it is going to do her?" said St. Clare.

"Why, it always has done children good. It 's what children always have to learn, you know," said Miss Ophelia.

"Understand it or not," said St. Clare.

"O, children never understand it at the time; but, after they are grown up, it 'll come to them."

"Mine has n't come to me yet," said St. Clare, "though I 'll bear testimony that you put it into me pretty thoroughly when I was a boy."

"Ah, you were always good at learning, Augustine. I used to have great hopes of you," said Miss Ophelia.

"Well, have n't you now?" said St. Clare.

"I wish you were as good as you were when you were a boy, Augustine."

"So do I, that 's a fact, Cousin," said St. Clare. "Well, go ahead and catechize Topsy; may be you 'll make out something yet."

Topsy, who had stood like a black statue during this discussion, with hands decently folded, now, at a signal from Miss Ophelia, went on:

"Our first parents, being left to the freedom of their own will, fell from the state wherein they were created."

Topsy's eyes twinkled, and she looked inquiringly.

"What is it, Topsy?" said Miss Ophelia.

"Please, Missis, was dat ar state Kintuck?"

"What state, Topsy?"

"Dat state dey fell out of. I used to hear Mas'r tell how we came down from Kintuck."

St. Clare laughed.

"You'll have to give her a meaning, or she'll make one," said he. "There seems to be a theory of emigration suggested there."

"O! Augustine, be still," said Miss Ophelia; "how can I do anything, if you will be laughing?"

"Well, I won't disturb the exercises again, on my honor;" and St. Clare took his paper into the parlor, and sat down, till Topsy had finished her recitations. They were all very well, only that now and then she would oddly transpose some important words, and persist in the mistake, in spite of every effort to the contrary; and St. Clare, after all his promises of goodness, took a wicked pleasure in these mistakes, calling Topsy to him whenever he had a mind to amuse himself, and getting her to repeat the offending passages, in spite of Miss Ophelia's remonstrances.

"How do you think I can do anything with the child, if you will go on so, Augustine?" she would say.

"Well, it is too bad,—I won't again; but I do like to hear the droll little image stumble over those big words!"

"But you confirm her in the wrong way."

"What's the odds? One word is as good as another to her."

"You wanted me to bring her up right; and you ought to remember she is a reasonable creature, and be careful of your influence over her."

"O, dismal! so I ought; but, as Topsy herself says, 'I's so wicked!'"

In very much this way Topsy's training proceeded, for a year or two,—Miss Ophelia worrying herself, from day to day, with her, as a kind of chronic plague, to whose inflictions she became, in time, as accustomed, as persons sometimes do to the neuralgia or sick head-ache.

St. Clare took the same kind of amusement in the child that a man might in the tricks of a parrot or a pointer. Topsy, whenever her sins brought her into disgrace in other quarters, always took refuge behind his chair; and St. Clare, in one way or other, would make peace for her. From him she got many a stray picayune, which she laid out in nuts and candies, and distributed, with careless generosity, to all the children in the family; for Topsy, to do her justice, was good-natured and liberal, and only spiteful in self-defence. She is fairly introduced into our *corps de ballet*, and will figure, from time to time, in her turn, with other performers.

XXI.

Kentuck

Our readers may not be unwilling to glance back, for a brief interval, at Uncle Tom's Cabin, on the Kentucky farm, and see what has been transpiring among those whom he had left behind.

It was late in the summer afternoon, and the doors and windows of the large parlor all stood open, to invite any stray breeze, that might feel in a good humor, to enter. Mr. Shelby sat in a large hall opening into the room, and running through the whole length of the house, to a balcony on either end. Leisurely tipped back in one chair, with his heels in another, he was enjoying his after-dinner cigar. Mrs. Shelby sat in the door, busy about some fine sewing; she seemed like one who had something on her mind, which she was seeking an opportunity to introduce.

"Do you know," she said, "that Chloe has had a letter from Tom?"

"Ah! has she? Tom 's got some friend there, it seems. How is the old boy?"

"He has been bought by a very fine family, I should think," said Mrs. Shelby,—"is kindly treated, and has not much to do."

"Ah! well, I 'm glad of it,—very glad," said Mr. Shelby, heartily. "Tom, I suppose, will get reconciled to a Southern residence;—hardly want to come up here again."

"On the contrary, he inquires very anxiously," said Mrs. Shelby, "when the money for his redemption is to be raised."

"I 'm sure *I* don't know," said Mr. Shelby. "Once get business running wrong, there does seem to be no end to it. It 's like jumping from one bog to another, all through a swamp; borrow of one to pay another, and then borrow of another to pay one,—and these confounded notes falling due before a man has time to smoke a cigar and turn round,—dunning letters and dunning messages,—all scamper and hurry-scurry."

"It does seem to me, my dear, that something might be done to straighten matters. Suppose we sell off all the horses, and sell one of your farms, and pay up square?"

"O, ridiculous, Emily! You are the finest woman in Kentucky; but still you have n't sense to know that you don't understand business;—women never do, and never can."

"But, at least," said Mrs. Shelby, "could not you give me some little insight into yours; a list of all your debts, at least, and of all that is owed to you, and let me try and see if I can't help you to economize."

"O, bother! don't plague me, Emily!—I can't tell exactly. I know somewhere about what things are likely to be; but there 's no trimming and squaring my affairs, as Chloe trims crust off her pies. You don't know anything about business, I tell you."

And Mr. Shelby, not knowing any other way of enforcing his ideas, raised his voice,—a mode of arguing very convenient and convincing, when a gentleman is discussing matters of business with his wife.

Mrs. Shelby ceased talking, with something of a sigh. The fact was, that though her husband had stated she was a woman, she had a clear, energetic, practical mind, and a force of character every way superior to that of her husband; so that it would not have been so very absurd a supposition, to have allowed her capable of managing, as Mr. Shelby supposed. Her heart was set on performing her promise to Tom and Aunt Chloe, and she sighed as discouragements thickened around her.

"Don't you think we might in some way contrive to raise that money? Poor Aunt Chloe! her heart is so set on it!"

"I 'm sorry, if it is. I think I was premature in promising. I 'm not sure, now, but it 's the best way to tell Chloe, and let her make up her mind to it. Tom 'll have another wife, in a year or two; and she had better take up with somebody else."

"Mr. Shelby, I have taught my people that their marriages are as sacred as ours. I never could think of giving Chloe such advice."

"It 's a pity, wife, that you have burdened them with a morality above their condition and prospects. I always thought so."

"It 's only the morality of the Bible, Mr. Shelby."

"Well, well, Emily, I don't pretend to interfere with your religious notions; only they seem extremely unfitted for people in that condition."

"They are, indeed," said Mrs. Shelby, "and that is why, from my soul, I hate the whole thing. I tell you, my dear, *I* cannot absolve myself from the promises I make to these helpless creatures. If I can get the money no other way, I will take music-scholars;—I could get enough, I know, and earn the money myself."

"You would n't degrade yourself that way, Emily? I never could consent to it."

"Degrade! would it degrade me as much as to break my faith with the helpless? No, indeed!"

"Well, you are always heroic and transcendental," said Mr. Shelby, "but I think you had better think before you undertake such a piece of Quixotism."

Here the conversation was interrupted by the appearance of Aunt Chloe, at the end of the verandah.

"If you please, Missis," said she.

"Well, Chloe, what is it?" said her mistress, rising, and going to the end of the balcony.

"If Missis would come and look at dis yer lot o' poetry."

Chloe had a particular fancy for calling poultry poetry,— an application of language in which she always persisted, notwithstanding frequent corrections and advisings from the young members of the family.

"La sakes!" she would say, "I can't see; one jis good as turry,—poetry suthin good, any how;" and so poetry Chloe continued to call it.

Mrs. Shelby smiled as she saw a prostrate lot of chickens and ducks, over which Chloe stood, with a very grave face of consideration.

"I 'm a thinkin whether Missis would be a havin a chicken pie o' dese yer."

"Really, Aunt Chloe, I don't much care;—serve them any way you like."

Chloe stood handling them over abstractedly; it was quite evident that the chickens were not what she was thinking of. At last, with the short laugh with which her tribe often introduced a doubtful proposal, she said,

"Laws me, Missis! what should Mas'r and Missis be a troublin theirselves 'bout de money, and not a usin what 's right in der hands?" and Chloe laughed again.

"I don't understand you, Chloe," said Mrs. Shelby, nothing doubting, from her knowledge of Chloe's manner, that she had heard every word of the conversation that had passed between her and her husband.

"Why, laws me, Missis!" said Chloe, laughing again, "other folks hires out der niggers and makes money on 'em! Don't keep sich a tribe eatin 'em out of house and home."

"Well, Chloe, who do you propose that we should hire out?"

"Laws! I an't a proposin nothin; only Sam he said der was one of dese yer *perfectioners*, dey calls 'em, in Louisville, said he wanted a good hand at cake and pastry; and said he 'd give four dollars a week to one, he did."

"Well, Chloe."

"Well, laws, I 's a thinkin, Missis, it 's time Sally was put along to be doin' something. Sally 's been under my care, now, dis some time, and she does most as well as me, considerin; and if Missis would only let me go, I would help fetch up de money. I an't afraid to put my cake, nor pies nother, 'long side no *perfectioner's*."

"Confectioner's, Chloe."

"Law sakes, Missis! 't an't no odds;—words is so curis, can't never get 'em right!"

"But, Chloe, do you want to leave your children?"

"Laws, Missis! de boys is big enough to do day's works; dey does well enough; and Sally, she 'll take de baby,—she 's such a peart young un, she won't take no lookin arter."

"Louisville is a good way off."

"Law sakes! who 's afeard?—it 's down river, somer near my old man, perhaps?" said Chloe, speaking the last in the tone of a question, and looking at Mrs. Shelby.

"No, Chloe; it 's many a hundred miles off," said Mrs. Shelby.

Chloe's countenance fell.

"Never mind; your going there shall bring you nearer, Chloe. Yes, you may go; and your wages shall every cent of them be laid aside for your husband's redemption."

As when a bright sunbeam turns a dark cloud to silver, so Chloe's dark face brightened immediately,—it really shone.

"Laws! if Missis is n't too good! I was thinking of dat ar very thing; cause I should n't need no clothes, nor shoes, nor nothin,—I could save every cent. How many weeks is der in a year, Missis?"

"Fifty-two," said Mrs. Shelby.

"Laws! now, dere is? and four dollars for each on 'em. Why, how much 'd dat ar be?"

"Two hundred and eight dollars," said Mrs. Shelby.

"Why-e!" said Chloe, with an accent of surprise and delight; "and how long would it take me to work it out, Missis?"

"Some four or five years, Chloe; but, then, you need n't do it all,—I shall add something to it."

"I would n't hear to Missis' givin lessons nor nothin. Mas'r's quite right in dat ar;—'t would n't do, no ways. I hope none our family ever be brought to dat ar, while I 's got hands."

"Don't fear, Chloe; I 'll take care of the honor of the family," said Mrs. Shelby, smiling. "But when do you expect to go?"

"Well, I want spectin nothin; only Sam, he 's a gwine to de river with some colts, and he said I could go long with him; so I jes put my things together. If Missis was willin, I 'd go with Sam to-morrow morning, if Missis would write my pass, and write me a commendation."

"Well, Chloe, I 'll attend to it, if Mr. Shelby has no objections. I must speak to him."

Mrs. Shelby went up stairs, and Aunt Chloe, delighted, went out to her cabin, to make her preparation.

"Law sakes, Mas'r George! ye did n't know I 's a gwine to Louisville to-morrow!" she said to George, as, entering her cabin, he found her busy in sorting over her baby's clothes. "I thought I 'd jis look over sis's things, and get 'em straightened up. But I 'm gwine, Mas'r George,—gwine to have four dollars a week; and Missis is gwine to lay it all up, to buy back my old man agin!"

"Whew!" said George, "here 's a stroke of business, to be sure! How are you going?"

"To-morrow, wid Sam. And now, Mas'r George, I knows you 'll jis sit down and write to my old man, and tell him all about it,—won't ye?"

"To be sure," said George; "Uncle Tom 'll be right glad to hear from us. I 'll go right in the house, for paper and ink; and then, you know, Aunt Chloe, I can tell about the new colts and all."

"Sartin, sartin, Mas'r George; you go 'long, and I 'll get ye up a bit o' chicken, or some sich; ye won't have many more suppers wid yer poor old aunty."

XXII.

"The Grass Withereth—The Flower Fadeth"

LIFE passes, with us all, a day at a time; so it passed with our friend Tom, till two years were gone. Though parted from all his soul held dear, and though often yearning for what lay beyond, still was he never positively and consciously miserable; for, so well is the harp of human feeling strung, that nothing but a crash that breaks every string can wholly mar its harmony; and, on looking back to seasons which in review appear to us as those of deprivation and trial, we can remember that each hour, as it glided, brought its diversions and alleviations, so that, though not happy wholly, we were not, either, wholly miserable.

Tom read, in his only literary cabinet, of one who had "learned in whatsoever state he was, therewith to be content." It seemed to him good and reasonable doctrine, and accorded well with the settled and thoughtful habit which he had acquired from the reading of that same book.

His letter homeward, as we related in the last chapter, was in due time answered by Master George, in a good, round, school-boy hand, that Tom said might be read "most acrost the room." It contained various refreshing items of home intelligence, with which our reader is fully acquainted: stated how Aunt Chloe had been hired out to a confectioner in Louisville, where her skill in the pastry line was gaining wonderful sums of money, all of which, Tom was informed, was to be laid up to go to make up the sum of his redemption money; Mose and Pete were thriving, and the baby was trotting all about the house, under the care of Sally and the family generally.

Tom's cabin was shut up for the present; but George expatiated brilliantly on ornaments and additions to be made to it when Tom came back.

The rest of this letter gave a list of George's school studies, each one headed by a flourishing capital; and also told the names of four new colts that appeared on the premises since Tom left; and stated, in the same connection, that father and mother were well. The style of the letter was decidedly concise and terse; but Tom thought it the most wonderful specimen of composition that had appeared in modern times. He was never tired of looking at it, and even held a council with Eva on the expediency of getting it framed, to hang up in his room. Nothing but the difficulty of arranging it so that both sides of the page would show at once stood in the way of this undertaking.

The friendship between Tom and Eva had grown with the child's growth. It would be hard to say what place she held in the soft, impressible heart of her faithful attendant. He loved her as something frail and earthly, yet almost worshipped her as something heavenly and divine. He gazed on her as the Italian sailor gazes on his image of the child Jesus,—with a mixture of reverence and tenderness; and to humor her graceful fancies, and meet those thousand simple wants which invest childhood like a many-colored rainbow, was Tom's chief delight. In the market, at morning, his eyes were always on the flower-stalls for rare bouquets for her, and the choicest peach or orange was slipped into his pocket to give to her when he came back; and the sight that pleased him most was her sunny head looking out the gate for his distant approach, and her childish question,—"Well, Uncle Tom, what have you got for me to-day?"

Nor was Eva less zealous in kind offices, in return. Though a child, she was a beautiful reader;—a fine musical ear, a quick poetic fancy, and an instinctive sympathy with what is grand and noble, made her such a reader of the Bible as Tom had never before heard. At first, she read to please her humble friend; but soon her own earnest nature threw out its tendrils, and wound itself around the majestic book; and Eva loved it, because it woke in her strange yearnings, and strong, dim emotions, such as impassioned, imaginative children love to feel.

The parts that pleased her most were the Revelations and the Prophecies,—parts whose dim and wondrous imagery, and fervent language, impressed her the more, that she questioned vainly of their meaning;—and she and her simple friend, the old child and the young one, felt just alike about it. All that they knew was, that they spoke of a glory to be revealed,—a wondrous something yet to come, wherein their soul rejoiced, yet knew not why; and though it be not so in the physical, yet in moral science that which cannot be understood is not always profitless. For the soul awakes, a trembling stranger, between two dim eternities,—the eternal past, the eternal future. The light shines only on a small space around her; therefore, she needs must yearn towards the unknown; and the voices and shadowy movings which come to her from out the cloudy pillar of inspiration have each one echoes and answers in her own expecting nature. Its mystic imagery are so many talismans and gems inscribed with unknown hieroglyphics; she folds them in her bosom, and expects to read them when she passes beyond the veil.

At this time in our story, the whole St. Clare establishment is, for the time being, removed to their villa on Lake Pontchartrain. The heats of summer had driven all who were able to leave the sultry and unhealthy city, to seek the shores of the lake, and its cool sea-breezes.

St. Clare's villa was an East Indian cottage, surrounded by light verandahs of bamboo-work, and opening on all sides into gardens and pleasure-grounds. The common sitting-room opened on to a large garden, fragrant with every picturesque plant and flower of the tropics, where winding paths ran down to the very shores of the lake, whose silvery sheet of water lay there, rising and falling in the sunbeams, —a picture never for an hour the same, yet every hour more beautiful.

It is now one of those intensely golden sunsets which kindles the whole horizon into one blaze of glory, and makes the water another sky. The lake lay in rosy or golden streaks, save where white-winged vessels glided hither and thither, like so many spirits, and little golden stars twinkled through the glow, and looked down at themselves as they trembled in the water.

Tom and Eva were seated on a little mossy seat, in an arbor, at the foot of the garden. It was Sunday evening, and Eva's Bible lay open on her knee. She read,—"And I saw a sea of glass, mingled with fire."

"Tom," said Eva, suddenly stopping, and pointing to the lake, "there 't is."

"What, Miss Eva?"

"Don't you see,—there?" said the child, pointing to the glassy water, which, as it rose and fell, reflected the golden glow of the sky. "There 's a 'sea of glass, mingled with fire.' "

"True enough, Miss Eva," said Tom; and Tom sang—

"O, had I the wings of the morning,
    I 'd fly away to Canaan's shore;
Bright angels should convey me home,
    To the new Jerusalem."

"Where do you suppose new Jerusalem is, Uncle Tom?" said Eva.

"O, up in the clouds, Miss Eva."

"Then I think I see it," said Eva. "Look in those clouds!— they look like great gates of pearl; and you can see beyond them—far, far off—it 's all gold. Tom, sing about 'spirits bright.' "

Tom sung the words of a well-known Methodist hymn,

"I see a band of spirits bright,
    That taste the glories there;
They all are robed in spotless white,
    And conquering palms they bear."

"Uncle Tom, I 've seen *them*," said Eva.

Tom had no doubt of it at all; it did not surprise him in the least. If Eva had told him she had been to heaven, he would have thought it entirely probable.

"They come to me sometimes in my sleep, those spirits;" and Eva's eyes grew dreamy, and she hummed, in a low voice,

"They are all robed in spotless white,
    And conquering palms they bear."

"Uncle Tom," said Eva, "I 'm going there."

"Where, Miss Eva?"

The child rose, and pointed her little hand to the sky; the

Little Eva reading the Bible to Uncle Tom in the arbor

glow of evening lit her golden hair and flushed cheek with a kind of unearthly radiance, and her eyes were bent earnestly on the skies.

"I'm going *there*," she said, "to the spirits bright, Tom; *I'm going, before long*."

The faithful old heart felt a sudden thrust; and Tom thought how often he had noticed, within six months, that Eva's little hands had grown thinner, and her skin more transparent, and her breath shorter; and how, when she ran or played in the garden, as she once could for hours, she became soon so tired and languid. He had heard Miss Ophelia speak often of a cough, that all her medicaments could not cure; and even now that fervent cheek and little hand were burning with hectic fever; and yet the thought that Eva's words suggested had never come to him till now.

Has there ever been a child like Eva? Yes, there have been; but their names are always on grave-stones, and their sweet smiles, their heavenly eyes, their singular words and ways, are among the buried treasures of yearning hearts. In how many families do you hear the legend that all the goodness and graces of the living are nothing to the peculiar charms of one who *is not*. It is as if heaven had an especial band of angels, whose office it was to sojourn for a season here, and endear to them the wayward human heart, that they might bear it upward with them in their homeward flight. When you see that deep, spiritual light in the eye,—when the little soul reveals itself in words sweeter and wiser than the ordinary words of children,—hope not to retain that child; for the seal of heaven is on it, and the light of immortality looks out from its eyes.

Even so, beloved Eva! fair star of thy dwelling! Thou art passing away; but they that love thee dearest know it not.

The colloquy between Tom and Eva was interrupted by a hasty call from Miss Ophelia.

"Eva—Eva!—why, child, the dew is falling; you must n't be out there!"

Eva and Tom hastened in.

Miss Ophelia was old, and skilled in the tactics of nursing. She was from New England, and knew well the first guileful footsteps of that soft, insidious disease, which sweeps away so many of the fairest and loveliest, and, before one fibre of life seems broken, seals them irrevocably for death.

She had noted the slight, dry cough, the daily brightening cheek; nor could the lustre of the eye, and the airy buoyancy born of fever, deceive her.

She tried to communicate her fears to St. Clare; but he threw back her suggestions with a restless petulance, unlike his usual careless good-humor.

"Don't be croaking, Cousin,—I hate it!" he would say; "don't you see that the child is only growing. Children always lose strength when they grow fast."

"But she has that cough!"

"O! nonsense of that cough!—it is not anything. She has taken a little cold, perhaps."

"Well, that was just the way Eliza Jane was taken, and Ellen and Maria Sanders."

"O! stop these hobgoblin' nurse legends. You old hands got so wise, that a child cannot cough, or sneeze, but you see desperation and ruin at hand. Only take care of the child, keep her from the night air, and don't let her play too hard, and she 'll do well enough."

So St. Clare said; but he grew nervous and restless. He watched Eva feverishly day by day, as might be told by the frequency with which he repeated over that "the child was quite well"—that there was n't anything in that cough,—it was only some little stomach affection, such as children often had. But he kept by her more than before, took her oftener to ride with him, brought home every few days some receipt or strengthening mixture,—"not," he said, "that the child *needed* it, but then it would not do her any harm."

If it must be told, the thing that struck a deeper pang to his heart than anything else was the daily increasing maturity of the child's mind and feelings. While still retaining all a child's fanciful graces, yet she often dropped, unconsciously, words of such a reach of thought, and strange unworldly wisdom, that they seemed to be an inspiration. At such times, St. Clare would feel a sudden thrill, and clasp her in his arms, as if that fond clasp could save her; and his heart rose up with wild determination to keep her, never to let her go.

The child's whole heart and soul seemed absorbed in works

of love and kindness. Impulsively generous she had always been; but there was a touching and womanly thoughtfulness about her now, that every one noticed. She still loved to play with Topsy, and the various colored children; but she now seemed rather a spectator than an actor of their plays, and she would sit for half an hour at a time, laughing at the odd tricks of Topsy, — and then a shadow would seem to pass across her face, her eyes grew misty, and her thoughts were afar.

"Mamma," she said, suddenly, to her mother, one day, "why don't we teach our servants to read?"

"What a question, child! People never do."

"Why don't they?" said Eva.

"Because it is no use for them to read. It don't help them to work any better, and they are not made for anything else."

"But they ought to read the Bible, mamma, to learn God's will."

"O! they can get that read to them all *they* need."

"It seems to me, mamma, the Bible is for every one to read themselves. They need it a great many times when there is nobody to read it."

"Eva, you are an odd child," said her mother.

"Miss Ophelia has taught Topsy to read," continued Eva.

"Yes, and you see how much good it does. Topsy is the worst creature I ever saw!"

"Here 's poor Mammy!" said Eva. "She does love the Bible so much, and wishes so she could read! And what will she do when I can't read to her?"

Marie was busy, turning over the contents of a drawer, as she answered,

"Well, of course, by and by, Eva, you will have other things to think of, besides reading the Bible round to servants. Not but that is very proper; I 've done it myself, when I had health. But when you come to be dressing and going into company, you won't have time. See here!" she added, "these jewels I 'm going to give you when you come out. I wore them to my first ball. I can tell you, Eva, I made a sensation."

Eva took the jewel-case, and lifted from it a diamond necklace. Her large, thoughtful eyes rested on them, but it was plain her thoughts were elsewhere.

"How sober you look, child!" said Marie.

"Are these worth a great deal of money, mamma?"

"To be sure, they are. Father sent to France for them. They are worth a small fortune."

"I wish I had them," said Eva, "to do what I pleased with!"

"What would you do with them?"

"I'd sell them, and buy a place in the free states, and take all our people there, and hire teachers, to teach them to read and write."

Eva was cut short by her mother's laughing.

"Set up a boarding-school! Wouldn't you teach them to play on the piano, and paint on velvet?"

"I'd teach them to read their own Bible, and write their own letters, and read letters that are written to them," said Eva, steadily. "I know, mamma, it does come very hard on them, that they can't do these things. Tom feels it,—Mammy does,—a great many of them do. I think it's wrong."

"Come, come, Eva; you are only a child! You don't know anything about these things," said Marie; "besides, your talking makes my head ache."

Marie always had a head-ache on hand for any conversation that did not exactly suit her.

Eva stole away; but after that, she assiduously gave Mammy reading lessons.

XXIII.

Henrique

ABOUT this time, St. Clare's brother Alfred, with his eldest son, a boy of twelve, spent a day or two with the family at the lake.

No sight could be more singular and beautiful than that of these twin brothers. Nature, instead of instituting resemblances between them, had made them opposites on every point; yet a mysterious tie seemed to unite them in a closer friendship than ordinary.

They used to saunter, arm in arm, up and down the alleys and walks of the garden. Augustine, with his blue eyes and golden hair, his ethereally flexible form and vivacious features; and Alfred, dark-eyed, with haughty Roman profile, firmly-knit limbs, and decided bearing. They were always abusing each other's opinions and practices, and yet never a whit the less absorbed in each other's society; in fact, the very contrariety seemed to unite them, like the attraction between opposite poles of the magnet.

Henrique, the eldest son of Alfred, was a noble, dark-eyed, princely boy, full of vivacity and spirit; and, from the first moment of introduction, seemed to be perfectly fascinated by the spirituelle graces of his cousin Evangeline.

Eva had a little pet pony, of a snowy whiteness. It was easy as a cradle, and as gentle as its little mistress; and this pony was now brought up to the back verandah by Tom, while a little mulatto boy of about thirteen led along a small black Arabian, which had just been imported, at a great expense, for Henrique.

Henrique had a boy's pride in his new possession; and, as he advanced and took the reins out of the hands of his little groom, he looked carefully over him, and his brow darkened.

"What's this, Dodo, you little lazy dog! you have n't rubbed my horse down, this morning."

"Yes, Mas'r," said Dodo, submissively; "he got that dust on his own self."

"You rascal, shut your mouth!" said Henrique, violently raising his riding-whip. "How dare you speak?"

The boy was a handsome, bright-eyed mulatto, of just Henrique's size, and his curling hair hung round a high, bold forehead. He had white blood in his veins, as could be seen by the quick flush in his cheek, and the sparkle of his eye, as he eagerly tried to speak.

"Mas'r Henrique!—" he began.

Henrique struck him across the face with his riding-whip, and, seizing one of his arms, forced him on to his knees, and beat him till he was out of breath.

"There, you impudent dog! Now will you learn not to answer back when I speak to you? Take the horse back, and clean him properly. I'll teach you your place!"

"Young Mas'r," said Tom, "I specs what he was gwine to say was, that the horse would roll when he was bringing him up from the stable; he's so full of spirits,—that's the way he got that dirt on him; I looked to his cleaning."

"You hold your tongue till you're asked to speak!" said Henrique, turning on his heel, and walking up the steps to speak to Eva, who stood in her riding-dress.

"Dear Cousin, I'm sorry this stupid fellow has kept you waiting," he said. "Let's sit down here, on this seat, till they come. What's the matter, Cousin?—you look sober."

"How could you be so cruel and wicked to poor Dodo?" said Eva.

"Cruel,—wicked!" said the boy, with unaffected surprise. "What do you mean, dear Eva?"

"I don't want you to call me dear Eva, when you do so," said Eva.

"Dear Cousin, you don't know Dodo; it's the only way to manage him, he's so full of lies and excuses. The only way is to put him down at once,—not let him open his mouth; that's the way papa manages."

"But Uncle Tom said it was an accident, and he never tells what is n't true."

"He's an uncommon old nigger, then!" said Henrique. "Dodo will lie as fast as he can speak."

"You frighten him into deceiving, if you treat him so."

"Why, Eva, you 've really taken such a fancy to Dodo, that I shall be jealous."

"But you beat him,—and he did n't deserve it."

"O, well, it may go for some time when he does, and don't get it. A few cuts never come amiss with Dodo,—he 's a regular spirit, I can tell you; but I won't beat him again before you, if it troubles you."

Eva was not satisfied, but found it in vain to try to make her handsome cousin understand her feelings.

Dodo soon appeared, with the horses.

"Well, Dodo, you 've done pretty well, this time," said his young master, with a more gracious air. "Come, now, and hold Miss Eva's horse, while I put her on to the saddle."

Dodo came and stood by Eva's pony. His face was troubled; his eyes looked as if he had been crying.

Henrique, who valued himself on his gentlemanly adroitness in all matters of gallantry, soon had his fair cousin in the saddle, and, gathering the reins, placed them in her hands.

But Eva bent to the other side of the horse, where Dodo was standing, and said, as he relinquished the reins,— "That 's a good boy, Dodo;—thank you!"

Dodo looked up in amazement into the sweet young face; the blood rushed to his cheeks, and the tears to his eyes.

"Here, Dodo," said his master, imperiously.

Dodo sprang and held the horse, while his master mounted.

"There 's a picayune for you to buy candy with, Dodo," said Henrique; "go get some."

And Henrique cantered down the walk after Eva. Dodo stood looking after the two children. One had given him money; and one had given him what he wanted far more,— a kind word, kindly spoken. Dodo had been only a few months away from his mother. His master had bought him at a slave warehouse, for his handsome face, to be a match to the handsome pony; and he was now getting his breaking in, at the hands of his young master.

The scene of the beating had been witnessed by the two brothers St. Clare, from another part of the garden.

Augustine's cheek flushed; but he only observed, with his

usual sarcastic carelessness,

"I suppose that's what we may call republican education, Alfred?"

"Henrique is a devil of a fellow, when his blood's up," said Alfred, carelessly.

"I suppose you consider this an instructive practice for him," said Augustine, drily.

"I could n't help it, if I did n't. Henrique is a regular little tempest;—his mother and I have given him up, long ago. But, then, that Dodo is a perfect sprite,—no amount of whipping can hurt him."

"And this by way of teaching Henrique the first verse of a republican's cathecism, 'All men are born free and equal!' "

"Poh!" said Alfred; "one of Tom Jefferson's pieces of French sentiment and humbug. It's perfectly ridiculous to have that going the rounds among us, to this day."

"I think it is," said St. Clare, significantly.

"Because," said Alfred, "we can see plainly enough that all men are *not* born free, nor born equal; they are born anything else. For my part, I think half this republican talk sheer humbug. It is the educated, the intelligent, the wealthy, the refined, who ought to have equal rights, and not the canaille."

"If you can keep the canaille of that opinion," said Augustine. "They took *their* turn once, in France."

"Of course, they must be *kept down*, consistently, steadily, as I *should*," said Alfred, setting his foot hard down, as if he were standing on somebody.

"It makes a terrible slip when they get up," said Augustine,—"in St. Domingo, for instance."

"Poh!" said Alfred, "we'll take care of that, in this country. We must set our face against all this educating, elevating talk, that is getting about now; the lower class must not be educated."

"That is past praying for," said Augustine; "educated they will be, and we have only to say how. Our system is educating them in barbarism and brutality. We are breaking all humanizing ties, and making them brute beasts; and, if they get the upper hand, such we shall find them."

"They never shall get the upper hand!" said Alfred.

"That's right," said St. Clare; "put on the steam, fasten down the escape-valve, and sit on it, and see where you'll land."

"Well," said Alfred, "we *will* see. I'm not afraid to sit on the escape-valve, as long as the boilers are strong, and the machinery works well."

"The nobles in Louis XVI.'s time thought just so; and Austria and Pius IX. think so now; and, some pleasant morning, you may all be caught up to meet each other in the air, *when the boilers burst*."

"*Dies declarabit*," said Alfred, laughing.

"I tell you," said Augustine, "if there is anything that is revealed with the strength of a divine law in our times, it is that the masses are to rise, and the under class become the upper one."

"That's one of your red republican humbugs, Augustine! Why didn't you ever take to the stump;—you'd make a famous stump orator! Well, I hope I shall be dead before this millennium of your greasy masses comes on."

"Greasy or not greasy, they will govern *you*, when their time comes," said Augustine; "and they will be just such rulers as you make them. The French noblesse chose to have the people '*sans culottes*,' and they had '*sans culotte*' governors to their hearts' content. The people of Hayti—"

"O, come, Augustine! as if we hadn't had enough of that abominable, contemptible Hayti! The Haytiens were not Anglo Saxons; if they had been, there would have been another story. The Anglo Saxon is the dominant race of the world, and *is to be so*."

"Well, there is a pretty fair infusion of Anglo Saxon blood among our slaves, now," said Augustine. "There are plenty among them who have only enough of the African to give a sort of tropical warmth and fervor to our calculating firmness and foresight. If ever the San Domingo hour comes, Anglo Saxon blood will lead on the day. Sons of white fathers, with all our haughty feelings burning in their veins, will not always be bought and sold and traded. They will rise, and raise with them their mother's race."

"Stuff!—nonsense!"

"Well," said Augustine, "there goes an old saying to this effect, 'As it was in the days of Noah, so shall it be;—they ate, they drank, they planted, they builded, and knew not till the flood came and took them.' "

"On the whole, Augustine, I think your talents might do for a circuit rider," said Alfred, laughing. "Never you fear for us; possession is our nine points. We 've got the power. This subject race," said he, stamping firmly, "is down, and shall *stay* down! We have energy enough to manage our own powder."

"Sons trained like your Henrique will be grand guardians of your powder-magazines," said Augustine,—"so cool and self-possessed! The proverb says, 'They that cannot govern themselves cannot govern others.' "

"There is a trouble there," said Alfred, thoughtfully; "there 's no doubt that our system is a difficult one to train children under. It gives too free scope to the passions, altogether, which, in our climate, are hot enough. I find trouble with Henrique. The boy is generous and warm-hearted, but a perfect fire-cracker when excited. I believe I shall send him North for his education, where obedience is more fashionable, and where he will associate more with equals, and less with dependants."

"Since training children is the staple work of the human race," said Augustine, "I should think it something of a consideration that our system does not work well there."

"It does not for some things," said Alfred; "for others, again, it does. It makes boys manly and courageous; and the very vices of an abject race tend to strengthen in them the opposite virtues. I think Henrique, now, has a keener sense of the beauty of truth, from seeing lying and deception the universal badge of slavery."

"A Christian-like view of the subject, certainly!" said Augustine.

"It 's true, Christian-like or not; and is about as Christian-like as most other things in the world," said Alfred.

"That may be," said St. Clare.

"Well, there 's no use in talking, Augustine. I believe we 've been round and round this old track five hundred times, more or less. What do you say to a game of backgammon?"

The two brothers ran up the verandah steps, and were soon seated at a light bamboo stand, with the backgammon-board between them. As they were setting their men, Alfred said,

"I tell you, Augustine, if I thought as you do, I should do something."

"I dare say you would,—you are one of the doing sort,—but what?"

"Why, elevate your own servants, for a specimen," said Alfred, with a half-scornful smile.

"You might as well set Mount Ætna on them flat, and tell them to stand up under it, as tell me to elevate my servants under all the superincumbent mass of society upon them. One man can do nothing, against the whole action of a community. Education, to do anything, must be a state education; or there must be enough agreed in it to make a current."

"You take the first throw," said Alfred; and the brothers were soon lost in the game, and heard no more till the scraping of horses' feet was heard under the verandah.

"There come the children," said Augustine, rising. "Look here, Alf! Did you ever see anything so beautiful?" And, in truth, it *was* a beautiful sight. Henrique, with his bold brow, and dark, glossy curls, and glowing cheek, was laughing gayly, as he bent towards his fair cousin, as they came on. She was dressed in a blue riding-dress, with a cap of the same color. Exercise had given a brilliant hue to her cheeks, and heightened the effect of her singularly transparent skin, and golden hair.

"Good heavens! what perfectly dazzling beauty!" said Alfred. "I tell you, Auguste, won't she make some hearts ache, one of these days?"

"She will, too truly,—God knows I'm afraid so!" said St. Clare, in a tone of sudden bitterness, as he hurried down to take her off her horse.

"Eva, darling! you're not much tired?" he said, as he clasped her in his arms.

"No, papa," said the child; but her short, hard breathing alarmed her father.

"How could you ride so fast, dear?—you know it's bad for you."

"I felt so well, papa, and liked it so much, I forgot."

St. Clare carried her in his arms into the parlor, and laid her on the sofa.

"Henrique, you must be careful of Eva," said he; "you must n't ride fast with her."

"I 'll take her under my care," said Henrique, seating himself by the sofa, and taking Eva's hand.

Eva soon found herself much better. Her father and uncle resumed their game, and the children were left together.

"Do you know, Eva, I 'm so sorry papa is only going to stay two days here, and then I shan't see you again for ever so long! If I stay with you, I 'd try to be good, and not be cross to Dodo, and so on. I don't mean to treat Dodo ill; but, you know, I 've got such a quick temper. I 'm not really bad to him, though. I give him a picayune, now and then; and you see he dresses well. I think, on the whole, Dodo 's pretty well off."

"Would you think you were well off, if there were not one creature in the world near you to love you?"

"I?—Well, of course not."

"And you have taken Dodo away from all the friends he ever had, and now he has not a creature to love him;—nobody can be good that way."

"Well, I can't help it, as I know of. I can't get his mother, and I can't love him myself, nor anybody else, as I know of."

"Why can't you?" said Eva.

"*Love* Dodo! Why, Eva, you would n't have me! I may *like* him well enough; but you don't *love* your servants."

"I do, indeed."

"How odd!"

"Don't the Bible say we must love everybody?"

"O, the Bible! To be sure, it says a great many such things; but, then, nobody ever thinks of doing them,—you know, Eva, nobody does."

Eva did not speak; her eyes were fixed and thoughtful, for a few moments.

"At any rate," she said, "dear Cousin, do love poor Dodo, and be kind to him, for my sake!"

"I could love anything, for your sake, dear Cousin; for I really think you are the loveliest creature that I ever saw!" And Henrique spoke with an earnestness that flushed his handsome face. Eva received it with perfect simplicity, without even a change of feature; merely saying, "I'm glad you feel so, dear Henrique! I hope you will remember."

The dinner-bell put an end to the interview.

XXIV.

Foreshadowings

Two days after this, Alfred St. Clare and Augustine parted; and Eva, who had been stimulated, by the society of her young cousin, to exertions beyond her strength, began to fail rapidly. St. Clare was at last willing to call in medical advice,—a thing from which he had always shrunk, because it was the admission of an unwelcome truth.

But, for a day or two, Eva was so unwell as to be confined to the house; and the doctor was called.

Marie St. Clare had taken no notice of the child's gradually decaying health and strength, because she was completely absorbed in studying out two or three new forms of disease to which she believed she herself was a victim. It was the first principle of Marie's belief that nobody ever was or could be so great a sufferer as *herself*; and, therefore, she always repelled quite indignantly any suggestion that any one around her could be sick. She was always sure, in such a case, that it was nothing but laziness, or want of energy; and that, if they had had the suffering *she* had, they would soon know the difference.

Miss Ophelia had several times tried to awaken her maternal fears about Eva; but to no avail.

"I don't see as anything ails the child," she would say; "she runs about, and plays."

"But she has a cough."

"Cough! you don't need to tell *me* about a cough. I 've always been subject to a cough, all my days. When I was of Eva's age, they thought I was in a consumption. Night after night, Mammy used to sit up with me. O! Eva's cough is not anything."

"But she gets weak, and is short-breathed."

"Law! I 've had that, years and years; it 's only a nervous affection."

"But she sweats so, nights!"

"Well, I have, these ten years. Very often, night after night, my clothes will be wringing wet. There won't be a dry thread in my night-clothes, and the sheets will be so that Mammy has to hang them up to dry! Eva does n't sweat anything like that!"

Miss Ophelia shut her mouth for a season. But, now that Eva was fairly and visibly prostrated, and a doctor called, Marie, all on a sudden, took a new turn.

"She knew it," she said; "she always felt it, that she was destined to be the most miserable of mothers. Here she was, with her wretched health, and her only darling child going down to the grave before her eyes;"—and Marie routed up Mammy nights, and rumpussed and scolded, with more energy than ever, all day, on the strength of this new misery.

"My dear Marie, don't talk so!" said St. Clare. "You ought not to give up the case so, at once."

"You have not a mother's feelings, St. Clare! You never could understand me!—you don't now."

"But don't talk so, as if it were a gone case!"

"I can't take it as indifferently as you can, St. Clare. If *you* don't feel when your only child is in this alarming state, *I* do. It 's a blow too much for me, with all I was bearing before."

"It 's true," said St. Clare, "that Eva is very delicate, *that* I always knew; and that she has grown so rapidly as to exhaust her strength; and that her situation is critical. But just now she is only prostrated by the heat of the weather, and by the excitement of her cousin's visit, and the exertions she made. The physician says there is room for hope."

"Well, of course, if you can look on the bright side, pray do; it 's a mercy if people have n't sensitive feelings, in this world. I am sure I wish I did n't feel as I do; it only makes me completely wretched! I wish I *could* be as easy as the rest of you!"

And the "rest of them" had good reason to breathe the same prayer, for Marie paraded her new misery as the reason and apology for all sorts of inflictions on every one about her. Every word that was spoken by anybody, everything that was done or was not done everywhere, was only a new proof that she was surrounded by hard-hearted, insensible beings, who were unmindful of her peculiar sorrows. Poor Eva heard some of these speeches; and nearly cried her little eyes out, in pity for her mamma, and in sorrow that she should make her so much distress.

In a week or two, there was a great improvement of symptoms,—one of those deceitful lulls, by which her inexorable disease so often beguiles the anxious heart, even on the verge of the grave. Eva's step was again in the garden,—in the balconies; she played and laughed again,—and her father, in a transport, declared that they should soon have her as hearty as anybody. Miss Ophelia and the physician alone felt no encouragement from this illusive truce. There was one other heart, too, that felt the same certainty, and that was the little heart of Eva. What is it that sometimes speaks in the soul so calmly, so clearly, that its earthly time is short? Is it the secret instinct of decaying nature, or the soul's impulsive throb, as immortality draws on? Be it what it may, it rested in the heart of Eva, a calm, sweet, prophetic certainty that Heaven was near; calm as the light of sunset, sweet as the bright stillness of autumn, there her little heart reposed, only troubled by sorrow for those who loved her so dearly.

For the child, though nursed so tenderly, and though life was unfolding before her with every brightness that love and wealth could give, had no regret for herself in dying.

In that book which she and her simple old friend had read so much together, she had seen and taken to her young heart the image of one who loved the little child; and, as she gazed and mused, He had ceased to be an image and a picture of the distant past, and come to be a living, all-surrounding reality. His love enfolded her childish heart with more than mortal tenderness; and it was to Him, she said, she was going, and to his home.

But her heart yearned with sad tenderness for all that she was to leave behind. Her father most,—for Eva, though she never distinctly thought so, had an instinctive perception that she was more in his heart than any other. She loved her mother because she was so loving a creature, and all the selfishness that she had seen in her only saddened and perplexed her; for she had a child's implicit trust that her mother could not do wrong. There was something about her that Eva never could make out; and she always smoothed it over with thinking that, after all, it was mamma, and she loved her very dearly indeed.

She felt, too, for those fond, faithful servants, to whom she was as daylight and sunshine. Children do not usually generalize; but Eva was an uncommonly mature child, and the things that she had witnessed of the evils of the system under which they were living had fallen, one by one, into the depths of her thoughtful, pondering heart. She had vague longings to do something for them,—to bless and save not only them, but all in their condition,—longings that contrasted sadly with the feebleness of her little frame.

"Uncle Tom," she said, one day, when she was reading to her friend, "I can understand why Jesus *wanted* to die for us."

"Why, Miss Eva?"

"Because I 've felt so, too."

"What is it, Miss Eva?—I don't understand."

"I can't tell you; but, when I saw those poor creatures on the boat, you know, when you came up and I,—some had lost their mothers, and some their husbands, and some mothers cried for their little children,—and when I heard about poor Prue,—oh, was n't that dreadful!—and a great many other times, I 've felt that I would be glad to die, if my dying could stop all this misery. I *would die* for them, Tom, if I could," said the child, earnestly, laying her little thin hand on his.

Tom looked at the child with awe; and when she, hearing her father's voice, glided away, he wiped his eyes many times, as he looked after her.

"It 's jest no use tryin' to keep Miss Eva here," he said to Mammy, whom he met a moment after. "She 's got the Lord's mark in her forehead."

"Ah, yes, yes," said Mammy, raising her hands; "I 've allers said so. She was n't never like a child that 's to live—there was allers something deep in her eyes. I 've told Missis so, many the time; it 's a comin' true,—we all sees it,—dear, little, blessed lamb!"

Eva came tripping up the verandah steps to her father. It was late in the afternoon, and the rays of the sun formed a kind of glory behind her, as she came forward in her white dress, with her golden hair and glowing cheeks, her eyes unnaturally bright with the slow fever that burned in her veins.

St. Clare had called her to show a statuette that he had been buying for her; but her appearance, as she came on, impressed him suddenly and painfully. There is a kind of beauty so intense, yet so fragile, that we cannot bear to look at it. Her father folded her suddenly in his arms, and almost forgot what he was going to tell her.

"Eva, dear, you are better now-a-days,—are you not?"

"Papa," said Eva, with sudden firmness, "I've had things I wanted to say to you, a great while. I want to say them now, before I get weaker."

St. Clare trembled as Eva seated herself in his lap. She laid her head on his bosom, and said,

"It's all no use, papa, to keep it to myself any longer. The time is coming that I am going to leave you. I am going, and never to come back!" and Eva sobbed.

"O, now, my dear little Eva!" said St. Clare, trembling as he spoke, but speaking cheerfully, "you've got nervous and low-spirited; you mustn't indulge such gloomy thoughts. See here, I've bought a statuette for you!"

"No, papa," said Eva, putting it gently away, "don't deceive yourself!—I am *not* any better, I know it perfectly well,—and I am going, before long. I am not nervous,—I am not low-spirited. If it were not for you, papa, and my friends, I should be perfectly happy. I want to go,—I long to go!"

"Why, dear child, what has made your poor little heart so sad? You have had everything, to make you happy, that could be given you."

"I had rather be in heaven; though, only for my friends' sake, I would be willing to live. There are a great many things here that make me sad, that seem dreadful to me; I had rather be there; but I don't want to leave you,—it almost breaks my heart!"

"What makes you sad, and seems dreadful, Eva?"

"O, things that are done, and done all the time. I feel sad for our poor people; they love me dearly, and they are all good and kind to me. I wish, papa, they were all *free*."

"Why, Eva, child, don't you think they are well enough off now?"

"O, but, papa, if anything should happen to you, what would become of them? There are very few men like you, papa. Uncle Alfred is n't like you, and mamma is n't; and then, think of poor old Prue's owners! What horrid things people do, and can do!" and Eva shuddered.

"My dear child, you are too sensitive. I 'm sorry I ever let you hear such stories."

"O, that 's what troubles me, papa. You want me to live so happy, and never to have any pain,—never suffer anything,— not even hear a sad story, when other poor creatures have nothing but pain and sorrow, all their lives;—it seems selfish. I ought to know such things, I ought to feel about them! Such things always sunk into my heart; they went down deep; I 've thought and thought about them. Papa, is n't there any way to have all slaves made free?"

"That 's a difficult question, dearest. There 's no doubt that this way is a very bad one; a great many people think so; I do myself. I heartily wish that there were not a slave in the land; but, then, I don't know what is to be done about it!"

"Papa, you are such a good man, and so noble, and kind, and you always have a way of saying things that is so pleasant, could n't you go all round and try to persuade people to do right about this? When I am dead, papa, then you will think of me, and do it for my sake. I would do it, if I could."

"When you are dead, Eva," said St. Clare, passionately. "O, child, don't talk to me so! You are all I have on earth."

"Poor old Prue's child was all that she had,—and yet she had to hear it crying, and she could n't help it! Papa, these poor creatures love their children as much as you do me. O! do something for them! There 's poor Mammy loves her children; I 've seen her cry when she talked about them. And Tom loves his children; and it 's dreadful, papa, that such things are happening, all the time!"

"There, there, darling," said St. Clare, soothingly; "only don't distress yourself, and don't talk of dying, and I will do anything you wish."

"And promise me, dear father, that Tom shall have his free- dom as soon as"—she stopped, and said, in a hesitating tone—"I am gone!"

"Yes, dear, I will do anything in the world,—anything you could ask me to."

"Dear papa," said the child, laying her burning cheek against his, "how I wish we could go together!"

"Where, dearest?" said St. Clare.

"To our Saviour's home; it's so sweet and peaceful there— it is all so loving there!" The child spoke unconsciously, as of a place where she had often been. "Don't you want to go, papa?" she said.

St. Clare drew her closer to him, but was silent.

"You will come to me," said the child, speaking in a voice of calm certainty which she often used unconsciously.

"I shall come after you. I shall not forget you."

The shadows of the solemn evening closed round them deeper and deeper, as St. Clare sat silently holding the little frail form to his bosom. He saw no more the deep eyes, but the voice came over him as a spirit voice, and, as in a sort of judgment vision, his whole past life rose in a moment before his eyes: his mother's prayers and hymns; his own early yearnings and aspirings for good; and, between them and this hour, years of worldliness and scepticism, and what man calls respectable living. We can think *much*, very much, in a mo-ment. St. Clare saw and felt many things, but spoke nothing; and, as it grew darker, he took his child to her bed-room; and, when she was prepared for rest, he sent away the atten-dants, and rocked her in his arms, and sung to her till she was asleep.

XXV.

The Little Evangelist

IT was Sunday afternoon. St. Clare was stretched on a bamboo lounge in the verandah, solacing himself with a cigar. Marie lay reclined on a sofa, opposite the window opening on the verandah, closely secluded, under an awning of transparent gauze, from the outrages of the mosquitos, and languidly holding in her hand an elegantly bound prayer-book. She was holding it because it was Sunday, and she imagined she had been reading it,—though, in fact, she had been only taking a succession of short naps, with it open in her hand.

Miss Ophelia, who, after some rummaging, had hunted up a small Methodist meeting within riding distance, had gone out, with Tom as driver, to attend it; and Eva had accompanied them.

"I say, Augustine," said Marie after dozing a while, "I must send to the city after my old Doctor Posey; I'm sure I've got the complaint of the heart."

"Well; why need you send for him? This doctor that attends Eva seems skilful."

"I would not trust him in a critical case," said Marie; "and I think I may say mine is becoming so! I've been thinking of it, these two or three nights past; I have such distressing pains, and such strange feelings."

"O, Marie, you are blue; I don't believe it's heart complaint."

"I dare say *you* don't," said Marie; "I was prepared to expect *that*. You can be alarmed enough, if Eva coughs, or has the least thing the matter with her; but you never think of me."

"If it's particularly agreeable to you to have heart disease, why, I'll try and maintain you have it," said St. Clare; "I didn't know it was."

"Well, I only hope you won't be sorry for this, when it's too late!" said Marie; "but, believe it or not, my distress about Eva, and the exertions I have made with that dear child, have developed what I have long suspected."

What the *exertions* were which Marie referred to, it would have been difficult to state. St. Clare quietly made this commentary to himself, and went on smoking, like a hard-hearted wretch of a man as he was, till a carriage drove up before the verandah, and Eva and Miss Ophelia alighted.

Miss Ophelia marched straight to her own chamber, to put away her bonnet and shawl, as was always her manner, before she spoke a word on any subject; while Eva came, at St. Clare's call, and was sitting on his knee, giving him an account of the services they had heard.

They soon heard loud exclamations from Miss Ophelia's room, which, like the one in which they were sitting, opened on to the verandah, and violent reproof addressed to somebody.

"What new witchcraft has Tops been brewing?" asked St. Clare. "That commotion is of her raising, I 'll be bound!"

And, in a moment after, Miss Ophelia, in high indignation, came dragging the culprit along.

"Come out here, now!" she said. "I *will* tell your master!"

"What 's the case now?" asked Augustine.

"The case is, that I cannot be plagued with this child, any longer! It 's past all bearing; flesh and blood cannot endure it! Here, I locked her up, and gave her a hymn to study; and what does she do, but spy out where I put my key, and has gone to my bureau, and got a bonnet-trimming, and cut it all to pieces, to make dolls' jackets! I never saw anything like it, in my life!"

"I told you, Cousin," said Marie, "that you 'd find out that these creatures can't be brought up, without severity. If I had *my* way, now," she said, looking reproachfully at St. Clare, "I 'd send that child out, and have her thoroughly whipped; I 'd have her whipped till she could n't stand!"

"I don't doubt it," said St. Clare. "Tell me of the lovely rule of woman! I never saw above a dozen women that would n't half kill a horse, or a servant, either, if they had their own way with them!—let alone a man."

"There is no use in this shilly-shally way of yours, St.

Clare!" said Marie. "Cousin is a woman of sense, and she sees it now, as plain as I do."

Miss Ophelia had just the capability of indignation that belongs to the thorough-paced housekeeper, and this had been pretty actively roused by the artifice and wastefulness of the child; in fact, many of my lady readers must own that they should have felt just so in her circumstances; but Marie's words went beyond her, and she felt less heat.

"I would n't have the child treated so, for the world," she said; "but, I am sure, Augustine, I don't know what to do. I 've taught and taught; I 've talked till I 'm tired; I 've whipped her; I 've punished her in every way I can think of, and still she 's just what she was at first."

"Come here, Tops, you monkey!" said St. Clare, calling the child up to him.

Topsy came up; her round, hard eyes glittering and blinking with a mixture of apprehensiveness and their usual odd drollery.

"What makes you behave so?" said St. Clare, who could not help being amused with the child's expression.

"Spects it 's my wicked heart," said Topsy, demurely; "Miss Feely says so."

"Don't you see how much Miss Ophelia has done for you? She says she has done everything she can think of."

"Lor, yes, Mas'r! old Missis used to say so, too. She whipped me a heap harder, and used to pull my har, and knock my head agin the door; but it did n't do me no good! I spects, if they 's to pull every spire o' har out o' my head, it would n't do no good, neither,—I 's so wicked! Laws! I 's nothin but a nigger, no ways!"

"Well, I shall have to give her up," said Miss Ophelia; "I can't have that trouble any longer."

"Well, I 'd just like to ask one question," said St. Clare.

"What is it?"

"Why, if your Gospel is not strong enough to save one heathen child, that you can have at home here, all to yourself, what 's the use of sending one or two poor missionaries off with it among thousands of just such? I suppose this child is about a fair sample of what thousands of your heathen are."

Miss Ophelia did not make an immediate answer; and Eva, who had stood a silent spectator of the scene thus far, made a silent sign to Topsy to follow her. There was a little glass-room at the corner of the verandah, which St. Clare used as a sort of reading-room; and Eva and Topsy disappeared into this place.

"What's Eva going about, now?" said St. Clare; "I mean to see."

And, advancing on tiptoe, he lifted up a curtain that covered the glass-door, and looked in. In a moment, laying his finger on his lips, he made a silent gesture to Miss Ophelia to come and look. There sat the two children on the floor, with their side faces towards them. Topsy, with her usual air of careless drollery and unconcern; but, opposite to her, Eva, her whole face fervent with feeling, and tears in her large eyes.

"What does make you so bad, Topsy? Why won't you try and be good? Don't you love *anybody,* Topsy?"

"Donno nothing 'bout love; I loves candy and sich, that's all," said Topsy.

"But you love your father and mother?"

"Never had none, ye know. I telled ye that, Miss Eva."

"O, I know," said Eva, sadly; "but had n't you any brother, or sister, or aunt, or—"

"No, none on 'em,—never had nothing nor nobody."

"But, Topsy, if you'd only try to be good, you might—"

"Could n't never be nothin' but a nigger, if I was ever so good," said Topsy. "If I could be skinned, and come white, I'd try then."

"But people can love you, if you are black, Topsy. Miss Ophelia would love you, if you were good."

Topsy gave the short, blunt laugh that was her common mode of expressing incredulity.

"Don't you think so?" said Eva.

"No; she can't bar me, 'cause I'm a nigger!—she'd's soon have a toad touch her! There can't nobody love niggers, and niggers can't do nothin'! *I* don't care," said Topsy, beginning to whistle.

"O, Topsy, poor child, *I* love you!" said Eva, with a sudden burst of feeling, and laying her little thin, white hand on Topsy's shoulder; "I love you, because you have n't had any father, or mother, or friends;—because you 've been a poor, abused child! I love you, and I want you to be good. I am very unwell, Topsy, and I think I shan't live a great while; and it really grieves me, to have you be so naughty. I wish you would try to be good, for my sake;—it 's only a little while I shall be with you."

The round, keen eyes of the black child were overcast with tears;—large, bright drops rolled heavily down, one by one, and fell on the little white hand. Yes, in that moment, a ray of real belief, a ray of heavenly love, had penetrated the darkness of her heathen soul! She laid her head down between her knees, and wept and sobbed,—while the beautiful child, bending over her, looked like the picture of some bright angel stooping to reclaim a sinner.

"Poor Topsy!" said Eva, "don't you know that Jesus loves all alike? He is just as willing to love you, as me. He loves you just as I do,—only more, because he is better. He will help you to be good; and you can go to Heaven at last, and be an angel forever, just as much as if you were white. Only think of it, Topsy!—*you* can be one of those spirits bright, Uncle Tom sings about."

"O, dear Miss Eva, dear Miss Eva!" said the child; "I will try, I will try; I never did care nothin' about it before."

St. Clare, at this instant, dropped the curtain. "It puts me in mind of mother," he said to Miss Ophelia. "It is true what she told me; if we want to give sight to the blind, we must be willing to do as Christ did,—call them to us, and *put our hands on them*."

"I 've always had a prejudice against negroes," said Miss Ophelia, "and it 's a fact, I never could bear to have that child touch me; but, I don't think she knew it."

"Trust any child to find that out," said St. Clare; "there 's no keeping it from them. But I believe that all the trying in the world to benefit a child, and all the substantial favors you can do them, will never excite one emotion of gratitude, while that feeling of repugnance remains in the heart;—it 's a queer kind of a fact,—but so it is."

"I don't know how I can help it," said Miss Ophelia; "they *are* disagreeable to me,—this child in particular,—how can I help feeling so?"

"Eva does, it seems."

"Well, she's so loving! After all, though, she's no more than Christ-like," said Miss Ophelia; "I wish I were like her. She might teach me a lesson."

"It wouldn't be the first time a little child had been used to instruct an old disciple, if it *were* so," said St. Clare.

XXVI.

Death

Weep not for those whom the veil of the tomb,
In life's early morning, hath hid from our eyes.

E VA'S bed-room was a spacious apartment, which, like all
the other rooms in the house, opened on to the broad
verandah. The room communicated, on one side, with her
father and mother's apartment; on the other, with that appropriated to Miss Ophelia. St. Clare had gratified his own
eye and taste, in furnishing this room in a style that had a
peculiar keeping with the character of her for whom it was
intended. The windows were hung with curtains of rose-
colored and white muslin, the floor was spread with a mat-
ting which had been ordered in Paris, to a pattern of his
own device, having round it a border of rose-buds and
leaves, and a centre-piece with full-blown roses. The bedstead, chairs, and lounges, were of bamboo, wrought in peculiarly graceful and fanciful patterns. Over the head of the
bed was an alabaster bracket, on which a beautiful sculptured angel stood, with drooping wings, holding out a
crown of myrtle-leaves. From this depended, over the bed,
light curtains of rose-colored gauze, striped with silver, supplying that protection from mosquitos which is an indispensable addition to all sleeping accommodation in that climate. The graceful bamboo lounges were amply supplied
with cushions of rose-colored damask, while over them, de-
pending from the hands of sculptured figures, were gauze curtains similar to those of the bed. A light, fanciful bamboo
table stood in the middle of the room, where a Parian vase,
wrought in the shape of a white lily, with its buds, stood,
ever filled with flowers. On this table lay Eva's books and
little trinkets, with an elegantly wrought alabaster writing-
stand, which her father had supplied to her when he saw her
trying to improve herself in writing. There was a fireplace in

the room, and on the marble mantle above stood a beautifully
wrought statuette of Jesus receiving little children, and on either side marble vases, for which it was Tom's pride and delight to offer bouquets every morning. Two or three exquisite
paintings of children, in various attitudes, embellished the
wall. In short, the eye could turn nowhere without meeting
images of childhood, of beauty, and of peace. Those little eyes
never opened, in the morning light, without falling on something which suggested to the heart soothing and beautiful
thoughts.

The deceitful strength which had buoyed Eva up for a little
while was fast passing away; seldom and more seldom her
light footstep was heard in the verandah, and oftener and oftener she was found reclined on a little lounge by the open
window, her large, deep eyes fixed on the rising and falling
waters of the lake.

It was towards the middle of the afternoon, as she was so
reclining,—her Bible half open, her little transparent fingers
lying listlessly between the leaves,—suddenly she heard her
mother's voice, in sharp tones, in the verandah.

"What now, you baggage!—what new piece of mischief!
You've been picking the flowers, hey?" and Eva heard the
sound of a smart slap.

"Law, Missis!—they's for Miss Eva," she heard a voice
say, which she knew belonged to Topsy.

"Miss Eva! A pretty excuse!—you suppose she wants *your*
flowers, you good-for-nothing nigger! Get along off with
you!"

In a moment, Eva was off from her lounge, and in the
verandah.

"O, don't, mother! I should like the flowers; do give them
to me; I want them!"

"Why, Eva, your room is full now."

"I can't have too many," said Eva. "Topsy, do bring them
here."

Topsy, who had stood sullenly, holding down her head,
now came up and offered her flowers. She did it with a look
of hesitation and bashfulness, quite unlike the eldrich boldness and brightness which was usual with her.

"It's a beautiful bouquet!" said Eva, looking at it.

It was rather a singular one,—a brilliant scarlet geranium, and one single white japonica, with its glossy leaves. It was tied up with an evident eye to the contrast of color, and the arrangement of every leaf had carefully been studied.

Topsy looked pleased, as Eva said,—"Topsy, you arrange flowers very prettily. Here," she said, "is this vase I have n't any flowers for. I wish you 'd arrange something every day for it."

"Well, that 's odd!" said Marie. "What in the world do you want that for?"

"Never mind, mamma; you 'd as lief as not Topsy should do it,—had you not?"

"Of course, anything you please, dear! Topsy, you hear your young mistress;—see that you mind."

Topsy made a short courtesy, and looked down; and, as she turned away, Eva saw a tear roll down her dark cheek.

"You see, mamma, I knew poor Topsy wanted to do something for me," said Eva to her mother.

"O, nonsense! it 's only because she likes to do mischief. She knows she must n't pick flowers,—so she does it; that 's all there is to it. But, if you fancy to have her pluck them, so be it."

"Mamma, I think Topsy is different from what she used to be; she 's trying to be a good girl."

"She 'll have to try a good while before *she* gets to be good," said Marie, with a careless laugh.

"Well, you know, mamma, poor Topsy! everything has always been against her."

"Not since she 's been here, I 'm sure. If she has n't been talked to, and preached to, and every earthly thing done that anybody could do;—and she 's just so ugly, and always will be; you can't make anything of the creature!"

"But, mamma, it 's so different to be brought up as I 've been, with so many friends, so many things to make me good and happy; and to be brought up as she 's been, all the time, till she came here!"

"Most likely," said Marie, yawning,—"dear me, how hot it is!"

"Mamma, you believe, don't you, that Topsy could become an angel, as well as any of us, if she were a Christian?"

"Topsy! what a ridiculous idea! Nobody but you would ever think of it. I suppose she could, though."

"But, mamma, is n't God her father, as much as ours? Is n't Jesus her Saviour?"

"Well, that may be. I suppose God made everybody," said Marie. "Where is my smelling-bottle?"

"It 's such a pity,—oh! *such* a pity!" said Eva, looking out on the distant lake, and speaking half to herself.

"What 's a pity?" said Marie.

"Why, that any one, who could be a bright angel, and live with angels, should go all down, down, down, and nobody help them!—oh, dear!"

"Well, we can't help it; it 's no use worrying, Eva! I don't know what 's to be done; we ought to be thankful for our own advantages."

"I hardly can be," said Eva, "I 'm so sorry to think of poor folks that have n't any."

"That 's odd enough," said Marie;—"I 'm sure my religion makes me thankful for my advantages."

"Mamma," said Eva, "I want to have some of my hair cut off,—a good deal of it."

"What for?" said Marie.

"Mamma, I want to give some away to my friends, while I am able to give it to them myself. Won't you ask aunty to come and cut it for me?"

Marie raised her voice, and called Miss Ophelia, from the other room.

The child half rose from her pillow as she came in, and, shaking down her long golden-brown curls, said, rather playfully, "Come, aunty, shear the sheep!"

"What 's that?" said St. Clare, who just then entered with some fruit he had been out to get for her.

"Papa, I just want aunty to cut off some of my hair;—there 's too much of it, and it makes my head hot. Besides, I want to give some of it away."

Miss Ophelia came, with her scissors.

"Take care,—don't spoil the looks of it!" said her father; "cut underneath, where it won't show. Eva's curls are my pride."

"O, papa!" said Eva, sadly.

"Yes, and I want them kept handsome against the time I take you up to your uncle's plantation, to see Cousin Henrique," said St. Clare, in a gay tone.

"I shall never go there, papa;—I am going to a better country. O, do believe me! Don't you see, papa, that I get weaker, every day?"

"Why do you insist that I shall believe such a cruel thing, Eva?" said her father.

"Only because it is *true*, papa: and, if you will believe it now, perhaps you will get to feel about it as I do."

St. Clare closed his lips, and stood gloomily eying the long, beautiful curls, which, as they were separated from the child's head, were laid, one by one, in her lap. She raised them up, looked earnestly at them, twined them around her thin fingers, and looked, from time to time, anxiously at her father.

"It 's just what I 've been foreboding!" said Marie; "it 's just what has been preying on my health, from day to day, bringing me downward to the grave, though nobody regards it. I have seen this, long. St. Clare, you will see, after a while, that I was right."

"Which will afford you great consolation, no doubt!" said St. Clare, in a dry, bitter tone.

Marie lay back on a lounge, and covered her face with her cambric handkerchief.

Eva's clear blue eye looked earnestly from one to the other. It was the calm, comprehending gaze of a soul half loosed from its earthly bonds; it was evident she saw, felt, and appreciated, the difference between the two.

She beckoned with her hand to her father. He came, and sat down by her.

"Papa, my strength fades away every day, and I know I must go. There are some things I want to say and do,—that I ought to do; and you are so unwilling to have me speak a word on this subject. But it must come; there 's no putting it off. Do be willing I should speak now!"

"My child, I *am* willing!" said St. Clare, covering his eyes with one hand, and holding up Eva's hand with the other.

"Then, I want to see all our people together. I have some things I *must* say to them," said Eva.

"*Well*," said St. Clare, in a tone of dry endurance.

Miss Ophelia despatched a messenger, and soon the whole of the servants were convened in the room.

Eva lay back on her pillows; her hair hanging loosely about her face, her crimson cheeks contrasting painfully with the intense whiteness of her complexion and the thin contour of her limbs and features, and her large, soul-like eyes fixed earnestly on every one.

The servants were struck with a sudden emotion. The spiritual face, the long locks of hair cut off and lying by her, her father's averted face, and Marie's sobs, struck at once upon the feelings of a sensitive and impressible race; and, as they came in, they looked one on another, sighed, and shook their heads. There was a deep silence, like that of a funeral.

Eva raised herself, and looked long and earnestly round at every one. All looked sad and apprehensive. Many of the women hid their faces in their aprons.

"I sent for you all, my dear friends," said Eva, "because I love you. I love you all; and I have something to say to you, which I want you always to remember. . . . . . I am going to leave you. In a few more weeks, you will see me no more—"

Here the child was interrupted by bursts of groans, sobs, and lamentations, which broke from all present, and in which her slender voice was lost entirely. She waited a moment, and then, speaking in a tone that checked the sobs of all, she said,

"If you love me, you must not interrupt me so. Listen to what I say. I want to speak to you about your souls. . . . . . Many of you, I am afraid, are very careless. You are thinking only about this world. I want you to remember that there is a beautiful world, where Jesus is. I am going there, and you can go there. It is for you, as much as me. But, if you want to go there, you must not live idle, careless, thoughtless lives. You must be Christians. You must remember that each one of you can become angels, and be angels forever. . . . . If you want to be Christians, Jesus will help you. You must pray to him; you must read—"

The child checked herself, looked piteously at them, and said, sorrowfully,

"O, dear! you *can't* read,—poor souls!" and she hid her face in the pillow and sobbed, while many a smothered sob from those she was addressing, who were kneeling on the floor, aroused her.

"Never mind," she said, raising her face and smiling brightly through her tears, "I have prayed for you; and I know Jesus will help you, even if you can't read. Try all to do the best you can; pray every day; ask Him to help you, and get the Bible read to you whenever you can; and I think I shall see you all in heaven."

"Amen," was the murmured response from the lips of Tom and Mammy, and some of the elder ones, who belonged to the Methodist church. The younger and more thoughtless ones, for the time completely overcome, were sobbing, with their heads bowed upon their knees.

"I know," said Eva, "you all love me."

"Yes; oh, yes! indeed we do! Lord bless her!" was the involuntary answer of all.

"Yes, I know you do! There is n't one of you that has n't always been very kind to me; and I want to give you something that, when you look at, you shall always remember me. I 'm going to give all of you a curl of my hair; and, when you look at it, think that I loved you and am gone to heaven, and that I want to see you all there."

It is impossible to describe the scene, as, with tears and sobs, they gathered round the little creature, and took from her hands what seemed to them a last mark of her love. They fell on their knees; they sobbed, and prayed, and kissed the hem of her garment; and the elder ones poured forth words of endearment, mingled in prayers and blessings, after the manner of their susceptible race.

As each one took their gift, Miss Ophelia, who was apprehensive for the effect of all this excitement on her little patient, signed to each one to pass out of the apartment.

At last, all were gone but Tom and Mammy.

"Here, Uncle Tom," said Eva, "is a beautiful one for you. O, I am so happy, Uncle Tom, to think I shall see you in heaven,—for I 'm sure I shall; and Mammy,—dear, good, kind Mammy!" she said, fondly throwing her arms round her old nurse,—"I know you 'll be there, too."

"O, Miss Eva, don't see how I can live without ye, no how!" said the faithful creature. " 'Pears like it 's just taking everything off the place to oncet!" and Mammy gave way to a passion of grief.

Miss Ophelia pushed her and Tom gently from the apartment, and thought they were all gone; but, as she turned, Topsy was standing there.

"Where did you start up from?" she said, suddenly.

"I was here," said Topsy, wiping the tears from her eyes. "O, Miss Eva, I 've been a bad girl; but won't you give *me* one, too?"

"Yes, poor Topsy! to be sure, I will. There—every time you look at that, think that I love you, and wanted you to be a good girl!"

"O, Miss Eva, I *is* tryin!" said Topsy, earnestly; "but, Lor, it 's so hard to be good! 'Pears like I an't used to it, no ways!"

"Jesus knows it, Topsy; he is sorry for you; he will help you."

Topsy, with her eyes hid in her apron, was silently passed from the apartment by Miss Ophelia; but, as she went, she hid the precious curl in her bosom.

All being gone, Miss Ophelia shut the door. That worthy lady had wiped away many tears of her own, during the scene; but concern for the consequence of such an excitement to her young charge was uppermost in her mind.

St. Clare had been sitting, during the whole time, with his hand shading his eyes, in the same attitude. When they were all gone, he sat so still.

"Papa!" said Eva, gently, laying her hand on his.

He gave a sudden start and shiver; but made no answer.

"Dear papa!" said Eva.

"I *cannot*," said St. Clare, rising, "I *cannot* have it so! The Almighty hath dealt *very bitterly* with me!" and St. Clare pronounced these words with a bitter emphasis, indeed.

"Augustine! has not God a right to do what he will with his own?" said Miss Ophelia.

"Perhaps so; but that does n't make it any easier to bear," said he, with a dry, hard, tearless manner, as he turned away.

"Papa, you break my heart!" said Eva, rising and throwing herself into his arms; "you must not feel so!" and the child sobbed and wept with a violence which alarmed them all, and turned her father's thoughts at once to another channel.

"There, Eva,—there, dearest! Hush! hush! I was wrong; I was wicked. I will feel any way, do any way,—only don't distress yourself; don't sob so. I will be resigned; I was wicked to speak as I did."

Eva soon lay like a wearied dove in her father's arms; and he, bending over her, soothed her by every tender word he could think of.

Marie rose and threw herself out of the apartment into her own, when she fell into violent hysterics.

"You did n't give me a curl, Eva," said her father, smiling sadly.

"They are all yours, papa," said she, smiling,—"yours and mamma's; and you must give dear aunty as many as she wants. I only gave them to our poor people myself, because you know, papa, they might be forgotten when I am gone, and because I hoped it might help them remember. . . . . You are a Christian, are you not, papa?" said Eva, doubtfully.

"Why do you ask me?"

"I don't know. You are so good, I don't see how you can help it."

"What is being a Christian, Eva?"

"Loving Christ most of all," said Eva.

"Do you, Eva?"

"Certainly I do."

"You never saw him," said St. Clare.

"That makes no difference," said Eva. "I believe him, and in a few days I shall *see* him;" and the young face grew fervent, radiant with joy.

St. Clare said no more. It was a feeling which he had seen before in his mother; but no chord within vibrated to it.

Eva, after this, declined rapidly; there was no more any doubt of the event; the fondest hope could not be blinded. Her beautiful room was avowedly a sick room; and Miss Ophelia day and night performed the duties of a nurse,—and never did her friends appreciate her value more than in that capacity. With so well-trained a hand and eye, such perfect adroitness and practice in every art which could promote neatness and comfort, and keep out of sight every disagreeable incident of sickness,—with such a perfect sense of time, such a clear, untroubled head, such exact ac-

curacy in remembering every prescription and direction of
the doctors,—she was everything to him. They who had
shrugged their shoulders at her little peculiarities and set-
nesses, so unlike the careless freedom of southern manners,
acknowledged that now she was the exact person that was
wanted.

Uncle Tom was much in Eva's room. The child suffered
much from nervous restlessness, and it was a relief to her to
be carried; and it was Tom's greatest delight to carry her little
frail form in his arms, resting on a pillow, now up and down
her room, now out into the verandah; and when the fresh
sea-breezes blew from the lake,—and the child felt freshest in
the morning,—he would sometimes walk with her under the
orange-trees in the garden, or, sitting down in some of their
old seats, sing to her their favorite old hymns.

Her father often did the same thing; but his frame was
slighter, and when he was weary, Eva would say to him,

"O, papa, let Tom take me. Poor fellow! it pleases him;
and you know it's all he can do now, and he wants to do
something!"

"So do I, Eva!" said her father.

"Well, papa, you can do everything, and are everything to
me. You read to me,—you sit up nights,—and Tom has only
this one thing, and his singing; and I know, too, he does it
easier than you can. He carries me so strong!"

The desire to do something was not confined to Tom.
Every servant in the establishment showed the same feeling,
and in their way did what they could.

Poor Mammy's heart yearned towards her darling; but she
found no opportunity, night or day, as Marie declared that
the state of her mind was such, it was impossible for her to
rest; and, of course, it was against her principles to let any
one else rest. Twenty times in a night, Mammy would be
roused to rub her feet, to bathe her head, to find her pocket-
handkerchief, to see what the noise was in Eva's room, to let
down a curtain because it was too light, or to put it up because it was too dark; and, in the day-time, when she longed
to have some share in the nursing of her pet, Marie seemed
unusually ingenious in keeping her busy anywhere and everywhere all over the house, or about her own person; so that

stolen interviews and momentary glimpses were all she could obtain.

"I feel it my duty to be particularly careful of myself, now," she would say, "feeble as I am, and with the whole care and nursing of that dear child upon me."

"Indeed, my dear," said St. Clare, "I thought our cousin relieved you of that."

"You talk like a man, St. Clare,—just as if a mother *could* be relieved of the care of a child in that state; but, then, it's all alike,—no one ever knows what I feel! I can't throw things off, as you do."

St. Clare smiled. You must excuse him, he couldn't help it,—for St. Clare could smile yet. For so bright and placid was the farewell voyage of the little spirit,—by such sweet and fragrant breezes was the small bark borne towards the heavenly shores,—that it was impossible to realize that it was death that was approaching. The child felt no pain,—only a tranquil, soft weakness, daily and almost insensibly increasing; and she was so beautiful, so loving, so trustful, so happy, that one could not resist the soothing influence of that air of innocence and peace which seemed to breathe around her. St. Clare found a strange calm coming over him. It was not hope,—that was impossible; it was not resignation; it was only a calm resting in the present, which seemed so beautiful that he wished to think of no future. It was like that hush of spirit which we feel amid the bright, mild woods of autumn, when the bright hectic flush is on the trees, and the last lingering flowers by the brook; and we joy in it all the more, because we know that soon it will all pass away.

The friend who knew most of Eva's own imaginings and foreshadowings was her faithful bearer, Tom. To him she said what she would not disturb her father by saying. To him she imparted those mysterious intimations which the soul feels, as the cords begin to unbind, ere it leaves its clay forever.

Tom, at last, would not sleep in his room, but lay all night in the outer verandah, ready to rouse at every call.

"Uncle Tom, what alive have you taken to sleeping anywhere and everywhere, like a dog, for?" said Miss Ophelia. "I thought you was one of the orderly sort, that liked to lie in bed in a Christian way."

"I do, Miss Feely," said Tom, mysteriously. "I do, but now—"

"Well, what now?"

"We must n't speak loud; Mas'r St. Clare won't hear on 't; but Miss Feely, you know there must be somebody watchin' for the bridegroom."

"What do you mean, Tom?"

"You know it says in Scripture, 'At midnight there was a great cry made. Behold, the bridegroom cometh.' That 's what I 'm spectin now, every night, Miss Feely,—and I could n't sleep out o' hearin, no ways."

"Why, Uncle Tom, what makes you think so?"

"Miss Eva, she talks to me. The Lord, he sends his messenger in the soul. I must be thar, Miss Feely; for when that ar blessed child goes into the kingdom, they 'll open the door so wide, we 'll all get a look in at the glory, Miss Feely."

"Uncle Tom, did Miss Eva say she felt more unwell than usual to-night?"

"No; but she told me, this morning, she was coming nearer,—thar 's them that tells it to the child, Miss Feely. It 's the angels,—'it 's the trumpet sound afore the break o' day,'" said Tom, quoting from a favorite hymn.

This dialogue passed between Miss Ophelia and Tom, between ten and eleven, one evening, after her arrangements had all been made for the night, when, on going to bolt her outer door, she found Tom stretched along by it, in the outer verandah.

She was not nervous or impressible; but the solemn, heartfelt manner struck her. Eva had been unusually bright and cheerful, that afternoon, and had sat raised in her bed, and looked over all her little trinkets and precious things, and designated the friends to whom she would have them given; and her manner was more animated, and her voice more natural, than they had known it for weeks. Her father had been in, in the evening, and had said that Eva appeared more like her former self than ever she had done since her sickness; and when he kissed her for the night, he said to Miss Ophelia,— "Cousin, we may keep her with us, after all; she is certainly better;" and he had retired with a lighter heart in his bosom than he had had there for weeks.

But at midnight,—strange, mystic hour!—when the veil between the frail present and the eternal future grows thin,—then came the messenger!

There was a sound in that chamber, first of one who stepped quickly. It was Miss Ophelia, who had resolved to sit up all night with her little charge, and who, at the turn of the night, had discerned what experienced nurses significantly call "a change." The outer door was quickly opened, and Tom, who was watching outside, was on the alert, in a moment.

"Go for the doctor, Tom! lose not a moment," said Miss Ophelia; and, stepping across the room, she rapped at St. Clare's door.

"Cousin," she said, "I wish you would come."

Those words fell on his heart like clods upon a coffin. Why did they? He was up and in the room in an instant, and bending over Eva, who still slept.

What was it he saw that made his heart stand still? Why was no word spoken between the two? Thou canst say, who hast seen that same expression on the face dearest to thee;— that look indescribable, hopeless, unmistakable, that says to thee that thy beloved is no longer thine.

On the face of the child, however, there was no ghastly imprint,—only a high and almost sublime expression,—the overshadowing presence of spiritual natures, the dawning of immortal life in that childish soul.

They stood there so still, gazing upon her, that even the ticking of the watch seemed too loud. In a few moments, Tom returned, with the doctor. He entered, gave one look, and stood silent as the rest.

"When did this change take place?" said he, in a low whisper, to Miss Ophelia.

"About the turn of the night," was the reply.

Marie, roused by the entrance of the doctor, appeared, hurriedly, from the next room.

"Augustine! Cousin!—O!—what!" she hurriedly began.

"Hush!" said St. Clare, hoarsely; *"she is dying!"*

Mammy heard the words, and flew to awaken the servants. The house was soon roused,—lights were seen, footsteps heard, anxious faces thronged the verandah, and looked tearfully through the glass doors; but St. Clare heard and said nothing,

—he saw only *that look* on the face of the little sleeper.

"O, if she would only wake, and speak once more!" he said; and, stooping over her, he spoke in her ear,—"Eva, darling!"

The large blue eyes unclosed,—a smile passed over her face;—she tried to raise her head, and to speak.

"Do you know me, Eva?"

"Dear papa," said the child, with a last effort, throwing her arms about his neck. In a moment they dropped again; and, as St. Clare raised his head, he saw a spasm of mortal agony pass over the face,—she struggled for breath, and threw up her little hands.

"O, God, this is dreadful!" he said, turning away in agony, and wringing Tom's hand, scarce conscious what he was doing. "O, Tom, my boy, it is killing me!"

Tom had his master's hands between his own; and, with tears streaming down his dark cheeks, looked up for help where he had always been used to look.

"Pray that this may be cut short!" said St. Clare,—"this wrings my heart."

"O, bless the Lord! it's over,—it's over, dear Master!" said Tom; "look at her."

The child lay panting on her pillows, as one exhausted,— the large clear eyes rolled up and fixed. Ah, what said those eyes, that spoke so much of heaven? Earth was past, and earthly pain; but so solemn, so mysterious, was the triumphant brightness of that face, that it checked even the sobs of sorrow. They pressed around her, in breathless stillness.

"Eva," said St. Clare, gently.

She did not hear.

"O, Eva, tell us what you see! What is it?" said her father.

A bright, a glorious smile passed over her face, and she said, brokenly,—"O! love,—joy,—peace!" gave one sigh, and passed from death unto life!

"Farewell, beloved child! the bright, eternal doors have closed after thee; we shall see thy sweet face no more. O, woe for them who watched thy entrance into heaven, when they shall wake and find only the cold gray sky of daily life, and thou gone forever!"

XXVII.

"This is the Last of Earth."
—*John Q. Adams*

THE statuettes and pictures in Eva's room were shrouded in white napkins, and only hushed breathings and muffled foot-falls were heard there, and the light stole in solemnly through windows partially darkened by closed blinds.

The bed was draped in white; and there, beneath the drooping angel-figure, lay a little sleeping form,—sleeping never to waken!

There she lay, robed in one of the simple white dresses she had been wont to wear when living; the rose-colored light through the curtains cast over the icy coldness of death a warm glow. The heavy eyelashes drooped softly on the pure cheek; the head was turned a little to one side, as if in natural sleep, but there was diffused over every lineament of the face that high celestial expression, that mingling of rapture and repose, which showed it was no earthly or temporary sleep, but the long, sacred rest which "He giveth to his beloved."

There is no death to such as thou, dear Eva! neither darkness nor shadow of death; only such a bright fading as when the morning star fades in the golden dawn. Thine is the victory without the battle,—the crown without the conflict.

So did St. Clare think, as, with folded arms, he stood there gazing. Ah! who shall say what he did think? for, from the hour that voices had said, in the dying chamber, "she is gone," it had been all a dreary mist, a heavy "dimness of anguish." He had heard voices around him; he had had questions asked, and answered them; they had asked him when he would have the funeral, and where they should lay her; and he had answered, impatiently, that he cared not.

Adolph and Rosa had arranged the chamber; volatile, fickle and childish, as they generally were, they were soft-hearted and full of feeling; and, while Miss Ophelia presided over the general details of order and neatness, it was their hands that added those soft, poetic touches to the arrangements, that

347

took from the death-room the grim and ghastly air which too often marks a New England funeral.

There were still flowers on the shelves,—all white, delicate and fragrant, with graceful, drooping leaves. Eva's little table, covered with white, bore on it her favorite vase, with a single white moss rose-bud in it. The folds of the drapery, the fall of the curtains, had been arranged and rearranged, by Adolph and Rosa, with that nicety of eye which characterizes their race. Even now, while St. Clare stood there thinking, little Rosa tripped softly into the chamber with a basket of white flowers. She stepped back when she saw St. Clare, and stopped respectfully; but, seeing that he did not observe her, she came forward to place them around the dead. St. Clare saw her as in a dream, while she placed in the small hands a fair cape jessamine, and, with admirable taste, disposed other flowers around the couch.

The door opened again, and Topsy, her eyes swelled with crying, appeared, holding something under her apron. Rosa made a quick, forbidding gesture; but she took a step into the room.

"You must go out," said Rosa, in a sharp, positive whisper; "*you* have n't any business here!"

"O, do let me! I brought a flower,—such a pretty one!" said Topsy, holding up a half-blown tea rose-bud. "Do let me put just one there."

"Get along!" said Rosa, more decidedly.

"Let her stay!" said St. Clare, suddenly stamping his foot. "She shall come."

Rosa suddenly retreated, and Topsy came forward and laid her offering at the feet of the corpse; then suddenly, with a wild and bitter cry, she threw herself on the floor alongside the bed, and wept, and moaned aloud.

Miss Ophelia hastened into the room, and tried to raise and silence her; but in vain.

"O, Miss Eva! oh, Miss Eva! I wish I 's dead, too,—I do!"

There was a piercing wildness in the cry; the blood flushed into St. Clare's white, marble-like face, and the first tears he had shed since Eva died stood in his eyes.

"Get up, child," said Miss Ophelia, in a softened voice; "don't cry so. Miss Eva is gone to heaven; she is an angel."

"But I can't see her!" said Topsy. "I never shall see her!" and she sobbed again.

They all stood a moment in silence.

"*She* said she *loved* me," said Topsy,—"she did! O, dear! oh, dear! there an't *nobody* left now,—there an't!"

"That 's true enough," said St. Clare; "but do," he said to Miss Ophelia, "see if you can't comfort the poor creature."

"I jist wish I had n't never been born," said Topsy. "I did n't want to be born, no ways; and I don't see no use on 't."

Miss Ophelia raised her gently, but firmly, and took her from the room; but, as she did so, some tears fell from her eyes.

"Topsy, you poor child," she said, as she led her into her room, "don't give up! *I* can love you, though I am not like that dear little child. I hope I 've learnt something of the love of Christ from her. I can love you; I do, and I 'll try to help you to grow up a good Christian girl."

Miss Ophelia's voice was more than her words, and more than that were the honest tears that fell down her face. From that hour, she acquired an influence over the mind of the destitute child that she never lost.

"O, my Eva, whose little hour on earth did so much of good," thought St. Clare, "what account have I to give for my long years?"

There were, for a while, soft whisperings and foot-falls in the chamber, as one after another stole in, to look at the dead; and then came the little coffin; and then there was a funeral, and carriages drove to the door, and strangers came and were seated; and there were white scarfs and ribbons, and crape bands, and mourners dressed in black crape; and there were words read from the Bible, and prayers offered; and St. Clare lived, and walked, and moved, as one who has shed every tear;—to the last he saw only one thing, that golden head in the coffin; but then he saw the cloth spread over it, the lid of the coffin closed; and he walked, when he was put beside the others, down to a little place at the bottom of the garden, and there, by the mossy seat where she and Tom had talked, and sung, and read so often, was the little grave. St. Clare stood beside it,—looked vacantly down; he saw them lower the lit-

tle coffin; he heard, dimly, the solemn words, "I am the resurrection and the Life; he that believeth in me, though he
were dead, yet shall he live;" and, as the earth was cast in and
filled up the little grave, he could not realize that it was his
Eva that they were hiding from his sight.

Nor was it!—not Eva, but only the frail seed of that
bright, immortal form with which she shall yet come forth, in
the day of the Lord Jesus!

And then all were gone, and the mourners went back to
the place which should know her no more; and Marie's room
was darkened, and she lay on the bed, sobbing and moaning
in uncontrollable grief, and calling every moment for the attentions of all her servants. Of course, they had no time to
cry,—why should they? the grief was *her* grief, and she was
fully convinced that nobody on earth did, could, or would
feel it as she did.

"St. Clare did not shed a tear," she said; "he did n't sympathize with her; it was perfectly wonderful to think how
hard-hearted and unfeeling he was, when he must know how
she suffered."

So much are people the slave of their eye and ear, that
many of the servants really thought that Missis was the principal sufferer in the case, especially as Marie began to have
hysterical spasms, and sent for the doctor, and at last declared
herself dying; and, in the running and scampering, and bringing up hot bottles, and heating of flannels, and chafing, and
fussing, that ensued, there was quite a diversion.

Tom, however, had a feeling at his own heart, that drew
him to his master. He followed him wherever he walked,
wistfully and sadly; and when he saw him sitting, so pale and
quiet, in Eva's room, holding before his eyes her little open
Bible, though seeing no letter or word of what was in it,
there was more sorrow to Tom in that still, fixed, tearless eye,
than in all Marie's moans and lamentations.

In a few days the St. Clare family were back again in the
city; Augustine, with the restlessness of grief, longing for another scene, to change the current of his thoughts. So they
left the house and garden, with its little grave, and came back
to New Orleans; and St. Clare walked the streets busily, and
strove to fill up the chasm in his heart with hurry and bustle,

and change of place; and people who saw him in the street, or met him at the café, knew of his loss only by the weed on his hat; for there he was, smiling and talking, and reading the newspaper, and speculating on politics, and attending to business matters; and who could see that all this smiling outside was but a hollowed shell over a heart that was a dark and silent sepulchre?

"Mr. St. Clare is a singular man," said Marie to Miss Ophelia, in a complaining tone. "I used to think, if there was anything in the world he did love, it was our dear little Eva; but he seems to be forgetting her very easily. I cannot ever get him to talk about her. I really did think he would show more feeling!"

"Still waters run deepest, they used to tell me," said Miss Ophelia, oracularly.

"O, I don't believe in such things; it's all talk. If people have feeling, they will show it,—they can't help it; but, then, it's a great misfortune to have feeling. I'd rather have been made like St. Clare. My feelings prey upon me so!"

"Sure, Missis, Mas'r St. Clare is gettin' thin as a shader. They say, he don't never eat nothin'," said Mammy. "I know he don't forget Miss Eva; I know there could n't be nobody,— dear, little, blessed cretur!" she added, wiping her eyes.

"Well, at all events, he has no consideration for me," said Marie; "he has n't spoken one word of sympathy, and he must know how much more a mother feels than any man can."

"The heart knoweth its own bitterness," said Miss Ophelia, gravely.

"That's just what I think. I know just what I feel,—nobody else seems to. Eva used to, but she is gone!" and Marie lay back on her lounge, and began to sob disconsolately.

Marie was one of those unfortunately constituted mortals, in whose eyes whatever is lost and gone assumes a value which it never had in possession. Whatever she had, she seemed to survey only to pick flaws in it; but, once fairly away, there was no end to her valuation of it.

While this conversation was taking place in the parlor, another was going on in St. Clare's library.

Tom, who was always uneasily following his master about,

had seen him go to his library, some hours before; and, after vainly waiting for him to come out, determined, at last, to make an errand in. He entered softly. St. Clare lay on his lounge, at the further end of the room. He was lying on his face, with Eva's Bible open before him, at a little distance. Tom walked up, and stood by the sofa. He hesitated; and, while he was hesitating, St. Clare suddenly raised himself up. The honest face, so full of grief, and with such an imploring expression of affection and sympathy, struck his master. He laid his hand on Tom's, and bowed down his forehead on it.

"O, Tom, my boy, the whole world is as empty as an egg-shell."

"I know it, Mas'r,—I know it," said Tom; "but, oh, if Mas'r could only look up,—up where our dear Miss Eva is,—up to the dear Lord Jesus!"

"Ah, Tom! I do look up; but the trouble is, I don't see anything, when I do. I wish I could."

Tom sighed heavily.

"It seems to be given to children, and poor, honest fellows, like you, to see what we can't," said St. Clare. "How comes it?"

"Thou hast 'hid from the wise and prudent, and revealed unto babes,'" murmured Tom; "'even so, Father, for so it seemed good in thy sight.'"

"Tom, I don't believe,—I can't believe,—I 've got the habit of doubting," said St. Clare. "I want to believe this Bible,—and I can't."

"Dear Mas'r, pray to the good Lord,—'Lord, I believe; help thou my unbelief.'"

"Who knows anything about anything?" said St. Clare, his eyes wandering dreamily, and speaking to himself. "Was all that beautiful love and faith only one of the ever-shifting phases of human feeling, having nothing real to rest on, passing away with the little breath? And is there no more Eva,—no heaven,—no Christ,—nothing?"

"O, dear Mas'r, there is! I know it; I 'm sure of it," said Tom, falling on his knees. "Do, do, dear Mas'r, believe it!"

"How do you know there 's any Christ, Tom? You never saw the Lord."

"Felt Him in my soul, Mas'r,—feel Him now! O, Mas'r,

when I was sold away from my old woman and the children, I was jest a'most broke up. I felt as if there warn't nothin' left; and then the good Lord, he stood by me, and he says, 'Fear not, Tom;' and he brings light and joy into a poor feller's soul,—makes all peace; and I 's so happy, and loves everybody, and feels willin' jest to be the Lord's, and have the Lord's will done, and be put jest where the Lord wants to put me. I know it could n't come from me, cause I 's a poor, complainin' cretur; it comes from the Lord; and I know He 's willin' to do for Mas'r."

Tom spoke with fast-running tears and choking voice. St. Clare leaned his head on his shoulder, and wrung the hard, faithful, black hand.

"Tom, you love me," he said.

"I 's willin' to lay down my life, this blessed day, to see Mas'r a Christian."

"Poor, foolish boy!" said St. Clare, half-raising himself. "I 'm not worth the love of one good, honest heart, like yours."

"O, Mas'r, dere 's more than me loves you,—the blessed Lord Jesus loves you."

"How do you know that, Tom?" said St. Clare.

"Feels it in my soul. O, Mas'r! 'the love of Christ, that passeth knowledge.' "

"Singular!" said St. Clare, turning away, "that the story of a man that lived and died eighteen hundred years ago can affect people so yet. But he was no man," he added, suddenly. "No man ever had such long and living power! O, that I could believe what my mother taught me, and pray as I did when I was a boy!"

"If Mas'r pleases," said Tom, "Miss Eva used to read this so beautifully. I wish Mas'r 'd be so good as read it. Don't get no readin', hardly, now Miss Eva 's gone."

The chapter was the eleventh of John,—the touching account of the raising of Lazarus. St. Clare read it aloud, often pausing to wrestle down feelings which were roused by the pathos of the story. Tom knelt before him, with clasped hands, and with an absorbed expression of love, trust, adoration, on his quiet face.

"Tom," said his Master, "this is all *real* to you!"

"I can jest fairly *see* it, Mas'r," said Tom.

"I wish I had your eyes, Tom."

"I wish, to the dear Lord, Mas'r had!"

"But, Tom, you know that I have a great deal more knowledge than you; what if I should tell you that I don't believe this Bible?"

"O, Mas'r!" said Tom, holding up his hands, with a deprecating gesture.

"Would n't it shake your faith some, Tom?"

"Not a grain," said Tom.

"Why, Tom, you must know I know the most."

"O, Mas'r, have n't you jest read how he hides from the wise and prudent, and reveals unto babes? But Mas'r was n't in earnest, for sartin, now?" said Tom, anxiously.

"No, Tom, I was not. I don't disbelieve, and I think there is reason to believe; and still I don't. It 's a troublesome bad habit I 've got, Tom."

"If Mas'r would only pray!"

"How do you know I don't, Tom?"

"Does Mas'r?"

"I would, Tom, if there was anybody there when I pray; but it 's all speaking unto nothing, when I do. But come, Tom, you pray, now, and show me how."

Tom's heart was full; he poured it out in prayer, like waters that have been long suppressed. One thing was plain enough; Tom thought there was somebody to hear, whether there were or not. In fact, St. Clare felt himself borne, on the tide of his faith and feeling, almost to the gates of that heaven he seemed so vividly to conceive. It seemed to bring him nearer to Eva.

"Thank you, my boy," said St. Clare, when Tom rose. "I like to hear you, Tom; but go, now, and leave me alone; some other time, I 'll talk more."

Tom silently left the room.

XXVIII.

Reunion

WEEK after week glided away in the St. Clare mansion, and the waves of life settled back to their usual flow, where that little bark had gone down. For how imperiously, how coolly, in disregard of all one's feeling, does the hard, cold, uninteresting course of daily realities move on! Still must we eat, and drink, and sleep, and wake again,—still bargain, buy, sell, ask and answer questions,—pursue, in short, a thousand shadows, though all interest in them be over; the cold mechanical habit of living remaining, after all vital interest in it has fled.

All the interests and hopes of St. Clare's life had unconsciously wound themselves around this child. It was for Eva that he had managed his property; it was for Eva that he had planned the disposal of his time; and, to do this and that for Eva,—to buy, improve, alter, and arrange, or dispose something for her,—had been so long his habit, that now she was gone, there seemed nothing to be thought of, and nothing to be done.

True, there was another life,—a life which, once believed in, stands as a solemn, significant figure before the otherwise unmeaning ciphers of time, changing them to orders of mysterious, untold value. St. Clare knew this well; and often, in many a weary hour, he heard that slender, childish voice calling him to the skies, and saw that little hand pointing to him the way of life; but a heavy lethargy of sorrow lay on him,— he could not arise. He had one of those natures which could better and more clearly conceive of religious things from its own perceptions and instincts, than many a matter-of-fact and practical Christian. The gift to appreciate and the sense to feel the finer shades and relations of moral things, often seems an attribute of those whose whole life shows a careless disregard of them. Hence Moore, Byron, Goethe, often speak words more wisely descriptive of the true religious sentiment, than another man, whose whole life is governed by it. In such minds, disregard of religion is a more fearful treason,—a more deadly sin.

St. Clare had never pretended to govern himself by any religious obligation; and a certain fineness of nature gave him such an instinctive view of the extent of the requirements of Christianity, that he shrank, by anticipation, from what he felt would be the exactions of his own conscience, if he once did resolve to assume them. For, so inconsistent is human nature, especially in the ideal, that not to undertake a thing at all seems better than to undertake and come short.

Still St. Clare was, in many respects, another man. He read his little Eva's Bible seriously and honestly; he thought more soberly and practically of his relations to his servants,— enough to make him extremely dissatisfied with both his past and present course; and one thing he did, soon after his return to New Orleans, and that was to commence the legal steps necessary to Tom's emancipation, which was to be perfected as soon as he could get through the necessary formalities. Meantime, he attached himself to Tom more and more, every day. In all the wide world, there was nothing that seemed to remind him so much of Eva; and he would insist on keeping him constantly about him, and, fastidious and unapproachable as he was with regard to his deeper feelings, he almost thought aloud to Tom. Nor would any one have wondered at it, who had seen the expression of affection and devotion with which Tom continually followed his young master.

"Well, Tom," said St. Clare, the day after he had commenced the legal formalities for his enfranchisement, "I 'm going to make a free man of you;—so, have your trunk packed, and get ready to set out for Kentuck."

The sudden light of joy that shone in Tom's face as he raised his hands to heaven, his emphatic "Bless the Lord!" rather discomposed St. Clare; he did not like it that Tom should be so ready to leave him.

"You have n't had such very bad times here, that you need be in such a rapture, Tom," he said, drily.

"No, no, Mas'r! 'tan't that,—it 's bein' a *free man!* That 's what I 'm joyin' for."

"Why, Tom, don't you think, for your own part, you 've been better off than to be free?"

"*No, indeed,* Mas'r St. Clare," said Tom, with a flash of energy. "No, indeed!"

"Why, Tom, you could n't possibly have earned, by your work, such clothes and such living as I have given you."

"Knows all that, Mas'r St. Clare; Mas'r 's been too good; but, Mas'r, I 'd rather have poor clothes, poor house, poor everything, and have 'em *mine,* than have the best, and have 'em any man's else,—I had *so,* Mas'r; I think it 's natur, Mas'r."

"I suppose so, Tom, and you'll be going off and leaving me, in a month or so," he added, rather discontentedly. "Though why you should n't, no mortal knows," he said, in a gayer tone; and, getting up, he began to walk the floor.

"Not while Mas'r is in trouble," said Tom. "I 'll stay with Mas'r as long as he wants me,—so as I can be any use."

"Not while I 'm in trouble, Tom?" said St. Clare, looking sadly out of the window. . . . . "And when will *my* trouble be over?"

"When Mas'r St. Clare 's a Christian," said Tom.

"And you really mean to stay by till that day comes?" said St. Clare, half smiling, as he turned from the window, and laid his hand on Tom's shoulder. "Ah, Tom, you soft, silly boy! I won't keep you till that day. Go home to your wife and children, and give my love to all."

"I 's faith to believe that day will come," said Tom, earnestly, and with tears in his eyes; "the Lord has a work for Mas'r."

"A work, hey?" said St. Clare; "well, now, Tom, give me your views on what sort of a work it is;—let 's hear."

"Why, even a poor fellow like me has a work from the Lord; and Mas'r St. Clare, that has larnin, and riches, and friends,—how much he might do for the Lord!"

"Tom, you seem to think the Lord needs a great deal done for him," said St. Clare, smiling.

"We does for the Lord when we does for his critturs," said Tom.

"Good theology, Tom; better than Dr. B. preaches, I dare swear," said St. Clare.

The conversation was here interrupted by the announcement of some visitors.

Marie St. Clare felt the loss of Eva as deeply as she could feel anything; and, as she was a woman that had a great faculty of making everybody unhappy when she was, her immediate attendants had still stronger reason to regret the loss of their young mistress, whose winning ways and gentle intercessions had so often been a shield to them from the tyrannical and selfish exactions of her mother. Poor old Mammy, in particular, whose heart, severed from all natural domestic ties, had consoled itself with this one beautiful being, was almost heart-broken. She cried day and night, and was, from excess of sorrow, less skilful and alert in her ministrations on her mistress than usual, which drew down a constant storm of invectives on her defenceless head.

Miss Ophelia felt the loss; but, in her good and honest heart, it bore fruit unto everlasting life. She was more softened, more gentle; and, though equally assiduous in every duty, it was with a chastened and quiet air, as one who communed with her own heart not in vain. She was more diligent in teaching Topsy,—taught her mainly from the Bible,—did not any longer shrink from her touch, or manifest an ill-repressed disgust, because she felt none. She viewed her now through the softened medium that Eva's hand had first held before her eyes, and saw in her only an immortal creature, whom God had sent to be led by her to glory and virtue. Topsy did not become at once a saint; but the life and death of Eva did work a marked change in her. The callous indifference was gone; there was now sensibility, hope, desire, and the striving for good,—a strife irregular, interrupted, suspended oft, but yet renewed again.

One day, when Topsy had been sent for by Miss Ophelia, she came, hastily thrusting something into her bosom.

"What are you doing there, you limb? You 've been stealing something, I 'll be bound," said the imperious little Rosa, who had been sent to call her, seizing her, at the same time, roughly by the arm.

"You go 'long, Miss Rosa!" said Topsy, pulling from her; " 'tan't none o' your business!"

"None o' your sa'ce!" said Rosa. "I saw you hiding something,—I know yer tricks," and Rosa seized her arm, and tried to force her hand into her bosom, while Topsy, enraged, kicked and fought valiantly for what she considered her rights. The clamor and confusion of the battle drew Miss Ophelia and St. Clare both to the spot.

"She's been stealing!" said Rosa.

"I han't, neither!" vociferated Topsy, sobbing with passion.

"Give me that, whatever it is!" said Miss Ophelia, firmly.

Topsy hesitated; but, on a second order, pulled out of her bosom a little parcel done up in the foot of one of her own old stockings.

Miss Ophelia turned it out. There was a small book, which had been given to Topsy by Eva, containing a single verse of Scripture, arranged for every day in the year, and in a paper the curl of hair that she had given her on that memorable day when she had taken her last farewell.

St. Clare was a good deal affected at the sight of it; the little book had been rolled in a long strip of black crape, torn from the funeral weeds.

"What did you wrap *this* round the book for?" said St. Clare, holding up the crape.

"Cause,—cause,—cause 't was Miss Eva. O, don't take 'em away, please!" she said; and, sitting flat down on the floor, and putting her apron over her head, she began to sob vehemently.

It was a curious mixture of the pathetic and the ludicrous,—the little old stocking,—black crape,—text-book, —fair, soft curl,—and Topsy's utter distress.

St. Clare smiled; but there were tears in his eyes, as he said,

"Come, come,—don't cry; you shall have them!" and, putting them together, he threw them into her lap, and drew Miss Ophelia with him into the parlor.

"I really think you can make something of that concern," he said, pointing with his thumb backward over his shoulder. "Any mind that is capable of a *real sorrow* is capable of good. You must try and do something with her."

"The child has improved greatly," said Miss Ophelia. "I have great hopes of her; but, Augustine," she said, laying her hand on his arm, "one thing I want to ask; whose is this child to be?—yours or mine?"

"Why, I gave her to *you*," said Augustine.

"But not legally;—I want her to be mine legally," said Miss Ophelia.

"Whew! cousin," said Augustine. "What will the Abolition Society think? They 'll have a day of fasting appointed for this backsliding, if you become a slave-holder!"

"O, nonsense! I want her mine, that I may have a right to take her to the free States, and give her her liberty, that all I am trying to do be not undone."

"O, cousin, what an awful 'doing evil that good may come'! I can't encourage it."

"I don't want you to joke, but to reason," said Miss Ophelia. "There is no use in my trying to make this child a Christian child, unless I save her from all the chances and reverses of slavery; and, if you really are willing I should have her, I want you to give me a deed of gift, or some legal paper."

"Well, well," said St. Clare, "I will;" and he sat down, and unfolded a newspaper to read.

"But I want it done now," said Miss Ophelia.

"What 's your hurry?"

"Because now is the only time there ever is to do a thing in," said Miss Ophelia. "Come, now, here 's paper, pen, and ink; just write a paper."

St. Clare, like most men of his class of mind, cordially hated the present tense of action, generally; and, therefore, he was considerably annoyed by Miss Ophelia's downrightness.

"Why, what 's the matter?" said he. "Can't you take my word? One would think you had taken lessons of the Jews, coming at a fellow so!"

"I want to make sure of it," said Miss Ophelia. "You may die, or fail, and then Topsy be hustled off to auction, spite of all I can do."

"Really, you are quite provident. Well, seeing I 'm in the hands of a Yankee, there is nothing for it but to concede;" and St. Clare rapidly wrote off a deed of gift, which, as he was well versed in the forms of law, he could easily do, and signed his name to it in sprawling capitals, concluding by a tremendous flourish.

"There, is n't that black and white, now, Miss Vermont?" he said, as he handed it to her.

"Good boy," said Miss Ophelia, smiling. "But must it not be witnessed?"

"O, bother!—yes. Here," he said, opening the door into Marie's apartment, "Marie, Cousin wants your autograph; just put your name down here."

"What 's this?" said Marie, as she ran over the paper. "Ridiculous! I thought Cousin was too pious for such horrid things," she added, as she carelessly wrote her name; "but, if she has a fancy for that article, I am sure she 's welcome."

"There, now, she 's yours, body and soul," said St. Clare, handing the paper.

"No more mine now than she was before," said Miss Ophelia. "Nobody but God has a right to give her to me; but I can protect her now."

"Well, she 's yours by a fiction of law, then," said St. Clare, as he turned back into the parlor, and sat down to his paper.

Miss Ophelia, who seldom sat much in Marie's company, followed him into the parlor, having first carefully laid away the paper.

"Augustine," she said, suddenly, as she sat knitting, "have you ever made any provision for your servants, in case of your death?"

"No," said St. Clare, as he read on.

"Then all your indulgence to them may prove a great cruelty, by and by."

St. Clare had often thought the same thing himself; but he answered, negligently,

"Well, I mean to make a provision, by and by."

"When?" said Miss Ophelia.

"O, one of these days."

"What if you should die first?"

"Cousin, what 's the matter?" said St. Clare, laying down his paper and looking at her. "Do you think I show symptoms of yellow fever or cholera, that you are making post mortem arrangements with such zeal?"

" 'In the midst of life we are in death,' " said Miss Ophelia.

St. Clare rose up, and laying the paper down, carelessly, walked to the door that stood open on the verandah, to put an end to a conversation that was not agreeable to him. Mechanically, he repeated the last word again,—*"Death!"*—

and, as he leaned against the railings, and watched the sparkling water as it rose and fell in the fountain; and, as in a dim and dizzy haze, saw flowers and trees and vases of the courts, he repeated again the mystic word so common in every mouth, yet of such fearful power,—"DEATH!" "Strange that there should be such a word," he said, "and such a thing, and we ever forget it; that one should be living, warm and beautiful, full of hopes, desires and wants, one day, and the next be gone, utterly gone, and forever!"

It was a warm, golden evening; and, as he walked to the other end of the verandah, he saw Tom busily intent on his Bible, pointing, as he did so, with his finger to each successive word, and whispering them to himself with an earnest air.

"Want me to read to you, Tom?" said St. Clare, seating himself carelessly by him.

"If Mas'r pleases," said Tom, gratefully, "Mas'r makes it so much plainer."

St. Clare took the book and glanced at the place, and began reading one of the passages which Tom had designated by the heavy marks around it. It ran as follows:

"When the Son of man shall come in his glory, and all his holy angels with him, then shall he sit upon the throne of his glory: and before him shall be gathered all nations; and he shall separate them one from another, as a shepherd divideth his sheep from the goats." St. Clare read on in an animated voice, till he came to the last of the verses.

"Then shall the king say unto them on his left hand, Depart from me, ye cursed, into everlasting fire: for I was an hungered, and ye gave me no meat: I was thirsty, and ye gave me no drink: I was a stranger, and ye took me not in: naked, and ye clothed me not: I was sick, and in prison, and ye visited me not. Then shall they answer unto Him, Lord when saw we thee an hungered, or athirst, or a stranger, or naked, or sick, or in prison, and did not minister unto thee? Then shall he say unto them, Inasmuch as ye did it not to one of the least of these my brethren, ye did it not to me."

St. Clare seemed struck with this last passage, for he read it twice,—the second time slowly, and as if he were revolving the words in his mind.

"Tom," he said, "these folks that get such hard measure

seem to have been doing just what I have,—living good, easy, respectable lives; and not troubling themselves to inquire how many of their brethren were hungry or athirst, or sick, or in prison."

Tom did not answer.

St. Clare rose up and walked thoughtfully up and down the verandah, seeming to forget everything in his own thoughts; so absorbed was he, that Tom had to remind him twice that the tea-bell had rung, before he could get his attention.

St. Clare was absent and thoughtful, all tea-time. After tea, he and Marie and Miss Ophelia took possession of the parlor, almost in silence.

Marie disposed herself on a lounge, under a silken mosquito curtain, and was soon sound asleep. Miss Ophelia silently busied herself with her knitting. St. Clare sat down to the piano, and began playing a soft and melancholy movement with the Æolian accompaniment. He seemed in a deep reverie, and to be soliloquizing to himself by music. After a little, he opened one of the drawers, took out an old music-book whose leaves were yellow with age, and began turning it over.

"There," he said to Miss Ophelia, "this was one of my mother's books,—and here is her handwriting,—come and look at it. She copied and arranged this from Mozart's Requiem." Miss Ophelia came accordingly.

"It was something she used to sing often," said St. Clare. "I think I can hear her now."

He struck a few majestic chords, and began singing that grand old Latin piece, the "Dies Iræ."

Tom, who was listening in the outer verandah, was drawn by the sound to the very door, where he stood earnestly. He did not understand the words, of course; but the music and manner of singing appeared to affect him strongly, especially when St. Clare sang the more pathetic parts. Tom would have sympathized more heartily, if he had known the meaning of the beautiful words:

> Recordare Jesu pie
> Quod sum causa tuæ viæ
> No me perdas, illa die

Querens me sedisti lassus
Redemisti crucem passus
Tantus labor non sit cassus.*

St. Clare threw a deep and pathetic expression into the words; for the shadowy veil of years seemed drawn away, and he seemed to hear his mother's voice leading his. Voice and instrument seemed both living, and threw out with vivid sympathy those strains which the ethereal Mozart first conceived as his own dying requiem.

When St. Clare had done singing, he sat leaning his head upon his hand a few moments, and then began walking up and down the floor.

"What a sublime conception is that of a last judgment!" said he,—"a righting of all the wrongs of ages!—a solving of all moral problems, by an unanswerable wisdom! It is, indeed, a wonderful image."

"It is a fearful one to us," said Miss Ophelia.

"It ought to be to me, I suppose," said St Clare, stopping, thoughtfully. "I was reading to Tom, this afternoon, that chapter in Matthew that gives an account of it, and I have been quite struck with it. One should have expected some terrible enormities charged to those who are excluded from Heaven, as the reason; but no,—they are condemned for *not* doing positive good, as if that included every possible harm."

"Perhaps," said Miss Ophelia, "it is impossible for a person who does no good not to do harm."

"And what," said St. Clare, speaking abstractedly, but with deep feeling, "what shall be said of one whose own heart, whose education, and the wants of society, have called in vain to some noble purpose; who has floated on, a dreamy, neutral spectator of the struggles, agonies, and wrongs of man, when he should have been a worker?"

*These lines have been thus rather inadequately translated:

Think, O Jesus, for what reason
Thou endured'st earth's spite and treason,
Nor me lose, in that dread season;
Seeking me, thy worn feet hasted,
On the cross thy soul death tasted,
Let not all these toils be wasted.

"I should say," said Miss Ophelia, "that he ought to repent, and begin now."

"Always practical and to the point!" said St. Clare, his face breaking out into a smile. "You never leave me any time for general reflections, Cousin; you always bring me short up against the actual present; you have a kind of eternal *now*, always in your mind."

"*Now* is all the time I have anything to do with," said Miss Ophelia.

"Dear little Eva,—poor child!" said St. Clare, "she had set her little simple soul on a good work for me."

It was the first time since Eva's death that he had ever said as many words as these of her, and he spoke now evidently repressing very strong feeling.

"My view of Christianity is such," he added, "that I think no man can consistently profess it without throwing the whole weight of his being against this monstrous system of injustice that lies at the foundation of all our society; and, if need be, sacrificing himself in the battle. That is, I mean that *I* could not be a Christian otherwise, though I have certainly had intercourse with a great many enlightened and Christian people who did no such thing; and I confess that the apathy of religious people on this subject, their want of perception of wrongs that filled me with horror, have engendered in me more scepticism than any other thing."

"If you knew all this," said Miss Ophelia, "why did n't you do it?"

"O, because I have had only that kind of benevolence which consists in lying on a sofa, and cursing the church and clergy for not being martyrs and confessors. One can see, you know, very easily, how others ought to be martyrs."

"Well, are you going to do differently now?" said Miss Ophelia.

"God only knows the future," said St. Clare. "I am braver than I was, because I have lost all; and he who has nothing to lose can afford all risks."

"And what are you going to do?"

"My duty, I hope, to the poor and lowly, as fast as I find it out," said St. Clare, "beginning with my own servants, for whom I have yet done nothing; and, perhaps, at some future day, it may appear that I can do something for a whole class; something to save my country from the disgrace of that false position in which she now stands before all civilized nations."

"Do you suppose it possible that a nation ever will voluntarily emancipate?" said Miss Ophelia.

"I don't know," said St. Clare. "This is a day of great deeds. Heroism and disinterestedness are rising up, here and there, in the earth. The Hungarian nobles set free millions of serfs, at an immense pecuniary loss; and, perhaps, among us may be found generous spirits, who do not estimate honor and justice by dollars and cents."

"I hardly think so," said Miss Ophelia.

"But, suppose we should rise up to-morrow and emancipate, who would educate these millions, and teach them how to use their freedom? They never would rise to do much among us. The fact is, we are too lazy and unpractical, ourselves, ever to give them much of an idea of that industry and energy which is necessary to form them into men. They will have to go north, where labor is the fashion,—the universal custom; and tell me, now, is there enough Christian philanthropy, among your northern states, to bear with the process of their education and elevation? You send thousands of dollars to foreign missions; but could you endure to have the heathen sent into your towns and villages, and give your time, and thoughts, and money, to raise them to the Christian standard? That 's what I want to know. If we emancipate, are you willing to educate? How many families, in your town, would take in a negro man and woman, teach them, bear with them, and seek to make them Christians? How many merchants would take Adolph, if I wanted to make him a clerk; or mechanics, if I wanted him taught a trade? If I wanted to put Jane and Rosa to a school, how many schools are there in the northern states that would take them in? how many families that would board them? and yet they are as white as many a woman, north or south. You see, Cousin, I want justice done us. We are in a bad position. We are the more *obvious* oppressors of the negro; but the unchristian prejudice of the north is an oppressor almost equally severe."

"Well, Cousin, I know it is so," said Miss Ophelia,—"I know it was so with me, till I saw that it was my duty to overcome it; but, I trust I have overcome it; and I know there are many good people at the north, who in this matter need only to be *taught* what their duty is, to do it. It would certainly be a greater self-denial to receive heathen among us, than to send missionaries to them; but I think we would do it."

"*You* would, I know," said St. Clare. "I'd like to see anything you would n't do, if you thought it your duty!"

"Well, I'm not uncommonly good," said Miss Ophelia. "Others would, if they saw things as I do. I intend to take Topsy home, when I go. I suppose our folks will wonder, at first; but I think they will be brought to see as I do. Besides, I know there are many people at the north who do exactly what you said."

"Yes, but they are a minority; and, if we should begin to emancipate to any extent, we should soon hear from you."

Miss Ophelia did not reply. There was a pause of some moments; and St. Clare's countenance was overcast by a sad, dreamy expression.

"I don't know what makes me think of my mother so much, to-night," he said. "I have a strange kind of feeling, as if she were near me. I keep thinking of things she used to say. Strange, what brings these past things so vividly back to us, sometimes!"

St. Clare walked up and down the room for some minutes more, and then said,

"I believe I'll go down street, a few moments, and hear the news, to-night."

He took his hat, and passed out.

Tom followed him to the passage, out of the court, and asked if he should attend him.

"No, my boy," said St. Clare. "I shall be back in an hour."

Tom sat down in the verandah. It was a beautiful moonlight evening, and he sat watching the rising and falling spray of the fountain, and listening to its murmur. Tom thought of his home, and that he should soon be a free man, and able to return to it at will. He thought how he should work to buy his wife and boys. He felt the muscles of his brawny arms with a sort of joy, as he thought they would soon belong to himself, and how much they could do to work out the free-

dom of his family. Then he thought of his noble young master, and, ever second to that, came the habitual prayer that he
had always offered for him; and then his thoughts passed on
to the beautiful Eva, whom he now thought of among the
angels; and he thought till he almost fancied that that bright
face and golden hair were looking upon him, out of the spray
of the fountain. And, so musing, he fell asleep, and dreamed
he saw her coming bounding towards him, just as she used to
come, with a wreath of jessamine in her hair, her cheeks
bright, and her eyes radiant with delight; but, as he looked,
she seemed to rise from the ground; her cheeks wore a paler
hue,—her eyes had a deep, divine radiance, a golden halo
seemed around her head,—and she vanished from his sight;
and Tom was awakened by a loud knocking, and a sound of
many voices at the gate.

He hastened to undo it; and, with smothered voices and
heavy tread, came several men, bringing a body, wrapped in
a cloak, and lying on a shutter. The light of the lamp fell full
on the face; and Tom gave a wild cry of amazement and despair, that rung through all the galleries, as the men advanced,
with their burden, to the open parlor door, where Miss
Ophelia still sat knitting.

St. Clare had turned into a café, to look over an evening
paper. As he was reading, an affray arose between two gentlemen in the room, who were both partially intoxicated. St.
Clare and one or two others made an effort to separate them,
and St. Clare received a fatal stab in the side with a bowie-
knife, which he was attempting to wrest from one of them.

The house was full of cries and lamentations, shrieks and
screams; servants frantically tearing their hair, throwing themselves on the ground, or running distractedly about, lament-
ing. Tom and Miss Ophelia alone seemed to have any
presence of mind; for Marie was in strong hysteric convulsions. At Miss Ophelia's direction, one of the lounges in the
parlor was hastily prepared, and the bleeding form laid upon
it. St. Clare had fainted, through pain and loss of blood;
but, as Miss Ophelia applied restoratives, he revived, opened
his eyes, looked fixedly on them, looked earnestly around
the room, his eyes travelling wistfully over every object, and

finally they rested on his mother's picture.

The physician now arrived, and made his examination. It was evident, from the expression of his face, that there was no hope; but he applied himself to dressing the wound, and he and Miss Ophelia and Tom proceeded composedly with this work, amid the lamentations and sobs and cries of the affrighted servants, who had clustered about the doors and windows of the verandah.

"Now," said the physician, "we must turn all these creatures out; all depends on his being kept quiet."

St. Clare opened his eyes, and looked fixedly on the distressed beings, whom Miss Ophelia and the doctor were trying to urge from the apartment. "Poor creatures!" he said, and an expression of bitter self-reproach passed over his face. Adolph absolutely refused to go. Terror had deprived him of all presence of mind; he threw himself along on the floor, and nothing could persuade him to rise. The rest yielded to Miss Ophelia's urgent representations, that their master's safety depended on their stillness and obedience.

St. Clare could say but little; he lay with his eyes shut, but it was evident that he wrestled with bitter thoughts. After a while, he laid his hand on Tom's, who was kneeling beside him, and said, "Tom! poor fellow!"

"What, Mas'r?" said Tom, earnestly.

"I am dying!" said St. Clare, pressing his hand; "pray!"

"If you would like a clergyman—" said the physician.

St. Clare hastily shook his head, and said again to Tom, more earnestly, "Pray!"

And Tom did pray, with all his mind and strength, for the soul that was passing,—the soul that seemed looking so steadily and mournfully from those large, melancholy blue eyes. It was literally prayer offered with strong crying and tears.

When Tom ceased to speak, St. Clare reached out and took his hand, looking earnestly at him, but saying nothing. He closed his eyes, but still retained his hold; for, in the gates of eternity, the black hand and the white hold each other with an equal clasp. He murmured softly to himself, at broken intervals,

"Recordare Jesu pie—

* * *

Ne me perdas—ille die
Querens me—sedisti lassus."

It was evident that the words he had been singing that evening were passing through his mind,—words of entreaty addressed to Infinite Pity. His lips moved at intervals, as parts of the hymn fell brokenly from them.

"His mind is wandering," said the doctor.

"No! it is coming HOME, at last!" said St. Clare, energetically; "at last! at last!"

The effort of speaking exhausted him. The sinking paleness of death fell on him; but with it there fell, as if shed from the wings of some pitying spirit, a beautiful expression of peace, like that of a wearied child who sleeps.

So he lay for a few moments. They saw that the mighty hand was on him. Just before the spirit parted, he opened his eyes, with a sudden light, as of joy and recognition, and said *"Mother!"* and then he was gone!

XXIX.

The Unprotected

WE hear often of the distress of the negro servants, on the loss of a kind master; and with good reason, for no creature on God's earth is left more utterly unprotected and desolate than the slave in these circumstances.

The child who has lost a father has still the protection of friends, and of the law; he is something, and can do something,—has acknowledged rights and position; the slave has none. The law regards him, in every respect, as devoid of rights as a bale of merchandise. The only possible acknowledgment of any of the longings and wants of a human and immortal creature, which are given to him, comes to him through the sovereign and irresponsible will of his master; and when that master is stricken down, nothing remains.

The number of those men who know how to use wholly irresponsible power humanely and generously is small. Everybody knows this, and the slave knows it best of all; so that he feels that there are ten chances of his finding an abusive and tyrannical master, to one of his finding a considerate and kind one. Therefore is it that the wail over a kind master is loud and long, as well it may be.

When St. Clare breathed his last, terror and consternation took hold of all his household. He had been stricken down so in a moment, in the flower and strength of his youth! Every room and gallery of the house resounded with sobs and shrieks of despair.

Marie, whose nervous system had been enervated by a constant course of self-indulgence, had nothing to support the terror of the shock, and, at the time her husband breathed his last, was passing from one fainting fit to another; and he to whom she had been joined in the mysterious tie of marriage passed from her forever, without the possibility of even a parting word.

Miss Ophelia, with characteristic strength and self-control, had remained with her kinsman to the last,—all eye, all ear, all attention; doing everything of the little that could be done, and joining with her whole soul in the tender and impassioned prayers which the poor slave had poured forth for the soul of his dying master.

When they were arranging him for his last rest, they found upon his bosom a small, plain miniature case, opening with a spring. It was the miniature of a noble and beautiful female face; and on the reverse, under a crystal, a lock of dark hair. They laid them back on the lifeless breast,—dust to dust,— poor mournful relics of early dreams, which once made that cold heart beat so warmly!

Tom's whole soul was filled with thoughts of eternity; and while he ministered around the lifeless clay, he did not once think that the sudden stroke had left him in hopeless slavery. He felt at peace about his master; for in that hour, when he had poured forth his prayer into the bosom of his Father, he had found an answer of quietness and assurance springing up within himself. In the depths of his own affectionate nature, he felt able to perceive something of the fulness of Divine love; for an old oracle hath thus written,—"He that dwelleth in love dwelleth in God, and God in him." Tom hoped and trusted, and was at peace.

But the funeral passed, with all its pageant of black crape, and prayers, and solemn faces; and back rolled the cool, muddy waves of every-day life; and up came the everlasting hard inquiry of "What is to be done next?"

It rose to the mind of Marie, as, dressed in loose morning-robes, and surrounded by anxious servants, she sat up in a great easy-chair, and inspected samples of crape and bombazine. It rose to Miss Ophelia, who began to turn her thoughts towards her northern home. It rose, in silent terrors, to the minds of the servants, who well knew the unfeeling, tyrannical character of the mistress in whose hands they were left. All knew, very well, that the indulgences which had been accorded to them were not from their mistress, but from their master; and that, now he was gone, there would be no screen between them and every tyrannous infliction which a temper soured by affliction might devise.

It was about a fortnight after the funeral, that Miss Ophelia, busied one day in her apartment, heard a gentle tap at the door. She opened it, and there stood Rosa, the pretty young quadroon, whom we have before often noticed, her hair in disorder, and her eyes swelled with crying.

"O, Miss Feely," she said, falling on her knees, and catching the skirt of her dress, "*do, do go* to Miss Marie for me! do plead for me! She's goin' to send me out to be whipped,— look there!" And she handed to Miss Ophelia a paper.

It was an order, written in Marie's delicate Italian hand, to the master of a whipping-establishment, to give the bearer fifteen lashes.

"What have you been doing?" said Miss Ophelia.

"You know, Miss Feely, I've got such a bad temper; it's very bad of me. I was trying on Miss Marie's dress, and she slapped my face; and I spoke out before I thought, and was saucy; and she said that she'd bring me down, and have me know, once for all, that I wasn't going to be so topping as I had been; and she wrote this, and says I shall carry it. I'd rather she'd kill me, right out."

Miss Ophelia stood considering, with the paper in her hand.

"You see, Miss Feely," said Rosa, "I don't mind the whipping so much, if Miss Marie or you was to do it; but, to be sent to a *man*! and such a horrid man,—the shame of it, Miss Feely!"

Miss Ophelia well knew that it was the universal custom to send women and young girls to whipping-houses, to the hands of the lowest of men,—men vile enough to make this their profession,—there to be subjected to brutal exposure and shameful correction. She had *known* it before; but hitherto she had never realized it, till she saw the slender form of Rosa almost convulsed with distress. All the honest blood of womanhood, the strong New England blood of liberty, flushed to her cheeks, and throbbed bitterly in her indignant heart; but, with habitual prudence and self-control, she mastered herself, and, crushing the paper firmly in her hand, she merely said to Rosa,

"Sit down, child, while I go to your mistress."

"Shameful! monstrous! outrageous!" she said to herself, as she was crossing the parlor.

She found Marie sitting up in her easy-chair, with Mammy standing by her, combing her hair; Jane sat on the ground before her, busy in chafing her feet.

"How do you find yourself, to-day?" said Miss Ophelia.

A deep sigh, and a closing of the eyes, was the only reply, for a moment; and then Marie answered, "O, I don't know, Cousin; I suppose I 'm as well as I ever shall be!" and Marie wiped her eyes with a cambric handkerchief, bordered with an inch deep of black.

"I came," said Miss Ophelia, with a short, dry cough, such as commonly introduces a difficult subject,—"I came to speak with you about poor Rosa."

Marie's eyes were open wide enough now, and a flush rose to her sallow cheeks, as she answered, sharply,

"Well, what about her?"

"She is very sorry for her fault."

"She is, is she? She 'll be sorrier, before I 've done with her! I 've endured that child's impudence long enough; and now I 'll bring her down,—I 'll make her lie in the dust!"

"But could not you punish her some other way,—some way that would be less shameful?"

"I mean to shame her; that 's just what I want. She has all her life presumed on her delicacy, and her good looks, and her lady-like airs, till she forgets who she is;—and I 'll give her one lesson that will bring her down, I fancy!"

"But, Cousin, consider that, if you destroy delicacy and a sense of shame in a young girl, you deprave her very fast."

"Delicacy!" said Marie, with a scornful laugh,—"a fine word for such as she! I 'll teach her, with all her airs, that she 's no better than the raggedest black wench that walks the streets! She 'll take no more airs with me!"

"You will answer to God for such cruelty!" said Miss Ophelia, with energy.

"Cruelty,—I 'd like to know what the cruelty is! I wrote orders for only fifteen lashes, and told him to put them on lightly. I 'm sure there 's no cruelty there!"

"No cruelty!" said Miss Ophelia. "I 'm sure any girl might rather be killed outright!"

"It might seem so to anybody with your feeling; but all these creatures get used to it; it 's the only way they can be kept in order. Once let them feel that they are to take any airs about delicacy, and all that, and they 'll run all over you, just as my servants always have. I 've begun now to bring them under; and I 'll have them all to know that I 'll send one out to be whipped, as soon as another, if they don't mind themselves!" said Marie, looking around her decidedly.

Jane hung her head and cowered at this, for she felt as if it was particularly directed to her. Miss Ophelia sat for a moment, as if she had swallowed some explosive mixture, and were ready to burst. Then, recollecting the utter uselessness of contention with such a nature, she shut her lips resolutely, gathered herself up, and walked out of the room.

It was hard to go back and tell Rosa that she could do nothing for her; and, shortly after, one of the man-servants came to say that her mistress had ordered him to take Rosa with him to the whipping-house, whither she was hurried, in spite of her tears and entreaties.

A few days after, Tom was standing musing by the balconies, when he was joined by Adolph, who, since the death of his master, had been entirely crest-fallen and disconsolate. Adolph knew that he had always been an object of dislike to Marie; but while his master lived he had paid but little attention to it. Now that he was gone, he had moved about in daily dread and trembling, not knowing what might befall him next. Marie had held several consultations with her lawyer; after communicating with St. Clare's brother, it was determined to sell the place, and all the servants, except her own personal property, and these she intended to take with her, and go back to her father's plantation.

"Do ye know, Tom, that we 've all got to be sold?" said Adolph.

"How did you hear that?" said Tom.

"I hid myself behind the curtains when Missis was talking with the lawyer. In a few days we shall all be sent off to auction, Tom."

"The Lord's will be done!" said Tom, folding his arms and sighing heavily.

"We 'll never get another such a master," said Adolph, apprehensively; "but I 'd rather be sold than take my chance under Missis."

Tom turned away; his heart was full. The hope of liberty, the thought of distant wife and children, rose up before his patient soul, as to the mariner shipwrecked almost in port rises the vision of the church-spire and loving roofs of his native village, seen over the top of some black wave only for one last farewell. He drew his arms tightly over his bosom, and choked back the bitter tears, and tried to pray. The poor old soul had such a singular, unaccountable prejudice in favor of liberty, that it was a hard wrench for him; and the more he said, "Thy will be done," the worse he felt.

He sought Miss Ophelia, who, ever since Eva's death, had treated him with marked and respectful kindness.

"Miss Feely," he said, "Mas'r St. Clare promised me my freedom. He told me that he had begun to take it out for me; and now, perhaps, if Miss Feely would be good enough to speak about it to Missis, she would feel like goin' on with it, as it was Mas'r St. Clare's wish."

"I'll speak for you, Tom, and do my best," said Miss Ophelia; "but, if it depends on Mrs. St. Clare, I can't hope much for you; — nevertheless, I will try."

This incident occurred a few days after that of Rosa, while Miss Ophelia was busied in preparations to return north.

Seriously reflecting within herself, she considered that perhaps she had shown too hasty a warmth of language in her former interview with Marie; and she resolved that she would now endeavor to moderate her zeal, and to be as conciliatory as possible. So the good soul gathered herself up, and, taking her knitting, resolved to go into Marie's room, be as agreeable as possible, and negotiate Tom's case with all the diplomatic skill of which she was mistress.

She found Marie reclining at length upon a lounge, supporting herself on one elbow by pillows, while Jane, who had been out shopping, was displaying before her certain samples of thin black stuffs.

"That will do," said Marie, selecting one; "only I'm not sure about its being properly mourning."

"Laws, Missis," said Jane, volubly, "Mrs. General Derbennon wore just this very thing, after the General died, last summer; it makes up lovely!"

"What do you think?" said Marie to Miss Ophelia.

"It's a matter of custom, I suppose," said Miss Ophelia. "You can judge about it better than I."

"The fact is," said Marie, "that I have n't a dress in the world that I can wear; and, as I am going to break up the establishment, and go off, next week, I must decide upon something."

"Are you going so soon?"

"Yes. St. Clare's brother has written, and he and the lawyer think that the servants and furniture had better be put up at auction, and the place left with our lawyer."

"There's one thing I wanted to speak with you about," said Miss Ophelia. "Augustine promised Tom his liberty, and began the legal forms necessary to it. I hope you will use your influence to have it perfected."

"Indeed, I shall do no such thing!" said Marie, sharply. "Tom is one of the most valuable servants on the place,— it could n't be afforded, any way. Besides, what does he want of liberty? He's a great deal better off as he is."

"But he does desire it, very earnestly, and his master promised it," said Miss Ophelia.

"I dare say he does want it," said Marie; "they all want it, just because they are a discontented set,— always wanting what they have n't got. Now, I'm principled against emancipating, in any case. Keep a negro under the care of a master, and he does well enough, and is respectable; but set them free, and they get lazy, and won't work, and take to drinking, and go all down to be mean, worthless fellows. I've seen it tried, hundreds of times. It's no favor to set them free."

"But Tom is so steady, industrious, and pious."

"O, you need n't tell me! I've seen a hundred like him. He'll do very well, as long as he's taken care of,— that's all."

"But, then, consider," said Miss Ophelia, "when you set him up for sale, the chances of his getting a bad master."

"O, that's all humbug!" said Marie; "it is n't one time in a hundred that a good fellow gets a bad master; most masters are good, for all the talk that is made. I've lived and grown up here, in the South, and I never yet was acquainted with a master that did n't treat his servants well,— quite as well as is worth while. I don't feel any fears on that head."

"Well," said Miss Ophelia, energetically, "I know it was

one of the last wishes of your husband that Tom should have his liberty; it was one of the promises that he made to dear little Eva on her death-bed, and I should not think you would feel at liberty to disregard it."

Marie had her face covered with her handkerchief at this appeal, and began sobbing and using her smelling-bottle, with great vehemence.

"Everybody goes against me!" she said. "Everybody is so inconsiderate! I should n't have expected that *you* would bring up all these remembrances of my troubles to me,—it's so inconsiderate! But nobody ever does consider,—my trials are so peculiar! It's so hard, that when I had only one daughter, she should have been taken!—and when I had a husband that just exactly suited me,—and I'm so hard to be suited!—he should be taken! And you seem to have so little feeling for me, and keep bringing it up to me so carelessly,—when you know how it overcomes me! I suppose you mean well; but it is very inconsiderate,—very!" And Marie sobbed, and gasped for breath, and called Mammy to open the window, and to bring her the camphor-bottle, and to bathe her head, and un-hook her dress. And, in the general confusion that ensued, Miss Ophelia made her escape to her apartment.

She saw, at once, that it would do no good to say anything more; for Marie had an indefinite capacity for hysteric fits; and, after this, whenever her husband's or Eva's wishes with regard to the servants were alluded to, she always found it convenient to set one in operation. Miss Ophelia, therefore, did the next best thing she could for Tom,—she wrote a let-ter to Mrs. Shelby for him, stating his troubles, and urging them to send to his relief.

The next day, Tom and Adolph, and some half a dozen other servants, were marched down to a slave-warehouse, to await the convenience of the trader, who was going to make up a lot for auction.

XXX.

The Slave Warehouse

A SLAVE warehouse! Perhaps some of my readers conjure up horrible visions of such a place. They fancy some foul, obscure den, some horrible *Tartarus "informis, ingens, cui lumen ademptum."* But no, innocent friend; in these days men have learned the art of sinning expertly and genteelly, so as not to shock the eyes and senses of respectable society. Human property is high in the market; and is, therefore, well fed, well cleaned, tended, and looked after, that it may come to sale sleek, and strong, and shining. A slave-warehouse in New Orleans is a house externally not much unlike many others, kept with neatness; and where every day you may see arranged, under a sort of shed along the outside, rows of men and women, who stand there as a sign of the property sold within.

Then you shall be courteously entreated to call and examine, and shall find an abundance of husbands, wives, brothers, sisters, fathers, mothers, and young children, to be "sold separately, or in lots to suit the convenience of the purchaser;" and that soul immortal, once bought with blood and anguish by the Son of God, when the earth shook, and the rocks rent, and the graves were opened, can be sold, leased, mortgaged, exchanged for groceries or dry goods, to suit the phases of trade, or the fancy of the purchaser.

It was a day or two after the conversation between Marie and Miss Ophelia, that Tom, Adolph, and about half a dozen others of the St. Clare estate, were turned over to the loving kindness of Mr. Skeggs, the keeper of a depot on——street, to await the auction, next day.

Tom had with him quite a sizable trunk full of clothing, as had most others of them. They were ushered, for the night, into a long room, where many other men, of all ages, sizes, and shades of complexion, were assembled, and from which roars of laughter and unthinking merriment were proceeding.

379

"Ah, ha! that's right. Go it, boys,—go it!" said Mr. Skeggs, the keeper. "My people are always so merry! Sambo, I see!" he said, speaking approvingly to a burly negro who was performing tricks of low buffoonery, which occasioned the shouts which Tom had heard.

As might be imagined, Tom was in no humor to join these proceedings; and, therefore, setting his trunk as far as possible from the noisy group, he sat down on it, and leaned his face against the wall.

The dealers in the human article make scrupulous and systematic efforts to promote noisy mirth among them, as a means of drowning reflection, and rendering them insensible to their condition. The whole object of the training to which the negro is put, from the time he is sold in the northern market till he arrives south, is systematically directed towards making him callous, unthinking, and brutal. The slave-dealer collects his gang in Virginia or Kentucky, and drives them to some convenient, healthy place,—often a watering place,—to be fattened. Here they are fed full daily; and, because some incline to pine, a fiddle is kept commonly going among them, and they are made to dance daily; and he who refuses to be merry—in whose soul thoughts of wife, or child, or home, are too strong for him to be gay—is marked as sullen and dangerous, and subjected to all the evils which the ill will of an utterly irresponsible and hardened man can inflict upon him. Briskness, alertness, and cheerfulness of appearance, especially before observers, are constantly enforced upon them, both by the hope of thereby getting a good master, and the fear of all that the driver may bring upon them, if they prove unsalable.

"What dat ar nigger doin here?" said Sambo, coming up to Tom, after Mr. Skeggs had left the room. Sambo was a full black, of great size, very lively, voluble, and full of trick and grimace.

"What you doin here?" said Sambo, coming up to Tom, and poking him facetiously in the side. "Meditatin', eh?"

"I am to be sold at the auction, to-morrow!" said Tom, quietly.

"Sold at auction,—haw! haw! boys, an't this yer fun? I wish't I was gwine that ar way!—tell ye, would n't I make em laugh? But how is it,—dis yer whole lot gwine to-morrow?" said Sambo, laying his hand freely on Adolph's shoulder.

"Please to let me alone!" said Adolph, fiercely, straightening himself up, with extreme disgust.

"Law, now, boys! dis yer 's one o' yer white niggers,—kind o' cream color, ye know, scented!" said he, coming up to Adolph and snuffing. "O, Lor! he 'd do for a tobaccer-shop; they could keep him to scent snuff! Lor, he 'd keep a whole shop agwine,—he would!"

"I say, keep off, can't you?" said Adolph, enraged.

"Lor, now, how touchy we is,—we white niggers! Look at us, now!" and Sambo gave a ludicrous imitation of Adolph's manner; "here 's de airs and graces. We 's been in a good family, I specs."

"Yes," said Adolph; "I had a master that could have bought you all for old truck!"

"Laws, now, only think," said Sambo, "the gentlemens that we is!"

"I belonged to the St. Clare family," said Adolph, proudly.

"Lor, you did! Be hanged if they ar' n't lucky to get shet of ye. Spects they 's gwine to trade ye off with a lot o' cracked tea-pots and sich like!" said Sambo, with a provoking grin.

Adolph, enraged at this taunt, flew furiously at his adversary, swearing and striking on every side of him. The rest laughed and shouted, and the uproar brought the keeper to the door.

"What now, boys? Order,—order!" he said, coming in and flourishing a large whip.

All fled in different directions, except Sambo, who, presuming on the favor which the keeper had to him as a licensed wag, stood his ground, ducking his head with a facetious grin, whenever the master made a dive at him.

"Lor, Mas'r, 'tan't us,—we 's reglar stiddy,—it 's these yer new hands; they 's real aggravatin',—kinder pickin' at us, all time!"

The keeper, at this, turned upon Tom and Adolph, and distributing a few kicks and cuffs without much inquiry, and leaving general orders for all to be good boys and go to sleep, left the apartment.

While this scene was going on in the men's sleeping-room,

the reader may be curious to take a peep at the corresponding apartment allotted to the women. Stretched out in various attitudes over the floor, he may see numberless sleeping forms of every shade of complexion, from the purest ebony to white, and of all years, from childhood to old age, lying now asleep. Here is a fine bright girl, of ten years, whose mother was sold out yesterday, and who to-night cried herself to sleep when nobody was looking at her. Here, a worn old negress, whose thin arms and callous fingers tell of hard toil, waiting to be sold to-morrow, as a cast-off article, for what can be got for her; and some forty or fifty others, with heads variously enveloped in blankets or articles of clothing, lie stretched around them. But, in a corner, sitting apart from the rest, are two females of a more interesting appearance than common. One of these is a respectably-dressed mulatto woman between forty and fifty, with soft eyes and a gentle and pleasing physiognomy. She has on her head a high-raised turban, made of a gay red Madras handkerchief, of the first quality, and her dress is neatly fitted, and of good material, showing that she has been provided for with a careful hand. By her side, and nestling closely to her, is a young girl of fifteen,—her daughter. She is a quadroon, as may be seen from her fairer complexion, though her likeness to her mother is quite discernible. She has the same soft, dark eye, with longer lashes, and her curling hair is of a luxuriant brown. She also is dressed with great neatness, and her white, delicate hands betray very little acquaintance with servile toil. These two are to be sold to-morrow, in the same lot with the St. Clare servants; and the gentleman to whom they belong, and to whom the money for their sale is to be transmitted, is a member of a Christian church in New York, who will receive the money, and go thereafter to the sacrament of his Lord and theirs, and think no more of it.

These two, whom we shall call Susan and Emmeline, had been the personal attendants of an amiable and pious lady of New Orleans, by whom they had been carefully and piously instructed and trained. They had been taught to read and write, diligently instructed in the truths of religion, and their lot had been as happy an one as in their condition it was possible to be. But the only son of their protectress had the management of her property; and, by carelessness and extravagance involved it to a large amount, and at last failed. One of the largest creditors was the respectable firm of B. & Co., in New York. B. & Co. wrote to their lawyer in New Orleans, who attached the real estate (these two articles and a lot of plantation hands formed the most valuable part of it), and wrote word to that effect to New York. Brother B., being, as we have said, a Christian man, and a resident in a free State, felt some uneasiness on the subject. He did n't like trading in slaves and souls of men,—of course, he did n't; but, then, there were thirty thousand dollars in the case, and that was rather too much money to be lost for a principle; and so, after much considering, and asking advice from those that he knew would advise to suit him, Brother B. wrote to his lawyer to dispose of the business in the way that seemed to him the most suitable, and remit the proceeds.

The day after the letter arrived in New Orleans, Susan and Emmeline were attached, and sent to the depot to await a general auction on the following morning; and as they glimmer faintly upon us in the moonlight which steals through the grated window, we may listen to their conversation. Both are weeping, but each quietly, that the other may not hear.

"Mother, just lay your head on my lap, and see if you can't sleep a little," says the girl, trying to appear calm.

"I have n't any heart to sleep, Em; I can't; it 's the last night we may be together!"

"O, mother, don't say so! perhaps we shall get sold together,—who knows?"

"If 't was anybody's else case, I should say so, too, Em," said the woman; "but I 'm so feard of losin' you that I don't see anything but the danger."

"Why, mother, the man said we were both likely, and would sell well."

Susan remembered the man's looks and words. With a deadly sickness at her heart, she remembered how he had looked at Emmeline's hands, and lifted up her curly hair, and pronounced her a first-rate article. Susan had been trained as a Christian, brought up in the daily reading of the Bible, and had the same horror of her child's being sold to a life of shame that any other Christian mother might have; but she had no hope,—no protection.

"Mother, I think we might do first rate, if you could get a place as cook, and I as chamber-maid or seamstress, in some family. I dare say we shall. Let's both look as bright and lively as we can, and tell all we can do, and perhaps we shall," said Emmeline.

"I want you to brush your hair all back straight, to-morrow," said Susan.

"What for, mother? I don't look near so well, that way."

"Yes, but you 'll sell better so."

"I don't see why!" said the child.

"Respectable families would be more apt to buy you, if they saw you looked plain and decent, as if you was n't trying to look handsome. I know their ways better 'n you do," said Susan.

"Well, mother, then I will."

"And, Emmeline, if we should n't ever see each other again, after to-morrow,—if I 'm sold way up on a plantation somewhere, and you somewhere else,—always remember how you 've been brought up, and all Missis has told you; take your Bible with you, and your hymn-book; and if you 're faithful to the Lord, he 'll be faithful to you."

So speaks the poor soul, in sore discouragement; for she knows that to-morrow any man, however vile and brutal, however godless and merciless, if he only has money to pay for her, may become owner of her daughter, body and soul; and then, how is the child to be faithful? She thinks of all this, as she holds her daughter in her arms, and wishes that she were not handsome and attractive. It seems almost an aggravation to her to remember how purely and piously, how much above the ordinary lot, she has been brought up. But she has no resort but to *pray*; and many such prayers to God have gone up from those same trim, neatly-arranged, respectable slave-prisons,—prayers which God has not forgotten, as a coming day shall show; for it is written, "Who causeth one of these little ones to offend, it were better for him that a mill-stone were hanged about his neck, and that he were drowned in the depths of the sea."

The soft, earnest, quiet moonbeam looks in fixedly, marking the bars of the grated windows on the prostrate, sleeping forms. The mother and daughter are singing together a wild and melancholy dirge, common as a funeral hymn among the slaves:

> "O, where is weeping Mary?
> O, where is weeping Mary?
>   'Rived in the goodly land.
> She is dead and gone to Heaven;
> She is dead and gone to Heaven;
>   'Rived in the goodly land."

These words, sung by voices of a peculiar and melancholy sweetness, in an air which seemed like the sighing of earthly despair after heavenly hope, floated through the dark prison rooms with a pathetic cadence, as verse after verse was breathed out:

> "O, where are Paul and Silas?
> O, where are Paul and Silas?
>   Gone to the goodly land.
> They are dead and gone to Heaven;
> They are dead and gone to Heaven;
>   'Rived in the goodly land."

Sing on, poor souls! The night is short, and the morning will part you forever!

But now it is morning, and everybody is astir; and the worthy Mr. Skeggs is busy and bright, for a lot of goods is to be fitted out for auction. There is a brisk look-out on the toilet; injunctions passed around to every one to put on their best face and be spry; and now all are arranged in a circle for a last review, before they are marched up to the Bourse.

Mr. Skeggs, with his palmetto on and his cigar in his mouth, walks around to put farewell touches on his wares.

"How 's this?" he said, stepping in front of Susan and Emmeline. "Where 's your curls, gal?"

The girl looked timidly at her mother, who, with the smooth adroitness common among her class, answers,

"I was telling her, last night, to put up her hair smooth and neat, and not havin' it flying about in curls; looks more respectable so."

"Bother!" said the man, peremptorily, turning to the girl; "you go right along, and curl yourself real smart!" He added, giving a crack to a rattan he held in his hand, "And be back in quick time, too!"

"You go and help her," he added, to the mother. "Them curls may make a hundred dollars difference in the sale of her."

———

Beneath a splendid dome were men of all nations, moving to and fro, over the marble pave. On every side of the circular area were little tribunes, or stations, for the use of speakers and auctioneers. Two of these, on opposite sides of the area, were now occupied by brilliant and talented gentlemen, enthusiastically forcing up, in English and French commingled, the bids of connoisseurs in their various wares. A third one, on the other side, still unoccupied, was surrounded by a group, waiting the moment of sale to begin. And here we may recognize the St. Clare servants,—Tom, Adolph, and others; and there, too, Susan and Emmeline, awaiting their turn with anxious and dejected faces. Various spectators, intending to purchase, or not intending, as the case might be, gathered around the group, handling, examining, and commenting on their various points and faces with the same freedom that a set of jockeys discuss the merits of a horse.

"Hulloa, Alf! what brings you here?" said a young exquisite, slapping the shoulder of a sprucely-dressed young man, who was examining Adolph through an eye-glass.

"Well, I was wanting a valet, and I heard that St. Clare's lot was going. I thought I 'd just look at his—"

"Catch me ever buying any of St. Clare's people! Spoilt niggers, every one. Impudent as the devil!" said the other.

"Never fear that!" said the first. "If I get 'em, I 'll soon have their airs out of them; they 'll soon find that they 've another kind of master to deal with than Monsieur St. Clare. 'Pon my word, I 'll buy that fellow. I like the shape of him."

"You 'll find it 'll take all you 've got to keep him. He 's deucedly extravagant!"

"Yes, but my lord will find that he *can't* be extravagant with *me*. Just let him be sent to the calaboose a few times, and thoroughly dressed down! I 'll tell you if it don't bring him to a sense of his ways! O, I 'll reform him, up hill and down,—you 'll see. I buy him, that 's flat!"

Tom had been standing wistfully examining the multitude of faces thronging around him, for one whom he would wish to call master. And if you should ever be under the necessity, sir, of selecting, out of two hundred men, one who was to become your absolute owner and disposer, you would, per-haps, realize, just as Tom did, how few there were that you would feel at all comfortable in being made over to. Tom saw abundance of men,—great, burly, gruff men; little, chirping, dried men; long-favored, lank, hard men; and every variety of stubbed-looking, commonplace men, who pick up their fel-low-men as one picks up chips, putting them into the fire or a basket with equal unconcern, according to their conve-nience; but he saw no St. Clare.

A little before the sale commenced, a short, broad, muscu-lar man, in a checked shirt considerably open at the bosom, and pantaloons much the worse for dirt and wear, elbowed his way through the crowd, like one who is going actively into a business; and, coming up to the group, began to ex-amine them systematically. From the moment that Tom saw him approaching, he felt an immediate and revolting horror at him, that increased as he came near. He was evidently, though short, of gigantic strength. His round, bullet head, large, light-gray eyes, with their shaggy, sandy eye-brows, and stiff, wiry, sun-burned hair, were rather unprepossessing items, it is to be confessed; his large, coarse mouth was dis-tended with tobacco, the juice of which, from time to time, he ejected from him with great decision and explosive force; his hands were immensely large, hairy, sun-burned, freckled,

and very dirty, and garnished with long nails, in a very foul
condition. This man proceeded to a very free personal examination of the lot. He seized Tom by the jaw, and pulled open
his mouth to inspect his teeth; made him strip up his sleeve,
to show his muscle; turned him round, made him jump and
spring, to show his paces.

"Where was you raised?" he added, briefly, to these investigations.

"In Kintuck, Mas'r," said Tom, looking about, as if for deliverance.

"What have you done?"

"Had care of Mas'r's farm," said Tom.

"Likely story!" said the other, shortly, as he passed on. He
paused a moment before Dolph; then spitting a discharge of
tobacco-juice on his well-blacked boots, and giving a contemptuous umph, he walked on. Again he stopped before Susan and Emmeline. He put out his heavy, dirty hand, and
drew the girl towards him; passed it over her neck and bust,
felt her arms, looked at her teeth, and then pushed her back
against her mother, whose patient face showed the suffering
she had been going through at every motion of the hideous
stranger.

The girl was frightened, and began to cry.

"Stop that, you minx!" said the salesman; "no whimpering
here,—the sale is going to begin." And accordingly the sale
begun.

Adolph was knocked off, at a good sum, to the young gentleman who had previously stated his intention of buying
him; and the other servants of the St. Clare lot went to various bidders.

"Now, up with you, boy! d 'ye hear?" said the auctioneer
to Tom.

Tom stepped upon the block, gave a few anxious looks
round; all seemed mingled in a common, indistinct noise,—
the clatter of the salesman crying off his qualifications in
French and English, the quick fire of French and English
bids; and almost in a moment came the final thump of the
hammer, and the clear ring on the last syllable of the word
"*dollars,*" as the auctioneer announced his price, and Tom was
made over.—He had a master!

He was pushed from the block;—the short, bullet-headed man seizing him roughly by the shoulder, pushed him to one side, saying, in a harsh voice, "Stand there, *you*!"

Tom hardly realized anything; but still the bidding went on,—rattling, clattering, now French, now English. Down goes the hammer again,—Susan is sold! She goes down from the block, stops, looks wistfully back,—her daughter stretches her hands towards her. She looks with agony in the face of the man who has bought her,—a respectable middle-aged man, of benevolent countenance.

"O, Mas'r, please do buy my daughter!"

"I 'd like to, but I 'm afraid I can't afford it!" said the gentleman, looking, with painful interest, as the young girl mounted the block, and looked around her with a frightened and timid glance.

The blood flushes painfully in her otherwise colorless cheek, her eye has a feverish fire, and her mother groans to see that she looks more beautiful than she ever saw her before. The auctioneer sees his advantage, and expatiates volubly in mingled French and English, and bids rise in rapid succession.

"I 'll do anything in reason," said the benevolent-looking gentleman, pressing in and joining with the bids. In a few moments they have run beyond his purse. He is silent; the auctioneer grows warmer; but bids gradually drop off. It lies now between an aristocratic old citizen and our bullet-headed acquaintance. The citizen bids for a few turns, contemptuously measuring his opponent; but the bullet-head has the advantage over him, both in obstinacy and concealed length of purse, and the controversy lasts but a moment; the hammer falls,—he has got the girl, body and soul, unless God help her!

Her master is Mr. Legree, who owns a cotton plantation on the Red river. She is pushed along into the same lot with Tom and two other men, and goes off, weeping as she goes.

The benevolent gentleman is sorry; but, then, the thing happens every day! One sees girls and mothers crying, at these sales, *always*! it can't be helped, &c.; and he walks off, with his acquisition, in another direction.

Two days after, the lawyer of the Christian firm of B. &

Co., New York, sent on their money to them. On the reverse of that draft, so obtained, let them write these words of the great Paymaster, to whom they shall make up their account in a future day: *"When he maketh inquisition for blood, he forgetteth not the cry of the humble!"*

XXXI.

The Middle Passage

"Thou art of purer eyes than to behold evil, and canst not look upon iniquity: wherefore lookest thou upon them that deal treacherously, and holdest thy tongue when the wicked devoureth the man that is more righteous than he?"—HAB. 1:13.

O N the lower part of a small, mean boat, on the Red river, Tom sat,—chains on his wrists, chains on his feet, and a weight heavier than chains lay on his heart. All had faded from his sky,—moon and star; all had passed by him, as the trees and banks were now passing, to return no more. Kentucky home, with wife and children, and indulgent owners; St. Clare home, with all its refinements and splendors; the golden head of Eva, with its saint-like eyes; the proud, gay, handsome, seemingly careless, yet ever-kind St. Clare; hours of ease and indulgent leisure,—all gone! and in place thereof, *what* remains?

It is one of the bitterest apportionments of a lot of slavery, that the negro, sympathetic and assimilative, after acquiring, in a refined family, the tastes and feelings which form the atmosphere of such a place, is not the less liable to become the bond-slave of the coarsest and most brutal,—just as a chair or table, which once decorated the superb saloon, comes, at last, battered and defaced, to the bar-room of some filthy tavern, or some low haunt of vulgar debauchery. The great difference is, that the table and chair cannot feel, and the *man* can; for even a legal enactment that he shall be "taken, reputed, adjudged in law, to be a chattel personal," cannot blot out his soul, with its own private little world of memories, hopes, loves, fears, and desires.

Mr. Simon Legree, Tom's master, had purchased slaves at one place and another, in New Orleans, to the number of eight, and driven them, handcuffed, in couples of two and two, down to the good steamer Pirate, which lay at the levee, ready for a trip up the Red river.

Having got them fairly on board, and the boat being off, he came round, with that air of efficiency which ever characterized him, to take a review of them. Stopping opposite to Tom, who had been attired for sale in his best broadcloth suit, with well-starched linen and shining boots, he briefly expressed himself as follows:

"Stand up."

Tom stood up.

"Take off that stock!" and, as Tom, encumbered by his fetters, proceeded to do it, he assisted him, by pulling it, with no gentle hand, from his neck, and putting it in his pocket.

Legree now turned to Tom's trunk, which, previous to this, he had been ransacking, and, taking from it a pair of old pantaloons and a dilapidated coat, which Tom had been wont to put on about his stable-work, he said, liberating Tom's hands from the handcuffs, and pointing to a recess in among the boxes,

"You go there, and put these on."

Tom obeyed, and in a few moments returned.

"Take off your boots," said Mr. Legree.

Tom did so.

"There," said the former, throwing him a pair of coarse, stout shoes, such as were common among the slaves, "put these on."

In Tom's hurried exchange, he had not forgotten to transfer his cherished Bible to his pocket. It was well he did so; for Mr. Legree, having refitted Tom's handcuffs, proceeded deliberately to investigate the contents of his pockets. He drew out a silk handkerchief, and put it into his own pocket. Several little trifles, which Tom had treasured, chiefly because they had amused Eva, he looked upon with a contemptuous grunt, and tossed them over his shoulder into the river.

Tom's Methodist hymn-book, which, in his hurry, he had forgotten, he now held up and turned over.

"Humph! pious, to be sure. So, what's yer name,—you belong to the church, eh?"

"Yes, Mas'r," said Tom, firmly.

"Well, I'll soon have *that* out of you. I have none o' yer bawling, praying, singing niggers on my place; so remember. Now, mind yourself," he said, with a stamp and a fierce glance of his gray eye, directed at Tom, "*I 'm* your church now! You understand,—you 've got to be as *I* say."

Something within the silent black man answered *No!* and, as if repeated by an invisible voice, came the words of an old prophetic scroll, as Eva had often read them to him,—"Fear not! for I have redeemed thee. I have called thee by my name. Thou art MINE!"

But Simon Legree heard no voice. That voice is one he never shall hear. He only glared for a moment on the downcast face of Tom, and walked off. He took Tom's trunk, which contained a very neat and abundant wardrobe, to the forecastle, where it was soon surrounded by various hands of the boat. With much laughing, at the expense of niggers who tried to be gentlemen, the articles very readily were sold to one and another, and the empty trunk finally put up at auction. It was a good joke, they all thought, especially to see how Tom looked after his things, as they were going this way and that; and then the auction of the trunk, that was funnier than all, and occasioned abundant witticisms.

This little affair being over, Simon sauntered up again to his property.

"Now, Tom, I 've relieved you of any extra baggage, you see. Take mighty good care of them clothes. It 'll be long enough 'fore you get more. I go in for making niggers careful; one suit has to do for one year, on my place."

Simon next walked up to the place where Emmeline was sitting, chained to another woman.

"Well, my dear," he said, chucking her under the chin, "keep up your spirits."

The involuntary look of horror, fright and aversion, with which the girl regarded him, did not escape his eye. He frowned fiercely.

"None o' your shines, gal! you 's got to keep a pleasant face, when I speak to ye,—d' ye hear? And you, you old yellow poco moonshine!" he said, giving a shove to the mulatto woman to whom Emmeline was chained, "don't you carry that sort of face! You 's got to look chipper, I tell ye!"

"I say, all on ye," he said retreating a pace or two back, "look at me,—look at me,—look me right in the eye,—*straight*, now!" said he, stamping his foot at every pause.

As by a fascination, every eye was now directed to the glaring greenish-gray eye of Simon.

"Now," said he, doubling his great, heavy fist into something resembling a blacksmith's hammer, "d' ye see this fist? Heft it!" he said, bringing it down on Tom's hand. "Look at these yer bones! Well, I tell ye this yer fist has got as hard as iron *knocking down niggers*. I never see the nigger, yet, I could n't bring down with one crack," said he, bringing his fist down so near to the face of Tom that he winked and drew back. "I don't keep none o' yer cussed overseers; I does my own overseeing; and I tell you things *is* seen to. You 's every one on ye got to toe the mark, I tell ye; quick,—straight,— the moment I speak. That 's the way to keep in with me. Ye won't find no soft spot in me, nowhere. So, now, mind yerselves; for I don't show no mercy!"

The women involuntarily drew in their breath, and the whole gang sat with downcast, dejected faces. Meanwhile, Simon turned on his heel, and marched up to the bar of the boat for a dram.

"That 's the way I begin with my niggers," he said, to a gentlemanly man, who had stood by him during his speech. "It 's my system to begin strong,—just let 'em know what to expect."

"Indeed!" said the stranger, looking upon him with the curiosity of a naturalist studying some out-of-the-way specimen.

"Yes, indeed. I 'm none o' yer gentlemen planters, with lily fingers, to slop round and be cheated by some old cuss of an overseer! Just feel of my knuckles, now; look at my fist. Tell ye, sir, the flesh on 't has come jest like a stone, practising on niggers,—feel on it."

The stranger applied his fingers to the implement in question, and simply said,

" 'T is hard enough; and, I suppose," he added, "practice has made your heart just like it."

"Why, yes, I may say so," said Simon, with a hearty laugh. "I reckon there 's as little soft in me as in any one going. Tell you, nobody comes it over me! Niggers never gets round me, neither with squalling nor soft soap,—that 's a fact."

"You have a fine lot there."

"Real," said Simon. "There's that Tom, they telled me he was suthin' uncommon. I paid a little high for him, tendin' him for a driver and a managing chap; only get the notions out that he's larnt by bein' treated as niggers never ought to be, he'll do prime! The yellow woman I got took in. I rayther think she's sickly, but I shall put her through for what she's worth; she may last a year or two. I don't go for savin' niggers. Use up, and buy more, 's my way;—makes you less trouble, and I'm quite sure it comes cheaper in the end;" and Simon sipped his glass.

"And how long do they generally last?" said the stranger.

"Well, donno; 'cordin' as their constitution is. Stout fellers last six or seven years; trashy ones gets worked up in two or three. I used to, when I fust begun, have considerable trouble fussin' with 'em and trying to make 'em hold out,—doctorin' on 'em up when they's sick, and givin' on 'em clothes and blankets, and what not, tryin' to keep 'em all sort o' decent and comfortable. Law, 't was n't no sort o' use; I lost money on 'em, and 't was heaps o' trouble. Now, you see, I just put 'em straight through, sick or well. When one nigger's dead, I buy another; and I find it comes cheaper and easier, every way."

The stranger turned away, and seated himself beside a gentleman, who had been listening to the conversation with repressed uneasiness.

"You must not take that fellow to be any specimen of Southern planters," said he.

"I should hope not," said the young gentleman, with emphasis.

"He is a mean, low, brutal fellow!" said the other.

"And yet your laws allow him to hold any number of human beings subject to his absolute will, without even a shadow of protection; and, low as he is, you cannot say that there are not many such."

"Well," said the other, "there are also many considerate and humane men among planters."

"Granted," said the young man; "but, in my opinion, it is you considerate, humane men, that are responsible for all the brutality and outrage wrought by these wretches; because, if it were not for your sanction and influence, the whole system

could not keep foot-hold for an hour. If there were no planters except such as that one," said he, pointing with his finger
to Legree, who stood with his back to them, "the whole thing
would go down like a mill-stone. It is your respectability and
humanity that licenses and protects his brutality."

"You certainly have a high opinion of my good nature,"
said the planter, smiling; "but I advise you not to talk quite
so loud, as there are people on board the boat who might not
be quite so tolerant to opinion as I am. You had better wait
till I get up to my plantation, and there you may abuse us all,
quite at your leisure."

The young gentleman colored and smiled, and the two
were soon busy in a game of backgammon. Meanwhile, another conversation was going on in the lower part of the
boat, between Emmeline and the mulatto woman with whom
she was confined. As was natural, they were exchanging with
each other some particulars of their history.

"Who did you belong to?" said Emmeline.

"Well, my Mas'r was Mr. Ellis,—lived on Levee-street.
P'raps you 've seen the house."

"Was he good to you?" said Emmeline.

"Mostly, till he tuk sick. He 's lain sick, off and on, more
than six months, and been orful oneasy. 'Pears like he warnt
willin' to have nobody rest, day nor night; and got so curous,
there could n't nobody suit him. 'Pears like he just grew crosser, every day; kep me up nights till I got farly beat out, and
could n't keep awake no longer; and cause I got to sleep, one
night, Lors, he talk so orful to me, and he tell me he 'd sell
me to just the hardest master he could find; and he 'd promised me my freedom, too, when he died."

"Had you any friends?" said Emmeline.

"Yes, my husband,—he 's a blacksmith. Mas'r gen'ly hired
him out. They took me off so quick, I did n't even have time
to see him; and I 's got four children. O, dear me!" said the
woman, covering her face with her hands.

It is a natural impulse, in every one, when they hear a
tale of distress, to think of something to say by way of consolation. Emmeline wanted to say something, but she could
not think of anything to say. What was there to be said?
As by a common consent, they both avoided, with fear and

dread, all mention of the horrible man who was now their master.

True, there is religious trust for even the darkest hour. The mulatto woman was a member of the Methodist church, and had an unenlightened but very sincere spirit of piety. Emmeline had been educated much more intelligently,—taught to read and write, and diligently instructed in the Bible, by the care of a faithful and pious mistress; yet, would it not try the faith of the firmest Christian, to find themselves abandoned, apparently, of God, in the grasp of ruthless violence? How much more must it shake the faith of Christ's poor little ones, weak in knowledge and tender in years!

The boat moved on,—freighted with its weight of sorrow,—up the red, muddy, turbid current, through the abrupt, tortuous windings of the Red river; and sad eyes gazed wearily on the steep red-clay banks, as they glided by in dreary sameness. At last the boat stopped at a small town, and Legree, with his party, disembarked.

XXXII.

Dark Places

"The dark places of the earth are full of the
habitations of cruelty."

TRAILING wearily behind a rude wagon, and over a ruder
road, Tom and his associates faced onward.

In the wagon was seated Simon Legree; and the two
women, still fettered together, were stowed away with some
baggage in the back part of it, and the whole company were
seeking Legree's plantation, which lay a good distance off.

It was a wild, forsaken road, now winding through dreary
pine barrens, where the wind whispered mournfully, and now
over log causeways, through long cypress swamps, the doleful
trees rising out of the slimy, spongy ground, hung with long
wreaths of funereal black moss, while ever and anon the
loathsome form of the moccasin snake might be seen sliding
among broken stumps and shattered branches that lay here
and there, rotting in the water.

It is disconsolate enough, this riding, to the stranger, who,
with well-filled pocket and well-appointed horse, threads the
lonely way on some errand of business; but wilder, drearier,
to the man enthralled, whom every weary step bears further
from all that man loves and prays for.

So one should have thought, that witnessed the sunken and
dejected expression on those dark faces; the wistful, patient
weariness with which those sad eyes rested on object after
object that passed them in their sad journey.

Simon rode on, however, apparently well pleased, occasionally pulling away at a flask of spirit, which he kept in his
pocket.

"I say, *you!*" he said, as he turned back and caught a glance
at the dispirited faces behind him! "Strike up a song, boys,—
come!"

The men looked at each other, and the *"come"* was re-

peated, with a smart crack of the whip which the driver carried in his hands. Tom began a Methodist hymn,

> "Jerusalem, my happy home!
>   Name ever dear to me!
> When shall my sorrows have an end,
>   Thy joys when shall—"

"Shut up, you black cuss!" roared Legree; "did ye think I
wanted any o' yer infernal old Methodism? I say, tune up,
now, something real rowdy,—quick!"

One of the other men struck up one of those unmeaning
songs, common among the slaves.

> "Mas'r see'd me cotch a coon,
>   High boys, high!
> He laughed to split,—d' ye see the moon,
>   Ho! ho! ho! boys, ho!
> Ho! yo! hi—e! oh!"

The singer appeared to make up the song to his own pleasure, generally hitting on rhyme, without much attempt at
reason; and all the party took up the chorus, at intervals,

> "Ho! ho! ho! boys, ho!
> High—e—oh! high—e—oh!"

It was sung very boisterously, and with a forced attempt at
merriment; but no wail of despair, no words of impassioned
prayer, could have had such a depth of woe in them as the
wild notes of the chorus. As if the poor, dumb heart, threatened,—prisoned,—took refuge in that inarticulate sanctuary
of music, and found there a language in which to breathe its
prayer to God! There was a prayer in it, which Simon could
not hear. He only heard the boys singing noisily, and was
well pleased; he was making them "keep up their spirits."

"Well, my little dear," said he, turning to Emmeline, and
laying his hand on her shoulder, "we 're almost home!"

When Legree scolded and stormed, Emmeline was terri-
fied; but when he laid his hand on her, and spoke as he now

did, she felt as if she had rather he would strike her. The expression of his eyes made her soul sick, and her flesh creep. Involuntarily she clung closer to the mulatto woman by her side, as if she were her mother.

"You did n't ever wear ear-rings," he said, taking hold of her small ear with his coarse fingers.

"No, Mas'r!" said Emmeline, trembling and looking down.

"Well, I 'll give you a pair, when we get home, if you 're a good girl. You need n't be so frightened; I don't mean to make you work very hard. You 'll have fine times with me, and live like a lady,—only be a good girl."

Legree had been drinking to that degree that he was inclining to be very gracious; and it was about this time that the enclosures of the plantation rose to view. The estate had formerly belonged to a gentleman of opulence and taste, who had bestowed some considerable attention to the adornment of his grounds. Having died insolvent, it had been purchased, at a bargain, by Legree, who used it, as he did everything else, merely as an implement for money-making. The place had that ragged, forlorn appearance, which is always produced by the evidence that the care of the former owner has been left to go to utter decay.

What was once a smooth-shaven lawn before the house, dotted here and there with ornamental shrubs, was now covered with frowsy tangled grass, with horse-posts set up, here and there, in it, where the turf was stamped away, and the ground littered with broken pails, cobs of corn, and other slovenly remains. Here and there, a mildewed jessamine or honeysuckle hung raggedly from some ornamental support, which had been pushed to one side by being used as a horse-post. What once was a large garden was now all grown over with weeds, through which, here and there, some solitary exotic reared its forsaken head. What had been a conservatory had now no window-sashes, and on the mouldering shelves stood some dry, forsaken flower-pots, with sticks in them, whose dried leaves showed they had once been plants.

The wagon rolled up a weedy gravel walk, under a noble avenue of China trees, whose graceful forms and ever-springing foliage seemed to be the only things there that neglect could not daunt or alter,—like noble spirits, so deeply rooted in goodness, as to flourish and grow stronger amid discouragement and decay.

The house had been large and handsome. It was built in a manner common at the South; a wide verandah of two stories running round every part of the house, into which every outer door opened, the lower tier being supported by brick pillars.

But the place looked desolate and uncomfortable; some windows stopped up with boards, some with shattered panes, and shutters hanging by a single hinge,—all telling of coarse neglect and discomfort.

Bits of board, straw, old decayed barrels and boxes, garnished the ground in all directions; and three or four ferocious-looking dogs, roused by the sound of the wagon-wheels, came tearing out, and were with difficulty restrained from laying hold of Tom and his companions, by the effort of the ragged servants who came after them.

"Ye see what ye 'd get!" said Legree, caressing the dogs with grim satisfaction, and turning to Tom and his companions. "Ye see what ye 'd get, if ye try to run off. These yer dogs has been raised to track niggers; and they 'd jest as soon chaw one on ye up as eat their supper. So, mind yerself! How now, Sambo!" he said, to a ragged fellow, without any brim to his hat, who was officious in his attentions. "How have things been going?"

"Fust rate, Mas'r."

"Quimbo," said Legree to another, who was making zealous demonstrations to attract his attention, "ye minded what I telled ye?"

"Guess I did, did n't I?"

These two colored men were the two principal hands on the plantation. Legree had trained them in savageness and brutality as systematically as he had his bull-dogs; and, by long practice in hardness and cruelty, brought their whole nature to about the same range of capacities. It is a common remark, and one that is thought to militate strongly against the character of the race, that the negro overseer is always more tyrannical and cruel than the white one. This is simply saying that the negro mind has been more crushed and debased than the white. It is no more true of this race than of every oppressed race, the world over. The slave is always a tyrant, if he can get a chance to be one.

Legree, like some potentates we read of in history, governed his plantation by a sort of resolution of forces. Sambo and Quimbo cordially hated each other; the plantation hands, one and all, cordially hated them; and, by playing off one against another, he was pretty sure, through one or the other of the three parties, to get informed of whatever was on foot in the place.

Nobody can live entirely without social intercourse; and Legree encouraged his two black satellites to a kind of coarse familiarity with him,—a familiarity, however, at any moment liable to get one or the other of them into trouble; for, on the slightest provocation, one of them always stood ready, at a nod, to be a minister of his vengeance on the other.

As they stood there now by Legree, they seemed an apt illustration of the fact that brutal men are lower even than animals. Their coarse, dark, heavy features; their great eyes, rolling enviously on each other; their barbarous, guttural, half-brute intonation; their dilapidated garments fluttering in the wind,—were all in admirable keeping with the vile and unwholesome character of everything about the place.

"Here, you Sambo," said Legree, "take these yer boys down to the quarters; and here's a gal I've got for *you*," said he, as he separated the mulatto woman from Emmeline, and pushed her towards him;—"I promised to bring you one, you know."

The woman gave a sudden start, and, drawing back, said, suddenly,

"O, Mas'r! I left my old man in New Orleans."

"What of that, you——; won't you want one here? None o' your words,—go long!" said Legree, raising his whip.

"Come, mistress," he said to Emmeline, "you go in here with me."

A dark, wild face was seen, for a moment, to glance at the window of the house; and, as Legree opened the door, a female voice said something, in a quick, imperative tone. Tom, who was looking, with anxious interest, after Emmeline, as she went in, noticed this, and heard Legree answer, angrily, "You may hold your tongue! I'll do as I please, for all you!"

Tom heard no more; for he was soon following Sambo to the quarters. The quarters was a little sort of street of rude shanties, in a row, in a part of the plantation, far off from the house. They had a forlorn, brutal, forsaken air. Tom's heart sunk when he saw them. He had been comforting himself with the thought of a cottage, rude, indeed, but one which he might make neat and quiet, and where he might have a shelf for his Bible, and a place to be alone out of his laboring hours. He looked into several; they were mere rude shells, destitute of any species of furniture, except a heap of straw, foul with dirt, spread confusedly over the floor, which was merely the bare ground, trodden hard by the tramping of innumerable feet.

"Which of these will be mine?" said he, to Sambo, submissively.

"Dunno; ken turn in here, I spose," said Sambo; "spects thar's room for another thar; thar's a pretty smart heap o' niggers to each on 'em, now; sure, I dunno what I's to do with more."

It was late in the evening when the weary occupants of the shanties came flocking home,—men and women, in soiled and tattered garments, surly and uncomfortable, and in no mood to look pleasantly on new-comers. The small village was alive with no inviting sounds; hoarse, guttural voices contending at the hand-mills where their morsel of hard corn was yet to be ground into meal, to fit it for the cake that was to constitute their only supper. From the earliest dawn of the day, they had been in the fields, pressed to work under the driving lash of the overseers; for it was now in the very heat and hurry of the season, and no means was left untried to press every one up to the top of their capabilities. "True," says the negligent lounger; "picking cotton is n't hard work." Is n't it? And it is n't much inconvenience, either, to have one drop of water fall on your head; yet the worst torture of the inquisition is produced by drop after drop, drop after drop, falling moment after moment, with monotonous succession, on the same spot; and work, in itself not hard, becomes so, by being pressed, hour after hour, with unvarying, unrelenting sameness, with not even the consciousness of free-will to take from its tediousness. Tom looked in vain among the gang, as they poured along, for companionable faces. He saw only sullen, scowling, imbruted men, and feeble, discouraged women, or women that were not women,—the strong pushing away the weak,—the gross, unrestricted animal selfishness of human beings, of whom nothing good was expected and desired; and who, treated in every way like brutes, had sunk as nearly to their level as it was possible for human beings to do. To a late hour in the night the sound of the grinding was protracted; for the mills were few in number compared with the grinders, and the weary and feeble ones were driven back by the strong, and came on last in their turn.

"Ho yo!" said Sambo, coming to the mulatto woman, and throwing down a bag of corn before her; "what a cuss yo name?"

"Lucy," said the woman.

"Wal, Lucy, yo my woman now. Yo grind dis yer corn, and get *my* supper baked, ye har?"

"I an't your woman, and I won't be!" said the woman, with the sharp, sudden courage of despair; "you go long!"

"I 'll kick yo, then!" said Sambo, raising his foot threateningly.

"Ye may kill me, if ye choose,—the sooner the better! Wish't I was dead!" said she.

"I say, Sambo, you go to spilin' the hands, I 'll tell Mas'r o' you," said Quimbo, who was busy at the mill, from which he had viciously driven two or three tired women, who were waiting to grind their corn.

"And I 'll tell him ye won't let the women come to the mills, yo old nigger!" said Sambo. "Yo jes keep to yo own row."

Tom was hungry with his day's journey, and almost faint for want of food.

"Thar, yo!" said Quimbo, throwing down a coarse bag, which contained a peck of corn; "thar, nigger, grab, take car on 't,—yo won't get no more, *dis* yer week."

Tom waited till a late hour, to get a place at the mills; and then, moved by the utter weariness of two women, whom he saw trying to grind their corn there, he ground for them, put together the decaying brands of the fire, where many had baked cakes before them, and then went about getting his own supper. It was a new kind of work there,—a deed of charity, small as it was; but it woke an answering touch in their hearts,—an expression of womanly kindness came over their hard faces; they mixed his cake for him, and tended its baking; and Tom sat down by the light of the fire, and drew out his Bible,—for he had need of comfort.

"What's that?" said one of the women.

"A Bible," said Tom.

"Good Lord! han't seen un since I was in Kentuck."

"Was you raised in Kentuck?" said Tom, with interest.

"Yes, and well raised, too; never 'spected to come to dis yer!" said the woman, sighing.

"What's dat ar book, any way?" said the other woman.

"Why, the Bible."

"Laws a me! what's dat?" said the woman.

"Do tell! you never hearn on 't?" said the other woman. "I used to har Missis a readin' on 't, sometimes, in Kentuck; but, laws o' me! we don't har nothin' here but crackin' and swarin'."

"Read a piece, anyways!" said the first woman, curiously, seeing Tom attentively poring over it.

Tom read,—"Come unto ME, all ye that labor and are heavy laden, and I will give you rest."

"Them's good words, enough," said the woman; "who says 'em?"

"The Lord," said Tom.

"I jest wish I know'd whar to find Him," said the woman. "I would go; 'pears like I never should get rested agin. My flesh is fairly sore, and I tremble all over, every day, and Sambo's allers a jawin' at me, 'cause I does n't pick faster; and nights it's most midnight 'fore I can get my supper; and den 'pears like I don't turn over and shut my eyes, 'fore I hear de horn blow to get up, and at it agin in de mornin'. If I knew whar de Lor was, I'd tell him."

"He's here, he's everywhere," said Tom.

"Lor, you an't gwine to make me believe dat ar! I know de Lord an't here," said the woman; "'t an't no use talking, though. I's jest gwine to camp down, and sleep while I ken."

The women went off to their cabins, and Tom sat alone, by the smouldering fire, that flickered up redly in his face.

The silver, fair-browed moon rose in the purple sky, and looked down, calm and silent, as God looks on the scene of misery and oppression,—looked calmly on the lone black man, as he sat, with his arms folded, and his Bible on his knee.

"Is God HERE?" Ah, how is it possible for the untaught heart to keep its faith, unswerving, in the face of dire misrule, and palpable, unrebuked injustice? In that simple heart waged a fierce conflict: the crushing sense of wrong, the foreshadowing of a whole life of future misery, the wreck of all past hopes, mournfully tossing in the soul's sight, like dead corpses of wife, and child, and friend, rising from the dark wave, and surging in the face of the half-drowned mariner! Ah, was it easy *here* to believe and hold fast the great password of Christian faith, that "God IS, and is the REWARDER of them that diligently seek Him"?

Tom rose, disconsolate, and stumbled into the cabin that had been allotted to him. The floor was already strewn with weary sleepers, and the foul air of the place almost repelled him; but the heavy night-dews were chill, and his limbs weary, and, wrapping about him a tattered blanket, which formed his only bed-clothing, he stretched himself in the straw and fell asleep.

In dreams, a gentle voice came over his ear; he was sitting on the mossy seat in the garden by Lake Pontchartrain, and Eva, with her serious eyes bent downward, was reading to him from the Bible; and he heard her read,

"When thou passest through the waters, I will be with thee, and the rivers they shall not overflow thee; when thou walkest through the fire, thou shalt not be burned, neither shall the flame kindle upon thee; for I am the Lord thy God, the Holy One of Israel, thy Saviour."

Gradually the words seemed to melt and fade, as in a divine music; the child raised her deep eyes, and fixed them lovingly on him, and rays of warmth and comfort seemed to go from them to his heart; and, as if wafted on the music, she seemed to rise on shining wings, from which flakes and spangles of gold fell off like stars, and she was gone.

Tom woke. Was it a dream? Let it pass for one. But who shall say that that sweet young spirit, which in life so yearned to comfort and console the distressed, was forbidden of God to assume this ministry after death?

> It is a beautiful belief,
>   That ever round our head
> Are hovering, on angel wings,
>   The spirits of the dead.

XXXIII.

Cassy

"And behold, the tears of such as were oppressed, and they had no comforter; and on the side of their oppressors there was *power*, but they had no comforter."—ECCL. 4:1.

IT took but a short time to familiarize Tom with all that was to be hoped or feared in his new way of life. He was an expert and efficient workman in whatever he undertook; and was, both from habit and principle, prompt and faithful. Quiet and peaceable in his disposition, he hoped, by unremitting diligence, to avert from himself at least a portion of the evils of his condition. He saw enough of abuse and misery to make him sick and weary; but he determined to toil on, with religious patience, committing himself to Him that judgeth righteously, not without hope that some way of escape might yet be opened to him.

Legree took silent note of Tom's availability. He rated him as a first-class hand; and yet he felt a secret dislike to him,— the native antipathy of bad to good. He saw, plainly, that when, as was often the case, his violence and brutality fell on the helpless, Tom took notice of it; for, so subtle is the atmosphere of opinion, that it will make itself felt, without words; and the opinion even of a slave may annoy a master. Tom in various ways manifested a tenderness of feeling, a commiseration for his fellow-sufferers, strange and new to them, which was watched with a jealous eye by Legree. He had purchased Tom with a view of eventually making him a sort of overseer, with whom he might, at times, intrust his affairs, in short absences; and, in his view, the first, second, and third requisite for that place, was *hardness*. Legree made up his mind, that, as Tom was not hard to his hand, he would harden him forthwith; and some few weeks after Tom had been on the place, he determined to commence the process.

One morning, when the hands were mustered for the field, Tom noticed, with surprise, a new comer among them, whose appearance excited his attention. It was a woman, tall and slenderly formed, with remarkably delicate hands and feet, and dressed in neat and respectable garments. By the appearance of her face, she might have been between thirty-five and forty; and it was a face that, once seen, could never be forgotten,—one of those that, at a glance, seem to convey to us an idea of a wild, painful, and romantic history. Her forehead was high, and her eyebrows marked with beautiful clearness. Her straight, well-formed nose, her finely-cut mouth, and the graceful contour of her head and neck, showed that she must once have been beautiful; but her face was deeply wrinkled with lines of pain, and of proud and bitter endurance. Her complexion was sallow and unhealthy, her cheeks thin, her features sharp, and her whole form emaciated. But her eye was the most remarkable feature,—so large, so heavily black, overshadowed by long lashes of equal darkness, and so wildly, mournfully despairing. There was a fierce pride and defiance in every line of her face, in every curve of the flexible lip, in every motion of her body; but in her eye was a deep, settled night of anguish,—an expression so hopeless and unchanging as to contrast fearfully with the scorn and pride expressed by her whole demeanor.

Where she came from, or who she was, Tom did not know. The first he did know, she was walking by his side, erect and proud, in the dim gray of the dawn. To the gang, however, she was known; for there was much looking and turning of heads, and a smothered yet apparent exultation among the miserable, ragged, half-starved creatures by whom she was surrounded.

"Got to come to it, at last,—glad of it!" said one.

"He! he! he!" said another; "you 'll know how good it is, Misse!"

"We 'll see her work!"

"Wonder if she 'll get a cutting up, at night, like the rest of us!"

"I 'd be glad to see her down for a flogging, I 'll bound!" said another.

The woman took no notice of these taunts, but walked on, with the same expression of angry scorn, as if she heard nothing. Tom had always lived among refined and cultivated people, and he felt intuitively, from her air and bearing, that she belonged to that class; but how or why she could be fallen to those degrading circumstances, he could not tell. The woman neither looked at him nor spoke to him, though, all the way to the field, she kept close at his side.

Tom was soon busy at his work; but, as the woman was at no great distance from him, he often glanced an eye to her, at her work. He saw, at a glance, that a native adroitness and handiness made the task to her an easier one than it proved to many. She picked very fast and very clean, and with an air of scorn, as if she despised both the work and the disgrace and humiliation of the circumstances in which she was placed.

In the course of the day, Tom was working near the mulatto woman who had been bought in the same lot with himself. She was evidently in a condition of great suffering, and Tom often heard her praying, as she wavered and trembled, and seemed about to fall down. Tom silently, as he came near to her, transferred several handfuls of cotton from his own sack to hers.

"O, don't, don't!" said the woman, looking surprised; "it 'll get you into trouble."

Just then Sambo came up. He seemed to have a special spite against this woman; and, flourishing his whip, said, in brutal, guttural tones, "What dis yer, Luce,—foolin' a'?" and, with the word, kicking the woman with his heavy cowhide shoe, he struck Tom across the face with his whip.

Tom silently resumed his task; but the woman, before at the last point of exhaustion, fainted.

"I 'll bring her to!" said the driver, with a brutal grin. "I 'll give her something better than camphire!" and, taking a pin from his coat-sleeve, he buried it to the head in her flesh. The woman groaned, and half rose. "Get up, you beast, and work, will yer, or I 'll show yer a trick more!"

The woman seemed stimulated, for a few moments, to an unnatural strength, and worked with desperate eagerness.

"See that you keep to dat ar," said the man, "or yer 'll wish yer 's dead to-night, I reckin!"

"That I do now!" Tom heard her say; and again he heard her say, "O, Lord, how long! O, Lord, why don't you help us?"

At the risk of all that he might suffer, Tom came forward again, and put all the cotton in his sack into the woman's.

"O, you must n't! you donno what they 'll do to ye!" said the woman.

"I can bar it!" said Tom, "better 'n you;" and he was at his place again. It passed in a moment.

Suddenly, the stranger woman whom we have described, and who had, in the course of her work, come near enough to hear Tom's last words, raised her heavy black eyes, and fixed them, for a second, on him; then, taking a quantity of cotton from her basket, she placed it in his.

"You know nothing about this place," she said, "or you would n't have done that. When you 've been here a month, you 'll be done helping anybody; you 'll find it hard enough to take care of your own skin!"

"The Lord forbid, Missis!" said Tom, using instinctively to his field companion the respectful form proper to the high bred with whom he had lived.

"The Lord never visits these parts," said the woman, bitterly, as she went nimbly forward with her work; and again the scornful smile curled her lips.

But the action of the woman had been seen by the driver, across the field; and, flourishing his whip, he came up to her.

"What! what!" he said to the woman, with an air of triumph, "YOU a foolin'? Go along! yer under me now,— mind yourself, or yer 'll cotch it!"

A glance like sheet-lightning suddenly flashed from those black eyes; and, facing about, with quivering lip and dilated nostrils, she drew herself up, and fixed a glance, blazing with rage and scorn, on the driver.

"Dog!" she said, "touch *me*, if you dare! I 've power enough, yet, to have you torn by the dogs, burnt alive, cut to inches! I 've only to say the word!"

"What de devil you here for, den?" said the man, evidently cowed, and sullenly retreating a step or two. "Did n't mean no harm, Misse Cassy!"

"Keep your distance, then!" said the woman. And, in truth, the man seemed greatly inclined to attend to something at the other end of the field, and started off in quick time.

The woman suddenly turned to her work, and labored with

a despatch that was perfectly astonishing to Tom. She seemed to work by magic. Before the day was through, her basket was filled, crowded down, and piled, and she had several times put largely into Tom's. Long after dusk, the whole weary train, with their baskets on their heads, defiled up to the building appropriated to the storing and weighing the cotton. Legree was there, busily conversing with the two drivers.

"Dat ar Tom 's gwine to make a powerful deal o' trouble; kept a puttin' into Lucy's basket.—One o' these yer dat will get all der niggers to feelin' 'bused, if Mas'r don't watch him!" said Sambo.

"Hey-dey! The black cuss!" said Legree. "He 'll have to get a breakin' in, won't he, boys?"

Both negroes grinned a horrid grin, at this intimation.

"Ay, ay! let Mas'r Legree alone, for breakin' in! De debil heself could n't beat Mas'r at dat!" said Quimbo.

"Wal, boys, the best way is to give him the flogging to do, till he gets over his notions. Break him in!"

"Lord, Mas'r 'll have hard work to get dat out o' him!"

"It 'll have to come out of him, though!" said Legree, as he rolled his tobacco in his mouth.

"Now, dar 's Lucy,—de aggravatinest, ugliest wench on de place!" pursued Sambo.

"Take care, Sam; I shall begin to think what 's the reason for your spite agin Lucy."

"Well, Mas'r knows she sot herself up agin Mas'r, and would n't have me, when he telled her to."

"I 'd a flogged her into 't," said Legree, spitting, "only there 's such a press o' work, it don't seem wuth a while to upset her jist now. She 's slender; but these yer slender gals will bear half killin' to get their own way!"

"Wal, Lucy was real aggravatin' and lazy, sulkin' round; would n't do nothin',—and Tom he tuck up for her."

"He did, eh! Wal, then, Tom shall have the pleasure of flogging her. It 'll be a good practice for him, and he won't put it on to the gal like you devils, neither."

"Ho, ho! haw! haw! haw!" laughed both the sooty wretches; and the diabolical sounds seemed, in truth, a not unapt expression of the fiendish character which Legree gave them.

"Wal, but, Mas'r, Tom and Misse Cassy, and dey among 'em, filled Lucy's basket. I ruther guess der weight 's in it, Mas'r!"

"*I do the weighing!*" said Legree, emphatically.

Both the drivers again laughed their diabolical laugh.

"So!" he added, "Misse Cassy did her day's work."

"She picks like de debil and all his angels!"

"She 's got 'em all in her, I believe!" said Legree; and, growling a brutal oath, he proceeded to the weighing-room.

Slowly the weary, dispirited creatures, wound their way into the room, and, with crouching reluctance, presented their baskets to be weighed.

Legree noted on a slate, on the side of which was pasted a list of names, the amount.

Tom's basket was weighed and approved; and he looked, with an anxious glance, for the success of the woman he had befriended.

Tottering with weakness, she came forward, and delivered her basket. It was of full weight, as Legree well perceived; but, affecting anger, he said,

"What, you lazy beast! short again! stand aside, you 'll catch it, pretty soon!"

The woman gave a groan of utter despair, and sat down on a board.

The person who had been called Misse Cassy now came forward, and, with a haughty, negligent air, delivered her basket. As she delivered it, Legree looked in her eyes with a sneering yet inquiring glance.

She fixed her black eyes steadily on him, her lips moved slightly, and she said something in French. What it was, no one knew; but Legree's face became perfectly demoniacal in its expression, as she spoke; he half raised his hand, as if to strike,—a gesture which she regarded with fierce disdain, as she turned and walked away.

"And now," said Legree, "come here, you Tom. You see,

I telled ye I did n't buy ye jest for the common work; I mean to promote ye, and make a driver of ye; and to-night ye may jest as well begin to get yer hand in. Now, ye jest take this yer gal and flog her; ye 've seen enough on 't to know how."

"I beg Mas'r's pardon," said Tom; "hopes Mas'r won't set me at that. It 's what I an't used to,—never did,—and can't do, no way possible."

"Ye 'll larn a pretty smart chance of things ye never did know, before I 've done with ye!" said Legree, taking up a cow-hide, and striking Tom a heavy blow across the cheek, and following up the infliction by a shower of blows.

"There!" he said, as he stopped to rest; "now, will ye tell me ye can't do it?"

"Yes, Mas'r," said Tom, putting up his hand, to wipe the blood, that trickled down his face. "I 'm willin' to work, night and day, and work while there 's life and breath in me; but this yer thing I can't feel it right to do;—and, Mas'r, I *never* shall do it,—*never!*"

Tom had a remarkably smooth, soft voice, and a habitually respectful manner, that had given Legree an idea that he would be cowardly, and easily subdued. When he spoke these last words, a thrill of amazement went through every one; the poor woman clasped her hands, and said, "O Lord!" and every one involuntarily looked at each other and drew in their breath, as if to prepare for the storm that was about to burst.

Legree looked stupefied and confounded; but at last burst forth,—

"What! ye blasted black beast! tell *me* ye don't think it *right* to do what I tell ye! What have any of you cussed cattle to do with thinking what 's right? I 'll put a stop to it! Why, what do ye think ye are? May be ye think ye 'r a gentleman master, Tom, to be a telling your master what 's right, and what an't! So you pretend it 's wrong to flog the gal!"

"I think so, Mas'r," said Tom; "the poor crittur 's sick and feeble; 't would be downright cruel, and it 's what I never will do, nor begin to. Mas'r, if you mean to kill me, kill me; but, as to my raising my hand agin any one here, I never shall,— I 'll die first!"

Tom spoke in a mild voice, but with a decision that could not be mistaken. Legree shook with anger; his greenish eyes glared fiercely, and his very whiskers seemed to curl with passion; but, like some ferocious beast, that plays with its victim before he devours it, he kept back his strong impulse to proceed to immediate violence, and broke out into bitter raillery.

"Well, here's a pious dog, at last, let down among us sinners!—a saint, a gentleman, and no less, to talk to us sinners about our sins! Powerful holy critter, he must be! Here, you rascal, you make believe to be so pious,—did n't you never hear, out of yer Bible, 'Servants, obey yer masters'? An't I yer master? Did n't I pay down twelve hundred dollars, cash, for all there is inside yer old cussed black shell? An't yer mine, now, body and soul?" he said, giving Tom a violent kick with his heavy boot; "tell me!"

In the very depth of physical suffering, bowed by brutal oppression, this question shot a gleam of joy and triumph through Tom's soul. He suddenly stretched himself up, and, looking earnestly to heaven, while the tears and blood that flowed down his face mingled, he exclaimed,

"No! no! no! my soul an't yours, Mas'r! You have n't bought it,—ye can't buy it! It's been bought and paid for, by one that is able to keep it;—no matter, no matter, you can't harm me!"

"I can't!" said Legree, with a sneer; "we'll see,—we'll see! Here, Sambo, Quimbo, give this dog such a breakin' in as he won't get over, this month!"

The two gigantic negroes that now laid hold of Tom, with fiendish exultation in their faces, might have formed no unapt personification of powers of darkness. The poor woman screamed with apprehension, and all rose, as by a general impulse, while they dragged him unresisting from the place.

XXXIV.

The Quadroon's Story

And behold the tears of such as are oppressed; and on the side
of their oppressors there was power. Wherefore I praised the
dead that are already dead more than the living that are yet
alive.—ECCL. 4:1.

IT was late at night, and Tom lay groaning and bleeding
alone, in an old forsaken room of the gin-house, among
pieces of broken machinery, piles of damaged cotton, and
other rubbish which had there accumulated.

The night was damp and close, and the thick air swarmed
with myriads of mosquitos, which increased the restless torture of his wounds; whilst a burning thirst—a torture beyond
all others—filled up the uttermost measure of physical anguish.

"O, good Lord! *Do* look down,—give me the victory!—
give me the victory over all!" prayed poor Tom, in his anguish.

A footstep entered the room, behind him, and the light of
a lantern flashed on his eyes.

"Who's there? O, for the Lord's massy, please give me
some water!"

The woman Cassy—for it was she—set down her lantern,
and, pouring water from a bottle, raised his head, and gave
him drink. Another and another cup were drained, with feverish eagerness.

"Drink all ye want," she said; "I knew how it would be. It
isn't the first time I've been out in the night, carrying water
to such as you."

"Thank you, Missis," said Tom, when he had done drinking.

"Don't call me Missis! I'm a miserable slave, like yourself,—a lower one than you can ever be!" said she, bitterly;
"but now," said she, going to the door, and dragging in a
small pallaise, over which she had spread linen cloths wet

Cassy ministering to Uncle Tom after his whipping

with cold water, "try, my poor fellow, to roll yourself on to this."

Stiff with wounds and bruises, Tom was a long time in accomplishing this movement; but, when done, he felt a sensible relief from the cooling application to his wounds.

The woman, whom long practice with the victims of brutality had made familiar with many healing arts, went on to make many applications to Tom's wounds, by means of which he was soon somewhat relieved.

"Now," said the woman, when she had raised his head on a roll of damaged cotton, which served for a pillow, "there's the best I can do for you."

Tom thanked her; and the woman, sitting down on the floor, drew up her knees, and embracing them with her arms, looked fixedly before her, with a bitter and painful expression of countenance. Her bonnet fell back, and long wavy streams of black hair fell around her singular and melancholy face.

"It's no use, my poor fellow!" she broke out, at last, "it's of no use, this you've been trying to do. You were a brave fellow,—you had the right on your side; but it's all in vain, and out of the question, for you to struggle. You are in the devil's hands;—he is the strongest, and you must give up!"

Give up! and, had not human weakness and physical agony whispered that, before? Tom started; for the bitter woman, with her wild eyes and melancholy voice, seemed to him an embodiment of the temptation with which he had been wrestling.

"O Lord! O Lord!" he groaned, "how can I give up?"

"There's no use calling on the Lord,—he never hears," said the woman, steadily; "there isn't any God, I believe; or, if there is, he's taken sides against us. All goes against us, heaven and earth. Everything is pushing us into hell. Why shouldn't we go?"

Tom closed his eyes, and shuddered at the dark, atheistic words.

"You see," said the woman, "*you* don't know anything about it;—I do. I've been on this place five years, body and soul, under this man's foot; and I hate him as I do the devil! Here you are, on a lone plantation, ten miles from any other, in the swamps; not a white person here, who could testify, if you were burned alive,—if you were scalded, cut into inch-pieces, set up for the dogs to tear, or hung up and whipped to death. There's no law here, of God or man, that can do you, or any one of us, the least good; and, this man! there's no earthly thing that he's too good to do. I could make any one's hair rise, and their teeth chatter, if I should only tell what I've seen and been knowing to, here,—and it's no use resisting! Did I *want* to live with him? Was n't I a woman delicately bred; and he—God in heaven! what was he, and is he? And yet, I've lived with him, these five years, and cursed every moment of my life,—night and day! And now, he's got a new one,—a young thing, only fifteen, and she brought up, she says, piously. Her good mistress taught her to read the Bible; and she's brought her Bible here—to hell with her!"—and the woman laughed a wild and doleful laugh, that rung, with a strange, supernatural sound, through the old ruined shed.

Tom folded his hands; all was darkness and horror.

"O Jesus! Lord Jesus! have you quite forgot us poor critturs?" burst forth, at last;—"help, Lord, I perish!"

The woman sternly continued:

"And what are these miserable low dogs you work with, that you should suffer on their account? Every one of them would turn against you, the first time they got a chance. They are all of 'em as low and cruel to each other as they can be; there's no use in your suffering to keep from hurting them."

"Poor critturs!" said Tom,—"what made 'em cruel?—and, if I give out, I shall get used to 't, and grow, little by little, just like 'em! No, no, Missis! I've lost everything,—wife, and children, and home, and a kind Mas'r,—and he would have set me free, if he'd only lived a week longer; I've lost everything in *this* world, and it's clean gone, forever,—and now I *can't* lose Heaven, too; no, I can't get to be wicked, besides all!"

"But it can't be that the Lord will lay sin to our account," said the woman; "he won't charge it to us, when we're forced to it; he'll charge it to them that drove us to it."

"Yes," said Tom; "but that won't keep us from growing wicked. If I get to be as hard-hearted as that ar' Sambo, and

as wicked, it won't make much odds to me how I come so;
it's the *bein' so*,—that ar's what I'm a dreadin'."

The woman fixed a wild and startled look on Tom, as if a
new thought had struck her; and then heavily groaning, said,

"O God a' mercy! you speak the truth! O—O—O!"—
and, with groans, she fell on the floor, like one crushed and
writhing under the extremity of mental anguish.

There was a silence, a while, in which the breathing of both
parties could be heard, when Tom faintly said, "O, please,
Missis!"

The woman suddenly rose up, with her face composed to
its usual stern, melancholy expression.

"Please, Missis, I saw 'em throw my coat in that ar' corner,
and in my coat-pocket is my Bible;—if Missis would please
get it for me."

Cassy went and got it. Tom opened, at once, to a heavily
marked passage, much worn, of the last scenes in the life of
Him by whose stripes we are healed.

"If Missis would only be so good as read that ar',—it's
better than water."

Cassy took the book, with a dry, proud air, and looked
over the passage. She then read aloud, in a soft voice, and
with a beauty of intonation that was peculiar, that touching
account of anguish and of glory. Often, as she read, her voice
faltered, and sometimes failed her altogether, when she would
stop, with an air of frigid composure, till she had mastered
herself. When she came to the touching words, "Father forgive them, for they know not what they do," she threw down
the book, and, burying her face in the heavy masses of her
hair, she sobbed aloud, with a convulsive violence.

Tom was weeping, also, and occasionally uttering a smothered ejaculation.

"If we only could keep up to that ar'!" said Tom;—"it
seemed to come so natural to him, and we have to fight so
hard for 't! O Lord, help us! O blessed Lord Jesus, do help
us!"

"Missis," said Tom, after a while, "I can see that, some
how, you're quite 'bove me in everything; but there's one
thing Missis might learn even from poor Tom. Ye said the

Lord took sides against us, because he lets us be 'bused and knocked round; but ye see what come on his own Son,—the blessed Lord of Glory,—wan't he allays poor? and have we, any on us, yet come so low as he come? The Lord han't forgot us,—I 'm sartin' o' that ar'. If we suffer with him, we shall also reign, Scripture says; but, if we deny Him, he also will deny us. Did n't they all suffer?—the Lord and all his? It tells how they was stoned and sawn asunder, and wandered about in sheep-skins and goat-skins, and was destitute, afflicted, tormented. Sufferin' an't no reason to make us think the Lord 's turned agin us; but jest the contrary, if only we hold on to him, and does n't give up to sin."

"But why does he put us where we can't help but sin?" said the woman.

"I think we *can* help it," said Tom.

"You 'll see," said Cassy; "what 'll you do? To-morrow they 'll be at you again. I know 'em; I 've seen all their doings; I can't bear to think of all they 'll bring you to;—and they 'll make you give out, at last!"

"Lord Jesus!" said Tom, "you *will* take care of my soul? O Lord, do!—don't let me give out!"

"O dear!" said Cassy; "I 've heard all this crying and praying before; and yet, they 've been broken down, and brought under. There 's Emmeline, she 's trying to hold on, and you 're trying,—but what use? You must give up, or be killed by inches."

"Well, then, I *will* die!" said Tom. "Spin it out as long as they can, they can't help my dying, some time!—and, after that, they can't do no more. I 'm clar, I 'm set! I *know* the Lord 'll help me, and bring me through."

The woman did not answer; she sat with her black eyes intently fixed on the floor.

"May be it 's the way," she murmured to herself; "but those that *have* given up, there 's no hope for them!—none! We live in filth, and grow loathsome, till we loathe ourselves! And we long to die, and we don't dare to kill ourselves!—No hope! no hope! no hope!—this girl now,—just as old as I was!

"You see me now," she said, speaking to Tom very rapidly; "see what I am! Well, I was brought up in luxury; the first I

remember is, playing about, when I was a child, in splendid
parlors;—when I was kept dressed up like a doll, and company and visiters used to praise me. There was a garden opening from the saloon windows; and there I used to play hide-
and-go-seek, under the orange-trees, with my brothers and
sisters. I went to a convent, and there I learned music, French
and embroidery, and what not; and when I was fourteen, I
came out to my father's funeral. He died very suddenly, and
when the property came to be settled, they found that there
was scarcely enough to cover the debts; and when the creditors took an inventory of the property, I was set down in it.
My mother was a slave woman, and my father had always
meant to set me free; but he had not done it, and so I was
set down in the list. I'd always known who I was, but never
thought much about it. Nobody ever expects that a strong,
healthy man is a going to die. My father was a well man only
four hours before he died;—it was one of the first cholera
cases in New Orleans. The day after the funeral, my father's
wife took her children, and went up to her father's plantation.
I thought they treated me strangely, but did n't know. There
was a young lawyer who they left to settle the business; and
he came every day, and was about the house, and spoke very
politely to me. He brought with him, one day, a young man,
whom I thought the handsomest I had ever seen. I shall never
forget that evening. I walked with him in the garden. I was
lonesome and full of sorrow, and he was so kind and gentle
to me; and he told me that he had seen me before I went to
the convent, and that he had loved me a great while, and that
he would be my friend and protector;—in short, though
he did n't tell me, he had paid two thousand dollars for me,
and I was his property,—I became his willingly, for I loved
him. Loved!" said the woman, stopping. "O, how I *did* love
that man! How I love him now,—and always shall, while I
breathe! He was so beautiful, so high, so noble! He put me
into a beautiful house, with servants, horses, and carriages,
and furniture, and dresses. Everything that money could buy,
he gave me; but I did n't set any value on all that,—I only
cared for him. I loved him better than my God and my own
soul; and, if I tried, I could n't do any other way from what
he wanted me to.

"I wanted only one thing—I did want him to *marry* me. I thought, if he loved me as he said he did, and if I was what he seemed to think I was, he would be willing to marry me and set me free. But he convinced me that it would be impossible; and he told me that, if we were only faithful to each other, it was marriage before God. If that is true, was n't I that man's wife? Was n't I faithful? For seven years, did n't I study every look and motion, and only live and breathe to please him? He had the yellow fever, and for twenty days and nights I watched with him. I alone,—and gave him all his medicine, and did everything for him; and then he called me his good angel, and said I 'd saved his life. We had two beautiful children. The first was a boy, and we called him Henry. He was the image of his father,—he had such beautiful eyes, such a forehead, and his hair hung all in curls around it; and he had all his father's spirit, and his talent, too. Little Elise, he said, looked like me. He used to tell me that I was the most beautiful woman in Louisiana, he was so proud of me and the children. He used to love to have me dress them up, and take them and me about in an open carriage, and hear the remarks that people would make on us; and he used to fill my ears constantly with the fine things that were said in praise of me and the children. O, those were happy days! I thought I was as happy as any one could be; but then there came evil times. He had a cousin come to New Orleans, who was his particular friend,—he thought all the world of him;—but, from the first time I saw him, I could n't tell why, I dreaded him; for I felt sure he was going to bring misery on us. He got Henry to going out with him, and often he would not come home nights till two or three o'clock. I did not dare say a word; for Henry was so high-spirited, I was afraid to. He got him to the gaming-houses; and he was one of the sort that, when he once got a going there, there was no holding back. And then he introduced him to another lady, and I saw soon that his heart was gone from me. He never told me, but I saw it,—I knew it, day after day,—I felt my heart breaking, but I could not say a word! At this, the wretch offered to buy me and the children of Henry, to clear off his gambling debts, which stood in the way of his marrying as he wished;—and *he sold us*. He told me, one day, that he had business in the country, and should be gone two or three weeks. He spoke kinder than usual, and said he should come back; but it did n't deceive me. I knew that the time had come; I was just like one turned into stone; I could n't speak, nor shed a tear. He kissed me and kissed the children, a good many times, and went out. I saw him get on his horse, and I watched him till he was quite out of sight; and then I fell down, and fainted.

"Then *he* came, the cursed wretch! he came to take possession. He told me that he had bought me and my children; and showed me the papers. I cursed him before God, and told him I 'd die sooner than live with him.

" 'Just as you please,' said he; 'but, if you don't behave reasonably, I 'll sell both the children, where you shall never see them again.' He told me that he always had meant to have me, from the first time he saw me; and that he had drawn Henry on, and got him in debt, on purpose to make him willing to sell me. That he got him in love with another woman; and that I might know, after all that, that he should not give up for a few airs and tears, and things of that sort.

"I gave up, for my hands were tied. He had my children;— whenever I resisted his will anywhere, he would talk about selling them, and he made me as submissive as he desired. O, what a life it was! to live with my heart breaking, every day,—to keep on, on, on, loving, when it was only misery; and to be bound, body and soul, to one I hated. I used to love to read to Henry, to play to him, to waltz with him, and sing to him; but everything I did for this one was a perfect drag,—yet I was afraid to refuse anything. He was very imperious, and harsh to the children. Elise was a timid little thing; but Henry was bold and high-spirited, like his father, and he had never been brought under, in the least, by any one. He was always finding fault, and quarrelling with him; and I used to live in daily fear and dread. I tried to make the child respectful;—I tried to keep them apart, for I held on to those children like death; but it did no good. *He sold both those children.* He took me to ride, one day, and when I came home, they were nowhere to be found! He told me he had sold them; he showed me the money, the price of their blood. Then it seemed as if all good forsook me. I raved and cursed,—cursed God and man; and, for a while, I believe, he really was afraid of me. But he did n't give up so. He told me that my children were sold, but whether I ever saw their faces again, depended on him; and that, if I was n't quiet, they should smart for it. Well, you can do anything with a woman, when you 've got her children. He made me submit; he made me be peaceable; he flattered me with hopes that, perhaps, he would buy them back; and so things went on, a week or two. One day, I was out walking, and passed by the calaboose; I saw a crowd about the gate, and heard a child's voice,—and suddenly my Henry broke away from two or three men who were holding him, and ran, screaming, and caught my dress. They came up to him, swearing dreadfully; and one man, whose face I shall never forget, told him that he would n't get away so; that he was going with him into the calaboose, and he 'd get a lesson there he 'd never forget. I tried to beg and plead,—they only laughed; the poor boy screamed and looked into my face, and held on to me, until, in tearing him off, they tore the skirt of my dress half away; and they carried him in, screaming 'Mother! mother! mother!' There was one man stood there seemed to pity me. I offered him all the money I had, if he 'd only interfere. He shook his head, and said that the boy had been impudent and disobedient, ever since he bought him; that he was going to break him in, once for all. I turned and ran; and every step of the way, I thought that I heard him scream. I got into the house; ran, all out of breath, to the parlor, where I found Butler. I told him, and begged him to go and interfere. He only laughed, and told me the boy had got his deserts. He 'd got to be broken in,— the sooner the better; 'what did I expect?' he asked.

"It seemed to me something in my head snapped, at that moment, I felt dizzy and furious. I remember seeing a great sharp bowie-knife on the table; I remember something about catching it, and flying upon him; and then all grew dark, and I did n't know any more—not for days and days.

"When I came to myself, I was in a nice room,—but not mine. An old black woman tended me; and a doctor came to see me, and there was a great deal of care taken of me. After a while, I found that he had gone away, and left me at this house to be sold; and that 's why they took such pains with me.

"I did n't mean to get well, and hoped I should n't; but, in spite of me, the fever went off, and I grew healthy, and finally got up. Then, they made me dress up, every day; and gentlemen used to come in and stand and smoke their cigars, and look at me, and ask questions, and debate my price. I was so gloomy and silent, that none of them wanted me. They threatened to whip me, if I was n't gayer, and did n't take some pains to make myself agreeable. At length, one day, came a gentleman named Stuart. He seemed to have some feeling for me; he saw that something dreadful was on my heart, and he came to see me alone, a great many times, and finally persuaded me to tell him. He bought me, at last, and promised to do all he could to find and buy back my children. He went to the hotel where my Henry was; they told him he had been sold to a planter up on Pearl river; that was the last that I ever heard. Then he found where my daughter was; an old woman was keeping her. He offered an immense sum for her, but they would not sell her. Butler found out that it was for me he wanted her; and he sent me word that I should never have her. Captain Stuart was very kind to me; he had a splendid plantation, and took me to it. In the course of a year, I had a son born. O, that child!—how I loved it! How just like my poor Henry the little thing looked! But I had made up my mind,—yes, I had. I would never again let a child live to grow up! I took the little fellow in my arms, when he was two weeks old, and kissed him, and cried over him; and then I gave him laudanum, and held him close to my bosom, while he slept to death. How I mourned and cried over it! and who ever dreamed that it was anything but a mistake, that had made me give it the laudanum? but it 's one of the few things that I 'm glad of, now. I am not sorry, to this day; he, at least, is out of pain. What better than death could I give him, poor child! After a while, the cholera came, and Captain Stuart died; everybody died that wanted to live,—and I,—I, though I went down to death's door,—*I lived!* Then I was sold, and passed from hand to hand, till I grew faded and wrinkled, and I had a fever; and then this wretch bought me, and brought me here,—and here I am!"

The woman stopped. She had hurried on through her story, with a wild, passionate utterance; sometimes seeming

to address it to Tom, and sometimes speaking as in a soliloquy. So vehement and overpowering was the force with
which she spoke, that, for a season, Tom was beguiled even
from the pain of his wounds, and, raising himself on one elbow, watched her as she paced restlessly up and down, her
long black hair swaying heavily about her, as she moved.

"You tell me," she said, after a pause, "that there is a
God,—a God that looks down and sees all these things. May
be it's so. The sisters in the convent used to tell me of a day
of judgment, when everything is coming to light;—won't
there be vengeance, then!

"They think it's nothing, what we suffer,—nothing, what
our children suffer! It's all a small matter; yet I've walked
the streets when it seemed as if I had misery enough in my
one heart to sink the city. I've wished the houses would fall
on me, or the stones sink under me. Yes! and, in the judgment day, I will stand up before God, a witness against those
that have ruined me and my children, body and soul!

"When I was a girl, I thought I was religious; I used to
love God and prayer. Now, I'm a lost soul, pursued by devils
that torment me day and night; they keep pushing me on and
on—and I'll do it, too, some of these days!" she said, clenching her hand, while an insane light glanced in her heavy black
eyes. "I'll send him where he belongs,—a short way, too,—
one of these nights, if they burn me alive for it!" A wild, long
laugh, rang through the deserted room, and ended in a hysteric sob; she threw herself on the floor, in convulsive sob-
bings and struggles.

In a few moments, the frenzy fit seemed to pass off; she
rose slowly, and seemed to collect herself.

"Can I do anything more for you, my poor fellow?" she
said, approaching where Tom lay; "shall I give you some
more water?"

There was a graceful and compassionate sweetness in her
voice and manner, as she said this, that formed a strange contrast with the former wildness.

Tom drank the water, and looked earnestly and pitifully
into her face.

"O, Missis, I wish you'd go to him that can give you living
waters!"

"Go to him! Where is he? Who is he?" said Cassy.

"Him that you read of to me,—the Lord."

"I used to see the picture of him, over the altar, when I was a girl," said Cassy, her dark eyes fixing themselves in an expression of mournful reverie; "but, *he is n't here!* there's nothing here, but sin and long, long, long despair! O!" She laid her hand on her breast and drew in her breath, as if to lift a heavy weight.

Tom looked as if he would speak again; but she cut him short, with a decided gesture.

"Don't talk, my poor fellow. Try to sleep, if you can." And, placing water in his reach, and making whatever little arrangements for his comfort she could, Cassy left the shed.

XXXV.

The Tokens

"And slight, withal, may be the things that bring
   Back on the heart the weight which it would fling
   Aside forever; it may be a sound,
   A flower, the wind, the ocean, which shall wound,—
   Striking the electric chain wherewith we 're darkly bound."
                                       Childe Harold's Pilgrimage, Can. 4.

T HE sitting-room of Legree's establishment was a large, long room, with a wide, ample fireplace. It had once been hung with a showy and expensive paper, which now hung mouldering, torn and discolored, from the damp walls. The place had that peculiar sickening, unwholesome smell, compounded of mingled damp, dirt and decay, which one often notices in close old houses. The wall-paper was defaced, in spots, by slops of beer and wine; or garnished with chalk memorandums, and long sums footed up, as if somebody had been practising arithmetic there. In the fireplace stood a brazier full of burning charcoal; for, though the weather was not cold, the evenings always seemed damp and chilly in that great room; and Legree, moreover, wanted a place to light his cigars, and heat his water for punch. The ruddy glare of the charcoal displayed the confused and unpromising aspect of the room,—saddles, bridles, several sorts of harness, riding-whips, overcoats, and various articles of clothing, scattered up and down the room in confused variety; and the dogs, of whom we have before spoken, had encamped themselves among them, to suit their own taste and convenience.

Legree was just mixing himself a tumbler of punch, pouring his hot water from a cracked and broken-nosed pitcher, grumbling, as he did so,

"Plague on that Sambo, to kick up this yer row between me and the new hands! The fellow won't be fit to work for a week, now,—right in the press of the season!"

"Yes, just like you," said a voice, behind his chair. It was the woman Cassy, who had stolen upon his soliloquy.

"Hah! you she-devil! you 've come back, have you?"

"Yes, I have," she said, coolly; "come to have my own way, too!"

"You lie, you jade! I 'll be up to my word. Either behave yourself, or stay down to the quarters, and fare and work with the rest."

"I 'd rather, ten thousand times," said the woman, "live in the dirtiest hole at the quarters, than be under your hoof!"

"But you *are* under my hoof, for all that," said he, turning upon her, with a savage grin; "that 's one comfort. So, sit down here on my knee, my dear, and hear to reason," said he, laying hold on her wrist.

"Simon Legree, take care!" said the woman, with a sharp flash of her eye, a glance so wild and insane in its light as to be almost appalling. "You 're afraid of me, Simon," she said, deliberately; "and you 've reason to be! But be careful, for I 've got the devil in me!"

The last words she whispered in a hissing tone, close to his ear.

"Get out! I believe, to my soul, you have!" said Legree, pushing her from him, and looking uncomfortably at her. "After all, Cassy," he said, "why can't you be friends with me, as you used to?"

"Used to!" said she, bitterly. She stopped short,—a world of choking feelings, rising in her heart, kept her silent.

Cassy had always kept over Legree the kind of influence that a strong, impassioned woman can ever keep over the most brutal man; but, of late, she had grown more and more irritable and restless, under the hideous yoke of her servitude, and her irritability, at times, broke out into raving insanity; and this liability made her a sort of object of dread to Legree, who had that superstitious horror of insane persons which is common to coarse and uninstructed minds. When Legree brought Emmeline to the house, all the smouldering embers of womanly feeling flashed up in the worn heart of Cassy, and she took part with the girl; and a fierce quarrel ensued between her and Legree. Legree, in a fury, swore she should be put to field service, if she would not be peaceable. Cassy, with proud scorn, declared she *would* go to the field. And she worked there one day, as we have described, to show how perfectly she scorned the threat.

Legree was secretly uneasy, all day; for Cassy had an influence over him from which he could not free himself. When she presented her basket at the scales, he had hoped for some concession, and addressed her in a sort of half conciliatory, half scornful tone; and she had answered with the bitterest contempt.

The outrageous treatment of poor Tom had roused her still more; and she had followed Legree to the house, with no particular intention, but to upbraid him for his brutality.

"I wish, Cassy," said Legree, "you 'd behave yourself decently."

"*You* talk about behaving decently! And what have you been doing?—you, who have n't even sense enough to keep from spoiling one of your best hands, right in the most pressing season, just for your devilish temper!"

"I was a fool, it 's a fact, to let any such brangle come up," said Legree; "but, when the boy set up his will, he had to be broke in."

"I reckon you won't break *him* in!"

"Won't I?" said Legree, rising, passionately. "I 'd like to know if I won't? He 'll be the first nigger that ever came it round me! I 'll break every bone in his body, but he *shall* give up!"

Just then the door opened, and Sambo entered. He came forward, bowing, and holding out something in a paper.

"What 's that, you dog?" said Legree.

"It 's a witch thing, Mas'r!"

"A what?"

"Something that niggers gets from witches. Keeps 'em from feelin' when they 's flogged. He had it tied round his neck, with a black string."

Legree, like most godless and cruel men, was superstitious. He took the paper, and opened it uneasily.

There dropped out of it a silver dollar, and a long, shining curl of fair hair,—hair which, like a living thing, twined itself round Legree's fingers.

"Damnation!" he screamed, in sudden passion, stamping

on the floor, and pulling furiously at the hair, as if it burned him. "Where did this come from? Take it off!—burn it up!—burn it up!" he screamed, tearing it off, and throwing it into the charcoal. "What did you bring it to me for?"

Sambo stood, with his heavy mouth wide open, and aghast with wonder; and Cassy, who was preparing to leave the apartment, stopped, and looked at him in perfect amazement.

"Don't you bring me any more of your devilish things!" said he, shaking his fist at Sambo, who retreated hastily towards the door; and, picking up the silver dollar, he sent it smashing through the window-pane, out into the darkness.

Sambo was glad to make his escape. When he was gone, Legree seemed a little ashamed of his fit of alarm. He sat doggedly down in his chair, and began sullenly sipping his tumbler of punch.

Cassy prepared herself for going out, unobserved by him; and slipped away to minister to poor Tom, as we have already related.

And what was the matter with Legree? and what was there in a simple curl of fair hair to appall that brutal man, familiar with every form of cruelty? To answer this, we must carry the reader backward in his history. Hard and reprobate as the godless man seemed now, there had been a time when he had been rocked on the bosom of a mother,—cradled with prayers and pious hymns,—his now seared brow bedewed with the waters of holy baptism. In early childhood, a fair-haired woman had led him, at the sound of Sabbath bell, to worship and to pray. Far in New England that mother had trained her only son, with long, unwearied love, and patient prayers. Born of a hard-tempered sire, on whom that gentle woman had wasted a world of unvalued love, Legree had followed in the steps of his father. Boisterous, unruly, and tyrannical, he despised all her counsel, and would none of her reproof; and, at an early age, broke from her, to seek his fortunes at sea. He never came home but once, after; and then, his mother, with the yearning of a heart that must love something, and has nothing else to love, clung to him, and sought, with passionate prayers and entreaties, to win him from a life of sin, to his soul's eternal good.

That was Legree's day of grace; then good angels called

him; then he was almost persuaded, and mercy held him by the hand. His heart inly relented,—there was a conflict,—but sin got the victory, and he set all the force of his rough nature against the conviction of his conscience. He drank and swore,—was wilder and more brutal than ever. And, one night, when his mother, in the last agony of her despair, knelt at his feet, he spurned her from him,—threw her senseless on the floor, and, with brutal curses, fled to his ship. The next Legree heard of his mother was, when, one night, as he was carousing among drunken companions, a letter was put into his hand. He opened it, and a lock of long, curling hair fell from it, and twined about his fingers. The letter told him his mother was dead, and that, dying, she blest and forgave him.

There is a dread, unhallowed necromancy of evil, that turns things sweetest and holiest to phantoms of horror and affright. That pale, loving mother,—her dying prayers, her forgiving love,—wrought in that demoniac heart of sin only as a damning sentence, bringing with it a fearful looking for of judgment and fiery indignation. Legree burned the hair, and burned the letter; and when he saw them hissing and crackling in the flame, inly shuddered as he thought of everlasting fires. He tried to drink, and revel, and swear away the memory; but often, in the deep night, whose solemn stillness arraigns the bad soul in forced communion with herself, he had seen that pale mother rising by his bedside, and felt the soft twining of that hair around his fingers, till the cold sweat would roll down his face, and he would spring from his bed in horror. Ye who have wondered to hear, in the same evangel, that God is love, and that God is a consuming fire, see ye not how, to the soul resolved in evil, perfect love is the most fearful torture, the seal and sentence of the direst despair?

"Blast it!" said Legree to himself, as he sipped his liquor; "where did he get that? If it did n't look just like—whoo! I thought I 'd forgot that. Curse me, if I think there 's any such thing as forgetting anything, any how,—hang it! I 'm lonesome! I mean to call Em. She hates me—the monkey! I don't care,—I 'll *make* her come!"

Legree stepped out into a large entry, which went up stairs, by what had formerly been a superb winding staircase; but the passage-way was dirty and dreary, encumbered with boxes and unsightly litter. The stairs, uncarpeted, seemed winding up, in the gloom, to nobody knew where! The pale moonlight streamed through a shattered fanlight over the door; the air was unwholesome and chilly, like that of a vault.

Legree stopped at the foot of the stairs, and heard a voice singing. It seemed strange and ghostlike in that dreary old house, perhaps because of the already tremulous state of his nerves. Hark! what is it?

A wild, pathetic voice, chants a hymn common among the slaves:

"O there 'll be mourning, mourning, mourning,
 O there 'll be mourning, at the judgment-seat of Christ!"

"Blast the girl!" said Legree. "I 'll choke her.—Em! Em!" he called, harshly; but only a mocking echo from the walls answered him. The sweet voice still sung on:

"Parents and children there shall part!
Parents and children there shall part!
Shall part to meet no more!"

And clear and loud swelled through the empty halls the refrain,

"O there 'll be mourning, mourning, mourning,
 O there 'll be mourning, at the judgment-seat of Christ!"

Legree stopped. He would have been ashamed to tell of it, but large drops of sweat stood on his forehead, his heart beat heavy and thick with fear; he even thought he saw something white rising and glimmering in the gloom before him, and shuddered to think what if the form of his dead mother should suddenly appear to him.

"I know one thing," he said to himself, as he stumbled back in the sitting-room, and sat down; "I 'll let that fellow alone, after this! What did I want of his cussed paper? I b'lieve I am bewitched, sure enough! I 've been shivering and sweating, ever since! Where did he get that hair? It could n't have been *that*! I burnt *that* up, I know I did! It would be a joke, if hair could rise from the dead!"

Ah, Legree! that golden tress *was* charmed; each hair had in it a spell of terror and remorse for thee, and was used by a mightier power to bind thy cruel hands from inflicting uttermost evil on the helpless!

"I say," said Legree, stamping and whistling to the dogs, "wake up, some of you, and keep me company!" but the dogs only opened one eye at him, sleepily, and closed it again.

"I'll have Sambo and Quimbo up here, to sing and dance one of their hell dances, and keep off these horrid notions," said Legree; and, putting on his hat, he went on to the verandah, and blew a horn, with which he commonly summoned his two sable drivers.

Legree was often wont, when in a gracious humor, to get these two worthies into his sitting-room, and, after warming them up with whiskey, amuse himself by setting them to singing, dancing or fighting, as the humor took him.

It was between one and two o'clock at night, as Cassy was returning from her ministrations to poor Tom, that she heard the sound of wild shrieking, whooping, halloing, and singing, from the sitting-room, mingled with the barking of dogs, and other symptoms of general uproar.

She came up on the verandah steps, and looked in. Legree and both the drivers, in a state of furious intoxication, were singing, whooping, upsetting chairs, and making all manner of ludicrous and horrid grimaces at each other.

She rested her small, slender hand on the window-blind, and looked fixedly at them;—there was a world of anguish, scorn, and fierce bitterness, in her black eyes, as she did so. "Would it be a sin to rid the world of such a wretch?" she said to herself.

She turned hurriedly away, and, passing round to a back door, glided up stairs, and tapped at Emmeline's door.

XXXVI.

Emmeline and Cassy

CASSY entered the room, and found Emmeline sitting, pale with fear, in the furthest corner of it. As she came in, the girl started up nervously; but, on seeing who it was, rushed forward, and catching her arm, said, "O, Cassy, is it you? I'm so glad you 've come! I was afraid it was—. O, you don't know what a horrid noise there has been, down stairs, all this evening!"

"I ought to know," said Cassy, dryly. "I 've heard it often enough."

"O Cassy! do tell me,—could n't we get away from this place? I don't care where,—into the swamp among the snakes,—anywhere! *Could n't* we get *somewhere* away from here?"

"Nowhere, but into our graves," said Cassy.

"Did you ever try?"

"I 've seen enough of trying, and what comes of it," said Cassy.

"I 'd be willing to live in the swamps, and gnaw the bark from trees. I an't afraid of snakes! I 'd rather have one near me than him," said Emmeline, eagerly.

"There have been a good many here of your opinion," said Cassy; "but you could n't stay in the swamps,—you 'd be tracked by the dogs, and brought back, and then—then—"

"What would he do?" said the girl, looking, with breathless interest, into her face.

"What *would n't* he do, you 'd better ask," said Cassy. "He 's learned his trade well, among the pirates in the West Indies. You would n't sleep much, if I should tell you things I 've seen,—things that he tells of, sometimes, for good jokes. I 've heard screams here that I have n't been able to get out of my head for weeks and weeks. There 's a place way out down by the quarters, where you can see a black, blasted tree, and the ground all covered with black ashes. Ask any one what was done there, and see if they will dare to tell you."

"O! what do you mean?"

"I won't tell you. I hate to think of it. And I tell you, the Lord only knows what we may see to-morrow, if that poor fellow holds out as he 's begun."

"Horrid!" said Emmeline, every drop of blood receding from her cheeks. "O, Cassy, do tell me what I shall do!"

"What I 've done. Do the best you can,—do what you must,—and make it up in hating and cursing."

"He wanted to make me drink some of his hateful brandy," said Emmeline; "and I hate it so—"

"You 'd better drink," said Cassy. "I hated it, too; and now I can't live without it. One must have something;—things don't look so dreadful, when you take that."

"Mother used to tell me never to touch any such thing," said Emmeline.

"*Mother* told you!" said Cassy, with a thrilling and bitter emphasis on the word mother. "What use is it for mothers to say anything? You are all to be bought and paid for, and your souls belong to whoever gets you. That 's the way it goes. I say, *drink* brandy; drink all you can, and it 'll make things come easier."

"O, Cassy! do pity me!"

"Pity you!—don't I? Have n't I a daughter,—Lord knows where she is, and whose she is, now,—going the way her mother went, before her, I suppose, and that her children must go, after her! There 's no end to the curse—forever!"

"I wish I 'd never been born!" said Emmeline, wringing her hands.

"That 's an old wish with me," said Cassy. "I 've got used to wishing that. I 'd die, if I dared to," she said, looking out into the darkness, with that still, fixed despair which was the habitual expression of her face when at rest.

"It would be wicked to kill one's self," said Emmeline.

"I don't know why,—no wickeder than things we live and do, day after day. But the sisters told me things, when I was in the convent, that make me afraid to die. If it would only be the end of us, why, then—"

Emmeline turned away, and hid her face in her hands.

While this conversation was passing in the chamber, Legree, overcome with his carouse, had sank to sleep in the room below. Legree was not an habitual drunkard. His coarse, strong nature craved, and could endure, a continual stimulation, that would have utterly wrecked and crazed a finer one. But a deep, underlying spirit of cautiousness prevented his often yielding to appetite in such measure as to lose control of himself.

This night, however, in his feverish efforts to banish from his mind those fearful elements of woe and remorse which woke within him, he had indulged more than common; so that, when he had discharged his sable attendants, he fell heavily on a settle in the room, and was sound asleep.

O! how dares the bad soul to enter the shadowy world of sleep?—that land whose dim outlines lie so fearfully near to the mystic scene of retribution! Legree dreamed. In his heavy and feverish sleep, a veiled form stood beside him, and laid a cold, soft hand upon him. He thought he knew who it was; and shuddered, with creeping horror, though the face was veiled. Then he thought he felt *that hair* twining round his fingers; and then, that it slid smoothly round his neck, and tightened and tightened, and he could not draw his breath; and then he thought voices *whispered* to him,—whispers that chilled him with horror. Then it seemed to him he was on the edge of a frightful abyss, holding on and struggling in mortal fear, while dark hands stretched up, and were pulling him over; and Cassy came behind him laughing, and pushed him. And then rose up that solemn veiled figure, and drew aside the veil. It was his mother; and she turned away from him, and he fell down, down, down, amid a confused noise of shrieks, and groans, and shouts of demon laughter,—and Legree awoke.

Calmly the rosy hue of dawn was stealing into the room. The morning star stood, with its solemn, holy eye of light, looking down on the man of sin, from out the brightening sky. O, with what freshness, what solemnity and beauty, is each new day born; as if to say to insensate man, "Behold! thou hast one more chance! *Strive* for immortal glory!" There is no speech nor language where this voice is not heard; but the bold, bad man heard it not. He woke with an oath and a curse. What to him was the gold and purple, the daily miracle of morning! What to him the sanctity of that star which the

Son of God has hallowed as his own emblem? Brute-like, he saw without perceiving; and, stumbling forward, poured out a tumbler of brandy, and drank half of it.

"I 've had a h—l of a night!" he said to Cassy, who just then entered from an opposite door.

"You 'll get plenty of the same sort, by and by," said she, dryly.

"What do you mean, you minx?"

"You 'll find out, one of these days," returned Cassy, in the same tone. "Now, Simon, I 've one piece of advice to give you."

"The devil, you have!"

"My advice is," said Cassy, steadily, as she began adjusting some things about the room, "that you let Tom alone."

"What business is 't of yours?"

"What? To be sure, I don't know what it should be. If you want to pay twelve hundred for a fellow, and use him right up in the press of the season, just to serve your own spite, it 's no business of mine. I 've done what I could for him."

"You have? What business have you meddling in my matters?"

"None, to be sure. I 've saved you some thousands of dollars, at different times, by taking care of your hands,—that 's all the thanks I get. If your crop comes shorter into market than any of theirs, you won't lose your bet, I suppose? Tompkins won't lord it over you, I suppose,—and you 'll pay down your money like a lady, won't you? I think I see you doing it!"

Legree, like many other planters, had but one form of ambition,—to have in the heaviest crop of the season,—and he had several bets on this very present season pending in the next town. Cassy, therefore, with woman's tact, touched the only string that could be made to vibrate.

"Well, I 'll let him off at what he 's got," said Legree; "but he shall beg my pardon, and promise better fashions."

"That he won't do," said Cassy.

"Won't,—eh?"

"No, he won't," said Cassy.

"I 'd like to know *why*, Mistress," said Legree, in the extreme of scorn.

"Because he 's done right, and he knows it, and won't say he 's done wrong."

"Who a cuss cares what he knows? The nigger shall say what I please, or—"

"Or, you 'll lose your bet on the cotton crop, by keeping him out of the field, just at this very press."

"But he *will* give up,—course, he will; don't I know what niggers is? He 'll beg like a dog, this morning."

"He won't, Simon; you don't know this kind. You may kill him by inches,—you won't get the first word of confession out of him."

"We 'll see;—where is he?" said Legree, going out.

"In the waste-room of the gin-house," said Cassy.

Legree, though he talked so stoutly to Cassy, still sallied forth from the house with a degree of misgiving which was not common with him. His dreams of the past night, mingled with Cassy's prudential suggestions, considerably affected his mind. He resolved that nobody should be witness of his encounter with Tom; and determined, if he could not subdue him by bullying, to defer his vengeance, to be wreaked in a more convenient season.

The solemn light of dawn—the angelic glory of the morning-star—had looked in through the rude window of the shed where Tom was lying; and, as if descending on that starbeam, came the solemn words, "I am the root and offspring of David, and the bright and morning star." The mysterious warnings and intimations of Cassy, so far from discouraging his soul, in the end had roused it as with a heavenly call. He did not know but that the day of his death was dawning in the sky; and his heart throbbed with solemn throes of joy and desire, as he thought that the wondrous *all*, of which he had often pondered,—the great white throne, with its ever radiant rainbow; the white-robed multitude, with voices as many waters; the crowns, the palms, the harps,—might all break upon his vision before that sun should set again. And, therefore, without shuddering or trembling, he heard the voice of his persecutor, as he drew near.

"Well, my boy," said Legree, with a contemptuous kick, "how do you find yourself? Did n't I tell yer I could larn yer a thing or two? How do yer like it,—eh? How did yer whal-

ing agree with yer, Tom? An't quite so crank as ye was last
night. Ye could n't treat a poor sinner, now, to a bit of a
sermon, could ye,—eh?"

Tom answered nothing.

"Get up, you beast!" said Legree, kicking him again.

This was a difficult matter for one so bruised and faint;
and, as Tom made efforts to do so, Legree laughed brutally.

"What makes ye so spry, this morning, Tom? Cotched
cold, may be, last night."

Tom by this time had gained his feet, and was confronting
his master with a steady, unmoved front.

"The devil, you can!" said Legree, looking him over. "I
believe you have n't got enough yet. Now, Tom, get right
down on yer knees and beg my pardon, for yer shines last
night."

Tom did not move.

"Down, you dog!" said Legree, striking him with his riding-whip.

"Mas'r Legree," said Tom, "I can't do it. I did only what I
thought was right. I shall do just so again, if ever the time
comes. I never will do a cruel thing, come what may."

"Yes, but ye don't know what may come, Master Tom. Ye
think what you 've got is something. I tell you 't an't anything,—nothing 't all. How would ye like to be tied to a tree,
and have a slow fire lit up around ye;—would n't that be
pleasant,—eh, Tom?"

"Mas'r," said Tom, "I know ye can do dreadful things;
but,"—he stretched himself upward and clasped his hands,—
"but, after ye 've killed the body, there an't no more ye can
do. And O, there 's all ETERNITY to come, after that!"

ETERNITY,—the word thrilled through the black man's
soul with light and power, as he spoke; it thrilled through the
sinner's soul, too, like the bite of a scorpion. Legree gnashed
on him with his teeth, but rage kept him silent; and Tom,
like a man disenthralled, spoke, in a clear and cheerful voice,

"Mas'r Legree, as ye bought me, I 'll be a true and faithful
servant to ye. I 'll give ye all the work of my hands, all my
time, all my strength; but my soul I won't give up to mortal
man. I will hold on to the Lord, and put his commands before all,—die or live; you may be sure on 't. Mas'r Legree,

The fugitives are safe in a free land

I an't a grain afeard to die. I'd as soon die as not. Ye may whip me, starve me, burn me,—it'll only send me sooner where I want to go."

"I'll make ye give out, though, 'fore I've done!" said Legree, in a rage.

"I shall have *help*," said Tom; "you'll never do it."

"Who the devil's going to help you?" said Legree, scornfully.

"The Lord Almighty," said Tom.

"D—n you!" said Legree, as with one blow of his fist he felled Tom to the earth.

A cold soft hand fell on Legree's, at this moment. He turned,—it was Cassy's; but the cold soft touch recalled his dream of the night before, and, flashing through the chambers of his brain, came all the fearful images of the night-watches, with a portion of the horror that accompanied them.

"Will you be a fool?" said Cassy, in French. "Let him go! Let me alone to get him fit to be in the field again. Is n't it just as I told you?"

They say the alligator, the rhinoceros, though enclosed in bullet-proof mail, have each a spot where they are vulnerable; and fierce, reckless, unbelieving reprobates, have commonly this point in superstitious dread.

Legree turned away, determined to let the point go for the time.

"Well, have it your own way," he said, doggedly, to Cassy.

"Hark, ye!" he said to Tom; "I won't deal with ye now, because the business is pressing, and I want all my hands; but I *never* forget. I'll score it against ye, and sometime I'll have my pay out o' yer old black hide,—mind ye!"

Legree turned, and went out.

"There you go," said Cassy, looking darkly after him; "your reckoning's to come, yet!—My poor fellow, how are you?"

"The Lord God hath sent his angel, and shut the lion's mouth, for this time," said Tom.

"For this time, to be sure," said Cassy; "but now you've got his ill will upon you, to follow you day in, day out, hanging like a dog on your throat,—sucking your blood, bleeding away your life, drop by drop. I know the man."

XXXVII.

Liberty

"No matter with what solemnities he may have been devoted upon the altar of slavery, the moment he touches the sacred soil of Britain, the altar and the God sink together in the dust, and he stands redeemed, regenerated, and disenthralled, by the irresistible genius of universal emancipation."—*Curran.*

A WHILE we must leave Tom in the hands of his persecutors, while we turn to pursue the fortunes of George and his wife, whom we left in friendly hands, in a farm-house on the road-side.

Tom Loker we left groaning and touzling in a most immaculately clean Quaker bed, under the motherly supervision of Aunt Dorcas, who found him to the full as tractable a patient as a sick bison.

Imagine a tall, dignified, spiritual woman, whose clear muslin cap shades waves of silvery hair, parted on a broad, clear forehead, which overarches thoughtful gray eyes. A snowy handkerchief of lisse crape is folded neatly across her bosom; her glossy brown silk dress rustles peacefully, as she glides up and down the chamber.

"The devil!" says Tom Loker, giving a great throw to the bed-clothes.

"I must request thee, Thomas, not to use such language," says Aunt Dorcas, as she quietly reärranged the bed.

"Well, I won't, granny, if I can help it," says Tom; "but it is enough to make a fellow swear,—so cursedly hot!"

Dorcas removed a comforter from the bed, straightened the clothes again, and tucked them in till Tom looked something like a chrysalis; remarking, as she did so,

"I wish, friend, thee would leave off cursing and swearing, and think upon thy ways."

"What the devil," said Tom, "should I think of *them* for? Last thing ever *I* want to think of—hang it all!" And Tom flounced over, untucking and disarranging everything, in a manner frightful to behold.

"That fellow and gal are here, I 'spose," said he, sullenly, after a pause.

"They are so," said Dorcas.

"They 'd better be off up to the lake," said Tom; "the quicker the better."

"Probably they will do so," said Aunt Dorcas, knitting peacefully.

"And hark ye," said Tom; "we 've got correspondents in Sandusky, that watch the boats for us. I don't care if I tell, now. I hope they *will* get away, just to spite Marks,—the cursed puppy!—d—n him!"

"Thomas!" said Dorcas.

"I tell you, granny, if you bottle a fellow up too tight, I shall split," said Tom. "But about the gal,—tell 'em to dress her up some way, so 's to alter her. Her description 's out in Sandusky."

"We will attend to that matter," said Dorcas, with characteristic composure.

As we at this place take leave of Tom Loker, we may as well say, that, having lain three weeks at the Quaker dwelling, sick with a rheumatic fever, which set in, in company with his other afflictions, Tom arose from his bed a somewhat sadder and wiser man; and, in place of slave-catching, betook himself to life in one of the new settlements, where his talents developed themselves more happily in trapping bears, wolves, and other inhabitants of the forest, in which he made himself quite a name in the land. Tom always spoke reverently of the Quakers. "Nice people," he would say; "wanted to convert me, but could n't come it, exactly. But, tell ye what, stranger, they do fix up a sick fellow first rate,—no mistake. Make jist the tallest kind o' broth and knicknacks."

As Tom had informed them that their party would be looked for in Sandusky, it was thought prudent to divide them. Jim, with his old mother, was forwarded separately; and a night or two after, George and Eliza, with their child, were driven privately into Sandusky, and lodged beneath a hospitable roof, preparatory to taking their last passage on the lake.

Their night was now far spent, and the morning star of liberty rose fair before them. Liberty!—electric word! What is it? Is there anything more in it than a name—a rhetorical flourish? Why, men and women of America, does your heart's blood thrill at that word, for which your fathers bled, and your braver mothers were willing that their noblest and best should die?

Is there anything in it glorious and dear for a nation, that is not also glorious and dear for a man? What is freedom to a nation, but freedom to the individuals in it? What is freedom to that young man, who sits there, with his arms folded over his broad chest, the tint of African blood in his cheek, its dark fires in his eye,—what is freedom to George Harris? To your fathers, freedom was the right of a nation to be a nation. To him, it is the right of a man to be a man, and not a brute; the right to call the wife of his bosom his wife, and to protect her from lawless violence; the right to protect and educate his child; the right to have a home of his own, a religion of his own, a character of his own, unsubject to the will of another. All these thoughts were rolling and seething in George's breast, as he was pensively leaning his head on his hand, watching his wife, as she was adapting to her slender and pretty form the articles of man's attire, in which it was deemed safest she should make her escape.

"Now for it," said she, as she stood before the glass, and shook down her silky abundance of black curly hair. "I say, George, it's almost a pity, isn't it," she said, as she held up some of it, playfully,—"pity it's all got to come off?"

George smiled sadly, and made no answer.

Eliza turned to the glass, and the scissors glittered as one long lock after another was detached from her head.

"There, now, that'll do," she said, taking up a hair-brush; "now for a few fancy touches."

"There, an't I a pretty young fellow?" she said, turning around to her husband, laughing and blushing at the same time.

"You always will be pretty, do what you will," said George.

"What does make you so sober?" said Eliza, kneeling on one knee, and laying her hand on his. "We are only within twenty-four hours of Canada, they say. Only a day and a night on the lake, and then—oh, then!—"

"O, Eliza!" said George, drawing her towards him; "that is it! Now my fate is all narrowing down to a point. To come so near, to be almost in sight, and then lose all. I should never live under it, Eliza."

"Don't fear," said his wife, hopefully. "The good Lord would not have brought us so far, if he did n't mean to carry us through. I seem to feel him with us, George."

"You are a blessed woman, Eliza!" said George, clasping her with a convulsive grasp. "But,—oh, tell me! can this great mercy be for us? Will these years and years of misery come to an end?—shall we be free?"

"I am sure of it, George," said Eliza, looking upward, while tears of hope and enthusiasm shone on her long, dark lashes. "I feel it in me, that God is going to bring us out of bondage, this very day."

"I will believe you, Eliza," said George, rising suddenly up. "I will believe,—come, let 's be off. Well, indeed," said he, holding her off at arm's length, and looking admiringly at her, "you *are* a pretty little fellow. That crop of little, short curls, is quite becoming. Put on your cap. So—a little to one side. I never saw you look quite so pretty. But, it 's almost time for the carriage;—I wonder if Mrs. Smyth has got Harry rigged?"

The door opened, and a respectable, middle-aged woman entered, leading little Harry, dressed in girl's clothes.

"What a pretty girl he makes," said Eliza, turning him round. "We call him Harriet, you see;—don't the name come nicely?"

The child stood gravely regarding his mother in her new and strange attire, observing a profound silence, and occasionally drawing deep sighs, and peeping at her from under his dark curls.

"Does Harry know mamma?" said Eliza, stretching her hands toward him.

The child clung shyly to the woman.

"Come, Eliza, why do you try to coax him, when you know that he has got to be kept away from you?"

"I know it 's foolish," said Eliza; "yet, I can't bear to have him turn away from me. But come,—where 's my cloak? Here,—how is it men put on cloaks, George?"

"You must wear it so," said her husband, throwing it over his shoulders.

"So, then," said Eliza, imitating the motion,—"and I must stamp, and take long steps, and try to look saucy."

"Don't exert yourself," said George. "There is, now and then, a modest young man; and I think it would be easier for you to act that character."

"And these gloves! mercy upon us!" said Eliza; "why, my hands are lost in them."

"I advise you to keep them on pretty strictly," said George. "Your little slender paw might bring us all out. Now, Mrs. Smyth, you are to go under our charge, and be our aunty,— you mind."

"I 've heard," said Mrs. Smyth, "that there have been men down, warning all the packet captains against a man and woman, with a little boy."

"They have!" said George. "Well, if we see any such people, we can tell them."

A hack now drove to the door, and the friendly family who had received the fugitives crowded around them with farewell greetings.

The disguises the party had assumed were in accordance with the hints of Tom Loker. Mrs. Smyth, a respectable woman from the settlement in Canada, whither they were fleeing, being fortunately about crossing the lake to return thither, had consented to appear as the aunt of little Harry; and, in order to attach him to her, he had been allowed to remain, the two last days, under her sole charge; and an extra amount of petting, joined to an indefinite amount of seed-cakes and candy, had cemented a very close attachment on the part of the young gentleman.

The hack drove to the wharf. The two young men, as they appeared, walked up the plank into the boat, Eliza gallantly giving her arm to Mrs. Smyth, and George attending to their baggage.

George was standing at the captain's office, settling for his party, when he overheard two men talking by his side.

"I 've watched every one that came on board," said one, "and I know they 're not on this boat."

The voice was that of the clerk of the boat. The speaker

whom he addressed was our sometime friend Marks, who, with that valuable perseverance which characterized him, had come on to Sandusky, seeking whom he might devour.

"You would scarcely know the woman from a white one," said Marks. "The man is a very light mulatto; he has a brand in one of his hands."

The hand with which George was taking the tickets and change trembled a little; but he turned coolly around, fixed an unconcerned glance on the face of the speaker, and walked leisurely toward another part of the boat, where Eliza stood waiting for him.

Mrs. Smyth, with little Harry, sought the seclusion of the ladies' cabin, where the dark beauty of the supposed little girl drew many flattering comments from the passengers.

George had the satisfaction, as the bell rang out its farewell peal, to see Marks walk down the plank to the shore; and drew a long sigh of relief, when the boat had put a returnless distance between them.

It was a superb day. The blue waves of Lake Erie danced, rippling and sparkling, in the sun-light. A fresh breeze blew from the shore, and the lordly boat ploughed her way right gallantly onward.

O, what an untold world there is in one human heart! Who thought, as George walked calmly up and down the deck of the steamer, with his shy companion at his side, of all that was burning in his bosom? The mighty good that seemed approaching seemed too good, too fair, even to be a reality; and he felt a jealous dread, every moment of the day, that something would rise to snatch it from him.

But the boat swept on. Hours fleeted, and, at last, clear and full rose the blessed English shores; shores charmed by a mighty spell,—with one touch to dissolve every incantation of slavery, no matter in what language pronounced, or by what national power confirmed.

George and his wife stood arm in arm, as the boat neared the small town of Amherstberg, in Canada. His breath grew thick and short; a mist gathered before his eyes; he silently pressed the little hand that lay trembling on his arm. The bell rang; the boat stopped. Scarcely seeing what he did, he looked out his baggage, and gathered his little party. The lit-

tle company were landed on the shore. They stood still till
the boat had cleared; and then, with tears and embracings,
the husband and wife, with their wondering child in their
arms, knelt down and lifted up their hearts to God!

> "'T was something like the burst from death to life;
>   From the grave's cerements to the robes of heaven;
> From sin's dominion, and from passion's strife,
>   To the pure freedom of a soul forgiven;
>   Where all the bonds of death and hell are riven,
> And mortal puts on immortality,
> When Mercy's hand hath turned the golden key,
> And Mercy's voice hath said, *Rejoice, thy soul is free*."

The little party were soon guided, by Mrs. Smyth, to the
hospitable abode of a good missionary, whom Christian charity has placed here as a shepherd to the out-cast and wandering, who are constantly finding an asylum on this shore.

Who can speak the blessedness of that first day of freedom?
Is not the *sense* of liberty a higher and a finer one than any of
the five? To move, speak and breathe,—go out and come in
unwatched, and free from danger! Who can speak the blessings of that rest which comes down on the free man's pillow,
under laws which insure to him the rights that God has given
to man? How fair and precious to that mother was that sleeping child's face, endeared by the memory of a thousand dangers! How impossible was it to sleep, in the exuberant possession of such blessedness! And yet, these two had not one
acre of ground,—not a roof that they could call their own,—
they had spent their all, to the last dollar. They had nothing
more than the birds of the air, or the flowers of the field,—
yet they could not sleep for joy. "O, ye who take freedom
from man, with what words shall ye answer it to God?"

XXXVIII.

The Victory

"Thanks be unto God, who giveth us the victory."

Have not many of us, in the weary way of life, felt, in some hours, how far easier it were to die than to live? The martyr, when faced even by a death of bodily anguish and horror, finds in the very terror of his doom a strong stimulant and tonic. There is a vivid excitement, a thrill and fervor, which may carry through any crisis of suffering that is the birth-hour of eternal glory and rest.

But to live,—to wear on, day after day, of mean, bitter, low, harassing servitude, every nerve dampened and depressed, every power of feeling gradually smothered,—this long and wasting heart-martyrdom, this slow, daily bleeding away of the inward life, drop by drop, hour after hour,—this is the true searching test of what there may be in man or woman.

When Tom stood face to face with his persecutor, and heard his threats, and thought in his very soul that his hour was come, his heart swelled bravely in him, and he thought he could bear torture and fire, bear anything, with the vision of Jesus and heaven but just a step beyond; but, when he was gone, and the present excitement passed off, came back the pain of his bruised and weary limbs,—came back the sense of his utterly degraded, hopeless, forlorn estate; and the day passed wearily enough.

Long before his wounds were healed, Legree insisted that he should be put to the regular field-work; and then came day after day of pain and weariness, aggravated by every kind of injustice and indignity that the ill-will of a mean and malicious mind could devise. Whoever, in *our* circumstances, has made trial of pain, even with all the alleviations which, for us, usually attend it, must know the irritation that comes with it. Tom no longer wondered at the habitual surliness of his associates; nay, he found the placid, sunny temper, which had been the habitude of his life, broken in on, and sorely strained, by the inroads of the same thing. He had flattered himself on leisure to read his Bible; but there was no such thing as leisure there. In the height of the season, Legree did not hesitate to press all his hands through, Sundays and week-days alike. Why should n't he?—he made more cotton by it, and gained his wager; and if it wore out a few more hands, he could buy better ones. At first, Tom used to read a verse or two of his Bible, by the flicker of the fire, after he had returned from his daily toil; but, after the cruel treatment he received, he used to come home so exhausted, that his head swam and his eyes failed when he tried to read; and he was fain to stretch himself down, with the others, in utter exhaustion.

Is it strange that the religious peace and trust, which had upborne him hitherto, should give way to tossings of soul and despondent darkness? The gloomiest problem of this mysterious life was constantly before his eyes,—souls crushed and ruined, evil triumphant, and God silent. It was weeks and months that Tom wrestled, in his own soul, in darkness and sorrow. He thought of Miss Ophelia's letter to his Kentucky friends, and would pray earnestly that God would send him deliverance. And then he would watch, day after day, in the vague hope of seeing somebody sent to redeem him; and, when nobody came, he would crush back to his soul bitter thoughts,—that it was vain to serve God, that God had forgotten him. He sometimes saw Cassy; and sometimes, when summoned to the house, caught a glimpse of the dejected form of Emmeline, but held very little communion with either; in fact, there was no time for him to commune with anybody.

One evening, he was sitting, in utter dejection and prostration, by a few decaying brands, where his coarse supper was baking. He put a few bits of brushwood on the fire, and strove to raise the light, and then drew his worn Bible from his pocket. There were all the marked passages, which had thrilled his soul so often,—words of patriarchs and seers, poets and sages, who from early time had spoken courage to man,—voices from the great cloud of witnesses who ever surround us in the race of life. Had the word lost its power, or could the failing eye and weary sense no longer answer to the touch of that mighty inspiration? Heavily sighing, he put it in his pocket. A coarse laugh roused him; he looked up,— Legree was standing opposite to him.

"Well, old boy," he said, "you find your religion don't work, it seems! I thought I should get that through your wool, at last!"

The cruel taunt was more than hunger and cold and nakedness. Tom was silent.

"You were a fool," said Legree; "for I meant to do well by you, when I bought you. You might have been better off than Sambo, or Quimbo either, and had easy times; and, instead of getting cut up and thrashed, every day or two, ye might have had liberty to lord it round, and cut up the other niggers; and ye might have had, now and then, a good warming of whiskey punch. Come, Tom, don't you think you 'd better be reasonable?—heave that ar old pack of trash in the fire, and join my church!"

"The Lord forbid!" said Tom, fervently.

"You see the Lord an't going to help you; if he had been, he would n't have let *me* get you! This yer religion is all a mess of lying trumpery, Tom. I know all about it. Ye 'd better hold to me; I 'm somebody, and can do something!"

"No, Mas'r," said Tom; "I 'll hold on. The Lord may help me, or not help; but I 'll hold to him, and believe him to the last!"

"The more fool you!" said Legree, spitting scornfully at him, and spurning him with his foot. "Never mind; I 'll chase you down, yet, and bring you under,—you 'll see!" and Legree turned away.

When a heavy weight presses the soul to the lowest level at which endurance is possible, there is an instant and desperate effort of every physical and moral nerve to throw off the weight; and hence the heaviest anguish often precedes a return tide of joy and courage. So was it now with Tom. The atheistic taunts of his cruel master sunk his before dejected soul to the lowest ebb; and, though the hand of faith still held to the eternal rock, it was with a numb, despairing grasp. Tom sat, like one stunned, at the fire. Suddenly everything around him seemed to fade, and a vision rose before him of one crowned with thorns, buffeted and bleeding. Tom gazed, in awe and wonder, at the majestic patience of the face; the deep, pathetic eyes thrilled him to his inmost heart; his soul woke, as, with floods of emotion, he stretched out his hands and fell upon his knees,—when, gradually, the vision changed: the sharp thorns became rays of glory; and, in splendor inconceivable, he saw that same face bending compassionately towards him, and a voice said, "He that overcometh shall sit down with me on my throne, even as I also overcame, and am set down with my Father on his throne."

How long Tom lay there, he knew not. When he came to himself, the fire was gone out, his clothes were wet with the chill and drenching dews; but the dread soul-crisis was past, and, in the joy that filled him, he no longer felt hunger, cold, degradation, disappointment, wretchedness. From his deepest soul, he that hour loosed and parted from every hope in the life that now is, and offered his own will an unquestioning sacrifice to the Infinite. Tom looked up to the silent, ever-living stars,—types of the angelic hosts who ever look down on man; and the solitude of the night rung with the triumphant words of a hymn, which he had sung often in happier days, but never with such feeling as now:

> "The earth shall be dissolved like snow,
>   The sun shall cease to shine;
> But God, who called me here below,
>   Shall be forever mine.
>
> "And when this mortal life shall fail,
>   And flesh and sense shall cease,
> I shall possess within the veil
>   A life of joy and peace.
>
> "When we 've been there ten thousand years,
>   Bright shining like the sun,
> We 've no less days to sing God's praise
>   Than when we first begun."

Those who have been familiar with the religious histories of the slave population know that relations like what we have narrated are very common among them. We have heard some from their own lips, of a very touching and affecting character. The psychologist tells us of a state, in which the affections and images of the mind become so dominant and overpowering, that they press into their service the outward senses, and make them give tangible shape to the inward imagining. Who shall measure what an all-pervading Spirit may do with these capabilities of our mortality, or the ways in which He may encourage the desponding souls of the desolate? If the poor forgotten slave believes that Jesus hath appeared and spoken to him, who shall contradict him? Did He not say that his mission, in all ages, was to bind up the broken-hearted, and set at liberty them that are bruised?

When the dim gray of dawn woke the slumberers to go forth to the field, there was among those tattered and shivering wretches one who walked with an exultant tread; for firmer than the ground he trod on was his strong faith in Almighty, eternal love. Ah, Legree, try all your forces now! Utmost agony, woe, degradation, want, and loss of all things, shall only hasten on the process by which he shall be made a king and a priest unto God!

From this time, an inviolable sphere of peace encompassed the lowly heart of the oppressed one,—an ever-present Saviour hallowed it as a temple. Past now the bleeding of earthly regrets; past its fluctuations of hope, and fear, and desire; the human will, bent, and bleeding, and struggling long, was now entirely merged in the Divine. So short now seemed the remaining voyage of life,—so near, so vivid, seemed eternal blessedness,—that life's uttermost woes fell from him unharming.

All noticed the change in his appearance. Cheerfulness and alertness seemed to return to him, and a quietness which no insult or injury could ruffle seemed to possess him.

"What the devil's got into Tom?" Legree said to Sambo. "A while ago he was all down in the mouth, and now he's peart as a cricket."

"Dunno, Mas'r; gwine to run off, mebbe."

"Like to see him try that," said Legree, with a savage grin, "would n't we, Sambo?"

"Guess we would! Haw! haw! ho!" said the sooty gnome,

laughing obsequiously. "Lord, de fun! To see him stickin' in de mud, — chasin' and tarin' through de bushes, dogs a holdin' on to him! Lord, I laughed fit to split, dat ar time we cotched Molly. I thought they 'd a had her all stripped up afore I could get 'em off. She car's de marks o' dat ar spree yet."

"I reckon she will, to her grave," said Legree. "But now, Sambo, you look sharp. If the nigger 's got anything of this sort going, trip him up."

"Mas'r, let me lone for dat," said Sambo. "I 'll tree de coon. Ho, ho, ho!"

This was spoken as Legree was getting on to his horse, to go to the neighboring town. That night, as he was returning, he thought he would turn his horse and ride round the quarters, and see if all was safe.

It was a superb moonlight night, and the shadows of the graceful China trees lay minutely pencilled on the turf below, and there was that transparent stillness in the air which it seems almost unholy to disturb. Legree was at a little distance from the quarters, when he heard the voice of some one singing. It was not a usual sound there, and he paused to listen. A musical tenor voice sang,

> "When I can read my title clear
>   To mansions in the skies,
> I 'll bid farewell to every fear,
>   And wipe my weeping eyes.
>
> "Should earth against my soul engage,
>   And hellish darts be hurled,
> Then I can smile at Satan's rage,
>   And face a frowning world.
>
> "Let cares like a wild deluge come,
>   And storms of sorrow fall,
> May I but safely reach my home,
>   My God, my Heaven, my All."

"So ho!" said Legree to himself, "he thinks so, does he? How I hate these cursed Methodist hymns! Here, you nigger," said he, coming suddenly out upon Tom, and raising his riding-whip, "how dare you be gettin' up this yer row, when you ought to be in bed? Shut yer old black gash, and get along in with you!"

"Yes, Mas'r," said Tom, with ready cheerfulness, as he rose to go in.

Legree was provoked beyond measure by Tom's evident happiness; and, riding up to him, belabored him over his head and shoulders.

"There, you dog," he said, "see if you 'll feel so comfortable, after that!"

But the blows fell now only on the outer man, and not, as before, on the heart. Tom stood perfectly submissive; and yet Legree could not hide from himself that his power over his bond thrall was somehow gone. And, as Tom disappeared in his cabin, and he wheeled his horse suddenly round, there passed through his mind one of those vivid flashes that often send the lightning of conscience across the dark and wicked soul. He understood full well that it was GOD who was standing, between him and his victim, and he blasphemed him. That submissive and silent man, whom taunts, nor threats, nor stripes, nor cruelties, could disturb, roused a voice within him, such as of old his Master roused in the demoniac soul, saying, "What have we to do with thee, thou Jesus of Nazareth?—art thou come to torment us before the time?"

Tom's whole soul overflowed with compassion and sympathy for the poor wretches by whom he was surrounded. To him it seemed as if his life-sorrows were now over, and as if, out of that strange treasury of peace and joy, with which he had been endowed from above, he longed to pour out something for the relief of their woes. It is true, opportunities were scanty; but, on the way to the fields, and back again, and during the hours of labor, chances fell in his way of extending a helping-hand to the weary, the disheartened and discouraged. The poor, worn-down, brutalized creatures, at first, could scarce comprehend this; but, when it was continued week after week, and month after month, it began to awaken long-silent chords in their benumbed hearts. Gradually and imperceptibly the strange, silent, patient man, who was ready to bear every one's burden, and sought help from none,—

who stood aside for all, and came last, and took least, yet was foremost to share his little all with any who needed,—the man who, in cold nights, would give up his tattered blanket to add to the comfort of some woman who shivered with sickness, and who filled the baskets of the weaker ones in the field, at the terrible risk of coming short in his own measure,—and who, though pursued with unrelenting cruelty by their common tyrant, never joined in uttering a word of reviling or cursing,—this man, at last, began to have a strange power over them; and, when the more pressing season was past, and they were allowed again their Sundays for their own use, many would gather together to hear from him of Jesus. They would gladly have met to hear, and pray, and sing, in some place, together; but Legree would not permit it, and more than once broke up such attempts, with oaths and brutal execrations,—so that the blessed news had to circulate from individual to individual. Yet who can speak the simple joy with which some of those poor outcasts, to whom life was a joyless journey to a dark unknown, heard of a compassionate Redeemer and a heavenly home? It is the statement of missionaries, that, of all races of the earth, none have received the Gospel with such eager docility as the African. The principle of reliance and unquestioning faith, which is its foundation, is more a native element in this race than any other; and it has often been found among them, that a stray seed of truth, borne on some breeze of accident into hearts the most ignorant, has sprung up into fruit, whose abundance has shamed that of higher and more skilful culture.

The poor mulatto woman, whose simple faith had been well-nigh crushed and overwhelmed, by the avalanche of cruelty and wrong which had fallen upon her, felt her soul raised up by the hymns and passages of Holy Writ, which this lowly missionary breathed into her ear in intervals, as they were going to and returning from work; and even the half-crazed and wandering mind of Cassy was soothed and calmed by his simple and unobtrusive influences.

Stung to madness and despair by the crushing agonies of a life, Cassy had often resolved in her soul an hour of retribution, when her hand should avenge on her oppressor all the injustice and cruelty to which she had been witness, or which *she* had in her own person suffered.

One night, after all in Tom's cabin were sunk in sleep, he was suddenly aroused by seeing her face at the hole between the logs, that served for a window. She made a silent gesture for him to come out.

Tom came out the door. It was between one and two o'clock at night,—broad, calm, still moonlight. Tom remarked, as the light of the moon fell upon Cassy's large, black eyes, that there was a wild and peculiar glare in them, unlike their wonted fixed despair.

"Come here, Father Tom," she said, laying her small hand on his wrist, and drawing him forward with a force as if the hand were of steel; "come here,—I 've news for you."

"What, Misse Cassy?" said Tom, anxiously.

"Tom, would n't you like your liberty?"

"I shall have it, Misse, in God's time," said Tom.

"Ay, but you may have it to-night," said Cassy, with a flash of sudden energy. "Come on."

Tom hesitated.

"Come!" said she, in a whisper, fixing her black eyes on him. "Come along! He 's asleep—sound. I put enough into his brandy to keep him so. I wish I 'd had more,—I should n't have wanted you. But come, the back door is unlocked; there 's an axe there, I put it there,—his room door is open; I 'll show you the way. I 'd a done it myself, only my arms are so weak. Come along!"

"Not for ten thousand worlds, Misse!" said Tom, firmly, stopping and holding her back, as she was pressing forward.

"But think of all these poor creatures," said Cassy. "We might set them all free, and go somewhere in the swamps, and find an island, and live by ourselves; I 've heard of its being done. Any life is better than this."

"No!" said Tom, firmly. "No! good never comes of wickedness. I 'd sooner chop my right hand off!"

"Then *I* shall do it," said Cassy, turning.

"O, Misse Cassy!" said Tom, throwing himself before her, "for the dear Lord's sake that died for ye, don't sell your precious soul to the devil, that way! Nothing but evil will come of it. The Lord has n't called us to wrath. We must suffer, and wait his time."

"Wait!" said Cassy. "Have n't I waited?—waited till my head is dizzy and my heart sick? What has he made me suffer? What has he made hundreds of poor creatures suffer? Is n't he wringing the life-blood out of you? I 'm called on; they call me! His time 's come, and I 'll have his heart's blood!"

"No, no, no!" said Tom, holding her small hands, which were clenched with spasmodic violence. "No, ye poor, lost soul, that ye must n't do. The dear, blessed Lord never shed no blood but his own, and that he poured out for us when we was enemies. Lord, help us to follow his steps, and love our enemies."

"Love!" said Cassy, with a fierce glare; "love *such* enemies! It is n't in flesh and blood."

"No, Misse, it is n't," said Tom, looking up; "but *He* gives it to us, and that 's the *victory*. When we can love and pray over all and through all, the battle 's past, and the victory 's come,—glory be to God!" And, with streaming eyes and choking voice, the black man looked up to heaven.

And this, oh Africa! latest called of nations,—called to the crown of thorns, the scourge, the bloody sweat, the cross of agony,—this is to be *thy* victory; by this shalt thou reign with Christ when his kingdom shall come on earth.

The deep fervor of Tom's feelings, the softness of his voice, his tears, fell like dew on the wild, unsettled spirit of the poor woman. A softness gathered over the lurid fires of her eye; she looked down, and Tom could feel the relaxing muscles of her hands, as she said,

"Did n't I tell you that evil spirits followed me? O! Father Tom, I can't pray,—I wish I could. I never have prayed since my children were sold! What you say must be right, I know it must; but when I try to pray, I can only hate and curse. I can't pray!"

"Poor soul!" said Tom, compassionately. "Satan desires to have ye, and sift ye as wheat. I pray the Lord for ye. O! Misse Cassy, turn to the dear Lord Jesus. He came to bind up the broken-hearted, and comfort all that mourn."

Cassy stood silent, while large, heavy tears dropped from her downcast eyes.

"Misse Cassy," said Tom, in a hesitating tone, after surveying her a moment in silence, "if ye only could get away from here,—if the thing was possible,—I 'd 'vise ye and Emmeline to do it; that is, if ye could go without blood-guiltiness,— not otherwise."

"Would you try it with us, Father Tom?"

"No," said Tom; "time was when I would; but the Lord 's given me a work among these yer poor souls, and I 'll stay with 'em and bear my cross with 'em till the end. It 's different with you; it 's a snare to you,—it 's more 'n you can stand,—and you 'd better go, if you can."

"I know no way but through the grave," said Cassy. "There 's no beast or bird but can find a home somewhere; even the snakes and the alligators have their places to lie down and be quiet; but there 's no place for us. Down in the darkest swamps, their dogs will hunt us out, and find us. Everybody and everything is against us; even the very beasts side against us,—and where shall we go?"

Tom stood silent; at length he said,

"Him that saved Daniel in the den of lions,—that saved the children in the fiery furnace,—Him that walked on the sea, and bade the winds be still,—He 's alive yet; and I 've faith to believe he can deliver you. Try it, and I 'll pray, with all my might, for you."

By what strange law of mind is it that an idea long overlooked, and trodden under foot as a useless stone, suddenly sparkles out in new light, as a discovered diamond?

Cassy had often revolved, for hours, all possible or probable schemes of escape, and dismissed them all, as hopeless and impracticable; but at this moment there flashed through her mind a plan, so simple and feasible in all its details, as to awaken an instant hope.

"Father Tom, I 'll try it!" she said, suddenly.

"Amen!" said Tom; "the Lord help ye!"

XXXIX.

The Stratagem

"The way of the wicked is as darkness; he knoweth not
at what he stumbleth."

THE garret of the house that Legree occupied, like most
other garrets, was a great, desolate space, dusty, hung
with cobwebs, and littered with cast-off lumber. The opulent
family that had inhabited the house in the days of its splendor
had imported a great deal of splendid furniture, some of
which they had taken away with them, while some remained
standing desolate in mouldering, unoccupied rooms, or
stored away in this place. One or two immense packing-
boxes, in which this furniture was brought, stood against the
sides of the garret. There was a small window there, which
let in, through its dingy, dusty panes, a scanty, uncertain light
on the tall, high-backed chairs and dusty tables, that had once
seen better days. Altogether, it was a weird and ghostly place;
but, ghostly as it was, it wanted not in legends among the
superstitious negroes, to increase its terrors. Some few years
before, a negro woman, who had incurred Legree's displeasure, was confined there for several weeks. What passed there,
we do not say; the negroes used to whisper darkly to each
other; but it was known that the body of the unfortunate
creature was one day taken down from there, and buried;
and, after that, it was said that oaths and cursings, and the
sound of violent blows, used to ring through that old garret,
and mingled with wailings and groans of despair. Once, when
Legree chanced to overhear something of this kind, he flew
into a violent passion, and swore that the next one that told
stories about that garret should have an opportunity of knowing what was there, for he would chain them up there for a
week. This hint was enough to repress talking, though, of
course, it did not disturb the credit of the story in the least.

Gradually, the staircase that led to the garret, and even the
passage-way to the staircase, were avoided by every one in the

house, from every one fearing to speak of it, and the legend was gradually falling into desuetude. It had suddenly occurred to Cassy to make use of the superstitious excitability, which was so great in Legree, for the purpose of her liberation, and that of her fellow-sufferer.

The sleeping-room of Cassy was directly under the garret. One day, without consulting Legree, she suddenly took it upon her, with some considerable ostentation, to change all the furniture and appurtenances of the room to one at some considerable distance. The under-servants, who were called on to effect this movement, were running and bustling about with great zeal and confusion, when Legree returned from a ride.

"Hallo! you Cass!" said Legree, "what 's in the wind now?"

"Nothing; only I choose to have another room," said Cassy, doggedly.

"And what for, pray?" said Legree.

"I choose to," said Cassy.

"The devil you do! and what for?"

"I 'd like to get some sleep, now and then."

"Sleep! well, what hinders your sleeping?"

"I could tell, I suppose, if you want to hear," said Cassy, dryly.

"Speak out, you minx!" said Legree.

"O! nothing. I suppose it would n't disturb *you*! Only groans, and people scuffling, and rolling round on the garret floor, half the night, from twelve to morning!"

"People up garret!" said Legree, uneasily, but forcing a laugh; "who are they, Cassy?"

Cassy raised her sharp, black eyes, and looked in the face of Legree, with an expression that went through his bones, as she said, "To be sure, Simon, who are they? I 'd like to have *you* tell me. You don't know, I suppose!"

With an oath, Legree struck at her with his riding-whip; but she glided to one side, and passed through the door, and looking back, said, "If you 'll sleep in that room, you 'll know all about it. Perhaps you 'd better try it!" and then immediately she shut and locked the door.

Legree blustered and swore, and threatened to break down the door; but apparently thought better of it, and walked uneasily into the sitting-room. Cassy perceived that her shaft had struck home; and, from that hour, with the most exquisite address, she never ceased to continue the train of influences she had begun.

In a knot-hole of the garret, that had opened, she had inserted the neck of an old bottle, in such a manner that when there was the least wind, most doleful and lugubrious wailing sounds proceeded from it, which, in a high wind, increased to a perfect shriek, such as to credulous and superstitious ears might easily seem to be that of horror and despair.

These sounds were, from time to time, heard by the servants, and revived in full force the memory of the old ghost legend. A superstitious creeping horror seemed to fill the house; and though no one dared to breathe it to Legree, he found himself encompassed by it, as by an atmosphere.

No one is so thoroughly superstitious as the godless man. The Christian is composed by the belief of a wise, all-ruling Father, whose presence fills the void unknown with light and order; but to the man who has dethroned God, the spirit-land is, indeed, in the words of the Hebrew poet, "a land of darkness and the shadow of death," without any order, where the light is as darkness. Life and death to him are haunted grounds, filled with goblin forms of vague and shadowy dread.

Legree had had the slumbering moral element in him roused by his encounters with Tom,—roused, only to be resisted by the determinate force of evil; but still there was a thrill and commotion of the dark, inner world, produced by every word, or prayer, or hymn, that reäcted in superstitious dread.

The influence of Cassy over him was of a strange and singular kind. He was her owner, her tyrant and tormentor. She was, as he knew, wholly, and without any possibility of help or redress, in his hands; and yet so it is, that the most brutal man cannot live in constant association with a strong female influence, and not be greatly controlled by it. When he first bought her, she was, as she had said, a woman delicately bred; and then he crushed her, without scruple, beneath the foot of his brutality. But, as time, and debasing influences, and despair, hardened womanhood within her, and waked the fires of fiercer passions, she had become in a measure his mistress, and he alternately tyrannized over and dreaded her.

This influence had become more harassing and decided, since partial insanity had given a strange, weird, unsettled cast to all her words and language.

A night or two after this, Legree was sitting in the old sitting-room, by the side of a flickering wood fire, that threw uncertain glances round the room. It was a stormy, windy night, such as raises whole squadrons of nondescript noises in rickety old houses. Windows were rattling, shutters flapping, the wind carousing, rumbling, and tumbling down the chimney, and, every once in a while, puffing out smoke and ashes, as if a legion of spirits were coming after them. Legree had been casting up accounts and reading newspapers for some hours, while Cassy sat in the corner, sullenly looking into the fire. Legree laid down his paper, and seeing an old book lying on the table, which he had noticed Cassy reading, the first part of the evening, took it up, and began to turn it over. It was one of those collections of stories of bloody murders, ghostly legends, and supernatural visitations, which, coarsely got up and illustrated, have a strange fascination for one who once begins to read them.

Legree poohed and pished, but read, turning page after page, till, finally, after reading some way, he threw down the book, with an oath.

"You don't believe in ghosts, do you, Cass?" said he, taking the tongs and settling the fire. "I thought you 'd more sense than to let noises scare *you*."

"No matter what I believe," said Cassy, sullenly.

"Fellows used to try to frighten me with their yarns at sea," said Legree. "Never come it round me that way. I 'm too tough for any such trash, tell ye."

Cassy sat looking intensely at him in the shadow of the corner. There was that strange light in her eyes that always impressed Legree with uneasiness.

"Them noises was nothing but rats and the wind," said Legree. "Rats will make a devil of a noise. I used to hear 'em sometimes down in the hold of the ship; and wind,—Lord's sake! ye can make anything out o' wind."

Cassy knew Legree was uneasy under her eyes, and, therefore, she made no answer, but sat fixing them on him, with that strange, unearthly expression, as before.

"Come, speak out, woman,—don't you think so?" said Legree.

"Can rats walk down stairs, and come walking through the entry, and open a door when you 've locked it and set a chair against it?" said Cassy; "and come walk, walk, walking right up to your bed, and put out their hand, so?"

Cassy kept her glittering eyes fixed on Legree, as she spoke, and he stared at her like a man in the nightmare, till, when she finished by laying her hand, icy cold, on his, he sprung back, with an oath.

"Woman! what do you mean? Nobody did?"—

"O, no,—of course not,—did I say they did?" said Cassy, with a smile of chilling derision.

"But—did—have you really seen?—Come, Cass, what is it, now,—speak out!"

"You may sleep there, yourself," said Cassy, "if you want to know."

"Did it come from the garret, Cassy?"

"*It*,—what?" said Cassy.

"Why, what you told of—"

"I did n't tell you anything," said Cassy, with dogged sullenness.

Legree walked up and down the room, uneasily.

"I 'll have this yer thing examined. I 'll look into it, this very night. I 'll take my pistols—"

"Do," said Cassy; "sleep in that room. I 'd like to see you doing it. Fire your pistols,—do!"

Legree stamped his foot, and swore violently.

"Don't swear," said Cassy; "nobody knows who may be hearing you. Hark! What was that?"

"What?" said Legree, starting.

A heavy old Dutch clock, that stood in the corner of the room, began, and slowly struck twelve.

For some reason or other, Legree neither spoke nor moved; a vague horror fell on him; while Cassy, with a keen, sneering glitter in her eyes, stood looking at him, counting the strokes.

"Twelve o'clock; well, *now* we 'll see," said she, turning, and opening the door into the passage-way, and standing as if listening.

"Hark! What 's that?" said she, raising her finger.

"It 's only the wind," said Legree. "Don't you hear how cursedly it blows?"

"Simon, come here," said Cassy, in a whisper, laying her hand on his, and leading him to the foot of the stairs: "do you know what *that* is? Hark!"

A wild shriek came pealing down the stairway. It came from the garret. Legree's knees knocked together; his face grew white with fear.

"Had n't you better get your pistols?" said Cassy, with a sneer that froze Legree's blood. "It 's time this thing was looked into, you know. I 'd like to have you go up now; *they 're at it.*"

"I won't go!" said Legree, with an oath.

"Why not? There an't any such thing as ghosts, you know! Come!" and Cassy flitted up the winding stairway, laughing, and looking back after him. "Come on."

"I believe you *are* the devil!" said Legree. "Come back, you hag,—come back, Cass! You shan't go!"

But Cassy laughed wildly, and fled on. He heard her open the entry doors that led to the garret. A wild gust of wind swept down, extinguishing the candle he held in his hand, and with it the fearful, unearthly screams; they seemed to be shrieked in his very ear.

Legree fled frantically into the parlor, whither, in a few moments, he was followed by Cassy, pale, calm, cold as an avenging spirit, and with that same fearful light in her eye.

"I hope you are satisfied," said she.

"Blast you, Cass!" said Legree.

"What for?" said Cassy. "I only went up and shut the doors. *What 's the matter with that garret*, Simon, do you suppose?" said she.

"None of your business!" said Legree.

"O, it an't? Well," said Cassy, "at any rate, I 'm glad *I* don't sleep under it."

Anticipating the rising of the wind, that very evening,

Cassy had been up and opened the garret window. Of course, the moment the doors were opened, the wind had drafted down, and extinguished the light.

This may serve as a specimen of the game that Cassy played with Legree, until he would sooner have put his head into a lion's mouth than to have explored that garret. Meanwhile, in the night, when everybody else was asleep, Cassy slowly and carefully accumulated there a stock of provisions sufficient to afford subsistence for some time; she transferred, article by article, a greater part of her own and Emmeline's wardrobe. All things being arranged, they only waited a fitting opportunity to put their plan in execution.

By cajoling Legree, and taking advantage of a good-natured interval, Cassy had got him to take her with him to the neighboring town, which was situated directly on the Red river. With a memory sharpened to almost preternatural clearness, she remarked every turn in the road, and formed a mental estimate of the time to be occupied in traversing it.

At the time when all was matured for action, our readers may, perhaps, like to look behind the scenes, and see the final *coup d' état*.

It was now near evening. Legree had been absent, on a ride to a neighboring farm. For many days Cassy had been unusually gracious and accommodating in her humors; and Legree and she had been, apparently, on the best of terms. At present, we may behold her and Emmeline in the room of the latter, busy in sorting and arranging two small bundles.

"There, these will be large enough," said Cassy. "Now put on your bonnet, and let 's start: it 's just about the right time."

"Why, they can see us yet," said Emmeline.

"I mean they shall," said Cassy, coolly. "Don't you know that they must have their chase after us, at any rate? The way of the thing is to be just this:—We will steal out of the back door, and run down by the quarters. Sambo or Quimbo will be sure to see us. They will give chase, and we will get into the swamp; then, they can't follow us any further till they go up and give the alarm, and turn out the dogs, and so on; and, while they are blundering round, and tumbling over each other, as they always do, you and I will just slip along to the creek, that runs back of the house, and wade along in it, till we get opposite the back door. That will put the dogs all at fault; for scent won't lie in the water. Every one will run out of the house to look after us, and then we 'll whip in at the back door, and up into the garret, where I 've got a nice bed made up in one of the great boxes. We must stay in that garret a good while; for, I tell you, he will raise heaven and earth after us. He 'll muster some of those old overseers on the other plantations, and have a great hunt; and they 'll go over every inch of ground in that swamp. He makes it his boast that nobody ever got away from him. So let him hunt at his leisure."

"Cassy, how well you have planned it!" said Emmeline. "Who ever would have thought of it, but you?"

There was neither pleasure nor exultation in Cassy's eyes, —only a despairing firmness.

"Come," she said, reaching her hand to Emmeline.

The two fugitives glided noiselessly from the house, and flitted, through the gathering shadows of evening, along by the quarters. The crescent moon, set like a silver signet in the western sky, delayed a little the approach of night. As Cassy expected, when quite near the verge of the swamps that encircled the plantation, they heard a voice calling to them to stop. It was not Sambo, however, but Legree, who was pursuing them with violent execrations. At the sound, the feebler spirit of Emmeline gave way; and, laying hold of Cassy's arm, she said, "O, Cassy, I 'm going to faint!"

"If you do, I 'll kill you!" said Cassy, drawing a small, glittering stiletto, and flashing it before the eyes of the girl.

The diversion accomplished the purpose. Emmeline did not faint, and succeeded in plunging, with Cassy, into a part of the labyrinth of swamp, so deep and dark that it was perfectly hopeless for Legree to think of following them, without assistance.

"Well," said he, chuckling brutally; "at any rate, they 've got themselves into a trap now—the baggages! They 're safe enough. They shall sweat for it!"

"Hulloa, there! Sambo! Quimbo! All hands!" called Legree, coming to the quarters, when the men and women were just returning from work. "There 's two runaways in the swamps. I'll give five dollars to any nigger as catches 'em. Turn out the dogs! Turn out Tiger, and Fury, and the rest!"

The sensation produced by this news was immediate. Many of the men sprang forward, officiously, to offer their services, either from the hope of the reward, or from that cringing subserviency which is one of the most baleful effects of slavery. Some ran one way, and some another. Some were for getting flambeaux of pine-knots. Some were uncoupling the dogs, whose hoarse, savage bay added not a little to the animation of the scene.

"Mas'r, shall we shoot 'em, if we can't cotch 'em?" said Sambo, to whom his master brought out a rifle.

"You may fire on Cass, if you like; it's time she was gone to the devil, where she belongs; but the gal, not," said Legree. "And now, boys, be spry and smart. Five dollars for him that gets 'em; and a glass of spirits to every one of you, anyhow."

The whole band, with the glare of blazing torches, and whoop, and shout, and savage yell, of man and beast, proceeded down to the swamp, followed, at some distance, by every servant in the house. The establishment was, of a consequence, wholly deserted, when Cassy and Emmeline glided into it the back way. The whooping and shouts of their pursuers were still filling the air; and, looking from the sitting-room windows, Cassy and Emmeline could see the troop, with their flambeaux, just dispersing themselves along the edge of the swamp.

"See there!" said Emmeline, pointing to Cassy; "the hunt is begun! Look how those lights dance about! Hark! the dogs! Don't you hear? If we were only *there,* our chance would n't be worth a picayune. O, for pity's sake, do let's hide ourselves. Quick!"

"There's no occasion for hurry," said Cassy, coolly; "they are all out after the hunt,—that's the amusement of the evening! We'll go up stairs, by and by. Meanwhile," said she, deliberately taking a key from the pocket of a coat that Legree had thrown down in his hurry, "meanwhile I shall take something to pay our passage."

She unlocked the desk, took from it a roll of bills, which she counted over rapidly.

"O, don't let 's do that!" said Emmeline.

"Don't!" said Cassy; "why not? Would you have us starve in the swamps, or have that that will pay our way to the free states? Money will do anything, girl." And, as she spoke, she put the money in her bosom.

"It would be stealing," said Emmeline, in a distressed whisper.

"Stealing!" said Cassy, with a scornful laugh. "They who steal body and soul need n't talk to us. Every one of these bills is stolen,—stolen from poor, starving, sweating creatures, who must go to the devil at last, for his profit. Let *him* talk about stealing! But come, we may as well go up garret; I 've got a stock of candles there, and some books to pass away the time. You may be pretty sure they won't come *there* to inquire after us. If they do, I 'll play ghost for them."

When Emmeline reached the garret, she found an immense box, in which some heavy pieces of furniture had once been brought, turned on its side, so that the opening faced the wall, or rather the eaves. Cassy lit a small lamp, and, creeping round under the eaves, they established themselves in it. It was spread with a couple of small mattresses and some pillows; a box near by was plentifully stored with candles, provisions, and all the clothing necessary to their journey, which Cassy had arranged into bundles of an astonishingly small compass.

"There," said Cassy, as she fixed the lamp into a small hook, which she had driven into the side of the box for that purpose; "this is to be our home for the present. How do you like it?"

"Are you sure they won't come and search the garret?"

"I 'd like to see Simon Legree doing that," said Cassy. "No, indeed; he will be too glad to keep away. As to the servants, they would any of them stand and be shot, sooner than show their faces here."

Somewhat reässured, Emmeline settled herself back on her pillow.

"What did you mean, Cassy, by saying you would kill me?" she said, simply.

"I meant to stop your fainting," said Cassy, "and I did do it. And now I tell you, Emmeline, you must make up your mind *not* to faint, let what will come; there's no sort of need of it. If I had not stopped you, that wretch might have had his hands on you now."

Emmeline shuddered.

The two remained some time in silence. Cassy busied herself with a French book; Emmeline, overcome with the exhaustion, fell into a doze, and slept some time. She was awakened by loud shouts and outcries, the tramp of horses' feet, and the baying of dogs. She started up, with a faint shriek.

"Only the hunt coming back," said Cassy, coolly; "never fear. Look out of this knot-hole. Don't you see 'em all down there? Simon has to give it up, for this night. Look, how muddy his horse is, flouncing about in the swamp; the dogs, too, look rather crest-fallen. Ah, my good sir, you'll have to try the race again and again,—the game is n't there."

"O, don't speak a word!" said Emmeline; "what if they should hear you?"

"If they do hear anything, it will make them very particular to keep away," said Cassy. "No danger; we may make any noise we please, and it will only add to the effect."

At length the stillness of midnight settled down over the house. Legree, cursing his ill luck, and vowing dire vengeance on the morrow, went to bed.

XL.

The Martyr

"Deem not the just by Heaven forgot!
　　Though life its common gifts deny,—
Though, with a crushed and bleeding heart,
　　And spurned of man, he goes to die!
For God hath marked each sorrowing day,
　　And numbered every bitter tear;
And heaven's long years of bliss shall pay
　　For all his children suffer here."—*Bryant*

THE longest way must have its close,—the gloomiest night will wear on to a morning. An eternal, inexorable lapse of moments is ever hurrying the day of the evil to an eternal night, and the night of the just to an eternal day. We have walked with our humble friend thus far in the valley of slavery; first through flowery fields of ease and indulgence, then through heart-breaking separations from all that man holds dear. Again, we have waited with him in a sunny island, where generous hands concealed his chains with flowers; and, lastly, we have followed him when the last ray of earthly hope went out in night, and seen how, in the blackness of earthly darkness, the firmament of the unseen has blazed with stars of new and significant lustre.

The morning-star now stands over the tops of the mountains, and gales and breezes, not of earth, show that the gates of day are unclosing.

The escape of Cassy and Emmeline irritated the before surly temper of Legree to the last degree; and his fury, as was to be expected, fell upon the defenceless head of Tom. When he hurriedly announced the tidings among his hands, there was a sudden light in Tom's eye, a sudden upraising of his hands, that did not escape him. He saw that he did not join the muster of the pursuers. He thought of forcing him to do it; but, having had, of old, experience of his inflexibility when commanded to take part in any deed of inhumanity, he would not, in his hurry, stop to enter into any conflict with him.

Tom, therefore, remained behind, with a few who had learned of him to pray, and offered up prayers for the escape of the fugitives.

When Legree returned, baffled and disappointed, all the long-working hatred of his soul towards his slave began to gather in a deadly and desperate form. Had not this man braved him,—steadily, powerfully, resistlessly,—ever since he bought him? Was there not a spirit in him which, silent as it was, burned on him like the fires of perdition?

"I *hate* him!" said Legree, that night, as he sat up in his bed; "I *hate* him! And is n't he MINE? Can't I do what I like with him? Who 's to hinder, I wonder?" And Legree clenched his fist, and shook it, as if he had something in his hands that he could rend in pieces.

But, then, Tom was a faithful, valuable servant; and, although Legree hated him the more for that, yet the consideration was still somewhat of a restraint to him.

The next morning, he determined to say nothing, as yet; to assemble a party, from some neighboring plantations, with dogs and guns; to surround the swamp, and go about the hunt systematically. If it succeeded, well and good; if not, he would summon Tom before him, and—his teeth clenched and his blood boiled—*then* he would break that fellow down, or——there was a dire inward whisper, to which his soul assented.

Ye say that the *interest* of the master is a sufficient safeguard for the slave. In the fury of man's mad will, he will wittingly, and with open eye, sell his own soul to the devil to gain his ends; and will he be more careful of his neighbor's body?

"Well," said Cassy, the next day, from the garret, as she reconnoitred through the knot-hole, "the hunt 's going to begin again, to-day!"

Three or four mounted horsemen were curvetting about, on the space front of the house; and one or two leashes of strange dogs were struggling with the negroes who held them, baying and barking at each other.

The men are, two of them, overseers of plantations in the vicinity; and others were some of Legree's associates at the tavern-bar of a neighboring city, who had come for the inter-

est of the sport. A more hard-favored set, perhaps, could not
be imagined. Legree was serving brandy, profusely, round
among them, as also among the negroes, who had been de-
tailed from the various plantations for this service; for it was
an object to make every service of this kind, among the negroes, as much of a holiday as possible.

Cassy placed her ear at the knot-hole; and, as the morning
air blew directly towards the house, she could overhear a
good deal of the conversation. A grave sneer overcast the
dark, severe gravity of her face, as she listened, and heard
them divide out the ground, discuss the rival merits of the
dogs, give orders about firing, and the treatment of each, in
case of capture.

Cassy drew back; and, clasping her hands, looked upward,
and said, "O, great Almighty God! we are *all* sinners; but
what have *we* done, more than all the rest of the world, that
we should be treated so?"

There was a terrible earnestness in her face and voice, as
she spoke.

"If it was n't for *you*, child," she said, looking at Emmeline,
"I 'd *go* out to them; and I 'd thank any one of them that
would shoot me down; for what use will freedom be to me?
Can it give me back my children, or make me what I used to
be?"

Emmeline, in her child-like simplicity, was half afraid of the
dark moods of Cassy. She looked perplexed, but made no
answer. She only took her hand, with a gentle, caressing
movement.

"Don't!" said Cassy, trying to draw it away; "you 'll get me
to loving you; and I never mean to love anything, again!"

"Poor Cassy!" said Emmeline, "don't feel so! If the Lord
gives us liberty, perhaps he 'll give you back your daughter;
at any rate, I 'll be like a daughter to you. I know I 'll never
see my poor old mother again! I shall love you, Cassy,
whether you love me or not!"

The gentle, child-like spirit conquered. Cassy sat down by
her, put her arm round her neck, stroked her soft, brown
hair; and Emmeline then wondered at the beauty of her magnificent eyes, now soft with tears.

"O, Em!" said Cassy, "I 've hungered for my children, and

thirsted for them, and my eyes fail with longing for them!
Here! here!" she said, striking her breast, "it 's all desolate, all
empty! If God would give me back my children, then I could
pray."

"You must trust him, Cassy," said Emmeline; "he is our
Father!"

"His wrath is upon us," said Cassy; "he has turned away in
anger."

"No, Cassy! He will be good to us! Let us hope in Him,"
said Emmeline,—"I always have had hope."

———————

The hunt was long, animated, and thorough, but unsuccessful; and, with grave, ironic exultation, Cassy looked down
on Legree, as, weary and dispirited, he alighted from his horse.

"Now, Quimbo," said Legree, as he stretched himself down
in the sitting-room, "you jest go and walk that Tom up here,
right away! The old cuss is at the bottom of this yer whole
matter; and I 'll have it out of his old black hide, or I 'll know
the reason why!"

Sambo and Quimbo, both, though hating each other, were
joined in one mind by a no less cordial hatred of Tom. Legree
had told them, at first, that he had bought him for a general
overseer, in his absence; and this had begun an ill will, on
their part, which had increased, in their debased and servile
natures, as they saw him becoming obnoxious to their master's displeasure. Quimbo, therefore, departed, with a will, to
execute his orders.

Tom heard the message with a forewarning heart; for he
knew all the plan of the fugitives' escape, and the place
of their present concealment;—he knew the deadly character
of the man he had to deal with, and his despotic power. But
he felt strong in God to meet death, rather than betray the
helpless.

He sat his basket down by the row, and, looking up, said,
"Into thy hands I commend my spirit! Thou hast redeemed
me, oh Lord God of truth!" and then quietly yielded himself
to the rough, brutal grasp with which Quimbo seized him.

"Ay, ay!" said the giant, as he dragged him along; "ye 'll
cotch it, now! I 'll boun' Mas'r's back 's up *high*! No sneaking

out, now! Tell ye, ye 'll get it, and no mistake! See how ye 'll look, now, helpin' Mas'r's niggers to run away! See what ye 'll get!"

The savage words none of them reached that ear!—a higher voice there was saying, "Fear not them that kill the body, and, after that, have no more that they can do." Nerve and bone of that poor man's body vibrated to those words, as if touched by the finger of God; and he felt the strength of a thousand souls in one. As he passed along, the trees and bushes, the huts of his servitude, the whole scene of his degradation, seemed to whirl by him as the landscape by the rushing car. His soul throbbed,—his home was in sight,—and the hour of release seemed at hand.

"Well, Tom!" said Legree, walking up, and seizing him grimly by the collar of his coat, and speaking through his teeth, in a paroxysm of determined rage, "do you know I 've made up my mind to KILL you?"

"It 's very likely, Mas'r," said Tom, calmly.

"I *have*," said Legree, with grim, terrible calmness, "*done—just—that—thing*, Tom, unless you 'll tell me what you know about these yer gals!"

Tom stood silent.

"D' ye hear?" said Legree, stamping, with a roar like that of an incensed lion. "Speak!"

"*I han't got nothing to tell, Mas'r,*" said Tom, with a slow, firm, deliberate utterance.

"Do you dare to tell me, ye old black Christian, ye don't *know?*" said Legree.

Tom was silent.

"Speak!" thundered Legree, striking him furiously. "Do you know anything?"

"I know, Mas'r; but I can't tell anything. *I can die!*"

Legree drew in a long breath; and, suppressing his rage, took Tom by the arm, and, approaching his face almost to his, said, in a terrible voice, "Hark 'e, Tom!—ye think, 'cause I 've let you off before, I don't mean what I say; but, this time, I 've *made up my mind*, and counted the cost. You 've always stood it out agin' me: now, I 'll *conquer ye; or kill ye!*—one or t' other. I 'll count every drop of blood there is in you, and take 'em, one by one, till ye give up!"

Tom looked up to his master, and answered, "Mas'r, if you was sick, or in trouble, or dying, and I could save ye, I 'd *give* ye my heart's blood; and, if taking every drop of blood in this poor old body would save your precious soul, I 'd give 'em freely, as the Lord gave his for me. O, Mas'r! don't bring this great sin on your soul! It will hurt you more than 't will me! Do the worst you can, my troubles 'll be over soon; but, if ye don't repent, yours won't *never* end!"

Like a strange snatch of heavenly music, heard in the lull of a tempest, this burst of feeling made a moment's blank pause. Legree stood aghast, and looked at Tom; and there was such a silence, that the tick of the old clock could be heard, measuring, with silent touch, the last moments of mercy and probation to that hardened heart.

It was but a moment. There was one hesitating pause,— one irresolute, relenting thrill,—and the spirit of evil came back, with seven-fold vehemence; and Legree, foaming with rage, smote his victim to the ground.

———

Scenes of blood and cruelty are shocking to our ear and heart. What man has nerve to do, man has not nerve to hear. What brother-man and brother-Christian must suffer, cannot be told us, even in our secret chamber, it so harrows up the soul! And yet, oh my country! these things are done under the shadow of thy laws! O, Christ! thy church sees them, almost in silence!

But, of old, there was One whose suffering changed an instrument of torture, degradation and shame, into a symbol of glory, honor, and immortal life; and, where His spirit is, neither degrading stripes, nor blood, nor insults, can make the Christian's last struggle less than glorious.

Was he alone, that long night, whose brave, loving spirit was bearing up, in that old shed, against buffeting and brutal stripes?

Nay! There stood by him ONE,—seen by him alone,— "like unto the Son of God."

The tempter stood by him, too,—blinded by furious, despotic will,—every moment pressing him to shun that agony by the betrayal of the innocent. But the brave, true heart was firm on the Eternal Rock. Like his Master, he knew that, if he saved others, himself he could not save; nor could utmost extremity wring from him words, save of prayer and holy trust.

"He 's most gone, Mas'r," said Sambo, touched, in spite of himself, by the patience of his victim.

"Pay away, till he gives up! Give it to him!—give it to him!" shouted Legree. "I 'll take every drop of blood he has, unless he confesses!"

Tom opened his eyes, and looked upon his master. "Ye poor miserable critter!" he said, "there an't no more ye can do! I forgive ye, with all my soul!" and he fainted entirely away.

"I b'lieve, my soul, he 's done for, finally," said Legree, stepping forward, to look at him. "Yes, he is! Well, his mouth 's shut up, at last,—that 's one comfort!"

Yes, Legree; but who shall shut up that voice in thy soul? that soul, past repentance, past prayer, past hope, in whom the fire that never shall be quenched is already burning!

Yet Tom was not quite gone. His wondrous words and pious prayers had struck upon the hearts of the imbruted blacks, who had been the instruments of cruelty upon him; and, the instant Legree withdrew, they took him down, and, in their ignorance, sought to call him back to life,—as if *that* were any favor to him.

"Sartin, we 's been doin' a drefful wicked thing!" said Sambo; "hopes Mas'r 'll have to 'count for it, and not we."

They washed his wounds,—they provided a rude bed, of some refuse cotton, for him to lie down on; and one of them, stealing up to the house, begged a drink of brandy of Legree, pretending that he was tired, and wanted it for himself. He brought it back, and poured it down Tom's throat.

"O, Tom!" said Quimbo, "we 's been awful wicked to ye!"

"I forgive ye, with all my heart!" said Tom, faintly.

"O, Tom! do tell us who is *Jesus*, anyhow?" said Sambo;— "Jesus, that 's been a standin' by you so, all this night!—Who is he?"

The word roused the failing, fainting spirit. He poured forth a few energetic sentences of that wondrous One,—his life, his death, his everlasting presence, and power to save.

They wept,—both the two savage men.

"Why did n't I never hear this before?" said Sambo; "but I do believe!—I can't help it! Lord Jesus, have mercy on us!"

"Poor critters!" said Tom, "I 'd be willing to bar' all I have, if it 'll only bring ye to Christ! O, Lord! give me these two more souls, I pray!"

That prayer was answered!

XLI.

The Young Master

Two days after, a young man drove a light wagon up through the avenue of china-trees, and, throwing the reins hastily on the horses' neck, sprang out and inquired for the owner of the place.

It was George Shelby; and, to show how he came to be there, we must go back in our story.

The letter of Miss Ophelia to Mrs. Shelby had, by some unfortunate accident, been detained, for a month or two, at some remote post-office, before it reached its destination; and, of course, before it was received, Tom was already lost to view among the distant swamps of the Red river.

Mrs. Shelby read the intelligence with the deepest concern; but any immediate action upon it was an impossibility. She was then in attendance on the sick-bed of her husband who lay delirious in the crisis of a fever. Master George Shelby, who, in the interval, had changed from a boy to a tall young man, was her constant and faithful assistant, and her only reliance in superintending his father's affairs. Miss Ophelia had taken the precaution to send them the name of the lawyer who did business for the St. Clares; and the most that, in the emergency, could be done, was to address a letter of inquiry to him. The sudden death of Mr. Shelby, a few days after, brought, of course, an absorbing pressure of other interests, for a season.

Mr. Shelby showed his confidence in his wife's ability, by appointing her sole executrix upon his estates; and thus immediately a large and complicated amount of business was brought upon her hands.

Mrs. Shelby, with characteristic energy, applied herself to the work of straightening the entangled web of affairs; and she and George were for some time occupied with collecting and examining accounts, selling property and settling debts;

for Mrs. Shelby was determined that everything should be brought into tangible and recognizable shape, let the consequences to her prove what they might. In the mean time, they received a letter from the lawyer to whom Miss Ophelia had referred them, saying that he knew nothing of the matter; that the man was sold at a public auction, and that, beyond receiving the money, he knew nothing of the affair.

Neither George nor Mrs. Shelby could be easy at this result; and, accordingly, some six months after, the latter, having business for his mother, down the river, resolved to visit New Orleans, in person, and push his inquiries, in hopes of discovering Tom's whereabouts, and restoring him.

After some months of unsuccessful search, by the merest accident, George fell in with a man, in New Orleans, who happened to be possessed of the desired information; and with his money in his pocket, our hero took steamboat for Red river, resolving to find out and re-purchase his old friend.

He was soon introduced into the house, where he found Legree in the sitting-room.

Legree received the stranger with a kind of surly hospitality.

"I understand," said the young man, "that you bought, in New Orleans, a boy, named Tom. He used to be on my father's place, and I came to see if I could n't buy him back."

Legree's brow grew dark, and he broke out, passionately: "Yes, I did buy such a fellow,—and a h—l of a bargain I had of it, too! The most rebellious, saucy, impudent dog! Set up my niggers to run away; got off two gals, worth eight hundred or a thousand dollars apiece. He owned to that, and, when I bid him tell me where they was, he up and said he knew, but he would n't tell; and stood to it, though I gave him the cussedest flogging I ever gave nigger yet. I b'lieve he's trying to die; but I don't know as he 'll make it out."

"Where is he?" said George, impetuously. "Let me see him." The cheeks of the young man were crimson, and his eyes flashed fire; but he prudently said nothing, as yet.

"He 's in dat ar shed," said a little fellow, who stood holding George's horse.

Legree kicked the boy, and swore at him; but George,

without saying another word, turned and strode to the spot.

Tom had been lying two days since the fatal night; not suffering, for every nerve of suffering was blunted and destroyed. He lay, for the most part, in a quiet stupor; for the laws of a powerful and well-knit frame would not at once release the imprisoned spirit. By stealth, there had been there, in the darkness of the night, poor desolated creatures, who stole from their scanty hours' rest, that they might repay to him some of those ministrations of love in which he had always been so abundant. Truly, those poor disciples had little to give,—only the cup of cold water; but it was given with full hearts.

Tears had fallen on that honest, insensible face,—tears of late repentance in the poor, ignorant heathen, whom his dying love and patience had awakened to repentance, and bitter prayers, breathed over him to a late-found Saviour, of whom they scarce knew more than the name, but whom the yearning ignorant heart of man never implores in vain.

Cassy, who had glided out of her place of concealment, and, by over-hearing, learned the sacrifice that had been made for her and Emmeline, had been there, the night before, defying the danger of detection; and, moved by the few last words which the affectionate soul had yet strength to breathe, the long winter of despair, the ice of years, had given way, and the dark, despairing woman had wept and prayed.

When George entered the shed, he felt his head giddy and his heart sick.

"Is it possible,—is it possible?" said he, kneeling down by him. "Uncle Tom, my poor, poor old friend!"

Something in the voice penetrated to the ear of the dying. He moved his head gently, smiled, and said,

> "Jesus can make a dying-bed
> Feel soft as downy pillows are."

Tears which did honor to his manly heart fell from the young man's eyes, as he bent over his poor friend.

"O, dear Uncle Tom! do wake,—do speak once more! Look up! Here's Mas'r George,—your own little Mas'r George. Don't you know me?"

"Mas'r George!" said Tom, opening his eyes, and speaking in a feeble voice; "Mas'r George!" He looked bewildered.

Slowly the idea seemed to fill his soul; and the vacant eye became fixed and brightened, the whole face lighted up, the hard hands clasped, and tears ran down the cheeks.

"Bless the Lord! it is,—it is,—it's all I wanted! They have n't forgot me. It warms my soul; it does my old heart good! Now I shall die content! Bless the Lord, oh my soul!"

"You shan't die! you *must n't* die, nor think of it! I 've come to buy you, and take you home," said George, with impetuous vehemence.

"O, Mas'r George, ye 're too late. The Lord 's bought me, and is going to take me home,—and I long to go. Heaven is better than Kintuck."

"O, don't die! It 'll kill me!—it 'll break my heart to think what you 've suffered,—and lying in this old shed, here! Poor, poor fellow!"

"Don't call me poor fellow!" said Tom, solemnly. "I *have* been poor fellow; but that 's all past and gone, now. I 'm right in the door, going into glory! O, Mas'r George! *Heaven has come!* I 've got the victory!—the Lord Jesus has given it to me! Glory be to His name!"

George was awe-struck at the force, the vehemence, the power, with which these broken sentences were uttered. He sat gazing in silence.

Tom grasped his hand, and continued,—"Ye must n't, now, tell Chloe, poor soul! how ye found me;—'t would be so dreful to her. Only tell her ye found me going into glory; and that I could n't stay for no one. And tell her the Lord 's stood by me everywhere and al'ays, and made everything light and easy. And oh, the poor chil'en, and the baby!—my old heart 's been most broke for 'em, time and agin! Tell 'em all to follow me—follow me! Give my love to Mas'r, and dear good Missis, and everybody in the place! Ye don't know! 'Pears like I loves 'em all! I loves every creatur', everywhar!— it 's nothing *but* love! O, Mas'r George! what a thing 't is to be a Christian!"

At this moment, Legree sauntered up to the door of the shed, looked in, with a dogged air of affected carelessness, and turned away.

"The old satan!" said George, in his indignation. "It 's a comfort to think the devil will pay *him* for this, some of these days!"

"O, don't!—oh, ye must n't!" said Tom, grasping his hand; "he 's a poor mis'able critter! it 's awful to think on 't! O, if he only could repent, the Lord would forgive him now; but I 'm 'feared he never will!"

"I hope he won't!" said George; "I never want to see *him* in heaven!"

"Hush, Mas'r George!—it worries me! Don't feel so! He an't done me no real harm,—only opened the gate of the kingdom for me; that 's all!"

At this moment, the sudden flush of strength which the joy of meeting his young master had infused into the dying man gave way. A sudden sinking fell upon him; he closed his eyes; and that mysterious and sublime change passed over his face, that told the approach of other worlds.

He began to draw his breath with long, deep inspirations; and his broad chest rose and fell, heavily. The expression of his face was that of a conqueror.

"Who,—who,—who shall separate us from the love of Christ?" he said, in a voice that contended with mortal weakness; and, with a smile, he fell asleep.

George sat fixed with solemn awe. It seemed to him that the place was holy; and, as he closed the lifeless eyes, and rose up from the dead, only one thought possessed him,—that expressed by his simple old friend,—"What a thing it is to be a Christian!"

He turned: Legree was standing, sullenly, behind him.

Something in that dying scene had checked the natural fierceness of youthful passion. The presence of the man was simply loathsome to George; and he felt only an impulse to get away from him, with as few words as possible.

Fixing his keen dark eyes on Legree, he simply said, pointing to the dead, "You have got all you ever can of him. What shall I pay you for the body? I will take it away, and bury it decently."

"I don't sell dead niggers," said Legree, doggedly. "You are welcome to bury him where and when you like."

"Boys," said George, in an authoritative tone, to two or

three negroes, who were looking at the body, "help me lift him up, and carry him to my wagon; and get me a spade."

One of them ran for a spade; the other two assisted George to carry the body to the wagon.

George neither spoke to nor looked at Legree, who did not countermand his orders, but stood, whistling, with an air of forced unconcern. He sulkily followed them to where the wagon stood at the door.

George spread his cloak in the wagon, and had the body carefully disposed of in it,—moving the seat, so as to give it room. Then he turned, fixed his eyes on Legree, and said, with forced composure,

"I have not, as yet, said to you what I think of this most atrocious affair;—this is not the time and place. But, sir, this innocent blood shall have justice. I will proclaim this murder. I will go to the very first magistrate, and expose you."

"Do!" said Legree, snapping his fingers, scornfully. "I 'd like to see you doing it. Where you going to get witnesses?— how you going to prove it?—Come, now!"

George saw, at once, the force of this defiance. There was not a white person on the place; and, in all southern courts, the testimony of colored blood is nothing. He felt, at that moment, as if he could have rent the heavens with his heart's indignant cry for justice; but in vain.

"After all, what a fuss, for a dead nigger!" said Legree.

The word was as a spark to a powder magazine. Prudence was never a cardinal virtue of the Kentucky boy. George turned, and, with one indignant blow, knocked Legree flat upon his face; and, as he stood over him, blazing with wrath and defiance, he would have formed no bad personification of his great namesake triumphing over the dragon.

Some men, however, are decidedly bettered by being knocked down. If a man lays them fairly flat in the dust, they seem immediately to conceive a respect for him; and Legree was one of this sort. As he rose, therefore, and brushed the dust from his clothes, he eyed the slowly-retreating wagon with some evident consideration; nor did he open his mouth till it was out of sight.

Beyond the boundaries of the plantation, George had noticed a dry, sandy knoll, shaded by a few trees: there they made the grave.

"Shall we take off the cloak, Mas'r?" said the negroes, when the grave was ready.

"No, no,—bury it with him! It 's all I can give you, now, poor Tom, and you shall have it."

They laid him in; and the men shovelled away, silently. They banked it up, and laid green turf over it.

"You may go, boys," said George, slipping a quarter into the hand of each. They lingered about, however.

"If young Mas'r would please buy us—" said one.

"We 'd serve him so faithful!" said the other.

"Hard times here, Mas'r!" said the first. "Do, Mas'r, buy us, please!"

"I can't!—I can't!" said George, with difficulty, motioning them off; "it 's impossible!"

The poor fellows looked dejected, and walked off in silence.

"Witness, eternal God!" said George, kneeling on the grave of his poor friend; "oh, witness, that, from this hour, I will do *what one man can* to drive out this curse of slavery from my land!"

There is no monument to mark the last resting-place of our friend. He needs none! His Lord knows where he lies, and will raise him up, immortal, to appear with him when he shall appear in his glory.

Pity him not! Such a life and death is not for pity! Not in the riches of omnipotence is the chief glory of God; but in self-denying, suffering love! And blessed are the men whom he calls to fellowship with him, bearing their cross after him with patience. Of such it is written, "Blessed are they that mourn, for they shall be comforted."

XLII.

An Authentic Ghost Story

F OR some remarkable reason, ghostly legends were uncommonly rife, about this time, among the servants on Legree's place.

It was whisperingly asserted that footsteps, in the dead of night, had been heard descending the garret stairs, and patrolling the house. In vain the doors of the upper entry had been locked; the ghost either carried a duplicate key in its pocket, or availed itself of a ghost's immemorial privilege of coming through the keyhole, and promenaded as before, with a freedom that was alarming.

Authorities were somewhat divided, as to the outward form of the spirit, owing to a custom quite prevalent among negroes,—and, for aught we know, among whites, too,—of invariably shutting the eyes, and covering up heads under blankets, petticoats, or whatever else might come in use for a shelter, on these occasions. Of course, as everybody knows, when the bodily eyes are thus out of the lists, the spiritual eyes are uncommonly vivacious and perspicuous; and, therefore, there were abundance of full-length portraits of the ghost, abundantly sworn and testified to, which, as is often the case with portraits, agreed with each other in no particular, except the common family peculiarity of the ghost tribe,—the wearing of a *white sheet*. The poor souls were not versed in ancient history, and did not know that Shakspeare had authenticated this costume, by telling how

> "The *sheeted* dead
> Did squeak and gibber in the streets of Rome."

And, therefore, their all hitting upon this is a striking fact in pneumatology, which we recommend to the attention of spiritual media generally.

Be it as it may, we have private reasons for knowing that a

tall figure in a white sheet did walk, at the most approved ghostly hours, around the Legree premises,—pass out the doors, glide about the house,—disappear at intervals, and, reäppearing, pass up the silent stair-way, into that fatal garret; and that, in the morning, the entry doors were all found shut and locked as firm as ever.

Legree could not help overhearing this whispering; and it was all the more exciting to him, from the pains that were taken to conceal it from him. He drank more brandy than usual; held up his head briskly, and swore louder than ever in the day-time; but he had bad dreams, and the visions of his head on his bed were anything but agreeable. The night after Tom's body had been carried away, he rode to the next town for a carouse, and had a high one. Got home late and tired; locked his door, took out the key, and went to bed.

After all, let a man take what pains he may to hush it down, a human soul is an awful ghostly, unquiet possession, for a bad man to have. Who knows the metes and bounds of it? Who knows all its awful perhapses,—those shudderings and tremblings, which it can no more live down than it can outlive its own eternity! What a fool is he who locks his door to keep out spirits, who has in his own bosom a spirit he dares not meet alone,—whose voice, smothered far down, and piled over with mountains of earthliness, is yet like the forewarning trumpet of doom!

But Legree locked his door and set a chair against it; he set a night-lamp at the head of his bed; and he put his pistols there. He examined the catches and fastenings of the windows, and then swore he "did n't care for the devil and all his angels," and went to sleep.

Well, he slept, for he was tired,—slept soundly. But, finally, there came over his sleep a shadow, a horror, an apprehension of something dreadful hanging over him. It was his mother's shroud, he thought; but Cassy had it, holding it up, and showing it to him. He heard a confused noise of screams and groanings; and, with it all, he knew he was asleep, and he struggled to wake himself. He was half awake. He was sure something was coming into his room. He knew the door was opening, but he could not stir hand or foot. At last he turned, with a start; the door *was* open, and he saw a hand putting out his light.

It was a cloudy, misty moonlight, and there he saw it!—something white, gliding in! He heard the still rustle of its ghostly garments. It stood still by his bed;—a cold hand touched his; a voice said, three times, in a low, fearful whisper, "Come! come! come!" And, while he lay sweating with terror, he knew not when or how, the thing was gone. He sprang out of bed, and pulled at the door. It was shut and locked, and the man fell down in a swoon.

After this, Legree became a harder drinker than ever before. He no longer drank cautiously, prudently, but imprudently and recklessly.

There were reports around the country, soon after, that he was sick and dying. Excess had brought on that frightful disease that seems to throw the lurid shadows of a coming retribution back into the present life. None could bear the horrors of that sick room, when he raved and screamed, and spoke of sights which almost stopped the blood of those who heard him; and, at his dying bed, stood a stern, white, inexorable figure, saying, "Come! come! come!"

By a singular coincidence, on the very night that this vision appeared to Legree, the house-door was found open in the morning, and some of the negroes had seen two white figures gliding down the avenue towards the high-road.

It was near sunrise when Cassy and Emmeline paused, for a moment, in a little knot of trees near the town.

Cassy was dressed after the manner of the Creole Spanish ladies,—wholly in black. A small black bonnet on her head, covered by a veil thick with embroidery, concealed her face. It had been agreed that, in their escape, she was to personate the character of a Creole lady, and Emmeline that of her servant.

Brought up, from early life, in connection with the highest society, the language, movements and air of Cassy, were all in agreement with this idea; and she had still enough remaining with her, of a once splendid wardrobe, and sets of jewels, to enable her to personate the thing to advantage.

She stopped in the outskirts of the town, where she had noticed trunks for sale, and purchased a handsome one. This she requested the man to send along with her. And, accordingly, thus escorted by a boy wheeling her trunk, and Emmeline behind her, carrying her carpet-bag and sundry bundles, she made her appearance at the small tavern, like a lady of consideration.

The first person that struck her, after her arrival, was George Shelby, who was staying there, awaiting the next boat.

Cassy had remarked the young man from her loop-hole in the garret, and seen him bear away the body of Tom, and observed, with secret exultation, his rencontre with Legree. Subsequently, she had gathered, from the conversations she had overheard among the negroes, as she glided about in her ghostly disguise, after nightfall, who he was, and in what relation he stood to Tom. She, therefore, felt an immediate accession of confidence, when she found that he was, like herself, awaiting the next boat.

Cassy's air and manner, address, and evident command of money, prevented any rising disposition to suspicion in the hotel. People never inquire too closely into those who are fair on the main point, of paying well,—a thing which Cassy had foreseen when she provided herself with money.

In the edge of the evening, a boat was heard coming along, and George Shelby handed Cassy aboard, with the politeness which comes naturally to every Kentuckian, and exerted himself to provide her with a good state-room.

Cassy kept her room and bed, on pretext of illness, during the whole time they were on Red river; and was waited on, with obsequious devotion, by her attendant.

When they arrived at the Mississippi river, George, having learned that the course of the strange lady was upward, like his own, proposed to take a state-room for her on the same boat with himself,—good-naturedly compassionating her feeble health, and desirous to do what he could to assist her.

Behold, therefore, the whole party safely transferred to the good steamer Cincinnati, and sweeping up the river under a powerful head of steam.

Cassy's health was much better. She sat upon the guards, came to the table, and was remarked upon in the boat as a lady that must have been very handsome.

From the moment that George got the first glimpse of her face, he was troubled with one of those fleeting and indefinite likenesses, which almost everybody can remember, and has been, at times, perplexed with. He could not keep himself from looking at her, and watching her perpetually. At table, or sitting at her state-room door, still she would encounter the young man's eyes fixed on her, and politely withdrawn, when she showed, by her countenance, that she was sensible of the observation.

Cassy became uneasy. She began to think that he suspected something; and finally resolved to throw herself entirely on his generosity, and intrusted him with her whole history.

George was heartily disposed to sympathize with any one who had escaped from Legree's plantation,—a place that he could not remember or speak of with patience,—and, with the courageous disregard of consequences which is characteristic of his age and state, he assured her that he would do all in his power to protect and bring them through.

The next state-room to Cassy's was occupied by a French lady, named De Thoux, who was accompanied by a fine little daughter, a child of some twelve summers.

This lady, having gathered, from George's conversation, that he was from Kentucky, seemed evidently disposed to cultivate his acquaintance; in which design she was seconded by the graces of her little girl, who was about as pretty a plaything as ever diverted the weariness of a fortnight's trip on a steamboat.

George's chair was often placed at her state-room door; and Cassy, as she sat upon the guards, could hear their conversation.

Madame de Thoux was very minute in her inquiries as to Kentucky, where she said she had resided in a former period of her life. George discovered, to his surprise, that her former residence must have been in his own vicinity; and her inquiries showed a knowledge of people and things in his vicinity, that was perfectly surprising to him.

"Do you know," said Madame de Thoux to him, one day, "of any man, in your neighborhood, of the name of Harris?"

"There is an old fellow, of that name, lives not far from my father's place," said George. "We never have had much inter-course with him, though."

"He is a large slave-owner, I believe," said Madame de Thoux, with a manner which seemed to betray more interest than she was exactly willing to show.

"He is," said George, looking rather surprised at her manner.

"Did you ever know of his having—perhaps, you may have heard of his having a mulatto boy, named George?"

"O, certainly,—George Harris,—I know him well; he married a servant of my mother's, but has escaped, now, to Canada."

"He has?" said Madame de Thoux, quickly. "Thank God!"

George looked a surprised inquiry, but said nothing.

Madame de Thoux leaned her head on her hand, and burst into tears.

"He is my brother," she said.

"Madame!" said George, with a strong accent of surprise.

"Yes," said Madame de Thoux, lifting her head, proudly, and wiping her tears; "Mr. Shelby, George Harris is my brother!"

"I am perfectly astonished," said George, pushing back his chair a pace or two, and looking at Madame de Thoux.

"I was sold to the South when he was a boy," said she. "I was bought by a good and generous man. He took me with him to the West Indies, set me free, and married me. It is but lately that he died; and I was coming up to Kentucky, to see if I could find and redeem my brother."

"I have heard him speak of a sister Emily, that was sold South," said George.

"Yes, indeed! I am the one," said Madame de Thoux;— "tell me what sort of a—"

"A very fine young man," said George, "notwithstanding the curse of slavery that lay on him. He sustained a first rate character, both for intelligence and principle. I know, you see," he said; "because he married in our family."

"What sort of a girl?" said Madame de Thoux, eagerly.

"A treasure," said George; "a beautiful, intelligent, amiable girl. Very pious. My mother had brought her up, and trained her as carefully, almost, as a daughter. She could read and write, embroider and sew, beautifully; and was a beautiful singer."

"Was she born in your house?" said Madame de Thoux.

"No. Father bought her once, in one of his trips to New Orleans, and brought her up as a present to mother. She was about eight or nine years old, then. Father would never tell mother what he gave for her; but, the other day, in looking over his old papers, we came across the bill of sale. He paid an extravagant sum for her, to be sure. I suppose, on account of her extraordinary beauty."

George sat with his back to Cassy, and did not see the absorbed expression of her countenance, as he was giving these details.

At this point in the story, she touched his arm, and, with a face perfectly white with interest, said, "Do you know the names of the people he bought her of?"

"A man of the name of Simmons, I think, was the principal in the transaction. At least, I think that was the name on the bill of sale."

"O, my God!" said Cassy, and fell insensible on the floor of the cabin.

George was wide awake now, and so was Madame de Thoux. Though neither of them could conjecture what was the cause of Cassy's fainting, still they made all the tumult which is proper in such cases;—George upsetting a wash-pitcher, and breaking two tumblers, in the warmth of his humanity; and various ladies in the cabin, hearing that somebody had fainted, crowded the state-room door, and kept out all the air they possibly could, so that, on the whole, everything was done that could be expected.

Poor Cassy! when she recovered, turned her face to the wall, and wept and sobbed like a child,—perhaps, mother, you can tell what she was thinking of! Perhaps you cannot,—but she felt as sure, in that hour, that God had had mercy on her, and that she should see her daughter,—as she did, months afterwards,—when—but we anticipate.

XLIII.

Results

THE rest of our story is soon told. George Shelby, interested, as any other young man might be, by the romance of the incident, no less than by feelings of humanity, was at the pains to send to Cassy the bill of sale of Eliza; whose date and name all corresponded with her own knowledge of facts, and left no doubt upon her mind as to the identity of her child. It remained now only for her to trace out the path of the fugitives.

Madame de Thoux and she, thus drawn together by the singular coincidence of their fortunes, proceeded immediately to Canada, and began a tour of inquiry among the stations, where the numerous fugitives from slavery are located. At Amherstberg they found the missionary with whom George and Eliza had taken shelter, on their first arrival in Canada; and through him were enabled to trace the family to Montreal.

George and Eliza had now been five years free. George had found constant occupation in the shop of a worthy machinist, where he had been earning a competent support for his family, which, in the mean time, had been increased by the addition of another daughter.

Little Harry—a fine bright boy—had been put to a good school, and was making rapid proficiency in knowledge.

The worthy pastor of the station, in Amherstberg, where George had first landed, was so much interested in the statements of Madame de Thoux and Cassy, that he yielded to the solicitations of the former, to accompany them to Montreal, in their search,—she bearing all the expense of the expedition.

The scene now changes to a small, neat tenement, in the outskirts of Montreal; the time, evening. A cheerful fire blazes on the hearth; a tea-table, covered with a snowy cloth, stands prepared for the evening meal. In one corner of the room was a table covered with a green cloth, where was an open writing-desk, pens, paper, and over it a shelf of well-selected books.

This was George's study. The same zeal for self-improvement, which led him to steal the much coveted arts of reading and writing, amid all the toils and discouragements of his early life, still led him to devote all his leisure time to self-cultivation.

At this present time, he is seated at the table, making notes from a volume of the family library he has been reading.

"Come, George," says Eliza, "you 've been gone all day. Do put down that book, and let 's talk, while I 'm getting tea,—do."

And little Eliza seconds the effort, by toddling up to her father, and trying to pull the book out of his hand, and install herself on his knee as a substitute.

"O, you little witch!" says George, yielding, as, in such circumstances, man always must.

"That 's right," says Eliza, as she begins to cut a loaf of bread. A little older she looks; her form a little fuller; her air more matronly than of yore; but evidently contented and happy as woman need be.

"Harry, my boy, how did you come on in that sum, to-day?" says George, as he laid his hand on his son's head.

Harry has lost his long curls; but he can never lose those eyes and eyelashes, and that fine, bold brow, that flushes with triumph, as he answers, "I did it, every bit of it, *myself*, father; and *nobody* helped me!"

"That 's right," says his father; "depend on yourself, my son. You have a better chance than ever your poor father had."

At this moment, there is a rap at the door; and Eliza goes and opens it. The delighted—"Why!—this you?"—calls up her husband; and the good pastor of Amherstberg is welcomed. There are two more women with him, and Eliza asks them to sit down.

Now, if the truth must be told, the honest pastor had arranged a little programme, according to which this affair was to develop itself; and, on the way up, all had very cautiously and prudently exhorted each other not to let things out, except according to previous arrangement.

What was the good man's consternation, therefore, just as he had motioned to the ladies to be seated, and was taking out his pocket-handkerchief to wipe his mouth, so as to proceed to his introductory speech in good order, when Madame de Thoux upset the whole plan, by throwing her arms around George's neck, and letting all out at once, by saying, "O, George! don't you know me? I 'm your sister Emily."

Cassy had seated herself more composedly, and would have carried on her part very well, had not little Eliza suddenly appeared before her in exact shape and form, every outline and curl, just as her daughter was when she saw her last. The little thing peered up in her face; and Cassy caught her up in her arms, pressed her to her bosom, saying, what, at the moment she really believed, "Darling, I 'm your mother!"

In fact, it was a troublesome matter to do up exactly in proper order; but the good pastor, at last, succeeded in getting everybody quiet, and delivering the speech with which he had intended to open the exercises; and in which, at last, he succeeded so well, that his whole audience were sobbing about him in a manner that ought to satisfy any orator, ancient or modern.

They knelt together, and the good man prayed,—for there are some feelings so agitated and tumultuous, that they can find rest only by being poured into the bosom of Almighty love,—and then, rising up, the new-found family embraced each other, with a holy trust in Him, who from such peril and dangers, and by such unknown ways, had brought them together.

The note-book of a missionary, among the Canadian fugitives, contains truth stranger than fiction. How can it be otherwise, when a system prevails which whirls families and scatters their members, as the wind whirls and scatters the leaves of autumn? These shores of refuge, like the eternal shore, often unite again, in glad communion, hearts that for long years have mourned each other as lost. And affecting beyond expression is the earnestness with which every new arrival among them is met, if, perchance, it may bring tidings of mother, sister, child or wife, still lost to view in the shadows of slavery.

Deeds of heroism are wrought here more than those of romance, when, defying torture, and braving death itself, the fugitive voluntarily threads his way back to the terrors and

perils of that dark land, that he may bring out his sister, or
mother, or wife.

One young man, of whom a missionary has told us, twice
re-captured, and suffering shameful stripes for his heroism,
had escaped again; and, in a letter which we heard read, tells
his friends that he is going back a third time, that he may, at
last, bring away his sister. My good sir, is this man a hero, or
a criminal? Would not you do as much for your sister? And
can you blame him?

But, to return to our friends, whom we left wiping their
eyes, and recovering themselves from too great and sudden a
joy. They are now seated around the social board, and are
getting decidedly companionable; only that Cassy, who keeps
little Eliza on her lap, occasionally squeezes the little thing, in
a manner that rather astonishes her, and obstinately refuses to
have her mouth stuffed with cake to the extent the little one
desires,—alleging, what the child rather wonders at, that she
has got something better than cake, and does n't want it.

And, indeed, in two or three days, such a change has passed
over Cassy, that our readers would scarcely know her. The
despairing, haggard expression of her face had given way to
one of gentle trust. She seemed to sink, at once, into the bosom of the family, and take the little ones into her heart, as
something for which it long had waited. Indeed, her love
seemed to flow more naturally to the little Eliza than to her
own daughter; for she was the exact image and body of the
child whom she had lost. The little one was a flowery bond
between mother and daughter, through whom grew up acquaintanceship and affection. Eliza's steady, consistent piety,
regulated by the constant reading of the sacred word, made
her a proper guide for the shattered and wearied mind of her
mother. Cassy yielded at once, and with her whole soul, to
every good influence, and became a devout and tender Christian.

After a day or two, Madame de Thoux told her brother
more particularly of her affairs. The death of her husband had
left her an ample fortune, which she generously offered to
share with the family. When she asked George what way she
could best apply it for him, he answered, "Give me an edu-

cation, Emily; that has always been my heart's desire. Then, I can do all the rest."

On mature deliberation, it was decided that the whole family should go, for some years, to France; whither they sailed, carrying Emmeline with them.

The good looks of the latter won the affection of the first mate of the vessel; and, shortly after entering the port, she became his wife.

George remained four years at a French university, and, applying himself with an unintermitted zeal, obtained a very thorough education.

Political troubles in France, at last, led the family again to seek an asylum in this country.

George's feelings and views, as an educated man, may be best expressed in a letter to one of his friends.

"I feel somewhat at a loss, as to my future course. True, as you have said to me, I might mingle in the circles of the whites, in this country, my shade of color is so slight, and that of my wife and family scarce perceptible. Well, perhaps, on sufferance, I might. But, to tell you the truth, I have no wish to.

"My sympathies are not for my father's race, but for my mother's. To him I was no more than a fine dog or horse; to my poor heart-broken mother I was a *child*; and, though I never saw her, after the cruel sale that separated us, till she died, yet I *know* she always loved me dearly. I know it by my own heart. When I think of all she suffered, of my own early sufferings, of the distresses and struggles of my heroic wife, of my sister, sold in the New Orleans slave-market, — though I hope to have no unchristian sentiments, yet I may be excused for saying, I have no wish to pass for an American, or to identify myself with them.

"It is with the oppressed, enslaved African race that I cast in my lot; and, if I wished anything, I would wish myself two shades darker, rather than one lighter.

"The desire and yearning of my soul is for an African *nationality*. I want a people that shall have a tangible, separate existence of its own; and where am I to look for it? Not in Hayti; for in Hayti they had nothing to start with. A stream

cannot rise above its fountain. The race that formed the character of the Haytiens was a worn-out, effeminate one; and, of
course, the subject race will be centuries in rising to anything.

"Where, then, shall I look? On the shores of Africa I see a
republic,—a republic formed of picked men, who, by energy
and self-educating force, have, in many cases, individually,
raised themselves above a condition of slavery. Having gone
through a preparatory stage of feebleness, this republic has, at
last, become an acknowledged nation on the face of the
earth,—acknowledged by both France and England. There it
is my wish to go, and find myself a people.

"I am aware, now, that I shall have you all against me; but,
before you strike, hear me. During my stay in France, I have
followed up, with intense interest, the history of my people
in America. I have noted the struggle between abolitionist
and colonizationist, and have received some impressions, as a
distant spectator, which could never have occurred to me as
a participator.

"I grant that this Liberia may have subserved all sorts of
purposes, by being played off, in the hands of our oppressors,
against us. Doubtless the scheme may have been used, in un-
justifiable ways, as a means of retarding our emancipation.
But the question to me is, Is there not a God above all man's
schemes? May He not have overruled their designs, and
founded for us a nation by them?

"In these days, a nation is born in a day. A nation starts,
now, with all the great problems of republican life and civilization wrought out to its hand;—it has not to discover, but
only to apply. Let us, then, all take hold together, with all
our might, and see what we can do with this new enterprise,
and the whole splendid continent of Africa opens before us
and our children. *Our nation* shall roll the tide of civilization
and Christianity along its shores, and plant there mighty republics, that, growing with the rapidity of tropical vegetation,
shall be for all coming ages.

"Do you say that I am deserting my enslaved brethren? I
think not. If I forget them one hour, one moment of my life,
so may God forget me! But, what can I do for them, here?
Can I break their chains? No, not as an individual; but, let
me go and form part of a nation, which shall have a voice in

the councils of nations, and then we can speak. A nation has a right to argue, remonstrate, implore, and present the cause of its race,—which an individual has not.

"If Europe ever becomes a grand council of free nations,—as I trust in God it will,—if, there, serfdom, and all unjust and oppressive social inequalities, are done away; and if they, as France and England have done, acknowledge our position,—then, in the great congress of nations, we will make our appeal, and present the cause of our enslaved and suffering race; and it cannot be that free, enlightened America will not then desire to wipe from her escutcheon that bar sinister which disgraces her among nations, and is as truly a curse to her as to the enslaved.

"But, you will tell me, our race have equal rights to mingle in the American republic as the Irishman, the German, the Swede. Granted, they have. We *ought* to be free to meet and mingle,—to rise by our individual worth, without any consideration of caste or color; and they who deny us this right are false to their own professed principles of human equality. We ought, in particular, to be allowed *here*. We have *more* than the rights of common men;—we have the claim of an injured race for reparation. But, then, *I do not want it*; I want a country, a nation, of my own. I think that the African race has peculiarities, yet to be unfolded in the light of civilization and Christianity, which, if not the same with those of the Anglo-Saxon, may prove to be, morally, of even a higher type.

"To the Anglo-Saxon race has been intrusted the destinies of the world, during its pioneer period of struggle and conflict. To that mission its stern, inflexible, energetic elements, were well adapted; but, as a Christian, I look for another era to arise. On its borders I trust we stand; and the throes that now convulse the nations are, to my hope, but the birthpangs of an hour of universal peace and brotherhood.

"I trust that the development of Africa is to be essentially a Christian one. If not a dominant and commanding race, they are, at least, an affectionate, magnanimous, and forgiving one. Having been called in the furnace of injustice and oppression, they have need to bind closer to their hearts that sublime doctrine of love and forgiveness, through which alone they are to conquer, which it is to be their mission to spread over the continent of Africa.

"In myself, I confess, I am feeble for this,—full half the blood in my veins is the hot and hasty Saxon; but I have an eloquent preacher of the Gospel ever by my side, in the person of my beautiful wife. When I wander, her gentler spirit ever restores me, and keeps before my eyes the Christian calling and mission of our race. As a Christian patriot, as a teacher of Christianity, I go to *my country*,—my chosen, my glorious Africa!—and to her, in my heart, I sometimes apply those splendid words of prophecy: 'Whereas thou hast been forsaken and hated, so that no man went through thee; *I* will make thee an eternal excellence, a joy of many generations!'

"You will call me an enthusiast: you will tell me that I have not well considered what I am undertaking. But I have considered, and counted the cost. I go to *Liberia*, not as to an Elysium of romance, but as to *a field of work*. I expect to work with both hands,—to work *hard*; to work against all sorts of difficulties and discouragements; and to work till I die. This is what I go for; and in this I am quite sure I shall not be disappointed.

"Whatever you may think of my determination, do not divorce me from your confidence; and think that, in whatever I do, I act with a heart wholly given to my people.

"GEORGE HARRIS."

George, with his wife, children, sister and mother, embarked for Africa, some few weeks after. If we are not mistaken, the world will yet hear from him there.

Of our other characters we have nothing very particular to write, except a word relating to Miss Ophelia and Topsy, and a farewell chapter, which we shall dedicate to George Shelby.

Miss Ophelia took Topsy home to Vermont with her, much to the surprise of that grave deliberative body whom a New Englander recognizes under the term *"Our folks."* "Our folks," at first, thought it an odd and unnecessary addition to their well-trained domestic establishment; but, so thoroughly efficient was Miss Ophelia in her conscientious endeavor to do her duty by her elève, that the child rapidly grew in grace and in favor with the family and neighborhood. At the age of womanhood, she was, by her own request baptized, and became a member of the Christian church in the place; and showed so much intelligence, activity and zeal, and desire to do good in the world, that she was at last recommended, and approved, as a missionary to one of the stations in Africa; and we have heard that the same activity and ingenuity which, when a child, made her so multiform and restless in her developments, is now employed, in a safer and wholesomer manner, in teaching the children of her own country.

P. S.—It will be a satisfaction to some mother, also, to state, that some inquiries, which were set on foot by Madame de Thoux, have resulted recently in the discovery of Cassy's son. Being a young man of energy, he had escaped, some years before his mother, and been received and educated by friends of the oppressed in the north. He will soon follow his family to Africa.

XLIV.

The Liberator

G EORGE SHELBY had written to his mother merely a line, stating the day that she might expect him home. Of the death scene of his old friend he had not the heart to write. He had tried several times, and only succeeded in half choking himself; and invariably finished by tearing up the paper, wiping his eyes, and rushing somewhere to get quiet.

There was a pleased bustle all through the Shelby mansion, that day, in expectation of the arrival of young Mas'r George.

Mrs. Shelby was seated in her comfortable parlor, where a cheerful hickory fire was dispelling the chill of the late autumn evening. A supper-table, glittering with plate and cut glass, was set out, on whose arrangements our former friend, old Chloe, was presiding.

Arrayed in a new calico dress, with clean, white apron, and high, well-starched turban, her black polished face glowing with satisfaction, she lingered, with needless punctiliousness, around the arrangements of the table, merely as an excuse for talking a little to her mistress.

"Laws, now! won't it look natural to him?" she said. "Thar,—I set his plate just whar he likes it,—round by the fire. Mas'r George allers wants de warm seat. O, go way!— why did n't Sally get out de *best* tea-pot,—de little new one, Mas'r George got for Missis, Christmas? I 'll have it out! And Missis has heard from Mas'r George?" she said, inquiringly.

"Yes, Chloe; but only a line, just to say he would be home to-night, if he could,—that 's all."

"Did n't say nothin' 'bout my old man, s'pose?" said Chloe, still fidgeting with the tea-cups.

"No, he did n't. He did not speak of anything, Chloe. He said he would tell all, when he got home."

"Jes like Mas'r George,—he 's allers so ferce for tellin' everything hisself. I allers minded dat ar in Mas'r George. Don't see, for my part, how white people gen'lly can bar to hev to write things much as they do, writin' 's such slow, oneasy kind o' work."

Mrs. Shelby smiled.

"I 'm a thinkin' my old man won't know de boys and de baby. Lor'! she 's de biggest gal, now,—good she is, too, and peart, Polly is. She 's out to the house, now, watchin' de hoe-cake. I 's got jist de very pattern my old man liked so much, a bakin'. Jist such as I gin him the mornin' he was took off. Lord bless us! how I felt, dat ar mornin'!"

Mrs. Shelby sighed, and felt a heavy weight on her heart, at this allusion. She had felt uneasy, ever since she received her son's letter, lest something should prove to be hidden behind the veil of silence which he had drawn.

"Missis has got dem bills?" said Chloe, anxiously.

"Yes, Chloe."

" 'Cause I wants to show my old man dem very bills de *perfectioner* gave me. 'And,' says he, 'Chloe, I wish you 'd stay longer.' 'Thank you, Mas'r,' says I, 'I would, only my old man 's coming home, and Missis,—she can't do without me no longer.' There 's jist what I telled him. Berry nice man, dat Mas'r Jones was."

Chloe had pertinaciously insisted that the very bills in which her wages had been paid should be preserved, to show to her husband, in memorial of her capability. And Mrs. Shelby had readily consented to humor her in the request.

"He won't know Polly,—my old man won't. Laws, it 's five year since they tuck him! She was a baby den,—could n't but jist stand. Remember how tickled he used to be, cause she would keep a fallin' over, when she sot out to walk. Laws a me!"

The rattling of wheels now was heard.

"Mas'r George!" said Aunt Chloe, starting to the window.

Mrs. Shelby ran to the entry door, and was folded in the arms of her son. Aunt Chloe stood anxiously straining her eyes out into the darkness.

"O, *poor* Aunt Chloe!" said George, stopping compassionately, and taking her hard, black hand between both his; "I 'd have given all my fortune to have brought him with me, but he 's gone to a better country."

There was a passionate exclamation from Mrs. Shelby, but Aunt Chloe said nothing.

The party entered the supper-room. The money, of which Chloe was so proud, was still lying on the table.

"Thar," said she, gathering it up, and holding it, with a trembling hand, to her mistress, "don't never want to see nor hear on 't again. Jist as I knew 't would be,—sold, and murdered on dem ar' old plantations!"

Chloe turned, and was walking proudly out of the room. Mrs. Shelby followed her softly, and took one of her hands, drew her down into a chair, and sat down by her.

"My poor, good Chloe!" said she.

Chloe leaned her head on her mistress' shoulder, and sobbed out, "O Missis! 'scuse me, my heart 's broke,—dat 's all!"

"I know it is," said Mrs. Shelby, as her tears fell fast; "and *I* cannot heal it, but Jesus can. He healeth the broken hearted, and bindeth up their wounds."

There was a silence for some time, and all wept together. At last, George, sitting down beside the mourner, took her hand, and, with simple pathos, repeated the triumphant scene of her husband's death, and his last messages of love.

About a month after this, one morning, all the servants of the Shelby estate were convened together in the great hall that ran through the house, to hear a few words from their young master.

To the surprise of all, he appeared among them with a bundle of papers in his hand, containing a certificate of freedom to every one on the place, which he read successively, and presented, amid the sobs and tears and shouts of all present.

Many, however, pressed around him, earnestly begging him not to send them away; and, with anxious faces, tendering back their free papers.

"We don't want to be no freer than we are. We 's allers had all we wanted. We don't want to leave de ole place, and Mas'r and Missis, and de rest!"

"My good friends," said George, as soon as he could get a silence, "there 'll be no need for you to leave me. The place wants as many hands to work it as it did before. We need the same about the house that we did before. But, you are now free men and free women. I shall pay you wages for your work, such as we shall agree on. The advantage is, that in case of my getting in debt, or dying,—things that might happen,—you cannot now be taken up and sold. I expect to carry on the estate, and to teach you what, perhaps, it will take you some time to learn,—how to use the rights I give you as free men and women. I expect you to be good, and willing to learn; and I trust in God that I shall be faithful, and willing to teach. And now, my friends, look up, and thank God for the blessing of freedom."

An aged, patriarchal negro, who had grown gray and blind on the estate, now rose, and, lifting his trembling hand said, "Let us give thanks unto the Lord!" As all kneeled by one consent, a more touching and hearty Te Deum never ascended to heaven, though borne on the peal of organ, bell and cannon, than came from that honest old heart.

On rising, another struck up a Methodist hymn, of which the burden was,

> "The year of Jubilee is come,—
> Return, ye ransomed sinners, home."

"One thing more," said George, as he stopped the congratulations of the throng; "you all remember our good old Uncle Tom?"

George here gave a short narration of the scene of his death, and of his loving farewell to all on the place, and added,

"It was on his grave, my friends, that I resolved, before God, that I would never own another slave, while it was possible to free him; that nobody, through me, should ever run the risk of being parted from home and friends, and dying on a lonely plantation, as he died. So, when you rejoice in your freedom, think that you owe it to that good old soul, and pay it back in kindness to his wife and children. Think of your freedom, every time you see UNCLE TOM'S CABIN; and let it be a memorial to put you all in mind to follow in his steps, and be as honest and faithful and Christian as he was."

XLV.

Concluding Remarks

THE writer has often been inquired of, by correspondents from different parts of the country, whether this narrative is a true one; and to these inquiries she will give one general answer.

The separate incidents that compose the narrative are, to a very great extent, authentic, occurring, many of them, either under her own observation, or that of her personal friends. She or her friends have observed characters the counterpart of almost all that are here introduced; and many of the sayings are word for word as heard herself, or reported to her.

The personal appearance of Eliza, the character ascribed to her, are sketches drawn from life. The incorruptible fidelity, piety and honesty, of Uncle Tom, had more than one development, to her personal knowledge. Some of the most deeply tragic and romantic, some of the most terrible incidents, have also their parallel in reality. The incident of the mother's crossing the Ohio river on the ice is a well-known fact. The story of "old Prue," in the second volume, was an incident that fell under the personal observation of a brother of the writer, then collecting-clerk to a large mercantile house, in New Orleans. From the same source was derived the character of the planter Legree. Of him her brother thus wrote, speaking of visiting his plantation, on a collecting tour: "He actually made me feel of his fist, which was like a blacksmith's hammer, or a nodule of iron, telling me that it was 'calloused with knocking down niggers.' When I left the plantation, I drew a long breath, and felt as if I had escaped from an ogre's den."

That the tragical fate of Tom, also, has too many times had its parallel, there are living witnesses, all over our land, to testify. Let it be remembered that in all southern states it is a principle of jurisprudence that no person of colored lineage can testify in a suit against a white, and it will be easy to see that such a case may occur, wherever there is a man whose passions outweigh his interests, and a slave who has manhood or principle enough to resist his will. There is, actually, nothing to protect the slave's life, but the *character* of the master. Facts too shocking to be contemplated occasionally force their way to the public ear, and the comment that one often hears made on them is more shocking than the thing itself. It is said, "Very likely such cases may now and then occur, but they are no sample of general practice." If the laws of New England were so arranged that a master could *now and then* torture an apprentice to death, without a possibility of being brought to justice, would it be received with equal composure? Would it be said, "These cases are rare, and no samples of general practice"? This injustice is an *inherent* one in the slave system,—it cannot exist without it.

The public and shameless sale of beautiful mulatto and quadroon girls has acquired a notoriety, from the incidents following the capture of the Pearl. We extract the following from the speech of Hon. Horace Mann, one of the legal counsel for the defendants in that case. He says: "In that company of seventy-six persons, who attempted, in 1848, to escape from the District of Columbia in the schooner Pearl, and whose officers I assisted in defending, there were several young and healthy girls, who had those peculiar attractions of form and feature which connoisseurs prize so highly. Elizabeth Russel was one of them. She immediately fell into the slave-trader's fangs, and was doomed for the New Orleans market. The hearts of those that saw her were touched with pity for her fate. They offered eighteen hundred dollars to redeem her; and some there were who offered to give, that would not have much left after the gift; but the fiend of a slave-trader was inexorable. She was despatched to New Orleans; but, when about half way there, God had mercy on her, and smote her with death. There were two girls named Edmundson in the same company. When about to be sent to the same market, an older sister went to the shambles, to plead with the wretch who owned them, for the love of God, to spare his victims. He bantered her, telling what fine dresses and fine furniture they would have. 'Yes,' she said, 'that may do very well in this life, but what will become of them in the next?' They too were sent to New Orleans; but were afterwards redeemed, at an enormous ransom, and brought back." Is it not plain, from this, that the histories of Emmeline and Cassy may have many counterparts?

Justice, too, obliges the author to state that the fairness of mind and generosity attributed to St. Clare are not without a parallel, as the following anecdote will show. A few years since, a young southern gentleman was in Cincinnati, with a favorite servant, who had been his personal attendant from a boy. The young man took advantage of this opportunity to secure his own freedom, and fled to the protection of a Quaker, who was quite noted in affairs of this kind. The owner was exceedingly indignant. He had always treated the slave with such indulgence, and his confidence in his affection was such, that he believed he must have been practised upon to induce him to revolt from him. He visited the Quaker, in high anger; but, being possessed of uncommon candor and fairness, was soon quieted by his arguments and representations. It was a side of the subject which he never had heard,—never had thought on; and he immediately told the Quaker that, if his slave would, to his own face, say that it was his desire to be free, he would liberate him. An interview was forthwith procured, and Nathan was asked by his young master whether he had ever had any reason to complain of his treatment, in any respect.

"No, Mas'r," said Nathan; "you 've always been good to me."

"Well, then, why do you want to leave me?"

"Mas'r may die, and then who get me?—I 'd rather be a free man."

After some deliberation, the young master replied, "Nathan, in your place, I think I should feel very much so, myself. You are free."

He immediately made him out free papers; deposited a sum of money in the hands of the Quaker, to be judiciously used in assisting him to start in life, and left a very sensible and kind letter of advice to the young man. That letter was for some time in the writer's hands.

The author hopes she has done justice to that nobility, generosity, and humanity, which in many cases characterize individuals at the South. Such instances save us from utter despair of our kind. But, she asks any person, who knows the world, are such characters *common*, anywhere?

For many years of her life, the author avoided all reading upon or allusion to the subject of slavery, considering it as too painful to be inquired into, and one which advancing light and civilization would certainly live down. But, since the legislative act of 1850, when she heard, with perfect surprise and consternation, Christian and humane people actually recommending the remanding escaped fugitives into slavery, as a duty binding on good citizens,—when she heard, on all hands, from kind, compassionate and estimable people, in the free states of the North, deliberations and discussions as to what Christian duty could be on this head,—she could only think, These men and Christians cannot know what slavery is; if they did, such a question could never be open for discussion. And from this arose a desire to exhibit it in a *living dramatic reality*. She has endeavored to show it fairly, in its best and its worst phases. In its *best* aspect, she has, perhaps, been successful; but, oh! who shall say what yet remains untold in that valley and shadow of death, that lies the other side?

To you, generous, noble-minded men and women, of the South,—you, whose virtue, and magnanimity, and purity of character, are the greater for the severer trial it has encountered,—to you is her appeal. Have you not, in your own secret souls, in your own private conversings, felt that there are woes and evils, in this accursed system, far beyond what are here shadowed, or can be shadowed? Can it be otherwise? Is *man* ever a creature to be trusted with wholly irresponsible power? And does not the slave system, by denying the slave all legal right of testimony, make every individual owner an irresponsible despot? Can anybody fail to make the inference what the practical result will be? If there is, as we admit, a public sentiment among you, men of honor, justice and humanity, is there not also another kind of public sentiment among the ruffian, the brutal and debased? And cannot the ruffian, the brutal, the debased, by slave law, own just as many slaves as the best and purest? Are the honorable, the just, the high-minded and compassionate, the majority anywhere in this world?

The slave-trade is now, by American law, considered as piracy. But a slave-trade, as systematic as ever was carried on on the coast of Africa, is an inevitable attendant and result of American slavery. And its heart-break and its horrors, *can* they be told?

The writer has given only a faint shadow, a dim picture, of the anguish and despair that are, at this very moment, riving thousands of hearts, shattering thousands of families, and driving a helpless and sensitive race to frenzy and despair. There are those living who know the mothers whom this accursed traffic has driven to the murder of their children; and themselves seeking in death a shelter from woes more dreaded than death. Nothing of tragedy can be written, can be spoken, can be conceived, that equals the frightful reality of scenes daily and hourly acting on our shores, beneath the shadow of American law, and the shadow of the cross of Christ.

And now, men and women of America, is this a thing to be trifled with, apologized for, and passed over in silence? Farmers of Massachusetts, of New Hampshire, of Vermont, of Connecticut, who read this book by the blaze of your winter-evening fire,—strong-hearted, generous sailors and ship-owners of Maine,—is this a thing for you to countenance and encourage? Brave and generous men of New York, farmers of rich and joyous Ohio, and ye of the wide prairie states,—answer, is this a thing for you to protect and countenance? And you, mothers of America,—you, who have learned, by the cradles of your own children, to love and feel for all mankind,—by the sacred love you bear your child; by your joy in his beautiful, spotless infancy; by the motherly pity and tenderness with which you guide his growing years; by the anxieties of his education; by the prayers you breathe for his soul's eternal good;—I beseech you, pity the mother who has all your affections, and not one legal right to protect, guide, or educate, the child of her bosom! By the sick hour of your child; by those dying eyes, which you can never forget; by those last cries, that wrung your heart when you could neither help nor save; by the desolation of that empty cradle, that silent nursery,—I beseech you, pity those mothers that are constantly made childless by the American slave-trade! And say, mothers of America, is this a thing to be defended, sympathized with, passed over in silence?

Do you say that the people of the free states have nothing to do with it, and can do nothing? Would to God this were true! But it is not true. The people of the free states have defended, encouraged, and participated; and are more guilty for it, before God, than the South, in that they have *not* the apology of education or custom.

If the mothers of the free states had all felt as they should, in times past, the sons of the free states would not have been the holders, and, proverbially, the hardest masters of slaves; the sons of the free states would not have connived at the extension of slavery, in our national body; the sons of the free states would not, as they do, trade the souls and bodies of men as an equivalent to money, in their mercantile dealings. There are multitudes of slaves temporarily owned, and sold again, by merchants in northern cities; and shall the whole guilt or obloquy of slavery fall only on the South?

Northern men, northern mothers, northern Christians, have something more to do than denounce their brethren at the South; they have to look to the evil among themselves.

But, what can any individual do? Of that, every individual can judge. There is one thing that every individual can do,— they can see to it that *they feel right*. An atmosphere of sympathetic influence encircles every human being; and the man or woman who *feels* strongly, healthily and justly, on the great interests of humanity, is a constant benefactor to the human race. See, then, to your sympathies in this matter! Are they in harmony with the sympathies of Christ? or are they swayed and perverted by the sophistries of worldly policy?

Christian men and women of the North! still further,—you have another power; you can *pray*! Do you believe in prayer? or has it become an indistinct apostolic tradition? You pray for the heathen abroad; pray also for the heathen at home. And pray for those distressed Christians whose whole chance of religious improvement is an accident of trade and sale; from whom any adherence to the morals of Christianity is, in many cases, an impossibility, unless they have given them, from above, the courage and grace of martyrdom.

But, still more. On the shores of our free states are emerging the poor, shattered, broken remnants of families,—men and women, escaped, by miraculous providences, from the surges of slavery,—feeble in knowledge, and, in many cases, infirm in moral constitution, from a system which confounds and confuses every principle of Christianity and morality. They come to seek a refuge among you; they come to seek education, knowledge, Christianity.

What do you owe to these poor unfortunates, oh Christians? Does not every American Christian owe to the African race some effort at reparation for the wrongs that the American nation has brought upon them? Shall the doors of churches and school-houses be shut upon them? Shall states arise and shake them out? Shall the church of Christ hear in silence the taunt that is thrown at them, and shrink away from the helpless hand that they stretch out; and, by her silence, encourage the cruelty that would chase them from our borders? If it must be so, it will be a mournful spectacle. If it must be so, the country will have reason to tremble, when it remembers that the fate of nations is in the hands of One who is very pitiful, and of tender compassion.

Do you say, "We don't want them here; let them go to Africa"?

That the providence of God has provided a refuge in Africa, is, indeed, a great and noticeable fact; but that is no reason why the church of Christ should throw off that responsibility to this outcast race which her profession demands of her.

To fill up Liberia with an ignorant, inexperienced, half-barbarized race, just escaped from the chains of slavery, would be only to prolong, for ages, the period of struggle and conflict which attends the inception of new enterprises. Let the church of the north receive these poor sufferers in the spirit of Christ; receive them to the educating advantages of Christian republican society and schools, until they have attained to somewhat of a moral and intellectual maturity, and then assist them in their passage to those shores, where they may put in practice the lessons they have learned in America.

There is a body of men at the north, comparatively small,

who have been doing this; and, as the result, this country has already seen examples of men, formerly slaves, who have rapidly acquired property, reputation, and education. Talent has been developed, which, considering the circumstances, is certainly remarkable; and, for moral traits of honesty, kindness, tenderness of feeling,—for heroic efforts and self-denials, endured for the ransom of brethren and friends yet in slavery,—they have been remarkable to a degree that, considering the influence under which they were born, is surprising.

The writer has lived, for many years, on the frontier-line of slave states, and has had great opportunities of observation among those who formerly were slaves. They have been in her family as servants; and, in default of any other school to receive them, she has, in many cases, had them instructed in a family school, with her own children. She has also the testimony of missionaries, among the fugitives in Canada, in coincidence with her own experience; and her deductions, with regard to the capabilities of the race, are encouraging in the highest degree.

The first desire of the emancipated slave, generally, is for *education*. There is nothing that they are not willing to give or do to have their children instructed; and, so far as the writer has observed herself, or taken the testimony of teachers among them, they are remarkably intelligent and quick to learn. The results of schools, founded for them by benevolent individuals in Cincinnati, fully establish this.

The author gives the following statement of facts, on the authority of Professor C. E. Stowe, then of Lane Seminary, Ohio, with regard to emancipated slaves, now resident in Cincinnati; given to show the capability of the race, even without any very particular assistance or encouragement.

The initial letters alone are given. They are all residents of Cincinnati.

"B——. Furniture maker; twenty years in the city; worth ten thousand dollars, all his own earnings; a Baptist.

"C——. Full black; stolen from Africa; sold in New Orleans; been free fifteen years; paid for himself six hundred dollars; a farmer; owns several farms in Indiana; Presbyterian; probably worth fifteen or twenty thousand dollars, all earned by himself.

"K——. Full black; dealer in real estate; worth thirty thousand dollars; about forty years old; free six years; paid eighteen hundred dollars for his family; member of the Baptist church; received a legacy from his master, which he has taken good care of, and increased.

"G——. Full black; coal dealer; about thirty years old; worth eighteen thousand dollars; paid for himself twice, being once defrauded to the amount of sixteen hundred dollars; made all his money by his own efforts—much of it while a slave, hiring his time of his master, and doing business for himself; a fine, gentlemanly fellow.

"W——. Three-fourths black; barber and waiter; from Kentucky; nineteen years free; paid for self and family over three thousand dollars; deacon in the Baptist church.

"G. D——. Three-fourths black; white-washer; from Kentucky; nine years free; paid fifteen hundred dollars for self and family; recently died, aged sixty; worth six thousand dollars."

Professor Stowe says, "With all these, except G——, I have been, for some years, personally acquainted, and make my statements from my own knowledge."

The writer well remembers an aged colored woman, who was employed as a washerwoman in her father's family. The daughter of this woman married a slave. She was a remarkably active and capable young woman, and, by her industry and thrift, and the most persevering self-denial, raised nine hundred dollars for her husband's freedom, which she paid, as she raised it, into the hands of his master. She yet wanted a hundred dollars of the price, when he died. She never recovered any of the money.

These are but few facts, among multitudes which might be adduced, to show the self-denial, energy, patience, and honesty, which the slave has exhibited in a state of freedom.

And let it be remembered that these individuals have thus bravely succeeded in conquering for themselves comparative wealth and social position, in the face of every disadvantage and discouragement. The colored man, by the law of Ohio, cannot be a voter, and, till within a few years, was even denied the right of testimony in legal suits with the white. Nor are these instances confined to the State of Ohio. In all states of the Union we see men, but yesterday burst from the shackles of slavery, who, by a self-educating force, which cannot be too much admired, have risen to highly respectable stations in society. Pennington, among clergymen, Douglas and Ward, among editors, are well known instances.

If this persecuted race, with every discouragement and disadvantage, have done thus much, how much more they might do, if the Christian church would act towards them in the spirit of her Lord!

This is an age of the world when nations are trembling and convulsed. A mighty influence is abroad, surging and heaving the world, as with an earthquake. And is America safe? Every nation that carries in its bosom great and unredressed injustice has in it the elements of this last convulsion.

For what is this mighty influence thus rousing in all nations and languages those groanings that cannot be uttered, for man's freedom and equality?

O, Church of Christ, read the signs of the times! Is not this power the spirit of HIM whose kingdom is yet to come, and whose will to be done on earth as it is in heaven?

But who may abide the day of his appearing? "for that day shall burn as an oven: and he shall appear as a swift witness against those that oppress the hireling in his wages, the widow and the fatherless, and that *turn aside the stranger in his right*: and he shall break in pieces the oppressor."

Are not these dread words for a nation bearing in her bosom so mighty an injustice? Christians! every time that you pray that the kingdom of Christ may come, can you forget that prophecy associates, in dread fellowship, the *day of vengeance* with the year of his redeemed?

A day of grace is yet held out to us. Both North and South have been guilty before God; and the *Christian church* has a heavy account to answer. Not by combining together, to protect injustice and cruelty, and making a common capital of sin, is this Union to be saved,—but by repentance, justice and mercy; for, not surer is the eternal law by which the millstone sinks in the ocean, than that stronger law, by which injustice and cruelty shall bring on nations the wrath of Almighty God!

THE MINISTER'S WOOING

Contents

CHAPTER I.
Pre-Railroad Times 527

CHAPTER II.
The Kitchen 535

CHAPTER III.
The Interview 544

CHAPTER IV.
Theological Tea 552

CHAPTER V.
The Letter 567

CHAPTER VI.
The Doctor 578

CHAPTER VII.
The Friends and Relations of James 587

CHAPTER VIII.
Which Treats of Romance 598

CHAPTER IX.
Which Treats of Things Seen 609

CHAPTER X.
The Test of Theology 618

CHAPTER XI.
The Practical Test 628

CHAPTER XII.
Miss Prissy 636

CHAPTER XIII.
The Party 652

CHAPTER XIV.
Aaron Burr 656

CHAPTER XV.
The Sermon 669

CHAPTER XVI.
The Garret-Boudoir 676

Chapter XVII.
  Polemics in the Kitchen 693

Chapter XVIII.
  Evidences 700

Chapter XIX.
  Madame de Frontignac 706

Chapter XX.
  Tidings from Over Sea 714

Chapter XXI.
  The Bruised Flax-Flower 720

Chapter XXII.
  The House of Mourning 722

Chapter XXIII.
  Views of Divine Government 727

Chapter XXIV.
  Mysteries 739

Chapter XXV.
  A Guest at the Cottage 753

Chapter XXVI.
  The Declaration 769

Chapter XXVII.
  Surprises 774

Chapter XXVIII.
  The Betrothed 782

Chapter XXIX.
  Bustle in the Parish 787

Chapter XXX.
  The Quilting 793

Chapter XXXI.
  An Adventure 805

Chapter XXXII.
  Plain Talk 812

Chapter XXXIII.
  New England in French Eyes 818

CHAPTER XXXIV.
Consultations and Confidences 823

CHAPTER XXXV.
Old Love and New Duty 832

CHAPTER XXXVI.
Jacob's Vow 838

CHAPTER XXXVII.
The Question of Duty 843

CHAPTER XXXVIII.
The Transfigured 852

CHAPTER XXXIX.
The Ice Broken 855

CHAPTER XL.
The Sacrifice 860

CHAPTER XLI.
The Wedding 864

CHAPTER XLII.
Last Words 870

I.

Pre-Railroad Times

M RS. KATY SCUDDER had invited Mrs. Brown, and Mrs. Jones, and Deacon Twitchel's wife to take tea with her on the afternoon of June second, A. D. 17—.

When one has a story to tell, one is always puzzled which end of it to begin at. You have a whole corps of people to introduce that *you* know and your reader doesn't; and one thing so presupposes another, that, whichever way you turn your patchwork, the figures still seem ill-arranged. The small item which I have given will do as well as any other to begin with, as it certainly will lead you to ask, "Pray, who was Mrs. Katy Scudder?"—and this will start me systematically on my story.

You must understand that in the then small seaport-town of Newport, at that time unconscious of its present fashion and fame, there lived nobody in those days who did not know "the Widow Scudder."

In New England settlements a custom has obtained, which is wholesome and touching, of ennobling the woman whom God has made desolate, by a sort of brevet rank which continually speaks for her as a claim on the respect and consideration of the community. The Widow Jones, or Brown, or Smith, is one of the fixed institutions of every New England village,—and doubtless the designation acts as a continual plea for one whom bereavement, like the lightning of heaven, has made sacred.

The Widow Scudder, however, was one of the sort of women who reign queens in whatever society they move; nobody was more quoted, more deferred to, or enjoyed more unquestioned position than she. She was not rich,—a small farm, with a modest, "gambrel-roofed," one-story cottage, was her sole domain; but she was one of the much-admired class who, in the speech of New England, are said to have "faculty,"—a gift which, among that shrewd people, com-

527

mands more esteem than beauty, riches, learning, or any other worldly endowment. *Faculty* is Yankee for *savoir faire*, and the opposite virtue to shiftlessness. Faculty is the greatest virtue, and shiftlessness the greatest vice, of Yankee man and woman. To her who has faculty nothing shall be impossible. She shall scrub floors, wash, wring, bake, brew, and yet her hands shall be small and white; she shall have no perceptible income, yet always be handsomely dressed; she shall have not a servant in her house,—with a dairy to manage, hired men to feed, a boarder or two to care for, unheard-of pickling and preserving to do,—and yet you commonly see her every afternoon sitting at her shady parlor-window behind the lilacs, cool and easy, hemming muslin cap-strings, or reading the last new book. She who hath faculty is never in a hurry, never behindhand. She can always step over to distressed Mrs. Smith, whose jelly won't come,—and stop to show Mrs. Jones how she makes her pickles so green,—and be ready to watch with poor old Mrs. Simpkins, who is down with the rheumatism.

Of this genus was the Widow Scudder,—or, as the neighbors would have said of her, she that *was* Katy Stephens. Katy was the only daughter of a shipmaster, sailing from Newport harbor, who was wrecked off the coast one cold December night, and left small fortune to his widow and only child. Katy grew up, however, a tall, straight, black-eyed girl, with eyebrows drawn true as a bow, a foot arched like a Spanish woman's, and a little hand which never saw the thing it could not do,—quick of speech, ready of wit, and, as such girls have a right to be, somewhat positive withal. Katy could harness a chaise, or row a boat; she could saddle and ride any horse in the neighborhood; she could cut any garment that ever was seen or thought of, make cake, jelly, and wine, from her earliest years, in most precocious style;—all without seeming to derange a sort of trim, well-kept air of ladyhood that sat jauntily on her.

Of course, being young and lively, she had her admirers, and some well-to-do in worldly affairs laid their lands and houses at Katy's feet; but, to the wonder of all, she would not even pick them up to look at them. People shook their heads, and wondered whom Katy Stephens expected to get, and talked about going through the wood to pick up a crooked stick,—till one day she astonished her world by marrying a man that nobody ever thought of her taking.

George Scudder was a grave, thoughtful young man,—not given to talking, and silent in the society of women, with that kind of reverential bashfulness which sometimes shows a pure, unworldly nature. How Katy came to fancy him everybody wondered,—for he never talked to her, never so much as picked up her glove when it fell, never asked her to ride or sail; in short, everybody said she must have wanted him from sheer wilfulness, because he of all the young men of the neighborhood never courted her. But Katy, having very sharp eyes, saw some things that nobody else saw. For example, you must know she discovered by mere accident that George Scudder always was looking at her, wherever she moved, though he looked away in a moment, if discovered,—and that an accidental touch of her hand or brush of her dress would send the blood into his cheek like the spirit in the tube of a thermometer; and so, as women are curious, you know, Katy amused herself with investigating the causes of these little phenomena, and, before she knew it, got her foot caught in a cobweb that held her fast, and constrained her, whether she would or no, to marry a poor man that nobody cared much for but herself.

George was, in truth, one of the sort who evidently have made some mistake in coming into this world at all, as their internal furniture is in no way suited to its general courses and currents. He was of the order of dumb poets,—most wretched when put to the grind of the hard and actual; for if he who would utter poetry stretches out his hand to a gainsaying world, he is worse off still who is possessed with the desire of living it. Especially is this the case, if he be born poor, and with a dire necessity upon him of making immediate efforts in the hard and actual. George had a helpless invalid mother to support; so, though he loved reading and silent thought above all things, he put to instant use the only convertible worldly talent he possessed, which was a mechanical genius, and shipped at sixteen as a ship-carpenter. He studied navigation in the forecastle, and found in its calm diagrams and tranquil eternal signs food for his thoughtful nature, and a refuge from the brutality and coarseness of sea-life. He had a healthful, kindly animal nature, and so his inwardness did not ferment and turn to Byronic sourness and bitterness; nor did he needlessly parade to everybody in his vicinity the great gulf which lay between him and them. He was called a good fellow,—only a little lumpish,—and as he was brave and faithful, he rose in time to be a shipmaster. But when came the business of making money, the aptitude for accumulating, George found himself distanced by many a one with not half his general powers.

What shall a man do with a sublime tier of moral faculties, when the most profitable business out of his port is the slave-trade? So it was in Newport in those days. George's first voyage was on a slaver, and he wished himself dead many a time before it was over,—and ever after would talk like a man beside himself, if the subject was named. He declared that the gold made in it was distilled from human blood, from mothers' tears, from the agonies and dying groans of gasping, suffocating men and women, and that it would sear and blister the soul of him that touched it; in short, he talked as whole-souled, unpractical fellows are apt to talk about what respectable people sometimes do. Nobody had ever instructed him that a slave-ship, with a procession of expectant sharks in its wake, is a missionary institution, by which closely-packed heathens are brought over to enjoy the light of the gospel.

So, though George was acknowledged to be a good fellow, and honest as the noon-mark on the kitchen floor, he let slip so many chances of making money as seriously to compromise his reputation among thriving folks. He was wastefully generous,—insisted on treating every poor dog that came in his way, in any foreign port, as a brother,—absolutely refused to be party in cheating or deceiving the heathen on any shore, or in skin of any color,—and also took pains, as far as in him lay, to spoil any bargains which any of his subordinates founded on the ignorance or weakness of his fellow-men. So he made voyage after voyage, and gained only his wages and the reputation among his employers of an incorruptibly honest fellow.

To be sure, it was said that he carried out books in his ship, and read and studied, and wrote observations on all the countries he saw, which Parson Smith told Miss Dolly Persimmon would really do credit to a printed book; but then they never *were* printed, or, as Miss Dolly remarked of them, they never seemed to come to anything,—and coming to anything, as she understood it, meant standing in definite relations to bread and butter.

George never cared, however, for money. He made enough to keep his mother comfortable, and that was enough for him, till he fell in love with Katy Stephens. He looked at her through those glasses which such men carry in their souls, and she was a mortal woman no longer, but a transfigured, glorified creature,—an object of awe and wonder. He was actually afraid of her; her glove, her shoe, her needle, thread, and thimble, her bonnet-string, everything, in short, she wore or touched, became invested with a mysterious charm. He wondered at the impudence of men that could walk up and talk to her,—that could ask her to dance with such an assured air. *Now* he wished he were rich; he dreamed impossible chances of his coming home a millionnaire to lay unknown wealth at Katy's feet; and when Miss Persimmon, the ambulatory dress-maker of the neighborhood, in making up a new black gown for his mother, recounted how Captain Blatherem had sent Katy Stephens " 'most the splendidest India shawl that ever she did see," he was ready to tear his hair at the thought of his poverty. But even in that hour of temptation he did not repent that he had refused all part and lot in the ship by which Captain Blatherem's money was made, for he knew every timber of it to be seasoned by the groans and saturated with the sweat of human agony. True love is a natural sacrament; and if ever a young man thanks God for having saved what is noble and manly in his soul, it is when he thinks of offering it to the woman he loves. Nevertheless, the India-shawl story cost him a night's rest; nor was it till Miss Persimmon had ascertained, by a private confabulation with Katy's mother, that she had indignantly rejected it, and that she treated the Captain "real ridiculous," that he began to take heart. "He ought not," he said, "to stand in her way now, when he had nothing to offer. No, he would leave Katy free to do better, if she could; he would try his luck; and if, when he came home from the next voyage, Katy was disengaged, why, then he would lay all at her feet."

And so George was going to sea with a secret shrine in his soul, at which he was to burn unsuspected incense.

But, after all, the mortal maiden whom he adored suspected this private arrangement, and contrived—as women will—to get her own key into the lock of his secret temple; because, as girls say, "she was *determined* to know what was there." So, one night, she met him quite accidentally on the sea-sands, struck up a little conversation, and begged him in such a pretty way to bring her a spotted shell from the South Sea, like the one on his mother's mantel-piece, and looked so simple and childlike in saying it, that our young man very imprudently committed himself by remarking, that, "When people had rich friends to bring them all the world from foreign parts, he never dreamed of her wanting so trivial a thing."

Of course Katy "didn't know what he meant,—she hadn't heard of any rich friends." And then came something about Captain Blatherem; and Katy tossed her head, and said, "If anybody wanted to insult her, they might talk to her about Captain Blatherem,"—and then followed this, that, and the other, till finally, as you might expect, out came all that never was to have been said; and Katy was almost frightened at the terrible earnestness of the spirit she had evoked. She tried to laugh, and ended by crying, and saying she hardly knew what; but when she came to herself in her own room at home, she found on her finger a ring of African gold that George had put there, which she did not send back like Captain Blatherem's presents.

Katy was like many intensely matter-of-fact and practical women, who have not in themselves a bit of poetry or a particle of ideality, but who yet worship these qualities in others with the homage which the Indians paid to the unknown tongue of the first whites. They are secretly weary of a certain conscious dryness of nature in themselves, and this weariness predisposes them to idolize the man who brings them this unknown gift. Naturalists say that every defect of organization has its compensation, and men of ideal natures find in the favor of women the equivalent for their disabilities among men.

Do you remember, at Niagara, a little cataract on the American side, which throws its silver sheeny veil over a cave called the Grot of Rainbows? Whoever stands on a rock in that grotto sees himself in the centre of a rainbow-circle, above, below, around. In like manner, merry, chatty, positive, busy, housewifely, Katy saw herself standing in a rainbow-shrine in her lover's inner soul, and liked to see herself so. A woman, by-the-by, must be very insensible, who is not moved to come upon a higher plane of being, herself, by seeing how undoubtingly she is insphered in the heart of a good and noble man. A good man's faith in you, fair lady, if you ever have it, will make you better and nobler even before you know it.

Katy made an excellent wife; she took home her husband's old mother and nursed her with a dutifulness and energy worthy of all praise, and made her own keen outward faculties and deft handiness a compensation for the defects in worldly estate. Nothing would make Katy's black eyes flash quicker than any reflections on her husband's want of luck in the material line. "She didn't know whose business it was, if *she* was satisfied. She hated these sharp, gimlet, gouging sort of men that would put a screw between body and soul for money. George had that in him that nobody understood. She would rather be his wife on bread and water than to take Captain Blatherem's house, carriages, and horses, and all,— and she *might* have had 'em fast enough, dear knows. She was sick of making money when she saw what sort of men could make it,"—and so on. All which talk did her infinite credit, because after all she *did* care, and was naturally as proud and ambitious a little minx as ever breathed, and was thoroughly grieved at heart at George's want of worldly success; but, like a nice little Robin Redbreast, she covered up the grave of her worldliness with the leaves of true love, and sung a "Who cares for that?" above it.

Her thrifty management of the money her husband brought her soon bought a snug little farm, and put up the little brown gambrel-roofed cottage to which we directed your attention in the first of our story. Children were born to them; and George found, in short intervals between voyages, his home an earthly paradise. He was still sailing, with the fond illusion, in every voyage, of making enough to remain at home,—when the yellow fever smote him under the line, and the ship returned to Newport without its captain.

George was a Christian man;—he had been one of the first to attach himself to the unpopular and unworldly ministry of the celebrated Dr. Hopkins, and to appreciate the sublime ideality and unselfishness of those teachings which then were awakening new sensations in the theological mind of New England. Katy, too, had become a professor with her husband in the same church, and her husband's death in the midst of life deepened the power of her religious impressions. She became absorbed in religion, after the fashion of New England, where devotion is doctrinal, not ritual. As she grew older, her energy of character, her vigor and good judgment, caused her to be regarded as a mother in Israel; the minister boarded at her house, and it was she who was first to be consulted in all matters relating to the well-being of the church. No woman could more manfully breast a long sermon, or bring a more determined faith to the reception of a difficult doctrine. To say the truth, there lay at the bottom of her doctrinal system this stable corner-stone,—"Mr. Scudder used to believe it,—*I* will." And after all that is said about independent thought, isn't the fact, that a just and good soul has thus or thus believed, a more respectable argument than many that often are adduced? If it be not, more's the pity,—since two thirds of the faith in the world is built on no better foundation.

In time, George's old mother was gathered to her son, and two sons and a daughter followed their father to the invisible,—one only remaining of the flock, and she a person with whom you and I, good reader, have joint concern in the further unfolding of our story.

II.

The Kitchen

As I before remarked, Mrs. Katy Scudder had invited company to tea. Strictly speaking, it is necessary to begin with the creation of the world, in order to give a full account of anything. But, for popular use, something less may serve one's turn, and therefore I shall let the past chapter suffice to introduce my story, and shall proceed to arrange my scenery and act my little play, on the supposition that you know enough to understand things and persons.

Being asked to tea in our New England in the year 17— meant something very different from the same invitation in our more sophisticated days. In those times, people held to the singular opinion that the night was made to sleep in; they inferred it from a general confidence they had in the wisdom of Mother Nature, supposing that she did not put out her lights and draw her bed-curtains and hush all noise in her great world-house without strongly intending that her children should go to sleep; and the consequence was, that very soon after sunset the whole community very generally set their faces bedward, and the tolling of the nine-o'clock evening-bell had an awful solemnity in it, announcing the end of all respectable proceedings in life for that day. Good society in New England in those days very generally took its breakfast at six, its dinner at twelve, and its tea at six. "Company tea," however, among thrifty, industrious folk, was often taken an hour earlier, because each of the *invitées* had children to put to bed, or other domestic cares at home; and, as in those simple times people were invited because you wanted to see them, a tea-party assembled themselves at three and held session till sundown, when each matron rolled up her knitting-work and wended soberly home.

Though Newport, even in those early times, was not without its families which affected state and splendor, rolled about in carriages with armorial emblazonments, and had servants in abundance to every turn within-doors, yet there, as else-where in New England, the majority of the people lived with the wholesome, thrifty simplicity of the olden time, when labor and intelligence went hand in hand in perhaps a greater harmony than the world has ever seen.

Our scene opens in the great, old-fashioned kitchen, which, on ordinary occasions, is the family dining and sitting-room of the Scudder family. I know fastidious moderns think that the working-room wherein are carried on the culinary operations of a large family, must necessarily be an untidy and comfortless sitting-place; but it is only because they are ignorant of the marvellous workings which pertain to the organ of "faculty," on which we have before insisted. The kitchen of a New England matron was her throne-room, her pride; it was the habit of her life to produce the greatest possible results there with the slightest possible discomposure; and what any woman could do, Mrs. Katy Scudder could do *par excellence*. Everything there seemed to be always done and never doing. Washing and baking, those formidable disturbers of the composure of families, were all over with in those two or three morning-hours when we are composing ourselves for a last nap,—and only the fluttering of linen over the green yard, on Monday mornings, proclaimed that the dreaded solemnity of a wash had transpired. A breakfast arose there as by magic; and in an incredibly short space after, every knife, fork, spoon, and trencher, clean and shining, was looking as innocent and unconscious in its place as if it never had been used and never expected to be.

The floor,—perhaps, Sir, you remember your grand-mother's floor, of snowy boards sanded with whitest sand; you remember the ancient fireplace stretching quite across one end,—a vast cavern, in each corner of which a cozy seat might be found, distant enough to enjoy the crackle of the great jolly wood-fire; across the room ran a dresser, on which was displayed great store of shining pewter dishes and plates, which always shone with the same mysterious brightness; and by the side of the fire, a commodious wooden "settee," or settle, offered repose to people too little accustomed to luxury to ask for a cushion. Oh, that kitchen of the olden times, the old, clean, roomy New England kitchen!—who that has breakfasted, dined, and supped in one has not cheery visions of its thrift, its warmth, its coolness? The noon-mark on its floor was a dial that told off some of the happiest days; thereby did we right up the short-comings of the solemn old clock that tick-tacked in the corner, and whose ticks seemed mysterious prophecies of unknown good yet to arise out of the hours of life. How dreamy the winter twilight came in there,—when as yet the candles were not lighted,—when the crickets chirped around the dark stone hearth, and shifting tongues of flame flickered and cast dancing shadows and elf-ish lights on the walls, while grandmother nodded over her knitting-work, and puss purred, and old Rover lay dreamily opening now one eye and then the other on the family group! With all our ceiled houses, let us not forget our grandmothers' kitchens!

But we must pause, however, and back to our subject-matter, which is in the kitchen of Mrs. Katy Scudder, who has just put into the oven, by the fireplace, some wondrous tea-rusks, for whose composition she is renowned. She has examined and pronounced perfect a loaf of cake, which has been prepared for the occasion, and which, as usual, is done exactly right. The best room, too, has been opened and aired,—the white window-curtains saluted with a friendly little shake, as when one says, "How d'ye do?" to a friend;—for you must know, clean as our kitchen is, we are genteel, and have something better for company. Our best room in here has a polished little mahogany tea-table, and six mahogany chairs, with claw talons grasping balls; the white sanded floor is crinkled in curious little waves, like those on the seabeach; and right across the corner stands the "buffet," as it is called, with its transparent glass doors, wherein are displayed the solemn appurtenances of company tea-table. There you may see a set of real China teacups, which George bought in Canton, and had marked with his and his wife's joint initials,—a small silver cream-pitcher, which has come down as an heirloom from unknown generations,—silver spoons and delicate China cake-plates, which have been all carefully reviewed and wiped on napkins of Mrs. Scudder's own weaving.

Her cares now over, she stands drying her hands on a roller-towel in the kitchen, while her only daughter, the gentle Mary, stands in the doorway with the afternoon sun streaming in spots of flickering golden light on her smooth pale-brown hair,—a *petite* figure in a full stuff petticoat and white short gown, she stands reaching up one hand and cooing to something among the apple-blossoms,—and now a Java dove comes whirring down and settles on her finger,— and we, that have seen pictures, think, as we look on her girlish face, with its lines of statuesque beauty, on the tremulous, half-infantine expression of her lovely mouth, and the general air of simplicity and purity, of some old pictures of the girlhood of the Virgin. But Mrs. Scudder was thinking of no such Popish matter, I can assure you,—not she! I don't think you could have done her a greater indignity than to mention her daughter in any such connection. She had never seen a painting in her life, and therefore was not to be reminded of them; and furthermore, the dove was evidently, for some reason, no favorite,—for she said, in a quick, imperative tone, "Come, come, child! don't fool with that bird,—it's high time we were dressed and ready,"—and Mary, blushing, as it would seem, even to her hair, gave a little toss, and sent the bird, like a silver fluttering cloud, up among the rosy apple-blossoms. And now she and her mother have gone to their respective little bedrooms for the adjustment of their toilettes; and while the door is shut and nobody hears us, we shall talk to you about Mary.

Newport at the present day blooms like a flower-garden with young ladies of the best *ton*,—lovely girls, hopes of their families, possessed of amiable tempers and immensely large trunks, and capable of sporting ninety changes of raiment in thirty days and otherwise rapidly emptying the purses of distressed fathers, and whom yet travellers and the world in general look upon as genuine specimens of the kind of girls formed by American institutions.

We fancy such a one lying in a rustling silk *négligée*, and, amid a gentle generality of rings, ribbons, puffs, laces, beaux, and dinner-discussion, reading our humble sketch;—and what favor shall our poor heroine find in her eyes? For though her mother was a world of energy and "faculty," in herself considered, and had bestowed on this one little lone chick all the vigor and all the care and all the training which would have sufficed for a family of sixteen, there were no results produced which could be made appreciable in the eyes of such company. She could not waltz or polk, or speak bad French, or sing Italian songs; but, nevertheless, we must proceed to say what was her education and what her accomplishments.

Well, then, she could both read and write fluently in the mother-tongue. She could spin both on the little and the great wheel; and there were numberless towels, napkins, sheets, and pillow-cases in the household store that could attest the skill of her pretty fingers. She had worked several samplers of such rare merit, that they hung framed in different rooms of the house, exhibiting every variety and style of possible letter in the best marking-stitch. She was skilful in all sewing and embroidery, in all shaping and cutting, with a quiet and deft handiness that constantly surprised her energetic mother, who could not conceive that so much could be done with so little noise. In fact, in all household lore she was a veritable good fairy; her knowledge seemed unerring and intuitive; and whether she washed or ironed, or moulded biscuit or conserved plums, her gentle beauty seemed to turn to poetry all the prose of life.

There was something in Mary, however, which divided her as by an appreciable line from ordinary girls of her age. From her father she had inherited a deep and thoughtful nature, predisposed to moral and religious exaltation. Had she been born in Italy, under the dissolving influences of that sunny dreamy clime, beneath the shadow of cathedrals, and where pictured saints and angels smiled in clouds of painting from every arch and altar, she might, like fair St. Catherine of Siena, have seen beatific visions in the sunset skies, and a silver dove descending upon her as she prayed; but, unfolding in the clear, keen, cold New England clime, and nurtured in its abstract and positive theologies, her religious faculties took other forms. Instead of lying entranced in mysterious raptures at the foot of altars, she read and pondered treatises on the Will, and listened in rapt attention, while her spiritual guide, the venerated Dr. Hopkins, unfolded to her the theories of the great Edwards on the nature of true virtue. Womanlike, she felt the subtile poetry of these sublime abstractions which dealt with such infinite and unknown quantities,—which spoke of the universe, of its great Architect, of man, of angels, as matters of intimate and daily contemplation; and her teacher, a grand-minded and simple-hearted man as ever lived, was often amazed at the tread with which this fair young child walked through these high regions of abstract thought,—often comprehending through an ethereal clearness of nature what he had laboriously and heavily reasoned out; and sometimes, when she turned her grave, childlike face upon him with some question or reply, the good man started as if an angel had looked suddenly out upon him from a cloud. Unconsciously to himself, he often seemed to follow her, as Dante followed the flight of Beatrice, through the ascending circles of the celestial spheres.

When her mother questioned him, anxiously, of her daughter's spiritual estate, he answered, that she was a child of a strange graciousness of nature, and of a singular genius; to which Katy responded with a woman's pride, that she was all her father over again. It is only now and then that a matter-of-fact woman is sublimated by a real love; but if she is, it is affecting to see how impossible it is for death to quench it; for in the child the mother feels that she has a mysterious and undying repossession of the father.

But, in truth, Mary was only a recast in feminine form of her father's nature. The elixir of the spirit that sparkled within her was of that quality of which the souls of poets and artists are made; but the keen New England air crystalizes emotions into ideas, and restricts many a poetic soul to the necessity of expressing itself only in practical living.

The rigid theological discipline of New England is fitted to produce rather strength and purity than enjoyment. It was not fitted to make a sensitive and thoughtful nature happy, however it might ennoble and exalt.

The system of Dr. Hopkins was one that could have had its origin in a soul at once reverential and logical—a soul, moreover, trained from its earliest years in the habits of thought engendered by monarchical institutions. For although he, like other ministers, took an active part as a patriot in the Revolution, still he was brought up under the shadow of a throne, and a man cannot ravel out the stitches in which early days have knit him. His theology was, in fact, the turning to an invisible Sovereign of that spirit of loyalty and unquestioning subjugation which is one of the noblest capabilities of our nature. And as a gallant soldier renounces life and personal aims in the case of his king and country, and holds himself ready to be drafted for a forlorn hope, to be shot down, or help make a bridge of his mangled body, over which the more fortunate shall pass to victory and glory, so he regarded himself as devoted to the King Eternal, ready in His hands to be used to illustrate and build up an Eternal Commonwealth, either by being sacrificed as a lost spirit or glorified as a redeemed one, ready to throw not merely his mortal life, but his immortality even, into the forlorn hope, to bridge with a never-dying soul the chasm over which white-robed victors should pass to a commonwealth of glory and splendor whose vastness should dwarf the misery of all the lost to an infinitesimal.

It is not in our line to imply the truth or the falsehood of those systems of philosophic theology which seem for many years to have been the principal outlet for the proclivities of the New England mind, but as psychological developments they have an intense interest. He who does not see a grand side to these strivings of the soul cannot understand one of the noblest capabilities of humanity.

No real artist or philosopher ever lived who has not at some hours risen to the height of utter self-abnegation for the glory of the invisible. There have been painters who would have been crucified to demonstrate the action of a muscle,— chemists who would gladly have melted themselves and all humanity in their crucible, if so a new discovery might arise out of its fumes. Even persons of mere artistic sensibility are at times raised by music, painting, or poetry to a momentary trance of self-oblivion, in which they would offer their whole being before the shrine of an invisible loveliness. These hard old New England divines were the poets of meta-physical philosophy, who built systems in an artistic fervor, and felt self exhale from beneath them as they rose into the higher regions of thought. But where theorists and philoso-phers tread with sublime assurance, woman often follows with bleeding footsteps;—women are always turning from the abstract to the individual, and feeling where the philosopher only thinks.

It was easy enough for Mary to believe in *self*-renunciation, for she was one with a born vocation for martyrdom; and so, when the idea was put to her of suffering eternal pains for the glory of God and the good of being in general, she responded to it with a sort of sublime thrill, such as it is given to some natures to feel in view of uttermost sacrifice. But when she looked around on the warm, living faces of friends, acquaintances and neighbors, viewing them as possible candidates for dooms so fearfully different, she sometimes felt the walls of her faith closing round her as an iron shroud,—she wondered that the sun could shine so brightly, that flowers could flaunt such dazzling colors, that sweet airs could breathe, and little children play, and youth love and hope, and a thousand intoxicating influences combine to cheat the victims from the thought that their next step might be into an abyss of horrors without end. The blood of youth and hope was saddened by this great sorrow, which lay ever on her heart,—and her life, unknown to herself, was a sweet tune in the minor key; it was only in prayer, or deeds of love and charity, or in rapt contemplation of that beautiful millennial day, which her spiritual guide most delighted to speak of, that the tone of her feelings ever rose to the height of joy.

Among Mary's young associates was one who had been as a brother to her childhood. He was her mother's cousin's son,—and so, by a sort of family immunity, had always a free access to her mother's house. He took to the sea, as the most bold and resolute young men will, and brought home from foreign parts those new modes of speech, those other eyes for received opinions and established things, which so often shock established prejudices,—so that he was held as little better than an infidel and a castaway by the stricter religious circles in his native place. Mary's mother, now that Mary was grown up to woman's estate, looked with a severe eye on her cousin. She warned her daughter against too free an association with him,—and so—— We all know what comes to pass when girls are constantly warned not to think of a man. The most conscientious and obedient little person in the world, Mary resolved to be very careful. She never would think of James, except, of course, in her prayers; but as these were constant, it may easily be seen it was not easy to forget him.

All that was so often told her of his carelessness, his trifling, his contempt of orthodox opinions, and his startling and bold expressions, only wrote his name deeper in her heart,—for was not his soul in peril? Could she look in his frank, joyous face and listen to his thoughtless laugh, and then think that a fall from mast-head, or one night's storm, might——Ah, with what images her faith filled the blank! Could she believe all this and forget him?

You see, instead of getting our tea ready, as we promised at the beginning of this chapter, we have filled it with descriptions and meditations,—and now we foresee that the next chapter will be equally far from the point. But have patience with us; for we can write only as we are driven, and never know exactly where we are going to land.

III.

The Interview

A QUIET, maiden-like place was Mary's little room. The window looked out under the over-arching boughs of a thick apple-orchard, now all in a blush with blossoms and pink-tipped buds, and the light came golden-green, strained through flickering leaves,—and an ever-gentle rustle and whirr of branches and blossoms, a chitter of birds, and an indefinite whispering motion, as the long heads of orchard-grass nodded and bowed to each other under the trees, seemed to give the room the quiet hush of some little side-chapel in a cathedral, where green and golden glass softens the sunlight, and only the sigh and rustle of kneeling wor-shippers break the stillness of the aisles. It was small enough for a nun's apartment, and dainty in its neatness as the waxen cell of a bee. The bed and low window were draped in spot-less white, with fringes of Mary's own knotting. A small table under the looking-glass bore the library of a well-taught young woman of those times. "The Spectator," "Paradise Lost," Shakspeare, and "Robinson Crusoe," stood for the ad-mitted secular literature, and beside them the Bible and the works then published of Mr. Jonathan Edwards. Laid a little to one side as if of doubtful reputation, was the only novel which the stricter people in those days allowed for the read-ing of their daughters: that seven-volumed, trailing, tedious, delightful old bore, "Sir Charles Grandison,"—a book whose influence in those times was so universal, that it may be traced in the epistolary style even of the gravest divines. Our little heroine was mortal, with all her divinity, and had an imagi-nation which sometimes wandered to the things of earth; and this glorious hero in lace and embroidery, who blended rank, gallantry, spirit, knowledge of the world, disinterestedness, constancy, and piety, sometimes stepped before her, while she sat spinning at her wheel, till she sighed, she hardly knew why, that no such men walked the earth now. Yet it is to be confessed, this occasional raid of the romantic into Mary's balanced and well-ordered mind was soon energetically put to rout, and the book, as we have said, remained on her table under protest,—protected by being her father's gift to her mother during their days of courtship. The small looking-glass was curiously wreathed with corals and foreign shells, so disposed as to indicate an artistic eye and skilful hand; and some curious Chinese paintings of birds and flowers gave rather a piquant and foreign air to the otherwise homely neatness of the apartment.

Here in this little retreat Mary spent those few hours which her exacting conscience would allow her to spare from her busy-fingered household-life; here she read and wrote and thought and prayed;—and here she stands now, arraying herself for the tea company that afternoon. Dress, which in our day is becoming in some cases the whole of woman, was in those times a remarkably simple affair. True, every person of a certain degree of respectability had state and festival robes; and a certain camphor-wood brass-bound trunk, which was always kept solemnly locked in Mrs. Katy Scudder's apartment, if it could have spoken, might have given off quite a catalogue of brocade satin and laces. The wedding-suit there slumbered in all the unsullied whiteness of its stiff ground broidered with heavy knots of flowers; and there were scarfs of wrought India muslin and embroidered crape, each of which had its history,—for each had been brought into the door with beating heart on some return voyage of one who, alas, should return no more! The old trunk stood with its histories, its imprisoned remembrances,—and a thousand tender thoughts seemed to be shaken out of every rustling fold of silk and embroidery, on the few yearly occasions when all were brought out to be aired, their history related and then solemnly locked up again. Nevertheless, the possession of these things gave to the women of an establishment a certain innate dignity, like a good conscience; so that in that larger portion of existence commonly denominated among them "every day," they were content with plain stuff and home-spun. Mary's toilette, therefore, was sooner made than those of Newport belles of the present day; it simply consisted in changing her ordinary "short gown and petticoat" for another of somewhat nicer materials,—a skirt of India chintz and a striped jacconet short-gown. Her hair was of the kind which always lies like satin; but, nevertheless, girls never think their toilette complete unless the smoothest hair has been shaken down and rearranged. A few moments, however, served to braid its shining folds and dispose them in their simple knot on the back of the head; and having given a final stroke to each side with her little dimpled hands, she sat down a moment at the window, thoughtfully watching where the afternoon sun was creeping through the slats of the fence in long lines of gold among the tall, tremulous orchard-grass, and unconsciously she began warbling, in a low, gurgling voice, the words of a familiar hymn, whose grave earnestness accorded well with the general tone of her life and education:—

> "Life is the time to serve the Lord,
>   The time to insure the great reward."

There was a swish and rustle in the orchard-grass, and a tramp of elastic steps; then the branches were brushed aside, and a young man suddenly emerged from the trees a little behind Mary. He was apparently about twenty-five, dressed in the holiday rig of a sailor on shore, which well set off his fine athletic figure, and accorded with a sort of easy, dashing, and confident air which sat not unhandsomely on him. For the rest, a high forehead shaded by rings of the blackest hair, a keen, dark eye, a firm and determined mouth, gave the impression of one who had engaged to do battle with life, not only with a will, but with shrewdness and ability.

He introduced the colloquy by stepping deliberately behind Mary, putting his arms round her neck, and kissing her.

"Why, James!" said Mary, starting up, and blushing. "Come, now!"

"I have come, haven't I?" said the young man, leaning his elbow on the window-seat and looking at her with an air of comic determined frankness, which yet had in it such wholesome honesty that it was scarcely possible to be angry. "The fact is, Mary," he added, with a sudden earnest darkening of the face, "I won't stand this nonsense any longer. Aunt Katy has been holding me at arm's length ever since I got home;

and what have I done? Haven't I been to every prayer-meet-ing and lecture and sermon, since I got into port, just as reg-ular as a psalm-book? and not a bit of a word could I get with you, and no chance even so much as to give you my arm. Aunt Kate always comes between us and says, 'Here, Mary, you take my arm.' What does she think I go to meeting for, and almost break my jaws keeping down the gapes? I never even go to sleep, and yet I'm treated in this way! It's too bad! What's the row? What's anybody been saying about me? I always have waited on you ever since you were that high. Didn't I always draw you to school on my sled? didn't we always use to do our sums together? didn't I always wait on you to singing-school? and I've been made free to run in and out as if I were your brother;—and now she is as glum and stiff, and always stays in the room every minute of the time that I am there, as if she was afraid I should be in some mischief. It's too bad!"

"Oh, James, I am sorry that you only go to meeting for the sake of seeing me; you feel no real interest in religious things; and besides, mother thinks now I'm grown so old, that——Why, you know things are different now,—at least, we mustn't, you know, always do as we did when we were chil-dren. But I wish you did feel more interested in good things."

"I *am* interested in one or two good things, Mary,—prin-cipally in you, who are the best I know of. Besides," he said quickly, and scanning her face attentively to see the effect of his words, "don't you think there is more merit in my sitting out all these meetings, when they bore me so confoundedly, than there is in your and Aunt Katy's doing it, who really seem to find something to like in them? I believe you have a sixth sense, quite unknown to me; for it's all a maze,—I can't find top, nor bottom, nor side, nor up, nor down to it,—it's you can and you can't, you shall and you sha'n't, you will and you won't,"——

"James!"

"You needn't look at me so. I'm not going to say the rest of it. But, seriously, it's all anywhere and nowhere to me; it don't touch me, it don't help me, and I think it rather makes me worse; and then they tell me it's because I'm a natural man, and the natural man understandeth not the things of the Spirit. Well, I *am* a natural man,—how's a fellow to help it?"

"Well, James, why need you talk everywhere as you do? You joke, and jest, and trifle, till it seems to everybody that you don't believe in anything. I'm afraid mother thinks you are an infidel, but I *know* that can't be; yet we hear of all sorts of things that you say."

"I suppose you mean my telling Deacon Twitchel that I had seen as good Christians among the Mahometans as any in Newport. *Didn't* I make him open his eyes? It's true, too!"

"In every nation, he that feareth God and worketh righteousness is accepted of Him," said Mary; "and if there are better Christians than we are among the Mahometans, I am sure I'm glad of it. But, after all, the great question is, 'Are we Christians ourselves?' Oh, James, if you only were a real, true, noble Christian!"

"Well, Mary, you have got into that harbor, through all the sandbars and rocks and crooked channels; and now do you think it right to leave a fellow beating about outside, and not go out to help him in? This way of drawing up, among you good people, and leaving us sinners to ourselves, isn't generous. You might care a little for the soul of an old friend, anyhow!"

"And don't I care, James? How many days and nights have been one prayer for you! If I could take my hopes of heaven out of my own heart and give them to you, I would. Dr. Hopkins preached last Sunday on the text, 'I could wish myself accursed from Christ for my brethren, my kinsmen'; and he went on to show how we must be willing to give up even our own salvation, if necessary, for the good of others. People said it was hard doctrine, but I could feel my way through it very well. Yes, I would give my soul for yours; I wish I could."

There was a solemnity and pathos in Mary's manner which checked the conversation. James was the more touched because he felt it all so real, from one whose words were always yea and nay, so true, so inflexibly simple. Her eyes filled with tears, her face kindled with a sad earnestness, and James thought, as he looked, of a picture he had once seen in a

European cathedral, where the youthful Mother of Sorrows is represented,

> "Radiant and grave, as pitying man's decline;
> All youth, but with an aspect beyond time;
> Mournful, but mournful of another's crime;
> She looked as if she sat by Eden's door,
> And grieved for those who should return no more."

James had thought he loved Mary; he had admired her remarkable beauty, he had been proud of a certain right in her before that of other young men, her associates; he had thought of her as the keeper of his home; he had wished to appropriate her wholly to himself;—but in all this there had been, after all, only the thought of what she was to be to him; and, for this poor measure of what he called love, she was ready to offer, an infinite sacrifice.

As a subtile flash of lightning will show in a moment a whole landscape, tower, town, winding stream, and distant sea, so that one subtile ray of feeling seemed in a moment to reveal to James the whole of his past life; and it seemed to him so poor, so meagre, so shallow, by the side of that child-like woman, to whom the noblest of feelings were unconscious matters of course, that a sort of awe awoke in him; like the Apostles of old, he "feared as he entered into the cloud"; it seemed as if the deepest string of some eternal sorrow had vibrated between them.

After a moment's pause, he spoke in a low and altered voice:—

"Mary, I am a sinner. No psalm or sermon ever taught it to me, but I see it now. Your mother is quite right, Mary; you are too good for me; I am no mate for you. Oh, what would you think of me, if you knew me wholly? I have lived a mean, miserable, shallow, unworthy life. You are worthy, you are a saint, and walk in white! Oh, what upon earth could ever make you care so much for me?"

"Well, then, James, you will be good? Won't you talk with Dr. Hopkins?"

"Hang Dr. Hopkins!" said James. "Now, Mary, I beg your

pardon, but I can't make head or tail of a word Dr. Hopkins says. I don't get hold of it, or know what he would be at. You girls and women don't know your power. Why, Mary, you are a living gospel. You have always had a strange power over us boys. You never talked religion much, but I have seen high fellows come away from being with you as still and quiet as one feels when one goes into a church. I can't understand all the hang of predestination, and moral ability, and natural ability, and God's efficiency, and man's agency, which Dr. Hopkins is so engaged about; but I can understand *you*,—*you* can do me good!"

"Oh, James, can I?"

"Mary, I'm going to confess my sins. I saw, that, somehow or other, the wind was against me in Aunt Katy's quarter, and you know we fellows who take up the world in both fists don't like to be beat. If there's opposition, it sets us on. Now I confess I never did care much about religion, but I thought, without being really a hypocrite, I'd just let you try to save my soul for the sake of getting you; for there's nothing surer to hook a woman than trying to save a fellow's soul. It's a dead-shot, generally, that. Now our ship sails to-night, and I thought I'd just come across this path in the orchard to speak to you. You know I used always to bring you peaches and juneatings across this way, and once I brought you a ribbon."

"Yes, I've got it yet, James."

"Well, now, Mary, all this seems mean to me,—mean, to try and trick and snare you, who are so much too good for me. I felt very proud this morning that I was to go out first mate this time, and that I should command a ship next voyage. I meant to have asked you for a promise, but I don't. Only, Mary, just give me your little Bible, and I'll promise to read it all through soberly, and see what it all comes to. And pray for me; and if, while I'm gone, a good man comes who loves you, and is worthy of you, why, take him, Mary,— that's my advice."

"James, I am not thinking of any such things; I don't ever mean to be married. And I'm glad you don't ask me for any promise,—because it would be wrong to give it; mother doesn't even like me to be much with you. But I'm sure all I have said to you to-day is right; I shall tell her exactly all I have said."

"If Aunt Katy knew what things we fellows are pitched into, who take the world headforemost, she wouldn't be so selfish. Mary, you girls and women don't know the world you live in; you ought to be pure and good; you are not tempted as we are. You don't know what men, what women,—no, they're not women!—what creatures, beset us in every foreign port, and boarding-houses that are gates of hell; and then, if a fellow comes back from all this and don't walk exactly straight, you just draw up the hems of your garments and stand close to the wall, for fear he should touch you when he passes. I don't mean you, Mary, for you are different from most; but if you would do what you could, you might save us.—But it's no use talking, Mary. Give me the Bible; and please be kind to my dove,—for I had a hard time getting him across the water, and I don't want him to die."

If Mary had spoken all that welled up in her little heart at that moment, she might have said too much; but duty had its habitual seal upon her lips. She took the little Bible from her table and gave it with a trembling hand, and James turned to go. In a moment he turned back, and stood irresolute.

"Mary," he said, "we are cousins; I may never come back; you might kiss me this once."

The kiss was given and received in silence, and James disappeared among the thick trees.

"Come, child," said Aunt Katy, looking in, "there is Deacon Twitchel's chaise in sight,—are you ready?"

"Yes, mother."

IV.

Theological Tea

At the call of her mother, Mary hurried into the "best room," with a strange discomposure of spirit she had never felt before. From childhood, her love for James had been so deep, equable, and intense, that it had never disturbed her with thrills and yearnings; it had grown up in sisterly calmness, and, quietly expanding, had taken possession of her whole nature, without her once dreaming of its power. But this last interview seemed to have struck some great nerve of her being,—and calm as she usually was, from habit, principle, and good health, she shivered and trembled, as she heard his retreating footsteps, and saw the orchard-grass fly back from under his feet. It was as if each step trod on a nerve,—as if the very sound of the rustling grass was stirring something living and sensitive in her soul. And, strangest of all, a vague impression of guilt hovered over her. *Had* she done anything wrong? She did not ask him there; she had not spoken love to him; no, she had only talked to him of his soul, and how she would give hers for his,—oh, so willingly!—and that was not love; it was only what Dr. Hopkins said Christians must always feel.

"Child, what *have* you been doing?" said Aunt Katy, who sat in full flowing chintz petticoat and spotless dimity short-gown, with her company knitting-work in her hands; "your cheeks are as red as peonies. Have you been crying? What's the matter?"

"There is the Deacon's wife, mother," said Mary, turning confusedly, and darting to the entry-door.

Enter Mrs. Twitchel,—a soft, pillowy little elderly lady, whose whole air and dress reminded one of a sack of feathers tied in the middle with a string. A large, comfortable pocket, hung upon the side, disclosed her knitting-work ready for operation; and she zealously cleansed herself with a checked handkerchief from the dust which had accumulated during her ride in the old "one-hoss shay," answering the hospitable salutation of Katy Scudder in that plaintive, motherly voice which belongs to certain nice old ladies, who appear to live in a state of mild chronic compassion for the sins and sorrows of this mortal life generally.

"Why, yes, Miss Scudder, I'm pretty tol'able. I keep goin', and goin'. That's my way. I's a-tellin' the Deacon, this mornin', I didn't see how I *was* to come here this afternoon; but then I *did* want to see Miss Scudder and talk a little about that precious sermon, Sunday. How *is* the Doctor? blessed man! Well, his reward must be great in heaven, if not on earth, as I was a-tellin' the Deacon; and he says to me, says he, 'Polly, we mustn't be man-worshippers.' There, dear," (*to Mary*,) "don't trouble yourself about my bonnet; it a'n't my Sunday one, but I thought 'twould do. Says I to Cerinthy Ann, 'Miss Scudder won't mind, 'cause her heart's set on better things.' I always like to drop a word in season to Cerinthy Ann, 'cause she's clean took up with vanity and dress. Oh, dear! oh, dear me! so different from your blessed daughter, Miss Scudder! Well, it's a great blessin' to be called in one's youth, like Samuel and Timothy; but then we doesn't know the Lord's ways. Sometimes I gets clean discouraged with my children,—but then ag'in I don't know; none on us does. Cerinthy Ann is one of the most master hands to turn off work; she takes hold and goes along like a woman, and nobody never knows when that gal finds the time to do all she does do; and I don't know nothin' what I *should* do without her. Deacon was saying, if ever she was called, she'd be a Martha, and not a Mary; but then she's dreadful opposed to the doctrines. Oh, dear me! oh, dear me! Somehow they seem to rile her all up; and she was a-tellin' me yesterday, when she was a-hangin' out clothes, that she never should get reconciled to Decrees and 'Lection, 'cause she can't see, if things is certain, how folks is to help 'emselves. Says I, 'Cerinthy Ann, folks a'n't to help themselves; they's to submit unconditional.' And she jest slammed down the clothes-basket and went into the house."

When Mrs. Twitchel began to talk, it flowed a steady stream, as when one turns a faucet, that never ceases running till some hand turns it back again; and the occasion that cut the flood short at present was the entrance of Mrs. Brown.

Mr. Simeon Brown was a thriving ship-owner of Newport, who lived in a large house, owned several negro-servants and a span of horses, and affected some state and style in his worldly appearance. A passion for metaphysical Orthodoxy had drawn Simeon to the congregation of Dr. Hopkins, and his wife of course stood by right in a high place there. She was a tall, angular, somewhat hard-favored body, dressed in a style rather above the simple habits of her neighbors, and her whole air spoke the great woman, who in right of her thousands expected to have her say in all that was going on in the world, whether she understood it or not.

On her entrance, mild little Mrs. Twitchel fled from the cushioned rocking-chair, and stood with the quivering air of one who feels she has no business to be anywhere in the world, until Mrs. Brown's bonnet was taken and she was seated, when Mrs. Twitchel subsided into a corner and rattled her knitting-needles to conceal her emotion.

New England has been called the land of equality; but what land upon earth is wholly so? Even the mites in a bit of cheese, naturalists say, have great tumblings and strivings about position and rank; he who has ten pounds will always be a nobleman to him who has but one, let him strive as manfully as he may; and therefore let us forgive meek little Mrs. Twitchel for melting into nothing in her own eyes when Mrs. Brown came in, and let us forgive Mrs. Brown that she sat down in the rocking-chair with an easy grandeur, as one who thought it her duty to be affable and meant to be. It was, however, rather difficult for Mrs. Brown, with her money, house, negroes, and all, to patronize Mrs. Katy Scudder, who was one of those women whose natures seem to sit on thrones, and who dispense patronage and favor by an inborn right and aptitude, whatever be their social advantages. It was one of Mrs. Brown's trials of life, this secret, strange quality in her neighbor, who stood apparently so far below her in worldly goods. Even the quiet, positive style of Mrs. Katy's knitting made her nervous; it was an implication of independence of her sway; and though on the present occasion every customary courtesy was bestowed, she still felt, as she always did when Mrs. Katy's guest, a secret uneasiness. She mentally contrasted the neat little parlor, with its white sanded floor and muslin curtains, with her own grand front-room, which boasted the then uncommon luxuries of Turkey carpet and Persian rug, and wondered if Mrs. Katy did really feel as cool and easy in receiving her as she appeared.

You must not understand that this was what Mrs. Brown *supposed* herself to be thinking about; oh, no! by no means! All the little, mean work of our nature is generally done in a small dark closet just a little back of the subject we are talking about, on which subject we suppose ourselves of course to be thinking;—of course we *are* thinking of it; how else could we talk about it?

The subject in discussion, and what Mrs. Brown supposed to be in her own thoughts, was the last Sunday's sermon on the doctrine of entire Disinterested Benevolence, in which good Doctor Hopkins had proclaimed to the citizens of Newport their duty of being so wholly absorbed in the general good of the universe as even to acquiesce in their own final and eternal destruction, if the greater good of the whole might thereby be accomplished.

"Well, now, dear me!" said Mrs. Twitchel, while her knitting-needles trotted contentedly to the mournful tone of her voice,—"I was tellin' the Deacon, if we only could get there! Sometimes I think I get a little way,—but then ag'in I don't know; but the Deacon he's quite down,—he don't see no evidences in himself. Sometimes he says he don't feel as if he ought to keep his place in the church,—but then ag'in he don't know. He keeps a-turnin' and turnin' on't over in his mind, and a-tryin' himself this way and that way; and he says he don't see nothin' but what's selfish, no way.

" 'Member one night last winter, after the Deacon got warm in bed, there come a rap at the door; and who should it be but old Beulah Ward, wantin' to see the Deacon?— 'twas her boy she sent, and he said Beulah was sick and hadn't no more wood nor candles. Now I know'd the Deacon had carried that crittur half a cord of wood, if he had one stick, since Thanksgivin', and I'd sent her two o' my best moulds of candles,—nice ones that Cerinthy Ann run when we killed a crittur; but nothin' would do but the Deacon must get right out his warm bed and dress himself, and hitch up his team to carry over some wood to Beulah. Says I, 'Father, you know you'll be down with the rheumatis for this; besides, Beulah is real aggravatin'. I know she trades off what we send her to the store for rum, and you never get no thanks. She expects, 'cause we has done for her, we always must; and more we do more we may do.' And says he to me, says he, 'That's jest the way we sarves the Lord, Polly; and what if He shouldn't hear us when we call on Him in our troubles?' So I shet up; and the next day he was down with the rheumatis. And Cerinthy Ann, says she, 'Well, father, *now* I hope you'll own you have got *some* disinterested benevolence,' says she; and the Deacon he thought it over a spell, and then he says, 'I'm 'fraid it's all selfish. I'm jest a-makin' a righteousness of it.' And Cerinthy Ann she come out, declarin' that the best folks never had no comfort in religion; and for her part she didn't mean to trouble her head about it, but have jest as good a time as she could while she's young, 'cause if she was 'lected to be saved she should be, and if she wa'n't she couldn't help it, any how."

"Mr. Brown says he came on to Dr. Hopkins's ground years ago," said Mrs. Brown, giving a nervous twitch to her yarn, and speaking in a sharp, hard, didatic voice, which made little Mrs. Twitchel give a gentle quiver, and look humble and apologetic. "Mr. Brown's a master thinker; there's nothing pleases that man better than a hard doctrine; he says you can't get 'em too hard for him. He don't find any difficulty in bringing his mind up; he just reasons it out all plain; and he says, people have no need to be in the dark; and that's *my* opinion. 'If folks know they ought to come up to anything, why *don't* they?' he says; and I say so too."

"Mr. Scudder used to say that it took great afflictions to bring his mind to that place," said Mrs. Katy. "He used to say that an old paper-maker told him once, that paper that was shaken only one way in the making would tear across the other, and the best paper had to be shaken every way; and so he said we couldn't tell, till we had been turned and shaken and tried every way, where we should tear."

Mrs. Twitchel responded to this sentiment with a gentle series of groans, such as were her general expression of approbation, swaying herself backward and forward; while Mrs. Brown gave a sort of toss and snort, and said that for her part she always thought people knew what they did know,—but she guessed she was mistaken.

The conversation was here interrupted by the civilities attendant on the reception of Mrs. Jones,—a broad, buxom, hearty soul, who had come on horseback from a farm about three miles distant.

Smiling with rosy content, she presented Mrs. Katy a small pot of golden butter,—the result of her forenoon's churning.

There are some people so evidently broadly and heartily of this world, that their coming into a room always materializes the conversation. We wish to be understood that we mean no disparaging reflection on such persons;—they are as necessary to make up a world as cabbages to make up a garden; the great healthy principles of cheerfulness and animal life seem to exist in them in the gross; they are wedges and ingots of solid, contented vitality. Certain kinds of virtues and Christian graces thrive in such people as the first crop of corn does in the bottom-lands of the Ohio. Mrs. Jones was a church-member, a regular church-goer, and planted her comely person plump in front of Dr. Hopkins every Sunday, and listened to his searching and discriminating sermons with broad, honest smiles of satisfaction. Those keen distinctions as to motives, those awful warnings and urgent expostulations, which made poor Deacon Twitchel weep, she listened to with great, round, satisfied eyes, making to all, and after all, the same remark,—that it was good, and she liked it, and the Doctor was a good man; and on the present occasion, she announced her pot of butter as one fruit of her reflections after the last discourse.

"You see," she said, "as I was a-settin' in the spring-house, this mornin', a-workin' my butter, I says to Dinah,—'I'm goin' to carry a pot of this down to Miss Scudder for the Doctor,—I got so much good out of his Sunday's sermon.' And Dinah she says to me, says she,—'Laws, Miss Jones, I thought you was asleep, for sartin!' But I wasn't; only I forgot to take any caraway-seed in the mornin', and so I kinder missed it; you know it 'livens one up. But I never lost myself so but what I kinder heerd him goin' on, on, sort o' like,— and it sounded *all* sort o' *good*; and so I thought of the Doctor to-day."

"Well, I'm sure," said Aunt Katy, "this will be a treat; we all know about your butter, Mrs. Jones. I sha'n't think of putting any of mine on table to-night, I'm sure."

"Law, now don't!" said Mrs. Jones. "Why, you re'lly make me ashamed, Miss Scudder. To be sure, folks does like our butter, and it always fetches a pretty good price,—*he's* very proud on't. I tell him he oughtn't to be,—we oughtn't to be proud of anything."

And now Mrs. Katy, giving a look at the old clock, told Mary it was time to set the tea-table; and forthwith there was a gentle movement of expectancy. The little mahogany tea-table opened its brown wings, and from a drawer came forth the snowy damask covering. It was etiquette, on such occasions, to compliment every article of the establishment successively, as it appeared; so the Deacon's wife began at the table-cloth.

"Well, I do declare, Miss Scudder beats us all in her table-cloths," she said, taking up a corner of the damask, admiringly; and Mrs. Jones forthwith jumped up and seized the other corner.

"Why, this 'ere must have come from the Old Country. It's 'most the beautiflest thing I ever did see."

"It's my own spinning," replied Mrs. Katy, with conscious dignity. "There was an Irish weaver came to Newport the year before I was married, who wove beautifully,—just the Old-Country patterns,—and I'd been spinning some uncommonly fine flax then. I remember Mr. Scudder used to read to me while I was spinning,"—and Aunt Katy looked afar, as one whose thoughts are in the past, and dropped out the last words with a little sigh, unconsciously, as if speaking to herself.

"Well, now, I must say," said Mrs. Jones, "this goes quite beyond me. I thought I could spin some; but I sha'n't never dare to show mine."

"I'm sure, Mrs. Jones, your towels that you had out bleaching, this spring, were wonderful," said Aunt Katy. "But I don't pretend to do much now," she continued, straightening her trim figure. "I'm getting old, you know; we must let the young folks take up these things. Mary spins better now than I ever did. Mary, hand out those napkins."

And so Mary's napkins passed from hand to hand.

"Well, well," said Mrs. Twitchel to Mary, "it's easy to see that *your* linen-chest will be pretty full by the time *he* comes along; won't it, Miss Jones?"—and Mrs. Twitchel looked pleasantly facetious, as elderly ladies generally do, when suggesting such possibilities to younger ones.

Mary was vexed to feel the blood boil up in her cheeks in a most unexpected and provoking way at the suggestion; whereat Mrs. Twitchel nodded knowingly at Mrs. Jones, and whispered something in a mysterious aside, to which plump Mrs. Jones answered,—"Why, do tell! now I never!"

"It's strange," said Mrs. Twitchel, taking up her parable again, in such a plaintive tone that all knew something pathetic was coming, "what mistakes some folks will make, a-fetchin' up girls. Now there's your Mary, Miss Scudder,— why, there a'n't nothin' she can't do; but law, I was down to Miss Skinner's, last week, a-watchin' with her, and re'lly it 'most broke my heart to see her. Her mother was a most amazin' smart woman; but she brought Suky up, for all the world, as if she'd been a wax doll, to be kept in the drawer,— and sure enough, she was a pretty creetur,—and now she's married, what is she? She ha'n't no more idee how to take hold than nothin'. The poor child means well enough, and she works so hard she most kills herself; but then she is in the suds from mornin' till night,—she's one the sort whose work's never done,—and poor George Skinner's clean discouraged."

"There's everything in *knowing how*," said Mrs. Katy. "Nobody ought to be always working; it's a bad sign. I tell Mary,—'Always do up your work in the forenoon.' Girls must learn that. I never work afternoons, after my dinner-dishes are got away; I never did and never would."

"Nor I, neither," chimed in Mrs. Jones and Mrs. Twitchel,—both anxious to show themselves clear on this leading point of New England housekeeping.

"There's another thing I always tell Mary," said Mrs. Katy, impressively. " 'Never say there isn't time for a thing that ought to be done. If a thing is *necessary*, why, life is long enough to find a place for it. That's my doctrine. When anybody tells me they can't *find time* for this or that, I don't think much of 'em. I think they don't know how to work,—that's all.' "

Here Mrs. Twitchel looked up from her knitting, with an apologetic giggle, at Mrs. Brown.

"Law, now, there's Miss Brown, she don't know nothin' about it, 'cause she's got her servants to every turn. I s'pose she thinks it queer to hear us talkin' about our work. Miss Brown must have her time all to herself. I was tellin' the Deacon the other day that she was a privileged woman."

"I'm sure, those that have servants find work enough following 'em 'round," said Mrs. Brown,—who, like all other human beings, resented the implication of not having as many trials in life as her neighbors. "As to getting the work done up in the forenoon, that's a thing I never can teach 'em; they'd rather not. Chloe likes to keep her work 'round, and do it by snacks, any time, day or night, when the notion takes her."

"And it was just for that reason I never would have one of those creatures 'round," said Mrs. Katy. "Mr. Scudder was principled against buying negroes,—but if he had *not* been, I should not have wanted any of *their* work. I know what's to be done, and most help is no help to me. I want people to stand out of my way and let me get done. I've tried keeping a girl once or twice, and I never worked so hard in my life. When Mary and I do all ourselves, we can calculate everything to a minute; and we get our time to sew and read and spin and visit, and live just as we want to."

Here, again, Mrs. Brown looked uneasy. To what use was it that she was rich and owned servants, when this Mordecai in her gate utterly despised her prosperity? In her secret heart she thought Mrs. Katy must be envious, and rather comforted herself on this view of the subject,—sweetly unconscious of any inconsistency in the feeling with her views of utter self-abnegation just announced.

Meanwhile the tea-table had been silently gathering on its snowy plateau the delicate china, the golden butter, the loaf of faultless cake, a plate of crullers or wonders, as a sort of sweet fried cake was commonly called,—tea-rusks, light as a puff, and shining on top with a varnish of egg,—jellies of apple and quince quivering in amber clearness,—whitest and purest honey in the comb,—in short, everything that could go to the getting-up of a most faultless tea.

"I don't see," said Mrs. Jones, resuming the gentle pæans of the occasion, "how Miss Scudder's loaf-cake always comes out jest so. It don't rise neither to one side nor t'other, but jest even all 'round; and it a'n't white one side and burnt the other, but jest a good brown all over; and it don't have no heavy streak in it."

"Jest what Cerinthy Ann was sayin', the other day," said Mrs. Twitchel. "She says she can't never be sure how hers is a-comin' out. Do what she can, it will be either too much or too little; but Miss Scudder's is always jest so. 'Law,' says I, 'Cerinthy Ann, it's *faculty*,—that's it;—them that has it has it, and them that hasn't—why, they've got to work hard, and not do half so well, neither.' "

Mrs. Katy took all these praises as matter of course. Since she was thirteen years old, she had never put her hand to anything that she had not been held to do better than other folks, and therefore she accepted her praises with the quiet repose and serenity of assured reputation; though, of course, she used the usual polite disclaimers of "Oh, it's nothing, nothing at all; I'm sure I don't know how I do it, and was not aware it was so good,"—and so on. All which things are proper for gentlewomen to observe in like cases, in every walk of life.

"Do you think the Deacon will be along soon?" said Mrs. Katy, when Mary, returning from the kitchen, announced the important fact, that the tea-kettle was boiling.

"Why, yes," said Mrs. Twitchel. "I'm a-lookin' for him every minute. He told me, that he and the men should be plantin' up to the eight-acre lot, but he'd keep the colt up there to come down on; and so I laid him out a clean shirt, and says I, 'Now, Father, you be sure and be there by five, so that Miss Scudder may know when to put her tea a-drawin'.'—There he is, I believe," she added, as a horse's tramp was heard without, and, after a few moments, the desired Deacon entered.

He was a gentle, soft-spoken man, low, sinewy, thin, with black hair showing lines and patches of silver. His keen, thoughtful, dark eye marked the nervous and melancholic temperament. A mild and pensive humility of manner seemed to brood over him, like the shadow of a cloud. Everything in his dress, air, and motions indicated punctilious exactness and accuracy, at times rising to the point of nervous anxiety.

Immediately after the bustle of his entrance had subsided, Mr. Simeon Brown followed. He was a tall, lank individual, with high cheek-bones, thin, sharp features, small, keen, hard eyes, and large hands and feet.

Simeon was, as we have before remarked, a keen theologian, and had the scent of a hound for a metaphysical distinction. True, he was a man of business, being a thriving trader to the coast of Africa, whence he imported negroes for the American market; and no man was held to understand that branch of traffic better,—he having, in his earlier days, commanded ships in the business, and thus learned it from the root. In his private life, Simeon was severe and dictatorial. He was one of that class of people who, of a freezing day, will plant themselves directly between you and the fire, and there stand and argue to prove that selfishness is the root of all moral evil. Simeon said he always had thought so; and his neighbors sometimes supposed that nobody could enjoy better experimental advantages for understanding the subject. He was one of those men who suppose themselves submissive to the Divine will, to the uttermost extent demanded by the extreme theology of that day, simply because they have no nerves to feel, no imagination to conceive what endless happiness or suffering is, and who deal therefore with the great question of the salvation or damnation of myriads as a problem of theological algebra, to be worked out by their inevitable *x*, *y*, *z*.

But we must not spend too much time with our analysis of character, for matters at the tea-table are drawing to a crisis. Mrs. Jones has announced that she does not think *"he"* can come this afternoon, by which significant mode of expression she conveyed the dutiful idea that there was for her but one male person in the world. And now Mrs. Katy says, "Mary, dear, knock at the Doctor's door and tell him that tea is ready."

The Doctor was sitting in his shady study, in the room on the other side of the little entry. The windows were dark and fragrant with the shade and perfume of blossoming lilacs, whose tremulous shadow, mingled with spots of afternoon sunlight, danced on the scattered papers of a great writing-table covered with pamphlets and heavily-bound volumes of theology, where the Doctor was sitting.

A man of gigantic proportions, over six feet in height, and built every way with an amplitude corresponding to his height, he bent over his writing, so absorbed that he did not hear the gentle sound of Mary's entrance.

"Doctor," said the maiden, gently, "tea is ready."

No motion, no sound, except the quick racing of the pen over the paper.

"Doctor! Doctor!"—a little louder, and with another step into the apartment,—"tea is ready."

The Doctor stretched his head forward to a paper which lay before him, and responded in a low, murmuring voice, as reading something.

"Firstly,—if underived virtue be peculiar to the Deity, can it be the duty of a creature to have it?"

Here a little waxen hand came with a very gentle tap on his huge shoulder, and "Doctor, tea is ready," penetrated drowsily to the nerve of his ear, as a sound heard in sleep. He rose suddenly with a start, opened a pair of great blue eyes, which shone abstractedly under the dome of a capacious and lofty forehead, and fixed them on the maiden, who by this time was looking up rather archly, and yet with an attitude of the most profound respect, while her venerated friend was assembling together his earthly faculties.

"Tea is ready, if you please. Mother wished me to call you."

"Oh!—ah!—yes!—indeed!" he said, looking confusedly about, and starting for the door, in his study-gown.

"If you please, Sir," said Mary, standing in his way, "would you not like to put on your coat and wig?"

The Doctor gave a hurried glance at his study-gown, put his hand to his head, which, in place of the ample curls of his full-bottomed wig, was decked only with a very ordinary cap, and seemed to come at once to full comprehension. He smiled a kind of conscious, benignant smile, which adorned his high cheek-bones and hard features as sunshine adorns the side of a rock, and said, kindly, "Ah, well, child, I understand now; I'll be out in a moment."

And Mary, sure that he was now on the right track, went back to the tea-room with the announcement that the Doctor was coming.

In a few moments he entered, majestic and proper, in all the dignity of full-bottomed, powdered wig, full, flowing coat, with ample cuffs, silver knee- and shoe-buckles, as became the gravity and majesty of the minister of those days.

He saluted all the company with a benignity which had a touch of the majestic, and also of the rustic in it; for at heart the Doctor was a bashful man,—that is, he had somewhere in his mental camp that treacherous fellow whom John Bunyan anathematizes under the name of Shame. The company rose on his entrance; the men bowed and the women curtsied, and all remained standing while he addressed to each with punctilious decorum those inquiries in regard to health and well-being which preface a social interview. Then, at a dignified sign from Mrs. Katy, he advanced to the table, and, all following his example, stood, while, with one hand uplifted, he went through a devotional exercise which, for length, more resembled a prayer than a grace,—after which the company were seated.

"Well, Doctor," said Mr. Brown, who, as a householder of substance, felt a conscious right to be first to open conversation with the minister, "people are beginning to make a noise about your views. I was talking with Deacon Timmins the other day down on the wharf, and he said Dr. Stiles said that it was entirely new doctrine,—entirely so,—and for his part he wanted the good old ways."

"They say so, do they?" said the Doctor, kindling up from an abstraction into which he seemed to be gradually subsiding. "Well, let them. I had rather publish *new* divinity than any other, and the more of it the better,—*if it be but true.* I should think it hardly worth while to write, if I had nothing *new* to say."

"Well," said Deacon Twitchel,—his meek face flushing with awe of his minister,—"Doctor, there's all sorts of things said about you. Now the other day I was at the mill with a load of corn, and while I was a-waitin', Amariah Wadsworth came along with his'n; and so while we were waitin', he says to me, 'Why they say your minister is gettin' to be an Arminian'; and he went on a-tellin' how old Ma'am Badger told him that you interpreted some parts of Paul's Epistles clear on the Arminian side. You know Ma'am Badger's a master-hand at doctrines, and she's 'most an uncommon Calvinist."

"That does not frighten me at all," said the sturdy Doctor. "Supposing I do interpret some texts like the Arminians. Can't Arminians have anything right about them? Who wouldn't rather go with the Arminians when they are *right*, than with the Calvinists when they are wrong?"

"That's it,—you've hit it, Doctor," said Simeon Brown. "That's what I always say. I say, 'Don't he *prove* it? and how are you going to answer him?' That gravels 'em."

"Well," said Deacon Twitchel, "Brother Seth,—you know Brother Seth,—he says you deny depravity. He's all for im-putation of Adam's sin, you know; and I have long talks with Seth about it, every time he comes to see me; and he says, that, if we did not sin in Adam, it's givin' up the whole ground altogether; and then he insists you're clean wrong about the unregenerate doings."

"Not at all,—not in the least," said the Doctor, promptly.

"I wish Seth could talk with you sometime, Doctor. Along in the spring, he was down helpin' me to lay stone fence,—it was when we was fencin' off the south-pastur' lot,—and we talked pretty nigh all day; and it re'lly did seem to me that the longer we talked, the sotter Seth grew. He's a master-hand at readin'; and when he heard that your remarks on Dr. Mayhew had come out, Seth tackled up o' purpose and come up to Newport to get them, and spent all his time, last win-ter, studyin' on it and makin' his remarks; and I tell you, Sir, he's a tight fellow to argue with. Why, that day, what with layin' stone wall and what with arguin' with Seth, I come home quite beat out,—Miss Twitchel will remember."

"That he was!" said his helpmeet. "I 'member, when he came home, says I, 'Father, you seem clean used up'; and I stirred 'round lively like, to get him his tea. But he jest went into the bedroom and laid down afore supper; and I says to Cerinthy Ann, 'That's a thing I ha'n't seen your father do since he was took with the typhus.' And Cerinthy Ann, she said she knew 'twa'n't anything but them old doctrines,—that it was always so when Uncle Seth come down. And after tea Father was kinder chirked up a little, and he and Seth sot by the fire, and was a-beginnin' it ag'in, and I jest spoke out and said,—'Now, Seth, these 'ere things doesn't hurt you; but the Deacon is weakly, and if he gets his mind riled after supper, he don't sleep none all night. So,' says I, 'you'd better jest let matters stop where they be; 'cause,' says I, ' 'twon't make no difference, for to-night, which on ye's got the right on't;— reckon the Lord 'll go on his own way without you; and we shall find out, by'm-by, what that is.' "

"Mr. Scudder used to think a great deal on these points," said Mrs. Katy, "and the last time he was home he wrote out his views. I haven't ever shown them to you, Doctor; but I should be pleased to know what you think of them."

"Mr. Scudder was a good man, with a clear head," said the Doctor; "and I should be much pleased to see anything that he wrote."

A flush of gratified feeling passed over Mrs. Katy's face;— for one flower laid on the shrine which we keep in our hearts for the dead, is worth more than any gift to our living selves.

We will not now pursue our party further, lest you, reader, get more theological tea than you can drink. We will not re-count the numerous nice points raised by Mr. Simeon Brown and adjusted by the Doctor,—and how Simeon invariably de-clared, that that was the way in which he disposed of them himself, and how he had thought it out ten years ago.

We will not relate, either, too minutely, how Mary changed color and grew pale and red in quick succession, when Mr. Simeon Brown incidentally remarked, that the "Monsoon" was going to set sail that very afternoon, for her three-years' voyage. Nobody noticed it in the busy amenities,—the sud-den welling and ebbing of that one poor little heart-fountain.

So we go,—so little knowing what we touch and what touches us as we talk! We drop out a common piece of news,—"Mr. So-and-so is dead,—Miss Such-a-one is mar-ried,—such a ship has sailed,"—and lo, on our right hand or our left, some heart has sunk under the news silently,—gone down in the great ocean of Fate, without even a bubble rising to tell its drowning pang. And this—God help us!—is what we call living!

V.

The Letter

M ARY returned to the quietude of her room. The red of
twilight had faded, and the silver moon, round and
fair, was rising behind the thick boughs of the apple-trees.
She sat down in the window, thoughtful and sad, and listened
to the crickets, whose ignorant jollity often sounds as mournfully to us mortals as ours may to superior beings. There the
little hoarse, black wretches were scraping and creaking, as if
life and death were invented solely for their pleasure, and the
world were created only to give them a good time in it. Now
and then a little wind shivered among the boughs and
brought down a shower of white petals which shimmered in
the slant beams of the moonlight; and now a ray touched
some tall head of grass, and forthwith it blossomed into silver, and stirred itself with a quiet joy, like a new-born saint
just awakening in paradise. And ever and anon came on the
still air the soft eternal pulsations of the distant sea,—sound
mournfulest, most mysterious, of all the harpings of Nature.
It was the sea,—the deep, eternal sea,—the treacherous, soft,
dreadful, inexplicable sea; and *he* was perhaps at this moment
being borne away on it,—away, away,—to what sorrows, to
what temptations, to what dangers, she knew not. She looked
along the old, familiar, beaten path by which he came, by
which he went, and thought, "What if he *never* should come
back?" There was a little path through the orchard out to a
small elevation in the pasture lot behind, whence the sea was
distinctly visible, and Mary had often used her low-silled window as a door when she wanted to pass out thither; so now
she stepped out, and, gathering her skirts back from the dewy
grass, walked thoughtfully along the path and gained the hill.
Newport harbor lay stretched out in the distance, with the
rising moon casting a long, wavering track of silver upon it;
and vessels, like silver-winged moths, were turning and shifting slowly to and fro upon it, and one stately ship in full sail

passing fairly out under her white canvas, graceful as some grand, snowy bird. Mary's beating heart told her that *there* was passing away from her one who carried a portion of her existence with him. She sat down under a lonely tree that stood there, and, resting her elbow on her knee, followed the ship with silent prayers, as it passed, like a graceful cloudy dream, out of her sight.

Then she thoughtfully retraced her way to her chamber; and as she was entering, observed in the now clearer moon-light what she had not seen before,—something white, like a letter, lying on the floor. Immediately she struck a light, and there, sure enough, it was,—a letter in James's handsome, dashing hand; and the little puss, before she knew what she was about, actually kissed it, with a fervor which would much have astonished the writer, could he at that moment have been clairvoyant. But Mary felt as one who finds, in the emptiness after a friend's death, an unexpected message or memento; and all alone in the white, calm stillness of her little room her heart took sudden possession of her. She opened the letter with trembling hands, and read what of course we shall let you read. We got it out of a bundle of old, smoky, yellow letters, years after all the parties concerned were gone on the eternal journey beyond earth.

"My dear Mary,—

"I cannot leave you so. I have about two hundred things to say to you, and it's a shame I could not have had longer to see you; but blessed be ink and paper! I am writing and seeing to fifty things besides; so you mustn't wonder if my letter has rather a confused appearance.

"I have been thinking that perhaps I gave you a wrong impression of myself, this afternoon. I am going to speak to you from my heart, as if I were confessing on my death-bed. Well, then, I do not confess to being what is commonly called a bad young man. I should be willing that men of the world generally, even strict ones, should look my life through and know all about it. It is only in your presence, Mary, that I feel that I am bad and low and shallow and mean, because you represent to me a sphere higher and holier than any in which I have ever moved, and stir up a sort of sighing and longing in my heart to come towards it. In all countries, in all temptations, Mary, your image has stood between me and low, gross vice. When I have been with fellows roaring drunken, beastly songs,—suddenly I have seemed to see you as you used to sit beside me in the singing-school, and your voice has been like an angel's in my ear, and I have got up and gone out sick and disgusted. Your face has risen up calm and white and still, between the faces of poor lost creatures who know no better way of life than to tempt us to sin. And sometimes, Mary, when I have seen girls that, had they been cared for by good pious mothers, might have been like you, I have felt as if I could cry for them. Poor women are abused all the world over; and it's no wonder they turn round and revenge themselves on us.

"No, I have not been bad, Mary, as the world calls badness. I have been kept by you. But do you remember you told me once, that, when the snow first fell and lay so dazzling and pure and soft, all about, you always felt as if the spreads and window-curtains that seemed white before were not clean? Well, it's just like that with me. Your presence makes me feel that I am not pure,—that I am low and unworthy,—not worthy to touch the hem of your garment. Your good Dr. Hopkins spent a whole half-day, the other Sunday, trying to tell us about the beauty of holiness; and he cut, and pared, and peeled, and sliced, and told us what it wasn't, and what was *like* it, and wasn't; and then he built up an exact definition, and fortified and bricked it up all round; and I thought to myself that he'd better tell 'em to look at Mary Scudder, and they'd understand all about it. That was what I was thinking when you talked to me for looking at you in church instead of looking towards the pulpit. It really made me laugh in myself to see what a good little ignorant, unconscious way you had of looking up at the Doctor, as if he knew more about that than you did.

"And now as to your Doctor that you think so much of, I like him for certain things, in certain ways. He is a great, grand, large pattern of a man,—a man who isn't afraid to think, and to speak anything he does think; but then I do believe, if he would take a voyage round the world in the forecastle of a whaler, he would know more about what to say to people than he does now; it would certainly give him several new points to be considered. Much of his preaching about men is as like live men as Chinese pictures of trees and rocks and gardens,—no nearer the reality than that. All I can say is, 'It isn't so; and you'd know it, Sir, if you knew men.' He has got what they call a *system*,—just so many bricks put together just so; but it is too narrow to take in all I see in my wanderings round this world of ours. Nobody that has a soul, and goes round the world as I do, can help feeling it at times, and thinking, as he sees all the races of men and their ways, who made them, and what they were made for. To doubt the existence of a God seems to me like a want of common sense. There is a Maker and a Ruler, doubtless; but then, Mary, all this invisible world of religion is unreal to me. I can see we must be good, somehow,—that if we are not, we shall not be happy here or hereafter. As to all the metaphysics of your good Doctor, you can't tell how they tire me. I'm not the sort of person that they can touch. I must have real things,— real people; abstractions are nothing to me. Then I think that he systematically contradicts on one Sunday what he preaches on another. One Sunday he tells us that God is the immediate efficient Author of every act of will; the next he tells us that we are entire free agents. I see no sense in it, and can't take the trouble to put it together. But then he and you have something in you that I call religion,—something that makes you *good*. When I see a man working away on an entirely honest, unworldly, disinterested pattern, as he does, and when I see you, Mary, as I said before, I should like at least to *be* as you are, whether I can believe as you do or not.

"How could you so care for me, and waste on one so unworthy of you such love? Oh, Mary, some better man must win you; I never shall and never can; but then you must not quite forget me; you must be my friend, my saint. If, through your prayers, your Bible, your friendship, you can bring me to your state, I am willing to be brought there,—nay, desirous. God has put the key of my soul into your hands.

"So, dear Mary, good-by! Pray still for your naughty, loving

"COUSIN JAMES."

Mary read this letter and re-read it, with more pain than pleasure. To feel the immortality of a beloved soul hanging upon us, to feel that its only communications with Heaven must be through us, is the most solemn and touching thought that can pervade a mind. It was without one particle of gratified vanity, with even a throb of pain, that she read such exalted praises of herself from one blind to the glories of a far higher loveliness.

Yet was she at that moment, unknown to herself, one of the great company scattered through earth who are priests unto God,—ministering between the Divine One, who has unveiled himself unto them, and those who as yet stand in the outer courts of the great sanctuary of truth and holiness. Many a heart, wrung, pierced, bleeding with the sins and sorrows of earth, longing to depart, stands in this mournful and beautiful ministry, but stands unconscious of the glory of the work in which it waits and suffers. God's kings and priests are crowned with thorns, walking the earth with bleeding feet, and comprehending not the work they are performing.

Mary took from a drawer a small pocket-book, from which dropped a lock of black hair,—a glossy curl, which seemed to have a sort of wicked, wilful life in every shining ring, just as she had often seen it shake naughtily on the owner's head. She felt a strange tenderness towards the little wilful thing, and, as she leaned over it, made in her heart a thousand fond apologies for every fault and error.

She was standing thus when Mrs. Scudder entered the room to see if her daughter had yet retired.

"What are you doing there, Mary?" she said, as her eye fell on the letter. "What is it you are reading?"

Mary felt herself grow pale; it was the first time in her whole life that her mother had asked her a question that she was not from the heart ready to answer. Her loyalty to her only parent had gone on even-handed with that she gave to her God; she felt, somehow, that the revelations of that afternoon had opened a gulf between them, and the consciousness overpowered her.

Mrs. Scudder was astonished at her evident embarrassment, her trembling, and paleness. She was a woman of prompt, imperative temperament, and the slightest hesitation in rendering to her a full, outspoken confidence had never before occurred in their intercourse. Her child was the core of her heart, the apple of her eye; and intense love is always near neighbor to anger; there was, therefore, an involuntary flash from her eye and a heightening of her color, as she said,—"Mary, are you concealing anything from your mother?"

In that moment, Mary had grown calm again. The wonted serene, balanced nature had found its habitual poise, and she looked up innocently, though with tears in her large, blue eyes, and said,—

"No, mother,—I have nothing that I do not mean to tell you fully. This letter came from James Marvyn; he came here to see me this afternoon."

"Here?—when? I did not see him."

"After dinner. I was sitting here in the window, and suddenly he came up behind me through the orchard-path."

Mrs. Katy sat down with a flushed cheek and a discomposed air; but Mary seemed actually to bear her down by the candid clearness of the large, blue eye which she turned on her, as she stood perfectly collected, with her deadly pale face and a brilliant spot burning on each cheek.

"James came to say good-by. He complained that he had not had a chance to see me alone since he came home."

"And what should he want to see you alone for?" said Mrs. Scudder, in a dry, disturbed tone.

"Mother,—everybody has things at times which they would like to say to some one person alone," said Mary.

"Well, tell me what he said."

"I will try. In the first place, he said that he always had been free, all his life, to run in and out of our house, and to wait on me like a brother."

"Hum!" said Mrs. Scudder; "but he isn't your brother, for all that."

"Well, then, he wanted to know why you were so cold to him, and why you never let him walk with me from meetings or see me alone, as he often used to. And I told him why,— that we were not children now, and that you thought it was not best; and then I talked with him about religion, and tried to persuade him to attend to the concerns of his soul, and I never felt so much hope for him as I do now."

Aunt Katy looked skeptical, and remarked,—"If he really felt a disposition for religious instruction, Dr. Hopkins could guide him much better than you could."

"Yes,—so I told him, and I tried to persuade him to talk with Dr. Hopkins; but he was very unwilling. He said, I could have more influence over him than anybody else,—that nobody could do him any good but me."

"Yes, yes,—I understand all that," said Aunt Katy,—"I have heard young men say *that* before, and I know just what it amounts to."

"But, mother, I do think James was moved very much, this afternoon. I never heard him speak so seriously; he seemed really in earnest, and he asked me to give him my Bible."

"Couldn't he read any Bible but yours?"

"Why, naturally, you know, mother, he would like my Bible better, because it would put him in mind of me. He promised faithfully to read it all through."

"And then, it seems, he wrote you a letter."

"Yes, mother."

Mary shrank from showing this letter, from the natural sense of honor which makes us feel it indelicate to expose to an unsympathizing eye the confidential outpourings of another heart; and then she felt quite sure that there was no such intercessor for James in her mother's heart as in her own. But over all this reluctance rose the determined force of duty; and she handed the letter in silence to her mother.

Mrs. Scudder took it, laid it deliberately in her lap, and then began searching in the pocket of her chintz petticoat for her spectacles. These being found, she wiped them, accurately adjusted them, opened the letter and spread it on her lap, brushing out its folds and straightening it, that she might read with the greater ease. After this she read it carefully and deliberately; and all this while there was such a stillness, that the sound of the tall varnished clock in the best room could be heard through the half-opened door.

After reading it with the most tiresome, torturing slowness, she rose, and laying it on the table under Mary's eye, and pressing down her finger on two lines in the letter, said, "Mary, have you told James that you loved him?"

"Yes, mother, always. I always loved him, and he always knew it."

"But, Mary, this that he speaks of is something different. What has passed between——"

"Why, mother, he was saying that we who were Christians drew to ourselves and did not care for the salvation of our friends; and then I told him how I had always prayed for him, and how I should be willing even to give up my hopes in heaven, if he might be saved."

"Child,—what do you mean?"

"I mean, if only one of us two could go to heaven, I had rather it should be him than me," said Mary.

"Oh, child! child!" said Mrs. Scudder, with a sort of groan,—"has it gone with you so far as this? Poor child!—after all my care, you *are* in love with this boy,—your heart is set on him."

"Mother, I am not. I never expect to see him much,—never expect to marry him or anybody else;—only he seems to me to have so much more life and soul and spirit than most people,—I think him so noble and grand,—that is, that he *could* be if he were all he ought to be,—that, somehow, I never think of myself in thinking of him, and his salvation seems worth more than mine;—men can do so much more!—they can live such splendid lives!—oh, a real noble man is so glorious!"

"And you would like to see him well married, would you not?" said Mrs. Scudder, sending, with a true woman's aim, this keen arrow into the midst of the cloud of enthusiasm which enveloped her daughter. "I think," she added, "that Jane Spencer would make him an excellent wife."

Mary was astonished at a strange, new pain that shot through her at these words. She drew in her breath and turned herself uneasily, as one who had literally felt a keen dividing blade piercing between soul and spirit. Till this moment, she had never been conscious of herself; but the shaft had torn the veil. She covered her face with her hands; the hot blood flushed scarlet over neck and brow; at last, with a beseeching look, she threw herself into her mother's arms.

"Oh, mother, mother, I am selfish, after all!"

Mrs. Scudder folded her silently to her heart, and said, "My daughter, this is not at all what I wished it to be; I see how it is;—but then you have been a good child; I don't blame you. We can't always help ourselves. We don't always really know how we do feel. I didn't know, for a long while, that I loved your father. I thought I was only curious about him, because he had a strange way of treating me, different from other men; but, one day, I remember, Julian Simons told me that it was reported that his mother was making a match for him with Susan Emery, and I was astonished to find how I felt. I saw him that evening, and the moment he looked at me I saw it wasn't true; all at once I knew something I never knew before,—and that was, that I should be very unhappy if he loved any one else better than me. But then, my child, your father was a different man from James;—he was as much better than I was as you are than James. I was a foolish, thoughtless young thing then. I never should have been any thing at all, but for him. Somehow, when I loved him, I grew more serious, and then he always guided and led me. Mary, your father was a wonderful man; he was one of the sort that the world knows not of;—sometime I must show you his letters. I always hoped, my daughter, that you would marry such a man."

"Don't speak of marrying, mother. I never shall marry."

"You certainly should not, unless you can marry in the Lord. Remember the words, 'Be ye not unequally yoked together with unbelievers. For what fellowship hath righteousness with unrighteousness? and what communion hath light with darkness? and what concord hath Christ with Belial? or what part hath he that believeth with an infidel?' "

"Mother, James is not an infidel."

"He certainly is an *unbeliever*, Mary, by his own confession;—but then God is a Sovereign and hath mercy on whom he will. You do right to pray for him; but if he does not come out on the Lord's side, you must not let your heart mislead you. He is going to be gone three years, and you must try to think as little of him as possible;—put your mind upon your duties, like a good girl, and God will bless you. Don't believe too much in your power over him;—young men, when they are in love, will promise anything, and really think they mean it; but nothing is a saving change, except what is wrought in them by sovereign grace."

"But, mother, does not God use the love we have to each other as a means of doing us good? Did you not say that it was by your love to father that you first were led to think seriously?"

"That is true, my child," said Mrs. Scudder, who, like many of the rest of the world, was surprised to meet her own words walking out on a track where she had not expected them, but was yet too true of soul to cut their acquaintance because they were not going the way of her wishes. "Yes, all that is true; but yet, Mary, when one has but one little ewe lamb in the world, one is jealous of it. I would give all the world, if you had never seen James. It is dreadful enough for a woman to love anybody as you can, but it is more to love a man of unsettled character and no religion. But then the Lord appoints all our goings; it is not in man that walketh to direct his steps;—I leave you, my child, in His hands." And, with one solemn and long embrace, the mother and daughter parted for the night.

It is impossible to write a story of New England life and manners for a thoughtless, shallow-minded person. If we represent things as they are, their intensity, their depth, their unworldly gravity and earnestness, must inevitably repel lighter spirits, as the reverse pole of the magnet drives off sticks and straws.

In no other country were the soul and the spiritual life ever such intense realities, and everything contemplated so much (to use a current New England phrase) "in reference to eternity." Mrs. Scudder was a strong, clear-headed, practical woman. No one had a clearer estimate of the material and outward life, or could more minutely manage its smallest item; but then a tremendous, eternal future had so weighed down and compacted the fibres of her very soul, that all earthly things were but as dust in comparison to it. That her child should be one elected to walk in white, to reign with Christ when earth was a forgotten dream, was her one absorbing wish; and she looked on all the events of life only with reference to this. The way of life was narrow, the chances in favor of any child of Adam infinitely small; the best, the most seemingly pure and fair, was by nature a child of wrath, and could be saved only by a sovereign decree, by which it should be plucked as a brand from the burning. Therefore it was, that, weighing all things in one balance, there was the sincerity of her whole being in the dread which she felt at the thought of her daughter's marriage with an unbeliever.

Mrs. Scudder, after retiring to her room, took her Bible, in preparation for her habitual nightly exercise of devotion, before going to rest. She read and re-read a chapter, scarce thinking what she was reading,—aroused herself,—and then sat with the book in her hand in deep thought. James Marvyn was her cousin's son, and she had a strong feeling of respect and family attachment for his father. She had, too, a real kindness for the young man, whom she regarded as a well-meaning, wilful youngster; but that *he* should touch her saint, her Mary, that *he* should take from her the daughter who was her all, really embittered her heart towards him.

"After all," she said to herself, "there are three years,— three years in which there will be no letters, or perhaps only one or two,—and a great deal may be done in three years, if one is wise";—and she felt within herself an arousing of all the shrewd womanly and motherly tact of her nature to meet this new emergency.

VI.

The Doctor

I T is seldom that man and woman come together in intimate association, unless influences are at work more subtile and mysterious than the subjects of them dream. Even in cases where the strongest ruling force of the two sexes seems out of the question, there is still something peculiar and insidious in their relationship. A fatherly old gentleman, who undertakes the care of a sprightly young girl, finds, to his astonishment, that little Miss spins all sorts of cobwebs round him. Grave professors and teachers cannot give lessons to their female pupils just as they give them to the coarser sex, and more than once has the fable of "Cadenus and Vanessa" been acted over by the most unlikely performers.

The Doctor was a philosopher, a metaphysician, a philanthropist, and in the highest and most earnest sense a minister of good on earth. The New England clergy had no sentimental affectation of sanctity that segregated them from wholesome human relations; and consequently our good Doctor had always resolved, in a grave and thoughtful spirit, at a suitable time in his worldly affairs, to choose unto himself a helpmeet. Love, as treated of in romances, he held to be a foolish and profane matter, unworthy the attention of a serious and reasonable creature. All the language of poetry on this subject was to him an unknown tongue. He contemplated the entrance on married life somewhat in this wise: — That at a time and place suiting, he should look out unto himself a woman of a pleasant countenance and of good repute, a zealous, earnest Christian, and well skilled in the items of household management, whom, accosting as a stranger and pilgrim to a better life, he should loyally and lovingly entreat, as Isaac did Rebekah, to come under the shadow of his tent and be a helpmeet unto him in what yet remained of this mortal journey. But straitened circumstances, and the unsettled times of the Revolution, in which he had taken an earnest

and zealous part, had delayed to a late bachelorhood the ful-
filment of this resolution.

When once received under the shadow of Mrs. Scudder's
roof, and within the provident sphere of her unfailing housekeeping, all material necessity for an immediate choice was
taken away; for he was exactly in that situation dearest to
every scholarly and thoughtful man, in which all that per-
tained to the outward life appeared to rise under his hand at
the moment he wished for it, without his knowing how or
why.

He was not at the head of a prosperous church and society,
rich and well-to-do in the world,—but, as the pioneer leader
of a new theology, in a country where theology was the all-
absorbing interest, he had to breast the reaction that ever attends the advent of new ideas. His pulpit talents, too, were
unattractive. His early training had been all logical, not in the
least æsthetic; for, like the ministry of his country generally,
he had been trained always to think more of what he should
say than of how he should say it. Consequently, his style,
though not without a certain massive greatness, which always
comes from largeness of nature, had none of those attractions
by which the common masses are beguiled into thinking. He
gave only the results of thought, not its incipient processes;
and the consequence was, that few could follow him. In like
manner, his religious teachings were characterized by an ideality so high as quite to discourage ordinary virtue.

There is a ladder to heaven, whose base God has placed in
human affections, tender instincts, symbolic feelings, sacraments of love, through which the soul rises higher and
higher, refining as she goes, till she outgrows the human, and
changes, as she rises, into the image of the divine. At the very
top of this ladder, at the threshold of paradise, blazes dazzling
and crystalline that celestial grade where the soul knows self
no more, having learned, through a long experience of devotion, how blest it is to lose herself in that eternal Love and
Beauty of which all earthly fairness and grandeur are but the
dim type, the distant shadow. This highest step, this saintly
elevation, which but few selectest spirits ever on earth attain,
to raise the soul to which the Eternal Father organized every
relation of human existence and strung every cord of human

love, for which this world is one long discipline, for which the soul's human education is constantly varied, for which it is now torn by sorrow, now flooded by joy, to which all its multiplied powers tend with upward hands of dumb and ignorant aspiration,—this Ultima Thule of virtue had been seized upon by our sage as the *all* of religion. He knocked out every round of the ladder but the highest, and then, pointing to its hopeless splendor, said to the world, "Go up thither and be saved!"

Short of that absolute self-abnegation, that unconditional surrender to the Infinite, there was nothing meritorious,—because, if *that* were commanded, every moment of refusal was rebellion. Every prayer, not based on such consecration, he held to be an insult to the Divine Majesty;—the reading of the Word, the conscientious conduct of life, the performance of the duties of man to man, being, without this, the deeds of a creature in conscious rebellion to its Eternal Sovereign, were all vitiated and made void. Nothing was to be preached to the sinner, but his ability and obligation to rise immediately to this height.

It is not wonderful that teaching of this sort should seem to many unendurable, and that the multitude should desert the preacher with the cry, "This is an hard saying; who can hear it?" The young and gay were wearied by the dryness of metaphysical discussions which to them were as unintelligible as a statement of the last results of the mathematician to the child commencing the multiplication table. There remained around him only a select circle,—shrewd, hard thinkers, who delighted in metaphysical subtilties,—deep-hearted, devoted natures, who sympathized with the unworldly purity of his life, his active philanthropy and untiring benevolence,—courageous men, who admired his independence of thought and freedom in breasting received opinion,—and those unperceiving, dull, good people who are content to go to church anywhere as convenience and circumstance may drift them,—people who serve, among the keen feeling and thinking portion of the world, much the same purpose as adipose matter in the human system, as a soft cushion between the nerves of feeling and the muscles of activity.

There was something affecting in the pertinacity with

which the good Doctor persevered in saying his say to his discouraging minority of hearers. His salary was small; his meeting-house, damaged during the Revolutionary struggle, was dilapidated and forlorn,—fireless in winter, and in summer admitting a flood of sun and dust through those great windows which formed so principal a feature in those first efforts of Puritan architecture.

Still, grand in his humility, he preached on,—and as a soldier never asks why, but stands at apparently the most useless post, so he went on from Sunday to Sunday, comforting himself with the reflection that no one could think more meanly of his ministrations than he did himself. "I am like Moses only in not being eloquent," he said, in his simplicity. "My preaching is barren and dull, my voice is hard and harsh; but then the Lord is a Sovereign, and may work through me. He fed Elijah once through a raven, and he may feed some poor wandering soul through me."

The only mistake made by the good man was that of supposing that the elaboration of theology was preaching the gospel. The gospel he was preaching constantly, by his pure, unworldly living, by his visitations to homes of poverty and sorrow, by his searching out of the lowly African slaves, his teaching of those whom no one else in those days had thought of teaching, and by the grand humanity, outrunning his age, in which he protested against the then admitted system of slavery and the slave-trade. But when, rising in the pulpit, he followed trains of thought suited only to the desk of the theological lecture-room, he did it blindly, following that law of self-development by which minds of a certain amount of fervor *must* utter what is in them, whether men will hear or whether they will forbear.

But the place where our Doctor was happiest was his study. There he explored, and wandered, and read, and thought, and lived a life as wholly ideal and intellectual as heart could conceive.

And could *Love* enter a reverend doctor's study, and find his way into a heart empty and swept of all those shreds of poetry and romance in which he usually finds the material of his incantations? Even so;—but he came so thoughtfully, so reverently, with so wise and cautious a footfall, that the good

Doctor never even raised his spectacles to see who was there. The first that he knew, poor man, he was breathing an air of strange and subtile sweetness,—from what paradise he never stopped his studies to inquire. He was like a great, rugged elm, with all its lacings and archings of boughs and twigs, which has stood cold and frozen against the metallic blue of winter sky, forgetful of leaves, and patient in its bareness, calmly content in its naked strength and crystalline definiteness of outline. But in April there is a rising and stirring within the grand old monster,—a whispering of knotted buds, a mounting of sap coursing ethereally from bough to bough with a warm and gentle life; and though the old elm knows it not, a new creation is at hand. Just so, ever since the good man had lived at Mrs. Scudder's, and had the gentle Mary for his catechumen, a richer life seemed to have colored his thoughts,—his mind seemed to work with a pleasure as never before.

Whoever looked on the forehead of the good Doctor must have seen the squareness of ideality giving marked effect to its outline. As yet ideality had dealt only with the intellectual and invisible, leading to subtile refinements of argument and exalted ideas of morals. But there was lying in him, crude and unworked, a whole mine of those artistic feelings and perceptions which are awakened and developed only by the touch of beauty. Had he been born beneath the shadow of the great Duomo of Florence, where Giotto's Campanile rises like the slender stalk of a celestial lily, where varied marbles and rainbow-glass and gorgeous paintings and lofty statuary call forth, even from childhood, the soul's reminiscences of the bygone glories of its pristine state, his would have been a soul as rounded and full in its sphere of faculties as that of Da Vinci or Michel Angelo. But of all that he was as ignorant as a child; and the first revelation of his dormant nature was to come to him through the face of woman,—that work of the Mighty Master which is to be found in all lands and ages.

What makes the love of a great mind something fearful in its inception is, that it is often the unsealing of a hitherto undeveloped portion of a large and powerful being; the woman may or may not seem to other eyes adequate to the effect produced, but the man cannot forget her, because with her came a change which makes him forever a different being. So it was with our friend. A woman it was that was destined to awaken in him all that consciousness which music, painting, poetry awaken in more evenly developed minds; and it is the silent breathing of her creative presence that is even now creating him anew, while as yet he knows it not.

He never thought, this good old soul, whether Mary were beautiful or not; he never even knew that he looked at her; nor did he know why it was that the truths of his theology, when uttered by her tongue, had such a wondrous beauty as he never felt before. He did not know why it was, that, when she silently sat by him, copying tangled manuscript for the press, as she sometimes did, his whole study seemed so full of some divine influence, as if, like St. Dorothea, she had worn in her bosom, invisibly, the celestial roses of paradise. He recorded honestly in his diary what marvellous freshness of spirit the Lord had given him, and how he seemed to be uplifted in his communings with heaven, without once thinking from the robes of what angel this sweetness had exhaled.

On Sundays, when he saw good Mrs. Jones asleep, and Simeon Brown's hard, sharp eyes, and Deacon Twitchel mournfully rocking to and fro, and his wife handing fennel to keep the children awake, his eye glanced across to the front gallery, where one earnest young face, ever kindling with feeling and bright with intellect, followed on his way, and he felt uplifted and comforted. On Sunday mornings, when Mary came out of her little room, in clean white dress, with her singing-book and psalm-book in her hands, her deep eyes solemn from recent prayer, he thought of that fair and mystical bride, the Lamb's wife, whose union with her Divine Redeemer in a future millennial age was a frequent and favorite subject of his musings; yet he knew not that this celestial bride, clothed in fine linen, clean and white, veiled in humility and meekness, bore in his mind those earthly features. No, he never had dreamed of that! But only after she had passed by, that mystical vision seemed to him more radiant, more easy to be conceived.

It is said, that, if a grape-vine be planted in the neighborhood of a well, its roots, running silently underground, wreathe themselves in a network around the cold, clear wa-

ters, and the vine's putting on outward greenness and unwonted clusters and fruit is all that tells where every root and
fibre of its being has been silently stealing. So those loves are
most fatal, most absorbing, in which, with unheeded quietness, every thought and fibre of our life twines gradually
around some human soul, to us the unsuspected wellspring
of our being. Fearful it is, because so often the vine must be
uprooted, and all its fibres wrenched away; but till the hour
of discovery comes, how is it transfigured by a new and beautiful life!

There is nothing in life more beautiful than that trance-like
quiet dawn which precedes the rising of love in the soul.
When the whole being is pervaded imperceptibly and tranquilly by another being, and we are happy, we know not and
ask not why, the soul is then receiving all and asking nothing.
At a later day she becomes self-conscious, and then come
craving exactions, endless questions,—the whole world of the
material comes in with its hard counsels and consultations,
and the beautiful trance fades forever.

Of course, all this is not so to *you*, my good friends, who
read it without the most distant idea what it can mean; but
there are people in the world to whom it has meant and will
mean much, and who will see in the present happiness of our
respectable friend something even ominous and sorrowful.

It had not escaped the keen eye of the mother how quickly
and innocently the good Doctor was absorbed by her daughter, and thereupon had come long trains of practical reflections.

The Doctor, though not popular indeed as a preacher, was
a noted man in his age. Her deceased husband had regarded
him with something of the same veneration which might have
been accorded to a divine messenger, and Mrs. Scudder had
received and kept this veneration as a precious legacy. Then,
although not handsome, the Doctor had decidedly a grand
and imposing appearance. There was nothing common or insignificant about him. Indeed, it had been said, that, when,
just after the declaration of peace, he walked through the
town in the commemorative procession side by side with
General Washington, the minister, in the majesty of his gown,

bands, cocked hat, and full flowing wig, was thought by many to be the more majestic and personable figure of the two.

In those days, the minister united in himself all those ideas of superior position and cultivation with which the theocratic system of the New England community had invested him. Mrs. Scudder's notions of social rank could reach no higher than to place her daughter on the throne of such preeminence.

Her Mary, she pondered, was no common girl. In those days, it was a rare thing for young persons to devote themselves to religion or make any professions of devout life. The church, or that body of people who professed to have passed through a divine regeneration, was almost entirely confined to middle-aged and elderly people, and it was looked upon as a singular and unwonted call of divine grace when young persons came forward to attach themselves to it. When Mary, therefore, at quite an early age, in all the bloom of her youthful beauty, arose, according to the simple and impressive New England rite, to consecrate herself publicly to a religious life, and to join the company of professing Christians, she was regarded with a species of deference amounting even to awe. Had it not been for the childlike, unconscious simplicity of her manners, the young people of her age would have shrunk away from her, as from one entirely out of their line of thought and feeling; but a certain natural and innocent playfulness and amiable self-forgetfulness made her a general favorite.

Nevertheless, Mrs. Scudder knew no young man whom she deemed worthy to have and hold a heart which she prized so highly. As to James, he stood at double disadvantage, because, as her cousin's son, he had grown up from childhood under her eye, and all those sins and iniquities into which gay and adventurous youngsters will be falling had come to her knowledge. She felt kindly to the youth; she wished him well; but as to giving him her Mary!—the very suggestion made her dislike him. She was quite sure he must have tried to beguile her,—he must have tampered with her feelings, to arouse in her pure and well-ordered mind so much emotion and devotedness as she had witnessed.

How encouraging a Providence, then, was it that he was

gone to sea for three years!—how fortunate that Mary had been prevented in any way from committing herself with him!—how encouraging that the only man in those parts, in the least fitted to appreciate her, seemed so greatly pleased and absorbed in her society!—how easily might Mary's dutiful reverence be changed to a warmer sentiment, when she should find that so great a man could descend from his lofty thoughts to think of her!

In fact, before Mrs. Scudder had gone to sleep the first night after James's departure, she had settled upon the house where the minister and his young wife were to live, had reviewed the window-curtains and bed-quilts for each room, and glanced complacently at an improved receipt for wedding-cake which might be brought out to glorify a certain occasion!

VII.

The Friends and Relations of James

M R. ZEBEDEE MARVYN, the father of James, was the sample of an individuality so purely the result of New England society and education, that he must be embodied in our story as a representative man of the times.

He owned a large farm in the immediate vicinity of Newport, which he worked with his own hands and kept under the most careful cultivation. He was a man past the middle of life, with a white head, a keen blue eye, and a face graven deeply with the lines of energy and thought. His was one of those clearly-cut minds which New England forms among her farmers, as she forms quartz crystals in her mountains, by a sort of gradual influence flowing through every pore of her soil and system.

His education, properly so called, had been merely that of those common schools and academies with which the States are thickly sown, and which are the springs of so much intellectual activity. Here he had learned to think and to inquire,—a process which had not ceased with his schooldays. Though toiling daily with his sons and hired man in all the minutiæ of a farmer's life, he kept an observant eye on the field of literature, and there was not a new publication heard of which he did not immediately find means to add to his yearly increasing stock of books. In particular was he a well-read and careful theologian, and all the controversial tracts, sermons, and books, with which then, (as ever since,) New England abounded, not only lay on his shelves, but had his pencilled annotations, queries, and comments thickly scattered along their margins. There was scarce an office of public trust which had not at one time or another been filled by him. He was deacon of the church, chairman of the school-committee, justice of the peace, had been twice representative in the State legislature, and was in permanence a sort of adviser-general in all cases between neighbor and neighbor. Among other acquisitions, he had gained some knowledge of the general forms of law, and his advice was often asked in preference to that of the regular practitioners.

His dwelling was one of those large, square, white, green-blinded mansions, cool, clean, and roomy, wherein the respectability of New England in those days rejoiced. The windows were shaded by clumps of lilacs; the deep yard with its white fence inclosed a sweep of clean, short grass, and a few fruit-trees. Opposite the house was a small blacksmith's-shed, which, of a wet day, was sparkling and lively with bellows and ringing forge, while Mr. Zebedee and his sons were hammering and pounding and putting in order anything that was out of the way in farming-tools or establishments. Not unfrequently the latest scientific work or the last tractate of theology lay open by his side, the contents of which would be discussed with a neighbor or two as they entered; for, to say the truth, many a neighbor, less forehanded and thrifty, felt the benefit of this arrangement of Mr. Zebedee, and would drop in to see if he "wouldn't just tighten that rivet," or "kind o' ease out that 'ere brace," or "let a feller have a turn with his bellows, or a stroke or two on his anvil,"—to all which the good man consented with a grave obligingness. The fact was, that, as nothing in the establishment of Mr. Marvyn was often broken or lost or out of place, he had frequent applications to lend to those less fortunate persons, always to be found, who supply their own lack of considerateness from the abundance of their neighbors.

He who is known always to be in hand, and always obliging, in a neighborhood, stands the chance sometimes of having nothing for himself. Mr. Zebedee reflected quietly on this subject, taking it, as he did all others, into grave and orderly consideration, and finally provided a complete set of tools, which he kept for the purpose of lending; and when any of these were lent, he told the next applicant quietly, that the axe or the hoe was already out, and thus he reconciled the Scripture which commanded him "to do good and lend" with that law of order which was written in his nature.

Early in life Mr. Marvyn had married one of the handsomest girls of his acquaintance, who had brought him a thriving and healthy family of children, of whom James was the youngest. Mrs. Marvyn was, at this time, a tall, sad-eyed, gentle-mannered woman, thoughtful, earnest, deep-natured, though sparing in the matter of words. In all her household arrangements, she had the same thrift and order which characterized her husband; but hers was a mind of a finer and higher stamp than his.

In her bedroom, near by her work-basket, stood a table covered with books,—and so systematic were her household arrangements, that she never any day missed her regular hours for reading. One who should have looked over this table would have seen there how eager and hungry a mind was hid behind the silent eyes of this quiet woman. History, biography, mathematics, volumes of the encyclopædia, poetry, novels, all alike found their time and place there,—and while she pursued her household labors, the busy, active soul within travelled cycles and cycles of thought, few of which ever found expression in words. What might be that marvellous music of the *Miserere*, of which she read, that it convulsed crowds and drew groans and tears from the most obdurate? What might be those wondrous pictures of Raphael and Leonardo da Vinci? What would it be to see the Apollo, the Venus? What was the charm that enchanted the old marbles,—charm untold and inconceivable to one who had never seen even the slightest approach to a work of art? Then those glaciers of Switzerland, that grand, unapproachable mixture of beauty and sublimity in her mountains!—what would it be to one who could see it? Then what were all those harmonies of which she read,—masses, fugues, symphonies? Oh, could she once hear the Miserere of Mozart, just to know what music was like! And the cathedrals, what were they? How wonderful they must be, with their forests of arches, many-colored as autumn-woods with painted glass, and the chants and anthems rolling down their long aisles! On all these things she pondered quietly, as she sat often on Sundays in the old staring, rattle-windowed meeting-house, and looked at the uncouth old pulpit, and heard the choir faw-sol-la-ing or singing fuguing tunes; but of all this she said nothing.

Sometimes, for days, her thoughts would turn from these subjects and be absorbed in mathematical or metaphysical studies. "I have been following that treatise on Optics for a week, and never understood it till to-day," she once said to her husband. "I have found now that there has been a mistake in drawing the diagrams. I have corrected it, and now the demonstration is complete. Dinah, take care, that wood is hickory, and it takes only seven sticks of that size to heat the oven."

It is not to be supposed that a woman of this sort was an inattentive listener to preaching so stimulating to the intellect as that of Dr. Hopkins. No pair of eyes followed the web of his reasonings with a keener and more anxious watchfulness than those sad, deep-set, hazel ones; and as she was drawn along the train of its inevitable logic, a close observer might have seen how the shadows deepened over them. For, while others listened for the clearness of the thought, for the acuteness of the argument, she listened as a soul wide, fine-strung, acute, repressed, whose every fibre is a nerve, listens to the problem of its own destiny,—listened as the mother of a family listens, to know what were the possibilities, the probabilities, of this mysterious existence of ours to herself and those dearer to her than herself.

The consequence of all her listening was a history of deep inward sadness. That exultant joy, or that entire submission, with which others seemed to view the scheme of the universe, as thus unfolded, did not visit her mind. Everything to her seemed shrouded in gloom and mystery; and that darkness she received as a token of unregeneracy, as a sign that she was one of those who are destined, by a mysterious decree, never to receive the light of the glorious gospel of Christ. Hence, while her husband was a deacon of the church, she, for years, had sat in her pew while the sacramental elements were distributed, a mournful spectator. Punctilious in every duty, exact, reverential, she still regarded herself as a child of wrath, an enemy to God, and an heir of perdition; nor could she see any hope of remedy, except in the sovereign, mysterious decree of an Infinite and Unknown Power, a mercy for which she waited with the sickness of hope deferred.

Her children had grown up successively around her, intelligent and exemplary. Her eldest son was mathematical professor in one of the leading colleges of New England. Her second son, who jointly with his father superintended the farm, was a man of wide literary culture and of fine mathematical genius; and not unfrequently, on winter evenings, the son, father, and mother worked together, by their kitchen fireside, over the calculations for the almanac for the ensuing year, which the son had been appointed to edit.

Everything in the family arrangements was marked by a sober precision, a grave and quiet self-possession. There was little demonstrativeness of affection between parents and children, brothers and sisters, though great mutual love and confidence. It was not pride, nor sternness, but a sort of habitual shamefacedness, that kept far back in each soul those feelings which are the most beautiful in their outcome; but after a while, the habit became so fixed a nature, that a caressing or affectionate expression could not have passed the lips of one to another without a painful awkwardness. Love was understood, once for all, to be the basis on which their life was built. Once for all, they loved each other, and after that, the less said, the better. It had cost the woman's heart of Mrs. Marvyn some pangs, in the earlier part of her wedlock, to accept of this *once for all* in place of those daily outgushings which every woman desires should be like God's loving-kindnesses, "new every morning;" but hers, too, was a nature strongly inclining inward, and, after a few tremulous movements, the needle of her soul settled, and her life-lot was accepted,—not as what she would like or could conceive, but as a reasonable and good one. Life was a picture painted in low, cool tones, but in perfect keeping; and though another and brighter style might have pleased better, she did not quarrel with this.

Into this steady, decorous, highly-respectable circle the youngest child, James, made a formidable irruption. One sometimes sees launched into a family-circle a child of so different a nature from all the rest, that it might seem as if, like an aërolite, he had fallen out of another sphere. All the other babies of the Marvyn family had been of that orderly, contented sort, who sleep till it is convenient to take them up, and while awake suck their thumbs contentedly and look up with large, round eyes at the ceiling when it is not convenient for their elders and betters that they should do anything else.

In farther advanced childhood, they had been quiet and decorous children, who could be all dressed and set up in chairs,
like so many dolls, of a Sunday morning, patiently awaiting
the stroke of the church-bell to be carried out and put into
the wagon which took them over the two-miles' road to
church. Possessed of such tranquil, orderly, and exemplary
young offshoots, Mrs. Marvyn had been considered eminent
for her "faculty" in bringing up children.

But James was destined to put "faculty," and every other
talent which his mother possessed, to rout. He was an infant
of moods and tenses, and those not of any regular verb. He
would cry of nights, and he would be taken up of mornings,
and he would not suck his thumb, nor a bundle of caraway-
seed tied in a rag and dipped in sweet milk, with which the
good gossips in vain endeavored to pacify him. He fought
manfully with his two great fat fists the battle of babyhood,
utterly reversed all nursery maxims, and reigned as baby over
the whole prostrate household. When old enough to run
alone, his splendid black eyes and glossy rings of hair were
seen flashing and bobbing in every forbidden place and occupation. Now trailing on his mother's gown, he assisted her
in salting her butter by throwing in small contributions of
snuff or sugar, as the case might be; and again, after one of
those mysterious periods of silence which are of most ominous significance in nursery experience, he would rise from
the demolition of her indigo-bag, showing a face ghastly with
blue streaks, and looking more like a gnome than the son of
a respectable mother. There was not a pitcher of any description of contents left within reach of his little tiptoes and busy
fingers that was not pulled over upon his giddy head without
in the least seeming to improve its steadiness. In short, his
mother remarked that she was thankful every night when she
had fairly gotten him into bed and asleep; James had really
got through one more day and killed neither himself nor any
one else.

As a boy, the case was little better. He did not take to
study,—yawned over books, and cut out moulds for running
anchors when he should have been thinking of his columns
of words in four syllables. No mortal knew how he learned to

read, for he never seemed to stop running long enough to learn anything; and yet he did learn, and used the talent in conning over travels, sea-voyages, and lives of heroes and naval commanders. Spite of father, mother, and brother, he seemed to possess the most extraordinary faculty of running up unsavory acquaintances. He was hale-fellow well-met with every Tom and Jack and Jim and Ben and Dick that strolled on the wharves, and astonished his father with minutest particulars of every ship, schooner, and brig in the harbor, together with biographical notes of the different Toms, Dicks, and Harrys by whom they were worked.

There was but one member of the family that seemed to know at all what to make of James, and that was their negro servant, Candace.

In those days, when domestic slavery prevailed in New England, it was quite a different thing in its aspects from the same institution in more southern latitudes. The hard soil, unyielding to any but the most considerate culture, the thrifty, close, shrewd habits of the people, and their untiring activity and industry, prevented, among the mass of the people, any great reliance on slave labor.

Added to this, there were from the very first, in New England, serious doubts in the minds of thoughtful and conscientious people in reference to the lawfulness of slavery; this scruple prevented many from availing themselves of it, and proved a restraint on all, so that nothing like plantation-life existed, and what servants were owned were scattered among different families, of which they came to be regarded and to regard themselves as a legitimate part and portion. Slavery was something foreign, grotesque, and picturesque in a life of the most matter-of-fact sameness; it was even as if one should see clusters of palm-trees scattered here and there among Yankee wooden meeting-houses, or open one's eyes on clumps of yellow-striped aloes growing among hardhack and huckleberry bushes in the pastures.

Mr. Marvyn, as a man of substance, numbered two or three in his establishment, among whom Candace reigned chief. The presence of these tropical specimens of humanity, with their wide, joyous, rich, physical abundance of nature, and their hearty *abandon* of outward expression, was a relief to the still clear-cut lines in which the picture of New England life was drawn, that an artist must appreciate.

No race has ever shown such infinite and rich capabilities of adaptation to varying soil and circumstances as the negro. Alike to them the snows of Canada, the hard, rocky land of New England, with its set lines and orderly ways, or the gorgeous profusion and loose abundance of the Southern States. Sambo and Cuffy expand under them all. New England yet preserves among her hills and valleys the lingering echoes of the jokes and jollities of various sable worthies, who saw alike in orthodoxy and heterodoxy, in Dr. This-side and Dr. That-side, only food for more abundant merriment;—in fact, the minister of those days not unfrequently had his black shadow, a sort of African Boswell, who powdered his wig, brushed his boots, defended and patronized his sermons, and strutted complacently about as if through virtue of his blackness he had absorbed every ray of his master's dignity and wisdom. In families, the presence of these exotics was a godsend to the children, supplying from the abundant outwardness and demonstrativeness of their nature that aliment of sympathy so dear to childhood, which the repressed and quiet habits of New England education denied. Many and many a New Englander counts among his pleasantest early recollections the memory of some of these genial creatures, who by their warmth of nature were the first and most potent mesmerizers of his childish mind.

Candace was a powerfully built, majestic black woman, corpulent, heavy, with a swinging majesty of motion like that of a ship in a ground-swell. Her shining black skin and glistening white teeth were indications of perfect physical vigor which had never known a day's sickness; her turban, of broad red and yellow bandanna stripes, had even a warm tropical glow; and her ample skirts were always ready to be spread over every childish transgression of her youngest pet and favorite, James.

She used to hold him entranced long winter-evenings, while she sat knitting in the chimney-corner, and crooned to him strange, wild African legends of the things that she had seen in her childhood and early days,—for she had been stolen when about fifteen years of age; and these weird, dreamy talks increased the fervor of his roving imagination, and his desire to explore the wonders of the wide and unknown world. When rebuked or chastised, it was she who had secret bowels of mercy for him, and hid doughnuts in her ample bosom to be secretly administered to him in mitigation of the sentence that sent him supperless to bed; and many a triangle of pie, many a wedge of cake, had conveyed to him surreptitious consolations which his more conscientious mother longed, but dared not, to impart. In fact, these ministrations, if suspected, were winked at by Mrs. Marvyn, for two reasons: first, that mothers are generally glad of any loving-kindness to an erring boy, which they are not responsible for; and second, that Candace was so set in her ways and opinions that one might as well come in front of a ship under full sail as endeavor to stop her in a matter where her heart was engaged.

To be sure, she had her own private and special quarrels with "Massa James" when he disputed any of her sovereign orders in the kitchen, and would sometimes pursue him with uplifted rolling-pin and floury hands when he had snatched a gingernut or cookey without suitable deference or supplication, and would declare, roundly, that there "never was sich an aggravatin' young un." But if, on the strength of this, any one else ventured a reproof, Candace was immediately round on the other side:—"Dat ar' chile gwin' to be spiled, 'cause dey's allers a-pickin' at him;—he's well enough, on'y let him alone."

Well, under this miscellaneous assortment of influences,— through the order and gravity and solemn monotone of life at home, with the unceasing tick-tack of the clock forever resounding through clean, empty-seeming rooms,—through the sea, ever shining, ever smiling, dimpling, soliciting, like a magical charger who comes saddled and bridled and offers to take you to fairyland,—through acquaintance with all sorts of foreign, outlandish ragamuffins among the ships in the harbor,—from disgust of slow-moving oxen, and long-drawn, endless furrows round the fifteen-acre lot,—from misunderstandings with grave elder brothers, and feeling somehow as if, he knew not why, he grieved his mother all the time just by being what he was and couldn't help being,—and, finally, by a bitter break with his father, in which came that last wrench for an individual existence which some time or other the young growing mind will give to old authority,—by all these united, was the lot at length cast; for one evening James was missing at supper, missing by the fireside, gone all night, not at home to breakfast,—till, finally, a strange, weird, most heathenish-looking cabin-boy, who had often been forbidden the premises by Mr. Marvyn, brought in a letter, half-defiant, half-penitent, which announced that James had sailed in the "Ariel" the evening before.

Mr. Zebedee Marvyn set his face as a flint, and said, "He went out from us because he was not of us,"—whereat old Candace lifted her great floury fist from the kneading-trough, and, shaking it like a large snowball, said, "Oh, you go 'long, Massa Marvyn; ye'll live to count dat ar' boy for de staff o' your old age yet, now I tell ye; got de makin' o' ten or'nary men in him; kittles dat's full allers will bile over; good yeast will blow out de cork,—lucky ef it don't bust de bottle. Tell ye, der's angels has der hooks in sich, and when de Lord wants him dey'll haul him in safe and sound." And Candace concluded her speech by giving a lift to her whole batch of dough and flinging it down in the trough with an emphasis that made the pewter on the dresser rattle.

This apparently irreverent way of expressing her mind, so contrary to the deferential habits studiously inculcated in family discipline, had grown to be so much a matter of course to all the family that nobody ever thought of rebuking it. There was a sort of savage freedom about her which they excused in right of her having been born and bred a heathen, and of course not to be expected to come at once under the yoke of civilization. In fact, you must all have noticed, my dear readers, that there are some sorts of people for whom everybody turns out as they would for a railroad-car, without stopping to ask why; and Candace was one of them.

Moreover, Mr. Marvyn was not displeased with this defence of James, as might be inferred from his mentioning it four or five times in the course of the morning, to say how foolish it was,—wondering why it was that Candace and everybody else got so infatuated with that boy,—and ending, at last, after a long period of thought, with the remark, that these poor African creatures often seemed to have a great deal of shrewdness in them, and that he was often astonished at the penetration that Candace showed.

At the end of the year James came home, more quiet and manly than he had ever been before,—so handsome with his sunburnt face, and his keen, dark eyes, and glossy curls, that half the girls in the front gallery lost their hearts the first Sunday he appeared in church. He was tender as a woman to his mother, and followed her with his eyes, like a lover, wherever she went; he made due and manly acknowledgments to his father, but declared his fixed and settled intention to abide by the profession he had chosen; and he brought home all sorts of strange foreign gifts for every member of the household. Candace was glorified with a flaming red and yellow turban of Moorish stuff, from Mogadore, together with a pair of gorgeous yellow morocco slippers with peaked toes, which, though there appeared no call to wear them in her common course of life, she would put on her fat feet and contemplate with daily satisfaction. She became increasingly strengthened thereby in the conviction that the angels who had their hooks in Massa James's jacket were already beginning to shorten the line.

VIII.

Which Treats of Romance

THERE is no word in the English language more uncere-moniously and indefinitely kicked and cuffed about, by what are called sensible people, than the word *romance*. When Mr. Smith or Mr. Stubbs has brought every wheel of life into such range and order that it is one steady, daily grind,—when they themselves have come into the habits and attitudes of the patient donkey, who steps round and round the end-lessly turning wheel of some machinery, then they fancy that they have gotten "the victory that overcometh the world."

All but this dead grind, and the dollars that come through the mill, is by them thrown into one waste "catch-all" and labelled *romance*. Perhaps there was a time in Mr. Smith's youth,—he remembers it now,—when he read poetry, when his cheek was wet with strange tears, when a little song, ground out by an organ-grinder in the street, had power to set his heart beating and bring a mist before his eyes. Ah, in those days he had a vision!—a pair of soft eyes stirred him strangely; a little weak hand was laid on his manhood, and it shook and trembled; and then came all the humility, the as-piration, the fear, the hope, the high desire, the troubling of the waters by the descending angel of love,—and a little more and Mr. Smith might have become a man, instead of a banker! He thinks of it now, sometimes, as he looks across the fireplace after dinner and sees Mrs. Smith asleep, inno-cently shaking the bouquet of pink bows and Brussels lace that waves over her placid red countenance.

Mrs. Smith wasn't his first love, nor, indeed, any love at all; but they agree reasonably well. And as for poor Nellie,—well, she is dead and buried,—all that was stuff and romance. Mrs. Smith's money set him up in business, and Mrs. Smith is a capital manager, and he thanks God that he isn't roman-tic, and tells Smith Junior not to read poetry or novels, and to stick to realities.

"This is the victory that overcometh the world,"—to learn to be fat and tranquil, to have warm fires and good dinners, to hang your hat on the same peg at the same hour every day, to sleep soundly all night, and never to trouble your head with a thought or imagining beyond.

But there are many people besides Mr. Smith who have gained this victory,—who have strangled their higher nature and buried it, and built over its grave the structure of their life, the better to keep it down.

The fascinating Mrs. T., whose life is a whirl between ball and opera, point-lace, diamonds, and schemings of admiration for herself, and of establishments for her daughters,—there was a time, if you will believe me, when that proud, worldly woman was so humbled, under the touch of some mighty power, that she actually thought herself capable of being a poor man's wife. She thought she could live in a little, mean house on no-matter-what-street, with one servant, and make her own bonnets and mend her own clothes, and sweep the house Mondays, while Betty washed,—all for what? All because she thought that there was a man so noble, so true, so good, so high-minded, that to live with him in poverty, to be guided by him in adversity, to lean on him in every rough place of life, was a something nobler, better, purer, more satisfying, than French laces, opera-boxes, and even Madame Roget's best gowns.

Unfortunately, this was all romance,—there was no such man. There was, indeed, a person of very common, self-interested aims and worldly nature, whom she had credited at sight with an unlimited draft on all her better nature; and when the hour of discovery came, she awoke from her dream with a start and a laugh, and ever since has despised aspiration, and been busy with the *realities* of life, and feeds poor little Mary Jane, who sits by her in the opera-box there, with all the fruit which she has picked from the bitter tree of knowledge. There is no end of the epigrams and witticisms which she can throw out, this elegant Mrs. T., on people who marry for love, lead prosy, worky lives, and put on their best cap with pink ribbons for Sunday. "Mary Jane shall never make a fool of herself;" but, even as she speaks, poor Mary Jane's heart is dying within her at the vanishing of a pair of whiskers from an opposite box,—which whiskers the poor little fool has credited with a *résumé* drawn from her own imaginings of all that is grandest and most heroic, most worshipful in man. By-and-by, when Mrs. T. finds the glamour has fallen on her daughter, she wonders; she has "tried to keep novels out of the girl's way,—where did she get these notions?"

All prosaic, and all bitter, disenchanted people talk as if poets and novelists *made* romance. They do,—just as much as craters make volcanoes,—no more. What is romance? whence comes it? Plato spoke to the subject wisely, in his quaint way, some two thousand years ago, when he said, "Man's soul, in a former state, was winged and soared among the gods; and so it comes to pass, that, in this life, when the soul, by the power of music or poetry, or the sight of beauty, hath her remembrance quickened, forthwith there is a struggling and a pricking pain as of wings trying to come forth,— even as children in teething." And if an old heathen, two thousand years ago, discoursed thus gravely of the romantic part of our nature, whence comes it that in Christian lands we think in so pagan a way of it, and turn the whole care of it to ballad-makers, romancers, and opera-singers?

Let us look up in fear and reverence and say, "GOD is the great maker of romance. HE, from whose hand came man and woman,—HE, who strung the great harp of Existence with all its wild and wonderful and manifold chords, and attuned them to one another,—HE is the great Poet of life." Every impulse of beauty, of heroism, and every craving for purer love, fairer perfection, nobler type and style of being than that which closes like a prison-house around us, in the dim, daily walk of life, is God's breath, God's impulse, God's reminder to the soul that there is something higher, sweeter, purer, yet to be attained.

Therefore, man or woman, when thy ideal is shattered,— as shattered a thousand times it must be,—when the vision fades, the rapture burns out, turn not away in skepticism and bitterness, saying, "There is nothing better for a man than that he should eat and drink," but rather cherish the revelations of those hours as prophecies and foreshadowings of something real and possible, yet to be attained in the man-

hood of immortality. The scoffing spirit that laughs at romance is an apple of the Devil's own handing from the bitter
tree of knowledge;—it opens the eyes only to see eternal nakedness.

If ever you have had a romantic, uncalculating friendship,
—a boundless worship and belief in some hero of your
soul,—if ever you have so loved, that all cold prudence, all
selfish worldly considerations have gone down like drift-wood
before a river flooded with new rain from heaven, so that you
even forgot yourself, and were ready to cast your whole being
into the chasm of existence, as an offering before the feet of
another, and all for nothing,—if you awoke bitterly betrayed
and deceived, still give thanks to God that you have had one
glimpse of heaven. The door now shut will open again. Rejoice that the noblest capability of your eternal inheritance has
been made known to you; treasure it, as the highest honor of
your being, that ever you could so feel,—that so divine a
guest ever possessed your soul.

By such experiences are we taught the pathos, the sacredness of life; and if we use them wisely, our eyes will ever after
be anointed to see what poems, what romances, what sublime
tragedies lie around us in the daily walk of life, "written not
with ink, but in fleshy tables of the heart." The dullest street
of the most prosaic town has matter in it for more smiles,
more tears, more intense excitement, than ever were written
in story or sung in poem; the reality is there, of which the
romancer is the second-hand recorder.

So much of a plea we put in boldly, because we foresee
grave heads beginning to shake over our history, and doubts
rising in reverend and discreet minds whether this history is
going to prove anything but a love-story, after all.

We do assure you, right reverend Sir, and you, most discreet Madam, that it is not going to prove anything else; and
you will find, if you will follow us, that there is as much romance burning under the snow-banks of cold Puritan precise-
ness as if Dr. Hopkins had been brought up to attend operas
instead of metaphysical preaching, and Mary had been nourished on Byron's poetry instead of "Edwards on the Affections."

The innocent credulities, the subtle deceptions, that were quietly at work under the grave, white curls of the Doctor's wig, were exactly of the kind which have beguiled man in all ages, when near the sovereign presence of her who is born for his destiny;—and as for Mary, what did it avail her that she could say the Assembly's Catechism from end to end without tripping, and that every habit of her life beat time to practical realities, steadily as the parlor clock? The wildest Italian singer or dancer, nursed on nothing but excitement from her cradle, never was more thoroughly possessed by the awful and solemn mystery of woman's life than this Puritan girl.

It is quite true, that, the next morning after James's departure, she rose as usual in the dim gray, and was to be seen opening the kitchen-door just at the moment when the birds were giving the first little drowsy stir and chirp,—and that she went on setting the breakfast-table for the two hired men, who were bound to the fields with the oxen,—and that then she went on skimming cream for the butter, and getting ready to churn, and making up biscuit for the Doctor's breakfast, when he and they should sit down together at a somewhat later hour; and as she moved about, doing all these things, she sung various scraps of old psalm-tunes; and the good Doctor, who was then busy with his early exercises of devotion, listened, as he heard the voice, now here, now there, and thought about angels and the Millennium. Solemnly and tenderly there floated in at his open study-window, through the breezy lilacs, mixed with low of kine and bleat of sheep and hum of early wakening life, the little silvery ripples of that singing, somewhat mournful in its cadence, as if a gentle soul were striving to hush itself to rest. The words were those of the rough old version of the Psalms then in use:—

> "Truly my waiting soul relies
>   In silence God upon;
> Because from him there doth arise
>   All my salvation."

And then came the busy patter of the little footsteps without, the moving of chairs, the clink of plates, as busy hands were arranging the table; and then again there was a pause, and he thought she seemed to come near to the open window of the adjoining room, for the voice floated in clearer and sadder:—

> "O God, to me be merciful,
>   Be merciful to me!
>   Because my soul for shelter safe
>   Betakes itself to thee.
>
> "Yea, in the shadow of thy wings
>   My refuge have I placed,
>   Until these sore calamities
>   Shall quite be overpast."

The tone of life in New England, so habitually earnest and solemn, breathed itself in the grave and plaintive melodies of the tunes then sung in the churches; and so these words, though in the saddest minor key, did not suggest to the listening ear of the auditor anything more than that pensive religious calm in which he delighted to repose. A contrast indeed they were, in their melancholy earnestness, to the exuberant carollings of a robin, who, apparently attracted by them, perched himself hard by in the lilacs, and struck up such a merry *roulade* as quite diverted the attention of the fair singer;—in fact, the intoxication breathed in the strain of this little messenger, whom God had feathered and winged and filled to the throat with ignorant joy, came in singular contrast with the sadder notes breathed by that creature of so much higher mould and fairer clay,—that creature born for an immortal life.

But the good Doctor was inly pleased when she sung,— and when she stopped, looked up from his Bible wistfully, as missing something, he knew not what; for he scarce thought how pleasant the little voice was, or knew he had been listening to it,—and yet he was in a manner enchanted by it, so thankful and happy that he exclaimed with fervor, "The lines are fallen unto me in pleasant places; yea, I have a goodly heritage."

So went the world with him, full of joy and praise, because the voice and the presence wherein lay his unsuspected life were securely near, so certainly and constantly a part of his daily walk that he had not even the trouble to wish for them. But in that other heart how was it?—how with the sweet saint that was talking to herself in psalms and hymns and spiritual songs?

The good child had remembered her mother's parting words the night before,—"Put your mind upon your duties," —and had begun her first conscious exercise of thought with a prayer that grace might be given her to do it. But even as she spoke, mingling and interweaving with that golden thread of prayer was another consciousness, a life in another soul, as she prayed that the grace of God might overshadow him, shield him from temptation, and lead him up to heaven; and this prayer so got the start of the other, that, ere she was aware, she had quite forgotten self, and was feeling, living, thinking in that other life.

The first discovery she made, when she looked out into the fragrant orchard, whose perfumes steamed in at her window, and listened to the first chirping of birds among the old apple-trees, was one that has astonished many a person before her; it was this: she found that all that had made life interesting to her was suddenly gone. She herself had not known, that, for the month past, since James came from sea, she had been living in an enchanted land,—that Newport harbor, and every rock and stone, and every mat of yellow seaweed on the shore, that the two-mile road between the cottage and the white house of Zebedee Marvyn, every mullein-stalk, every juniper-tree, had all had a light and a charm which were suddenly gone. There had not been an hour in the day for the last four weeks that had not had its unsuspected interest,— because he was at the white house, because, possibly, he might be going by, or coming in; nay, even in church, when she stood up to sing, and thought she was thinking only of God, had she not been conscious of that tenor voice that poured itself out by her side? and though afraid to turn her head that way, had she not felt that he was there every moment,—heard every word of the sermon and prayer for him? The very vigilant care which her mother had taken to prevent private interviews had only served to increase the interest by throwing over it the veil of constraint and mystery. Silent looks, involuntary starts, things indicated, not expressed,—

these are the most dangerous, the most seductive aliment of thought to a delicate and sensitive nature. If things were said out, they might not be said wisely,—they might repel by their freedom, or disturb by their unfitness; but what is only looked is sent into the soul through the imagination, which makes of it all that the ideal faculties desire.

In a refined and exalted nature, it is very seldom that the feeling of love, when once thoroughly aroused, bears any sort of relation to the reality of the object. It is commonly an enkindling of the whole power of the soul's love for whatever she considers highest and fairest; it is, in fact, the love of something divine and unearthly, which, by a sort of illusion, connects itself with a personality. Properly speaking, there is but One true, eternal Object of all that the mind conceives, in this trance of its exaltation. Disenchantment must come, of course; and in a love which terminates in happy marriage, there is a tender and gracious process, by which, without shock or violence, the ideal is gradually sunk in the real, which, though found faulty and earthly, is still ever tenderly remembered as it seemed under the morning light of that enchantment.

What Mary loved so passionately, that which came between her and God in every prayer, was not the gay, young, dashing sailor,—sudden in anger, imprudent of speech, and, though generous in heart, yet worldly in plans and schemings,—but her own ideal of a grand and noble man,—such a man as she thought he might become. He stood glorified before her, an image of the strength that overcomes things physical, of the power of command which controls men and circumstances, of the courage which disdains fear, of the honor which cannot lie, of constancy which knows no shadow of turning, of tenderness which protects the weak, and, lastly, of religious loyalty which should lay the golden crown of its perfected manhood at the feet of a Sovereign Lord and Redeemer. This was the man she loved, and with this regal mantle of glories she invested the person called James Marvyn; and all that she saw and felt to be wanting she prayed for with the faith of a believing woman.

Nor was she wrong;—for, as to every leaf and every flower there is an ideal to which the growth of the plant is constantly urging, so is there an ideal to every human being,—a perfect form in which it might appear, were every defect removed and every characteristic excellence stimulated to the highest point. Once in an age, God sends to some of us a friend who loves in us, *not* a false imagining, an unreal character, but, looking through all the rubbish of our imperfections, loves in us the divine ideal of our nature,—loves, not the man that we are, but the angel that we may be. Such friends seem inspired by a divine gift of prophecy,—like the mother of St. Augustine, who, in the midst of the wayward, reckless youth of her son, beheld him in a vision, standing, clothed in white, a ministering priest at the right hand of God,—as he has stood for long ages since. Could a mysterious foresight unveil to us this resurrection form of the friends with whom we daily walk, compassed about with mortal infirmity, we should follow them with faith and reverence through all the disguises of human faults and weaknesses, "waiting for the manifestation of the sons of God."

But these wonderful soul-friends, to whom God grants such perception, are the exceptions in life; yet sometimes are we blessed with one who sees through us, as Michel Angelo saw through a block of marble, when he attacked it in a divine fervor, declaring that an angel was imprisoned within it; and it is often the resolute and delicate hand of such a friend that sets the angel free.

There be soul-artists, who go through this world, looking among their fellows with reverence, as one looks amid the dust and rubbish of old shops for hidden works of Titian and Leonardo, and, finding them, however cracked or torn or painted over with tawdry daubs of pretenders, immediately recognize the divine original, and set themselves to cleanse and restore. Such be God's real priests, whose ordination and anointing are from the Holy Spirit; and he who hath not this enthusiasm is not ordained of God, though whole synods of bishops laid hands on him.

Many such priests there be among women;—for to this silent ministry their nature calls them, endowed, as it is, with fineness of fibre, and a subtile keenness of perception outrunning slow-footed reason;—and she of whom we write was one of these.

At this very moment, while the crimson wings of morning were casting delicate reflections on tree, and bush, and rock, they were also reddening innumerable waves round a ship that sailed alone, with a wide horizon stretching like an eternity around it; and in the advancing morning stood a young man thoughtfully looking off into the ocean, with a book in his hand,—James Marvyn,—as truly and heartily a creature of this material world as Mary was of the invisible and heavenly.

There are some who seem made to *live*;—life is such a joy to them, their senses are so fully *en rapport* with all outward things, the world is so keenly appreciable, so much a part of themselves, they are so conscious of power and victory in the government and control of material things,—that the moral and invisible life often seems to hang tremulous and unreal in their minds, like the pale, faded moon in the light of a gorgeous sunrise. When brought face to face with the great truths of the invisible world, they stand related to the higher wisdom much like the gorgeous, gay Alcibiades to the divine Socrates, or like the young man in Holy Writ to Him for whose appearing Socrates longed;—they gaze, imperfectly comprehending, and at the call of ambition or riches turn away sorrowing.

So it was with James;—in the full tide of worldly energy and ambition, there had been forming over his mind that hard crust, that skepticism of the spiritual and exalted, which men of the world delight to call practical sense; he had been suddenly arrested and humbled by the revelation of a nature so much nobler than his own that he seemed worthless in his own eyes. He had asked for love; but when *such* love unveiled itself, he felt like the disciple of old in the view of a diviner tenderness,—"Depart from me, for I am a sinful man."

But it is not often that all the current of a life is reversed in one hour; and now, as James stood on the ship's deck, with life passing around him, and everything drawing upon the strings of old habits, Mary and her religion recurred to his mind as some fair, sweet, inexplicable vision. Where she stood he saw; but how *he* was ever to get there seemed as incomprehensible as how a mortal man should pillow his form on sunset clouds.

He held the little Bible in his hand as if it were some amulet charmed by the touch of a superior being; but when he strove to read it, his thoughts wandered, and he shut it, troubled and unsatisfied. Yet there were within him yearnings and cravings, wants never felt before, the beginning of that trouble which must ever precede the soul's rise to a higher plane of being.

There we leave him. We have shown you now our three different characters, each one in its separate sphere, feeling the force of that strongest and holiest power with which it has pleased our great Author to glorify this mortal life.

IX.

Which Treats of Things Seen

As, for example, the breakfast. It is six o'clock,—the hired men and oxen are gone,—the breakfast-table stands before the open kitchen-door, snowy with its fresh cloth, the old silver coffee-pot steaming up a refreshing perfume,—and the Doctor sits on one side, sipping his coffee and looking across the table at Mary, who is innocently pleased at the kindly beaming in his placid blue eyes,—and Aunt Katy Scudder discourses of housekeeping, and fancies something must have disturbed the rising of the cream, as it is not so thick and yellow as wont.

Now the Doctor, it is to be confessed, was apt to fall into a way of looking at people such as pertains to philosophers and scholars generally, that is, as if he were looking through them into the infinite,—in which case his gaze became so earnest and intent that it would quite embarrass an uninitiated person; but Mary, being used to this style of contemplation, was only quietly amused, and waited till some great thought should loom up before his mental vision,—in which case she hoped to hear from him.

The good man swallowed his first cup of coffee and spoke:—

"In the Millennium, I suppose, there will be such a fulness and plenty of all the necessaries and conveniences of life, that it will not be necessary for men and women to spend the greater part of their lives in labor in order to procure a living. It will not be necessary for each one to labor more than two or three hours a day,—not more than will conduce to health of body and vigor of mind; and the rest of their time they will spend in reading and conversation, and such exercises as are necessary and proper to improve their minds and make progress in knowledge."

New England presents probably the only example of a successful commonwealth founded on a theory, as a distinct experiment in the problem of society. It was for this reason that the minds of its great thinkers dwelt so much on the final solution of that problem in this world. The fact of a future Millennium was a favorite doctrine of the great leading theologians of New England, and Dr. Hopkins dwelt upon it with a peculiar partiality. Indeed, it was the solace and refuge of his soul, when oppressed with the discouragements which always attend things actual, to dwell upon and draw out in detail the splendors of this perfect future which was destined to glorify the world.

Nobody, therefore, at the cottage was in the least surprised when there dropped into the flow of their daily life these sparkling bits of ore, which their friend had dug in his explorations of a future Canaan,—in fact, they served to raise the hackneyed present out of the level of mere commonplace.

"But how will it be possible," inquired Mrs. Scudder, "that so much less work will suffice in those days to do all that is to be done?"

"Because of the great advance of arts and sciences which will take place before those days," said the Doctor, "whereby everything shall be performed with so much greater ease,—also the great increase of disinterested love, whereby the skill and talents of those who have much shall make up for the weakness of those who have less.

"Yes,"—he continued, after a pause,—"all the careful Marthas in those days will have no excuse for not sitting at the feet of Jesus; there will be no cumbering with much serving; the Church will have only Maries in those days."

This remark, made without the slightest personal intention, called a curious smile into Mrs. Scudder's face, which was reflected in a slight blush from Mary's, when the crack of a whip and the rattling of wagon-wheels disturbed the conversation and drew all eyes to the door.

There appeared the vision of Mr. Zebedee Marvyn's farm-wagon, stored with barrels, boxes, and baskets, over which Candace sat throned triumphant, her black face and yellow-striped turban glowing in the fresh morning with a hearty, joyous light, as she pulled up the reins, and shouted to the horse to stop with a voice that might have done credit to any man living.

"Dear me, if there isn't Candace!" said Mary.

"Queen of Ethiopia," said the Doctor, who sometimes adventured a very placid joke.

The Doctor was universally known in all the neighborhood as a sort of friend and patron-saint of the negro race; he had devoted himself to their interests with a zeal unusual in those days. His church numbered more of them than any in Newport; and his hours of leisure from study were often spent in lowliest visitations among them, hearing their stories, consoling their sorrows, advising and directing their plans, teaching them reading and writing, and he often drew hard on his slender salary to assist them in their emergencies and distresses.

This unusual condescension on his part was repaid on theirs with all the warmth of their race; and Candace, in particular, devoted herself to the Doctor with all the force of her being.

There was a legend current in the neighborhood, that the first efforts to catechize Candace were not eminently successful, her modes of contemplating theological tenets being so peculiarly from her own individual point of view that it was hard to get her subscription to a received opinion. On the venerable clause in the Catechism, in particular, which declares that all men sinned in Adam and fell with him, Candace made a dead halt:—

"I didn't do dat ar', for one, I knows. I's got good mem'ry,—allers knows what I does,—nebber did eat dat ar' apple,—nebber eat a bit ob him. Don't tell me!"

It was of no use, of course, to tell Candace of all the explanations of this redoubtable passage,—of potential presence, and representative presence, and representative identity, and federal headship. She met all with the dogged,—

"Nebber did it, I knows; should 'ave 'membered, if I had. Don't tell me!"

And even in the catechizing class of the Doctor himself, if this answer came to her, she sat black and frowning in stony silence even in his reverend presence.

Candace was often reminded that the Doctor believed the Catechism, and that she was differing from a great and good man; but the argument made no manner of impression on her, till, one day, a far-off cousin of hers, whose condition under a hard master had often moved her compassion, came in overjoyed to recount to her how, owing to Dr. Hopkins's exertions, he had gained his freedom. The Doctor himself had in person gone from house to house, raising the sum for his redemption; and when more yet was wanting, supplied it by paying half his last quarter's limited salary.

"He do dat ar'?" said Candace, dropping the fork wherewith she was spearing doughnuts. "Den I'm gwine to b'liebe ebery word *he* does!"

And accordingly, at the next catechizing, the Doctor's astonishment was great when Candace pressed up to him, exclaiming,—

"De Lord bress you, Doctor, for opening de prison for dem dat is bound! I b'liebes in you now, Doctor. I's gwine to b'liebe every word you say. I'll say de Catechize now,—fix it any way you like. I *did* eat dat ar' apple,—I eat de whole tree, an' swallowed ebery bit ob it, if you say so."

And this very thorough profession of faith was followed, on the part of Candace, by years of the most strenuous orthodoxy. Her general mode of expressing her mind on the subject was short and definitive.

"Law me! what's de use? I's set out to b'liebe de Catechize, an' I'm gwine to b'liebe it,—so!"

While we have been telling you all this about her, she has fastened her horse, and is swinging leisurely up to the house with a basket on either arm.

"Good morning, Candace," said Mrs. Scudder. "What brings you so early?"

"Come down 'fore light to sell my chickens an' eggs,—got a lot o' money for 'em, too. Missy Marvyn she sent Miss Scudder some turkey-eggs, an' I brought down some o' my doughnuts for de Doctor. Good folks must lib, you know, as well as wicked ones,"—and Candace gave a hearty, unctuous laugh. "No reason why Doctors shouldn't hab good tings as well as sinners, is dere?"—and she shook in great billows, and showed her white teeth in the *abandon* of her laugh. "Lor' bress ye honey, chile!" she said, turning to Mary, "why ye looks like a new rose, ebery bit! Don't wonder *somebody* was allers pryin' an' spyin' about here!"

"How is your mistress, Candace?" said Mrs. Scudder, by way of changing the subject.

"Well, porly,—rader porly. When Massa Jim goes, 'pears like takin' de light right out her eyes. Dat ar' boy trains roun' arter his mudder like a cosset, he does. Lor', de house seems so still widout him!—can't a fly scratch his ear but it starts a body. Missy Marvyn she sent down, an' says, would you an' de Doctor an' Miss Mary please come to tea dis arternoon."

"Thank your mistress, Candace," said Mrs. Scudder; "Mary and I will come,—and the Doctor, perhaps," looking at the good man, who had relapsed into meditation, and was eating his breakfast without taking note of anything going on. "It will be time enough to tell him of it," she said to Mary, "when we have to wake him up to dress; so we won't disturb him now."

To Mary the prospect of the visit was a pleasant one, for reasons which she scarce gave a definite form to. Of course, like a good girl, she had come to a fixed and settled resolution to think of James as little as possible; but when the path of duty lay directly along scenes and among people fitted to re-call him, it was more agreeable than if it had lain in another direction. Added to this, a very tender and silent friendship subsisted between Mrs. Marvyn and Mary; in which, besides similarity of mind and intellectual pursuits, there was a deep, unspoken element of sympathy.

Candace watched the light in Mary's eyes with the instinctive shrewdness by which her race seem to divine the thoughts and feelings of their superiors, and chuckled to herself internally. Without ever having been made a *confidante* by any party, or having a word said to or before her, still the whole position of affairs was as clear to her as if she had seen it on a map. She had appreciated at once Mrs. Scudder's coolness, James's devotion, and Mary's perplexity,—and inly resolved, that, if the little maiden did not think of James in his absence, it should not be her fault.

"Laws, Miss Scudder," she said, "I's right glad you's comin'; 'cause you hasn't seen how we's kind o' splendified since Massa Jim come home. You wouldn't know it. Why, he's got mats from Mogadore on all de entries, and a great big 'un on de parlor; and ye ought to see de shawl he brought

Missus, an' all de cur'us kind o' tings to de squire. 'Tell ye, dat ar' boy honors his fader and mudder, ef he don't do nuffin else,—an' dats de fus' commandment wid promise, Ma'am; an' to see him a-settin' up ebery day in prayer-time, so handsome, holdin' Missus's han', an' lookin' right into her eyes all de time! Why, dat ar' boy is one of de 'lect,—it's jest as clare to me; and de 'lect has got to come in,—dat's what I say. My faith's strong,—real clare, 'tell ye," she added, with the triumphant laugh which usually chorused her conversation, and turning to the Doctor, who, aroused by her loud and vigorous strain, was attending with interest to her.

"Well, Candace," he said, "we all hope you are right."

"*Hope*, Doctor!—I don't hope,—I *knows*. 'Tell ye, when I pray for him, don't I feel enlarged? 'Tell ye, it goes wid a rush. I can feel it gwine up like a rushin', mighty wind. I feels strong, I do."

"That's right, Candace," said the Doctor, "keep on; your prayers stand as much chance with God as if you were a crowned queen. The Lord is no respecter of persons."

"Dat's what he a'n't, Doctor,—an' dere's where I 'gree wid him," said Candace, as she gathered her baskets vigorously together, and, after a sweeping curtsy, went sailing down to her wagon, full laden with content, shouting a hearty "Good mornin', Missus," with the full power of her cheerful lungs, as she rode off.

As the Doctor looked after her, the simple, pleased expression with which he had watched her gradually faded, and there passed over his broad, good face a shadow, as of a cloud on a mountain-side.

"What a shame it is," he said, "what a scandal and disgrace to the Protestant religion, that Christians of America should openly practise and countenance this enslaving of the Africans! I have for a long time holden my peace,—may the Lord forgive me!—but I believe the time is coming when I must utter my voice. I cannot go down to the wharves or among the shipping, without these poor dumb creatures look at me so that I am ashamed,—as if they asked me what I, a Christian minister, was doing, that I did not come to their help. I must testify."

Mrs. Scudder looked grave at this earnest announcement;

she had heard many like it before, and they always filled her with alarm, because——Shall we tell you why?

Well, then, it was not because she was not a thoroughly indoctrinated anti-slavery woman. Her husband, who did all her thinking for her, had been a man of ideas beyond his day, and never for a moment countenanced the right of slavery so far as to buy or own a servant or attendant of any kind; and Mrs. Scudder had always followed decidedly along the path of his opinions and practice, and never hesitated to declare the reasons for the faith that was in her. But if any of us could imagine an angel dropped down out of heaven, with wings, ideas, notions, manners, and customs all fresh from that very different country, we might easily suppose that the most pious and orthodox family might find the task of presenting him in general society and piloting him along the courses of this world a very delicate and embarrassing one. However much they might reverence him on their own private account, their hearts would probably sink within them at the idea of allowing him to expand himself according to his previous nature and habits in the great world without. In like manner, men of high, unworldly natures are often reverenced by those who are somewhat puzzled what to do with them practically.

Mrs. Scudder considered the Doctor as a superior being, possessed by a holy helplessness in all things material and temporal, which imposed on her the necessity of thinking and caring for him, and prevising the earthly and material aspects of his affairs.

There was not in Newport a more thriving and reputable business at that time than the slave-trade. Large fortunes were constantly being turned out in it, and what better providential witness of its justice could most people require?

Besides this, in their own little church, she reflected with alarm, that Simeon Brown, the richest and most liberal supporter of the society, had been, and was then, drawing all his wealth from this source; and rapidly there flashed before her mind a picture of one and another, influential persons, who were holders of slaves. Therefore, when the Doctor announced, "I must testify," she rattled her tea-spoon uneasily, and answered,—

"In what way, Doctor, do you think of bearing testimony? The subject, I think, is a very difficult one."

"Difficult? I think no subject can be clearer. If we were right in our war for liberty, we are wrong in making slaves or keeping them."

"Oh, I did not mean," said Mrs. Scudder, "that it was difficult to understand the subject; the *right* of the matter is clear, but what to *do* is the thing."

"I shall preach about it," said the Doctor; "my mind has run upon it some time. I shall show to the house of Judah their sin in this matter."

"I fear there will be great offence given," said Mrs. Scudder. "There's Simeon Brown, one of our largest supporters,—he is in the trade."

"Ah, yes,—but he will come out of it,—of course he will,—he is all right, all clear. I was delighted with the clearness of his views the other night, and thought then of bringing them to bear on this point,—only, as others were present, I deferred it. But I can show him that it follows logically from his principles; I am confident of that."

"I think you'll be disappointed in him, Doctor;—I think he'll be angry, and get up a commotion, and leave the church."

"Madam," said the Doctor, "do you suppose that a man who would be willing even to give up his eternal salvation for the greatest good of the universe could hesitate about a few paltry thousands that perish in the using?"

"He may feel willing to give up his soul," said Mrs. Scudder, naïvely, "but I don't think he'll give up his ships,—that's quite another matter,—he won't see it to be his duty."

"Then, Ma'am, he'll be a hypocrite, a gross hypocrite, if he won't," said the Doctor. "It is not Christian charity to think it of him. I shall call upon him this morning and tell him my intentions."

"But, Doctor," exclaimed Mrs. Scudder, with a start, "pray, think a little more of it. You know a great many things depend on him. Why! he has subscribed for twenty copies of your 'System of Theology.' I hope you'll remember that."

"And why should I remember that?" said the Doctor,—hastily turning round, suddenly enkindled, his blue eyes flashing out of their usual misty calm,—"what has my 'System of Theology' to do with the matter?"

"Why," said Mrs. Scudder, "it's of more importance to get right views of the gospel before the world than anything else, is it not?—and if, by any imprudence in treating influential people, this should be prevented, more harm than good would be done."

"Madam," said the Doctor, "I'd sooner my system should be sunk in the sea than it should be a millstone round my neck to keep me from my duty. Let God take care of my theology; I must do my duty."

And as the Doctor spoke, he straightened himself to the full dignity of his height, his face kindling with an unconscious majesty, and, as he turned, his eye fell on Mary, who was standing with her slender figure dilated, her large blue eye wide and bright, in a sort of trance of solemn feeling, half smiles, half tears,—and the strong, heroic man started, to see this answer to his higher soul in the sweet, tremulous mirror of womanhood. One of those lightning glances passed between his eyes and hers which are the freemasonry of noble spirits,—and, by a sudden impulse, they approached each other. He took both her outstretched hands, looked down into her face with a look full of admiration, and a sort of naïve wonder,—then, as if her inspired silence had been a voice to him, he laid his hand on her head, and said,—

"God bless you, child! 'Out of the mouth of babes and sucklings hast thou ordained strength because of thine enemies, that thou mightest still the enemy and the avenger!'"

In a moment he was gone.

"Mary," said Mrs. Scudder, laying her hand on her daughter's arm, "the Doctor loves you!"

"I know he does, mother," said Mary, innocently; "and I love him,—dearly!—he is a noble, grand man!"

Mrs. Scudder looked keenly at her daughter. Mary's eye was as calm as a June sky, and she began, composedly, gathering up the teacups.

"She did not understand me," thought the mother.

X.

The Test of Theology

THE Doctor went immediately to his study and put on his best coat and his wig, and, surmounting them by his cocked hat, walked manfully out of the house, with his gold-headed cane in his hand.

"There he goes!" said Mrs. Scudder, looking regretfully after him. "He is *such* a good man!—but he has not the least idea how to get along in the world. He never thinks of anything but what is true; he hasn't a particle of management about him."

"Seems to me," said Mary, "that is like an Apostle. You know, mother, St. Paul says, 'In simplicity and godly sincerity, not with fleshly wisdom, but by the grace of God, we have had our conversation in the world.'"

"To be sure,—that is just the Doctor," said Mrs. Scudder; "that's as like him as if it had been written for him. But that kind of way, somehow, don't seem to do in our times; it won't answer with Simeon Brown,—I know the man. I know just as well, now, how it will all seem to him, and what will be the upshot of this talk, if the Doctor goes there! It won't do any good; if it would, I would be willing. I feel as much desire to have this horrid trade in slaves stopped as anybody; your father, I'm sure, said enough about it in his time; but then I know it's no use trying. Just as if Simeon Brown, when he is making his hundreds of thousands in it, is going to be persuaded to give it up! He won't,—he'll only turn against the Doctor, and won't pay his part of the salary, and will use his influence to get up a party against him, and our church will be broken up and the Doctor driven away,—that's all that will come of it; and all the good that he is doing now to these poor negroes will be overthrown,—and they never will have so good a friend. If he would stay here and work gradually, and get his System of Theology printed,—and Simeon

618

Brown would help at that,—and only drop words in season here and there, till people are brought along with him,
why, by-and-by something might be done; but now, it's
just the most imprudent thing a man could undertake."

"But, mother, if it really is a sin to trade in slaves and hold
them, I don't see how he can help himself. I quite agree with
him. I don't see how he came to let it go so long as he has."

"Well," said Mrs. Scudder, "if worst comes to worst, and
he will do it, I, for one, shall stand by him to the last."

"And I, for another," said Mary.

"I would like him to talk with Cousin Zebedee about it,"
said Mrs. Scudder. "When we are up there this afternoon, we
will introduce the conversation. He is a good, sound man,
and the Doctor thinks much of him, and perhaps he may shed
some light upon this matter."

Meanwhile the Doctor was making the best of his way, in
the strength of his purpose to test the orthodoxy of Simeon
Brown.

Honest old granite boulder that he was, no sooner did he
perceive a truth than he rolled after it with all the massive
gravitation of his being, inconsiderate as to what might lie in
his way;—from which it is to be inferred, that, with all his
intellect and goodness, he would have been a very clumsy and
troublesome inmate of the modern American Church. How
many societies, boards, colleges, and other good institutions,
have reason to congratulate themselves that he has long been
among the saints!

With him logic was everything, and to perceive a truth and
not act in logical sequence from it a thing so incredible, that
he had not yet enlarged his capacity to take it in as a possibility. That a man should refuse to hear truth, he could understand. In fact, he had good reason to think the majority of
his townsmen had no leisure to give to that purpose. That
men hearing truth should dispute it and argue stoutly against
it, he could also understand; but that a man could admit a
truth and not admit the plain practice resulting from it was
to him a thing incomprehensible. Therefore, spite of Mrs.
Katy Scudder's discouraging observations, our good Doctor
walked stoutly and with a trusting heart.

At the moment when the Doctor, with a silent uplifting of

his soul to his invisible Sovereign, passed out of his study, on this errand, where was the disciple whom he went to seek?

In a small, dirty room, down by the wharf, the windows veiled by cobwebs and dingy with the accumulated dust of ages, he sat in a greasy, leathern chair by a rickety office-table, on which was a great pewter inkstand, an account-book, and divers papers tied with red tape.

Opposite to him was seated a square-built individual,—a man of about forty, whose round head, shaggy eyebrows, small, keen eyes, broad chest, and heavy muscles showed a preponderance of the animal and brutal over the intellectual and spiritual. This was Mr. Scroggs, the agent of a rice-plantation, who had come on, bringing an order for a new relay of negroes to supply the deficit occasioned by fever, dysentery, and other causes, in their last year's stock.

"The fact is," said Simeon, "this last ship-load wasn't as good a one as usual; we lost more than a third of it, so we can't afford to put them a penny lower."

"Ay," said the other,—"but then there are so many women!"

"Well," said Simeon, "women a'n't so strong, perhaps, to start with,—but then they stan' it out, perhaps, in the long run, better. They're more patient;—some of these men, the Mandingoes, particularly, are pretty troublesome to manage. We lost a splendid fellow, coming over, on this very voyage. Let 'em on deck for air, and this fellow managed to get himself loose and fought like a dragon. He settled one of our men with his fist, and another with a marlinspike that he caught,—and, in fact, they had to shoot him down. You'll have his wife; there's his son, too,—fine fellow, fifteen year old by his teeth."

"What! that lame one?"

"Oh, he a'n't lame!—it's nothing but the cramps from stowing. You know, of course, they are more or less stiff. He's as sound as a nut."

"Don't much like to buy relations, on account of their hatching up mischief together," said Mr. Scroggs.

"Oh, that's all humbug! You must keep 'em from coming together, anyway. It's about as broad as 'tis long. There'll be wives and husbands and children among 'em before long, start 'em as you will. And then this woman will work better for having the boy; she's kinder set on him; she jabbers lots of lingo to him, day and night."

"Too much, I doubt," said the overseer, with a shrug.

"Well, well,—I'll tell you," said Simeon, rising. "I've got a few errands up-town, and you just step over with Matlock and look over the stock;—just set aside any that you want, and when I see 'em all together, I'll tell you just what you shall have 'em for. I'll be back in an hour or two."

And so saying, Simeon Brown called an underling from an adjoining room, and, committing his customer to his care, took his way up-town, in a serene frame of mind, like a man who comes from the calm performance of duty.

Just as he came upon the street where was situated his own large and somewhat pretentious mansion, the tall figure of the Doctor loomed in sight, sailing majestically down upon him, making a signal to attract his attention.

"Good morning, Doctor," said Simeon.

"Good morning, Mr. Brown," said the Doctor. "I was looking for you. I did not quite finish the subject we were talking about at Mrs. Scudder's table last night. I thought I should like to go on with it a little."

"With all my heart, Doctor," said Simeon, not a little flattered. "Turn right in. Mrs. Brown will be about her house-business, and we will have the keeping-room all to ourselves. Come right in."

The "keeping-room" of Mr. Simeon Brown's house was an intermediate apartment between the ineffable glories of the front-parlor and that court of the gentiles, the kitchen; for the presence of a large train of negro servants made the latter apartment an altogether different institution from the throne-room of Mrs. Katy Scudder.

This keeping-room was a low-studded apartment, finished with the heavy oaken beams of the wall left full in sight, boarded over and painted. Two windows looked out on the street, and another into a sort of court-yard, where three black wenches, each with a broom, pretended to be sweeping, but were, in fact, chattering and laughing, like so many crows.

On one side of the room stood a heavy mahogany sideboard, covered with decanters, labelled Gin, Brandy, Rum, etc.,—for Simeon was held to be a provider of none but the best, in his house-keeping. Heavy mahogany chairs, with crewel coverings, stood sentry about the room; and the fire-place was flanked by two broad arm-chairs, covered with stamped leather.

On ushering the Doctor into this apartment, Simeon courteously led him to the sideboard.

"We mus'n't make our discussions too *dry*, Doctor," he said. "What will you take?"

"Thank you, Sir," said the Doctor, with a wave of his hand,—"nothing this morning."

And depositing his cocked hat in a chair, he settled himself into one of the leathern easy-chairs, and, dropping his hands upon his knees, looked fixedly before him, like a man who is studying how to enter upon an inwardly absorbing subject.

"Well, Doctor," said Simeon, seating himself opposite, sipping comfortably at a glass of rum-and-water, "our views appear to be making a noise in the world. Everything is preparing for your volumes; and when they appear, the battle of New Divinity, I think, may fairly be considered as won."

Let us consider, that, though a woman may forget her first-born, yet a man cannot forget his own system of theology,—because therein, if he be a true man, is the very elixir and essence of all that is valuable and hopeful to the universe; and considering this, let us appreciate the settled purpose of our friend, whom even this tempting bait did not swerve from the end which he had in view.

"Mr. Brown," he said, "all our theology is as a drop in the ocean of God's majesty, to whose glory we must be ready to make any and every sacrifice."

"Certainly," said Mr. Brown, not exactly comprehending the turn the Doctor's thoughts were taking.

"And the glory of God consisteth in the happiness of all his rational universe, each in his proportion, according to his separate amount of being; so that, when we devote ourselves to God's glory, it is the same as saying that we devote ourselves to the highest happiness of his created universe.

"That's clear, Sir," said Simeon, rubbing his hands, and taking out his watch to see the time.

The Doctor hitherto had spoken in a laborious manner, like a man who is slowly lifting a heavy bucket of thought out of an internal well.

"I am glad to find your mind so clear on this all-important point, Mr. Brown,—the more so as I feel that we must immediately proceed to apply our principles, at whatever sacrifice of worldly goods; and I trust, Sir, that you are one who at the call of your Master would not hesitate even to lay down all your worldly possessions for the greater good of the universe."

"I trust so, Sir," said Simeon, rather uneasily, and without the most distant idea what could be coming next in the mind of his reverend friend.

"Did it never occur to you, my friend," said the Doctor, "that the enslaving of the African race is a clear violation of the great law which commands us to love our neighbor as ourselves,—and a dishonor upon the Christian religion, more particularly in us Americans, whom the Lord hath so marvellously protected, in our recent struggle for our own liberty?"

Simeon started at the first words of this address, much as if some one had dashed a bucket of water on his head, and after that rose uneasily, walking the room and playing with the seals of his watch.

"I—I never regarded it in this light," he said.

"Possibly not, my friend," said the Doctor,—"so much doth established custom blind the minds of the best of men. But since I have given more particular attention to the case of the poor negroes here in Newport, the thought has more and more labored in my mind,—more especially as our own struggles for liberty have turned my attention to the rights which every human creature hath before God,—so that I find much in my former blindness and the comparative dumbness I have heretofore maintained on this subject wherewith to reproach myself; for, though I have borne somewhat of a testimony, I have not given it that force which so important a subject required. I am humbled before God for my neglect, and resolved now, by His grace, to leave no stone unturned till this iniquity be purged away from our Zion."

"Well, Doctor," said Simeon, "you are certainly touching on a very dark and difficult subject, and one in which it is hard to find out the path of duty. Perhaps it will be well to bear it in mind, and by looking at it prayerfully some light may arise. There are such great obstacles in the way, that I do not see at present what can be done; do you, Doctor?"

"I intend to preach on the subject next Sunday, and hereafter devote my best energies in the most public way to this great work," said the Doctor.

"You, Doctor?—and now, immediately? Why, it appears to me you cannot do it. You are the most unfit man possible. Whosever duty it may be, it does not seem to me to be yours. You already have more on your shoulders than you can carry; you are hardly able to keep your ground now, with all the odium of this new theology upon you. Such an effort would break up your church,—destroy the chance you have to do good here,—prevent the publication of your system."

"If it's nobody's system but mine, the world won't lose much, if it never be published; but if it be God's system, nothing can hinder its appearing. Besides, Mr. Brown, I ought not to be one man alone. I count on your help. I hold it as a special providence, Mr. Brown, that in our own church an opportunity will be given to testify to the reality of disinterested benevolence. How glorious the opportunity for a man to come out and testify by sacrificing his worldly living and business! If you, Mr. Brown, will at once, at whatever sacrifice, quit all connection with this detestable and diabolical slave-trade, you will exhibit a spectacle over which angels will rejoice, and which will strengthen and encourage me to preach and write and testify."

Mr. Simeon Brown's usual demeanor was that of the most leathery imperturbability. In calm theological reasoning, he could demonstrate, in the dryest tone, that, if the eternal torment of six bodies and souls were absolutely the necessary means for preserving the eternal blessedness of thirty-six, benevolence would require us to rejoice in it, not in itself considered, but in view of greater good. And when he spoke, not a nerve quivered; the great mysterious sorrow with which the creation groaneth and travaileth, the sorrow from which angels veil their faces, never had touched one vibrating chord either of body or soul; and he laid down the obligations of man to unconditional submission in a style which would have

affected a person of delicate sensibility much like being mentally sawn in sunder. Benevolence, when Simeon Brown
spoke of it, seemed the grimmest and unloveliest of Gorgons;
for his mind seemed to resemble those fountains which pet-
rify everything that falls into them. But the hardest-shelled
animals have a vital and sensitive part, though only so large
as the point of a needle; and the Doctor's innocent proposition to Simeon, to abandon his whole worldly estate for his
principles, touched this spot.

When benevolence required but the acquiescence in certain
possible things which might be supposed to happen to his
soul, which, after all, he was comfortably certain never would
happen, or the acquiescence in certain suppositious sacrifices
for the good of that most intangible of all abstractions, Being
in general, it was a dry, calm subject. But when it concerned
the immediate giving-up of his slave-ships and a transfer of
business, attended with all that confusion and loss which he
foresaw at a glance, then he *felt*, and felt too much to see
clearly. His swarthy face flushed, his little blue eye kindled,
he walked up to the Doctor and began speaking in the short,
energetic sentences of a man thoroughly awake to what he is
talking about.

"Doctor, you're too fast. You are not a practical man, Doctor. You are good in your pulpit;—nobody better. Your theology is clear;—nobody can argue better. But come to practical matters, why, business has its laws, Doctor. Ministers are
the most unfit men in the world to talk on such subjects; it's
departing from their sphere; they talk about what they don't
understand. Besides, you take too much for granted. I'm not
sure that this trade is an evil. I want to be convinced of it.
I'm sure it's a favor to these poor creatures to bring them to
a Christian land. They are a thousand times better off. Here
they can hear the gospel and have some chance of salvation."

"If we want to get the gospel to the Africans," said the
Doctor, "why not send whole ship-loads of missionaries to
them, and carry civilization and the arts and Christianity to
Africa, instead of stirring up wars, tempting them to ravage
each other's territories, that we may get the booty? Think of
the numbers killed in the wars,—of all that die on the passage? Is there any need of killing ninety-nine men to give the

hundredth one the gospel, when we could give the gospel to them all? Ah, Mr. Brown, what if all the money spent in fitting out ships to bring the poor negroes here, so prejudiced against Christianity that they regard it with fear and aversion, had been spent in sending it to them, Africa would have been covered with towns and villages, rejoicing in civilization and Christianity?"

"Doctor, you are a dreamer," replied Simeon, "an unpractical man. Your situation prevents your knowing anything of real life."

"Amen! the Lord be praised therefor!" said the Doctor, with a slowly increasing flush mounting to his cheek, showing the burning brand of a smouldering fire of indignation.

"Now let me just talk common-sense, Doctor,—which has its time and place, just as much as theology;—and if you have the most theology, I flatter myself I have the most common-sense; a business-man must have it. Now just look at your situation,—how you stand. You've got a most important work to do. In order to do it, you must keep your pulpit, you must keep our church together. We are few and weak. We are a minority. Now there's not an influential man in your society that don't either hold slaves or engage in the trade; and if you open upon this subject as you are going to do, you'll just divide and destroy the church. All men are not like you;— men are men, and will be, till they are thoroughly sanctified, which never happens in this life,—and there will be an instant and most unfavorable agitation. Minds will be turned off from the discussion of the great saving doctrines of the gospel to a side issue. You will be turned out,—and you know, Doctor, you are not appreciated as you ought to be, and it won't be easy for you to get a new settlement; and then subscriptions will all drop off from your book, and you won't be able to get that out; and all this good will be lost to the world, just for want of common-sense."

"There is a kind of wisdom in what you say, Mr. Brown," replied the Doctor, naïvely; "but I fear much that it is the wisdom spoken of in James, iii. 15, which 'descendeth not from above, but is earthly, sensual, devilish.' You avoid the very point of the argument, which is, Is this a sin against God? That it is, I am solemnly convinced; and shall I 'use lightness? or the things that I purpose do I purpose according to the flesh, that with me there should be yea, yea, and nay, nay?' No, Mr. Brown, immediate repentance, unconditional submission, these are what I must preach as long as God gives me a pulpit to stand in, whether men will hear or whether they will forbear."

"Well, Doctor," said Simeon, shortly, "you can do as you like; but I give you fair warning, that I, for one, shall stop my subscription, and go to Dr. Stiles's church."

"Mr. Brown," said the Doctor, solemnly, rising, and drawing his tall figure to its full height, while a vivid light gleamed from his blue eye, "as to that, you can do as you like; but I think it my duty, as your pastor, to warn you that I have perceived, in my conversation with you this morning, such a want of true spiritual illumination and discernment as leads me to believe that you are yet in the flesh, blinded by that 'carnal mind' which 'is not subject to the law of God, neither indeed can be.' I much fear you have no part nor lot in this matter, and that you have need, seriously, to set yourself to search into the foundations of your hope; for you may be like him of whom it is written, (Isaiah, xliv. 20,) 'he feedeth on ashes: a deceived heart hath turned him aside, that he cannot deliver his soul, nor say, Is there not a lie in my right hand?' "

The Doctor delivered this address to his man of influence with the calmness of an ambassador charged with a message from a sovereign, for which he is no otherwise responsible than to speak it in the most intelligible manner; and then, taking up his hat and cane, he bade him good morning, leaving Simeon Brown in a tumult of excitement which no previous theological discussion had ever raised in him.

XI.

The Practical Test

THE hens cackled drowsily in the barnyard of the white Marvyn-house; in the blue June-afternoon sky sported great sailing islands of cloud, whose white, glistening heads looked in and out through the green apertures of maple and blossoming apple-boughs; the shadows of the trees had already turned eastward, when the one-horse wagon of Mrs. Katy Scudder appeared at the door, where Mrs. Marvyn stood, with a pleased, quiet welcome in her soft, brown eyes. Mrs. Scudder herself drove, sitting on a seat in front, while the Doctor, apparelled in the most faultless style, with white wrist-ruffles, plaited shirt-bosom, immaculate wig, and well-brushed coat, sat by Mary's side, serenely unconscious how many feminine cares had gone to his getting-up. He did not know of the privy consultations, the sewings, stitchings, and starchings, the ironings, the brushings, the foldings and unfoldings and timely arrangements, that gave such dignity and respectability to his outer man, any more than the serene moon rising tranquilly behind a purple mountain-top troubles her calm head with treatises on astronomy; it is enough for her to shine,—she thinks not how or why.

There is a vast amount of latent gratitude to women lying undeveloped in the hearts of men, which would come out plentifully, if they only knew what they did for them. The Doctor was so used to being well dressed, that he never asked why. That his wig always sat straight and even around his ample forehead, not facetiously poked to one side, nor assuming rakish airs, unsuited to clerical dignity, was entirely owing to Mrs. Katy Scudder. That his best broadcloth coat was not illustrated with shreds and patches, fluff and dust, and hanging in ungainly folds, was owing to the same. That his long silk stockings never had a treacherous stitch allowed to break out into a long running ladder was due to her watchfulness; and that he wore spotless ruffles on his wrists or at his bosom

628

was her doing also. The Doctor little thought, while he, in common with good ministers generally, gently traduced the Scriptural Martha and insisted on the duty of heavenly abstractedness, how much of his own leisure for spiritual contemplation was due to the Martha-like talents of his hostess. But then, the good soul had it in him to be grateful, and would have been unboundedly so, if he had known his indebtedness,—as, we trust, most of our magnanimous masters would be.

Mr. Zebedee Marvyn was quietly sitting in the front summer parlor, listening to the story of two of his brother church-members, between whom some difficulty had arisen in the settling of accounts: Jim Bigelow, a small, dry, dapper little individual, known as general jobber and factotum, and Abram Griswold, a stolid, wealthy, well-to-do farmer. And the fragments of conversation we catch are not uninteresting, as showing Mr. Zebedee's habits of thought and mode of treating those who came to him for advice.

"I could 'ave got along better, if he'd 'a' paid me regular every night," said the squeaky voice of little Jim;—"but he was allers puttin' me off till it come even change, he said."

"Well, 'ta'n't always handy," replied the other, "one doesn't like to break into a five-pound note for nothing; and I like to let it run till it comes even change."

"But, brother," said Mr. Zebedee, turning over the great Bible that lay on the mahogany stand in the corner, "we must go to the law and to the testimony,"—and, turning over the leaves, he read from Deuteronomy, xxiv.:—

"Thou shalt not oppress an hired servant that is poor and needy, whether he be of thy brethren or of thy strangers that are in thy land within thy gates. At his day thou shalt give him his hire, neither shall the sun go down upon it; for he is poor, and setteth his heart upon it: lest he cry against thee unto the Lord, and it be sin unto thee."

"You see what the Bible has to say on the matter," he said.

"Well, now, Deacon, I rather think you've got me in a tight place," said Mr. Griswold, rising; and turning confusedly round, he saw the placid figure of the Doctor, who had entered the room unobserved in the midst of the conversation, and was staring with that look of calm, dreamy abstraction which often led people to suppose that he heard and saw nothing of what was going forward.

All rose reverently; and while Mr. Zebedee was shaking hands with the Doctor, and welcoming him to his house, the other two silently withdrew, making respectful obeisance.

Mrs. Marvyn had drawn Mary's hand gently under her arm and taken her to her own sleeping-room, as it was her general habit to do, that she might show her the last book she had been reading, and pour into her ear the thoughts that had been kindled up by it.

Mrs. Scudder, after carefully brushing every speck of dust from the Doctor's coat and seeing him seated in an arm-chair by the open window, took out a long stocking of blue-mixed yarn which she was knitting for his winter wear, and, pinning her knitting-sheath on her side, was soon trotting her needles contentedly in front of him.

The ill-success of the Doctor's morning attempt at enforcing his theology in practice rather depressed his spirits. There was a noble innocence of nature in him which looked at hypocrisy with a puzzled and incredulous astonishment. How a man *could* do so and be so was to him a problem at which his thoughts vainly labored. Not that he was in the least discouraged or hesitating in regard to his own course. When he had made up his mind to perform a duty, the question of success no more entered his thoughts than those of the granite boulder to which we have before compared him. When the time came for him to roll, he did roll with the whole force of his being;—where he was to land was not his concern.

Mildly and placidly he sat with his hands resting on his knees, while Mr. Zebedee and Mrs. Scudder compared notes respecting the relative prospects of corn, flax, and buckwheat, and thence passed to the doings of Congress and the last proclamation of General Washington, pausing once in a while, if, peradventure, the Doctor might take up the conversation. Still he sat dreamily eyeing the flies as they fizzed down the panes of the half-open window.

"I think," said Mr. Zebedee, "the prospects of the Federal party were never brighter."

The Doctor was a stanch Federalist, and generally warmed to this allurement; but it did not serve this time.

Suddenly drawing himself up, a light came into his blue eyes, and he said to Mr. Marvyn,—

"I'm thinking, Deacon, if it is wrong to keep back the wages of a servant till after the going down of the sun, what those are to do who keep them back all their lives."

There was a way the Doctor had of hearing and seeing when he looked as if his soul were afar off, and bringing suddenly into present conversation some fragment of the past on which he had been leisurely hammering in the quiet chambers of his brain, which was sometimes quite startling.

This allusion to a passage of Scripture which Mr. Marvyn was reading when he came in, and which nobody supposed he had attended to, startled Mrs. Scudder, who thought, mentally, "Now for it!" and laid down her knitting-work, and eyed her cousin anxiously. Mrs. Marvyn and Mary, who had glided in and joined the circle, looked interested; and a slight flush rose and overspread the thin cheeks of Mr. Marvyn, and his blue eyes deepened in a moment with a thoughtful shadow, as he looked inquiringly at the Doctor, who proceeded:—

"My mind labors with this subject of the enslaving of the Africans, Mr. Marvyn. We have just been declaring to the world that all men are born with an inalienable right to liberty. We have fought for it, and the Lord of Hosts has been with us; and can we stand before Him with our foot upon our brother's neck?"

A generous, upright nature is always more sensitive to blame than another,—sensitive in proportion to the amount of its reverence for good,—and Mr. Marvyn's face flushed, his eye kindled, and his compressed respiration showed how deeply the subject moved him. Mrs. Marvyn's eyes turned on him an anxious look of inquiry. He answered, however, calmly:—

"Doctor, I have thought of the subject myself. Mrs. Marvyn has lately been reading a pamphlet of Mr. Thomas Clarkson's on the slave-trade, and she was saying to me only last night, that she did not see but the argument extended equally to holding slaves. One thing, I confess, stumbles me:—Was there not an express permission given to Israel to buy and hold slaves of old?"

"Doubtless," said the Doctor; "but many permissions were given to them which were local and temporary; for if we hold them to apply to the human race, the Turks might quote the Bible for making slaves of us, if they could,—and the Algerines have the Scripture all on their side,—and our own blacks, at some future time, if they can get the power, might justify themselves in making slaves of us."

"I assure you, Sir," said Mr. Marvyn, "if I speak, it is not to excuse myself. But I am quite sure my servants do not desire liberty, and would not take it, if it were offered."

"Call them in and try it," said the Doctor. "If they refuse, it is their own matter."

There was a gentle movement in the group at the directness of this personal application; but Mr. Marvyn replied, calmly,—

"Cato is up at the eight-acre lot, but you may call in Candace. My dear, call Candace, and let the Doctor put the question to her."

Candace was at this moment sitting before the ample fireplace in the kitchen, with two iron kettles before her, nestled each in its bed of hickory coals, which gleamed out from their white ashes like sleepy, red eyes, opening and shutting. In one was coffee, which she was burning, stirring vigorously with a pudding-stick,—and in the other, puffy doughnuts, in shapes of rings, hearts, and marvellous twists, which Candace had such a special proclivity for making, that Mrs. Marvyn's table and closets never knew an intermission of their presence.

"Candace, the Doctor wishes to see you," said Mrs. Marvyn.

"Bress his heart!" said Candace, looking up, perplexed. "Wants to see me, does he? Can't nobody hab me till dis yer coffee's done; a minnit's a minnit in coffee;—but I'll be in dereckly," she added, in a patronizing tone. "Missis, you jes' go 'long in, an' I'll be dar dereckly."

A few moments after, Candace joined the group in the sitting-room, having hastily tied a clean, white apron over her blue linsey working-dress, and donned the brilliant Madras which James had lately given her, and which she had a barbaric fashion of arranging so as to give to her head the air of a gigantic butterfly. She sunk a dutiful curtsy, and stood twirling her thumbs, while the Doctor surveyed her gravely.

"Candace," said he, "do you think it right that the black race should be slaves to the white?"

The face and air of Candace presented a curious picture at this moment; a sort of rude sense of delicacy embarrassed her, and she turned a deprecating look, first on Mrs. Marvyn and then on her master.

"Don't mind us, Candace," said Mrs. Marvyn; "tell the Doctor the exact truth."

Candace stood still a moment, and the spectators saw a deeper shadow roll over her sable face, like a cloud over a dark pool of water, and her immense person heaved with her labored breathing.

"Ef I must speak, I must," she said. "No,—I neber did tink 'twas right. When Gineral Washington was here, I hearn 'em read de Declaration ob Independence and Bill o' Rights; an' I tole Cato den, says I, 'Ef dat ar' true, you an' I are as free as anybody.' It stands to reason. Why, look at me,—I a'n't a critter. I's neider huffs nor horns. I's a reasonable bein',—a woman,—as much a woman as anybody," she said, holding up her head with an air as majestic as a palm-tree;—"an' Cato,—he's a man, born free an' equal, ef dar's any truth in what you read,—dat's all."

"But, Candace, you've always been contented and happy with us, have you not?" said Mr. Marvyn.

"Yes, Mass'r,—I ha'n't got nuffin to complain ob in dat matter. I couldn't hab no better friends 'n you an' Missis."

"Would you like your liberty, if you could get it, though?" said Mr. Marvyn. "Answer me honestly."

"Why, to be sure I should! Who wouldn't? Mind ye," she said, earnestly raising her black, heavy hand, " 'ta'n't dat I want to go off, or want to shirk work; but I want to *feel free*. Dem dat isn't free has nuffin to gib to nobody;—dey can't show what dey would do."

"Well, Candace, from this day you are free," said Mr. Marvyn, solemnly.

Candace covered her face with both her fat hands, and shook and trembled, and, finally, throwing her apron over her head, made a desperate rush for the door, and threw herself down in the kitchen in a perfect tropical torrent of tears and sobs.

"You see," said the Doctor, "what freedom is to every human creature. The blessing of the Lord will be on this deed, Mr. Marvyn. 'The steps of a just man are ordered by the Lord, and he delighteth in his way.' "

At this moment, Candace reappeared at the door, her butterfly turban somewhat deranged with the violence of her prostration, giving a whimsical air to her portly person.

"I want ye all to know," she said, with a clearing-up snuff, "dat it's my will an' pleasure to go right on doin' my work jes' de same; an', Missis, please, I'll allers put three eggs in de crullers, now; an' I won't turn de wash-basin down in de sink, but hang it jam-up on de nail; an' I won't pick up chips in a milk-pan, ef I'm in ever so big a hurry;—I'll do eberyting jes' as ye tells me. Now you try me an' see ef I won't!"

Candace here alluded to some of the little private wilfulnesses which she had always obstinately cherished as reserved rights, in pursuing domestic matters with her mistress.

"I intend," said Mr. Marvyn, "to make the same offer to your husband, when he returns from work to-night."

"Laus, Mass'r,—why, Cato he'll do jes' as I do,—dere a'n't no kind o' need o' askin' him. 'Course he will."

A smile passed round the circle, because between Candace and her husband there existed one of those whimsical contrasts which one sometimes sees in married life. Cato was a small-built, thin, softly-spoken negro, addicted to a gentle chronic cough; and, though a faithful and skilful servant, seemed, in relation to his better half, much like a hill of potatoes under a spreading apple-tree. Candace held to him with a vehement and patronizing fondness, so devoid of conjugal reverence as to excite the comments of her friends.

"You must remember, Candace," said a good deacon to her one day, when she was ordering him about at a catechizing, "you ought to give honor to your husband; the wife is the weaker vessel."

"*I* de weaker vessel?" said Candace, looking down from the tower of her ample corpulence on the small, quiet man whom she had been fledging with the ample folds of a worsted comforter, out of which his little head and shining bead-eyes looked, much like a blackbird in a nest,—"*I* de weaker vessel? Umph!"

A whole woman's-rights' convention could not have expressed more in a day than was given in that single look and word. Candace considered a husband as a thing to be taken care of,—a rather inconsequent and somewhat troublesome species of pet, to be humored, nursed, fed, clothed, and guided in the way that he was to go,—an animal that was always losing off buttons, catching colds, wearing his best coat every day, and getting on his Sunday hat in a surreptitious manner for week-day occasions; but she often condescended to express it as her opinion that he was a blessing, and that she didn't know what she should do, if it wasn't for Cato. In fact, he seemed to supply her that which we are told is the great want in woman's situation,—an object in life. She sometimes was heard expressing herself very energetically in disapprobation of the conduct of one of her sable friends, named Jinny Stiles, who, after being presented with her own freedom, worked several years to buy that of her husband, but became afterwards so disgusted with her acquisition that she declared she would "neber buy anoder nigger."

"Now Jinny don't know what she's talkin' about," she would say. "S'pose he does cough and keep her awake nights, and take a little too much sometimes, a'n't he better'n no husband at all? A body wouldn't seem to hab nuffin to lib for, ef dey hadn't an ole man to look arter. Men is nate'lly foolish about some tings,—but dey's good deal better'n nuffin."

And Candace, after this condescending remark, would lift off with one hand a brass kettle in which poor Cato might have been drowned, and fly across the kitchen with it as if it were a feather.

XII.

Miss Prissy

WILL our little Mary really fall in love with the Doctor?—The question reaches us in anxious tones from all the circle of our readers; and what especially shocks us is, that grave doctors of divinity, and serious, stocking-knitting matrons seem to be the class who are particularly set against the success of our excellent orthodox hero, and bent on reminding us of the claims of that unregenerate James, whom we have sent to sea on purpose that our heroine may recover herself of that foolish partiality for him which all the Christian world seems bent on perpetuating.

"Now, really," says the Rev. Mrs. Q., looking up from her bundle of Sewing-Society work, "you are *not* going to let Mary marry the Doctor?"

My dear Madam, is not that just what you did, yourself, after having turned off three or four fascinating young sinners as good as James any day? Don't make us believe that you are sorry for it now!

"Is it possible," says Dr. Theophrastus, who is himself a stanch Hopkinsian divine, and who is at present recovering from his last grand effort on Natural and Moral Ability,—"is it possible that you are going to let Mary forget that poor young man and marry Dr. Hopkins? That will never do in the world!"

Dear Doctor, consider what would have become of you, if some lady at a certain time had not had the sense and discernment to fall in love with the *man* who came to her disguised as a theologian.

"But he's so old!" says Aunt Maria.

Not at all. Old? What do you mean? Forty is the very season of ripeness,—the very meridian of manly lustre and splendor.

"But he wears a wig."

My dear Madam, so did Sir Charles Grandison, and Lovelace, and all the other fine fellows of those days; the wig was the distinguishing mark of a gentleman.

No,—spite of all you may say and declare, we do insist that our Doctor is a very proper and probable subject for a young lady to fall in love with.

If women have one weakness more marked than another, it is towards veneration. They are born worshippers,—makers of silver shrines for some divinity or other, which, of course, they always think fell straight down from heaven.

The first step towards their falling in love with an ordinary mortal is generally to dress him out with all manner of real or fancied superiority; and having made him up, they worship him.

Now a truly great man, a man really grand and noble in heart and intellect, has this advantage with women, that he is an idol ready-made to hand; and so that very painstaking and ingenious sex have less labor in getting him up, and can be ready to worship him on shorter notice.

In particular is this the case where a sacred profession and a moral supremacy are added to the intellectual. Just think of the career of celebrated preachers and divines in all ages. Have they not stood like the image that "Nebuchadnezzar the king set up," and all womankind, coquettes and flirts not excepted, been ready to fall down and worship, even before the sound of cornet, flute, harp, sackbut, and so forth? Is not the faithful Paula, with her beautiful face, prostrate in reverence before poor, old, lean, haggard, dying St. Jerome, in the most splendid painting of the world, an emblem and sign of woman's eternal power of self-sacrifice to what she deems noblest in man? Does not old Richard Baxter tell us, with delightful single-heartedness, how his wife fell in love with him first, spite of his long, pale face,—and how she confessed, dear soul, after many years of married life, that she had found him *less* sour and bitter than she had expected?

The fact is, women are burdened with fealty, faith, reverence, more than they know what to do with; they stand like a hedge of sweet-peas, throwing out fluttering tendrils everywhere for something high and strong to climb by,—and when they find it, be it ever so rough in the bark, they catch upon it. And instances are not wanting of those who have

turned away from the flattery of admirers to prostrate themselves at the feet of a genuine hero who never wooed them,
except by heroic deeds and the rhetoric of a noble life.

Never was there a distinguished man whose greatness could
sustain the test of minute domestic inspection better than our
Doctor. Strong in a single-hearted humility, a perfect unconsciousness of self an honest and sincere absorption in high
and holy themes and objects, there was in him what we so
seldom see,—a perfect logic of life; his minutest deeds were
the true results of his sublimest principles. His whole nature,
moral, physical and intellectual, was simple, pure, and cleanly.
He was temperate as an anchorite in all matters of living,—
avoiding, from a healthy instinct, all those intoxicating stimuli
then common among the clergy. In his early youth, indeed,
he had formed an attachment to the almost universal clerical
pipe,—but, observing a delicate woman once nauseated by
coming into the atmosphere which he and his brethren had
polluted, he set himself gravely to reflect that that which
could so offend a woman must needs be uncomely and unworthy a Christian man; wherefore he laid his pipe on the
mantelpiece, and never afterwards resumed the indulgence.

In all his relations with womanhood he was delicate and
reverential, forming his manners by that old precept, "The
elder women entreat as mothers, the younger as sisters,"—
which rule, short and simple as it is, is, nevertheless, the most
perfect *résumé* of all true gentlemanliness. Then, as for person,
the Doctor was not handsome, to be sure; but he was what
sometimes serves with woman better,—majestic and manly;
and, when animated by thought and feeling, having even a
commanding grandeur of mien. Add to all this, that our valiant hero is now on the straight road to bring him into that
situation most likely to engage the warm partisanship of a
true woman,—namely, that of a man unjustly abused for
right-doing,—and one may see that it is ten to one our Mary
may fall in love with him yet before she knows it.

If it were not for this mysterious selfness-and-sameness
which makes this wild, wandering, uncanonical sailor, James
Marvyn, so intimate and internal,—if his thread were not knit
up with the thread of her life,—were it not for the old habit
of feeling for him, thinking for him, praying for him, hoping

for him, fearing for him, which—wo is us!—is the unfortunate habit of womankind,—if it were not for that fatal something which neither judgment, nor wishes, nor reason, nor common sense shows any great skill in unravelling,—we are quite sure that Mary would be in love with the Doctor within the next six months; as it is, we leave you all to infer from your own heart and consciousness what his chances are.

A new sort of scene is about to open on our heroine, and we shall show her to you, for an evening at least, in new associations, and with a different background from that homely and rural one in which she has fluttered as a white dove amid leafy and congenial surroundings.

As we have before intimated, Newport presented a *résumé* of many different phases of society, all brought upon a social level by the then universally admitted principle of equality.

There were scattered about in the settlement lordly mansions, whose owners rolled in emblazoned carriages, and whose wide halls were the scenes of a showy and almost princely hospitality. By her husband's side, Mrs. Katy Scudder was allied to one of these families of wealthy planters, and often recognized the connection with a quiet undertone of satisfaction, as a dignified and self-respecting woman should. She liked, once in a while, quietly to let people know, that, although they lived in the plain little cottage, and made no pretensions, yet they had good blood in their veins,—that Mr. Scudder's mother was a Wilcox, and that the Wilcoxes were, she supposed, as high as anybody,—generally ending the remark with the observation, that "all these things, to be sure, were matters of small consequence, since at last it would be of far more importance to have been a true Christian than to have been connected with the highest families of the land."

Nevertheless, Mrs. Scudder was not a little pleased to have in her possession a card of invitation to a splendid wedding-party that was going to be given, on Friday, at the Wilcox Manor. She thought it a very becoming mark of respect to the deceased Mr. Scudder that his widow and daughter should be brought to mind,—so becoming and praiseworthy, in fact, that, "though an old woman," as she said, with a complacent straightening of her tall, lithe figure, she really thought she must make an effort to go.

Accordingly, early one morning, after all domestic duties had been fulfilled, and the clock, loudly ticking through the empty rooms, told that all needful bustle had died down to silence, Mrs. Katy, Mary, and Miss Prissy Diamond, the dressmaker, might have been observed sitting in solemn senate around the camphor-wood trunk, before spoken of, and which exhaled vague foreign and Indian perfumes of silk and sandal-wood.

You may have heard of dignitaries, my good reader,—but, I assure you, you know very little of a situation of trust or importance compared to that of *the* dressmaker in a small New England town.

What important interests does she hold in her hands! How is she besieged, courted, deferred to! Three months beforehand, all her days and nights are spoken for; and the simple statement, that *only* on that day you can have Miss Clippers, is of itself an apology for any omission of attention elsewhere,—it strikes home at once to the deepest consciousness of every woman, married or single. How thoughtfully is everything arranged, weeks beforehand, for the golden, important season when Miss Clippers can come! On that day, there is to be no extra sweeping, dusting, cleaning, cooking, no visiting, no receiving, no reading or writing, but all with one heart and soul are to wait upon her, intent to forward the great work which she graciously affords a day's leisure to direct. Seated in her chair of state, with her well-worn cushion bristling with pins and needles at her side, her ready roll of patterns and her scissors, she hears, judges, and decides *ex cathedrá* on the possible or not possible, in that important art on which depends the right of presentation of the floral part of Nature's great horticultural show. She alone is competent to say whether there is any available remedy for the stained breadth in Jane's dress,—whether the fatal spot by any magical hocus-pocus can be cut out from the fulness, or turned up and smothered from view in the gathers, or concealed by some new fashion of trimming falling with generous appropriateness exactly across the fatal weak point. She can tell you whether that remnant of velvet will make you a basque,— whether Mamma's old silk can reappear in juvenile grace for Miss Lucy. What marvels follow her, wherever she goes!

What wonderful results does she contrive from the most un-likely materials, as everybody after her departure wonders to see old things become so much better than new!

Among the most influential and happy of her class was Miss Prissy Diamond,—a little, dapper, doll-like body, quick in her motions and nimble in her tongue, whose delicate complexion, flaxen curls, merry flow of spirits, and ready abundance of gayety, song, and story, apart from her profes-sional accomplishments, made her a welcome guest in every family in the neighborhood. Miss Prissy laughingly boasted being past forty, sure that the avowal would always draw down on her quite a storm of compliments, on the freshness of her sweet-pea complexion and the brightness of her merry blue eyes. She was well pleased to hear dawning girls won-dering why, with so many advantages, she had never married. At such remarks, Miss Prissy always laughed loudly, and de-clared that she had always had such a string of engagements with the women that she never found half an hour to listen to what any *man* living would say to her, supposing she could stop to hear him. "Besides, if I were to get married, nobody else could," she would say. "What would become of all the wedding-clothes for everybody else?" But sometimes, when Miss Prissy felt extremely gracious, she would draw out of her little chest just the faintest tip-end of a sigh, and tell some young lady, in a confidential undertone, that one of these days she would tell her something,—and then there would come a wink of her blue eyes and a fluttering of the pink ribbons in her cap quite stimulating to youthful inquisitive-ness, though we have never been able to learn by any of our antiquarian researches that the expectations thus excited were ever gratified.

In her professional prowess she felt a pardonable pride. What feats could she relate of wonderful dresses got out of impossibly small patterns of silk! what marvels of silks turned that could not be told from new! what reclaimings of waists that other dressmakers had hopelessly spoiled. Had not Mrs. General Wilcox once been obliged to call in her aid on a dress sent to her from Paris? and did not Miss Prissy work three days and nights on that dress, and make every stitch of that trimming over with her own hands, before it was fit to be

seen? And when Mrs. Governor Dexter's best silver-gray brocade was spoiled by Miss Pimlico, and there wasn't another
scrap to pattern it with, didn't she make a new waist out of
the cape and piece one of the sleeves twenty-nine times, and
yet nobody would ever have known that there was a joining
in it?

In fact, though Miss Prissy enjoyed the fair average plain-
sailing of her work, she might be said to *revel* in difficulties.
A full pattern with trimming, all ample and ready, awoke a
moderate enjoyment; but the resurrection of anything half-
worn or imperfectly made, the brilliant success, when, after
turning, twisting, piecing, contriving, and, by unheard-of in-
ventions of trimming, a dress faded and defaced was restored
to more than pristine splendor,—*that* was a triumph worth
enjoying.

It was true, Miss Prissy, like most of her nomadic compeers, was a little given to gossip; but, after all, it was innocent gossip,—not a bit of malice in it; it was only all the
particulars about Mrs. Thus-and-So's wardrobe,—all the sta-
tistics of Mrs. That-and-T'other's china-closet,—all the minute items of Miss Simkins's wedding-clothes,—and how her
mother cried, the morning of the wedding, and said that she
didn't know anything how she could spare Louisa Jane, only
that Edward was such a good boy that she felt she could love
him like an own son,—and what a providence it seemed that
the very ring that was put into the bride-loaf was the one that
he gave her when he first went to sea, when she wouldn't be
engaged to him because she thought she loved Thomas
Strickland better, but that was only because she hadn't found
him out, you know,—and so forth, and so forth. Sometimes,
too, her narrations assumed a solemn cast, and brought to
mind the hush of funerals, and told the words spoken in faint
whispers, when hands were clasped for the last time,—and of
utterances crushed out from hearts, when the hammer of a
great sorrow strikes out sparks of the divine, even from common stone; and there would be real tears in the little blue
eyes, and the pink bows would flutter tremulously, like the
last three leaves on a bare scarlet maple in autumn. In fact,
dear reader, *gossip*, like romance, has its noble side to it. How
can you love your neighbor as yourself and not feel a little

curiosity as to how he fares, what he wears, where he goes, and how he takes the great life tragi-comedy at which you and he are both more than spectators? Show me a person who lives in a country village absolutely without curiosity or interest on these subjects, and I will show you a cold, fat oyster, to whom the tide-mud of propriety is the whole of existence.

As one of our esteemed collaborators in the ATLANTIC remarks,—"A dull town, where there is neither theatre nor circus nor opera, must have some excitement, and the real tragedy and comedy of life *must* come in place of the second-hand. Hence the noted gossiping propensities of country-places, which, so long as they are not poisoned by envy or ill-will, have a respectable and picturesque side to them,—an undoubted leave to be, as probably has almost everything, which obstinately and always insists on being, except sin!"

As it is, it must be confessed that the arrival of Miss Prissy in a family was much like the setting up of a domestic show-case, through which you could look into all the families of the neighborhood, and see the never-ending drama of life,—births, marriages, deaths,—joy of new-made mothers, whose babes weighed just eight pounds and three quarters, and had hair that would part with a comb,—and tears of Rachels who wept for their children, and would not be comforted because they were not. Was there a tragedy, a mystery, in all Newport, whose secret closet had not been unlocked by Miss Prissy? She thought not; and you always wondered, with an uncertain curiosity, what those things might be over which she gravely shook her head, declaring, with such a look,—"Oh, if you only *could* know!"—and ending with a general sigh and lamentation, like the confidential chorus of a Greek tragedy.

We have been thus minute in sketching Miss Prissy's portrait, because we rather like her. She has great power, we admit; and were she a sour-faced, angular, energetic body, with a heart whose secretions had all become acrid by disappointment and dyspepsia, she might be a fearful gnome, against whose family visitations one ought to watch and pray. As it was, she came into the house rather like one of those breezy days of spring, which burst all the blossoms, set all the doors and windows open, make the hens cackle and the turtles peep,—filling a solemn Puritan dwelling with as much bustle and chatter as if a box of martins were setting up housekeeping in it.

Let us now introduce you to the sanctuary of Mrs. Scudder's own private bedroom, where the committee of exigencies, with Miss Prissy at their head, are seated in solemn session around the camphor-wood trunk.

"Dress, you know, is of *some* importance, after all," said Mrs. Scudder, in that apologetic way in which sensible people generally acknowledge a secret leaning towards anything so very mundane. While the good lady spoke, she was reverentially unpinning and shaking out of their fragrant folds creamy crape shawls of rich Chinese embroidery,—India muslin, scarfs, and aprons; and already her hands were undoing the pins of a silvery damask linen in which was wrapped her own wedding-dress. "I have always told Mary," she continued, "that, though our hearts ought not to be set on these things, yet they had their importance."

"Certainly, certainly, Ma'am," chimed in Miss Prissy. "I was saying to Miss General Wilcox, the other day, *I* didn't see how we could 'consider the lilies of the field,' without seeing the importance of looking pretty. I've got a flower-de-luce in my garden now, from one of the new roots that old Major Seaforth brought over from France, which is just the most beautiful thing you ever did see; and I was thinking, as I looked at it to-day, that, if women's dresses only grew on 'em as handsome and well-fitting as that, why, there wouldn't be any need of me; but as it is, why, we *must think*, if we want to look well. Now, peach-trees, I s'pose, might bear just as good peaches without the pink blows, but then who would want 'em to? Miss Deacon Twitchel, when I was up there the other day, kept kind o' sighin' 'cause Cerintha Ann is getting a new pink silk made up, 'cause she said it was such a dying world it didn't seem right to call off our attention: but I told her it wasn't any pinker than the apple-blossoms; and what with robins and blue-birds and one thing or another, the Lord is always calling off our attention; and I think we ought to observe the Lord's works and take a lesson from 'em."

"Yes, you are quite right," said Mrs. Scudder, rising and

shaking out a splendid white brocade, on which bunches of moss-roses were looped to bunches of violets by graceful fillets of blue ribbons. "This was my wedding-dress," she said.

Little Miss Prissy sprang up and clapped her hands in an ecstasy.

"Well, now, Miss Scudder, really!—did I ever see anything more beautiful? It really goes beyond anything *I* ever saw. I don't think, in all the brocades I ever made up, I ever saw so pretty a pattern as this."

"Mr. Scudder chose it for me, himself, at the silk-factory in Lyons," said Mrs. Scudder, with pardonable pride, "and I want it tried on to Mary."

"Really, Miss Scudder, this ought to be kept for *her* wedding-dress," said Miss Prissy, as she delightedly bustled about the congenial task. "I was up to Miss Marvyn's, a-working, last week," she said, as she threw the dress over Mary's head, "and she said that James expected to make his fortune in that voyage, and come home and settle down."

Mary's fair head emerged from the rustling folds of the brocade, her cheeks crimson as one of the moss-roses,—while her mother's face assumed a severe gravity, as she remarked that she believed James had been much pleased with Jane Spencer, and that, for her part, she should be very glad, when he came home, if he could marry such a steady, sensible girl, and settle down to a useful, Christian life.

"Ah, yes,—just so,—a very excellent idea, certainly," said Miss Prissy. "It wants a little taken in here on the shoulders, and a little under the arms. The biases are all right; the sleeves will want altering, Miss Scudder. I hope you will have a hot iron ready for pressing."

Mrs. Scudder rose immediately, to see the command obeyed; and as her back was turned, Miss Prissy went on in a low tone,—

"Now, *I*, for my part, don't think there's a word of truth in that story about James Marvyn and Jane Spencer; for I was down there at work one day when he called, and I *know* there couldn't have been anything between them,—besides, Miss Spencer, her mother, told me there wasn't.—There, Miss Scudder, you see that is a good fit. It's astonishing how near it comes to fitting, just as it was. I didn't think Mary was so near what you were, when you were a girl, Miss Scudder. The other day, when I was up to General Wilcox's, the General he was in the room when I was a-trying on Miss Wilcox's cherry velvet, and she was asking couldn't I come this week for her, and I mentioned I was coming to Miss Scudder, and the General says he,—'I used to know her when she was a girl. I tell you, she was one of the handsomest girls in Newport, by George!' says he. And says I,—'General, you ought to see her daughter.' And the General,—you know his jolly way,—he laughed, and says he,—'If she is as handsome as her mother was, I don't want to see her,' says he. 'I tell you, wife,' says he, 'I but just missed falling in love with Katy Stephens.'"

"I could have told her more than that," said Mrs. Scudder, with a flash of her old coquette girlhood for a moment lighting her eyes and straightening her lithe form. "I guess, if I should show a letter he wrote me once——But what am I talking about?" she said, suddenly stiffening back into a sensible woman. "Miss Prissy, do you think it will be necessary to cut it off at the bottom? It seems a pity to cut such rich silk."

"So it does, I declare. Well, I believe it will do to turn it up."

"I depend on you to put it a little into modern fashion, you know," said Mrs. Scudder. "It is many a year, you know, since it was made."

"Oh, never you fear! You leave all that to me," said Miss Prissy. "Now, there never was anything so lucky as, that, just before all these wedding-dresses had to be fixed, I got a letter from my sister Martha, that works for all the first families of Boston. And Martha she is really unusually privileged, because she works for Miss Cranch, and Miss Cranch gets letters from Miss Adams,—you know Mr. Adams is Ambassador now at the Court of St. James, and Miss Adams writes home all the particulars about the court-dresses; and Martha she heard one of the letters read, and she told Miss Cranch that she would give the best five-pound-note she had, if she could just copy that description to send to Prissy. Well, Miss Cranch let her do it, and I've got a copy of the letter here in my work-pocket. I read it up to Miss General Wilcox's, and to Major Seaforth's, and I'll read it to you."

Mrs. Katy Scudder was a born subject of a crown, and, though now a republican matron, had not outlived the reverence, from childhood implanted, for the high and stately doings of courts, lords, ladies, queens, and princesses, and therefore it was not without some awe that she saw Miss Prissy produce from her little black work-bag the well-worn epistle.

"Here it is," said Miss Prissy, at last. "I only copied out the parts about being presented at Court. She says:—

" 'One is obliged here to attend the circles of the Queen, which are held once a fortnight; and what renders it very expensive is, that you cannot go twice in the same dress, and a court-dress you cannot make use of elsewhere. I directed my mantua-maker to let my dress be elegant, but plain as I could possibly appear with decency. Accordingly, it is white lute-string, covered and full-trimmed with white crape, festooned with lilac ribbon and mock point-lace, over a hoop of enormous size. There is only a narrow train, about three yards in length to the gown-waist, which is put into a ribbon on the left side,—the Queen only having her train borne. Ruffled cuffs for married ladies,—treble lace ruffles, a very dress cap with long lace lappets, two white plumes, and a blonde lace handkerchief. This is my rigging.' "

Miss Prissy here stopped to adjust her spectacles. Her audience expressed a breathless interest.

"You see," she said, "I used to know her when she was Nabby Smith. She was Parson Smith's daughter, at Weymouth, and as handsome a girl as ever I wanted to see,—just as graceful as a sweet-brier bush. I don't believe any of those English ladies looked one bit better than she did. She was always a master-hand at writing. Everything she writes about, she puts it right before you. You feel as if you'd been there. Now, here she goes on to tell about her daughter's dress. She says:—

" 'My head is dressed for St. James's, and in my opinion looks very tasty. Whilst my daughter is undergoing the same operation, I set myself down composedly to write you a few lines. Well, methinks I hear Betsey and Lucy say, "What is cousin's dress?" *White*, my dear girls, like your aunt's, only differently trimmed and ornamented,—her train being wholly of white crape, and trimmed with white ribbon; the petticoat, which is the most showy part of the dress, covered and drawn up in what are called festoons, with light wreaths of beautiful flowers; the sleeves, white crape drawn over the silk, with a row of lace round the sleeve near the shoulder, another half-way down the arm, and a third upon the top of the ruffle,—a little stuck between,—a kind of hat-cap with three large feathers and a bunch of flowers,—a wreath of flowers on the hair.' "

Miss Prissy concluded this relishing description with a little smack of the lips, such as people sometimes give when reading things that are particularly to their taste.

"Now, I was a-thinking," she added, "that it would be an excellent way to trim Mary's sleeves,—three rows of lace, with a sprig to each row."

All this while, our Mary, with her white short-gown and blue stuff-petticoat, her shining pale brown hair and serious large blue eyes, sat innocently looking first at her mother, then at Miss Prissy, and then at the finery.

We do not claim for her any superhuman exemption from girlish feelings. She was innocently dazzled with the vision of courtly halls and princely splendors, and thought Mrs. Adams's descriptions almost a perfect realization of things she had read in "Sir Charles Grandison." If her mother thought it right and proper she should be dressed and made fine, she was glad of it; only there came a heavy, leaden feeling in her little heart, which she did not understand, but we who know womankind will translate it for you; it was, that a certain pair of dark eyes would not see her after she was dressed; and so, after all, what was the use of looking pretty?

"I wonder what James *would* think," passed through her head; for Mary had never changed a ribbon, or altered the braid of her hair, or pinned a flower in her bosom, that she had not quickly seen the effect of the change mirrored in those dark eyes. It was a pity, of course, now she had found out that she ought not to think about him, that so many thought-strings were twisted round him.

So while Miss Prissy turned over her papers, and read out of others extracts about Lord Caermarthen and Sir Clement Cotterel Dormer and the Princess Royal and Princess Augusta, in black and silver, with a silver netting upon the coat, and a head stuck full of diamond pins,—and Lady Salisbury and Lady Talbot and the Duchess of Devonshire, and scarlet satin sacks and diamonds and ostrich-plumes, and the King's kissing Mrs. Adams,—little Mary's blue eyes grew larger and larger, seeing far off on the salt green sea, and her ears heard only the ripple and murmur of those waters that carried her heart away,—till, by-and-by, Miss Prissy gave her a smart little tap, which awakened her to the fact that she was wanted again to try on the dress which Miss Prissy's nimble fingers had basted.

So passed the day,—Miss Prissy busily chattering, clipping, basting,—Mary patiently trying on to an unheard-of extent, —and Mrs. Scudder's neat room whipped into a perfect froth and foam of gauze, lace, artificial flowers, linings, and other aids, accessories, and abetments.

At dinner, the Doctor, who had been all the morning studying out his Treatise on the Millennium, discoursed tranquilly as usual, innocently ignorant of the unusual cares which were distracting the minds of his listeners. What should he know of dress-makers, good soul? Encouraged by the respectful silence of his auditors, he calmly expanded and soliloquized on his favorite topic, the last golden age of Time, the Marriage-Supper of the Lamb, when the purified Earth, like a repentant Psyche, shall be restored to the long-lost favor of a celestial Bridegroom, and glorified saints and angels shall walk familiarly as wedding-guests among men.

"Sakes alive!" said little Miss Prissy, after dinner, "did I ever hear any one go on like that blessed man?—such a spiritual mind! Oh, Miss Scudder, how you are privileged in having him here! I do really think it is a shame such a blessed man a'n't thought more of. Why, I could just sit and hear him talk all day. Miss Scudder, I wish sometimes you'd just let me make a ruffled shirt for him, and do it all up myself, and put a stitch in the hem that I learned from my sister Martha, who learned it from a French young lady who was educated in a convent;—nuns, you know, poor things, can do *some* things right; and I think *I* never saw such hemstitching as they do there;—and I should like to hemstitch the Doctor's ruffles; he is *so* spiritually-minded, it really makes me love him. Why, hearing him talk put me in mind of a real beautiful song of Mr. Watts,—I don't know as I could remember the tune."

And Miss Prissy, whose musical talent was one of her special *fortes*, tuned her voice, a little cracked and quavering, and sang, with a vigorous accent on each accented syllable,—

> "From *the* third heaven, where God resides,
>   That holy, happy place,
> The New Jerusalem comes down,
>   Adorned with shining grace.
>
> "Attending angels shout for joy,
>   And the bright armies sing,—
> 'Mortals! behold the sacred seat
>   Of your descending King!'"

"Take care, Miss Scudder!—that silk must be cut exactly on the bias"; and Miss Prissy, hastily finishing her last quaver, caught the silk and the scissors out of Mrs. Scudder's hand, and fell down at once from the Millennium into a discourse on her own particular way of covering piping-cord.

So we go, dear reader,—so long as we have a body and a soul. Two worlds must mingle,—the great and the little, the solemn and the trivial, wreathing in and out, like the grotesque carvings on a Gothic shrine;—only, did we know it rightly, nothing is trivial; since the human soul, with its awful shadow, makes all things sacred. Have not ribbons, cast-off flowers, soiled bits of gauze, trivial, trashy fragments of millinery, sometimes had an awful meaning, a deadly power, when they belonged to one who should wear them no more, and whose beautiful form, frail and crushed as they, is a hidden and a vanished thing for all time? For so sacred and individual is a human being, that, of all the million-peopled earth, no one form ever restores another. The mould of each mortal type is broken at the grave; and never, never, though you look through all the faces on earth, shall the exact form you mourn ever meet your eyes again! You are living your daily life among trifles that one death-stroke may make relics. One false step, one luckless accident, an obstacle on the track of a train, the tangling of the cord in shifting a sail, and the penknife, the pen, the papers, the trivial articles of dress and clothing, which to-day you toss idly and jestingly from hand to hand, may become dread memorials of that awful tragedy whose deep abyss ever underlies our common life.

XIII.

The Party

WELL, let us proceed to tell how the eventful evening drew on,—how Mary, by Miss Prissy's care, stood at last in a long-waisted gown flowered with rose-buds and violets, opening in front to display a white satin skirt trimmed with lace and flowers,—how her little feet were put into high-heeled shoes, and a little jaunty cap with a wreath of moss-rose-buds was fastened over her shining hair,—and how Miss Prissy, delighted, turned her round and round, and then declared that she must go and get the Doctor to look at her. She knew he must be a man of taste, he talked so beautifully about the Millennium; and so, bursting into his study, she actually chattered him back into the visible world, and, leading the blushing Mary to the door, asked him, point-blank, if he ever saw anything prettier.

The Doctor, being now wide awake, gravely gave his mind to the subject, and, after some consideration, said, gravely, "No,—he didn't think he ever did." For the Doctor was not a man of compliment, and had a habit of always thinking, before he spoke, whether what he was going to say was exactly true; and having lived some time in the family of President Edwards, renowned for beautiful daughters, he naturally thought them over.

The Doctor looked innocent and helpless, while Miss Prissy, having got him now quite into her power, went on volubly to expatiate on the difficulties overcome in adapting the ancient wedding-dress to its present modern fit. He told her that it was very nice,—said, "Yes, Ma'am," at proper places,—and, being a very obliging man, looked at whatever he was directed to, with round, blank eyes; but ended all with a long gaze on the laughing, blushing face, that, half in shame and half in perplexed mirth, appeared and disappeared as Miss Prissy in her warmth turned her round and showed her.

"Now don't she look beautiful?" Miss Prissy reiterated for the twentieth time, as Mary left the room.

The Doctor, looking after her musingly, said to himself,—
" 'The king's daughter is all glorious within; her clothing is
of wrought gold; she shall be brought unto the king in raiment of needle-work.' "

"Now, did I ever?" said Miss Prissy, rushing out. "How
that good man does turn everything! I believe you couldn't
get anything, that he wouldn't find a text right out of the
Bible about it. I mean to get the linen for that shirt this very
week, with the Miss Wilcox's money; they always pay well,
those Wilcoxes,—and I've worked for them, off and on, sixteen days and a quarter. To be sure, Miss Scudder, there's no
real need of my doing it, for I must say you keep him looking
like a pink,—but only I feel as if I must do something for
such a good man."

The good doctor was brushed up for the evening with zealous care and energy; and if he did *not* look like a pink, it was
certainly no fault of his hostess.

Well, we cannot reproduce in detail the faded glories of
that entertainment, nor relate how the Wilcox Manor and
gardens were illuminated,—how the bride wore a veil of real
point-lace,—how carriages rolled and grated on the gravel
walks, and negro servants, in white kid gloves, handed out
ladies in velvet and satin.

To Mary's inexperienced eye it seemed like an enchanted
dream,—a realization of all she had dreamed of grand and
high society. She had her little triumph of an evening; for
everybody asked who that beautiful girl was, and more than
one gallant of the old Newport first families felt himself
adorned and distinguished to walk with her on his arm. Busy,
officious dowagers repeated to Mrs. Scudder the applauding
whispers that followed her wherever she went.

"Really, Mrs. Scudder," said gallant old General Wilcox,
"where have you kept such a beauty all this time? It's a sin
and a shame to hide such a light under a bushel."

And Mrs. Scudder, though, of course, like you and me,
sensible reader, properly apprised of the perishable nature of
such fleeting honors, was, like us, too, but a mortal, and
smiled condescendingly on the follies of the scene.

The house was divided by a wide hall opening by doors,
the front one upon the street, the back into a large garden,

the broad central walk of which, edged on each side with high clipped hedges of box, now resplendent with colored lamps, seemed to continue the prospect in a brilliant vista.

The old-fashioned garden was lighted in every part, and the company dispersed themselves about it in picturesque groups.

We have the image in our mind of Mary as she stood with her little hat and wreath of rose-buds, her fluttering ribbons and rich brocade, as it were a picture framed in the door-way, with her back to the illuminated garden, and her calm, inno-cent face regarding with a pleased wonder the unaccustomed gayeties within.

Her dress, which, under Miss Prissy's forming hand, had been made to assume that appearance of style and fashion which more particularly characterized the mode of those times, formed a singular, but not unpleasing contrast to the sort of dewy freshness of air and mien which was character-istic of her style of beauty. It seemed so to represent a being who was in the world, yet not of it,—who, though living habitually in a higher region of thought and feeling, was art-lessly curious, and innocently pleased with a fresh experience in an altogether untried sphere. The feeling of being in a cir-cle to which she did not belong, where her presence was in a manner an accident, and where she felt none of the responsi-bilities which come from being a component part of a society, gave to her a quiet, disengaged air, which produced all the effect of the perfect ease of high breeding.

While she stands there, there comes out of the door of the bridal reception-room a gentleman with a stylishly-dressed lady on either arm, with whom he seems wholly absorbed. He is of middle height, peculiarly graceful in form and moulding, with that indescribable air of high breeding which marks the polished man of the world. His beautifully-formed head, delicate profile, fascinating sweetness of smile, and, above all, an eye which seemed to have an almost mesmeric power of attraction, were traits which distinguished one of the most celebrated men of the time, and one whose peculiar history yet lives not only in our national records, but in the private annals of many an American family.

"Good Heavens!" he said, suddenly pausing in conversation, as his eye accidentally fell upon Mary. "Who is that lovely creature?"

"Oh, that," said Mrs. Wilcox,—"why, that is Mary Scudder. Her father was a family connection of the General's. The family are in rather modest circumstances, but highly respectable."

After a few moments more of ordinary chit-chat, in which from time to time he darted upon her glances of rapid and piercing observation, the gentleman might have been observed to disembarrass himself of one of the ladies on his arm, by passing her with a compliment and a bow to another gallant, and, after a few moments more, he spoke something to Mrs. Wilcox, in a low voice, and with that gentle air of deferential sweetness which always made everybody well satisfied to do his will. The consequence was, that in a few moments Mary was startled from her calm speculations by the voice of Mrs. Wilcox, saying at her elbow, in a formal tone,—

"Miss Scudder, I have the honor to present to your acquaintance Colonel Burr, of the United States Senate."

XIV.

Aaron Burr

A<small>T</small> the period of which we are speaking, no name in the New Republic was associated with ideas of more brilliant promise, and invested with a greater *prestige* of popularity and success, than that of Colonel Aaron Burr.

Sprung of a line distinguished for intellectual ability, the grandson of a man whose genius has swayed New England from that day to this, the son of parents eminent in their day for influential and popular talents, he united in himself the quickest perceptions and keenest delicacy of fibre with the most diamond hardness and unflinching steadiness of purpose;—apt, subtle, adroit, dazzling, no man in his time ever began life with fairer chances of success and fame.

His name, as it fell on the ear of our heroine, carried with it the suggestion of all this; and when, with his peculiarly engaging smile, he offered his arm, she felt a little of the flutter natural to a modest young person unexpectedly honored with the notice of one of the great ones of the earth, whom it is seldom the lot of humble individuals to know, except by distant report.

But, although Mary was a blushing and sensitive person, she was not what is commonly called a diffident girl;—her nerves had that healthy, steady poise which gave her presence of mind in the most unwonted circumstances.

The first few sentences addressed to her by her new companion were in a tone and style altogether different from any in which she had ever been approached,—different from the dashing frankness of her sailor lover, and from the rustic gallantry of her other admirers.

That indescribable mixture of ease and deference, guided by refined tact, which shows the practised, high-bred man of the world, made its impression on her immediately, as a breeze on the chords of a wind-harp. She felt herself pleasantly swayed and breathed upon;—it was as if an atmosphere were around her in which she felt a perfect ease and freedom, an assurance that her lightest word might launch forth safely, as a tiny boat, on the smooth, glassy mirror of her listener's pleased attention.

"I came to Newport only on a visit of business," he said, after a few moments of introductory conversation. "I was not prepared for its many attractions."

"Newport has a great deal of beautiful scenery," said Mary.

"I have heard that it was celebrated for the beauty of its scenery, and of its ladies," he answered; "but," he added, with a quick flash of his dark eye, "I never realized the fact before."

The glance of the eye pointed and limited the compliment, and, at the same time, there was a wary shrewdness in it;— he was measuring how deep his shaft had sunk, as he always instinctively measured the person he talked with.

Mary had been told of her beauty since her childhood, not-withstanding her mother had essayed all that transparent, re-spectable hoaxing by which discreet mothers endeavor to blind their daughters to the real facts of such cases; but, in her own calm, balanced mind, she had accepted what she was so often told, as a quiet verity; and therefore she neither flut-tered nor blushed on this occasion, but regarded the speaker with a pleased attention, as one who was saying obliging things.

"Cool!" he thought to himself,—"hum!—a little rustic belle, I suppose,—well aware of her own value;—rather piquant, on my word!"

"Shall we walk in the garden?" he said,—"the evening is so beautiful."

They passed out of the door and began promenading the long walk. At the bottom of the alley he stopped, and, turn-ing, looked up the vista of box ending in the brilliantly-lighted rooms, where gentlemen, with powdered heads, lace ruffles, and glittering knee-buckles, were handing ladies in stiff brocades, whose towering heads were shaded by ostrich-feathers and sparkling with gems.

"Quite court-like, on my word!" he said. "Tell me, do you often have such brilliant entertainments as this?"

"I suppose they do," said Mary. "I never was at one before, but I sometimes hear of them."

"And *you* do not attend?" said the gentleman, with an accent which made the inquiry a marked compliment.

"No, I do not," said Mary; "these people generally do not visit us."

"What a pity," he said, "that their parties should want such an ornament! But," he added, "this night must make them aware of their oversight;—if you are not always in society after this, it will surely not be for want of solicitation."

"You are very kind to think so," replied Mary; "but even if it were to be so, I should not see my way clear to be often in such scenes as this."

Her companion looked at her with a glance a little doubtful and amused, and said, "And pray, why not? if the inquiry be not too presumptuous."

"Because," said Mary, "I should be afraid they would take too much time and thought, and lead me to forget the great object of life."

The simple gravity with which this was said, as if quite assured of the sympathy of her auditor, appeared to give him a secret amusement. His bright, dark eyes danced, as if he suppressed some quick repartee; but, drooping his long lashes deferentially, he said, in gentle tones, "I should like to know what so beautiful a young lady considers the great object of life."

Mary answered reverentially, in those words then familiar from infancy to every Puritan child, "To glorify God, and enjoy Him forever."

"*Really?*" he said, looking straight into her eyes with that penetrating glance with which he was accustomed to take the gauge of every one with whom he conversed.

"Is it *not?*" said Mary, looking back, calm and firm, into the sparkling, restless depths of his eyes.

At that moment, two souls, going with the whole force of their being in opposite directions, looked out of their windows at each other with a fixed and earnest recognition.

Burr was practised in every art of gallantry,—he had made womankind a study,—he never saw a beautiful face and form without a sort of restless desire to experiment upon it and try his power over the interior inhabitant; but, just at this moment, something streamed into his soul from those blue, earnest eyes, which brought back to his mind what pious people had so often told him of his mother, the beautiful and early-sainted Esther Burr. He was one of those persons who systematically managed and played upon himself and others, as a skilful musician, and on an instrument. Yet one secret of his fascination was the *naïveté* with which, at certain moments, he would abandon himself to some little impulse of a nature originally sensitive and tender. Had the strain of feeling which now awoke in him come over him elsewhere, he would have shut down some spring in his mind, and excluded it in a moment; but, talking with a beautiful creature whom he wished to please, he gave way at once to the emotion; — real tears stood in his fine eyes, and he raised Mary's hand to his lips, and kissed it, saying, —

"Thank you, my beautiful child, for so good a thought. It is truly a noble sentiment, though practicable only to those gifted with angelic natures."

"Oh, I trust not," said Mary, earnestly touched and wrought upon, more than she herself knew, by the beautiful eyes, the modulated voice, the charm of manner, which seemed to enfold her like an Italian summer.

Burr sighed, — a real sigh of his better nature, but passed out with all the more freedom that he felt it would interest his fair companion, who, for the time being, was the one woman of the world to him.

"Pure and artless souls like yours," he said, "cannot measure the temptations of those who are called to the real battle of life in a world like this. How many nobler aspirations fall withered in the fierce heat and struggle of the conflict!"

He was saying then what he really felt, often bitterly felt, — but *using* this real feeling advisedly, and with skilful tact, for the purpose of the hour.

What was this purpose? To win the regard, the esteem, the tenderness of a religious, exalted nature shrined in a beautiful form, — to gain and hold ascendency. It was a life-long habit, — one of those forms of refined self-indulgence which he pursued, thoughtless and reckless of consequences. He had found now the key-note of the character; it was a beautiful instrument, and he was well pleased to play on it.

"I think, Sir," said Mary, modestly, "that you forget the great provision made for our weakness."

"How?" he said.

"They that *wait on the Lord* shall renew their strength," she replied, gently.

He looked at her, as she spoke these words, with a pleased, artistic perception of the contrast between her worldly attire and the simple, religious earnestness of her words.

"She is entrancing!" he thought to himself,— "so altogether fresh and *naïve!*"

"My sweet saint," he said, "such as you are the appointed guardians of us coarser beings. The prayers of souls given up to worldliness and ambition effect little. You must intercede for us. I am very orthodox, you see," he added, with that subtle smile which sometimes irradiated his features. "I am fully aware of all that your reverend doctor tells you of the worthlessness of unregenerate doings; and so, when I see angels walking below, I try to secure 'a friend at court.' "

He saw that Mary looked embarrassed and pained at this banter, and therefore added, with a delicate shading of earnestness,—

"In truth, my fair young friend, I hope you *will* sometimes pray for me. I am sure, if I have any chance of good, it will come in such a way."

"Indeed I will," said Mary, fervently,—her little heart full, tears in her eyes, her breath coming quick,—and she added, with a deepening color, "I am sure, Mr. Burr, that there should be a covenant blessing for you, if for any one, for you are the son of a holy ancestry."

"*Eh, bien, mon ami, qu'est ce que tu fais ici?*" said a gay voice behind a clump of box; and immediately there started out, like a French picture from its frame, a dark-eyed figure, dressed like a Marquise of Louis XIV.'s time, with powdered hair, sparkling with diamonds.

"*Rien que m'amuser,*" he replied, with ready presence of mind, in the same tone, and then added,—"Permit me, Madame, to present to you a charming specimen of our genuine New England flowers. Miss Scudder, I have the honor to present you to the acquaintance of Madame de Frontignac."

"I am very happy," said the lady, with that sweet, lisping

accentuation of English which well became her lovely mouth. "Miss Scudder, I hope, is very well."

Mary replied in the affirmative,—her eyes resting the while with pleased admiration on the graceful, animated face and diamond-bright eyes which seemed looking her through.

"Monsieur la trouve bien séduisante apparemment," said the stranger, in a low, rapid voice, to the gentleman, in a manner which showed a mingling of pique and admiration.

"Petite jalouse! rassure-toi," he replied, with a look and manner into which, with that mobile force which was peculiar to him, he threw the most tender and passionate devotion. *"Ne suis-je pas à toi tout à fait?"*—and as he spoke, he offered her his other arm. "Allow me to be an unworthy link between the beauty of France and America."

The lady swept a proud curtsy backward, bridled her beautiful neck, and signed for them to pass her. "I am waiting here for a friend," she said.

"Whatever is your will is mine," replied Burr, bowing with proud humility, and passing on with Mary to the supper-room.

Here the company were fast assembling, in that high tide of good-humor which generally sets in at this crisis of the evening.

The scene, in truth, was a specimen of a range of society which in those times could have been assembled nowhere else but in Newport. There stood Dr. Hopkins in the tranquil majesty of his lordly form, and by his side, the alert, compact figure of his contemporary and theological opponent, Dr. Stiles, who, animated by the social spirit of the hour, was dispensing courtesies to right and left with the debonair grace of the trained gentleman of the old school. Near by, and engaging from time to time in conversation with them, stood a Jewish Rabbin, whose olive complexion, keen eye, and flowing beard gave a picturesque and foreign grace to the scene. Colonel Burr, one of the most brilliant and distinguished men of the New Republic, and Colonel de Frontignac, who had won for himself laurels in the corps of La Fayette, during the recent revolutionary struggle, with his brilliant, accomplished wife, were all unexpected and distinguished additions to the circle.

Burr gently cleared the way for his fair companion, and, purposely placing her where the full light of the wax chandeliers set off her beauty to the best advantage, devoted himself to her with a subserviency as deferential as if she had been a goddess.

For all that, he was not unobservant, when, a few moments after, Madame de Frontignac was led in, on the arm of a Senator, with whom she was presently in full flirtation.

He observed, with a quiet, furtive smile, that, while she rattled and fanned herself, and listened with apparent attention to the flatteries addressed to her, she darted every now and then a glance, keen as a steel blade towards him and his companion. He was perfectly adroit in playing off one woman against another, and it struck him with a pleasant sense of oddity, how perfectly unconscious his sweet and saintly neighbor was of the position in which she was supposed to stand by her rival; and poor Mary, all this while, in her simplicity, really thought that she had seen traces of what she would have called the "strivings of the spirit" in his soul. Alas! that a phrase weighed down with such mysterious truth and meaning should ever come to fall on the ear as mere empty cant!

With Mary it was a living form,—as were all her words; for in nothing was the Puritan education more marked than in the earnest *reality* and truthfulness which it gave to language; and even now, as she stands by his side, her large blue eye is occasionally fixed in dreamy reverie as she thinks what a triumph of Divine grace it would be, if these inward movings of her companion's mind *should* lead him, as all the pious of New England hoped, to follow in the footsteps of President Edwards, and forms wishes that she could see him some time when she could talk to him undisturbed.

She was too humble and too modest fully to accept the delicious flattery which he had breathed, in implying that her hand had had power to unseal the fountains of good in his soul; but still it thrilled through all the sensitive strings of her nature a tremulous flutter of suggestion.

She had read instances of striking and wonderful conversions from words dropped by children and women,—and suppose some such thing should happen to her! and that this so charming and distinguished and powerful being should be called into the fold of Christ's Church by her means! No, it was too much to be hoped,—but the very possibility was thrilling.

When, after supper, Mrs. Scudder and the Doctor made their adieus, Burr's devotion was still unabated. With an enchanting mixture of reverence and fatherly protection, he waited on her to the last,—shawled her with delicate care, and handed her into the small, one-horse wagon,—as if it had been the coach of a duchess.

"I have pleasant recollections connected with this kind of establishment," he said, as, after looking carefully at the harness, he passed the reins into Mrs. Scudder's hands. "It reminds me of school-days and old times. I hope your horse is quite safe, Madam."

"Oh, yes," said Mrs. Scudder, "I perfectly understand him."

"Pardon the suggestion," he replied;—"what is there that a New England matron does *not* understand? Doctor, I must call by-and-by, and have a little talk with you,—my theology, you know, needs a little straightening."

"We should all be happy to see you, Colonel Burr," said Mrs. Scudder; "we live in a very plain way, it is true,"——

"But can always find place for a friend,—that, I trust, is what you meant to say," he replied, bowing, with his own peculiar grace, as the carriage drove off.

"Really, a most charming person is this Colonel Burr," said Mrs. Scudder.

"He seems a very frank, ingenuous young person," said the Doctor; "one cannot but mourn that the son of such gracious parents should be left to wander into infidelity."

"Oh, he is not an infidel," said Mary; "he is far from it, though I think his mind is a little darkened on some points."

"Ah," said the Doctor, "have you had any special religious conversation with him?"

"A little," said Mary blushing; "and it seems to me that his mind is perplexed somewhat in regard to the doings of the unregenerate,—I fear that it has rather proved a stumbling-block in his way; but he showed *so* much feeling!—I could really see the tears in his eyes!"

"His mother was a most godly woman, Mary," said the Doctor. "She was called from her youth, and her beautiful person became a temple for the indwelling of the Holy Spirit. Aaron Burr is a child of many prayers, and therefore there is hope that he may yet be effectually called. He studied awhile with Bellamy," he added, musingly, "and I have often doubted whether Bellamy took just the right course with him."

"I hope he *will* call and talk with you," said Mary, earnestly; "what a blessing to the world, if such talents as his could become wholly consecrated!"

"Not many wise, not many mighty, not many noble are called," said the Doctor; "yet if it would please the Lord to employ my instrumentality and prayers, how much should I rejoice! I was struck," he added, "to-night, when I saw those Jews present, with the thought that it was, as it were, a type of that last ingathering, when both Jew and Gentile shall sit down lovingly together to the gospel feast. It is only by passing over and forgetting these present years, when so few are called and the gospel makes such slow progress, and looking unto that glorious time, that I find comfort. If the Lord but use me as a dumb stepping-stone to that heavenly Jerusalem, I shall be content."

Thus they talked while the wagon jogged soberly homeward, and the frogs and the turtles and the distant ripple of the sea made a drowsy, mingling concert in the summer-evening air.

Meanwhile Colonel Burr had returned to the lighted rooms, and it was not long before his quick eye espied Madame de Frontignac standing pensively in a window-recess, half hid by the curtain. He stole softly up behind her and whispered something in her ear.

In a moment she turned on him a face glowing with anger, and drew back haughtily; but Burr remarked the glitter of tears, not quite dried even by the angry flush of her eyes.

"In what have I had the misfortune to offend?" he said, crossing his arms upon his breast. "I stand at the bar, and plead, Not guilty."

He spoke in French, and she replied in the same smooth accents, —

"It was not for her to dispute Monsieur's right to amuse himself."

Burr drew nearer, and spoke in those persuasive, pleading tones which he had ever at command, and in that language whose very structure in its delicate *tutoiement* gives such opportunity for gliding on through shade after shade of intimacy and tenderness, till gradually the haughty fire of the eyes was quenched in tears, and, in the sudden revulsion of a strong, impulsive nature, she said what she called words of friendship, but which carried with them all the warmth of that sacred fire which is given to woman to light and warm the temple of home, and which sears and scars when kindled for any other shrine.

And yet this woman was the wife of his friend and associate!

Colonel de Frontignac was a grave and dignified man of forty-five. Virginie de Frontignac had been given him to wife when but eighteen,—a beautiful, generous, impulsive, wilful girl. She had accepted him gladly, for very substantial reasons. First, that she might come out of the convent where she was kept for the very purpose of educating her in ignorance of the world she was to live in. Second, that she might wear velvet, lace, cashmere, and jewels. Third, that she might be a Madame, free to go and come, ride, walk, and talk, without surveillance. Fourth,—and consequent upon this,—that she might go into company and have admirers and adorers.

She supposed, of course, that she loved her husband;— whom else should she love? He was the only man, except her father and brothers, that she had ever seen; and in the fortnight that preceded their marriage did he not send her the most splendid *bon-bons* every day, with bouquets of every pattern that ever taxed the brain of a Parisian *artiste?*—was not the *corbeille de mariage* a wonder and an envy to all her acquaintance?—and after marriage had she not found him always a steady, indulgent friend, easy to be coaxed as any grave papa?

On his part, Monsieur de Frontignac cherished his young wife as a beautiful, though somewhat absurd little pet, and amused himself with her frolics and gambols, as the gravest person often will with those of a kitten.

It was not until she knew Aaron Burr that poor Virginie de Frontignac came to that great awakening of her being which teaches woman what she is, and transforms her from a careless child to a deep-hearted, thinking, suffering human being.

For the first time, in his society she became aware of the charm of a polished and cultivated mind, able with exquisite tact to adapt itself to hers, to draw forth her inquiries, to excite her tastes, to stimulate her observation. A new world awoke around her,—the world of literature and taste, of art and of sentiment; she felt somehow, as if she had gained the growth of years in a few months. She felt within herself the stirring of dim aspiration, the uprising of a new power of self-devotion and self-sacrifice, a trance of hero-worship, a cloud of high ideal images,—the lighting up, in short, of all that God has laid, ready to be enkindled, in a woman's nature, when the time comes to sanctify her as the pure priestess of a domestic temple. But, alas! it was kindled by one who did it only for an experiment, because he felt an artistic pleasure in the beautiful light and heat, and cared not, though it burned a soul away.

Burr was one of those men willing to play with any charming woman the game of those navigators who give to simple natives glass beads and feathers in return for gold and diamonds,—to accept from a woman her heart's blood in return for such odds and ends and clippings as he can afford her from the serious ambition of life.

Look in with us one moment, now that the party is over, and the busy hum of voices and blaze of lights has died down to midnight silence and darkness; we make you clairvoyant, and you may look through the walls of this stately old mansion, still known as that where Rochambeau held his head-quarters, into this room, where two wax candles are burning on a toilette table, before an old-fashioned mirror. The slumberous folds of the curtains are drawn with stately gloom around a high bed, where Colonel de Frontignac has been for many hours quietly asleep; but opposite, resting with one elbow on the toilette table, her long black hair hanging down over her night-dress, and the brush lying listlessly in her hand, sits Virginie, looking fixedly into the dreamy depths of the mirror.

Scarcely twenty yet, all unwarned of the world of power and passion that lay slumbering in her girl's heart, led in the

meshes of custom and society to utter vows and take responsibilities of whose nature she was no more apprised than is a
slumbering babe, and now at last fully awake, feeling the
whole power of that mysterious and awful force which we
call love, yet shuddering to call it by its name, but by its light
beginning to understand all she is capable of, and all that
marriage should have been to her! She struggles feebly and
confusedly with her fate, still clinging to the name of duty,
and baptizing as friendship this strange new feeling which
makes her tremble through all her being. How can she dream
of danger in such a feeling, when it seems to her the awakening of all that is highest and noblest within her? She remembers when she thought of nothing beyond an opera-
ticket or a new dress, and now she feels that there might be
to her a friend for whose sake she would try to be noble and
great and good,—for whom all self-denial, all high endeavor,
all difficult virtue would become possible,—who would be to
her life, inspiration, order, beauty.

She sees him as woman always sees the man she loves,—
noble, great, and good;—for when did a loving woman ever
believe a man otherwise?—too noble, too great, too high,
too good, she thinks, for her,—poor, trivial, ignorant
coquette,—poor, childish, trifling Virginie! Has he not commanded armies? she thinks,—is he not eloquent in the senate? and yet what interest he has taken in her, a poor,
unformed, ignorant creature!—she never tried to improve
herself till since she knew him. And he is so considerate,
too,—so respectful, so thoughtful and kind, so manly and
honorable, and has such a tender friendship for her, such a
brotherly and fatherly solicitude! and yet, if she is haughty or
imperious or severe, how humbled and grieved he looks!
How strange that she could have power over such a man!

It is one of the saddest truths of this sad mystery of life,
that woman is, often, never so much an angel as just the moment before she falls into an unsounded depth of perdition.
And what shall we say of the man who leads her on as an
experiment,—who amuses himself with taking woman after
woman up these dazzling, delusive heights, knowing, as he
certainly must, where they lead?

We have been told, in extenuation of the course of Aaron

Burr, that he was not a man of gross passions or of coarse indulgence, but, in the most consummate and refined sense, *a man of gallantry*. This, then, is the descriptive name which polite society has invented for the man who does this thing!

Of old, it was thought that one who administered poison in the sacramental bread and wine had touched the very height of impious sacrilege; but this crime is white, by the side of his who poisons God's eternal sacrament of love and destroys a woman's soul through her noblest and purest affections.

We have given you the after-view of most of the actors of our little scene to-night, and therefore it is but fair that you should have a peep over the Colonel's shoulder, as he sums up the evening in a letter to a friend.

"My dear—— —

"As to the business, it gets on rather slowly. L—— and S—— are away, and the coalition cannot be formed without them; they set out a week ago from Philadelphia, and are yet on the road.

"Meanwhile, we have some providential alleviations,—as, for example, a wedding-party to-night, at the Wilcoxes', which was really quite an affair. I saw the prettiest little Puritan there that I have set eyes on for many a day. I really couldn't help getting up a flirtation with her, although it was much like flirting with a small copy of the 'Assembly's Catechism,'—of which last I had enough years ago, Heaven knows.

"But, really, such a *naïve*, earnest little saint, who has such real deadly belief, and opens such pitying blue eyes on one, is quite a stimulating novelty. I got myself well scolded by the fair Madame, (as angels scold,) and had to plead like a lawyer to make my peace;—after all, that woman really enchains me. Don't shake your head wisely,—'What's going to be the end of it?' I'm sure I don't know; we'll see, when the time comes.

"Meanwhile, push the business ahead with all your might. I shall not be idle. D—— must canvass the Senate thoroughly. I wish I could be in two places at once,—I would do it myself. *Au revoir.*

"*Ever yours,*
"BURR."

XV.

The Sermon

"AND now, Mary," said Mrs. Scudder, at five o'clock the next morning, "to-day, you know, is the Doctor's fast; so we won't get any regular dinner, and it will be a good time to do up all our little odd jobs. Miss Prissy promised to come in for two or three hours this morning, to alter the waist of that black silk; and I shouldn't be surprised if we should get it all done and ready to wear by Sunday."

We will remark, by way of explanation to a part of this conversation, that our Doctor, who was a specimen of life in earnest, made a practice, through the greater part of his pulpit course, of spending every Saturday as a day of fasting and retirement, in preparation for the duties of the Sabbath.

Accordingly, the early breakfast things were no sooner disposed of than Miss Prissy's quick footsteps might have been heard pattering in the kitchen.

"Well, Miss Scudder, how *do* you do this morning? and how do you do, Mary? Well, if you a'n't the beaters! up just as early as ever, and everything cleared away! I was telling Miss Wilcox there didn't ever seem to be anything done in Miss Scudder's kitchen, and I did verily believe you made your beds before you got up in the morning.

"Well, well, wasn't that a party last night?" she said, as she sat down with the black silk and prepared her ripping-knife.—"I must rip this myself, Miss Scudder; for there's a great deal in ripping silk so as not to let anybody know where it has been sewed.—You didn't know that I was at the party, did you? Well, I was. You see, I thought I'd just step round there, to see about that money to get the Doctor's shirt with, and there I found Miss Wilcox with so many things on her mind, and says she, 'Miss Prissy, you don't know how much it would help me, if I had somebody like you just to look after things a little here.' And says I, 'Miss Wilcox, you just go right to your room and dress, and don't you give yourself

669

one minute's thought about anything, and you see if I don't have everything just right.' And so, there I was, in for it; and I just staid through, and it was well I did,—for Dinah, she wouldn't have put near enough egg into the coffee, if it hadn't been for me; why, I just went and beat up four eggs with my own hands and stirred 'em into the grounds.

"Well,—but, really, wasn't I behind the door, and didn't I peep into the supper-room? I saw who was a-waitin' on Miss Mary. Well, they do say he's the handsomest, most fascinating man. Why, they say all the ladies in Philadelphia are in a perfect quarrel about him; and I heard he said he hadn't seen such a beauty he didn't remember when."

"We all know that beauty is of small consequence," said Mrs. Scudder. "I hope Mary has been brought up to feel that."

"Oh, of course," said Miss Prissy, "it's just like a fading flower; all is to be good and useful,—and that's what she is. I told 'em that her beauty was the least part of her; though I must say, that dress did fit like a biscuit,—if 'twas my own fitting.

"But, Miss Scudder, what do you think I heard 'em saying about the good Doctor?"

"I'm sure I don't know," said Mrs. Scudder; "I only know they couldn't say anything bad."

"Well, not bad exactly," said Miss Prissy,—"but they say he's getting such strange notions in his head. Why, I heard some of 'em say, he's going to come out and preach against the slave-trade; and I'm sure I don't know what Newport folks will do, if that's wicked. There a'n't hardly any money here that's made any other way; and I hope the Doctor a'n't a-going to do anything of that sort."

"I believe he is," said Mrs. Scudder; "he thinks it's a great sin, that ought to be rebuked;—and I think so too," she added, bracing herself resolutely; "that was Mr. Scudder's opinion when I first married him, and it's mine."

"Oh,—ah,—yes,—well,—if it's a sin, of course," said Miss Prissy; "but then—dear me!—it don't seem as if it could be. Why, just think how many great houses are living on it;— why, there's General Wilcox himself, and he's a very nice man; and then there's Major Seaforth; why, I could count

you off a dozen,—all our very first people. Why, Doctor
Stiles doesn't think so, and I'm sure he's a good Christian.
Doctor Stiles thinks it's a dispensation for giving the light of
the gospel to the Africans. Why, now I'm sure, when I was
a-working at Deacon Stebbins's, I stopped over Sunday once
'cause Miss Stebbins she was weakly,—'twas when she was
getting up, after Samuel was born,—no, on the whole, I believe it was Nehemiah,—but, any way, I remember I staid
there, and I remember, as plain as if 'twas yesterday, just after
breakfast, how a man went driving by in a chaise, and the
Deacon he went out and stopped him ('cause you know he
was justice of the peace) for travelling on the Lord's day,
and who should it be but Tom Seaforth?—he told the
Deacon his father had got a ship-load of negroes just come
in,—and the Deacon he just let him go; 'cause I remember
he said that was a plain work of necessity and mercy.*
Well, now who would 'a' thought it? I believe the Doctor
is better than most folks, but then the best people may be
mistaken, you know."

"The Doctor has made up his mind that it's his duty," said
Mrs. Scudder. "I'm afraid it will make him very unpopular;
but I, for one, shall stand by him."

"Oh, certainly, Miss Scudder, you are doing just right exactly. Well, there's one comfort, he'll have a great crowd to
hear him preach; 'cause as I was going round through the
entries last night, I heard 'em talking about it,—and Colonel
Burr said he should be there, and so did the General, and so
did Mr. What's-his-name there, that Senator from Philadelphia. I tell you, you'll have a full house."

It was to be confessed that Mrs. Scudder's heart rather sunk
than otherwise at this announcement; and those who have
felt what it is to stand almost alone in the right, in the face of
all the first families of their acquaintance, may perhaps find
some compassion for her,—since, after all, truth is invisible,
but "first families" are very evident. First families are often
very agreeable, undeniably respectable, fearfully virtuous, and
it takes great faith to resist an evil principle which incarnates
itself in the suavities of their breeding and amiability; and
therefore it was that Mrs. Scudder felt her heart heavy within

*A fact.

her, and could with a very good grace have joined in the Doctor's Saturday fast.

As for the Doctor, he sat the while tranquil in his study, with his great Bible and his Concordance open before him, culling, with that patient assiduity for which he was remarkable, all the terrible texts which that very unceremonious and old-fashioned book rains down so unsparingly on the sin of oppressing the weak.

First families, whether in Newport or elsewhere, were as invisible to him as they were to Moses during the forty days that he spent with God on the mount; he was merely thinking of his message,—thinking only how he should shape it, so as not to leave one word of it unsaid,—not even imagining in the least what the result of it was to be. He was but a voice, but an instrument,—the passive instrument through which an almighty will was to reveal itself; and the sublime fatalism of his faith made him as dead to all human considerations as if he had been a portion of the immutable laws of Nature herself.

So, the next morning, although all his friends trembled for him when he rose in the pulpit, he never thought of trembling for himself; he had come in the covered way of silence from the secret place of the Most High, and felt himself still abiding under the shadow of the Almighty. It was alike to him, whether the house was full or empty,—whoever were decreed to hear the message would be there; whether they would hear or forbear was already settled in the counsels of a mightier will than his,—he had the simple duty of utterance.

The ruinous old meeting-house was never so radiant with station and gentility as on that morning. A June sun shone brightly; the sea sparkled with a thousand little eyes; the birds sang all along the way; and all the notables turned out to hear the Doctor. Mrs. Scudder received into her pew, with dignified politeness, Colonel Burr and Colonel and Madame de Frontignac. General Wilcox and his portly dame, Major Seaforth, and we know not what of Vernons and De Wolfs, and other grand old names, were represented there; stiff silks rustled, Chinese fans fluttered, and the last court fashions stood revealed in bonnets.

Everybody was looking fresh and amiable,—a charming

and respectable set of sinners, come to hear what the Doctor would find to tell them about their transgressions.

Mrs. Scudder was calculating consequences; and, shutting her eyes on the too evident world about her, prayed that the Lord would overrule all for good. The Doctor prayed that he might have grace to speak the truth, and the whole truth. We have yet on record, in his published works, the great argument of that day, through which he moved with that calm appeal to the reason which made his results always so weighty.

"If these things be true," he said, after a condensed statement of the facts of the case, "then the following terrible consequences, which may well make all shudder and tremble who realize them, force themselves upon us, namely: that all who have had any hand in this iniquitous business, whether directly or indirectly, or have used their influence to promote it, or have consented to it, or even connived at it, or have not opposed it by all proper exertions of which they are capable,—all these are, in a greater or less degree, chargeable with the injuries and miseries which millions have suffered and are suffering, and are guilty of the blood of millions who have lost their lives by this traffic in the human species. Not only the merchants who have been engaged in this trade, and the captains who have been tempted by the love of money to engage in this cruel work, and the slave-holders of every description, are guilty of shedding rivers of blood, but all the legislatures who have authorized, encouraged, or even neglected to suppress it to the utmost of their power, and all the individuals in private stations who have in any way aided in this business, consented to it, or have not opposed it to the utmost of their ability, have a share in this guilt.

"This trade in the human species has been the first wheel of commerce in Newport, on which every other movement in business has chiefly depended; this town has been built up, and flourished in times past, at the expense of the blood, the liberty, and the happiness of the poor Africans; and the inhabitants have lived on this, and by it have gotten most of their wealth and riches. If a bitter woe is pronounced on him 'that buildeth his house by unrighteousness and his chambers by wrong,' Jer. xxii. 13,—to him 'that buildeth a town with blood, and stablisheth a city by iniquity,' Hab. ii. 12,—to 'the bloody city,' Ezek. xxiv. 6,—what a heavy, dreadful woe hangs over the heads of all those whose hands are defiled by the blood of the Africans, especially the inhabitants of this State and this town, who have had a distinguished share in this unrighteous and bloody commerce!"

He went over the recent history of the country, expatiated on the national declaration so lately made, that all men are born equally free and independent and have natural and in-alienable rights to liberty, and asked with what face a nation declaring such things could continue to hold thousands of their fellow-men in abject slavery. He pointed out signs of national disaster which foreboded the wrath of Heaven,—the increase of public and private debts, the spirit of murmuring and jealousy of rulers among the people, divisions and con-tentions and bitter party alienations, the jealous irritation of England constantly endeavoring to hamper our trade, the In-dians making war on the frontiers, the Algerines taking cap-tive our ships and making slaves of our citizens,—all evident tokens of the displeasure and impending judgment of an of-fended Justice.

The sermon rolled over the heads of the gay audience, deep and dark as a thunder-cloud, which in a few moments changes a summer sky into heaviest gloom. Gradually an expression of intense interest and deep concern spread over the listeners; it was the magnetism of a strong mind, which held them for a time under the shadow of his own awful sense of God's almighty justice.

It is said that a little child once described his appearance in the pulpit by saying, "I saw God there, and I was afraid."

Something of the same effect was produced on his audience now; and it was not till after sermon, prayer, and benediction were all over, that the respectables of Newport began gradu-ally to unstiffen themselves from the spell, and to look into each other's eyes for comfort, and to reassure themselves that after all they were the first families, and going on the way the world had always gone, and that the Doctor, of course, was a radical and a fanatic.

When the audience streamed out, crowding the broad aisle, Mary descended from the singers, and stood with her psalm-book in hand, waiting at the door to be joined by her mother and the Doctor. She overheard many hard words from people who, an evening or two before, had smiled so graciously upon them. It was therefore with no little determination of manner that she advanced and took the Doctor's arm, as if anxious to associate herself with his well-earned unpopularity,—and just at this moment she caught the eye and smile of Colonel Burr, as he bowed gracefully, yet not without a suggestion of something sarcastic in his eye.

XVI.

The Garret-Boudoir

WE suppose the heroine of a novel, among other privileges and immunities, has a prescriptive right to her own private boudoir, where, as a French writer has it, "she appears like a lovely picture in its frame."

Well, our little Mary is not without this luxury, and to its sacred precincts we will give you this morning a ticket of admission. Know, then, that the garret of this gambrel-roofed cottage had a projecting window on the seaward side, which opened into an immensely large old apple-tree, and was a look-out as leafy and secluded as a robin's nest.

Garrets are delicious places in any case, for people of thoughtful, imaginative temperament. Who has not loved a garret in the twilight days of childhood, with its endless stores of quaint, cast-off, suggestive antiquity,—old worm-eaten chests,—rickety chairs,—boxes and casks full of odd comminglings, out of which, with tiny, childish hands, we fished wonderful hoards of fairy treasure? What peep-holes, and hiding-places, and undiscoverable retreats we made to ourselves,—where we sat rejoicing in our security, and bidding defiance to the vague, distant cry which summoned us to school, or to some unsavory every-day task! How deliciously the rain came pattering on the roof over our head, or the red twilight streamed in at the window, while we sat snugly ensconced over the delicious pages of some romance, which careful aunts had packed away at the bottom of all things, to be sure we should never read it! If you have anything, beloved friends, which you wish your Charley or your Susie to be sure and read, pack it mysteriously away at the bottom of a trunk of stimulating rubbish, in the darkest corner of your garret;—in that case, if the book be at all readable, one that by any possible chance can make its way into a young mind, you may be sure that it will not only be read, but remembered to the longest day they have to live.

Mrs. Katy Scudder's garret was not an exception to the general rule. Those quaint little people who touch with so airy a grace all the lights and shadows of great beams, bare rafters, and unplastered walls, had not failed in their work there. Was there not there a grand easy-chair of stamped-leather, minus two of its hinder legs, which had genealogical associations through the Wilcoxes with the Vernons and through the Vernons quite across the water with Old England? and was there not a dusky picture, in an old tarnished frame, of a woman of whose tragic end strange stories were whispered,—one of the sufferers in the time when witches were unceremoniously helped out of the world, instead of being, as now-a-days, helped to make their fortune in it by table-turning?

Yes, there were all these things, and many more which we will not stay to recount, but bring you to the boudoir which Mary has constructed for herself around the dormer-window which looks into the whispering old apple-tree.

The inclosure was formed by blankets and bed-spreads, which, by reason of their antiquity, had been pensioned off to an undisturbed old age in the garret,—not *common* blankets or bed-spreads, either,—bought, as you buy yours, out of a shop,—spun or woven by machinery,—without individuality or history. Every one of these curtains had its story. The one on the right, nearest the window, and already falling into holes, is a Chinese linen, and even now displays unfaded, quaint patterns of sleepy-looking Chinamen, in conical hats, standing on the leaves of most singular herbage, and with hands forever raised in act to strike bells, which never are struck and never will be till the end of time. These, Mrs. Katy Scudder had often instructed Mary, were brought from the Indies by her great-great-grandfather, and were her grandmother's wedding-curtains,—the grandmother who had blue eyes like hers and was just about her height.

The next spread was spun and woven by Mrs. Katy's beloved Aunt Eunice,—a mythical personage, of whom Mary gathered vague accounts that she was disappointed in love, and that this very article was part of a bridal outfit, prepared in vain, against the return of one from sea, who never came back,—and she heard of how she sat wearily and patiently at

her work, this poor Aunt Eunice, month after month, starting
every time she heard the gate shut, every time she heard the
tramp of a horse's hoof, every time she heard the news of a
sail in sight,—her color, meanwhile, fading and fading as life
and hope bled away at an inward wound,—till at last she
found comfort and reunion beyond the veil.

Next to this was a bed-quilt pieced in tiny blocks, none of
them bigger than a sixpence, containing, as Mrs. Katy said,
pieces of the gowns of all her grandmothers, aunts, cousins,
and female relatives for years back,—and mated to it was one
of the blankets which had served Mrs. Scudder's uncle in his
bivouac at Valley Forge, when the American soldiers went on
the snows with bleeding feet, and had scarce anything for
daily bread except a morning message of patriotism and hope
from George Washington.

Such were the memories woven into the tapestry of our
little boudoir. Within, fronting the window, stands the large
spinning-wheel, one end adorned with a snowy pile of fleecy
rolls,—and beside it, a reel and a basket of skeins of yarn,—
and open, with its face down on the beam of the wheel, lay
always a book, with which the intervals of work were beguiled.

The dusky picture of which we have spoken hung against
the rough wall in one place, and in another appeared an old
engraved head of one of the Madonnas of Leonardo da Vinci,
a picture which to Mary had a mysterious interest, from the
fact of its having been cast on shore after a furious storm, and
found like a waif lying in the sea-weed; and Mrs. Marvyn,
who had deciphered the signature, had not ceased exploring
till she found for her, in an Encyclopædia, a life of that wonderful man, whose greatness enlarges our ideas of what is possible to humanity,—and Mary pondering thereon, felt the
seaworn picture as a constant vague inspiration.

Here our heroine spun for hours and hours,—with intervals, when, crouched on a low seat in the window, she pored
over her book, and then, returning again to her work,
thought of what she had read to the lulling burr of the sound-
ing wheel.

By chance a robin had built its nest so that from her retreat
she could see the five little blue eggs, whenever the patient

brooding mother left them for a moment uncovered. And sometimes, as she sat in dreamy reverie, resting her small, round arms on the window-sill, she fancied that the little feathered watcher gave her familiar nods and winks of a confidential nature,—cocking the small head first to one side and then to the other, to get a better view of her gentle human neighbor.

I dare say it seems to you, reader, that we have travelled in our story, over a long space of time, because we have talked so much and introduced so many personages and reflections; but, in fact, it is only Wednesday week since James sailed, and the eggs which were brooded when he went are still unhatched in the nest, and the apple-tree has changed only in having now a majority of white blossoms over the pink buds.

This one week has been a critical one to our Mary;—in it, she has made the great discovery, that she loves; and she has made her first step into the gay world; and now she comes back to her retirement to think the whole over by herself. It seems a dream to her, that she who sits there now reeling yarn in her stuff petticoat and white short-gown is the same who took the arm of Colonel Burr amid the blaze of wax-lights and the sweep of silks and rustle of plumes. She wonders dreamily as she remembers the dark, lovely face of the foreign Madame, so brilliant under its powdered hair and flashing gems,—the sweet, foreign accents of the voice,—the tiny, jewelled fan, with its glancing pictures and sparkling tassels, whence exhaled vague and floating perfumes; then she hears again that manly voice, softened to tones so seductive, and sees those fine eyes with the tears in them, and wonders within herself that *he* could have kissed her hand with such veneration, as if she had been a throned queen.

But here the sound of busy, pattering footsteps is heard on the old, creaking staircase, and soon the bows of Miss Prissy's bonnet part the folds of the boudoir drapery, and her merry, May-day face looks in.

"Well, really, Mary, how do you do, to be sure? You wonder to see me, don't you? but I thought I must just run in, a minute, on my way up to Miss Marvyn's. I promised her at least a half-a-day, though I didn't see how I was to spare it,— for I tell Miss Wilcox I just run and run till it does seem as if my feet would drop off; but I thought I must just step in to say, that I, for my part, *do admire* the Doctor more than ever, and I was telling your mother we mus'n't mind too much what people say. I 'most made Miss Wilcox angry, standing up for him; but I put it right to her, and says I, 'Miss Wilcox, you know folks *must* speak what's on their mind,—in particular ministers must; and you know, Miss Wilcox,' I says, 'that the Doctor *is* a good man, and lives up to his teaching, if anybody in this world does, and gives away every dollar he can lay hands on to those poor negroes, and works over 'em and teaches 'em as if they were his brothers'; and says I, 'Miss Wilcox, you know I don't spare myself, night nor day, trying to please you and do your work to give satisfaction; but when it comes to my conscience,' says I, 'Miss Wilcox, you know I always must speak out, and if it was the last word I had to say on my dying bed, I'd say that I think the Doctor is right.' Why! what things he told about the slave-ships, and packing those poor creatures so that they couldn't move nor breathe!—why, I declare, every time I turned over and stretched in bed, I thought of it;—and says I, 'Miss Wilcox, I do believe that the judgments of God will come down on us, if something a'n't done, and I shall always stand by the Doctor,' says I;—and, if you'll believe me, just then I turned round and saw the General; and the General, he just haw-hawed right out, and says he, 'Good for you, Miss Prissy! that's real grit,' says he, 'and I like you better for it.'—Laws," added Miss Prissy, reflectively, "I sha'n't lose by it, for Miss Wilcox knows she never can get anybody to do the work for her that I will."

"Do you think," said Mary, "that there are a great many made angry?"

"Why, bless your heart, child, haven't you heard?—Why, there never was such a talk in all Newport. Why, you know Mr. Simeon Brown is gone clear off to Dr. Stiles; and Miss Brown, I was making up her plum-colored satin o' Monday, and you ought to 'a' heard her talk. But, I tell you, I fought her. She used to talk to me," said Miss Prissy, sinking her voice to a mysterious whisper, "'cause I never could come to it to say that I was willin' to be lost, if it was for the glory of God; and she always told me folks could just bring their

minds right up to anything they knew they must; and I just
got the tables turned on her, for they talked and abused the
Doctor till they fairly wore me out, and says I, 'Well, Miss
Brown, I'll give in, that you and Mr. Brown *do* act up to your
principles; you certainly *act* as if you were willing to be
damned';—and so do all those folks who will live on the
blood and groans of the poor Africans, as the Doctor said;
and I should think, by the way Newport people are making
their money, that they were all pretty willing to go that
way,—though, whether it's for the glory of God, or not, I'm
doubting.—But you see, Mary," said Miss Prissy, sinking her
voice again to a solemn whisper, "I never was *clear* on that
point; it always did seem to me a dreadful high place to come
to, and it didn't seem to be given to me; but I thought, perhaps, if it *was* necessary, it would be given, you know,—for
the Lord always has been so good to me that I've faith to
believe that, and so I just say, 'The Lord is my shepherd, I
shall not want' ";—and Miss Prissy hastily whisked a little
drop out of her blue eye with her handkerchief.

At this moment, Mrs. Scudder came into the boudoir with
a face expressive of some anxiety.

"I suppose Miss Prissy has told you," she said, "the news
about the Browns. That'll make a great falling off in the Doctor's salary; and I feel for him, because I know it will come
hard to him not to be able to help and do, especially for these
poor negroes, just when he will. But then we must put everything on the most economical scale we can, and just try, all
of us, to make it up to him. I was speaking to Cousin Zebedee about it, when he was down here, on Monday, and he is
all clear;—he has made out free papers for Candace and Cato
and Dinah, and they couldn't, one of 'em, be hired to leave
him; and he says, from what he's seen already, he has no
doubt but they'll do enough more to pay for their wages."

"Well," said Miss Prissy, "I haven't got anybody to care for
but myself. I was telling sister Elizabeth, one time, (she's married and got four children,) that I could take a storm a good
deal easier than she could, 'cause I hadn't near so many sails
to pull down; and now, you just look to me for the Doctor's
shirts, 'cause, after this, they shall all come in ready to put on,
if I have to sit up till morning. And I hope, Miss Scudder,

you can trust me to make them; for if I do say it myself, I a'n't afraid to do fine stitching 'longside of anybody,—and hemstitching ruffles, too; and I haven't shown you yet that French stitch I learned of the nuns;—but you just set your heart at rest about the Doctor's shirts. I always thought," continued Miss Prissy, laughing, "that I should have made a famous hand about getting up that tabernacle in the wilderness, with the blue and the purple and fine-twined linen; it's one of my favorite passages, that is;—different things, you know, are useful to different people."

"Well," said Mrs. Scudder, "I see that it's our call to be a remnant small and despised, but I hope we sha'n't shrink from it. I thought, when I saw all those fashionable people go out Sunday, tossing their heads and looking so scornful, that I hoped grace would be given me to be faithful."

"And what does the Doctor say?" said Miss Prissy.

"He hasn't said a word; his mind seems to be very much lifted above all these things."

"La, yes," said Miss Prissy, "that's one comfort; he'll never know where his shirts come from; and besides that, Miss Scudder," she said, sinking her voice to a whisper, "as you know, I haven't any children to provide for,—though I was telling Elizabeth t'other day, when I was making up frocks for her children, that I believed old maids, first and last, did more providing for children than married women; but still I do contrive to slip away a pound-note, now and then, in my little old silver tea-pot that was given to me when they settled old Mrs. Simpson's property, (I nursed her all through her last sickness, and laid her out with my own hands,) and, as I was saying, if ever the Doctor should want money, you just let me know."

"Thank you, Miss Prissy," said Mrs. Scudder; "we all know where your heart is."

"And now," added Miss Prissy, "what do you suppose they say? Why, they say Colonel Burr is struck dead in love with our Mary; and you know his wife's dead, and he's a widower; and they do say that he'll get to be the next President. Sakes alive! Well, Mary must be careful, if she don't want to be carried off; for they do say that there can't any woman resist him, that sees enough of him. Why, there's that poor French

woman, Madame——what do you call her, that's staying
with the Vernons?—they say she's over head and ears in love
with him."

"But she's a married woman," said Mary; "it can't be possible."

Mrs. Scudder looked reprovingly at Miss Prissy, and for a
few moments there was great shaking of heads and a whispered conference between the two ladies, ending in Miss
Prissy's going off, saying, as she went down stairs,—

"Well, if women will do so, I, for my part, can't blame the
men."

In a few moments Miss Prissy rushed back as much discomposed as a clucking hen who has seen a hawk.

"Well, Miss Scudder, what do you think? Here's Colonel
Burr come to call on the ladies!"

Mrs. Scudder's first movement, in common with all middle-aged gentlewomen, was to put her hand to her head and
reflect that she had not on her best cap; and Mary looked
down at her dimpled hands, which were blue from the contact with mixed yarn she had just been spinning.

"Now, I'll tell you what," said Miss Prissy,—"wasn't it
lucky you had me here? for I first saw him coming in at the
gate, and I whipped in quick as a wink and opened the best-
room window-shutters, and then I was back at the door, and
he bowed to me as if I'd been a queen, and says he, 'Miss
Prissy, how fresh you're looking this morning!' You see, I
was in working at the Vernons', but I never thought as he'd
noticed me. And then he inquired in the handsomest way for
the ladies and the Doctor, and so I took him into the parlor
and settled him down, and then I ran into the study, and you
may depend upon it I flew round lively for a few minutes. I
got the Doctor's study-gown off, and got his best coat on,
and put on his wig for him, and started him up kinder
lively,—you know it takes me to get him down into this
world,—and so there he's in talking with him; and so you
can just slip down and dress yourselves,—easy as not."

Meanwhile Colonel Burr was entertaining the simple-
minded Doctor with all the grace of a young neophyte come
to sit at the feet of superior truth. There are some people who
receive from Nature as a gift a sort of graceful facility of sym-

pathy, by which they incline to take on, for the time being, the sentiments and opinions of those with whom they converse, as the chameleon was fabled to change its hue with every surrounding. Such are often supposed to be wilfully acting a part, as exerting themselves to flatter and deceive, when in fact they are only framed so sensitive to the sphere of mental emanation which surrounds others that it would require an exertion *not* in some measure to harmonize with it. In approaching others in conversation, they are like a musician who joins a performer on an instrument,—it is impossible for them to strike a discord; their very nature urges them to bring into play faculties according in vibration with those which another is exerting. It was as natural as possible for Burr to commence talking with the Doctor on scenes and incidents in the family of President Edwards, and his old tutor, Dr. Bellamy,—and thence to glide on to the points of difference and agreement in theology, with a suavity and deference which acted on the good man like a June sun on a budding elm-tree. The Doctor was soon wide awake, talking with fervent animation on the topic of disinterested benevolence,—Burr the mean while studying him with the quiet interest of an observer of natural history, who sees a new species developing before him. At all the best possible points he interposed suggestive questions, and set up objections in the quietest manner for the Doctor to knock down, smiling ever the while as a man may who truly and genuinely does not care a *sou* for truth on any subject not practically connected with his own schemes in life. He therefore gently guided the Doctor to sail down the stream of his own thoughts till his bark glided out into the smooth waters of the Millennium, on which, with great simplicity, he gave his views at length.

It was just in the midst of this that Mary and her mother entered. Burr interrupted the conversation to pay them the compliments of the morning,—to inquire for their health, and hope they suffered no inconvenience from their night-ride from the party; then, seeing the Doctor still looking eager to go on, he contrived with gentle dexterity to tie again the broken thread of conversation.

"Our excellent friend," he said, "was explaining to me his views of a future Millennium. I assure you, ladies, that we sometimes find ourselves in company which enables us to believe in the perfectibility of the human species. We see family retreats, so unaffected, so charming in their simplicity, where industry and piety so go hand in hand! One has only to suppose all families such, to imagine a Millennium."

There was no disclaiming this compliment, because so delicately worded, that, while perfectly clear to the internal sense, it was, in a manner, veiled and unspoken.

Meanwhile the Doctor, who sat ready to begin where he left off, turned to his complaisant listener and resumed an exposition of the Apocalypse.

"To my mind, it is certain," he said, "as it is now three hundred years since the fifth vial was poured out, there is good reason to suppose that the sixth vial began to be poured out at the beginning of the last century, and has been running for a hundred years or more, so that it is run nearly out; the seventh and last vial will begin to run early in the next century."

"You anticipate, then, no rest for the world for some time to come?" said Burr.

"Certainly not," said the Doctor, definitively; "there will be no rest from overturnings till He whose right it is shall come.

"The passage," he added, "concerning the drying up of the river Euphrates, under the sixth vial, has a distinct reference, I think, to the account in ancient writers of the taking of Babylon, and prefigures, in like manner, that the resources of that modern Babylon, the Popish power, shall continue to be drained off, as they have now been drying up for a century or more, till, at last, there will come a sudden and final downfall of that power. And after that will come the first triumphs of truth and righteousness,—the marriage-supper of the Lamb."

"These investigations must undoubtedly possess a deep interest for you, Sir," said Burr; "the hope of a future as well as the tradition of a past age of gold seems to have been one of the most cherished conceptions of the human breast."

"In those times," continued the Doctor, "the whole earth will be of one language."

"Which language, Sir, do you suppose will be considered worthy of such preëminence?" inquired his listener.

"That will probably be decided by an amicable conference

of all nations," said the Doctor; "and the one universally considered most valuable will be adopted; and the literature of all other nations being translated into it, they will gradually drop all other tongues. Brother Stiles thinks it will be the Hebrew. I am not clear on that point. The Hebrew seems to me too inflexible, and not sufficiently copious. I do not think," he added, after some consideration, "that it will be the Hebrew tongue."

"I am most happy to hear it, Sir," said Burr, gravely; "I never felt much attracted to that language. But, ladies," he added, starting up with animation, "I must improve this fine weather to ask you to show me the view of the sea from this little hill beyond your house, it is evidently so fine;—I trust I am not intruding too far on your morning?"

"By no means, Sir," said Mrs. Scudder, rising; "we will go with you in a moment."

And soon Colonel Burr, with one on either arm, was to be seen on the top of the hill beyond the house,—the very one from which Mary, the week before, had seen the retreating sail we all wot of. Hence, though her companion contrived, with the adroitness of a practised man of gallantry, to direct his words and looks as constantly to her as if they had been in a *tête-a-tête,* and although nothing could be more graceful, more delicately flattering, more engaging, still the little heart kept equal poise; for where a true love has once bolted the door, a false one serenades in vain under the window.

Some fine, instinctive perceptions of the real character of the man beside her seemed to have dawned on Mary's mind in the conversation of the morning;—she had felt the covert and subtle irony that lurked beneath his polished smile, felt the utter want of faith or sympathy in what she and her revered friend deemed holiest, and therefore there was a calm dignity in her manner of receiving his attentions which rather piqued and stimulated his curiosity. He had been wont to boast that he could subdue any woman, if he could only see enough of her; in the first interview in the garden, he had made her color come and go and brought tears to her eyes in a manner that interested his fancy, and he could not resist the impulse to experiment again. It was a new sensation to him, to find himself quietly studied and calmly measured by those thoughtful blue eyes; he felt, with his fine, instinctive tact, that the soul within was infolded in some crystalline sphere of protection, transparent, but adamantine, so that he could not touch it. What was that secret poise, that calm, immutable centre on which she rested, that made her, in her rustic simplicity, so unapproachable and so strong?

Burr remembered once finding in his grandfather's study, among a mass of old letters, one in which that great man, in early youth, described his future wife, then known to him only by distant report. With his keen natural sense of everything fine and poetic, he had been struck with this passage, as so beautifully expressing an ideal womanhood, that he had in his earlier days copied it in his private *recueil*.

"They say," it ran, "that there is a young lady who is beloved of that Great Being who made and rules the world, and that there are certain seasons in which this Great Being, in some way or other invisible, comes to her and fills her mind with such exceeding sweet delight, that she hardly cares for anything except to meditate on him; that she expects, after a while, to be received up where he is, to be raised up out of the world and caught up into heaven, being assured that he loves her too well to let her remain at a distance from him always. Therefore, if you present all the world before her, with the richest of its treasures, she disregards it. She has a strange sweetness in her mind, and singular purity in her affections; and you could not persuade her to do anything wrong or sinful, if you should give her all the world. She is of a wonderful sweetness, calmness, and universal benevolence of mind, especially after this great God has manifested himself to her mind. She will sometimes go from place to place singing sweetly, and seems to be always full of joy and pleasure; and no one knows for what. She loves to be alone, walking in fields and groves, and seems to have some invisible one always conversing with her."

A shadowy recollection of this description crossed his mind more than once, as he looked into those calm and candid eyes. Was there, then, a truth in that inner union of chosen souls with God, of which his mother and her mother before her had borne meek witness,—their souls shining out as sacred lamps through the alabaster walls of a temple?

But then, again, had he not logically met and demonstrated, to his own satisfaction, the nullity of the religious dogmas on which New England faith was based? There could be no such inner life, he said to himself,—he had demonstrated it as an absurdity. What was it, then,—this charm, so subtle and so strong, by which this fair child, his inferior in age, cultivation, and knowledge of the world, held him in a certain awe, and made him feel her spirit so unapproachable? His curiosity was piqued. He felt stimulated to employ all his powers of pleasing. He was determined, that, sooner or later, she should feel his power.

With Mrs. Scudder his success was immediate; she was completely won over by the deferential manner with which he constantly referred himself to her matronly judgments; and, on returning to the house, she warmly pressed him to stay to dinner.

Burr accepted the invitation with a frank and almost boyish *abandon*, declaring that he had not seen anything, for years, that so reminded him of old times. He praised everything at table,—the smoking brown-bread, the baked beans steaming from the oven, where they had been quietly simmering during the morning walk, and the Indian pudding, with its gelatinous softness, matured by long and patient brooding in the motherly old oven. He declared that there was no style of living to be compared with the simple, dignified order of a true New England home, where servants were excluded, and everything came direct from the polished and cultured hand of a lady. It realized the dreams of Arcadian romance. A man, he declared, must be unworthy the name, who did not rise to lofty sentiments and heroic deeds, when even his animal wants were provided for by the ministrations of the most delicate and exalted portion of the creation.

After dinner he would be taken into all the family interests. Gentle and pliable as oil, he seemed to penetrate every joint of the *ménage* by a subtle and seductive sympathy. He was interested in the spinning, in the weaving,—and in fact, nobody knows how it was done, but, before the afternoon shadows had turned, he was sitting in the cracked arm-chair of Mary's garret-boudoir, gravely giving judgment on several specimens of her spinning, which Mrs. Scudder had presented to his notice.

With that ease with which he could at will glide into the character of the superior and elder brother, he had, without seeming to ask questions, drawn from Mary an account of her reading, her studies, her acquaintances.

"You read French, I presume?" he said to her, with easy negligence.

Mary colored deeply, and then, as one who recollects one's self, answered, gravely,—

"No, Mr. Burr, I know no language but my own."

"But you should learn French, my child," said Burr, with that gentle dictatorship which he could at times so gracefully assume.

"I should be delighted to learn," said Mary, "but have no opportunity."

"Yes," said Mrs. Scudder,—"Mary has always had a taste for study, and would be glad to improve in any way."

"Pardon me, Madam, if I take the liberty of making a suggestion. There is a most excellent man, the Abbé Léfon, now in Newport, driven here by the political disturbances in France; he is anxious to obtain a few scholars, and I am interested that he should succeed, for he is a most worthy man."

"Is he a Roman Catholic?"

"He is, Madam; but there could be no manner of danger with a person so admirably instructed as your daughter. If you please to see him, Madam, I will call with him some time."

"Mrs. Marvyn will, perhaps, join me," said Mary. "She has been studying French by herself for some time, in order to read a treatise on astronomy, which she found in that language. I will go over to-morrow and see her about it."

Before Colonel Burr departed, the Doctor requested him to step a moment with him into his study. Burr, who had had frequent occasions during his life to experience the sort of paternal freedom which the clergy of his country took with him in right of his clerical descent, began to summon together his faculties of address for the avoidance of a kind of conversation which he was not disposed to meet. He was agreeably disappointed, however, when, taking a paper from the table, and presenting it to him, the Doctor said,—

"I feel myself, my dear Sir, under a burden of obligation for benefits received from your family, so that I never see a member of it without casting about in my own mind how I may in some measure express my good-will towards him. You are aware that the papers of your distinguished grandfather have fallen into my hands, and from them I have taken the liberty to make a copy of those maxims by which he guided a life which was a blessing to his country and to the world. May I ask the favor that you will read them with attention? and if you find anything contrary to right reason or sober sense, I shall be happy to hear of it on a future occasion."

"Thank you, Doctor," said Burr, bowing. "I shall always be sensible of the kindness of the motive which has led you to take this trouble on my account. Believe me, Sir, I am truly obliged to you for it."

And thus the interview terminated.

That night, the Doctor, before retiring, offered fervent prayers for the grandson of his revered master and friend, praying that his father's and mother's God might bless him and make him a living stone in the Eternal Temple.

Meanwhile, the object of these prayers was sitting by a table in dressing-gown and slippers, thinking over the events of the day. The paper which Doctor Hopkins had handed him contained the celebrated "Resolutions" by which his ancestor led a life nobler than any mere dogmas can possibly be. By its side lay a perfumed note from Madame de Frontignac,—one of those womanly notes, so beautiful, so sacred in themselves, but so mournful to a right-minded person who sees whither they are tending. Burr opened and perused it,—laid it by,—opened the document that the Doctor had given, and thoughtfully read the first of the "Resolutions":—

"Resolved, That I will do whatsoever I think to be most to God's glory, and my own good profit and pleasure *in the whole of my duration*, without any consideration of time, whether now or never so many myriad ages hence.

"Resolved, To do whatever I think to be my duty and most for the good and advantage of mankind in general.

"Resolved, To do this, whatsoever difficulties I meet with, and how many and how great soever."

Burr read the whole paper through attentively once or

twice, and paused thoughtfully over many parts of it. He sat for some time after, lost in reflection; the paper dropped from his hand, and then followed one of those long, deep seasons of fixed reverie, when the soul thinks by pictures and goes over endless distances in moments. In him, originally, every moral faculty and sensibility was as keenly strung as in any member of that remarkable family from which he was descended, and which has, whether in good or ill, borne no common stamp. Two possible lives flashed before his mind at that moment, rapidly as when a train sweeps by with flashing lamps in the night. The life of worldly expediency, the life of eternal rectitude,—the life of seventy years, and that life eternal in which the event of death is no disturbance. Suddenly he roused himself, picked up the paper, filed and dated it carefully, and laid it by; and in that moment was renewed again that governing purpose which sealed him, with all his beautiful capabilities, as the slave of the fleeting and the temporary, which sent him at last, a shipwrecked man, to a nameless, dishonored grave.

He took his pen and gave to a friend his own views of the events of the day.

"My dear,——We are still in Newport, conjugating the verb *s'ennuyer*, which I, for one, have put through all the moods and tenses. *Pour passer le temps*, however, I have *la belle Française* and my sweet little Puritan. I visited there this morning. She lives with her mother, a little walk out toward the seaside, in a cottage quite prettily sequestered among blossoming apple-trees, and the great hierarch of modern theology, Dr. Hopkins, keeps guard over them. No chance here for any indiscretions, you see.

"By-the-by, the good Doctor astonished our *monde* here on Sunday last, by treating us to a solemn onslaught on slavery and the slave-trade. He had all the chief captains and counsellors to hear him, and smote them hip and thigh, and pursued them even unto Shur.

"He is one of those great, honest fellows, without the smallest notion of the world we live in, who think, in dealing with men, that you must go to work and prove the right or the wrong of a matter; just as if anybody cared for that! Sup-

posing he is right,—which appears very probable to me,—
what is he going to do about it? No moral argument, since
the world began, ever prevailed over twenty-five per cent.
profit.

"However, he is the spiritual director of *la belle Puritaine*,
and was a resident in my grandfather's family, so I did the
agreeable with him as well as such an uncircumcised Ishmael-
ite could. I discoursed theology,—sat with the most docile
air possible while he explained to me all the ins and outs in
his system of the universe, past, present, and future,—heard
him dilate calmly on the Millennium, and expound prophetic
symbols, marching out before me his whole apocalyptic me-
nagerie of beasts and dragons with heads and horns innumerable, to all which I gave edifying attention, taking occasion
now and then to turn a compliment in favor of the ladies,—
never lost, you know.

"Really, he is a worthy old soul, and actually believes all
these things with his whole heart, attaching unheard-of importance to the most abstract ideas, and embarking his whole
being in his ideal view of a grand Millennial *finale* to the
human race. I look at him and at myself, and ask, Can human
beings be made so unlike?

"My little Mary to-day was in a mood of 'sweet austere
composure' quite becoming to her style of beauty; her *naïve
nonchalance* at times is rather stimulating. What a contrast between her and *la belle Française!*—all the difference that there
is between a diamond and a flower. I find the little thing has
a cultivated mind, enriched by reading, and more by a still,
quaint habit of thinking, which is new and charming. But a
truce to this.

"I have seen our friends at last. We have had three or four
meetings, and are waiting to hear from Philadelphia,—matters are getting in train. If Messrs. T. and S. dare to repeat
what they said again, let me know; they will find in me a man
not to be trifled with. I shall be with you in a week or ten
days at farthest. Meanwhile stand to your guns.

"*Ever yours,*

"BURR."

XVII.

Polemics in the Kitchen

THE next morning, before the early dews had yet dried off
the grass, Mary started to go and see her friend Mrs.
Marvyn. It was one of those charming, invigorating days, familiar to those of Newport experience, when the sea lies
shimmering and glittering in deep blue and gold, and the sky
above is firm and cloudless, and every breeze that comes landward seems to bear health and energy upon its wings.

As Mary approached the house, she heard loud sounds of
discussion from the open kitchen-door, and, looking in, saw
a rather original scene acting.

Candace, armed with a long oven-shovel, stood before the
open door of the oven, whence she had just been removing
an army of good things which appeared ranged around on
the dresser. Cato, in the undress of a red flannel shirt and
tow-cloth trousers, was cuddled, in a consoled and protected
attitude, in the corner of the wooden settle, with a mug of
flip in his hand, which Candace had prepared, and, calling
him in from his work, authoritatively ordered him to drink,
on the showing that he had kept her awake the night before
with his cough, and she was sure he was going to be sick. Of
course, worse things may happen to a man than to be vigorously taken care of by his wife, and Cato had a salutary conviction of this fact, so that he resigned himself to his comfortable corner and his flip with edifying serenity.

Opposite to Candace stood a well-built, corpulent negro
man, dressed with considerable care, and with the air of a
person on excellent terms with himself. This was no other
than Digo, the house-servant and factotum of Dr. Stiles, who
considered himself as the guardian of his master's estate, his
title, his honor, his literary character, his professional position, and his religious creed.

Digo was ready to assert before all the world, that one and
all of these were under his special protection, and that

whoever had anything to say to the contrary of any of these must expect to take issue with him. Digo not only swallowed all his master's opinions whole, but seemed to have the stomach of an ostrich in their digestion. He believed everything, no matter what, the moment he understood that the Doctor held it. He believed that Hebrew was the language of heaven,—that the ten tribes of the Jews had reappeared in the North American Indians,—that there was no such thing as disinterested benevolence, and that the doings of the unregenerate had some value,—that slavery was a divine ordinance, and that Dr. Hopkins was a radical, who did more harm than good,—and, finally, that there never was so great a man as Dr. Stiles; and as Dr. Stiles belonged to him in the capacity of master, why, he, Digo, owned the greatest man in America. Of course, as Candace held precisely similar opinions in regard to Dr. Hopkins, the two never could meet without a discharge of the opposite electricities. Digo had, it is true, come ostensibly on a mere worldly errand from his mistress to Mrs. Marvyn, who had promised to send her some turkeys' eggs, but he had inly resolved with himself that he would give Candace his opinion,—that is, what Dr. Stiles had said at dinner the day before about Dr. Hopkins' Sunday's discourse. Dr. Stiles had not heard it, but Digo had. He had felt it due to the responsibilities of his position to be present on so very important an occasion.

Therefore, after receiving his eggs, he opened hostilities by remarking, in a general way, that he had attended the Doctor's preaching on Sunday, and that there was quite a crowded house. Candace immediately began mentally to bristle her feathers like a hen who sees a hawk in the distance, and responded with decision:—

"Den you *heard* sometin', for once in your life!"

"I must say," said Digo, with suavity, "dat I can't give my 'proval to such sentiments."

"More shame for you," said Candace, grimly. "*You* a man, and not stan' by your color, and flunk under to mean white ways! Ef you was *half* a man, your heart would 'a' bounded like a cannon-ball at dat ar' sermon."

"Dr. Stiles and me we talked it over after church," said

Digo,—"and de Doctor was of my 'pinion, dat Providence didn't intend"——

"Oh, you go 'long wid your Providence! Guess, ef white folks had let us alone, Providence wouldn't trouble us."

"Well," said Digo, "Dr. Stiles is clear dat dis yer's a-fulfillin' de prophecies and bringin' in de fulness of the Gentiles."

"Fulness of de fiddlesticks!" said Candace, irreverently. "Now what a way dat ar' is of talkin'! Go look at one o' dem ships we come over in,—sweatin' and groanin',—in the dark and dirt,—cryin' and dyin',—howlin' for breath till de sweat run off us,—livin' and dead chained together,—prayin' like de rich man in hell for a drop o' water to cool our tongues! Call dat ar' a-bringin' de fulness of de Gentiles, do ye? Ugh!"

And Candace ended with a guttural howl, and stood frowning and gloomy over the top of her long kitchen-shovel, like a black Bellona leaning on her spear of battle.

Digo recoiled a little, but stood too well in his own esteem to give up; so he shifted his attack.

"Well, for my part, I must say I never was 'clined to your Doctor's 'pinions. Why, now, Dr. Stiles says, notin' couldn't be more absurd dan what he says 'bout disinterested benevolence. *My* Doctor says, dere a'n't no such ting!"

"I should tink it's likely!" said Candace, drawing herself up with superb disdain. "*Our* Doctor knows dere *is*,—and why? 'cause he's got it IN HERE," said she, giving her ample chest a knock which resounded like the boom from a barrel.

"Candace," said Cato, gently, "you's gittin' too hot."

"Cato, you shut up!" said Candace, turning sharp round. "What did I make you dat ar' flip for, 'cept you was so hoarse you oughtn' for to say a word? Pooty business, you go to agitatin' *your*self wid dese yer! Ef you wear out your poor old throat talkin', you may get de 'sumption; and den what'd become o' me?"

Cato, thus lovingly pitched *hors de combat*, sipped the sweetened cup in quietness of soul, while Candace returned to the charge.

"Now, I tell ye what," she said to Digo,—"jest cause you wear your master's old coats and hats, you tink you must go in for all dese yer old, mean white 'pinions. A'n't ye 'shamed—you, a black man—to have no more pluck and make cause wid de Egyptians? Now, 'ta'n't what my Doctor gives me,—he never giv' me the snip of a finger-nail,—but it's what he does for *mine*; and when de poor critturs lands dar tumbled out like bales on de wharves, ha'n't dey seen his great cocked hat, like a lighthouse, and his big eyes lookin' sort o' pitiful at 'em as ef he felt o' one blood wid 'em? Why, de very looks of de man is worth everyting; and who ever thought o' doing anyting for deir souls, or cared ef dey had souls, till he begun it?"

"Well, at any rate," said Digo, brightening up, "I don't believe his doctrine about de doings of de unregenerate,—it's quite clear he's wrong dar."

"Who cares?" said Candace,—"generate or unregenerate, it's all one to me. I believe a man dat *acts* as he does. Him as stands up for the poor,—him as pleads for de weak,—he's my man. I'll believe straight through anyting he's a mind to put at me."

At this juncture, Mary's fair face appearing at the door put a stop to the discussion.

"Bress *you*, Miss Mary! comin' here like a fresh June rose! it makes a body's eyes dance in deir head! Come right in! I got Cato up from de lot, 'cause he's rader poorly dis mornin'; his cough makes me a sight o' concern; he's allers a-pullin' off his jacket de wrong time, or doin' sometin' I tell him not to,—and it just keeps him hack, hack, hackin', all de time."

During this speech, Cato stood meekly bowing, feeling that he was being apologized for in the best possible manner; for long years of instruction had fixed the idea in his mind, that he was an ignorant sinner, who had not the smallest notion how to conduct himself in this world, and that, if it were not for his wife's distinguishing grace, he would long since have been in the shades of oblivion.

"Missis is spinnin' up in de north chamber," said Candace; "but I'll run up and fetch her down."

Candace, who was about the size of a puncheon, was fond of this familiar manner of representing her mode of ascending the stairs; but Mary, suppressing a smile, said, "Oh, no, Candace! don't for the world disturb her. I know just where she is." And before Candace could stop her, Mary's light foot was on the top step of the staircase that led up from the kitchen.

The north room was a large chamber, overlooking a splendid reach of sea-prospect. A moving panorama of blue water and gliding sails was unrolled before its three windows, so that stepping into the room gave one an instant and breezy sense of expansion. Mrs. Marvyn was standing at the large wheel, spinning wool,—a reel and basket of spools on her side. Her large brown eyes had an eager joy in them when Mary entered; but they seemed to calm down again, and she received her only with that placid, sincere air which was her habit. Everything about this woman showed an ardent soul, repressed by timidity and by a certain dumbness in the faculties of outward expression; but her eyes had, at times, that earnest, appealing language which is so pathetic in the silence of inferior animals.—One sometimes sees such eyes, and wonders whether the story they intimate will ever be spoken in mortal language.

Mary began eagerly detailing to her all that had interested her since they last met:—the party,—her acquaintance with Burr,—his visit to the cottage,—his inquiries into her education and reading,—and, finally, the proposal, that they should study French together.

"My dear," said Mrs. Marvyn, "let us begin at once;—such an opportunity is not to be lost. I studied a little with James, when he was last at home."

"With James?" said Mary, with an air of timid surprise.

"Yes,—the dear boy has become, what I never expected, quite a student. He employs all his spare time now in reading and studying;—the second mate is a Frenchman, and James has got so that he can both speak and read. He is studying Spanish, too."

Ever since the last conversation with her mother on the subject of James, Mary had felt a sort of guilty constraint when any one spoke of him;—instead of answering frankly, as she once did, when anything brought his name up, she fell at once into a grave, embarrassed silence.

Mrs. Marvyn was so constantly thinking of him, that it was difficult to begin on any topic that did not in some manner or other knit itself into the one ever present in her thoughts.

None of the peculiar developments of the female nature have a more exquisite vitality than the sentiment of a frail, delicate, repressed, timid woman for a strong, manly, generous son. There is her ideal expressed; there is the out-speaking and out-acting of all she trembles to think, yet burns to say or do; here is the hero that shall speak for her, the heart into which she has poured her's, and that shall give to her tremulous and hidden aspirations a strong and victorious expression. "I have gotten a *man* from the Lord," she says to herself; and each outburst of his manliness, his vigor, his self-confidence, his superb vitality, fills her with a strange, wondering pleasure, and she has a secret tenderness and pride even in his wilful-ness and waywardness. "What a creature he is!" she says, when he flouts at sober argument and pitches all received opinions hither and thither in the wild capriciousness of youthful paradox. She looks grave and reproving; but he reads the concealed triumph in her eyes,—he knows that in her heart she is full of admiration all the time. First love of womanhood is something wonderful and mysterious,—but in this second love it rises again, idealized and refined; she loves the father and herself united and made one in this young heir of life and hope.

Such was Mrs. Marvyn's still intense, passionate love for her son. Not a tone of his manly voice, not a flash of his dark eyes, not one of the deep, shadowy dimples that came and went as he laughed, not a ring of his glossy black hair, that was not studied, got by heart, and dwelt on in the inner shrine of her thoughts; he was the romance of her life. His strong, daring nature carried her with it beyond those nar-row, daily bounds where her soul was weary of treading; and just as his voyages had given to the trite prose of her *ménage* a poetry of strange, foreign perfumes, of quaint objects of interest, speaking of many a far-off shore, so his mind and life were a constant channel of outreach through which her soul held converse with the active and stirring world. Mrs. Marvyn had known all the story of her son's love, and to no other woman would she have been willing to resign him; but her love to Mary was so deep, that she thought of his union with her more as gaining a daughter than as losing a son. She would not speak of the subject; she knew the feelings of

Mary's mother; and the name of James fell so often from her lips, simply because it was so ever-present in her heart that it could not be helped.

Before Mary left, it was arranged that they should study together, and that the lessons should be given alternately at each other's houses; and with this understanding they parted.

XVIII.

Evidences

THE Doctor sat at his study-table. It was evening, and the slant beams of the setting sun shot their golden arrows through the healthy purple clusters of lilacs that veiled the windows. There had been a shower that filled them with drops of rain, which every now and then tattooed with a slender rat-tat on the window-sill, as a breeze would shake the leaves and bear in perfume on its wings. Sweet, fragrance-laden airs tripped stirringly to and fro about the study-table, making gentle confusions, fluttering papers on moral ability, agitating treatises on the great end of creation, mixing up subtile distinctions between amiable instincts and true holiness, and, in short, conducting themselves like very unappreciative and unphilosophical little breezes.

The Doctor patiently smoothed back and rearranged, while opposite to him sat Mary, bending over some copying she was doing for him. One stray sunbeam fell on her light brown hair, tinging it to gold; her long, drooping lashes lay over the wax-like pink of her cheeks, as she wrote on.

"Mary," said the Doctor, pushing the papers from him.

"Sir," she answered, looking up, the blood just perceptibly rising in her cheeks.

"Do you ever have any periods in which your evidences seem not altogether clear?"

Nothing could show more forcibly the grave, earnest character of thought in New England at this time than the fact that this use of the term "evidences" had become universally significant and understood as relating to one's right of citizenship in a celestial, invisible commonwealth.

So Mary understood it, and it was with a deepening flush she answered gently, "No, Sir."

"What! never any doubts?" said the Doctor.

"I am sorry," said Mary, apologetically; "but I do not see how I *can* have; I never could."

"Ah!" said the Doctor, musingly, "would I could say so! There are times, indeed, when I hope I have an interest in the precious Redeemer, and behold an infinite loveliness and beauty in Him, apart from anything I expect or hope. But even then how deceitful is the human heart! how insensibly might a mere selfish love take the place of that disinterested complacency which regards Him for what He is in Himself, apart from what He is to us! Say, my dear friend, does not this thought sometimes make you tremble?"

Poor Mary was truth itself, and this question distressed her; she must answer the truth. The fact was, that it had never come into her blessed little heart to tremble, for she was one of those children of the bride-chamber who cannot mourn because the bridegroom is ever with them; but then, when she saw the man for whom her reverence was almost like that for her God thus distrustful, thus lowly, she could not but feel that her too calm repose might, after all, be the shallow, treacherous calm of an ignorant, ill-grounded spirit, and therefore, with a deep blush and a faltering voice, she said,—

"Indeed, I am afraid something must be wrong with me. I *cannot* have any fears,—I never could; I try sometimes, but the thought of God's goodness comes all around me, and I am so happy before I think of it!"

"Such exercises, my dear friend, I have also had," said the Doctor; "but before I rest on them as evidences, I feel constrained to make the following inquiries:—Is this gratitude that swells my bosom the result of a mere natural sensibility? Does it arise in a particular manner because God has done me good? or do I love God for what He *is*, as well as for what He has done? and for what He has done for others, as well as for what He has done for me? Love to God which is built on nothing but good received is not incompatible with a disposition so horrid as even to curse God to His face. If God is not to be loved except when He does good, then in affliction we are free. If doing *us* good is all that renders God lovely to us, then not doing us good divests Him of His glory, and dispenses us from obligation to love Him. But there must be, undoubtedly, some permanent reason why God is to be loved by all; and if not doing us good divests Him of His glory so as to free *us* from our obligation to love, it equally frees the universe; so that, in fact, the universe of happiness, if ours be not included, reflects no glory on its Author."

The Doctor had practised his subtile mental analysis till his instruments were so fine-pointed and keen-edged that he scarce ever allowed a flower of sacred emotion to spring in his soul without picking it to pieces to see if its genera and species were correct. Love, gratitude, reverence, benevolence,—which all moved in mighty tides in his soul,—were all compelled to pause midway while he rubbed up his optical instruments to see whether they were rising in right order. Mary, on the contrary, had the blessed gift of womanhood,— that vivid life in the soul and sentiment which resists the chills of analysis, as a healthful human heart resists cold; yet still, all humbly, she thought this perhaps was a defect in herself, and therefore, having confessed, in a depreciating tone, her habits of unanalyzed faith and love, she added,—

"But, my dear Sir, you are my best friend. I trust you will be faithful to me. If I am deceiving myself, undeceive me; you cannot be too severe with me."

"Alas!" said the Doctor, "I fear that I may be only a blind leader of the blind. What, after all, if I be only a miserable self-deceiver? What if some thought of self has come in to poison all my prayers and strivings? It is true, I think,—yes, I *think*," said the Doctor, speaking very slowly, and with intense earnestness,—"I think, that, if I knew at this moment that my name never would be written among those of the elect, I could still see God to be infinitely amiable and glorious, and could feel sure that He *could* not do me wrong, and that it was infinitely becoming and right that He should dispose of me according to His sovereign pleasure. I *think* so;—but still my deceitful heart!—after all, I might find it rising in rebellion. Say, my dear friend, are you sure, that, should you discover yourself to be forever condemned by His justice, you would not find your heart rising up against Him?"

"Against *Him*?" said Mary, with a tremulous, sorrowful expression on her face,—"against my Heavenly Father?"

Her face flushed, and faded; her eyes kindled eagerly, as if she had something to say, and then grew misty with tears. At last she said,—

"Thank you, my dear, faithful friend! I will think about this; *perhaps* I may have been deceived. How very difficult it must be to know one's self perfectly!"

Mary went into her own little room, and sat leaning for a long time with her elbow on the window-seat, watching the pale shells of the apple-blossoms as they sailed and fluttered downward into the grass, and listened to a chippering conversation in which the birds in the nest above were settling up their small housekeeping accounts for the day.

After awhile, she took her pen and wrote the following, which the Doctor found the next morning lying on his study-table:—

"MY DEAR, HONORED FRIEND,—How can I sufficiently thank you for your faithfulness with me? All you say to me seems true and excellent; and yet, my dear Sir, permit me to try to express to you some of the many thoughts to which our conversation this evening has given rise. To love God because He is good to me you seem to think is not a right kind of love; and yet every moment of my life I have experienced His goodness. When recollection brings back the past, where can I look that I see not His goodness? What moment of my life presents not instances of merciful kindness to me, as well as to every creature, more and greater than I can express, than my mind is able to take in? How, then, can I help loving God because He is good to me? Were I not an object of God's mercy and goodness, I cannot have any conception what would be my feeling. Imagination never yet placed me in a situation not to experience the goodness of God in some way or other; and if I do love Him, how can it be but because He is good, and to me good? Do not God's children love Him because He first loved them?

"If I called nothing goodness which did not happen to suit my inclination, and could not believe the Deity to be gracious and merciful except when the course of events was so ordered as to agree with my humor, so far from imagining that I had any love to God, I must conclude myself wholly destitute of anything good. A love founded on nothing but good received is not, you say, incompatible with a disposition so horrid as even to curse God. I am not sensible that I ever in my life imagined anything *but* good could come from the hand of God. From a Being infinite in goodness everything *must* be good, though we do not always comprehend how it is so. Are not afflictions good? Does He not even in judgment remember mercy? Sensible that 'afflictions are but blessings in disguise,' I would bless the hand that, with infinite kindness, wounds only to heal, and love and adore the goodness of God equally in suffering as in rejoicing.

"The disinterested love to God, which you think is alone the genuine love, I see not how we can be certain we possess, when our love of happiness and our love of God are so inseparably connected. The joys arising from a consciousness that God is a benefactor to me and my friends, (and when I think of God, every creature is my friend,) if arising from a selfish motive, it does not seem to me possible could be changed into hate, even supposing God my enemy, whilst I regarded Him as a Being infinitely just as well as good. If God is my enemy, it must be because I deserve that He should be such; and it does not seem to me *possible* that I should hate Him, even if I knew He would always be so.

"In what you say of willingness to suffer eternal punishment, I don't know that I understand what the feeling is. Is it wickedness in me that I do not feel a willingness to be left to eternal sin? Can any one joyfully acquiesce in being thus left? When I pray for a new heart and a right spirit, must I be willing to be denied, and rejoice that my prayer is not heard? Could any real Christian rejoice in this? But he fears it not,—he knows it will never be,—he therefore can cheerfully leave it with God; and so can I.

"Such, my dear friend, are my thoughts, poor and unworthy; yet they seem to me as certain as my life, or as anything I see. Am I unduly confident? I ask your prayers that I may be guided aright.

"Your affectionate friend,
"MARY."

There are in this world two kinds of natures,—those that have wings, and those that have feet,—the winged and the walking spirits. The walking are the logicians; the winged are the instinctive and poetic. Natures that must always walk find many a bog, many a thicket, many a tangled brake, which God's happy little winged birds flit over by one noiseless flight. Nay, when a man has toiled till his feet weigh too heavily with the mud of earth to enable him to walk another step, these little birds will often cleave the air in a right line towards the bosom of God, and show the way where he could never have found it.

The Doctor paused in his ponderous and heavy reasonings to read this real woman's letter; and being a loving man, he felt as if he could have kissed the hem of her garment who wrote it. He recorded it in his journal, and after it this significant passage from Canticles: —

"I charge you, O ye daughters of Jerusalem, by the roes, and by the hinds of the field, that ye stir not up nor awake this lovely one till she please."

Mrs. Scudder's motherly eye noticed, with satisfaction, these quiet communings. "Let it alone," she said to herself; "before she knows it, she will find herself wholly under his influence." Mrs. Scudder was a wise woman.

XIX.

Madame de Frontignac

IN the course of a day or two, a handsome carriage drew up in front of Mrs. Scudder's cottage, and a brilliant party alighted. They were Colonel and Madame de Frontignac, the Abbé Léfon, and Colonel Burr. Mrs. Scudder and her daughter, being prepared for the call, sat in afternoon dignity and tranquillity, in the best room, with their knitting-work.

Madame de Frontignac had divined, with the lightning-like tact which belongs to women in the positive, and to French women in the superlative degree, that there was something in the cottage-girl, whom she had passingly seen at the party, which powerfully affected the man whom she loved with all the jealous intensity of a strong nature, and hence she embraced eagerly the opportunity to see her,—yes, to see her, to study her, to dart her keen French wit through her, and detect the secret of her charm, that she, too, might practise it.

Madame de Frontignac was one of those women whose beauty is so striking and imposing, that they seem to kindle up, even in the most prosaic apartment, an atmosphere of enchantment. All the pomp and splendor of high life, the wit, the refinements, the nameless graces and luxuries of courts, seemed to breathe in invisible airs around her, and she made a Faubourg St. Germain of the darkest room into which she entered. Mary thought, when she came in, that she had never seen anything so splendid. She was dressed in a black velvet riding-habit, buttoned to the throat with coral; her riding-hat drooped with its long plumes so as to cast a shadow over her animated face, out of which her dark eyes shone like jewels, and her pomegranate cheeks glowed with the rich shaded radiance of one of Rembrandt's pictures. Something quaint and foreign, something poetic and strange, marked each turn of her figure, each article of her dress, down to the sculptured hand on which glittered singular and costly rings,—and the riding-glove, embroidered with seed-pearls, that fell carelessly beside her on the floor.

In Antwerp one sees a picture in which Rubens, who felt more than any other artist the glory of the physical life, has embodied his conception of the Madonna, in opposition to the faded, cold ideals of the Middle Ages, from which he revolted with such a bound. *His* Mary is a superb Oriental sultana, with lustrous dark eyes, redundant form, jewelled turban, standing leaning on the balustrade of a princely terrace, and bearing on her hand, *not* the silver dove, but a gorgeous paroquet. The two styles, in this instance, were both in the same room; and as Burr sat looking from one to the other, he felt, for a moment, as one would who should put a sketch of Overbeck's beside a splendid painting of Titian's.

For a few moments, everything in the room seemed faded and cold, in contrast with the tropical atmosphere of this regal beauty. Burr watched Mary with a keen eye, to see if she were dazzled and overawed. He saw nothing but the most innocent surprise and delight. All the slumbering poetry within her seemed to awaken at the presence of her beautiful neighbor,—as when one, for the first time, stands before the great revelations of Art. Mary's cheek glowed, her eyes seemed to grow deep with the enthusiasm of admiration, and, after a few moments, it seemed as if her delicate face and figure reflected the glowing loveliness of her visitor, just as the virgin snows of the Alps become incarnadine as they stand opposite the glorious radiance of a sunset sky.

Madame de Frontignac was accustomed to the effect of her charms; but there was so much love in the admiration now directed towards her, that her own warm nature was touched, and she threw out the glow of her feelings with a magnetic power. Mary never felt the cold, habitual reserve of her education so suddenly melt, never felt herself so naturally falling into language of confidence and endearment with a stranger; and as her face, so delicate and spiritual, grew bright with love, Madame de Frontignac thought she had never seen anything so beautiful, and, stretching out her hands towards her, she exclaimed, in her own language,—

"*Mais, mon Dieu! mon enfant, que tu es belle!*"

Mary's deep blush, at her ignorance of the language in which her visitor spoke, recalled her to herself;—she laughed a clear, silvery laugh, and laid her jewelled little hand on Mary's with a caressing movement.

"*He* shall not teach you French, *ma toute belle*," she said, indicating the Abbé, by a pretty, wilful gesture; "*I* will teach you;—and you shall teach me English. Oh, I shall try *so* hard to learn!" she said.

There was something inexpressibly pretty and quaint in the childish lisp with which she pronounced English. Mary was completely won over. She could have fallen into the arms of this wondrously beautiful fairy princess, expecting to be carried away by her to Dream-land.

Meanwhile, Mrs. Scudder was gravely discoursing with Colonel Burr and M. de Frontignac; and the Abbé, a small and gentlemanly personage, with clear black eye, delicately-cut features, and powdered hair, appeared to be absorbed in his efforts to follow the current of a conversation imperfectly understood. Burr, the while, though seeming to be entirely and politely absorbed in the conversation he was conducting, lost not a glimpse of the picturesque aside which was being enacted between the two fair ones whom he had thus brought together. He smiled quietly when he saw the effect Madame de Frontignac produced on Mary.

"After all, the child has flesh and blood!" he thought, "and may feel that there are more things in heaven and earth than she has dreamed of yet. A few French ideas won't hurt her."

The arrangements about lessons being completed, the party returned to the carriage. Madame de Frontignac was enthusiastic in Mary's praise.

"*Cependant,*" she said, leaning back, thoughtfully, after having exhausted herself in superlatives,—"*cependant elle est dévote,—et à dix-neuf comment cela se peut il?*"

"It is the effect of her austere education," said Burr. "It is not possible for you to conceive how young people are trained in the religious families of this country."

"But yet," said Madame, "it gives her a grace altogether peculiar; something in her looks went to my heart. I could find it very easy to love her, because she is really good."

"The Queen of Hearts should know all that is possible in loving," said Burr.

Somehow, of late, the compliments which fell so readily

from those graceful lips had brought with them an unsatisfying pain. Until a woman really *loves*, flattery and compliment
are often like her native air; but when that deeper feeling has
once awakened in her, her instincts become marvellously
acute to detect the false from the true. Madame de Frontignac
longed for one strong, unguarded, real, earnest word from
the man who had stolen from her her whole being. She was
beginning to feel in some dim wise what an untold treasure
she was daily giving for tinsel and dross. She leaned back in
the carriage, with a restless, burning cheek, and wondered
why she was born to be so miserable. The thought of Mary's
saintly face and tender eyes rose before her as the moon rises
on the eyes of some hot and fevered invalid, inspiring vague
yearnings after an unknown, unattainable peace.

Could some friendly power have made her at that time
clairvoyant and shown her the *reality* of the man whom she
was seeing through the prismatic glass of her own enkindled
ideality! Could she have seen the calculating quietness in
which, during the intervals of a restless and sleepless ambition,
he played upon her heart-strings, as one uses a musical instrument to beguile a passing hour,—how his only embarrassment was the fear that the feelings he was pleased to excite
might become too warm and too strong, while as yet his relations to her husband were such as to make it dangerous to
arouse his jealousy! And if he could have seen that pure ideal
conception of himself which alone gave him power in the
heart of this woman,—that spotless, glorified image of a hero
without fear, without reproach,—would he have felt a moment's shame and abasement at its utter falsehood?

The poet says that the Evil Spirit stood abashed when he
saw virtue in an angel form! How would a man, then, stand,
who meets face to face his own glorified, spotless ideal, made
living by the boundless faith of some believing heart? The
best must needs lay his hand on his mouth at this apparition;
but woe to him who feels no redeeming power in the sacredness of this believing dream,—who with calculating shrewdness *uses* this most touching miracle of love only to corrupt
and destroy the loving! For him there is no sacrifice for sin,
no place for repentance. His very mother might shrink in her
grave to have him laid beside her.

Madame de Frontignac had the high, honorable nature of the old blood of France, and a touch of its romance. She was strung heroically, and educated according to the notions of her caste and church, purely and religiously. True it is, that one can scarcely call *that* education which teaches woman everything except herself,—*except* the things that relate to her own peculiar womanly destiny, and, on plea of the holiness of ignorance, sends her without one word of just counsel into the temptations of life. Incredible as it may seem, Virginie de Frontignac had never read a romance or work of fiction of which love was the staple; the *régime* of the convent in this regard was inexorable; at eighteen she was more thoroughly a child than most American girls at thirteen. On entrance into life, she was at first so dazzled and bewildered by the mere contrast of fashionable excitement with the quietness of the scenes in which she had hitherto grown up, that she had no time for reading or thought,—all was one intoxicating frolic of existence, one dazzling, bewildering dream.

He whose eye had measured her for his victim verified, if ever man did, the proverbial expression of the iron hand under the velvet glove. Under all his gentle suavities there was a fixed, inflexible will, a calm self-restraint, and a composed philosophical measurement of others, that fitted him to bear despotic rule over an impulsive, unguarded nature. The position, at once accorded to him, of her instructor in the English language and literature, gave him a thousand daily opportunities to touch and stimulate all that class of finer faculties, so restless and so perilous, and which a good man approaches always with a certain awe. It is said that he once asserted that he never beguiled a woman who did not come half-way to meet him,—an observation much the same as a serpent might make in regard to his birds.

The visit of the morning was followed by several others. Madame de Frontignac seemed to conceive for Mary one of those passionate attachments which women often conceive for anything fair and sympathizing, at those periods when their whole inner being is made vital by the approaches of a grand passion. It took only a few visits to make her as familiar as a child at the cottage; and the whole air of the Faubourg St. Germain seemed to melt away from her, as, with the pliability peculiar to her nation, she blended herself with the quiet pursuits of the family. Sometimes, in simple straw hat and white wrapper, she would lie down in the grass under the apple-trees, or join Mary in an expedition to the barn for hen's eggs, or a run along the sea-beach for shells; and her childish eagerness and delight on these occasions used to arouse the unqualified astonishment of Mrs. Katy Scudder.

The Doctor she regarded with a *naïve* astonishment, slightly tinctured with apprehension. She knew he was very religious, and stretched her comprehension to imagine what he might be like. She thought of Bossuet's sermons walking about under a Protestant coat, and felt vaguely alarmed and sinful in his presence, as she used to when entering under the shadows of a cathedral. In her the religious sentiment, though vague, was strong. Nothing in the character of Burr had ever awakened so much disapprobation as his occasional sneers at religion. On such occasions she always reproved him with warmth, but excused him in her heart, because he was brought up a heretic. She held a special theological conversation with the Abbé, whether salvation were possible to one outside of the True Church,—and had added to her daily prayer a particular invocation to the Virgin for him.

The French lessons, with her assistance, proceeded prosperously. She became an inmate in Mrs. Marvyn's family also. The brown-eyed, sensitive woman loved her as a new poem; she felt enchanted by her; and the prosaic details of her household seemed touched to poetic life by her innocent interest and admiration. The young Madame insisted on being taught to spin at the great wheel; and a very pretty picture she made of it, too, with her earnest gravity of endeavor, her deepening cheek, her graceful form, with some strange foreign scarf or jewelry waving and flashing in odd contrast with her work.

"Do you know," she said, one day, while thus employed in the north room at Mrs. Marvyn's,—"do you know Burr told me that princesses used to spin? He read me a beautiful story from the 'Odyssey,' about how Penelope cheated her lovers with her spinning, while she was waiting for her husband to come home;—*he* was gone to sea, Mary,—her *true* love,— you understand."

She turned on Mary a wicked glance, so full of intelligence that the snowdrop grew red as the inside of a sea-shell.

"*Mon enfant!* thou hast a thought *deep in here!*" she said to Mary, one day, as they sat together in the grass under the apple-trees.

"Why, what?" said Mary, with a startled and guilty look.

"Why, what? *petite!*" said the fairy princess, whimsically mimicking her accent. "*Ah! ah! ma belle!* you think I have no eyes;—Virginie sees deep in here!" she said, laying her hand playfully on Mary's heart. "*Ah, petite!*" she said, gravely, and almost sorrowfully, "if you love him, wait for him,—*don't marry another!* It is dreadful not to have one's heart go with one's duty."

"I shall never marry anybody," said Mary.

"Nevare marrie anybodie!" said the lady, imitating her accents in tones much like those of a bobolink. "Ah! ah! my little saint, you cannot always live on nothing but the prayers, though prayers are verie good. But, *ma chère,*" she added, in a low tone, "don't you ever marry that good man in there; priests should not marry."

"Ours are not priests,—they are ministers," said Mary. "But why do you speak of him?—he is like my father."

"Virginie sees something!" said the lady, shaking her head gravely; "she sees he loves little Mary."

"Of course he does!"

"Of-course-he-does?—ah, yes; and by-and-by comes the mamma, and she takes this little hand, and she says, 'Come, Mary!' and then she gives it to him; and then the poor *jeune homme,* when he comes back, finds not a bird in his poor little nest. *Oh, c'est ennuyeux cela!*" she said, throwing herself back in the grass till the clover-heads and buttercups closed over her.

"I do assure you, dear Madame!"——

"I do assure you, dear Mary, *Virginie knows.* So lock up her words in your little heart; you will want them some day."

There was a pause of some moments, while the lady was watching the course of a cricket through the clover. At last, lifting her head, she spoke very gravely,—

"My little cat! it is *dreadful* to be married to a good man, and want to be good, and want to love him, and yet never like to have him take your hand, and be more glad when he is away than when he is at home; and then to think how different it would all be, if it was only somebody else. That will be the way with you, if you let them lead you into this; so don't you do it, *mon enfant*."

A thought seemed to cross Mary's mind, as she turned to Madame de Frontignac, and said, earnestly,—

"If a good man were my husband, I would never think of another,—I wouldn't let myself."

"How could you help it, *mignonne*? Can you stop your thinking?"

Mary said, after a moment's blush,—

"I can *try*!"

"Ah, yes! But to try all one's life,—oh, Mary, that is too hard! Never do it, darling!"

And then Madame de Frontignac broke out into a carolling little French song, which started all the birds around into a general orchestral accompaniment.

This conversation occurred just before Madame de Frontignac started for Philadelphia, whither her husband had been summoned as an agent in some of the ambitious intrigues of Burr.

It was with a sigh of regret that she parted from her friends at the cottage. She made them a hasty good-bye call,—alighting from a splendid barouche with two white horses, and filling their simple best-room with the light of her presence for a last half-hour. When she bade good-bye to Mary, she folded her warmly to her heart, and her long lashes drooped heavily with tears.

After her absence, the lessons were still pursued with the gentle, quiet little Abbé, who seemed the most patient and assiduous of teachers; but, in both houses, there was that vague *ennui*, that sense of want, which follows the fading of one of life's beautiful dreams! We bid her adieu for a season; —we may see her again.

XX.

Tidings from Over Sea

THE summer passed over the cottage, noiselessly as our summers pass. There were white clouds walking in saintly troops over blue mirrors of sea,—there were purple mornings, choral with bird-singing,—there were golden evenings, with long, eastward shadows. Apple-blossoms died quietly in the deep orchard-grass, and tiny apples waxed and rounded and ripened and gained stripes of gold and carmine; and the blue eggs broke into young robins, that grew from gaping, yellow-mouthed youth to fledged and outflying maturity. Came autumn, with its long Indian summer, and winter, with its flinty, sparkling snows, under which all Nature lay a sealed and beautiful corpse. Came once more the spring winds, the lengthening days, the opening flowers, and the ever-renewing miracle of buds and blossoms on the apple-trees around the cottage. A year had passed since the June afternoon when first we showed you Mary standing under the spotty shadows of the tree, with the white dove on her hand,—a year in which not many outward changes have been made in the relations of the actors of our story.

Mary calmly spun and read and thought; now and then composing with care very English-French letters, to be sent to Philadelphia to Madame de Frontignac, and receiving short missives of very French-English in return.

The cautions of Madame, in regard to the Doctor, had not rippled the current of their calm, confiding intercourse; and the Doctor, so very satisfied and happy in her constant society and affection, scarcely as yet mediated distinctly that he needed to draw her more closely to himself. If he had a passage to read, a page to be copied, a thought to express, was she not ever there, gentle, patient, unselfish? and scarce by the absence of a day did she let him perceive that his need of her was becoming so absolute that his hold on her must needs be made permanent.

As to his salary and temporal concerns, they had suffered somewhat for his unpopular warfare with reigning sins,—a fact which had rather reconciled Mrs. Scudder to the dilatory movement of her cherished hopes. Since James was gone, what need to press imprudently to new arrangements? Better give the little heart time to grow over before starting a subject which a certain womanly instinct told her might be met with a struggle. Somehow she never thought without a certain heart-sinking of Mary's look and tone the night she spoke with her about James; she had an awful presentiment that that tone of voice belonged to the things that cannot be shaken. But yet, Mary seemed so even, so quiet, her delicate form filled out and rounded so beautifully, and she sang so cheerfully at her work, and, above all, she was so entirely silent about James, that Mrs. Scudder had hope.

Ah, that silence! Do not listen to hear whom a woman praises, to know where her heart is! do not ask for whom she expresses the most earnest enthusiasm! but if there be one she once knew well, whose name she never speaks,—if she seem to have an instinct to avoid every occasion of its mention,— if, when you speak, she drops into silence and changes the subject,—why, look there for something! just as, when going through deep meadow-grass, a bird flies ostentatiously up before you, you may know her nest is not there, but far off, under distant tufts of fern and buttercup, through which she has crept with a silent flutter in her spotted breast, to act her pretty little falsehood before you.

Poor Mary's little nest was along the sedgy margin of the sea-shore, where grow the tufts of golden rod, where wave the reeds, where crimson, green, and purple seaweeds float up, like torn fringes of Nereid vestures, and gold and silver shells lie on the wet wrinkles of the sands.

The sea had become to her like a friend, with its ever-varying monotony. Somehow she loved this old, fresh, blue, babbling, restless giant, who had carried away her heart's love to hide him in some far-off palmy island, such as she had often heard him tell of in his sea-romances. Sometimes she would wander out for an afternoon's stroll on the rocks, and pause by the great Spouting Cave, now famous to Newport *dilettanti*, but then a sacred and impressive solitude. There the rising tide bursts with deafening strokes through a narrow opening into some inner cavern, which, with a deep thunder-boom, like the voice of an angry lion, casts it back in a high jet of foam into the sea.

Mary often sat and listened to this hollow noise, and watched the ever-rising columns of spray as they reddened with the transpiercing beams of the afternoon sun; and thence her eye travelled far, far off over the shimmering starry blue, where sails looked no bigger than miller's wings; and it seemed sometimes as if a door were opening by which her soul might go out into some eternity,—some abyss, so wide and deep, that fathomless lines of thought could not sound it. She was no longer a girl in a mortal body, but an infinite spirit, the adoring companion of Infinite Beauty and Infinite Love.

As there was an hour when the fishermen of Galilee saw their Master transfigured, his raiment white and glistening, and his face like the light, so are there hours when our whole mortal life stands forth in a celestial radiance. From our daily lot falls off every weed of care,—from our heart-friends every speck and stain of earthly infirmity. Our horizon widens, and blue, and amethyst, and gold touch every object. Absent friends and friends gone on the last long journey stand once more together, bright with an immortal glow, and, like the disciples who saw their Master floating in the clouds above them, we say, "Lord, it is good to be here!" How fair the wife, the husband, the absent mother, the gray-haired father, the manly son, the bright-eyed daughter! Seen in the actual present, all have some fault, some flaw; but absent, we see them in their permanent and better selves. Of our distant home we remember not one dark day, not one servile care, nothing but the echo of its holy hymns and the radiance of its brightest days,—of our father, not one hasty word, but only the fulness of his manly vigor and noble tenderness,—of our mother, nothing of mortal weakness, but a glorified form of love,—of our brother, not one teasing, provoking word of brotherly freedom, but the proud beauty of his noblest hours,—of our sister, our child, only what is fairest and sweetest.

This is to life the true ideal, the calm glass, wherein looking, we shall see, that, whatever defects cling to us, they are not, after all, permanent, and that we are tending to something nobler than we yet are;—it is "the earnest of our inheritance until the redemption of the purchased possession." In the resurrection we shall see our friends forever as we see them in these clairvoyant hours.

We are writing thus on and on, linking image and thought and feeling, and lingering over every flower, and listening to every bird, because just before us there lies a dark valley, and we shrink and tremble to enter it.

But it *must* come, and why do we delay?

Towards evening, one afternoon in the latter part of June, Mary returned from one of these lonely walks by the sea, and entered the kitchen. It was still in its calm and sober cleanness;—the tall clock ticked with a startling distinctness. From the half-closed door of her mother's bedroom, which stood ajar, she heard the chipper of Miss Prissy's voice. She stayed her light footsteps, and the words that fell on her ear were these:—

"Miss Marvyn fainted dead away;—she stood it till it came to *that*; but then she just clapped both hands together, as if she'd been shot, and fell right forward on the floor in a faint!"

What could this be? There was a quick, intense whirl of thoughts in Mary's mind, and then came one of those awful moments when the powers of life seem to make a dead pause and all things stand still; and then all seemed to fail under her, and the life to sink down, down, down, till nothing was but one dim, vague, miserable consciousness.

Mrs. Scudder and Miss Prissy were sitting, talking earnestly, on the foot of the bed, when the door opened noiselessly, and Mary glided to them like a spirit,—no color in cheek or lip,—her blue eyes wide with calm horror; and laying her little hand, with a nervous grasp, on Miss Prissy's arm, she said,—

"Tell me,—what is it?—is it?—is he—dead?"

The two women looked at each other, and then Mrs. Scudder opened her arms.

"My daughter!"

"Oh! mother! mother!"

Then fell that long, hopeless silence, broken only by hysteric sobs from Miss Prissy, and answering ones from the mother; but *she* lay still and quiet, her blue eyes wide and clear, making an inarticulate moan.

"Oh! are they *sure?*—*can* it be?—*is* he dead?" at last she gasped.

"My child, it is too true; all we can say is, 'Be still, and know that I am God!' "

"I shall *try* to be still, mother," said Mary with a piteous, hopeless voice, like the bleat of a dying lamb; "but I did not think he *could* die! I never thought of that!—I never *thought* of it!—Oh! mother! mother! mother! oh! what shall I do?"

They laid her on her mother's bed,—the first and last resting-place of broken hearts,—and the mother sat down by her in silence. Miss Prissy stole away into the Doctor's study, and told him all that had happened.

"It's the same to her," said Miss Prissy, with womanly reserve, "as if he'd been an own brother."

"What was his spiritual state?" said the Doctor, musingly.

Miss Prissy looked blank, and answered mournfully,—

"I don't know."

The Doctor entered the room where Mary was lying with closed eyes. Those few moments seemed to have done the work of years,—so pale, and faded, and sunken she looked; nothing but the painful flutter of the eyelids and lips showed that she yet breathed. At a sign from Mrs. Scudder, he kneeled by the bed, and began to pray,—"Lord, thou hast been our dwelling-place in all generations,"—prayer deep, mournful, upheaving like the swell of the ocean, surging upward, under the pressure of mighty sorrows, toward an Almighty heart.

The truly good are of one language in prayer. Whatever lines or angles of thought may separate them in other hours, *when they pray in extremity*, all good men pray alike. The Emperor Charles V. and Martin Luther, two great generals of opposite faiths, breathed out their dying struggle in the self-same words.

There be many tongues and many languages of men,—but the language of prayer is one by itself, *in* all and *above* all. It is the inspiration of that Spirit that is ever working with our spirit, and constantly lifting us higher than we know, and, by our wants, by our woes, by our tears, by our yearnings, by our poverty, urging us, with mightier and mightier force, against those chains of sin which keep us from our God. We speak not of *things* conventionally called prayers,—vain mutterings of unawakened spirits talking drowsily in sleep,—but of such prayers as come when flesh and heart fail, in mighty straits;—*then* he who prays is a prophet, and a Mightier than he speaks in him; for the "*Spirit* helpeth our infirmities; for we know not what we should pray for as we ought; but the Spirit itself maketh intercession for us, with groanings which cannot be uttered."

So the voice of supplication, upheaving from that great heart, so childlike in its humility, rose with a wisdom and a pathos beyond what he dreamed in his intellectual hours; it uprose even as a strong angel, whose brow is solemnly calm, and whose wings shed healing dews of paradise.

XXI.

The Bruised Flax-Flower

THE next day broke calm and fair. The robins sang re-morselessly in the apple-tree, and were answered by bob-olink, oriole, and a whole tribe of ignorant little bits of feath-ered happiness that danced among the leaves. Golden and glorious unclosed those purple eyelids of the East, and regally came up the sun; and the treacherous sea broke into ten thou-sand smiles, laughing and dancing with every ripple, as un-consciously as if no form dear to human hearts had gone down beneath it. Oh! treacherous, deceiving beauty of out-ward things! beauty, wherein throbs not one answering nerve to human pain!

Mary rose early and was about her morning work. Her ed-ucation was that of the soldier, who must know himself no more, whom no personal pain must swerve from the slightest minutiæ of duty. So she was there, at her usual hour, dressed with the same cool neatness, her brown hair parted in satin bands, and only the colorless cheek and lip differing from the Mary of yesterday.

How strange this external habit of living! One thinks how to stick in a pin, and how to tie a string,—one busies one's self with folding robes, and putting away napkins, the day after some stroke that has cut the inner life in two, with the heart's blood dropping quietly at every step.

Yet it is better so! Happy those whom stern principle or long habit or hard necessity calls from the darkened room, the languid trance of pain, in which the wearied heart longs to indulge, and gives this trite prose of common life, at which our weak and wearied appetites so revolt! Mary never thought of such a thing as self-indulgence;—this daughter of the Puritans had her seed within her. Aerial in her delicacy, as the blue-eyed flax-flower with which they sowed their fields, she had yet its strong fibre, which no stroke of the flail could break; bruising and hackling only made it fitter for uses of homely utility. Mary, therefore, opened the kitchen-door at dawn, and, after standing one moment to breathe the freshness, began spreading the cloth for an early breakfast. Mrs. Scudder, the mean while, was kneading the bread that had been set to rise over-night; and the oven was crackling and roaring with a large-throated, honest garrulousness.

But, ever and anon, as the mother worked, she followed the motions of her child anxiously.

"Mary, my dear," she said, "the eggs are giving out; hadn't you better run to the barn and get a few?"

Most mothers are instinctive philosophers. No treatise on the laws of nervous fluids could have taught Mrs. Scudder a better *rôle* for this morning, than her tender gravity, and her constant expedients to break and ripple, by changing employments, that deep, deadly under-current of thoughts which she feared might undermine her child's life.

Mary went into the barn, stopped a moment, and took out a handful of corn to throw to her hens, who had a habit of running towards her and cocking an expectant eye to her little hand, whenever she appeared. All came at once flying towards her,—speckled, white, and gleamy with hues between of tawny orange-gold,—the cocks, magnificent with the blade-like waving of their tails,—and, as they chattered and cackled and pressed and crowded about her, pecking the corn, even where it lodged in the edge of her little shoes, she said, "Poor things, I am glad they enjoy it!"—and even this one little act of love to the ignorant fellowship below her carried away some of the choking pain which seemed all the while suffocating her heart. Then, climbing into the hay, she sought the nest and filled her little basket with eggs, warm, translucent, pinky-white in their freshness. She felt, for a moment, the customary animation in surveying her new treasures; but suddenly, like a vision rising before her, came a remembrance of once when she and James were children together and had been seeking eggs just there. He flashed before her eyes, the bright boy with the long black lashes, the dimpled cheeks, the merry eyes, just as he stood and threw the hay over her when they tumbled and laughed together,—and she sat down with a sick faintness, and then turned and walked wearily in.

XXII.

The House of Mourning

MARY returned to the house with her basket of warm, fresh eggs, which she set down mournfully upon the table. In her heart there was one conscious want and yearning, and that was to go to the friends of him she had lost,— to go to his mother. The first impulse of bereavement is to stretch out the hands towards what was nearest and dearest to the departed.

Her dove came fluttering down out of the tree, and settled on her hand, and began asking in his dumb way to be noticed. Mary stroked his white feathers, and bent her head down over them, till they were wet with tears. "Oh, birdie, you live, but he is gone!" she said. Then suddenly putting it gently from her, and going near and throwing her arms around her mother's neck,—"Mother," she said, "I want to go up to Cousin Ellen's." (This was the familiar name by which she always called Mrs. Marvyn.) "Can't you go with me, mother?"

"My daughter, I have thought of it. I hurried about my baking this morning, and sent word to Mr. Jenkyns that he needn't come to see about the chimney, because I expected to go as soon as breakfast should be out of the way. So, hurry, now, boil some eggs, and get on the cold beef and potatoes; for I see Solomon and Amaziah coming in with the milk. They'll want their breakfast immediately."

The breakfast for the hired men was soon arranged on the table, and Mary sat down to preside while her mother was going on with her baking,—introducing various loaves of white and brown bread into the capacious oven by means of a long iron shovel, and discoursing at intervals with Solomon, with regard to the different farming operations which he had in hand for the day.

Solomon was a tall, large-boned man, brawny and angular; with a face tanned by the sun, and graven with those considerate lines which New England so early writes on the faces of her sons. He was reputed an oracle in matters of agriculture and cattle, and, like oracles generally, was prudently sparing of his responses. Amaziah was one of those uncouth overgrown boys of eighteen whose physical bulk appears to have so suddenly developed that the soul has more matter than she has learned to recognize, so that the hapless individual is always awkwardly conscious of too much limb; and in Amaziah's case, this consciousness grew particularly distressing when Mary was in the room. He liked to have her there, he said,—"but, somehow, she was so white and pretty, she made him feel sort o' awful-like."

Of course, as such poor mortals always do, he must, on this particular morning, blunder into precisely the wrong subject.

"S'pose you've heerd the news that Jeduthun Pettibone brought home in the 'Flying Scud,' 'bout the wreck o' the 'Monsoon'; it's an awful providence, that 'ar' is,—a'n't it? Why, Jeduthun says she jest crushed like an egg-shell";—and with that Amaziah illustrated the fact by crushing an egg in his great brown hand.

Mary did not answer. She could not grow any paler than she was before; a dreadful curiosity came over her, but her lips could frame no question. Amaziah went on:—

"Ye see, the cap'en he got killed with a spar when the blow fust come on, and Jim Marvyn he commanded; and Jeduthun says that he seemed to have the spirit of ten men in him; he worked and he watched, and he was everywhere at once, and he kep' 'em all up for three days, till finally they lost their rudder, and went drivin' right onto the rocks. When they come in sight, he come up on deck, and says he, 'Well, my boys, we're headin' right into eternity,' says he, 'and our chances for this world a'n't worth mentionin', any on us, but we'll all have one try for our lives. Boys, I've tried to do my duty by you and the ship,—but God's will be done! All I have to ask now is, that, if any of you git to shore, you'll find my mother and tell her I died thinkin' of her and father and my dear friends.' That was the last Jeduthun saw of him; for in a few minutes more the ship struck, and then it was every man for himself. Laws! Jeduthun says there couldn't nobody have stood beatin' agin them rocks, unless they was all leather and inger-rubber like him. Why, he says the waves would take strong men and jest crush 'em against the rocks like smashin' a pie-plate!"

Here Mary's paleness became livid; she made a hasty motion to rise from the table, and Solomon trod on the foot of the narrator.

"You seem to forget that friends and relations has feelin's," he said, as Mary hastily went into her own room.

Amaziah, suddenly awakened to the fact that he had been trespassing, sat with mouth half open and a stupefied look of perplexity on his face for a moment, and then, rising hastily, said, "Well, Sol, I guess I'll go an' yoke up the steers."

At eight o'clock all the morning toils were over, the wide kitchen cool and still, and the one-horse wagon standing at the door, into which climbed Mary, her mother, and the Doctor; for, though invested with no spiritual authority, and charged with no ritual or form for hours of affliction, the religion of New England always expects her minister as a first visitor in every house of mourning.

The ride was a sorrowful and silent one. The Doctor, propped upon his cane, seemed to reflect deeply.

"Have you been at all conversant with the exercises of our young friend's mind on the subject of religion?" he asked.

Mrs. Scudder did not at first reply. The remembrance of James's last letter flashed over her mind, and she felt the vibration of the frail child beside her, in whom every nerve was quivering. After a moment, she said,—"It does not become us to judge the spiritual state of any one. James's mind was in an unsettled way when he left; but who can say what wonders may have been effected by divine grace since then?"

This conversation fell on the soul of Mary like the sound of clods falling on a coffin to the ear of one buried alive;—she heard it with a dull, smothering sense of suffocation. *That* question to be raised?—and about one, too, for whom she could have given her own soul? At this moment she felt how idle is the mere hope or promise of personal salvation made to one who has passed beyond the life of self, and struck deep the roots of his existence in others. She did not utter a word;—how could she? A doubt,—the faintest shadow of a doubt,—in such a case, falls on the soul with the weight of mountain certainty; and in that short ride she felt what an infinite pain may be locked in one small, silent breast.

The wagon drew up to the house of mourning. Cato stood at the gate, and came forward, officiously, to help them out. "Mass'r and Missis will be glad to see you," he said. "It's a dreffel stroke has come upon 'em."

Candace appeared at the door. There was a majesty of sorrow in her bearing, as she received them. She said not a word, but pointed with her finger towards the inner room; but as Mary lifted up her faded, weary face to hers, her whole soul seemed to heave towards her like a billow, and she took her up in her arms and broke forth into sobbing, and, carrying her in, as if she had been a child, set her down in the inner room and sat down beside her.

Mrs. Marvyn and her husband sat together, holding each other's hands, the open Bible between them. For a few moments nothing was to be heard but sobs and unrestrained weeping, and then all kneeled down to pray.

After they rose up, Mr. Zebedee Marvyn stood for a moment thoughtfully, and then said,—"If it had pleased the Lord to give me a sure evidence of my son's salvation, I could have given him up with all my heart; but now, whatever there may be, I have seen none." He stood in an attitude of hopeless, heart-smitten dejection, which contrasted painfully with his usual upright carriage and the firm lines of his face.

Mrs. Marvyn started as if a sword had pierced her, passed her arm round Mary's waist, with a strong, nervous clasp, unlike her usual calm self, and said,—"Stay with me, daughter, to-day!—stay with me!"

"Mary can stay as long as you wish, cousin," said Mrs. Scudder; "we have nothing to call her home."

"*Come* with me!" said Mrs. Marvyn to Mary, opening an adjoining door into her bedroom, and drawing her in with a sort of suppressed vehemence,—"I want you!—I must have you!"

"Mrs. Marvyn's state alarms me," said her husband, looking apprehensively after her when the door was closed; "she has not shed any tears, nor slept any, since she heard this news. You know that her mind has been in a peculiar and unhappy state with regard to religious things for many years. I was in hopes she might feel free to open her exercises of mind to the Doctor."

"Perhaps she will feel more freedom with Mary," said the Doctor. "There is no healing for such troubles except in unconditional submission to Infinite Wisdom and Goodness. The Lord reigneth, and will at last bring infinite good out of evil, whether *our* small portion of existence be included or not."

After a few moments more of conference, Mrs. Scudder and the Doctor departed, leaving Mary alone in the house of mourning.

XXIII.

Views of Divine Government

WE have said before, what we now repeat, that it is impossible to write a story of New England life and manners for superficial thought or shallow feeling. They who would fully understand the springs which moved the characters with whom we now associate must go down with us to the very depths.

Never was there a community where the roots of common life shot down so deeply, and were so intensely grappled around things sublime and eternal. The founders of it were a body of confessors and martyrs, who turned their backs on the whole glory of the visible, to found in the wilderness a republic of which the God of Heaven and Earth should be the sovereign power. For the first hundred years grew this community, shut out by a fathomless ocean from the existing world, and divided by an antagonism not less deep from all the reigning ideas of nominal Christendom.

In a community thus unworldly must have arisen a mode of thought, energetic, original, and sublime. The leaders of thought and feeling were the ministry, and we boldly assert that the spectacle of the early ministry of New England was one to which the world gives no parallel. Living an intense, earnest, practical life, mostly tilling the earth with their own hands, they yet carried on the most startling and original religious investigations with a simplicity that might have been deemed audacious, were it not so reverential. All old issues relating to government, religion, ritual, and forms of church organization having for them passed away, they went straight to the heart of things, and boldly confronted the problem of universal being. They had come out from the world as witnesses to the most solemn and sacred of human rights. They had accustomed themselves boldly to challenge and dispute all sham pretensions and idolatries of past ages, — to question the right of kings in the State, and of prelates in the Church;

and now they turned the same bold inquiries towards the Eternal Throne, and threw down their glove in the lists as authorized defenders of every mystery in the Eternal Government. The task they proposed to themselves was that of reconciling the most tremendous facts of sin and evil, present and eternal, with those conceptions of Infinite Power and Benevolence which their own strong and generous natures enabled them so vividly to realize. In the intervals of planting and harvesting, they were busy with the toils of adjusting the laws of a universe. Solemnly simple, they made long journeys in their old one-horse chaises, to settle with each other some nice point of celestial jurisprudence, and to compare their maps of the Infinite. Their letters to each other form a literature altogether unique. Hopkins sends to Edwards the younger his scheme of the universe, in which he starts with the proposition, that God is infinitely above all obligations of any kind to his creatures. Edwards replies with the brusque comment,—"This is wrong; God has no more right to injure a creature than a creature has to injure God;" and each probably about that time preached a sermon on his own views, which was discussed by every farmer, in intervals of plough and hoe, by every woman and girl, at loom, spinning-wheel, or wash-tub. New England was one vast sea, surging from depths to heights with thought and discussion on the most insoluble of mysteries. And it is to be added, that no man or woman accepted any theory or speculation simply *as* theory or speculation; all was profoundly real and vital,—a foundation on which actual life was based with intensest earnestness.

The views of human existence which resulted from this course of training were gloomy enough to oppress any heart which did not rise above them by triumphant faith or sink below them by brutish insensibility; for they included every moral problem of natural or revealed religion, divested of all those softening poetries and tender draperies which forms, ceremonies, and rituals had thrown around them in other parts and ages of Christendom. The human race, without exception, coming into existence "under God's wrath and curse," with a nature so fatally disordered, that, although perfect free agents, men were infallibly certain to do nothing to Divine acceptance until regenerated by the supernatural aid of

God's Spirit,—this aid being given only to a certain decreed number of the human race, the rest, with enough free agency to make them responsible, but without this indispensable assistance exposed to the malignant assaults of evil spirits versed in every art of temptation, were sure to fall hopelessly into perdition. The standard of what constituted a true regeneration, as presented in such treatises as Edwards on the Affections, and others of the times, made this change to be something so high, disinterested, and superhuman, so removed from all natural and common habits and feelings, that the most earnest and devoted, whose whole life had been a constant travail of endeavor, a tissue of almost unearthly disinterestedness, often lived and died with only a glimmering hope of its attainment.

According to any views then entertained of the evidences of a true regeneration, the number of the whole human race who could be supposed as yet to have received this grace was so small, that, as to any numerical valuation, it must have been expressed as an infinitesimal. Dr. Hopkins in many places distinctly recognizes the fact, that the greater part of the human race, up to his time, had been eternally lost,—and boldly assumes the ground, that this amount of sin and suffering, being the best and most necessary means of the greatest final amount of happiness, was not merely permitted, but distinctly chosen, decreed, and provided for, as essential in the schemes of Infinite Benevolence. He held that this decree not only *permitted* each individual act of sin, but also took measures to make it certain, though, by an exercise of infinite skill, it accomplished this result without violating human free agency.

The preaching of those times was animated by an unflinching consistency which never shrank from carrying an idea to its remotest logical verge. The sufferings of the lost were not kept from view, but proclaimed with a terrible power. Dr. Hopkins boldly asserts, that "all the use which God will have for them is to suffer; this is all the end they can answer; therefore all their faculties, and their whole capacities, will be employed and used for this end. . . . . . The body can by omnipotence be made capable of suffering the greatest imaginable pain, without producing dissolution, or abating the least degree of life or sensibility. . . . . . One way in which God will show his power in punishing the wicked will be in strengthening and upholding their bodies and souls in torments which otherwise would be intolerable."

The sermons preached by President Edwards on this subject are so terrific in their refined poetry of torture, that very few persons of quick sensibility could read them through without agony; and it is related, that, when, in those calm and tender tones which never rose to passionate enunciation, he read these discourses, the house was often filled with shrieks and wailings, and that a brother minister once laid hold of his skirts, exclaiming, in an involuntary agony, "Oh! Mr. Edwards! Mr. Edwards! is God not a God of mercy?"

Not that these men were indifferent or insensible to the dread words they spoke; their whole lives and deportment bore thrilling witness to their sincerity. Edwards set apart special days of fasting, in view of the dreadful doom of the lost, in which he was wont to walk the floor, weeping and wringing his hands. Hopkins fasted every Saturday. David Brainerd gave up every refinement of civilized life to weep and pray at the feet of hardened savages, if by any means he might save *one*. All, by lives of eminent purity and earnestness, gave awful weight and sanction to their words.

If we add to this statement the fact, that it was always proposed to every inquiring soul, as an evidence of regeneration, that it should truly and heartily accept all the ways of God thus declared right and lovely, and from the heart submit to Him as the only just and good, it will be seen what materials of tremendous internal conflict and agitation were all the while working in every bosom. Almost all the histories of religious experience of those times relate paroxysms of opposition to God and fierce rebellion, expressed in language which appalls the very soul,—followed, at length, by mysterious elevations of faith and reactions of confiding love, the result of Divine interposition, which carried the soul far above the region of the intellect, into that of direct spiritual intuition.

President Edwards records that he was once in this state of enmity,—that the facts of the Divine administration seemed horrible to him,—and that this opposition was overcome by no course of reasoning, but by an *"inward and sweet sense,"* which came to him once when walking alone in the fields, and, looking up into the blue sky, he saw the blending of the Divine majesty with a calm, sweet, and almost infinite meekness.

The piety which grew up under such a system was, of necessity, energetic,—it was the uprousing of the whole energy of the human soul, pierced and wrenched and probed from her lowest depths to her topmost heights with every awful life-force possible to existence. He whose faith in God came clear through these terrible tests would be sure never to know greater ones. He might certainly challenge earth or heaven, things present or things to come, to swerve him from this grand allegiance.

But it is to be conceded, that these systems, so admirable in relation to the energy, earnestness, and acuteness of their authors, when received as absolute truth, and as a basis of actual life, had, on minds of a certain class, the effect of a slow poison, producing life-habits of morbid action very different from any which ever followed the simple reading of the Bible. They differ from the New Testament as the living embrace of a friend does from his lifeless body, mapped out under the knife of the anatomical demonstrator;—every nerve and muscle is there, but to a sensitive spirit there is the very chill of death in the analysis.

All systems that deal with the infinite are, besides, exposed to danger from small, unsuspected admixtures of human error, which become deadly when carried to such vast results. The smallest speck of earth's dust, in the focus of an infinite lens, appears magnified among the heavenly orbs as a frightful monster.

Thus it happened, that, while strong spirits walked, palm-crowned, with victorious hymns, along these sublime paths, feebler and more sensitive ones lay along the track, bleeding away in life-long despair. Fearful to them were the shadows that lay over the cradle and the grave. The mother clasped her babe to her bosom, and looked with shuddering to the awful coming trial of free agency, with its terrible responsibilities and risks; and, as she thought of the infinite chances against her beloved, almost wished it might die in infancy. But when the stroke of death came, and some young, thoughtless head was laid suddenly low, who can say what silent anguish of loving hearts sounded the dread depths of eternity with the awful question, *Where?*

In no other time or place of Christendom have so fearful issues been presented to the mind. Some church interposed its protecting shield; the Christian born and baptized child was supposed in some wise rescued from the curse of the fall, and related to the great redemption,—to be a member of Christ's family, and, if ever so sinful, still infolded in some vague sphere of hope and protection. Augustine solaced the dread anxieties of trembling love by prayers offered for the dead, in times when the Church above and on earth presented itself to the eye of the mourner as a great assembly with one accord lifting interceding hands for the parted soul.

But the clear logic and intense individualism of New England deepened the problems of the Augustinian faith, while they swept away all those softening provisions so earnestly clasped to the throbbing heart of that great poet of theology. No rite, no form, no paternal relation, no faith or prayer of church, earthly or heavenly, interposed the slightest shield between the trembling spirit and Eternal Justice. The individual entered eternity alone, as if he had no interceding relation in the universe.

This, then, was the awful dread which was constantly underlying life. This it was which caused the tolling bell in green hollows and lonely dells to be a sound which shook the soul and searched the heart with fearful questions. And this it was that was lying with mountain weight on the soul of the mother, too keenly agonized to feel that doubt in such a case was any less a torture than the most dreadful certainty.

Hers was a nature more reasoning than creative and poetic; and whatever she believed bound her mind in strictest chains to its logical results. She delighted in the regions of mathematical knowledge, and walked them as a native home, but the commerce with abstract certainties fitted her mind still more to be stiffened and enchained by glacial reasonings, in regions where spiritual intuitions are as necessary as wings to birds.

Mary was by nature of the class who never reason abstractly, whose intellections all begin in the heart which sends

them colored with its warm life-tint to the brain. Her perceptions of the same subjects were as different from Mrs. Marvyn's as his who revels only in color from his who is busy
with the dry details of mere outline. The one mind was arranged like a map, and the other like a picture. In all the
system which had been explained to her, her mind selected
points on which it seized with intense sympathy, which it
dwelt upon and expanded till all else fell away. The sublimity
of disinterested benevolence,—the harmony and order of a
system tending in its final results to infinite happiness,—the
goodness of God,—the love of a self-sacrificing Redeemer,—
were all so many glorious pictures, which she revolved in her
mind with small care for their logical relations.

Mrs. Marvyn had never, in all the course of their intimacy,
opened her mouth to Mary on the subject of religion. It was
not an uncommon incident of those times for persons of great
elevation and purity of character to be familiarly known and
spoken of as living under a cloud of religious gloom; and it
was simply regarded as one more mysterious instance of the
workings of that infinite decree which denied to them the
special illumination of the Spirit.

When Mrs. Marvyn had drawn Mary with her into her
room, she seemed like a person almost in frenzy. She shut
and bolted the door, drew her to the foot of the bed, and,
throwing her arms round her, rested her hot and throbbing
forehead on her shoulder. She pressed her thin hand over her
eyes, and then, suddenly drawing back, looked her in the face
as one resolved to speak something long suppressed. Her soft
brown eyes had a flash of despairing wildness in them, like
that of a hunted animal turning in its death-struggle on its
pursuer.

"Mary," she said, "I can't help it,—don't mind what I say,
but I must speak or die! Mary, I cannot, will not, be resigned!—it is all hard, unjust, cruel!—to all eternity I will
say so! To me there is no goodness, no justice, no mercy in
anything! Life seems to me the most tremendous doom that
can be inflicted on a helpless being! *What had we done*, that it
should be sent upon us? Why were we made to love so, to
hope so,—our hearts so full of feeling, and all the laws of
Nature marching over us,—never stopping for our agony?

Why, we can suffer so in this life that we had better never have been born!

"But, Mary, think what a moment life is! think of those awful ages of eternity! and then think of all God's power and knowledge used on the lost to make them suffer! think that all but the merest fragment of mankind have gone into this,—are in it now! The number of the elect is so small we can scarce count them for anything! Think what noble minds, what warm, generous hearts, what splendid natures are wrecked and thrown away by thousands and tens of thousands! How we love each other! how our hearts weave into each other! how more than glad we should be to die for each other! And all this ends——O God, how must it end?— Mary! it isn't *my* sorrow only! What right have I to mourn? Is *my* son any better than any other mother's son? Thousands of thousands, whose mothers loved them as I love mine, are gone there!—Oh, my wedding-day! Why did they rejoice? Brides should wear mourning,—the bells should toll for every wedding; every new family is built over this awful pit of despair, and only one in a thousand escapes!"

Pale, aghast, horror-stricken, Mary stood dumb, as one who in the dark and storm sees by the sudden glare of lightning a chasm yawning under foot. It was amazement and dimness of anguish;—the dreadful words struck on the very centre where her soul rested. She felt as if the point of a wedge were being driven between her life and her life's life,— between her and her God. She clasped her hands instinctively on her bosom, as if to hold there some cherished image, and said, in a piercing voice of supplication, "*My* God! *my* God! oh, where art Thou?"

Mrs. Marvyn walked up and down the room with a vivid spot of red in each cheek, and a baleful fire in her eyes, talking in rapid soliloquy, scarcely regarding her listener, absorbed in her own enkindled thoughts.

"Dr. Hopkins says that this is all best,—better than it would have been in any other possible way,—that God *chose* it because it was for a greater final good,—that He not only chose it, but took means to make it certain,—that He ordains every sin, and does all that is necessary to make it certain,— that He creates the vessels of wrath and fits them for destruction, and that He has an infinite knowledge by which He can do it without violating their free agency.—So much the worse! What a use of infinite knowledge! What if men should do so? What if a father should take means to make it certain that his poor little child should be an abandoned wretch, without violating his free agency? So much the worse, I say!—They say He does this so that He may show to all eternity, by their example, the evil nature of sin and its consequences! This is all that the greater part of the human race have been used for yet; and it is all right, because an overplus of infinite happiness is yet to be wrought out by it!—It is *not* right! No possible amount of good to ever so many can make it right to deprave ever so few;—happiness and misery cannot be measured so! I never can think it right,—never!—Yet they say our salvation depends on our loving God,—loving Him better than ourselves,—loving Him better than our dearest friends.—It is impossible!—it is contrary to the laws of my nature! I can never love God! I can never praise Him!—I am lost! lost! lost! And what is worse, I cannot redeem my friends! Oh, I *could* suffer forever,—how willingly!—if I could save *him*!—But oh, eternity, eternity! Frightful, unspeakable woe! No end!—no bottom!—no shore!—no hope!—O God! O God!"

Mrs. Marvyn's eyes grew wilder,—she walked the floor, wringing her hands,—and her words, mingled with shrieks and moans, became whirling and confused, as when in autumn a storm drives the leaves in dizzy mazes.

Mary was alarmed,—the ecstacy of despair was just verging on insanity. She rushed out and called Mr. Marvyn.

"Oh! come in! do! quick!—I'm afraid her mind is going!" she said.

"It is what I feared," he said, rising from where he sat reading his great Bible, with an air of heartbroken dejection. "Since she heard this news, she has not slept nor shed a tear. The Lord hath covered us with a cloud in the day of his fierce anger."

He came into the room, and tried to take his wife into his arms. She pushed him violently back, her eyes glistening with a fierce light. "Leave me alone!" she said,—"I am a lost spirit!"

These words were uttered in a shriek that went through Mary's heart like an arrow.

At this moment, Candace, who had been anxiously listening at the door for an hour past, suddenly burst into the room.

"Lor' bress ye, Squire Marvyn, we won't hab her goin' on dis yer way," she said. "Do talk *gospel* to her, can't ye?—ef you can't, I will.

"Come, ye poor little lamb," she said, walking straight up to Mrs. Marvyn, "come to ole Candace!"—and with that she gathered the pale form to her bosom, and sat down and began rocking her, as if she had been a babe. "Honey, darlin', ye a'n't right,—dar's a drefful mistake somewhar," she said. "Why, de Lord a'n't like what ye tink,—He *loves* ye, honey! Why, jes' feel how *I* loves ye,—poor ole black Candace,—an' I a'n't better'n Him as made me! Who was it wore de crown o' thorns, lamb?—who was it sweat great drops o' blood?— who was it said, 'Father, forgive dem'? Say, honey!—wasn't it de Lord dat made ye?—Dar, dar, now ye'r' cryin'!—cry away, and ease yer poor little heart! He died for Mass'r Jim,—loved him and *died* for him,—jes' give up his sweet, precious body and soul for him on de cross! Laws, jes' *leave* him in Jesus's hands! Why, honey, dar's de very print o' de nails in his hands now!"

The flood-gates were rent; and healing sobs and tears shook the frail form, as a faded lily shakes under the soft rains of summer. All in the room wept together.

"Now, honey," said Candace, after a pause of some minutes, "I knows our Doctor's a mighty good man, an' larned, —an' in fair weather I ha'n't no 'bjection to yer hearin' all about dese yer great an' mighty tings he's got to say. But, honey, dey won't do for you now; sick folks mus'n't hab strong meat; an' times like dese, dar jest a'n't but one ting to come to, an' dat ar's *Jesus*. Jes' come right down to whar poor ole black Candace has to stay allers,—it's a good place, darlin'! *Look right at Jesus.* Tell ye, honey, ye can't live no other way now. Don't ye 'member how He looked on His mother, when she stood faintin' an' tremblin' under de cross, jes' like you? He knows all about mothers' hearts; He won't break yours. It was jes' 'cause He know'd we'd come into straits like dis yer, dat he went through all dese tings,—Him, de Lord o' Glory! Is dis Him you was a-talkin' about?—Him you can't love? Look at Him, an' see ef you can't. Look an' see what He is!—don't ask no questions, and don't go to no reasonin's,—jes' look at *Him*, hangin' dar, so sweet and patient, on de cross! All dey could do couldn't stop his lovin' 'em; he prayed for 'em wid all de breath he had. Dar's a God you can love, a'n't dar? Candace loves Him,—poor, ole, foolish, black, wicked Candace,—and she knows He loves her,"—and here Candace broke down into torrents of weeping.

They laid the mother, faint and weary, on her bed, and beneath the shadow of that suffering cross came down a healing sleep on those weary eyelids.

"Honey," said Candace, mysteriously, after she had drawn Mary out of the room, "don't ye go for to troublin' yer mind wid dis yer. I'm clar Mass'r James is one o' de 'lect; and I'm clar dar's consid'able more o' de 'lect dan people tink. Why, Jesus didn't die for nothin',—all dat love a'n't gwine to be wasted. De 'lect is more'n you or I knows, honey! Dar's de *Spirit*,—He'll give it to 'em; and ef Mass'r James *is* called an' took, depend upon it de Lord has got him ready,—course He has,—so don't ye go to layin' on your poor heart what no mortal creetur can live under; 'cause, as we's got to live in dis yer world, it's quite clar de Lord must ha' fixed it so we *can*; and ef tings was as some folks suppose, why, we *couldn't* live, and dar wouldn't be no sense in anyting dat goes on."

The sudden shock of these scenes was followed, in Mrs. Marvyn's case, by a low, lingering fever. Her room was darkened, and she lay on her bed, a pale, suffering form, with scarcely the ability to raise her hand. The shimmering twilight of the sick-room fell on white napkins, spread over stands, where constantly appeared new vials, big and little, as the physician made his daily visit, and prescribed now this drug and now that, for a wound that had struck through the soul.

Mary remained many days at the white house, because, to the invalid, no step, no voice, no hand was like hers. We see her there now, as she sits in the glimmering by the bed-curtains,—her head a little drooped, as droops a snowdrop over a grave;—one ray of light from a round hole in the closed shutters falls on her smooth-parted hair, her small hands are clasped on her knees, her mouth has lines of sad compression, and in her eyes are infinite questionings.

XXIV.

Mysteries

WHEN Mrs. Marvyn began to amend, Mary returned to the home cottage, and resumed the details of her industrious and quiet life.

Between her and her two best friends had fallen a curtain of silence. The subject that filled all her thoughts could not be named between them. The Doctor often looked at her pale cheeks and drooping form with a face of honest sorrow, and heaved deep sighs as she passed; but he did not find any power within himself by which he could approach her. When he would speak, and she turned her sad, patient eyes so gently on him, the words went back again to his heart, and there, taking a second thought, spread upward wing in prayer.

Mrs. Scudder sometimes came to her room after she was gone to bed, and found her weeping; and when gently she urged her to sleep, she would wipe her eyes so patiently and turn her head with such obedient sweetness, that her mother's heart utterly failed her. For hours Mary sat in her room with James's last letter spread out before her. How anxiously had she studied every word and phrase in it, weighing them to see if the hope of eternal life were in them! How she dwelt on those last promises! Had he kept them? Ah! to die without one word more! Would no angel tell her?—would not the loving God, who knew all, just whisper one word? He must have read the little Bible! What had he thought? What did he feel in that awful hour when he felt himself drifting on to that fearful eternity? Perhaps he had been regenerated,—perhaps there had been a sudden change;—who knows?—she had read of such things;—*perhaps*——Ah, in that perhaps lies a world of anguish! Love will not hear of it. Love *dies* for certainty. Against an uncertainty who can brace the soul? We put all our forces of faith and prayer against it, and it goes down just as a buoy sinks in the water, and the next moment it is up again. The soul fatigues itself with efforts which come and go in waves; and when with laborious care she has adjusted all things in the light of hope, back flows the tide, and sweeps all away. In such struggles life spends itself fast; an inward wound does not carry one deathward more surely than this worst wound of the soul. God has made us so mercifully that there is no *certainty*, however dreadful, to which life-forces do not in time adjust themselves,—but to uncertainty there is no possible adjustment. Where is he? Oh, question of questions!—question which we suppress, but which a power of infinite force still urges on the soul, who feels a part of herself torn away.

Mary sat at her window in evening hours, and watched the slanting sunbeams through the green blades of grass, and thought one year ago he stood there, with his well-knit, manly form, his bright eye, his buoyant hope, his victorious mastery of life! And where was he now? Was his heart as sick, longing for her, as hers for him? Was he looking back to earth and its joys with pangs of unutterable regret? or had a divine power interpenetrated his soul, and lighted there the flame of a celestial love which bore him far above earth? If he were among the lost, in what age of eternity could she ever be blessed? Could Christ be happy, if those who were one with Him were sinful and accursed? and could Christ's own loved ones be happy, when those with whom they have exchanged being, in whom they live and feel, are as wandering stars, for whom is reserved the mist of darkness forever? She had been taught that the agonies of the lost would be forever in sight of the saints, without abating in the least their eternal joys; nay, that they would find in it increasing motives to praise and adoration. Could it be so? Would the last act of the great Bridegroom of the Church be to strike from the heart of his purified Bride those yearnings of self-devoting love which His whole example had taught her, and in which she reflected, as in a glass, His own nature? If not, is there not some provision by which those roots of deathless love which Christ's betrothed ones strike into other hearts shall have a divine, redeeming power? Question vital as life-blood to ten thousand hearts,—fathers, mothers, wives, husbands,—to all who feel the infinite sacredness of love!

After the first interview with Mrs. Marvyn, the subject

which had so agitated them was not renewed. She had risen at last from her sick-bed, as thin and shadowy as a faded moon after sunrise. Candace often shook her head mournfully, as her eyes followed her about her daily tasks. Once only, with Mary, she alluded to the conversation which had passed between them;—it was one day when they were together, spinning, in the north upper room that looked out upon the sea. It was a glorious day. A ship was coming in under full sail, with white gleaming wings. Mrs. Marvyn watched it a few moments,—the gay creature, so full of exultant life,—and then smothered down an inward groan, and Mary thought she heard her saying, "Thy will be done!"

"Mary," she said, gently, "I hope you will forget all I said to you that dreadful day. It had to be said, or I should have died. Mary, I begin to think that it is not best to stretch our minds with reasonings where we are so limited, where we can know so little. I am quite sure there must be dreadful mistakes somewhere.

"It seems to me irreverent and shocking that a child should oppose a father, or a creature its Creator. I never should have done it, only that, where direct questions are presented to the judgment, one cannot help judging. If one is required to praise a being as just and good, one must judge of his actions by some standard of right,—and we have no standard but such as our Creator has placed in us. I have been told it was my duty to attend to these subjects, and I have tried to,—and the result has been that the facts presented seem wholly irreconcilable with any notions of justice or mercy that I am able to form. If these be the facts, I can only say that my nature is made entirely opposed to them. If I followed the standard of right they present, and acted according to my small mortal powers on the same principles, I should be a very bad person. Any father, who should make such use of power over his children as they say the Deity does with regard to us, would be looked upon as a monster by our very imperfect moral sense. Yet I cannot say that the facts are not so. When I heard the Doctor's sermons on 'Sin a Necessary Means of the Greatest Good,' I could not extricate myself from the reasoning.

"I have thought, in desperate moments, of giving up the Bible itself. But what do I gain? Do I not see the same diffi-

culty in Nature? I see everywhere a Being whose main ends
seem to be beneficent, but whose good purposes are worked
out at terrible expense of suffering, and apparently by the total sacrifice of myriads of sensitive creatures. I see unflinching
order, general good-will, but no sympathy, no mercy. Storms,
earthquakes, volcanoes, sickness, death, go on without regarding us. Everywhere I see the most hopeless, unrelieved
suffering,—and for aught I see, it may be eternal. Immortality
is a dreadful chance, and I would rather never have been.—
The Doctor's dreadful system is, I confess, much like the laws
of Nature,—about what one might reason out from them.

"There is but just one thing remaining, and that is, as Candace said, the cross of Christ. If God so loved us,—if He
died for us,—greater love hath no man than this. It seems to
me that love is shown here in the two highest forms possible
to our comprehension. We see a Being who gives himself for
us,—and more than that, harder than that, a Being who con-
sents to the suffering of a dearer than self. Mary, I feel that I
must love more, to give up one of my children to suffer, than
to consent to suffer myself. There is a world of comfort to
me in the words, 'He that spared not his own Son, but delivered him up for us all, how shall he not with him also freely
give us all things?' These words speak to my heart. I can interpret them by my own nature, and I rest on them. If there
is a fathomless mystery of sin and sorrow, there is a deeper
mystery of God's love. So, Mary, I try Candace's way,—I
look at Christ,—I pray to Him. If he that hath seen Him
hath seen the Father, it is enough. I rest there,—I wait. What
I know not now I shall know hereafter."

Mary kept all things and pondered them in her heart. She
could speak to no one,—not to her mother, nor to her spiritual guide; for had she not passed to a region beyond theirs?
As well might those on the hither side of mortality instruct
the souls gone beyond the veil as souls outside a great affliction guide those who are struggling in it. That is a mighty
baptism, and only Christ can go down with us into those
waters.

Mrs. Scudder and the Doctor only marked that she was
more than ever conscientious in every duty, and that she
brought to life's daily realities something of the calmness and

disengagedness of one whose soul has been wrenched by a mighty shock from all moorings here below. Hopes did not excite, fears did not alarm her; life had no force strong enough to awaken a thrill within; and the only subjects on which she ever spoke with any degree of ardor were religious subjects.

One who should have seen moving about the daily ministrations of the cottage a pale girl, whose steps were firm, whose eye was calm, whose hands were ever busy, would scarce imagine that through that silent heart were passing tides of thought that measured a universe; but it was even so. Through that one gap of sorrow flowed in the whole awful mystery of existence, and silently, as she spun and sewed, she thought over and over again all that she had ever been taught, and compared and revolved it by the light of a dawning inward revelation.

Sorrow is the great birth-agony of immortal powers,—sorrow is the great searcher and revealer of hearts, the great test of truth; for Plato has wisely said, sorrow will not endure sophisms,—all shams and unrealities melt in the fire of that awful furnace. Sorrow reveals forces in ourselves we never dreamed of. The soul, a bound and sleeping prisoner, hears her knock on her cell-door, and wakens. Oh, how narrow the walls! oh, how close and dark the grated window! how the long useless wings beat against the impassable barriers! Where are we? What *is* this prison? What *is* beyond? Oh for more air, more light! When will the door be opened? The soul seems to itself to widen and deepen; it trembles at its own dreadful forces; it gathers up in waves that break with wailing only to flow back into the everlasting void. The calmest and most centred natures are sometimes thrown by the shock of a great sorrow into a tumultuous amazement. All things are changed. The earth no longer seems solid, the skies no longer secure; a deep abyss seems underlying every joyous scene of life. The soul, struck with this awful inspiration, is a mournful Cassandra; she sees blood on every threshold, and shudders in the midst of mirth and festival with the weight of a terrible wisdom.

Who shall dare be glad any more, that has once seen the frail foundations on which love and joy are built? Our brighter hours, have they only been weaving a network of agonizing remembrances for this day of bereavement? The heart is pierced with every past joy, with every hope of its ignorant prosperity. Behind every scale in music, the gayest and cheeriest, the grandest, the most triumphant, lies its dark relative minor; the notes are the same, but the change of a semitone changes all to gloom;—all our gayest hours are tunes that have a modulation into these dreary keys ever possible; at any moment the key-note may be struck.

The firmest, best-prepared natures are often beside themselves with astonishment and dismay, when they are called to this dread initiation. They thought it a very happy world before,—a glorious universe. Now it is darkened with the shadow of insoluble mysteries. Why this everlasting tramp of inevitable laws on quivering life? If the wheels must roll, why must the crushed be so living and sensitive?

And yet sorrow is godlike, sorrow is grand and great, sorrow is wise and far-seeing. Our own instinctive valuations, the intense sympathy which we give to the tragedy which God has inwoven into the laws of Nature, show us that it is with no slavish dread, no cowardly shrinking, that we should approach her divine mysteries. What are the natures that cannot suffer? Who values them? From the fat oyster, over which the silver tide rises and falls without one pulse upon its fleshy ear, to the hero who stands with quivering nerve parting with wife and child and home for country and God, all the way up is an ascending scale, marked by increasing power to suffer; and when we look to the Head of all being, up through principalities and powers and princedoms, with dazzling orders and celestial blazonry, to behold by what emblem the Infinite Sovereign chooses to reveal himself, we behold, in the midst of the throne, "a lamb as it had been slain."

Sorrow is divine. Sorrow is reigning on the throne of the universe, and the crown of all crowns has been one of thorns. There have been many books that treat of the mystery of sorrow, but only one that bids us glory in tribulation, and count it all joy when we fall into divers afflictions, that so we may be associated with that great fellowship of suffering of which the Incarnate God is the head, and through which He is carrying a redemptive conflict to a glorious victory over evil. If we suffer with Him, we shall also reign with Him.

Even in the very making up of our physical nature, God puts suggestions of such a result. "Weeping may endure for a night, but joy cometh in the morning." There are victorious powers in our nature which are all the while working for us in our deepest pain. It is said, that, after the sufferings of the rack, there ensues a period in which the simple repose from torture produces a beatific trance; it is the reaction of Nature, asserting the benignant intentions of her Creator. So, after great mental conflicts and agonies must come a reaction, and the Divine Spirit, co-working with our spirit, seizes the favorable moment, and, interpenetrating natural laws with a celestial vitality, carries up the soul to joys beyond the ordinary possibilities of mortality.

It is said that gardeners, sometimes, when they would bring a rose to richer flowering, deprive it, for a season, of light and moisture. Silent and dark it stands, dropping one fading leaf after another, and seeming to go down patiently to death. But when every leaf is dropped, and the plant stands stripped to the uttermost, a new life is even then working in the buds, from which shall spring a tender foliage and a brighter wealth of flowers. So, often in celestial gardening, every leaf of earthly joy must drop, before a new and divine bloom visits the soul.

Gradually, as months passed away, the floods grew still; the mighty rushes of the inner tides ceased to dash. There came first a delicious calmness, and then a celestial inner clearness, in which the soul seemed to lie quiet as an untroubled ocean, reflecting heaven. Then came the fulness of mysterious communion given to the pure in heart,—that advent of the Comforter in the soul, teaching all things and bringing all things to remembrance; and Mary moved in a world transfigured by a celestial radiance. Her face, so long mournfully calm, like some chiselled statue of Patience, now wore a radiance, as when one places a light behind some alabaster screen sculptured with mysterious and holy emblems, and words of strange sweetness broke from her, as if one should hear snatches of music from a door suddenly opened in heaven. Something wise and strong and sacred gave an involuntary impression of awe in her looks and words;—it was not the childlike loveliness of early days, looking with dovelike, ignorant eyes on sin and sorrow; but the victorious sweetness of that great multitude who have come out of great tribulation, having washed their robes and made them white in the blood of the Lamb. In her eyes there was that nameless depth that one sees with awe in the Sistine Madonna,—eyes that have measured infinite sorrow and looked through it to an infinite peace.

"My dear Madam," said the Doctor to Mrs. Scudder, "I cannot but think that there must be some uncommonly gracious exercises passing in the mind of your daughter; for I observe, that, though she is not inclined to conversation, she seems to be much in prayer; and I have, of late, felt the sense of a Divine Presence with her in a most unusual degree. Has she opened her mind to you?"

"Mary was always a silent girl," said Mrs. Scudder, "and not given to speaking of her own feelings; indeed, until she gave you an account of her spiritual state, on joining the church, I never knew what her exercises were. Hers is a most singular case. I never knew the time when she did not seem to love God more than anything else. It has disturbed me sometimes,—because I did not know but it might be mere natural sensibility, instead of gracious affection."

"Do not disturb yourself, Madam," said the Doctor. "The Spirit worketh when, where, and how He will; and, undoubtedly, there have been cases where His operations commence exceedingly early. Mr. Edwards relates a case of a young person who experienced a marked conversion when three years of age; and Jeremiah was called from the womb. (Jeremiah, i. 5) In all cases we must test the quality of the evidence without relation to the time of its commencement. I do not generally lay much stress on our impressions, which are often uncertain and delusive; yet I have had an impression that the Lord would be pleased to make some singular manifestations of His grace through this young person. In the economy of grace there is neither male nor female; and Peter says (Acts, ii. 17) that the Spirit of the Lord shall be poured out and your sons and your daughters shall prophesy. Yet if we consider that the Son of God, as to his human nature, was made of a woman, it leads us to see that in matters of grace God sets a special value on woman's nature and designs to put special honor upon it. Accordingly, there have been in the Church, in all ages, holy women who have received the Spirit and been called to a ministration in the things of God,—such as Deborah, Huldah, and Anna, the prophetess. In our own days, most uncommon manifestations of divine grace have been given to holy women. It was my privilege to be in the family of President Edwards at a time when Northampton was specially visited, and his wife seemed and spoke more like a glorified spirit than a mortal woman,—and multitudes flocked to the house to hear her wonderful words. She seemed to have such a sense of the Divine love as was almost beyond the powers of nature to endure. Just to speak the words, 'Our Father who art in heaven,' would overcome her with such a manifestation that she would become cold and almost faint; and though she uttered much, yet she told us that the divinest things she saw could not be spoken. These things could not be fanaticism, for she was a person of a singular evenness of nature, and of great skill and discretion in temporal matters, and of an exceeding humility, sweetness, and quietness of disposition."

"I have observed of late," said Mrs. Scudder, "that, in our praying circles, Mary seemed much carried out of herself, and often as if she would speak, and with difficulty holding herself back. I have not urged her, because I thought it best to wait till she should feel full liberty."

"Therein you do rightly, Madam," said the Doctor; "but I am persuaded you will hear from her yet."

It came at length, the hour of utterance. And one day, in a praying circle of the women of the church, all were startled by the clear silver tones of one who sat among them and spoke with the unconscious simplicity of an angel child, calling God her Father, and speaking of an ineffable union in Christ, binding all things together in one, and making all complete in Him. She spoke of a love passing knowledge,— passing all love of lovers or of mothers,—a love forever spending, yet never spent,—a love ever pierced and bleeding, yet ever constant and triumphant, rejoicing with infinite joy to bear in its own body the sins and sorrows of a universe,—

conquering, victorious love, rejoicing to endure, panting to give, and offering its whole self with an infinite joyfulness for our salvation. And when, kneeling, she poured out her soul in prayer, her words seemed so many winged angels, musical with unearthly harpings of an untold blessedness. They who heard her had the sensation of rising in the air, of feeling a celestial light and warmth descending into their souls; and when, rising, she stood silent and with downcast drooping eyelids, there were tears in all eyes, and a hush in all movements as she passed, as if something celestial were passing out.

Miss Prissy came rushing homeward, to hold a private congratulatory talk with the Doctor and Mrs. Scudder, while Mary was tranquilly setting the tea-table and cutting bread for supper.

"To see her now, certainly," said Miss Prissy, "moving round so thoughtful, not forgetting anything, and doing everything so calm, you wouldn't 'a' thought it could be her that spoke those blessed words and made that prayer! Well, certainly that prayer seemed to take us all right up and put us down in heaven! and when I opened my eyes, and saw the roses and asparagus-bushes on the manteltree-piece, I had to ask myself, 'Where have I been?' Oh, Miss Scudder, her afflictions have been sanctified to her!—and really, when I see her going on so, I feel she can't be long for us. They say, dying grace is for dying hours, and I'm sure this seems more like dying grace than anything that I ever yet saw."

"She is a precious gift," said the Doctor; "let us thank the Lord for his grace through her. She has evidently had a manifestation of the Beloved, and feedeth among the lilies (Canticles, vi. 3); and we will not question the Lord's further dispensations concerning her."

"Certainly," said Miss Prissy, briskly, "it's never best to borrow trouble; 'sufficient unto the day' is enough, to be sure.—And now, Miss Scudder, I thought I'd just take a look at that dove-colored silk of yours to-night, to see what would have to be done with it, because I must make every minute tell; and you know I lose half a day every week for the prayer-meeting. Though I ought not to say I lose it, either; for I was telling Miss General Wilcox I wouldn't give up that meeting for bags and bags of gold. She wanted me to come and sew for her one Wednesday, and says I, 'Miss Wilcox, I'm poor and have to live by my work, but I a'n't so poor but what I have some comforts, and I can't give up my prayer-meeting for any money,'—for you see, if one gets a little lift there, it makes all the work go lighter,—but then I have to be particular to save up every scrap and end of time."

Mrs. Scudder and Miss Prissy crossed the kitchen and entered the bedroom, and soon had the dove-colored silk under consideration.

"Well, Miss Scudder," said Miss Prissy, after mature investigation, "here's a broad hem, not cut at all on the edge, as I see, and that might be turned down, and so cut off the worn spot up by the waist,—and then, if it is turned, it will look every bit and grain as well as a new silk;—I'll sit right down now and go to ripping. I put my ripping-knife into my pocket when I put on this dress to go to prayer-meeting, because, says I to myself, there'll be something to do at Miss Scudder's to-night. You just get an iron to the fire, and we'll have it all ripped and pressed out before dark."

Miss Prissy seated herself at the open window, as cheery as a fresh apple-blossom, and began busily plying her knife, looking at the garment she was ripping with an astute air, as if she were about to circumvent it into being a new dress by some surprising act of legerdemain. Mrs. Scudder walked to the looking-glass and began changing her bonnet cap for a tea-table one.

Miss Prissy, after a while, commenced in a mysterious tone.

"Miss Scudder, I know folks like me shouldn't have their eyes open too wide, but then I can't help noticing some things. Did you see the Doctor's face when we was talking to him about Mary? Why, he colored all up and the tears came into his eyes. It's my belief that that blessed man worships the ground she treads on. I don't mean *worships*, either,— 'cause that would be wicked, and he's too good a man to make a graven image of anything,—but it's clear to see that there a'n't anybody in the world like Mary to him. I always did think so; but I used to think Mary was such a little poppet— that she'd do better for——Well, you know, I thought about some younger man;—but, laws, now I see how she rises up to be ahead of every body, and is so kind of solemn-like. I can't but see the leadings of Providence. What a minister's wife she'd be, Miss Scudder!—why, all the ladies coming out of prayer-meeting were speaking of it. You see, they want the Doctor to get married;—it seems more comfortable-like to have ministers married; one feels more free to open their exercises of mind, and as Miss Deacon Twitchel said to me,—'If the Lord had made a woman o' purpose, as he did for Adam, he wouldn't have made her a bit different from Mary Scudder.' Why, the oldest of us would follow her lead,—'cause she goes before us without knowing it."

"I feel that the Lord has greatly blessed me in such a child," said Mrs. Scudder, "and I feel disposed to wait the leadings of Providence."

"Just exactly," said Miss Prissy, giving a shake to her silk; "and as Miss Twitchel said, in this case every providence seems to p'int. I felt dreadfully for her along six months back; but now I see how she's been brought out, I begin to see that things are for the best, perhaps, after all. I can't help feeling that Jim Marvyn is gone to heaven, poor fellow! His father is a deacon,—and such a good man!—and Jim, though he did make a great laugh wherever he went, and sometimes laughed where he hadn't ought to, was a noble-hearted fellow. Now, to be sure, as the Doctor says, 'amiable instincts a'n't true holiness'; but then they are better than unamiable ones, like Simeon Brown's. I do think, if that man is a Christian, he is a dreadful ugly one; he snapped me short up about my change, when he settled with me last Tuesday; and if I hadn't felt that it was a sinful rising, I should have told him I'd never put foot in his house again; I'm glad, for my part, he's gone out of our church. Now Jim Marvyn was like a prince to poor people; and I remember once his mother told him to settle with me, and he gave me 'most double, and wouldn't let me make change. 'Confound it all, Miss Prissy,' says he, 'I wouldn't stitch as you do from morning to night for double that money.' Now I know we can't do anything to recommend ourselves to the Lord, but then I can't help feeling some sorts of folks must be by nature more pleasing to Him than others. David was a man after God's own heart, and he was a generous, whole-souled fellow, like Jim Marvyn, though he did get carried away by his spirits sometimes and do wrong things; and so I hope the Lord saw fit to make Jim one of the elect. We don't ever know what God's grace has done for folks. I think a great many are converted when we know nothing about it, as Miss Twitchel told poor old Miss Tyrel, who was mourning about her son, a dreadful wild boy, who was killed falling from mast-head; she says, that from the mast-head to the deck was time enough for divine grace to do the work."

"I have always had a trembling hope for poor James," said Mrs. Scudder,—"not on account of any of his good deeds or amiable traits, because election is without foresight of any good works,—but I felt he was a child of the covenant, at least by the father's side, and I hope the Lord has heard his prayer. These are dark providences; the world is full of them; and all we can do is to have faith that the Lord will bring infinite good out of finite evil, and make everything better than if the evil had not happened. That's what our good Doctor is always repeating; and we must try to rejoice, in view of the happiness of the universe, without considering whether we or our friends are to be included in it or not."

"Well, dear me!" said Miss Prissy, "I hope, if that is necessary, it will please the Lord to give it to me; for I don't seem to find any powers in me to get up to it. But all's for the best, at any rate,—and that's a comfort."

Just at this moment Mary's clear voice at the door announced that tea was on the table.

"Coming, this very minute," said Miss Prissy, bustling up and pulling off her spectacles. Then, running across the room, she shut the door mysteriously, and turned to Mrs. Scudder with the air of an impending secret. Miss Prissy was subject to sudden impulses of confidence, in which she was so very cautious that not the thickest oak-plank door seemed secure enough, and her voice dropped to its lowest key. The most important and critical words were entirely omitted, or supplied by a knowing wink and a slight stamp of the foot.

In this mood she now approached Mrs. Scudder, and, holding up her hand on the door-side to prevent consequences, if, after all, she should be betrayed into a loud word, she said, "I thought I'd just say, Miss Scudder, that, in case

Mary should——the Doctor,—in case, you know, there should be a——in the house, you *must* just contrive it so as to give me a month's notice, so that I could give you a whole fortnight to fix her up as such a good man's——ought to be. Now I know how spiritually-minded our blessed Doctor is; but bless you, Ma'am, he's got eyes. I tell you, Miss Scudder, these men, the best of 'em, *feel* what's what, though they don't *know* much. I saw the Doctor look at Mary that night I dressed her for the wedding-party. I tell you he'd like to have his wife look pretty well, and he'll get up some blessed text or other about it, just as he did that night about being brought unto the king in raiment of needle-work. That is an encouraging thought to us sewing-women.

"But this thing was spoken of after the meeting. Miss Twitchel and Miss Jones were talking about it; and they all say that there would be the best setting-out got for her that was ever seen in Newport, if it should happen. Why, there's reason in it. She ought to have at least two real good India silks that will stand alone,—and you'll see she'll have 'em too; you let me alone for that, and I was thinking, as I lay awake last night, of a new way of making up, that you will say is just the sweetest that ever you did see. And Miss Jones was saying that she hoped there wouldn't anything happen without her knowing it, because her husband's sister in Philadelphia has sent her a new receipt for cake, and she has tried it and it came out beautifully, and she says she'll send some in."

All the time that this stream was flowing, Mrs. Scudder stood with the properly reserved air of a discreet matron, who leaves all such matters to Providence, and is not supposed unduly to anticipate the future; and, in reply, she warmly pressed Miss Prissy's hand, and remarked, that no one could tell what a day might bring forth,—and other general observations on the uncertainty of mortal prospects, which form a becoming shield when people do not wish to say more exactly what they are thinking of.

XXV.

A Guest at the Cottage

NOTHING is more striking, in the light and shadow of the human drama, than to compare the inner life and thoughts of elevated and silent natures with the thoughts and plans which those by whom they are surrounded have of and for them. Little thought Mary of any of the speculations that busied the friendly head of Miss Prissy, or that lay in the provident forecastings of her prudent mother. When a life into which all our life-nerves have run is cut suddenly away, there follows, after the first long bleeding is stanched, an internal paralysis of certain portions of our nature. It was so with Mary: the thousand fibres that bind youth and womanhood to earthly love and life were all in her as still as the grave, and only the spiritual and divine part of her being was active. Her hopes, desires, and aspirations were all such as she could have had in greater perfection as a disembodied spirit than as a mortal woman. The small stake for self which she had invested in life was gone,—and henceforward all personal matters were to her so indifferent that she scarce was conscious of a wish in relation to her own individual happiness. Through the sudden crush of a great affliction, she was in that state of self-abnegation to which the mystics brought themselves by fastings and self-imposed penances,—a state not purely healthy, nor realizing the divine ideal of a perfect human being made to exist in the relations of human life,—but one of those exceptional conditions, which, like the hours that often precede dissolution, seem to impart to the subject of them a peculiar aptitude for delicate and refined spiritual impressions. We could not afford to have it always night,—and we must think that the broad, gay morning-light, when meadow-lark and robin and bobolink are singing in chorus and a thousand insects and the waving of a thousand breezes, is on the whole the most in accordance with the average wants of those who have a material life to live and material work to do. But then we reverence that clear-obscure of midnight, when everything is still and dewy;—then sing the nightingales, which cannot be heard by day; then shine the mysterious stars. So when all earthly voices are hushed in the soul, all earthly lights darkened, music and color float in from a higher sphere.

No veiled nun, with her shrouded forehead and downcast eyes, ever moved about a convent with a spirit more utterly divided from the world than Mary moved about her daily employments. Her care about the details of life seemed more than ever minute; she was always anticipating her mother in every direction, and striving by a thousand gentle preveniences to save her from fatigue and care; there was even a tenderness about her ministrations, as if the daughter had changed feelings and places with the mother.

The Doctor, too, felt a change in her manner towards him, which, always considerate and kind, was now invested with a tender thoughtfulness and anxious solicitude to serve which often brought tears to his eyes. All the neighbors who had been in the habit of visiting at the house received from her, almost daily, in one little form or another, some proof of her thoughtful remembrance.

She seemed in particular to attach herself to Mrs. Marvyn, —throwing her care around that fragile and wounded nature, as a generous vine will sometimes embrace with tender leaves and flowers a dying tree.

But her heart seemed to have yearnings beyond even the circle of home and friends. She longed for the sorrowful and the afflicted,—she would go down to the forgotten and the oppressed,—and made herself the companion of the Doctor's secret walks and explorings among the poor victims of the slave-ships, and entered with zeal as teacher among his African catechumens.

Nothing but the limits of bodily strength could confine her zeal to do and suffer for others; a river of love had suddenly been checked in her heart, and it needed all these channels to drain off the waters that must otherwise have drowned her in the suffocating agonies of repression.

Sometimes, indeed, there would be a returning thrill of the old wound,—one of those overpowering moments when some turn in life brings back anew a great anguish. She would find unexpectedly in a book a mark that he had placed there,—or a turn in conversation would bring back a tone of his voice,—or she would see on some thoughtless young head curls just like those which were swaying to and fro down among the wavering seaweeds,—and then her heart gave one great throb of pain, and turned for relief to some immediate act of love to some living being. They who saw her in one of these moments felt a surging of her heart towards them, a moisture of the eye, a sense of some inexpressible yearning, and knew not from what pain that love was wrung, nor how that poor heart was seeking to still its own throbbings in blessing them.

By what name shall we call this beautiful twilight, this night of the soul, so starry with heavenly mysteries? *Not* happiness,—but blessedness. They who have it walk among men "as sorrowful, yet always rejoicing,—as poor, yet making many rich,—as having nothing, and yet possessing all things."

The Doctor, as we have seen, had always that reverential spirit towards women which accompanies a healthy and great nature; but in the constant converse which he now held with a beautiful being, from whom every particle of selfish feeling or mortal weakness seemed sublimed, he appeared to yield his soul up to her leading with a wonderful humility, as to some fair, miraculous messenger of Heaven. All questions of internal experience, all delicate shadings of the spiritual history with which his pastoral communings in his flock made him conversant, he brought to her to be resolved with the purest simplicity of trust.

"She is one of the Lord's rarities," he said, one day to Mrs. Scudder, "and I find it difficult to maintain the bounds of Christian faithfulness in talking with her. It is a charm of the Lord's hidden ones that they know not their own beauty, and God forbid that I should tempt a creature made so perfect by divine grace to self-exaltation, or lay my hand unadvisedly, as Uzzah did, upon the ark of God, by my inconsiderate praises!"

"Well, Doctor," said Miss Prissy, who sat in the corner, sewing on the dove-colored silk, "I do wish you could come into one of our meetings and hear those blessed prayers. I don't think you nor anybody else ever heard anything like 'em."

"I would, indeed, that I might with propriety enjoy the privilege," said the Doctor.

"Well, I'll tell you what," said Miss Prissy, "next week they're going to meet here; and I'll leave the door just ajar, and you can hear every word, just by standing in the entry."

"Thank you, Madam," said the Doctor; "it would certainly be a blessed privilege, but I cannot persuade myself that such an act would be consistent with Christian propriety."

"Ah, now do hear that good man!" said Miss Prissy, after he had left the room; "if he ha'n't got the making of a real gentleman in him, as well as a real Christian!—though I always did say, for my part, that a real Christian will be a gentleman. But I don't believe all the temptations in the world could stir that blessed man one jot or grain to do the least thing that he thinks is wrong or out of the way. Well, I must say, I never saw such a good man; he is the only man I ever saw good enough for our Mary."

Another spring came round, and brought its roses, and the apple-trees blossomed for the third time since the commencement of our story; and the robins had rebuilt their nest, and began to lay their blue eggs in it; and Mary still walked her calm course, as a sanctified priestess of the great worship of sorrow. Many were the hearts now dependent on her, the spiritual histories, the threads of which were held in her loving hand,—many the souls burdened with sins, or oppressed with sorrow, who found in her bosom at once confessional and sanctuary. So many sought her prayers, that her hours of intercession were full, and often needed to be lengthened to embrace all for whom she would plead. United to the good Doctor by a constant friendship and fellowship, she had gradually grown accustomed to the more and more intimate manner in which he regarded her,—which had risen from a simple "dear child," and "dear Mary," to "dear friend," and at last "dearest of all friends," which he frequently called her, encouraged by the calm, confiding sweetness of those still, blue eyes, and that gentle smile, which came without one varying flutter of the pulse or the rising of the slightest flush on the marble cheek.

One day a letter was brought in, post-marked "Philadelphia." It was from Madame de Frontignac; it was in French, and ran as follows:—

"MY DEAR LITTLE WHITE ROSE:—

"I am longing to see you once more, and before long I shall be in Newport. Dear little Mary, I am sad, very sad;— the days seem all of them too long; and every morning I look out of my window and wonder why I was born. I am not so happy as I used to be, when I cared for nothing but to sing and smooth my feathers like the birds. That is the best kind of life for us women;—if we love anything better than our clothes, it is sure to bring us great sorrow. For all that, I can't help thinking it is very noble and beautiful to love;—love is very beautiful, but very, very sad. My poor dear little white cat, I should like to hold you a little while to my heart;—it is so cold all the time, and aches so, I wish I were dead; but then I am not good enough to die. The Abbé says, we must offer up our sorrow to God as a satisfaction for our sins. I have a good deal to offer, because my nature is strong and I can feel a great deal.

"But I am very selfish, dear little Mary, to think only of myself, when I know how you must suffer. Ah! but you knew he loved you truly, the poor dear boy!—that is something. I pray daily for his soul; don't think it wrong of me; you know it is our religion;—we should all do our best for each other.

"Remember me tenderly to Mrs. Marvyn. Poor mother!— the bleeding heart of the Mother of God alone can understand such sorrows.

"I am coming in a week or two, and then I have many things to say to *ma belle rose blanche;* till then I kiss her little hands.

"VIRGINIE DE FRONTIGNAC."

One beautiful afternoon, not long after, a carriage stopped at the cottage, and Madame de Frontignac alighted. Mary was spinning in her garret-boudoir, and Mrs. Scudder was at that moment at a little distance from the house, sprinkling some linen, which was laid out to bleach on the green turf of the clothes-yard.

Madame de Frontignac sent away the carriage, and ran up the stairway, pursuing the sound of Mary's spinning-wheel, mingled with her song; and in a moment, throwing aside the curtain, she seized Mary in her arms, and kissed her on either cheek, laughing and crying both at once.

"I knew where I should find you, *ma blanche*! I heard the wheel of my poor little princess! It's a good while since we spun together, *mimi*! Ah, Mary, darling, little do we know what we spin! life is hard and bitter, is n't it? Ah, how white your cheeks are, poor child!"

Madame de Frontignac spoke with tears in her own eyes, passing her hand caressingly over the fair cheeks.

"And you have grown pale, too, dear Madame," said Mary, looking up, and struck with the change in the once brilliant face.

"Have I, *petite*? I don't know why not. We women have secret places where our life runs out. At home I wear *rouge*; that makes all right;—but I don't put it on for you, Mary; you see me just as I am."

Mary could not but notice the want of that brilliant color and roundness in the cheek, which once made so glowing a picture; the eyes seemed larger and tremulous with a pathetic depth, and around them those bluish circles that speak of languor and pain. Still, changed as she was, Madame de Frontignac seemed only more strikingly interesting and fascinating than ever. Still she had those thousand pretty movements, those nameless graces of manner, those wavering shades of expression, that irresistibly enchained the eye and the imagination,—true Frenchwoman as she was, always in one rainbow shimmer of fancy and feeling, like one of those cloud-spotted April days which give you flowers and rain, sun and shadow, and snatches of bird-singing, all at once.

"I have sent away my carriage, Mary, and come to stay with you. You want me,—*n'est ce pas?*" she said, coaxingly, with her arms round Mary's neck; "if you don't, *tant pis*! for I am the bad penny you English speak of,—you cannot get me off."

"I am sure, dear friend," said Mary, earnestly, "we don't want to put you off."

"I know it; you are true; you *mean* what you say; you are

all good real gold, down to your hearts; that is why I love you. But you, my poor Mary, your cheeks are very white; poor little heart, you suffer!"

"No," said Mary; "I do not suffer now. Christ has given me the victory over sorrow."

There was something sadly sublime in the manner in which this was said,—and something so sacred in the expression of Mary's face that Madame de Frontignac crossed herself, as she had been wont before a shrine; and then said, "Sweet Mary, pray for me; I am not at peace; I cannot get the victory over sorrow."

"What sorrow can you have?" said Mary,—"you, so beautiful, so rich, so admired, whom everybody must love?"

"That is what I came to tell you; I came to confess to you. But you must sit down *there*," she said, placing Mary on a low seat in the garret-window; "and Virginie will sit here," she said, drawing a bundle of uncarded wool towards her, and sitting down at Mary's feet.

"Dear Madame," said Mary, "let me get you a better seat."

"No, no, *mignonne*, this is best; I want to lay my head in your lap";—and she took off her riding-hat with its streaming plume, and tossed it carelessly from her, and laid her head down on Mary's lap. "Now don't call me Madame any more. Do you know," she said, raising her head with a sudden brightening of cheek and eye, "do you know that there are two *mes* to this person?—one is Virginie, and the other is Madame de Frontignac. Everybody in Philadelphia knows Madame de Frontignac;—she is very gay, very careless, very happy; she never has any serious hours, or any sad thoughts; she wears powder and diamonds, and dances all night, and never prays;—that is Madame. But Virginie is quite another thing. She is tired of all this,—tired of the balls, and the dancing, and the diamonds, and the beaux; and she likes true people, and would like to live very quiet with somebody that she loved. She is very unhappy; and she prays, too, sometimes, in a poor little way,—like the birds in your nest out there, who don't know much, but chipper and cry because they are hungry. This is your Virginie. Madame never comes here,—never call me Madame."

"Dear Virginie," said Mary, "how I love you!"

"Do you Mary,—*bien sûr*? You are my good angel! I felt a good impulse from you when I first saw you, and have always been stronger to do right when I got one of your pretty little letters. Oh, Mary, darling, I have been very foolish and very miserable, and sometimes tempted to be very, very bad! Oh, sometimes I thought I would not care for God or anything else!—it was very bad of me,—but I was like a foolish little fly caught in a spider's net before he knows it."

Mary's eyes questioned her companion with an expression of eager sympathy, somewhat blended with curiosity.

"I can't make you understand me quite," said Madame de Frontignac, "unless I go back a good many years. You see, dear Mary, my dear angel mamma died when I was very little, and I was sent to be educated at the Sacré Cœur in Paris. I was very happy and very good in those days; the sisters loved me, and I loved them; and I used to be so pious, and loved God dearly. When I took my first communion, Sister Agatha prepared me. She was a true saint, and is in heaven now; and I remember, when I came to her, all dressed like a bride, with my white crown and white veil, that she looked at me so sadly, and said she hoped I would never love anybody better than God, and then I should be happy. I didn't think much of those words then; but, oh, I have since, many times! They used to tell me always that I had a husband who was away in the army, and who would come to marry me when I was seventeen, and that he would give me all sorts of beautiful things, and show me everything I wanted to see in the world, and that I must love and honor him.

"Well, I was married at last; and Monsieur de Frontignac is a good brave man, although he seemed to me very old and sober; but he was always kind to me, and gave me nobody knows how many sets of jewelry, and let me do everything I wanted to, and so I liked him very much; but I thought there was no danger I should love him, or anybody else, better than God. I didn't *love* anybody in those days; I only liked people, and some people more than others. All the men I saw professed to be lovers, and I liked to lead them about and see what foolish things I could make them do, because it pleased my vanity; but I laughed at the very idea of love.

"Well, Mary, when we came to Philadelphia, I heard everybody speaking of Colonel Burr, and what a fascinating man he was; and I thought it would be a pretty thing to have him in my train,—and so I did all I could to charm him. I tried all my little arts,—and if it is a sin for us women to do such things, I am sure I have been punished for it. Mary, he was stronger than I was. These men, they are not satisfied with having the whole earth under their feet, and having all the strength and all the glory, but they must even take away our poor little reign;—it's too bad!

"I can't tell you how it was; I didn't know myself; but it seemed to me that he took my very life away from me; and it was all done before I knew it. He called himself my friend, my brother; he offered to teach me English; he read with me; and by-and-by he controlled my whole life. I, that used to be so haughty, so proud,—I, that used to laugh to think how independent I was of everybody,—I was entirely under his control, though I tried not to show it. I didn't well know where I was; for he talked friendship, and I talked friendship; he talked about sympathetic natures that are made for each other, and I thought how beautiful it all was; it was living in a new world. Monsieur de Frontignac was as much charmed with him as I was; he often told me that he was his best friend,—that he was his hero, his model man; and I thought,——oh, Mary, you would wonder to hear me say what I thought! I thought he was a Bayard, a Sully, a Montmorenci,—everything grand and noble and good. I loved him with a religion; I would have died for him; I sometimes thought how I might lay down my life to save his, like women I read of in history. I did not know myself; I was astonished I could feel so; and I did not dream that this could be wrong. How could I, when it made me feel more religious than anything in my whole life? Everything in the world seemed to grow sacred. I thought, if men could be so good and admirable, life was a holy thing, and not to be trifled with.

"But our good Abbé is a faithful shepherd, and when I told him these things in confession, he told me I was in great danger,—danger of falling into mortal sin. Oh, Mary, it was as if the earth had opened under me! He told me, too, that this noble man, this man so dear, was a heretic, and that, if he died, he would go to dreadful pains. Oh, Mary, I dare not tell you half what he told me,—dreadful things that make me shiver when I think of them! And then he said that I must offer myself a sacrifice for him; that, if I would put down all this love and overcome it, God would perhaps accept it as a satisfaction, and bring him into the True Church at last.

"Then I began to try. Oh, Mary, we never know how we love till we try to unlove! It seemed like taking my heart out of my breast, and separating life from life. How can one do it? I wish any one would tell me. The Abbé said I must do it by prayer; but it seemed to me prayer only made me think the more of him.

"But at last I had a great shock; everything broke up like a great, grand, noble dream,—and I waked out of it just as weak and wretched as one feels when one has overslept. Oh, Mary, I found I was mistaken in him,—all, all, wholly!"

Madame de Frontignac laid her forehead on Mary's knee, and her long chestnut hair drooped down over her face.

"He was going somewhere with my husband to explore, out in the regions of the Ohio, where he had some splendid schemes of founding a state; and I was all interest. And one day, as they were preparing, Monsieur de Frontignac gave me a quantity of papers to read and arrange, and among them was a part of a letter;—I never could imagine how it got there; it was from Burr to one of his confidential friends. I read it, at first, wondering what it meant, till I came to two or three sentences about me."

Madame de Frontignac paused a moment, and then said, rising with sudden energy,—

"Mary, that man never loved me; he cannot love; he does not know what love is. What I felt he cannot know; he cannot even dream of it, because he never felt anything like it. Such men never know us women; we are as high as heaven above them. It is true enough that my heart was wholly in his power,—but why? Because I adored him as something divine, incapable of dishonor, incapable of selfishness, incapable of even a thought that was not perfectly noble and heroic. If he had been all that, I should have been proud to be even a poor little flower that should exhale away to give him an hour's pleasure; I would have offered my whole life to God as a sacrifice for such a glorious soul;—and all this time what was he thinking of me?

"He was *using* my feelings to carry his plans; he was admiring me like a picture; he was considering what he should do with me; and but for his interests with my husband, he would have tried his power to make me sacrifice this world and the next to his pleasure. But he does not know me. My mother was a Montmorenci, and I have the blood of her house in my veins; we are princesses;—we can give all; but he must be a god that we give it for."

Mary's enchanted eye followed the beautiful narrator, as she enacted before her this poetry and tragedy of real life, so much beyond what dramatic art can ever furnish. Her eyes grew splendid in their depth and brilliancy; sometimes they were full of tears, and sometimes they flashed out like lightnings; her whole form seemed to be a plastic vehicle which translated every emotion of her soul; and Mary sat and looked at her with the intense absorption that one gives to the highest and deepest in Art or Nature.

"*Enfin,—que faire!*" she said at last, suddenly stopping, and drooping in every limb. "Mary, I have lived on this dream so long!—never thought of anything else!—now all is gone, and what shall I do?

"I think, Mary," she added, pointing to the nest in the tree, "I see my life in many things. My heart was once still and quiet, like the round little eggs that were in your nest;—now it has broken out of its shell, and cries with cold and hunger. I want my dream again,—I wish it all back,—or that my heart could go back into its shell. If I only could drop this year out of my life, and care for nothing, as I used to! I have tried to do that; I can't; I cannot get back where I was before."

"*Would* you do it, dear Virginie?" said Mary; "would you, if you could?"

"It was very noble and sweet, all that," said Virginie; "it gave me higher thoughts than ever I had before; I think my feelings were beautiful;—but now they are like little birds that have no mother; they kill me with their crying."

"Dear Virginie, there is a real Friend in heaven, who is all you can ask or think,—nobler, better, purer,—who cannot change, and cannot die, and who loved you and gave himself for you."

"You mean Jesus," said Virginie. "Ah, I know it; and I say the offices to him daily, but my heart is very wild and starts away from my words. I say, 'My God, I give myself to you!'—and after all, I don't give myself, and I don't feel comforted. Dear Mary, you must have suffered, too,—for you loved really,—I saw it;—when we feel a thing ourselves, we can see very quick the same in others;—and it was a dreadful blow to come so all at once."

"Yes, it was," said Mary; "I thought I must die; but Christ has given me peace."

These words were spoken with that long-breathed sigh with which we always speak of peace,—a sigh that told of storms and sorrows past,—the sighing of the wave that falls spent and broken on the shores of eternal rest.

There was a little pause in the conversation, and then Virginie raised her head and spoke in a sprightlier tone.

"Well, my little fairy cat, my white doe, I have come to you. Poor Virginie wants something to hold to her heart; let me have you," she said, throwing her arms round Mary.

"Dear, dear Virginie, indeed you shall!" said Mary. "I will love you dearly, and pray for you. I always have prayed for you, ever since the first day I knew you."

"I knew it,—I felt your prayers in my heart. Mary, I have many thoughts that I dare not tell to any one, lately,—but I cannot help feeling that some are real Christians who are not in the True Church. You are as true a saint as Saint Catharine; indeed, I always think of you when I think of our dear Lady; and yet they say there is no salvation out of the Church."

This was a new view of the subject to Mary, who had grown up with the familiar idea that the Romish Church was Babylon and Antichrist, and who, during the conversation, had been revolving the same surmises with regard to her friend. She turned her grave, blue eyes on Madame de Frontignac with a somewhat surprised look, which melted into a half-smile. But the latter still went on with a puzzled air, as if trying to talk herself out of some mental perplexity.

"Now, Burr is a heretic,—and more than that, he is an

infidel; he has no religion in his heart.—I saw that often,— it made me tremble for him,—it ought to have put me on my guard. But you, dear Mary, you love Jesus as your life. I think you love him just as much as Sister Agatha, who was a saint. The Abbé says that there is nothing so dangerous as to begin to use our reason in religion,—that, if we once begin, we never know where it may carry us; but I can't help using mine a very little. I must think there are some saints that are not in the True Church."

"All are one who love Christ," said Mary; "we are one in Him."

"I should not dare to tell the Abbé," said Madame de Frontignac; and Mary queried in her heart, whether Dr. Hopkins would feel satisfied that she could bring this wanderer to the fold of Christ without undertaking to batter down the walls of her creed; and yet, there they were, the Catholic and the Puritan, each strong in her respective faith, yet melting together in that embrace of love and sorrow, joined in the great communion of suffering. Mary took up her Testament, and read the fourteenth chapter of John:—

"Let not your heart be troubled; ye believe in God, believe also in me. In my Father's house are many mansions; if it were not so, I would have told you. I go to prepare a place for you; and if I go and prepare a place for you, I will come again and receive you unto myself, that where I am, there ye may be also."

Mary read on through the chapter,—through the next wonderful prayer; her face grew solemnly transparent, as of an angel; for her soul was lifted from earth by the words, and walked with Christ far above all things, over that starry pavement where each footstep is on a world.

The greatest moral effects are like those of music,—not wrought out by sharp-sided intellectual propositions, but melted in by a divine fusion, by words that have mysterious, indefinite fulness of meaning, made living by sweet voices, which seem to be the out-throbbings of angelic hearts. So one verse in the Bible read by a mother in some hour of tender prayer has a significance deeper and higher than the most elaborate of sermons, the most acute of arguments.

Virginie Frontignac sat as one divinely enchanted, while

that sweet voice read on; and when the silence fell between them, she gave a long sigh, as we do when sweet music stops. They heard between them the soft stir of summer leaves, the distant songs of birds, the breezy hum when the afternoon wind shivered through many branches, and the silver sea chimed in. Virginie rose at last, and kissed Mary on the forehead.

"That is a beautiful book," she said, "and to read it all by one's self must be lovely. I cannot understand why it should be dangerous; it has not injured you.

"Sweet saint," she added, "let me stay with you; you shall read to me every day. Do you know I came here to get you to take me? I want you to show me how to find peace where you do; will you let me be your sister?"

"Yes, indeed," said Mary, with a cheek brighter than it had been for many a day; her heart feeling a throb of more real human pleasure than for long months.

"Will you get your mamma to let me stay?" said Virginie, with the bashfulness of a child; "haven't you a little place like yours, with white curtains and sanded floor, to give to poor little Virginie to learn to be good in?"

"Why, do you really want to stay here with us," said Mary, "in this little house?"

"Do I really?" said Virginie, mimicking her voice with a start of her old playfulness;—"*don't* I really? Come now, *mimi*, coax the good mamma for me,—tell her I shall try to be very good. I shall help you with the spinning,—you know I spin beautifully,—and I shall make butter, and milk the cow, and set the table. Oh, I will be so useful, you can't spare me!"

"I should love to have you dearly," said Mary, warmly; "but you would soon be dull for want of society here."

"*Quelle idée! ma petite drôle!*" said the lady,—who, with the mobility of her nation, had already recovered some of the saucy mocking grace that was habitual to her, as she began teasing Mary with a thousand little childish motions. "Indeed, *mimi*, you must keep me hid up here, or may be the wolf will find me and eat me up; who knows?"

Mary looked at her with inquiring eyes.

"What do you mean?"

"I mean, Mary,—I mean, that, when *he* comes back to Philadelphia, he thinks he shall find me there; he thought I should stay while my husband was gone; and when he finds I am gone, he may come to Newport; and I never want to see him again without you;—you must let me stay with you."

"Have you told him," said Mary, "what you think?"

"I wrote to him, Mary,—but, oh, I can't trust my heart! I want so much to believe him, it kills me so to think evil of him, that it will never do for me to see him. If he looks at me with those eyes of his, I am all gone; I shall believe anything he tells me; he will draw me to him as a great magnet draws a poor little grain of steel."

"But now you know his unworthiness, his baseness," said Mary, "I should think it would break all his power."

"*Should* you think so? Ah, Mary, we cannot unlove in a minute; love is a great while dying. I do not worship him now as I did. I know what he is. I know he is bad, and I am sorry for it. I should like to cover it from all the world,— even from you, Mary, since I see it makes you dislike him; it hurts me to hear any one else blame him. But sometimes I do so long to think I am mistaken, that I know, if I should see him, I should catch at anything he might tell me, as a drowning man at straws; I should shut my eyes, and think, after all, that it was all my fault, and ask a thousand pardons for all the evil he has done. No,—Mary, you must keep your blue eyes upon me, or I shall be gone."

At this moment Mrs. Scudder's voice was heard, calling Mary below.

"Go down now, darling, and tell mamma; make a good little talk to her, *ma reine!* Ah, you are queen here! all do as you say,—even the good priest there; you have a little hand, but it leads all; so go, *petite.*"

Mrs. Scudder was somewhat flurried and discomposed at the proposition;—there were the *pros* and the *cons* in her nature, such as we all have. In the first place, Madame de Frontignac belonged to high society,—and that was *pro;* for Mrs. Scudder prayed daily against worldly vanities, because she felt a little traitor in her heart that was ready to open its door to them, if not constantly talked down. In the second place, Madame de Frontignac was French,—there was a *con;* for

Mrs. Scudder had enough of her father John Bull in her heart to have a very wary look-out on anything French. But then, in the third place, she was out of health and unhappy,—and there was a *pro* again; for Mrs. Scudder was as kind and motherly a soul as ever breathed. But then she was a Catholic,—*con*. But the Doctor and Mary might convert her,—*pro*. And then Mary wanted her,—*pro*. And she was a pretty, bewitching, lovable creature,—*pro*.—The *pros* had it; and it was agreed that Madame de Frontignac should be installed as proprietress of the spare chamber, and she sat down to the tea-table that evening in the great kitchen.

XXVI.

The Declaration

THE domesticating of Madame de Frontignac as an inmate of the cottage added a new element of vivacity to that still and unvaried life. One of the most beautiful traits of French nature is that fine gift of appreciation, which seizes at once the picturesque side of every condition of life, and finds in its own varied storehouse something to assort with it. As compared with the Anglo-Saxon, the French appear to be gifted with a *naïve* childhood of nature, and to have the power that children have of gilding every scene of life with some of their own poetic fancies.

Madame de Frontignac was in raptures with the sanded floor of her little room, which commanded, through the apple-boughs, a little morsel of a sea view. She could fancy it was a nymph's cave, she said.

"Yes, *ma Marie*, I will play Calypso, and you shall play Telemachus, and Dr. Hopkins shall be Mentor. Mentor was so very, very good!—only a bit—*dull*," she said, pronouncing the last word with a wicked accent, and lifting her hands with a whimsical gesture like a naughty child who expects a correction.

Mary could not but laugh; and as she laughed, more color rose in her waxen cheeks than for many days before.

Madame de Frontignac looked as triumphant as a child who has made its mother laugh, and went on laying things out of her trunk into her drawers with a zeal that was quite amusing to see.

"You see, *ma blanche*, I have left all Madame's clothes at Philadelphia, and brought only those that belong to Virginie,—no *tromperie*, no feathers, no gauzes, no diamonds,— only white dresses, and my straw hat *en bergère*. I brought one string of pearls that was my mother's; but pearls, you know, belong to the sea-nymphs. I will trim my hat with seaweed and buttercups together, and we will go out on the

beach to-night and get some gold and silver shells to dress
mon miroir."

"Oh, I have ever so many now," said Mary, running into
her room, and coming back with a little bag.

They both sat on the bed together, and began pouring
them out,—Madame de Frontignac showering childish exclamations of delight.

Suddenly Mary put her hand to her heart as if she had been
struck with something; and Madame de Frontignac heard her
say, in a low voice of sudden pain, "Oh, dear!"

"What is it, *mimi?*" she said, looking up quickly.

"Nothing," said Mary, turning her head.

Madame de Frontignac looked down, and saw among the
sea-treasures a necklace of Venetian shells, that she knew
never grew on the shores of Newport. She held it up.

"Ah, I see," she said. "He gave you this. Ah, *ma pauvrette,*"
she said, clasping Mary in her arms, "thy sorrow meets thee
everywhere! May I be a comfort to thee!—just a little one!"

"Dear, dear friend!" said Mary, weeping. "I know not how
it is. Sometimes I think this sorrow is all gone; but then, for
a moment, it comes back again. But I am at peace; it is all
right, all right; I would not have it otherwise. But, oh, if he
could have spoken one word to me before! He gave me this,"
she added, "when he came home from his first voyage to the
Mediterranean. I did not know it was in this bag. I had
looked for it everywhere."

"Sister Agatha would have told you to make a rosary of it,"
said Madame de Frontignac; "but you pray without a rosary.
It is all one," she added; "there will be a prayer for every
shell, though you do not count them. But come, *ma chère,*
get your bonnet, and let us go out on the beach."

That evening, before going to bed, Mrs. Scudder came into
Mary's room. Her manner was grave and tender; her eyes had
tears in them; and although her usual habits were not caressing, she came to Mary and put her arms around her and
kissed her. It was an unusual manner, and Mary's gentle eyes
seemed to ask the reason of it.

"My daughter," said her mother, "I have just had a long
and very interesting talk with our dear good friend, the Doctor; ah, Mary, very few people know how good he is!"

"True, mother," said Mary, warmly; "he is the best, the noblest, and yet the humblest man in the world."

"You love him very much, do you not?" said her mother.

"Very dearly," said Mary.

"Mary, he has asked me, this evening, if you would be willing to be his wife."

"His *wife*, mother?" said Mary, in the tone of one confused with a new and strange thought.

"Yes, daughter; I have long seen that he was preparing to make you this proposal."

"You have, mother?"

"Yes, daughter; have you never thought of it?"

"Never, mother."

There was a long pause,—Mary standing, just as she had been interrupted, in her night toilette, with her long, light hair streaming down over her white dress, and the comb held mechanically in her hand. She sat down after a moment, and, clasping her hands over her knees, fixed her eyes intently on the floor; and there fell between the two a silence so profound, that the tickings of the clock in the next room seemed to knock upon the door. Mrs. Scudder sat with anxious eyes watching that silent face, pale as sculptured marble.

"Well, Mary," she said at last.

A deep sigh was the only answer. The violent throbbings of her heart could be seen undulating the long hair as the moaning sea tosses the rock-weed.

"My daughter," again said Mrs. Scudder.

Mary gave a great sigh, like that of a sleeper awakening from a dream, and, looking at her mother, said,—"Do you suppose he really *loves* me, mother?"

"Indeed he does, Mary, as much as man ever loved woman!"

"Does he indeed?" said Mary, relapsing into thoughtfulness.

"And you love him, do you not?" said her mother.

"Oh, yes, I love him."

"You love him better than any man in the world, don't you?"

"Oh, mother, mother! yes!" said Mary, throwing herself

passionately forward, and bursting into sobs; "yes, there is no one else now that I love better,—no one!—no one!"

"My darling! my daughter!" said Mrs. Scudder, coming and taking her in her arms.

"Oh, mother, mother!" she said, sobbing distressfully, "let me cry, just for a little,—oh, mother, mother, mother!"

What was there hidden under that despairing wail?—It was the parting of the last strand of the cord of youthful hope.

Mrs. Scudder soothed and caressed her daughter, but maintained still in her breast a tender pertinacity of purpose, such as mothers will, who think they are conducting a child through some natural sorrow into a happier state.

Mary was not one, either, to yield long to emotion of any kind. Her rigid education had taught her to look upon all such outbursts as a species of weakness, and she struggled for composure, and soon seemed entirely calm.

"If he really loves me, mother, it would give him great pain if I refused," said Mary thoughtfully.

"Certainly it would; and, Mary, you have allowed him to act as a very near friend for a long time; and it is quite natural that he should have hopes that you loved him."

"I do love him, mother,—better than anybody in the world except you. Do you think that will do?"

"Will do?" said her mother; "I don't understand you."

"Why, is that loving enough to marry? I shall love him more, perhaps, after,—shall I, mother?"

"Certainly you will; every one does."

"I wish he did not want to marry me, mother," said Mary, after a pause. "I liked it a great deal better as we were before."

"All girls feel so, Mary, at first; it is very natural."

"Is that the way you felt about father, mother?"

Mrs. Scudder's heart smote her when she thought of her own early love,—that great love that asked no questions,—that had no doubts, no fears, no hesitations,—nothing but one great, outsweeping impulse, which swallowed her life in that of another. She was silent; and after a moment, she said,—

"I was of a different disposition from you, Mary. I was of a strong, wilful, positive nature. I either liked or disliked with all my might. And besides, Mary, there never was a man like your father."

The matron uttered this first article in the great confession of woman's faith with the most unconscious simplicity.

"Well, mother, I will do whatever is my duty. I want to be guided. If I can make that good man happy, and help him to do some good in the world——After all, life is short, and the great thing is to do for others."

"I am sure, Mary, if you could have heard how he spoke, you would be sure you could make him happy. He had not spoken before, because he felt so unworthy of such a blessing; he said I was to tell you that he should love and honor you all the same, whether you could be his wife or not,—but that nothing this side of heaven would be so blessed a gift,—that it would make up for every trial that could possibly come upon him. And you know, Mary, he has a great many discouragements and trials;—people don't appreciate him; his efforts to do good are misunderstood and misconstrued; they look down on him, and despise him, and tell all sorts of evil things about him; and sometimes he gets quite discouraged."

"Yes, mother, I will marry him," said Mary;—"yes, I will."

"My darling daughter!" said Mrs. Scudder,—"this has been the hope of my life!"

"Has it, mother?" said Mary, with a faint smile; "I shall make you happier then?"

"Yes, dear, you will. And think what a prospect of usefulness opens before you! You can take a position, as his wife, which will enable you to do even more good than you do now; and you will have the happiness of seeing, every day, how much you comfort the hearts and encourage the hands of God's dear people."

"Mother, I ought to be very glad I can do it," said Mary; "and I trust I am. God orders all things for the best."

"Well, my child, sleep to-night, and to-morrow we will talk more about it."

XXVII.

Surprises

M RS. SCUDDER kissed her daughter, and left her. After a
moment's thought, Mary gathered the long silky folds
of hair around her head, and knotted them for the night.
Then leaning forward on her toilet-table, she folded her
hands together, and stood regarding the reflection of herself
in the mirror.

Nothing is capable of more ghostly effect than such a silent, lonely contemplation of that mysterious image of ourselves which seems to look out of an infinite depth in the
mirror, as if it were our own soul beckoning to us visibly
from unknown regions. Those eyes look into our own with
an expression sometimes vaguely sad and inquiring. The face
wears weird and tremulous lights and shadows; it asks us
mysterious questions, and troubles us with the suggestions of
our relations to some dim unknown. The sad, blue eyes that
gazed into Mary's had that look of calm initiation, of melancholy comprehension, peculiar to eyes made clairvoyant by
"great and critical" sorrow. They seemed to say to her, "Fulfil
thy mission; life is made for sacrifice; the flower must fall
before fruit can perfect itself." A vague shuddering of mystery
gave intensity to her reverie. It seemed as if those mirror-
depths were another world; she heard the far-off dashing of
sea-green waves; she felt a yearning impulse towards that dear
soul gone out into the infinite unknown.

Her word just passed had in her eyes all the sacred force of
the most solemnly attested vow; and she felt as if that vow
had shut some till then open door between her and him; she
had a kind of shadowy sense of a throbbing and yearning
nature that seemed to call on her,—that seemed surging towards her with an imperative, protesting force that shook her
heart to its depths.

Perhaps it is so, that souls, once intimately related, have
ever after this a strange power of affecting each other,—a

power that neither absence nor death can annul. How else can we interpret those mysterious hours in which the power of departed love seems to overshadow us, making our souls vital with such longings, with such wild throbbings, with such unutterable sighings, that a little more might burst the mortal bond? Is it not deep calling unto deep? the free soul singing outside the cage to her mate beating against the bars within?

Mary even, for a moment, fancied that a voice called her name, and started, shivering. Then the habits of her positive and sensible education returned at once, and she came out of her reverie as one breaks from a dream, and lifted all these sad thoughts with one heavy sigh from her breast; and opening her Bible, she read: "They that trust in the Lord shall be as Mount Zion, which cannot be removed, but abideth forever. As the mountains are round about Jerusalem, so the Lord is round about his people from henceforth, even forever."

Then she kneeled by her bedside, and offered her whole life a sacrifice to the loving God who had offered his life a sacrifice for her. She prayed for grace to be true to her promise,— to be faithful to the new relation she had accepted. She prayed that all vain regrets for the past might be taken away, and that her soul might vibrate without discord in unison with the will of Eternal Love. So praying, she rose calm, and with that clearness of spirit which follows an act of uttermost self-sacrifice; and so calmly she laid down and slept, with her two hands crossed upon her breast, her head slightly turned on the pillow, her cheek pale as marble, and her long dark lashes lying drooping, with a sweet expression, as if under that mystic veil of sleep the soul were seeing things forbidden to the waking eye. Only the gentlest heaving of the quiet breast told that the heavenly spirit within had not gone whither it was hourly aspiring to go.

Meanwhile Mrs. Scudder had left Mary's room, and entered the Doctor's study, holding a candle in her hand. The good man was sitting alone in the dark, with his head bowed upon his Bible. When Mrs. Scudder entered, he rose, and regarded her wistfully, but did not speak. He had something just then in his heart for which he had no words; so he only looked as a man does who hopes and fears for the answer of a decisive question.

Mrs. Scudder felt some of the natural reserve which becomes a matron coming charged with a gift in which lies the whole sacredness of her own existence, and which she puts from her hands with a jealous reverence. She therefore measured the man with her woman's and mother's eye, and said, with a little stateliness,—

"My dear Sir, I come to tell you the result of my conversation with Mary."

She made a little pause,—and the Doctor stood before her as humbly as if he had not weighed and measured the universe; because he knew, that, though he might weigh the mountains in scales and the hills in a balance, yet it was a far subtiler power which must possess him of one small woman's heart. In fact, he felt to himself like a great, awkward, clumsy mountainous earthite asking of a white-robed angel to help him up a ladder of cloud. He was perfectly sure, for the moment, that he was going to be refused; and he looked humbly firm,—he would take it like a man. His large blue eyes, generally so misty in their calm, had a resolute clearness, rather mournful than otherwise. Of course, no such celestial experience was going to happen to him.

He cleared his throat, and said,—

"Well, Madam?"

Mrs. Scudder's womanly dignity was appeased; she reached out her hand, cheerfully, and said,—

"She has accepted."

The Doctor drew his hand suddenly away, turned quickly round, and walked to the window,—although, as it was ten o'clock at night and quite dark, there was evidently nothing to be seen there. He stood there, quietly, swallowing very hard, and raising his handkerchief several times to his eyes. There was enough going on under the black coat just then to make quite a little figure in a romance, if it had been uttered; but he belonged to a class who *lived* romance, but never spoke it. In a few moments he returned to Mrs. Scudder, and said,—

"I trust, dear Madam, that this very dear friend may never have reason to think me ungrateful for her wonderful goodness; and whatever sins my evil heart may lead me into, I *hope* I may never fall so low as to forget the undeserved mercy of this hour. If ever I shrink from duty or murmur at trials, while so sweet a friend is mine, I shall be vile indeed."

The Doctor, in general, viewed himself on the discouraging side, and had berated and snubbed himself all his life as a most flagitious and evil-disposed individual,—a person to be narrowly watched, and capable of breaking at any moment into the most flagrant iniquity; and therefore it was that he received his good fortune in so different a spirit from many of the lords of creation in similar circumstances.

"I am sensible," he added, "that a poor minister, without much power of eloquence, and commissioned of the Lord to speak unpopular truths, and whose worldly condition, in consequence, is never likely to be very prosperous,—that such an one could scarcely be deemed a suitable partner for so very beautiful a young woman, who might expect proposals, in a temporal point of view, of a much more advantageous nature; and I am therefore the more struck and overpowered with this blessed result."

These last words caught in the Doctor's throat, as if he were overpowered in very deed.

"In regard to *her* happiness," said the Doctor, with a touch of awe in his voice, "I would not have presumed to become the guardian of it, were it not that I am persuaded it is assured by a Higher Power; for 'when He giveth quietness, who then can make trouble?' (Job, xxxiv. 29.) But I trust I may say no effort on my part shall be wanting to secure it."

Mrs. Scudder was a mother, and had come to that stage in life where mothers always feel tears rising behind their smiles. She pressed the Doctor's hand silently, and they parted for the night.

We know not how we can acquit ourselves to our friends of the great world for the details of such an unfashionable courtship, so well as by giving them, before they retire for the night, a dip into a more modish view of things.

The Doctor was evidently green,—green in his faith, green in his simplicity, green in his general belief of the divine in woman, green in his particular humble faith in one small Puritan maiden, whom a knowing fellow might at least have manœuvred so skilfully as to break up her saintly superiority, discompose her, rout her ideas, and lead her up and down a swamp of hopes and fears and conjectures, till she was wholly bewildered and ready to take him at last—if he made up his mind to have her at all—as a great bargain, for which she was to be sensibly grateful.

Yes, the Doctor was green,—*immortally* green, as a cedar of Lebanon, which, waving its broad archangel wings over some fast-rooted, eternal old solitude, and seeing from its sublime height the vastness of the universe, veils its kingly head with humility before God's infinite majesty.

He has gone to bed now,—simple old soul!—first apologizing to Mrs. Scudder for having kept her up to so dissipated and unparalleled an hour as ten o'clock on his personal matters.

Meanwhile our Asmodeus shall transport us to a handsomely furnished apartment in one of the most fashionable hotels of Philadelphia, where Colonel Aaron Burr, just returned from his trip to the then aboriginal wilds of Ohio, is seated before a table covered with maps, letters, books, and papers. His keen eye runs over the addresses of the letters, and he eagerly seizes one from Madame de Frontignac, and reads it; and as no one but ourselves is looking at him now, his face has no need to wear its habitual mask. First comes an expression of profound astonishment; then of chagrin and mortification; then of deepening concern; there were stops where the dark eyelashes flashed together, as if to brush a tear out of the view of the keen-sighted eyes; and then a red flush rose even to his forehead, and his delicate lips wore a sarcastic smile. He laid down the letter, and made one or two turns through the room.

The man had felt the dashing against his own of a strong, generous, indignant woman's heart fully awakened, and speaking with that impassioned vigor with which a French regiment charges in battle. There were those picturesque, winged words, those condensed expressions, those subtile piercings of meaning, and, above all, that simple pathos, for which the French tongue has no superior; and for the moment the woman had the victory; she shook his heart. But Burr resembled the marvel with which chemists amuse themselves. His heart was a vase filled with boiling passions,—while his *will*, a still, cold, unmelted lump of ice, lay at the bottom.

Self-denial is not peculiar to Christians. He who goes downward often puts forth as much force to kill a noble nature as another does to annihilate a sinful one. There was something in this letter so keen, so searching, so self-revealing, that it brought on one of those interior crises in which a man is convulsed with the struggle of two natures, the godlike and the demoniac, and from which he must pass out more wholly to the dominion of the one or the other.

Nobody knew the true better than Burr. He *knew* the godlike and the pure; he had *felt* its beauty and its force to the very depths of his being, as the demoniac knew at once the fair Man of Nazareth; and even now he felt the voice within that said, "What have I to do with thee?" and the rending of a struggle of heavenly life with fast-coming eternal death.

That letter had told him what he might be, and what he was. It was as if his dead mother's hand had held up before him a glass in which he saw himself white-robed and crowned, and so dazzling in purity that he loathed his present self.

As he walked up and down the room perturbed, he sometimes wiped tears from his eyes, and then set his teeth and compressed his lips. At last his face grew calm and settled in its expression, his mouth wore a sardonic smile; he came and took the letter, and, folding it leisurely, laid it on the table, and put a heavy paper-weight over it, as if to hold it down and bury it. Then drawing to himself some maps of new territories, he set himself vigorously to some columns of arithmetical calculations on the margin; and thus he worked for an hour or two, till his mind was as dry and his pulse as calm as a machine; then he drew the inkstand towards him, and scribbled hastily the following letter to his most confidential associate,—a letter which told no more of the conflict that preceded it than do the dry sands and the civil gossip of the sea-waves to-day of the storm and wreck of last week.

"Dear——. *Nous voici*—once more in Philadelphia. Our schemes in Ohio prosper. Frontignac remains there to superintend. He answers our purpose *passablement*. On the whole, I don't see that we could do better than retain him; he is, besides, a gentlemanly, agreeable person, and wholly devoted to me,—a point certainly not to be overlooked.

"As to your railleries about the fair Madame, I must say, in justice both to her and myself, that any grace with which she has been pleased to honor me is not to be misconstrued. You are not to imagine any but the most Platonic of *liaisons*. She is as high-strung as an Arabian steed,—proud, heroic, romantic, and *French!* and such must be permitted to take their own time and way, which we in our *gaucherie* can only humbly wonder at. I have ever professed myself her abject slave, ready to follow any whim, and obeying the slightest signal of the jewelled hand. As that is her sacred pleasure, I have been inhabiting the most abstract realms of heroic sentiment, living on the most diluted moonshine, and spinning out elaborately all those charming and seraphic distinctions between tweedle-dum and tweedle-dee with which these ecstatic creatures delight themselves in certain stages of *affaires du cœur*.

"The last development, on the part of my goddess, is a fit of celestial anger, of the cause of which I am in the most innocent ignorance. She writes me three pages of French sublimities, writing as only a French woman can,—bids me an eternal adieu, and informs me she is going to Newport.

"Of course the affair becomes stimulating. I am not to presume to dispute her sentence, or doubt a lady's perfect sincerity in wishing never to see me again; but yet I think I shall try to pacify the

'tantas in animis cœlestibus iras.'

If a woman hates you, it is only her love turned wrong side out, and you may turn it back with due care. The pretty creatures know how becoming a *grande passion* is, and take care to keep themselves in mind; a quarrel serves their turn, when all else fails.

"To another point. I wish you to advertise S——, that his insinuations in regard to me in the 'Aurora' have been observed, and that I require that they be promptly retracted. He knows me well enough to attend to this hint. I am in earnest when I speak; if the word does nothing, the blow will come,—and if I strike once, no second blow will be needed. Yet I do not wish to get him on my hands needlessly; a duel and a love affair and hot weather, coming on together, might prove too much even for me.—N. B. Thermometer stands at 85. I am resolved on Newport next week.

"Yours ever,

BURR.

"P. S. I forgot to say, that, oddly enough, my goddess has gone and placed herself under the wing of the pretty Puritan I saw in Newport. Fancy the *mélange*! Could anything be more piquant?—that cart-load of goodness, the old Doctor, that sweet little saint, and Madame Faubourg St. Germain shaken up together! Fancy her listening with well-bred astonishment to a *critique* on the doings of the unregenerate, or flirting that little jewelled fan of hers in Mrs. Scudder's square pew of a Sunday! Probably they will carry her to the weekly prayer-meeting, which of course she will contrive some fine French subtilty for admiring, and find *ravissant*. I fancy I see it."

When Burr had finished this letter, he had actually written himself into a sort of persuasion of its truth. When a finely constituted nature wishes to go into baseness, it has first to bribe itself. Evil is never embraced undisguised, as evil, but under some fiction which the mind accepts and with which it has the singular power of blinding itself in the face of daylight. The power of imposing on one's self is an essential preliminary to imposing on others. The man first argues himself down, and then he is ready to put the whole weight of his nature to deceiving others. This letter ran so smoothly, so plausibly, that it produced on the writer of it the effect of a work of fiction, which we *know* to be unreal, but *feel* to be true. Long habits of this kind of self-delusion in time produce a paralysis in the vital nerves of truth, so that one becomes habitually unable to see things in their verity, and realizes the awful words of Scripture,—"He feedeth on ashes; a deceived heart hath turned him aside, that he cannot deliver his soul, nor say, Is there not a lie in my right hand?"

XXVIII.

The Betrothed

ETWEEN three and four the next morning, the robin in
the nest above Mary's window stretched out his left
wing, opened one eye, and gave a short and rather drowsy
chirp, which broke up his night's rest and restored him to the
full consciousness that he was a bird with wings and feathers,
with a large apple-tree to live in, and all heaven for an estate,—and so, on these fortunate premises, he broke into a
gush of singing, clear and loud, which Mary, without waking,
heard in her slumbers.

Scarcely conscious, she lay in that dim clairvoyant state,
when the half-sleep of the outward senses permits a delicious
dewy clearness of the soul, that perfect ethereal rest and freshness of faculties, comparable only to what we imagine of the
spiritual state,—season of celestial enchantment, in which the
heavy weight "of all this unintelligible world" drops off, and
the soul, divinely charmed, nestles like a wind-tossed bird in
the protecting bosom of the One All-Perfect, All-Beautiful.
What visions then come to the inner eye have often no words
corresponding in mortal vocabularies. The poet, the artist,
and the prophet in such hours become possessed of divine
certainties which all their lives they struggle with pencil or
song or burning words to make evident to their fellows. The
world around wonders; but they are unsatisfied, because they
have seen the glory and know how inadequate the copy.

And not merely to selectest spirits come these hours, but to
those humbler poets, ungifted with utterance, who are among
men as fountains sealed, whose song can be wrought out only
by the harmony of deeds, the patient, pathetic melodies of
tender endurance, or the heroic chant of undiscouraged labor.
The poor slave-woman, last night parted from her only boy,
and weary with the cotton-picking,—the captive pining in his
cell,—the patient wife of the drunkard, saddened by a consciousness of the growing vileness of one so dear to her

once,—the delicate spirit doomed to harsh and uncongenial surroundings,—all in such hours feel the soothings of a celestial harmony, the tenderness of more than a mother's love.

It is by such seasons as these, more often than by reasonings or disputings, that doubts are resolved in the region of religious faith. The All-Father treats us as the mother does her "infant crying in the dark;" He does not reason with our fears, or demonstrate their fallacy, but draws us silently to His bosom, and we are at peace. Nay, there have been those, undoubtedly, who have known God falsely with the intellect, yet felt Him truly with the heart,—and there be many, principally among the unlettered little ones of Christ's flock, who positively know that much that is dogmatically propounded to them of their Redeemer is cold, barren, unsatisfying, and utterly false, who yet can give no account of their certainties better than that of the inspired fisherman, "We know Him, and have seen Him." It was in such hours as these that Mary's deadly fears for the soul of her beloved had passed all away,—passed out of her,—as if some warm, healing nature of tenderest vitality had drawn out of her heart all pain and coldness, and warmed it with the breath of an eternal summer.

So, while the purple shadows spread their gauzy veils inwoven with fire along the sky, and the gloom of the sea broke out here and there into lines of light, and thousands of birds were answering to each other from apple-tree and meadow-grass, and top of jagged rock, or trooping in bands hither and thither, like angels on loving messages, Mary lay there with the flickering light through the leaves fluttering over her face, and the glow of dawn warming the snow-white draperies of the bed and giving a tender rose-hue to the calm cheek. She lay half-conscious, smiling the while, as one who sleeps while the heart waketh, and who hears in dreams the voice of the One Eternally Beautiful and Beloved.

Mrs. Scudder entered her room, and, thinking that she still slept, stood and looked down on her. She felt as one does who has parted with some precious possession, a sudden sense of its value coming over her; she queried in herself whether any living mortal were worthy of so perfect a gift; and nothing but a remembrance of the Doctor's prostrate humility at all reconciled her to the sacrifice she was making.

"Mary, dear!" she said, bending over her, with an unusual infusion of emotion in her voice,—"darling child!"

The arms moved instinctively, even before the eyes unclosed, and drew her mother down to her with a warm, clinging embrace. Love in Puritan families was often like latent caloric,—an all-pervading force, that affected no visible thermometer, shown chiefly by a noble silent confidence, a ready helpfulness, but seldom outbreathed in caresses; yet natures like Mary's always craved these outward demonstrations, and leaned towards them as a trailing vine sways to the nearest support. It was delightful for once fully to feel how much her mother loved her, as well as to know it.

"Dear, precious mother! do you love me so very much?"

"I live and breathe in you, Mary!" said Mrs. Scudder,—giving vent to herself in one of those trenchant shorthand expressions, wherein positive natures incline to sum up everything, if they must speak at all.

Mary held her mother silently to her breast, her heart shining through her face with a quiet radiance.

"Do you feel happy this morning?" said Mrs. Scudder.

"Very, very, very happy, mother!"

"I am so glad to hear you say so!" said Mrs. Scudder,—who, to say the truth, had entertained many doubts on her pillow the night before.

Mary began dressing herself in a state of calm exaltation. Every trembling leaf on the tree, every sunbeam, was like a living smile of God,—every fluttering breeze like His voice, full of encouragement and hope.

"Mother, did you tell the Doctor what I said last night?"

"I did, my darling."

"Then, mother, I would like to see him a few moments alone."

"Well, Mary, he is in his study, at his morning devotions."

"That is just the time. I will go to him."

The Doctor was sitting by the window; and the honest-hearted, motherly lilacs, abloom for the third time since our story began, were filling the air with their sweetness.

Suddenly the door opened, and Mary entered, in her simple white short-gown and skirt, her eyes calmly radiant, and her whole manner having something serious and celestial. She came directly towards him and put out both her little hands, with a smile half childlike, half angelic; and the Doctor bowed his head and covered his face with his hands.

"Dear friend," said Mary, kneeling and taking his hands, "if you want me, I am come. Life is but a moment,—there is an eternal blessedness just beyond us,—and for the little time between I will be all I can to you, if you will only show me how."

And the Doctor——

No, young man,—the study-door closed just then, and no one heard those words from a quaint old Oriental book which told that all the poetry of that grand old soul had burst into flower, as the aloe blossoms once in a hundred years. The feelings of that great heart might have fallen unconsciously into phrases from that one love-poem of the Bible which such men as he read so purely and devoutly, and which warm the icy clearness of their intellection with the myrrh and spices of ardent lands, where earthly and heavenly love meet and blend in one indistinguishable horizon-line, like sea and sky.

"Who is she that looketh forth as the morning, fair as the moon, clear as the sun? My dove, my undefiled, is but one; she is the only one of her mother. Thou art all fair, my love; there is no spot in thee!"

The Doctor might have said all this; we will not say he did, nor will we say he did not; all we know is, that, when the breakfast-table was ready, they came out cheerfully together. Madame de Frontignac stood in a fresh white wrapper, with a few buttercups in her hair, waiting for the breakfast. She was startled to see the Doctor entering all-radiant, leading in Mary by the hand, and looking as if he thought she were some dream-miracle which might dissolve under his eyes, unless he kept fast hold of her.

The keen eyes shot their arrowy glance, which went at once to the heart of the matter. Madame de Frontignac knew they were affianced, and regarded Mary with attention.

The calm, sweet, elevated expression of her face struck her; it struck her also that *that* was not the light of any earthly love,—that it had no thrill, no blush, no tremor, but only the calmness of a soul that knows itself no more; and she sighed involuntarily.

She looked at the Doctor, and seemed to study attentively a face which happiness made this morning as genial and attractive as it was generally strong and fine.

There was little said at the breakfast-table; and yet the loud singing of the birds, the brightness of the sunshine, the life and vigor of all things, seemed to make up for the silence of those who were too well pleased to speak.

"Eh bien, ma chère," said Madame, after breakfast, drawing Mary into her little room,—*"c'est donc fini?"*

"Yes," said Mary, cheerfully.

"Thou art content?" said Madame, passing her arm around her. "Well, then, I should be. But, Mary, it is like a marriage with the altar, like taking the veil, is it not?"

"No," said Mary; "it is not taking the veil; it is beginning a cheerful, reasonable life with a kind, noble friend, who will always love me truly, and whom I hope to make as happy as he deserves."

"I think well of him, my little cat," said Madame, reflectively; but she stopped something she was going to say, and kissed Mary's forehead. After a moment's pause, she added, "One must have love or refuge, Mary;—this is thy refuge, child; thou wilt have peace in it." She sighed again. *"Enfin,"* she said, resuming her gay tone, "what shall be *la toilette de noces*? Thou shalt have Virginie's pearls, my fair one, and look like a sea-born Venus. *Tiens*, let me try them in thy hair."

And in a few moments she had Mary's long hair down, and was chattering like a blackbird, wreathing the pearls in and out, and saying a thousand pretty little nothings,—weaving grace and poetry upon the straight thread of Puritan life.

XXIX.

Bustle in the Parish

THE announcement of the definite engagement of two such bright particular stars in the hemisphere of the Doctor's small parish excited the interest that such events usually create among the faithful of the flock.

There was a general rustle and flutter, as when a covey of wild pigeons has been started; and all the little elves who rejoice in the name of "says he" and "says I" and "do tell" and "have you heard" were speedily flying through the consecrated air of the parish.

The fact was discussed by matrons and maidens, at the spinning-wheel, in the green clothes-yard, and at the foamy wash-tub, out of which rose weekly a new birth of freshness and beauty. Many a rustic Venus of the foam, as she splashed her dimpled elbows in the rainbow-tinted froth, talked of what should be done for the forthcoming solemnities, and wondered what Mary would have on when she was married, and whether she (the Venus) should get an invitation to the wedding, and whether Ethan would go,—not, of course, that she cared in the least whether he did or not.

Grave, elderly matrons talked about the prosperity of Zion, which they imagined intimately connected with the event of their minister's marriage; and descending from Zion, speculated on bed-quilts and table-cloths, and rummaged their own clean, sweet-smelling stores, fragrant with balm and rose-leaves, to lay out a bureau-cover, or a pair of sheets, or a dozen napkins for the wedding outfit.

The solemnest of solemn quiltings was resolved upon. Miss Prissy declared that she fairly couldn't sleep nights with the responsibility of the wedding-dresses on her mind, but yet she must give one day to getting on that quilt.

The *grand monde* also was in motion. Mrs. General Wilcox called in her own particular carriage, bearing present of a Cashmere shawl for the bride, with the General's best compliments,—also an oak-leaf pattern for quilting, which had been sent her from England, and which was authentically established to be that used on a petticoat belonging to the Princess Royal. And Mrs. Major Seaforth came also, bearing a scarf of wrought India muslin; and Mrs. Vernon sent a splendid China punch-bowl. Indeed, to say the truth, the notables high and mighty of Newport, whom the Doctor had so unceremoniously accused of building their houses with blood and establishing their city with iniquity, considering that nobody seemed to take his words to heart, and that they were making money as fast as old Tyre, rather assumed the magnanimous, and patted themselves on the shoulder for this opportunity to show the Doctor that after all they were good fellows, though they did make money at the expense of thirty *per cent.* on human life.

Simeon Brown was the only exception. He stood aloof, grim and sarcastic, and informed some good middle-aged ladies who came to see if he would, as they phrased it, "esteem it a privilege to add his mite" to the Doctor's outfit, that he would give him a likely negro boy, if he wanted him, and, if he was too conscientious to keep him, he might sell him at a fair profit,—a happy stroke of humor which he was fond of relating many years after.

The quilting was in those days considered the most solemn and important recognition of a betrothal. And for the benefit of those not to the manner born, a little preliminary instruction may be necessary.

The good wives of New England, impressed with that thrifty orthodoxy of economy which forbids to waste the merest trifle, had a habit of saving every scrap clipped out in the fashioning of household garments, and these they cut into fanciful patterns and constructed of them rainbow shapes and quaint traceries, the arrangement of which became one of their few fine arts. Many a maiden, as she sorted and arranged fluttering bits of green, yellow, red, and blue, felt rising in her breast a passion for somewhat vague and unknown, which came out at length in a new pattern of patchwork. Collections of these tiny fragments were always ready to fill an hour when there was nothing else to do; and as the maiden chattered with her beau, her busy flying needle stitched together those pretty bits, which, little in themselves, were destined, by gradual unions and accretions, to bring about at last substantial beauty, warmth, and comfort,—emblems thus of that household life which is to be brought to stability and beauty by reverent economy in husbanding and tact in arranging the little useful and agreeable morsels of daily existence.

When a wedding was forthcoming, there was a solemn review of the stores of beauty and utility thus provided, and the patchwork-spread best worthy of such distinction was chosen for the quilting. Thereto, duly summoned, trooped all intimate female friends of the bride, old and young; and the quilt being spread on a frame, and wadded with cotton, each vied with the others in the delicacy of the quilting she could put upon it. For the quilting also was a fine art, and had its delicacies and nice points,—which grave elderly matrons discussed with judicious care. The quilting generally began at an early hour in the afternoon, and ended at dark with a great supper and general jubilee, at which that ignorant and incapable sex which could not quilt was allowed to appear and put in claims for consideration of another nature. It may, perhaps, be surmised that this expected reinforcement was often alluded to by the younger maidens, whose wickedly coquettish toilettes exhibited suspicious marks of that willingness to get a chance to say "No" which has been slanderously attributed to mischievous maidens.

In consideration of the tremendous responsibilities involved in this quilting, the reader will not be surprised to learn, that, the evening before, Miss Prissy made her appearance at the brown cottage, armed with thimble, scissors, and pincushion, in order to relieve her mind by a little preliminary confabulation.

"You see me, Miss Scudder, run 'most to death," she said; "but I thought I would just run up to Miss Major Seaforth's and see her best bedroom quilt, 'cause I wanted to have all the ideas we possibly could, before I decided on the pattern. Her's is in shells,—just common shells,—nothing to be compared with Miss Wilcox's oak-leaves; and I suppose there isn't the least doubt that Miss Wilcox's sister, in London, did get that from a lady who had a cousin who was governess in the royal family; and I just quilted a little bit to-day on an old piece of silk, and it comes out beautiful; and so I thought I would just come and ask you if you did not think it was best for us to have the oak-leaves."

"Well, certainly, Miss Prissy, if you think so," said Mrs. Scudder, who was as pliant to the opinions of this wise woman of the parish as New England matrons generally are to a reigning dress-maker and *factotum*.

Miss Prissy had the happy consciousness, always, that her early advent under any roof was considered a matter of especial grace; and therefore it was with rather a patronizing tone that she announced that she would stay and spend the night with them.

"I knew," she added, "that your spare chamber was full, with that Madame de——, what do you call her?—if I was to die, I could not remember the woman's name. Well, I thought I could curl in with you, Mary, 'most anywhere."

"That's right, Miss Prissy," said Mary; "you shall be welcome to half my bed any time."

"Well, I knew you would say so, Mary; I never saw the thing you would not give away one half of, since you was that high," said Miss Prissy,—illustrating her words by placing her hand about two feet from the floor.

Just at this moment, Madame de Frontignac entered and asked Mary to come into her room and give her advice as to a piece of embroidery. When she was gone out, Miss Prissy looked after her and sunk her voice once more to the confidential whisper which we before described.

"I have heard strange stories about that French woman," she said; "but as she is here with you and Mary, I suppose there cannot be any truth in them. Dear me! the world is so censorious about women! But then, you know, we don't expect much from French women. I suppose she is a Roman Catholic, and worships pictures and stone images; but then, after all, she has got an immortal soul, and I can't help hoping Mary's influence may be blest to her. They say, when she speaks French, she swears every few minutes; and if that is the way she was brought up, may-be she isn't accountable. I think we can't be too charitable for people that a'n't privileged as we are. Miss Vernon's Polly told me she had seen her sew Sundays,—sew Sabbath-day! She came into her room sudden, and she was working on her embroidery there; and she never winked nor blushed, nor offered to put it away, but sat there just as easy! Polly said she never was so beat in all her life; she felt kind o' scared, every time she thought of it. But now she has come here, who knows but she may be converted?"

"Mary has not said much about her state of mind," said Mrs. Scudder; "but something of deep interest has passed between them. Mary is such an uncommon child, that I trust everything to her."

We will not dwell further on the particulars of this evening,—nor describe how Madame de Frontignac reconnoitered Miss Prissy with keen, amused eyes,—nor how Miss Prissy assured Mary, in the confidential solitude of her chamber, that her fingers just itched to get hold of that trimming on Madame de Frog— something's dress, because she was pretty nigh sure she could make some just like it, for she never saw any trimming she could not make.

The robin that lived in the apple-tree was fairly outgeneralled the next morning; for Miss Prissy was up before him, tripping about the chamber on the points of her toes, knocking down all the movable things in the room, in her efforts to be still, so as not to wake Mary; and it was not until she had finally upset the stand by the bed, with the candlestick, snuffers, and Bible on it, that Mary opened her eyes.

"Miss Prissy! dear me! what is it you are doing?"

"Why, I am trying to be still, Mary, so as not to wake you up; and it seems to me as if everything was possessed, to tumble down so. But it is only half past three,—so you turn over and go to sleep."

"But, Miss Prissy," said Mary, sitting up in bed, "you are all dressed; where are you going?"

"Well, to tell the truth, Mary, I am just one of those people that can't sleep when they have got responsibility on their minds; and I have been lying awake more than an hour here, thinking about that quilt. There is a new way of getting it on to the frame that I want to try; 'cause, you know, when we quilted Cerinthy Stebbins's, it *would* trouble us in the rolling; and I have got a new way that I want to try, and I mean just to get it on to the frame before breakfast. I was in hopes I should get out without waking any of you. I am in hopes I shall get by your mother's door without waking her,—'cause I know she works hard and needs her rest,—but that bedroom door squeaks like a cat, enough to raise the dead!

"Mary," she added, with sudden energy, "If I had the least drop of oil in a teacup, and a bit of quill, I'd stop that door making such a noise." And Miss Prissy's eyes glowed with resolution.

"I don't know where you could find any at this time," said Mary.

"Well, never mind; I'll just go and open the door as slow and careful as I can," said Miss Prissy, as she trotted out of the apartment.

The result of her carefulness was very soon announced to Mary by a protracted sound resembling the mewing of a hoarse cat, accompanied by sundry audible grunts from Miss Prissy, terminating in a grand finale of clatter, occasioned by her knocking down all the pieces of the quilting-frame that stood in the corner of the room, with a concussion that roused everybody in the house.

"What is that?" called out Mrs. Scudder, from her bedroom.

She was answered by two streams of laughter,—one from Mary, sitting up in bed, and the other from Miss Prissy, holding her sides, as she sat dissolved in merriment on the sanded floor.

XXX.

The Quilting

B Y six o'clock in the morning, Miss Prissy came out of the
best room to the breakfast-table, with the air of a general who has arranged a campaign,—her face glowing with
satisfaction. All sat down together to their morning meal. The
outside door was open into the green, turfy yard, and the
apple-tree, now nursing stores of fine yellow jeannetons,
looked in at the window. Every once in a while, as a breeze
shook the leaves, a fully ripe apple might be heard falling to
the ground, at which Miss Prissy would bustle up from the
table and rush to secure the treasure.

As the meal waned to its close, the rattling of wheels was
heard at the gate, and Candace was discerned, seated aloft in
the one-horse wagon, with her usual complement of baskets
and bags.

"Well, now, dear me! if there isn't Candace!" said Miss
Prissy; "I do believe Miss Marvyn has sent her with something for the quilting!" and out she flew as nimble as a
humming-bird, while those in the house heard various exclamations of admiration, as Candace, with stately dignity,
disinterred from the wagon one basket after another, and
exhibited to Miss Prissy's enraptured eyes sly peeps under the
white napkins with which they were covered. And then,
hanging a large basket on either arm, she rolled majestically
towards the house, like a heavy-laden Indiaman, coming in
after a fast voyage.

"Good-mornin', Miss Scudder! good-mornin', Doctor!" she
said, dropping her curtsy on the door-step; "good-mornin',
Miss Mary! Ye see our folks was stirrin' pootty early dis
mornin', an' Miss Marvyn sent me down wid two or tree little
tings."

Setting down her baskets on the floor, and seating herself
between them, she proceeded to develop their contents with
ill-concealed triumph. One basket was devoted to cakes of

every species, from the great Mont-Blanc loaf-cake, with its snowy glaciers of frosting, to the twisted cruller and puffy doughnut. In the other basket lay pots of golden butter curiously stamped, reposing on a bed of fresh, green leaves,— while currants, red and white, and delicious cherries and raspberries, gave a final finish to the picture. From a basket which Miss Prissy brought in from the rear appeared cold fowl and tongue delicately prepared, and shaded with feathers of parsley. Candace, whose rollicking delight in the good things of this life was conspicuous in every emotion, might have furnished to a painter, as she sat in her brilliant turban, an idea for an African Genius of Plenty.

"Why, really, Candace," said Mrs. Scudder, "you are overwhelming us!"

"Ho! ho! ho!" said Candace, "I's tellin' Miss Marvyn folks don't git married but once in der lives, (gin'ally speakin', dat is,) an' den dey oughter hab plenty to do it wid."

"Well, I must say," said Miss Prissy, taking out the loaf-cake with busy assiduity,—"I must say, Candace, this does beat all!"

"I should rader tink it oughter," said Candace, bridling herself with proud consciousness; "ef it don't, 'ta'n't 'cause ole Candace ha'n't put enough into it. I tell ye, I didn't do nothin' all day yisterday but jes' make dat ar cake. Cato, when he got up, he begun to talk someh'n' 'bout his shirt-buttons, an' I jes' shet him right up. Says I, 'Cato, when I's r'ally got cake to make for a great 'casion, I wants my mind *jest* as quiet an' *jest* as serene as ef I was a-goin' to de sacrament. I don't want no 'arthly cares on't. Now,' says I, 'Cato, de ole Doctor's gwine to be married, an' dis yer's his quiltin'-cake,—an' Miss Mary, she's gwine to be married, an' dis yer's *her* quiltin'-cake. An' dar'll be eberybody to dat ar quiltin'; an' ef de cake a'n't right, why, 'twould be puttin' a candle under a bushel. An' so,' says I, 'Cato, your buttons mus' wait.' An' Cato, he sees de 'priety ob it, 'cause, dough he can't make cake like me, he's a 'mazin' good judge on't, an' is dre'ful tickled when I slips out a little loaf for his supper."

"How is Mrs. Marvyn?" said Mrs. Scudder.

"Kinder thin and shimmery; but she's about,—habin' her eyes eberywar 'n' lookin' into eberyting. She jes' touches tings wid de tips ob her fingers an' dey seem to go like. She'll be down to de quiltin' dis arternoon. But she tole me to take de tings an' come down an' spen' de day here; for Miss Marvyn an' I both knows how many steps mus' be taken sech times, an' we agreed you oughter favor yourselves all you could."

"Well, now," said Miss Prissy, lifting up her hands, "if that a'n't what 'tis to have friends! Why, that was one of the things I was thinking of, as I lay awake last night; because, you know, at times like these, people run their feet off before the time begins, and then they are all limpsey and lop-sided when the time comes. Now, I say, Candace, all Miss Scudder and Mary have to do is to give everything up to us, and we'll put it through straight."

"Dat's what we will!" said Candace. "Jes' show me what's to be done, an' I'll do it."

Candace and Miss Prissy soon disappeared together into the pantry with the baskets, whose contents they began busily to arrange. Candace shut the door, that no sound might escape, and began a confidential outpouring to Miss Prissy.

"Ye see," she said, "I's *feelin's* all de while for Miss Marvyn; 'cause, ye see, she was expectin', ef eber Mary was married,— well—dat 'twould be to somebody else, ye know."

Miss Prissy responded with a sympathetic groan.

"Well," said Candace, "ef 't had ben anybody but de Doctor, I wouldn't 'a' been resigned. But arter all he has done for my color, dar a'n't nothin' I could find it in my heart to grudge him. But den I was tellin' Cato t'oder day, says I, 'Cato, I dunno 'bout de rest o' de world, but I ha'n't neber felt it in my bones dat Mass'r James is r'ally dead, for sartin.' Now I feels tings *gin'ally*, but *some* tings I feels *in my bones*, and dem allers comes true. And dat ar's a feelin' I ha'n't had 'bout Mass'r Jim yit, an' dat ar's what I'm waitin' for 'fore I clar make up my mind. Though I know, 'cordin' to all white folks' way o' tinkin', dar a'n't no hope, 'cause Squire Marvyn he had dat ar Jeduth Pettibone up to his house, a-questionin' on him, off an' on, nigh about tree hours. An' r'ally I didn't see no hope no way, 'xcept jes' dis yer, as I was tellin' Cato,— *I can't feel it in my bones*."

Candace was not versed enough in the wisdom of the world to know that she belonged to a large and respectable school of philosophers in this particular mode of testing evidence, which, after all, the reader will perceive has its conveniences.

"Anoder ting," said Candace, "as much as a dozen times, dis yer last year, when I's been a-scourin' knives, a fork has fell an' stuck straight up in de floor; an' de las' time I pinted it out to Miss Marvyn, an' she on'y jes' said, 'Why, what o' dat, Candace?'"

"Well," said Miss Prissy, "I don't believe in *signs*, but then strange things do happen. Now about dogs howling under windows,—why, I don't believe in it a bit, but I never knew it fail that there was a death in the house after."

"Ah, I tell ye what," said Candace, looking mysterious, "dogs knows a heap more'n dey likes to tell!"

"Jes' so," said Miss Prissy. "Now I remember, one night, when I was watching with Miss Colonel Andrews, after Marthy Ann was born, that we heard the *mournfulest* howling that ever you did hear. It seemed to come from right under the front stoop; and Miss Andrews she just dropped the spoon in her gruel, and says she, 'Miss Prissy, do, for pity's sake, just go down and see what that noise is.' And I went down and lifted up one of the loose boards of the stoop, and what should I see there but their Newfoundland pup?—there that creature had dug a grave and was a-sitting by it, crying!"

Candace drew near to Miss Prissy, dark with expressive interest, as her voice, in this awful narration, sank to a whisper.

"Well," said Candace, after Miss Prissy had made something of a pause.

"Well, I told Miss Andrews I didn't think there was anything in it," said Miss Prissy; "but," she added, impressively, "she lost a very dear brother, six months after, and I laid him out with my own hands,—yes, laid him out in white flannel."

"Some folks say," said Candace, "dat dreamin' 'bout white horses is a sartin sign. Jinny Styles is berry strong 'bout dat. Now she come down one mornin' cryin', 'cause she'd been dreamin' 'bout white horses, an' she was sure she should hear some friend was dead. An' sure enough, a man come in dat bery day an' tole her her son was drownded out in de harbor. An' Jinny said, 'Dar! she was sure dat sign neber would fail.' But den, ye see, dat night he come home. Jinny wa'n't r'ally disappinted, but she allers insisted he was *as good as drownded*, any way, 'cause he sunk tree times."

"Well, I tell you," said Miss Prissy, "there are a great many more things in this world than folks know about."

"So dey are," said Candace. "Now, I ha'n't neber opened my mind to nobody; but dar's a dream I's had, tree mornin's runnin', lately. I dreamed I see Jim Marvyn a-sinkin' in de water, an' stretchin' up his hands. An' den I dreamed I see de Lord Jesus come a-walkin' on de water an' take hold ob his hand, an' says he, 'O thou of little faith, wherefore didst thou doubt?' An' den he lifted him right out. An' I ha'n't said nothin' to nobody, 'cause, you know, de Doctor, he says people mus'n't mind nothin' 'bout der dreams, 'cause dreams belongs to de ole 'spensation."

"Well, well, well!" said Miss Prissy, "I am sure I don't know what to think. What time in the morning was it that you dreamed it?"

"Why," said Candace, "it was jest arter bird-peep. I kinder allers wakes myself den, an' turns ober, an' what comes arter dat is apt to run clar."

"Well, well, well!" said Miss Prissy, "I don't know what to think. You see, it may have reference to the state of his soul."

"I know dat," said Candace; "but as nigh as I could judge in my dream," she added, sinking her voice and looking mysterious, "as nigh as I can judge, *dat boy's soul was in his body*!"

"Why, how do you know?" said Miss Prissy, looking astonished at the confidence with which Candace expressed her opinion.

"Well, ye see," said Candace, rather mysteriously, "de Doctor, he don't like to hab us talk much 'bout dese yer tings, 'cause he tinks it's kind o' heathenish. But den, folks as is used to seein' sech tings knows de look ob a sperit *out* o' de body from de look ob a sperit *in* de body, jest as easy as you can tell Mary from de Doctor."

At this moment Mrs. Scudder opened the pantry-door and put an end to this mysterious conversation, which had already so affected Miss Prissy, that, in the eagerness of her interest, she had rubbed up her cap border and ribbon into rather an elfin and goblin style, as if they had been ruffled up by a breeze from the land of spirits; and she flew around for a few moments in a state of great nervous agitation, upsetting dishes, knocking down plates, and huddling up contrary suggestions as to what ought to be done first, in such impossible relations that Mrs. Katy Scudder stood in dignified surprise at this strange freak of conduct in the wise woman of the parish.

A dim consciousness of something not quite canny in herself seemed to strike her, for she made a vigorous effort to appear composed; and facing Mrs. Scudder, with an air of dignified suavity, inquired if it would not be best to put Jim Marvyn in the oven now, while Candace was getting the pies ready,—meaning, of course, a large turkey, which was to be the first in an indefinite series to be baked that morning; and discovering, by Mrs. Scudder's dazed expression and a vigorous pinch from Candace, that somehow she had not improved matters, she rubbed her spectacles into a diagonal position across her eyes, and stood glaring, half through, half over them, with a helpless expression, which in a less judicious person might have suggested the idea of a state of slight intoxication.

But the exigencies of an immediate temporal dispensation put an end to Miss Prissy's unwonted vagaries, and she was soon to be seen flying round like a meteor, dusting, shaking curtains, counting napkins, wiping and sorting china, all with such rapidity as to give rise to the notion that she actually existed in forty places at once.

Candace, whom the limits of her corporeal frame restricted to an altogether different style of locomotion, often rolled the whites of her eyes after her and gave vent to her views of her proceedings in sententious expressions.

"Do you know why *dat ar* neber was married?" she said to Mary, as she stood looking after her. Miss Prissy had made one of those rapid transits through the apartment.

"No," answered Mary, innocently. "Why wasn't she?"

" 'Cause neber was a man could run fast enough to cotch her," said Candace; and then her portly person shook with the impulse of her own wit.

By two o'clock a goodly company began to assemble. Mrs. Deacon Twitchel arrived, soft, pillowy, and plaintive as ever, accompanied by Cerinthy Ann, a comely damsel, tall and

trim, with a bright black eye, and a most vigorous and determined style of movement. Good Mrs. Jones, broad, expan-
sive, and solid, having vegetated tranquilly on in the cabbage-
garden of the virtues since three years ago, when she graced
our tea-party, was now as well preserved as ever, and brought
some fresh butter, a tin pail of cream, and a loaf of cake made
after a new Philadelphia receipt. The tall, spare, angular figure
of Mrs. Simeon Brown alone was wanting; but she patronized Mrs. Scudder no more, and tossed her head with a becoming pride when her name was mentioned.

The quilt-pattern was gloriously drawn in oak-leaves, done
in indigo; and soon all the company, young and old, were
passing busy fingers over it, and conversation went on briskly.

Madame de Frontignac, we must not forget to say, had
entered with hearty *abandon* into the spirit of the day. She
had dressed the tall china vases on the mantel-pieces, and,
departing from the usual rule of an equal mixture of roses and
asparagus-bushes, had constructed two quaint and graceful
bouquets, where garden-flowers were mingled with drooping
grasses and trailing wild vines, forming a graceful combina-
tion which excited the surprise of all who saw it.

"It's the very first time in my life that I ever saw grass put
into a flower-pot," said Miss Prissy; "but I must say it looks
as handsome as a picture. Mary, I must say," she added, in an
aside, "I think that Madame de Frongenac is the sweetest
dressing and appearing creature I ever saw; she don't dress up
nor put on airs, but she seems to see in a minute how things
ought to go; and if it's only a bit of grass, or leaf, or wild
vine, that she puts in her hair, why, it seems to come just
right. I should like to make her a dress, for I know she would
understand my fit; do speak to her, Mary, in case she should
want a dress fitted here, to let me try it."

At the quilting, Madame de Frontignac would have her
seat, and soon won the respect of the party by the dexterity
with which she used her needle; though, when it was whispered that she learned to quilt among the nuns, some of the
elderly ladies exhibited a slight uneasiness, as being rather
doubtful whether they might not be encouraging Papistical
opinions by allowing her an equal share in the work of getting up their minister's bed-quilt; but the younger part of the

company were quite captivated by her foreign air, and the pretty manner in which she lisped her English; and Cerinthy Ann even went so far as to horrify her mother by saying that she wished she'd been educated in a convent herself,—a declaration which arose less from native depravity than from a certain vigorous disposition, which often shows itself in young people, to shock the current opinions of their elders and betters. Of course, the conversation took a general turn, somewhat in unison with the spirit of the occasion; and whenever it flagged, some allusion to a forthcoming wedding, or some sly hint at the future young Madame of the parish, was sufficient to awaken the dormant animation of the company.

Cerinthy Ann contrived to produce an agreeable electric shock by declaring, that, for her part, she never could see into it, how any girl could marry a minister,—that she should as soon think of setting up housekeeping in a meeting-house.

"Oh, Cerinthy Ann!" exclaimed her mother, "how can you go on so?"

"It's a fact," said the adventurous damsel; "now other men let you have some peace,—but a minister's always round under your feet."

"So you think, the less you see of a husband, the better?" said one of the ladies.

"Just my views," said Cerinthy, giving a decided snip to her thread with her scissors; "I like the Nantucketers, that go off on four-years' voyages, and leave their wives a clear field. If ever I get married, I'm going up to have one of those fellows."

It is to be remarked, in passing, that Miss Cerinthy Ann was at this very time receiving surreptitious visits from a consumptive-looking, conscientious, young theological candidate, who came occasionally to preach in the vicinity, and put up at the house of the Deacon, her father. This good young man, being violently attacked on the doctrine of Election by Miss Cerinthy, had been drawn on to illustrate it in a most practical manner, to her comprehension; and it was the consciousness of the weak and tottering state of the internal garrison that added vigor to the young lady's tones. As Mary had been the chosen confidante of the progress of this affair, she was quietly amused at the demonstration.

"You'd better take care, Cerinthy Ann," said her mother; "they say that 'those who sing before breakfast will cry before supper.' Girls talk about getting married," she said, relapsing into a gentle didactic melancholy, "without realizing its awful responsibilities."

"Oh, as to that," said Cerinthy, "I've been practising on my pudding now these six years, and I shouldn't be afraid to throw one up chimney with any girl."

This speech was founded on a tradition, current in those times, that no young lady was fit to be married till she could construct a boiled Indian-pudding of such consistency that it could be thrown up chimney and come down on the ground, outside, without breaking; and the consequence of Cerinthy Ann's sally was a general laugh.

"Girls a'n't what they used to be in my day," sententiously remarked an elderly lady. "I remember my mother told me when she was thirteen she could knit a long cotton stocking in a day."

"I haven't much faith in these stories of old times,—have you, girls?" said Cerinthy, appealing to the younger members at the frame.

"At any rate," said Mrs. Twitchel, "our minister's wife will be a pattern; I don't know anybody that goes beyond her either in spinning or fine stitching."

Mary sat as placid and disengaged as the new moon, and listened to the chatter of old and young with the easy quietness of a young heart that has early outlived life, and looks on everything in the world from some gentle, restful eminence far on towards a better home. She smiled at everybody's word, had a quick eye for everybody's wants, and was ready with thimble, scissors, or thread, whenever any one needed them; but once, when there was a pause in the conversation, she and Mrs. Marvyn were both discovered to have stolen away. They were seated on the bed in Mary's little room, with their arms around each other, communing in low and gentle tones.

"Mary, my dear child," said her friend, "this event is very

pleasant to me, because it places you permanently near me. I did not know but eventually this sweet face might lead to my losing you, who are in some respects the dearest friend I have."

"You might be sure," said Mary, "I never would have married, except that my mother's happiness and the happiness of so good a friend seemed to depend on it. When we renounce self in anything, we have reason to hope for God's blessing; and so I feel assured of a peaceful life in the course I have taken. You will always be as a mother to me," she added, laying her head on her friend's shoulder.

"Yes," said Mrs. Marvyn; "and I must not let myself think a moment how dear it might have been to have you *more* my own. If you feel really, truly happy,—if you can enter on this life without any misgivings——"

"I can," said Mary, firmly.

At this instant, very strangely, the string which confined a wreath of sea-shells around her glass, having been long undermined by moths, suddenly broke and fell down, scattering the shells upon the floor.

Both women started, for the string of shells had been placed there by James; and though neither was superstitious, this was one of those odd coincidences that make hearts throb.

"Dear boy!" said Mary, gathering the shells up tenderly; "wherever he is, I shall never cease to love him. It makes me feel sad to see this come down; but it is only an accident; nothing of him will ever fail out of my heart."

Mrs. Marvyn clasped Mary closer to her, with tears in her eyes.

"I'll tell you what, Mary; it must have been the moths did that," said Miss Prissy, who had been standing, unobserved, at the door for a moment back; "moths will eat away strings just so. Last week Miss Vernon's great family-picture fell down because the moths eat through the cord; people ought to use twine or cotton string always. But I came to tell you that the supper is all set, and the Doctor out of his study, and all the people are wondering where you are."

Mary and Mrs. Marvyn gave a hasty glance at themselves in the glass, to be assured of their good keeping, and went into the great kitchen, where a long table stood exhibiting all that plenitude of provision which the immortal description of Washington Irving has saved us the trouble of recapitulating in detail.

The husbands, brothers, and lovers had come in, and the scene was redolent of gayety. When Mary made her appearance, there was a moment's pause, till she was conducted to the side of the Doctor; when, raising his hand, he invoked a grace upon the loaded board.

Unrestrained gayeties followed. Groups of young men and maidens chatted together, and all the gallantries of the times were enacted. Serious matrons commented on the cake, and told each other high and particular secrets in the culinary art, which they drew from remote family-archives. One might have learned in that instructive assembly how best to keep moths out of blankets,—how to make fritters of Indian corn undistinguishable from oysters,—how to bring up babies by hand,—how to mend a cracked teapot,—how to take out grease from a brocade,—how to reconcile absolute decrees with free will, how to make five yards of cloth answer the purpose of six,—and how to put down the Democratic party. All were busy, earnest, and certain,—just as a swarm of men and women, old and young, are in 1859.

Miss Prissy was in her glory; every bow of her best cap was alive with excitement, and she presented to the eyes of the astonished Newport gentry an animated receipt-book. Some of the information she communicated, indeed, was so valuable and important that she could not trust the air with it, but whispered the most important portions in a confidential tone. Among the crowd, Cerinthy Ann's theological admirer was observed in deeply reflective attitude; and that high-spirited young lady added further to his convictions of the total depravity of the species by vexing and discomposing him in those thousand ways in which a lively, ill-conditioned young woman will put to rout a serious, well-disposed young man,—comforting herself with the reflection, that by-and-by she would repent of all her sins in a lump together.

Vain, transitory splendors! Even this evening, so glorious, so heart-cheering, so fruitful in instruction and amusement, could not last forever. Gradually the company broke up; the

804 THE MINISTER'S WOOING
804

matrons mounted soberly on horseback behind their spouses; and Cerinthy consoled her clerical friend by giving him an opportunity to read her a lecture on the way home, if he found the courage to do so.

Mr. and Mrs. Marvyn and Candace wound their way soberly homeward; the Doctor returned to his study for nightly devotions; and before long, sleep settled down on the brown cottage.

"I'll tell you what, Cato," said Candace, before composing herself to sleep, "I can't feel it in my bones dat dis yer weddin's gwine to come off yit."

XXXI.

An Adventure

A DAY or two after, Madame de Frontignac and Mary
went out to gather shells and seaweed on the beach. It
was four o'clock; and the afternoon sun was hanging in the
sultry sky of July with a hot and vaporous stillness. The whole
air was full of blue haze, that softened the outlines of objects
without hiding them. The sea lay like so much glass; every
ship and boat was double; every line and rope and spar had
its counterpart; and it seemed hard to say which was the more
real, the under or the upper world.

Madame de Frontignac and Mary had brought a little basket with them, which they were filling with shells and sea-
mosses. The former was in high spirits. She ran, and shouted,
and exclaimed, and wondered at each new marvel thrown out
upon the shore, with the *abandon* of a little child. Mary could
not but wonder whether this indeed were she whose strong
words had pierced and wrung her sympathies the other night,
and whether a deep life-wound could lie bleeding under those
brilliant eyes and that infantine exuberance of gayety; yet,
surely, all that which seemed so strong, so true, so real could
not be gone so soon,—and it could not be so soon consoled.
Mary wondered at her, as the Anglo-Saxon constitution, with
its strong, firm intensity, its singleness of nature, wonders at
the mobile, many-sided existence of warmer races, whose versatility of emotion on the surface is not incompatible with the
most intense persistency lower down.

Mary's was one of those indulgent and tolerant natures
which seem to form the most favorable base for the play of
other minds, rather than to be itself salient,—and something
about her tender calmness always seemed to provoke the
spirit of frolic in her friend. She would laugh at her, kiss her,
gambol round her, dress her hair with fantastic coiffures, and
call her all sorts of fanciful and poetic names in French or
English,—while Mary surveyed her with a pleased and inno-

cent surprise, as a revelation of character altogether new and different from anything to which she had been hitherto accustomed. She was to her a living pantomime, and brought into her unembellished life the charms of opera and theatre and romance.

After wearying themselves with their researches, they climbed round a point of rock that stretched some way out into the sea, and attained to a little kind of grotto, where the high cliffs shut out the rays of the sun. They sat down to rest upon the rocks. A fresh breeze of declining day was springing up, and bringing the rising tide landward,—each several line of waves with its white crests coming up and breaking gracefully on the hard, sparkling sand-beach at their feet.

Mary's eyes fixed themselves, as they were apt to do, in a mournful reverie, on the infinite expanse of waters, which was now broken and chopped into a thousand incoming waves by the fresh afternoon breeze. Madame de Frontignac noticed the expression, and began to play with her as if she had been a child. She pulled the comb from her hair, and let down its long silky waves upon her shoulders.

"Now," said she, "let us make a Miranda of thee. This is our cave. I will be Prince Ferdinand. Burr told me all about that,—he reads beautifully, and explained it all to me. What a lovely story that is!—you must be so happy, who know how to read Shakspeare without learning! *Tenez!* I will put this shell on your forehead,—it has a hole here, and I will pass this gold chain through,—now! What a pity this seaweed will not be pretty out of water! it has no effect; but there is some green that will do;—let me fasten it so. Now, fair Miranda, look at thyself!"

Where is the girl so angelic as not to feel a slight curiosity to know how she shall look in a new and strange costume? Mary bent over the rock, where a little pool of water lay in a brown hollow above the fluctuations of the tide, dark and still, like a mirror,—and saw a fair face, with a white shell above the forehead and drooping wreaths of green seaweed in the silken hair; and a faint blush and smile rose on the cheek, giving the last finish to the picture.

"How do you find yourself?" said Madame. "Confess now that I have a true talent in coiffure. Now I will be Ferdinand."

She turned quickly, and her eye was caught by something that Mary did not see; she only saw the smile fade suddenly from Madame de Frontignac's cheek, and her lips grow deadly white, while her heart beat so that Mary could discern its flutterings under her black silk bodice.

"Will the sea-nymphs punish the rash presumption of a mortal who intrudes?" said Colonel Burr, stepping before them with a grace as invincible and assured as if he had never had any past history with either.

Mary started with a guilty blush, like a child detected in an unseemly frolic, and put her hand to her head to take off the unwonted adornments.

"Let me protest, in the name of the Graces," said Burr, who by that time stood with easy calmness at her side; and as he spoke, he stayed her hand with that gentle air of authority which made it the natural impulse of most people to obey him. "It would be treason against the picturesque," he added, "to spoil that toilette, so charmingly uniting the wearer to the scene."

Mary was taken by surprise, and discomposed as every one is who finds himself masquerading in attire foreign to his usual habits and character; and therefore, when she would persist in taking it to pieces, Burr found sufficient to alleviate the embarrassment of Madame de Frontignac's utter silence in a playful run of protestations and compliments.

"I think, Mary," said Madame de Frontignac, "that we had better be returning to the house."

This was said in the haughtiest and coolest tone imaginable, looking at the place where Burr stood, as if there were nothing there but empty air. Mary rose to go; Madame de Frontignac offered her arm.

"Permit me to remark, ladies," said Burr, with the quiet suavity which never forsook him, "that your very agreeable occupations have caused time to pass more rapidly than you are aware. I think you will find that the tide has risen so as to intercept the path by which you came here. You will hardly be able to get around the point of rocks without some assistance."

Mary looked a few paces ahead, and saw, a little before them, a fresh afternoon breeze driving the rising tide high on to the side of the rocks, at whose foot their course had lain. The nook in which they had been sporting formed part of a shelving ledge which inclined over their heads, and which it was just barely possible could be climbed by a strong and agile person, but which would be wholly impracticable to a frail, unaided woman.

"There is no time to be lost," said Burr, coolly, measuring the possibilities with that keen eye that was never discomposed by any exigency. "I am at your service, ladies; I can either carry you in my arms around this point, or assist you up these rocks."

He paused and waited for their answer.

Madame de Frontignac stood pale, cold, and silent, hearing only the wild beating of her heart.

"I think," said Mary, "that we should try the rocks."

"Very well," said Burr; and placing his gloved hand on a fragment of rock somewhat above their heads, he swung himself up to it with an easy agility; from this he stretched himself down as far as possible towards them, and, extending his hand, directed Mary, who stood foremost, to set her foot on a slight projection, and give him both her hands; she did so, and he seemed to draw her up as easily as if she had been a feather. He placed her by him on a shelf of rock, and turned again to Madame de Frontignac; she folded her arms and turned resolutely away towards the sea.

Just at that moment a coming wave broke at her feet.

"There is no time to be lost," said Burr; "there's a tremendous surf coming in, and the next wave may carry you out."

"*Tant mieux!*" she responded, without turning her head.

"Oh, Virginie! Virginie!" exclaimed Mary, kneeling and stretching her arms over the rock; but another voice called Virginie, in a tone which went to her heart. She turned and saw those dark eyes full of tears.

"Oh, come!" he said, with that voice which she never could resist.

She put her cold, trembling hands into his, and he drew her up and placed her safely beside Mary. A few moments of difficult climbing followed, in which his arm was thrown now around one and then around the other, and they felt them-

selves carried with a force as if the slight and graceful form
were strung with steel.

Placed in safety on the top of the bank, there was a natural
gush of grateful feeling towards their deliverer. The severest
resentment, the coolest moral disapprobation, are necessarily
somewhat softened, when the object of them has just laid one
under a personal obligation.

Burr did not seem disposed to press his advantage, and
treated the incident as the most matter-of-course affair in the
world. He offered an arm to each lady, with the air of a well-
bred gentleman who offers a necessary support; and each took
it, because neither wished, under the circumstances, to refuse.

He walked along leisurely homeward, talking in that easy,
quiet, natural way in which he excelled, addressing no very
particular remark to either one, and at the door of the cottage
took his leave, saying, as he bowed, that he hoped neither of
them would feel any inconvenience from their exertions, and
that he should do himself the pleasure to call soon and inquire after their health.

Madame de Frontignac made no reply; but curtsied with a
stately grace, turned and went into her little room, whither
Mary, after a few minutes, followed her.

She found her thrown upon the bed, her face buried in the
pillow, her breast heaving as if she were sobbing; but when,
at Mary's entrance, she raised her head, her eyes were bright
and dry.

"It is just as I told you, Mary,—that man holds me. I love
him yet, in spite of myself. It is in vain to be angry. What is
the use of striking your right hand with your left? When we
love one more than ourselves, we only hurt ourselves with our
anger."

"But," said Mary, "love is founded on respect and esteem;
and when that is gone"——

"Why, then," said Madame, "we are very sorry,—but we
love yet. Do we stop loving ourselves when we have lost our
own self-respect? No! it is so disagreeable to see, we shut our
eyes and ask to have the bandage put on,—you know *that*,
poor little heart! You can think how it would have been with
you, if you had found that *he* was not what you thought."

The word struck home to Mary's consciousness,—but she sat down and took her friend in her arms with an air self-controlled, serious, rational.

"I see and feel it all, dear Virginie, but I must stand firm for you. You are in the waves, and I on the shore. If you are so weak at heart, you must not see this man any more."

"But he will call."

"I will see him for you."

"What will you tell him, my heart?—tell him that I am ill, perhaps?"

"No; I will tell him the truth,—that you do not wish to see him."

"That is hard;—he will wonder."

"I think not," said Mary, resolutely; "and furthermore, I shall say to him, that, while Madame de Frontignac is at the cottage, it will not be agreeable for us to receive calls from him."

"Mary, *ma chère*, you astonish me!"

"My dear friend," said Mary, "it is the only way. This man—this cruel, wicked, deceitful man—must not be allowed to trifle with you in this way. I will protect you."

And she rose up with flashing eye and glowing cheek, looking as her father looked when he protested against the slave-trade.

"Thou art my Saint Catharine," said Virginie, rising up, excited by Mary's enthusiasm, "and hast the sword as well as the palm; but, dear saint, don't think so very, very badly of him;—he has a noble nature; he has the angel in him."

"The greater his sin," said Mary; "he sins against light and love."

"But I think his heart is touched,—I think he is sorry. Oh, Mary, if you had only seen how he looked at me when he put out his hands on the rocks!—there were tears in his eyes."

"Well there might be!" said Mary; "I do not think he is quite a fiend; no one could look at those cheeks, dear Virginie, and not feel sad, that saw you a few months ago."

"Am I so changed?" she said, rising and looking at herself in the mirror. "Sure enough,—my neck used to be quite round;—now you can see those two little bones, like rocks at low tide. Poor Virginie! her summer is gone, and the leaves are falling; poor little cat!"—and Virginie stroked her own chestnut head, as if she had been pitying another, and began humming a little Norman air, with a refrain that sounded like the murmur of a brook over the stones.

The more Mary was touched by these little poetic ways, which ran just on an even line between the gay and the pathetic, the more indignant she grew with the man that had brought all this sorrow. She felt a saintly vindictiveness, and a determination to place herself as an adamantine shield between him and her friend. There is no courage and no anger like that of a gentle woman, when once fully roused; if ever you have occasion to meet it, you will certainly remember the hour.

XXXII.

Plain Talk

MARY revolved the affairs of her friend in her mind, during the night. The intensity of the mental crisis through which she had herself just passed had developed her in many inward respects, so that she looked upon life no longer as a timid girl, but as a strong, experienced woman. She had thought, and suffered, and held converse with eternal realities, until thousands of mere earthly hesitations and timidities, that often restrain a young and untried nature, had entirely lost their hold upon her. Besides, Mary had at heart the true Puritan seed of heroism,—never absent from the souls of true New England women. Her essentially Hebrew education, trained in daily converse with the words of prophets and seers, and with the modes of thought of a people essentially grave and heroic, predisposed her to a kind of exaltation, which, in times of great trial, might rise to the heights of the religious-sublime, in which the impulse of self-devotion took a form essentially commanding. The very intensity of the repression under which her faculties had developed seemed, as it were, to produce a surplus of hidden strength, which came out in exigencies. Her reading, though restricted to a few volumes, had been of the kind that vitalized and stimulated a poetic nature, and laid up in its chambers vigorous words and trenchant phrases, for the use of an excited feeling,—so that eloquence came to her as a native gift. She realized, in short, in her higher hours, the last touch with which Milton finishes his portrait of an ideal woman:—

> "Greatness of mind and nobleness their seat
> Build in her loftiest, and create an awe
> About her as a guard angelic placed."

The next morning, Colonel Burr called at the cottage. Mary was spinning in the garret, and Madame de Frontignac was reeling yarn, when Mrs. Scudder brought this announcement.

"Mother," said Mary, "I wish to see Mr. Burr alone. Madame de Frontignac will not go down."

Mrs. Scudder looked surprised, but asked no questions. When she was gone down, Mary stood a moment reflecting; Madame de Frontignac looked eager and agitated.

"Remember and notice all he says, and just how he looks, Mary, so as to tell me; and be sure and say that I thank him for his kindness yesterday. We must own, he appeared very well there; did he not?"

"Certainly," said Mary; "but no man could have done less."

"Ah! but, Mary, not every man could have done it *as* he did. Now don't be too hard on him, Mary;—I have said dreadful things to him; I am afraid I have been too severe. After all, these distinguished men are so tempted! we don't know how much they are tempted; and who can wonder that they are a little spoiled? So, my angel, you must be merciful."

"Merciful!" said Mary, kissing the pale cheek, and feeling the cold little hands that trembled in hers.

"So you will go down in your little spinning-toilette, *mimi*? I fancy you look as Joan of Arc did, when she was keeping her sheep at Domremy. Go, and God bless thee!" and Madame de Frontignac pushed her playfully forward.

Mary entered the room where Burr was seated, and wished him good-morning, in a serious and placid manner, in which there was not the slightest trace of embarrassment or discomposure.

"Shall I have the pleasure of seeing your fair companion this morning?" said Burr, after some moments of indifferent conversation.

"No, Sir; Madame de Frontignac desires me to excuse her to you."

"Is she ill?" said Burr, with a look of concern.

"No, Mr. Burr, she prefers not to see you."

Burr gave a start of well-bred surprise, and Mary added,—

"Madame de Frontignac has made me familiar with the history of your acquaintance with her; and you will therefore understand what I mean, Mr. Burr, when I say, that, during the time of her stay with us, we should prefer not to receive calls from you."

"Your language, Miss Scudder, has certainly the merit of explicitness."

"I intend it shall have, Sir," said Mary, tranquilly; "half the misery in the world comes of want of courage to speak and to hear the truth plainly and in a spirit of love."

"I am gratified that you add the last clause, Miss Scudder; I might not otherwise recognize the gentle being whom I have always regarded as the impersonation of all that is softest in woman. I have not the honor of understanding in the least the reason of this apparently capricious sentence, but I bow to it in submission."

"Mr. Burr," said Mary, walking up to him, and looking him full in the eyes, with an energy that for the moment bore down his practised air of easy superiority, "I wish to speak to you for a moment, as one immortal soul should to another, without any of those false glosses and deceits which men call ceremony and good manners. You have done a very great injury to a lovely lady, whose weakness ought to have been sacred in your eyes. Precisely because you are what you are,— strong, keen, penetrating, and able to control and govern all who come near you,—because you have the power to make yourself agreeable, interesting, fascinating, and to win esteem and love,—just for that reason you ought to hold yourself the guardian of every woman, and treat her as you would wish any man to treat your own daughter. I leave it to your conscience, whether this is the manner in which you have treated Madame de Frontignac."

"Upon my word, Miss Scudder," began Burr, "I cannot imagine what representations our mutual friend may have been making. I assure you, our intercourse has been as irreproachable as the most scrupulous could desire."

" 'Irreproachable!—scrupulous!'—Mr. Burr, you know that you have taken the very life out of her. You men can have everything,—ambition, wealth, power; a thousand ways are open to you: women have nothing but their heart; and when that is gone, all is gone. Mr. Burr, you remember the rich man who had flocks and herds, but nothing would do for him but he must have the one little ewe-lamb which was all his poor neighbor had. Thou art the man! You have stolen all the love she had to give,—all that she had to make a happy home; and you can never give her anything in return, without endangering her purity and her soul,—and you knew you could not. I know you men *think* this is a light matter; but it is death to us. What will this woman's life be? one long struggle to forget; and when you have forgotten her, and are going on gay and happy,—when you have thrown her very name away as a faded flower, she will be praying, hoping, fearing for you; though all men deny you, yet will not she. Yes, Mr. Burr, if ever your popularity and prosperity should leave you, and those who now flatter should despise and curse you, she will always be interceding with her own heart and with God for you, and making a thousand excuses where she cannot deny; and if you die, as I fear you have lived, unreconciled to the God of your fathers, it will be in her heart to offer up her very soul for you, and to pray that God will impute all your sins to her, and give you heaven. Oh, I know this, because I have felt it in my own heart!" and Mary threw herself passionately down into a chair, and broke into an agony of uncontrolled sobbing.

Burr turned away, and stood looking through the window; tears were dropping silently, unchecked by the cold, hard pride which was the evil demon of his life.

It is due to our human nature to believe that no man could ever have been so passionately and enduringly loved and revered by both men and women as he was, without a beautiful and lovable nature;—no man ever demonstrated more forcibly the truth, that it is not a man's natural constitution, but the *use* he makes of it, which stamps him as good or vile.

The diviner part of him was weeping, and the cold, proud demon was struggling to regain his lost ascendency. Every sob of the fair, inspired child who had been speaking to him seemed to shake his heart,—he felt as if he could have fallen on his knees to her; and yet that stoical habit which was the boast of his life, which was the sole wisdom he taught to his only and beautiful daughter, was slowly stealing back round his heart,—and he pressed his lips together, resolved that no word should escape till he had fully mastered himself.

In a few moments Mary rose with renewed calmness and dignity, and, approaching him, said,—

"Before I wish you good-morning, Mr. Burr, I must ask pardon for the liberty I have taken in speaking so very plainly."

"There is no pardon needed, my dear child," said Burr, turning and speaking very gently, and with a face expressive of a softened concern; "if you have told me harsh truths, it was with gentle intentions;—I only hope that I may prove, at least by the future, that I am not altogether so bad as you imagine. As to the friend whose name has been passed between us, no man can go beyond me in a sense of her real nobleness; I am sensible how little I can ever deserve the sentiment with which she honors me. I am ready, in my future course, to obey any commands that you and she may think proper to lay upon me."

"The only kindness you can now do her," said Mary, "is to leave her. It is impossible that you should be merely friends; —it is impossible, without violating the holiest bonds, that you should be more. The injury done is irreparable; but you *can* avoid adding another and greater one to it."

Burr looked thoughtful.

"May I say one thing more?" said Mary, the color rising in her cheeks.

Burr looked at her with that smile that always drew out the confidence of every heart.

"Mr. Burr," she said, "you will pardon me, but I cannot help saying this: You have, I am told, wholly renounced the Christian faith of your fathers, and build your whole life on quite another foundation. I cannot help feeling that this is a great and terrible mistake. I cannot help wishing that you would examine and reconsider."

"My dear child, I am extremely grateful to you for your remark, and appreciate fully the purity of the source from which it springs. Unfortunately, our intellectual beliefs are not subject to the control of our will. I have examined, and the examination has, I regret to say, not had the effect you would desire."

Mary looked at him wistfully; he smiled and bowed,—all

himself again; and stopping at the door, he said, with a proud humility,—

"Do me the favor to present my devoted regard to your friend; believe me, that hereafter you shall have less reason to complain of me."

He bowed, and was gone.

An eye-witness of the scene has related, that, when Burr resigned his seat as President of his country's Senate, an object of peculiar political bitterness and obloquy, almost all who listened to him had made up their minds that he was an utterly faithless, unprincipled man; and yet, such was his singular and peculiar personal power, that his short farewell-address melted the whole assembly into tears, and his most embittered adversaries were charmed into a momentary enthusiasm of admiration.

It must not be wondered at, therefore, if our simple-hearted, loving Mary strangely found all her indignation against him gone, and herself little disposed to criticize the impassioned tenderness with which Madame de Frontignac still regarded him.

We have one thing more that we cannot avoid saying, of two men so singularly in juxtaposition as Aaron Burr and Dr. Hopkins. Both had a perfect *logic* of life, and guided themselves with an inflexible rigidity by it. Burr assumed individual pleasure to be the great object of human existence; Dr. Hopkins placed it in a life altogether beyond self. Burr rejected all sacrifice; Hopkins considered sacrifice as the foundation of all existence. To live as far as possible without a disagreeable sensation was an object which Burr proposed to himself as the *summum bonum*, for which he drilled down and subjugated a nature of singular richness. Hopkins, on the other hand, smoothed the asperities of a temperament naturally violent and fiery by a rigid discipline which guided it entirely above the plane of self-indulgence; and, in the pursuance of their great end, the one watched against his better nature as the other did against his worse. It is but fair, then, to take their lives as the practical workings of their respective ethical creeds.

XXXIII.

New England in French Eyes

WE owe our readers a digression at this point, while we return for a few moments to say a little more of the fortunes of Madame de Frontignac, whom we left waiting with impatience for the termination of the conversation between Mary and Burr.

"*Enfin, chère Sybille,*" said Madame de Frontignac, when Mary came out of the room, with her cheeks glowing and her eye flashing with a still unsubdued light, "*te voilà encore!* What did he say, *mimi?*—did he ask for me?"

"Yes," said Mary, "he asked for you."

"What did you tell him?"

"I told him that you wished me to excuse you."

"How did he look then?—did he look surprised?"

"A good deal so, I thought," said Mary.

"*Allons, mimi,*—tell me all you said, and all he said."

"Oh," said Mary, "I am the worst person in the world; in fact, I cannot remember anything that I have said; but I told him that he must leave you, and never see you any more."

"Oh, *mimi,* never!"

Madame de Frontignac sat down on the side of the bed with such a look of utter despair as went to Mary's heart.

"You know that it is best, Virginie; do you not?"

"Oh, yes, I know it; *mais pourtant, c'est dur comme la mort.* Ah, well, what shall Virginie do now?"

"You have your husband," said Mary.

"*Je ne l'aime point,*" said Madame de Frontignac.

"Yes, but he is a good and honorable man, and you should love him."

"Love is not in our power," said Madame de Frontignac.

"Not every kind of love," said Mary, "but some kinds. If you have a kind, indulgent friend who protects you and cares for you, you can be grateful to him, you can try to make him happy, and in time you may come to love him very much. He is a thousand times nobler man, if what you say is true, than the one who has injured you so."

"Oh, Mary!" said Madame de Frontignac, "there are some cases where we find it too easy to love our enemies."

"More than that," said Mary; "I believe, that, if you go on patiently in the way of duty, and pray daily to God, He will at last take out of your heart this painful love, and give you a true and healthy one. As you say, such feelings are very sweet and noble; but they are not the only ones we have to live by;—we can find happiness in duty, in self-sacrifice, in calm, sincere, honest friendship. That is what you can feel for your husband."

"Your words cool me," said Madame de Frontignac; "thou art a sweet snow-maiden, and my heart is hot and tired. I like to feel thee in my arms," she said, putting her arms around Mary, and resting her head upon her shoulder. "Talk to me so every day, and read me good cool verses out of that beautiful Book, and perhaps by-and-by I shall grow still and quiet like you."

Thus Mary soothed her friend; but every few days this soothing had to be done over, as long as Burr remained in Newport. When he was finally gone, she grew more calm. The simple, homely ways of the cottage, the healthful routine of daily domestic toils, into which she delighted to enter, brought refreshment to her spirit. That fine tact and exquisite social sympathy, which distinguish the French above other nations, caused her at once to enter into the spirit of the life in which she moved; so that she no longer shocked any one's religious feelings by acts forbidden by the Puritan idea of Sunday, or failed in any of the exterior proprieties of religious life. She also read and studied with avidity the English Bible, which came to her with the novelty of a wholly new book in a new language; nor was she without a certain artistic appreciation of the austere precision and gravity of the religious life by which she was surrounded.

"It is sublime, but a little *glaciale*, like the Alps," she sometimes said to Mary and Mrs. Marvyn, when speaking of it; "but then," she added, playfully, "there are the flowers,—*les roses des Alpes,*— and the air is very strengthening, and it is near to heaven,—*faut avouer.*"

We have shown how she appeared to the eye of New England life; it may not be uninteresting to give a letter to one of her friends, which showed how the same appeared to her. It was not a friend with whom she felt on such terms, that her intimacy with Burr would appear at all in the correspondence.

"You behold me, my charming Gabrielle, quite pastoral, recruiting from the dissipations of my Philadelphia life in a quiet cottage, with most worthy, excellent people, whom I have learned to love very much. They are good and true, as pious as the saints themselves, although they do not belong to the Church,—a thing which I am sorry for; but then let us hope, that, if the world is wide, heaven is wider, and that all worthy people will find room at last. This is Virginie's own little, pet, private heresy; and when I tell it to the Abbé, he only smiles, and so I think, somehow, that it is not so very bad as it might be.

"We have had a very gay life in Philadelphia, and now I am growing tired of the world, and think I shall retire to my cheese, like Lafontaine's rat.

"These people in the country here in America have a character quite their own, very different from the life of cities, where one sees, for the most part, only a continuation of the forms of good society which exist in the Old World.

"In the country, these people seem simple, grave, severe, always industrious, and, at first, cold and reserved in their manners towards each other, but with great warmth of heart. They are all obedient to the word of their minister, who lives among them just like any other man, and marries and has children.

"Everything in their worship is plain and austere; their churches are perfectly desolate; they have no chants, no pictures, no carvings,—only a most disconsolate, bare-looking building, where they meet together, and sing one or two hymns, and the minister makes one or two prayers, all out of his own thoughts, and then gives them a long, long discourse about things which I cannot understand enough English to comprehend.

"There is a very beautiful, charming young girl here, the

daughter of my hostess, who is as lovely and as saintly as St. Catharine, and has such a genius for religion, that, if she had been in our Church, she would certainly have been made a saint.

"Her mother is a good, worthy matron; and the good priest lives in the family. I think he is a man of very sublime religion, as much above this world as a great mountain; but he has the true sense of liberty and fraternity; for he has dared to oppose with all his might this detestable and cruel trade in poor negroes, which makes us, who are so proud of the example of America in asserting the rights of men, so ashamed for her inconsistencies.

"Well, now, there is a little romance getting up in the cottage; for the good priest has fixed his eyes on the pretty saint, and discovered, what he must be blind not to see, that she is very lovely,—and so, as he can marry, he wants to make her his wife; and her mamma, who adores him as if he were God, is quite set upon it. The sweet Marie, however, has had a lover of her own in her little heart, a beautiful young man, who went to sea, as heroes always do, to seek his fortune. And the cruel sea has drowned him; and the poor little saint has wept and prayed, till she is so thin and sweet and mournful that it makes one's heart ache to see her smile. In our Church, Gabrielle, she would have gone into a convent; but she makes a vocation of her daily life, and goes round the house so sweetly, doing all the little work that is to be done, as sacredly as the nuns pray at the altar. For you must know, here in New England, the people, for the most part, keep no servants, but perform all the household work themselves, with no end of spinning and sewing besides. It is the true Arcadia, where you find cultivated and refined people busying themselves with the simplest toils. For these people are well-read and well-bred, and truly ladies in all things. And so my little Marie and I, we feed the hens and chickens together, and we search for eggs in the hay in the barn. And they have taught me to spin at their great wheel, and at a little one too, which makes a noise like the humming of a bee.

"But where am I? Oh, I was telling about the romance. Well, so the good priest has proposed for my Marie, and the dear little soul has accepted him as the nun accepts the veil;

for she only loves him filially and religiously. And now they are going on, in their way, with preparations for the wedding. They had what they call 'a quilting' here the other night, to prepare the bride's quilt,—and all the friends in the neighborhood came;—it was very amusing to see.

"The morals of this people are so austere, that young men and girls are allowed the greatest freedom. They associate and talk freely together, and the young men walk home alone with the girls after evening parties. And most generally, the young people, I am told, arrange their marriages among themselves before the consent of the parents is asked. This is very strange to us. I must not weary you, however, with the details. I watch my little romance daily, and will let you hear further as it progresses.

"With a thousand kisses, I am, ever, your loving
"Virginie."

XXXIV.

Consultations and Confidences

MEANWHILE, the wedding-preparations were going on at the cottage with that consistent vigor with which Yankee people always drive matters when they know precisely what they are about.

The wedding-day was definitely fixed for the first of August; and each of the two weeks between had its particular significance and value precisely marked out and arranged in Mrs. Katy Scudder's comprehensive and systematic schemes.

It was settled that the newly wedded pair were, for a while at least, to reside at the cottage. It might have been imagined, therefore, that no great external changes were in contemplation; but it is astonishing, the amount of discussion, the amount of advising, consulting, and running to and fro, which can be made to result out of an apparently slight change in the relative position of two people in the same house.

Dr. Hopkins really opened his eyes with calm amazement. Good, modest soul! he had never imagined himself the hero of so much preparation. From morning to night, he heard his name constantly occurring in busy consultations that seemed to be going on between Miss Prissy and Mrs. Deacon Twitchel and Mrs. Scudder and Mrs. Jones, and quietly wondered what they could have so much more than usual to say about him. For a while it seemed to him that the whole house was about to be torn to pieces. He was even requested to step out of his study, one day, into which immediately entered, in his absence, two of the most vigorous women of the parish, who proceeded to uttermost measures,—first pitching everything into pi, so that the Doctor, who returned disconsolately to look for a book, at once gave up himself and his system of divinity as entirely lost, until assured by one of the ladies, in a condescending manner, that he knew nothing about the matter, and that, if he would return after half a day, he would find everything right again,—a declaration in which he tried to have unlimited faith, and which made him feel the advantage of a mind accustomed to believing in mysteries. And it is to be remarked, that on his return he actually found his table in most perfect order, with not a single one of his papers missing; in fact, to his ignorant eye the room looked exactly as it did before; and when Miss Prissy eloquently demonstrated to him, that every inch of that paint had been scrubbed, and the windows taken out, and washed inside and out, and rinsed through three waters, and that the curtains had been taken down, and washed, and put through a blue water, and starched, and ironed, and put up again,—he only innocently wondered, in his ignorance, what there was in a man's being married that made all these ceremonies necessary. But the Doctor was a wise man, and in cases of difficulty kept his mind to himself; and therefore he only informed these energetic practitioners that he was extremely obliged to them, accepting it by simple faith,—an example which we recommend to all good men in similar circumstances.

The house throughout was subjected to similar renovation. Everything in every chest or box was vigorously pulled out and hung out on lines in the clothes-yard to air; for when once the spirit of enterprise has fairly possessed a group of women, it assumes the form of a "prophetic fury," and carries them beyond themselves. Let not any ignorant mortal of the masculine gender, at such hours, rashly dare to question the promptings of the genius that inspires them. Spite of all the treatises that have lately appeared, to demonstrate that there are no particular inherent diversities between men and women, we hold to the opinion that one thorough season of house-cleaning is sufficient to prove the existence of awful and mysterious difference between the sexes, and of subtile and reserved forces in the female line, before which the lords of creation can only veil their faces with a discreet reverence, as our Doctor has done.

In fact, his whole deportment on the occasion was characterized by humility so edifying as really to touch the hearts of the whole synod of matrons; and Miss Prissy rewarded him by declaring impressively her opinion, that he was worthy to have a voice in the choosing of the wedding-dress; and she actually swooped him up, just in a very critical part of a distinction between natural and moral ability, and conveyed him bodily, as fairy sprites knew how to convey the most ponderous of mortals, into the best room, where three specimens of brocade lay spread out upon a table for inspection.

Mary stood by the side of the table, her pretty head bent reflectively downward, her cheek just resting upon the tip of one of her fingers, as she stood looking thoughtfully *through* the brocades at something deeper that seemed to lie under them; and when the Doctor was required to give judgment on the articles, it was observed by the matrons that his large blue eyes were resting upon Mary, with an expression that almost glorified his face; and it was not until his elbow was repeatedly shaken by Miss Prissy, that he gave a sudden start, and fixed his attention, as was requested, upon the silks. It had been one of Miss Prissy's favorite theories, that *"that dear blessed man had taste enough, if he would only give his mind to things"*; and, in fact, the Doctor rather verified the remark on the present occasion, for he looked very conscientiously and soberly at the silks, and even handled them cautiously and respectfully with his fingers, and listened with grave attention to all that Miss Prissy told him of their price and properties, and then laid his finger down on one whose snow-white ground was embellished with a pattern representing lillies of the valley on a background of green leaves. "This is the one," he said, with an air of decision; and then he looked at Mary, and smiled, and a murmur of universal approbation broke out.

"Il a de la délicatesse," said Madame de Frontignac, who had been watching this scene with bright, amused eyes,—while a chorus of loud acclamations, in which Miss Prissy's voice took the lead, conveyed to the innocent-minded Doctor the idea, that in some mysterious way he had distinguished himself in the eyes of his feminine friends; whereat he retired to his study slightly marvelling, but on the whole well pleased, as men generally are when they do better than they expect; and Miss Prissy, turning out all profaner persons from the apartment, held a solemn consultation, to which only Mary, Mrs. Scudder, and Madame de Frontignac were admitted. For it is to be observed that the latter had risen daily and hourly in

Miss Prissy's esteem, since her entrance into the cottage; and she declared, that, if she only would give her a few hints, she didn't believe but that she could make that dress look just like a Paris one; and rather intimated that in such a case she might almost be ready to resign all mortal ambitions.

The afternoon of this day, just at that cool hour when the clock ticks so quietly in a New England kitchen, and everything is so clean and put away that there seems to be nothing to do in the house, Mary sat quietly down in her room to hem a ruffle. Everybody had gone out of the house on various errands. The Doctor, with implicit faith, had surrendered himself to Mrs. Scudder and Miss Prissy, to be conveyed up to Newport, and attend to various appointments in relation to his outer man, which he was informed would be indispensable in the forthcoming solemnities. Madame de Frontignac had also gone to spend the day with some of her Newport friends. And Mary, quite well pleased with the placid and orderly stillness which reigned through the house, sat pleasantly murmuring a little tune to her sewing, when suddenly the trip of a very brisk foot was heard in the kitchen, and Miss Cerinthy Ann Twitchel made her appearance at the door, her healthy glowing cheek wearing a still brighter color from the exercise of a three-mile walk in a July day.

"Why, Cerinthy," said Mary, "how glad I am to see you!"

"Well," said Cerinthy, "I have been meaning to come down all this week, but there's so much to do in haying-time,—but to-day I told mother I *must* come. I brought these down," she said, unfolding a dozen snowy damask napkins, "that I spun myself, and was thinking of you almost all the while I spun them, so I suppose they aren't quite so wicked as they might be."

We will observe here, that Cerinthy Ann, in virtue of having a high stock of animal spirits and great fulness of physical vigor, had very small proclivities towards the unseen and spiritual, but still always indulged a secret resentment at being classed as a sinner above many others, who, as church-members, made such professions, and were, as she remarked, "not a bit better than she was." She had always, however, cherished an unbounded veneration for Mary, and had made her the confidante of most of her important secrets. It soon became very evident that she had come with one on her mind now.

"Don't you want to come and sit out in the lot?" she said, after sitting awhile, twirling her bonnet-strings with the air of one who has something to say and doesn't know exactly how to begin upon it.

Mary cheerfully gathered up her thread, scissors, and ruffling, and the two stepped over the window-sill, and soon found themselves seated cozily under the boughs of a large apple-tree, whose descending branches, meeting the tops of the high grass all around, formed a seclusion as perfect as heart could desire.

They sat down, pushing away a place in the grass; and Cerinthy Ann took off her bonnet, and threw it among the clover, exhibiting to view her black hair, always trimly arranged in shining braids, except where some glossy curls fell over the rich high color of her cheeks. Something appeared to discompose her this afternoon. There were those evident signs of a consultation impending, which, to an experienced eye, are as unmistakable as the coming up of a shower in summer.

Cerinthy began by passionately demolishing several heads of clover, remarking, as she did so, that she "didn't see, for her part, how Mary could keep so calm when things were coming so near." And as Mary answered to this only with a quiet smile, she broke out again:—

"I don't see, for my part, how a young girl *could* marry a minister, anyhow; but then I think *you* are just cut out for it. But what would anybody say, if *I* should do such a thing?"

"I don't know," said Mary, innocently.

"Well, I suppose everybody would hold up their hands; and yet, if I *do* say it myself,"—she added, coloring,—"there are not many girls who could make a better minister's wife than I could, if I had a mind to try."

"That I am sure of," said Mary, warmly.

"I guess you are the only one that ever thought so," said Cerinthy, giving an impatient toss. "There's father and mother all the while mourning over me; and yet I don't see but what I do pretty much all that is done in the house, and they say I am a great comfort in a temporal point of view. But, oh, the groanings and the sighings that there are over me! I don't think it is pleasant to know that your best friends are thinking such awful things about you, when you are working your fingers off to help them. It is kind o' discouraging, but I don't know what to do about it;"—and for a few moments Cerinthy sat demolishing buttercups, and throwing them up in the air till her shiny black head was covered with golden flakes, while her cheeks grew redder with something that she was going to say next.

"Now, Mary, there is *that creature*. Well, you know, he won't take '*No*' for an answer. What shall I do?"

"Suppose, then, you try '*Yes*,'" said Mary, rather archly.

"Oh, pshaw! Mary Scudder, you know better than that, now. I look like it, don't I?"

"Why, yes," said Mary, looking at Cerinthy, deliberately; "on the whole, I think you do."

"Well! one thing I must say," said Cerinthy,—"I can't see what *he* finds in me. I think he is a thousand times too good for me. Why, you have no idea, Mary, how I *have* plagued him. I believe that man *really is a Christian*," she added, while something like a penitent tear actually glistened in those sharp, saucy, black eyes. "Besides," she added, "I have told him everything I could think of to discourage him. I told him that I had a bad temper, and didn't believe the doctrines, and couldn't promise that I ever should; and after all, that creature keeps right on, and I don't know what to tell him."

"Well," said Mary, mildly, "do you think you really love him?"

"Love him?" said Cerinthy, giving a great flounce, "to be sure I don't! Catch me loving any man! I told him last night I didn't; but it didn't do a bit of good. I used to think that man was bashful, but I declare I have altered my mind; he will talk and talk till I don't know what to do. I tell you, Mary, he talks beautifully, too, sometimes."

Here Cerinthy turned quickly away, and began reaching passionately after clover-heads. After a few moments, she resumed:—

"The fact is, Mary, that man *needs* somebody to take care of him; for he never thinks of himself. They say he has got the consumption; but he hasn't, any more than I have. It is just the way he neglects himself,—preaching, talking, and visiting; nobody to take care of him, and see to his clothes, and nurse him up when he gets a little hoarse and run down. Well, I suppose if I *am* unregenerate, I do know how to keep things in order; and if I should keep *such* a man's soul in his body, I should be doing some good in the world; because, if ministers don't live, of course they can't convert anybody. Just think of his saying that I could be a comfort to *him*! I told him that it was perfectly ridiculous. 'And besides,' says I, 'what will everybody think?' I thought that I had really talked him out of the notion of it last night; but there he was in again this morning, and told me he had derived great encouragement from what I had said. Well, the poor man really is lonesome,—his mother's dead, and he hasn't any sisters. I asked him why he didn't go and take Miss Olladine Slocum: everybody says she would make a first-rate minister's wife."

"Well, and what did he say to that?" said Mary.

"Well, something really silly,—about my looks," said Cerinthy, looking down.

Mary looked up, and remarked the shining black hair, the long dark lashes lying down over the glowing cheek, where two arch dimples were nestling, and said, quietly,—

"Probably he is a man of taste, Cerinthy; I advise you to leave the matter entirely to his judgment."

"You don't, really, Mary!" said the damsel, looking up. "Don't you think it would injure *him*, if I should?"

"I think not, materially," said Mary.

"Well," said Cerinthy, rising, "the men will be coming home from the mowing, before I get home, and want their supper. Mother has got one of her headaches on this afternoon, so I can't stop any longer. There isn't a soul in the house knows where anything is, when I am gone. If I should ever take it into my head to go off, I don't know what would become of father and mother. I was telling mother, the other day, that I thought unregenerate folks were of some use in *this* world, any way."

"Does your mother know anything about it?" said Mary.

"Oh, as to mother, I believe she has been hoping and praying about it these three months. She thinks that I am such a desperate case, it is the only way I am to be brought in, as she calls it. That's what set me against him at first; but the fact is, if girls will let a man argue with them, he always contrives to get the best of it. I am kind of provoked about it, too. But, mercy on us! he is so meek, there is no use of getting provoked at him. Well, I guess I will go home and think about it."

As she turned to go, she looked really pretty. Her long lashes were wet with a twinkling moisture, like meadow-grass after a shower; and there was a softened, childlike expression stealing over the careless gayety of her face.

Mary put her arms round her with a gentle caressing movement, which the other returned with a hearty embrace. They stood locked in each other's arms,—the glowing, vigorous, strong-hearted girl, with that pale, spiritual face resting on her breast, as when the morning, songful and radiant, clasps the pale silver moon to her glowing bosom.

"Look here now, Mary," said Cerinthy; "your folks are all gone. You may as well walk with me. It's pleasant now."

"Yes, I will," said Mary; "wait a minute, till I get my bonnet."

In a few moments the two girls were walking together in one of those little pasture foot-tracks which run so cozily among huckleberry and juniper bushes, while Cerinthy eagerly pursued the subject she could not leave thinking of. Their path now wound over high ground that overlooked the distant sea, now lost itself in little copses of cedar and pitch-pine, and now there came on the air the pleasant breath of new hay, which mowers were harvesting in adjoining meadows.

They walked on and on, as girls will; because, when a young lady has once fairly launched into the enterprise of telling another all that *he* said, and just how *he* looked, for the last three months, walks are apt to be indefinitely extended.

Mary was, besides, one of the most seductive little confidantes in the world. She was so pure from selfishness, so heartily and innocently interested in what another was telling her, that people in talking with her found the subject constantly increasing in interest,—although, if they really had been called upon afterwards to state the exact portion in words which she added to the conversation, they would have been surprised to find it so small.

In fact, before Cerinthy Ann had quite finished her confessions, they were more than a mile from the cottage, and Mary began to think of returning, saying that her mother would wonder where she was, when she came home.

XXXV.

Old Love and New Duty

THE sun was just setting, and the whole air and sea seemed flooded with rosy rays. Even the crags and rocks of the sea-shore took purple and lilac tints, and savins and junipers, had a painter been required to represent them, would have been found not without a suffusion of the same tints. And through the tremulous rosy sea of the upper air, the silver full-moon looked out like some calm superior presence which waits only for the flush of a temporary excitement to die away, to make its tranquillizing influence felt.

Mary, as she walked homeward with this dreamy light around her, moved with a slower step than when borne along by the vigorous arm and determined motion of her young friend.

It is said that a musical sound uttered with decision by one instrument always makes the corresponding chord of another vibrate; and Mary felt, as she left her positive but warm-hearted friend, a plaintive vibration of something in her own self, of which she was conscious her calm friendship for her future husband had no part. She fell into one of those reveries which she thought she had forever forbidden to herself, and there rose before her mind the picture of a marriage-ceremony,—but the eyes of the bridegroom were dark, and his curls were clustering in raven ringlets, and her hand throbbed in his as it had never throbbed in any other.

It was just as she was coming out of a little grove of cedars, where the high land overlooks the sea, and the dream which came to her overcame her with a vague and yearning sense of pain. Suddenly she heard footsteps behind her, and some one said, "Mary!" It was spoken in a choked voice, as one speaks in the crises of a great emotion; and she turned and saw those very eyes, that very hair, yes, and the cold little hand throbbed with that very throb in that strong, living, manly hand; and, whether in the body or out of the body God knoweth, she felt herself borne in those arms, and words that spoke themselves in her inner heart, words profaned by being repeated, were on her ear.

"Oh! is this a dream? is this a dream? James! are we in heaven? Oh, I have lived through such an agony! I have been so worn out! Oh, I thought you never would come!" And then the eyes closed, and heaven and earth faded away together in a trance of blissful rest.

But it was no dream; for an hour later you might have seen a manly form sitting in that self-same place, bearing in his arms a pale figure which he cherished as tenderly as a mother her babe. And they were talking together,—talking in low tones; and in all this wide universe neither of them knew or felt anything but the great joy of being thus side by side.

They spoke of love mightier than death, which many waters cannot quench. They spoke of yearnings, each for the other,—of longing prayers,—of hopes deferred,—and then of this great joy,—for *one* had hardly yet returned to the visible world.

Scarce wakened from deadly faintness, she had not come back fully to the realm of life,—only to that of love,—to love which death cannot quench. And therefore it was, that, without knowing that she spoke, she had said all, and compressed the history of those three years into one hour.

But at last, thoughtful of her health, provident of her weakness, he rose up and passed his arm around her to convey her home. And as he did so, he spoke *one* word that broke the whole charm.

"You will allow me, Mary, the right of a future husband, to watch over your life and health."

Then came back the visible world,—recollection, consciousness, and the great battle of duty,—and Mary drew away a little, and said,—

"Oh, James, you are too late! that can never be!"

He drew back from her.

"Mary, are you married?"

"Before God, I am," she said. "My word is pledged. I cannot retract it. I have suffered a good man to place his whole faith upon it,—a man who loves me with his whole soul."

"But, Mary, you do not love *him*. *That* is impossible!" said

James, holding her off from him, and looking at her with an agonized eagerness. "After what you have just said, it is not possible."

"Oh, James! I am sure I don't know what I have said,—it was all so sudden, and I didn't know what I was saying,—but things that I must never say again. The day is fixed for next week. It is all the same as if you had found me his wife."

"Not quite," said James, his voice cutting the air with a decided manly ring. "I have some words to say to that yet."

"Oh, James, will you be selfish? will *you* tempt me to do a mean, dishonorable thing? to be false to my word deliberately given?"

"But," said James, eagerly, "you know, Mary, you *never* would have given it, if you had known that I was living."

"That is true, James; but I *did* give it. I have suffered him to build all his hopes of life upon it. I *beg* you not to tempt me,—help me to do right!"

"But, Mary, did you not get my letter?"

"Your letter?"

"Yes,—that long letter that I wrote you."

"I never got any letter, James."

"Strange!" he said. "No wonder it seems sudden to you!"

"Have you seen your mother?" said Mary, who was conscious this moment only of a dizzy instinct to turn the conversation from where she felt too weak to bear it.

"No; do you suppose I should see anybody before you?"

"Oh, then, you must go to her!" said Mary. "Oh, James, you don't know how she has suffered!"

They were drawing near to the cottage-gate.

"Do, pray!" said Mary. "Go, hurry to your mother! Don't be too sudden, either, for she's very weak; she is almost worn out with sorrow. Go, my dear brother! *Dear* you always will be to me."

James helped her into the house, and they parted. All the house was yet still. The open kitchen-door let in a sober square of moonlight on the floor. The very stir of the leaves on the trees could be heard. Mary went into her little room, and threw herself upon the bed, weak, weary, yet happy,—for deep and high above all other feeling was the great relief that *he* was living still. After a little while she heard the rattling of the wagon, and then the quick patter of Miss Prissy's feet, and her mother's considerate tones, and the Doctor's grave voice,—and quite unexpectedly to herself, she was shocked to find herself turning with an inward shudder from the idea of meeting him. "How very wicked!" she thought,— "how ungrateful!"—and she prayed that God would give her strength to check the first rising of such feelings.

Then there was her mother, so ignorant and innocent, busy putting away baskets of things that she had bought in provision for the wedding-ceremony.

Mary almost felt as if she had a guilty secret. But when she looked back upon the last two hours, she felt no wish to take them back again. Two little hours of joy and rest they had been,—so pure, so perfect! she thought God must have given them to her as a keepsake to remind her of His love, and to strengthen her in the way of duty.

Some will, perhaps, think it an unnatural thing that Mary should have regarded her pledge to the Doctor as of so absolute and binding force; but they must remember the rigidity of her education. Self-denial and self-sacrifice had been the daily bread of her life. Every prayer, hymn, and sermon, from her childhood, had warned her to distrust her inclinations, and regard her feelings as traitors. In particular had she been brought up to regard the sacredness of a promise with a superstitious tenacity; and in this case the promise involved so deeply the happiness of a friend whom she had loved and revered all her life, that she never thought of any way of escape from it. She had been taught that there was no feeling so strong but that it might be immediately repressed at the call of duty; and if the thought arose to her of this great love to another, she immediately answered it by saying, "How would it have been if I had been married? As I could have overcome then, so I can now."

Mrs. Scudder came into her room with a candle in her hand, and Mary, accustomed to read the expression of her mother's face, saw at a glance a visible discomposure there. She held the light so that it shone upon Mary's face.

"Are you asleep?" she said.

"No, mother."

"Are you unwell?"

"No, mother,—only a little tired."

Mrs. Scudder set down the candle, and shut the door, and, after a moment's hesitation, said,—

"My daughter, I have some news to tell you, which I want you to prepare your mind for. Keep yourself quite quiet."

"Oh, mother!" said Mary, stretching out her hands towards her, "I know it. James has come home."

"How did you hear?" said her mother, with astonishment.

"I have seen him, mother."

Mrs. Scudder's countenance fell.

"Where?"

"I went to walk home with Cerinthy Twitchel, and as I was coming back he came up behind me, just at Savin Rock."

Mrs. Scudder sat down on the bed and took her daughter's hand.

"I trust, my dear child," she said. She stopped.

"I think I know what you are going to say, mother. It is a great joy, and a great relief; but of course I shall be true to my engagement with the Doctor."

Mrs. Scudder's face brightened.

"That is my own daughter! I might have known that you would do so. You would not, certainly, so cruelly disappoint a noble man who has set his whole faith upon you."

"No, mother, I shall not disappoint him. I told James that I should be true to my word."

"He will probably see the justice of it," said Mrs. Scudder, in that easy tone with which elderly people are apt to dispose of the feelings of young persons. "Perhaps it may be something of a trial at first."

Mary looked at her mother with incredulous blue eyes. The idea that feelings which made her hold her breath when she thought of them could be so summarily disposed of! She turned her face wearily to the wall, with a deep sigh, and said,—

"After all, mother, it is mercy enough and comfort enough to think that he is living. Poor Cousin Ellen, too,—what a relief to her! It is like life from the dead. Oh, I shall be happy enough; no fear of that!"

"And you know," said Mrs. Scudder, "that there has never existed any engagement of any kind between you and James.

He had no right to found any expectations on anything you ever told him."

"That is true also, mother," said Mary. "I had never thought of such a thing as marriage, in relation to James."

"Of course," pursued Mrs. Scudder, "he will always be to you as a near friend."

Mary assented.

"There is but a week now, before your wedding," continued Mrs. Scudder; "and I think Cousin James, if he is reasonable, will see the propriety of your mind being kept as quiet as possible. I heard the news this afternoon in town," pursued Mrs. Scudder, "from Captain Staunton, and, by a curious coincidence, I received from him this letter from James, which came from New York by post. The brig that brought it must have been delayed out of the harbor."

"Oh, please, mother, give it to me!" said Mary, rising up with animation; "he mentioned having sent me one."

"Perhaps you had better wait till morning," said Mrs. Scudder; "you are tired and excited."

"Oh, mother, I think I shall be more composed when I know all that is in it," said Mary, still stretching out her hand.

"Well, my daughter, you are the best judge," said Mrs. Scudder; and she set down the candle on the table, and left Mary alone.

It was a very thick letter of many pages, dated in Canton, and ran as follows:—

XXXVI.

Jacob's Vow

"M Y DEAREST MARY:—"I have lived through many wonderful scenes since I saw you last. My life has been so adventurous, that I scarcely know myself when I think of it. But it is not of *that* I am going now to write. I have written all that to mother, and she will show it to you. But since I parted from you, there has been another history going on within me; and that is what I wish to make you understand, if I can.

"It seems to me that I have been a changed man from that afternoon when I came to your window, and where we parted. I have never forgot how you looked then, nor what you said. Nothing in my life ever had such an effect upon me. I thought that I loved you before; but I went away feeling that love was something so deep and high and sacred, that I was not worthy to name it to you. I cannot think of the man in the world who is worthy of what you said you felt for me.

"From *that* hour there was a new purpose in my soul,—a purpose which has led me upward ever since. I thought to myself in this way: 'There is some secret source from whence this inner life springs,'—and I knew that it was connected with the Bible which you gave me; and so I thought I would read it carefully and deliberately, to see what I could make of it.

"I began with the beginning. It impressed me with a sense of something quaint and strange,—something rather fragmentary; and yet there were spots all along that went right to the heart of a man who had to deal with life and things as I did. Now I must say that the Doctor's preaching, as I told you, never impressed me much in any way. I could not make any connection between it and the men I had to manage and the things I had to do in my daily life. But there were things in the Bible that struck me otherwise. There was *one* passage in particular, and that was where Jacob started off from all his friends to go off and seek his fortune in a strange country, and laid down to sleep all alone in the field, with only a stone

838

for his pillow. It seemed to me exactly the image of what
every young man is like, when he leaves his home and goes
out to shift for himself in this hard world. I tell you, Mary,
that one man alone on the great ocean of life feels himself a
very weak thing. We are held up by each other more than we
know till we go off by ourselves into this great experiment.
Well, there he was as lonesome as *I* upon the deck of my
ship. And so lying with the stone under his head, he saw a
ladder in his sleep between him and heaven, and angels going
up and down. That was a sight which came to the very point
of his necessities. He saw that there was a way between him
and God, and that there were those above who did care for
him, and who could come to him to help him. Well, so the
next morning he got up, and set up the stone to mark the
place; and it says Jacob vowed a vow, saying, 'If God will be
with me, and will keep me in this way that I go, and will give
me bread to eat and raiment to put on, so that I come again
to my father's house in peace, *then* shall the Lord be my
God.' Now *there* was something that looked to me like a tangible foundation to begin upon.

"If I understand Dr. Hopkins, I believe he would have
called that all selfishness. At first sight it does look a little so;
but then I thought of it in this way: 'Here he was all alone.
God was entirely invisible to him; and how could he feel certain that He really existed, unless he could come into some
kind of connection with Him? the point that he wanted to be
sure of, more than merely to know that there was a God who
made the world;—he wanted to know whether He cared anything about men, and would do anything to help them. And
so, in fact, it was saying, 'If there is a God who interests Himself at all in me, and will be my Friend and Protector, I will
obey Him, so far as I can find out His will.'

"I thought to myself, 'This is the great experiment, and I
will try it.' I made in my heart exactly the same resolution,
and just quietly resolved to assume for a while as a fact that
there *was* such a God, and, whenever I came to a place where
I could not help myself, just to ask His help honestly in so
many words, and see what would come of it.

"Well, as I went on reading through the Old Testament, I
was more and more convinced that all the men of those times

had tried this experiment, and found that it would bear them; and in fact, I did begin to find, in my own experience, a great many things happening so remarkably that I could not but think that *Somebody* did attend even to my prayers,—I began to feel a trembling faith that *Somebody* was guiding me, and that the events of my life were not happening by accident, but working themselves out by His will.

"Well, as I went on in this way, there were other and higher thoughts kept rising in my mind. I wanted to be better than I was. I had a sense of a life much nobler and purer than anything I had ever lived, that I wanted to come up to. But in the world of men, as I found it, such feelings are always laughed down as romantic, and impracticable, and impossible. But about this time I began to read the New Testament, and then the idea came to me, that the same Power that helped me in the lower sphere of life would help me carry out those higher aspirations. Perhaps the Gospels would not have interested me so much, if I had begun with them first; but my Old Testament life seemed to have schooled me, and brought me to a place where I wanted something higher; and I began to notice that my prayers now were more that I might be noble, and patient, and self-denying, and constant in my duty, than for any other kind of help. And then I understood what met me in the very first of Matthew: 'Thou shalt call his name Jesus, for he shall save his people from their sins.'

"I began now to live a new life,—a life in which I felt myself coming into sympathy with you; for, Mary, when I began to read the Gospels, I took knowledge of you, that you had been with Jesus.

"The crisis of my life was that dreadful night of the shipwreck. It was as dreadful as the Day of Judgment. No words of mine can describe to you what I felt when I knew that our rudder was gone, and saw those hopeless rocks before us. What I felt for our poor men! But, in the midst of it all, the words came into my mind, 'And Jesus was in the hinder part of the ship asleep on a pillow,' and at once I felt He *was* there; and when the ship struck I was only conscious of an intense going out of my soul to Him, like Peter's when he threw himself from the ship to meet Him in the waters.

"I will not recapitulate what I have already written,—the wonderful manner in which I was saved, and in which friends and help and prosperity and worldly success came to me again, after life had seemed all lost; but now I am ready to return to my country, and I feel as Jacob did when he said, 'With my staff I passed over this Jordan, and now I am become two bands.'

"I do not need any arguments now to convince me that the Bible is from above. There is a great deal in it that I cannot understand, a great deal that seems to me inexplicable; but all I can say is, that I have tried its directions, and find that in my case they do work,—that it is a book that I can live by; and that is enough for me.

"And now, Mary, I am coming home again, quite another man from what I went out,—with a whole new world of thought and feeling in my heart, and a new purpose, by which, please God, I mean to shape my life. All this, under God, I owe to you; and if you will let me devote my whole life to you, it will be a small return for what you have done for me.

"You know I left you wholly free. Others must have seen your loveliness, and felt your worth; and you may have learnt to love some better man than me. But I know not what hope tells me that this will not be; and I shall find true what the Bible says of love, that 'many waters cannot quench it, nor floods drown.' In any case, I shall be always, from my very heart, yours, and yours only.

                                        "JAMES MARVYN."

Mary rose, after reading this letter, rapt into a divine state of exaltation,—the pure joy, in contemplating an infinite good to another, in which the question of self was utterly forgotten.

He was, then, what she had always hoped and prayed he would be, and she pressed the thought triumphantly to her heart. He was that true and victorious man, that Christian able to subdue life, and to show, in a perfect and healthy manly nature, a reflection of the image of the superhuman excellence. Her prayers that night were aspirations and praises, and she felt how possible it might be so to appropriate the good and the joy and the nobleness of others as to have in them an eternal and satisfying treasure. And with this came the dearer thought, that she, in her weakness and solitude, had been permitted to put her hand to the beginning of a work so noble. The consciousness of good done to an immortal spirit is wealth that neither life nor death can take away.

And so, having prayed, she lay down to that sleep which God giveth to his beloved.

XXXVII.

The Question of Duty

IT is a hard condition of our existence here, that every exaltation must have its depression. God will not let us have heaven here below, but only such glimpses and faint showings as parents sometimes give to children, when they show them beforehand the jewelry and pictures and stores of rare and curious treasures which they hold for the possession of their riper years. So it very often happens that the man who has gone to bed an angel, feeling as if all sin were forever vanquished, and he himself immutably grounded in love, may wake the next morning with a sick-headache and, if he be not careful, may scold about his breakfast like a miserable sinner.

We will not say that our dear little Mary rose in this condition next morning,—for, although she had the headache, she had one of those natures in which, somehow or other, the combative element seems to be left out, so that no one ever knew her to speak a fretful word. But still, as we have observed, she had the headache and the depression,—and there came the slow, creeping sense of waking up, through all her heart and soul, of a thousand, thousand things that could be said only to one person, and that person one that it would be temptation and danger to say them to.

She came out of her room to her morning work with a face resolved and calm, but expressive of languor, with slight signs of some inward struggle.

Madame de Frontignac, who had already heard the intelligence, threw two or three of her bright glances upon her at breakfast, and at once divined how the matter stood. She was of a nature so delicately sensitive to the most refined shades of honor, that she apprehended at once that there must be a conflict,—though, judging by her own impulsive nature, she made no doubt that all would at once go down before the mighty force of re-awakened love.

After breakfast she would insist upon following Mary

about through all her avocations. She possessed herself of a
towel, and would wipe the teacups and saucers, while Mary
washed. She clinked the glasses, and rattled the cups and
spoons, and stepped about as briskly as if she had two or
three breezes to carry her train, and chattered half English
and half French, for the sake of bringing into Mary's cheek
the shy, slow dimples that she liked to watch. But still Mrs.
Scudder was around, with an air as provident and forbidding
as that of a sitting hen who watches her nest; nor was it till
after all things had been cleared away in the house, and Mary
had gone up into her little attic to spin, that the long-sought
opportunity came of diving to the bottom of this mystery.

"*Enfin, Marie, nous voici!* Are you not going to tell me anything, when I have turned my heart out to you like a bag?
Chère enfant! how happy you must be!" she said, embracing
her.

"Yes, I am very happy," said Mary, with calm gravity.

"*Very happy!*" said Madame de Frontignac, mimicking her
manner. "Is that the way you American girls show it, when
you are very happy? Come, come, *ma belle!* tell little Virginie
something. Thou hast seen this hero, this wandering Ulysses.
He has come back at last; the tapestry will not be quite as
long as Penelope's? Speak to me of him. Has he beautiful
black eyes, and hair that curls like a grape-vine? Tell me, *ma
belle!*"

"I only saw him a little while," said Mary, "and I felt a
great deal more than I saw. He could not have been any
clearer to me than he always has been in my mind."

"But I think," said Madame de Frontignac, seating Mary,
as was her wont, and sitting down at her feet,—"I think you
are a little *triste* about this. Very likely you pity the good
priest. It is sad for him; but a good priest has the Church for
his bride, you know."

"You do not think," said Mary, speaking seriously, "that I
shall break my promise given before God to this good man?"

"*Mon Dieu, mon enfant!* you do not mean to marry the
priest, after all? *Quelle idée!*"

"But I *promised* him," said Mary.

Madame de Frontignac threw up her hands with an expression of vexation.

"What a pity, my little one, you are not in the True Church! Any good priest could dispense you from that."

"I do not believe," said Mary, "in any earthly power that can dispense us from solemn obligations which we have assumed before God, and on which we have suffered others to build the most precious hopes. If James had won the affections of some girl, thinking as I do, I should not think it right for him to leave her and come to me. The Bible says, that the just man is 'he that sweareth to his own hurt, and changeth not.'"

"*C'est le sublime de devoir!*" said Madame de Frontignac, who, with the airy frailty of her race never lost her appreciation of the fine points of anything that went on under her eyes. But, nevertheless, she was inwardly resolved, that, picturesque as this "sublime of duty" was, it must not be allowed to pass beyond the limits of a fine art, and so she recommenced.

"*Mais c'est absurde.* This beautiful young man, with his black eyes, and his curls,—a real hero,—a Theseus, Mary,— just come home from killing a Minotaur,—and loves you with his whole heart,—and this dreadful promise! Why, haven't you any sort of people in your Church that can unbind you from promises? I should think the good priest himself would do it!"

"Perhaps he would," said Mary, "if I should ask him; but that would be equivalent to a breach of it. Of course, no man would marry a woman that asked to be dispensed."

"You are an angel of delicacy, my child; *c'est admirable!* but, after all, Mary, this is not well. Listen now to me. You are a very sweet saint, and very strong in goodness. I think you must have a very strong angel that takes care of you. But think, *chère enfant*,—think what it is to marry one man, while you love another!"

"But I love the Doctor," said Mary, evasively.

"*Love!*" said Madame de Frontignac. "Oh, Marie! you may love him well, but you and I both know that there is something deeper than that. What will you *do* with this young man? Must he move away from this place, and not be with his poor mother any more? Or can you see him, and hear him, and be with him, after your marriage, and not feel that you love him more than your husband?"

"I should hope that God would help me to feel right," said Mary.

"I am very much afraid He will not, *ma chère*. I asked Him a great many times to help *me*, when I found how wrong it all was; and He did not. You remember what you told me the other day,—that, if I would do right, I must not *see* that man any more. You will have to ask him to go away from this place; you can never see him; for this love will never die till you die;—that you may be sure of. Is it wise? is it right, dear little one? *Must* he leave his home forever for you? or must you struggle always, and grow whiter and whiter, and fall away into heaven, like the moon this morning, and nobody know what is the matter? People will say you have the liver-complaint, or the consumption, or something. Nobody ever knows what we women die of."

Poor Mary's conscience was fairly posed. This appeal struck upon her sense of right as having its grounds. She felt inexpressibly confused and distressed.

"Oh, I wish somebody would tell me exactly what is right!" she said.

"Well, *I* will," said Madame de Frontignac. "Go down to the dear priest, and tell him the whole truth. My dear child, do you think, if he should ever find it out after your marriage, he would think you used him right?"

"And yet *mother* does not think so; mother does not wish me to tell him."

"*Pauvrette, toujours les mères!* Yes, it is always the mothers that stand in the way of the lovers. Why cannot she marry the priest herself?" she said between her teeth, and then looked up, startled and guilty, to see if Mary had heard her.

"I *cannot*," said Mary,—"I cannot go against my conscience, and my mother, and my best friend."

At this moment, the conference was cut short by Mrs. Scudder's provident footsteps on the garret-stairs. A vague suspicion of something French had haunted her during her dairy-work, and she resolved to come and put a stop to the interview, by telling Mary that Miss Prissy wanted her to come and be measured for the skirt of her dress.

Mrs. Scudder, by the use of that sixth sense peculiar to mothers, had divined that there had been some agitating conference, and, had she been questioned about it, her guesses as to what it might have been would probably have given no bad *résumé* of the real state of the case. She was inwardly resolved that there should be no more such for the present, and kept Mary employed about various matters relating to the dresses, so scrupulously that there was no opportunity for anything more of the sort that day.

In the evening James Marvyn came down, and was welcomed with the greatest demonstrations of joy by all but Mary, who sat distant and embarrassed, after the first salutations had passed.

The Doctor was innocently paternal; but we fear that on the part of the young man there was small reciprocation of the sentiments he expressed.

Miss Prissy, indeed, had had her heart somewhat touched, as good little women's hearts are apt to be by a true love-story, and had hinted something of her feelings to Mrs. Scudder, in a manner which brought such a severe rejoinder as quite humbled and abashed her, so that she coweringly took refuge under her former declaration, that, "to be sure, there couldn't be any man in the world better *worthy* of Mary than the Doctor," while still at her heart she was possessed with that troublesome preference for unworthy people which stands in the way of so many excellent things. But she went on vigorously sewing on the wedding-dress, and pursing up her small mouth into the most perfect and guarded expression of non-committal; though she said afterwards, "it went to her heart to see how that poor young man did look, sitting there just as noble and as handsome as a picture. She didn't see, for *her* part, how anybody's heart *could* stand it; though, to be sure, as Miss Scudder said, the poor Doctor ought to be thought about, dear blessed man! What a pity it was things *would* turn out so! Not that it was a pity that Jim came home,—that was a great providence,—but a pity they hadn't known about it sooner. Well, for her part, she didn't pretend to say; the path of duty did have a great many hard places in it."

As for James, during his interview at the cottage, he waited and tried in vain for one moment's private conversation. Mrs. Scudder was immovable in her motherly kindness, sitting there, smiling and chatting with him, but never stirring from her place by Mary.

Madame de Frontignac was out of all patience, and determined, in her small way, to do something to discompose the fixed state of things. So, retreating to her room, she contrived, in very desperation, to upset and break a water-pitcher, shrieking violently in French and English at the deluge which came upon the sanded floor and the little piece of carpet by the bedside.

What housekeeper's instincts are proof against the crash of breaking china?

Mrs. Scudder fled from her seat, followed by Miss Prissy.

"Ah! then and there was hurrying to and fro," while Mary sat quiet as a statue, bending over her sewing, and James, knowing that it must be now or never, was, like a flash, in the empty chair by her side, with his black moustache very near to the bent brown head.

"Mary," he said, "you *must* let me see you once more. All is not said, is it? Just hear me,—hear me once alone!"

"Oh, James, I am too weak!—I dare not!—I am afraid of myself!"

"You think," he said, "that you *must* take this course, because it is right. But *is* it right? Is it right to marry one man, when you love another better? I don't put this to your inclination, Mary,—I know it would be of no use,—I put it to your conscience."

"Oh, I was never so perplexed before!" said Mary. "I don't know what I *do* think. I must have time to reflect. And you,—oh, James!—you *must* let me do right! There will never be any happiness for me, if I do wrong,—nor for you, either."

All this while the sounds of running and hurrying in Madame de Frontignac's room had been unintermitted; and Miss Prissy, not without some glimmerings of perception, was holding tight on to Mrs. Scudder's gown, detailing to her a most capital receipt for mending broken china, the history of which she traced regularly through all the families in which she had ever worked, varying the details with small items of family history, and little incidents as to the births, marriages, and deaths of different people for whom it had been employed, with all the particulars of how, where, and when, so that the time of James for conversation was by this means indefinitely extended.

"Now," he said to Mary, "let me propose one thing. Let *me* go to the Doctor, and tell him the truth."

"James, it does not seem to me that I can. A friend who has been so considerate, so kind, so self-sacrificing and disinterested, and whom I have allowed to go on with this implicit faith in me so long. Should you, James, think of *yourself* only?"

"I do not, I trust, think of myself only," said James; "I hope that I am calm enough, and have a heart to think for others. But, I ask you, is it doing right to *him* to let him marry you in ignorance of the state of your feelings? Is it a kindness to a good and noble man to give yourself to him only seemingly, when the best and noblest part of your affections is gone wholly beyond your control? I am quite sure of *that*, Mary. I know you do love him very well,—that you would make a most true, affectionate, constant wife to him, but what I know you feel for me is something wholly out of your power to give to him,—is it not, now?"

"I think it is," said Mary, looking gravely and deeply thoughtful. "But then, James, I ask myself, 'What if this had happened a week hence?' My feelings would have been just the same, because they are feelings over which I have no more control than over my existence. I can only control the expression of them. But in *that* case you would not have asked me to break my marriage-vow; and why now shall I break a solemn vow deliberately made before God? If what I can give him will content him, and he never knows that which would give him pain, what wrong is done him?"

"I should think the deepest possible wrong done me," said James, "if, when I thought I had married a wife with a whole heart, I found that the greater part of it had been before that given to another. If you tell him, or if I tell him, or your mother,—who is the proper person,—and he chooses to hold you to your promise, then, Mary, I have no more to say. I shall sail in a few weeks again, and carry your image forever in my heart;—nobody can take that away; that dear shadow will be the only wife I shall ever know."

At this moment Miss Prissy came rattling along towards

the door, talking—we suspect designedly—on quite a high
key. Mary hastily said,—

"Wait, James,—let me think,—to-morrow is the Sabbath-
day. Monday I will send you word, or see you."

And when Miss Prissy returned into the best room, James
was sitting at one window and Mary at another,—he making
remarks, in a style of most admirable commonplace, on a
copy of Milton's "Paradise Lost," which he had picked up in
the confusion of the moment, and which, at the time Mrs.
Katy Scudder entered, he was declaring to be a most excellent
book,—a really, truly, valuable work.

Mrs. Scudder looked keenly from one to the other, and saw
that Mary's cheek was glowing like the deepest heart of a
pink shell, while, in all other respects, she was as cold and
calm. On the whole, she felt satisfied that no mischief had
been done.

We hope our readers will do Mrs. Scudder justice. It is true
that she yet wore on her third finger the marriage-ring of a
sailor lover, and his memory was yet fresh in her heart; but
even mothers who have married for love themselves somehow
so blend a daughter's existence with their own as to conceive
that she must marry their love, and not her own. Besides this,
Mrs. Scudder was an Old Testament woman, brought up
with that scrupulous exactitude of fidelity in relation to promises which would naturally come from familiarity with a book
in which covenant-keeping is represented as one of the highest attributes of Deity, and covenant-breaking as one of the
vilest sins of humanity. To break the word that had gone
forth out of one's mouth was to lose self-respect, and all claim
to the respect of others, and to sin against eternal rectitude.

As we have said before, it is almost impossible to make our
light-minded times comprehend the earnestness with which
those people lived. It was, in the beginning, no vulgar nor
mercenary ambition that made her seek the Doctor as a husband for her daughter. He was poor, and she had had offers
from richer men. He was often unpopular; but he was the
man in the world she most revered, the man she believed in
with the most implicit faith, the man who embodied her
highest ideas of the good; and therefore it was that she was
willing to resign her child to him.

As to James, she had felt truly sympathetic with his mother, and with Mary, in the dreadful hour when they supposed him lost; and had it not been for the great perplexity occasioned by his return, she would have received him, as a relative, with open arms. But now she felt it her duty to be on the defensive,—an attitude not the most favorable for cherishing pleasing associations in regard to another. She had read the letter giving an account of his spiritual experience with very sincere pleasure, as a good woman should, but not without an internal perception how very much it endangered her favorite plans. When Mary, however, had calmly reiterated her determination, she felt sure of her; for had she ever known her to say a thing she did not do?

The uneasiness she felt at present was not the doubt of her daughter's steadiness, but the fear that she might have been unsuitably harrassed or annoyed.

XXXVIII.

The Transfigured

THE next morning rose calm and fair. It was the Sabbath-day,—the last Sabbath in Mary's maiden life, if her promises and plans were fulfilled.

Mary dressed herself in white,—her hands trembling with unusual agitation, her sensitive nature divided between two opposing consciences and two opposing affections. Her devoted filial love toward the Doctor made her feel the keenest sensitiveness at the thought of giving him pain. At the same time, the questions which James had proposed to her had raised serious doubts in her mind whether it was altogether right to suffer him blindly to enter into this union. So, after she was all prepared, she bolted the door of her chamber, and, opening her Bible, read, "If any of you lack wisdom, let him ask of God, that giveth to all men liberally, and upbraideth not, and it shall be given him"; and then, kneeling down by the bedside, she asked that God would give her some immediate light in her present perplexity. So praying, her mind grew calm and steady, and she rose up at the sound of the bell, which marked that it was time to set forward for church.

Everybody noticed, as she came into church that morning, how beautiful Mary Scudder looked. It was no longer the beauty of the carved statue, the pale alabaster shrine, the sainted virgin, but a warm, bright, living light, that spoke of some summer breath breathing within her soul.

When she took her place in the singers' seat, she knew, without turning her head, that *he* was in his old place, not far from her side; and those whose eyes followed her to the gallery marvelled at her face there,—

> "her pure and eloquent blood
> Spoke in her cheeks, and so distinctly wrought
> That you might almost say her body thought;"

for a thousand delicate nerves were becoming vital once more, —the holy mystery of womanhood had wrought within her.

When they rose to sing, the tune must needs be one which they had often sung together, out of the same book, at the singing-school,—one of those wild, pleading tunes, dear to the heart of New England,—born, if we may credit the report, in the rocky hollows of its mountains, and whose notes have a kind of grand and mournful triumph in their warbling wail, and in which different parts of the harmony, set contrary to all the canons of musical Pharisaism, had still a singular and romantic effect, which a true musical genius would not have failed to recognize. The four parts, tenor, treble, bass, and counter, as they were then called, rose and swelled and wildly mingled, with the fitful strangeness of an Æolian harp, or of winds in mountain-hollows, or the vague moanings of the sea on lone, forsaken shores. And Mary, while her voice rose over the waves of the treble, and trembled with a pathetic richness, felt, to her inmost heart, the deep accord of that other voice which rose to meet hers, so wildly melancholy, as if the soul in that manly breast had come to meet her soul in the disembodied, shadowy verity of eternity. The grand old tune, called by our fathers "China," never, with its dirge-like melody, drew two souls more out of themselves, and entwined them more nearly with each other.

The last verse of the hymn spoke of the resurrection of the saints with Christ,—

> "Then let the last dread trumpet sound
>   And bid the dead arise;
> Awake, ye nations under ground!
>   Ye saints, ascend the skies!"

And as Mary sang, she felt sublimely upborne with the idea that life is but a moment and love is immortal, and seemed, in a shadowy trance, to feel herself and him past this mortal fane, far over on the shores of that other life, ascending with Christ, all-glorified, all tears wiped away, and with full permission to love and to be loved forever. And as she sang, the Doctor looked upward, and marvelled at the light in her eyes and the rich bloom on her cheek; for where she stood, a sunbeam, streaming aslant through the dusty panes of the window, touched her head with a kind of glory, and the thought he then received out-breathed itself in the yet more fervent adoration of his prayer.

XXXIX.

The Ice Broken

Our fathers believed in special answers to prayer. They were not stumbled by the objection about the inflexibility of the laws of Nature; because they had the idea, that, when the Creator of the world promised to answer human prayers, He probably understood the laws of Nature as well as they did. At any rate, the laws of Nature were His affair, and not theirs. They were men, very apt, as the Duke of Wellington said, to "look to their marching-orders,"—which, being found to read, "Be careful for nothing, but in everything by prayer and supplication with thanksgiving let your requests be made known unto God," they did it. "They looked unto Him and were lightened, and their faces were not ashamed." One reads, in the Memoirs of Dr. Hopkins, of Newport Gardner, one of his African catechumens, a negro of singular genius and ability, who, being desirous of his freedom, that he might be a missionary to Africa, and having long worked without being able to raise the amount required, was counselled by Dr. Hopkins that it might be a shorter way to seek his freedom from the Lord, by a day of solemn fasting and prayer. The historical fact is, that, on the evening of a day so consecrated, his master returned from church, called Newport to him, and presented him with his freedom. Is it not possible that He who made the world may have established laws for prayer as invariable as those for the sowing of seed and raising of grain? Is it not as legitimate a subject of inquiry, when petitions are not answered, which of these laws has been neglected?

But be that as it may, certain it is, that Candace, who on this morning in church sat where she could see Mary and James in the singers' seat, had certain thoughts planted in her mind which bore fruit afterwards in a solemn and select consultation held with Miss Prissy at the end of the horse-shed by the meeting-house, during the intermission between the morning and afternoon services.

Candace sat on a fragment of granite boulder which lay there, her black face relieved against a clump of yellow mulleins, then in majestic altitude. On her lap was spread a checked pocket-handkerchief, containing rich slices of cheese, and a store of her favorite brown doughnuts.

"Now, Miss Prissy," she said, "dar's *reason* in all tings, an' a good deal *more* in some tings dan dar is in oders. Dar's a good deal more reason in two young, handsome folks comin' togeder dan dar is in"——

Candace finished the sentence by an emphatic flourish of her doughnut.

"Now, as long as eberybody thought Jim Marvyn was dead, dar wa'n't nothin' else in de world *to* be done *but* marry de Doctor. But, good lan'! I hearn him a-talkin' to Miss Marvyn las' night; it kinder 'mos' broke my heart. Why, dem two poor creeturs, dey's jest as onhappy's dey can be! An' she's got too much feelin' for de Doctor to say a word; an' *I* say *he oughter be told on't!* dat's what *I* say," said Candace, giving a decisive bite to her doughnut.

"I say so, too," said Miss Prissy. "Why, I never had such bad feelings in my life as I did yesterday, when that young man came down to our house. He was just as pale as a cloth. I tried to say a word to Miss Scudder, but she snapped me up so! She's an awful decided woman when her mind's made up. I was telling Cerinthy Ann Twitchel,—she came round me this noon,—that it didn't exactly seem to me right that things should go on as they are going. And says I, 'Cerinthy Ann, I don't know anything what to do.' And says she, 'If I was you, I know what *I'd* do,—I'd tell the Doctor,' says she. 'Nobody ever takes offense at anything *you* do, Miss Prissy.' To be sure," added Miss Prissy, "I have talked to people about a good many things that it's rather strange I should; 'cause I a'n't one, somehow, that can let things go that seem to want doing. I always told folks that I should spoil a novel before it got half-way through the first volume, by blurting out some of those things that they let go trailing on so, till everybody gets so mixed up they don't know what they're doing."

"Well, now, honey," said Candace, authoritatively, "ef you's got any notions o' dat kind, I tink it mus' come from de good Lord, an' I 'dvise you to be 'tendin' to't, right away. You jes' go 'long an' tell de Doctor yourself all you know, an' den le's see what'll come on't. I tell you, I b'liebe it'll be one o' de bes' day's works you eber did in your life!"

"Well," said Miss Prissy, "I guess to-night, before I go to bed, I'll make a dive at him. When a thing's once out, it's out, and can't be got in again, even if people don't like it; and that's a mercy, anyhow. It really makes me feel 'most wicked to think of it, for he is the most blessedest man!"

"Dat's what he is," said Candace. "But de blessedest man in de world oughter know de truth; dat's what I tink!"

"Yes,—true enough!" said Miss Prissy. "I'll tell him, any-way."

Miss Prissy was as good as her word; for that evening, when the Doctor had retired to his study, she took her life in her hand, and, walking swiftly as a cat, tapped rather timidly at the study-door, which the Doctor opening said, benignantly,—

"Ah, Miss Prissy!"

"If you please, Sir," said Miss Prissy, "I'd like a little conversation."

The Doctor was well enough used to such requests from the female members of his church, which, generally, were the prelude to some disclosures of internal difficulties or spiritual experiences. He therefore graciously motioned her to a chair.

"I thought I must come in," she began, busily twirling a bit of her Sunday gown. "I thought—that is—I felt it my duty—I thought—perhaps—I ought to tell you—that perhaps you ought to know."

The Doctor looked civilly concerned. He did not know but Miss Prissy's wits were taking leave of her. He replied, however, with his usual honest stateliness,—

"I trust, dear Madam, that you will feel at perfect freedom to open to me any exercises of mind that you may have."

"It isn't about myself," said Miss Prissy. "If you please, it's about you and Mary!"

The Doctor *now* looked awake in right earnest, and very much astonished besides; and he looked eagerly at Miss Prissy, to have her go on.

"I don't know how you would view such a matter," said Miss Prissy; "but the fact is, that James Marvyn and Mary always did love each other, ever since they were children."

Still the Doctor was unawakened to the real meaning of the words, and he answered, simply,—

"I should be far from wishing to interfere with so very natural and universal a sentiment, which, I make no doubt, is all quite as it should be."

"No,—but," said Miss Prissy, "you don't understand what I mean. I mean that James Marvyn wanted to marry Mary, and that she was—well—she wasn't engaged to him, but"——

"Madam!" said the Doctor, in a voice that frightened Miss Prissy out of her chair, while a blaze like sheet-lightning shot from his eyes, and his face flushed crimson.

"Mercy on us! Doctor, I hope you'll excuse me; but there the fact is,—I've said it out,—the fact is, they wa'n't engaged; but that Mary loved him ever since he was a boy, as she never will and never can love any man again in this world, is what I am just as sure of as that I'm standing here; and I've felt you ought to know it; 'cause I'm quite sure, that, if he'd been alive, she'd never given the promise she has,—the promise that she means to keep, if her heart breaks, and his too. They wouldn't anybody tell you, and I thought I must tell you; 'cause I thought you'd know what was right to do about it."

During all this latter speech the Doctor was standing with his back to Miss Prissy, and his face to the window, just as he did some time before, when Mrs. Scudder came to tell him of Mary's consent. He made a gesture backward, without speaking, that she should leave the apartment; and Miss Prissy left, with a guilty kind of feeling, as if she had been striking a knife into her pastor, and, rushing distractedly across the entry into Mary's little bedroom, she bolted the door, threw herself on the bed, and began to cry.

"Well, I've done it!" she said to herself. "He's a very strong, hearty man," she soliloquized, "so I hope it won't put him in a consumption;—men do go into a consumption about such things sometimes. I remember Abner Seaforth did; but then he was always narrow-chested, and had the liver-complaint, or something. I don't know what Miss Scudder will say;—but I've done it. Poor man! such a good man, too! I declare, I feel just like Herod taking off John the Baptist's head. Well, well! it's done, and can't be helped."

Just at this moment Miss Prissy heard a gentle tap at the door, and started, as if it had been a ghost,—not being able to rid herself of the impression, that, somehow, she had committed a great crime, for which retribution was knocking at the door.

It was Mary, who said, in her sweetest and most natural tones, "Miss Prissy, the Doctor would like to see you."

Mary was much astonished at the frightened, discomposed manner with which Miss Prissy received this announcement, and said,—

"I'm afraid I've waked you up out of sleep. I don't think there's the least hurry."

Miss Prissy didn't, either; but she reflected afterwards that she might as well get through with it at once; and therefore, smoothing her tumbled cap-border, she went to the Doctor's study. This time he was quite composed, and received her with a mournful gravity, and requested her to be seated.

"I beg, Madam," he said, "you will excuse the abruptness of my manner in our late interview. I was so little prepared for the communication you had to make, that I was, perhaps, unsuitably discomposed. Will you allow me to ask whether you were requested by any of the parties to communicate to me what you did?"

"No, Sir," said Miss Prissy.

"Have any of the parties ever communicated with you on the subject at all?" said the Doctor.

"No, Sir," said Miss Prissy.

"That is all," said the Doctor. "I will not detain you. I am very much obliged to you, Madam."

He rose, and opened the door for her to pass out,—and Miss Prissy, overawed by the stately gravity of his manner, went out in silence.

XL.

The Sacrifice

WHEN Miss Prissy left the room, the Doctor sat down by the table and covered his face with his hands. He had a large, passionate, determined nature; and he had just come to one of those cruel crises in life in which it is apt to seem to us that the whole force of our being, all that we can hope, wish, feel, enjoy, has been suffered to gather itself into one great wave, only to break upon some cold rock of inevitable fate, and go back, moaning, into emptiness.

In such hours men and women have cursed God and life, and thrown violently down and trampled under their feet what yet was left of life's blessings, in the fierce bitterness of despair. "This, or nothing!" the soul shrieks, in her frenzy. At just such points as these, men have plunged into intemperance and wild excess,—they have gone to be shot down in battle,—they have broken life, and thrown it away, like an empty goblet, and gone, like wailing ghosts, out into the dread unknown.

The possibility of all this lay in that heart which had just received that stunning blow. Exercised and disciplined as he had been, by years of sacrifice, by constant, unsleeping self-vigilance, there was rising there, in that great heart, an ocean-tempest of passion, and for a while his cries unto God seemed as empty and as vague as the screams of birds tossed and buffeted in the clouds of mighty tempests.

The will that he thought wholly subdued seemed to rise under him as a rebellious giant. A few hours before, he thought himself established in an invincible submission to God's will that nothing could shake. Now he looked into himself as into a seething vortex of rebellion, and against all the passionate cries of his lower nature could, in the language of an old saint, cling to God only by the naked force of his will. That will rested unmelted amid the boiling sea of pas-

sion, waiting its hour of renewed sway. He walked the room
for hours, and then sat down to his Bible, and roused once
or twice to find his head leaning on its pages, and his mind
far gone in thoughts, from which he woke with a bitter
throb. Then he determined to set himself to some definite
work, and, taking his Concordance, began busily tracing out
and numbering all the proof-texts for one of the chapters of
his theological system! till, at last, he worked himself down
to such calmness that he could pray; and then he schooled
and reasoned with himself, in a style not unlike, in its spirit,
to that in which a great modern author has addressed suffering humanity:—

"What is it that thou art fretting and self-tormenting
about? Is it because thou art not happy? Who told thee that
thou wast to be happy? Is there any ordinance of the universe
that thou shouldst be happy? Art thou nothing but a vulture
screaming for prey? Canst thou not do without happiness?
Yea, thou canst do without happiness, and, instead thereof,
find blessedness."

The Doctor came, lastly, to the conclusion, that blessedness, which was all the portion his Master had on earth,
might do for him also; and therefore he kissed and blessed
that silver dove of happiness, which he saw was weary of sailing in his clumsy old ark, and let it go out of his hand without a tear.

He slept little that night; but when he came to breakfast,
all noticed an unusual gentleness and benignity of manner,
and Mary, she knew not why, saw tears rising in his eyes
when he looked at her.

After breakfast he requested Mrs. Scudder to step with him
into his study, and Miss Prissy shook in her little shoes as she
saw the matron entering. The door was shut for a long time,
and two voices could be heard in earnest conversation.

Meanwhile James Marvyn entered the cottage, prompt to
remind Mary of her promise that she would talk with him
again this morning.

They had talked with each other but a few moments, by
the sweetbrier-shaded window in the best room, when Mrs.
Scudder appeared at the door of the apartment, with traces of
tears upon her cheeks.

"Good morning, James," she said. "The Doctor wishes to see you and Mary a moment, together."

Both looked sufficiently astonished, knowing, from Mrs. Scudder's looks, that something was impending. They followed her, scarcely feeling the ground they trod on.

The Doctor was sitting at his table, with his favorite large-print Bible open before him. He rose to receive them, with a manner at once gentle and grave.

There was a pause of some minutes, during which he sat with his head leaning upon his hand.

"You all know," he said, turning toward Mary, who sat very near him, "the near and dear relation in which I have been expected to stand towards this friend. I should not have been worthy of that relation, if I had not felt in my heart the true love of a husband, as set forth in the New Testament,—who should love his wife even as Christ loved the Church, and gave himself for it; and in case any peril or danger threatened this dear soul, and I could not give myself for her, I had never been worthy the honor she has done me. For, I take it, whenever there is a cross or burden to be borne by one or the other, that the man, who is made in the image of God as to strength and endurance, should take it upon himself, and not lay it upon her that is weaker; for he is therefore strong, not that he may tyrannize over the weak, but bear their burdens for them, even as Christ for his Church.

"I have just discovered," he added, looking kindly upon Mary, "that there is a great cross and burden which must come, either on this dear child or on myself, through no fault of either of us, but through God's good providence; and therefore let me bear it.

"Mary, my dear child," he said, "I will be to thee as a father, but I will not force thy heart."

At this moment, Mary, by a sudden, impulsive movement, threw her arms around his neck and kissed him, and lay sobbing on his shoulder.

"No! no!" she said,—"I will marry you, as I said!"

"Not if I will not," he replied, with a benign smile. "Come here, young man," he said, with some authority, to James. "I give thee this maiden to wife." And he lifted her from his shoulder, and placed her gently in the arms of the young man, who, overawed and overcome, pressed her silently to his heart.

"There, children, it is over," he said. "God bless you!"

"Take her away," he added; "she will be more composed soon."

Before James left, he grasped the Doctor's hand in his, and said,—

"Sir, this tells on my heart more than any sermon you ever preached. I shall never forget it. God bless you, Sir!"

The Doctor saw them slowly quit the apartment, and, following them, closed the door; and thus ended THE MINISTER'S WOOING.

XLI.

The Wedding

O F the events which followed this scene we are happy to
give our readers more minute and graphic details than
we ourselves could furnish, by transcribing for their edification an autograph letter of Miss Prissy's, still preserved in a
black oaken cabinet of our great-grandmother's; and with
which we take no further liberties than the correction of a
somewhat peculiar orthography. It is written to that sister
"Lizabeth," in Boston, of whom she made such frequent
mention, and whom, it appears, it was her custom to keep
well-informed in all the gossip of her immediate sphere.

"MY DEAR SISTER:—

"You wonder, I s'pose, why I haven't written you; but the
fact is, I've been run just off my feet, and worked till the flesh
aches so it seems as if it would drop off my bones, with this
wedding of Mary Scudder's. And, after all, you'll be astonished to hear that she ha'n't married the Doctor, but that Jim
Marvyn that I told you about. You see, he came home a week
before the wedding was to be, and Mary, she was so conscientious she thought 'twa'n't right to break off with the Doctor, and so she was for going right on with it; and Mrs. Scudder, she was for going on more yet; and the poor young man,
he couldn't get a word in edgeways, and there wouldn't anybody tell the Doctor a word about it, and there 'twas drifting
along, and both on 'em feeling dreadful, and so I thought to
myself, 'I'll just take my life in my hand, like Queen Esther,
and go in and tell the Doctor all about it.' And so I did. I'm
scared to death always when I think of it. But that dear
blessed man, he took it like a saint. He just gave her up as
serene and calm as a psalm-book, and called Jim in and told
him to take her.

"Jim was fairly overcrowed,—it really made him feel
small,—and he says he'll agree that there is more in the Doc-

tor's religion than most men's: which shows how important it is for professing Christians to bear testimony in their works,—as I was telling Cerinthy Ann Twitchel; and she said there wa'n't anything made her want to be a Christian so much, if that was what religion would do for people.

"Well, you see, when this came out, it wanted just three days of the wedding, which was to be Thursday, and that wedding-dress I told you about that had lilies of the valley on a white ground was pretty much made, except puffing the gauze round the neck, which I do with white satin piping-cord, and it looks beautiful too; and so Mrs. Scudder and I, we were thinking 'twould do just as well, when in come Jim Marvyn, bringing the sweetest thing you ever saw, that he had got in China, and I think I never did see anything lovelier. It was a white silk, as thick as a board, and so stiff that it would stand alone, and overshot with little fine dots of silver, so that it shone, when you moved it, just like frostwork; and when I saw it, I just clapped my hands, and jumped up from the floor, and says I, 'If I have to sit up all night, that dress shall be made, and made well, too.' For, you know, I thought I could get Miss Olladine Hocum to run the breadths and do such parts, so that I could devote myself to the fine work. And that French woman I told you about, she said she'd help, and she's a master-hand for touching things up. There seems to be work provided for all kinds of people, and French people seem to have a gift in all sorts of dressy things, and 'tisn't a bad gift either.

"Well, as I was saying, we agreed that this was to be cut open with a train, and a petticoat of just the palest, sweetest, loveliest blue that ever you saw, and gauze puffings down the edgings each side, fastened in, every once in a while, with lilies of the valley; and 'twas cut square in the neck, with puffings and flowers to match, and then tight sleeves, with full ruffles of that old Mechlin lace that you remember Mrs. Katy Scudder showed you once in that great camphor-wood trunk.

"Well, you see, come to get all things together that were to be done, we concluded to put off the wedding till Tuesday; and Madame de Frontignac, she would dress the best room for it herself, and she spent nobody knows what time in going round and getting evergreens and making wreaths, and putting up green boughs over the pictures, so that the room looked just like the Episcopal church at Christmas. In fact, Mrs. Scudder said, if it had been Christmas, she shouldn't have felt it right, but, as it was, she didn't think anybody would think it any harm.

"Well, Tuesday night, I and Madame de Frontignac, we dressed Mary ourselves, and, I tell you, the dress fitted as if it was grown on her; and Madame de Frontignac, she dressed her hair; and she had on a wreath of lilies of the valley, and a gauze veil that came a'most down to her feet, and came all around her like a cloud, and you could see her white shining dress through it every time she moved, and she looked just as white as a snow-berry; but there were two little pink spots that kept coming and going in her cheeks, that kind of lightened up when she smiled, and then faded down again. And the French lady put a string of real pearls round her neck, with a cross of pearls, which went down and lay hid in her bosom.

"She was mighty calm-like while she was being dressed; but just as I was putting in the last pin, she heard the rumbling of a coach down-stairs, for Jim Marvyn had got a real elegant carriage to carry her over to his father's in, and so she knew he was come. And pretty soon Mrs. Marvyn came in the room, and when she saw Mary, her brown eyes kind of danced, and she lifted up both hands, to see how beautiful she looked. And Jim Marvyn, he was standing at the door, and they told him it wasn't proper that he should see till the time come; but he begged so hard that he might just have one peep, that I let him come in, and he looked at her as if she was something he wouldn't dare to touch; and he said to me softly, says he, 'I'm 'most afraid she has got wings somewhere that will fly away from me, or that I shall wake up and find it is a dream.'

"Well, Cerinthy Ann Twitchel was the bridesmaid, and she came next with that young man she is engaged to. It is all out now, that she is engaged, and she don't deny it. And Cerinthy, she looked handsomer than I ever saw her, in a white brocade, with rosebuds on it, which I guess she got in reference to the future, for they say she is going to be married next month.

"Well, we all filled up the room pretty well, till Mrs. Scudder came in to tell us that the company were all together; and then they took hold of arms, and they had a little time practising how they must stand, and Cerinthy Ann's beau would always get her on the wrong side, 'cause he's rather bashful, and don't know very well what he's about; and Cerinthy Ann declared she was afraid that she should laugh out in prayer-time, 'cause she always did laugh when she knew she mus'n't. But finally Mrs. Scudder told us we must go in, and looked so reproving at Cerinthy that she had to hold her mouth with her pocket-handkerchief.

"Well, the old Doctor was standing there in the very silk gown that the ladies gave him to be married in himself,— poor, dear man!—and he smiled kind of peaceful on 'em when they came in, and walked up to a kind of bower of evergreens and flowers that Madame de Frontignac had fixed for them to stand in. Mary grew rather white, as if she was going to faint; but Jim Marvyn stood up just as firm, and looked as proud and handsome as a prince, and he kind of looked down at her,—'cause, you know, he is a great deal taller,—kind of wondering, as if he wanted to know if it was really so. Well, when they got all placed, they let the doors stand open, and Cato and Candace came and stood in the door. And Candace had on her great splendid Mogadore turban, and a crimson and yellow shawl, that she seemed to take comfort in wearing, although it was pretty hot.

"Well, so when they were all fixed, the Doctor, he begun his prayer,—and as 'most all of us knew what a great sacrifice he had made, I don't believe there was a dry eye in the room; and when he had done, there was a great time,—people blowing their noses and wiping their eyes, as if it had been a funeral. Then Cerinthy Ann, she pulled off Mary's glove pretty quick; but that poor beau of hers, he made such work of James's that he had to pull it off himself, after all, and Cerinthy Ann, she liked to have laughed out loud. And so when the Doctor told them to join hands, Jim took hold of Mary's hand as if he didn't mean to let go very soon, and so they were married.

"I was the first one that kissed the bride after Mrs. Scudder,—I got that promise out of Mary when I was making the

dress. And Jim Marvyn, he insisted upon kissing me,—
' 'Cause,' says he, 'Miss Prissy, you are as young and handsome as any of 'em'; and I told him he was a saucy fellow,
and I'd box his ears, if I could reach them.

"That French lady looked lovely, dressed in pale pink silk,
with long pink wreaths of flowers in her hair; and she came
up and kissed Mary, and said something to her in French.

"And after a while old Candace came up, and Mary kissed
her; and then Candace put her arms round Jim's neck, and
gave him a real hearty smack, so that everybody laughed.

"And then the cake and the wine was passed round, and
everybody had good times till we heard the nine-o'clock-bell
ring. And then the coach came up to the door, and Mrs.
Scudder, she wrapped Mary up, kissing her, and crying over
her, while Mrs. Marvyn stood stretching her arms out of the
coach after her. And then Cato and Candace went after in the
wagon behind, and so they all went off together; and that
was the end of the wedding; and ever since then we ha'n't
any of us done much but rest, for we were pretty much beat
out. So no more at present from your affectionate sister,

"PRISSY.

"P.S.—I forgot to tell you that Jim Marvyn has come home
quite rich. He fell in with a man in China who was at the
head of one of their great merchant-houses, whom he nursed
through a long fever, and took care of his business, and so,
when he got well, nothing would do but he must have him
for a partner; and now he is going to live in this country and
attend to the business of the house here. They say he is going
to build a house as grand as the Vernons'. And we hope he
has experienced religion; and he means to join our church,
which is a providence, for he is twice as rich and generous as
that old Simeon Brown that snapped me up so about my
wages. I never believed in him, for all his talk. I was down to
Mrs. Scudder's when the Doctor examined Jim about his evidences. At first the Doctor seemed a little anxious, 'cause he
didn't talk in the regular way; for you know Jim always did
have his own way of talking, and never could say things in
other people's words; and sometimes he makes folks laugh,
when he himself don't know what they laugh at, because he

hits the nail on the head in some strange way they aren't expecting. If I was to have died, I couldn't help laughing at some things he said; and yet I don't think I ever felt more solemnized. He sat up there in a sort of grand, straightforward, noble way, and told all the way the Lord had been leading of him, and all the exercises of his mind, and all about the dreadful shipwreck, and how he was saved, and the loving-kindness of the Lord, till the Doctor's spectacles got all blinded with tears, and he couldn't see the notes he made to examine him by; and we all cried, Mrs. Scudder, and Mary, and I; and as to Mrs. Marvyn, she just sat with her hands clasped, looking into her son's eyes, like a picture of the Virgin Mary. And when Jim got through, there wa'n't nothing to be heard for some minutes; and the Doctor he wiped his eyes and wiped his glasses, and he looked over his papers, but he couldn't bring out a word, and at last says he, "Let us pray,"—for that was all there was to be said; for I think sometimes things so kind of fills folks up that there a'n't nothing to be done but pray, which, the Lord be praised, we are privileged to do always. Between you and I, Martha, I never could understand all the distinctions our dear, blessed Doctor sets up; but when he publishes his system, if I work my fingers to the bone, I mean to buy one and study it out, because he is such a blessed man; though, after all's said, I have to come back to my old place, and trust to the loving-kindness of the Lord, who takes care of the sparrow on the house-top, and all small, lone creatures like me; though I can't say I'm lone either, because nobody need say that, so long as there's folks to be done for. So if I *don't* understand the Doctor's theology, or don't get eyes to read it, on account of the fine stitching on his shirt-ruffles I've been trying to do, still I hope I may be accepted on account of the Lord's great goodness; for if we can't trust that, it's all over with us all."

XLII.

Last Words

WE know it is fashionable to drop the curtain over a newly married pair, as they recede from the altar; but we cannot but hope our readers may by this time have enough of interest in our little history to wish for a few words on the lot of the personages whose acquaintance they have thereby made.

The conjectures of Miss Prissy in regard to the grand house which James was to build for his bride were as speedily as possible realized. On a beautiful elevation, a little out of the town of Newport, rose a fair and stately mansion, whose windows overlooked the harbor, and whose wide, cool rooms were adorned by the constant presence of the sweet face and form which has been the guiding star of our story. The fair poetic maiden, the seeress, the saint, has passed into that appointed shrine for woman, more holy than cloister, more saintly and pure than church or altar,—*a Christian home.* Priestess, wife, and mother, there she ministers daily in holy works of household peace, and by faith and prayer and love redeems from grossness and earthliness the common toils and wants of life.

The gentle guiding force that led James Marvyn from the maxims and habits and ways of this world to the higher conception of an heroic and Christ-like manhood was still ever present with him, gently touching the springs of life, brooding peacefully with dovelike wings over his soul, and he grew up under it noble in purpose and strong in spirit. He was one of the most energetic and fearless supporters of the Doctor in his life-long warfare against an inhumanity which was intrenched in all the mercantile interests of the day, and which at last fell before the force of conscience and moral appeal.

Candace in time transferred her allegiance to the growing family of her young master and mistress, and predominated proudly in gorgeous raiment with her butterfly turban over a

rising race of young Marvyns. All the care not needed by
them was bestowed on the somewhat querulous old age of
Cato, whose never-failing cough furnished occupation for all
her spare hours and thought.

As for our friend the Doctor, we trust our readers will appreciate the magnanimity with which he proved a real and
disinterested love, in a point where so many men experience
only the graspings of a selfish one. A mind so severely trained
as his had been brings to a great crisis, involving severe self-
denial, an amount of reserved moral force quite inexplicable
to those less habituated to self-control. He was like a warrior
whose sleep even was in armor, always ready to be roused to
the conflict.

In regard to his feelings for Mary, he made the sacrifice of
himself to her happiness so wholly and thoroughly that there
was not a moment of weak hesitation,—no going back over
the past,—no vain regret. Generous and brave souls find a
support in such actions, because the very exertion raises them
to a higher and purer plane of existence.

His diary records the event only in these very calm and
temperate words:—"It was a trial to me,—a *very great* trial;
but as she did not deceive me, I shall never lose my friendship
for her."

The Doctor was always a welcome inmate in the house of
Mary and James, as a friend revered and dear. Nor did he
want in time a hearthstone of his own, where a bright and
loving face made him daily welcome; for we find that he married at last a woman of a fair countenance, and that sons and
daughters grew up around him.

In time, also, his theological system was published. In that
day, it was customary to dedicate new or important works to
the patronage of some distinguished or powerful individual.
The Doctor had no earthly patron. Four or five simple lines
are found in the commencement of his work, in which, in a
spirit reverential and affectionate, he dedicates it to our Lord
Jesus Christ, praying Him to accept the good, and to overrule
the errors to His glory.

Quite unexpectedly to himself, the work proved a success,
not only in public acceptance and esteem, but even in a temporal view, bringing to him at last a modest competence,

which he accepted with surprise and gratitude. To the last of a very long life, he was the same steady, undiscouraged worker, the same calm witness against popular sins and proclaimer of unpopular truths, ever saying and doing what he saw to be eternally right, without the slightest consultation with worldly expediency or earthly gain; nor did his words cease to work in New England till the evils he opposed were finally done away.

Colonel Burr leaves the scene of our story to pursue those brilliant and unscrupulous political intrigues so well known to the historian of those times, and whose results were so disastrous to himself. His duel with the ill-fated Hamilton, the awful retribution of public opinion that followed, and the slow downward course of a doomed life are all on record. Chased from society, pointed at everywhere by the finger of hatred, so accursed in common esteem that even the publican who lodged him for a night refused to accept his money when he knew his name, heart-stricken in his domestic relations, his only daughter taken by pirates and dying amid untold horrors,—one seems to see in a doom so much above that of other men the power of an avenging Nemesis for sins beyond those of ordinary humanity.

But we who have learned of Christ may humbly hope that these crushing miseries in this life came not because he was a sinner above others, not in wrath alone,—but that the prayers of the sweet saint who gave him to God even before his birth brought to him those friendly adversities, that thus might be slain in his soul the evil demon of pride, which had been the opposing force to all that was noble within him. Nothing is more affecting than the account of the last hours of this man, whom a woman took in and cherished in his poverty and weakness with that same heroic enthusiasm with which it was his lot to inspire so many women. This humble keeper of lodgings was told, that, if she retained Aaron Burr, all her other lodgers would leave. "Let them do it, then," she said; "but he shall remain." In the same uncomplaining and inscrutable silence in which he had borne the reverses and miseries of his life did this singular being pass through the shades of the dark valley. The New Testament was always under his pillow, and when alone he was often found reading it attentively; but of the result of that communion with higher powers he said nothing. Patient, gentle, and grateful, he was, as to all his inner history, entirely silent and impenetrable. He died with the request, which has a touching significance, that he might be buried at the feet of those parents whose lives had finished so differently from his own.

> "No farther seek his errors to disclose,
>   Or draw his frailties from their dread abode."

Shortly after Mary's marriage, Madame de Frontignac sailed with her husband for home, where they lived in a very retired way on a large estate in the South of France. An intimate correspondence was kept up between her and Mary for many years, from which we shall give our readers a few extracts. Her first letter is dated shortly after her return to France.

"At last, my sweet Marie, you behold us in peace after our wanderings. I wish you could see our lovely nest in the hills, which overlook the Mediterranean, whose blue waters remind me of Newport harbor and our old days there. Ah, my sweet saint, blessed was the day I first learned to know you! for it was you, more than anything else, that kept me back from sin and misery. I call you my Sibyl, dearest, because the Sibyl was a prophetess of divine things out of the Church; and so are you. The Abbé says, that all true, devout persons in all persuasions belong to the True Catholic Apostolic Church, and will in the end be enlightened to know it; what do you think of that, *ma belle*? I fancy I see you look at me with your grave, innocent eyes, just as you used to; but you say nothing.

"I am far happier, *ma Marie*, than I ever thought I could be. I took your advice, and told my husband all I had felt and suffered. It was a very hard thing to do; but I felt how true it was, as you said, that there could be no real friendship without perfect truth at bottom; so I told him all, and he was very good and noble and helpful to me; and since then he has been so gentle and patient and thoughtful, that no mother could be kinder; and I should be a very bad woman, if I did not love him truly and dearly,—as I do.

"I must confess that there is still a weak, bleeding place in my heart that aches yet, but I try to bear it bravely; and when I am tempted to think myself very miserable, I remember how patiently you used to go about your house-work and spinning, in those sad days when you thought your heart was drowned in the sea; and I try to do like you. I have many duties to my servants and tenants, and mean to be a good *châtelaine*; and I find, when I nurse the sick and comfort the poor, that my sorrows are lighter. For, after all, Mary, I have lost nothing that ever was mine,—only my foolish heart has grown to something that it should not, and bleeds at being torn away. Nobody but Christ and His dear Mother can tell what this sorrow is; but they know, and that is enough."

The next letter is dated some three years after.

"You see me now, my Marie, a proud and happy woman. I was truly envious, when you wrote me of the birth of your little son; but now the dear good God has sent a sweet little angel to me, to comfort my sorrows and lie close to my heart; and since he came, all pain is gone. Ah, if you could see him! he has black eyes and lashes like silk, and such little hands!— even his finger-nails are all perfect, like little gems; and when he puts his little hand on my bosom, I tremble with joy. Since he came, I pray always, and the good God seems very near to me. Now I realize, as I never did before, the sublime thought that God revealed Himself in the infant Jesus; and I bow before the manger of Bethlehem where the Holy Babe was laid. What comfort, what adorable condescension for us mothers in that scene!—My husband is so moved, he can scarce stay an hour from the cradle. He seems to look at me with a sort of awe, because I know how to care for this precious treasure that he adores without daring to touch. We are going to call him Henri, which is my husband's name and that of his ancestors for many generations back. I vow for him an eternal friendship with the son of my little Marie; and I shall try and train him up to be a brave man and a true Christian. Ah, Marie, this gives me something to live for! My heart is full,— a whole new life opens before me!"

Somewhat later, another letter announces the birth of a daughter,—and later still, the birth of another son; but we shall only add one more, written some years after, on hearing of the great reverses of popular feeling towards Burr, subsequently to his duel with the ill-fated Hamilton.

"*Ma chère Marie,*—Your letter has filled me with grief. My noble Henri, who already begins to talk of himself as my protector, (these boys feel their manhood so soon, *ma Marie!*) saw by my face, when I read your letter, that something pained me, and he would not rest till I told him something about it. Ah, Marie, how thankful I then felt that I had nothing to blush for before my son! how thankful for those dear children whose little hands had healed all the morbid places of my heart, so that I could think of all the past without a pang! I told Henri that the letter brought bad news of an old friend, but that it pained me to speak of it; and you would have thought, by the grave and tender way he talked to his mamma, that the boy was an experienced man of forty, to say the least.

"But, Marie, how unjust is the world! how unjust both in praise and blame! Poor Burr was the petted child of society; yesterday she doted on him, flattered him, smiled on his faults, and let him do what he would without reproof; today she flouts and scorns and scoffs him, and refuses to see the least good in him. I know that man, Mary,—and I know, that, sinful as he may be before Infinite Purity, he is not so much more sinful than all the other men of his time. Have I not been in America? I know Jefferson; I knew poor Hamilton,—peace be with the dead! Neither of them had a life that could bear the sort of trial to which Burr's is subjected. When every secret fault, failing, and sin is dragged out, and held up without mercy, what man can stand?

"But I know what irritates the world is that proud, disdainful calm which will neither give sigh nor tear. It was not that he killed poor Hamilton, but that he never seemed to care! Ah, there is that evil demon of his life,—that cold, stoical pride, which haunts him like a fate! But I know he *does* feel; I know he is *not* as hard at heart as he tries to be; I have seen too many real acts of pity to the unfortunate, of tenderness to the weak, of real love to his friends, to believe that. Great have been his sins against our sex, and God forbid that the mothers of children should speak lightly of them; but is not so susceptible a temperament, and so singular a power to charm as he possessed, to be taken into account in estimating his temptations? Because he is a sinning man, it does not follow that he is a demon. If any should have cause to think bitterly of him, I should. He trifled inexcusably with my deepest feelings; he caused me years of conflict and anguish, such as he little knows; I was almost shipwrecked; yet I will still say to the last that what I loved in him was a better self,—something really noble and good, however concealed and perverted by pride, ambition, and self-will. Though all the world reject him, I still have faith in this better nature, and prayers that he may be led right at last. There is at least one heart that will always intercede with God for him."

It is well known, that, for many years after Burr's death, the odium that covered his name was so great that no monument was erected, lest it should become a mark for popular violence. Subsequently, however, in a mysterious manner, a plain granite slab marked his grave; by whom erected has been never known. It was placed in the night by some friendly, unknown hand. A laborer in the vicinity, who first discovered it, found lying near the spot a small *porte-monnaie*, which had perhaps been used in paying for the workmanship. It contained no papers that could throw any light on the subject, except the fragment of the address of a letter on which was written "Henri de Frontignac."

THE END.

OLDTOWN FOLKS

Contents

Preface 883

CHAPTER I.
   Oldtown and the Minister 885

CHAPTER II.
   My Father 894

CHAPTER III.
   My Grandmother 901

CHAPTER IV.
   The Village Do-Nothing 910

CHAPTER V.
   The Old Meeting-House 921

CHAPTER VI.
   Fire-Light Talks in My Grandmother's Kitchen 943

CHAPTER VII.
   Old Crab Smith 966

CHAPTER VIII.
   Miss Asphyxia 977

CHAPTER IX.
   Harry's First Day's Work 989

CHAPTER X.
   Miss Asphyxia's System 995

CHAPTER XI.
   The Crisis 1008

CHAPTER XII.
   The Lion's Mouth Shut 1014

CHAPTER XIII.
   The Empty Bird's-Nest 1021

CHAPTER XIV.
   The Day in Fairy-Land. 1025

CHAPTER XV.
   The Old Manor-House 1037

Chapter XVI.
  Sam Lawson's Discoveries 1046

Chapter XVII.
  The Visit to the Haunted House 1055

Chapter XVIII.
  Tina's Adoption 1074

Chapter XIX.
  *Miss Mehitable's Letter, and the Reply, Giving Further Hints
  of the Story* 1087

Chapter XX.
  *Miss Asphyxia Goes in Pursuit, and My Grandmother Gives
  Her Views on Education* 1108

Chapter XXI.
  What Is to Be Done with the Boy? 1122

Chapter XXII.
  Daily Living in Oldtown 1134

Chapter XXIII.
  We Take a Step up in the World 1147

Chapter XXIV.
  We Behold Grandeur 1162

Chapter XXV.
  Easter Sunday 1176

Chapter XXVI.
  What "Our Folks" Said at Oldtown 1196

Chapter XXVII.
  How We Kept Thanksgiving at Oldtown 1207

Chapter XXVIII.
  The Raid on Oldtown, and Uncle Fliakim's Bravery 1224

Chapter XXIX.
  My Grandmother's Blue Book 1237

Chapter XXX.
  We Begin to Be Grown-up People 1260

Chapter XXXI.
  What Shall We Do with Tina? 1273

CHAPTER XXXII.
The Journey to Cloudland 1281

CHAPTER XXXIII.
School-Life in Cloudland 1288

CHAPTER XXXIV.
Our Minister in Cloudland 1308

CHAPTER XXXV.
The Revival of Religion 1324

CHAPTER XXXVI.
After the Revival 1334

CHAPTER XXXVII.
The Minister's Wood-Spell 1344

CHAPTER XXXVIII.
Ellery Davenport 1353

CHAPTER XXXIX.
Last Days in Cloudland 1363

CHAPTER XL.
We Enter College 1372

CHAPTER XLI.
Night Talks 1383

CHAPTER XLII.
Spring Vacation at Oldtown 1388

CHAPTER XLIII.
What Our Folks Thought about It 1397

CHAPTER XLIV.
Marriage Preparations 1409

CHAPTER XLV.
Wedding Bells 1419

CHAPTER XLVI.
Wedding After-Talks at Oldtown 1430

CHAPTER XLVII.
Behind the Curtain 1436

CHAPTER XLVIII.
Tina's Solution 1444

Chapter XLIX.
  What Came of It 1452
Chapter L.
  The Last Chapter 1462

Preface

GENTLE READER,—It is customary to omit prefaces. I beg you to make an exception in my particular case; I have something I really want to say. I have an object in this book, more than the mere telling of a story, and you can always judge of a book better if you compare it with the author's object. My object is to interpret to the world the New England life and character in that particular time of its history which may be called the seminal period. I would endeavor to show you New England in its *seed-bed*, before the hot suns of modern progress had developed its sprouting germs into the great trees of to-day.

New England has been to these United States what the Dorian hive was to Greece. It has always been a capital country to emigrate from, and North, South, East, and West have been populated largely from New England, so that the seed-bed of New England was the seed-bed of this great American Republic, and of all that is likely to come of it.

New England people cannot be thus interpreted without calling into view many grave considerations and necessitating some serious thinking.

In doing this work, I have tried to make my mind as still and passive as a looking-glass, or a mountain lake, and then to give you merely the images reflected there. I desire that you should see the characteristic persons of those times, and hear them talk; and sometimes I have taken an author's liberty of explaining their characters to you, and telling you why they talked and lived as they did.

My studies for this object have been Pre-Raphaelite,—taken from real characters, real scenes, and real incidents. And some of those things in the story which may appear most romantic and like fiction are simple renderings and applications of facts.

Any one who may be curious enough to consult Rev. Elias Nason's book, called "Sir Charles Henry Frankland, or Boston in the Colonial Times," will there see a full description of the old manor-house which in this story is called the Dench

House. It was by that name I always heard it spoken of in my boyhood.

In portraying the various characters which I have introduced, I have tried to maintain the part simply of a sympathetic spectator. I propose neither to teach nor preach through them, any farther than any spectator of life is preached to by what he sees of the workings of human nature around him.

Though Calvinist, Arminian, High-Church Episcopalian, sceptic, and simple believer all speak in their turn, I merely listen, and endeavor to understand and faithfully represent the inner life of each. I myself am but the observer and reporter, seeing much, doubting much, questioning much, and believing with all my heart in only a very few things.

And so I take my leave of you.

Horace Holyoke.

I.

Oldtown and the Minister

It has always been a favorite idea of mine, that there is so much of the human in every man, that the life of any one individual, however obscure, if really and vividly perceived in all its aspirations, struggles, failures, and successes, would command the interest of all others. This is my only apology for offering my life as an open page to the reading of the public.

Besides this, however, every individual is part and parcel of a great picture of the society in which he lives and acts, and his life cannot be painted without reproducing the picture of the world he lived in; and it has appeared to me that my life might recall the image and body of a period in New England most peculiar and most interesting, the impress of which is now rapidly fading away. I mean the ante-railroad times,—the period when our own hard, rocky, sterile New England was a sort of half Hebrew theocracy, half ultra-democratic republic of little villages, separated by a pathless ocean from all the civilization and refinement of the Old World, forgotten and unnoticed, and yet burning like live coals under this obscurity with all the fervid activity of an intense, newly kindled, peculiar, and individual life.

My early life lies in one of these quiet little villages,—that of Oldtown, in Massachusetts. It was as pretty a village as ever laid itself down to rest on the banks of a tranquil river. The stream was one of those limpid children of the mountains, whose brown, clear waters ripple with a soft yellow light over many-colored pebbles, now brawling and babbling on rocky bottoms, dashing hither and thither in tiny cascades, throwing white spray over green mossed rocks, and then again sweeping silently, with many a winding curve, through soft green meadows, nursing on its bosom troops of water-lilies, and bordering its banks with blue and white violets, snow-flaked meadow-sweet, and wild iris. Hither and thither,

in the fertile tracts of meadow or upland through which this
little stream wound, were some two dozen farm-houses, hid
in green hollows, or perched on breezy hill-tops; while close
alongside of the river, at its widest and deepest part, ran one
rustic street, thickly carpeted with short velvet green grass,
where stood the presiding buildings of the village.

First among these was the motherly meeting-house, with
its tall white spire, its ample court of sheds and stalls for the
shelter of the horses and the various farm-wagons which came
in to Sunday services. There was also the school-house, the
Academy, and Israel Scran's store, where everything was sold,
from hoe-handles up to cambric needles, where the post-office was kept, and where was a general exchange of news, as
the different farm-wagons stood hitched around the door,
and their owners spent a leisure moment in discussing politics
or theology from the top of codfish or mackerel barrels, while
their wives and daughters were shopping among the dress
goods and ribbons, on the other side of the store. Next to the
store was the tavern,—with a tall sign-post which used to
creak and flap in the summer winds, with a leisurely, rich,
easy sort of note of invitation,—a broad veranda in front,
with benches,—an open tap-room, where great barrels of
beer were kept on draft, and a bar where the various articles
proscribed by the temperance society were in those days allowed an open and respectable standing. This tavern veranda
and tap-room was another general exchange, not in those
days held in the ill repute of such resorts now. The minister
himself, in all the magnificence of his cocked hat and ample
clerical wig, with his gold-headed cane in his hand, would
sometimes step into the tap-room of a cold winter morning,
and order a mug of flip from obsequious Amaziah the host,
and, while he sipped it, would lecture with a severe gravity a
few idle, ragged fellows who were spending too much time
in those seductive precincts. The clergy in those days felt that
they never preached temperance with so warm a fervor as between the comfortable sips of a beverage of whose temperate
use they intended to be shining examples. The most vivid image of respectability and majesty which a little boy born in a
Massachusetts village in those early days could form was the
minister. In the little theocracy which the Pilgrims established

in the wilderness, the ministry was the only order of nobility. They were the only privileged class, and their voice it was that decided *ex cathedra* on all questions both in Church and State, from the choice of a Governor to that of the district-school teacher.

Our minister, as I remember him, was one of the cleanest, most gentlemanly, most well bred of men,—never appearing without all the decorums of silk stockings, shining knee and shoe buckles, well-brushed shoes, immaculately powdered wig, out of which shone his clear, calm, serious face, like the moon out of a fleecy cloud.

Oldtown was originally an Indian town, and one of the most numerous and powerful of the Indian tribes had possessed the beautiful tracts of meadow and upland farms that bordered the Sepaug River. Here the great apostle of the Indians had established the first missionary enterprise among them, under the patronage of a society in England for the propagation of the Gospel in foreign parts; here he had labored and taught and prayed with a fervor which bowed all hearts to his sway, and gathered from the sons of the forest a church of devoted Christians. The harsh guttural Indian language, in the fervent alembic of his loving study, was melted into a written dialect; a Bible and hymn-book and spelling-book seemed to open a path to an Indian literature. He taught them agriculture, and many of the arts and trades of civilized life. But he could not avert the doom which seems to foreordain that those races shall dry up and pass away with their native forests, as the brook dries up when the pines and hemlocks which shaded its source are torn away.

In my boyhood, three generations had passed since the apostle died. The elms which two grateful Indian catechumens had set out as little saplings on either side of his gateway were now two beautiful pillars, supporting each its firmament of leafy boughs, and giving a grand air of scholarly retirement to the plain, old-fashioned parsonage; but the powerful Indian tribe had dwindled to a few scattered families, living an uncertain and wandering life on the outskirts of the thrift and civilization of the whites.

Our minister was one of those cold, clear-cut, polished crystals that are formed in the cooling-down of society, after it has been melted and purified by a great enthusiasm. No-body can read Dr. Cotton Mather's biography of the first ministers of Massachusetts, without feeling that they were men whose whole souls were in a state of fusion, by their conceptions of an endless life; that the ruling forces which impelled them were the sublimities of a world to come; and that, if there be such a thing possible as perfect faith in the eternal and invisible, and perfect loyalty to God and to con-science, these men were pervaded by it.

More than this, many of them were men of a softened and tender spirit, bowed by past afflictions, who had passed through the refining fires of martyrdom, and come to this country, counting not home or kindred dear to them, that they might found a commonwealth for the beloved name and honor of One who died for them. *Christo et Ecclesiæ*, was the seal with which they consecrated all their life-work, from the founding of Harvard College down to the district school in every village. These men lived in the full spirit of him who said, "I am crucified with Christ, nevertheless I live: yet not I, but Christ liveth in me"; and the power of this invisible and mighty love shed a softening charm over the austere grandeur of their lives. They formed a commonwealth where vice was wellnigh impossible; where such landmarks and boundaries and buttresses and breastworks hedged in and de-fended the morality of a community, that to go very far out of the way would require some considerable ingenuity and enterprise.

The young men grew up grave and decorous through the nursing of church, catechism, and college, all acting in one line; and in due time many studious and quiet youths stepped, in regular succession, from the college to the theo-logical course, and thence to the ministry, as their natural and appointed work. They received the articles of faith as taught in their catechism without dispute, and took their places calmly and without opposition to assist in carrying on a so-ciety where everything had been arranged to go under their direction, and they were the recognized and appointed leaders and governors.

The Rev. Mr. Lothrop had come of good ministerial blood for generations back. His destination had always been for the pulpit. He was possessed of one of those calm, quiet, sedate natures, to whom the temptations of turbulent nerves or vehement passions are things utterly incomprehensible.

Now, however stringent and pronounced may be the forms in which one's traditional faith may have been expressed, it is certain that temperament gradually, and with irresistible power, modifies one's creed. Those features of a man's professed belief which are unsympathetic with his nature become to his mind involved in a perpetual haze and cloud of disuse; while certain others, which are congenial, become vivid and pronounced; and thus, practically, the whole faith of the man changes without his ever being aware of the fact himself.

Parson Lothrop belonged to a numerous class in the third generation of Massachusetts clergy, commonly called Arminian,—men in whom this insensible change had been wrought from the sharply defined and pronounced Calvinism of the early fathers. They were mostly scholarly, quiet men, of calm and philosophic temperament, who, having from infancy walked in all the traditions of a virtuous and pious education, and passed from grade to grade of their progress with irreproachable quiet and decorum, came to regard the spiritual struggles and conflicts, the wrestlings and tears, the fastings and temptations of their ancestors with a secret scepticism,—to dwell on moralities, virtues, and decorums, rather than on those soul-stirring spiritual mysteries which still stood forth unquestioned and uncontradicted in their confessions of faith.

Parson Lothrop fulfilled with immaculate precision all the properties exacted in his station. Oldtown having been originally an Indian missionary station, an annual stipend was paid the pastor of this town from a fund originally invested in England for the conversion of the Indians; and so Parson Lothrop had the sounding-board of Eliot's pulpit put up over the great arm-chair in his study, and used to call thither weekly the wandering remnants of Indian tribes to be catechised. He did not, like his great predecessor, lecture them on the original depravity of the heart, the need of a radical and thorough regeneration by the Holy Spirit of God, or the power of Jesus as a Saviour from sin, but he talked to them of the evil of drunkenness and lying and idleness, and exhorted them to be temperate and industrious; and when they, notwithstanding his exhortations, continued to lead an unthrifty, wandering life, he calmly expressed his conviction that they were children of the forest, a race destined to extinction with the progress of civilization, but continued his labors for them with automatic precision.

His Sunday sermons were well-written specimens of the purest and most elegant Addisonian English, and no mortal could find fault with a word that was in them, as they were sensible, rational, and religious, as far as they went. Indeed, Mr. Lothrop was quite an elegant scholar and student in literature, and more than once surprise had been expressed to him that he should be willing to employ his abilities in so obscure a town and for so inconsiderable a salary. His reply was characteristic. "My salary is indeed small, but it is as certain as the Bank of England, and retirement and quiet give me leisure for study."

He, however, mended his worldly prospects by a matrimonial union with a widow lady of large property, from one of the most aristocratic families of Boston. Mrs. Dorothea Lucretia Dixwell was the widow of a Tory merchant, who, by rare skill in trimming his boat to suit the times, had come through the Revolutionary war with a handsome property unimpaired, which, dying shortly after, he left to his widow. Mrs. Dixwell was in heart and soul an Englishwoman, an adorer of church and king, a worshipper of aristocracy and all the powers that be. She owned a pew in King's Chapel, and clung more punctiliously than ever to her prayer-book, when all other memorials of our connection with the mother country had departed.

Could it be thought that the elegant and rich widow would smile on the suit of an obscure country Congregational clergyman? Yet she did; and for it there were many good reasons. Parson Lothrop was a stately, handsome, well-proportioned man, and had the formal and ceremonious politeness of a gentleman of the old school, and by family descent Mrs. Dorothea's remembrance could trace back his blood to that of some very solid families among the English gentry, and as there were no more noblemen to be had in America, marrying a minister in those days was the next best thing to it; and so Mrs. Dixwell became Mrs. Parson Lothrop, and made a processional entrance into Oldtown in her own coach, and came therein to church the first Sunday after her marriage, in all the pomp of a white brocade, with silver flowers on it of life-size, and white-satin slippers with heels two inches high. This was a great grace to show to a Congregational church, but Mrs. Lothrop knew the duty of a wife, and conformed to it heroically. Nor was Parson Lothrop unmindful of the courtesies of a husband in this matrimonial treaty, for it was stipulated and agreed that Madam Lothrop should have full liberty to observe in her own proper person all the festivals and fasts of the Church of England, should be excused from all company and allowed to keep the seclusion of her own apartment on Good Friday, and should proceed immediately thereafter in her own coach to Boston, to be present at the Easter services in King's Chapel. The same procession to Boston in her own coach took place also on Whitsunday and Christmas. Moreover she decked her house with green boughs and made mince-pies at Christmas time, and in short conducted her housekeeping in all respects as a zealous member of the Church of England ought.

In those days of New England, the minister and his wife were considered the temporal and spiritual superiors of everybody in the parish. The idea which has since gained ground, of regarding the minister and his family as a sort of stipendiary attachment and hired officials of the parish, to be overlooked, schooled, advised, rebuked, and chastened by every deacon and deacon's wife or rich and influential parishioner, had not then arisen. Parson Lothrop was so calmly awful in his sense of his own position and authority, that it would have been a sight worth seeing to witness any of his parish coming to him, as deacons and influential parishioners now-a-days feel at liberty to come to their minister, with suggestions and admonitions. His manner was ever gracious and affable, as of a man who habitually surveys every one from above, and is disposed to listen with indulgent courtesy, and has advice in reserve for all seekers; but there was not the slightest shadow of anything which encouraged the most presuming to offer counsel in return. And so the marriage with the rich Episcopal widow, her processional entry into Oldtown, the coach and outriders, the brocade and satin slippers, were all submitted to on the part of the Oldtown people without a murmur.

The fact is, that the parson himself felt within his veins the traditional promptings of a far-off church and king ancestry, and relished with a calm delight a solemn trot to the meeting-house behind a pair of fat, decorous old family horses, with a black coachman in livery on the box. It struck him as sensible and becoming. So also he liked a sideboard loaded with massive family plate, warmed up with the ruby hues of old wines of fifty years' ripening, gleaming through crystal decanters, and well-trained man-servants and maid-servants, through whom his wig, his shoes, and all his mortal belongings, received daily and suitable care. He was to Mrs. Dorothea the most deferential of husbands, always rising with stately courtesy to offer her a chair when she entered an apartment, and hastening to open the door for her if she wished to pass out, and passing every morning and evening the formal gallantries and inquiries in regard to her health and well-being which he felt that her state and condition required.

Fancy if you can the magnificent distance at which this sublime couple stood above a little ten-year-old boy, who wore a blue checked apron, and every day pattered barefoot after the cows, and who, at the time this story of myself begins, had just, by reaching up on his little bare tiptoes, struck the great black knocker on their front door.

The door was opened by a stately black servant, who had about him an indistinct and yet perceptible atmosphere of ministerial gravity and dignity, looking like a black doctor of divinity.

"Is Mr. Lothrop at home," I said, blushing to the roots of my hair.

"Yes, sonny," said the black condescendingly.

"Won't you please tell him father's dying, and mother wants him to come quick?" and with that, what with awe, and what with grief, I burst into tears.

The kind-hearted black relaxed from his majesty at once, and said: "Lord bress yer soul! why, don't cry now, honey, and I'll jes' call missis";—and in fact, before I knew it, he had opened the parlor door, and ushered me into the august presence of Lady Lothrop, as she used to be familiarly called in our village.

She was a tall, thin, sallow woman, looking very much like those portraits by Copley that still adorn some old houses in Boston; but she had a gentle voice, and a compassionate, womanly way with her. She comforted me with a cake, which she drew from the closet in the sideboard; decanted some very choice old wine into a bottle, which she said I was to carry to my mother, and be sure and tell her to take a little of it herself. She also desired me to give her a small book which she had found of use in times of affliction, called "The Mourner's Companion," consisting mainly of choice selections from the English Book of Common Prayer.

When the minister came into the room I saw that she gave a conjugal touch to the snowy plaited frill of his ruffled shirt, and a thoughtful inspection to the wide linen cambric frills which set off his well-formed hand, and which were a little discomposed by rubbing over his writing-table,—nay, even upon one of them a small stain of ink was visible, as the minister, unknown to himself, had drawn his ruffles over an undried portion of his next Sunday's sermon.

"Dinah must attend to this," she said; "here's a spot requiring salts of lemon; and, my dear," she said, in an insinuating tone, holding out a richly bound velvet prayer-book, "would you not like to read our service for the Visitation of the Sick,—it is so excellent."

"I am well aware of that, my love," said the minister, repelling her prayer-book with a gentle stateliness, "but I assure you, Dorothea, it would not do,—no, it would not do."

I thought the good lady sighed as her husband left the house, and looked longingly after him through the window as he walked down the yard. She probably consoled herself with the reflection that one could not have everything, and that her spouse, if not in the Established Church of England, was every way fitted to adorn it had he only been there.

II.

My Father

M Y good reader, it must sometimes have fallen under
your observation that there is a class of men who go
through life under a cloud, for no other reason than that,
being born with the nature of gentlemen, they are nevertheless poor. Such men generally live under a sense of the dissat-
isfaction and rebuke of our good mother world; and yet it is
easy to see all the while that even a moderate competence
would at any moment turn their faults into virtues, and make
them in everybody's opinion model characters.

Now you know there are plants to whom poor soil or rich
soil seems to make no manner of difference. Your mullein and
your burdock do admirably on a gravelly hillside, and admirably in rich garden soil. Nothing comes amiss with them.
But take a saffrano rose or a hyacinth and turn it out to shift
for itself by the roadside, and it soon dwindles and pines, and
loses its color and shape, till everybody thinks such a
wretched, ragged specimen of vegetation had better be out of
the world than in it.

From all I remember of my poor father, he had the organization and tastes of a scholar and a gentleman; but he was
born the son of a poor widow, who hardly knew from week
to week where the few hard-earned dollars were to come from
which kept her and her boy in the very plainest food and
clothing. So she thought herself happy when she apprenticed
him to a paper-maker. Thence he had fought his way up with
his little boy hands towards what to him was light and life,—
an education. Harvard College, to his eyes, was like the distant vision of the New Jerusalem to the Christian. Thither he
aspired, thither he meant to go. Through many a self-denial,
many an hour of toil,—studying his Latin grammar by night
in the paper-mill, saving his odd pennies, and buying book
after book, and treasuring each one as a mine of wealth,—he
went on, till finally he gained enough of a standing to teach,
first the common school, and then the Academy.

While he was teacher of the Academy he made his first false step, which was a false step only because he was poor,—he fell in love with my mother. If he had been well to do in the world, everybody would have said that it was the most natural and praiseworthy thing possible. It was some extenuation of his fault that my poor mother was very pretty and attractive,—she was, in fact, one of my father's prettiest scholars. He saw her daily, and so the folly grew upon him, till he was ready to sacrifice his life's object, and consent to be all his days a poor academy teacher in Oldtown, that he might marry her.

One must be very much of a woman for whom a man can sacrifice the deepest purpose of his life without awaking to regret it. I do not say that my father did so; and yet I could see, from the earliest of my recollection, that ours was a household clouded by suppressed regrets, as well as embarrassed by real wants.

My mother was one of those bright, fair, delicate New England girls who remind us of the shell-pink of the wood-anemone, or the fragile wind-flower; and every one must remember how jauntily they toss their gay little heads as they grow in their own mossy dells, at the root of old oaks or beeches, but how quickly they become withered and bedraggled when we gather them.

My mother's gayety of animal spirits, her sparkle and vivacity, all went with the first year of marriage. The cares of housekeeping, the sicknesses of maternity and nursing, drained her dry of all that was bright and attractive; and my only recollections of her are of a little quiet, faded, mournful woman, who looked on my birth and that of my brother Bill as the greatest of possible misfortunes, and took care of us with a discouraged patience, more as if she pitied us for being born than as if she loved us.

My father seemed to regard her with a half-remorseful tenderness, as he strove by extra reading and study to make up for the loss of that education the prospect of which he had sacrificed in his marriage. In common with a great many scholars of that day and of this, he ignored his body altogether, and tasked and strained his brain with night studies till his health sank under it; and Consumption, which in New

England stands ever waiting for victims, took his cold hand in hers, and led him quietly but irresistibly downward.

Such, to this moment, was my father's history; and you will see the truth of what I have been saying,—that a modest little property would have changed all his faults and mistakes into proprieties and virtues.

He had been sick so long, so very long, it seemed to my child-mind! and now there was approaching him that dark shadow so terrible to flesh and heart, in whose dimness every one feels an instinctive longing for aid. That something must be done for the dying to prepare them for their last lonesome journey is a strong instinct of every soul; and I had heard my mother pathetically urging my father that morning to send for the minister.

"What good will it do, Susy?" had been his answer, given with a sort of weary despondence; but still he had assented, and I had gone eagerly to bring him.

I was, for my part, strong in faith. I wanted to do something for my father, and I felt certain that the minister would know what was the right thing; and when I set forth with him, in his full panoply,—wig and ruffles and gold-headed cane,—I felt somehow as if the ark of the covenant was moving down the street to our house.

My mother met the minister at the door, with tears yet undried in her eyes, and responded in the fullest manner to the somewhat stately, but yet gracious, inquiries which he made as to my father's health and condition, and thanked him for the kindly messages and gifts of Lady Lothrop, which I had brought.

Then he was shown into the sick-room. My father was lying propped up by pillows, and with the bright flush of his afternoon fever on his cheeks. He was always a handsome man, fastidious about his person and belongings; and as he lay with his long thin hands folded together over the bed-clothes, his hair clinging in damp curls round his high white forehead, and his large, clear hazel eyes kindled with an unnatural brightness, he formed on my childish memory a picture that will never fade. There was in his eyes at this moment that peculiar look of deep suffering which I have sometimes seen in the eyes of wounded birds or dying animals,—something that spoke of a quiet, unutterable anguish.

My father had been not only a scholar, but a thinker,—one of those silent, peculiar natures whose thoughts and reasonings too often wander up and down the track of commonly received opinion, as Noah's dove of old, without finding rest for the sole of their foot. When a mind like this is approaching the confines of the eternal unknown, there is often a conflict of thought and emotion, the utterance of which to a receptive and sympathizing soul might bring relief. Something there was of intense yearning and inquiry in the first glance he threw on the minister, and then it changed to one of weary languor. With the quick spiritual instincts of that last dying hour, he had seen into the soul of the man,—that there was nothing there for him. Even the gold-headed cane was not the rod and staff for him in the dark valley.

There was, in fact, something in the tranquil, calm, unpathetic nature of that good man, which rendered him peculiarly inapt to enter into the secret chamber of souls that struggle and suffer and doubt. He had a nature so evenly balanced, his course in life had been so quiet and unruffled, his speculations and doubts had been of so philosophical and tranquil a kind, that he was not in the least fitted to become father confessor to a sick and wounded spirit.

His nature was one that inclined to certain stately formalities and proprieties; and although he had, in accordance with his station in the Congregational church, put from him the forms of the Church of England, and was supposed to rely on the extemporaneous movements of the hour, his devotional exercises, nevertheless, had as much a stereotype form as if they had been printed in a book. We boys always knew when the time for certain familiar phrases and expressions would occur in his Sunday morning prayer, and exactly the welcome words which heralded the close of the afternoon exercise.

I remember now, as he knelt by my father's bedside, how far off and distant the usual opening formula of his prayer made the Great Helper to appear. "Supremely great, infinitely glorious, and ever-blessed God," it said, "grant that we may suitably realize the infinite distance between us, worms of the dust, and thy divine majesty."

I was gazing earnestly at my father, as he lay with his bright, yearning, troubled eyes looking out into the misty shadows of the eternal world, and I saw him close them wearily, and open them again, with an expression of quiet endurance. The infinite distance was a thing that he realized only too well; but who should tell him of an infinite *nearness* by which those who are far off are made nigh?

After the prayer, the minister expressed the hope that my father would be resigned to the decrees of infinite wisdom, and my father languidly assented; and then, with a ministerial benediction, the whole stately apparition of ghostly aid and comfort departed from our house.

One thing, at all events, had been gained,—my father had had the minister and been prayed with, and nobody in Oldtown could say that everything had not been properly done, according to the code of spiritual etiquette generally established. For our town, like other little places, always kept a wide-awake eye on the goings and doings of her children. Oldtown had had its own opinion of my father for a great while, and expressed it freely in tea-drinkings, quiltings, at the store, and at the tavern. If Oldtown's advice had been asked, there were a hundred things that he did which would have been left undone, and a hundred things done which he did not do. Oldtown knew just whom he ought to have married instead of marrying my mother, and was certain he could have had her too. Oldtown knew just how and when he might have made himself a rich man, and did n't. Oldtown knew exactly when, how, and why he caught the cold that set him into a consumption, and what he ought to have taken to cure it, and did n't. And now he was, so to speak, dying under a cloud, just as Oldtown always knew he would. But one thing was certain, and Oldtown was glad to hear of it,—he was n't an infidel, as had been at different times insinuated, for he had had the minister and been prayed with; and so, though he never had joined the church, Oldtown indulged some hope for his hereafter.

When the minister was gone, my father said, with a weary smile: "There, Susy dear, I hope you are satisfied now. My poor child," he added, gently drawing her to sit down by him, and looking at her with the strange, solemn dispassionateness of dying people, who already begin to feel that they are of another sphere,—"my poor dear little girl! You were so pretty and so gay! I did you a great wrong in marrying you."

"O, don't say that Horace," said my mother.

"It's true, though," said my father. "With a richer and more prosperous man, you might have been blooming and happy yet. And this poor little man," said my father, stroking my head,—"perhaps fate may have something better in store for him. If I had had but the ghost of a chance, such as some men have,—some who do not value it, who only throw it away,—I might have been something. I had it in me; but no one will ever know it now. My life is a miserable, disgusting failure. Burn all my papers, Susy. Promise me that."

"I will do just what you say, Horace."

"And, Susy, when I am gone, don't let all the old gossips of Oldtown come to croak and croon over me, and make their stupid remarks on my helpless body. I hate country funerals. Don't make a vulgar show of me for their staring curiosity. Death is dreary enough at best, but I never could see any sense in aggravating its horrors by stupid funeral customs. Instead of dressing me in those ghostly, unnatural grave-clothes that people seem to delight in, just let me be buried in my clothes and let the last look my poor children have of me be as natural and familiar as possible. The last look of the dead ought to be sacred to one's friends alone. Promise, now, Susy," he said earnestly, "promise to do as I say."

"O Horace, I do promise,—I promise to do all you say. You know I always have."

"Yes, poor dear child, you have; you have been only too good for me."

"O Horace, how can you say so!" and my poor mother fell on my father's neck in a paroxysm of weeping.

But his great, bright eyes gathered no tears; they were fixed in an awful stillness. "My darling, you must not," he said tenderly, but with no answering emotion. "Calm yourself. And now, dear, as I am sure that to-morrow I shall not be with you, you must send for your mother to be with you to-night. You know she will come."

"Father," said I earnestly, "where are you going?"

"Where?" said he, looking at me with his clear, mournful eyes. "God knows, my son. I do not. It ought to be enough for me that God does know."

III.

My Grandmother

"Now, Horace," said my mother, "you must run right up to your grandfather's, and tell your grandmother to come down and stay with us to-night; and you and Bill must stay there."

Bill, my brother, was a year or two older than I was; far more healthy, and consequently, perhaps, far more noisy. At any rate, my mother was generally only too glad to give her consent to his going anywhere of a leisure afternoon which would keep him out of the house, while I was always retained as her own special waiter and messenger.

My father had a partiality for me, because I was early an apt reader, and was fond of the quiet of his study and his books. He used to take pride and pleasure in hearing me read, which I did with more fluency and understanding than many children of twice my age; and thus it happened that, while Bill was off roaming in the woods this sunny autumn afternoon, I was the attendant and waiter in the sick-room. My little soul was oppressed and sorrowful, and so the message that sent me to my grandmother was a very welcome one, for my grandmother was, in my view, a tower of strength and deliverance. My mother was, as I have said, a frail, mournful, little, discouraged woman; but my grandmother belonged to that tribe of strong-backed, energetic, martial mothers in Israel, who brought to our life in America the vigorous bone and muscle and hearty blood of the yeomanry of Old England. She was a valiant old soul, who fearlessly took any bull in life by the horns, and was ready to shake him into decorum.

My grandfather, a well-to-do farmer, was one of the chief magnates of the village, and carried on a large farm and certain mills at the other end of it. The great old-fashioned farmhouse where they lived was at some distance from my father's cottage, right on the banks of that brown, sparkling, clear stream I have spoken of.

My grandfather was a serene, moderate, quiet man, upward of sixty, with an affable word and a smile for everybody,—a man of easy habits, never discomposed, and never in a hurry, —who had a comfortable faith that somehow or other the affairs of this world in general, and his own in particular, would turn out all right, without much seeing to on his part.

My grandmother, on the contrary, was one of those wide-awake, earnest, active natures, whose days were hardly ever long enough for all that she felt needed to be done and attended to. She had very positive opinions on every subject, and was not at all backward in the forcible and vigorous expression of them; and evidently considering the apostolic gift of exhortation as having come straight down to her, she failed not to use it for the benefit of all whom it might concern.

Oldtown had in many respects a peculiar sort of society. The Indian tribe that once had been settled in its vicinity had left upon the place the tradition of a sort of wandering, gypsy, tramping life, so that there was in the town an unusual number of that roving, uncertain class of people, who are always falling into want, and needing to be helped, hanging like a tattered fringe on the thrifty and well-kept petticoat of New England society.

The traditions of tenderness, pity, and indulgence which the apostle Eliot had inwrought into the people of his day in regard to the Indians, had descended through all the families, and given to that roving people certain established rights in every household, which in those days no one ever thought of disowning. The wandering Indian was never denied a good meal, a seat by the kitchen fire, a mug of cider, and a bed in the barn. My grandfather, out of his ample apple-orchard, always made one hogshead of cider which was called the Indian hogshead, and which was known to be always on tap for them; and my grandmother not only gave them food, but more than once would provide them with blankets, and allow them to lie down and sleep by her great kitchen fire. In those days New England was such a well-watched, and schooled and catechised community, and so innocent in the general tone of its society, that in the rural villages no one ever locked the house doors of a night. I have lain awake many a night hearing the notes of the whippoorwills and the frogs, and listening to the sighing of the breeze, as it came through the great wide-open front-door of the house, and swept up the staircase. Nobody ever thought of being afraid that the tramper whom he left asleep on the kitchen floor would rouse up in the night and rob the house. In fact, the poor vagrants were themselves tolerably innocent, not being guilty of very many sins darker than occasional drunkenness and habitual unthrift. They were a simple, silly, jolly set of rovers, partly Indian and partly whites who had fallen into Indian habits, who told stories, made baskets, drank cider, and raised puppies, of which they generally carried a supply in their wanderings, and from which came forth in due time an ample supply of those yellow dogs of old, one of whom was a standing member of every well-regulated New England family. Your yellow dog had an important part to act in life, as much as any of his masters. He lay in the kitchen door and barked properly at everything that went by. He went out with the children when they went roving in the woods Saturday afternoon, and was always on hand with a sober face to patter on his four solemn paws behind the farm-wagon as it went to meeting of a Sunday morning. And in meeting, who can say what an infinite fund of consolation their yellow, honest faces and great, soft eyes were to the children tired of the sermon, but greatly consoled by getting a sly opportunity to stroke Bose's yellow back? How many little eyes twinkled sympathetically through the slats of the high-backed pews, as the tick of their paws up and down the broad aisle announced that they were treating themselves to that meditative locomotion allowed to good dogs in sermon-time!

Surrounded by just such a community as I have described, my grandmother's gifts never became rusty for want of exercise. Somebody always needed straightening up and attending to. Somebody was to be exhorted, rebuked, or admonished, with all long-suffering and doctrine; and it was cheering to behold, after years of labors that had appeared to produce no very brilliant results on her disciples, how hale and vigorous her faith yet remained in the power of talking to people. She seemed to consider that evil-doers fell into sins and evils of all sorts merely for want of somebody to talk to them, and would fly at some poor, idle, loafing, shiftless object who staggered past her house from the tavern, with the same earnestness and zeal for the fortieth time as if she had not exhorted him vainly for the thirty-nine before.

In fact, on this very Saturday afternoon, as I was coming down the hill, whence I could see the mill and farm-house, I caught sight of her standing in the door, with cap-border erect, and vigorous gesticulation, upbraiding a poor miserable dog commonly called Uncle Eph, who stood swaying on the bridge, holding himself up by the rails with drunken gravity, only answering her expostulations by shaking his trembling fist at her, irreverently replying in every pause of her expostulation, "You—darned—old sheep you!"

"I do wonder now, mother, that you can't let Uncle Eph alone," said my Aunt Lois, who was washing up the kitchen floor behind her. "What earthly good does it do to be talking to him? He always has drank, and always will."

"I can't help it," quoth my grandmother; "it 's a shame to him, and his wife lying there down with rheumatism. I don't see how folks can do so."

"And I don't see as it 's any of our business," said Aunt Lois. "What is it to us? We are not our brother's keeper."

"Well, it was Cain that said that to begin with," said my grandmother; "and I think it 's the spirit of Cain not to care what becomes of our neighbors!"

"I can't help it if it is. I don't see the use of fussing and caring about what you can't help. But there comes Horace Holyoke, to be sure. I suppose, mother, you 're sent for; I 've been expecting it all along.—Stand still there!" she called to me as I approached the door, "and don't come in to track my floor."

I stood without the door, therefore, and delivered my message; and my grandmother promptly turned into her own bedroom, adjoining the kitchen, to make herself ready to go. I stood without the door, humbly waiting Aunt Lois's permission to enter the house.

"Well," said Aunt Lois, "I suppose we 've got to have both boys down here to-night. They 've got to come here, I suppose, and we may as well have 'em first as last. It 's just what I told Susy, when she would marry Horace Holyoke. I saw it just as plain as I see it now, that we should have to take care of 'em. It 's aggravating, because Susy neglected her opportunities. She might have been Mrs. Captain Shawmut, and had her carriage and horses, if she 'd only been a mind to."

"But," said my Aunt Keziah, who sat by the chimney, knitting,—"but if she could n't love Captain Shawmut, and *did* love Horace Holyoke—"

"Fiddlestick about that. Susy would 'a' loved him well enough if she 'd 'a' married him. She 'd 'a' loved anybody that she married well enough,—she 's one of the kind; and he 's turned out a very rich man, just as I told her. Susy was the only handsome one in our family, and she might have done something with herself if she 'd had sense."

"For my part," said Aunt Keziah, "I can't blame people for following their hearts. I never saw the money yet that would 'a' tempted *me* to marry the man I did n't love."

Poor Aunt Keziah had the reputation of being, on the whole, about the homeliest woman in Oldtown. She was fat and ill-shaped and clumsy, with a pale, greenish tinge to her complexion, watery, whitish-blue eyes, very rough thin hair, and ragged, scrubby eyebrows. Nature had been peculiarly unkind to her; but far within her ill-favored body she had the most exalted and romantic conceptions. She was fond of reading Young's Night Thoughts, Mrs. Rowe's Meditations, and Sir Charles Grandison, and always came out strong on the immaterial and sentimental side of every question. She had the most exalted ideas of a lofty, disinterested devotion, which she, poor soul! kept always simmering on a secret altar, ready to bestow on some ideal hero, if ever he should call for it. But, alas! her want of external graces prevented any such application. The princess was enchanted behind a hedge of ragged and unsightly thorns.

She had been my mother's aid and confidante in her love affair, and was therefore regarded with a suppressed displeasure by Aunt Lois, who rejoined, smartly: "I don't think, Kezzy, that you are likely to be tempted with offers of any sort; but Susy did have 'em,—plenty of 'em,—and took Horace Holyoke when she might 'a' done better. Consequence is, we 've got to take her and her children home and take care of 'em. It 's just our luck. Your poor folks are the ones that are sure to have children,—the less they have to give 'em, the more they have. I think, for my part, that people that can't provide for children ought not to have 'em. Susy 's no more fit to bring up those boys than a white kitten. There never was a great deal to Susy," added Aunt Lois, reflectively, as, having finished the ablution of the floor, she took the dish of white sand to sand it.

"Well, for my part," said Aunt Kezzy, "I don't blame Susy a mite. Horace Holyoke was a handsome man, and the Holyokes are a good family. Why, his grandfather was a minister, and Horace certainly was a man of talents. Parson Lothrop said, if he 'd 'a' had early advantages, there were few men would have surpassed him. If he 'd only been able to go to college."

"And why was n't he able to go to college? Because he must needs get married. Now, when people set out to do a thing, I like to see 'em do it. If he 'd a let Susy alone and gone to college, I dare say he might have been distinguished, and all that. I would n't have had the least objection. But no, nothing would do but he must get married, and have two boys, and then study himself into his grave, and leave 'em to us to take care of."

"Well now, Lois," said my grandmother, coming out with her bonnet on, and her gold-headed cane in her hand, "if I were you, I would n't talk so. What do you always want to fight Providence for?"

"Providence!" said my Aunt Lois, with a sniff. "I don't call it Providence. I guess, if folks would behave themselves, Providence would let them alone."

"Why, everything is ordered and foreordained," said Aunt Keziah.

"Besides that," said my grandmother, setting down her stick hard on the floor, "there 's no use in such talk, Lois. What 's done 's done; and if the Lord let it be done, we may. We can't always make people do as we would. There 's no use in being dragged through the world like a dog under a cart, hanging back and yelping. What we must do, we may as well do willingly,—as well walk as be dragged. Now we 've got Susy and her children to take care of, and let 's do it. They 've got to come here, and they shall come,—should come if there were forty-eleven more of 'em than there be,—so now you just shut up."

"Who said they should n't come?" said Aunt Lois. "I want to know now if I have n't moved out of the front room and gone into the little back chamber, and scoured up every inch of that front-room chamber on my hands and knees, and brought down the old trundle-bed out of the garret and cleaned it up, on purpose to be all ready for Susy and those children. If I have n't worked hard for them, I'd like to have any one tell me; and I don't see, for my part, why I should be scolded."

"She was n't scolding you, Lois," said Aunt Keziah, pacifically.

"She was, too; and I never open my mouth," said Lois, in an aggrieved tone, "that you all don't come down on me. I'm sure I don't see the harm of wishing Susy had married a man that could 'a' provided for her; but some folks feel so rich, nothing comes amiss with 'em. I suppose we are able to send both boys to college, and keep 'em like gentlemen, are n't we?"

My grandmother had not had the benefit of this last volley, as she prudently left the house the moment she had delivered herself of her reproof to Aunt Lois.

I was listening at the door with a troubled spirit. Gathering from the conversation that my father and mother, somehow, had been improperly conducted people, and that I and my brother Bill had no business to have been born, and that our presence on the earth was, somehow or other, of the nature of an impertinence, making everybody a vast deal of trouble. I could not bear to go in; and as I saw my grandmother's stately steppings in the distance, I ran after her as fast as my little bare feet could patter, and seized fast hold of her gown with the same feeling that makes a chicken run under a hen.

"Why, Horace," said my grandmother, "why didn't you stay down at the house?"

"I did n't want to, grandma; please let me go with you."

"You must n't mind Aunt Lois's talk,—she means well."

I snuffled and persisted, and so had my own way, for my grandmother was as soft-hearted to children as any of the meekest of the tribe who bear that revered name; and so she did n't mind it that I slid back into the shadows of my father's room, under cover of her ample skirts, and sat down disconsolate in a dark corner.

My grandmother brought to the sick-room a heavier responsibility than any mere earthly interest could have laid on her. With all her soul, which was a very large one, she was an earnest Puritan Calvinist. She had been nourished in the sayings and traditions of the Mathers and the Eliots, and all the first generation of the saints who had possessed Massachusetts. To these she had added the earnest study of the writings of Edwards and Bellamy, and others of those brave old thinkers who had broken up the crust of formalism and mechanical piety that was rapidly forming over the New England mind.

My remembrances of her are always as a reader. In her private chamber was always a table covered with books; and though performing personally the greater share of the labors of a large family, she never failed to have her quiet hour every afternoon for reading. History and biography she delighted in, but she followed with a keen relish the mazes of theology.

During the days of my father's health and vigor, he had one of those erratic, combative minds that delight in running logical tilts against received opinions, and was skilled in finding the weak point in all assertions. My grandmother, who believed with heart and soul and life-blood everything that she believed at all, had more than once been worsted by him in arguments where her inconsiderate heat outran her logic. These remembrances had pressed heavily on her soul during the time of his sickness, and she had more than once earnestly sought to bring him to her ways of thinking,—ways which to her view were the only possible or safe ones; but during his illness he had put such conversation from him with the quick, irritable impatience of a sore and wounded spirit.

On some natures theology operates as a subtle poison; and the New England theology in particular, with its intense clearness, its sharp-cut crystalline edges and needles of thought, has had in a peculiar degree the power of lacerating the nerves of the soul, and producing strange states of morbid horror and repulsion. The great unanswerable questions which must perplex every thinking soul that awakes to consciousness in this life are there posed with the severest and most appalling distinctness. These awful questions underlie all religions,—they belong as much to Deism as to the strictest orthodoxy,—in fact, they are a part of human perception and consciousness, since it cannot be denied that Nature in her teaching is a more tremendous and inexorable Calvinist than the Cambridge Platform or any other platform that ever was invented.

But in New England society, where all poetic forms, all the draperies and accessories of religious ritual, have been rigidly and unsparingly retrenched, there was nothing between the soul and these austere and terrible problems; it was constantly and severely brought face to face with their infinite mystery. When my grandmother came into the room, it was with an evident and deep emotion working in her strong but plain features. She came up to the bed and grasped my father's hand earnestly.

"Well, mother," he said, "my time is come, and I have sent for you to put Susy and the children into your hands."

"I 'll take 'em and welcome,—you know that," said my grandmother heartily.

"God bless you, mother,—I do know it," he said; "but do have a special eye on poor little Horace. He has just my passion for books and study; and if he could be helped to get an education, he might do what I have failed to do. I leave him my books,—you will try and help him, mother?"

"Yes, my son, I will; but O my son, my son!" she added with trembling eagerness, "how is it with you now? Are you prepared for this great change?"

"Mother," he said in a solemn voice, yet speaking with a great effort, "no sane man ever comes to my age, and to this place where I lie, without thinking a great deal on all these things. I have thought,—God knows how earnestly,—but I cannot talk of it. We see through a glass darkly here. There perhaps we shall see clearly. You must be content to leave me where I leave myself,—in the hands of my Creator. He can do no wrong."

IV.

The Village Do-Nothing

"WAL naow, Horace, don't ye cry so. Why, I'm railly concerned for ye. Why, don't you s'pose your daddy's better off? Why, sartin *I* do. Don't cry, there's a good boy, now. I'll give ye my jack-knife now."

This was addressed to me the day after my father's death, while the preparations for the funeral hung like a pall over the house, and the terror of the last cold mystery, the tears of my mother, and a sort of bustling dreariness on the part of my aunts and grandmother, all conspired to bear down on my childish nerves with fearful power. It was a doctrine of those good old times, no less than of many in our present days, that a house invaded by death should be made as forlorn as hands could make it. It should be rendered as cold and stiff, as unnatural, as dead and corpse-like as possible, by closed shutters, looking-glasses pinned up in white sheets, and the locking up and hiding out of sight of any pleasant little familiar object which would be thought out of place in a sepulchre. This work had been driven through with unsparing vigor by Aunt Lois, who looked like one of the Fates as she remorselessly cleared away every little familiar object belonging to my father, and reduced every room to the shrouded stillness of a well-kept tomb.

Of course no one thought of looking after me. It was not the fashion of those days to think of children, if only they would take themselves off out of the way of the movements of the grown people; and so I had run out into the orchard back of the house, and, throwing myself down on my face under an apple-tree in the tall clover, I gave myself up to despair, and was sobbing aloud in a nervous paroxysm of agony, when these words were addressed to me. The speaker was a tall, shambling, loose-jointed man, with a long, thin visage, prominent watery blue eyes, very fluttering and seedy habiliments, who occupied the responsible position of first do-nothing-in-ordinary in our village of Oldtown, and as such I must introduce him to my readers' notice.

Every New England village, if you only think of it, must have its do-nothing as regularly as it has its school-house or meeting-house. Nature is always wide awake in the matter of compensation. Work, thrift, and industry are such an incessant steam-power in Yankee life, that society would burn itself out with intense friction were there not interposed here and there the lubricating power of a decided do-nothing,—a man who won't be hurried, and won't work, and will take his ease in his own way, in spite of the whole protest of his neighborhood to the contrary. And there is on the face of the whole earth no do-nothing whose softness, idleness, general inaptitude to labor, and everlasting, universal shiftlessness can compare with that of this worthy, as found in a brisk Yankee village.

Sam Lawson filled this post with ample honor in Oldtown. He was a fellow dear to the souls of all "us boys" in the village, because, from the special nature of his position, he never had anything more pressing to do than croon and gossip with us. He was ready to spend hours in tinkering a boy's jack-knife, or mending his skate, or start at the smallest notice to watch at a woodchuck's hole, or give incessant service in tending a dog's sprained paw. He was always on hand to go fishing with us on Saturday afternoons; and I have known him to sit hour after hour on the bank, surrounded by a troop of boys, baiting our hooks and taking off our fish. He was a soft-hearted old body, and the wrigglings and contortions of our prey used to disturb his repose so that it was a regular part of his work to kill the fish by breaking their necks when he took them from the hook.

"Why, lordy massy, boys," he would say, "I can't bear to see no kind o' critter in torment. These 'ere pouts ain't to blame for bein' fish, and ye ought to put 'em out of their misery. Fish hes their rights as well as any on us."

Nobody but Sam would have thought of poking through the high grass and clover on our back lot to look me up, as I lay sobbing under the old apple-tree, the most insignificant little atom of misery that ever bewailed the inevitable.

Sam was of respectable family, and not destitute of educa-

tion. He was an expert in at least five or six different kinds of
handicraft, in all of which he had been pronounced by the
knowing ones to be a capable workman, "if only he would
stick to it." He had a blacksmith's shop, where, when the fit
was on him, he would shoe a horse better than any man in
the county. No one could supply a missing screw, or apply a
timely brace, with more adroitness. He could mend cracked
china so as to be almost as good as new; he could use carpenter's tools as well as a born carpenter, and would doctor a
rheumatic door or a shaky window better than half the
professional artisans in wood. No man could put a refractory
clock to rights with more ingenuity than Sam,—that is, if
you would give him his time to be about it.

I shall never forget the wrath and dismay which he roused
in my Aunt Lois's mind by the leisurely way in which, after
having taken our own venerable kitchen clock to pieces, and
strewn the fragments all over the kitchen, he would roost over
it in endless incubation, telling stories, entering into long-
winded theological discussions, smoking pipes, and giving
histories of all the other clocks in Oldtown, with occasional
memoirs of those in Needmore, the North Parish, and Podunk, as placidly indifferent to all her volleys of sarcasm and
contempt, her stinging expostulations and philippics, as the
sailing old moon is to the frisky, animated barking of some
puppy dog of earth.

"Why, ye see, Miss Lois," he would say, "clocks can't be
druv; that 's jest what they can't. Some things can be druv,
and then agin some things can't, and clocks is that kind. They
's jest got to be humored. Now this 'ere 's a 'mazin' good
clock; give me my time on it, and I 'll have it so 't will keep
straight on to the Millennium."

"Millennium!" says Aunt Lois, with a snort of infinite contempt.

"Yes, the Millennium," says Sam, letting fall his work in a
contemplative manner. "That 'ere 's an interestin' topic now.
Parson Lothrop, he don't think the Millennium will last a
thousand years. What 's your 'pinion on that pint, Miss Lois?"

"My opinion is," said Aunt Lois, in her most nipping
tones, "that if folks don't mind their own business, and do

with their might what their hand finds to do, the Millennium won't come at all."

"Wal, you see, Miss Lois, it 's just here,—one day is with the Lord as a thousand years, and a thousand years as one day."

"I should think you thought a day was a thousand years, the way you work," said Aunt Lois.

"Wal," says Sam, sitting down with his back to his desperate litter of wheels, weights, and pendulums, and meditatively caressing his knee as he watched the sailing clouds in abstract meditation, "ye see, ef a thing 's ordained, why it 's got to be, ef you don't lift a finger. That 'ere 's *so* now, ain't it?"

"Sam Lawson, you are about the most aggravating creature I ever had to do with. Here you 've got our clock all to pieces, and have been keeping up a perfect hurrah's nest in our kitchen for three days, and there you sit maundering and talking with your back to your work, fussin' about the Millennium, which is none of your business, or mine, as I know of! Do either put that clock together or let it alone!"

"Don't you be a grain uneasy, Miss Lois. Why, I 'll have your clock all right in the end, but I can't be druv. Wal, I guess I 'll take another spell on 't to-morrow or Friday."

Poor Aunt Lois, horror-stricken, but seeing herself actually in the hands of the imperturbable enemy, now essayed the tack of conciliation. "Now do, Lawson, just finish up this job, and I 'll pay you down, right on the spot; and you need the money."

"I 'd like to 'blige ye, Miss Lois; but ye see money ain't everything in this world. Ef I work tew long on one thing, my mind kind o' gives out, ye see; and besides, I 've got some 'sponsibilities to 'tend to. There 's Mrs. Captain Brown, she made me promise to come to-day and look at the nose o' that 'ere silver teapot o' hern; it 's kind o' sprung a leak. And then I 'greed to split a little oven-wood for the Widdah Pedee, that lives up on the Shelburn road. Must visit the widdahs in their affliction, Scriptur' says. And then there 's Hepsy: she 's allers a castin' it up at me that I don't do nothing for her and the chil'en; but then, lordy massy, Hepsy hain't no sort o' patience. Why jest this mornin' I was a tellin' her to count up

her marcies, and I 'clare for 't if I did n't think she 'd a
throwed the tongs at me. That 'ere woman's temper railly
makes me consarned. Wal, good day, Miss Lois. I 'll be along
again to-morrow or Friday, or the first o' next week." And
away he went with long, loose strides down the village street,
while the leisurely wail of an old fuguing tune floated back
after him, —

> "Thy years are an
> Etarnal day,
> Thy years are an
> Etarnal day."

"An eternal torment," said Aunt Lois, with a snap. "I 'm
sure, if there 's a mortal creature on this earth that I pity, it 's
Hepsy Lawson. Folks talk about her scolding, — that Sam
Lawson is enough to make the saints in Heaven fall from
grace. And you can't *do* anything with him: it 's like charging
bayonet into a woolsack."

Now, the Hepsy thus spoken of was the luckless woman
whom Sam's easy temper, and a certain youthful reputation
for being a capable fellow, had led years before into the snares
of matrimony with him, in consequence of which she was
encumbered with the bringing up of six children on very
short rations. She was a gnarly, compact, efficient little pepper-box of a woman, with snapping black eyes, pale cheeks,
and a mouth always at half-cock, ready to go off with some
sharp crack of reproof at the shoreless, bottomless, and tide-
less inefficiency of her husband. It seemed to be one of those
facts of existence that she could not get used to, nor find anywhere in her brisk, fiery little body a grain of cool resignation
for. Day after day she fought it with as bitter and intense a
vigor, and with as much freshness of objurgation, as if it had
come upon her for the first time, — just as a sharp, wiry little
terrier will bark and bark from day to day, with never-ceasing
pertinacity, into an empty squirrel-hole. She seemed to have
no power within her to receive and assimilate the great truth
that her husband was essentially, and was to be and always
would be, only a do-nothing.

Poor Hepsy was herself quite as essentially a do-some-
thing, — an early-rising, bustling, driving, neat, efficient, ca-

pable little body,—who contrived, by going out to day's
works,—washing, scrubbing, cleaning,—by making vests for
the tailor, or closing and binding shoes for the shoemaker, by
hoeing corn and potatoes in the garden at most unseasonable
hours, actually to find bread to put into the mouths of the six
young ravens aforesaid, and to clothe them decently. This
might all do very well; but when Sam—who believed with
all his heart in the modern doctrines of woman's rights so far
as to have no sort of objection to Hepsy's sawing wood or
hoeing potatoes if she chose—would make the small degree
of decency and prosperity the family had attained by these
means a text on which to preach resignation, cheerfulness,
and submission, then Hepsy's last cobweb of patience gave
out, and she often became, for the moment, really dangerous,
so that Sam would be obliged to plunge hastily out of doors
to avoid a strictly personal encounter.

It was not to be denied that poor Hepsy really was a scold,
in the strong old Saxon acceptation of the word. She had
fought life single-handed, tooth and nail, with all the ferocity
of outraged sensibilities, and had come out of the fight
scratched and dishevelled, with few womanly graces. The
good wives of the village, versed in the outs and ins of their
neighbors' affairs, while they admitted that Sam was not all
he should be, would sometimes roll up the whites of their
eyes mysteriously, and say, "But then, poor man, what could
you expect when he has n't a happy home? Hepsy's temper
is, you know," etc., etc.

The fact is, that Sam's softly easy temper and habits of miscellaneous handiness caused him to have a warm corner in
most of the households. No mothers ever are very hard on a
man who always pleases the children; and every one knows
the welcome of a universal gossip, who carries round a district a wallet of choice bits of neighborhood information.

Now Sam knew everything about everybody. He could tell
Mrs. Major Broad just what Lady Lothrop gave for her best
parlor carpet, that was brought over from England, and just
on what occasions she used the big silver tankard, and on
what they were content with the little one, and how many
pairs of long silk stockings the minister had, and how many
rows of stitching there were on the shoulders of his Sunday

shirts. He knew just all that was in Deacon Badger's best room, and how many silver table-spoons and teaspoons graced the beaufet in the corner; and when each of his daughters was born, and just how Miss Susy came to marry as she did, and who wanted to marry her and could n't. He knew just the cost of Major Broad's scarlet cloak and shoe-buckles, and how Mrs. Major had a real *Ingy* shawl up in her "camphire" trunk, that cost nigh as much as Lady Lothrop's. Nobody had made love, or married, or had children born, or been buried, since Sam was able to perambulate the country, without his informing himself minutely of every available particular; and his unfathomable knowledge on these subjects was an unfailing source of popularity.

Besides this, Sam was endowed with no end of idle accomplishments. His indolence was precisely of a turn that enjoyed the excitement of an occasional odd bit of work with which he had clearly no concern, and which had no sort of tendency toward his own support or that of his family. Something so far out of the line of practical utility as to be in a manner an artistic labor would awaken all the energies of his soul. His shop was a perfect infirmary for decayed articles of *virtu* from all the houses for miles around. Cracked china, lame tea-pots, broken shoe-buckles, rickety tongs, and decrepit fire-irons, all stood in melancholy proximity, awaiting Sam's happy hours of inspiration; and he was always happy to sit down and have a long, strictly confidential conversation concerning any of these with the owner, especially if Hepsy were gone out washing, or on any other work which kept her at a safe distance.

Sam could shave and cut hair as neatly as any barber, and was always in demand up and down the country to render these offices to the sick. He was ready to go for miles to watch with invalids, and a very acceptable watcher he made, beguiling the night hours with endless stories and legends. He was also an expert in psalmody, having in his youth been the pride of the village singing-school. In those days he could perform reputably on the bass-viol in the choir of a Sunday with a dolefulness and solemnity of demeanor in the highest degree edifying,—though he was equally ready of a week-evening in scraping on a brisk little fiddle, if any of the thoughtless ones wanted a performer at a husking or a quilting frolic. Sam's obligingness was many-sided, and he was equally prepared at any moment to raise a funeral psalm or whistle the time of a double-shuffle.

But the more particular delight of Sam's heart was in funerals. He would walk miles on hearing the news of a dangerous illness, and sit roosting on the fence of the premises, delighted to gossip over the particulars, but ready to come down at any moment to do any of the odd turns which sickness in a family makes necessary; and when the last earthly scene was over, Sam was more than ready to render those final offices from which the more nervous and fastidious shrink, but in which he took almost a professional pride.

The business of an undertaker is a refinement of modern civilization. In simple old days neighbors fell into one another's hands for all the last wants of our poor mortality; and there were men and women of note who took a particular and solemn pride in these mournful offices. Sam had in fact been up all night in our house, and having set me up in the clover, and comforted me with a jack-knife, he proceeded to inform me of the particulars.

"Why, ye see, Horace, I ben up with 'em pretty much all night; and I laid yer father out myself, and I never see a better-lookin' corpse. It's a 'mazin' pity your daddy hed such feelin's 'bout havin' people come to look at him, 'cause he does look beautiful, and it's been a long time since we've hed a funeral, anyway, and everybody was expectin' to come to his 'n, and they'll all be dissipinted if the corpse ain't show'd; but then, lordy massy, folks ought n't to think hard on 't ef folks hes their own way 'bout their own funeral. That 'ere's what I've been a tellin' on 'em all, over to the tavern and round to the store. Why, you never see such a talk as there was about it. There was Aunt Sally Morse, and Betsey and Patsy Sawin, and Mis' Zeruiah Bacon, come over early to look at the corpse, and when they was n't let in, you never heerd sich a jawin'. Betsey and Patsy Sawin said that they allers suspected your father was an infidel, or some sich, and now they was clear; and Aunt Sally, she asked who made his shroud, and when she heerd there was n't to be none, he was laid out in his clothes, she said she never heerd such unchris-

tian doin's,—that she always had heerd he had strange opinions, but she never thought it would come to that."

"My father is n't an infidel, and I wish I could kill 'em for
talking so," said I, clenching my jack-knife in my small fist,
and feeling myself shake with passion.

"Wal, wal, I kind o' spoke up to 'em about it. I was n't a-
goin' to hear no sich jaw; and says I, 'I think ef there is any
body that knows what's what about funerals I'm the man,
fur I don't s'pose there's a man in the county that's laid out
more folks, and set up with more corpses, and ben sent for
fur and near, than I have, and my opinion is that mourners
must always follow the last directions gi'n to 'em by the person. Ef a man has n't a right to have the say about his own
body, what hes he a right to?' Wal, they said that it was putty
well of me to talk so, when I had the privilege of sittin' up
with him, and seein' all that was to be seen. 'Lordy massy,'
says I, 'I don't see why ye need envi me; 't ain't my fault that
folks thinks it's agreeable to have me round. As to bein' buried in his clothes, why, lordy massy, 't ain't nothin' so extraordinary. In the old country great folks is very often laid out in
their clothes. 'Member, when I was a boy, old Mr. Sanger,
the minister in Deerbrook, was laid out in his gown and
bands, with a Bible in his hands, and he looked as nateral as
a pictur. I was at Parson Rider's funeral, down to Wrentham.
He was laid out in white flannel. But then there was old Captain Bigelow, down to the Pint there, he was laid out regular
in his rigimentals, jest as he wore 'em in the war, epaulets and
all.' Wal now, Horace, your daddy looks jest as peaceful as a
psalm-tune. Now, you don't know,—jest as nateral as if he'd
only jest gone to sleep. So ye may set your heart at rest 'bout
him."

It was one of those beautiful serene days of October, when
the earth lies as bright and still as anything one can dream of
in the New Jerusalem, and Sam's homely expressions of sympathy had quieted me somewhat. Sam, tired of his discourse,
lay back in the clover, with his hands under his head, and
went on with his moralizing.

"Lordy massy, Horace, to think on 't,—it's so kind o' sol-
emnizin'! It's one's turn to-day, and another's to-morrow.

We never know when our turn 'll come." And Sam raised a
favorite stave,—

> "And must these active limbs of mine
> Lie moulderin' in the clay?"

"Active limbs! I guess so!" said a sharp voice, which came
through the clover-heads like the crack of a rifle. "Well, I 've
found you at last. Here you be, Sam Lawson, lyin' flat on
your back at eleven o'clock in the morning, and not a potato
dug, and not a stick of wood cut to get dinner with; and I
won't cut no more if we never have dinner. It 's no use a
humorin' you,—doin' your work for you. The more I do, the
more I may do; so come home, won't you?"

"Lordy massy, Hepsy," said Sam, slowly erecting himself
out of the grass, and staring at her with white eyes, "you
don't ought to talk so. I ain't to blame. I had to sit up with
Mr. Holyoke all night, and help 'em lay him out at four
o'clock this mornin'."

"You 're always everywhere but where you 've business to
be," said Hepsy; "and helpin' and doin' for everybody but
your own. For my part, I think charity ought to begin at
home. You 're everywhere, up and down and round,—over
to Shelbun, down to Podunk, up to North Parish; and here
Abram and Kiah Stebbins have been waitin' all the morning
with a horse they brought all the way from Boston to get you
to shoe."

"Wal now, that 'ere shows they know what 's what. I told
Kiah that ef they 'd bring that 'ere hoss to me I 'd 'tend to his
huffs."

"And be off lying in the mowing, like a patridge, when
they come after ye. That 's one way to do business," said
Hepsy.

"Hepsy, I was just a miditatin'. Ef we don't miditate sometimes on all these 'ere things, it 'll be wus for us by and by."

"Meditate! I 'll help your meditations in a way you won't
like, if you don't look out. So now you come home, and stop
your meditatin', and go to doin' somethin'. I told 'em to
come back this afternoon, and I 'd have you on the spot if

't was a possible thing," said the very practical Hepsy, laying firm hold of Sam's unresisting arm, and leading him away captive.

I stole into the darkened, silent room where my father had lain so long. Its desolate neatness struck a chill to my heart. Not even a bottle remained of the many familiar ones that used to cover the stand and the mantel-piece; but he, lying in his threadbare Sunday coat, looked to me as I had often seen him in later days, when he had come from school exhausted, and fallen asleep on the bed. I crept to his side and nestled down on the floor as quietly as a dog lies down by the side of his master.

V.

The Old Meeting-House

THE next day was the funeral, and I have little remembrance in it of anything but what was dreary. Our Puritan ancestors, in the decision of their reaction from a dead formalism, had swept away from the solemn crises of life every symbolic expression; and this severe bareness and rigid restriction were nowhere more striking than in funeral services, as conducted in these early times in Massachusetts.

There was at the house of mourning simply a prayer, nothing more; and then the procession of relatives, friends, and towns-people walked silently to the grave, where, without text, prayer, or hymn, the dust was forever given to its fellow-dust. The heavy thud of the clods on the coffin, the rattling of spades, and the fall of the earth, were the only voices that spoke in that final scene. Yet that austere stillness was not without its majesty, since it might be interpreted, not as the silence of indifference, but as the stillness of those whose thoughts are too mighty for words. It was the silence of the unutterable. From the grave my mother and her two boys were conducted to my grandfather's house,—the asylum ever ready for the widowed daughter.

The next day after was Sunday, and a Sunday full of importance in the view of Aunt Lois, Aunt Keziah, and, in fact, of every one in the family. It was the custom, on the first Sabbath after a bereavement, for the whole family circle to be present together in church, to request, in a formal note, the prayers of the congregation that the recent death might be sanctified to them. It was a point of honor for all family connections to be present at this service, even though they should not attend the funeral; and my Uncle Bill, a young Sophomore in Cambridge College, had come down duly to be with us on the occasion. He was a joyous, spirited, jolly, rollicking young fellow, not in the slightest degree given to funereal reflections, and his presence in the house always brought a certain busy cheerfulness which I felt to lighten my darkness.

One thing certainly had a tendency in that direction, which was that Aunt Lois was always perceptibly ameliorated by Uncle Bill's presence. Her sharp, spare features wore a relaxed and smiling aspect, her eyes had a softer light, and she belied her own frequent disclaimer, that she never had any beauty, by looking almost handsome.

Poor Aunt Lois! I am afraid my reader will not do justice to her worth by the specimens of her ways and words which I have given. Any one that has ever pricked his fingers in trying to force open a chestnut-burr may perhaps have moralized at the satin lining, so smooth and soft, that lies inside of that sharpness. It is an emblem of a kind of nature very frequent in New England, where the best and kindest and most desirable of traits are enveloped in an outside wrapping of sharp austerity.

No person rendered more deeds of kindness in the family and neighborhood than Aunt Lois. She indeed bore the cares of the whole family on her heart; she watched and prayed and fretted and scolded for all. Had she cared less, she might perhaps have appeared more amiable. She *invested* herself, so to speak, in others; and it was vital to her happiness, not only that they should be happy, but that they should be happy precisely on her pattern and in her way. She had drawn out the whole family chart, and if she had only had power to make each one walk tractably in the path she foreordained, her sharp, thin face might have had a few less wrinkles. It seemed to her so perfectly evident that the ways she fixed upon for each one were ways of pleasantness and paths of peace, that she scarcely could have patience with Providence for allowing things to fall out in a way so entirely different from her designs.

Aunt Lois was a good Christian, but she made that particular mistake in repeating the Lord's Prayer which so many of us quite unconsciously do,—she always said, *My* will be done, instead of Thy will. Not in so many words, of course,—it was the secret inner voice of her essential nature that spoke and said one thing, while her tongue said another. But then who can be sure enough of himself in this matter, to cast the first stone at Aunt Lois?

It was the fashion of the Calvinistic preaching of that time to put the doctrine of absolute and unconditional submission to God in the most appalling forms, and to exercise the conscience with most severe supposititious tests. After many struggles and real agonies, Aunt Lois had brought herself to believe that she would be willing to resign her eternal salvation to the Divine glory; that she could consent to the eternal perdition of those on whom her heart was most particularly set, were it God's will; and thus her self-will, as she supposed, had been entirely annihilated, whereas it was only doubled back on itself, and ready to come out with tenfold intensity in the unsuspected little things of this life, where she looked less at Divine agency than human instrumentality. No law, as she supposed, required her to submit to people's acting foolishly in their worldly matters, particularly when she was able and willing to show them precisely how they ought to act.

Failing of a prosperous marriage for my mother, Aunt Lois's heart was next set upon a college education for my Uncle Bill, the youngest and brightest of the family. For this she toiled and economized in family labor, and eked it out by vest-making at the tailor's, and by shoe-binding at the shoe-maker's,—all that she might have something to give to Bill for spending-money, to keep up his standing respectably in college. Her antagonistic attitude toward my brother and myself proceeded less from hardness of heart than from an anxious, worrying fear that we should trench on the funds that at present were so heavily taxed to bring Uncle Bill through college. Especially did she fear that my father had left me the legacy of his own ungratified desire for an education, and that my grandmother's indulgence and bountifulness might lead her to encourage me in some such expectations, and then where was the money to come from? Aunt Lois foresaw contingencies afar off. Not content with the cares of the present day and hour, she dived far into the future, and carried all sorts of imaginary loads that would come in supposititious cases. As the Christian by the eye of faith sees all sorts of possible good along the path of future duty, so she by the eye of cautiousness saw every possible future evil that could arise in every supposable contingency. Aunt Lois's friends often had particular reason to wish that she cared less for them, for then, perhaps, she might give them some peace. But nothing is so hopeless as your worthy domestic house-dog, every hair of whose fur bristles with watchfulness, and who barks at you incessantly from behind a most terrible intrenchment of faithful labors and loving-kindnesses heaped up on your behalf.

These dear good souls who wear their life out for you, have they not a right to scold you, and dictate to you, and tie up your liberty, and make your life a burden to you? If they have not, who has? If you complain, you break their worthy old hearts. They insist on the privilege of seeking your happiness by thwarting you in everything you want to do, and putting their will instead of yours in every step of your life.

Between Aunt Lois and my father there had been that constant antagonism which is often perceptible between two human beings, each good enough in himself, but of a quality to act destructively upon the other. A satin vest and a nutmeg-grater are both perfectly harmless, and even worthy existences, but their close proximity on a jolting journey is not to be recommended.

My father never could bear my Aunt Lois in his house; and her presence had such an instant effect in developing all the combative element in him, that really the poor woman never saw him long enough under an agreeable aspect to enable her even to understand why my mother should regard him with affection; and it is not to be wondered at, therefore, that she was not a deep mourner at his death. She regarded her sister's love for my father as an unfortunate infatuation, and was more satisfied with the ways of Providence than she usually was, when its object was withdrawn.

It was according to all the laws of moral gravitation that, as soon as my father died, my mother became an obedient satellite in Aunt Lois's orbit. She was one of those dear, helpless little women, who, like flowers by the wayside, seem to be at the disposal of the first strong hand that wants to gather them. She was made to be ruled over; and so we all felt this first Sunday morning that we had come home to be under the dominion of Aunt Lois. She put on my mother's mourning-bonnet and tied it under her meek, unresisting chin, turning her round and round to get views of her from different points, and arranging her ribbons and veil and pins as if she had been a lay figure going to exhibition; and then she tied

our collars, and gave a final twitch to our jackets, and warned
us not to pull out the pins from the crape bands on our new
hats, nor to talk and look round in meeting, strengthening
the caution with, "Just so sure as you do, there 's Mr. Israel
Scran, the tithing-man, will come and take you and set you
on the pulpit stairs."

Now Mr. Israel Scran on week-days was a rather jolly, sec-
ular-looking individual, who sat on the top of a barrel in his
store, and told good stories; but Israel Scran on Sundays was
a tithing-man, whose eyes were supposed to be as a flame of
fire to search out little boys that played in meeting, and bring
them to awful retribution. And I must say that I shook in my
shoes at the very idea of his entering into judgment with me
for any misdemeanor.

Going to church on the present occasion was rather a severe and awful ceremony to my childish mind, second only to
the dreary horror of the time when we stood so dreadfully
still around the grave, and heard those heavy clods thud upon
the coffin. I ventured a timid inquiry of my mother as to what
was going to be done there.

Aunt Lois took the word out of her mouth. "Now, Horace, hush your talk, and don't worry your mother. She 's
going to put up a note to be prayed for to-day, and we are
all going to join; so you be a good boy, and don't talk."

Being good was so frequently in those days represented to
me as synonymous with keeping silence, that I screwed my
little mouth up firmly as I walked along to the meeting-house,
behind my mother, holding my brother Bill's hand, and spoke
not a word, though he made several overtures towards conversation by informing me that he saw a chipmunk, and that
if it was only Monday he 'd hit him smack; and also telling
me that Sam Lawson had promised to go pout-fishing with
us on Tuesday, with other boy temporalities of a nature
equally worldly.

The meeting-house to which our steps were tending was
one of those huge, shapeless, barn-like structures, which our
fathers erected apparently as a part of that well-arranged system by which they avoided all resemblance to those fair, poetic ecclesiastical forms of the Old World, which seemed in
their view as "garments spotted by the flesh."

The interior of it was revealed by the light of two staring rows of windows, which let in the glare of the summer sun, and which were so loosely framed, that, in wintry and windy weather, they rattled and shook, and poured in a perfect whirlwind of cold air, which disported itself over the shivering audience.

It was a part of the theory of the times never to warm these buildings by a fire; and the legend runs that once in our meeting-house the communion was administered under a temperature which actually froze the sacred elements while they were being distributed. Many a remembrance of winter sessions in that old meeting-house rose to my mind, in which I sat with my poor dangling feet perfectly numb and paralyzed with cold, and blew my finger-ends to keep a little warmth in them, and yet I never thought of complaining; for everybody was there,—mother, aunts, grandmother, and all the town. We all sat and took our hardships in common, as a plain, necessary fact of existence.

Going to meeting, in that state of society into which I was born, was as necessary and inevitable a consequence of waking up on Sunday morning as eating one's breakfast. Nobody thought of staying away,—and, for that matter, nobody wanted to stay away. Our weekly life was simple, monotonous, and laborious; and the chance of seeing the whole neighborhood together in their best clothes on Sunday was a thing which, in the dearth of all other sources of amusement, appealed to the idlest and most unspiritual of loafers. They who did not care for the sermon or the prayers wanted to see Major Broad's scarlet coat and laced ruffles, and his wife's brocade dress, and the new bonnet which Lady Lothrop had just had sent up from Boston. Whoever had not seen these would be out of society for a week to come, and not be able to converse understandingly on the topics of the day.

The meeting on Sunday united in those days, as nearly as possible, the whole population of a town,—men, women, and children. There was then in a village but one fold and one shepherd, and long habit had made the tendency to this one central point so much a necessity to every one, that to stay away from "meetin' " for any reason whatever was always a secret source of uneasiness. I remember in my early days,

sometimes when I had been left at home by reason of some
of the transient ailments of childhood, how ghostly and supernatural the stillness of the whole house and village outside
the meeting-house used to appear to me, how loudly the
clock ticked and the flies buzzed down the window-pane, and
how I listened in the breathless stillness to the distant psalm-
singing, the solemn tones of the long prayer, and then to the
monotone of the sermon, and then again to the closing
echoes of the last hymn, and thought sadly, what if some day
I should be left out, when all my relations and friends had
gone to meeting in the New Jerusalem, and hear afar the music from the crystal walls.

As our Sunday gathering at meeting was a complete picture
of the population of our village, I shall, as near as possible,
daguerreotype our Sunday audience, as the best means of
placing my readers in sympathy with the scene and actors of
this history.

The arrangement of our house of worship in Oldtown was
somewhat peculiar, owing to the fact of its having originally
been built as a mission church for the Indians. The central
portion of the house, usually appropriated to the best pews,
was in ours devoted to them; and here were arranged benches
of the simplest and most primitive form, on which were collected every Sunday the thin and wasted remnants of what
once was a numerous and powerful tribe. There were four or
five respectable Indian families, who owned comfortable
farms in the neighborhood, and came to meeting in their
farm-wagons, like any of their white neighbors.

Conspicuous among these, on the front bench, facing the
pulpit, sat the Indian head-magistrate, Justice Waban,—tall
and erect as an old pine-tree, and of a grave and reverend
aspect. Next to him was seated the ecclesiastical superior of
that portion of the congregation, Deacon Ephraim. Mild, intelligent, and devout, he was the perfect model of the praying
Indian formed in the apostolic traditions of the good Eliot.
By his side sat his wife, Keturah, who, though she had received Christian baptism, still retained in most respects the
wild instincts and untamed passions of the savage. Though
she attended church and allowed her children to be baptized,
yet, in spite of minister, elder, and tithing-man, she obsti-

nately held on to the practice of many of her old heathen
superstitions.

Old Keturah was one of the wonders of my childhood. She
was spoken of among the gossips with a degree of awe, as
one who possessed more knowledge than was good for her;
and in thunder-storms and other convulsions of nature she
would sit in her chimney-corner and chant her old Indian incantations, to my mingled terror and delight. I remember distinctly three syllables that occurred very often,—"ah-mah-ga,
ah-mah-ga,"—sometimes pronounced in wild, plaintive
tones, and sometimes in tones of menace and denunciation.
In fact, a century before, Keturah must have had a hard time
of it with her Christian neighbors; but our minister was a
gentleman and a scholar, and only smiled benignly when certain elderly ladies brought him terrible stories of Keturah's
proceedings.

Next to Keturah was seated Deborah Kummacher, an Indian woman, who had wisely forsaken the unprofitable gods
of the wild forest, and taken to the Christian occupation of
fruit-growing, and kept in nice order a fruit farm near my
grandfather's, where we children delighted to resort in the
season, receiving from her presents of cherries, pears, peaches,
or sweet apples, which she informed us she was always ready
to give to good children who said their prayers and made
their manners when they came into her house. Next behind
her came Betty Poganut, Patty Pegan, and old Sarah Wonsamug,—hard-visaged, high-cheek-boned females, with snaky-
black eyes, principally remarkable, in my mind, for the quantity of cider they could drink. I had special reason to remember this, as my grandmother's house was their favorite resort,
and drawing cider was always the work of the youngest boy.

Then there was Lem Sudock, a great, coarse, heavy-
moulded Indian, with gigantic limbs and a savage face, but
much in request for laying stone walls, digging wells, and
other tasks for which mere physical strength was the chief
requisite. Beside him was Dick Obscue, a dull, leering, lazy,
drinking old fellow, always as dry as an empty sponge, but
with an endless capacity for imbibing. Dick was of a class
which our modern civilization would never see inside of a
church, though he was in his seat in our meeting-house as

regularly as any of the deacons; but on week-days his principal employment seemed to be to perambulate the country, making stations of all the kitchen firesides, where he would tell stories, drink cider, and moralize, till the patience or cider-pitchers of his hosts ran dry, when he would rise up slowly, adjust his old straw hat, hitch up his dangling nether garments a little tighter, and, with a patronizing nod, say, "Wal, naow, 'f you can spare me I 'll go."

Besides our Indian population, we had also a few negroes, and a side gallery was appropriated to them. Prominent there was the stately form of old Boston Foodah, an African prince, who had been stolen from the coast of Guinea in early youth, and sold in Boston at some period of antiquity whereto the memory of man runneth not. All the Oldtown people, and their fathers and grandfathers, remembered old Boston just as he then existed, neither older nor younger. He was of a majestic stature, slender and proudly erect, and perfectly graceful in every movement, his woolly hair as white as the driven snow. He was servant to General Hull in the Revolutionary war, and at its close was presented by his master with a full suit of his military equipments, including three-cornered hat, with plume, epaulets, and sword. Three times a year,— at the spring training, the fall muster, and on Thanksgiving day,—Boston arrayed himself in full panoply, and walked forth a really striking and magnificent object. In the eyes of us boys, on these days, he was a hero, and he patronized us with a condescension which went to our hearts. His wife, Jinny, was a fat, roly-poly little body, delighting in red and yellow bonnets, who duly mustered into meeting a troop of black-eyed, fat, woolly-headed little negroes, whom she cuffed and disciplined during sermon-time with a matronly ferocity designed to show white folks that she was in earnest in their religious training.

Near by was old Primus King, a gigantic, retired whaleman, black as a coal, with enormous hands and feet, universally in demand in all the region about as assistant in butchering operations.

Besides these, let me not forget dear, jolly old Cæsar, my grandfather's own negro, the most joyous creature on two feet. What could not Cæsar do? He could gobble like a turkey so perfectly as to deceive the most experienced old gobbler on the farm; he could crow so like a cock that all the cocks in the neighborhood would reply to him; he could mew like a cat, and bark like a dog; he could sing and fiddle, and dance the double-shuffle, and was *au fait* in all manner of jigs and hornpipes; and one need not wonder, therefore, that old Cæsar was hugged and caressed and lauded by me in my childhood as the most wonderful of men.

There were several other colored families, of less repute, who also found seats in the negro gallery. One of them was that of Aunt Nancy Prime, famous for making election-cake and ginger-pop, and who was sent for at all the great houses on occasions of high festivity, as learned in all mysteries relating to the confection of cakes and pies. A tight, trig, bustling body she, black and polished as ebony, smooth-spoken and respectful, and quite a favorite with everybody. Nancy had treated herself to an expensive luxury in the shape of a husband,—an idle, worthless mulatto man, who was owned as a slave in Boston. Nancy bought him by intense labors in spinning flax, but found him an undesirable acquisition, and was often heard to declare, in the bitterness of her soul, when he returned from his drinking bouts, that she should never buy another nigger, she knew.

The only thing she gained by this matrimonial speculation was an abundant crop of noisy children, who, as she often declared, nearly wore the life out of her. I remember once, when I was on a visit to her cottage, while I sat regaling myself with a slice of cake, Nancy lifted the trap-door which went down into the cellar below. Forthwith the whole skirmishing tribe of little darkies, who had been rolling about the floor, seemed suddenly to unite in one coil, and, with a final flop, disappeared in the hole. Nancy gave a kick to the door, and down it went; when she exclaimed, with a sigh of exhausted patience, "Well, now then, I hope you 'll be still a minute, anyway!"

The houses of the colored people formed a little settlement by themselves in the north part of the village, where they lived on most amicable terms with all the inhabitants.

In the front gallery of the meeting-house, opposite the pulpit, was seated the choir of the church. The leader of our music was old Mump Morse, a giant of a man, in form not unlike a cider-hogshead, with a great round yellow head, and a voice like the rush of mighty winds, who was wont to boast that he could chord with thunder and lightning better than any man in the parish. Next to him came our friend Sam Lawson, whose distinguishing peculiarity it was, that he could strike into any part where his voice seemed most needed; and he often showed the miscellaneous nature of his accomplishments by appearing as tenor, treble, or counter, successively, during the rendering of one psalm. If we consider that he also pitched the tunes with his pitch-pipe, and played on his bass-viol, we shall see increasing evidence of that versatility of genius for which he was distinguished.

Another principal bass-singer was old Joe Stedman, who asserted his democratic right to do just as he had a mind to by always appearing every Sunday in a clean leather apron of precisely the form he wore about his weekly work. Of course all the well-conducted upper classes were scandalized, and Joe was privately admonished of the impropriety, which greatly increased his satisfaction, and caused him to regard himself as a person of vast importance. It was reported that the minister had told him that there was more pride in his leather apron than in Captain Browne's scarlet cloak; but Joe settled the matter by declaring that the apron was a matter of conscience with him, and of course after that there was no more to be said.

These leading characters, with a train of young men and maidens who practised in the weekly singing-school, used to conduct the musical devout exercises much to their own satisfaction, if not always to that of our higher circle.

And now, having taken my readers through the lower classes in our meeting-house, I must, in order of climax, represent to them our higher orders.

Social position was a thing in those days marked by lines whose precision and distinctness had not been blurred by the rough handling of democracy. Massachusetts was, in regard to the aroma and atmosphere of her early days, an aristocratic community. The seeds of democratic social equality lay as yet ungerminated in her soil. The State was a garden laid out with the old formal parallelograms and clipped hedges of princely courts and titled ranks, but sown with seeds of a new and rampant quality, which were destined to overgrow them all.

Even our little town had its court circle, its House of Lords and House of Commons, with all the etiquette and solemn observances thereto appertaining. At the head stood the minister and his wife, whose rank was expressed by the pew next the pulpit. Then came Captain Browne, a retired English merchant and ship-owner, who was reported to have ballasted himself with a substantial weight of worldly substance. Captain Browne was a tall, upright, florid man, a little on the shady side of life, but carrying his age with a cheerful greenness. His long, powdered locks hung in a well-tended queue down his back, and he wore a scarlet coat, with a white vest and stock, and small-clothes, while long silk stockings with knee and shoe buckles of the best paste, sparkling like real diamonds, completed his attire. His wife rustled by his side in brocade which might almost stand alone for stiffness, propped upon heels that gave a majestic altitude to her tall, thin figure.

Next came the pew of Miss Mehitable Rossiter, who, in right of being the only surviving member of the family of the former minister, was looked upon with reverence in Oldtown, and took rank decidedly in the Upper House, although a very restricted and limited income was expressed in the quality of her attire. Her Sunday suit in every article spoke of ages past, rather than of the present hour. Her laces were darned, though still they were laces; her satin gown had been turned and made over, till every possible capability of it was exhausted; and her one Sunday bonnet exhibited a power of coming out in fresh forms, with each revolving season, that was quite remarkable, particularly as each change was somewhat odder than the last. But still, as everybody knew that it was Miss Mehitable Rossiter, and no meaner person, her queer bonnets and dyed gowns were accepted as a part of those inexplicable dispensations of the Providence that watches over the higher classes, which are to be received by faith alone.

In the same pew with Miss Mehitable sat Squire Jones, once, in days of colonial rule, rejoicing in the dignity of Sheriff of the County. During the years of the Revolutionary war, he had mysteriously vanished from view, as many good Tories did; but now that the new social status was well established, he suddenly reappeared in the neighborhood, and took his place as an orderly citizen, unchallenged and unquestioned. It was enough that the Upper House received him. The minister gave him his hand, and Lady Lothrop courtesied to him, and called on his wife, and that, of course, settled the manner in which the parish were to behave; and, like an obedient flock, they all jumped the fence after their shepherd. Squire Jones, besides, was a well-formed, well-dressed man, who lived in a handsome style, and came to meeting in his own carriage; and these are social virtues not to be disregarded in any well-regulated community.

There were certain well-established ranks and orders in social position in Oldtown, which it is important that I should distinctly define. People who wore ruffles round their hands, and rode in their own coaches, and never performed any manual labor, might be said to constitute in Oldtown our House of Lords,—and they might all have been counted on two or three of my fingers. It was, in fact, confined to the personages already enumerated. There were the minister, Captain Browne, and Sheriff Jones.

But below these, yet associating with them on terms of strict equality, were a more numerous body of Commons,—men of substance and influence, but who tilled the earth with their own hands, or pursued some other active industrial calling.

Distinguished among these, sitting in the next pew to the Sheriff, was Major Broad, a practical farmer, who owned a large and thriving farm of the best New England type, and presented that true blending of the laboring man and the gentleman which is nowhere else found. He had received his military rank for meritorious services in the late Revolutionary war, and he came back to his native village with that indefinable improvement in air and manner which is given by the habits of military life. With us he owed great prestige to a certain personal resemblance to General Washington which he was asserted to have by one of our townsfolk, who had often seen him and the General on the same field, and who sent the word abroad in the town that whoever wanted to know how General Washington looked had only to look upon Major Broad. The Major was too much of a real man to betray the slightest consciousness of this advantage, but it invested him with an air of indefinable dignity in the eyes of all his neighbors, especially those of the lower ranks.

Next came my grandfather's family pew; and in our Old-town House of Commons I should say that none stood higher than he. In his Sunday suit my grandfather was quite a well-made, handsome man. His face was marked by grave, shrewd reflection, and a certain gentle cast of humor, which rarely revealed itself even in a positive smile, and yet often made me feel as if he were quietly and interiorly smiling at his own thoughts. His well-brushed Sunday coat and small-clothes, his bright knee and shoe buckles, his long silk stockings, were all arranged with a trim neatness refreshing to behold. His hair, instead of being concealed by a wig, or powdered and tied in a queue, after the manner of the aristocracy, fell in long curls on his shoulders, and was a not unbecoming silvery frame to the placid picture of his face. He was a man by nature silent and retiring, indisposed to anything like hurry or tumult, rather easy and generously free in his business habits, and quietly sanguine in his expectations. In point of material possessions he was reputed well to do, as he owned a large farm and two mills, and conducted the business thereof with a quiet easiness which was often exceedingly provoking to my grandmother and Aunt Lois. No man was more popular in the neighborhood, and the confidence of his fellow-townsmen was yearly expressed in town-meeting by his reappointment to every office of trust which he could be induced to accept. He was justice of the peace, deacon of the church, selectman,—in short, enjoyed every spiritual and temporal office by the bestowal of which his fellow-men could express confidence in him. This present year, indeed, he bore the office of tithing-man, in association with Mr. Israel Scran. It had been thought that it would be a good thing, in order to check the increasing thoughtlessness of the rising generation in regard to Sunday-keeping, to enlist in this office an authority so much respected as Deacon Badger; but the manner in which he performed its duties was not edifying to the minds of strictly disposed people. The Deacon in his official capacity was expected to stalk forth at once as a terror to evil-doers, whereas he seemed to have no capacity for terrifying anybody. When a busy individual informed him that this or that young person was to be seen walking out in the fields, or picking flowers in their gardens of a Sabbath afternoon, the Deacon always placidly answered that he had n't seen them; from which the ill-disposed would infer that he looked another way, of set purpose, and the quiet internal smile that always illuminated the Deacon's face gave but too much color to this idea.

In those days the great war of theology which has always divided New England was rife, and every man was marked and ruled as to his opinions, and the theologic lines passed even through the conjugal relation, which often, like everything else, had its Calvinistic and its Arminian side.

My grandfather was an Arminian, while my grandmother was, as I have said, an earnest, ardent Calvinist. Many were the controversies I have overheard between them, in which the texts of Scripture flew thick and fast, until my grandfather at last would shut himself up in that final fortress of calm and smiling silence which is so provoking to feminine ardor. There intrenched, he would look out upon his assailants with a quiet, imperturbable good-humor which quite drove them to despair.

It was a mystery to my grandmother how a good man, as she knew my grandfather to be, *could* remain years unmoved in the very hearing of such unanswerable arguments as she had a thousand times brought up, and still, in the very evening of his days, go on laying his serene old head on an Arminian pillow! My grandfather was a specimen of that class of men who can walk amid the opinions of their day, encircled by a halo of serene and smiling individuality which quarrels with nobody, and, without shocking any one's prejudices, preserves intact the liberty of individual dissent. He silently went on thinking and doing exactly as he pleased, and yet was always spoken of as the *good* Deacon. His calm, serene, benignant figure was a sort of benediction as he sat in his pew of a Sunday; and if he did not see the little boys that played, or, seeing them, only smilingly brought them to a sense of duty by passing them a head of fennel through the slats of the pews, still Deacon Badger was reckoned about the best man in the world.

By the side of my grandfather sat his eldest born, Uncle Jacob, a hale, thrifty young farmer, who, with his equally hale and thrifty wife, was settled on a well-kept farm at some distance from ours. Uncle Jacob was a genuine son of the soil, whose cheeks were ruddy as clover, and teeth as white as new milk. He had grown up on a farm, as quietly as a tree grows, and had never been ten miles from his birthplace. He was silent, contented, and industrious. He was in his place to be prayed for as one of a bereaved family, of course, this morning; but there was scarcely more capability of mourning in his plump, healthy body than there is in that of a well-fed, tranquil steer. But he took his weekly portion of religion kindly. It was the thing to do on Sunday, as much as making hay or digging potatoes on Monday. His wife by his side displayed no less the aspect of calm, respectable, well-to-do content. Her Sunday bonnet was without spot, her Sunday gown without wrinkle; and she had a great bunch of fennel in her pocket-handkerchief, which, from time to time, she imparted to us youngsters with a benevolent smile.

Far otherwise was the outward aspect of my grandmother's brother, Eliakim Sheril. He was a nervous, wiry, thin, dry little old man, every part of whose body appeared to be hung together by springs that were in constant vibration. He had small, keen black eyes, a thin, sharp hooked nose, which he was constantly buffeting, and blowing, and otherwise maltreating, in the fussy uneasiness which was the habit of the man.

Uncle 'Liakim was a man known as Uncle to all the village,—the kindest-souled, most untiringly benevolent, singlehearted old body that could be imagined; but his nervous activity was such as to have procured among the boys a slight change in the rendering of his name, which was always popularly given as Uncle Fliakim, and, still more abbreviated, Uncle Fly.

"Can you tell me where Mr. Sheril is," says an inquirer at the door of my grandfather's mill.

"If you want to find 'Liakim," says my grandfather, with

his usual smile, "never go after him,—you 'll never catch him;
but stand long enough on any one spot on earth, and he 's
sure to go by."

Uncle 'Liakim had his own particular business,—the overseeing of a soap and candle factory; but, besides that, he had
on his mind the business of everybody else in town,—the
sorrows of every widow, the lonely fears of every spinster, the
conversion of every reprobate, the orthodoxy of every minister, the manners and morals of all the parish,—all of which
caused him to be up early and down late, and flying about
confusedly at all hours, full of zeal, full of kindness, abounding in suggestions, asking questions the answers to which he
could not stop to hear, making promises which he did not
remember, and which got him into no end of trouble with
people who did, telling secrets, and letting innumerable cats
out of countless bags, to the dismay and affright of all reserved and well-conducted people. Uncle Fliakim, in fact,
might be regarded in our village of Oldtown as a little brown
pudding-stick that kept us in a perpetual stir. To be sure, it
was a general stir of loving-kindness and good intentions, yet
it did not always give unlimited satisfaction.

For instance, some of the more strictly disposed members
of the congregation were scandalized that Uncle Fliakim,
every stormy Sunday, nearly destroyed the solemnity of the
long prayer by the officious zeal which he bestowed in getting
sundry forlorn old maids, widows, and other desolate women
to church. He had a horse of that immortal species well
known in country villages,—made of whalebone and india-
rubber, with a long neck, a hammer-head, and one blind
eye,—and a wagon which rattled and tilted and clattered in
every part, as if infected with a double portion of its owner's
spirits; and, mounting in this, he would drive miles in the
rain or the snow, all for the pleasure of importing into the
congregation those dry, forlorn, tremulous specimens of female mortality which abound in every village congregation.

Uncle Fliakim had been talked to on this subject, and duly
admonished. The benevolence of his motives was allowed;
but why, it was asked, must he always drive his wagon with
a bang against the doorstep just as the congregation rose to
the first prayer? It was a fact that the stillness which followed

the words, "Let us pray," was too often broken by the thump
of the wagon and the sound, "Whoa, whoa! take care, there!"
from without, as Uncle Fly's blind steed rushed headlong
against the meeting-house door, as if he were going straight
in, wagon and all; and then there would be a further most
unedifying giggle and titter of light-minded young men and
damsels when Aunt Bathsheba Sawin and Aunt Jerusha Pettibone, in their rusty black-crape bonnets, with their big black
fans in their hands, slowly rustled and creaked into their seats,
while the wagon and Uncle 'Liakim were heard giggiting
away. Then the boys, if the tithing-man was not looking at
them, would bet marbles whether the next load would be old
Mother Chris and Phœbe Drury, or Hetty Walker and old
Mother Hopestill Loker.

It was a great offence to all the stricter classes that Uncle
Fly should demean his wagon by such an unedifying character
as Mother Hopestill Loker; for, though her name intimated
that she ought to have charity, still she was held no better
than a publican and sinner; and good people in those days
saw the same impropriety in such people having too much to
do with reputable Christians that they used to years ago in a
country called Palestine.

For all these reasons Uncle Fliakim was often dealt with as
one of good intentions, but wanting the wisdom which is
profitable to direct. One year his neighbors thought to employ his superfluous activity by appointing him tithing-man;
and great indeed in this department were his zeal and activity;
but it was soon found that the dear man's innocent sincerity
of heart made him the prey of every village good-for-naught
who chose to take him in. All the naughty boys in town were
agog with expectancy when Joe Valentine declared, with a
wink, that he'd drive a team Sunday right by Uncle Fly's
house, over to Hopkinton, with his full consent. Accordingly,
the next Sunday he drove leisurely by, with a solemn face and
a broad weed on his hat. Uncle Fly ran panting, half dressed,
and threw himself distractedly on the neck of the horse. "My
young friend, I cannot permit it. You must turn right back."

"My dear sir," said Joe, "have n't you heard that my mother
is lying dead in Hopkinton at this very moment?"

"Is it possible?" said my uncle, with tears in his eyes. "I beg your pardon. I had n't heard it. Proceed, by all means. I 'm sorry I interrupted you."

The next morning wicked Joe careered by again. "Good morning, Mr. Sheril. I s'pose you know my mother 's been lying dead these five years; but I 'm equally obliged for your politeness."

Vain was Uncle Fly's indignation. Greater men than he have had to give up before the sovereign power of a laugh, and erelong he resigned the office of tithing-man as one requiring a sterner metal than he possessed. In fact, an unsavory character, who haunted the tavern and was called by the boys Old Mopshear, gave a *résumé* of his opinions of tithing-men as seen from the camp of the enemy.

"Old Deacon Badger," he said, "was always lookin' 't other way, and never saw nothin' 't' was goin' on. But there was Uncle Fliakim,—wal, to be sure the gals could n't tie up their shoes without he was a lookin'; but then, come to railly doin' anythin', it was only a snap, and he was off again. He wa' n't much more 'n a middlin'-sized grasshopper, arter all. Tell you what," said Mopshear, "it takes a fellow like Israel Scran, that knows what he 's about, and 's got some *body* to do with. When old Jerusalem Ben swore he 'd drive the stage through the town a Sunday, I tell you it was fun to see Israel Scran. He jest stood out by the road and met the hosses smack, and turned 'em so quick that the stage flopped over like a wink, and Ben was off rolling over and over in the sand. Ben got the wust on 't that time. I tell you, it takes Israel Scran to be tithing-man!"

Good Uncle Fliakim had made himself extremely busy in my father's last sickness, dodging out of one door and in at another, at all hours; giving all manner of prescriptions for his temporal and spiritual state, but always in too much of a hurry to stop a minute,—a consideration which, I heard my father say, was the only one which made him tolerable. But, after all, I liked him, though he invariably tumbled over me, either in coming into or going out of the house, and then picked me up and gave me a cent, and went on rejoicing. The number of cents I acquired in this way became at last quite a little fortune.

But time would fail me to go on and describe all the quiddities and oddities of our Sunday congregation. Suffice it to say, that we all grew in those days like the apple-trees in our back lot. Every man had his own quirks and twists, and threw himself out freely in the line of his own individuality; and so a rather jerky, curious, original set of us there was. But such as we were, high and low, good and bad, refined and illiterate, barbarian and civilized, negro and white, the old meeting-house united us all on one day of the week, and its solemn services formed an insensible but strong bond of neighborhood charity.

We may rail at Blue Laws and Puritan strictness as much as we please, but certainly those communities where our fathers carried out their ideas fully had their strong points; and, rude and primitive as our meeting-houses were, this weekly union of all classes in them was a most powerful and efficient means of civilization. The man or woman cannot utterly sink who on every seventh day is obliged to appear in decent apparel, and to join with all the standing and respectability of the community in a united act of worship.

Nor were our Sunday services, though simple, devoid of their solemn forms. The mixed and motley congregation came in with due decorum during the ringing of the first bell, and waited in their seats the advent of the minister. The tolling of the bell was the signal for him that his audience were ready to receive him, and he started from his house. The clerical dress of the day, the black silk gown, the spotless bands, the wig and three-cornered hat and black gloves, were items of professional fitness which, in our minister's case, never failed of a due attention. When, with his wife leaning on his arm, he entered at the door of the meeting-house, the whole congregation rose and remained reverently standing until he had taken his seat in the pulpit. The same reverential decorum was maintained after service was over, when all remained standing and uncovered while the minister and his family passed down the broad aisle and left the house. Our fathers were no man-worshippers, but they regarded the minister as an ambassador from the great Sovereign of the universe, and paid reverence to Him whose word he bore in their treatment of him.

On the Sunday following the funeral of any one in the parish, it was customary to preach a sermon having immediate reference to the event which had occurred, in the course of which the nearest friends and relatives were directly addressed, and stood up in their seats to receive the pastoral admonition and consolation. I remember how wan and faded, like a shimmering flower, my poor mother rose in her place, while I was forcibly held down by Aunt Lois's grasp on my jacket till the "orphan children" were mentioned, when I was sent up on my feet with an impetus like a Jack in a box; and afterward the whole family circle arose and stood, as the stream of admonition and condolence became more general. We were reminded that the God of the widow and orphan never dies,—that this life is the shadow, and the life to come the substance,—that there is but one thing needful,—that as our departed friend is to-day, so we may all be to-morrow; and then the choir sung, to the tune of old Darwen,

> "Shall man, O God of life and light,
>   Forever moulder in the grave?
> Hast thou forgot thy glorious work,
>   Thy promise and thy power to save?"

I cannot say much for our country psalmody. Its execution was certainly open to severe criticism; and Uncle Fliakim, on every occasion of especial solemnity, aggravated its peculiarities by tuning up in a high, cracked voice a weird part, in those days called "counter," but which would in our days insure his being taken out of the house as a possessed person. But, in spite of all this, those old minor-keyed funeral hymns in which our fathers delighted always had a quality in them that affected me powerfully. The music of all barbarous nations is said to be in the minor key, and there is in its dark combinations something that gives piercing utterance to that undertone of doubt, mystery, and sorrow by which a sensitive spirit always is encompassed in this life.

I was of a peculiarly sensitive organization; my nerves shivered to every touch, like harp-strings. What might have come over me had I heard the solemn chants of cathedrals, and the deep pulsations of the old organ-hearts that beat there, I cannot say, but certain it is that the rude and primitive singing in our old meeting-house always excited me powerfully. It brought over me, like a presence, the sense of the infinite and eternal, the yearning and the fear and the desire of the poor finite being, so ignorant and so helpless. I left the church lifted up as if walking on air, with the final words of the psalm floating like an illuminated cloud around me,—

> "Faith sees the bright eternal doors
>   Unfold to make His children way;
> They shall be crowned with endless life,
>   And shine in everlasting day."

VI.

Fire-Light Talks in My Grandmother's Kitchen

M Y grandmother's kitchen was a great, wide, roomy apartment, whose white-sanded floor was always as clean as hands could make it. It was resplendent with the sheen of a set of scoured pewter plates and platters, which stood arranged on a dresser on one side. The great fireplace swept quite across another side. There we burned cord-wood, and the fire was built up on architectural principles known to those days. First came an enormous back-log, rolled in with the strength of two men, on the top of which was piled a smaller log; and then a fore-stick, of a size which would en- title it to rank as a log in our times, went to make the front foundation of the fire. The rearing of the ample pile there- upon was a matter of no small architectural skill, and all the ruling members of our family circle had their own opinions about its erection, which they maintained with the zeal and pertinacity which become earnest people. My grandfather, with his grave smile, insisted that he was the only reasonable fire-builder of the establishment; but when he had arranged his sticks in the most methodical order, my grandmother would be sure to rush out with a thump here and a twitch there, and divers incoherent exclamations tending to imply that men never knew how to build a fire. Frequently her in- tense zeal for immediate effect would end in a general rout and roll of the sticks in all directions, with puffs of smoke down the chimney, requiring the setting open of the outside door; and then Aunt Lois would come to the rescue, and, with a face severe with determination, tear down the whole structure and rebuild from the foundation with exactest pre- cision, but with an air that cast volumes of contempt on all that had gone before. The fact is, that there is no little nook of domestic life which gives snug harbor to so much self-will and self-righteousness as the family hearth; and this is particularly the case with wood fires, because, from the miscellaneous nature of the material, and the sprightly activity of the combustion, there is a constant occasion for tending and alteration, and so a vast field for individual opinion.

We had come home from our second Sunday service. Our evening meal of smoking brown bread and baked beans had been discussed, and the supper-things washed and put out of sight. There was an uneasy, chill moaning and groaning out of doors, showing the coming up of an autumn storm,—just enough chill and wind to make the brightness of a social hearth desirable,—and my grandfather had built one of his most methodical and splendid fires.

The wide, ample depth of the chimney was aglow in all its cavernous length with the warm leaping light that burst out in lively jets and spirts from every rift and chasm. The great black crane that swung over it, with its multiplicity of pot-hooks and trammels, seemed to have a sort of dusky illumination, like that of old Cæsar's black, shining face, as he sat on his block of wood in the deep recess of the farther corner, with his hands on the knees of his Sunday pantaloons, gazing lovingly into the blaze with all the devotion of a fire-worshipper. On week-day evenings old Cæsar used to have his jack-knife in active play in this corner, and whistles and pop-guns and squirrel-traps for us youngsters grew under his plastic hand; but on Sunday evening he was too good a Christian even to think of a jack-knife, and if his hand casually encountered it in his pocket, he resisted it as a temptation of the Devil, and sat peacefully winking and blinking, and occasionally breaking out into a ripple of private giggles which appeared to spring purely from the overflow of bodily contentment. My Uncle Bill was in that condition which is peculiarly apt to manifest itself in the youth of well-conducted families on Sunday evenings,—a kind of friskiness of spirits which appears to be a reactionary state from the spiritual tension of the day, inclining him to skirmish round on all the borders and outskirts of permitted pleasantry, and threatening every minute to burst out into most unbecoming uproariousness. This state among the youngsters of a family on Sunday evening is a familiar trial of all elders who have had the task of keeping them steady during the sacred hours.

My Uncle Bill, in his week-day frame, was the wit and buffoon of the family,—an adept in every art that could shake the sides, and bring a laugh out on the gravest face. His features were flexible, his powers of grimace and story-telling at times irresistible. On the present occasion it was only my poor mother's pale, sorrowful face that kept him in any decent bounds. He did not wish to hurt his sister's feelings, but he was boiling over with wild and elfish impulses, which he vented now by a sly tweak at the cat's tail, then by a surreptitious dig at black Cæsar's sides, which made the poor black a helpless, quivering mass of giggle, and then he would slyly make eyes and mouths at Bill and me behind Aunt Lois's chair, which almost slew us with laughter, though all the while he appeared with painful effort to keep on a face of portentous gravity.

On the part of Aunt Lois, however, there began to be manifested unequivocal symptoms that it was her will and pleasure to have us all leave our warm fireside and establish ourselves in the best room,—for we had a best room, else wherefore were we on tea-drinking terms with the high aristocracy of Oldtown? We had our best room, and kept it as cold, as uninviting and stately, as devoid of human light or warmth, as the most fashionable shut-up parlor of modern days. It had the tallest and brightest pair of brass andirons conceivable, and a shovel and tongs to match, that were so heavy that the mere lifting them was work enough, without doing anything with them. It had also a bright-varnished mahogany tea-table, over which was a looking-glass in a gilt frame, with a row of little architectural balls on it; which looking-glass was always kept shrouded in white muslin at all seasons of the year, on account of a tradition that flies might be expected to attack it for one or two weeks in summer. But truth compels me to state, that I never saw or heard of a fly whose heart could endure Aunt Lois's parlor. It was so dark, so cold, so still, that all that frisky, buzzing race, who delight in air and sunshine, universally deserted and seceded from it; yet the looking-glass, and occasionally the fire-irons, were rig-

orously shrouded, as if desperate attacks might any moment
be expected.

Now the kitchen was my grandmother's own room. In one
corner of it stood a round table with her favorite books, her
great work-basket, and by it a rickety rocking-chair, the bottom of which was of ingenious domestic manufacture, being
in fact made by interwoven strips of former coats and pantaloons of the home circle; but a most comfortable and easy
seat it made. My grandfather had also a large splint-bottomed
arm-chair, with rockers to it, in which he swung luxuriously
in the corner of the great fireplace. By the side of its ample
blaze we sat down to our family meals, and afterwards, while
grandmother and Aunt Lois washed up the tea-things, we all
sat and chatted by the firelight. Now it was a fact that nobody
liked to sit in the best room. In the kitchen each member of
the family had established unto him or her self some little pet
private snuggery, some chair or stool, some individual nook,
—forbidden to gentility, but dear to the ungenteel natural
heart,—that we looked back to regretfully when we were
banished to the colder regions of the best room.

There the sitting provisions were exactly one dozen stuffed-
seated cherry chairs, with upright backs and griffin feet, each
foot terminating in a bony claw, which resolutely grasped a
ball. These chairs were high and slippery, and preached decorum in the very attitudes which they necessitated, as no
mortal could ever occupy them except in the exercise of a
constant and collected habit of mind.

Things being thus, when my Uncle Bill saw Aunt Lois take
up some coals on a shovel, and look towards the best-room
door, he came and laid his hand on hers directly, with, "Now,
Lois, what are you going to do?"

"Going to make up a fire in the best room."

"Now, Lois, I protest. You 're not going to do any such
thing. Hang grandeur and all that.

> ' 'Mid pleasures and palaces though we may roam,
>   Be it ever so humble, there 's no place like home,'

you know; and home means right here by mother's kitchen-
fire, where she and father sit, and want to sit. You know

nobody ever wants to go into that terrible best room of yours."

"Now, Bill, how you talk!" said Aunt Lois, smiling, and putting down her shovel.

"But then, you see," she said, the anxious cloud again settling down on her brow,—"you see, we 're exposed to calls, and who knows who may come in? I should n't wonder if Major Broad, or Miss Mehitable, might drop in, as they saw you down from College."

"Let 'em come; never fear. They all know we 've got a best room, and that 's enough. Or, if you 'd rather, I 'll pin a card to that effect upon the door; and then we 'll take our ease. Or, better than that, I 'll take 'em all in and show 'em our best chairs, andirons, and mahogany table, and then we can come out and be comfortable."

"Bill, you 're a saucy boy," said Aunt Lois, looking at him indulgently as she subsided into her chair.

"Yes, that he always was," said my grandfather, with a smile of the kind that fathers give to frisky sophomores in college.

"Well, come sit down, anyway," said my grandmother, "and let 's have a little Sunday-night talk."

"Sunday-night talk, with all my heart," said Bill, as he seated himself comfortably right in front of the cheerful blaze. "Well, it must be about 'the meetin',' of course. Our old meeting-house looks as elegant as ever. Of all the buildings I ever saw to worship any kind of a being in, that meeting-house certainly is the most extraordinary. It really grows on me every time I come home!"

"Come, now, Bill," said Aunt Lois.

"Come, now! Ain't I coming? Have n't said anything but what you all know. Said our meeting-house was extraordinary, and you all know it is; and there 's extraordinary folks in it. I don't believe so queer a tribe could be mustered in all the land of Israel as we congregate. I hope some of our oddities will be in this evening after cider. I need to study a little, so that I can give representations of nature in our club at Cambridge. Nothing like going back to nature, you know. Old Obscue, seems to me, was got up in fine fancy this morning; and Sam Lawson had an extra touch of the hearse about him. Hepsy must have been disciplining him this morning,

before church. I always know when Sam is fresh from a matrimonial visitation: he 's peculiarly pathetic about the gills at
those times. Why don't Sam come in here?"

"I 'm sure I hope he won't," said Aunt Lois. "One reason why
I wanted to sit in the best room to-night was that every old tramper and queer object sees the light of our kitchen fire, and comes
in for a lounge and a drink; and then, when one has genteel persons calling, it makes it unpleasant."

"O, we all know you 're aristocratic, Lois; but, you see, you
can't be indulged. You must have your purple and fine linen and
your Lazarus at the gate come together some time, just as they
do in the meeting-house and the graveyard. Good for you all, if
not agreeable."

Just at this moment the conversation was interrupted by a
commotion in the back sink-room, which sounded much like a
rush of a flight of scared fowl. It ended with a tumble of a row of
milk-pans toward chaos, and the door flew open and Uncle Fly
appeared.

"What on earth!" said my grandmother, starting up. "That
you, 'Liakim? Why on earth *must* you come in the back way and
knock down all my milk-pans?"

"Why, I came 'cross lots from Aunt Bathsheba Sawin's," said
Uncle Fly, dancing in, "and I got caught in these pesky blackberry-bushes in the graveyard, and I do believe I 've torn my
breeches all to pieces," he added, pirouetting and frisking with
very airy gyrations, and trying vainly to get a view of himself behind, in which operation he went round and round as a cat does
after her tail.

"Laws a-massy, 'Liakim!" said my grandmother, whose ears
were startled by a peculiar hissing sound in the sink-room,
which caused her to spring actively in that direction. "Well,
now, you have been and done it! You 've gone and fidgeted the
tap out of my beer-barrel, and here 's the beer all over the floor. I
hope you 're satisfied now."

"Sorry for it. Did n't mean to. I 'll wipe it right up. Where 's a
towel, or floor-cloth, or something?" cried Uncle Fly, whirling
in more active circles round and round, till he seemed to me to
have a dozen pairs of legs.

"Do sit down, 'Liakim," said my grandmother. "Of course
you did n't mean to; but next time don't come bustling and

whirligigging through my back sink-room after dark. I do believe you never will be quiet till you 're in your grave."

"Sit down, uncle," said Bill. "Never mind mother,—she 'll come all right by and by. And never mind your breeches,—all things earthly are transitory, as Parson Lothrop told us to-day. Now let 's come back to our Sunday talk. Did ever anybody see such an astonishing providence as Miss Mehitable Rossiter's bonnet to-day? Does it belong to the old or the new dispensation, do you think?"

"Bill, I 'm astonished at you!" said Aunt Lois.

"Miss Mehitable is of a most respectable family," said Aunt Keziah, reprovingly. "Her father and grandfather and great-grandfather were all ministers; and two of her mother's brothers, Jeduthun and Amariah."

"Now, take care, youngster," said Uncle Fly. "You see you young colts must n't be too airy. When a fellow begins to speak evil of bonnets, nobody knows where he may end."

"Bless me, one and all of you," said Bill, "I have the greatest respect for Miss Mehitable. Furthermore, I like her. She 's a real spicy old concern. I 'd rather talk with her than any dozen of modern girls. But I do wish she 'd give me that bonnet to put in our Cambridge cabinet. I 'd tell 'em it was the wing of a Madagascar bat. Blessed old soul, how innocent she sat under it!—never knowing to what wandering thoughts it was giving rise. Such bonnets interfere with my spiritual progress."

At this moment, by the luck that always brings in the person people are talking of, Miss Mehitable came in, with the identical old wonder on her head. Now, outside of our own blood-relations, no one that came within our doors ever received a warmer welcome than Miss Mehitable. Even the children loved her, with that instinctive sense by which children and dogs learn the discerning of spirits. To be sure she was as gaunt and brown as the Ancient Mariner, but hers was a style of ugliness that was neither repulsive nor vulgar. Personal uncomeliness has its differing characters, and there are some very homely women who have a style that amounts to something like beauty. I know that this is not the common view of the matter; but I am firm in the faith that some very homely women have a certain attraction about them which is increased by their homeliness. It is like the quaintness of Japanese china,—not beautiful, but having a strong, pronounced character, as far remote as possible from the ordinary and vulgar, and which, in union with vigorous and agreeable traits of mind, is more stimulating than any mere insipid beauty.

In short, Miss Mehitable was a specimen of what I should call the good-goblin style of beauty. And people liked her so much that they came to like the singularities which individualized her from all other people. Her features were prominent and harsh; her eyebrows were shaggy, and finished abruptly half across her brow, leaving but half an eyebrow on each side. She had, however, clear, trustworthy, steady eyes, of a greenish gray, which impressed one with much of that idea of steadfast faithfulness that one sees in the eyes of some good, homely dogs. "Faithful and true," was written in her face as legibly as eyes could write it.

For the rest, Miss Mehitable had a strong mind, was an omnivorous reader, apt, ready in conversation, and with a droll, original way of viewing things, which made her society ever stimulating. To me her house was always full of delightful images,—a great, calm, cool, shady, old-fashioned house, full of books and of quaint old furniture, with a garden on one side where were no end of lilies, hollyhocks, pinks, and peonies, to say nothing of currants, raspberries, apples, and pears, and other carnal delights, all of which good Miss Mehitable was free to dispense to her child-visitors. It was my image of heaven to be allowed to go to spend an afternoon with Miss Mehitable, and establish myself, in a shady corner of the old study which contained her father's library, over an edition of Æsop's Fables illustrated with plates, which, opened, was an endless field of enchantment to me.

Miss Mehitable lived under the watch and charge of an ancient female domestic named Polly Shubel. Polly was a representative specimen of the now extinct species of Yankee serving-maids. She had been bred up from a child in the Rossiter family of some generations back. She was of that peculiar kind of constitution, known in New England, which merely becomes drier and tougher with the advance of time, without giving any other indications of old age. The exact number of her years was a point unsettled even among the most skilful genealogists of Oldtown. Polly was a driving, thrifty, doctrinal and practical female, with strong bones and muscles, and strong opinions, believing most potently in early rising, soap and sand, and the Assembly's Catechism, and knowing *certainly* all that she did know. Polly considered Miss Mehitable as a sort of child under her wardship, and conducted the whole business of life for her with a sovereign and unanswerable authority. As Miss Mehitable's tastes were in the world of books and ideas, rather than of physical matters, she resigned herself to Polly's sway with as good a grace as possible, though sometimes she felt that it rather abridged her freedom of action.

Luckily for my own individual self, Polly patronized me, and gave me many a piece of good advice, sweetened with gingerbread, when I went to visit Miss Rossiter. I counted Miss Mehitable among my personal friends; so to-night, when she came in, I came quickly and laid hold of the skirt of her gown, and looked admiringly upon her dusky face, under the portentous shadow of a great bonnet shaded by nodding bows of that preternatural color which people used to call olive-green. She had a word for us all, a cordial grasp of the hand for my mother, who sat silent and thoughtful in her corner, and a warm hand-shake all round.

"You see," she said, drawing out an old-fashioned snuff-box, and tapping upon it, "my house grew so stupid that I must come and share my pinch of snuff with you. It's windy out to-night, and I should think a storm was brewing; and the rattling of one's own window-blinds, as one sits alone, is n't half so amusing as some other things."

"You know, Miss Rossiter, we 're always delighted to have you come in," said my grandmother, and my Aunt Lois, and my Aunt Keziah, all at once. This, by the way, was a little domestic trick that the females of our family had; and, as their voices were upon very different keys, the effect was somewhat peculiar. My Aunt Lois's voice was high and sharp, my grandmother's a hearty chest-tone, while Aunt Keziah's had an uncertain buzz between the two, like the vibrations of a loose string; but as they all had corresponding looks and smiles of welcome, Miss Mehitable was pleased.

"I always indulge myself in thinking I am welcome," she

said. "And now pray how is our young scholar, Master William Badger? What news do you bring us from old Harvard?"

"Almost anything you want to hear, Miss Mehitable. You
know that I am your most devoted slave."

"Not so sure of that, sir," she said, with a whimsical twinkle of her eye. "Don't you know that your sex are always
treacherous? How do I know that you don't serve up old
Miss Rossiter when you give representations of the Oldtown
curiosities there at Cambridge? We are a set here that might
make a boy's fortune in that line,—now are n't we?"

"How do you know that I do serve up Oldtown curiosities?" said Bill, somewhat confused, and blushing to the roots
of his hair.

"How do I know? Can the Ethiopian change his skin, or
the leopard his spots? and can you help being a mimic, as you
were born, always were and always will be?"

"O, but I 'm sure, Miss Mehitable, Bill never would,—he
has too much respect," said Aunt Keziah and Aunt Lois, simultaneously again.

"Perhaps not; but if he wants to, he 's welcome. What are
queer old women for, if young folks may not have a good
laugh out of them now and then? If it 's only a friendly laugh,
it 's just as good as crying, and better too. I 'd like to be made
to laugh at myself. I think generally we take ourselves altogether too seriously. What now, bright eyes?" she added, as
I nestled nearer to her. "Do you want to come up into an old
woman's lap? Well, here you come. Bless me, what a tangle
of curls we have here! Don't your thoughts get caught in
these curls sometimes?"

I looked bashful and wistful at this address, and Miss Mehitable went on twining my curls around her fingers, and
trotting me on her knee, lulling me into a delicious dreami-
ness, in which she seemed to me to be one of those nice, odd-
looking old fairy women that figure to such effect in stories.

The circle all rose again as Major Broad came in. Aunt Lois
thought, with evident anguish, of the best room. Here was
the Major, sure enough, and we all sitting round the kitchen
fire! But my grandfather and grandmother welcomed him
cheerfully to their corner, and enthroned him in my grand-

father's splint-bottomed rocking-chair, where he sat far more comfortably than if he had been perched on a genteel, slippery-bottomed stuffed chair with claw feet.

The Major performed the neighborly kindnesses of the occasion in an easy way. He spoke a few words to my mother of the esteem and kindness he had felt for my father, in a manner that called up the blood into her thin cheeks, and made her eyes dewy with tears. Then he turned to the young collegian, recognizing him as one of the rising lights of Oldtown.

"Our only nobility now," he said to my grandfather. "We 've cut off everything else: no distinction now, sir, but educated and uneducated."

"It is a hard struggle for our human nature to give up titles and ranks, though," said Miss Mehitable. "For my part, I have a ridiculous kindness for them yet. I know it 's all nonsense; but I can't help looking back to the court we used to have at the Government House in Boston. You know it was something to hear of the goings and doings of my Lord this and my Lady that, and of Sir Thomas and Sir Peter and Sir Charles, and all the rest of 'em."

"Yes," said Bill; "the Oldtown folks call their minister's wife Lady yet."

"Well, that 's a little comfort," said Miss Mehitable; "one don't want life an entire dead level. Do let us have one titled lady among us."

"And a fine lady she is," said the Major. "Our parson did a good thing in that alliance."

While the conversation was thus taking a turn of the most approved genteel style, Aunt Keziah's ears heard alarming premonitory sounds outside the door. "Who 's that at the scraper?" said she.

"O, it 's Sam Lawson," said Aunt Lois, with a sort of groan. "You may be sure of that."

"Come in, Sam, my boy," said Uncle Bill, opening the door. "Glad to see you."

"Wal now, Mr. Badger," said Sam, with white eyes of veneration, "I 'm real glad to see ye. I told Hepsy you 'd want to see me. You 're the fust one of my Saturday arternoon fishin' boys that 's got into college, and I 'm 'mazing proud on 't. I tell you I walk tall,—ask 'em if I don't, round to the store."

"You always were gifted in that line," said Bill. "But come, sit down in the corner and tell us what you 've been about."

"Wal, you see, I thought I 'd jest go over to North Parish this arternoon, jest for a change, like, and I wanted to hear one of them *Hopkintinsians* they tell so much about; and Parson Simpson, he 's one on 'em."

"You ought not to be roving off on Sunday, leaving your own meeting," said my grandfather.

"Wal, you see, Deacon Badger, I 'm interested in these 'ere new doctrines. I met your Polly a goin' over, too," he said to Miss Mehitable.

"O yes," said Miss Mehitable, "Polly is a great Hopkinsian. She can hardly have patience to sit under our Parson Lothrop's preaching. It 's rather hard on me, because Polly makes it a point of conscience to fight every one of his discourses over to me in my parlor. Somebody gave Polly an Arminian tract last Sunday, entitled, 'The Apostle Paul an Arminian.' It would have done you good to hear Polly's comments. ''Postle Paul an Arminian! He 's the biggest 'lectioner of 'em all.' "

"That he is," said my grandmother, warmly. "Polly 's read her Bible to some purpose."

"Well, Sam, what did you think of the sermon?" said Uncle Bill.

"Wal," said Sam, leaning over the fire, with his long, bony hands alternatively raised to catch the warmth, and then dropped with an utter laxness, when the warmth became too pronounced, "Parson Simpson 's a smart man; but, I tell ye, it 's kind o' discouragin'. Why, he said our state and condition by natur was just like this. We was clear down in a well fifty feet deep, and the sides all round nothin' but glare ice; but we was under immediate obligations to get out, 'cause we was free, voluntary agents. But nobody ever had got out, and nobody would, unless the Lord reached down and took 'em. And whether he would or not nobody could tell; it was all sovereignty. He said there wa' n't one in a hundred,—not one in a thousand,—not one in ten thousand,—that would be saved. Lordy massy, says I to myself, ef that 's so they 're any of 'em welcome to my chance. And so I kind o' ris up and come out, 'cause I 'd got a pretty long walk home, and I wanted to go round by South Pond, and inquire about Aunt Sally Morse's toothache."

"I heard the whole sermon over from Polly," said Miss Mehitable, "and as it was not a particularly cheerful subject to think of, I came over here." These words were said with a sort of chilly, dreary sigh, that made me turn and look up in Miss Mehitable's face. It looked haggard and weary, as of one tired of struggling with painful thoughts.

"Wal," said Sam Lawson, "I stopped a minute round to your back door, Miss Rossiter, to talk with Polly about the sermon. I was a tellin' Polly that that 'ere was puttin' inability a leetle too strong."

"Not a bit, not a bit," said Uncle Fly, "so long as it 's moral inability. There 's the point, ye see, — *moral*, — that 's the word. That makes it all right."

"Wal," said Sam, "I was a puttin' it to Polly this way. Ef a man 's cut off his hands, it ain't right to require him to chop wood. Wal, Polly, she says he 'd no business to cut his hands off; and so he ought to be required to chop the wood all the same. Wal, I telled her it was Adam chopped our hands off. But she said, no; it was we did it *in* Adam, and she brought up the catechise plain enough, — '*We sinned in him,* and fell with him.' "

"She had you there, Sam," said Uncle Fly, with great content. "You won't catch Polly tripping on the catechism."

"Well, for my part," said Major Broad, "I don't like these doctrinal subtilties, Deacon Badger. Now I 've got a volume of Mr. Addison's religious writings that seem to me about the right thing. They 're very pleasing reading. Mr. Addison is my favorite author of a Sunday."

"I 'm afraid Mr. Addison had nothing but just mere morality and natural religion," said my grandmother, who could not be withheld from bearing her testimony. "You don't find any of the discriminating doctrines in Mr. Addison. Major Broad, did you ever read Mr. Bellamy's 'True Religion Delineated and Distinguished from all Counterfeits'?"

"No, madam, I never did," said Major Broad.

"Well, I earnestly hope you will read *that* book," said my grandmother.

"My wife is always at me about one good book or another," said my grandfather; "but I manage to do with my old Bible. I have n't used that up yet."

"I should know about Dr. Bellamy's book by this time," said Miss Mehitable, "for Polly intrenches herself in that, and preaches out of it daily. Polly certainly missed her vocation when she was trained for a servant. She is a born professor of theology. She is so circumstantial about all that took place at the time the angels fell, and when the covenant was made with Adam in the Garden of Eden, that I sometimes question whether she really might not have been there personally. Polly is particularly strong on Divine sovereignty. She thinks it applies to everything under the sun except my affairs. Those she chooses to look after herself."

"Well," said Major Broad, "I am not much of a theologian. I want to be taught my duty. Parson Lothrop's discourses are generally very clear and practical, and they suit me."

"They are good as far as they go," said my grandmother; "but I like good, strong, old-fashioned doctrine. I like such writers as Mr. Edwards and Dr. Bellamy and Dr. Hopkins. It 's all very well, your essays on cheerfulness and resignation, and all that; but I want something that takes strong hold of you, so that you feel something has got you that *can* hold."

"The Cambridge Platform, for instance," said Uncle Bill.

"Yes, my son, the Cambridge Platform. I ain't ashamed of it. It was made by men whose shoe-latchet we are n't worthy to unloose. I believe it,—every word on 't. I believe it, and I 'm going to believe it."

"And would if there was twice as much of it," said Uncle Bill. "That 's right, mother, stand up for your colors. I admire your spirit. But, Sam, what does Hepsy think of all this? I suppose you enlighten her when you return from your investigations."

"Wal, I try to. But lordy massy, Mr. Badger, Hepsy don't take no kind o' interest in the doctrines, no more 'n nothin' at all. She 's so kind o' worldly, Hepsy is. It 's allers meat and drink, meat and drink, with her. That 's all she 's thinkin' of."

"And if *you* would think more of such things, she would n't have to think so much," said Aunt Lois, sharply. "Don't you know the Bible says, that the man that provideth not for his own household hath denied the faith, and is worse than an infidel?"

"I don't see," said Sam, slowly flopping his great hands up and down over the blaze,—"I railly don't see why folks are allers a throwin' up that 'ere text at me. I 'm sure I work as hard as a man ken. Why, I was a workin' last night till nigh twelve o'clock, doin' up odd jobs o' blacksmithin'. They kind o' 'cumulate, ye know."

"Mr. Lawson," said my grandmother, with a look of long-suffering patience, "how often and often must I tell you, that if you 'd be steadier round your home, and work in regular hours, Hepsy would be more comfortable, and things would go on better?"

"Lordy massy, Mis' Badger, bless your soul and body, ye don't know nothin' about it;—ye don't know nothin' what I undergo. Hepsy, she 's at me from morning till night. First it 's one thing, and then another. One day it rains, and her clothes-line breaks. She 's at me 'bout that. Now I tell her, 'Hepsy, I ain't to blame,—I don't make the rain.' And then another day she 's at me agin 'cause the wind 's east, and fetches the smoke down chimbley. I tell her, 'Hepsy, now look here,—*do* I make the wind blow?' But it 's no use talkin' to Hepsy."

"Well, Sam, I take your part," said Bill. "I always knew you was a regular martyr. Come, boys, go down cellar and draw a pitcher of cider. We 'll stay him with flagons, and comfort him with apples. Won't we, Sam?"

As Sam was prime favorite with all boys, my brother Bill and I started willingly enough on this errand, one carrying the candle and the other a great stone pitcher of bountiful proportions, which always did hospitable duty on similar occasions.

Just as we returned, bearing our pitcher, there came another rap at the outside door of the kitchen, and Old Betty Poganut and Sally Wonsamug stood at the door.

"Well, now, Mis' Badger," said Betty, "Sally and me, we thought we must jest run in, we got so scar't. We was coming through that Bill Morse's woods, and there come such a flash o' lightnin' it most blinded us, and the wind blew enough to blow a body over; and we thought there was a storm right down on us, and we run jest as fast as we could. We did n't know what to do, we was so scar't. I 'm mortal 'fraid of lightning."

"Why, Betty, you forgot the sermon to-day. You should have said your prayers, as Parson Lothrop tells you," said my grandfather.

"Well, I did kind o' put up a sort o' silent 'jaculation, as a body may say. That is, I jest said, 'O Lord,' and kind o' gin him a wink, you know."

"O, you did?" said my grandfather.

"Yes, I kind o' thought He 'd know what I meant."

My grandfather turned with a smile to Miss Mehitable. "These Indians have their own wild ways of looking at things, after all."

"Well, now, I s'pose you have n't had a bit of supper, either of you," said my grandmother, getting up. "It 's commonly the way of it."

"Well, to tell the truth, I was sayin' to Sarah that if we come down to Mis' Deacon Badger's I should n't wonder if we got something good," said Betty, her broad, coarse face and baggy cheeks beginning to be illuminated with a smile.

"Here, Horace, you come and hold the candle while I go into the buttery and get 'em some cold pork and beans," said my grandmother, cheerily. "The poor creturs don't get a good meal of victuals very often; and I baked a good lot on purpose."

If John Bunyan had known my grandmother, he certainly would have introduced her in some of his histories as "the housekeeper whose name was Bountiful"; and under her care an ample meal of brown bread and pork and beans was soon set forth on the table in the corner of the kitchen, to which the two hungry Indian women sat down with the appetite of wolves. A large mug was placed between them, which Uncle Bill filled to the brim with cider.

"I s'pose you 'd like twice a mug better than once a mug, Sally," he said, punning on her name.

"O, if the mug 's only big enough," said Sally, her snaky

eyes gleaming with appetite; "and it's always a good big mug one gets here."

Sam Lawson's great white eyes began irresistibly to wander in the direction of the plentiful cheer which was being so liberally dispensed at the other side of the room.

"Want some, Sam, my boy?" said Uncle Bill, with a patronizing freedom.

"Why, bless your soul, Master Bill, I would n't care a bit if I took a plate o' them beans and some o' that 'ere pork. Hepsy did n't save no beans for me; and, walkin' all the way from North Parish, I felt kind o' empty and windy, as a body may say. You know Scriptur' tells about bein' filled with the east wind; but I never found it noways satisfyin', — it sets sort o' cold on the stomach."

"Draw up, Sam, and help yourself," said Uncle Bill, putting plate and knife and fork before him; and Sam soon showed that he had a vast internal capacity for the stowing away of beans and brown bread.

Meanwhile Major Broad and my grandfather drew their chairs together, and began a warm discussion of the Constitution of the United States, which had been recently presented for acceptance in a Convention of the State of Massachusetts.

"I have n't seen you, Major Broad," said my grandfather, "since you came back from the Convention. I 'm very anxious to have our State of Massachusetts accept that Constitution. We 're in an unsettled condition now; we don't know fairly where we are. If we accept this Constitution, we shall be a nation, — we shall have something to go to work on."

"Well, Deacon Badger, to say the truth, I could not vote for this Constitution in Convention. They have adopted it by a small majority; but I shall be bound to record my dissent from it."

"Pray, Major, what are your objections?" said Miss Mehitable.

"I have two. One is, it gives too much power to the President. There's an appointing power and a power of patronage that will play the mischief some day in the hands of an ambitious man. That 's one objection. The other is the recognizing and encouraging of slavery in the Constitution. That is such a dreadful wrong,—such a shameful inconsistency,—when we have just come through a battle for the doctrine that all men are free and equal, to turn round and found our national government on a recognition of African slavery. It cannot and will not come to good."

"O, well," said my grandfather, "slavery will gradually die out. You see how it is going in the New England States."

"I cannot think so," said the Major. "I have a sort of feeling about this that I cannot resist. If we join those States that still mean to import and use slaves, our nation will meet some dreadful punishment. I am certain of it."*

"Well, really," said my grandfather, "I 'm concerned to hear you speak so. I have felt such anxiety to have something settled. You see, without a union we are all afloat,—we are separate logs, but no raft."

"Yes," said Miss Mehitable, "but nothing can be settled that is n't founded on right. We ought to dig deep, and lay our foundations on a rock, when we build for posterity."

"Were there many of your way of thinking in the Convention, Major?" said my grandfather.

"Well, we had a pretty warm discussion, and we came very near to carrying it. Now, in Middlesex County, for instance, where we are, there were only seventeen in favor of the Constitution, and twenty-five against; and in Worcester County there were only seven in favor and forty-three against. Well, they carried it at last by a majority of nineteen; but the minority recorded their protest. Judge Widgery of Portland, General Thompson of Topsham, and Dr. Taylor of Worcester, rather headed the opposition. Then the town of Andover instructed its representative, Mr. Symmes, to vote against it, but he did n't, he voted on the other side, and I understand they are dreadfully indignant about it. I saw a man from Andover last week who said that he actually thought Symmes would be obliged to leave the town, he was so dreadfully unpopular."

*The dissent of Major Broad of Natick, and several others, on the grounds above stated, may still be read in the report of the proceedings of the Convention that ratified the Constitution.

"Well, Major Broad, I agree with you," said my grandmother, heartily, "and I honor you for the stand you took. Slavery is a sin and a shame; and I say, with Jacob, 'O my soul, come not thou into their secret,—unto their assembly, mine honor, be not thou united.' I wish we may keep clear on 't. I don't want anything that we can't ask God's blessing on heartily, and we certainly can't on this. Why, anybody that sees that great scar on Cæsar's forehead sees what slavery comes to."

My grandmother always pointed her anti-slavery arguments with an appeal to this mark of ill-usage which old Cæsar had received at the hands of a brutal master years before, and the appeal never failed to convince the domestic circle.

"Well," said my grandfather, after some moments of silence, in which he sat gazing fixedly at the great red coals of a hickory log, "you see, Major, it 's done, and can't be helped."

"It 's done," said the Major, "but in my opinion mischief will come of it as sure as there is a God in heaven."

"Let 's hope not," said my grandfather, placidly.

Outside the weather was windy and foul, the wind rattling doors, shaking and rumbling down the chimney, and causing the great glowing circle lighted by the fire to seem warmer and brighter. The Indian women and Sam Lawson, having finished their meal and thoroughly cleaned out the dishes, grouped themselves about the end of the ingle already occupied by black Cæsar, and began a little private gossip among themselves.

"I say," says Sam, raising his voice to call my grandfather's attention, "do you know, Deacon Badger, whether anybody is living in the Dench house now?"

"There was n't, the last I knew about it," said my grandfather.

"Wal, you won't make some folks believe but what that 'ere house is haunted."

"Haunted!" said Miss Mehitable; "nothing more likely. What old house is n't?—if one only knew it; and that certainly ought to be if ever a house was."

"But this 'ere 's a regular *haunt*," said Sam. "I was a talkin' the other night with Bill Payne and Jake Marshall, and they both on 'em said that they'd seen strange things in them grounds,—they'd seen a figger of a man—"

"With his head under his arm," suggested Uncle Bill.

"No, a man in a long red cloak," said Sam Lawson, "such as Sir Harry Frankland used to wear."

"Poor Sir Harry!" said Miss Mehitable, "has he come to that?"

"Did you know Sir Harry?" said Aunt Lois.

"I have met him once or twice at the Governor's house," said Miss Mehitable. "Lady Lothrop knew Lady Frankland very well."

"Well, Sam," said Uncle Bill, "do let's hear the end of this haunting."

"Nothin', only the other night I was a goin' over to watch with Lem Moss, and I passed pretty nigh the Dench place, and I thought I'd jest look round it a spell. And as sure as you're alive I see smoke a comin' out of the chimbley."

"I didn't know as ghosts ever used the fireplaces," said Uncle Bill. "Well, Sam, did you go in?"

"No, I was pretty much in a hurry; but I telled Jake and Bill, and then they each on 'em had something to match that they'd seen. As nigh as I can make it out, there's that 'ere boy that they say was murdered and thrown down that 'ere old well walks sometimes. And then there's a woman appears to some, and this 'ere man in a red cloak; and they think it's Sir Harry in his red cloak."

"For my part," said Aunt Lois, "I never had much opinion of Sir Harry Frankland, or Lady Frankland either. I don't think such goings on ever ought to be countenanced in society."

"They both repented bitterly,—repented in sackcloth and ashes," said Miss Mehitable. "And if God forgives such sins, why should n't we?"

"What was the story?" said Major Broad.

"Why," said Aunt Lois, "have n't you heard of Agnes Surridge, of Marblehead? She was housemaid in a tavern there, and Sir Harry fell in love with her, and took her and educated her. That was well enough; but when she'd done going to school he took her home to his house in Boston, and called her his daughter; although people became pretty sure that the connection was not what it should be, and they refused to have anything to do with her. So he bought this splendid place out in the woods, and built a great palace of a house, and took Miss Agnes out there. People that wanted to be splendidly entertained, and that were not particular as to morals, used to go out to visit them."

"I used to hear great stories of their wealth and pomp and luxury," said my grandmother, "but I mourned over it, that it should come to this in New England, that people could openly set such an example and be tolerated. It would n't have been borne a generation before, I can tell you. No, indeed,—the magistrates would have put a stop to it. But these noblemen, when they came over to America, seemed to think themselves lords of God's heritage, and free to do just as they pleased."

"But," said Miss Mehitable, "they repented, as I said. He took her to England, and there his friends refused to receive her; and then he was appointed Ambassador to Lisbon, and he took her there. On the day of the great earthquake Sir Harry was riding with a lady of the court when the shock came, and in a moment, without warning, they found themselves buried under the ruins of a building they were passing. He wore a scarlet cloak, as was the fashion; and they say that in her dying agonies the poor creature bit through this cloak and sleeve into the flesh of his arm, and made a mark that he carried to his dying day. Sir Harry was saved by Agnes Surridge. She came over the ruins, calling and looking for him, and he heard her voice and answered, and she got men to come and dig him out. When he was in that dreadful situation, he made a vow to God, if he would save his life, that he would be a different man. And he was a changed man from that day. He was married to Agnes Surridge as soon as they could get a priest to perform the ceremony; and when he took her back to England all his relations received her, and she was presented in court and moved in society with perfect acceptance."

"I don't think it ever ought to have been," said Aunt Lois. "Such women never ought to be received."

"What! is there no place of repentance for a woman?" said

Miss Mehitable. "Christ said, 'Neither do I condemn thee; go and sin no more.'"

I noticed again that sort of shiver of feeling in Miss Mehitable; and there was a peculiar thrill in her voice, as she said these words, that made me sensible that she was speaking from some inward depth of feeling.

"Don't you be so hard and sharp, Lois," said my grandmother; "sinners must have patience with sinners."

"Especially with sinners of quality, Lois," said Uncle Bill. "By all accounts Sir Harry and Lady Frankland swept all before them when they came back to Boston."

"Of course," said Miss Mehitable; "what was done in court would be done in Boston, and whom Queen Charlotte received would be received in our upper circles. Lady Lothrop never called on her till she was Lady Frankland, but after that I believe she has visited out at their place."

"Wal, I've heerd 'em say," said Sam Lawson, "that it would take a woman two days jest to get through cleaning the silver that there was in that 'ere house, to say nothing about the carpets and the curtains and the tapestry. But then, when the war broke out, Lady Frankland, she took most of it back to England, I guess, and the house has been back and forward to one and another. I never could rightly know jest who did live in it. I heard about some French folks that lived there one time. I thought some day, when I had n't nothin' else to do, I'd jest walk over to old Granny Walker's, that lives over the other side of Hopkinton. She used to be a housekeeper to Lady Frankland, and I could get particulars out o' her."

"Well," said Miss Mehitable, "I know one woman that must go back to a haunted house, and that is this present one." So saying, she rose and put me off her knee.

"Send this little man over to see me to-morrow," she said to my mother. "Polly has a cake for him, and I shall find something to amuse him."

Major Broad, with old-fashioned gallantry, insisted on waiting on Miss Mehitable home; and Sam Lawson reluctantly tore himself from the warm corner to encounter the asperities of his own fireside.

"Here, Sam," said good-natured Bill,—"here's a great red apple for Hepsy."

"Ef I dares to go nigh enough to give it to her," said Sam, with a grimace. "She's allers a castin' it up at me that I don't want to set with her at home. But lordy massy, she don't consider that a fellow don't want to set and be hectored and lectured when he can do better elsewhere."

"True enough, Sam; but give my regards to her."

As to the two Indian women, they gave it as their intention to pass the night by the kitchen fire; and my grandmother, to whom such proceedings were not at all strange, assented,—producing for each a blanket, which had often seen similar service. My grandfather closed the evening by bringing out his great Bible and reading a chapter. Then we all knelt down in prayer.

So passed an evening in my grandmother's kitchen,—where religion, theology, politics, the gossip of the day, and the legends of the supernatural all conspired to weave a fabric of thought quaint and various. Intense earnestness, a solemn undertone of deep mournful awe, was overlaid with quaint traceries of humor, strange and weird in their effect. I was one of those children who are all ear,—dreamy listeners, who brood over all that they hear, without daring to speak of it; and in this evening's conversation I had heard enough to keep my eyes broad open long after my mother had laid me in bed. The haunted house and its vague wonders filled my mind, and I determined to question Sam Lawson yet more about it.

But now that I have fairly introduced myself, the scene of my story, and many of the actors in it, I must take my reader off for a while, and relate a history that must at last blend with mine in one story.

VII.

Old Crab Smith

O N the brow of yonder hill you see that old, red farm-house, with its slanting back roof relieved against the golden sky of the autumn afternoon. The house lifts itself up dark and clear under the shadow of two great elm-trees that droop over it, and is the first of a straggling, irregular cluster of farm-houses that form the village of Needmore. A group of travellers, sitting on a bit of rock in the road below the hill on which the farm-house stands, are looking up to it, in earnest conversation.

"Mother, if you can only get up there, we 'll ask them to let you go in and rest," said a little boy of nine years to a weary, pale, sick-looking woman who sat as in utter exhaustion and discouragement on the rock. A little girl two years younger than the boy sat picking at the moss at her feet, and earnestly listening to her older brother with the air of one who is attending to the words of a leader.

"I don't feel as if I could get a step farther," said the woman; and the increasing deadly paleness of her face confirmed her words.

"O mother, don't give up," said the boy; "just rest here a little and then lean on me, and we 'll get you up the hill; and then I 'm sure they 'll take you in. Come, now; I 'll run and get you some water in our tin cup, and you 'll feel better soon." And the boy ran to a neighboring brook and filled a small tin cup, and brought the cool water to his mother.

She drank it, and then, fixing a pair of dark, pathetic eyes on the face of her boy, she said: "My dear child, you have always been such a blessing to me! What should I do without you?"

"Well, mother, now, if you feel able, just rest on my shoulder, and Tina will take the bundle. You take it, Tina, and we 'll find a place to rest."

And so, slowly and with difficulty, the three wound their

way up to the grassy top of the hill where stood the red house. This house belonged to a man named Caleb Smith, whose character had caused the name he bore to degenerate into another which was held to be descriptive of his nature, namely, "Crab"; and the boys of the vicinity commonly expressed the popular idea of the man by calling him "Old Crab Smith." His was one of those sour, cross, gnarly natures that now and then are to be met with in New England, which, like knotty cider-apples, present a compound of hardness, sourness, and bitterness. It was affirmed that a continual free indulgence in very hard cider as a daily beverage was one great cause of this churlishness of temper; but be that as it may, there was not a boy in the village that did not know and take account of it in all his estimates and calculations, as much as of northeast storms and rainy weather. No child ever willingly carried a message to him; no neighbor but dreaded to ask a favor of him; nobody hoped to borrow or beg of him; nobody willingly hired themselves out to him, or did him cheerful service. In short, he was a petrified man, walled out from all neighborhood sympathies, and standing alone in his crabbedness. And it was to this man's house that the wandering orphan boy was leading his poor sick mother.

The three travellers approached a neat back porch on the shady side of the house, where an old woman sat knitting. This was Old Crab Smith's wife, or, more properly speaking, his life-long bond-slave,—the only human being whom he could so secure to himself that she should be always at hand for him to vent that residue of ill-humor upon which the rest of the world declined to receive. Why half the women in the world marry the men they do, is a problem that might puzzle any philosopher; how any woman could marry Crab Smith, was the standing wonder of all the neighborhood. And yet Crab's wife was a modest, industrious, kindly creature, who uncomplainingly toiled from morning till night to serve and please him, and received her daily allowance of grumbling and fault-finding with quiet submission. She tried all she could to mediate between him and the many whom his ill-temper was constantly provoking. She did surreptitious acts of kindness here and there, to do away the effects of his hardness, and shrunk and quivered for fear of being detected in goodness, as much as many another might for fear of being discovered in sin. She had been many times a mother,—had passed through all the trials and weaknesses of maternity without one tender act of consideration, one encouraging word. Her children had grown up and gone from her, always eager to leave the bleak, ungenial home, and go out to shift for themselves in the world, and now, in old age, she was still working. Worn to a shadow,—little, old, wrinkled, bowed,— she was still about the daily round of toil, and still the patient recipient of the murmurs and chidings of her tyrant.

"My mother is so sick she can't get any farther," said a little voice from under the veranda; "won't you let her come in and lie down awhile?"

"Massy, child," said the little old woman, coming forward with a trembling, uncertain step. "Well, she does look beat eout, to be sure. Come up and rest ye a bit."

"If you 'll only let me lie down awhile and rest me," said a faint, sweet voice.

"Come up here," said the old woman, standing quivering like a gray shadow on the top doorstep; and, shading her wrinkled forehead with her hand, she looked with a glance of habitual apprehension along the road where the familiar cart and oxen of her tyrant might be expected soon to appear on their homeward way, and rejoiced in her little old heart that he was safe out of sight. "Yes, come in," she said, opening the door of a small ground-floor bedroom that adjoined the apartment known in New England houses as the sink-room, and showing them a plain bed.

The worn and wasted stranger sunk down on it, and, as she sunk, her whole remaining strength seemed to collapse, and something white and deathly fell, as if it had been a shadow, over her face.

"Massy to us! she 's fainted clean away," said the poor old woman, quiveringly. "I must jest run for the camphire."

The little boy seemed to have that unchildlike judgment and presence of mind that are the precocious development of want and sorrow. He ran to a water-pail, and, dipping his small tin cup, he dashed the water in his mother's face, and fanned her with his little torn straw hat. When the old woman returned, the invalid was breathing again, and able to take a few swallows of camphor and water which had been mixed for her.

"Sonny," said the old woman, "you are a nice little nurse,— a good boy. You jest take care now; and here 's a turkey-feather fan to fan her with; and I 'll get on the kettle to make her a cup of tea. We 'll bring her round with a little nursing. Been walking a long way, I calculate?"

"Yes," said the boy, "she was trying to get to Boston."

"What, going afoot?"

"We did n't mind walking, the weather is so pleasant," said the boy; "and Tina and I like walking; but mother got sick a day or two ago, and ever since she has been so tired!"

"Jes' so," said the old woman, looking compassionately on the bed. "Well, I 'll make up the fire and get her some tea."

The fire was soon smoking in the great, old-fashioned kitchen chimney, for the neat, labor-saving cook-stove had as yet no being; and the thin, blue smoke, curling up in the rosy sunset air, received prismatic coloring which a painter would have seized with enthusiasm.

Far otherwise, however, was its effect on the eye of Old Crab Smith, as, coming up the hill, his eye detected the luminous vapor going up from his own particular chimney.

"So, burning out wood,—always burning out wood. I told her that I would n't have tea got at night. These old women are crazy and bewitched after tea, and they don't care if they burn up your tables and chairs to help their messes. Why a plague can't she eat cold pork and potatoes as well as I, and drink her mug of cider? but must go to getting up her fire and biling her kettle. I 'll see to that. Halloa there," he said, as he stamped up on to the porch, "what the devil you up to now? I s'pose you think I hain't got nothing else to do but split up wood for you to burn out."

"Father, it 's nothing but a little brush and a few chips, jest to bile the kettle."

"Bile the kettle, bile the kettle! Jest like yer lazy, shif'less ways. What must you be a bilin' the kettle for?"

"Father, I jest want to make a little tea for a sick woman."

"A sick woman! What sick woman?"

"There was a poor sick woman came along this afternoon with two little children."

"Wal, I s'pose you took 'em in. I s'pose you think we keep
the poor-house, and that all the trampers belong to us. We
shall have to go to the poor-house ourselves before long, I
tell ye. But you never believe anything I say. Why could n't
you 'a' sent her to the selectmen? I don't know why I must
keep beggars' tavern."

"Father, father, don't speak so loud. The poor critter
wa' n't able to stir another step, and fainted dead away, and
we had to get her on to a bed."

"And we shall have her and her two brats through a fit of
sickness. That 's just like you. Wal, we shall all go to the poor-
house together before long, and then you 'll believe what I
say, won't ye? But I won't have it so. She may stay to-night,
but to-morrow morning I 'll cart her over to Joe Seran's,
bright and early, brats and all."

There was within hearing of this conversation a listener
whose heart was dying within her, — sinking deeper and
deeper at every syllable, — a few words will explain why.

A younger son of a family belonging to the English gentry
had come over to America as a commissioned officer near the
close of the Revolutionary war. He had persuaded to a private marriage the daughter of a poor country curate, a beautiful young girl, whom he induced to elope with him, and
share the fortunes of an officer's life in America. Her parents
died soon after; her husband proved a worthless, drunken,
dissipated fellow; and this poor woman had been through all
the nameless humiliations and agonies which beset helpless
womanhood in the sole power of such a man. Submissive,
gentle, trusting, praying, entreating, hoping against hope, she
had borne with him many vicissitudes and reverses, — always
believing that at last the love of his children, if not of her,
would awaken a better nature within him. But the man steadily went downward instead of upward, and the better part of
him by slow degrees died away, till he came to regard his wife
and children only as so many clogs on his life, and to meditate
night and day on a scheme to abandon them, and return,
without their encumbrance, to his own country. It was with
a distant outlook to some such result that he had from the
first kept their marriage an entire secret from his own friends.
When the English army, at the close of the war, re-embarked

for England, he carried his cowardly scheme into execution. He had boarded his wife and children for a season in a country farm-house in the vicinity of Boston, with the excuse of cheapness of lodgings. Then one day his wife received a letter enclosing a sum of money, and saying, in such terms as bad men can find to veil devilish deeds, that all was over between them, and that ere she got this he should be on the ocean. The sorest hurt of all was that the letter denied the validity of their marriage; and the poor child found, to her consternation, that the marriage certificate, which she had always kept among her papers, was gone with her husband.

The first result of this letter had been a fit of sickness, wherein her little stock of money had melted almost away, and then she had risen from her bed determined to find her way to Boston, and learn, if possible, from certain persons with whom he had lodged before his departure, his address in England, that she might make one more appeal to him. But before she had walked far the sickness returned upon her, till, dizzy and faint, she had lain down, as we have described, on the bed of charity.

She had thought, ever since she received that letter, that she had reached the bottom of desolation,—that nothing could be added to her misery; but the withering, harsh sounds which reached her ear revealed a lower deep in the lowest depths. Hitherto on her short travels she had met only that kindly country hospitality which New England, from one end to the other, always has shown to the stranger. No one had refused a good meal of brown bread and rich milk to her and her children, and more often the friendly housewife, moved by her delicate appearance, had unlocked the sanctum where was deposited her precious tea-caddy, and brewed an amber cup of tea to sustain the sickly-looking wanderer. She and her children had been carried here and there, as occasion offered, a friendly mile or two, when Noah or Job or Sol "hitched up the critter" to go to mill or country store. The voice of harsh, pitiless rejection smote on her ear for the first time, and it seemed to her the drop too much in her cup. She turned her face to the wall and said, "O my God, I cannot bear this! I cannot, I cannot!" She would have said, "Let me die," but that she was tied to life by the two helpless, inno-

cent ones who shared her misery. The poorest and most desolate mother feels that her little children are poorer and more
desolate than she; and, however much her broken spirit may
long for the rest of Paradise, she is held back by the thought
that to abide in the flesh is needful to them. Even in her uttermost destitution the approaching shadow of the dark valley
was a terror to the poor soul,— not for her own sake, but for
theirs. The idea of a harsh, unpitiful world arose before her
for the first time, and the thought of leaving her little ones in
it unprotected was an anguish which rent her heart.

The little girl, over-weary, had eaten her supper and fallen
asleep beside her, with the trusting, ignorant rest of early
childhood; but her boy sat by her bedside with that look of
precocious responsibility, that air of anxious thought, which
seems unnatural in early childhood, and contrasted painfully
with the slight childish figure, the little hands, and little voice.
He was, as we have said, but nine years of age, well grown
for his years, but with that style of growth which indicates
delicacy of fibre rather than strength of organization. His
finely formed head, with its clustering curls of yellow hair, his
large, clear blue eyes, his exquisitely delicate skin, and the sensitiveness betrayed by his quivering lips, spoke of a lineage of
gentle blood, and an organization fitted rather to æsthetic and
intellectual development than to sturdy material toil. The little girl, as she lay sleeping, was a beautiful picture. Her head
was a wilderness of curls of a golden auburn, and the defined
pencilling of the eyebrows, and the long silken veil of the
lashes that fell over the sleeping eyes, the delicate polished
skin, and the finely moulded limbs, all indicated that she was
one who ought to have been among the jewels, rather than
among the potsherds of this mortal life. And these were the
children that she was going to leave alone, without a single
friend and protector in this world. For there are intuitions
that come to the sick and dying which tell them when the end
is near; and as this wanderer sunk down upon her bed this
night, there had fallen upon her mind a perfect certainty that
she should never be carried thence till carried to the grave;
and it was this which had given her soul so deadly a wrench,
and caused her to cry out in such utter agony.

What happens to desolate souls, who, thus forsaken by all

the world, cry out to God, is a mystery, good brother and sister, which you can never fathom until you have been exactly where they are. But certain it is that there is a very near way to God's heart, and so to the great heart of all comfort, that sometimes opens like a shaft of light between heaven and the soul, in hours when everything earthly falls away from us. A quaint old writer has said, "God keeps his choicest cordials for the time of our deepest faintings." And so it came to pass that, as this poor woman closed her eyes and prayed earnestly, there fell a strange clearness into her soul, which calmed every fear, and hushed the voice of every passion, and she lay for a season as if entranced. Words of holy writ, heard years ago in church-readings, in the hours of unconscious girlhood, now seemed to come back, borne in with a living power on her soul. It seemed almost as if a voice within was saying to her: "The Lord hath called thee as a woman forsaken and grieved in spirit, and a wife of youth, when thou wast refused, saith thy God. For a small moment have I forsaken thee, but with great mercies will I gather thee. In a little wrath I hid my face from thee for a moment, but with everlasting kindness will I have mercy on thee, saith the Lord thy Redeemer. O thou afflicted, tossed with tempest, and not comforted, behold, I will lay thy stones with fair colors, and thy foundations with sapphires. And all thy children shall be taught of the Lord, and great shall be the peace of thy children."

It is fashionable now to speak of words like these as fragments of ancient Hebrew literature, interesting and curious indeed, but relating to scenes, events, and states of society long gone by. But it is a most remarkable property of this old Hebrew literature, that it seems to be enchanted with a divine and living power, which strikes the nerve of individual consciousness in every desolate and suffering soul. It may have been Judah or Jerusalem ages ago to whom these words first came, but as they have travelled down for thousands of years, they have seemed to tens of thousands of sinking and desolate souls as the voice of God to them individually. They have raised the burden from thousands of crushed spirits; they have been as the day-spring to thousands of perplexed wanderers. Ah! let us treasure these old words, for as of old Jehovah chose to dwell in a tabernacle in the wilderness, and between the cherubim in the temple, so now he dwells in them; and to the simple soul that seeks for him here he will look forth as of old from the pillar of cloud and of fire.

The poor, ill-used, forsaken, forgotten creature who lay there trembling on the verge of life felt the presence of that mighty and generous, that godlike spirit that inspired these words. And surely if Jehovah ever did speak to man, no words were ever more worthy of Him. She lay as in a blessed trance, as passage after passage from the Scriptures rolled over her mind, like bright waves from the ocean of eternal peace.

"Fear thou not, for I am with thee; be not dismayed, for I am thy God. When thou passest through the waters I will be with thee, and through the rivers, they shall not overflow thee. When thou walkest through the fire, thou shalt not be burned, neither shall the flame kindle upon thee; for I am the Lord thy God, the Holy One of Israel, thy Saviour."

The little boy, who had heard his mother's first distressful cry, sat by her anxiously watching the changes of her face as she lay there. He saw her brow gradually grow clear and calm, and every line of trouble fade from her face, as shadows and clouds roll up from the landscape at day-dawn, till at last there was a rapt, peaceful expression, an evenness of breathing, as if she slept, and were dreaming some heavenly dream. It lasted for more than an hour, and the child sat watching her with the old, grave, tender look which had come to be the fashion of his little face when he looked upon his mother.

This boy had come to this mother as a second harvest of heart, hope, and joy, after the first great love and hope of womanhood had vanished. She felt herself broken-hearted, lonely, and unloved, when her first-born son was put into her arms, and she received him as did the first mother, saying, "I have gotten a man from the Lord." To him her desolate heart had unfolded its burden of confidence from the first dawning hours of intelligence. His tiny faculties had been widened to make room for her sorrows, and his childish strength increased by her leaning. There had been hours when this boy had stood between the maniac rage of a drunken father and the cowering form of his mother, with an unchildlike courage and steadiness that seemed almost like an inspiration. In days of desertion and poverty he had gone out with their slender

stock of money and made bargains such as it is pitiful to think
that a little child should know how to make; and often, in
moments when his mother's heart was overwhelmed, he
would come to her side with the little prayers and hymns
which she had taught him, and revive her faith and courage
when it seemed entirely gone.

Now, as he thought her sleeping, he began with anxious
care to draw the coverlet over her, and to move his little sister
back upon the bed. She opened her eyes,—large, clear blue
eyes, the very mirror of his own,—and, smiling with a
strange sweetness, stretched out her hand and drew him towards her. "Harry, my dear good boy, my dear, dear child,
nobody knows what a comfort you have been to me."

Then holding him from her, and looking intently in his eyes,
she seemed to hesitate for words to tell him something that
lay on her mind. At last she said, "Harry, say your prayers
and psalms."

The child knelt by the bed, with his hands clasped in his
mother's, and said the Lord's Prayer, and then, standing up,
repeated the beautiful psalm beginning, "The Lord is my
shepherd." Then followed a hymn, which the Methodists had
made familiar in those times:—

> "One there is above all others
>   Well deserves the name of Friend;
>   His is love beyond a brother's,
>   Costly, free, and knows no end.
>
> "Which of all our friends, to save us,
>   Could or would have shed his blood?
>   But this Saviour died to have us
>   Reconciled in him to God.
>
> "When he lived on earth abased,
>   Friend of Sinners was his name;
>   Now, above all glory raised,
>   He rejoiceth in the same.
>
> "O for grace our hearts to soften!
>   Teach us, Lord, at length to love;
>   We, alas! forget too often
>   What a friend we have above."

"Harry," said his mother, looking at him with an intense earnestness, "I want to tell you something. God, our Father, has called me to come home to him; and I am going. In a little while—perhaps to-morrow—I shall be gone, and you cannot find me. My soul will go to God, and they will put my body in the ground; and then you will have no friend but Jesus, and no father but the Father in heaven."

The child looked at her with solemn, dilated gaze, not really comprehending the full mystery of that which she was trying to explain; yet the tears starting in his eyes, and the twitching of the muscles of his mouth, showed that he partly understood.

"Mother," he said, "will papa never come back?"

"No, Harry, never. He has left us and gone away. He does not love us,—nobody loves us but our Father in heaven; but He does. You must always believe this. Now, Harry, I am going to leave your little sister to your care. You must always keep with her and take care of her, for she is a very little girl."

"Yes, mother."

"This is a great charge for a little boy like you; but you will live and grow up to be a man, and I want you never, as long as you live, to forget what I say to you now. Promise me, Harry, all your life to say these prayers and hymns that you have just been saying, every morning and every night. They are all I have to leave you; but if you only believe them, you will never be without comfort, no matter what happens to you. Promise me, dear."

"Yes, mother, I will."

"And, Harry, no matter *what* happens, never doubt that God loves you,—never forget that you have a Friend in heaven. Whenever you have a trouble, just pray to Him, and He will help you. Promise this."

"Yes, mother."

"Now lie down by me; I am very, very tired."

The little boy lay down by his mother; she threw her arms around him, and both sunk to sleep.

VIII.

Miss Asphyxia

"THERE won't be no great profit in this 'ere these ten year."

The object denominated "this 'ere" was the golden-haired child whom we have spoken of before,—the little girl whose mother lay dying. That mother is dead now; and the thing to be settled is, What is to be done with the children? The morning after the scene we have described looked in at the window and saw the woman, with a pale, placid face, sleeping as one who has found eternal rest, and the two weeping children striving in vain to make her hear.

Old Crab had been up early in his design of "carting the 'hull lot over to the poor-house," but made a solemn pause when his wife drew him into the little chamber. Death has a strange dignity, and whatsoever child of Adam he lays his hand on is for the time ennobled,—removed from the region of the earthly and commonplace to that of the spiritual and mysterious. And when Crab found, by searching the little bundle of the deceased, that there was actually money enough in it to buy a coffin and pay 'Zekiel Stebbins for digging the grave, he began to look on the woman as having made a respectable and edifying end, and the whole affair as coming to a better issue than he had feared.

And so the event was considered in the neighborhood, in a melancholy way, rather an interesting and auspicious one. It gave something to talk about in a region where exciting topics were remarkably scarce. The Reverend Jabez Periwinkle found in it a moving Providence which started him favorably on a sermon, and the funeral had been quite a windfall to all the gossips about; and now remained the question, What was to be done with the children?

"Now that we are diggin' the 'taters," said old Crab, "that 'ere chap might be good for suthin', pickin' on 'em out o' the hills. Poor folks like us can't afford to keep nobody jest to look at, and so he 'll have to step spry and work smart to airn his keep." And so at early dawn, the day after the funeral, the little boy was roused up and carried into the fields with the men.

But "this 'ere"—that is to say, a beautiful little girl of seven years—had greatly puzzled the heads of the worthy gossips of the neighborhood. Miss Asphyxia Smith, the elder sister of old Crab, was at this moment turning the child round, and examining her through a pair of large horn spectacles, with a view to "taking her to raise," as she phrased it.

Now all Miss Asphyxia's ideas of the purpose and aim of human existence were comprised in one word,—work. She was herself a working machine, always wound up and going,—up at early cock-crowing, and busy till bedtime, with a rampant and fatiguing industry that never paused for a moment. She conducted a large farm by the aid of a hired man, and drove a flourishing dairy, and was universally respected in the neighborhood as a smart woman.

Latterly, as her young cousin, who had shared the toils of the house with her, had married and left her, Miss Asphyxia had talked of "takin' a child from the poor-house, and so raisin' her own help"; and it was with the view of this "raisin' her help," that she was thus turning over and inspecting the little article which we have spoken of.

Apparently she was somewhat puzzled, and rather scandalized, that Nature should evidently have expended so much in a merely ornamental way on an article which ought to have been made simply for service. She brushed up a handful of the clustering curls in her large, bony hand, and said, with a sniff, "These 'll have to come right off to begin with; gracious me, what a tangle!"

"Mother always brushed them out every day," said the child.

"And who do you suppose is going to spend an hour every day brushing your hair, Miss Pert?" said Miss Asphyxia. "That ain't what I take ye for, I tell you. You 've got to learn to work for your living; and you ought to be thankful if I 'm willing to show you how."

The little girl did not appear particularly thankful. She bent her soft, pencilled eyebrows in a dark frown, and her great hazel eyes had gathering in them a cloud of sullen gloom. Miss Asphyxia did not mind her frowning,—perhaps did not notice it. She had it settled in her mind, as a first principle, that children never liked anything that was good for them, and that, of course, if she took a child, it would have to be made to come to her by forcible proceedings promptly instituted. So she set her little subject before her by seizing her by her two shoulders and squaring her round and looking in her face, and opened direct conversation with her in the following succinct manner.

"What 's your name?"

Then followed a resolved and gloomy silence, as the large bright eyes surveyed, with a sort of defiant glance, the inquisitor.

"Don't you hear?" said Miss Asphyxia, giving her a shake.

"Don't be so ha'sh with her," said the little old woman. "Say, my little dear, tell Miss Asphyxia your name," she added, taking the child's hand.

"Eglantine Percival," said the little girl, turning towards the old woman, as if she disdained to answer the other party in the conversation.

"Wh—a—t?" said Miss Asphyxia. "If there ain't the beatin'est name ever I heard. Well, I tell you *I* ain't got time to fix *my* mouth to say all that 'ere every time I want ye, now I tell ye."

"Mother and Harry called me Tina," said the child.

"Teny! Well, I should think so," said Miss Asphyxia. "That showed she 'd got a grain o' sense left, anyhow. She 's tol'able strong and well-limbed for her age," added that lady, feeling of the child's arms and limbs; "her flesh is solid. I think she 'll make a strong woman, only put her to work early and keep her at it. I could rub out clothes at the wash-tub afore I was at her age."

"O, she can do considerable many little chores," said Old Crab's wife.

"Yes," said Miss Asphyxia; "there can a good deal be got out of a child if you keep at 'em, hold 'em in tight, and never let 'em have their head a minute; push right hard on behind 'em, and you get considerable. That 's the way I was raised."

"But I want to play," said the little girl, bursting out in a sobbing storm of mingled fear and grief.

"Want to play, do you? Well, you must get over that. Don't you know that that 's as bad as stealing? You have n't got any money, and if you eat folks's bread and butter, you 've got to work to pay for it; and if folks buy your clothes, you 've got to work to pay for them."

"But I 've got some clothes of my own," persisted the child, determined not to give up her case entirely.

"Well, so you have; but there ain't no sort of wear in 'em," said Miss Asphyxia, turning to Mrs. Smith. "Them two dresses o' hern might answer for Sundays and sich, but I 'll have to make her up a regular linsey working dress this fall, and check aprons; and she must set right about knitting every minute she is n't doing anything else. Did you ever learn how to knit?"

"No," said the child.

"Or to sew?" said Miss Asphyxia.

"Yes; mother taught me to sew," said the child.

"No! Yes! Hain't you learned manners? Do you say yes and no to people?"

The child stood a moment, swelling with suppressed feeling, and at last she opened her great eyes full on Miss Asphyxia, and said, "I don't like you. You ain't pretty, and I won't go with you."

"O now," said Mrs. Smith, "little girls must n't talk so; that 's naughty."

"Don't like me?—ain't I pretty?" said Miss Asphyxia, with a short, grim laugh. "May be I ain't; but I know what I 'm about, and you 'd as goods know it first as last. I 'm going to take ye right out with me in the waggin, and you 'd best not have none of your cuttin's up. I keep a stick at home for naughty girls. Why, where do you suppose you 're going to get your livin' if I don't take you?"

"I want to live with Harry," said the child, sobbing. "Where is Harry?"

"Harry 's to work,—and there 's where he 's got to be," said Miss Asphyxia. "He 's got to work with the men in the fields, and you 've got to come home and work with me."

"I want to stay with Harry,—Harry takes care of me," said the child, in a piteous tone.

Old Mother Smith now toddled to her milk-room, and, with a melting heart, brought out a doughnut. "There now, eat that," she said; "and mebbe, if you 're good, Miss Asphyxia will bring you down here some time."

"O laws, Polly, you allers was a fool!" said Miss Asphyxia. "It 's all for the child's good, and what 's the use of fussin' on her up? She 'll come to it when she knows she 's got to. 'T ain't no more than I was put to at her age, only the child 's been fooled with and babied."

The little one refused the doughnut, and seemed to gather herself up in silent gloom.

"Come, now, don't stand sulking; let me put your bonnet on," said Miss Asphyxia, in a brisk, metallic voice. "I can't be losin' the best part of my day with this nonsense!" And forthwith she clawed up the child in her bony grasp, as easily as an eagle might truss a chick-sparrow.

"Be a good little girl, now," said the little gray woman, who felt a strange swelling and throbbing in her poor old breast. To be sure, she knew she was a fool; her husband had told her so at least three times every day for years; and Miss Asphyxia only confirmed what she accepted familiarly as the truth. But yet she could not help these unprofitable longings to coddle and comfort something,—to do some of those little motherly tendernesses for children which go to no particular result, only to make them happy; so she ran out after the wagon with a tempting seed-cake, and forced it into the child's hand.

"Take it, do take it," she said; "eat it, and be a good girl, and do just as she tells you to."

"I 'll see to that," said Miss Asphyxia, as she gathered up the reins and gave a cut to her horse, which started that quadruped from a dream of green grass into a most animated pace. Every creature in her service—horse, cow, and pig—knew at once the touch of Miss Asphyxia, and the necessity of being up and doing when she was behind them; and the horse, who under other hands would have been the slowest and most reflective of beasts, now made the little wagon spin and bounce over the rough, stony road, so that the child's short legs flew up in the air every few moments.

"You must hold on tight," was Miss Asphyxia's only comment on this circumstance. "If you fall out, you 'll break your neck!"

It was a glorious day of early autumn, the sun shining as only an autumn sun knows how to shine. The blue fields of heaven were full of fleecy flocks of clouds, drifting hither and thither at their lazy will. The golden-rod and the aster hung their plumage over the rough, rocky road; and now and then it wound through a sombre piece of woods, where scarlet sumachs and maples flashed out among the gloomy green hemlocks with a solemn and gorgeous light. So very fair was the day, and so full of life and beauty was the landscape, that the child, who came of a beauty-loving lineage, felt her little heart drawn out from under its burden of troubles, and springing and bounding with that elastic habit of happiness which seems hard to kill in children.

Once she laughed out as a squirrel, with his little chops swelled with a nut on each side, sat upon the fence and looked after them, and then whisked away behind the stone wall; and once she called out, "O, how pretty!" at a splendid clump of blue fringed gentian, which stood holding up its hundred azure vases by the wayside. "O, I do wish I could get some of that!" she cried out, impulsively.

"Some of what?" said Miss Asphyxia.

"O, those *beautiful* flowers!" said the child, leaning far out to look back.

"O, that 's nothing but gentian," said Miss Asphyxia; "can't stop for that. Them blows is good to dry for weakness," she added. "By and by, if you 're good, mebbe I 'll let you get some of 'em."

Miss Asphyxia had one word for all flowers. She called them all "blows," and they were divided in her mind, in a manner far more simple than any botanical system, into two classes; namely, blows that were good to dry, and blows that were not. Elder-blow, catnip, hoarhound, hardhack, gentian, ginseng, and various other vegetable tribes, she knew well and had a great respect for; but all the other little weeds that put on obtrusive colors and flaunted in the summer breeze, without any pretensions to further usefulness, Miss Asphyxia completely ignored. It would not be describing her state to say she had a contempt for them: she simply never saw or thought of them at all. The idea of beauty as connected with any of them never entered her mind,—it did not exist there.

The young cousin who shared her housework had, to be sure, planted a few flowers in a corner of the garden; there were some peonies and pinks and a rose-bush, which often occupied a spare hour of the girl's morning or evening; but Miss Asphyxia watched these operations with a sublime contempt, and only calculated the loss of potatoes and carrots caused by this unproductive beauty. Since the marriage of this girl, Miss Asphyxia had often spoken to her man about "clearing out them things"; but somehow he always managed to forget it, and the thriftless beauties still remained.

It wanted but about an hour of noon when Miss Asphyxia set down the little girl on the clean-scrubbed floor of a great kitchen, where everything was even desolately orderly and neat. She swung her at once into a chair. "Sit there," she said, "till I 'm ready to see to ye." And then, marching up to her own room, she laid aside her bonnet, and, coming down, plunged into active preparations for the dinner.

An irrepressible feeling of desolation came over the child. The elation produced by the ride died away; and, as she sat dangling her heels from the chair, and watching the dry, grim form of Miss Asphyxia, a sort of terror of her began slowly to usurp the place of that courage which had at first inspired the child to rise up against the assertion of so uncongenial a power.

All the strange, dreadful events of the last few days mingled themselves, in her childish mind, in a weird mass of uncomprehended gloom and mystery. Her mother, so changed,—cold, stiff, lifeless, neither smiling nor speaking nor looking at her: the people coming to the house, and talking and singing and praying, and then putting her in a box in the ground, and saying that she was dead; and then, right upon that, to be torn from her brother, to whom she had always looked for protection and counsel,—all this seemed a weird, inexplicable cloud coming over her heart and darkening all her little life.

Where was Harry? Why did he let them take her? Or perhaps equally dreadful people had taken him, and would never bring him back again.

There was a tall black clock in a corner of the kitchen, that kept its invariable monotone of tick-tack, tick-tack, with a persistence that made her head swim; and she watched the quick, decisive movements of Miss Asphyxia with somewhat of the same respectful awe with which one watches the course of a locomotive engine.

It was late for Miss Asphyxia's dinner preparations, but she instituted prompt measures to make up for lost time. She flew about the kitchen with such long-armed activity and fearful celerity, that the child began instinctively to duck and bob her little head when she went by, lest she should hit her and knock her off her chair.

Miss Asphyxia raked open the fire in the great kitchen chimney, and built it up with a liberal supply of wood; then she rattled into the back room, and a sound was heard of a bucket descending into a well with such frantic haste as only an oaken bucket under Miss Asphyxia's hands could be frightened into. Back she came with a stout black iron tea-kettle, which she hung over the fire; and then, flopping down a ham on the table, she cut off slices with a martial and determined air, as if she would like to see the ham try to help itself; and, before the child could fairly see what she was doing, the slices of ham were in the frying-pan over the coals, the ham hung up in its place, the knife wiped and put out of sight, and the table drawn out into the middle of the floor, and invested with a cloth for dinner.

During these operations the child followed every movement with awe-struck eyes, and studied with trembling attention every feature of this wonderful woman.

Miss Asphyxia was tall and spare. Nature had made her, as she often remarked of herself, entirely for use. She had allowed for her muscles no cushioned repose of fat, no redundant smoothness of outline. There was nothing to her but good, strong, solid bone, and tough, wiry, well-strung muscle. She was past fifty, and her hair was already well streaked with gray, and so thin that, when tightly combed and tied, it still showed bald cracks, not very sightly to the eye. The only thought that Miss Asphyxia ever had had in relation to the *coiffure* of her hair was that it was to be got out of her way. Hair she considered principally as something that might get into people's eyes, if not properly attended to; and accordingly, at a very early hour every morning, she tied all hers in a very tight knot, and then secured it by a horn comb on the top of her head. To tie this knot so tightly that, once done, it should last all day, was Miss Asphyxia's only art of the toilet, and she tried her work every morning by giving her head a shake, before she left her looking-glass, not unlike that of an unruly cow. If this process did not start the horn comb from its moorings, Miss Asphyxia was well pleased. For the rest, her face was dusky and wilted,—guarded by gaunt, high cheek-bones, and watched over by a pair of small gray eyes of unsleeping vigilance. The shaggy eyebrows that overhung them were grizzled, like her hair.

It would not be proper to say that Miss Asphyxia looked ill-tempered; but her features could never, by any stretch of imagination, be supposed to wear an expression of tenderness. They were set in an austere, grim gravity, whose lines had become more deeply channelled by every year of her life. As related to her fellow-creatures, she was neither passionate nor cruel. We have before described her as a working machine, forever wound up to high-pressure working-point; and this being her nature, she trod down and crushed whatever stood in the way of her work, with as little compunction as if she had been a steam-engine or a power-loom.

Miss Asphyxia had a full conviction of what a recent pleasant writer has denominated the total depravity of matter. She was not given to many words, but it might often be gathered from her brief discourses that she had always felt herself, so to speak, sword in hand against a universe where everything was running to disorder,—everything was tending to slackness, shiftlessness, unthrift, and she alone was left on the earth to keep things in their places. Her hired men were always too late up in the morning,—always shirking,—always taking too long a nap at noon; everybody was watching to cheat her in every bargain; her horse, cow, pigs,—all her possessions,— were ready at the slightest winking of her eye, or relaxing of her watch, to fall into all sorts of untoward ways and gyrations; and therefore she slept, as it were, in her armor, and spent her life as a sentinel on duty.

In taking a child, she had had her eyes open only to one patent fact,—that a child was an animal who would always be wanting to play, and that she must make all her plans and calculations to keep her from playing. To this end she had beforehand given out word to her brother, that, if she took the girl, the boy must be kept away. "Got enough on my hands now, without havin' a boy trainin' round my house, and upsettin' all creation," said the grim virgin.

"Wal, wal," said Old Crab, "'t ain't best; they 'll be a consultin' together, and cuttin' up didos. I 'll keep the boy tight enough, I tell you."

Little enough was the dinner that the child ate that day. There were two hulking, square-shouldered men at the table, who stared at her with great round eyes like oxen; and so, though Miss Asphyxia dumped down Indian pudding, ham, and fried potatoes before her, the child's eating was scarcely that of a blackbird.

Marvellous to the little girl was the celerity with which Miss Asphyxia washed and cleared up the dinner-dishes. How the dishes rattled, the knives and forks clinked, as she scraped and piled and washed and wiped and put everything in a trice back into such perfect place, that it looked as if nothing had ever been done on the premises!

After this Miss Asphyxia produced thimble, thread, needle, and scissors, and, drawing out of a closet a bale of coarse blue home-made cloth, proceeded to measure the little girl for a petticoat and short gown of the same. This being done to her mind, she dumped her into a chair beside her, and, putting a brown towel into her hands to be hemmed, she briefly said, "There, keep to work"; while she, with great despatch and resolution, set to work on the little garments aforesaid.

The child once or twice laid down her work to watch the chickens who came up around the door, or to note a bird which flew by with a little ripple of song. The first time, Miss Asphyxia only frowned, and said, "Tut, tut." The second time, there came three thumps of Miss Asphyxia's thimble down on the little head, with the admonition, "Mind your work." The child now began to cry, but Miss Asphyxia soon put an end to that by displaying a long birch rod, with a threatening movement, and saying succinctly, "Stop that, this minute, or I 'll whip you." And the child was so certain of this that she swallowed her grief and stitched away as fast as her little fingers could go.

As soon as supper was over that night, Miss Asphyxia seized upon the child, and, taking her to a tub in the sink-room, proceeded to divest her of her garments and subject her to a most thorough ablution.

"I 'm goin' to give you one good scrubbin' to start with," said Miss Asphyxia; and, truth to say, no word could more thoroughly express the character of the ablution than the term "scrubbing." The poor child was deluged with soap and water, in mouth, nose, ears, and eyes, while the great bony hands rubbed and splashed, twisted her arms, turned her ears wrong side out, and dashed on the water with unsparing vigor. Nobody can tell the torture which can be inflicted on a child in one of these vigorous old New England washings, which used to make Saturday night a terror in good families. But whatever they were, the little martyr was by this time so thoroughly impressed with the awful reality of Miss Asphyxia's power over her, that she endured all with only a few long-drawn and convulsed sighs, and an inaudible "O dear!"

When well scrubbed and wiped, Miss Asphyxia put on a coarse homespun nightgown, and, pinning a cloth round the child's neck, began with her scissors the work of cutting off her hair. Snip, snip, went the fatal shears, and down into the towel fell bright curls, once the pride of a mother's heart, till finally the small head was despoiled completely. Then Miss Asphyxia, shaking up a bottle of camphor, proceeded to rub some vigorously upon the child's head. "There," she said, "that 's to keep ye from catchin' cold."

She then proceeded to the kitchen, raked open the fire, and shook the golden curls into the bed of embers, and stood grimly over them while they seethed and twisted and writhed, as if they had been living things suffering a fiery torture, meanwhile picking diligently at the cloth that had contained them, that no stray hair might escape.

"I wonder now," she said to herself, "if any of this will rise and get into the next pudding?" She spoke with a spice of bitterness, poor woman, as if it would be just the way things usually went on, if it did.

She buried the fire carefully, and then, opening the door of a small bedroom adjoining, which displayed a single bed, she said, "Now get into bed."

The child immediately obeyed, thankful to hide herself under the protecting folds of a blue checked coverlet, and feeling that at last the dreadful Miss Asphyxia would leave her to herself.

Miss Asphyxia clapped to the door, and the child drew a long breath. In a moment, however, the door flew open. Miss Asphyxia had forgotten something. "Can you say your prayers?" she demanded.

"Yes, ma'am," said the child.

"Say 'em, then," said Miss Asphyxia; and bang went the door again.

"There, now, if I hain't done up my duty to that child, then I don't know," said Miss Asphyxia.

IX.

Harry's First Day's Work

IT was the fashion of olden times to consider children only as children pure and simple; not as having any special and individual nature which required special and individual adaptation, but as being simply so many little creatures to be washed, dressed, schooled, fed, and whipped, according to certain general and well-understood rules.

The philosophy of modern society is showing to parents and educators how delicate and how varied is their task; but in the days we speak of nobody had thought of these shadings and variations. It is perhaps true, that in that very primitive and simple state of society there were fewer of those individual peculiarities which are the result of the stimulated brains and nervous systems of modern society.

Be that as it may, the little parish of Needmore saw nothing in the fact that two orphan children had fallen into the hands of Crab Smith and his sister, Miss Asphyxia, which appeared to its moral sense as at all unsuitable. To be sure, there was a suppressed shrug of the shoulders at the idea of the little fair-haired, pleasant-mannered boy being given up to Old Crab. People said to each other, with a knowing grin: "That 'ere boy 'd have to toe the mark pretty handsome; but then, he might do wus. He 'd have enough to eat and drink anyhow, and old Ma'am Smith, she 'd mother him. As to Miss Asphyxia and the girl, why, 't was jest the thing. She was jest the hand to raise a smart girl."

In fact, we are not certain that Miss Asphyxia, with a few modifications and fashionable shadings suitable for our modern society, is not, after all, the ideal personage who would get all votes as just the proper person to take charge of an orphan asylum,—would be recommended to widowers with large families as just the woman to bring up their children.

Efficiency has always been, in our New England, the golden calf before which we have fallen down and wor-

shipped. The great granite formation of physical needs and
wants that underlie life in a country with a hard soil and a
severe climate gives an intensity to our valuation of what pertains to the working of the direct and positive force that controls the physical; and that which can keep in constant order
the eating, drinking, and wearing of this mortal body is always asserting itself in every department of life as the true
wisdom.

But what, in fact, were the two little children who had been
thus seized on and appropriated?

The boy was, as we have described, of a delicate and highly
nervous organization,—sensitive, æsthetic,—evidently fitted
by nature more for the poet or scholar than for the rough
grind of physical toil. There had been superinduced on this
temperament a precocious development from the circumstance of his having been made, during the earliest years of
his consciousness, the companion of his mother. Nothing un-
folds a child faster than being thus taken into the companionship of older minds in the first years of life. He was naturally
one of those manly, good-natured, even-tempered children
that are the delight of nurses and the staff and stay of mothers. Early responsibility and sorrow, and the religious teachings of his mother, had awakened the spiritual part of his
nature to a higher consciousness than usually exists in childhood. There was about him a steady, uncorrupted goodness
and faithfulness of nature, a simple, direct truthfulness, and a
loyal habit of prompt obedience to elders, which made him
one of those children likely, in every position of child-life, to
be favorites, and to run a smooth course.

The girl, on the contrary, had in her all the elements of a
little bundle of womanhood, born to rule and command in a
pure womanly way. She was affectionate, gay, pleasure-loving,
self-willed, imperious, intensely fond of approbation, with
great stores of fancy, imagination, and an under-heat of undeveloped passion that would, in future life, give warmth and
color to all her thoughts, as a volcanic soil is said to bright-
en the hues of flowers and warm the flavor of grapes. She
had, too, that capacity of secretiveness which enabled her to
carry out the dictates of a strong will, and an intuitive

sense of where to throw a tendril or strike a little fibre of persuasion or coaxing, which comes early to those fair parasites who are to live by climbing upon others, and to draw their hues and sweetness from the warmth of other hearts. The moral and religious faculties were as undeveloped in her as in a squirrel or a robin. She had lived, in fact, between her sorrowing mother and her thoughtful little brother, as a beautiful pet, whose little gladsome ways and gay pranks were the only solace of their poverty. Even the father, in good-natured hours, had caressed her, played with her, told her stories, and allowed all her little audacities and liberties with an indulgence that her brother could not dare to hope for. No service or self-denial had ever been required of her. She had been served, with a delicate and exact care, by both mother and brother.

Such were the two little specimens of mortality which the town of Needmore thought well provided for when they were consigned to Crab Smith and Miss Asphyxia.

The first day after the funeral of his mother, the boy had been called up before light in the morning, and been off at sunrise to the fields with the men; but he had gone with a heart of manly enterprise, feeling as if he were beginning life on his own account, and meaning, with straightforward simplicity, to do his best.

He assented to Old Crab's harsh orders with such obedient submission, and set about the work given him with such a steady, manly patience and good-will, as to win for himself, at the outset, golden opinions from the hired men, and to excite in Old Crab that discontented satisfaction which he felt in an employee in whom he could find nothing to scold. The work of merely picking up the potatoes from the hills which the men opened was so very simple as to give no chance for mistake or failure, and the boy was so cheerful and unintermitting in his work that no fault could be found under that head. He was tired enough, it is true, at night; but, as he rode home in the cart, he solaced himself with the idea that he was beginning to be a man, and that he should work and support his sister,—and he had many things to tell her of the result of his first day's labor. He wondered that she did not come to meet him as the cart drove up to the house, and his first inquiry, when he saw the friendly old woman, was, "Where is Tina?"

"She 's gone to live with *his* sister," said Mrs. Smith, in an undertone, pointing to her husband in the back yard. "Asphyxia 's took her to raise."

"To what?" said the boy, timidly.

"Why, to fetch her up,—teach her to work," said the little old woman. "But come, sonny, go wash your hands to the sink. Dear me! why, you 've fairly took the skin off your fingers."

"I 'm not much used to work," said the boy, "but I don't mind it." And he washed carefully the little hands, which, sure enough, had the skin somewhat abraded on the finger-ends.

"Do ye good," said Old Crab. "Must n't mind that. Can't have no lily-fingered boys workin' for me."

The child had not thought of complaining; but as soon as he was alone with Mrs. Smith, he came to her confidentially and said, "How far is it to where Tina lives?"

"Well, it 's the best part of two miles, I calculate."

"Can't I go over there to-night and see her?"

"Dear heart! no, you can't. Why, your little back must ache now, and he 'll have you routed up by four o'clock in the morning."

"I 'm not so very tired," said the boy; "but I want to see Tina. If you 'll show me the way, I 'll go."

"O, well, you see, they won't let you," said the old woman, confidentially. "They are a ha'sh pair of 'em, him and Sphyxy are; and they 've settled it that you ain't to see each other no more, for fear you 'd get to playin' and idlin'."

The blood flushed into the boy's face, and he breathed short. Something stirred within him, such as makes slavery bitter, as he said, "But that is n't right. She 's my only sister, and my mother told me to take care of her; and I *ought* to see her sometimes."

"Lordy massy!" said Goody Smith; "when you 're with some folks, it don't make no difference what 's right and what ain't. You 've jest got to do as ye ken. It won't do to rile *him*, I tell you. He 's awful, once git his back up." And Goody

Smith shook her little old head mysteriously, and hushed the boy, as she heard her husband's heavy tread coming in from the barn.

The supper of cold beef and pork, potatoes, turnips, and hard cider, which was now dispensed at the farm-house, was ample for all purposes of satisfying hunger; and the little Harry, tired as he was, ate with a vigorous relish. But his mind was still dwelling on his sister.

After supper was over he followed Goody Smith into her milk-room. "Please do ask *him* to let me go and see Tina," he said, persuasively.

"Laws a massy, ye poor dear! ye don't know the critter. If *I* ask him to do a thing, he's all the more set agin it. I found out that 'ere years ago. He never does nothin' *I* ask him to. But never mind; some of these days, we'll try and contrive it. When he's gone to mill, I'll speak to the men, and tell 'em to let ye slip off. But then the pester on 't is, there's Sphyxy; she's allers wide awake, and would n't let a boy come near her house no more than ef he was a bulldog."

"Why, what harm do boys do?" said the child, to whom this view presented an entirely new idea.

"O, well, she's an old maid, and kind o' set in her ways; and it ain't easy gettin' round Sphyxy; but I'll try and contrive it. Sometimes I can get round 'em, and get something done, when they don't know nothin' about it; but it's dreffull hard gettin' things done."

The view thus presented to the child's mind of the cowering, deceptive policy in which the poor old woman's whole married life had been spent gave him much to think of after he had gone to his bedroom.

He sat down on his little, lonely bed, and began trying to comprehend in his own mind the events of the last few days. He recalled his mother's last conversation with him. All had happened just as she had said. She was gone, just as she had told him, and left him and little Tina alone in the world. Then he remembered his promise, and, kneeling down by his bedside, repeated the simple litany—psalm, prayer, and hymn— which his mother had left him as her only parting gift. The words soothed his little lonesome heart; and he thought what his mother said,—he recalled the look of her dying eyes as she said it,—"Never doubt that God loves you, whatever happens; and, if you have any trouble, pray to him." Upon this thought, he added to his prayer these words: "O dear Father! they have taken away Tina; and she 's a very little girl, and cannot work, as I can. Please do take care of Tina, and make them let me go and see her."

X.

Miss Asphyxia's System

WHEN Miss Asphyxia shut the door finally on little Tina, the child began slowly to gather up her faculties from the stunning, benumbing influence of the change which had come over her life.

In former days her father had told her stories of little girls that were carried off to giants' houses, and there maltreated and dominated over in very dreadful ways; and Miss Asphyxia presented herself to her as one of these giants. She was so terribly strong, the child felt instinctively, in every limb, that there was no getting away from her. Her eyes were so keen and searching, her voice so sharp, all her movements so full of a vigor that might be felt, that any chance of getting the better of her by indirect ways seemed hopelessly small. If she should try to run away to find Harry, she was quite sure that Miss Asphyxia could make a long arm that would reach her before she had gone far; and then what she would do to her was a matter that she dared not think of. Even when she was not meaning to be cross to her, but merely seized and swung her into a chair, she had such a grip that it almost gave pain; and what would it be if she seized her in wrath? No; there was evidently no escape; and, as the thought came over the child, she began to cry,—first sobbing, and then, as her agitation increased, screaming audibly.

Miss Asphyxia opened the door. "Stop that!" she said. "What under the canopy ails ye?"

"I—want—Harry!" said the child.

"Well, you can't have Harry; and I won't have ye bawling. Now shut up and go to sleep, or I 'll whip you!" And, with that, Miss Asphyxia turned down the bedclothes with a resolute hand.

"I will be good,—I will stop," said the child, in mortal terror, compressing the sobs that seemed to tear her little frame.

Miss Asphyxia waited a moment, and then, going out, shut

the door, and went on making up the child's stuff gown outside.

"That 'ere 's goin' to be a regular limb," she said; "but I
must begin as I 'm goin' to go on with her, and mebbe she 'll
amount to suthin' by and by. A child 's pretty much dead loss
the first three or four years; but after that they more 'n pay,
if they 're fetched up right."

"Mebbe that 'ere child 's lonesome," said Sol Peters, Miss
Asphyxia's hired man, who sat in the kitchen corner, putting
in a new hoe-handle.

"Lonesome!" said Miss Asphyxia, with a sniff of contempt.

"All sorts of young critters is," said Sol, undismayed by this
sniff. "Puppies is. 'Member how our Spot yelped when I fust
got him? Kept me 'wake the biggest part of one night. And
kittens mews when ye take 'em from the cats. Ye see they 's
used to other critters; and it 's sort o' cold like, bein' alone
is."

"Well, she 'll have to get used to it, anyhow," said Miss
Asphyxia. "I guess 't won't kill her. Ef a child has enough to
eat and drink, and plenty of clothes, and somebody to take
care of 'em, they ain't very bad off, if they be lonesome."

Sol, though a big-fisted, hard-handed fellow, had still
rather a soft spot under his jacket in favor of all young, defenceless animals, and the sound of the little girl's cry had
gone right to this spot. So he still revolved the subject, as he
leisurely turned and scraped with a bit of broken glass the
hoe-handle that he was elaborating. After a considerable
pause, he shut up one eye, looked along his hoe-handle at
Miss Asphyxia, as if he were taking aim, and remarked, "That
'ere boy 's a nice, stiddy little chap; and mebbe, if he could
come down here once and a while after work-hours, 't would
kind o' reconcile her."

"I tell you what, Solomon Peters," said Miss Asphyxia, "I 'd
jest as soon have the great red dragon in the Revelations a
comin' down on my house as a boy! Ef I don't work hard
enough now, I 'd like to know, without havin' a boy raound
raisin' gineral Cain. Don't tell me! I 'll find work enough to
keep that 'ere child from bein' lonesome. Lonesome! — there
did n't nobody think of no such things when I was little. I
was jest put right along, and no remarks made; and was made

to mind when I was spoken to, and to take things as they come. O, I 'll find her work enough to keep her mind occupied, I promise ye."

Sol did not in the least doubt that, for Miss Asphyxia's reputation in the region was perfectly established. She was spoken of with applause under such titles as "a staver," "a pealer," "a roarer to work"; and Sol himself had an awful sense of responsibility to her in this regard. He had arrived at something of a late era in single life, and had sometimes been sportively jogged by his associates, at the village store, as to his opportunity of becoming master of Miss Asphyxia's person and property by matrimonial overtures; to all which he summarily responded by declaring that "a hoss might as soon go a courtin' to the hoss-whip as he court Miss Sphyxy." As to Miss Asphyxia, when rallied on the same subject, she expressed her views of the matrimonial estate in a sentence more terse and vigorous than elegant,—that "she knew t' much to put her nose into hot swill." Queen Elizabeth might have expressed her mind in a more courtly way, but certainly with no more decision.

The little head and heart in the next room were full of the rudiments of thoughts, desires, feelings, imaginations, and passions which either had never lived in Miss Asphyxia's nature, or had died so long ago that not a trace or memory of them was left. If she had had even the dawnings of certain traits and properties, she might have doubted of her ability to bring up a child; but she had not.

Yet Miss Asphyxia's faults in this respect were not so widely different from the practice of the hard, rustic inhabitants of Needmore as to have prevented her getting employment as a district-school teacher for several terms, when she was about twenty years of age. She was held to be a "smart," economical teacher, inasmuch as she was able to hold the winter term, and thrash the very biggest boys, and, while she did the duty of a man, received only the wages of a woman,—a recommendation in female qualification which has not ceased to be available in our modern days. Gradually, by incredible industries, by a faculty of pinching, saving, and accumulating hard to conceive of, Miss Asphyxia had laid up money till she had actually come to be the possessor of a small but neat house, and a farm and dairy in excellent condition; and she regarded herself, therefore, and was regarded by others, as a model for imitation. Did she have the least doubt that she was eminently fitted to bring up a girl? I trow not.

Miss Asphyxia, in her early childhood, had been taken to raise in the same manner that she had taken this child. She had been trained to early rising, and constant, hard, unintermitted work, without thought of respite or amusement. During certain seasons of the year she had been sent to the district school, where, always energetic in whatever she took in hand, she always stood at the head of the school in the few arts of scholarship in those days taught. She could write a good, round hand; she could cipher with quickness and adroitness; she had learned by heart all the rules of Murray's Grammar, notwithstanding the fact that, from the habits of early childhood, she habitually set at naught every one of them in her daily conversation,—always strengthening all her denials with those good, hearty double negatives which help out French and Italian sentences, and are unjustly denied to the purists in genteel English. How much of the droll quaintness of Yankee dialect comes from the stumbling of human nature into these racy mistakes will never be known.

Perhaps my readers may have turned over a great, flat stone some time in their rural rambles, and found under it little clovers and tufts of grass pressed to earth, flat, white, and bloodless, but still growing, stretching, creeping towards the edges, where their plant instinct tells them there is light and deliverance. The kind of life that the little Tina led, under the care of Miss Asphyxia, resembled that of these poor clovers. It was all shut down and repressed, but growing still. She was roused at the first glimmer of early dawn, dressing herself in the dark, and, coming out, set the table for breakfast. From that time through the day, one task followed another in immediate succession, with the sense of the ever-driving Miss Asphyxia behind her.

Once, in the course of her labors, she let fall a saucer, while Miss Asphyxia, by good fortune, was out of the room. To tell of her mischance, and expose herself to the awful consequences of her anger, was more than her childish courage was equal to; and, with a quick adroitness, she slipped the broken fragments in a crevice between the kitchen doorstep and the house, and endeavored to look as if nothing had occurred. Alas! she had not counted on Miss Asphyxia's unsleeping vigilance of hearing. She was down stairs in a trice.

"What have you been breaking?"

"Nothing, ma'am," was the trembling response.

"Don't tell me! I heard something fall."

"I think it must have been the tongs," said the little girl,— not over-wise or ingenious in her subterfuge.

"Tongs! likely story," said Miss Asphyxia, keenly running her eye over the cups and saucers.

"One, two,—here's one of the saucers gone. What have you done with it?"

The child, now desperate with fear, saw no refuge but in persistent denial, till Miss Asphyxia, seizing her, threatened immediate whipping if she did not at once confess.

"I dropped a saucer," at last said the frightened child.

"You did, you little slut?" said Miss Asphyxia, administering a box on her ear. "Where is it? what have you done with the pieces?"

"I dropped them down by the doorstep," said the sobbing culprit.

Miss Asphyxia soon fished them up, and held them up in awful judgment. "You've been telling me a lie,—a naughty, wicked lie," she said. "I'll soon cure you of lying. I'll scour your mouth out for you." And forthwith, taking a rag with some soap and sand, she grasped the child's head under her arm, and rubbed the harsh mixture through her mouth with a vengeful energy. "There, now, see if you'll tell me another lie," said she, pushing her from her. "Don't you know where liars go to, you naughty, wicked girl? 'All liars shall have their part in the lake that burns with fire and brimstone,'—that's what the Bible says; and you may thank me for keeping you from going there. Now go and get up the potatoes and wash 'em, and don't let me get another lie out of your mouth as long as you live."

There was a burning sense of shame—a smothered fury of resentment—in the child's breast, and, as she took the basket, she felt as if she would have liked to do some mischief to Miss Asphyxia. "I hate you, I hate you, I hate you," she said to herself when she got into the cellar, and fairly out of hearing. "I hate you, and when I get to be a woman, I 'll pay you for all this."

Miss Asphyxia, however, went on her way, in the testimony of a good conscience. She felt that she had been equal to the emergency, and had met a crisis in the most thorough and effectual manner.

The teachers of district schools in those days often displayed a singular ingenuity in the invention of punishments by which the different vices of childhood should be repressed; and Miss Asphyxia's housewifely confidence in soap and sand as a means of purification had suggested to her this expedient in her school-teaching days. "You can break any child o' lying, right off short," she was wont to say. "Jest scour their mouths out with soap and sand. They never want to try it more 'n once or twice, I tell you."

The intervals which the child had for play were, in Miss Asphyxia's calendar, few and far between. Sometimes, when she had some domestic responsibility on her mind which made the watching of the child a burden to her, she would say to her, "You may go and play till I call you," or, "You may play for half an hour; but you must n't go out of the yard."

Then the child, alone, companionless, without playthings, sought to appropriate to herself some little treasures and possessions for the instituting of that fairy world of imagination which belongs to childhood. She sighed for a doll that had once belonged to her in the days when she had a mother, but which Miss Asphyxia had contemptuously tossed aside in making up her bundle.

Left thus to her own resources, the child yet showed the unquenchable love of beauty, and the power of creating and gilding an imaginary little world, which is the birthright of childhood. She had her small store of what she had been wont to call pretty things,—a broken teapot handle, a fragment of colored glass, part of a goblet that had once belonged to Miss Asphyxia's treasures, one or two smooth pebbles, and some red berries from a wild rose-bush. These were the darlings, the dear delights of her heart,—hoarded in secret places, gazed on by stealth, taken out and arranged and rearranged, during the brief half-hours, or hours, when Miss Asphyxia allowed her to play. To these treasures the kindly Sol added another; for one day, when Miss Asphyxia was not looking, he drew from his vest-pocket a couple of milkweed pods, and said, "Them 's putty,—mebbe ye 'd like 'em; hide 'em up, though, or she 'll sweep 'em into the fire."

No gloss of satin and glimmer of pearls ever made bright eyes open wider than did the exploring the contents of these pods. It was silk and silver, fairy-spun glass,—something so bright and soft that it really seemed dear to her; and she took the shining silk fringes out and caressed them against her cheek, and wrapped them in a little bit of paper, and put them in her bosom. They felt so soft and downy,—they were so shining and bright,—and they were her own,—Sol had given them to her. She meditated upon them as possessions of mysterious beauty and unknown value. Unfortunately, one day Miss Asphyxia discovered her gazing upon this treasure by stealth during her working hours.

"What have you got there?" she said. "Bring it to me."

The child reluctantly placed her treasure in the great bony claw.

"Why, that 's milkweed silk," said Miss Asphyxia. "'T ain't good for nothin'. What you doing with that?"

"I like it because it 's pretty."

"Fiddlestick!" said Miss Asphyxia, giving it a contemptuous toss. "I can't have you making litter with such stuff round the house. Throw it in the fire."

To do Miss Asphyxia justice, she would never have issued this order if she had had the remotest conception how dear this apparent trash was to the hopeless little heart.

The child hesitated, and held her treasure firmly. Her breast heaved, and there was a desperate glare in her soft hazel eyes.

"Throw it in the fire," said Miss Asphyxia, stamping her foot, as she thought she saw risings of insubordination.

The child threw it in, and saw her dear, beautiful treasure slowly consumed, with a swelling and indignant heart. She was now sure that Miss Asphyxia hated her, and only sought occasion to torment her.

Miss Asphyxia did not hate the child, nor did she love her. She regarded her exactly as she did her broom and her rolling-pin and her spinning-wheel,—as an implement or instrument which she was to fashion to her uses. She had a general idea, too, of certain duties to her as a human being, which she expressed by the phrase, "doing right by her,"—that is, to feed and clothe and teach her. In fact, Miss Asphyxia believed fully in the golden rule of doing as she would be done by; but if a lioness should do to a young lamb exactly as she would be done by, it might be all the worse for the lamb.

The little mind and heart were awakened to a perfect burning conflict of fear, shame, anger, and a desire for revenge, which now overflowed with strange, bitter waters that hitherto ignorantly happy valley of child-life. She had never had any sense of moral or religious obligation, any more than a butterfly or a canary-bird. She had, it is true, said her little prayers every night; but, as she said to herself, she had always said them to mother or Harry, and now there was nobody to say them to. Every night she thought of this when she lay down in her joyless, lonesome bed; but the kindly fatigue which hard work brings soon weighed down her eyes, and she slept soundly all night, and found herself hungry at breakfast-time the next morning.

On Sunday Miss Asphyxia rested from her labors,—a strange rest for a soul that had nothing to do in the spiritual world. Miss Asphyxia was past middle life, and, as she said, had never experienced religion,—a point which she regarded with some bitterness, since, as she was wont to say, she had always been as honest in her dealings and kept Sunday as strict as most church-members. Still, she would do her best at giving religious instruction to the child; and accordingly the first Sunday she was dressed in her best frock, and set up in a chair to be kept still while the wagon was getting ready to "go to meetin'," and Miss Asphyxia tried to put into her head the catechism made by that dear, friendly old lover of children, Dr. Watts.

But somehow the first question, benignly as it is worded, had a grim and threatening sound as it came from the jaws of Miss Asphyxia, somewhat thus: "Stop playing with your frock, and look right at me, now. 'Can you tell me, dear child, who made you?'"

Now the little one had often heard this point explained,

but she felt small disposition to give up her knowledge at this demand; so she only looked at Miss Asphyxia in sulky silence.

"Say, now, after me," said Miss Asphyxia, " 'The great God that made heaven and earth.' "

The child repeated the words, in that mumbling, sulky manner which children use when they are saying what does not please them.

"Tina Percival," said Miss Asphyxia, in warlike tones, "do you speak out plain, or I'll box yer ears."

Thus warned, the child uttered her confession of faith audibly enough.

Miss Asphyxia was peculiarly harsh and emphatic on the answer which described the omnipresence of the Supreme Being, and her harsh voice, croaking, "If I tell a lie, He sees me,—if I speak an idle or wicked word, He hears me," seemed to the child to have a ghastly triumph in it to confirm the idea that Miss Asphyxia's awful tyranny was thoroughly backed up by that of a Being far more mighty, and from whom there was no possible escape. Miss Asphyxia enforced this truth with a coarse and homely eloquence, that there was no getting away from God,—that He could see in the night just as plain as in the daytime,—see her in the yard, see her in the barn, see her under the bed, see her down cellar; and that whenever she did anything wrong He would write it down in a dreadful book, and on the Day of Judgment she would have it all brought out upon her,—all which the child heard with a stony, sullen despair. Miss Asphyxia illustrated what became of naughty children by such legends as the story of the two she-bears which came out of a wood and tare forty-and-two children who mocked at old Elisha, till the rebellious auditor quaked in her little shoes, and wondered if the bears would get Harry, and if Harry, after all, would not find some way to get round the bears and come to her help.

At meeting she at last saw Harry, seated, however, in a distant part of the house; but her heart was ready to jump out of her breast to go to him; and when the services were over she contrived to elude Miss Asphyxia, and, passing through the throng, seized his hand just as he was going out, and whispered, "O Harry, Harry, I do want to see you so much! Why don't you come to see me?"

"They would n't let me, Tina," said Harry, drawing his sister into a little recess made between the church and the horseblock,—an old-fashioned structure that used to exist for the accommodation of those who came to church on horseback. "They won't let me come. I wanted to come,—I wanted to see you so much!"

"O Harry, I don't like her,—she is cross to me. Do take me away,—do, Harry! Let 's run away together."

"Where could we go, Tina?"

"O, somewhere,—no matter where. I hate her. I won't stay with her. Say, Harry, I sleep in a little room by the kitchen; come to my window some night and take me away."

"Well, perhaps I will."

"Here you are, you little minx," said Miss Asphyxia. "What you up to now? Come, the waggin 's waiting,"—and, with a look of severe suspicion directed to Harry, she seized the child and conveyed her to the wagon, and was soon driving off with all speed homeward.

That evening the boy pondered long and soberly. He had worked well and steadily during the week, and felt no disposition to complain of his lot on that account, being, as we have said, of a faithful and patient nature, and accepting what the friendly hired men told him,—that work was good for little boys, that it would make him grow strong, and that by and by he would be grown up and able to choose his own work and master. But this separation from his little sister, and her evident unhappiness, distressed him; he felt that she belonged to him, and that he must care for her, and so, when he came home, he again followed Goody Smith to the retirement of her milk-room.

The poor woman had found a perfect summer of delight in her old age in having around her the gentle-mannered, sweet-spoken, good boy, who had thus marvellously fallen to her lot; and boundless was the loving-kindness with which she treated him. Sweet-cakes were slipped into his hands at all odd intervals, choice morsels set away for his consumption in secret places of the buttery, and many an adroit lie told to Old Crab to secure for him extra indulgences, or prevent the imposition of extra tasks; and many a little lie did she recommend to him, at which the boy's honest nature and Christian education inclined him greatly to wonder.

That a grown-up, good old woman should tell lies, and advise little boys to tell them, was one of those facts of human experience which he turned over in his mind with wonder,— thinking it over with that quiet questioning which children practise who have nobody of whom they dare make many inquiries. But to-day he was determined to have something done about Tina, and so he began, "Please, won't you ask him to let me go and see Tina to-night? It 's Sunday, and there is n't any work to do."

"Lordy massy, child, he 's crabbeder Sundays than any other day, he has so much time to graowl round. He drinks more cider; and Sunday night it 's always as much as a body's life 's worth to go near him. I don't want you to get him sot agin ye. He got sot agin Obed; and no critter knows why, except mebbe 'cause he was some comfort to me. And ye oughter seen how he used that 'ere boy. Why, I 've stood here in the milk-room and heerd that 'ere boy's screeches clear from the stun pastur'. Finally the men, they said they could n't stan' it, nor they would n't."

"Who was Obed?" said Harry, fearfully.

"Lordy massy! wal, I forgot ye did n't know Obed. He was the baby, ye see. He was born the eighteenth of April, just about nine o'clock in the evening, and Aunt Jerusha Periwinkle and Granny Watkins, they said they had n't seen no sich child in all their nussing. Held up his head jest as lively, and sucked his thumb, he did,—jest the patientest, best baby ye ever did see,—and growed beautiful. And he was gettin' to be a real beautiful young man when he went off."

"Went off?" said Harry.

"Yes, he went off to sea, jest for nothin' but 'cause his father aggravated him so."

"What *was* the matter? what *did* he do it for?"

"Wal, Obed, he was allers round helpin' me,—he 'd turn the cheeses for me, and draw the water, and was always on hand when I wanted a turn. And he took up agin him, and said we was both lazy, and that I kept him round waitin' on me; and he was allers a throwin' it up at me that I thought more of Obed than I did of him; and one day flesh and blood could n't stan' it no longer. I got clear beat out, and says I, 'Well, father, why should n't I? Obed 's allers a tryin' to help me and make my work easy to me, and thinkin' what he can do for me; and he 's the greatest comfort of my life, and it ain't no sin if I do think more on him than I do of other folks.' Wal, that very day he went and picked a quarrel with him, and told him he was going to give him a stand-up thrashing. And Obed, says he, 'No, father, that you sha' n't. I 'm sixteen year old, and I 've made up my mind you sha' n't thrash me no more.' And with that he says to him, 'Get along out of my house, you lazy dog,' says he; 'you 've been eatin' of my bread too long,' says he. 'Well, father, I will,' says Obed. And he walks up to me and kisses me, and says he, 'Never mind, mother, I 'm going to come home one of these days and bring money enough to take care of you in your old age; and you shall have a house of your own, and sha' n't have to work; and you shall sit in your satin gown and drink your tea with white sugar every day, and you sha' n't be no man's slave. You see if I don't.' With that he turned and was off, and I hain't never seen him since."

"How long 's he been gone?"

"Wal, it 's four years come next April. I 've hed one or two letters from him, and he 's ris' to be mate. And he sent me his wages,—biggest part on 'em,—but he hed to git 'em to me round by sendin on em to Ebal Parker; else *he* 'd a took 'em, ye see. I could n't have nothin' decent to wear to meetin', nor my little caddy o' green tea, if it had n't been for Obed. He won't read Obed's letters, nor hear a word about him, and keeps a castin' it up at me that I think so much of Obed that I don't love him none."

"I should n't think you would," said the boy, innocently.

"Wal, folks seems to think that you must love 'em through thick and thin, and I try ter. I 've allers kep' his clothes mended, and his stockings darned up, and two or three good pair ahead, and done for him jest the best I know how; but as to lovin' folks when they 's so kind o' as he is, I don't reelly know how ter. Expect, ef he was to be killed, I should feel putty bad, too,—kind o' used to havin' on him round."

This conversation was interrupted by the voice of Crab, in

the following pleasing style of remark: "What the devil be you a doin' with that boy,—keepin' him from his work there? It 's time to be to the barn seein' to the critters. Here, you young scamp, go out and cut some feed for the old mare. Suppose I keep you round jest to eat up the victuals and be round under folks' feet?"

XI.

The Crisis

MATTERS between Miss Asphyxia and her little subject began to show evident signs of approaching some crisis, for which that valiant virgin was preparing herself with mind resolved. It was one of her educational tactics that children, at greater or less intervals, would require what she was wont to speak of as *good* whippings, as a sort of constitutional stimulus to start them in the ways of well-doing. As a school-teacher, she was often fond of rehearsing her experiences,—how she had her eye on Jim or Bob through weeks of growing carelessness or obstinacy or rebellion, suffering the measure of iniquity gradually to become full, until, in an awful hour, she pounced down on the culprit in the very blossom of his sin, and gave him such a lesson as he would remember, as she would assure him, the longest day he had to live.

The burning of rebellious thoughts in the little breast, of internal hatred and opposition, could not long go on without slight whiffs of external smoke, such as mark the course of subterranean fire. As the child grew more accustomed to Miss Asphyxia, while her hatred of her increased, somewhat of that native hardihood which had characterized her happier days returned; and she began to use all the subtlety and secretiveness which belonged to her feminine nature in contriving how *not* to do the will of her tyrant, and yet not to seem designedly to oppose. It really gave the child a new impulse in living to devise little plans for annoying Miss Asphyxia without being herself detected. In all her daily toils she made nice calculations how slow she could possibly be, how blundering and awkward, without really bringing on herself a punishment; and when an acute and capable child turns all its faculties in such a direction, the results may be very considerable.

Miss Asphyxia found many things going wrong in her establishment in most unaccountable ways. One morning her sensibilities were almost paralyzed, on opening her milk-room door, to find there, with creamy whiskers, the venerable Tom, her own model cat,—a beast who had grown up in the very sanctities of household decorum, and whom she was sure she had herself shut out of the house, with her usual punctuality, at nine o'clock the evening before. She could not dream that he had been enticed through Tina's window, caressed on her bed, and finally sped stealthily on his mission of revenge, while the child returned to her pillow to gloat over her success.

Miss Asphyxia also, in more than one instance, in her rapid gyrations, knocked down and destroyed a valuable bit of pottery or earthen-ware, that somehow had contrived to be stationed exactly in the wind of her elbow or her hand. It was the more vexatious because she broke them herself. And the child assumed stupid innocence: "How could she know Miss Sphyxy was coming that way?" or, "She did n't see her." True, she caught many a hasty cuff and sharp rebuke; but, with true Indian spirit, she did not mind singeing her own fingers if she only tortured her enemy.

It would be an endless task to describe the many vexations that can be made to arise in the course of household experience when there is a shrewd little elf watching with sharpened faculties for every opportunity to inflict an annoyance or do a mischief. In childhood the passions move with a simplicity of action unknown to any other period of life, and a child's hatred and a child's revenge have an intensity of bitterness entirely unalloyed by moral considerations; and when a child is without an object of affection, and feels itself unloved, its whole vigor of being goes into the channels of hate.

Religious instruction, as imparted by Miss Asphyxia, had small influence in restraining the immediate force of passion. That "the law worketh wrath" is a maxim as old as the times of the Apostles. The image of a dreadful Judge—a great God, with ever-watchful eyes, that Miss Asphyxia told her about— roused that combative element in the child's heart which says in the heart of the fool, "There is no God." "After all," thought the little sceptic, "how does she know? She never saw him." Perhaps, after all, then, it might be only a fabrication of her tyrant to frighten her into submission. There was a

dear Father that mamma used to tell her about; and perhaps
he was the one, after all. As for the bear story she had a private conversation with Sol, and was relieved by his confident
assurance that there "had n't been no bears seen round in
them parts these ten year"; so that she was safe in that regard,
even if she should call Miss Asphyxia a bald-head, which she
perfectly longed to do, just to see what would come of it.

In like manner, though the story of Ananias and Sapphira,
struck down dead for lying, had been told her in forcible and
threatening tones, yet still the little sinner thought within herself that such things must have ceased in our times, as she had
told more than one clever lie which neither Miss Asphyxia
nor any one else had found out.

In fact, the child considered herself and Miss Asphyxia as
in a state of warfare which suspends all moral rules. In the
stories of little girls who were taken captives by goblins or
giants or witches, she remembered many accounts of saga-
cious deceptions which they had practised on their captors.
Her very blood tingled when she thought of the success of
some of them,—how Hensel and Grettel had heated an oven
red-hot, and persuaded the old witch to get into it by some
cock-and-bull story of what she would find there; and how,
the minute she got in, they shut up the oven door, and burnt
her all up! Miss Asphyxia thought the child a vexatious, careless, troublesome little baggage, it is true; but if she could
have looked into her heart and seen her imaginings, she
would probably have thought her a little fiend.

At last, one day, the smothered fire broke out. The child
had had a half-hour of holiday, and had made herself happy
in it by furbishing up her little bedroom. She had picked a
peony, a yellow lily, and one or two blue irises, from the spot
of flowers in the garden, and put them in a tin dipper on the
table in her room, and ranged around them her broken bits
of china, her red berries and fragments of glass, in various
zigzags. The spirit of adornment thus roused within her, she
remembered having seen her brother make pretty garlands of
oak-leaves; and, running out to an oak hard by, she stripped
off an apronful of the leaves, and, sitting down in the kitchen
door, began her attempts to plait them into garlands. She
grew good-natured and happy as she wrought, and was be-

ginning to find herself in charity even with Miss Asphyxia, when down came that individual, broom in hand, looking vengeful as those old Greek Furies who used to haunt houses, testifying their wrath by violent sweeping.

"What under the canopy you up to now, making such a litter on my kitchen floor?" she said. "Can't I leave you a minute 'thout your gettin' into some mischief, I want to know? Pick 'em up, every leaf of 'em, and carry 'em and throw 'em over the fence; and don't you never let me find you bringing no such rubbish into my kitchen agin!"

In this unlucky moment she turned, and, looking into the little bedroom, whose door stood open, saw the arrangements there. "What!" she said; "you been getting down the tin cup to put your messes into? Take 'em all out!" she said, seizing the flowers with a grasp that crumpled them, and throwing them into the child's apron. "Take 'em away, every one of 'em! You 'd get everything out of place, from one end of the house to the other, if I did n't watch you!" And forthwith she swept off the child's treasures into her dust-pan.

In a moment all the smothered wrath of weeks blazed up in the little soul. She looked as if a fire had been kindled in her which reddened her cheeks and burned in her eyes; and, rushing blindly at Miss Asphyxia, she cried, "You are a wicked woman, a hateful old witch, and I hate you!"

"Hity-tity! I thought I should have to give you a lesson before long, and so I shall," said Miss Asphyxia, seizing her with stern determination. "You 've needed a good sound whipping for a long time, miss, and you are going to get it now. I 'll whip you so that you'll remember it, I 'll promise you."

And Miss Asphyxia kept her word, though the child, in the fury of despair, fought her with tooth and nail, and proved herself quite a dangerous little animal; but at length strength got the better in the fray, and, sobbing, though unsubdued, the little culprit was put to bed without her supper.

In those days the literal use of the rod in the education of children was considered as a direct Bible teaching. The wisest, the most loving parent felt bound to it in many cases, even though every stroke cut into his own heart. The laws of New England allowed masters to correct their apprentices, and

teachers their pupils,—and even the public whipping-post
was an institution of New England towns. It is not to be
supposed, therefore, that Miss Asphyxia regarded herself otherwise than as thoroughly performing a most necessary duty.
She was as ignorant of the blind agony of mingled shame,
wrath, sense of degradation, and burning for revenge, which
had been excited by her measures, as the icy east wind of
Boston flats is of the stinging and shivering it causes in its
course. Is it the wind's fault if your nose is frozen? There is
not much danger in these days that such measures will be the
fashionable ones in the bringing up of children. But there is
a class of coldly-conscientious, severe persons, who still, as a
matter of duty and conscience, justify measures like these in
education. *They,* at all events, are the ones who ought to be
forbidden to use them, and whose use of them with children
too often proves a soul-murder,—a dispensation of wrath and
death. Such a person is commonly both obtuse in sensibility
and unimaginative in temperament; but if his imagination
could once be thoroughly enlightened to see the fiend-like
passions, the terrific convulsions, which are roused in a child's
soul by the irritation and degradation of such correction, he
would shrink back appalled. With sensitive children left in the
hands of stolid and unsympathizing force, such convulsions
and mental agonies often are the beginning of a sort of slow
moral insanity which gradually destroys all that is good in the
soul. Such was the danger now hanging over the hapless little
one whom a dying mother had left to God. Is there no stirring among the angel wings on her behalf?

As the child lay sobbing in a little convulsed heap in her
bed, a hard, horny hand put back the curtain of the window,
and the child felt something thrown on the bed. It was Sol,
who, on coming in to his supper, had heard from Miss Asphyxia the whole story, and who, as a matter of course, sympathized entirely with the child. He had contrived to slip a
doughnut into his pocket, when his hostess was looking the
other way. When the child rose up in the bed and showed
her swelled and tear-stained face, Sol whispered: "There's a
doughnut I saved for ye. Darn her pictur'! Don't dare say a
word, ye know. She'll hear me."

"O Sol, can't you get Harry to come here and see me?" said the child, in an earnest whisper.

"Yes, I'll get him, if I have to go to thunder for 't," said Sol. "You jest lie down now, there's a good girl, and I'll work it,—ye see if I don't. To-morrow I'll make her go off to the store, and I'll get him down here, you see if I don't. It's a tarnal shame; that 'ere critter ain't got no more bowels than a file."

The child, however, was comforted, and actually went to sleep hugging the doughnut. She felt as if she loved Sol, and said so to the doughnut many times,—although he had great horny fists, and eyes like oxen. With these, he had a heart in his bosom, and the child loved him.

XII.

The Lion's Mouth Shut

"Now, where a plague is that boy?" said Old Crab, suddenly bearing down, as evil-disposed people are always apt to do, in a most unforeseen moment.

The fact was that there had been a silent conspiracy among Sol and Goody Smith and the hired men of Old Crab, to bring about a meeting between the children. Miss Asphyxia had been got to the country store and kept busy with various bargains which Sol had suggested, and Old Crab had been induced to go to mill, and then the boy had been sent by Goody Smith on an errand to Miss Asphyxia's house. Of course he was not to find her at home, and was to stay and see his sister, and be sure and be back again by four o'clock.

"Where a plague is that lazy shote of a boy?" he repeated.

"What, Harry?"

"Yes, Harry. Who do you suppose I mean? Harry,—where is he?"

"O, I sent him up to Sphyxy's."

"*You* sent him?" said Old Crab, with that kind of tone which sounds so much like a blow that one dodges one's head involuntarily. "*You* sent him? What business *you* got interfering in the work?"

"Lordy massy, father, I jest wanted Sphyxy's cards and some o' that 'ere fillin' she promised to give me. He won't be gone long."

Old Crab stood at this disadvantage in his fits of ill-temper with his wife, that there was no form of evil language or abuse that he had not tried so many times on her that it was quite a matter of course for her to hear it. He had used up the English language,—made it, in fact, absolutely of no effect,—while his fund of ill-temper was, after all, but half expressed.

"You 've begun with that 'ere boy jest as you allers did with all your own, gettin' 'em to be a waitin' round on you,—

jest 'cause you 're a lazy good-for-nothin'. We 're so rich, I wonder you don't hire a waiter for nothin' but to stan' behind your chair. I 'll teach him who his master is when he comes back."

"Now, father, 't ain't no fault o' his'n. *I* sent him."

"And *I* sot him to work in the fields, and I 'd like to know if he 's goin' to leave what I set him to do, and go round after your errands. Here 't is gettin' to be 'most five o'clock, and the critters want fodderin', and that 'ere boy a dancing 'tend-ance on you. But he ain't a doin' that. He 's jest off a berryin' or suthin' with that trollopin' sister o' his'n,—jes' what you bring on us, takin' in trampers. That 'ere gal, she pesters Sphyxy half to death."

"Sphyxy 's pretty capable of takin' care of herself," said Goody Smith, still keeping busy with her knitting, but look-ing uneasily up the road, where the form of the boy might be expected to appear.

The outbreak that she had long feared of her husband's evil nature was at hand. She knew it by as many signs as one foretells the approach of hurricanes or rain-storms. She knew it by the evil gleam in his small, gray eyes,—by the impatient pacing backward and forward in the veranda, like a caged wild animal. It made little matter to him what the occasion was: he had such a superfluity of evil temper to vent, that one thing for his purpose was about as good as another.

It grew later and later, and Old Crab went to the barn to attend to his cattle, and the poor little old woman knitted uneasily.

"What could 'a' kep' him?" she thought. "He can't 'a' run off." There was a sudden gleam of mingled pleasure and pain in the old woman's heart as this idea darted through her mind. "I should n't wonder if he would, but I kind o' hate to part with him."

At last she sees him coming along the road, and runs to meet him. "How could you be so late? He 's drefful mad with ye."

"I did n't know how late it was. Besides, all I could do, Tina would follow me, and I had to turn back and carry her home. Tina has bad times there. That woman is n't kind to her."

"No, dear, she ain't noways kind," said the old woman; "it ain't Sphyxy's way to be kind; but she 'll do middlin' well by her,—anyway, she won't let nobody hurt her but herself. It 's a hard world to live in; we have to take it as 't comes."

"Well, anyway," said the boy, "they *must* let us go to see each other. It is n't right to keep us apart."

"No, 't ain't, dear; but lordy massy, what can ye do?"

There was a great steady tear in the boy's large, blue eyes as he stopped at the porch, and he gave a sort of dreary shiver.

"Halleoah you there! you lazy little cuss," said Old Crab, coming from the barn, "where you been idling all the afternoon?"

"I 've been seeing my sister," said the boy, steadily.

"Thought so. Where 's them cards and the fillin' you was sent for?"

"There was n't anybody at home to get them."

"And why did n't you come right back, you little varmint?"

"Because I wanted to see Tina. She 's my sister; and my mother told me to take care of her; and it 's wicked to keep us apart so."

"Don't you give me none of yer saace," said Old Crab, seizing the boy by one ear, to which he gave a vicious wrench.

"Let me alone," said the boy, flushing up with the sudden irritation of pain and the bitter sense of injustice.

"Let you alone? I guess I won't; talking saace to me that 'ere way. Guess I 'll show you who 's master. It 's time you was walked off down to the barn, sir, and find out who 's your master," he said, as he seized the boy by the collar and drew him off.

"O Lord!" said the woman, running out and stretching her hands instinctively after them. "Father, do let the boy alone."

She could not help this cry any more than a bird can help a shriek when she sees the hawk pouncing down on her nest, though she knew perfectly well that she might as well have shouted a petition in the angry face of the northeast wind.

"Take off your jacket," said Old Crab, as soon as he had helped himself to a long cart-whip which stood there.

The boy belonged to that class of amiable, good-natured children who are not easily irritated or often provoked, but who, when moved by a great injustice or cruelty, are thrown into convulsions of passion. The smallest and most insignificant animal, in moments of utter despair, when every fibre of its being is made vital with the energy of desperate resistance, often has a force which will make the strongest and boldest stand at bay. The boy retreated a pace or two, braced his back against the manger, while his whole form trembled and appeared to dilate, and it seemed as if blue streams of light glared from his eyes like sparks struck from burning steel.

"Strike me if you dare, you wicked, dreadful man," he shouted. "Don't you know that God sees you? God is my Father, and my mother is gone to God; and if you hurt me He'll punish you. You know I have n't done anything wrong, and God knows it. Now strike me if you dare."

The sight of any human being in a singular and abnormal state has something appalling about it; and at this moment the child really appeared to Old Crab like something supernatural. He stood a moment looking at him, and then his eyes suddenly seemed fixed on something above and beyond him, for he gazed with a strange, frightened expression; and at last, pushing with his hands, called out, "Go along; get away, get away! I hain't touched him," and, turning, fled out of the barn.

He did not go to the house again, but to the village tavern, and, entering the bar-room with a sort of distraught air, called for a dram, and passed the evening in a cowering state of quiet in the corner, which was remarked on by many as singular.

The boy came back into the house.

"Massy to us, child," said the old woman, "I thought he'd half killed ye."

"No, he has n't touched me. God would n't let him," said the boy.

"Well, I declare for 't! he must have sent the angels that shut the lion's mouth when Daniel was in the den," said the woman. "I would n't 'a' had him struck ye, not for ten dollars."

The moon was now rising, large, white, and silvery, yet with a sort of tremulous, rosy flush, as it came up in the girdle of a burning autumn horizon. The boy stood a moment looking at it. His eyes were still dilated with that unnatural light, and his little breast heaving with waves of passion not yet tranquillized.

"Which way did he go?" said the woman.

"Up the road," said the boy.

"To the tavern," said the woman. "He 's been there before this afternoon. At any rate, then, he 'll let us alone awhile. There comes the men home to supper. Come in; I 've got a turnover I made a purpose for ye."

"No, I must bid you good by, now," said the boy. "I can't stay here any longer."

"Why, where be ye going?"

"Going to look for a better place, where I can take care of Tina," said the boy.

"Ye ain't a going to leave me?" said the old woman. "Yet I can't want ye to stay. *I* can't have nothin' nor nobody."

"I 'll come back one of these days," said the boy cheerfully,—"come and see you."

"Stay and get your supper, anyhow," pleaded the old woman. "I hate ter have ye go, drefful bad."

"I don't want any supper," said the child; "but if you 'll give me a little basket of things,—I want 'em for Tina."

The old soul ran to her buttery, and crammed a small splint basket with turnovers, doughnuts, and ample slices of rye bread and butter, and the boy took it and trudged off, just as the hired men were coming home.

"Hulloah, bub!" shouted they, "where ye goin'?"

"Going to seek my fortune," said the boy cheerfully.

"Jest the way they all go," said the old woman.

"Where do you suppose the young un 'll fetch up?" said one of the men to the other.

"No business of mine,—can't fetch up wus than he has ben a doin'."

"Old Crab a cuttin' up one of his shines, I s'pose?" said the other, interrogatively.

"Should n't wonder; 'bout time,—ben to the tavern this arternoon, I reckon."

The boy walked along the rough stony road towards Miss Asphyxia's farm. It was a warm, mellow evening in October.

The air had only a pleasant coolness. Everything was tender and bright. A clump of hickory-trees on a rocky eminence before him stood like pillars of glowing gold in the twilight; one by one little stars looked out, winking and twinkling at the lonely child, as it seemed to him, with a friendly, encouraging ray, like his mother's eyes.

That afternoon he had spent trying to comfort his little sister, and put into her soul some of the childlike yet sedate patience with which he embraced his own lot, and the good hopes which he felt of being able some time to provide for her when he grew bigger. But he found nothing but feverish impatience, which all his eloquence could scarcely keep within bounds. He had, however, arranged with her that he should come evenings after she had gone to bed, and talk to her at the window of her bedroom, that she should not be so lonesome nights. The perfectly demoniac violence which Old Crab had shown this night had determined him not to stay with him any longer. He would take his sister, and they would wander off, a long, long way, till they came to better people, and then he would try again to get work, and ask some good woman to be kind to Tina. Such, in substance, was the plan that occurred to the child; and accordingly that night, after little Tina had laid her head on her lonely pillow, she heard a whispered call at her window. The large, bright eyes opened very wide as she sat up in bed and looked towards the window, where Harry's face appeared.

"It's me, Tina,—I've come back,—be very still. I'm going to stay in the barn till everybody's asleep, and then I'll come and wake you, and you get out of the window and come with me."

"To be sure I will, Harry. Let me come now, and sleep with you in the barn."

"No, Tina, that would n't do; lie still. They'd see us. Wait till everybody's asleep. You just lie down and go to sleep. I'll get in at your window and waken you when it's time."

At this moment the door of the child's room was opened; the boy's face was gone in an instant from the window. The child's heart was beating like a trip-hammer; there was a tingling in her ears; but she kept her little eyes tightly shut.

"O, here 's that brown towel I gin her to hem," said Miss Asphyxia, peacefully. "She 's done her stent this arternoon. That 'ere whipping did some good."

"You 'll never whip me again," thought the defiant little heart under the bedclothes.

Old Crab came home that night thoroughly drunk,—a thing that did not very often occur in his experience. He commonly took only just enough to keep himself in a hyena's state of temper, but not enough to dull the edge of his cautious, grasping, money-saving faculties. But to-night he had had an experience that had frightened him, and driven him to deeper excess as a refuge from thought.

When the boy, upon whom he was meaning to wreak his diabolic passions, so suddenly turned upon him in the electric fury of enkindled passion, there was a sort of jar or vibration of the nervous element in the man's nature, that brought about a result not uncommon to men of his habits. As he was looking in a sort of stunned, stupid wonder at the boy, where he stood braced against the manger, he afterwards declared that he saw suddenly in the dark space above it, hovering in the air, the exact figure and form of the dead woman whom they had buried in the graveyard only a few weeks before. "Her eyes was looking right at me, like live coals," he said; "and she had up her hand as if she 'd 'a' struck me; and I grew all over cold as a stone."

"What do you suppose 't was?" said his auditor.

"How should I know," said Old Crab. "But there I was; and that very night the young 'un ran off. I would n't have tried to get him back, not for my right hand, I tell you. Tell you what," he added, rolling a quid of tobacco reflectively in his mouth, "I don't like dead folks. Ef dead folks 'll let me alone, I 'll let them alone. That 'ere 's fair, ain't it?"

XIII.

The Empty Bird's-Nest

THE next morning showed as brilliant a getting up of gold and purple as ever belonged to the toilet of a morning. There was to be seen from Miss Asphyxia's bedroom window a brave sight, if there had been any eyes to enjoy it,—a range of rocky cliffs with little pin-feathers of black pine upon them, and behind them the sky all aflame with bars of massy light,—orange and crimson and burning gold,—and long, bright rays, darting hither and thither, touched now the window of a farm-house, which seemed to kindle and flash back a morning salutation; now they hit a tall scarlet maple, and now they pierced between clumps of pine, making their black edges flame with gold; and over all, in the brightening sky, stood the morning star, like a great, tremulous tear of light, just ready to fall on a darkened world.

Not a bit of all this saw Miss Asphyxia, though she had looked straight out at it. Her eyes and the eyes of the cow, who, with her horned front, was serenely gazing out of the barn window on the same prospect, were equally unreceptive.

She looked at all this solemn pomp of gold and purple, and the mysterious star, and only said: "Good day for killin' the hog, and I must be up gettin' on the brass kettle. I should like to know why Sol ain't been a stirrin' an hour ago. I'd really like to know how long folks *would* sleep ef I'd let 'em."

Here an indistinct vision came into Miss Asphyxia's mind of what the world would be without her to keep it in order. She called aloud to her prime minister, who slept in the loft above, "Sol! Sol! You awake?"

"Guess I be," said Sol; and a thundering sound of cowhide boots on the stairs announced that Sol's matutinal toilet was complete.

"We're late this morning," said Miss Asphyxia, in a tone of virtuous indignation.

"Never knowed the time when we wa' n't late," said Sol, composedly.

"You thump on that 'ere child's door, and tell her to be lively," said Miss Asphyxia.

"Yaas 'm, I will," said Sol, while secretly he was indulging in a long and low chuckle, for Sol had been party to the fact that the nest of that young bird had been for many hours forsaken. He had instructed the boy what road to take, and bade him "walk spry and he would be out of the parish of Needmore afore daybreak. Walk on, then, and follow the road along the river," said Sol, "and it 'll bring you to Old-town, where our folks be. You can't miss your victuals and drink any day in Oldtown, call at what house you may; and ef you 's to get into Deacon Badger's, why, your fortin 's made. The Deacon he 's a soft-spoken man to everybody,— white folks, niggers, and Indians,— and Ma'am Badger keeps regular poor-man's tavern, and won't turn even a dog away that behaves himself. Ye could n't light on wus than ye have lit on,— for Old Crab's possessed of a devil, everybody knows; and as for Miss Asphyxia, she 's one of the kind of sperits that goes walkin' through dry places seekin' rest and findin' none. Lordy massy, an old gal like her ain't nobody to bring up a child. It takes a woman that 's got juice in her to do that. Why, that 'ere crittur 's drier 'n a two-year-old mullen-stalk. There ain't no sap ris in her these 'ere thirty years. She means well; but, lordy, you might jest as well give young turkey chicks to the old gobbler, and let him stram off in the mowin' grass with 'em, as give a delicate little gal like your sister to her to raise; so you jest go long and keep up your courage, like a brave boy as ye be, and you 'll come to some-thin' by daylight";— and Sol added to these remarks a minced pie, with a rye crust of a peculiarly solid texture, adapted to resist any of the incidents of time and travel, which pie had been set out as part of his own last night's supper.

When, therefore, he was exhorted to rap on the little girl's door, he gave sundry noisy, gleeful thumps,— pounding with both fists, and alternating with a rhythmical kick of the cow-hide boots, calling out in stentorian tones: "Come, little un,— time you 's up. Miss Sphyxy 's comin' down on ye. Bet-ter be lively! Bless me, how the gal sleeps!"

"Don't take the door off the hinges," said Miss Asphyxia, sweeping down stairs. "Let me come; I 'll wake her, I guess!"

and with a dipper of cold water in her hand, Miss Asphyxia burst into the little room. "What!—what!—where!" she said, looking under the bed, and over and around, with a dazed expression. "What's this mean? Do tell if the child's re'lly for once got up of herself afore I called her. Sol, see if she's out pickin' up chips!"

Sol opened the door and gazed out with well-affected stolidity at the wood-pile, which, garnished with a goodly show of large chips, was now being touched up and brightened by the first rays of the morning sun.

"Ain't here," he said.

"Ain't here? Why, where can she be then? There ain't nobody swallowed her, I s'pose; and if anybody's run off with her in the night, I guess they'd bring her back by daylight."

"She must 'a' run off," said Sol.

"Run! Where could she 'a' run to?"

"Mebbe she's gone to her brother's."

"I bet you," said Miss Asphyxia, "it's that 'ere boy that's the bottom of it all. You may always know that there's a boy at the bottom, when there's any deviltry up. He was here yesterday,—now wa'n't he?"

"Wal, I reckon he was," said Sol. "But, massy, Miss Sphyxy, ef the pigs is to be killed to-day, we can't stan' a talkin' about what you nor me can't help. Ef the child's gone, why she's somewhere in the Lord's world, and it's likely she'll keep,—she won't melt away like the manna in the wilderness; and when the pigs is killed, and the pork salted down and got out o' the way, it'll be time enough to think o' lookin' on her up. She wa'n't no gret actual use,—and with kettles o' hot water round, it's jest as well not to have a child under yer feet. Ef she got scalded, why, there's your time a taking care on her, and mebbe a doctor to pay; so it's jest as well that things be as they be. *I* call it kind o' providential," said Sol, giving a hoist to his breeches by means of a tug at his suspenders, which gesture was his usual indication that he was girding up the loins of his mind for an immediate piece of work; and, turning forthwith, he brought in a mighty armful of wood, with massive back-log and fore-stick, well grizzled and bearded with the moss that showed that they were but yesterday living children of the forest.

The fire soon leaped and crackled and roared, being well fed with choice split hickory sticks of last year, of which Sol kept ample store; and very soon the big brass kettle was swung over, upon the old iron crane, and the sacrificial water was beginning to simmer briskly, while Miss Asphyxia prepared breakfast, not only for herself and Sol, but for Primus King, a vigorous old negro, famed as a sort of high-priest in all manner of butchering operations for miles around. Primus lived in the debatable land between Oldtown and Needmore, and so was at the call of all who needed an extra hand in both parishes.

The appearance of Primus at the gate in his butcher's frock, knife in hand, in fact put an end, in Miss Asphyxia's mind, to all thoughts apart from the present eventful crisis; and she hastened to place upon the table the steaming sausages which, with her usual despatch, had been put down for their morning meal. A mighty pitcher of cider flanked this savory dish, to which Primus rolled delighted eyes at the moment of sitting down. The time had not yet dawned, in those simple, old New England days, when the black skin of the African was held to disqualify him from a seat at the social board with the men whom he joined in daily labor. The strength of the arm, and the skill of the hand, and the willingness of the mind of the workman, in those days, were his passport to equal social rights; and old Primus took rank, in the butchering season, as in fact a sort of leader and commander. His word was law upon all steps and stages of those operations which should transform the plethoric, obese inhabitants of the sty into barrels of pink-hued salt-pork or savory hams and tenderloins and spareribs, or immense messes of sausage-meat.

Concerning all these matters, Primus was an oracle. His fervid Ethiopian nature glowed with a broad and visible delight, his black face waxed luminous with the oil of gladness, while he dwelt on the savory subject, whereon, sitting at breakfast, he dilated with an unctuous satisfaction that soothed the raven down of darkness in Miss Asphyxia's perturbed mind, till something bearing a distant analogy to a smile played over her rugged features.

XIV.

The Day in Fairy-Land

O UR little travellers, meanwhile, had had a prosperous journey along the rocky road between Needmore and Oldtown, in which Sol had planted their feet. There was a great, round-orbed, sober-eyed October moon in the sky, that made everything as light as day; and the children were alive in every nerve with the keen interest of their escape.

"We are going just as Hensel and Grettel did," said the little girl. "You are Hensel, and I am Grettel, and Miss Asphyxia is the old witch. I wish only we could have burnt her up in her old oven before we came away!"

"Now, Tina, you must n't wish such things *really*," said the boy, somewhat shocked at such very extreme measures. "You see, what happens in stories would n't do *really* to happen."

"O, but Harry, you don't know how I *hate*—how I h— *ate*—Miss Sphyxy! I hate her—most as much as I love you!"

"But, Tina, mother always told us it was wicked to hate anybody. We must love our enemies."

"You don't love Old Crab Smith, do you?"

"No, I don't; but I try not to hate him," said the boy. "I won't think anything about him."

"I can't help thinking," said Tina; "and when I think, I am *so* angry! I feel such a burning in here!" she said, striking her little breast; "it 's just like fire!"

"Then don't think about her at all," said the boy; "it is n't pleasant to feel that way. Think about the whippoorwills singing in the woods over there,—how plain they say it, don't they?—and the frogs, all singing, with their little, round, yellow eyes looking up out of the water; and the moon looking down on us so pleasantly! she seems just like mother!"

"O Harry, I 'm so glad," said the girl, suddenly throwing herself on his neck and hugging him,—"I 'm so glad we 're together again! Was n't it wicked to keep us apart,—we poor children?"

"Yes, Tina, I *am* glad," said the boy, with a steady, quiet, inward sort of light in his eyes; "but, baby, we can't stop to say so much, because we must walk fast and get way, way, way off before daylight; and you know Miss Sphyxy always gets up early,—don't she?"

"O dear, yes! She always poked me out of bed before it was light,—hateful old thing! Let's run as fast as we can, and get away!"

And with that she sprang forward, with a brisk and onward race, over the pebbly road, down a long hill, laughing as she went, and catching now at a branch of sweetbrier that overhung the road, and now at the tags of sweet-fern, both laden and hoary with heavy autumnal dews, till finally, her little foot tripping over a stone, she fell and grazed her arm sadly. Her brother lifted her up, and wiped the tears from her great, soft eyes with her blue check apron, and talked to her in that grandfatherly way that older children take such delight in when they feel the care of younger ones.

"Now, Tina, darling, you should n't run so wild. We'd better go pretty fast steadily, than run and fall down. But I'll kiss the place, as mother used to."

"I don't mind it, Hensel,—I don't mind it," she said, controlling the quivering of her little resolute mouth. "That scratch came for *liberty;* but this," she said, showing a long welt on her other arm,—"this was *slavery.* She struck me there with her great ugly stick. O, I never *can* forgive her!"

"Don't let's talk any more, baby; let's hurry on. She *never* shall get you again; I'll fight for you till I die, first!"

"You'd kill 'em all, would n't you? You would have knocked her down, would n't you?" said Tina, kindling up with that inconsiderate exultation in the powers of an elder brother which belongs to childhood. "I knew you would get me away from here, Harry,—I knew you would."

"But now," said Harry, "you just keep hold of my hand, and let's run together, and I'll hold you up. We must run fast, after all, because maybe they will harness up the wagon when daylight comes, and come out to look for us."

"Well, if it's only Sol comes," said the little girl, "I sha' n't care; for he would only carry us on farther."

"Ay, but you may be sure Miss Asphyxia would come herself."

The suggestion seemed too probable, and the two little pairs of heels seemed winged by it as they flew along, their long shadows dancing before them on the moonlit road, like spiritual conductors. They made such good headway that the hour which we have already recorded, when Miss Asphyxia's slumbers were broken, found the pair of tiny pilgrims five miles away on the road to Oldtown.

"Now, Tina," said the boy, as he stopped to watch the long bars of crimson and gold that seemed to be drawing back and opening in the eastern sky, where the sun was flaring upward an expectant blaze of glory, "only look there! Is n't it so wonderful? It 's worth being out here only to see it. There! there! there! the sun is coming! Look! Only see that bright-red maple,—it seems all on fire!—now that yellow chestnut, and that old pine-tree! O, see, see those red leaves! They are like the story papa used to tell of the trees that bore rubies and emeralds. Are n't they beautiful?"

"Set me on the fence, so as I can see," said Tina. "O Harry, it 's beautiful! And to think that we can see it together!"

Just at this moment they caught the distant sound of wheels.

"Hurry, Tina! Let me lift you over the fence," said the boy; "they are coming!"

How the little hearts beat, as both children jumped down into a thicket of sweet-fern, heavy and wet with morning dew! The lot was one of those confused jungles which one often sees hedging the course of rivers in New England. Groups of pine and hemlock grew here and there, intermixed with low patches of swampy land, which were waving with late wild-flowers and nodding swamp-grasses. The children tore their way through golden-rods, asters, and cat-tails to a little elevated spot where a great, flat rock was surrounded by a hedge of white-pine. This was precisely the shelter they wanted; for the pines grew so thickly around it as completely to screen it from sight from the road, while it was open to the warm beams of the morning sun.

"Cuddle down here, Tina," said Harry, in a whispering

voice, as if he feared the driver in the rattling farm-wagon might hear them.

"O, what a nice little house the trees make here!" said Tina. "We are as snug here and as warm as can be; and only see what a nice white-and-green carpet there is all over the rock!"

The rock, to be sure, was all frothed over with a delicate white foam of moss, which, later in the day, would have crackled and broken in brittle powder under their footsteps, but which now, saturated by the heavy night-dews, only bent under them, a soft, elastic carpet.

Their fears were soon allayed when, peeping like scared partridges from their cover, they saw a farm-wagon go rattling by from the opposite direction to that in which Miss Asphyxia lived.

"O, it's nobody for us; it comes the other way," said the boy.

It was, in fact, Primus King, going on his early way to preside over the solemnities of pig-killing.

"Then, Hensel, we are free," said the little girl; "nobody will catch us now. They could no more find us in this lot than they could find a little, little tiny pin in the hay-mow."

"No, indeed, Tina; we are safe now," said the boy.

"Why don't you call me Grettel? We will play be Hensel and Grettel; and who knows what luck will come to us?"

"Well, Grettel then," said the boy, obediently. "You sit now, and spread out your frock in the sun to dry, while I get out some breakfast for you. Old Aunty Smith has filled my basket with all sorts of good things."

"And nice old Sol,—he gave us his pie," said Tina. "I love Sol, though he is a funny-looking man. You ought to see Sol's hand, it's so big! And his feet,—why, one of his shoes would make a good boat for me! But he's a queer old dear, though, and I love him."

"What shall we eat first?" said the boy,—"the bread and butter, or the cookies, or the doughnuts, or the pie?"

"Let's try a little of all of them," said young madam.

"You know, Tina," said the boy, in a slow, considerate way, "that we must take care of this, because we don't know when we'll get any more. There's got to be a dinner and a supper got out of this at any rate."

"O, well, Hensel, you do just as you please with it, then; only let's begin with Sol's pie and some of that nice cheese, for I am so hungry! And then, when we have had our breakfast, I mean to lie down in the sun, and have a nap on this pretty white moss. O Harry, how pretty this moss is! There are bright little red things in it, as bright as mother's scarlet cloak. But, O Harry, look, quick! don't say a word! There's a squirrel! How bright his little eyes are! Let's give him some of our breakfast."

Harry broke off a crumb of cake and threw it to the little striped-backed stranger.

"Why, he's gone like a wink," said the girl. "Come back, little fellow; we sha'n't hurt you."

"O, hush, Tina, he's coming! I see his bright eyes. He's watching that bit of cake."

"There, he's got it and is off!" said Tina, with a shriek of delight. "See him race up that tree with it!"

"He's going to take it home to his wife."

"His wife!" said Tina, laughing so hard at Harry's wit that she was obliged to lay down her pie. "Has he got a wife?"

"Why, of course he has," said Harry, with superior wisdom.

"I'm *your* wife, ain't I?" said Tina, contentedly.

"No. You're my little sister, and I take care of you," said the boy. "But people can't have their sisters for wives; the Bible says so."

"Well, I can be just *like* your wife; and I'll mend your clothes and knit your stockings when I get bigger."

To which practical view of matrimonial duties Harry gave a grave assent.

Not a striped-backed squirrel, or a bobolink, or a cat-bird, in the whole pasture-lot, had better spirits than our two little travellers. They were free; they were together; the sun was shining and birds were singing; and as for the future, it was with them as with the birds. The boy, to be sure, had a share of forethought and care, and deemed himself a grown man acting with most serious responsibility for his light-headed little sister; but even in him this was only a half-awakening from the dream-land of childhood.

When they had finished their breakfast, he bethought him

of his morning prayers, and made Tina kneel down beside
him while he repeated psalm and hymn and prayer, in which
she joined with a very proper degree of attention. When he
had finished, she said, "Do you know, Hensel, I have n't said
my prayers a single once since I 've been at Miss Asphyxia's?"

"Why, Tina!"

"Well, you see, there was n't anybody to say them to, now
mother is gone; and you were not there."

"But you say them to God, Tina."

"O, he 's so far off, and I 'm so little, I can't say them to
him. I must say them to somebody I can see. Harry, where is
mother gone?"

"She is gone to heaven, Tina."

"Where is heaven?"

"It 's up in the sky, Tina," said the boy, looking up into the
deep, cloudless blue of an October sky, which, to say the
truth, is about as celestial a thing as a mortal child can look
into; and as he looked, his great blue eyes grew large and
serious with thoughts of his mother's last wonderful words.

"If it 's up in the sky, why did they dig down into the
ground, and put her in that hole?" said the little sceptic.

"It is her soul that went up. Her body is planted like a
beautiful flower. She will come up by and by; and we shall
see her again, if we are good children."

Tina lay back on the white moss, with only a fringy bough
of white-pine between her and the deep, eternal blue, where
the thinnest films of white clouds were slowly sailing to and
fro. Her spiritual musings grew, to say the truth, rather confused. She was now very tired with her night tramp; and the
long fringes fell over her great, dark eyes, as a flower shuts
itself, and she was soon asleep.

The boy sat watching her awhile, feeling soothed by the
calm, soft sunshine, and listening to the thousand sweet
lullaby-notes which Nature is humming to herself, while
about her great world-housework, in a calm October morning. The locusts and katydids grated a drowsy, continuous
note to each other from every tree and bush; and from a
neighboring thicket a lively-minded cat-bird was giving original variations and imitations of all sorts of bird voices and
warblings; while from behind the tangled thicket which

fringed its banks came the prattle of a hidden river, whose bright brown waters were gossiping, in a pleasant, constant chatter, with the many-colored stones on the bottom; and when the light breezes wandered hither and thither, as your idle breezes always will be doing, they made little tides and swishes of sound among the pine-trees, like the rising and falling of sunny waters on the sea-shore.

Altogether, it was not long before Harry's upright watch over his sister subsided into a droop upon one elbow, and finally the little curly head went suddenly down on to his sister's shoulder; and then they were fast asleep,—as nice a little pair of babes in the wood as ever the robins could cover up. They did not awake till it was almost noon. The sun was shining warm and cloudless, and every bit of dew had long been dried; and Tina, in refreshed spirits, proposed that they should explore the wonders of the pasture-lot,—especially that they should find out where the river was whose waters they heard gurgling behind the leafy wall of wild vines.

"We can leave our basket here in our little house, Hensel. See, I set it in here, way, way in among the pine-trees; and that's my little green closet."

So the children began picking their way through the thicket, guided by the sound of the water.

"O Tina!" said the boy; "look there, over your head!"

The object pointed out was a bough of a wild grape-vine, heavily laden with ripe purple grapes.

"O, wild grapes!" said Tina. "Harry, do get them!"

Harry soon pulled the bough down within reach, and the children began helping themselves.

"I'm going to take an apronful up to the tree, and put into our closet," said Tina; "and we shall have a nice store there."

"But, Tina, we can't live there on the rock," said the boy; "we must walk on and get to Oldtown some time."

"O, well, we have the whole long, long day for it," said the girl, "and we may as well have a good time now; so, when I've put up these grapes, we'll see where the river is."

A little scrambling and tearing through vines soon brought the children down to the banks of a broad, rather shallow river, whose waters were of that lustrous yellow-brown which makes every stone gleam up from the bottom in mellow colors, like the tints through the varnish of an old picture. The banks were a rampart of shrubbery and trees hung with drapery of wild vines, now in the brilliancy of autumnal coloring. It is not wonderful that exclamations of delight and wonder burst from both children. An old hemlock that hung slantwise over the water opposite was garlanded and interwoven, through all its dusky foliage, with wreaths and pendants of the Virginia creeper, now burning in the brilliant carmine and scarlet hues of autumn. Great, soft, powdery clumps of golden-rod projected their heads from the closely interwoven thicket, and leaned lovingly over the stream, while the royal purple of tall asters was displayed in bending plumage at their side. Here and there, a swamp-maple seemed all one crimson flame; while greener shrubbery and trees, yet untouched by frosts, rose up around it, as if purposely to give background and relief to so much color. The rippling surface of the waters, as they dashed here and there over the stones, gave back colored flashes from the red, yellow, crimson, purple, and green of the banks; while ever and anon little bright leaves came sailing down the stream, all moist and brilliant, like so many floating gems. The children clapped their hands, and began, with sticks, fishing them towards the shore. "These are our little boats," they said. So they were,—fairy boats, coming from the land of nowhere, and going on to oblivion, shining and fanciful, like the little ones that played with them.

"I declare," said Tina, "I mean to take off my shoes and stockings, and wade out to that little island where those pretty white stones are. You go with me."

"Well, Tina, wait till I can hold you."

And soon both the little pairs of white feet were slipping and spattering among the pebbles at the bottom. On the way, Tina made many efforts to entrap the bright rings of sunlight on the bottom, regardless of the logic with which Harry undertook to prove to her that it was nothing but the light, and that she could not catch it; and when they came to the little white gravelly bank, they sat down and looked around them with great content.

"We 're on a desolate island, are n't we, Hensel?" said Tina. "I like desolate islands," she added, looking around her, with the air of one who had had a wide experience of the article.

"The banks here are so high, and the bushes so thick, that Miss Asphyxia could not find us if she were to try. We 'll make our home here."

"Well, I think, Tina, darling, that it won't do for us to stay here very long," said Harry. "We must try to get to some place where I can find something to do, and some good, kind woman to take care of you."

"O Harry, what 's the use of thinking of that,—it 's so bright and pleasant, and it 's so long since I 've had you to play with! Do let 's have one good, pleasant day alone among the flowers! See how beautiful everything is!" she added, "and it 's so warm and quiet and still, and all the birds and squirrels and butterflies are having such a good time. I don't want anything better than to play about out in the woods with you."

"But where shall we sleep nights, Tina?"

"O, it was so pleasant last night, and the moon shone so bright, I would not be afraid to cuddle down under a bush with you, Harry."

"Ah, Tina! you don't know what may come. The moon don't shine all night, and there may be cold and wind and rain, and then where would we be? Come, darling, let 's go on; we can walk in the fields by the river, and so get down to the place Sol told us about."

So at last the little fanciful body was persuaded to wade back from her desolate island, and to set out once more on her pilgrimage. But even an older head than hers might have been turned by the delights of that glorious October day, and gone off into a vague trance of bliss, in which the only good of life seemed to be in luxurious lounging and dreamy enjoyment of the passing hour. Nature in New England is, for the most part, a sharp, determined matron, of the Miss Asphyxia school. She is shrewd, keen, relentless, energetic. She runs through the seasons a merciless express-train, on which you may jump if you can, at her hours, but which knocks you down remorselessly if you come in her way, and leaves you hopelessly behind if you are late. Only for a few brief weeks in the autumn does this grim, belligerent female condescend to be charming; but when she does set about it, the veriest Circe of enchanted isles could not do it better. Airs more dreamy, more hazy, more full of purple light and lustre, never lay over Cyprus or Capri than those which each October overshadow the granite rocks and prickly chestnuts of New England. The trees seem to run no longer sap, but some strange liquid glow; the colors of the flowers flame up, from the cold, pallid delicacy of spring, into royal tints wrought of the very fire of the sun and the hues of evening clouds. The humblest weed, which we trod under our foot unnoticed in summer, changes with the first frost into some colored marvel, and lifts itself up into a study for a painter,—just as the touch of death or adversity often strikes out in a rough nature traits of nobleness and delicacy before wholly undreamed of.

The children travelled onward along the winding course of the river, through a prairie-land of wild-flowers. The whole tribe of asters—white, lilac, pale blue, and royal purple— were rolling in perfect billows of blossoms around them, and the sprays of golden-rod often rose above their heads, as they crackled their way through the many-colored thickets. The children were both endowed with an organization exquisitely susceptible to beauty, and the flowers seemed to intoxicate them with their variety and brilliancy. They kept gathering from right to left without any other object than the possession of a newer and fairer spray, till their little arms were full; and then they would lay them down to select from the mass the choicest, which awhile after would be again thrown by for newer and fairer treasures. Their motion through the bushes often disturbed clouds of yellow butterflies, which had been hanging on the fringes of the tall purple asters, and which rose toying with each other, and fluttering in ethereal dances against the blue sky, looking like whirls and eddies of air-flowers. One of the most brilliant incidents in the many-colored pictures of October days is given by these fluttering caprices of the butterflies. Never in any other part of the season are these airy tribes so many and so brilliant. There are, in particular, whole armies of small, bright yellow ones, which seem born for no other purpose than to make effective and brilliant contrasts with those royal-purple tints of asters, and they hang upon them as if drawn to them by some law of affinity in their contrasting colors.

Tina was peculiarly enchanted with the fanciful fellowship

of these butterflies. They realized exactly her ideal of existence, and she pointed them out to Harry as proof positive that her own notion of living on sunshine and flowers was not a bad one. She was quite sure that they could sleep out all night if the butterflies could, and seemed not to doubt that they would fancy her as a bedfellow.

Towards sundown, when the children were somewhat weary of wandering, and had consumed most of the provisions in their basket, they came suddenly on a little tent pitched in the field, at the door of which sat an old Indian woman weaving baskets. Two or three red-skinned children, of about the same age as our wanderers, were tumbling and kicking about on the ground, in high frolic, with about as many young puppies, who were scratching, rolling, and biting, with their human companions, in admirable spirits. There was a fire before the door, over which a pot was swung from a frame of crossed sticks, the odor of which steamed up, suggestive of good cheer.

The old Indian woman received the children with a broad, hearty grin, while Harry inquired of her how far it was to Oldtown. The old squaw gave it as her opinion, in very Indian English, that it was "muchee walkee" for little white boy, and that he had best stay with her that night and go on to-morrow.

"There, Harry," said Tina, "now you see just how it is. This is a nice little house for us to sleep in, and oh! I see such pretty baskets in it."

The old woman drew out a stock of her wares, from which she selected a small, gayly-painted one, which she gave to the children; in short, it was very soon arranged that they were to stop to supper and spend the night with her. The little Indians gathered around them and surveyed them with grins of delight; and the puppies, being in that state of ceaseless effervescence of animal spirits which marks the indiscreet era of puppyhood, soon had the whole little circle in a state of uproarious laughter.

By and by, the old woman poured the contents of the pot into a wooden trough, and disclosed a smoking mess of the Indian dish denominated succotash,—to wit, a soup of corn and beans, with a generous allowance of salt pork. Offering a large, clean clam-shell to each of the children, she invited them to help themselves.

Whether it was the exhilarating effect of a whole day spent on foot in the open air, or whether it was owing to the absolute perfection of the cookery, we cannot pretend to say, but certain it is that the children thought they had never tasted anything better; and Tina's spirits became so very airy and effervescent, that she laughed perpetually,—a state which set the young barbarians to laughing for sympathy; and this caused all the puppies to bark at once, which made more fun; so that, on the whole, a jollier supper company could nowhere be found.

After sundown, when the whole party had sufficiently fatigued themselves with play and laughing, the old woman spread a skin inside the tent, where Tina lay down contentedly between Harry and one of the puppies, which she insisted upon having as her own particular bedfellow. Harry kneeled down to his prayers outside the tent, which being observed by the Indian woman, she clasped her hands, and seemed to listen with great devotion; and when he had finished, she said, "Me praying Indian; me much love Jesus."

The words were said with a tender gleam over the rough, hard, swarthy features; and the child felt comforted by them as he nestled down to his repose.

"Harry," said Tina, decisively, "let 's we live here. I like to play with the puppies, and the old woman is good to us."

"We 'll see, Tina," said wise little Harry.

XV.

The Old Manor-House

Alas! the next morning dawned wet and rainy. The wind flapped the tent-cover, and the rain put out the fire; and, what was worse, a cross, surly Indian man came home, who beat the poor old woman, and scattered the children and puppies, like partridges, into the bushes.

The poor old squaw took it all patiently, and seemed only intent on protecting the children from injuries and inconveniences on which she calculated as part of her daily lot. She beckoned them to her, and pointed across a field. "Go dat way. White folks dere be good to you." And she insisted on giving them the painted basket and some coarse corn bread.

They set off through the fields; but the wind was chilly and piercing, and the bushes and grass were wet, and Tina was in a doleful state. "O Harry, I wish we had a house to live in! Where do you suppose all the butterflies are staying that we saw yesterday? I 'd like to go where they stay."

"Never mind, Tina; by and by we 'll come to a house."

They passed a spot where evidently some Indians had been camping, for there were the remains of a fire; and Harry picked up some dry brush and refuse sticks around, and kindled it up bright for Tina to warm and dry herself. They sat there awhile and fed the fire, till they began to feel quite warm. In one of Harry's excursions for sticks, he came back and reported a house in sight.

Sure enough, concealed from view behind a pine thicket was a large, stately mansion, the approach to which was through an avenue of majestic trees. The path to this was all grown over with high grass, and a wilderness of ornamental shrubbery seemed to have twined and matted itself together in a wild labyrinth of utter desertion and neglect. The children made their way up the avenue through dripping grass, and bushes that reached almost to their shoulders, and that drizzled water upon their partially dried garments in a way that made Tina shiver. "I 'm so cold!" she said, pitifully. "The folks must let us come in to dry us."

They at last stood before the front door, in a sort of porch which overshadowed it, and which rested on Corinthian pillars of some architectural pretension. The knocker was a black serpent with its tail in its mouth. Tina shuddered with some vague, inward dread, as Harry, rising on tiptoe, struck several loud blows upon it, and then waited to see who would appear.

The wind now rose, and tossed and swung the branches of the great trees in the avenue with a creaking, groaning sound. The shrubbery had grown around the house in a dense and tangled mass, that produced, in the dismal stormy weather, a sense of oppression and darkness. Huge lilacs had climbed above the chamber windows, and clumps of syringas billowed outward from the house in dense cascades; while roses and various kinds of more tender shrubbery, which had been deprived of light and air by their more hardy neighbors, filled up the space below with bare, dead branches, through which the wind sighed dolefully.

"Harry, do knock again," said Tina, when they had waited some time.

"It 's no use," said the boy; "I don't think anybody lives here."

"Perhaps, if we go round to the back of the house, we shall find somebody," said Tina; "it 's storming worse and worse." And the little girl plunged resolutely into the thicket of dead shrubbery, and began tearing her way through.

There was a door on the side of the house, much like that in front; and there were spacious back buildings, which, joining the house, stretched far away in the shrubbery. Harry tried this side door. It was firmly locked. The children then began regularly trying every door that presented itself to their view. At last one, after considerable effort, gave way before their united exertions, and opened to them a shelter from the storm, which was now driving harder and harder. It was a place that had evidently been used for the storing of wood, for there was then quite a pile of fuel systematically arranged against the wall. An ancient axe, perfectly red with rust, was also hanging there.

"Well, we 're in at last," said Tina, "but wet through. What a storm it is!"

"Perhaps we can get to some better place in the house," said Harry; "here is wood, and we might make a fire and dry our clothes, and wait here till the storm is over."

He accordingly pushed against a door at the farther end of the wood-shed, and it opened before him into a large old kitchen. There was the ample fireplace of olden times, extending quite across one side, garnished with a crane having various hooks and other paraphernalia for the convenience of culinary operations.

"There, now," said Harry, "is a fireplace, and here is wood. Now we can dry ourselves. Just you wait here, and I 'll go back and bring a brand from our fire, if the rain has n't put it all out." And Harry turned, and hastily made the best of his way out of the house, to secure his treasure before it should be too late.

Tina now resolved to explore some of the other rooms. She opened a door which seemed to lead into a large dining-hall. A heavy dining-table of dark wood stood in the middle of this room, and a large, old-fashioned carved sideboard filled up an arched recess. Heavy mahogany chairs with stuffed leathern bottoms stood against the wall, but the brass nails with which they had been finished were green with rust. The windows of this room were so matted over with cobwebs, and so darkened by the dense shrubbery outside, as to give the apartment a most weird and forlorn appearance. One of the panes of the window had been broken, perhaps by the striking of the shrubbery against it; and the rain and snow beating in there had ruined the chair that stood below, for the seat of it was all discolored with mould.

Tina shivered as she looked at this dreary room, and the tapping of her own little heels seemed to her like something ghostly; so she hastened to open another door. This led to a small apartment, which had evidently been a lady's boudoir. The walls were hung with tapestry of a dark-green ground, on which flowers and fruits and birds were represented in colors that yet remained brilliant, notwithstanding the dilapidated air of some portions of it. There was a fireplace in this room, and the mantel was choicely carved, of white Italian marble, and upon it were sundry flasks and vases of Venetian glass, of quaint and strange shapes, which the child eyed with awe-struck curiosity. By the side of the fireplace was a broad lounge or sofa, with a pile of cushions, covered with a rich but faded brocade, of a pattern evidently made to carry out the same design with the tapestry on the wall.

A harpsichord occupied another side of the room, and upon it were piled music-books and manuscript music yellow with age. There was a sort of Oriental guitar or lute suspended from the wall, of which one of the strings, being broken, vibrated with the air of the door when the child made her way into the room, and continued quivering in a way that seemed to her nervous and ghostly. Still she was a resolute and enterprising little body; and though her heart was beating at a terrible rate, she felt a sort of mixture of gratified curiosity and exultation in her discovery.

"I wish Harry would come back," she said to herself. "We might make a fire in this pretty little room, and it would be quite snug, and we could wait here till the folks come home." How glad she was when the sound of his voice and footsteps broke the terrible loneliness! She ran out to him, exclaiming, "O Harry, we won't make a fire in this great, doleful old kitchen. I 've found such a nice little room full of pretty things! Let me bring in some wood";—and, running to the wood-pile, she filled her arms.

"It was all I could do to find a brand with a bit of fire on it," said Harry. "There was only the least spark left, but I put it under my jacket and blew and blew, and now we have quite a bright spot in it," he said, showing with exultation a black brand with a round, fiery eye in it, which had much the appearance of a knowing old goblin winking at the children.

The desolate boudoir was soon a scene of much animation, as the marble hearth was strewn with chips and splinters.

"Let me blow, Harry," said Tina, "while you go and look for some more of this brushwood. I saw a heap in that wood-house. I 'll tend the fire while you are gone. See," she said triumphantly to him, when he returned, dragging in a heavy pile of brushwood, "we 'll soon have such a fire!"—and she stooped down over the hearth, laying the burnt ends of sticks together, and blowing till her cheeks were so aflame with zeal and exertion that she looked like a little live coal herself. "Now for it!" she said, as she broke bit after bit of the brushwood. "See now, it's beginning to burn,—hear it crackle! Now put on more and more."

Very soon, in fact, the brushwood crackled and roared in a wide sheet of flame up the old chimney; and being now reinforced with stout sticks of wood, the fire took a solid and settled and companionable form,—the brightest, most hopeful companion a mortal could ask for in a chill, stormy day in autumn.

"Now, Harry," said Tina, "let's dry our clothes, and then we will see what we can do in our house."

"But is it really ours?" said thoughtful Harry. "Who knows who it may belong to?"

"Do you think," said Tina, apprehensively, "that any giant lives here that has gone out and will come home again? Father used to tell us a story like that."

"There are n't really giants now-a-days, Tina," said Harry; "those are only stories. I don't think that it looks as if anybody had lived here for a great while. Things don't look as if anybody lived here, or was expecting to come back."

"Then we may as well live here as anybody," said Tina, "and I will keep house for you. I will roast some apples for our dinner,—I saw ever so many out here on the tree. Roast apples with our corn bread will be so good! And then we can sleep to-night on this great, wide sofa,—can't we? Here, let me sweep up the chips we have made, and make our little house look nice."

"It must be a long time since any one has lived here," said Harry, looking up at the cobwebbed window, against which the shrubbery was dashing and beating in the fury of the storm, "and there can't be the least harm in our staying here till the storm is over."

"Such a strange, pretty room this is!" said Tina, "and so many strange, pretty things in it! Do you know, Harry, I was almost afraid to be here while you were gone; but this bright, warm fire makes such a difference. Fire is company, is n't it?"

When the little one had dried her clothes, she began, with a restless, butterfly sort of motion, to investigate more closely the various objects of the apartment. She opened the harpsi-

chord, and struck a few notes, which sounded rather discor-
dantly, as an instrument which chill and solitude had smitten
with a lasting hoarseness.

"O, horrid! This is n't pretty," she said. "I wonder who
ever played on it? But, O Harry! come and look here! I
thought this was another room in here, with a fire in it," she
said, as she lifted a curtain which hung over a recess. "Look!
it 's only looking-glass in a door. Where does it go to? Let 's
see." And with eager curiosity she turned the knob, and the
door opened, disclosing only a sort of inner closet, which had
been evidently employed for a writing-cabinet, as a writing-
table stood there, and book-cases filled with books.

What most attracted the attention of the children was a
picture, which was hung exactly opposite the door, so that it
met the children face to face. It was the image of a young
girl, dressed in white, with long, black, curling hair falling
down over her neck and shoulders. The dark eyes had an
expression both searching and melancholy; and it was painted
in that peculiar manner, which produces such weird effects on
the beholder, in which the eyes seem to be fixed upon the
spectator, and to follow him on whichever side he stands.

"What a pretty lady! But she looks at us so!" said Tina,
covering her eyes. "I almost thought it was a real woman."

"Whichever way we move, she looks after us," said Harry.

"She looks as if she would speak to us," said Tina; "she
surely wants to say something."

"It is something very sad, then," said the boy, studying the
picture attentively. "She was not sad as mother was," said he,
with a delicate, spiritual instinct reading the impression of the
face. "Mother used to look very, very sad, but in a different
way,—a better way, I think."

"Of course it is n't in the least like mother," said Tina.
"Mother had soft, bright hair,—not black, like this; and her
eyes were blue, like yours, Harry."

"I don't mean her hair or her eyes," said Harry; "but when
mother was sad, she always used to pray. I don't think this
one looks as if she would pray," said the boy, rather under
his breath.

There was, in fact, a lurking sparkle of haughty determination in the depths of the mournful eyes, and a firm curve to

the lines of the mouth, an arching of the neck, and a proud carriage of the head, that confirmed the boy's strictures, and indicated that, whatever sorrows might have crushed the poor heart that beat beneath that fair form, they were borne in her own strength, with no uplooking for aid.

Tina longed to open the drawers of the cabinet beneath the picture, but Harry held her hand. "Tina, dear, what would mother say?" he said, reprovingly. "This is n't our house. Whoever owns it would n't think it was wrong for us to stay here in such a storm, but we certainly ought not to touch their things."

"But we may go through the house, and see all the rooms," said Tina, who had a genuine feminine passion for rummaging, and whose curiosity was piqued to the extreme point by the discoveries already made. "I shall be afraid to sleep here to-night, unless I know all that is in the house."

So the children went, hand in hand, through the various apartments. The house was one of those stately manors which, before the Revolutionary war, the titled aristocracy of England delighted to reproduce on the virgin soil of America. Even to this modern time, some of the old provincial towns in New England preserve one or two of these monuments of the pride and pomp of old colonial days, when America was one of the ante-chambers of the English throne and aristocracy.

The histories of these old houses, if searched into, present many romantic incidents, in which truth may seem wilder than fiction. In the breaking of the ties between the mother country and America, many of these stately establishments were suddenly broken up, and the property, being subject to governmental claims yet undecided, lay a long time unoccupied; the real claimants being in England, and their possessions going through all the processes of deterioration and decay incident to property in the hands of agents at a distance from the real owners. The moss of legend and tradition grew upon these deserted houses. Life in New England, in those days, had not the thousand stimulants to the love of excitement which are to be found in the throng and rush of modern society, and there was a great deal more of story-telling and romancing in real life than exists now; and the simple villagers by their firesides delighted to plunge into the fathomless abyss of incident that came from the histories of grand, unknown people across the water, who had established this incidental connection with their neighborhood. They exaggerated the records of the pomp and wealth that had environed them. They had thrilling legends of romantic and often tragic incidents, of which such houses had been the theatres. More than one of them had its well-attested ghosts, which, at all proper hours, had been veritably seen to go through all those aimless ghostly perambulations and performances which, according to village legends, diversify the leisure of the spiritual state.

The house into which the children's wandering fortunes had led them was one whose legends and history formed the topic of many an excited hour of my childhood, as crooned over to me by different story-telling gossips; and it had, in its structure and arrangements, the evident impress of days nevermore to be reproduced in New England. Large and lofty apartments, some of them still hung with tapestry, and some adorned with arches and columns, were closed in from air and light by strong shutters, although a dusky glimmer came through the heart-shaped holes cut in them. Some of these apartments were quite dismantled and bare. In others the furniture was piled together in confusion, as if for the purpose of removal. One or two chambers were still thoroughly furnished, and bore the marks of having been, at some recent period, occupied; for there were mattresses and pillows and piles of bedclothing on the great, stately bedsteads.

"We might sleep in one of these rooms," said Harry.

"O, no, no!" said the child, clinging to him; "I should be afraid. That great, dreadful-looking, dark bed! And who knows what might be behind the curtains! Let me sleep in the bright little room, where we can see all around us. I should be afraid that lady in the closet would walk about these rooms in the night."

"Perhaps she did once," said Harry. "But come, let us go down. The wind blows and howls so about these lonesome rooms, it makes me afraid."

"How it rumbles down the chimneys!" said Tina; "and now it squeals just as if somebody was hurting it. It's a terrible storm, is n't it?"

"Yes, it's well we are in a house at any rate," said Harry; "but let's go down and bring in wood, and I'll get some apples and pears off the trees out by the back door."

And so the two poor little swallows chittered as they built their small, innocent nest in the deserted house, as ignorant of the great Before and After, as if they had had wings and feathers, and round, bright bird-eyes, instead of curly, golden heads. Harry brought in a quantity of fruit in Tina's little checked apron, and, like two squirrels, they stored it under the old brocade sofa.

"Now ever so much wood in the hall here," said Tina, with the providence of a little housewife; "because when the dark night comes we shall be afraid to go into the wood-house."

Harry felt very large and very provident, and quite like a householder, as he brought armful after armful and laid it outside the door, while Tina arranged some apples to roast on the marble hearth. "If we only could get something to eat every day, we might live here always," she said.

And so that evening, when the night shadows came down darkly on the house, though the storm without thundered and beat and groaned amid the branches of the old trees, and rumbled and shook the chimneys of the solitary manor-house, there was one nook that presented as bright and warm a picture as two fair child-faces, with a background of strange antique furniture and surroundings, could furnish. The fire had burned down into great splendid glowing coals, in which the children, seated before it on the tapestried hearth-rug, saw all sorts of strange faces. Tina had insisted on keeping open the door of the cabinet where the beautiful lady was, because, she said, she must be lonesome in that dark closet by herself.

"I wish she would only smile," she said, as the sharp spires of flame from a new stick of wood which she had just laid on, dancing up, made the face seem to become living and tremulous as if with emotion. "See, Hensel, she looks as if she were going to speak to us."

And hours later the fire still burned in the little boudoir; but the two pretty child-faces lay cheek to cheek in the wide, motherly arms of the sofa, and the shadowy lady seemed to watch over them silently from her lonely recess.

XVI.

Sam Lawson's Discoveries

THE evening was closing in sharp and frosty, with a lowering of wind and cloud that rendered fire-light doubly dear and welcome, as we all drew our chairs round the great, glowing fire in my grandmother's kitchen. I had my little block of wood, which served as a footstool, far in the cavernous depths of one end of the fireplace, close by Black Cæsar, who was busy making me a popgun, while my grandmother sat at the other end in her rocking-chair, rattling her knitting-needles. Uncle Fly had just frisked in, and was perched, as was his wont, on the very tip of his chair, where he sat fussily warming and rubbing his hands, much as a meditative blue-bottle performs the same operation with his fore feet.

"So," said my grandmother to my grandfather, in reproachful tones, "you 've gone and shut the calf up from its mother."

"To be sure," said my grandfather; "that was foreordained and freely predetermined."

"Well, I say it 's a shame," sputtered my grandmother,— "poor creturs!"

It was a part of the farming ordinance, when the calf was fated to be killed, to separate it for a day from its mother, a proceeding which never failed to excite the indignation of my grandmother, which she expressed always with as much life and freshness as if she had never heard of such a matter before in her life. She was not, to be sure, precisely aware what was to be done about it; but in a general way she considered calf-killing as an abominable cruelty, and the parting of calf and cow for a day beforehand as an aggravation. My grandfather was fond of meeting her with a sly use of some of the Calvinistic theological terms which abounded in her favorite writers. The most considerate of husbands often enjoy any quiet method of giving a sly tweak to some cherished peculiarity of their yokefellows; and there was the least suggestion of a smile hovering over my grandfather's face,—which smile, in your quiet man, means two things,—first, that he is going to have his own way in spite of all you can say, and, secondly, that he is quietly amused by your opposition.

"I say it's a shame," quoth my grandmother, "and I always shall. Hear that poor cow low! She feels as bad as I should."

"Mother," said Aunt Lois, in an impatient tone, "I wonder that you can't learn to let things go on as they must. What would you have? We must have fresh meat sometimes, and you eat as much as any of us."

"I don't care, it's too bad," said my grandmother, "and I always shall think so. If I had things *my* way, folks should n't eat creatures at all."

"You 'd be a Brahmin," said my grandfather.

"No, I should n't be a Brahmin, either; but I know an old cow's feelings, and I would n't torment her just to save myself a little trouble."

The conversation was here interrupted by the entrance of Sam Lawson, who came in with a long, lugubrious face, and an air of solemn, mysterious importance, which usually was the herald of some communication.

"Well, Sam," said my grandfather, "how are you?"

"Middlin', Deacon," said Sam, mournfully,—"only middlin'."

"Sit down, sit down," said my grandfather, "and tell us the news."

"Wal, I guess I will. How kind o' revivin' and cheerful it does look here," said Sam, seating himself in his usual attitude, with his hands over the fire. "Lordy massy, it's so different to our house! Hepsy hain't spoke a railly decent word to me since the gineral trainin'. You know, Deacon, Monday, a week ago, was gineral trainin' day over to Hopkinton, and Hepsy, she was set in the idee that I should take her and the young uns to muster. 'All right, Hepsy,' says I, 'ef I can borrow a hoss.' Wal, I walked and walked clean up to Captain Brown's to borrow a hoss, and I could n't get none, and I walked clean down to Bill Peters's, and I could n't get none. Finally, Ned Parker, he lent me his'n. Wal, to be sure, his hoss has got the spring-halt, that kind o' twitches up the waggin, and don't look so genteel as some; but, lordy massy, 't was all I could get. But Hepsy, she blamed me all the same. And then she was at me 'cause she had n't got no gloves. Wal, I had n't no gret o' change in my pocket, and I wanted to keep it for gingerbread and sich for the young uns, so I thought I 'd jest borrow a pair for her, and say nothin'; and I went over and asked Mis' Captain Brown, and over to Mis' Dana's, and round to two or three places; and finally Lady Lothrop, she said she 'd *give* me a old pair o' hern. And I brought 'em to Hepsy; and do you believe, she throwed 'em right smack in my face. 'S'pose I 'm goin' to wear such an old dirty pair as that?' says she. Wal, arter all, we sot out, and Hepsy, she got clear beat out; and when Hepsy does get beat out she has *spells*, and she goes on awful, and they last day arter day. Hepsy's spells is jest like these 'ere northeast storms,—they never do railly clear off, but kind o' wear out, as 't were,—and this 'ere seems to be about one of her longest. She was at me this mornin' fust thing 'fore I was out o' bed, cryin' and goin' on, and castin' on it up at me the men she might 'a hed if she had n't 'a hed me, and the things they 'd 'a done for her, jest as if 't was my fault. 'Lordy massy, Hepsy,' says I, 'I ain't t' blame. I wish with all my heart you hed 'a hed any on 'em you 'd ruther.' You see I wa' n't meanin' no 'fence, you know, but just a bein' kind o' sympathizin' like, and she flew at me 't oncet. Massy to us! why, you 'd 'a thought all them old Sodom and Gomorrah sinners biled down wa' n't nothin' to me. She did talk ridiculous. I tried to reason with her. Says I, 'Hepsy, see here now. Here you be in a good bed, in your own house, and your kindlin's all split to make your fire,—and I split every one on 'em after twelve o'clock last night,—and you a goin' on at this 'ere rate. Hepsy,' says I, 'it 's awful.' But lordy massy, how that 'ere woman can talk! She begun agin, and I could n't get in a word edgeways nor crossways nor noways; and so I jest got up and went round to the tavern, and there I met Bill Moss and Jake Marshall, and we had some crackers and cheese and a little suthin' hot with it, and it kind o' 'curred to me, as Hepsy was in one o' her spells, it would be a good time to go kind o' Indianing round the country a spell till she kind o' come to, ye know. And so I thought I 'd jest go t' other side o' Hopkinton and see Granny Walkers,—her that was housekeeper to Lady Frankland, ye know,—and see if I could n't rake out the pertickelars of that 'ere Dench house. That 'ere house has been a lyin' on my mind considerable, along back."

My ears began to prick up with great liveliness and animation at this sound; and, deserting Cæsar, I went over and stood by Sam, and surveyed him with fixed attention, wondering in the mean time how a house could lie on his mind.

"Well," said my grandfather, "what did you hear?"

"Wal, I did n't get over to her house; but when I 'd walked a pretty good piece I came across Widdah Peters's son, Sol Peters,—you know him, Mis' Badger, he lives over in Needmore with a great, spankin' old gal they call Miss Asphyxy Smith. You 've heard of Miss Sphyxy Smith, hain't you, Mis' Badger?"

"Certainly I have," said my grandmother.

"Miss Asphyxia Smith is a smart, industrious woman," said Aunt Lois; "it is n't worth while to talk so about her. The world would be better off," she continued, eying Sam with an air of didactic severity, "if there were more people in it that keep to their own business, like Miss Sphyxy."

"Wal, spuz so," said Sam Lawson, with an innocent and virtuous droop, not in the slightest degree recognizing the hint; "but now, you see, I 'm coming to a pint. Sol, he asked me if anybody over to Oldtown had seen or heard anything of a couple of children that had run away from Needmore. There was a boy and a gal about nine or ten or under, that had been put out by the parish. The boy was livin' with Old Crab Smith, and the gal with Miss Sphyxy."

"Well, I pity the child that Miss Sphyxy Smith has taken to bring up, I must say," said my grandmother. "What business have old maids a taking children to bring up, I want to know? Why, it is n't every hen that 's fit to bring up chickens. How came the children there, anyway?"

"Wal, you see, there come a woman along to Crab Smith's with these 'ere children. Sol says they 're real putty children, —putty-behaved as ever he see. The woman, she was took down and died there. And so Old Crab, he took the boy; and Miss Sphyxy, she took the gal."

"Too bad," said my grandmother; "poor motherless babes, and nobody but Crab and Sphyxy Smith to do for 'em! Somebody ought to see about it."

"Wal, ye see, Sol, he said that Miss Sphyxy was as hard as a grindstone on this gal, and they kep' the boy and gal apart, and would n't let 'em see nor speak to each other; and Sol says he never did pity any poor, lonesome little critter as he did that 'ere little gal. She used to lie abed nights, and sob and cry fit to break her little heart."

"I should like to go and talk to that woman!" said my grandmother, vengefully. "I wonder folks can be so mean! I wonder what such folks think of themselves, and where they expect to go to!"

"Wal, you see," continued Sam, "the young un was spicy; and when Miss Sphyxy was down on her too hard, the child, she fit her,—you know a rat 'll bite, a hen will peck, and a worm will turn,—and finally it come to a fight between 'em; and Miss Sphyxy, she gin her an awful whippin'. 'Lordy massy, Sol,' says I, when Sol was a tellin' me, 'you need n't say nothin' about it. That 'ere gal 's got arms like a windmill; she 's a regular brown thrasher, she is, only she ain't got no music in her; and ef she undertook to thrash me, she 'd make out.' "

"Well, what became of the children?" said my grandmother.

"Wal, you see, they run off together; fact is, Sol says he helped 'em off, and told 'em to come over to Oldtown. He says he told 'em to inquire for Deacon Badger's."

"I believe so," said Aunt Lois, severely. "Every man, woman, and child that wants taking care of is sent straight to our house."

"And good reason they should, Lois," said my grand-mother, who was wide awake. "I declare, people ought to be out looking for them. 'Liakim, you are always flying about; why don't you look 'em up?"

Uncle Fly jumped up with alacrity. "To be sure, they ought to be looked after," he said, running to the window. "They ought to be looked after right off; they must be attended to." And Uncle Fly seemed to have an indefinite intention of pitching straight through the window in pursuit.

Sam Lawson eyed him with a serene gravity. He felt the

importance of being possessed of all the information the subject in question admitted of, which he was determined to develop in an easy and leisurely manner, without any undue
hurry or heat. "Mr. Sheril," he said, "the fust thing you 'll hev
to find out is *where they be*. It 's no use tearin' round gen'lly.
Where be they?—that 's the question."

"To be sure, to be sure," said Uncle Fly. "Well, what you
got to say about that?"

"Wal, you jest set down now, and be kind o' composed.
I 'm a comin' to that 'ere pint in time," said Sam. "That 'ere 's
jest what I says to Sol. 'Sol,' says I, 'where be they?' And Sol,
he says to me, 'I dunno. They might 'a' gone with the Indians,' says Sol, 'or they might 'a' got lost in the Oldtown
woods';—and jest as we was a talkin', we see old Obscue a
comin' along. He was out on a tramp over to Hopkinton,
Obscue was, and we asked him about 'em. Wal, Obscue, he
says that a gal and boy like what we talked of had slep' in his
wife's hut not long sence. You know Obscue's wife; she
makes baskets, and goes round sellin' on 'em. I could n't fairly
get out o' Obscue what day 't was, nor which way they went
arter; but it was clear that them was the ones."

"Then," said Uncle Fly, "they must be somewhere. They
may have lost their way in the Oldtown woods, and wandered up and down. There ought to be a party started out to
look for 'em to-morrow morning."

"Now look here, Mr. Sheril," said Sam, "I think we 'd
better kind o' concentrate our idees on some one pint
afore we start out, and I 'll tell you what I 'm a thinkin' of.
You know I was a tellin' you that I 'd seen smoke coming
out o' the chimbly of the Dench house. Now I jest thought
them poor little robins might have jest got in there.
You know it stormed like vengeance last week, and the little
critters might have took shelter in that 'ere lonesome old
house."

"Poor babes!" said my grandmother. "'Liakim, you go up
there and see."

"Well, I tell you," said Uncle Eliakim, "I 'll be up bright
and early with my old horse and wagon, and go over to the
Dench house and see about it."

"Wal, now," said Sam, "if you would n't mind, I 'll just

ride over with you. I wanted to kind o' go over that 'ere house. I 've had it on my mind a good while."

"Is that the haunted house?" said I, in a whisper.

"Wal, it 's the one they call haunted, but 't ain't best to be 'fraid of nothin'," said Sam, surveying me paternally, and winking very obviously with one eye at Uncle Eliakim; quite forgetting the long roll of terrible suggestions he had made on the same subject a few evenings before.

"But you told about the man in a long red cloak, and the boy they threw in a well, and a woman in white."

"Lordy massy, what ears young ones has!" said Sam, throwing up his hands pathetically. "I never thought as you was round, Horace; but you must n't never mind nothin' about it. There ain't really no such thing as ghosts."

"I want to go over and see the house," said I.

"Well, well, you shall," said Uncle Fly; "but you must wake up bright and early. I shall be off by six o'clock."

"Well, now, mother," said Aunt Lois, "I just want to know if you are going to make our house an asylum for all the trampers and all the stray children in the neighboring parishes? Have we got to keep these children, or are we going to send 'em back where they belong?"

"Send 'em back to Old Crab Smith and Miss Sphyxy?" said my grandmother. "I 'd like to see myself doing that."

"Well, then, are *we* going to maintain 'em?" said Aunt Lois; "because I want to know definitely what this is coming to."

"We 'll see," said my grandmother. "It 's our business to do good as we have opportunity. *We* must n't reap the corners of our fields, nor beat off all our olive-berries, but leave 'em for the poor, the fatherless, and the widow, Scripture says."

"Well, I guess our olive-berries are pretty well beaten off now, and our fields reaped, corners and all," said Lois; "and I don't see why we needs must intermeddle with children that the selectmen in Needmore have put out."

Now Aunt Lois was a first-rate belligerent power in our family circle, and in many cases carried all before her; but my grandmother always bore her down on questions like these, and it was agreed, *nem. con.*, that the expedition to look up the wanderers should take place the next morning.

The matter being thus arranged, Sam settled back with a

jocular freedom of manner, surveying the fire, and flopping his hands over it, smiling to himself in a manner that made it evident that he had a further reserve of something on his mind to communicate. "This 'ere Miss Sphyxy Smith 's a rich old gal, and 'mazin' smart to work," he began. "Tell you, she holds all she gets. Old Sol, he told me a story 'bout her that was a pretty good un."

"What was it?" said my grandmother.

"Wal, ye see, you 'member old Parson Jeduthun Kendall, that lives up in Stonytown: he lost his wife a year ago last Thanksgiving, and he thought 't was about time he hed another; so he comes down and consults our Parson Lothrop. Says he, 'I want a good, smart, neat, economical woman, with a good property. I don't care nothin' about her bein' handsome. In fact, I ain't particular about anything else,' says he. Wal, Parson Lothrop, says he, 'I think, if that 's the case, I know jest the woman to suit ye. She owns a clear, handsome property, and she 's neat and economical; but she 's no beauty.' 'O, beauty is nothin' to me,' says Parson Kendall; and so he took the direction. Wal, one day he hitched up his old one-hoss shay, and kind o' brushed up, and started off a courtin'. Wal, the parson he come to the house, and he was tickled to pieces with the looks o' things outside, 'cause the house is all well shingled and painted, and there ain't a picket loose nor a nail wantin' nowhere. 'This 'ere 's the woman for me,' says Parson Kendall. So he goes up and raps hard on the front door with his whip-handle. Wal, you see, Miss Sphyxy, she was jest goin' out to help get in her hay. She had on a pair o' clompin' cowhide boots, and a pitchfork in her hand, just goin' out when she heard the rap. So she come jest as she was to the front door. Now you know Parson Kendall 's a little midget of a man; but he stood there on the step kind o' smilin' and genteel, lickin' his lips and lookin' *so* agreeable! Wal, the front door kind o' stuck,—front doors gen'ally do, ye know, 'cause they ain't opened very often,—and Miss Sphyxy, she had to pull and haul and put to all her strength, and finally it come open with a bang, and she 'peared to the parson, pitchfork and all, sort o' frownin' like.

" 'What do you want?' says she; for you see Miss Sphyxy ain't no ways tender to the men.

"'I want to see Miss Asphyxia Smith,' says he, very civil, thinking she was the hired gal.

"'*I* 'm Miss Asphyxia Smith,' says she. 'What do you want o' me?'

"Parson Kendall, he jest took one good look on her, from top to toe. '*Nothin',*' says he, and turned right round and went down the steps like lightnin'.

"The way she banged that 'ere door, Sol said, was lively. He jumped into his shay, and I tell you his old hoss was waked up for once. The way that 'ere old shay spun and bounced was a sight. And when he come to Oldtown, Parson Lothrop was walkin' out in his wig and cocked hat and ruffles, as serene as a pictur, and he took off his hat to him as handsome as a gentleman could; but Parson Kendall, he driv right by and never bowed. He was awful riled, Parson Kendall was; but he could n't say nothin', 'cause he 'd got all he asked for. But the story got out, and Sol and the men heard it, and you 'd a thought they 'd never be done laughin' about it. Sol says, if he was to be hung for it the next minute, he never can help laughin' when he thinks how kind o' scared little Parson Kendall looked when Miss Asphyxia 'peared to him on the doorstep."

"Well, well, well," said Uncle Eliakim, "if we are going to the Dench house to-morrow morning, you must all be up early, for I mean to be off by daylight; and we 'd better all go to bed." With which remark he fluttered out of the kitchen.

"'Liakim 'll be along here by ten o'clock to-morrow," said my grandfather, quietly. "I don't suppose he 's promised more than forty people to do something for them to-morrow morning."

"Yes," said Aunt Lois, "and the linch-pins of the wagon are probably lost, and the tire of the wheels sprung; but he 'll be up before daylight, and maybe get along some time in the forenoon."

XVII.

The Visit to the Haunted House

My story now approaches a point in which I am soon to meet and begin to feel the force of a train of circumstances which ruled and shaped my whole life. That I had been hitherto a somewhat exceptional child may perhaps have been made apparent in the incidents I have narrated. I was not, in fact, in the least like what an average healthy boy ought to be. My brother Bill was exactly that, and nothing more. He was a good, growing, well-limbed, comfortably disposed animal, reasonably docile, and capable, under fair government, of being made to go exactly in any paths his elders chose to mark out for him.

It had been settled, the night after my father's funeral, that my Uncle Jacob was to have him for a farm-boy, to work in the summer on the farm, and to pick up his education as he might at the district school in the winter season; and thus my mother was relieved of the burden of his support, and Aunt Lois of his superfluous activity in our home department. To me the loss was a small one; for except a very slight sympathy of souls in the matter of fish-hooks and popguns, there was scarcely a single feeling that we had in common. I had a perfect passion for books, and he had a solid and well-pronounced horror of them, which seems to belong to the nature of a growing boy. I could read, as by a kind of preternatural instinct, as soon as I could walk; and reading was with me at ten years a devouring passion. No matter what the book was that was left in my vicinity, I read it as by an irresistible fascination. To be sure, I preferred stories, history, and lively narrative, where such material was to be had; but the passion for reading was like hunger,—it must be fed, and, in the absence of palatable food, preyed upon what it could find. So it came to pass that theological tracts, treatises on agriculture, old sermons,—anything, in short, that could be raked out of the barrels and boxes in my grandfather's garret,—would

hold me absorbed in some shady nook of the house when I
ought to have been out playing as a proper boy should. I did
not, of course, understand the half of what I read, and mis-
called the words to myself in a way that would have been
laughable had anybody heard me; but the strange, unknown
sounds stimulated vague and dreamy images in my mind,
which were continually seething, changing, and interweaving,
like fog-wreaths by moonlight, and formed a phantasmagoria
in which I took a quaint and solemn delight.

But there was one peculiarity of my childhood which I
have hesitated with an odd sort of reluctance to speak of, and
yet which so powerfully influenced and determined my life,
and that of all with whom I was connected, that it must find
some place here. I was, as I said, dreamy and imaginative,
with a mind full of vague yearnings. But beside that, through
an extreme delicacy of nervous organization, my childish steps
were surrounded by a species of vision or apparition so clear
and distinct that I often found great difficulty in discriminating between the forms of real life and these shifting shapes,
that had every appearance of reality, except that they dissolved at the touch. All my favorite haunts had their particular shapes and forms, which it afforded me infinite amusement to watch in their varying movements.

Particularly at night, after I had gone to bed and the candle
was removed from my room, the whole atmosphere around
my bed seemed like that which Raphael has shadowed forth
around his Madonna San Sisto,—a palpitating crowd of faces
and forms changing in dim and gliding quietude. I have often
wondered whether any personal experience similar to mine
suggested to the artist this living background to his picture.
For the most part, these phantasms were agreeable to me, and
filled me with a dreamy delight. Sometimes distinct scenes or
visions would rise before my mind, in which I seemed to look
far beyond the walls of the house, and to see things passing
wherein were several actors. I remember one of these, which
I saw very often, representing a venerable old white-headed
man playing on a violin. He was always accompanied by a
tall, majestic woman, dressed in a strange, outlandish costume, in which I particularly remarked a high fur cap of a
peculiar form. As he played, the woman appeared to dance in

time to the music. Another scene which frequently presented itself to my eyes was that of a green meadow by the side of a lake of very calm water. From a grove on one side of the lake would issue a miniature form of a woman clothed in white, with a wide golden girdle around her waist, and long, black hair hanging down to her middle, which she constantly smoothed down with both her hands, with a gentle, rhythmical movement, as she approached me. At a certain point of approach, she always turned her back, and began a rapid retreat into the grove; and invariably as she turned there appeared behind her the image of a little misshapen dwarf, who pattered after her with ridiculous movements which always made me laugh. Night after night, during a certain year of my life, this pantomime never failed to follow the extinguishment of the candle, and it was to me a never-failing source of delight. One thing was peculiar about these forms,—they appeared to cause a vibration of the great central nerves of the body, as when a harp-string is struck. So I could feel in myself the jar of the dwarf's pattering feet, the soft, rhythmic movement of the little woman stroking down her long hair, the vibrations of the violin, and the steps of the dancing old woman. Nobody knew of this still and hidden world of pleasure which was thus nightly open to me. My mother used often to wonder, when, hours after she put me to bed, she would find me lying perfectly quiet, with my eyes widely and calmly open. Once or twice I undertook to tell her what I saw, but was hushed up with, "Nonsense, child! there has n't been anybody in the room; you should n't talk so."

The one thing that was held above all things sacred and inviolable in a child's education in those old Puritan days was to form habits of truth. Every statement received an immediate and unceremonious sifting, and anything that looked in the least like a departure from actual verity was met with prompt and stringent discouragement. When my mother repeated before Aunt Lois some of my strange sayings, she was met with the downright declaration: "That child will be an awful liar, Susy, if you don't keep a strict lookout on him. Don't you let him tell you any stories like that."

So I early learned silence; but my own confidence in the reality of my secondary world was not a whit diminished.

Like Galileo, who said, "It does move, nevertheless," so I, when I once had the candle out at night, snapped my fingers mentally at Aunt Lois, and enjoyed my vision.

One peculiarity of these appearances was that certain of them seemed like a sort of *genii loci*,—shapes belonging to certain places. The apparition of the fairy woman with the golden girdle only appeared in a certain room where I slept one year, and which had across one of its corners a sort of closet called a buffet. From this buffet the vision took its rise, and when my parents moved to another house it never appeared again.

A similar event in my shadow-world had marked our coming to my grandmother's to live. The old violin-player and his wife had for a long time been my nightly entertainers; but the first night after we were established in the apartment given up to our use by Aunt Lois, I saw them enter as they usually did, seeming to come right through the wall of the room. They, however, surveyed the apartment with a sort of confused, discontented movement, and seemed to talk to each other with their backs to me; finally I heard the old woman say, "We can't stay here," and immediately I saw them passing through the wall of the house. I saw after them as clearly as if the wall had dissolved and given my eyes the vision of all out of doors. They went to my grandfather's wood-pile and looked irresolutely round; finally they mounted on the pile, and seemed to sink gradually through it and disappear, and I never saw them afterwards.

But another of the companions of my solitude was more constant to me. This was the form of a young boy of about my own age, who for a year past had frequently come to me at night, and seemed to look lovingly upon me, and with whom I used to have a sort of social communion, without words, in a manner which seemed to me far more perfect than human language. I *thought* to him, and in return I received silent demonstrations of sympathy and fellowship from him. I called him Harvey, and used, as I lay looking in his face, mentally to tell him many things about the books I read, the games I played, and the childish joys and griefs I had; and in return he seemed to express affection and sympathy by a strange communication, as lovers sometimes talk to each other by distant glances.

Attendant on all these exceptional experiences, perhaps resulting from them, was a peculiar manner of viewing the human beings by whom I was surrounded. It is common now-a-days to speak of the sphere or emanation that surrounds a person. To my childish mind there was a vivid perception of something of this nature with regard to every one whom I approached. There were people for whom I had a violent and instinctive aversion, whose presence in the room gave me a pain so positive that it seemed almost physical, and others, again, to whom I was strongly attracted, and whose presence near me filled me with agreeable sensations, of which I could give no very definite account. For this reason, I suppose, the judgments which different people formed concerning me varied extremely. Miss Mehitable, for example, by whom I was strongly attracted, thought me one of the most amiable of boys; while my poor Aunt Lois was certain I was one of the most trying children that ever were born.

My poor mother! I surely loved her, and yet her deficient vital force, her continual sadness and discouragement, acted on my nerves as a constant weight and distress, against which I blindly and instinctively struggled; while Aunt Lois's very footstep on the stair seemed to rouse every nerve of combativeness in my little body into a state of bristling tension. I remember that when I was about six or seven years old I had the scarlet-fever, and Aunt Lois, who was a most rampant and energetic sick-nurse, undertook to watch with me; but my cries and resistance were so terrible that I was thought to be going deranged. Finally the matter was adjusted by Sam Lawson's offering to take the place, upon which I became perfectly tranquil, and resigned myself into his hands with the greatest composure and decorum. Sam was to me, during my childhood, a guide, philosopher, and friend. The lazy, easy, indefinite atmosphere of being that surrounded him was to me like the haze of Indian summer over a landscape, and I delighted to bask in it. Nothing about him was any more fixed than the wavering shadows of clouds; he was a boundless world of narrative and dreamy suggestion, tending to no point and having no end, and in it I delighted. Sam, besides, had a partiality for all those haunts in which I took pleasure. Near our house was the old town burying-ground, where reposed the bones of generations of Indian sachems, elders, pastors, and teachers, converted from the wild forests, who, Christianized and churched, died in the faith, and were gathered into Christian burial. On its green hillocks I loved to sit and watch and dream long after sundown or moonrise, and fancy I saw bands of wavering shapes, and hope that some one out of the crowd might have a smile of recognition or a spiritual word for me.

My mother and grandmother and Aunt Lois were horror-stricken by such propensities, indicating neither more nor less than indefinite coughs and colds, with early death in the rear; and however much in the way a little boy always seemed in those times in the active paths of his elders, yet it was still esteemed a primary duty to keep him in the world. "Horace, what do you go and sit in the graveyard for?" would my grandmother say. "I should think you 'd be 'fraid something would 'pear to you."

"I want something to appear, grandmother."

"Pshaw, pshaw! no, you don't. What do you want to be so odd for? Don't you ever say such things."

Sam, however, was willing to aid and abet me in strolling and lounging anywhere and at any hour, and lent a willing ear to my tales of what I saw, and had in his capacious wallet a pendent story or a spiritual precedent for anything that I could mention.

On this night, after he had left me, I went to bed with my mind full of the haunted house, and all that was to be hoped or feared from its exploration. Whether this was the cause or not, the result was that Harvey appeared nearer and more friendly than ever; and he held by his hand another boy, whose figure appeared to me like a faintly discerned form in a mist. Sometimes the mist seemed to waver and part, and I caught indistinct glimpses of bright yellow curls and clear blue eyes, and then Harvey smiled and shook his head. When he began to disappear, he said to me, "Good by"; and I felt an inward assurance that he was about to leave me. I said my "Good by" aloud, and stretched out my hands.

"Why, Horace, Horace!" said my mother, waking suddenly at the sound of my voice,—"Horace, wake up; you 've been dreaming."

I had not even been asleep, but I did not tell her so, and turning over, as I usually did when the curtain fell over my dream-land, I was soon asleep. I was wide awake with the earliest peep of dawn the next morning, and had finished dressing myself before my mother awoke.

Ours was an early household, and the brisk tap of Aunt Lois's footsteps, and the rattling of chairs and dishes in the kitchen, showed that breakfast was in active preparation.

My grandfather's prediction with regard to my Uncle Eliakim proved only too correct. The fact was, that the poor man lived always in the whirl of a perfect Maelstrom of promises and engagements, which were constantly converging towards every hour of his unoccupied time. His old wagon and horse both felt the effects of such incessant activity, and such deficient care and attention as were consequent upon it, and were at all times in a state of dilapidation. Therefore it was that the next morning nine, ten, and eleven o'clock appeared, and no Uncle Eliakim.

Sam Lawson had for more than two hours been seated in an expectant attitude on our doorstep; but as the sun shone warm, and he had a large mug of cider between his hands, he appeared to enjoy his mind with great equanimity.

Aunt Lois moved about the house with an air and manner of sharp contempt, which exhibited itself even in the way she did her household tasks. She put down plates as if she despised them, and laid sticks of wood on the fire with defiant thumps, as much as to say that she knew some things that had got to be in time and place if others were not; but she spake no word.

Aunt Lois, as I have often said before, was a good Christian, and held it her duty to govern her tongue. True, she said many sharp and bitter things; but nobody but herself and her God knew how many more she would have said had she not reined herself up in conscientious silence. But never was there a woman whose silence could express more contempt and displeasure than hers. You could feel it in the air about you, though she never said a word. You could feel it in the rustle of her dress, in the tap of her heels over the floor, in the occasional flash of her sharp, black eye. She was like a thunder-cloud whose quiet is portentous, and from which you every moment expect a flash or an explosion. This whole morning's excursion was contrary to her mind and judgment, — an ill-advised, ill-judged, shiftless proceeding, and being entered on in a way as shiftless.

"What time do you suppose it is, mother?" she at last said to my grandmother, who was busy in her buttery.

"Massy, Lois! I dare n't look," called out my grandmother, who was apt to fall behindhand of her desires in the amount of work she could bring to pass of a morning. "I don't want to know."

"Well, it 's eleven o'clock," said Lois, relentlessly, "and no signs of Uncle 'Liakim yet; and there 's Sam Lawson, I s'pose he's going to spend the day on our doorstep."

Sam Lawson looked after my Aunt Lois as she went out of the kitchen. "Lordy massy, Horace, I would n't be so kind o' unreconciled as she is all the time for nothin'. Now *I* might get into a fluster 'cause *I* 'm kep' a waitin', but I don't. I think it 's our duty to be willin' to wait quiet till things come round; this 'ere 's a world where things can't be driv', and folks must n't set their heart on havin' everything come out jes' so, 'cause ef they do they 'll allers be in a stew, like Hepsy and Miss Lois there. Let 'em jest wait quiet, and things allers do come round in the end as well or better 'n ef you worried."

And as if to illustrate and justify this train of thought, Uncle Eliakim's wagon at this moment came round the corner of the street, driving at a distracted pace. The good man came with such headlong speed and vivacity that his straw hat was taken off by the breeze, and flew far behind him, and he shot up to our door, as he usually did to that of the meeting-house, as if he were going to drive straight in.

"Lordy massy, Mr. Sheril," said Sam, "don't get out; I 'll get your hat. Horace, you jest run and pick it up; that 's a good boy."

I ran accordingly, but my uncle had sprung out as lively as an autumn grasshopper. "I 've been through a sea of troubles this morning," he said. "I lent my waggin to Jake Marshall yesterday afternoon, to take his wife a ride. I thought if Jake was a mind to pay the poor woman any attention, I'd help; but when he brought it back last night, one of the bolts was broken, and the harness gave out in two places."

"Want to know?" said Sam, leisurely examining the establishment. "I think the neighbors ought to subscribe to keep up your team, Mr. Sheril, for it's free to the hull on 'em."

"And what thanks does he get?" said Aunt Lois, sharply. "Well, Uncle 'Liakim, it's almost dinner-time."

"I know it, I know it, I know it, Lois. But there's been a lot o' things to do this morning. Just as I got the waggin mended come Aunt Bathsheba Sawin's boy and put me in mind that I promised to carry her corn to grind; and I had to stop and take that round to mill; and then I remembered the pills that was to go to Hannah Dexter—"

"I dare say, and forty more things like it," said Aunt Lois.

"Well, jump in now," said Uncle Fly; "we'll be over and back in no time."

"You may as well put it off till after dinner now," said Aunt Lois.

"Could n't stop for that," said Uncle 'Liakim; "my afternoon is all full now. I've got to be in twenty places before night." And away we rattled, while Aunt Lois stood looking after us in silent, unutterable contempt.

"Stop! stop! stop! Whoa! whoa!" said Uncle 'Liakim, drawing suddenly up. "There's that plaster for Widdah Peters, after all. I wonder if Lois would n't just run up with it." By this time he had turned the horse, who ran, with his usual straightforward, blind directness, in a right line, against the doorstep again.

"Well, what now?" said Aunt Lois, appearing at the door.

"Why, Lois, I've just come back to tell you I forgot I promised to carry Widdah Peters that plaster for lumbago; could n't you just find time to run up there with it?"

"Well, give it to me," said Aunt Lois, with sharp precision, and an air of desperate patience.

"Yes, yes, I will," said Uncle Fly, standing up and beginning a rapid search into that series of pockets which form a distinguishing mark of masculine habiliments,—searching with such hurried zeal that he really seemed intent on tearing himself to pieces. "Here 't is!—no, pshaw, pshaw! that 's my handkerchief! O, here!—pshaw, pshaw! Why, where is it? Did n't I put it in?—or did I— O, here it is in my vest-pocket; no, though. Where a plague!" and Uncle Fly sprang from the wagon and began his usual active round-and-round chase after himself, slapping his pockets, now before and now behind, and whirling like a dancing dervis, while Aunt Lois stood regarding him with stony composure.

"If you *could* ever think where anything was, before you began to talk about it, it would be an improvement," she said.

"Well, fact is," said Uncle Eliakim, "now I think of it, Mis' Sheril made me change my coat just as I came out, and that 's the whole on 't. You just run up, Lois, and tell Mis' Sheril to send one of the boys down to Widdah Peters's with the plaster she 'll find in the pocket,—right-hand side. Come now, get up."

These last words were addressed, not to Aunt Lois, but to the horse, who, kept in rather a hungry and craving state by his master's hurrying manner of life, had formed the habit of sedulously improving every spare interval in catching at a mouthful of anything to eat, and had been accordingly busy in cropping away a fringe of very green grass that was growing up by the kitchen doorstep, from which occupation he was remorselessly twitched up and started on an impetuous canter.

"Wal, now I hope we 're fairly started," said Sam Lawson; "and, Mr. Sheril, you may as well, while you are about it, take the right road as the wrong one, 'cause that 'ere saves time. It 's pleasant enough anywhere, to be sure, to-day; but when a body 's goin' to a place, a body likes to get there, as it were."

"Well, well, well," said Uncle Fly, "we 're on the right road, ain't we?"

"Wal, so fur you be; but when you come out on the plains, you must take the fust left-hand road that drives through the woods, and you may jest as well know as much aforehand."

"Much obliged to you," said my uncle. "I reely had n't thought particularly about the way."

"S'pose not," said Sam, composedly; "so it 's jest as well you took me along. Lordy massy, there ain't a road nor a cart-path round Oldtown that I hain't been over, time and time agin. I believe I could get through any on 'em the darkest night that ever was hatched. Jake Marshall and me has been Indianing round these 'ere woods more times 'n you could count. It 's kind o' pleasant, a nice bright day like this 'ere, to be a joggin' along in the woods. Everything so sort o' still, ye know; and ye hear the chestnuts a droppin', and the wa'nuts. Jake and me, last fall, went up by Widdah Peters's one day, and shuck them trees, and got nigh about a good bushel o' wa'nuts. I used to kind o' like to crack 'em for the young uns, nights, last winter, when Hepsy 'd let em sit up. Though she 's allers for drivin' on 'em all off to bed, and makin' it kind o' solitary, Hepsy is." And Sam concluded the conjugal allusion with a deep sigh.

"Have you ever been into the grounds of the Dench house?" said Uncle Fly.

"Wal, no, not reely; but Jake, he has; and ben into the house too. There was a fellow named 'Biah Smith that used to be a kind o' servant to the next family that come in after Lady Frankland went out, and he took Jake all over it once when there wa' n't nobody there. 'Biah, he said that when Sir Harry lived there, there was one room that was always kept shet up, and wa' n't never gone into, and in that 'ere room there was the long red cloak, and the hat and sword, and all the clothes he hed on when he was buried under the ruins in that 'ere earthquake. They said that every year, when the day of the earthquake come round, Sir Harry used to spend it a fastin' and prayin' in that 'ere room, all alone. 'Biah says that he had talked with a fellow that was one of Sir Harry's body-servants, and he told him that Sir Harry used to come out o' that 'ere room lookin' more like a ghost than a live man, when he' d fasted and prayed for twenty-four hours there. Nobody knows what might have 'peared to him there."

I wondered much in my own quiet way at this story, and marvelled whether, in Sir Harry's long, penitential watchings, he had seen the air of the room all tremulous with forms and faces such as glided around me in my solitary hours.

"Naow, you see," said Sam Lawson, "when the earthquake come, Sir Harry, he was a driving with a court lady; and she, poor soul, went into 'tarnity in a minit,—'thout a minit to prepare. And I 'spect there ain't no reason to s'pose but what she was a poor, mis'able Roman Catholic. So her prospects could n't have been noways encouragin'. And it must have borne on Sir Harry's mind to think she should be took and he spared, when he was a cuttin' up just in the way he was. I should n't wonder but she should 'pear to him. You know they say there is a woman in white walks them grounds, and 'Biah, he says, as near as he can find out, it 's that 'ere partic-ular chamber as she allers goes to. 'Biah said he 'd seen her at the windows a wringin' her hands and a cryin' fit to break her heart, poor soul. Kind o' makes a body feel bad, 'cause, arter all, 't wa' n't her fault she was born a Roman Catholic,— now was it?"

The peculiarity of my own mental history had this effect on me from a child, that it wholly took away from me all dread of the supernatural. A world of shadowy forms had always been as much a part of my short earthly experience as the more solid and tangible one of real people. I had just as quiet and natural a feeling about one as the other. I had not the slightest doubt, on hearing Sam's story, that the form of the white lady did tenant those deserted apartments; and so far from feeling any chill or dread in the idea, I felt only a sort of curiosity to make her acquaintance.

Our way to the place wound through miles of dense forest. Sir Harry had chosen it, as a retreat from the prying eyes and slanderous tongues of the world, in a region of woodland solitude. And as we trotted leisurely under the bright scarlet and yellow boughs of the forest, Uncle Eliakim and Sam dis-coursed of the traditions of the place we were going to.

"Who was it bought the place after Lady Frankland went to England?" said Uncle Eliakim.

"Wal, I believe 't was let a spell. There was some French folks hed it 'long through the war. I heerd tell that they was pretty high people. I never could quite make out when they went off; there was a good many stories round about it. I did n't clearly make out how 't was, till Dench got it. Dench, you know, got his money in a pretty peculiar way, ef all they say 's true."

"How 's that?" said my uncle.

"Wal, they do say he got the great carbuncle that was at

the bottom of Sepaug River. You 've heard about the great carbuncle, I s'pose?"

"O, no! do pray tell me about it," said I, interrupting with fervor.

"Why, did n't you never hear 'bout that? want to know. Wal, I 'll tell ye, then. I know all 'bout it. Jake Marshall, he told me that Dench fust told him, and he got it from old Mother Ketury, ye know,—a regelar old heathen Injun Ketury is,—and folks do go so fur as to say that in the old times Ketury 'd 'a' ben took up for a witch, though I never see no harm in her ways. Ef there be sperits, and we all know there is, what 's the harm o' Ketury 's seein' on 'em?"

"Maybe she can't help seeing them," suggested I.

"Jes' so, jes' so; that 'ere 's what I telled Jake when we 's a talkin' it over, and he said he did n't like Dench's havin' so much to do with old Ketury. But la, old Ketury could say the Lord's Prayer in Injun, cause I 've heard her; though she would n't say it when she did n't want to and she would say it when she did,—jest as the fit took her. But lordy massy, them wild Injuns, they ain't but jest half folks, they 're so kind o' wild, and birchy and bushy as a body may say. Ef they take religion at all, it 's got to be in their own way. Ef you get the wild beast all out o' one on 'em, there don't somehow seem to be enough left to make an ordinary smart man of, so much on 'em 's wild. Anyhow, Dench, he was thick with Ketury, and she told him all about the gret carbuncle, and gin him directions how to get it."

"But I don't know what a great carbuncle is," I interrupted.

"Lordy massy, boy, did n't you never read in your Bible about the New Jerusalem, and the precious stones in the foundation, that shone like the sun? Wal, the carbuncle was one on 'em."

"Did it fall down out of heaven into the river?" said I.

"Mebbe," said Sam. "At any rate Ketury, she told 'em what they had to do to get it. They had to go out arter it jest exactly at twelve o'clock at night, when the moon was full. You was to fast all the day before, and go fastin', and say the Lord's Prayer in Injun afore you went; and when you come to where 't was, you was to dive after it. But there wa' n't to be a word spoke; if there was, it went right off."

"What did they have to say the prayer in Indian for?" said I.

"Lordy massy, boy, I s'pose 't was 'cause 't was Indian sper-its kep' a watch over it. Any rate 't was considerable of a pull on 'em, 'cause Ketury, she had to teach 'em; and she wa' n't allers in the sperit on 't. Sometimes she 's crosser 'n torment, Ketury is. Dench, he gin her fust and last as much as ten dollars,—so Jake says. However, they got all through with it, and then come a moonlight night, and they went out. Jake says it was the splendidest moonlight ye ever did see,—all jest as still,—only the frogs and the turtles kind o' peepin'; and they did n't say a word, and rowed out past the pint there, where the water 's ten feet deep, and he looked down and see it a shinin' on the bottom like a great star, making the waters all light like a lantern. Dench, he dived for it, Jake said; and he saw him put his hand right on it; and he was so tickled, you know, to see he 'd got it, that he could n't help hollerin' right out, 'There, you got it!' and it was gone. Dench was mad enough to 'a' killed him; 'cause, when it goes that 'ere way, you can't see it agin for a year and a day. But two or three years arter, all of a sudden, Dench, he seemed to kind o' spruce up and have a deal o' money to spend. He said an uncle had died and left it to him in England; but Jake Marshall says you 'll never take him in that 'ere way. He says he thinks it 's no better 'n witchcraft, getting money that 'ere way. Ye see Jake was to have had half if they 'd 'a' got it, and not gettin' nothin' kind o' sot him to thinkin' on it in a moral pint o' view, ye know.—But, lordy massy, where be we, Mr. Sheril? This 'ere 's the second or third time we 've come round to this 'ere old dead chestnut. We ain't makin' no progress."

In fact there were many and crossing cart-paths through this forest, which had been worn by different farmers of the vicinity in going after their yearly supply of wood; and, not-withstanding Sam's assertion of superior knowledge in these matters, we had, in the negligent inattention of his narrative, become involved in this labyrinth, and driven up and down, and back and forward, in the wood, without seeming at all to advance upon our errand.

"Wal, I declare for 't, I never did see nothing beat it," said Sam. "We 've been goin' jest round and round for this hour or more, and come out again at exactly the same place. I 've heerd of places that 's kep' hid, and folks allers gets sort o' struck blind and confused that undertakes to look 'em up. Wal, I don't say I believe in sich stories, but this 'ere is curous. Why, I 'd 'a' thought I could 'a' gone straight to it blindfolded, any day. Ef Jake Marshall was here, he 'd go straight to it."

"Well, Sam," said Uncle Eliakim, "it 's maybe because you and me got so interested in telling stories that we 've missed the way."

"That 'ere 's it, 'thout a doubt," said Sam. "Now I 'll just hush up, and kind o' concentrate my 'tention. I 'll just git out and walk a spell, and take an observation."

The result of this improved attention to the material facts of the case was, that we soon fell into a road that seemed to wind slowly up a tract of rising ground, and to disclose to our view, through an interlacing of distant boughs, the western horizon, toward which the sun was now sinking with long, level beams. We had been such a time in our wanderings, that there seemed a prospect of night setting in before we should be through with our errand and ready to return.

"The house stan's on the top of a sort o' swell o' ground," said Sam; "and as nigh as I can make it out, it must be somewhere about there."

"There is a woman a little way before us," said I; "why don't you ask her?"

I saw very plainly in a turn of the road a woman whose face was hidden by a bonnet, who stood as if waiting for us. It was not the white woman of ghostly memory, but apparently a veritable person in the every-day habiliments of common life, who stood as if waiting for us.

"I don't see no woman," said Sam; "where is she?"

I pointed with my finger, but as I did so the form melted away. I remember distinctly the leaves of the trees back of it appearing through it as through a gauze veil, and then it disappeared entirely.

"There is n't any woman that I can see," said Uncle Eliakim, briskly. "The afternoon sun must have got into your eyes, boy."

I had been so often severely checked and reproved for stating what I saw, that I now determined to keep silence, whatever might appear to me. At a little distance before us the road forked, one path being steep and craggy, and the other easier of ascent, and apparently going in much the same general direction. A little in advance, in the more rugged path, stood the same female form. Her face was hidden by a branch of a tree, but she beckoned to us. "Take *that* path, Uncle 'Liakim," said I; "it 's the right one."

"Lordy massy," said Sam Lawson, "how in the world should you know that? That 'ere is the shortest road to the Dench house, and the other leads away from it."

I kept silence as to my source of information, and still watched the figure. As we passed it, I saw a beautiful face with a serene and tender expression, and her hands were raised as if in blessing. I looked back earnestly and she was gone.

A few moments after, we were in the grounds of the place, and struck into what had formerly been the carriage way, though now overgrown with weeds, and here and there with a jungle of what was once well-kept ornamental shrubbery. A tree had been uprooted by the late tempest, and blown down across the road, and we had to make quite a little detour to avoid it.

"Now how are we to get into this house?" said Uncle Eliakim. "No doubt it 's left fastened up."

"Do you see *that*?" said Sam Lawson, who had been gazing steadily upward at the chimneys of the house, with his eyes shaded by one of his great hands. "Look at that smoke from the middle chimbly."

"There 's somebody in the house, to be sure," said Uncle Eliakim; "suppose we knock at the front door here?"—and with great briskness, suiting the action to the word, he lifted the black serpent knocker, and gave such a rat tat tat as must have roused all the echoes of the old house, while Sam Lawson and I stood by him, expectant, on the front steps.

Sam then seated himself composedly on a sort of bench which was placed under the shadow of the porch, and awaited the result with the contentment of a man of infinite leisure. Uncle Eliakim, however, felt pressed for time, and therefore gave another long and vehement rap. Very soon a chirping of childish voices was heard behind the door, and a pattering of feet; there appeared to be a sort of consultation.

"There they be now," said Sam Lawson, "jest as I told you."

"Please go round to the back door," said a childish voice; "this is locked, and I can't open it."

We all immediately followed Sam Lawson, who took enormous strides over the shrubbery, and soon I saw the vision of a curly-headed, blue-eyed boy holding open the side door of the house.

I ran up to him. "Are you Harvey?" I said.

"No," he answered; "my name is n't Harvey, it 's Harry; and this is my sister Tina,"—and immediately a pair of dark eyes looked out over his shoulder.

"Well, we 've come to take you to my grandmother's house," said I.

I don't know how it was, but I always spoke of our domestic establishment under the style and title of the female ruler. It was grandmother's house.

"I am glad of it," said the boy, "for we have tried two or three times to find our way to Oldtown, and got lost in the woods and had to come back here again."

Here the female partner in the concern stepped a little forward, eager for her share in the conversation. "Do you know old Sol?" she said.

"Lordy massy, I do," said Sam Lawson, quite delighted at this verification of the identity of the children. "Yes, I see him only day afore yesterday, and he was 'quirin' arter you, and we thought we 'd find you over in this 'ere house, 'cause I 'd seen smoke a comin' out o' the chimblies. Had a putty good time in the old house, I reckon. Ben all over it pretty much, hain't ye?"

"O yes," said Tina; "and it 's such a strange old place,—a great big house with ever so many rooms in it!"

"Wal, we 'll jest go over it, being as we 're here," said Sam; and into it we all went.

Now there was nothing in the world that little Miss Tina took more native delight in than in playing the hostess. To entertain was her dearest instinct, and she hastened with all speed to open before us all in the old mansion that her own rummaging and investigating talents had brought to light, chattering meanwhile with the spirit of a bobolink.

"You don't know," she said to Sam Lawson, "what a curious little closet there is in here, with book-cases and drawers, and a looking-glass in the door, with a curtain over it."

"Want to know?" said Sam. "Wal, that 'ere does beat all. It 's some of them old English folks's grander, I s'pose."

"And here 's a picture of such a beautiful lady, that always looks at you, whichever way you go,—just see."

"Lordy massy, so 't does. Wal, now, them drawers, mebbe, have got curous things in 'em," suggested Sam.

"O yes, but Harry never would let me look in them. I tried, though, once, when Harry was gone; but, if you 'll believe me, they 're all locked."

"Want to know?" said Sam. "That 'ere 's a kind o' pity, now."

"Would *you* open them? You would n't, would you?" said the little one, turning suddenly round and opening her great wide eyes full on him. "Harry said the place was n't ours, and it would n't be proper."

"Wal, he 's a nice boy; quite right in him. Little folks must n't touch things that ain't theirn," said Sam, who was strong on the moralities; though, after all, when all the rest had left the apartment, I looked back and saw him giving a sly tweak to the drawers of the cabinet on his own individual account.

"I was just a makin' sure, you know, that 't was all safe," he said, as he caught my eye, and saw that he was discovered.

Sam revelled and expatiated, however, in the information that lay before him in the exploration of the house. No tourist with Murray's guide-book in hand, and with travels to prepare for publication, ever went more patiently through the doing of a place. Not a door was left closed that could be opened; not a passage unexplored. Sam's head came out dusty and cobwebby between the beams of the ghostly old garret, where mouldy relics of antique furniture were reposing, and disappeared into the gloom of the spacious cellars, where the light was as darkness. He found none of the marks of the traditional haunted room; but he prolonged the search till there seemed a prospect that poor Uncle Eliakim would have to get him away by physical force, if we meant to get home in time for supper.

"Mr. Lawson, you don't seem to remember we have n't any of us had a morsel of dinner, and the sun is actually going down. The folks 'll be concerned about us. Come, let 's take the children and be off."

And so we mounted briskly into the wagon, and the old horse, vividly impressed with the idea of barn and hay at the end of his toils, seconded the vigorous exertions of Uncle Fly, and we rattled and spun on our homeward career, and arrived at the farm-house a little after moonrise.

XVIII.

Tina's Adoption

DURING the time of our journey to the enchanted ground, my Aunt Lois, being a woman of business, who always knew precisely what she was about, had contrived not only to finish meritoriously her household tasks, and to supplement Uncle Eliakim's forgetful benevolence, but also to make a call on Miss Mehitable Rossiter, for the sake of unburdening to her her oppressed heart. For Miss Mehitable bore in our family circle the repute of being a woman of counsel and sound wisdom. The savor of ministerial stock being yet strong about her, she was much resorted to for advice in difficult cases.

"I don't object, of course, to doing for the poor and orphaned, and all that," said Aunt Lois, quite sensibly; "but I like to see folks seem to know what they are doing, and where they are going, and not pitch and tumble into things without asking what 's to come of them. Now, we 'd just got Susy and the two boys on our hands, and here will come along a couple more children to-night; and I must say I don't see what 's to be done with them."

"It 's a pity you don't take snuff," said Miss Mehitable, with a whimsical grimace. "Now, when I come to any of the cross-places of life, where the road is n't very clear, I just take a pinch of snuff and wait; but as you don't, just stay and get a cup of tea with me, in a quiet, Christian way, and after it we will walk round to your mother's and look at these children."

Aunt Lois was soothed in her perturbed spirit by this proposition; and it was owing to this that, when we arrived at home, long after dark, we found Miss Mehitable in the circle around the blazing kitchen fire. The table was still standing, with ample preparations for an evening meal,—a hot smoking loaf of rye-and-Indian bread, and a great platter of cold boiled beef and pork, garnished with cold potatoes and turnips, the sight of which, to a party who had had no dinner all day, was most appetizing.

My grandmother's reception of the children was as motherly as if they had been of her own blood. In fact, their beauty and evident gentle breeding won for them immediate favor in all eyes.

The whole party sat down to the table, and, after a long and somewhat scattering grace, pronounced by Uncle Eliakim, fell to with a most amazing appearance of enjoyment. Sam's face waxed luminous as he buttered great blocks of smoking brown bread with the fruits of my grandmother's morning churning, and refreshed himself by long and hearty pulls at the cider-mug.

"I tell *you*," he said, "when folks hes been a ridin' on an empty stomach ever since breakfast, victuals is victuals; we learn how to be thankful for 'em; so I 'll take another slice o' that 'ere beef, and one or two more cold potatoes, and the vinegar, Mr. Sheril. Wal, chillen, this ere 's better than bein' alone in that 'ere old house, ain't it?"

"Yes, indeed," piped Tina; "I had begun to be quite discouraged. We tried and tried to find our way to Oldtown, and always got lost in the woods." Seeing that this remark elicited sympathy in the listeners, she added, "I was afraid we should die there, and the robins would have to cover us up, like some children papa used to tell about."

"Poor babes! just hear 'em," said my grandmother, who seemed scarcely able to restrain herself from falling on the necks of the children, in the ardor of her motherly kindness, while she doubled up an imaginary fist at Miss Asphyxia Smith, and longed to give her a piece of her mind touching her treatment of them.

Harry remained modestly silent; but he and I sat together, and our eyes met every now and then with that quiet amity to which I had been accustomed in my spiritual friend. I felt a cleaving of spirit to him that I had never felt towards any human being before,—a certainty that something had come to me in him that I had always been wanting,—and I was too glad for speech.

He was one of those children who retreat into themselves and make a shield of quietness and silence in the presence of many people, while Tina, on the other hand, was electrically excited, waxed brilliant in color, and rattled and chattered with as fearless confidence as a cat-bird.

"Come hither to me, little maiden," said Miss Mehitable, with a whimsical air of authority, when the child had done her supper. Tina came to her knee, and looked up into the dusky, homely face, in that still, earnest fashion in which children seem to study older people.

"Well, how do you like me?" said Miss Mehitable, when this silent survey had lasted an appreciable time.

The child still considered attentively, looking long into the great, honest, open eyes, and then her face suddenly rippled and dimpled all over like a brook when a sunbeam strikes it. "I do like you. I think you are good," she said, putting out her hands impulsively.

"Then up you come," said Miss Mehitable, lifting her into her lap. "It 's well you like me, because, for aught you know, I may be an old fairy; and if I did n't like you, I might turn you into a mouse or a cricket. Now how would you like that?"

"You could n't do it," said Tina, laughing.

"How do you know I could n't?"

"Well, if you did turn me into a mouse, I 'd gnaw your knitting-work," said Tina, laying hold of Miss Mehitable's knitting. "You 'd be glad to turn me back again."

"Heyday! I must take care how I make a mouse of you, I see. Perhaps I 'll make you into a kitten."

"Well, I 'd like to be a kitten, if you 'll keep a ball for me to play with, and give me plenty of milk," said Tina, to whom no proposition seemed to be without possible advantages.

"Will you go home and live with me, and be my kitten?"

Tina had often heard her brother speak of finding a good woman who should take care of her; and her face immediately became grave at this proposal. She seemed to study Miss Mehitable in a new way. "Where do you live?" she said.

"O, my house is only a little way from here."

"And may Harry come to see me?"

"Certainly he may."

"Do you want me to work for you all the time?" said Tina; "because," she added, in a low voice, "I like to play sometimes, and Miss Asphyxia said that was wicked."

"Did n't I tell you I wanted you for my little white kitten," said Miss Mehitable, with an odd twinkle. "What work do you suppose kittens do?"

"Must I grow up and catch rats?" said the child.

"Certainly you will be likely to," said Miss Mehitable, solemnly. "I shall pity the poor rats when you are grown up."

Tina looked in the humorous, twinkling old face with a gleam of mischievous comprehension, and, throwing her arms around Miss Mehitable, said, "Yes, I like you, and I will be your kitten."

There was a sudden, almost convulsive pressure of the little one to the kind old breast, and Miss Mehitable's face wore a strange expression, that looked like the smothered pang of some great anguish blended with a peculiar tenderness. One versed in the reading of spiritual histories might have seen that, at that moment, some inner door of that old heart opened, not without a grating of pain, to give a refuge to the little orphan; but opened it was, and a silent inner act of adoption had gone forth. Miss Mehitable beckoned my grandmother and Aunt Lois into a corner of the fireplace by themselves, while Sam Lawson was entertaining the rest of the circle by reciting the narrative of our day's explorations.

"Now I suppose I'm about as fit to undertake to bring up a child as the old Dragon of Wantley," said Miss Mehitable; "but as you seem to have a surplus on your hands, I'm willing to take the girl and do what I can for her."

"Dear Miss Mehitable, what a mercy it'll be to her!" said my grandmother and Aunt Lois, simultaneously;—"if you feel that you can afford it," added Aunt Lois, considerately.

"Well, the fowls of the air and the lilies of the field are taken care of somehow, as we are informed," said Miss Mehitable. "My basket and store are not much to ask a blessing on, but I have a sort of impression that an orphan child will make it none the less likely to hold out."

"There'll always be a handful of meal in the barrel and a little oil in the cruse for you, I'm sure," said my grandmother; "the word of the Lord stands sure for that."

A sad shadow fell over Miss Mehitable's face at these words, and then the usual expression of quaint humor stole over it. "It's to be hoped that Polly will take the same view of the subject that you appear to," said she. "My authority over Polly is, you know, of an extremely nominal kind."

"Still," said my grandmother, "you must be mistress in your own house. Polly, I am sure, knows her duty to you."

"Polly's idea of allegiance is very much like that of the old Spanish nobles to their king; it used to run somewhat thus: 'We, who are every way as good as you are, promise obedience to your government if you maintain our rights and liberties, but if not, not.' Now Polly's ideas of 'rights and liberties' are of a very set and particular nature, and I have found her generally disposed to make a good fight for them. Still, after all," she added, "the poor old thing loves me, and I think will be willing to indulge me in having a doll, if I really am set upon it. The only way I can carry my point with Polly is, to come down on her with a perfect avalanche of certainty, and so I have passed my word to you that I will be responsible for this child. Polly may scold and fret for a fortnight; but she is too good a Puritan to question whether people shall keep their promises. Polly abhors covenant-breaking with all her soul, and so in the end she will have to help me through."

"It's a pretty child," said my grandmother, "and an engaging one, and Polly may come to liking her."

"There's no saying," said Miss Mehitable. "You never know what you may find in the odd corners of an old maid's heart, when you fairly look into them. There are often unused hoards of maternal affection enough to set up an orphan-asylum; but it's like iron filings and a magnet, — you must try them with a live child, and if there is anything in 'em you find it out. That little object," she said, looking over her shoulder at Tina, "made an instant commotion in the dust and rubbish of my forlorn old garret, and brought to light a deal that I thought had gone to the moles and the bats long ago. She will do me good, I can feel, with her little pertnesses and her airs and fancies. If you could know how chilly and lonesome an old house gets sometimes, particularly in autumn, when the equinoctial storm is brewing! A lively child is a godsend, even if she turns the whole house topsy-turvy."

"Well, a child can't always be a plaything," said Aunt Lois; "it's a solemn and awful responsibility."

"And if I don't take it, who will?" said Miss Mehitable,

gravely. "If a better one would, I would n't. I 've no great confidence in myself. I profess no skill in human cobbling. I can only give house-room and shelter and love, and let come what will come. 'A man cannot escape what is written on his forehead,' the Turkish proverb says, and this poor child's history is all forewritten."

"The Lord will bless you for your goodness to the orphan," said my grandmother.

"I don't know about its being goodness. I take a fancy to her. I hunger for the child. There 's no merit in wanting your bit of cake, and maybe taking it when it is n't good for you; but let 's hope all 's well that ends well. Since I have fairly claimed her for mine, I begin to feel a fierce right of property in her, and you 'd see me fighting like an old hen with anybody that should try to get her away from me. You 'll see me made an old fool of by her smart little ways and speeches; and I already am proud of her beauty. Did you ever see a brighter little minx?"

We looked across to the other end of the fireplace, where Miss Tina sat perched, with great contentment, on Sam Lawson's knee, listening with wide-open eyes to the accounts he was giving of the haunted house. The beautiful hair that Miss Asphyxia had cut so close had grown with each day, till now it stood up in half rings of reddish gold, through which the fire shone with a dancing light; and her great eyes seemed to radiate brightness from as many points as a diamond.

"Depend upon it, those children are of good blood," said Miss Mehitable, decisively. "You 'll never make me believe that they will not be found to belong in some way to some reputable stock."

"Well, we know nothing about their parents," said my grandmother, "except what we heard second-hand through Sam Lawson. It was a wandering woman, sick and a stranger, who was taken down and died in Old Crab Smith's house, over in Needmore."

"One can tell, by the child's manner of speaking, that she has been brought up among educated people," said Miss Mehitable. "She is no little rustic. The boy, too, looks of the fine clay of the earth. But it 's time for me to take little Miss Rattlebrain home with me, and get her into bed. Sleep is a gracious state for children, and the first step in my new duties is a plain one." So saying, Miss Mehitable rose, and, stepping over to the other side of the fireplace, tapped Tina lightly on the shoulder. "Come, Pussy," she said, "get your bonnet, and we will go home."

Harry, who had watched all the movements between Miss Mehitable and his sister with intense interest, now stepped forward, blushing very much, but still with a quaint little old-fashioned air of manliness. "Is my sister going to live with you?"

"So we have agreed, my little man," said Miss Mehitable. "I hope you have no objection?"

"Will you let me come and see her sometimes?"

"Certainly; you will always be quite welcome."

"I want to see her sometimes, because my mother left her under my care. I sha' n't have a great deal of time to come in the daytime, because I must work for my living," he said, "but a little while sometimes at night, if you would let me."

"And what do you work at?" said Miss Mehitable, surveying the delicate boy with an air of some amusement.

"I used to pick up potatoes, and fodder the cattle, and do a great many things; and I am growing stronger every day, and by and by can do a great deal more."

"Well said, sonny," said my grandfather, laying his hand on Harry's head. "You speak like a smart boy. We can have you down to help tend sawmill."

"I wonder how many more boys will be wanted to help tend sawmill," said Aunt Lois.

"Well, good night, all," said Miss Mehitable, starting to go home.

Tina, however, stopped and left her side, and threw her arms round Harry's neck and kissed him. "Good night now. You 'll come and see me to-morrow," she said.

"May I come too?" I said, almost before I thought.

"O, certainly, do come," said Tina, with that warm, earnest light in her eyes which seemed the very soul of hospitality. "*She* 'll like to have you, I know."

"The child is taking possession of the situation at once," said Miss Mehitable. "Well, Brighteyes, you may come too," she added, to me. "A precious row there will be among the

old books when you all get together there";—and Miss Mehitable with the gay, tripping figure by her side, left the room.

"Is this great, big, dark house yours?" said the child, as they
came under the shadow of a dense thicket of syringas and
lilacs that overhung the front of the house.

"Yes, this is Doubting Castle," said Miss Mehitable.

"And does Giant Despair live here?" said Tina. "Mamma
showed me a picture of him once in a book."

"Well, he has tried many times to take possession," said
Miss Mehitable, "but I do what I can to keep him out, and
you must help me."

Saying this she opened the door of a large, old-fashioned
room, that appeared to have served both the purposes of a
study and parlor. It was revealed to view by the dusky, uncertain glimmer of a wood fire that had burned almost down on
a pair of tall brass andirons. The sides of the room were filled
to the ceiling with book-cases full of books. Some dark portraits of men and women were duskily revealed by the flickering light, as well as a wide, ample-bosomed chintz sofa and
a great chintz-covered easy-chair. A table draped with a green
cloth stood in a corner by the fire, strewn over with books
and writing-materials, and sustaining a large work-basket.

"How dark it is!" said the child.

Miss Mehitable took a burning splinter of the wood, and
lighted a candle in a tall, plated candlestick, that stood on the
high, narrow mantel-piece over the fireplace. At this moment
a side door opened, and a large-boned woman, dressed in a
homespun stuff petticoat, with a short, loose sack of the same
material, appeared at the door. Her face was freckled; her
hair, of a carroty-yellow, was plastered closely to her head and
secured by a horn comb; her eyes were so sharp and searching, that, as she fixed them on Tina, she blinked involuntarily.
Around her neck she wore a large string of gold beads, the
brilliant gleam of which, catching the firelight, revealed itself
at once to Tina's eye, and caused her to regard the woman
with curiosity.

She appeared to have opened the door with an intention of
asking a question; but stopped and surveyed the child with a
sharp expression of not very well-pleased astonishment. "I
thought you spoke to me," she said, at last, to Miss Mehitable.

"You may warm my bed now, Polly," said Miss Mehitable; "I shall be ready to go up in a few moments."

Polly stood a moment more, as if awaiting some communication about the child; but as Miss Mehitable turned away, and appeared to be busying herself about the fire, Polly gave a sudden windy dart from the room, and closed the door with a bang that made the window-casings rattle.

"Why, what did she do that for?" said Tina.

"O, it 's Polly's way; she does everything with all her might," said Miss Mehitable.

"Don't she like *me*?" said the child.

"Probably not. She knows nothing about you, and she does not like new things."

"But won't she *ever* like me?" persisted Tina.

"*That,* my dear, will depend in a great degree on yourself. If she sees that you are good and behave well, she will probably end by liking you; but old people like her are afraid that children will meddle with their things, and get them out of place."

"I mean to be good," said Tina, resolutely. "When I lived with Miss Asphyxia, I wanted to be bad, I tried to be bad; but now I am changed. I mean to be good, because you are good to me," and the child laid her head confidingly in Miss Mehitable's lap.

The dearest of all flattery to the old and uncomely is this caressing, confiding love of childhood, and Miss Mehitable felt a glow of pleasure about her dusky old heart at which she really wondered. "Can anything so fair really love *me*?" she asked herself. Alas! how much of this cheap-bought happiness goes to waste daily! While unclaimed children grow up loveless, men and women wither in lonely, craving solitude.

Polly again appeared at the door. "Your bed 's all warm, and you 'd better go right up, else what 's the use of warming it?"

"Yes, I 'll come immediately," said Miss Mehitable, endeavoring steadfastly to look as if she did not see Polly's looks, and to act as if there had of course always been a little girl to sleep with her.

"Come, my little one." *My* little one! Miss Mehitable's heart gave a great throb at this possessive pronoun. It all seemed as strange to her as a dream. A few hours ago, and she sat in the old windy, lonesome house, alone with the memories of dead friends, and feeling herself walking to the grave in a dismal solitude. Suddenly she awoke as from a dark dream, and found herself sole possessor of beauty, youth, and love, in a glowing little form, all her own, with no mortal to dispute it. She had a mother's right in a child. She might have a daughter's love. The whole house seemed changed. The dreary, lonesome great hall, with its tall, solemn-ticking clock, the wide, echoing staircase, up which Miss Mehitable had crept, shivering and alone, so many sad nights, now gave back the chirpings of Tina's rattling gayety and the silvery echoes of her laugh, as, happy in her new lot, she danced up the stairway, stopping to ask eager questions on this and that, as anything struck her fancy. For Miss Tina had one of those buoyant, believing natures, born to ride always on the very top crest of every wave,—one fully disposed to accept of good fortune in all its length and breadth, and to make the most of it at once.

"This is *our* home," she said, "is n't it?"

"Yes, darling," said Miss Mehitable, catching her in her arms fondly; "it is *our* home; we will have good times here together."

Tina threw her arms around Miss Mehitable's neck and kissed her. "I 'm so glad! Harry said that God would find us a home as soon as it was best, and now here it comes."

Miss Mehitable set the child down by the side of a great dark wooden bedstead, with tall, carved posts, draped with curious curtains of India linen, where strange Oriental plants and birds, and quaint pagodas and figures in turbans, were all mingled together, like the phantasms in a dream. Then going to a tall chest of drawers, resplendent with many brass handles, which reached almost to the ceiling, she took a bunch of keys from her pocket and unlocked a drawer. A spasm as of pain passed over her face as she opened it, and her hands trembled with some suppressed emotion as she took up and laid down various articles, searching for something. At last she found what she wanted, and shook it out. It was a child's nightgown, of just the size needed by Tina. It was yellow with age, but made with dainty care. She sat down by the child and began a movement towards undressing her.

"Shall I say my prayers to you," said Tina, "before I go to bed?"

"Certainly," said Miss Mehitable; "by all means."

"They are rather long," said the child, apologetically,— "that is, if I say all that Harry does. Harry said mamma wanted us to say them all every night. It takes some time."

"O, by all means say all," said Miss Mehitable.

Tina kneeled down by her and put her hands in hers, and said the Lord's Prayer, and the psalm, "The Lord is my shepherd." She had a natural turn for elocution, this little one, and spoke her words with a grace and an apparent understanding not ordinary in childhood.

"There 's a hymn, besides," she said. "It belongs to the prayer."

"Well, let us have that," said Miss Mehitable.

Tina repeated,—

> "One there is above all others
>   Well deserves the name of Friend;
> His is love beyond a brother's,
>   Costly, free, and knows no end."

She had an earnest, half-heroic way of repeating, and as she gazed into her listener's eyes she perceived, by a subtile instinct, that what she was saying affected her deeply. She stopped, wondering.

"Go on, my love," said Miss Mehitable.

Tina continued, with enthusiasm, feeling that she was making an impression on her auditor:—

> "Which of all our friends, to save us,
>   Could or would have shed his blood?
> But the Saviour died to have us
>   Reconciled in him to God.

> "When he lived on earth abaséd,
>   Friend of sinners was his name;
> Now, above all glory raiséd,
>   He rejoiceth in the same."

"O my child, where did you learn that hymn?" said Miss Mehitable, to whom the words were new. Simple and homely as they were, they had struck on some inner nerve, which was vibrating with intense feeling. Tears were standing in her eyes.

"It was mamma's hymn," said Tina. "She always used to say it. There is one more verse," she added.

> "O for grace our hearts to soften!
>   Teach us, Lord, at length to love;
>   We, alas! forget too often
>   What a Friend we have above."

"Is that the secret of all earthly sorrow, then?" said Miss Mehitable aloud, in involuntary soliloquy. The sound of her own voice seemed to startle her. She sighed deeply, and kissed the child. "Thank you, my darling. It does me good to hear you," she said.

The child had entered so earnestly, so passionately even, into the spirit of the words she had been repeating, that she seemed to Miss Mehitable to be transfigured into an angel messenger, sent to inspire faith in God's love in a darkened, despairing soul. She put her into bed; but Tina immediately asserted her claim to an earthly nature by stretching herself exultingly in the warm bed, with an exclamation of vivid pleasure.

"How different this seems from my cold old bed at Miss Asphyxia's!" she said. "O, that horrid woman! how I *hate* her!" she added, with a scowl and a frown, which made the angelhood of the child more than questionable.

Miss Mehitable's vision melted. It was not a child of heaven, but a little mortal sinner, that she was tucking up for the night; and she felt constrained to essay her first effort at moral training.

"My dear," she said, "did you not say, to-night, 'Forgive us our trespasses, *as* we forgive those who trespass against us'? Do you know what that means?"

"O yes," said Tina, readily.

"Well, if your Heavenly Father should forgive your sins just *as* you forgive Miss Asphyxia, how would you like that?"

There was a silence. The large bright eyes grew round and reflective, as they peered out from between the sheets and the pillow. At last she said, in a modified voice: "Well, I won't hate her any more. But," she added, with increased vivacity, "I may think she's hateful, may n't I?"

Is there ever a hard question in morals that children do not drive straight at, in their wide-eyed questioning?

Miss Mehitable felt inclined to laugh, but said, gravely: "I would n't advise you to think evil about her. Perhaps she is a poor woman that never had any one to love her, or anything to love, and it has made her hard."

Tina looked at Miss Mehitable earnestly, as if she were pondering the remark. "She told me that she was put to work younger than I was," she said, "and kept at it all the time."

"And perhaps, if you had been kept at work all your life in that hard way, you would have grown up to be just like her."

"Well, then, I 'm sorry for her," said Tina. "There 's nobody loves her, that' s a fact. Nobody can love her, unless it 's God. He loves every one, Harry says."

"Well, good night, my darling," said Miss Mehitable, kissing her. "I shall come to bed pretty soon. I will leave you a candle," she added; "because this is a strange place."

"How good you are!" said Tina. "I used to be so afraid in the dark, at Miss Asphyxia's; and I was so wicked all day, that I was afraid of God too, at night. I used sometimes to think I heard something chewing under my bed; and I thought it was a wolf, and would eat me up."

"Poor little darling!" said Miss Mehitable. "Would you rather I sat by you till you went to sleep?"

"No, thank you; I don't like to trouble you," said the child. "If you leave a candle I sha' n't be afraid. And, besides, I 've said my prayers now. I did n't use to say them one bit at Miss Asphyxia's. She would tell me to say my prayers, and then bang the door so hard, and I would feel cross, and think I would n't. But I am better now, because you love me."

Miss Mehitable returned to the parlor, and sat down to ponder over her fire; and the result of her ponderings shall be given in a letter which she immediately began writing at the green-covered table.

XIX.

Miss Mehitable's Letter, and the Reply, Giving Further Hints of the Story

M Y DEAR BROTHER:—Since I wrote you last, so strange a change has taken place in my life that even now I walk about as in a dream, and hardly know myself. The events of a few hours have made everything in the world seem to me as different from what it ever seemed before as death is from life.

Not to keep you waiting, after so solemn a preface, I will announce to you first, briefly, what it is, and then, secondly, how it happened.

Well, then, *I have adopted a child*, in my dry and wilted old age. She is a beautiful and engaging little creature, full of life and spirits,—full of warm affections,—thrown an absolute waif and stray on the sands of life. Her mother was an unknown Englishwoman,—probably some relict of the retired English army. She died in great destitution, in the neighboring town of Needmore, leaving on the world two singularly interesting children, a boy and a girl. They were, of course, taken in charge by the parish, and fell to the lot of old Crab Smith and his sister, Miss Asphyxia,—just think of it! I think I need say no more than this about their lot.

In a short time they ran away from cruel treatment; lived in a desolate little housekeeping way in the old Dench house; till finally Sam Lawson, lounging about in his general and universal way, picked them up. He brought them, of course, where every wandering, distressed thing comes,—to Deacon Badger's.

Now I suppose the Deacon is comfortably off in the world, as our New England farmers go, but his ability to maintain general charges of housekeeping for all mankind may seriously be doubted. Lois Badger, who does the work of Martha in that establishment, came over to me, yesterday afternoon, quite distressed in her mind about it. Lois is a worthy creature,—rather sharp, to be sure, but, when her edge is turned the right way, none the worse for that,—and really I thought she had the right of it, to some extent.

People in general are so resigned to have other folks made burnt sacrifices, that it did not appear to me probable that there was a creature in Oldtown who would do anything more than rejoice that Deacon Badger felt able to take the children. After I had made some rather bitter reflections on the world, and its selfishness, in the style that we all practise, the thought suddenly occurred to me, What do you, more than others? and that idea, together with the beauty and charms of the poor little waif, decided me to take this bold step. I shut my eyes, and took it,—not without quaking in my shoes for fear of Polly; but I have carried my point in her very face, without so much as saying by your leave.

The little one has just been taken up stairs and tucked up warmly in my own bed, with one of our poor little Emily's old nightgowns on. They fit her exactly, and I exult over her as one that findeth great spoil.

Polly has not yet declared herself, except by slamming the door very hard when she first made the discovery of the child's presence in the house. I presume there is an equinoctial gale gathering, but I say nothing; for, after all, Polly is a good creature, and will blow herself round into the right quarter, in time, as our northeast rain-storms generally do. People always accommodate themselves to certainties.

I cannot but regard the coming of this child to me at this time as a messenger of mercy from God, to save me from sinking into utter despair. I have been so lonely, so miserable, so utterly, inexpressibly wretched of late, that it has seemed that, if something did not happen to help me, I must lose my reason. Our family disposition to melancholy is a hard enough thing to manage under the most prosperous circumstances. I remember my father's paroxysms of gloom: they used to frighten me when I was a little girl, and laid a heavy burden on the heart of our dear angel mother. Whatever that curse is, we all inherit it. In the heart of every one of us children there is that fearful *black drop*, like that which the Koran says the angel showed to Mahomet. It is an inexplicable something which always predisposes us to sadness, but in which any real, appreciable sorrow strikes a terribly deep and long root. Shakespeare describes this thing, as he does everything else:—

> "In sooth, I know not why I am so sad:
> It wearies me,—you say it wearies you;
> But how I caught it, found it, or came by it,
> What stuff 't is made of, whereof it is born,
> I am to learn."

You have struggled with it by the most rational means,—an active out-of-door life, by sea voyages and severe manual labor. A *man* can fight this dragon as a woman cannot. We women are helpless,—tied to places, forms, and rules,—chained to our stake. We must meet him as we can.

Of late I have not been able to sleep, and, lying awake all night long in darkness and misery, have asked, if *this* be life, whether an immortal existence is not a curse to be feared, rather than a blessing to be hoped, and if the wretchedness we fear in the eternal world can be worse than what we sometimes suffer now,—such sinking of heart, such helplessness of fear, such a vain calling for help that never comes. Well, I will not live it over again, for I dare say you know it all too well. I think I finally wore myself out in trying to cheer poor brother Theodore's darksome way down to death. Can you wonder that he would take opium? God alone can judge people that suffer as he did, and, let people say what they please, I must, I will, think that God has some pity for the work of his hands.

Now, brother, I must, I will, write to you about Emily; though you have said you never wished to hear her name again. What right had you, her brother, to give her up so, and to let the whole burden of this dreadful mystery and sorrow come down on me alone? You are not certain that she has gone astray in the worst sense that a woman can. We only know that she has broken away from us and gone,—but where, how, and with whom, you cannot say, nor I. And certainly there was great excuse for her. Consider how the peculiar temperament and constitution of our family wrought upon her. Consider the temptations of her wonderful beauty, her highly nervous, wildly excitable organization. Her genius was extraordinary; her strength and vigor of character quite as much so. Altogether, she was a perilously constituted human being,—and what did we do with her? A good, common girl might have been put with Uncle and Aunt Farnsworth with great advantage. We put her there for the simple reason that they were her aunt and uncle, and had money enough to educate her. But in all other respects they were about the most unsuited that could be conceived. I must say that I think that glacial, gloomy, religious training in Uncle Farnsworth's family was, for her, peculiarly unfortunate. She sat from Sunday to Sunday under Dr. Stern's preaching. With a high-keyed, acute mind, she could not help listening and thinking; and such thinking is unfortunate, to say the least.

It always seemed to me that he was one of those who experiment on the immortal soul as daring doctors experiment on the body,—using the most violent and terrible remedies, —remedies that must kill or cure. His theory was, that a secret enemy to God was lying latent in every soul, which, like some virulent poisons in the body, could only be expelled by being brought to the surface; and he had sermon after sermon, whose only object appeared to be to bring into vivid consciousness what he calls the natural opposition of the human heart.

But, alas! in some cases the enmity thus aroused can never be subdued; and Emily's was a nature that would break before it would bow. Nothing could have subdued her but love,—and love she never heard. These appalling doctrines were presented with such logical clearness, and apparently so established from the Scriptures, that, unable to distinguish between the word of God and the cruel deductions of human logic, she trod both under foot in defiant despair. Then came in the French literature, which is so fascinating, and which just now is having so wide an influence on the thinking of our country. Rousseau and Voltaire charmed her, and took her into a new world. She has probably gone to France for liberty, with no protection but her own virgin nature. Are we at once to infer the worst, when we know so little? I, for one, shall love her and trust in her to the end; and if ever she should fall, and do things that I and all the world must condemn, I shall still say, that it will be less her fault than that of others; that she will be one of those who fall by their higher, rather than their lower nature.

I have a prophetic instinct in my heart that some day, poor, forlorn, and forsaken, she will look back with regret to the old house where she was born: and then she shall be welcome here. This is why I keep this solitary old place, full of bitter and ghostly memories; because, as long as I keep it, there is one refuge that Emily may call her own, and one heart that will be true to her, and love her and believe in her to the end.

I think God has been merciful to me in sending me this child, to be to me as a daughter. Already her coming has been made a means of working in me that great moral change for which all my life I have been blindly seeking. I have sought that *conversion* which our father taught us to expect as alchemists seek the philosopher's stone.

What have I not read and suffered at the hands of the theologians? How many lonely hours, day after day, have I bent the knee in fruitless prayer that God would grant me this great, unknown grace! for without it how dreary is life!

We are in ourselves so utterly helpless,—life is so hard, so inexplicable, that we stand in perishing need of some helping hand, some sensible, appreciable connection with God. And yet for years every cry of misery, every breath of anguish, has been choked by the logical proofs of theology;—that God is my enemy, or that I am his; that every effort I make toward Him but aggravates my offence; and that this unknown gift, which no child of Adam ever did compass of himself, is so completely in my own power, that I am every minute of my life to blame for not possessing it.

How many hours have I gone round and round this dreary track,—chilled, weary, shivering, seeing no light, and hearing no voice! But within this last hour it seems as if a divine ray had shone upon me, and the great gift had been given me by the hand of a little child. It came in the simplest and most unexpected manner, while listening to a very homely hymn, repeated by this dear little one. The words themselves were not much in the way of poetry; it was merely the simplest statement of the truth that in Jesus Christ, ever living, ever present, every human soul has a personal friend, divine and almighty.

This thought came over me with such power, that it seemed as if all my doubts, all my intricate, contradictory theologies, all those personal and family sorrows which had made a burden on my soul greater than poor Christian ever staggered under, had gone where his did, when, at the sight of the Cross, it loosed from his back and rolled down into the sepulchre, to be seen no more. Can it be, I asked myself, that this mighty love, that I feel so powerfully and so sweetly, has been near me all these dark, melancholy years? Has the sun been shining behind all these heavy clouds, under whose shadows I have spent my life?

When I laid my little Tina down to sleep to-night, I came down here to think over this strange, new thought,—that I, even I, in my joyless old age, my poverty, my perplexities, my loneliness, am no longer alone! I am beloved. There is One who does love me,—the One Friend, whose love, like the sunshine, can be the portion of each individual of the human race, without exhaustion. This is the great mystery of faith, which I am determined from this hour to keep whole and undefiled.

My dear brother, I have never before addressed to you a word on this subject. It has been one in which I saw only perplexity. I have, it is true, been grieved and disappointed that you did not see your way clear to embrace the sacred ministry, which has for so many generations been the appointed work of our family. I confess for many years I did hope to see you succeed, not only to the library, but to the work of our honored, venerated father and grandfather. It was my hope that, in this position, I should find in you a spiritual guide to resolve my doubts and lead me aright. But I have gathered from you at times, by chance words dropped, that you could not exactly accept the faith of our fathers. Perhaps difficulties like my own have withheld you. I know you too well to believe that the French scepticism that has blown over here with the breath of our political revolution can have had the least influence over you. Whatever your views of doctrines may be, you are not a doubter. You are not—as poor Emily defiantly called herself—a deist, an alien from all that our fathers came to this wilderness to maintain. Yet when I see you burying your talents in a lonely mountain village, satisfied with the work of a poor schoolmaster, instead of standing forth to lead our New England in the pulpit, I ask myself, Why is this?

Speak to me, brother! tell me your innermost thoughts, as I have told you mine. Is not life short and sad and bitter enough, that those who could help each other should neglect the few things they can do to make it tolerable? Why do we travel side by side, lonely and silent,—each, perhaps, hiding in that silence the bread of life that the other needs? Write to me as I have written to you, and let me know that I have a brother in soul, as I have in flesh.

Your affectionate sister,
M. R.

My dear Sister:—I have read your letter. Answer it justly and truly how can I? How little we know of each other in outside intimacy! but when we put our key into the door of the secret chamber, who does not tremble and draw back?—*that* is the true haunted chamber!

First, about Emily, I will own I am wrong. It is from no want of love, though, but from too much. I was and am too sore and bitter on that subject to trust myself. I have a heart full of curses, but don't know exactly where to fling them; and, for aught I see, we are utterly helpless. Every clew fails; and what is the use of torturing ourselves? It is a man's nature to act, to do, and, where nothing can be done, to forget. It is a woman's nature to hold on to what can only torture, and live all her despairs over. Women's tears are their meat; men find the diet too salt, and won't take it.

Tell me anything I can *do*, and I'll do it; but talk I cannot,—every word burns me. I admit every word you say of Emily. We were mistaken in letting her go to the Farnsworths, and be baited and tortured with ultra-Calvinism; but we were blind, as we mortals always are,—fated never to see what we should have done, till seeing is too late.

I am glad you have taken that child,—first, because it 's a good deed in itself, and, secondly, because it 's good for you. That it should have shed light on your relations to God is strictly philosophical. You have been trying to find your way

to Him by definitions and by logic; one might as well make
love to a lady by the first book of Euclid. "He that loveth not
his brother whom he hath seen, how can he love God whom
he hath not seen?" That throb of protecting, all-embracing
love which thrilled through your heart for this child taught
you more of God than father's whole library. "He that loveth
not knoweth not God." The old Bible is philosophical, and
eminent for its common sense. Of course this child will make
a fool of you. Never mind; the follies of love are remedial.

As to a system of education, it will be an amusement for
you to get that up. Every human being likes to undertake to
dictate for some other one. Go at it with good cheer. But,
whatever you do, don't teach her *French*. Give her a good
Saxon-English education; and, if she needs a pasture-land of
foreign languages, let her learn Latin, and, more than that,
Greek. Greek is the morning-land of languages, and has the
freshness of early dew in it which will never exhale.

The French helped us in our late war: for that I thank
them; but from French philosophy and French democracy,
may the good Lord deliver us. They slew their Puritans in the
massacre of St. Bartholomew, and the nation ever since has
been without a moral sense. French literature is like an eagle
with one broken wing. What the Puritans did for us English
people, in bringing in civil liberty, they lacked. Our revolutions have been gradual. I predict that theirs will come by and
by with an explosion.

Meanwhile, our young men who follow after French literature become rakes and profligates. Their first step in liberty
is to repeal the ten commandments, especially the seventh.
Therefore I consider a young woman in our day misses nothing who does not read French. Decorous French literature is
stupid, and bright French literature is too wicked for anything. So let French alone.

She threatens to be pretty, does she? So much the worse
for you and her. If she makes you too much trouble by and
by, send her up to my academy, and I will drill her, and make
a Spartan of her.

As to what you say about religion, and the ministry, and
the schoolmaster, what can I say on this sheet of paper?
Briefly then. No, I am *not* in any sense an unbeliever in the

old Bible; I would as soon disbelieve my own mother. And I am in my nature a thorough Puritan. I am a Puritan as thoroughly as a hound is a hound, and a pointer a pointer, whose pedigree of unmixed blood can be traced for generations back. I feel within me the preaching instinct, just as the hound snuffs, and the pointer points; but as to the pulpit in these days,—well, thereby hangs a tale.

What should I preach, supposing I were a minister, as my father, and grandfather, and great-grandfather were before me? What they preached was true to them, was fitted for their times, was loyally and sincerely said, and of course did a world of good. But when I look over their sermons, I put an interrogation point to almost everything they say; and what was true to them is not true to me; and if I should speak out as honestly as they did what *is* true to me, the world would not understand or receive it, and I think it would do more harm than good. I believe I am thinking ahead of the present generation, and if I should undertake to push my thoughts I should only bother people,—just as one of my bright boys in the latter part of the algebra sometimes worries a new beginner with his advanced explanations.

Then again, our late Revolution has wrought a change in the ministry that will soon become more and more apparent. The time when ministers were noblemen by divine right, and reigned over their parishes by the cocked hat and gold-headed cane, is passing away. Dr. Lothrop, and Dr. Stern, and a few others, keep up the prestige, but that sort of thing is going by; and in the next generation the minister will be nothing but a citizen; his words will come without prestige, and be examined and sifted just like the words of any other citizen.

There is a race of ministers rising up who are fully adequate to meet this exigency; and these men are going to throw Calvinism down into the arena, and discuss every inch of it, hand to hand and knee to knee, with the common people; and we shall see what will come of this.

I, for my part, am not prepared to be a minister on these terms. Still, as I said, I have the born instinct of preaching; I am dictatorial by nature, and one of those who need constantly to see themselves reflected in other people's eyes; and so I have got an academy here, up in the mountains, where I have a set of as clear, bright-eyed, bright-minded boys and girls as you would wish to see, and am in my way a pope. Well, I enjoy being a pope. It is one of my weaknesses.

As to society, we have the doctor,—a quiet little wrinkled old man, a profound disbeliever in medicines, who gives cream-of-tartar for ordinary cases, and camomile tea when the symptoms become desperate, and reads Greek for his own private amusement. Of course he does n't get very rich, but here in the mountains one can afford to be poor. One of our sunsets is worth half a Boston doctor's income.

Then there 's the lawyer and squire, who draws the deeds, and makes the wills, and settles the quarrels; and the minister, who belongs to the new dispensation. He and I are sworn friends; he is my Fidus Achates. His garden joins mine, and when I am hoeing my corn he is hoeing his, and thence comes talk. As it gets more eager I jump the fence and hoe in his garden, or he does the same to mine. We have a strife on the matter of garden craft, who shall with most skill outwit our Mother Nature, and get cantelopes and melons under circumstances in which she never intended them to grow. This year I beat the parson, but I can see that he is secretly resolved to revenge himself on me when the sweet corn comes in. One evening every week we devote to reading the newspaper and settling the affairs of the country. We are both stanch Federalists, and make the walls ring with our denunciations of Jacobinism and Democracy. Once a month we have the Columbian Magazine and the foreign news from Europe, and then we have a great deal on our hands; we go over affairs, every country systematically, and settle them for the month. In general we are pretty well agreed, but now and then our lines of policy differ, and then we fight it out with good courage, not sparing the adjectives. The parson has a sly humor of his own, and our noisiest discussions generally end in a hearty laugh.

So much for the man and friend,—now for the clergyman. He is neither the sentimental, good parson of Goldsmith, nor the plaintive, ascetic parish priest of Romanism, nor the cocked hat of the theocracy, but a lively, acute, full-blooded *man*, who does his duty on equal terms among men. He is as single-hearted as an unblemished crystal, and in some matters sacredly simple; but yet not without a thrifty practical shrewdness, both in things temporal and things spiritual. He has an income of about two hundred and fifty dollars, with his wood. The farmers about here consider him as rolling in wealth, and I must say that, though the parsonage is absolutely bare of luxuries, one is not there often unpleasantly reminded that the parson is a poor man. He has that golden faculty of enjoying the work he does so utterly, and believing in it so entirely, that he can quite afford to be poor. He whose daily work is in itself a pleasure ought not to ask for riches: so I tell myself about my school-keeping, and him about his parish. He takes up the conversion of sinners as an immediate practical business, to be done and done now; he preaches in all the little hills and dales and hollows and brown school-houses for miles around, and chases his sinners up and down so zealously, that they have, on the whole, a lively time of it. He attacks drinking and all our small forms of country immorality with a vigor sufficient to demolish sins of double their size, and gives nobody even a chance to sleep in meeting. The good farmers around here, some of whom would like to serve Mammon comfortably, are rather in a quandary what to do. They never would bear the constant hounding which he gives them, and the cannonades he fires at their pet sins, and the way he chases them from pillar to post, and the merciless manner in which he breaks in upon their comfortable old habit of sleeping in meeting, were it not that they feel that they are paying him an enormous salary, and ought to get their money's worth out of him, which they are certain they are doing most fully. Your Yankee has such a sense of values, that, if he pays a man to thrash him, he wants to be thrashed thoroughly.

My good friend preaches what they call New Divinity, by which I understand the Calvinism which our fathers left us, in the commencing process of disintegration. He is thoroughly and enthusiastically in earnest about it, and believes that the system, as far as Edwards and Hopkins have got it, is almost absolute truth; but, for all that, is cheerfully busy in making some little emendations and corrections, upon which he values himself, and which he thinks of the greatest consequence. What is to the credit of his heart is, that these emendations are generally in favor of some original-minded sheep who can't be got into the sheep-fold without some alteration in the paling. In these cases I have generally noticed that he will loosen a rail or tear off a picket, and let the sheep in, it being his impression, after all, that the sheep are worth more than the sheep-fold.

In his zeal to catch certain shy sinners, he has more than once preached sermons which his brethren about here find fault with, as wandering from old standards; and it costs abundance of bustle and ingenuity to arrange his system so as to provide for exceptional cases, and yet to leave it exactly what it was before the alterations were made.

It is, I believe, an admitted thing among theologians, that, while theology must go on improving from age to age, it must also remain exactly what it was a hundred years ago.

The parson is my intimate friend, and it is easy for me to see that he has designs for the good of my soul, for which I sincerely love him. I can see that he is lying in wait for me patiently, as sometimes we do for trout, when we go out fishing together. He reconnoitres me, approaches me carefully, makes nice little logical traps to catch me in, and baits them with very innocent-looking questions, which I, being an old theological rat, skilfully avoid answering.

My friend's forte is logic. Between you and me, if there is a golden calf worshipped in our sanctified New England, its name is Logic; and my good friend the parson burns incense before it with a most sacred innocence of intention. He believes that sinners can be converted by logic, and that, if he could once get me into one of these neat little traps aforesaid, the salvation of my soul would be assured. He has caught numbers of the shrewdest infidel foxes among the farmers around, and I must say that there is no trap for the Yankee like the logic-trap.

I must tell you a story about this that amused me greatly. You know everybody's religious opinions are a matter of discussion in our neighborhood, and Ezekiel Scranton, a rich farmer who lives up on the hill, enjoys the celebrity of being an atheist, and rather values himself on the distinction. It takes a man of courage, you know, to live without a God; and Ezekiel gives himself out as a plucky dog, and able to hold the parson at bay. The parson, however, had privately prepared a string of questions which he was quite sure would drive Ezekiel into strait quarters. So he meets him the other day in the store.

"How's this, Mr. Scranton? they tell me that you're an atheist!"

"Well I guess I be, Parson," says Ezekiel, comfortably.

"Well, Ezekiel, let's talk about this. You believe in your own existence, don't you?"

"No, I don't."

"What! not believe in your own existence?"

"No, I don't." Then, after a moment, "Tell you what, Parson, ain't a going to be twitched up by none o' your syllogisms."

Ezekiel was quite in the right of it; for I must do my friend the parson the justice to say, that, if you answer one of his simple-looking questions, you are gone. You must say B after saying A, and the whole alphabet after that.

For my part, I do not greatly disbelieve the main points of Calvinism. They strike me, as most hard and disagreeable things do, as quite likely to be true, and very much in accordance with a sensible man's observation of facts as they stand in life and nature. My doubts come up, like bats, from a dark and dreadful cavern that underlies all religion, natural or revealed. They are of a class abhorrent to myself, smothering to my peace, imbittering to my life.

What must he be who is tempted to deny the very right of his Creator to the allegiance of his creatures?—who is tempted to feel that his own conscious existence is an inflicted curse, and that the whole race of men have been a set of neglected, suffering children, bred like fish-spawn on a thousand shores, by a Being who has never interested himself to care for their welfare, to prevent their degradation, to interfere with their cruelties to each other, as they have writhed and wrangled into life, through life, and out of life again? Does this look like being a Father in any sense in which we poor mortals think of fatherhood? After seeing nature, can we reason against any of the harshest conclusions of Calvinism, from the character of its Author?

Do we not consider a man unworthy the name of a good

father who, from mere blind reproductive instinct, gives birth to children for whose improvement, virtue, and happiness he makes no provision? and yet does not this seem to be the way more than half of the human race actually comes into existence?

Then the laws of nature are an inextricable labyrinth,—puzzling, crossing, contradictory; and ages of wearisome study have as yet hardly made a portion of them clear enough for human comfort; and doctors and ministers go on torturing the body and the soul, with the most devout good intentions. And so forth, for there is no end to this sort of talk.

Now my friend the parson is the outgrowth of the New England theocracy, about the simplest, purest, and least objectionable state of society that the world ever saw. He has a good digestion, a healthy mind in a healthy body; he lives in a village where there is no pauperism, and hardly any crime,—where all the embarrassing, dreadful social problems and mysteries of life scarcely exist. But I, who have been tumbled up and down upon all the shores of earth, lived in India, China, and Polynesia, and seen the human race as they breed like vermin, in their filth and their contented degradation,—how can I think of applying the measurements of any theological system to a reality like this?

Now the parts of their system on which my dear friend the parson, and those of his school, specially value themselves, are their explanations of the reasons why evil was permitted, and their vindications of the Divine character in view of it. They are specially earnest and alert in giving out their views here, and the parson has read to me more than one sermon, hoping to medicate what he supposes to be my secret wound. To me their various theories are, as my friend the doctor once said to me, "putting their bitter pill in a chestnut-burr; the pill is bad,—there is no help for that,—but the chestnut-burr is impossible."

It is incredible, the ease and cheerfulness with which a man in his study, who never had so much experience of suffering as even a toothache would give him, can arrange a system in which the everlasting torture of millions is casually admitted as an item. But I, to whom, seriously speaking, existence has been for much of my life nothing but suffering, and who always looked on my existence as a misfortune, must necessarily feel reasonings of this kind in a different way. This soul-ache, this throb of pain, that seems as if it were an actual anguish of the immaterial part itself, is a dreadful teacher, and gives a fearful sense of what the chances of an immortal existence might be, and what the responsibilities of originating such existence.

I am not one of the shallow sort, who think that everything for everybody must or ought to end with perfect bliss at death. On the contrary, I do not see how anything but misery in eternal ages is to come from the outpouring into their abyss, of wrangling, undisciplined souls, who were a torment to themselves and others here, and who would make this world unbearable, were they not all swept off in their turn by the cobweb brush of Death.

So you see it's all a hopeless muddle to me. Do I then believe nothing? Yes, I believe in Jesus Christ with all my heart, all my might. He stands before me the one hopeful phenomenon of history. I adore him as Divine, or all of the Divine that I can comprehend; and when he bids me say to God, "Our Father which art in heaven," I smother all my doubts and say it. Those words are the rope thrown out to me, choking in the waters,—the voice from the awful silence. "God *so* loved the world that he gave his own Son." I try to believe that he *loves* this world, but I have got only so far as "Help thou mine unbelief."

Now, as to talking out all this to the parson, what good would it do? He is preaching well and working bravely. His preaching suits the state of advancement to which New England has come; and the process which he and ministers of his sort institute, of having every point in theology fully discussed by the common people, is not only a capital drill for their minds, but it will have its effect in the end on their theologies, and out of them all the truth of the future will arise.

So you see my position, and why I am niched here for life, as a schoolmaster. Come up and see me some time. I have a housekeeper who is as ugly as Hecate, but who reads Greek. She makes the best bread and cake in town, keeps my stockings mended and my shirt-ruffles plaited and my house like wax, and hears a class in Virgil every day, after she has "done

her dinner-dishes." I shall not fall in love with her, though.
Come some time to see me, and bring your new acquisition.

Your brother,

JONATHAN ROSSITER.

I have given these two letters as the best means of showing
to the reader the character of the family with whom my destiny and that of Tina became in future life curiously intertwisted.

Among the peculiarly English ideas which the Colonists
brought to Massachusetts, which all the wear and tear of democracy have not been able to obliterate, was that of *family*.
Family feeling, family pride, family hope and fear and desire,
were, in my early day, strongly-marked traits. Genealogy was
a thing at the tip of every person's tongue, and in every person's mind; and it is among my most vivid remembrances,
with what a solemn air of intense interest my mother, grandmother, Aunt Lois, and Aunt Keziah would enter into minute and discriminating particulars with regard to the stock,
intermarriages, and family settlements of the different persons
whose history was under their consideration. "Of a very respectable family," was a sentence so often repeated at the old
fireside that its influence went in part to make up my character. In our present days, when every man is emphatically the
son of his own deeds, and nobody cares who his mother or
grandmother or great-aunt was, there can scarcely be an understanding of this intense feeling of race and genealogy
which pervaded simple colonial Massachusetts.

As I have often before intimated, the aristocracy of Massachusetts consisted of two classes, the magistracy and the ministry; and these two, in this theocratic State, played into each
other's hands continually. Next to the magistrate and the
minister, in the esteem of that community, came the schoolmaster; for education might be said to be the ruling passion
of the State.

The history of old New England families is marked by
strong lights and deep shadows of personal peculiarity. We
appeal to almost every old settler in New England towns, if
he cannot remember stately old houses, inhabited by old families, whose histories might be brought to mind by that of

Miss Mehitable and her brother. There was in them a sort of intellectual vigor, a ceaseless activity of thought, a passion for reading and study, and a quiet brooding on the very deepest problems of mental and moral philosophy. The characteristic of such families is the greatly disproportioned force of the internal, intellectual, and spiritual life to the external one. Hence come often morbid and diseased forms of manifestation. The threads which connect such persons with the real life of the outer world are so fine and so weak, that they are constantly breaking and giving way here and there, so that, in such races, oddities and eccentricities are come to be accepted only as badges of family character. Yet from stock of this character have come some of the most brilliant and effective minds in New England; and from them also have come hermits and recluses,—peculiar and exceptional people,—people delightful to the student of human nature, but excessively puzzling to the every-day judgment of mere conventional society.

The Rossiter family had been one of these. It traced its origin to the colony which came out with Governor Winthrop. The eldest Rossiter had been one of the ejected ministers, and came from a good substantial family of the English gentry. For several successive generations there had never been wanting a son in the Rossiter family to succeed to the pulpit of his father. The Rossiters had been leaned on by the magistrates and consulted by the governors, and their word had been law down to the time of Miss Mehitable's father.

The tendency of the stately old families of New England to constitutional melancholy has been well set forth by Dr. Cotton Mather, that delightful old New England grandmother, whose nursery tales of its infancy and childhood may well be pondered by those who would fully understand its far-reaching maturity. As I have before remarked, I have high ideas of the wisdom of grandmothers, and therefore do our beloved gossip, Dr. Cotton Mather, the greatest possible compliment in granting him the title.

The ministers of the early colonial days of New England, though well-read, scholarly men, were more statesmen than theologians. Their minds ran upon the actual arrangements of society, which were in a great degree left in their hands, rather than on doctrinal and metaphysical subtilties. They took their confession of faith just as the great body of Protestant reformers left it, and acted upon it as a practical foundation, without much further discussion, until the time of President Edwards. He was the first man who began the disintegrating process of applying rationalistic methods to the accepted doctrines of religion, and he rationalized far more boldly and widely than any publishers of his biography have ever dared to let the world know. He sawed the great dam and let out the whole waters of discussion over all New England, and that free discussion led to all the shades of opinion of our modern days. Little as he thought it, yet Waldo Emerson and Theodore Parker were the last results of the current set in motion by Jonathan Edwards.

Miss Mehitable Rossiter's father, during the latter part of his life, had dipped into this belt of New Divinity, and been excessively and immoderately interested in certain speculations concerning them. All the last part of his life had been consumed in writing a treatise in opposition to Dr. Stern, another rigorous old cocked-hat of his neighborhood, who maintained that the Deity had created sin on purpose, because it was a necessary means of the greatest good. Dr. Rossiter thought that evil had only *been permitted*, because it could be overruled for the greatest good; and each of them fought their battle as if the fate of the universe was to be decided by its results.

Considered as a man, in his terrestrial and mundane relations, Dr. Rossiter had that wholesome and homely interest in the things of this mortal life which was characteristic of the New England religious development. While the Puritans were intensely interested in the matters of the soul, they appeared to have a realizing sense of the fact that a soul without a body, in a material world, is at a great disadvantage in getting on. So they exhibited a sensible and commendable sense of the worth of property. They were especially addicted to lawful matrimony, and given to having large families of children; and, if one wife died, they straightway made up the loss by another,—a compliment to the virtues of the female sex which womankind appear always gratefully to appreciate.

Parson Rossiter had been three times married; first, to a

strong-grained, homely, highly intellectual woman of one of
the first Boston families, of whom Miss Mehitable Rossiter
was the only daughter. The Doctor was said to be one of the
handsomest men of his times. Nature, with her usual perver-
sity in these matters, made Miss Mehitable an exact reproduction of all the homely traits of her mother, with the addition
of the one or two physical defects of her handsome father.
No woman with a heart in her bosom ever feels marked personal uncomeliness otherwise than as a great misfortune. Miss
Mehitable bore it with a quaint and silent pride. Her brother
Jonathan, next to herself in age, the son of a second and more
comely wife, was far more gifted in personal points, though
not equal to his father. Finally, late in life, after a somewhat
prolonged widowhood, Parson Rossiter committed the folly
of many men on the downhill side of life, that of marrying a
woman considerably younger than himself. She was a pretty,
nervous, excitable, sensitive creature, whom her homely elder
daughter, Miss Mehitable, no less than her husband, petted
and caressed on account of her beauty, as if she had been a
child. She gave birth to two more children, a son named
Theodore, and a daughter named Emily, and then died.

All the children had inherited from their father the peculiar
constitutional tendency to depression of spirits of which we
have spoken. In these last two, great beauty and brilliant
powers of mind were united with such a singular sensitiveness
and waywardness of nature as made the prospect for happiness in such a life as this, and under the strict requirements of
New England society, very problematical.

Theodore ran through a brilliant course in college, notwithstanding constant difficulties with the college authorities,
but either could not or would not apply himself to any of the
accepted modes of getting bread and butter which a young
man must adopt who means to live and get on with other
men. He was full of disgusts, and repulsions, and dislikes;
everything in life wounded and made him sore; he could or
would do nothing reasonably or rationally with human
beings, and, to deaden the sense of pain in existence, took to
the use of opiates, which left him a miserable wreck on his
sister's hands, the father being dead.

Thus far the reader has the history of this family, and inti-

mations of the younger and more beautiful one whose after
fate was yet to be connected with ours.

Miss Mehitable Rossiter has always been to me a curious
study. Singularly plain as she was in person, old, withered,
and poor, she yet commanded respect, and even reverence,
through the whole of a wide circle of acquaintance; for she
was well known to some of the most considerable families in
Boston, with whom, by her mother's side, she was connected.
The interest in her was somewhat like that in old lace, old
china, and old cashmere shawls; which, though often excessively uncomely, and looking in the eyes of uninterested people like mere rubbish, are held by connoisseurs to be beyond
all price.

Miss Mehitable herself had great pride of character, in the
sense in which pride is an innocent weakness, if not a species
of virtue. She had an innate sense that she belonged to a good
family,—a perfectly quiet conviction that she was a Bradford
by her mother's side, and a Rossiter by her father's side,
come what might in this world. She was too well versed in
the duties of good blood not to be always polite and considerate to the last degree to all well-meaning common people,
for she felt the *noblesse oblige* as much as if she had been a
duchess. And, for that matter, in the circles of Oldtown
everything that Miss Mehitable did and said had a certain
weight, quite apart from that of her really fine mental powers.
It was the weight of past generations, of the whole Colony of
Massachusetts; all the sermons of five generations of ministers
were in it, which to a God-fearing community is a great deal.

But in her quaint, uncomely body was lodged, not only a
most active and even masculine mind, but a heart capable of
those passionate extremes of devotion which belong to the
purely feminine side of woman. She was capable of a romantic excess of affection, of an extravagance of hero-worship,
which, had she been personally beautiful, might perhaps have
made her the heroine of some poem of the heart. It was
among the quietly accepted sorrows of her life, that for her
no such romance was possible.

Men always admired her as they admired other men, and
talked to her as they talked with each other. Many, during
the course of her life, had formed friendships with her, which

were mere relations of comradeship, but which never touched the inner sphere of the heart. That heart, so warm, so tender, and so true, she kept, with a sort of conscious shame, hidden far behind the intrenchments of her intellect. With an instinctive fear of ridicule, she scarcely ever spoke a tender word, and generally veiled a soft emotion under some quaint phrase of drollery. She seemed forever to feel the strange contrast between the burning, romantic heart and the dry and withered exterior.

Like many other women who have borne the curse of marked plainness, Miss Mehitable put an extravagant valuation on personal beauty. Her younger sister, whose loveliness was uncommon, was a sort of petted idol to her, during all her childish years. At the time of her father's death, she would gladly have retained her with her, but, like many other women who are strong on the intellectual side of their nature, Miss Mehitable had a sort of weakness and helplessness in relation to mere material matters, which rendered her, in the eyes of the family, unfit to be trusted with the bringing up of a bright and wilful child. In fact, as regarded all the details of daily life, Miss Mehitable was the servant of Polly, who had united the offices of servant-of-all-work, housekeeper, nurse, and general factotum in old Parson Rossiter's family, and between whom and the little wilful Emily grievous quarrels had often arisen. For all these reasons, and because Mrs. Farnsworth of the neighboring town of Adams was the only sister of the child's mother, was herself childless, and in prosperous worldly circumstances, it would have been deemed a flying in the face of Providence to refuse her, when she declared her intention of adopting her sister's child as her own.

Of what came of this adoption I shall have occasion to speak hereafter.

XX.

Miss Asphyxia Goes in Pursuit, and My Grandmother Gives Her Views on Education

WHEN Miss Asphyxia Smith found that both children really had disappeared from Needmore so completely that no trace of them remained, to do her justice, she felt some solicitude to know what had become of them. There had not been wanting instances in those early days, when so large a part of Massachusetts was unbroken forest, of children who had wandered away into the woods and starved to death; and Miss Asphyxia was by no means an ill-wisher to any child, nor so utterly without bowels as to contemplate such a possibility without some anxiety.

Not that she in the least doubted the wisdom and perfect propriety of her own mode of administration, which she had full faith would in the end have made a "smart girl" of her little charge. "That 'ere little limb did n't know what was good for herself," she said to Sol, over their evening meal of cold potatoes and boiled beef.

Sol looked round-eyed and stupid, and squared his shoulders, as he always did when this topic was introduced. He suggested, "You don't s'pose they could 'a' wandered off to the maountains where Bijah Peters' boy got lost?"

There was a sly satisfaction in observing the anxious, brooding expression which settled down over Miss Asphyxia's dusky features at the suggestion.

"When they found that 'ere boy," continued Sol, "he was all worn to skin and bone; he 'd kep' himself a week on berries and ches'nuts and sich, but a boy can't be kep' on what a squirrel can."

"Well," said Miss Asphyxia, "I know one thing; it ain't my fault if they do starve to death. Silly critters, they was; well provided for, good home, good clothes, plenty and plenty to eat. I 'm sure you can bear witness ef I ever stinted that 'ere child in her victuals."

"I 'll bear you out on that 'ere," said Sol.

"And well you may; I 'd scorn not to give any one in my house a good bellyful," quoth Miss Asphyxia.

"That 's true enough," said Sol; "everybody 'll know that."

"Well, it 's jest total depravity," said Miss Asphyxia. "How can any one help bein' convinced o' that, that has anything to do with young uns?"

But the subject preyed upon the severe virgin's mind; and she so often mentioned it, with that roughening of her scrubby eyebrows which betokened care, that Sol's unctuous good-nature was somewhat moved, and he dropped at last a hint of having fallen on a trace of the children. He might as well have put the tips of his fingers into a rolling-mill. Miss Asphyxia was so wide-awake and resolute about anything that she wanted to know, that Sol at last was obliged to finish with informing her that he had heard of the children as hav- ing been taken in at Deacon Badger's, over in Oldtown. Sol internally chuckled, as he gave the information, when he saw how immediately Miss Asphyxia bristled with wrath. Even the best of human beings have felt that transient flash when anxiety for the fate of a child supposed to be in fatal danger gives place to unrestrained vexation at the little culprit who has given such a fright.

"Well, I shall jest tackle up and go over and bring them children home agin, at least the girl. Brother, he says he don't want the boy; he wa 'n't nothin' but a plague; but I 'm one o' them persons that when I undertake a thing I mean to go through with it. Now I undertook to raise that 'ere girl, and I mean to. She need n't think she 's goin' to come round me with any o' her shines, going over to Deacon Badger's with lying stories about me. Mis' Deacon Badger need n't think she 's goin' to hold up her head over me, if she *is* a deacon's wife and I *ain't* a perfessor of religion. I guess I *could* be a perfessor if I chose to do as some folks do. That 's what I told Mis' Deacon Badger once when she asked me why I did n't jine the church. 'Mis' Badger,' says I, 'perfessin ain't possessin, and I 'd ruther stand outside the church than go on as some people do inside on 't.' "

Therefore it was that a day or two after, when Miss Me- hitable was making a quiet call at my grandmother's, and the party, consisting of my grandmother, Aunt Lois, and Aunt Keziah, were peacefully rattling their knitting-needles, while Tina was playing by the river-side, the child's senses were suddenly paralyzed by the sight of Miss Asphyxia driving with a strong arm over the bridge near my grandmother's.

In a moment the little one's heart was in her throat. She had such an awful faith in Miss Asphyxia's power to carry through anything she undertook, that all her courage withered at once at sight of her. She ran in at the back door, perfectly pale with fright, and seized hold imploringly of Miss Mehitable's gown.

"O, she's coming! she's coming after me. Don't let her get me!" she exclaimed.

"What's the matter now?" said my grandmother. "What ails the child?"

Miss Mehitable lifted her in her lap, and began a soothing course of inquiry; but the child clung to her, only reiterating, "Don't let her have me! she is dreadful! don't!"

"As true as you live, mother," said Aunt Lois, who had tripped to the window, "there's Miss Asphyxia Smith hitching her horse at our picket fence."

"She is?" said my grandmother, squaring her shoulders, and setting herself in fine martial order. "Well, let her come in; she's welcome, I'm sure. I'd like to talk to that woman! It's a free country, and everybody's got to speak their minds,"—and my grandmother rattled her needles with great energy.

In a moment more Miss Asphyxia entered. She was arrayed in her best Sunday clothes, and made the neighborly salutations with an air of grim composure. There was silence, and a sense of something brooding in the air, as there often is before the outburst of a storm.

Finally, Miss Asphyxia opened the trenches. "I come over, Mis' Badger, to see about a gal o' mine that has run away." Here her eye rested severely on Tina.

"Run away!" quoth my grandmother, briskly; "and good reason she should run away; all I wonder at is that you have the face to come to a Christian family after her,—that's all. Well, she is provided for, and you've no call to be inquiring anything about *her*. So I advise you to go home, and attend

to your own affairs, and leave children to folks that know
how to manage them better than you do."

"I expected this, Mis' Badger," said Miss Asphyxia, in a
towering wrath, "but I 'd have you to know that I ain't a
person that 's going to take sa'ace from no one. No deacon
nor deacon's wife, nor perfesser of religion, 's a goin' to turn
up their noses at me! I can hold up my head with any on 'em,
and I think your religion might teach you better than takin'
up stories agin your neighbors, as a little lyin', artful hussy 'll
tell." Here there was a severe glance at Miss Tina, who
quailed before it, and clung to Miss Mehitable's gown. "Yes,
indeed, you may hide your head," she continued, "but you
can't git away from the truth; not when I 'm round to bring
you out. Yes, Mis' Badger, I defy her to say I hain't done well
by her, if she says the truth; for I say it now, this blessed
minute, and would say it on my dyin' bed, and you can ask
Sol ef that 'ere child hain't had everything pervided for her
that a child could want,—a good clean bed and plenty o'
bedclothes, and good whole clothes to wear, and her belly
full o' good victuals every day; an' me a teachin' and a trainin'
on her, enough to wear the very life out o' me,—for I always
hated young uns, and this ere 's a perfect little limb as I ever
did see. Why, what did she think I was a goin' to do for her?
I did n't make a lady on her; to be sure I did n't: I was a
fetchin' on her up to work for her livin' as I was fetched up.
I had n't nothin' more 'n she; an' just look at me now; there
ain't many folks that can turn off as much work in a day as I
can, though I say it that should n't. And I 've got as pretty a
piece of property, and as well seen to, as most any round; and
all I 've got—house and lands—is my own arnin's, honest,
so there! There 's folks, I s'pose, that thinks they can afford
to keep tavern for all sorts of stragglers and runaways, Injun
and white. I never was one o' them sort of folks, an' I should
jest like to know ef those folks is able,—that's all. I guess if
'counts was added up, my 'counts would square up better 'n
theirn."

Here Miss Asphyxia elevated her nose and sniffed over my
grandmother's cap-border in a very contemptuous manner,
and the cap-border bristled defiantly, but undismayed, back
again.

"Come now, Mis' Badger, have it out; I ain't afraid of you! I'd just like to have you tell me what I could ha' done more nor better for this child."

"Done!" quoth my grandmother, with a pop like a roasted chestnut bursting out of the fire. "Why, you've done what you'd no business to. You'd no business to take a child at all; you have n't got a grain of motherliness in you. Why, look at natur', that might teach you that more than meat and drink and clothes is wanted for a child. Hens brood their chickens, and keep 'em warm under their wings; and cows lick their calves and cosset 'em, and it's a mean shame that folks will take 'em away from them. There's our old cat will lie an hour on the kitchen floor and let her kittens lug and pull at her, atween sleeping and waking, just to keep 'em warm and comfortable, you know. 'T ain't just feedin' and clothin' back and belly that's all; it's *broodin'* that young creeturs wants; and you hain't got a bit of broodin' in you; your heart's as hard as the nether mill-stone. Sovereign grace may soften it some day, but nothin' else can; you're a poor, old, hard, worldly woman, Miss Asphyxia Smith: that's what *you* are! If Divine grace could have broken in upon you, and given you a heart to love the child, you might have brought her up, 'cause you are a smart woman, and an honest one; that nobody denies."

Here Miss Mehitable took up the conversation, surveying Miss Asphyxia with that air of curious attention with which one studies a human being entirely out of the line of one's personal experience. Miss Mehitable was, as we have shown, in every thread of her being and education an aristocrat, and had for Miss Asphyxia that polite, easy tolerance which a sense of undoubted superiority gives, united with a shrewd pleasure in the study of a new and peculiar variety of the human species.

"My good Miss Smith," she observed, in conciliatory tones, "by your own account you must have had a great deal of trouble with this child. Now I propose for the future to relieve you of it altogether. I do not think you would ever succeed in making as efficient a person as yourself of her. It strikes me," she added, with a humorous twinkle of her eye, "that there are radical differences of nature, which would pre-

vent her growing up like yourself. I don't doubt you conscientiously intended to do your duty by her, and I beg you to
believe that you need have no further trouble with her."

"Goodness gracious knows," said Miss Asphyxia, "the child
ain't much to fight over,—she was nothin' but a plague; and
I'd rather have done all she did any day, than to 'a' had her
round under my feet. I hate young uns, anyway."

"Then why, my good woman, do you object to parting
with her?"

"Who said I did object? I don't care nothin' about parting
with her; all is, when I begin a thing I like to go through
with it."

"But if it is n't worth going through with," said Miss Mehitable, "it 's as well to leave it, is it not?"

"And I 'd got her clothes made,—not that they 're worth
so very much, but then they 're worth just what they *are*
worth, anyway," said Miss Asphyxia.

Here Tina made a sudden impulsive dart from Miss Mehitable's lap, and ran out of the back door, and over to her new
home, and up into the closet of the chamber where was hanging the new suit of homespun in which Miss Asphyxia had
arrayed her. She took it down and rolled the articles all together in a tight bundle, which she secured with a string, and,
before the party in the kitchen had ceased wondering at her
flight, suddenly reappeared, with flushed cheeks and dilated
eyes, and tossed the bundle into Miss Asphyxia's lap.
"There 's every bit you ever gave me," she said; "I don't want
to keep a single thing."

"My dear, is that a proper way to speak?" said Miss Mehitable, reprovingly; but Tina saw my grandmother's broad
shoulders joggling with a secret laugh, and discerned twinkling lines in the reproving gravity which Miss Mehitable
tried to assume. She felt pretty sure of her ground by this
time.

"Well, it 's no use talkin'," said Miss Asphyxia, rising. "If
folks think they 're able to bring up a beggar child like a lady,
it 's their lookout and not mine. I was n't aware," she added,
with severe irony, "that Parson Rossiter left so much of an
estate that you could afford to bring up other folks' children
in silks and satins."

"Our estate is n't much," said Miss Mehitable, good-naturedly, "but we shall make the best of it."

"Well, now, you just mark my words, Miss Rossiter," said Miss Asphyxia, "that 'ere child will never grow up a smart woman with *your* bringin' up; she 'll jest run right over *you*, and you 'll let her have her head in everything. I see jest how 't 'll be; I don't want nobody to tell me."

"I dare say you are quite right, Miss Smith," said Miss Mehitable; "I have n't the slightest opinion of my own powers in that line; but she may be happy with me, for all that."

"Happy?" repeated Miss Asphyxia, with an odd intonation, as if she were repeating a sound of something imperfectly comprehended, and altogether out of her line. "O, well, if folks is goin' to begin to talk about *that*, I hain't got time; it don't seem to me that *that* 's what this 'ere world 's for."

"What is it for, then?" said Miss Mehitable, who felt an odd sort of interest in the human specimen before her.

"Meant for? Why, for hard work, I s'pose; that 's all I ever found it for. Talk about coddling! it 's little we get o' that, the way the Lord fixes things in this world, dear knows. He 's pretty up and down with us, by all they tell us. You must take things right off, when they 're goin'. Ef you don't, so much the worse for you; they won't wait for you. Lose an hour in the morning, and you may chase it till ye drop down, you never 'll catch it! That 's the way things goes, and I should like to know who 's a going to stop to quiddle with young uns? 'T ain't me, that 's certain; so, as there 's no more to be made by this 'ere talk, I may 's well be goin'. You 're welcome to the young un, ef you say so; I jest wanted you to know that what I begun I 'd 'a' gone through with, ef you had n't stepped in; and I did n't want no reflections on my good name, neither, for I had my ideas of what 's right, and can have 'em yet, I s'pose, if Mis' Badger does think I 've got a heart of stone. I should like to know how I 'm to have any other when I ain't elected, and I don't see as I am, or likely to be, and I don't see neither why I ain't full as good as a good many that be."

"Well, well, Miss Smith," said Miss Mehitable, "we can't any of us enter into those mysteries, but I respect your motives, and would be happy to see you any time you will call, and I 'm in hopes to teach this little girl to treat you properly," she said, taking the child's hand.

"Likely story," said Miss Asphyxia, with a short, hard laugh. "She 'll get ahead o' you, you 'll see that: but I don't hold malice, so good morning,"—and Miss Asphyxia suddenly and promptly departed, and was soon seen driving away at a violent pace.

"Upon my word, that woman is n't so bad, now," said Miss Mehitable, looking after her, while she leisurely inhaled a pinch of snuff.

"O, I 'm so glad you did n't let her have me!" said Tina.

"To think of a creature so dry and dreary, so devoid even of the conception of enjoyment in life," said Miss Mehitable, "hurrying through life without a moment's rest,—without even the capacity of resting if she could,—and all for what?"

"For my part, mother, I think you were down too hard on her," said Aunt Lois.

"Not a bit," said my grandmother, cheerily. "Such folks ought to be talked to; it may set her to thinking, and do her good. I 've had it on my heart to give that woman a piece of my mind ever since the children came here. Come here, my poor little dear," said she to Tina, with one of her impulsive outgushes of motherliness. "I know you must be hungry by this time; come into the buttery, and see what I 've got for you."

Now there was an indiscreet championship of Miss Tina, a backing of her in her treatment of Miss Asphyxia, in this overflow, which Aunt Lois severely disapproved, and which struck Miss Mehitable as not being the very best thing to enforce her own teachings of decorum and propriety.

The small young lady tilted into the buttery after my grandmother, with the flushed cheeks and triumphant air of a victor, and they heard her little tongue running with the full assurance of having a sympathetic listener.

"Now mother will spoil that child, if you let her," said Aunt Lois. "She 's the greatest hand to spoil children; she always lets 'em have what they ask for. I expect Susy's boys 'll be raising Cain round the house; they would if it was n't for

me. They have only to follow mother into that buttery, and
out they come with great slices of bread and butter, any time
of day,—yes, and even sugar on it, if you'll believe me."

"And does 'em good, too," said my grandmother, who
reappeared from the buttery, with Miss Tina tilting and dancing before her, with a confirmatory slice of bread and butter
and sugar in her hand. "Tastes good, don't it, dear?" said she,
giving the child a jovial chuck under her little chin.

"Yes, indeed," said Miss Tina; "I'd like to have old nasty
Sphyxy see me now."

"Tut, tut! my dear," said grandmother; "good little girls
don't call names";—but at the same time the venerable gen-
tlewoman nodded and winked in the most open manner
across the curly head at Miss Mehitable, and her portly shoulders shook with laughter, so that the young culprit was not
in the least abashed at the reproof.

"Mother, I do wonder at you!" said Aunt Lois, indignantly.

"Never you mind, Lois; I guess I've brought up more children than ever you did," said my grandmother, cheerily.
"There, my little dear," she added, "you may run down to
your play now, and never fear that anybody's going to get
you."

Miss Tina, upon this hint, gladly ran off to finish an architectural structure of pebbles by the river, which she was busy
in building at the time when the awful vision of Miss Asphyxia appeared; and my grandmother returned to her buttery to attend to a few matters which had been left unfinished
in the morning's work.

"It is a very serious responsibility," said Miss Mehitable,
when she had knit awhile in silence, "at my time of life, to
charge one's self with the education of a child. One treats
one's self to a child as one buys a picture or a flower, but the
child will not remain a picture or a flower, and then comes
the awful question, what it may grow to be, and what share
you may have in determining its future."

"Well, old Parson Moore used to preach the best sermons
on family government that ever I heard," said Aunt Lois. "He
said you must begin in the very beginning and break a child's
will,—short off,—nothing to be done without that. I remem-

ber he whipped little Titus, his first son, off and on, nearly a whole day, to make him pick up a pocket-handkerchief."

Here the edifying conversation was interrupted by a loud explosive expletive from the buttery, which showed that my grandmother was listening with anything but approbation.

"FIDDLESTICKS!" quoth she.

"And did he succeed in entirely subduing the child's will in that one effort?" said Miss Mehitable, musingly.

"Well, no. Mrs. Moore told me he had to have twenty or thirty just such spells before he brought him under; but he persevered, and he broke his will at last,—at least so far that he always minded when his father was round."

"FIDDLESTICKS!" quoth my grandmother, in a yet louder and more explosive tone.

"Mrs. Badger does not appear to sympathize with your views," said Miss Mehitable.

"O, mother? Of course she don't; she has her own ways and doings, and she won't hear to reason," said Aunt Lois.

"Come, come, Lois; I never knew an old maid who did n't think she knew just how to bring up children," said my grandmother. "Wish you could have tried yourself with that sort of doxy when you was little. Guess if I 'd broke your will, I should ha' had to break you for good an' all, for your will is about all there is of you! But I tell you, I had too much to do to spend a whole forenoon making you pick up a pocket-handkerchief. When you did n't mind, I hit you a good clip, and picked it up myself; and when you would n't go where I wanted you, I picked you up, neck and crop, and put you there. That was my government. I let your will take care of itself. I thought the Lord had given you a pretty strong one, and he knew what 't was for, and could take care of it in his own time, which hain't come yet, as I see."

Now this last was one of those personal thrusts with which dear family friends are apt to give arguments a practical application; and Aunt Lois's spare, thin cheeks flushed up as she said, in an aggrieved tone: "Well, I s'pose I 'm dreadful, of course. Mother always contrives to turn round on me."

"Well, Lois, I hate to hear folks talk nonsense," said my grandmother, who by this time had got a pot of cream under her arm, which she was stirring with the pudding-stick; and this afforded her an opportunity for emphasizing her sentences with occasional dumps of the same.

"People don't need to talk to me," she said, "about Parson Moore's government. Tite Moore was n't any great shakes, after all the row they made about him. He was well enough while his father was round, but about the worst boy that ever I saw when his eye was off from him. Good or bad, my children was about the same behind my back that they were before my face, anyway."

"Well, now, there was Aunt Sally Morse," said Aunt Lois, steadily ignoring the point of my grandmother's discourse. "There was a woman that brought up children exactly to suit me. Everything went like clock-work with her babies; they were nursed just so often, and no more; they were put down to sleep at just such a time, and nobody was allowed to rock 'em, or sing to 'em, or fuss with 'em. If they cried, she just whipped them till they stopped; and when they began to toddle about, she never put things out of their reach, but just slapped their hands whenever they touched them, till they learnt to let things alone."

"Slapped their hands!" quoth my grandmother, "and learnt them to let things alone! I 'd like to ha' seen that tried on my children. Sally had a set of white, still children, that were all just like dipped candles by natur', and she laid it all to her management; and look at 'em now they're grown up. They're decent, respectable folks, but noways better than other folks' children. Lucinda Morse ain't a bit better than you are, Lois, if she was whipped and made to lie still when she was a baby, and you were taken up and rocked when you cried. All is, they had hard times when they were little, and cried themselves to sleep nights, and were hectored and worried when they ought to have been taking some comfort. Ain't the world hard enough, without fighting babies, I want to know? I hate to see a woman that don't want to rock her own baby, and is contriving ways all the time to shirk the care of it. Why, if all the world was that way, there would be no sense in Scriptur'. 'As one whom his mother comforteth, so will I comfort you,' the Bible says, taking for granted that mothers were made to comfort children and give them good times when they are little. Sally Morse was always talking about her system. She thought she did wonders, 'cause she got so much time to piece bedquilts, and work counterpanes, and make pickles, by turning off her children; but I took my comfort in mine, and let them have their comfort as they went along. It 's about all the comfort there is in this world, anyway, and they 're none the worse for it now, as I see."

"Well, in all these cases there is a medium, if we could hit it," said Miss Mehitable. "There must be authority over these ignorant, helpless little folks in early years, to keep them from ruining themselves."

"O yes. Of course there must be government," said my grandmother. "I always made my children mind me; but I would n't pick quarrels with 'em, nor keep up long fights to break their will; if they did n't mind, I came down on 'em and had it over with at once, and then was done with 'em. They turned out pretty fair, too," said my grandmother complacently, giving an emphatic thump with her pudding-stick.

"I was reading Mr. John Locke's treatise on education yesterday," said Miss Mehitable. "It strikes me there are many good ideas in it."

"Well, one live child puts all your treatises to rout," said my grandmother. "There ain't any two children alike; and what works with one won't with another. Folks have just got to open their eyes, and look and see what the Lord meant when he put the child together, if they can, and not stand in his way; and after all we must wait for sovereign grace to finish the work: if the Lord don't keep the house, the watchman waketh but in vain. Children are the heritage of the Lord,—that 's all you can make of it."

My grandmother, like other warm-tempered, impulsive, dictatorial people, had formed her theories of life to suit her own style of practice. She was, to be sure, autocratic in her own realm, and we youngsters knew that, at certain times when her blood was up, it was but a word and a blow for us, and that the blow was quite likely to come first and the word afterward; but the temporary severities of kindly-natured, generous people never lessen the affection of children or servants, any more than the too hot rays of the benignant sun, or the too driving patter of the needful rain. When my grand-

mother detected us in a childish piece of mischief, and
soundly cuffed our ears, or administered summary justice
with immediate polts of her rheumatic crutch, we never felt
the least rising of wrath or rebellion, but only made off as fast
as possible, generally convinced that the good woman was in
the right of it, and that we got no more than we deserved.

I remember one occasion when Bill had been engaged in
making some dressed chickens dance, which she had left
trussed up with the liver and lights duly washed and replaced
within them. Bill set them up on their pins, and put them
through active gymnastics, in course of which these interior
treasures were rapidly scattered out upon the table. A howl of
indignation from grandmother announced coming wrath, and
Bill darted out of the back door, while I was summarily seized
and chastised.

"Grandmother, grandmother! *I* did n't do it,—it was Bill."

"Well, but I can't catch Bill, you see," said my venerable
monitor, continuing the infliction.

"But I did n't do it."

"Well, let it stand for something you did do, then," quoth
my grandmother, by this time quite pacified: "you do bad
things enough that you ain't whipped for, any day."

The whole resulted in a large triangle of pumpkin pie, administered with the cordial warmth of returning friendship,
and thus the matter was happily adjusted. Even the prodigal
son Bill, when, returning piteously, and standing penitent under the milk-room window, he put in a submissive plea,
"Please, grandmother, I won't do so any more," was allowed
a peaceable slice of the same comfortable portion, and bid to
go in peace.

I remember another funny instance of my grandmother's
discipline. It was when I was a little fellow, seated in the
chimney-corner at my grandfather's side. I had discovered a
rising at the end of my shoe-sole, which showed that it was
beginning to come off. It struck me as a funny thing to do to
tear up the whole sole, which piece of mischief my grandfather perceiving, he raised his hand to chastise.

"Come here, Horace, quick!" said my grandmother, imper-
atively, that she might save me from the impending blow.

I lingered, whereat she made a dart at me, and seized me. Just as my grandfather boxed my ear on one side, she hit me a similar cuff on the other.

"Why did n't you come when I called you," she said; "now you 've got your ears boxed both sides."

Somewhat bewildered, I retreated under her gown in disgrace, but I was after a relenting moment lifted into her lap, and allowed to go to sleep upon her ample bosom.

"Mother, why don't you send that boy to bed nights?" said Aunt Lois. "You never have any regular rules about anything."

"Law, he likes to sit up and see the fire as well as any of us, Lois; and do let him have all the comfort he can as he goes along, poor boy! there ain't any too much in this world, anyway."

"Well, for my part, I think there ought to be *system* in bringing up children," said Aunt Lois.

"Wait till you get 'em of your own, and then try it, Lois," said my grandmother, laughing with a rich, comfortable laugh which rocked my little sleepy head up and down, as I drowsily opened my eyes with a delicious sense of warmth and security.

From all these specimens it is to be inferred that the theorists on education will find no improvement in the contemplation of my grandmother's methods, and will pronounce her a pig-headed, passionate, impulsive, soft-hearted body, as entirely below the notice of a rational, inquiring mind as an old brooding hen, which model of maternity in many respects she resembled. It may be so, but the longer I live, the more faith I have in grandmothers and grandmotherly logic, of which, at some future time, I shall give my views at large.

XXI.

What Is to Be Done with the Boy?

"Well," said my Aunt Lois, as she gave the last sweep to the hearth, after she had finished washing up the supper-dishes; "I 've been up to Ebal Scran's store this afternoon, to see about soling Horace's Sunday shoes. Ebal will do 'em as reasonable as any one; and he spoke to me to know whether I knew of any boy that a good family would like to bind out to him for an apprentice, and I told him I 'd speak to you about Horace. It 'll be time pretty soon to think of putting him at something."

Among the many unexplained and inexplicable woes of childhood, are its bitter antagonisms, so perfectly powerless, yet often so very decided, against certain of the grown people who control it. Perhaps some of us may remember respectable, well-meaning people, with whom in our mature years we live in perfect amity, but who in our childhood appeared to us bitter enemies. Children are remarkably helpless in this respect, because they cannot choose their company and surroundings as grown people can; and are sometimes entirely in the power of those with whom their natures are so unsympathetic that they may be almost said to have a constitutional aversion to them. Aunt Lois was such a one to me, principally because of her forecasting, untiring, pertinacious, care-taking propensities. She had already looked over my lot in life, and set down in her own mind what was to be done with me, and went at it with a resolute energy that would not wait for the slow development of circumstances.

That I should want to study, as my father did,—that I should for this cause hang as an unpractical, unproductive, dead weight on the family,—was the evil which she saw in prospective, against which my grandfather's placid, easy temper, and my grandmother's impulsive bountifulness, gave her no security. A student in the family, and a son in college, she felt to be luxuries to which a poor widow in dependent circumstances had no right to look forward, and therefore she opened the subject betimes, with prompt energy, by the proposition above stated.

My mother, who sat on the other side of the fireplace, looked at me with a fluttering look of apprehension. I flushed up in a sort of rage that somehow Aunt Lois always succeeded in putting me into. "I don't want to be a shoemaker, and I won't neither," I said.

"Tut, tut," said my grandfather, placidly, from his corner; "we don't let little boys say 'won't' here."

I now burst out crying, and ran to my grandmother, sobbing as if my heart would break.

"Lois, *can't* you let this boy alone?" said my grandmother, vengefully; "I do wonder at you. Poor little fellow! his father ain't quite cold in his grave yet, and you want to pitch him out into the world,"—and my grandmother seized me in her strong arms, and lulled me against her ample bosom. "There, poor boy, don't you cry; you sha' n't, no, you sha' n't; you shall stay and help grandma, so you shall."

"Great help he is," said Aunt Lois, contemptuously; "gets a book in his hand and goes round with his head in a bag; never gives a message right, and is always stumbling over things that are right in his way. There's Harry, now, is as handy as a girl, and if he says he 'll do a thing, I know 't 'll be done,"—and Aunt Lois illustrated her doctrine by calling up Harry, and making him stretch forth his arms for a skein of blue-mixed yarn which she was going to wind. The fire-light shone full on his golden curls and clear blue eyes, as he stood obediently and carefully yielding to Aunt Lois's quick, positive movements. As she wound, and twitched, and pulled, with certainly twice the energy that the work in hand required, his eyes followed her motions with a sort of quiet drollery; there was a still, inward laugh in them, as if she amused him greatly.

Such open comparisons between two boys might have gone far to destroy incipient friendship; but Harry seemed to be in a wonderful degree gifted with the faculties that made him a universal favorite. All the elders of the family liked him, because he was quiet and obedient, always doing with cheerful promptness exactly what he was bidden, unless, as sometimes happened in our family circle, he was bidden to do two or three different things at one and the same time, when he would stand looking innocently puzzled, till my grandmother and Aunt Lois and Aunt Keziah had settled it among them whose was to be the ruling will. He was deft and neat-handed as a girl about any little offices of a domestic nature; he was thoughtful and exact in doing errands; he was delicately clean and neat in his personal habits; he never tracked Aunt Lois's newly scoured floor with the traces of unwiped shoes; he never left shavings and litter on a cleanly swept hearth, or tumbled and deranged anything, so that he might safely be trusted on errands even to the most sacred precincts of a housekeeper's dominions. What boy with all these virtues is not held a saint by all women-folk? Yet, though he was frequently commended in all those respects, to my marked discredit, Harry was to me a sort of necessary of life. There was something in his nature that was wanting to mine, and I attached myself to him with a pertinacity which had never before marked my intercourse with any boy.

A day or two after the arrival of the children, the minister and Lady Lothrop had called on my grandmother in all the dignity of their station, and taken an approving view of the boy. Lady Lothrop had engaged to take him under her care, and provide a yearly sum for his clothing and education. She had never had a child of her own, and felt that diffidence about taking the entire charge of a boy which would be natural to a person of fastidious and quiet habits, and she therefore signified that it would be more agreeable to her if my grandmother would allow him to make one of her own family circle,—a proposal to which she cheerfully assented, saying, that "one more chick makes little difference to an old hen."

I immediately petitioned that I might have Harry for a bedfellow, and he and I were allowed a small bedroom to ourselves at the head of the back stairs. It was a rude little crib, roughly fenced off from the passage-way by unplaned boards of different heights. A pine table, two stools, a small trundle-bed, and a rude case of drawers, were all its furniture. Harry's love of order was strikingly manifest in the care which he took of this little apartment. His few articles of clothing and personal belongings all had their exact place, and always were bestowed there with scrupulous regularity. He would adjust the furniture, straighten the bed-clothing, and quietly place and replace the things that I in my fitful, nervous eagerness was always disarranging; and when, as often happened in one of my spasms of enthusiasm, I turned everything in the room topsy-turvy, searching for something I had lost, or projecting some new arrangement, he would wait peaceably till I had finished, and then noiselessly get everything back again into its former order. He never quarrelled with me, or thwarted me in my turbulent or impatient moods, but seemed to wait for me to get through whatever I was doing, when he would come in and silently rearrange. He was, on the whole, a singularly silent child, but with the kind of silence which gives a sense of companionship. It was evident that he was always intensely observant and interested in whatever was going on before him, and ready at any moment to take a friendly part when he was wanted; but for the most part his place in the world seemed that of an amused listener and observer. Life seemed to present itself to him as a curious spectacle, and he was never tired of looking and listening, watching the ways and words of all our family circle, and often smiling to himself as if they afforded him great diversion. Aunt Lois, with her quick, sharp movements, her determined, outspoken ways, seemed to amuse him as much as she irritated me, and I would sometimes see him turn away with a droll smile when he had been watching one of her emphatic courses round the room. He had a certain tact in avoiding all the sharp corners and angles of her character, which, in connection with his handiness and his orderly ways, caused him at last to become a prime favorite with her. With his quiet serviceableness and manual dexterity, he seemed to be always the one that was exactly wanting to do an odd turn, so that at last he came to be depended on for many little inferior offices, which he rendered with a good-will none the less cheerful because of his silence.

"There 's time enough to think about what Horace is to do another year," said my grandfather, having reflected some moments after the passage of arms between my grandmother and Aunt Lois. "He 's got to have some schooling. The boys had both better go to school for this winter, and then we 'll see what next."

"Well, I just mentioned about Ebal Scran, because he 's a good man to take a boy, and he wants one now. If we don't take that chance it may not come again."

"Wal, Miss Lois," said Sam Lawson, who had sat silent in a dark corner of the chimney, "ef I was to say about Horace, I 'd say he 'd do better for somethin' else 'n shoemakin'. He 's the most amazin' little fellow to read I ever see. As much as a year ago Jake Marshall and me and the other fellers round to the store used to like to get him to read the Columbian Sentinel to us; he did it off slicker than any on us could, he did,—there wa' n't no kind o' word could stop him. I should say such a boy as that ought to have a liberal education."

"And who 's going to pay for it?" said Aunt Lois, turning round on him sharply. "I suppose you know it costs something to get a man through college. *We* never can afford to send him to college. It 's all we can do to bring his Uncle Bill through."

"Well, well," said my grandmother, "there 's no use worrying the child, one way or the other."

"They can both go to district school this winter," said my grandfather.

"Well," said Aunt Lois, "the other day I found him down in a corner humping his back out over a Latin grammar that I 'd put away with all the rest of his father's books on the back side of the upper shelf in our closet, and I took it away from him. If he was going to college, why, it 's well enough to study for it; but if he is n't we don't want him idlin' round with scraps of Latin in his head like old Jock Twitchel,—got just Latin enough to make a fool of his English, and he 's neither one thing nor another."

"I do wonder, Lois, what there is under the sun that you don't feel called to see to," said my grandmother. "What do you want to quarrel with the child for? He shall have his Latin grammar if he wants it, and any of the rest of his father's books, poor child. I s'pose he likes 'em because they were his poor father's."

I leaped for joy in my grandmother's lap, for my father's

precious books had been in a state of blockade ever since we had been in the house, and it was only by putting a chair on a table one day, when Aunt Lois and my mother were out, that I had managed to help myself to the Latin grammar, out of which my father had begun to teach me before he died.

"Well, well," said Aunt Lois, "at any rate it's eight o'clock, and time these boys went to bed."

Upon this hint Harry and I went to our little bedroom without the ceremony of a candle. It was a frosty autumn night, but a good, clear square of moonlight lay on the floor.

Now Harry, in common with many other very quiet-natured people, was remarkable for a peculiar persistency in all his ways and manners. Ever since I had roomed with him, I had noticed with a kind of silent wonder the regularity of his nightly devotional exercises, to which he always addressed himself before he went to bed, with an appearance of simple and absorbed fervor, kneeling down by the bed, and speaking in a low, earnest tone of voice, never seeming to hurry or to abbreviate, as I was always inclined to do whenever I attempted similar performances. In fact, as usually I said no prayers at all, there was often an awkward pause and stillness on my part, while I watched and waited for Harry to be through with his devotions, so that I might resume the thread of worldly conversation.

Now to me the perseverance with which he performed these nightly exercises was unaccountable. The doctrines which in that day had been gaining ground in New England, with regard to the utter inutility and unacceptableness of any prayers or religious doings of the unregenerate, had borne their legitimate fruits in causing parents to become less and less particular in cultivating early habits of devotion in children; and so, when I had a room to myself, my mother had ceased to take any oversight of my religious exercises; and as I had overheard my Aunt Lois maintaining very stringently that there was no use in it so long as my heart was not changed, I very soon dropped the form. So, when night after night I noticed Harry going on with his devotions, it seemed to me, from my more worldly point of view, that he gave himself a great deal of unnecessary trouble, particularly if, after all, his prayers did no good. I thought I would speak with him about it, and accordingly this night I said to him, "Harry, do you think it does any good to say your prayers?"

"To be sure I do," he said.

"But if your heart has n't been changed, your prayer is an abomination to the Lord. Aunt Lois says so," I said, repeating a Scriptural form I had often heard quoted.

Harry turned over, and in the fading daylight I saw his eyes, large, clear, and tranquil. There was not the shadow of a cloud in them. "I don't know anything about that," he said quietly. "You see I don't believe that sort of talk. God is our Father; he loves us. If we want things, and ask him for them, he will give them to us if it is best; mother always told me so, and I find it is so. I promised her always to say these prayers, and to believe that God loves us. I always shall."

"Do you *really* think so, Harry?" I said.

"Why, yes; to be sure I do."

"I mean, do you ever ask God for things you want? I don't mean saying prayers, but asking for anything."

"Of course I do. I always have, and he gives them to me. He always has taken care of me, and he always will."

"Now, Harry," said I, "I want to go to college, and Aunt Lois says there is n't any money to send me there. She wants mother to bind me out to a shoemaker; and I 'd rather die than do that. I love to study, and I mean to learn. Now do you suppose if I ask God he will help me?"

"Certainly he will," said Harry, with an incredible firmness and quietness of manner. "Just you try it."

"Don't you want to study and go to college?" said I.

"Certainly I do. I ask God every night that I may *if it is best*," he said with simplicity.

"It will be a great deal harder for you than for me," I said, "because you have n't any relations."

"Yes, but God *can* do anything he pleases," said Harry, with a sort of energetic simplicity.

The confidence expressed in his manner produced a kind of effect upon me. I had urgent needs, too,—longings which I was utterly helpless ever to fulfil,—particularly that visionary desire to go to college and get an education. "Harry," I said, "you ask God that I may go to college."

"Yes, I will," he answered,—"I 'll ask every night. But

then," he added, turning over and looking at me, "why don't you ask yourself, Horace?"

It was difficult for me to answer that question. I think that the differences among human beings in the natural power of *faith* are as great as any other constitutional diversity, and that they begin in childhood. Some are born believers, and some are born sceptics. I was one of the latter. There was an eternal query,—an habitual interrogation-point to almost every proposition in my mind, even from childhood,—a habit of looking at everything from so many sides, that it was difficult to get a settled assent to anything.

Perhaps the curious kind of double life that I led confirmed this sceptical tendency. I was certain that I constantly saw and felt things, the assertion of whose existence as I saw them drew down on me stinging reproofs and radical doubts of my veracity. This led me to distrust my own perceptions on all subjects, for I was no less certain of what I saw and felt in the spiritual world than of what I saw and felt in the material; and, if I could be utterly mistaken in the one, I could also be in the other.

The repression and silence about this which became the habit of my life formed a covering for a constant wondering inquiry. The habit of reserve on these subjects had become so intense, that even to Harry I never spoke of it. I think I loved Harry more than I loved anything; in fact, before he came to us, I do not think I knew anything of love as a sentiment. My devotion to my father resembled the blind, instinctive worship of a dog for his master. My feeling toward my mother and grandmother was that impulse of want that induces a chicken to run to a hen in any of its little straits. It was an animal instinct,—a commerce of helplessness with help.

For Harry I felt a sort of rudimentary, poetical tenderness, like the love of man for woman. I admired his clear blue eyes, his curling golden hair, his fair, pure complexion, his refined and quiet habits, and a sort of unconsciousness of self that there was about him. His simplicity of nature was incorruptible; he seemed always to speak, without disguise, exactly what he thought, without the least apparent consideration of anything but its truth; and this gave him a strange air of innocency. A sort of quaint humor always bubbling up in little quiet looks and ways, and in harmless practical jokes, gave me a constant sense of amusement in his society.

As the reader may have observed, we were a sharp-cut and peculiar set in our house, and sometimes, when the varied scenes of family life below stairs had amused Harry more than common, he would, after we had got into our chamber by ourselves, break into a sudden flow of mimicry,—imitating now Aunt Lois's sharp, incisive movements and decided tones, or flying about like my venerated grandmother in her most confused and hurried moments, or presenting a perfect image of Uncle Fliakim's frisky gyrations, till he would set me into roars of laughter; when he would turn gravely round and ask what I was laughing at. He never mentioned a name, or made remarks about the persons indicated,—the sole reflection on them was the absurd truthfulness of his imitation; and when I would call out the name he would look at me with eyes brimful of mischief, but in utter silence.

Generally speaking, his language was characterized by a peculiar nicety in the selection of words, and an avoidance of clownish or vulgar phraseology, and was such as marks a child whose early years have all been passed in the intercourse of refined society; but sometimes he would absurdly introduce into his conversation scraps from Sam Lawson's vocabulary, with flashes of mimicry of his shambling gait, and the lanky droop of his hands; yet these shifting flashes of imitation were the only comment he ever made upon him.

After Harry began to share my apartment, my nightly visions became less frequent, because, perhaps, instead of lying wide-awake expecting them, I had him to talk to. Once or twice, indeed, I saw standing by him, after he had fallen asleep, that same woman whose blue eyes and golden hair I had remarked when we were lost in the forest. She looked down on him with an inexpressible tenderness, and seemed to bless him; and I used to notice that he spoke oftener of his mother the next day, and quoted her words to me with the simple, unquestioning veneration which he always showed for them.

One thing about Harry which was striking to me, and which he possessed in common with many still, retiring people, was great vigor in maintaining his individuality. It has been the experience of my life that it is your quiet people who, above all other children of men, are set in their ways and intense in their opinions. Their very reserve and silence are a fortification behind which all their peculiarities grow and thrive at their leisure, without encountering those blows and shocks which materially modify more outspoken natures. It is owing to the peculiar power of quietness that one sometimes sees characters fashioning themselves in a manner the least to be expected from the circumstances and associates which surround them. As a fair white lily grows up out of the bed of meadow muck, and, without note or comment, rejects all in the soil that is alien from her being, and goes on fashioning her own silver cup side by side with weeds that are drawing coarser nutriment from the soil, so we often see a refined and gentle nature by some singular internal force unfolding itself by its own laws, and confirming itself in its own beliefs, as wholly different from all that surround it as is the lily from the rag-weed. There are persons, in fact, who seem to grow almost wholly from within, and on whom the teachings, the doctrines, and the opinions of those around them produce little or no impression.

Harry was modest in his bearing; he never put forth an opinion opposed to those around him, unless a special question was asked him; but, even from early childhood, the opinion of no human being seemed to have much power to modify or alter certain convictions on which his life was based.

I remember, one Sunday, our good Parson Lothrop took it into his head to preach one of those cool, philosophical sermons in which certain scholarly and rational Christians in easy worldly circumstances seem to take delight,—a sort of preaching which removes the providence of God as far off from human sympathy as it is possible to be. The amount of the matter as he stated it seemed to be, that the Creator had devised a very complicated and thorough-working machine, which he had wound up and set going ages ago, which brought out results with the undeviating accuracy of clockwork. Of course there was the declaration that "not a sparrow falleth to the ground without our Father," and that "the very hairs of our head are numbered," standing square across his way. But we all know that a text of Scripture is no embarrassment at all in the way of a thorough-paced theologian, when he has a favorite idea to establish.

These declarations were explained as an Oriental, metaphorical way of stating that the All-wise had started a grand world-machine on general laws which included the greatest good to the least of his creation.

I noticed that Harry sat gazing at him with clear, wide-open eyes and that fixed attention which he always gave to anything of a religious nature. The inference that I drew from it was, that Harry must be mistaken in his confidence in prayer, and that the kind of Fatherly intervention he looked for and asked for in his affairs was out of the question. As we walked home I expected him to say something about it, but he did not. When we were in our room at night, and he had finished his prayers, I said, "Harry, did you notice Dr. Lothrop's sermon?"

"Yes, I noticed it," he said.

"Well, if that is true, what good does it do to pray?"

"It is n't true," he said, simply.

"How do you know it is n't?"

"O, I *know* better," he said.

"But, Harry,—Dr. Lothrop, you know,—why, he 's the minister,"—and what could a boy of that day say more?

"He 's mistaken there, though," said Harry, quietly, as he would speak of a man who denied the existence of the sun or moon. He was too positive and too settled to be in any frame to argue about it, and the whole of the discourse, which had seemed to me so damaging to his opinions, melted over him like so much moonshine. He fell asleep saying to himself, "The Lord is my shepherd, I shall not want," and I lay awake, wondering in my own mind whether this was the way to live, and, if it were, why my grandmother and Aunt Lois, and my father and mother, and all the good people I had ever known, had so many troubles and worries.

Ages ago, in the green, flowery hollows of the hills of Bethlehem, a young shepherd boy took this view of life, and began his days singing, "The Lord is my shepherd, I shall not want," and ended them by saying, "Thou hast taught me from my youth up, and hitherto have I declared thy wondrous works"; and his tender communings with an unseen

Father have come down to our days as witnesses of green pastures and still waters to be found in this weary work-a-day world, open ever to those who are simple-hearted enough to seek them. It would seem to be the most natural thing in the world that the child of an ever-present Father should live in this way,—that weakness and ignorance, standing within call and reach of infinite grace and strength, should lay hold of that divine helpfulness, and grow to it and by it, as the vine climbs upon the rock; but yet such lives are the exception rather than the rule, even among the good. But the absolute faith of Harry's mind produced about him an atmosphere of composure and restfulness which was, perhaps, the strongest attraction that drew me to him. I was naturally nervous, sensitive, excitable, and needed the repose which he gave me. His quiet belief that all would be right had a sort of effect on me, and, although I did not fall into his way of praying, I came to have great confidence in it for him, and to indulge some vague hopes that something good might come of it for me.

XXII.

Daily Living in Oldtown

HENCEFORTH my story must be a cord with three strands, inexplicably intertwisted, and appearing and disappearing in their regular intervals, as each occupies for the moment the prominent place. And this threefold cord is composed of myself, Harry, and Tina. To show how the peculiar life of old Massachusetts worked upon us, and determined our growth and character and destinies, is a theme that brings in many personages, many subjects, many accessories. It is strange that no human being grows up who does not so intertwist in his growth the whole idea and spirit of his day, that rightly to dissect out his history would require one to cut to pieces and analyze society, law, religion, the metaphysics and the morals of his times; and, as all these things run back to those of past days, the problem is still further complicated. The humblest human being is the sum total of a column of figures which go back through centuries before he was born.

Old Crab Smith and Miss Asphyxia, if their biographies were rightly written, would be found to be the result and outcome of certain moral and social forces, justly to discriminate which might puzzle a philosopher. But be not alarmed, reader; I am not going to puzzle you, but to return in the briefest time possible to my story.

Harry was adopted into our family circle early in the autumn; and, after much discussion, it was resolved in the family synod that he and I should go to the common school in the neighborhood that winter, and out of school-hours share between us certain family tasks or "chores," as they were called at home.

Our daily life began at four o'clock in the morning, when the tapping of Aunt Lois's imperative heels on the back stairs, and her authoritative rap at our door, dispelled my slumbers. I was never much of a sleeper; my slumbers at best were light and cat-like; but Harry required all my help and my nervous wakefulness to get him to open his drowsy blue eyes, which he always did with the most perfectly amiable temper. He had that charming gift of physical good-humor which is often praised as a virtue in children and in grown people, but which is a mere condition of the animal nature. We all know that there are good-natured animals and irritable animals,—that the cow is tranquil and gentle, and the hyena snarly and fretful; but we never think of praising and rewarding the one, or punishing the other, for this obvious conformation. But in the case of the human animal it always happens that he who has the good luck to have a quiet, imperturbable nature has also the further good luck of being praised for it as for a Christian virtue, while he who has the ill fortune to be born with irritable nerves has the further ill fortune of being always considered a sinner on account of it.

Nobody that has not suffered from such causes can tell the amount of torture that a child of a certain nervous formation undergoes in the mere process of getting accustomed to his body, to the physical forces of life, and to the ways and doings of that world of grown-up people who have taken possession of the earth before him, and are using it, and determined to go on using it, for their own behoof and convenience, in spite of his childish efforts to push in his little individuality and seize his little portion of existence. He is at once laid hold upon by the older majority as an instrument to work out their views of what is fit and proper for himself and themselves; and if he proves a hard-working or creaking instrument, has the further capability of being rebuked and chastened for it.

My first morning feeling was generally one of anger at the sound of Aunt Lois's heels, worthy soul! I have lived to see the day when the tap of those efficient little instruments has seemed to me a most praiseworthy and desirable sound; but in those days they seemed only to be the reveille by which I was awakened to that daily battle of my will with hers which formed so great a feature in my life. It imposed in the first place the necessity of my quitting my warm bed in a room where the thermometer must have stood below zero, and where the snow, drifting through the loosely framed window, often lay in long wreaths on the floor.

As Aunt Lois always opened the door and set in a lighted candle, one of my sinful amusements consisted in lying and admiring the forest of glittering frost-work which had been made by our breath freezing upon the threads of the blanket. I sometimes saw rainbow colors in this frost-work, and went off into dreams and fancies about it, which ended in a doze, from which I was awakened, perhaps, by some of the snow from the floor rubbed smartly on my face, and the words, "How many times must you be called?" and opened my eyes to the vision of Aunt Lois standing over me indignant and admonitory.

Then I would wake Harry. We would spring from the bed and hurry on our clothes, buttoning them with fingers numb with cold, and run down to the back sink-room, where, in water that flew off in icy spatters, we performed our morning ablutions, refreshing our faces and hands by a brisk rub upon a coarse rolling-towel of brown homespun linen. Then with mittens, hats, and comforters, we were ready to turn out with old Cæsar to the barn to help him fodder the cattle. I must say that, when it came to this, on the whole it began to be grand fun for us. As Cæsar went ahead of us with his snow-shovel, we plunged laughing and rolling into the powdery element, with which we plentifully pelted him. Arrived at the barn we climbed, like cats, upon the mow, whence we joyously threw down enough for all his foddering purposes, and with such superabundant good-will in our efforts, that, had need so required, we would have stayed all day and flung off all the hay upon the mow; in fact, like the broomstick in the fable, which would persist in bringing water without rhyme or reason, so we overwhelmed our sable friend with avalanches of hay, which we cast down upon him in an inconsiderate fury of usefulness, and out of which we laughed to see him tear his way, struggling, gesticulating and remonstrating, till his black face shone with perspiration, and his woolly head bristled with hay-seeds and morsels of clover.

Then came the feeding of the hens and chickens and other poultry, a work in which we especially delighted, going altogether beyond Cæsar in our largesses of corn, and requiring

a constant interposition of his authority to prevent our emptying the crib on every single occasion.

In very severe weather we sometimes found hens or turkeys
so overcome with the cold as to require, in Cæsar's view,
hospital treatment. This awoke our sympathies, and stimulated our sense of personal importance, and we were never so
happy as when trudging back through the snow, following
Cæsar with a great cock-turkey lying languidly over his shoulder like a sick baby, his long neck drooping, his wattles, erst
so fiery red with pride and valor, now blue and despairing.
Great on such occasions were our zeal and excitement, as the
cavalcade burst into the kitchen with much noise, and upturn-
ing of everything, changing Aunt Lois's quiet arrangements
into an impromptu sanitary commission. My grandmother
bestirred herself promptly, compounding messes of Indian-
meal enlivened with pepper-corns, which were forced incon-
tinently down the long throat, and which in due time acted
as a restorative.

A turkey treated in this way soon recovered his wonted
pride of demeanor, and, with an ingratitude which is like the
ways of this world, would be ready to bully my grandmother
and fly at her back when she was picking up chips, and charge
down upon us children with vociferous gobblings, the very
first warm day afterwards. Such toils as these before breakfast
gave a zest to the smoking hot brown bread, the beans and
sausages, which formed our morning meal.

The great abundance of *food* in our New England life is one
subject quite worthy of reflection, if we consider the hardness
of the soil, the extreme severity of the climate, and the short-
ness of the growing season between the late frosts of spring
and those of early autumn. But, as matter of fact, good, plain
food was everywhere in New England so plentiful, that at the
day I write of nobody could really suffer for the want of it.
The theocracy of New England had been so thoroughly saturated with the humane and charitable spirit of the old laws
of Moses, in which, dealing "bread to the hungry" is so often
reiterated and enforced as foremost among human duties,
that no one ever thought of refusing food to any that appeared to need it; and a traveller might have walked on foot
from one end of New England to the other, as sure of a meal

in its season as he was that he saw a farm-house. Even if there
was now and then a Nabal like Crab Smith, who, from a
native viciousness, hated to do kindness, there was always
sure to be in his family an Abigail, ashamed of his baseness,
who redeemed the credit of the house by a surreptitious practice of the Christian virtues.

I mention all this because it strikes me, in review of my
childhood, that, although far from wealth, and living in many
respects in a hard and rough way, I remember great enjoyment in that part of our physical life so important to a
child,—the eating and drinking. Our bread, to be sure, was
the black compound of rye and Indian which the economy of
Massachusetts then made the common form, because it was
the result of what could be most easily raised on her hard and
stony soil; but I can inform all whom it may concern that rye
and Indian bread smoking hot, on a cold winter morning,
together with savory sausages, pork, and beans, formed a
breakfast fit for a king, if the king had earned it by getting
up in a cold room, washing in ice-water, tumbling through
snow-drifts, and foddering cattle. We partook of it with a
thorough cheeriness; and black Cæsar, seated on his block in
the chimney-corner, divided his rations with Bose, the yellow
dog of our establishment, with a contentment which it was
pleasant to behold.

After breakfast grandfather conducted family prayers, commencing always by reading his chapter in the Bible. He read
regularly through in course, as was the custom in those days,
without note, comment, or explanation. Among the many insensible forces which formed the minds of New England children, was this constant, daily familiarity with the letter of the
Bible. It was for the most part read twice a day in every family of any pretensions to respectability, and it was read as a
reading-book in every common school,—in both cases without any attempt at explanation. Such parts as explained themselves were left to do so. Such as were beyond our knowledge
were still read, and left to make what impression they would.
For my part, I am impatient of the theory of those who think
that nothing that is not understood makes any valuable
impression on the mind of a child. I am certain that the constant contact of the Bible with my childish mind was a very

great mental stimulant, as it certainly was a cause of a singular and vague pleasure. The wild, poetic parts of the prophecies, with their bold figures, vivid exclamations, and strange Oriental names and images, filled me with a quaint and solemn delight. Just as a child brought up under the shadow of the great cathedrals of the Old World, wandering into them daily, at morning, or eventide, beholding the many-colored windows flamboyant with strange legends of saints and angels, and neither understanding the legends, nor comprehending the architecture, is yet stilled and impressed, till the old minster grows into his growth and fashions his nature, so this wonderful old cathedral book insensibly wrought a sort of mystical poetry into the otherwise hard and sterile life of New England. Its passionate Oriental phrases, its quaint, pathetic stories, its wild, transcendent bursts of imagery, fixed an indelible mark in my imagination. Where Kedar and Tarshish and Pul and Lud, Chittim and the Isles, Dan and Beersheba, were, or what they were, I knew not, but they were fixed stations in my realm of cloud-land. I knew them as well as I knew my grandmother's rocking-chair, yet the habit of hearing of them only in solemn tones, and in the readings of religious hours, gave to them a mysterious charm. I think no New-Englander, brought up under the *régime* established by the Puritans, could really estimate how much of himself had actually been formed by this constant face-to-face intimacy with Hebrew literature. It is worthy of remark, too, that, although in details relating to human crime and vice, the Old Bible is the most plain-spoken book conceivable, it never violated the chastity of a child's mind, or stimulated an improper curiosity. I have been astonished in later years to learn the real meaning of passages to which, in family prayers, I listened with innocent gravity.

My grandfather's prayers had a regular daily form, to which, in time, I became quite accustomed. No man of not more than ordinary capacity ever ministered twice a day the year round, in the office of priest to his family, without soon learning to repeat the same ideas in the same phrases, forming to himself a sort of individual liturgy. My grandfather always prayed standing, and the image of his mild, silvery head, leaning over the top of the high-backed chair, always rises before

me as I think of early days. There was no great warmth or
fervor in these daily exercises, but rather a serious and decorous propriety. They were Hebraistic in their form; they
spoke of Zion and Jerusalem, of the God of Israel, the God
of Jacob, as much as if my grandfather had been a veritable
Jew; and except for the closing phrase, "for the sake of thy
Son, our Saviour," might all have been uttered in Palestine by
a well-trained Jew in the time of David.

When prayers were over every morning, the first move of
the day, announced in Aunt Lois's brief energetic phrases,
was to "get the boys out of the way." Our dinner was packed
in a small splint basket, and we were started on our way to
the district school, about a mile distant. We had our sleds
with us,—dear winter companions of boys,—not the gayly
painted, genteel little sledges with which Boston boys in these
days enliven the Common, but rude, coarse fabrics, got up by
Cæsar in rainy days out of the odds and ends of old sleigh-
runners and such rough boards as he could rudely fashion
with saw and hatchet. Such as they were, they suited us
well,—mine in particular, because upon it I could draw Tina
to school; for already, children as we were, things had naturally settled themselves between us. She was supreme mistress, and I the too happy slave, only anxious to be permitted
to do her bidding. With Harry and me she assumed the negligent airs of a little empress. She gave us her books to carry,
called on us to tie her shoes, charged us to remember her
errands, got us to learn her lessons for her, and to help her
out with whatever she had no mind to labor at; and we were
only too happy to do it. Harry was the most doting of brothers, and never could look on Tina in any other light than as
one whom he must at any price save from every care and
every exertion; and as for me, I never dreamed of disputing
her supremacy.

One may, perhaps, wonder how a person so extremely aristocratic in all her ideas of female education as Miss Mehitable
should commit her little charge to the chance comradeship
and unselect society of the district school. But Miss Mehitable, like many another person who has undertaken the task
of bringing up a human being, found herself reduced to the
doing of a great many things which she had never expected

to do. She prepared for her work in the most thorough manner; she read Locke and Milton, and Dr. Gregory's "Legacy to his Daughter," and Mrs. Chapone on the bringing up of girls, to say nothing of Miss Hannah More and all the other wise people; and, after forming some of the most carefully considered and select plans of operation for herself and her little charge, she was at length driven to the discovery that in education, as in all other things, people who cannot do as they would must do as they can. She discovered that a woman between fifty and sixty years of age, of a peculiar nature, and with very fixed, set habits, could not undertake to be the sole companion and educator of a lively, wilful, spirited little pilgrim of mortality, who was as active as a squirrel, and as inconsequent and uncertain in all her movements as a butterfly.

By some rare good fortune of nature or of grace, she found her little *protégée* already able to read with fluency, and a tolerable mistress of the use of the needle and thimble. Thus she possessed the key of useful knowledge and of useful feminine practice. But truth compels us to state that there appeared not the smallest prospect, during the first few weeks of Miss Mehitable's educational efforts, that she would ever make a good use of either. In vain Miss Mehitable had written a nice card, marking out regular hours for sewing, for reading, for geography and grammar, with suitable intervals of amusement; and in vain Miss Tina, with edifying enthusiasm, had promised, with large eyes and most abundant eloquence, and with many overflowing caresses, to be "so good." Alas! when it came to carrying out the programme, all alone in the old house, Mondays, Tuesdays, Wednesdays, Thursdays, Fridays, and all days, Tina gaped and nestled, and lost her thimble and her needle, and was infinite in excuses, and infinite in wheedling caresses, and arguments, enforced with flattering kisses, in favor of putting off the duties now of this hour and then of that, and substituting something more to her fancy. She had a thousand plans of her own for each passing hour, and no end of argument and eloquence to persuade her old friend to follow her ways,—to hear her read an old ballad instead of applying herself to her arithmetic lesson, or listen to her recital of something that she had just picked out of English history, or let her finish a drawing that she was just inspired

to commence, or spend a bright, sunny hour in flower-gath-
erings and rambles by the brown river-side; whence she
would return laden with flowers, and fill every vase in the old,
silent room till it would seem as if the wilderness had literally
blossomed as the rose. Tina's knack for the arranging of vases
and twining of vines and sorting of wild-flowers amounted to
a species of genius; and, as it was something of which Miss
Mehitable had not the slightest comprehension, the child
took the lead in this matter with a confident assurance. And,
after all, the effect was so cheerful and so delightful, that Miss
Mehitable could not find it in her heart to call to the mind of
the little wood-fairy how many hours these cheerful decorations had cost.

Thus poor Miss Mehitable found herself daily being drawn,
by the leash that held this gay bird, into all sorts of unseemly
gyrations and wanderings, instead of using it to tether the
bird to her own well-considered purposes. She could not
deny that the child was making her old days pass in a very
amusing manner, and it was so much easier to follow the
lively little sprite in all her airy ways and caprices, seeing her
lively and spirited and happy, than to watch the *ennui* and
the yawns and the restlessness that came over her with every
effort to conform to the strict letter of the programme, that
good Miss Mehitable was always yielding. Every night she
went to bed with an unquiet conscience, sensible that, though
she had had an entertaining day, she had been letting Tina
govern her, instead of governing Tina.

Over that grave supposed necessity of governing Tina, this
excellent woman groaned in spirit on many a night after the
little wheedling tongue had become silent, and the bright,
deluding eyes had gone down under their fringy lashes. "The
fact is," said the sad old woman, "Miss Asphyxia spoke the
truth. It is a fact, I am not fit to bring up a child. She does
rule over me, just as she said she would, and I 'm a poor old
fool; but then, what am I to do? She is so bright and sweet
and pretty, and I 'm a queer-looking, dry, odd old woman,
with nobody to love me if she does n't. If I cross her and tie
her to rules, and am severe with her, she won't love me, and
I am too selfish to risk that. Besides, only think what came of
using severe measures with poor Emily! people can be spoilt

by severity just as much as by indulgence, and more hopelessly. But what shall I do?"

Miss Mehitable at first had some hope of supporting and
backing up the weaknesses of her own heart by having recourse to Polly's well-known energy. Polly was a veritable
dragon of education, and strong in the most efficient articles
of faith. Children must have their wills *broken*, as she expressed it, "short off"; they must mind the very first time you
speak; they must be kept under and made to go according to
rule, and, if they swerved, Polly recommended measures of
most sanguinary severity.

But somehow or other Tina had contrived to throw over
this grimmest and most Calvinistic of virgins the glamour of
her presence, so that she ruled, reigned, and predominated in
the most awful sanctuaries of Polly's kitchen, with a fearfully
unconcerned and negligent freedom. She dared to peep into
her yeast-jug in the very moment of projection, and to pinch
off from her downy puffs of newly raised bread sly morsels
for her own cooking experiments; she picked from Polly's
very hand the raisins which the good woman was stoning for
the most awfully sacred election cake, and resolutely persisted
in hanging on her chair and chattering in her ear during the
evolution of high culinary mysteries with which the Eleusin-
ian, or any other heathen trumperies of old, were not to be
named. Had n't the receipt for election cake been in the family for one hundred years? and was not Polly the sacred ark
and tabernacle in which that divine secret resided? Even Miss
Mehitable had always been politely requested to step out of
the kitchen when Polly was composing her mind for this serious work, but yet Tina neglected her geography and sewing
to be present, chattered all the time, as Polly remarked, like a
grist-mill, tasted the sugar and spices, and helped herself at
intervals to the savory composition as it was gradually being
put together, announcing her opinions, and giving Polly her
advice, with an effrontery to which Polly's submission was
something appalling.

It really used to seem to Miss Mehitable, as she listened to
Polly's dissonant shrieks of laughter from the kitchen, as if
that venerable old girl must be slightly intoxicated. Polly's
laughter was in truth something quite formidable. All the or-

gans in her which would usually be employed in this exercise were so rusty for want of use, so choked up with theological dust and *débris*, that when brought into exercise they had a wild, grating, dissonant sound, rather calculated to alarm. Miss Mehitable really wondered if this could be the same Polly of whom she herself stood in a certain secret awe, whose premises she never invaded, and whose will over and about her had been always done instead of her own; but if she ventured to open the kitchen door and recall Tina, she was sure to be vigorously snubbed by Polly, who walked over all her own precepts and maxims in the most shameless and astonishing manner.

Polly, however, made up for her own compliances by heaping up censures on poor Miss Mehitable when Tina had gone to bed at night. When the bright eyes were fairly closed, and the little bewitching voice hushed in sleep, Polly's conscience awoke like an armed man, and she atoned for her own sins of compliance and indulgence by stringently admonishing Miss Mehitable that she must be more particular about that child, and not let her get her own head so much,—most unblushingly ignoring her own share in abetting her transgressions, and covering her own especial sins under the declaration that "*she* never had undertaken to bring the child up,—she had to get along with her the best way she could,—but the child never would make anything if she was let to go on so." Yet, in any particular case that arose, Polly was always sure to go over to Tina's side and back her usurpations.

For example, it is to be confessed that Tina never could or would be got to bed at those hours which are universally admitted to be canonical for well-brought-up children. As night drew on, the little one's tongue ran with increasing fluency, and her powers of entertainment waxed more dizzy and dazzling; and so, oftentimes, as the drizzling, freezing night shut in, and the wind piped and howled lonesomely round the corners of the dusky old mansion, neither of the two forlorn women could find it in her heart to extinguish the little cheerful candle of their dwelling in bed; and so she was to them ballet and opera as she sung and danced, mimicked the dog, mimicked the cat and the hens and the tom-turkey, and at last

talked and flew about the room like Aunt Lois, stirred up
butter and pshawed like grandma, or invented imaginary
scenes and conversations, or improvised unheard-of costumes
out of strange old things she had rummaged out of Miss
Mehitable's dark closets. Neither of the two worthy women
had ever seen the smallest kind of dramatic representation, so
that Tina's histrionic powers fascinated them by touching
upon dormant faculties, and seemed more wonderful for their
utter novelty; and more than once, to the poignant self-
reproach of Miss Mehitable, and Polly's most moral indignation, nine o'clock struck, in the inevitable tones of the old
family time-piece, before they were well aware what they were
doing. Then Tina would be hustled off to bed, and Polly
would preach Miss Mehitable a strenuous discourse on the
necessity of keeping children to regular hours, interspersed
with fragments of quotations from one of her venerable father's early sermons on the Christian bringing up of households. Polly would grow inexorable as conscience on these
occasions, and when Miss Mehitable humbly pleaded in extenuation how charming a little creature it was, and what a
pleasant evening she had given, Polly would shake her head,
and declare that the ways of sin were always pleasant for a
time, but at the last it would "bite like a serpent and sting like
an adder"; and when Miss Mehitable, in the most delicate
manner, would insinuate that Polly had been sharing the forbidden fruit, such as it was, Polly would flare up in sudden
wrath, and declare that "everything that went wrong was always laid to her."

In consequence of this, though Miss Mehitable found the
first few weeks with her little charge altogether the gayest and
brightest that had diversified her dreary life, yet there was a
bitter sense of self-condemnation and perplexity with it all.
One day she opened her mind to my grandmother.

"Laws a massy! don't try to teach her yourself," said that
plain-spoken old individual,—"send her to school with the
boys. Children have to go in droves. What's the use of
fussing with 'em all day? let the schoolmaster take a part of
the care. Children have to be got rid of sometimes, and we
come to them all the fresher for having them out of our
sight."

The consequence was, that Tina rode to school on our sleds in triumph, and made more fun, and did more mischief, and learned less, and was more adored and desired, than any other scholar of us all.

XXIII.

We Take a Step up in the World

ONE of my most vivid childish remembrances is the length of our winters, the depth of the snows, the raging fury of the storms that used to whirl over the old farmhouse, shrieking and piping and screaming round each angle and corner, and thundering down the chimney in a way that used to threaten to topple all down before it.

The one great central kitchen fire was the only means of warming known in the house, and duly at nine o'clock every night *that* was raked up, and all the family took their way to bed-chambers that never knew a fire, where the very sheets and blankets seemed so full of stinging cold air that they made one's fingers tingle; and where, after getting into bed, there was a prolonged shiver, until one's own internal heat-giving economy had warmed through the whole icy mass. Delicate people had these horrors ameliorated by the application of a brass warming-pan,—an article of high respect and repute in those days, which the modern conveniences for warmth in our houses have entirely banished.

Then came the sleet storms, when the trees bent and creaked under glittering mail of ice, and every sprig and spray of any kind of vegetation was reproduced in sparkling crystals. These were cold days *par excellence,* when everybody talked of the weather as something exciting and tremendous, —when the cider would freeze in the cellar, and the bread in the milk-room would be like blocks of ice,—when not a drop of water could be got out of the sealed well, and the very chimney-back over the raked-up fire would be seen in the morning sparkling with a rime of frost crystals. How the sledges used to squeak over the hard snow, and the breath freeze on the hair, and beard, and woolly comforters around the necks of the men, as one and another brought in news of the wonderful, unheard-of excesses of Jack Frost during the foregone night! There was always something exhilarating about those extremely cold days, when a very forest of logs, heaped up and burning in the great chimney, could not warm the other side of the kitchen; and when Aunt Lois, standing with her back so near the blaze as to be uncomfortably warm, yet found her dish-towel freezing in her hand, while she wiped the teacup drawn from the almost boiling water. When things got to this point, we little folks were jolly. It was an excitement, an intoxication; it filled life full of talk. People froze the tips of their noses, their ears, their toes; we froze our own. Whoever touched a door-latch incautiously, in the early morning, received a skinning bite from Jack. The axe, the saw, the hatchet, all the iron tools, in short, were possessed of a cold devil ready to snap out at any incautious hand that meddled with him. What ponderous stalactites of ice used to hang from the eaves, and hung unmelted days, weeks, and months, dripping a little, perhaps, towards noon, but hardening again as night came on! and how long all this lasted! To us children it seemed ages.

Then came April with here and there a sunny day. A bluebird would be vaguely spoken of as having appeared. Sam Lawson was usually the first to announce the fact, to the sharp and sceptical contempt of his helpmeet.

On a shimmering April morning, with a half-mind to be sunshiny, Sam saw Harry and myself trotting by his door, and called to us for a bit of gossip.

"Lordy massy, boys, ain't it pleasant? Why, bless your soul and body, I do believe spring 's a comin', though Hepsy she won't believe it," he said, as he leaned over the fence contemplatively, with the axe in his hand. "I heard a bluebird last week, Jake Marshall and me, when we was goin' over to Hopkinton to see how Ike Saunders is. You know he is down with the measles. I went over to offer to sit up with him. Where be ye goin' this mornin'?"

"We 're going to the minister's. Grandfather is n't well, and Lady Lothrop told us to come for some wine."

"Jes' so," said Sam. "Wal, now, he orter take something for his stomach's sake, Scriptur' goes in for that. A little good hot spiced wine, it 's jest the thing; and Ma'am Lothrop, she has the very best. Why, some o' that 'ere wine o' hern come over from England years ago, when her fust husband was living;

and he was a man that knew where to get his things. Wal, you must n't stop to play; allers remember when you 're sent on errands not to be a idlin' on the road."

"Sam Lawson, will you split me that oven-wood or won't you?" said a smart, cracking voice, as the door flew open and Hepsy's thin face and snapping black eyes appeared, as she stood with a weird, wiry, sharp-visaged baby exalted on one shoulder, while in the other hand she shook a dish-cloth.

"Lordy massy, Hepsy, I 'm splittin' as fast as I can. There, run along, boys; don't stop to play."

We ran along, for, truth to say, the vision of Hepsy's sharp features always quickened our speed, and we heard the loud, high-pitched storm of matrimonial objurgation long after we had left them behind.

Timidly we struck the great knocker, and with due respect and modesty told our errand to the black doctor of divinity who opened the door.

"I 'll speak to Missis," he said; "but this 'ere 's Missis' great day; it 's Good Friday, and she don't come out of her room the whole blessed day."

"But she sent word that we should come," we both answered in one voice.

"Well, you jest wait here while I go up and see,"—and the important messenger creaked up stairs on tiptoe with infinite precaution, and knocked at a chamber door.

Now there was something in all this reception that was vaguely solemn and impressive to us. The minister's house of itself was a dignified and august place. The minister was in our minds great and greatly to be feared, and to be had in reverence of them that were about him. The minister's wife was a very great lady, who wore very stiff silks, and rode in a coach, and had no end of unknown wealth at her control, so ran the village gossip. And now what this mysterious Good Friday was, and why the house was so still, and why the black doctor of divinity tiptoed up stairs so stealthily, and knocked at her door so timidly, we could not exactly conjecture;—it was all of a piece with the general marvellous and supernatural character of the whole establishment.

We heard above the silvery well-bred tones that marked Lady Lothrop.

"Tell the children to come up."

We looked at each other, and each waited a moment for the other to lead the way; finally I took the lead, and Harry followed. We entered a bedroom shaded in a sombre gloom which seemed to our childish eyes mysterious and impressive. There were three windows in the room, but the shutters were closed, and the only light that came in was from heart-shaped apertures in each one. There was in one corner a tall, solemn-looking, high-post bedstead with heavy crimson draperies. There were heavy carved bureaus and chairs of black, solid oak.

At a table covered with dark cloth sat Lady Lothrop, dressed entirely in black, with a great Book of Common Prayer spread out before her. The light from the heart-shaped hole streamed down upon this prayer-book in a sort of dusky shaft, and I was the more struck and impressed because it was not an ordinary volume, but a great folio bound in parchment, with heavy brass knobs and clasps, printed in black-letter, of that identical old edition first prepared in King Edward's time, and appointed to be read in churches. Its very unusual and antique appearance impressed me with a kind of awe.

There was at the other end of the room a tall, full-length mirror, which, as we advanced, duplicated the whole scene, giving back faithfully the image of the spare figure of Lady Lothrop, her grave and serious face, and the strange old book over which she seemed to be bending, with a dusky gleaming of crimson draperies in the background.

"Come here, my children," she said, as we hesitated; "how is your grandfather?"

"He is not so well to-day; and grandmamma said—"

"Yes, yes; I know," she said, with a gentle little wave of the hand; "I desired that you might be sent for some wine; Pompey shall have it ready for you. But tell me, little boys, do you know what day this is?"

"It's Friday, ma'am," said I, innocently.

"Yes, my child; but do you know *what* Friday it is?" she said.

"No, ma'am," said I, faintly.

"Well, my child, it is Good Friday; and do you know why it is called Good Friday?"

"No, ma'am."

"This is the day when our Lord and Saviour Jesus Christ died on the cross for our salvation; so we call it Good Friday."

I must confess that these words struck me with a strange and blank amazement. That there had been in this world a personage called "Our Lord and Saviour Jesus Christ," I had learned from the repetition of his name as the usual ending of prayers at church and in the family; but the real literal fact that he had lived on earth had never presented itself to me in any definite form before; but this solemn and secluded room, this sombre woman shut out from all the ordinary ways of the world, devoting the day to lonely musing, gave to her words a strange reality.

"When did he die?" I said.

"More than a thousand years ago," she answered.

Insensibly Harry had pressed forward till he stood in the shaft of light, which fell upon his golden curls, and his large blue eyes now had that wide-open, absorbed expression with which he always listened to anything of a religious nature, and, as if speaking involuntarily, he said eagerly, "But he is not dead. He is living; and we pray to him."

"Why, yes, my son," said Lady Lothrop, turning and looking with pleased surprise, which became more admiring as she gazed,—"yes, he rose from the dead."

"I know. Mother told me all about that. Day after to-morrow will be Easter day," said Harry; "I remember."

A bright flush of pleased expression passed over Lady Lothrop's face as she said, "I am glad, my boy, that *you* at least have been taught. Tell me, boys," she said at last, graciously, "should you like to go with me in my carriage to Easter Sunday, in Boston?"

Had a good fairy offered to take us on the rainbow to the palace of the sunset, the offer could not have seemed more unworldly and dream-like. What Easter Sunday was I had not the faintest idea, but I felt it to be something vague, strange, and remotely suggestive of the supernatural.

Harry, however, stood the thing in the simple, solemn, gentlemanlike way which was habitual with him.

"Thank you, ma'am, I shall be very happy, if grandmamma is willing."

It will be seen that Harry slid into the adoptive familiarity which made my grandmother his, with the easy good faith of childhood.

"Tell your grandmamma if she is willing I shall call for you in my coach to-morrow,"—and we were graciously dismissed.

We ran home in all haste with our bottle of wine, and burst into the kitchen, communicating our message both at once to Aunt Lois and Aunt Keziah. The two women looked at each other mysteriously; there was a slight flush on Aunt Lois's keen, spare face.

"Well, if she's a mind to do it, Kezzy, I don't see how we can refuse."

"Mother never would consent in the world," said Aunt Keziah.

"Mother *must*," said Aunt Lois, with decision. "We can't afford to offend Lady Lothrop, with both these boys on our hands. Besides, now father is sick, what a mercy to have 'em both out of the house for a Sunday!"

Aunt Lois spoke this with an intensive earnestness that deepened my already strong convictions that we boys were a daily load upon her life, only endured by a high and protracted exercise of Christian fortitude.

She rose and tapped briskly into the bedroom where my grandmother was sitting reading by my grandfather's bed. I heard her making some rapid statements in a subdued, imperative tone. There were a few moments of a sort of suppressed, earnest hum of conversation, and soon we heard sundry vehement interjections from my grandmother,—"Good Friday! —Easter!—pish, Lois!—don't tell me!—old cast-off rags of the scarlet woman,—nothing else.

'Abhor the arrant whore of Rome.
And all her blasphemies;
Drink not of her accursed cup,
Obey not her decrees.' "

"Now, mother, how absurd!" I heard Aunt Lois say. "Who's talking about Rome? I'm sure, if Dr. Lothrop can allow it, we can. It's all nonsense to talk so. We don't want to offend our minister's wife; we must do the things that make for peace"; and then the humming went on for a few moments more and more earnestly, till finally we heard grandmother break out:—

"Well, well, have it your own way, Lois,—you always did and always will, I suppose. Glad the boys 'll have a holiday, anyhow. She means well, I dare say,—thinks she's doing right."

I must say that this was a favorite formula with which my grandmother generally let herself down from the high platform of her own sharply defined opinions to the level of Christian charity with her neighbors.

"Who is the whore of Rome?" said Harry to me, confidentially, when we had gone to our room to make ready for our jaunt the next day.

"Don't you know?" said I. "Why, it's the one that burnt John Rogers, in the Catechism. I can show it to you"; and, forthwith producing from my small stock of books my New England Primer, I called his attention to the picture of Mr. John Rogers in gown and bands, standing in the midst of a brisk and voluminous coil of fire and smoke, over which an executioner, with a supernatural broadaxe upon his shoulders, seemed to preside with grim satisfaction. There was a woman with a baby in her arms and nine children at her side, who stood in a row, each head being just a step lower than the preceding, so that they made a regular flight of stairs. The artist had represented the mother and all the children with a sort of round bundle on each of their heads, of about the same size as the head itself,—a thing which I always interpreted as a further device of the enemy in putting stones on their heads to crush them down; and I pointed it out to Harry as an aggravating feature of the martyrdom.

"Did the whore of Rome do that?" said Harry, after a few moments' reflection.

"Yes, she did, and it tells about it in the poetry which he wrote here to his children the night before his execution"; and forthwith I proceeded to read to Harry that whole poetical production, delighted to find a gap in his education which I was competent to fill. We were both wrought up into a highly Protestant state by reading this.

"Horace," said Harry, timidly, "*she* would n't like such things, would she? she is such a good woman."

"What, Lady Lothrop? of course she 's a good woman; else she would n't be our minister's wife."

"What was grandma talking about?" said Harry.

"O, I don't know; grandmother talks about a great many things," said I. "At any rate, we shall see Boston, and I 've always wanted to see Boston. Only think, Harry, we shall go in a coach!"

This projected tour to Boston was a glorification of us children in the eyes of the whole family. To go, on the humblest of terms, *to Boston*,—but to be taken thither in Lady Lothrop's coach, to be trotted in magnificently behind her fat pair of carriage-horses,—that was a good fortune second only to translation.

Boston lay at an easy three hours' ride from Oldtown, and Lady Lothrop had signified to my grandmother that we were to be called for soon after dinner. We were to spend the night and the Sunday following at the house of Lady Lothrop's mother, who still kept the old family mansion at the north end, and Lady Lothrop was graciously pleased to add that she would keep the children over Easter Monday, to show them Boston. Faithful old soul, she never omitted the opportunity of reminding the gainsaying community among whom her lot was cast of the solemn days of her church and for one *I* have remembered Easter Sunday and Monday to this day.

Our good fortune received its crowning stroke in our eyes when, running over to Miss Mehitable's with the news, we found that Lady Lothrop had considerately included Tina in the invitation.

"Well, she must like children better than I do," was Aunt Lois's comment upon the fact, when we announced it. "Now, boys, mind and behave yourselves like young gentlemen," she added, "for you are going to one of the oldest families of Boston, among real genteel people."

"They 're Tories, Lois," put in Aunt Keziah, apprehensively.

"Well, what of that? that thing 's over and gone now," said

Aunt Lois, "and nobody lays it up against the Kitterys, and everybody knows they were in the very first circles in Boston before the war, and connected with the highest people in England, so it was quite natural they should be Tories."

"I should n't wonder if Lady Widgery should be there," said Aunt Keziah, musingly, as she twitched her yarn; "she always used to come to Boston about this time o' the year."

"Very likely she will," said my mother. "What relation is she to Lady Lothrop?"

"Why, bless me, don't you know?" said Aunt Lois. "Why, she was Polly Steadman, and sister to old Ma'am Kittery's husband's first wife. She was second wife to Sir Thomas; his first wife was one of the Keatons of Penshurst, in England; she died while Sir Thomas was in the custom-house; she was a poor, sickly thing. Polly was a great beauty in her day. People said he admired her rather too much before his wife died, but I don't know how that was."

"I wonder what folks want to say such things for," quoth my grandmother. "I hate backbiters, for my part."

"We are n't backbiting, mother. I only said how the story ran. It was years ago, and poor Sir Thomas is in his grave long ago."

"Then you might let him rest there," said my grandmother. "Lady Widgery was a pleasant-spoken woman, I remember."

"She 's quite an invalid now, I heard," said Aunt Lois. "Our Bill was calling at the Kitterys' the other day, and Miss Deborah Kittery spoke of expecting Lady Widgery. The Kitterys have been very polite to Bill; they 've invited him there to dinner once or twice this winter. That was one reason why I thought we ought to be careful how we treat Lady Lothrop's invitation. It 's entirely through her influence that Bill gets these attentions."

"I don't know about their being the best thing for him," said my grandmother, doubtfully.

"Mother, how can you talk so? What can be better than for a young man to have the run of good families in Boston?" said Aunt Lois.

"I 'd rather see him have intimacy with one godly minister of old times," said my grandmother.

"Well, that 's what Bill is n't likely to do," quoth Aunt

Lois, with a slight shade of impatience. "We must take boys as we find 'em."

"I have n't anything against Tories or Episcopalians," said my grandmother; "but they ain't our sort of folks. I dare say they mean as well as they know how."

"Miss Mehitable visits the Kitterys when she is in Boston," said Aunt Lois, "and thinks everything of them. She says that Deborah Kittery is a very smart, intelligent woman,—a woman of a very strong mind."

"I dare say they 're well enough," said my grandmother. "I 'm sure I wish 'em well with all my heart."

"Now, Horace," said Aunt Lois, "be careful you don't sniff, and be sure and wipe your shoes on the mat when you come in, and never on any account speak a word unless you are spoken to. Little boys should be seen and not heard; and be very careful you never touch anything you see. It is very good of Lady Lothrop to be willing to take all the trouble of having you with her, and you must make her just as little as possible."

I mentally resolved to reduce myself to a nonentity, to go out of existence, as it were, to be nobody and nowhere, if only I might escape making trouble.

"As to Harry, he is always a good, quiet boy, and never touches things, or forgets to wipe his shoes," said my aunt. "I 'm sure he will behave himself."

My mother colored slightly at this undisguised partiality for Harry, but she was too much under Aunt Lois's discipline to venture a word.

"Lordy massy, Mis' Badger, how do ye all do?" said Sam Lawson, this moment appearing at the kitchen door. "I saw your winders so bright, I thought I 'd jest look in and ask after the Deacon. I ben into Miss Mehitable's, and there 's Polly, she told me about the chillen goin' to Boston to-morrow. Tiny, she 's jest flying round and round like a lightning-bug, most out of her head, she 's so tickled; and Polly, she was a i'nin' up her white aprons to get her up smart. Polly, she says it 's all pagan flummery about Easter, but she 's glad the chillen are goin' to have the holiday." And with this Sam Lawson seated himself on his usual evening roost in the corner, next to black Cæsar, and we both came and stood by his knee.

"Wal, boys, now you 're goin' among real, old-fashioned gentility. Them Kitterys used to hold their heads 'mazin' high afore the war, and they 've managed by hook and crook to hold on to most what they got, and now by-gones is by-gones. But I believe they don't go out much, or go into company. Old Ma'am Kittery, she 's kind o' broke up about her son that was killed at the Delaware."

"Fighting on the wrong side, poor woman," said my grandmother. "Well, I s'pose he thought he was doing right."

"Yes, yes," said Sam, "there 's all sorts o' folks go to make up a world, and, lordy massy, we must n't be hard on no-body; can't 'spect everybody to be right all round; it 's what I tell Polly when she sniffs at Lady Lothrop keepin' Christmas and Easter and sich. 'Lordy massy, Polly,' says I, 'if she reads her Bible, and 's good to the poor, and don't speak evil o' nobody, why, let her have her Easter; what 's the harm on 't?' But, lordy massy bless your soul an' body! there 's no kind o' use talkin' to Polly. She fumed away there, over her i'nin' table; she did n't believe in folks that read their prayers out o' books; and then she hed it all over about them tew thousan' ministers that was all turned out o' the church in one day in old King Charles's time. Now, raily, Mis' Badger, I don't see why Lady Lothrop should be held 'sponsible for that are, if she is 'Piscopalian."

"Well, well," said my grandmother; "they did turn out the very best men in England, but the Lord took 'em for seed to plant America with. But no wonder we feel it: burnt children dread the fire. I 've nothing against Lady Lothrop, and I don't wish evil to the Episcopalians nor to the Tories. There 's good folks among 'em all, and 'the Lord knoweth them that are his.' But I do hope, Horace, that, when you get to Boston, you will go out on to Copps Hill and see the graves of the Saints. There are the men that I want my children to remember. You come here, and let me read you about them in my 'Magnaly'* here." And with this my grandmother produced her well-worn copy; and, to say the truth, we were never tired of hearing what there was in it. What legends, wonderful and stirring, of the solemn old forest life,—of fights with the Indians, and thrilling adventures, and captivi-

*Dr. Cotton Mather's "Magnalia."

ties, and distresses,—of encounters with panthers and serpents, and other wild beasts, which made our very hair stand
on end! Then there were the weird witch-stories, so wonderfully attested; and how Mr. Peter So-and-so did visibly see,
when crossing a river, a cat's head swimming in front of the
boat, and the tail of the same following behind; and how
worthy people had been badgered and harassed by a sudden
friskiness in all their household belongings, in a manner not
unknown in our modern days. Of all these fascinating legends
my grandmother was a willing communicator, and had, to
match them, numbers of corresponding ones from her own
personal observation and experience; and sometimes Sam
Lawson would chime in with long-winded legends, which,
being told by flickering firelight, with the wind rumbling and
tumbling down the great chimney, or shrieking and yelling
and piping around every corner of the house, like an army of
fiends trying with tooth and claw to get in upon us, had
power to send cold chills down our backs in the most charming manner.

For my part, I had not the slightest fear of the supernatural; it was to me only a delightful stimulant, just crisping the
surface of my mind with a pleasing horror. I had not any
doubt of the stories of apparitions related by Dr. Cotton, because I had seen so many of them myself; and I did not doubt
that many of the witnesses who testified in these cases really
did see what they said they saw, as plainly as I had seen similar
appearances. The consideration of the fact that there really are
people in whose lives such phenomena are of frequent occurrence seems to have been entirely left out of the minds of
those who have endeavored to explain that dark passage in
our history.

In my maturer years I looked upon this peculiarity as something resulting from a physical idiosyncrasy, and I have supposed that such affections may become at times epidemics in
communities, as well as any other affection of the brain and
nervous system. Whether the things thus discerned have an
objective reality or not, has been one of those questions at
which, all my life, the interrogation point has stood unerased.

On this evening, however, my grandmother thought fit to
edify us by copious extracts from "The Second Part, entituled

Sepher-Jearim, i. e. *Liber Deum Timentium*; or, Dead Abels;—
yet speaking and spoken of."

The lives of several of these "Dead Abels" were her favorite
reading, and to-night she designed especially to fortify our
minds with their biographies; so she gave us short dips and
extracts here and there from several of them, as, for example:
"*Janus Nov.-Anglicus*; or, The Life of Mr. Samuel Higginson";—"*Cadmus Americanus*; or, Life of Mr. Charles Chaun-
cey";—"*Cygnea Cantio*; or, The Death of Mr. John Avery";—
"*Fulgentius*; or, The Life of Mr. Richard Mather"; and
"*Elisha's Bones*; or, Life of Mr. Henry Whitefield."

These Latin titles stimulated my imagination like the sound
of a trumpet, and I looked them out diligently in my father's
great dictionary, and sometimes astonished my grandmother
by telling her what they meant.

In fact, I was sent to bed that night thoroughly fortified
against all seductions of the gay and worldly society into
which I was about to be precipitated; and my reader will see
that there was need enough of this preparation.

All these various conversations in regard to differences of
religion went on before us children with the freedom with
which older people generally allow themselves to go on in the
presence of the little non-combatants of life. In those days,
when utter silence and reserve in the presence of elders was
so forcibly inculcated as one of the leading virtues of childhood, there was little calculation made for the effect of such
words on the childish mind. With me it was a perfect hazy
mist of wonder and bewilderment; and I went to sleep and
dreamed that John Rogers was burning Lady Lothrop at the
stake, and Polly, as executioner, presided with a great broadaxe over her shoulder, while grandmother, with nine small
children, all with stone bundles on their heads, assisted at the
ceremony.

Our ride to Boston was performed in a most proper and
edifying manner. Lady Lothrop sat erect and gracious on the
back seat, and placed Harry, for whom she seemed to have
conceived a special affection, by her side. Tina was perched
on the knee of my lady's maid, a starched, prim woman who
had grown up and dried in all the most sacred and sanctified
essences of genteel propriety. She was the very crispness of

old-time decorum, brought up to order herself lowly and reverently to all her betters, and with a secret conviction that, aside from Lady Lothrop, the whole of the Oldtown population were rather low Dissenters, whom she was required by the rules of Christian propriety to be kind to. To her master, as having been honored with the august favor of her mistress's hand, she looked up with respect, but her highest mark of approbation was in the oft-repeated burst which came from her heart in moments of confidential enthusiasm,—"Ah, ma'am, depend upon it, master is a churchman in his heart. If 'e 'ad only 'ad the good fortune to be born in Hengland, 'e would 'ave been a bishop!"

Tina had been talked to and schooled rigorously by Miss Mehitable as to propriety of manner during this ride; and, as Miss Mehitable well knew what a chatterbox she was, she exacted from her a solemn promise that she would only speak when she was spoken to. Being perched in Mrs. Margery's lap, she felt still further the stringent and binding power of that atmosphere of frosty decorum which encircled this immaculate waiting-maid. A more well-bred, inoffensive, reverential little trio never surrounded a lady patroness; and as Lady Lothrop was not much of a talker, and, being a childless woman, had none of those little arts of drawing out children which the maternal instinct alone teaches, our ride, though undoubtedly a matter of great enjoyment, was an enjoyment of a serious and even awful character. Lady Lothrop addressed a few kind inquiries to each one of us in turn, to which we each of us replied, and then the conversation fell into the hands of Mrs. Margery, and consisted mainly in precise details as to where and how she had packed her mistress's Sunday cap and velvet dress; in doing which she evinced the great fluency and fertility of language with which women of her class are gifted on the one subject of their souls. Mrs. Margery felt as if the Sunday cap of the only supporter of the true Church in the dark and heathen parish of Oldtown was a subject not to be lightly or unadvisedly considered; and, therefore, she told at great length how she had intended to pack it first all together,—how she had altered her mind and taken off the bow, and packed that in a little box by itself, and laid the strings out flat in the box,—what difficulties had met her in folding the velvet dress,—and how she had at first laid it on top of the trunk, but had decided at last that the black lutestring might go on top of that, because it was so much lighter, &c., &c., &c.

Lady Lothrop was so much accustomed to this species of monologue, that it is quite doubtful if she heard a word of it; but poor Tina, who felt within herself whole worlds of things to say, from the various objects upon the road, of which she was dying to talk and ask questions, wriggled and twisted upon Mrs. Margery's knee, and finally gave utterance to her pent-up feelings in deep sighs.

"What's the matter, little dear?" said Lady Lothrop.

"O dear! I was just wishing I could go to church."

"Well, you are going to-morrow, dear."

"I just wish I could go now to say *one* prayer."

"And what is that, my dear?"

"I just want to say, 'O Lord, open thou my lips,'" said Tina, with effusion.

Lady Lothrop smiled with an air of innocent surprise, and Mrs. Margery winked over the little head.

"I'm *so* tired of not talking!" said Tina, pathetically; "but I promised Miss Mehitable I wouldn't speak unless I was spoken to," she added, with an air of virtuous resolution.

"Why, my little dear, you *may* talk," said Lady Lothrop. "It won't disturb me at all. Tell us now about anything that interests you."

"O, thank you ever so much," said Tina; and from this moment, as a little elfin butterfly bursts from a cold, gray chrysalis, Tina rattled and chattered and sparkled, and went on with *verve* and gusto that quite waked us all up. Lady Lothrop and Mrs. Margery soon found themselves laughing with a heartiness which surprised themselves; and, the icy chains of silence being once broken, we all talked, almost forgetting in whose presence we were. Lady Lothrop looked from one to another in a sort of pleased and innocent surprise. Her still, childless, decorous life covered and concealed many mute feminine instincts which now rose at the voice and touch of childhood; and sometimes in the course of our gambols she would sigh, perhaps thinking of her own childless hearth.

XXIV.

We Behold Grandeur

IT was just at dusk that our carriage stood before the door of a respectable mansion at the north end of Boston.

I remember our alighting and passing through a wide hall with a dark oaken staircase, into a low-studded parlor, lighted by the blaze of a fire of hickory logs, which threw out tongues of yellow flame, and winked at itself with a thousand fanciful flashes, in the crinkles and angles of a singularly high and mighty pair of brass andirons.

A lovely, peaceful old lady, whose silvery white hair and black dress were the most striking features of the picture, kissed Lady Lothrop, and then came to us with a perfect out-gush of motherly kindness. "Why, the poor little dears! the little darlings!" she said, as she began with her trembling fingers to undo Tina's bonnet-strings. "Did they want to come to Boston and see the great city? Well, they should. They must be cold; there, put them close by the fire, and grandma will get them a nice cake pretty soon. Here, I'll hold the little lady," she said, as she put Tina on her knee.

The child nestled her head down on her bosom as lovingly and confidingly as if she had known her all her days. "Poor babe," said the old lady to Lady Lothrop, "who could have had a heart to desert such a child? and this is the boy," she said, drawing Harry to her and looking tenderly at him. "Well, a father of the fatherless is God in his holy habitation." There was something even grand about the fervor of this sentence as she uttered it, and Tina put up her hand with a caressing gesture around the withered old neck.

"Debby, get these poor children a cake," said the lady to a brisk, energetic, rather high-stepping individual, who now entered the apartment.

"Come now, mother, do let it rest till supper-time. If we let you alone, you would murder all the children in your neighborhood with cake and sugar-plums; you'd be as bad as King Herod."

Miss Debby was a well-preserved, up-and-down, positive, cheery, sprightly maiden lady of an age lying somewhere in the indeterminate region between forty and sixty. There was a positive, brusque way about all her movements, and she advanced to the fire, rearranged the wood, picked up stray brands, and whisked up the coals with a brush, and then, seating herself bolt upright, took up the business of making our acquaintance in the most precise and systematic manner.

"So this is Master Horace Holyoke. How do you do, sir?"

As previously directed, I made my best bow with anxious politeness.

"And this is Master Harry Percival, is it?" Harry did the same.

"And this," she added, turning to Tina, "is Miss Tina Percival, I understand? Well, we are very happy to see *good* little children in this house always." There was a rather severe emphasis on the *good*, which, together with the somewhat martial and disciplinary air which invested all Miss Deborah's words and actions, was calculated to strike children with a wholesome awe.

Our resolution "to be very good indeed" received an immediate accession of strength. At this moment a serving-maid appeared at the door, and, with eyes cast down, and a stiff, respectful courtesy, conveyed the information, "If you please, ma'am, tea is ready."

This humble, self-abased figure—the utter air of self-abnegation with which the domestic seemed to intimate that, unless her mistress pleased, tea was not ready, and that everything in creation was to be either ready or not ready according to her sovereign will and good pleasure—was to us children a new lesson in decorum.

"Go tell Lady Widgery that tea is served," said Miss Deborah, in a loud, resounding voice. "Tell her that we will wait her ladyship's convenience."

The humble serving-maid courtesied, and closed the door softly with reverential awe. On the whole, the impression upon our minds was deeply solemn; we were about to see her ladyship.

Lady Widgery was the last rose of summer of the departed aristocracy. Lady Lothrop's title was only by courtesy; but Sir

Thomas Widgery was a live baronet; and as there were to be
no more of these splendid dispensations in America, one may
fancy the tenderness with which old Tory families cherished
the last lingering remnants.

The door was soon opened again, and a bundle of black
silk appeared, with a pale, thin face looking out of it. There
was to be seen the glitter of a pair of sharp, black eyes, and
the shimmer of a thin white hand with a diamond ring upon
it. These were the items that made up Lady Widgery, as she
dawned upon our childish vision.

Lest the reader should conceive any false hopes or impressions, I may as well say that it turned out, on further acquaintance, that these items were about all there was of Lady
Widgery. It was one of the cases where Nature had picked up
a very indifferent and commonplace soul, and shut it up in a
very intelligent-looking body. From her youth up, Lady
Widgery's principal attraction consisted in looking as if there
was a great deal more in her than there really was. Her eyes
were sparkling and bright, and had a habit of looking at
things in this world with keen, shrewd glances, as if she were
thinking about them to some purpose, which she never was.
Sometimes they were tender and beseeching, and led her distracted admirers to feel as if she were melting with emotions
that she never dreamed of. Thus Lady Widgery had always
been rushed for and contended for by the other sex; and one
husband had hardly time to be cold in his grave before the air
was filled with the rivalry of candidates to her hand; and after
all the beautiful little hoax had nothing for it but her attractive soul-case. In her old age she still looked elegant, shrewd,
and keen, and undeniably high-bred, and carried about her
the prestige of rank and beauty. Otherwise she was a little dry
bundle of old prejudices, of faded recollections of past con-
quests and gayeties, and weakly concerned about her own
health, which, in her view and that of everybody about her,
appeared a most sacred subject. She had a somewhat entertaining manner of rehearsing the gossip and scandals of the
last forty years, and was, so far as such a person could be,
religious: that is to say, she kept all the feasts and fasts of the
Church scrupulously. She had, in a weakly way, a sense of
some responsibility in this matter, because she was Lady

Widgery, and because infidelity was prevailing in the land, and it became Lady Widgery to cast her influence against it. Therefore it was that, even at the risk of her precious life, as she thought, she had felt it imperative to come to Boston to celebrate Easter Sunday.

When she entered the room there was an immediate bustle of welcome. Lady Lothrop ran up to her, saluting her with an appearance of great fondness, mingled, I thought, with a sort of extreme deference. Miss Deborah was pressing in her attentions. "Will you sit a moment before tea to get your feet warm, or will you go out at once? The dining-room is quite warm."

Lady Widgery's feet were quite warm, and everybody was *so* glad to hear it, that we were filled with wonder.

Then she turned and fixed her keen, dark eyes on us, as if she were reading our very destiny, and asked who we were. We were all presented circumstantially, and the brilliant eyes seemed to look through us shrewdly, as we made our bows and courtesies. One would have thought that she was studying us with a deep interest, which was not the case.

We were now marshalled out to the tea-table, where we children had our plates put in a row together, and were waited on with obsequious civility by Mrs. Margery and another equally starched and decorous female, who was the attendant of Lady Widgery. We stood at our places a moment, while the lovely old lady, raising her trembling hand, pronounced the words of the customary grace: "For what we are now about to receive, the Lord make us truly thankful." Her voice trembled as she spoke, and somehow the impression of fragility and sanctity that she made on me awoke in me a sort of tender awe. When the blessing was over, the maids seated us, and I had leisure to notice the entirely new scene about me.

It was all conducted with an inexpressible stateliness of propriety, and, in an undefined way, the impression was produced upon my mind that the frail, shivery, rather thin and withered little being, enveloped in a tangle of black silk wraps, was something inexpressibly sacred and sublime. Miss Deborah waited on her constantly, pressingly, energetically; and the dear, sweet old white-haired lady tended her with obsequiousness, which, like everything else that she did, was lost in lovingness; and Lady Lothrop, to me the most awe-inspiring of the female race, paled her ineffectual fires, and bowed her sacred head to the rustling little black silk bundle, in a way that made me inwardly wonder. The whole scene was so different from the wide, rough, noisy, free-and-easy democracy of my grandmother's kitchen, that I felt crusted all over with an indefinite stiffness of embarrassment, as if I had been dipped in an alum-bath. At the head of the table there was an old silver tea-urn, looking heavy enough to have the weight of whole generations in it, into which, at the moment of sitting down, a serious-visaged waiting-maid dropped a red-hot weight, and forthwith the noise of a violent boiling arose. We little folks looked at each other inquiringly, but said nothing. All was to us like an enchanted palace. The great, mysterious tea-urn, the chased silver tea-caddy, the precise and well-considered movements of Miss Deborah as she rinsed the old embossed silver teapots in the boiling water, the India-china cups and plates, painted with the family initials and family crest, all were to us solemn signs and symbols of that upper table-land of gentility, into which we were forewarned by Aunt Lois we were to enter.

"There," said Miss Deborah, with emphasis, as she poured and handed to Lady Widgery a cup of tea,—"there's some of the tea that my brother saved at the time of that disgraceful Boston riot, when Boston Harbor was floating with tea-chests. His cargo was rifled in the most scandalous manner, but he went out in a boat and saved some at the risk of his life."

Now my most sacred and enthusiastic remembrance was of the glow of patriotic fervor with which, seated on my grandfather's knee, I had heard the particulars of that event at a time when names and dates and dress, and time, place, and circumstance, had all the life and vividness of a recent transaction. I cannot describe the clarion tones in which Miss Deborah rung out the word *disgraceful*, in connection with an event which had always set my blood boiling with pride and patriotism. Now, as if convicted of sheep-stealing, I felt myself getting red to the very tips of my ears.

"It was a shameful proceeding," sighed Lady Widgery, in her pretty, high-bred tones, as she pensively stirred the amber fluid in her teacup. "I never saw Sir Thomas so indignant at anything in all my life, and I'm sure it gave me a sick-head-ache for three days, so that I had to stay shut up in a dark room, and could n't keep the least thing on my stomach. What a mysterious providence it is that such conduct should be suffered to lead to success!"

"Well," said Lady Lothrop, sipping her tea on the other side, "clouds and darkness are about the Divine dispensations; but let us hope it will be all finally overruled for the best."

"O, come," said Miss Debby, giving a cheerful, victorious crow of defiance from behind her teapots. "Dorothy will be down on us with the tip-end of one of her husband's ser-mons, of course. Having married a Continental Congress par-son, she has to say the best she can; but I, Deborah Kittery, who was never yet in bondage to any man, shall be free to have *my* say to the end of my days, and I *do* say that the Continental Congress is an abomination in the land, and the leaders of it, if justice had been done, they would all have been hanged high as Haman; and that there is one house in old Boston, at the North End, and not far from the spot where we have the honor to be, where King George now reigns as much as ever he did, and where law and order pre-vail in spite of General Washington and Mrs. Martha, with her court and train. It puts me out of all manner of patience to read the papers,—receptions to 'em here, there, and every-where;—I should like to give 'em a reception."

"Come, come, Deborah, my child, you must be patient," said the old lady. "The Lord's ways are not as our ways. He knows what is best."

"I dare say he does, mother, but we know he does let wickedness triumph to an awful extent. I think myself he's given this country up."

"Let us hope not," said the mother, fervently.

"Just look at it," said Miss Deborah. "Has not this misera-ble rebellion broken up the true Church in this country just as it was getting a foothold? has it not shaken hands with French infidelity? Thomas Jefferson is a scoffing infidel, and he drafted their old Declaration of Independence, which, I will say, is the most abominable and blasphemous document that ever sinners dared to sign."

"But General Washington was a Churchman," said Lady Widgery, "and they were always very careful about keeping the feasts and fasts. Why, I remember, in the old times, I have been there to Easter holidays, and we had a splendid ball."

"Well, then, if he was in the true Church, so much the worse for him," said Miss Deborah. "There is some excuse for men of Puritan families, because their ancestors were schismatics and disorganizers to begin with, and came over here because they did n't like to submit to lawful government. For my part, I have always been ashamed of having been born here. If I 'd been consulted I should have given my voice against it."

"Debby, child, how you do talk!" said the old lady.

"Well, mother, what can I do but talk? and it 's a pity if I should n't be allowed to do that. If I had been a man, I 'd have fought; and, if I could have my way now, I 'd go back to England and live, where there 's some religion and some government."

"I don't see," said the old lady, "but people are doing pretty well under the new government."

"Indeed, mother, how can you know anything about it? There 's a perfect reign of infidelity and immorality begun. Why, look here, in Boston and Cambridge things are going just as you might think they would. The college fellows call themselves D'Alembert, Rousseau, Voltaire, and other French heathen names; and there 's Ellery Davenport! just look at him, — came straight down from generations of Puritan ministers, and has n't half as much religion as my cat there; for Tom does know how to order himself lowly and reverently to all his betters."

Here there was such a burst of pleading feminine eloquence on all hands as showed that general interest which often pervades the female breast for some bright, naughty, wicked prodigal son. Lady Widgery and old Mrs. Kittery and Lady Lothrop all spoke at once. "Indeed, Miss Deborah," — "Come, come, Debby," — "You are too bad, — he goes to church with us sometimes."

"To church, does he?" said Miss Debby, with a toss; "and what does he go for? Simply to ogle the girls."

"We should be charitable in our judgments," said Lady Widgery.

"Especially of handsome young men," said Miss Debby, with strong irony. "You all know he does n't believe as much as a heathen. They say he reads and speaks French like a native, and that 's all I want to know of anybody. I 've no opinion of such people; a good honest Christian has no occasion to go out of his own language, and when he does you may be pretty sure it 's for no good."

"O, come now, Deborah, you are too sweeping altogether," said Lady Lothrop; "French is of course an elegant accomplishment."

"I never saw any good of the French language, for my part, I must confess," said Miss Debby, "nor, for that matter, of the French nation either; they eat frogs, and break the Sabbath, and are as immoral as the old Canaanites. It 's just exactly like them to aid and abet this unrighteous rebellion. They always hated England, and they take delight in massacres and rebellions, and every kind of mischief, ever since the massacre of St. Bartholomew. Well, well, we shall see what 'll come of these ungodly levelling principles in time. 'All men created free and equal,' forsooth. Just think of that! clearly against the church catechism."

"Of course that is all infidelity," said Lady Widgery, confidently. "Sir Thomas used to say it was the effect on the lower classes he dreaded. You see these lower classes are something dreadful; and what 's to keep them down if it is n't religion? as Sir Thomas used to say when he always would go to church Sundays. He felt such a responsibility."

"Well," said Miss Deborah, "you 'll see. I predict we shall see the time when your butcher and your baker, and your candlestick-maker will come into your parlor and take a chair as easy as if they were your equals, and every servant-maid will be thinking she must have a silk gown like her mistress. That 's what we shall get by our revolution."

"But let us hope it will be all overruled for good," said Lady Lothrop.

"O, overruled, overruled!" said Miss Deborah. "Of course it will be overruled. Sodom and Gomorrah were overruled for good, but 't was a great deal better not to be living there about those times." Miss Debby's voice had got upon so high a key, and her denunciations began to be so terrifying, that the dear old lady interposed.

"Well, children, do let 's love one another, whatever we do," she said; "and, Debby, you must n't talk so hard about Ellery, —he 's your cousin, you know."

"Besides, my dear," said Lady Widgery, "great allowances should be made for his domestic misfortunes."

"I don't see why a man need turn infidel and rebel because his wife has turned out a madwoman," said Miss Debby; "what did he marry her for?"

"O my dear, it was a family arrangement to unite the two properties," said Lady Widgery. "You see all the great Pierre-point estates came in through her, but then she was quite shocking,—very peculiar always, but after her marriage her temper was dreadful,—it made poor Ellery miserable, and drove him from home; it really was a mercy when it broke out into real insanity, so that they could shut her up. I 've always had great tenderness for Ellery on that account."

"Of course you have, because you 're a lady. Did I ever know a lady yet that did n't like Ellery Davenport, and was n't ready to go to the stake for him? For my part I hate him, because, after all, he humbugs me, and will make me like him in spite of myself. I have to watch and pray against him all the time."

And as if, by the odd law of attraction which has given birth to the proverb that somebody is always nearest when you are talking about him, at this moment the dining-room door was thrown open, and the old man-servant announced "Colonel Ellery Davenport."

"Colonel!" said Miss Debby, with a frown and an accent of contempt. "How often must I tell Hawkins not to use those titles of the old rebel mob army? Insubordination is begin-ning to creep in, I can see."

These words were lost in the bustle of the entrance of one on whom, after listening to all the past conversation, we chil-dren looked with very round eyes of attention. What we saw was a tall, graceful young man, whose air and movements gave a singular impression of both lightness and strength. He carried his head on his shoulders with a jaunty, slightly haughty air, like that of a thorough-bred young horse, and there was quality and breeding in every movement of his body. He was dressed in the imposing and picturesque fashion of those times, with a slight military suggestion in its arrangements. His hair was powdered to a dazzling whiteness, and brushed off his low Greek forehead, and the powder gave that peculiar effect to the eye and complexion which was one of the most distinctive traits of that style of costume. His eyes were of a deep violet blue, and of that lively, flashing brilliancy which a painter could only represent by double lights. They seemed to throw out light like diamonds. He entered the room bowing and smiling with the gay good-humor of one sure of pleasing. An inspiring sort of cheerfulness came in with him, that seemed to illuminate the room like a whole stream of sunshine. In short, he fully justified all Miss Deborah's fears.

In a moment he had taken a rapid survey of the party; he had kissed the hand of the dear old lady; he had complimented Lady Widgery; he had inquired with effusion after the health of Parson Lothrop, and ended all by an adroit attempt to kiss Miss Deborah's hand, which earned him a smart little cuff from that wary belligerent.

"No rebels allowed on these premises," said Miss Debby, sententiously.

"On my soul, cousin, you forget that peace has been declared," he said, throwing himself into a chair with a *nonchalant* freedom.

"Peace! not in our house. *I* have n't surrendered, if Lord Cornwallis has," said Miss Debby, "and I consider you as the enemy."

"Well, Debby, we must love our enemies," said the old lady, in a pleading tone.

"Certainly you must," he replied quickly; "and here I 've come to Boston on purpose to go to church with you to-morrow."

"That 's right, my boy," said the old lady. "I always knew you 'd come into right ways at last."

"O, there are hopes of me, certainly," he said; "if the gentler sex will only remember their mission, and be guardian angels, I think I shall be saved in the end."

"You mean that you are going to wait on pretty Lizzie Cabot to church to-morrow," said Miss Debby; "that's about all the religion there is in it."

"Mine is the religion of beauty, fair cousin," said he. "If I had had the honor of being one of the apostles, I should have put at least one article to that effect into our highly respectable creed."

"Ellery Davenport, you are a scoffer."

"What, I? because I believe in the beautiful? What is goodness but beauty? and what is sin but bad taste? I could prove it to you out of my grandfather Edwards's works, *passim*, and I think nobody in New England would dispute him."

"I don't know anything about him," said Miss Debby, with a toss. "He was n't in the Church."

"Mere matter of position, cousin. Could n't very well be when the Church was a thousand miles across the water; but he lived and died a stanch loyalist,—an aristocrat in the very marrow of his bones, as anybody may see. The whole of his system rests on the undisputed right of big folks to eat up little folks in proportion to their bigness, and the Creator, being biggest of all, is dispensed from all obligation to seek anything but his own glory. Here you have the root-doctrine of the divine right of kings and nobles, who have only to follow their Maker's example in their several spheres, as his blessed Majesty King George has of late been doing with his American colonies. If he had got the treatise on true virtue by heart, he could not have carried out its principles better."

"Well, now, I never knew that there was so much good in President Edwards before," said Lady Widgery, with simplicity. "I must get my maid to read me that treatise some time."

"Do, madam," said Ellery. "I think you will find it exactly adapted to your habits of thought, and extremely soothing."

"It will be a nice thing for her to read me to sleep with," said Lady Widgery, innocently.

"By all means," said Ellery, with an indescribable mocking light in his great blue eyes.

For my own part, having that strange, vibrating susceptibility of constitution which I have described as making me peculiarly impressible by the moral sphere of others, I felt in the presence of this man a singular and painful contest of attraction and repulsion, such as one might imagine to be produced by the near approach of some beautiful but dangerous animal. His singular grace and brilliancy awoke in me an undefined antagonism akin to antipathy, and yet, as if under some enchantment, I could not keep my eyes off from him, and eagerly listened to everything that he had to say.

With that quick insight into human nature which enabled him, as by a sort of instinct, to catch the reflex of every impression which he made on any human being, he surveyed the row of wide-open, wondering, admiring eyes, which followed him at our end of the table.

"Aha, what have we here?" he said, as he advanced and laid his hand on my head. I shuddered and shook it off with a feeling of pain and dislike amounting to hatred.

"How now, my little man?" he said; "what's the matter here?" and then he turned to Tina. "Here's a little lady will be more gracious, I know," and he stooped and attempted to kiss her.

The little lady drew her head back and repulsed him with the dignity of a young princess.

"Upon my word," he said, "we learn the tricks of our trade early, don't we? Pardon me, petite mademoiselle," he said as he retreated, laughing. "So you don't like to be kissed?"

"Only by proper persons," said Tina, with that demure gravity which she could at times so whimsically assume, but sending with the words a long mischievous flash from under her downcast eyelashes.

"Upon my word, if there is n't one that's perfect in Mother Eve's catechism at an early age," said Ellery Davenport. "Young lady, I hope for a better acquaintance with you one of these days."

"Come Ellery, let the child alone," said Miss Debby; "why should you be teaching all the girls to be forward? If you notice her so much she will be vain."

"That's past praying for, anyhow," said he, looking with admiration at the dimpling, sparkling face of Tina, who evidently was dying to answer him back. "Don't you see the monkey has her quiver full of arrows?" he said. "Do let her try her infant hand on me."

But Miss Debby, eminently proper, rose immediately, and

broke up the tea-table session by proposing adjournment to the parlor.

After this we had family prayers, the maid-servants and man-servant being called in and ranged in decorous order on a bench that stood prepared for exactly that occasion in a corner of the room. Miss Deborah placed a stand, with a great quarto edition of the Bible and prayer-book, before her mother, and the old lady read in a trembling voice the psalm, the epistle, and the gospel for Easter evening, and then, all kneeling, the evening prayers. The sound of her tremulous voice, and the beauty of the prayers themselves, which I vaguely felt, impressed me so much that I wept, without knowing why, as one sometimes does at plaintive music. One thing in particular filled me with a solemn surprise; and that was the prayers, which I had never heard before, for "The Royal Family of England." The trembling voice rose to fervent clearness on the words, "We beseech Thee, with Thy favor, to behold our most Sovereign Lord, King George, and so replenish him with the grace of Thy Holy Spirit, that he may always incline to Thy will, and walk in Thy way. Endue him plenteously with heavenly gifts, grant him in health and wealth long to live, strengthen him that he may vanquish and overcome all his enemies, and finally after this life may attain everlasting joy and felicity, through Jesus Christ our Lord."

The loud "Amen" from Miss Debby which followed this, heartily chorussed as it was by the well-taught man-servant and maid-servants, might have done any king's heart good. For my part, I was lost in astonishment; and when the prayer followed "for the gracious Queen Charlotte, their Royal Highnesses, George, Prince of Wales, the Princess Dowager of Wales, and all the Royal Family," my confusion of mind was at its height. All these unknown personages were to be endued with the Holy Spirit, enriched with heavenly grace, and brought to an everlasting kingdom, through Jesus Christ, our Lord. I must confess that all I had heard of them previously, in my education, had not prepared me to see the propriety of any peculiar celestial arrangements in their favor; but the sweet and solemn awe inspired by the trembling voice which pleaded went a long way towards making me feel as if there must have been a great mistake in my bringing up hitherto.

When the circle rose from their knees, Ellery Davenport said to Miss Debby, "It's a pity the king of England could n't know what stanch supporters he has in Boston."

"I don't see," said the old lady, "why they won't let us have that prayer read in churches now; it can't do any harm."

"I don't, either," said Ellery. "For my part, I don't know any one who needs praying for more than the King of England; but the prayers of the Church don't appear to have been answered in his case. If he had been in the slightest degree 'endowed with heavenly gifts,' he need n't have lost these American colonies."

"Come, Ellery, none of your profane talk," said Miss Debby; "*you* don't believe in anything good."

"On the contrary, I always insist on seeing the good before I believe; I should believe in prayer, if I saw any good come from it."

"For shame, Ellery, when children are listening to you!" said Miss Debby. "But come, my little folks," she added, rising briskly, "it's time for these little eyes to be shut."

The dear old lady called us all to her, and kissed us "good night," laying her hand gently on our heads as she did so. I felt the peaceful influence of that hand go through me like music, and its benediction even in my dreams.

XXV.

Easter Sunday

For a marvel, even in the stormy clime of Boston, our Easter Sunday was one of those celestial days which seem, like the New Jerusalem of the Revelations, to come straight down from God out of heaven, to show us mortals what the upper world may be like. Our poor old Mother Boston has now and then such a day given to her, even in the uncertain spring-time; and when all her bells ring together, and the old North Church chimes her solemn psalm-tunes, and all the people in their holiday garments come streaming out towards the churches of every name which line her streets, it seems as if the venerable dead on Copps Hill must dream pleasantly, for "Blessed are the dead that die in the Lord," and even to this day, in dear old Boston, their works do follow them.

At an early hour we were roused, and dressed ourselves with the most anxious and exemplary care. For the first time in my life I looked anxiously in the looking-glass, and scanned with some solicitude, as if it had been a third person, the little being who called himself "I." I saw a pair of great brown eyes, a face rather thin and pale, a high forehead, and a great profusion of dark curls,—the combing out of which, by the by, was one of the morning trials of my life. In vain Aunt Lois had cut them off repeatedly, in the laudable hope that my hair would grow out straight. It seemed a more inextricable mat at each shearing; but as Harry's flaxen poll had the same peculiarity, we consoled each other, while we labored at our morning toilet.

Down in the sunny parlor, a little before breakfast was on the table, we walked about softly with our hands behind us, lest Satan, who we were assured had always some mischief still for idle hands to do, should entice us into touching some of the many curious articles which we gazed upon now for the first time. There was the picture of a very handsome young man over the mantel-piece, and beneath it hung a soldier's sword in a large loop of black crape, a significant symbol of the last great sorrow which had overshadowed the household. On one side of the door, framed and glazed, was a large coat of arms of the Kittery family, worked in chenille and embroidery,—the labor of Miss Deborah's hands during the course of her early education. In other places on the walls hung oil paintings of the deceased master of the mansion, and of the present venerable mistress, as she was in the glow of early youth. They were evidently painted by a not unskilful hand, and their eyes always following us as we moved about the room gave us the impression of being overlooked, even while as yet there was nobody else in the apartment. Conspicuously hung on one side of the room was a copy of one of the Vandyck portraits of Charles the First, with his lace ruff and peaked beard. Underneath this was a printed document, framed and glazed; and I, who was always drawn to read any thing that could be read, stationed myself opposite to it and began reading aloud:—

"The Twelve Good Rules of the Most Blessed Martyr, King Charles First, of Blessed Memory."

I was reading these in a loud, clear voice, when Miss Debby entered the room. She stopped and listened to me, with a countenance beaming with approbation.

"Go on, sonny!" she said, coming up behind me, with an approving nod, when I blushed and stopped on seeing her. "Read them through; those are good rules for a man to form his life by."

I wish I could remember now what these so highly praised rules were. The few that I can recall are not especially in accordance with the genius of our modern times. They began:—

"1st. Profane no Divine Ordinances.

"2d. Touch no State Matter.

"3d. Pick no Quarrels.

"4th. Maintain no ill Opinions."

Here my memory fails me, but I remember that, stimulated by Miss Deborah's approbation, I did commit the whole of them to memory at the time, and repeated them with a readiness and fluency which drew upon me warm commendations from the dear old lady, and in fact from all in the house, though Ellery Davenport did shrug his shoulders contumaciously and give a sort of suppressed whistle of dissent.

"If we had minded those rules," he said, "we should n't be where we are now."

"No, indeed, you would n't; the more 's the pity you did n't." said Miss Debby. "If I 'd had the bringing of you up, you should be learning things like that, instead of trumpery French and democratic nonsense."

"Speaking of French," said Ellery, "I declare I forgot a package of gloves that I brought over especially for you and Aunty here,—the very best of Paris kid."

"You may spare yourself the trouble of bringing them, cousin," said Miss Deborah, coldly. "Whatever others may do, I trust *I* never shall be left to put a French glove on *my* hands. They may be all very fine, no doubt, but English gloves, made under her Majesty's sanction, will always be good enough for me."

"O, well, in that case I shall have the honor of presenting them to Lady Lothrop, unless her principles should be equally rigid."

"I dare say Dorothy will take them," said Miss Deborah. "When a woman has married a Continental parson, what can you expect of her? but, for *my* part, I should feel that I dishonored the house of the Lord to enter it with gloves on made by those atheistical French people. The fact is, we must put a stop to worldly conformities somewhere."

"And you draw the line at French gloves," said Ellery.

"No, indeed," said Miss Deborah; "by no means French gloves. French novels, French philosophy, and, above all, French morals, or rather want of morals,—*these* are what I go against, Cousin Ellery."

So saying, Miss Debby led the way to the breakfast-table, with an air of the most martial and determined moral principle.

I remember only one other incident of that morning before we went to church. The dear old lady had seemed sensibly affected by the levity with which Ellery Davenport generally spoke upon sacred subjects, and disturbed by her daughter's confident assertions of his infidel sentiments. So she adminis-

tered to him an admonition in her own way. A little before
church-time she was sitting on the sofa, reading in her great
Bible spread out on the table before her.

"Ellery," she said, "come here and sit down by me. I want
you to read me this text."

"Certainly, Aunty, by all means," he said, as he seated himself by her, bent his handsome head over the book, and, following the lead of her trembling finger, read: —

"And thou, Solomon, my son, know thou the God of thy
fathers, and serve him with a perfect heart and a willing mind.
If thou seek him, he will be found of thee, but if thou forsake
him, he will cast thee off forever."

"Ellery," she said, with trembling earnestness, "think of
that, my boy. O Ellery, remember!"

He turned and kissed her hand, and there certainly were
tears in his eyes. "Aunty," he said, "you must pray for me; I
may be a good boy one of these days, who knows?"

There was no more preaching, and no more said; she only
held his hand, looked lovingly at him, and stroked his forehead. "There have been a great many good people among
your fathers, Ellery."

"I know it," he said.

At this moment Miss Debby came in with the summons to
church. The family carriage came round for the old lady, but
we were better pleased to walk up the street under convoy of
Ellery Davenport, who made himself quite delightful to us.
Tina obstinately refused to take his hand, and insisted upon
walking only with Harry, though from time to time she cast
glances at him over her shoulder, and he called her "a little
chip of mother Eve's block,"—at which she professed to feel
great indignation.

The reader may remember my description of our meeting-
house at Oldtown, and therefore will not wonder that the
architecture of the Old North and its solemn-sounding
chimes, though by no means remarkable compared with European churches, appeared to us a vision of wonder. We
gazed with delighted awe at the chancel and the altar, with
their massive draperies of crimson looped back with heavy
gold cord and tassels, and revealing a cloud of little winged
cherubs, whereat Tina's eyes grew large with awe, as if she

had seen a vision. Above this there was a mystical Hebrew
word emblazoned in a golden halo, while around the galleries
of the house were marvellous little colored statuettes of angels
blowing long golden trumpets. These figures had been taken
from a privateer and presented to the church by a British
man-of-war, and no child that saw them would ever forget
them. Then there was the organ, whose wonderful sounds
were heard by me for the first time in my life. There was also
an indefinable impression of stately people that worshipped
there. They all seemed to me like Lady Lothrop, rustling in
silks and brocades; with gentlemen like Captain Brown, in
scarlet cloaks and powdered hair. Not a crowded house by
any means, but a well-ordered and select few, who performed
all the responses and evolutions of the service with immaculate propriety. I was struck with every one's kneeling and
bowing the head on taking a seat in the church; even gay
Ellery Davenport knelt down and hid his face in his hat,
though what he did it for was a matter of some speculation
with us afterward. Miss Debby took me under her special supervision. She gave me a prayer-book, found the places for
me, and took me up and down with her through the whole
service, giving her responses in such loud, clear, and energetic
tones as entirely to acquit herself of her share of responsibility
in the matter. The "true Church" received no detriment, so
far as she was concerned. I was most especially edified and
astonished by the deep courtesies which she and several dis-
tinguished-looking ladies made at the name of the Saviour in
the Creed; so much so, that she was obliged to tap me on the
head to indicate to me my own part in that portion of the
Church service.

I was surprised to observe that Harry appeared perfectly
familiar with the ceremony; and Lady Lothrop, who had him
under her particular surveillance, looked on with wonder and
approbation, as he quietly opened his prayer-book and went
through the service with perfect regularity. Tina, who stood
between Ellery Davenport and the old lady, seemed, to tell
the truth, much too conscious of the amused attention with
which he was regarding her little movements, notwithstanding the kindly efforts of her venerable guardian to guide her
through the service. She resolutely refused to allow him to

assist her, half-turning her back upon him, but slyly watching him from under her long eyelashes, in a way that afforded him great amusement.

The sermon which followed the prayers was of the most droning and sleepy kind. But as it was dispensed by a regularly ordained successor of the Apostles, Miss Deborah, though ordinarily the shrewdest and sharpest of womankind, and certainly capable of preaching a sermon far more to the point herself, sat bolt upright and listened to all those slumberous platitudes with the most reverential attention.

It yet remains a mystery to my mind, how a church which retains such a stimulating and inspiring liturgy *could* have such drowsy preaching,—how men could go through with the "Te Deum," and the "Gloria in Excelsis," without one thrill of inspiration, or one lift above the dust of earth, and, after uttering words which one would think might warm the frozen heart of the very dead, settle sleepily down into the quietest commonplace. Such, however, has been the sin of ritualism in all days, principally because human nature is, above all things, lazy, and needs to be thorned and goaded up those heights where it ought to fly.

Harry and I both had a very nice little nap during sermon-time, while Ellery Davenport made a rabbit of his pocket-handkerchief by way of paying his court to Tina, who sat shyly giggling and looking at him.

After the services came the Easter dinner, to which, as a great privilege, we were admitted from first to last; although children in those days were held to belong strictly to the dessert, and only came in with the nuts and raisins. I remember Ellery Davenport seemed to be the life of the table, and kept everybody laughing. He seemed particularly fond of rousing up Miss Debby to those rigorous and energetic statements concerning Church and King which she delivered with such freedom.

"I don't know how we are any of us to get to heaven now," he said to Miss Debby. "Supposing I wanted to be confirmed, there is n't a bishop in America."

"Well, don't you think they will send one over?" said Lady Widgery, with a face of great solicitude.

"Two, madam; it would take two in order to start the

succession in America. The apostolic electricity cannot come down through one."

"I heard that Dr. Franklin was negotiating with the Archbishop of Canterbury," said Lady Lothrop.

"Yes, but they are not in the best humor toward us over there," said Ellery. "You know what Franklin wrote back, don't you?"

"No," said Lady Widgery; "what was it?"

"Well, you see, he found Canterbury & Co. rather huffy, and somewhat on the high-and-mighty order with him, and, being a democratic American, he did n't like it. So he wrote over that he did n't see, for his part, why anybody that wanted to preach the Gospel could n't preach it, without sending a thousand miles across the water to ask leave of a cross old gentleman at Canterbury."

A shocked expression went round the table, and Miss Debby drew herself up. "That 's what I call a profane remark, Ellery Davenport," she said.

"I did n't make it, you understand."

"No, dear, you did n't," said the old lady. "Of course you would n't say such a thing."

"Of course I should n't, Aunty,—O no. I 'm only concerned to know how I shall be confirmed, if ever I want to be. Do you think there really is no other way to heaven, Miss Debby? Now, if the Archbishop of Canterbury won't repent, and I do,—if he won't send a bishop, and I become a good Christian,—don't you think now the Church might open the door a little crack for me?"

"Why, of course, Ellery," said Lady Lothrop. "We believe that many good people will be saved out of the Church."

"My dear madam, that 's because you married a Congregational parson; you are getting illogical."

"Ellery, you know better," said Miss Debby, vigorously. "You know we hold that many good persons out of the Church are saved, though they are saved by unconvenanted mercies. There are no direct promises to any but those in the Church; they have no authorized ministry or sacraments."

"What a dreadful condition these American colonies are in!" said Ellery; "it 's a result of our Revolution which never struck me before."

"You can sneer as much as you please, it 's a solemn fact, Ellery; it 's the chief mischief of this dreadful rebellion."

"Come, come, children," said the old lady; "let 's talk about something else. We 've been to the communion, and heard about 'peace on earth and good-will to men.' I always think of our blessed King George every time I take the communion wine out of those cups that he gave to our church."

"Yes, indeed," said Miss Debby; "it will be a long time before you get the American Congress to giving communion services, like our good, pious King George."

"It 's a pity pious folks are so apt to be pig-headed," said Ellery, in a tone just loud enough to stir up Miss Debby, but not to catch the ear of the old lady.

"I suppose there never was such a pious family as our royal family," said Lady Widgery. "I have been told that Queen Charlotte reads prayers with her maids regularly every night, and we all know how our blessed King read prayers beside a dying cottager."

"I do not know what the reason is," said Ellery Davenport, reflectively, "but political tyrants as a general thing are very pious men. The worse their political actions are, the more they pray. Perhaps it is on the principle of compensation, just as animals that are incapacitated from helping themselves in one way have some corresponding organ in another direction."

"I agree with you that kings are generally religious," said Lady Widgery, "and you must admit that, if monarchy makes men religious, it is an argument in its favor, because there is nothing so important as religion, you know."

"The argument, madam, is a profound one, and does credit to your discernment; but the question now is, since it has pleased Providence to prosper rebellion, and allow a community to be founded without any true church, or any means of getting at true ordinances and sacraments, what young fellows like us are to do about it."

"I 'll tell you, Ellery," said the old lady, laying hold of his arm. " 'Know the God of thy fathers, and serve him with a perfect heart and willing mind,' and everything will come right."

"But, even then, I could n't belong to 'the true Church,' " said Ellery.

"You 'd belong to the church of all good people," said the old lady, "and that 's the main thing."

"Aunty, you are always right," he said.

Now I listened with the sharpest attention to all this conversation, which was as bewildering to me as all the rest of the scenery and surroundings of this extraordinary visit had been.

Miss Debby's martial and declaratory air, the vigorous faith in her statements which she appeared to have, were quite a match, it seemed to me, for similar statements of a contrary nature which I had heard from my respected grandmother; and I could n't help wondering in my own mind what strange concussions of the elementary powers would result if ever these two should be brought together. To use a modern figure, it would be like the meeting of two full-charged railroad engines, from opposite directions, on the same track.

After dinner, in the evening, instead of the usual service of family prayers, Miss Debby catechised her family in a vigorous and determined manner. We children went and stood up with the row of men and maid servants, and Harry proved to have a very good knowledge of the catechism, but Tina and I only compassed our answers by repeating them after Miss Debby; and she applied herself to teaching us as if this were the only opportunity of getting the truth we were ever to have in our lives.

In fact, Miss Debby made a current of electricity that, for the time being, carried me completely away, and I exerted myself to the utmost to appear well before her, especially as I had gathered from Aunt Lois and Aunt Keziah's conversations, that whatever went on in this mansion belonged strictly to upper circles of society, dimly known and revered. American democracy had not in those days become a practical thing, so as to outgrow the result of generations of reverence for the upper classes. And the man-servant and the maid-servants seemed so humble, and Miss Debby so victorious and dominant, that I could n't help feeling what a grand thing the true Church must be, and find growing in myself the desires of a submissive catechumen.

As to the catechism itself, I don't recollect that I thought one moment what a word of it meant, I was so absorbed and busy in the mere effort of repeating it after Miss Debby's rapid dictation.

The only comparison I remember to have made with that which I had been accustomed to recite in school every Saturday respected the superior case of answering the first question; which required me, instead of relating in metaphysical terms what "man's chief end" was in time and eternity, to give a plain statement of what my own name was on this mortal earth.

This first question, as being easiest, was put to Tina, who dimpled and colored and flashed out of her eyes, as she usually did when addressed, looked shyly across at Ellery Davenport, who sat with an air of negligent amusement contemplating the scene, and then answered with sufficient precision and distinctness, "Eglantine Percival."

He gave a little start, as if some sudden train of recollection had been awakened, and looked at her with intense attention; and when Ellery Davenport fixed his attention upon anybody, there was so much fire and electricity in his eyes that they seemed to be felt, even at a distance; and I saw that Tina constantly colored and giggled, and seemed so excited that she scarcely knew what she was saying, till at last Miss Debby, perceiving this, turned sharp round upon him, and said, "Ellery Davenport, if you have n't any religion yourself, I wish you would n't interrupt my instructions."

"Bless my soul, cousin! what was I doing? I have been sitting here still as a mouse; but I 'll turn my back, and read a good book";—and round he turned, accordingly, till the catechising was finished.

When it was all over, and the servants had gone out, we grouped ourselves around the fire, and Ellery Davenport began: "Cousin Debby, I 'm going to come down handsomely to you. I admit that your catechism is much better for children than the one I was brought up on. I was well drilled in the formulas of the celebrated Assembly of *dry*vines of Westminster, and dry enough I found it. Now it 's a true proverb, 'Call a man a thief, and he 'll steal'; 'give a dog a bad name, and he 'll bite you'; tell a child that he is 'a member of Christ, a child of God, and an inheritor of the kingdom of heaven,' and he feels, to say the least, civilly disposed towards religion; tell him 'he is under God's wrath and curse, and so made liable to all the miseries of this life, to death itself, and the pains of hell forever,' because somebody ate an apple five thousand years ago, and his religious associations are not so agreeable,—especially if he has the answers whipped into him, or has to go to bed without his supper for not learning them."

"You poor dear!" said the old lady; "did they send you to bed without your supper? They ought to have been whipped themselves, every one of them."

"Well, you see, I was a little fellow when my parents died, and brought up under brother Jonathan, who was the bluest kind of blue; and he was so afraid that I should mistake my naturally sweet temper for religion, that he instructed me daily that I was a child of wrath, and could n't, and did n't, and never should do one right thing till I was regenerated, and when that would happen no mortal knew; so I thought, as my account was going to be scored off at that time, it was no matter if I did run up a pretty long one; so I lied and stole whenever it came handy."

"O Ellery, I hope not!" said the old lady; "certainly you never stole anything!"

"Have, though, my blessed aunt,—robbed orchards and watermelon patches; but then St. Augustine did that very thing himself, and he did n't turn about till he was thirty years old, and I 'm a good deal short of that yet; so you see there is a great chance for me."

"Ellery, why don't you come into the true Church?" said Miss Debby. "That 's what you need."

"Well," said Ellery, "I must confess that I like the idea of a nice old motherly Church, that sings to us, and talks to us, and prays with us, and takes us in her lap and coddles us when we are sick and says,—

'Hush, my dear, lie still and slumber.'

Nothing would suit me better, if I could get my reason to sleep; but the mischief of a Calvinistic education is, it wakes up your reason, and it never will go to sleep again, and you can't take a pleasant humbug if you would. Now, in this life, where nobody knows anything about anything, a capacity for humbugs would be a splendid thing to have. I wish to my heart I'd been brought up a Roman Catholic! but I have not,—I've been brought up a Calvinist, and so here I am."

"But if you'd try to come into the Church and believe," said Miss Debby, energetically, "grace would be given you. You've been baptized, and the Church admits your baptism. Now just assume your position."

Miss Debby spoke with such zeal and earnestness, that I, whom she was holding in her lap, looked straight across with the expectation of hearing Ellery Davenport declare his immediate conversion then and there. I shall never forget the expression of his face. There was first a flash of amusement, as he looked at Miss Debby's strong, sincere face, and then it faded into something between admiration and pity; and then he said to himself in a musing tone: "I a 'member of Christ, a child of God, and an inheritor of the kingdom of heaven.'" And then a strange, sarcastic expression broke over his face, as he added: "Could n't do it, cousin; not exactly my style. Besides, I should n't be much of a credit to any church, and whichever catches me would be apt to find a shark in the net. You see," he added, jumping up and walking about rapidly, "I have the misfortune to have an extremely exacting nature, and, if I set out to be religious at all, it would oblige me to carry the thing to as great lengths as did my grandfather Jonathan Edwards. I should have to take up the cross and all that, and I don't want to, and don't mean to; and as to all these pleasant, comfortable churches, where a fellow can get to heaven without it, I have the misfortune of not being able to believe in them; so there you see precisely my situation."

"These horrid old Calvinistic doctrines," said Miss Debby, "are the ruin of children."

"My dear, they are all in the Thirty-nine Articles as strong as in the Cambridge platform, and all the other platforms, for the good reason that John Calvin himself had the overlooking of them. And, what is worse, there is an abominable sight of truth in them. Nature herself is a high Calvinist, old jade; and there never was a man of energy enough to feel the force of the world he deals with that was n't a predestinarian, from the time of the Greek Tragedians down to the time of Oliver Cromwell, and ever since. The hardest doctrines are the things that a fellow sees with his own eyes going on in the world around him. If you had been in England, as I have, where the true Church prevails, you 'd see that pretty much the whole of the lower classes there are predestinated to be conceived and born in sin, and shapen in iniquity; and come into the world in such circumstances that to expect even decent morality of them is expecting what is contrary to all reason. This is your Christian country, after eighteen hundred years' experiment of Christianity. The elect, by whom I mean the bishops and clergy and upper classes, have attained to a position in which a decent and religious life is practicable, and where there is leisure from the claims of the body to attend to those of the soul. These, however, to a large extent are smothering in their own fat, or, as your service to-day had it, 'Their heart is fat as brawn'; and so they don't, to any great extent, make their calling and election sure. Then, as for heathen countries, they are a peg below those of Christianity. Taking the mass of human beings in the world at this hour, they are in such circumstances, that, so far from it 's being reasonable to expect the morals of Christianity of them, they are not within sight of ordinary human decencies. Talk of purity of heart to a Malay or Hottentot! Why, the doctrine of a clean shirt is an uncomprehended mystery to more than half the human race at this moment. That 's what I call visible election and reprobation, get rid of it as we may or can."

"Positively, Ellery, I am not going to have you talk so before these children," said Miss Debby, getting up and ringing the bell energetically. "This all comes of the vile democratic idea that people are to have opinions on all subjects, instead of believing what the Church tells them; and, as you say, it 's Calvinism that starts people out to be always reasoning and discussing and having opinions. I hate folks who are always speculating and thinking, and having new doctrines; all I want to know is *my duty*, and to do it. I want to know what *my* part is, and it 's none of my business whether the bishops and the kings and the nobility do theirs or not, if I only do mine. 'To do my duty in that state of life in which it has pleased God to call me,' is all I want, and I think it is all anybody need want."

"*Amen!*" said Ellery Davenport, "*and so be it.*"

Here Mrs. Margery appeared with the candles to take us to bed.

In bidding our adieus for the night, it was customary for good children to kiss all round; but Tina, in performing this ceremony both this night and the night before, resolutely ignored Ellery Davenport, notwithstanding his earnest petitions; and, while she would kiss with ostentatious affection those on each side of him, she hung her head and drew back whenever he attempted the familiarity, yet, by way of reparation, turned back at the door as she was going out, and made him a parting salutation with the air of a princess; and I heard him say, "Upon my word, how she does it!"

After we left the room (this being a particular which, like tellers of stories in general, I learned from other sources), he turned to Lady Lothrop and said: "Did I understand that she said her name was Eglantine Percival, and that she is a sort of foundling?"

"Certainly," said Lady Lothrop; "both these children are orphans, left on the parish by a poor woman who died in a neighboring town. They appear to be of good blood and breeding, but we have no means of knowing who they are."

"Well," said Ellery Davenport, "I knew a young English officer by the name of Percival, who was rather a graceless fellow. He once visited me at my country-seat, with several others. When he went away, being, as he often was, not very fit to take care of himself, he dropped and left a pocket-book, so some of the servants told me, which was thrown into one of the drawers, and for aught I know may be there now: it 's just barely possible that it may be, and that there may be some papers in it which will shed light on these children's parentage. If I recollect rightly, he was said to be connected with a good English family, and it might be possible, if we were properly informed, to shame him, or frighten him into doing something for these children. I will look into the matter myself, when I am in England next winter, where I shall have some business; that is to say, if we can get any clew. The probability is that the children are illegitimate."

"O, I hope not," said Lady Lothrop; "they appear to have been so beautifully educated."

"Well," said Ellery Davenport, "he may have seduced his curate's daughter; that's a very simple supposition. At any rate, he never produced her in society, never spoke of her, kept her in cheap, poor lodgings in the country, and the general supposition was that she was his mistress, not his wife."

"No," said a little voice near his elbow, which startled every one in the room,—"no, Mr. Davenport, my mother was my father's wife."

The fire had burnt low, and the candles had not been brought in, and Harry, who had been sent back by Mrs. Margery to give a message as to the night arrangements, had entered the room softly, and stood waiting to get a chance to deliver it. He now came forward, and stood trembling with agitation, pale yet bold. Of course all were very much shocked as he went on: "They took my mother's wedding-ring, and sold it to pay for her coffin; but she always wore it and often told me when it was put on. But," he added, "she told me, the night she died, that I had no father but God."

"And he is Father enough!" said the old lady, who, entirely broken down and overcome, clasped the little boy in her arms. "Never you mind it, dear, God certainly will take care of you."

"I know he will," said the boy, with solemn simplicity; "but I want you all to believe the truth about my mother."

It was characteristic of that intense inwardness and delicacy which were so peculiar in Harry's character, that, when he came back from this agitating scene, he did not tell me a word of what had occurred, nor did I learn it till years afterwards. I was very much in the habit of lying awake nights, long after he had sunk into untroubled slumbers, and this night I remember that he lay long but silently awake, so very still and quiet, that it was some time before I discovered that he was not sleeping.

The next day Ellery Davenport left us, but we remained to see the wonders of Boston. I remembered my grandmother's orders, and went on to Copps Hill, and to the old Granary burying-ground, to see the graves of the saints, and read the inscriptions. I had a curious passion for this sort of mortuary literature, even as a child,—a sort of nameless, weird, strange delight,—so that I accomplished this part of my grandmother's wishes *con amore*.

Boston in those days had not even arrived at being a city, but, as the reader may learn from contemporary magazines, was known as the Town of Boston. In some respects, however, it was even more attractive in those days for private residences than it is at present. As is the case now in some of our large rural towns, it had many stately old houses, which stood surrounded by gardens and grounds, where fruits and flowers were tended with scrupulous care. It was sometimes called "the garden town." The house of Madam Kittery stood on a high eminence overlooking the sea, and had connected with it a stately garden, which, just at the time of year I speak of, was gay with the first crocuses and snowdrops.

In the eyes of the New England people, it was always a sort of mother-town,—a sacred city, the shrine of that religious enthusiasm which founded the States of New England. There were the graves of her prophets and her martyrs,— those who had given their lives through the hardships of that enterprise in so ungenial a climate.

On Easter Monday Lady Lothrop proposed to take us all to see the shops and sights of Boston, with the bountiful intention of purchasing some few additions to the children's wardrobes. I was invited to accompany the expedition, and all parties appeared not a little surprised, and somewhat amused, that I preferred, instead of this lively tour among the living, to spend my time in a lonely ramble in the Copps Hill burying-ground.

I returned home after an hour or two spent in this way, and found the parlor deserted by all except dear old Madam Kittery. I remember, even now, the aspect of that sunny room, and the perfect picture of peace and love that she seemed to me, as she sat on the sofa with a table full of books drawn up to her, placidly reading.

She called me to her as soon as I came in, and would have me get on the sofa by her. She stroked my head, and looked lovingly at me, and called me "Sonny," till my whole heart opened toward her as a flower opens toward the sunshine.

Among all the loves that man has to woman, there is none

so sacred and saint-like as that toward these dear, white-haired angels, who seem to form the connecting link between heaven and earth, who have lived to get the victory over every sin and every sorrow, and live perpetually on the banks of the dark river, in that bright, calm land of Beulah, where angels daily walk to and fro, and sounds of celestial music are heard across the water.

Such have no longer personal cares, or griefs, or sorrows. The tears of life have all been shed, and therefore they have hearts at leisure to attend to every one else. Even the sweet, guileless childishness that comes on in this period has a sacred dignity; it is a seal of fitness for that heavenly kingdom which whosoever shall not receive as a little child, shall not enter therein.

Madam Kittery, with all her apparent simplicity, had a sort of simple shrewdness. She delighted in reading, and some of the best classical literature was always lying on her table. She began questioning me about my reading, and asking me to read to her, and seemed quite surprised at the intelligence and expression with which I did it.

I remember, in the course of the reading, coming across a very simple Latin quotation, at which she stopped me. "There," said she, "is one of those Latin streaks that always trouble me in books, because I can't tell what they mean. When George was alive, he used to read them to me."

Now, as this was very simple, I felt myself quite adequate to its interpretation, and gave it with a readiness which pleased her.

"Why! how came you to know Latin?" she said.

Then my heart opened, and I told her all my story, and how my poor father had always longed to go to college, "and died without the sight," and how he had begun to teach me Latin; but how he was dead, and my mother was poor, and grandpapa could only afford to keep Uncle Bill in college, and there was no way for me to go, and Aunt Lois wanted to bind me out to a shoemaker. And then I began to cry, as I always did when I thought of this.

I shall never forget the overflowing, motherly sympathy which had made it easy for me to tell all this to one who, but a few hours before, had been a stranger; nor how she comforted me, and cheered me, and insisted upon it that I should immediately eat a piece of cake, and begged me not to trouble myself about it, and she would talk to Debby, and something should be done.

Now I had not the slightest idea of what Madam Kittery could do in the situation, but I was exceedingly strengthened and consoled, and felt sure that there had come a favorable turn in my fortunes; and the dear old lady and myself forthwith entered into a league of friendship.

I was thus emboldened, now that we were all alone, and Miss Debby far away, to propound to her indulgent ear certain political doubts, raised by the conflict of my past education with the things I had been hearing for the last day or two.

"If King George was such a good man, what made him oppress the Colonies so?" said I.

"Why, dear, he did n't," she said, earnestly. "That 's all a great mistake. Our King is a dear, pious, good man, and wished us all well, and was doing just the best for us he knew how."

"Then was it because he did n't know how to govern us?" said I.

"My dear, you know the King can do no wrong; it was his ministers, if anybody. I don't know exactly how it was, but they got into a brangle, and everything went wrong; and then there was so much evil feeling and fighting and killing, and 'there was confusion, and every evil work.' There 's my poor boy," she said, pointing to the picture with a trembling hand, and to the sword hanging in its crape loop,—"he died for his King, doing his duty in that state of life in which it pleased God to call him. I must n't be sorry for that, but O, I wish there had n't been any war, and we could have had it all peaceful, and George could have stayed with us. I don't see, either, the use of all these new-fangled notions, but then I try to love everybody, and hope for the best."

So spoke my dear old friend; and has there ever been a step in human progress that has not been taken against the prayers of some good soul, and been washed by tears, sincerely and despondently shed? But, for all this, is there not a true unity of the faith in all good hearts? and when they have risen a

little above the mists of earth, may not both sides—the conqueror and the conquered—agree that God hath given them
the victory in advancing the cause of truth and goodness?

Only one other conversation that I heard during this memorable visit fixed itself very strongly in my mind. On the evening of this same day, we three children were stationed at a
table to look at a volume of engravings of beautiful birds,
while Miss Debby, Lady Widgery and Madam Kittery sat by
the fire. I heard them talking of Ellery Davenport, and,
though I had been instructed that it was not proper for children to listen when their elders were talking among themselves, yet it really was not possible to avoid hearing what
Miss Debby said, because all her words were delivered with
such a sharp and determinate emphasis.

As it appeared, Lady Widgery had been relating to them
some of the trials and sorrows of Ellery Davenport's domestic
life. And then there followed a buzz of some kind of story
which Lady Widgery seemed relating with great minuteness.
At last I heard Miss Deborah exclaim earnestly: "If I had a
daughter, catch me letting her be intimate with Ellery Davenport! I tell you that man has n't read French for nothing."

"I do assure you, his conduct has been marked with perfect
decorum," said Lady Widgery.

"So are your French novels," said Miss Deborah; "they are
always talking about decorum; they are full of decorum and
piety! why, the kingdom of heaven is nothing to them! but
somehow they all end in adultery."

"Debby," said the old lady, "I can't bear to hear you talk
so. I think your cousin's heart is in the right place, after all;
and he 's a good, kind boy as ever was."

"But, mother, he 's a liar! that 's just what he is."

"Debby, Debby! how can you talk so?"

"Well, mother, people have different names for different
things. I hear a great deal about Ellery Davenport's tact and
knowledge of the world, and all that; but he does a great deal
of what I call lying,—so there! Now there are some folks
who lie blunderingly, and unskilfully, but I 'll say for Ellery
Davenport that he can lie as innocently and sweetly and prettily as a French woman, and I can't say any more. And if a
woman does n't want to believe him, she just must n't listen

to him, that's all. I always believe him when he is around, but when he's away and I think him over, I know just what he is, and see just what an old fool he has made of me."

These words dropped into my childish mind as if you should accidentally drop a ring into a deep well. I did not think of them much at the time, but there came a day in my life when the ring was fished up out of the well, good as new.

XXVI.

What "Our Folks" Said at Oldtown

WE children returned to Oldtown, crowned with victory, as it were. Then, as now, even in the simple and severe Puritanical village, there was much incense burnt upon the altar of gentility,—a deity somewhat corresponding to the unknown god whose altar Paul found at Athens, and probably more universally worshipped in all the circles of this lower world than any other idol on record.

Now we had been taken notice of, put forward, and patronized, in undeniably genteel society. We had been to Boston and come back in a coach; and what well-regulated mind does not see that that was something to inspire respect?

Aunt Lois was evidently dying to ask us all manner of questions, but was restrained by a sort of decent pride. To exhibit any undue eagerness would be to concede that she was ignorant of good society, and that the ways and doings of upper classes were not perfectly familiar to her. That, my dear reader, is what no good democratic American woman can for a moment concede. Aunt Lois therefore, for once in her life, looked complacently on Sam Lawson, who continued to occupy his usual roost in the chimney-corner, and who, embarrassed with no similar delicate scruples, put us through our catechism with the usual Yankee thoroughness.

"Well, chillen, I suppose them Kitterys has everythin' in real grander, don't they? I 've heerd tell that they hes Turkey carpets on th' floors. You know Josh Kittery, he was in the Injy trade. Turkey carpets is that kind, you know, that lies all up thick like a mat. They had that kind, did n't they?"

We eagerly assured him that they did.

"Want to know, now," said Sam, who always moralized as he went along. "Wal, wal, some folks does seem to receive their good thin's in this life, don't they? S'pose the tea-things all on 'em was solid silver, wa' n't they? Yeh did n't ask them, did yeh?"

"O no," said I; "you know we were told we must n't ask questions."

"Jes so; very right,—little boys should n't ask questions. But I 've heerd a good 'eal about the Kittery silver. Jake Marshall, he knew a fellah that had talked with one of their servants, that helped bury it in the cellar in war-times, and he said theh was porringers an' spoons an' tankards, say nothing of table-spoons, an' silver forks, an' sich. That 'ere would ha' been a haul for Congress, if they could ha' got hold on 't in war-time, would n't it? S'pose yeh was sot up all so grand, and hed servants to wait on yeh, behind yer chairs, did n't yeh?"

"Yes," we assured him, "we did."

"Wal, wal; yeh must n't be carried away by these 'ere glories: they 's transitory, arter all: ye must jest come right daown to plain livin'. How many servants d' yeh say they kep'?"

"Why, there were two men and two women, besides Lady Widgery's maid and Mrs. Margery."

"And all used to come in to prayers every night," said Harry.

"Hes prayers reg'lar, does they?" said Sam. "Well, now, that 'ere beats all! Did n't know as these gran' families wus so pious as that comes to. Who prayed?"

"Old Madam Kittery," said I. "She used to read prayers out of a large book."

"O yis; these 'ere gran' Tory families is 'Piscopal, pretty much all on 'em. But now readin' prayers out of a book, that 'ere don' strike me as just the right kind o' thing. For my part, I like prayers that come right out of the heart better. But then, lordy massy, folks hes theh different ways; an' I ain't so set as Polly is. Why, I b'lieve, if that 'ere woman had her way, theh would n't nobody be 'lowed to do nothin', except just to suit her. Yeh did n't notice, did yeh, what the Kittery coat of arms was?"

Yes, we had noticed it; and Harry gave a full description of an embroidered set of armorial bearings which had been one of the ornaments of the parlor.

"So you say," said Sam, " 't was a lion upon his hind legs,—that 'ere is what they call 'the lion rampant,'—and then there was a key and a scroll. Wal! coats of arms is curus, and I don't wonder folks kind o' hangs onter um; but then, the Kitterys bein' Tories, they nat'ally has more interest in sech thin's. Do you know where Mis' Kittery keeps her silver nights?"

"No, really," said I; "we were sent to bed early, and did n't see."

Now this inquiry, from anybody less innocent than Sam Lawson, might have been thought a dangerous exhibition of burglarious proclivities; but from him it was received only as an indication of that everlasting thirst for general information which was his leading characteristic.

When the rigor of his cross-examination had somewhat abated, he stooped over the fire to meditate further inquiries. I seized the opportunity to propound to my grandmother a query which had been the result of my singular experiences for a day or two past. So, after an interval in which all had sat silently looking into the great coals of the fire, I suddenly broke out with the inquiry, "Grandmother, what is *The True Church*?"

I remember the expression on my grandfather's calm, benign face as I uttered this query. It was an expression of shrewd amusement, such as befits the face of an elder when a younger has propounded a well-worn problem; but my grandmother had her answer at the tip of her tongue, and replied, "It is the whole number of the elect, my son."

I had in my head a confused remembrance of Ellery Davenport's tirade on election, and of the elect who did or did not have clean shirts; so I pursued my inquiry by asking, "Who are the elect?"

"All good people," replied my grandfather. "In every nation he that feareth God and worketh righteousness is accepted of Him."

"Well, how came you to ask that question?" said my grandmother, turning on me.

"Why," said I, "because Miss Deborah Kittery said that the war destroyed the true Church in this country."

"O, pshaw!" said my grandmother; "that 's some of her Episcopal nonsense. I really should like to ask her, now, if she thinks there ain't any one going to heaven but Episcopalians."

"O no, she does n't think so," said I, rather eagerly. "She said a great many good people would be saved out of the Church, but they would be saved by uncovenanted mercies."

"Uncovenanted fiddlesticks!" said my grandmother, her very cap-border bristling with contempt and defiance. "Now, Lois, you just see what comes of sending children into Tory Episcopal families,—coming home and talking nonsense like that!"

"Mercy, mother! what odds does it make?" said Aunt Lois. "The children have got to learn to hear all sorts of things said,—may as well hear them at one time as another. Besides, it all goes into one ear and out at the other."

My grandmother was better pleased with the account that I hastened to give her of my visit to the graves of the saints and martyrs, in my recent pilgrimage. Her broad face glowed with delight, as she told over again to our listening ears the stories of the faith and self-denial of those who had fled from an oppressive king and church, that they might plant a new region where life should be simpler, easier, and more natural. And she got out her "Cotton Mather," and, notwithstanding Aunt Lois's reminder that she had often read it before, read to us again, in a trembling yet audible voice, that wonderful document, in which the reasons for the first planting of New England are set forth. Some of these reasons I remember from often hearing them in my childhood. They speak thus quaintly of the old countries of Europe:—

"Thirdly. The land grows weary of her inhabitants, insomuch that *man*, which is the most precious of all creatures, is here more vile than the earth he treads upon,—children, neighbors, and friends, especially the *poor*, which, if things were right, would be the greatest earthly blessings.

"Fourthly. We are grown to that intemperance in all *excess of riot*, as no mean estate will suffice a man to keep sail with his *equals*, and he that fails in it must live in scorn and contempt: hence it comes to pass that all *arts* and *trades* are carried in that deceitful manner and unrighteous course, as it is almost impossible for a good, upright man to maintain his constant charge, and live comfortably in them.

"Fifthly. The schools of learning and religion are so corrupted as (besides the insupportable charge of education) most children of the best, wittiest, and of the fairest hopes are

perverted, corrupted, and utterly overthrown by the multitude of evil examples and licentious behaviours in these *seminaries*.

"*Sixthly*. The *whole earth* is the Lord's *garden*, and he hath given it to the sons of Adam to be tilled and improved by them. Why then should we stand starving here for places of habitation, and in the mean time suffer whole countries as profitable for the use of man to lie waste without any improvement?"

Language like this, often repeated, was not lost upon us. The idea of self-sacrifice which it constantly inculcated,—the reverence for self-denial,—the conception of a life which should look, not mainly to selfish interests, but to the good of the whole human race, prevented the hardness and roughness of those early New England days from becoming mere stolid, material toil. It was toil and manual labor ennobled by a new motive.

Even in those very early times there was some dawning sense of what the great American nation was yet to be. And every man, woman, and child was constantly taught, by every fireside, to feel that he or she was part and parcel of a great new movement in human progress. The old aristocratic ideas, though still lingering in involuntary manners and customs, only served to give a sort of quaintness and grace of Old-World culture to the roughness of new-fledged democracy.

Our visit to Boston was productive of good to us such as we little dreamed of. In the course of a day or two Lady Lothrop called, and had a long private interview with the female portion of the family; after which, to my great delight, it was announced to us that Harry and I might begin to study Latin, if we pleased, and if we proved bright, good boys, means would be provided for the finishing of our education in college.

I was stunned and overwhelmed by the great intelligence, and Harry and I ran over to tell it to Tina, who jumped about and hugged and kissed us both with an impartiality which some years later she quite forgot to practice.

"I 'm glad, because you like it," she said; "but I should think it would be horrid to study Latin."

I afterwards learned that I was indebted to my dear old

friend Madam Kittery for the good fortune which had befall-en me. She had been interested in my story, as it appears, to some purpose, and, being wealthy and without a son, had resolved to console herself by appropriating to the education of a poor boy a portion of the wealth which should have gone to her own child.

The searching out of poor boys, and assisting them to a liberal education, had ever been held to be one of the appro-priate works of the minister in a New England town. The schoolmaster who taught the district school did not teach Latin; but Lady Lothrop was graciously pleased to say that, for the present, Dr. Lothrop would hear our lessons at a cer-tain hour every afternoon; and the reader may be assured that we studied faithfully in view of an ordeal like this.

I remember one of our favorite places for study. The brown, sparkling stream on which my grandfather's mill was placed had just below the mill-dam a little island, which a boy could easily reach by wading through the shallow waters over a bed of many-colored pebbles. The island was overshadowed by thick bushes, which were all wreathed and matted together by a wild grape-vine; but within I had hollowed out for my-self a green little arbor, and constructed a rude wigwam of poles and bark, after the manner of those I had seen among the Indians. It was one of the charms of this place, that no-body knew of it: it was utterly secluded; and being cut off from land by the broad belt of shallow water, and presenting nothing to tempt or attract anybody to its shores, it was mine, and mine alone. There I studied, and there I read; there I dreamed and saw visions.

Never did I find it in my heart to tell to any other boy the secret of this woodland shelter, this fairy-land, so near to the real outer world; but Harry, with his refinement, his qui-etude, his sympathetic silence, seemed to me as unobjection-able an associate as the mute spiritual companions whose presence had cheered my lonely, childish sleeping-room.

We moved my father's Latin books into a rough little closet that we constructed in our wigwam; and there, with the wa-ter dashing behind us, and the afternoon sun shining down through the green grape-leaves, with bluebirds and bobolinks singing to us, we studied our lessons. More than that, we spent many pleasant hours in reading; and I have now a *résumé*, in our boyish handwriting, of the greater part of Plutarch's Lives, which we wrote out during this summer.

As to Tina, of course she insisted upon it that we should occasionally carry her in a lady-chair over to this island, that she might inspect our operations and our housekeeping, and we read some of these sketches to her for her critical approbation; and if any of them pleased her fancy, she would immediately insist that we should come over to Miss Mehitable's, and have a dramatic representation of them up in the garret.

Saturday afternoon, in New England, was considered, from time immemorial, as the children's perquisite; and hardhearted must be that parent or that teacher who would wish to take away from them its golden hours. Certainly it was not Miss Mehitable, nor my grandmother, that could be capable of any such cruelty.

Our Saturday afternoons were generally spent as Tina dictated; and, as she had a decided taste for the drama, one of our most common employments was the improvising of plays, with Miss Tina for stage manager. The pleasure we took in these exercises was inconceivable; they had for us a vividness and reality past all expression.

I remember our acting, at one time, the Book of Esther, with Tina, very much be-trinketed and dressed out in an old flowered brocade that she had rummaged from a trunk in the garret, as Queen Esther. Harry was Mordecai, and I was Ahasuerus.

The great trouble was to find a Haman; but, as the hanging of Haman was indispensable to any proper moral effect of the tragedy, Tina petted and cajoled and coaxed old Bose, the yellow dog of our establishment, to undertake the part, instructing him volubly that he must sulk and look cross when Mordecai went by,—a thing which Bose, who was one of the best-natured of dogs, found difficulty in learning. Bose would always insist upon sitting on his haunches, in his free-and-easy, jolly manner, and lolling out his red tongue in a style so decidedly jocular as utterly to spoil the effect, till Tina, reduced to desperation, ensconced herself under an old quilted petticoat behind him, and brought out the proper expression at the right moment by a vigorous pull at his tail. Bose was a dog of great constitutional equanimity, but there were some things that transcended even his powers of endurance, and the snarl that he gave to Mordecai was held to be a triumphant success; but the thing was, to get him to snarl when Tina was in front of him, where she could see it; and now will it be believed that the all-conquering little mischief-maker actually kissed and flattered and bejuggled old Polly into taking this part behind the scenes?

No words can more fitly describe the abject state to which that vehemently moral old soul was reduced.

When it came to the hanging of Haman, the difficulties thickened. Polly warned us that we must by no means attempt to hang Bose by the neck, as "the crittur was heavy, and 't was sartin to be the death of him." So we compromised by passing the rope under his fore paws, or, as Tina called it, "under his arms." But Bose was rheumatic, and it took all Tina's petting and caressing, and obliged Polly to go down and hunt out two or three slices of meat from her larder, to induce him fairly to submit to the operation; but hang him we did, and he ki-hied with a vigor that strikingly increased the moral effect. So we soon let him down again, and plentifully rewarded him with cold meat.

In a similar manner we performed a patriotic drama, entitled "The Battle of Bunker Hill," in which a couple of old guns that we found in the garret produced splendid effects, and salvoes of artillery were created by the rolling across the garret of two old cannon-balls; but this was suppressed by order of the authorities, on account of the vigor of the cannonade. Tina, by the by, figured in this as the "Genius of Liberty," with some stars on her head cut out of gilt paper, and wearing an old flag which we had pulled out of one of the trunks.

We also acted the history of "Romulus and Remus," with Bose for the she-wolf. The difference in age was remedied by a vigorous effort of the imagination. Of course, operations of this nature made us pretty familiar with the topography of the old garret. There was, however, one quarter, fenced off by some barrels filled with pamphlets, where Polly strictly forbade us to go.

What was the result of such a prohibition, O reader? Can

you imagine it to be any other than that that part of the garret became at once the only one that we really cared about
investigating? How we hung about it, and considered it, and
peeped over and around and between the barrels at a pile of
pictures, that stood with their faces to the wall! What were
those pictures, we wondered. When we asked Polly this, she
drew on a mysterious face and said, "*Them* was things we
must n't ask about."

We talked it over among ourselves, and Tina assured us
that she dreamed about it nights; but Polly had strictly forbidden us even to mention that corner of the garret to Miss
Mehitable, or to ask her leave to look at it, alleging, as a
reason, that " 't would bring on her hypos."

We did n't know what "hypos" were, but we supposed of
course they must be something dreadful; but the very fear-
fulness of the consequences that might ensue from our getting behind those fatal barrels only made them still more
attractive. Finally, one rainy Saturday afternoon, when we
were tired of acting plays, and the rain pattered on the
roof, and the wind howled and shook the casings, and
there was a generally wild and disorganized state of affairs
out of doors, a sympathetic spirit of insubordination appeared to awaken in Tina's bosom. "I declare, I am going
inside of those barrels!" she said. "I don't care if Polly does
scold us; I know I can bring her all round again fast
enough. I can do about what I like with Polly. Now you boys
just move this barrel a little bit, and I 'll go in and see!"

Just at this moment there was one of those chance lulls in
the storm that sometimes occur, and as Tina went in behind
the barrels, and boldly turned the first picture, a ray of sunshine streamed through the dusky window and lit it up with
a watery light.

Harry and Tina both gave an exclamation of astonishment.
"O Tina! it 's the lady in the closet!"

The discovery seemed really to frighten the child. She retreated quickly to the outside of the barrels again, and stood
with us, looking at the picture.

It was a pastel of a young girl in a plain, low-necked white
dress, with a haughty, beautiful head, and jet-black curls flow-

ing down her neck, and deep, melancholy black eyes, that seemed to fix themselves reproachfully on us.

"O dear me, Harry, what shall we do?" said Tina. "How she looks at us! This certainly is the very same one that we saw in the old house."

"You ought not to have done it, Tina," said Harry, in a rather low and frightened voice; "but I 'll go in and turn it back again."

Just at this moment we heard what was still more appalling,—the footsteps of Polly on the garret stairs.

"Well! now I should like to know if there 's any mischief you would n't be up to, Tina Percival," she said, coming forward, reproachfully. "When I give you the run of the whole garret, and wear my life out a pickin' up and puttin' up after you, I sh'd think you might let this 'ere corner alone!"

"Oh! but, Polly, you 've no idea how I wanted to see it, and *do* pray tell me who it is, and how came it here? Is it anybody that 's dead?" said Tina, hanging upon Polly caressingly.

"Somebody that 's dead to us, I 'm afraid," said Polly, solemnly.

"Do tell us, Polly, *do*! who was she?"

"Well, child, you must n't *never* tell nobody, nor let a word about it come out of your lips; but it 's Parson Rossiter's daughter Emily, and where she 's gone to, the Lord only knows. I took that 'ere pictur' down myself, and put it up here with Mr. Theodore's, so 't Miss Mehitable need n't see 'em, 'cause they always give her the hypos."

"And don't anybody know where she is," said Tina, "or if she 's alive or dead?"

"Nobody," said Polly, shaking her head solemnly. "All I hope is, she may never come back here again. You see, children, what comes o' follerin' the natural heart; it 's deceitful above all things, and desperately wicked. She followed her natural heart, and nobody knows where she 's gone to."

Polly spoke with such sepulchral earnestness that, what with gloomy weather and the consciousness of having been accessory to an unlawful action, we all felt, to say the least, extremely sober.

"Do you think I have got such a heart as that?" said Tina, after a deep-drawn sigh.

"Sartain, you have," said the old woman. "We all on us has. Why, if the Lord should give any on us a sight o' our own heart just as it is, it would strike us down dead right on the spot."

"Mercy on us, Polly! I hope he won't, then," said Tina. "But, Polly," she added, getting her arms round her neck and playing with her gold beads, "*you* have n't got such a very bad heart now; I don't believe a word of it. I 'm sure you are just as *good* as can be."

"Law, Miss Tina, you don't see into me," said Polly, who, after all, felt a sort of ameliorating gleam stealing over her. "You must n't try to wheedle me into thinking better of myself than I be; that would just lead to carnal security."

"Well, Polly, don't tell Miss Mehitable, and I 'll try and not get you into carnal security."

Polly went behind the barrels, gently wiped the dust from the picture, and turned the melancholy, beseeching face to the wall again; but we pondered and talked many days as to what it might be.

XXVII.

How We Kept Thanksgiving at Oldtown

O N the whole, about this time in our life we were a reasonably happy set of children. The Thanksgiving festival
of that year is particularly impressed on my mind as a white
day.

Are there any of my readers who do not know what
Thanksgiving day is to a child? Then let them go back with
me, and recall the image of it as we kept it in Oldtown.

People have often supposed, because the Puritans founded
a society where there were no professed public amusements,
that therefore there was no fun going on in the ancient land
of Israel, and that there were no cakes and ale, because they
were virtuous. They were never more mistaken in their lives.
There was an abundance of sober, well-considered merriment;
and the hinges of life were well oiled with that sort of secret
humor which to this day gives the raciness to real Yankee wit.
Besides this, we must remember that life itself is the greatest
possible amusement to people who really believe they can do
much with it,—who have that intense sense of what can be
brought to pass by human effort, that was characteristic of
the New England colonies. To such it is not exactly proper to
say that life is an amusement, but it certainly is an engrossing
interest that takes the place of all amusements.

Looking over the world on a broad scale, do we not find
that public entertainments have very generally been the sops
thrown out by engrossing upper classes to keep lower classes
from inquiring too particularly into their rights, and to make
them satisfied with a stone, when it was not quite convenient
to give them bread? Wherever there is a class that is to be
made content to be plundered of its rights, there is an abundance of fiddling and dancing, and amusements, public and
private, are in great requisition. It may also be set down, I
think, as a general axiom, that people feel the need of amusements less and less, precisely in proportion as they have solid
reasons for being happy.

Our good Puritan fathers intended to form a state of society of such equality of conditions, and to make the means of securing the goods of life so free to all, that everybody should find abundant employment for his faculties in a prosperous seeking of his fortunes. Hence, while they forbade theatres, operas, and dances, they made a state of unparalleled peace and prosperity, where one could go to sleep at all hours of day or night with the house door wide open, without bolt or bar, yet without apprehension of any to molest or make afraid.

There were, however, some few national fêtes:—Election day, when the Governor took his seat with pomp and rejoicing, and all the housewives outdid themselves in election cake, and one or two training days, when all the children were refreshed, and our military ardor quickened, by the roll of drums, and the flash of steel bayonets, and marchings and evolutions,—sometimes ending in that sublimest of military operations, a sham fight, in which nobody was killed. The Fourth of July took high rank, after the Declaration of Independence; but the king and high priest of all festivals was the autumn Thanksgiving.

When the apples were all gathered and the cider was all made, and the yellow pumpkins were rolled in from many a hill in billows of gold, and the corn was husked, and the labors of the season were done, and the warm, late days of Indian Summer came in, dreamy and calm and still, with just frost enough to crisp the ground of a morning, but with warm trances of benignant, sunny hours at noon, there came over the community a sort of genial repose of spirit,—a sense of something accomplished, and of a new golden mark made in advance on the calendar of life,—and the deacon began to say to the minister, of a Sunday, "I suppose it 's about time for the Thanksgiving proclamation."

Rural dress-makers about this time were extremely busy in making up festival garments, for everybody's new dress, if she was to have one at all, must appear on Thanksgiving day.

Aunt Keziah and Aunt Lois and my mother talked over their bonnets, and turned them round and round on their hands, and discoursed sagely of ribbons and linings, and of all the kindred bonnets that there were in the parish, and how they would probably appear after Thanksgiving. My grand-mother, whose mind had long ceased to wander on such worldly vanities, was at this time officiously reminded by her daughters that her bonnet wasn't respectable, or it was an-nounced to her that she *must* have a new gown. Such were the distant horizon gleams of the Thanksgiving festival.

We also felt its approach in all departments of the house-hold,—the conversation at this time beginning to turn on high and solemn culinary mysteries and receipts of wondrous power and virtue. New modes of elaborating squash pies and quince tarts were now ofttimes carefully discussed at the eve-ning fireside by Aunt Lois and Aunt Keziah, and notes seri-ously compared with the experiences of certain other Aunties of high repute in such matters. I noticed that on these occa-sions their voices often fell into mysterious whispers, and that receipts of especial power and sanctity were communicated in tones so low as entirely to escape the vulgar ear. I still remem-ber the solemn shake of the head with which my Aunt Lois conveyed to Miss Mehitable Rossiter the critical properties of *mace*, in relation to its powers of producing in corn fritters a suggestive resemblance to oysters. As ours was an oyster-get-ting district, and as that charming bivalve was perfectly easy to come at, the interest of such an imitation can be accounted for only by the fondness of the human mind for works of art.

For as much as a week beforehand, "we children" were em-ployed in chopping mince for pies to a most wearisome fine-ness, and in pounding cinnamon, allspice, and cloves in a great lignum-vitæ mortar; and the sound of this pounding and chopping re-echoed through all the rafters of the old house with a hearty and vigorous cheer, most refreshing to our spirits.

In those days there were none of the thousand ameliora-tions of the labors of housekeeping which have since arisen,—no ground and prepared spices and sweet herbs; everything came into our hands in the rough, and in bulk, and the reducing of it into a state for use was deemed one of the appropriate labors of childhood. Even the very salt that we used in cooking was rock-salt, which we were required to wash and dry and pound and sift, before it became fit for use.

At other times of the year we sometimes murmured at

these labors, but those that were supposed to usher in the great Thanksgiving festival were always entered into with enthusiasm. There were signs of richness all around us,—stoning of raisins, cutting of citron, slicing of candied orange-peel. Yet all these were only dawnings and intimations of what was coming during the week of real preparation, after the Governor's proclamation had been read.

The glories of that proclamation! We knew beforehand the Sunday it was to be read, and walked to church with alacrity, filled with gorgeous and vague expectations.

The cheering anticipation sustained us through what seemed to us the long waste of the sermon and prayers; and when at last the auspicious moment approached,—when the last quaver of the last hymn had died out,—the whole house rippled with a general movement of complacency, and a satisfied smile of pleased expectation might be seen gleaming on the faces of all the young people, like a ray of sunshine through a garden of flowers.

Thanksgiving now was dawning! We children poked one another, and fairly giggled with unreproved delight as we listened to the crackle of the slowly unfolding document. That great sheet of paper impressed us as something supernatural, by reason of its mighty size, and by the broad seal of the State affixed thereto; and when the minister read therefrom, "By his Excellency, the Governor of the Commonwealth of Massachusetts, a Proclamation," our mirth was with difficulty repressed by admonitory glances from our sympathetic elders. Then, after a solemn enumeration of the benefits which the Commonwealth had that year received at the hands of Divine Providence, came at last the naming of the eventful day, and, at the end of all, the imposing heraldic words, "God save the Commonwealth of Massachusetts." And then, as the congregation broke up and dispersed, all went their several ways with schemes of mirth and feasting in their heads.

And now came on the week in earnest. In the very watches of the night preceding Monday morning, a preternatural stir below stairs, and the thunder of the pounding-barrel, announced that the washing was to be got out of the way before daylight, so as to give "ample scope and room enough" for the more pleasing duties of the season.

The making of *pies* at this period assumed vast proportions that verged upon the sublime. Pies were made by forties and fifties and hundreds, and made of everything on the earth and under the earth.

The pie is an English institution, which, planted on American soil, forthwith ran rampant and burst forth into an untold variety of genera and species. Not merely the old traditional mince pie, but a thousand strictly American seedlings from that main stock, evinced the power of American housewives to adapt old institutions to new uses. Pumpkin pies, cranberry pies, huckleberry pies, cherry pies, green-currant pies, peach, pear, and plum pies, custard pies, apple pies, Marlborough-pudding pies,—pies with top crusts, and pies without,—pies adorned with all sorts of fanciful flutings and architectural strips laid across and around, and otherwise varied, attested the boundless fertility of the feminine mind, when once let loose in a given direction.

Fancy the heat and vigor of the great pan-formation, when Aunt Lois and Aunt Keziah, and my mother and grandmother, all in ecstasies of creative inspiration, ran, bustled, and hurried,—mixing, rolling, tasting, consulting,—alternately setting us children to work when anything could be made of us, and then chasing us all out of the kitchen when our misinformed childhood ventured to take too many liberties with sacred mysteries. Then out we would all fly at the kitchen door, like sparks from a blacksmith's window.

On these occasions, as there was a great looseness in the police department over us children, we usually found a ready refuge at Miss Mehitable's with Tina, who, confident of the strength of her position with Polly, invited us into the kitchen, and with the air of a mistress led us around to view the proceedings there.

A genius for entertaining was one of Tina's principal characteristics; and she did not fail to make free with raisins, or citron, or whatever came to hand, in a spirit of hospitality at which Polly seriously demurred. That worthy woman occasionally felt the inconvenience of the state of subjugation to which the little elf had somehow or other reduced her, and sometimes rattled her chains fiercely, scolding with a vigor which rather alarmed us, but which Tina minded not a whit.

Confident of her own powers, she would, in the very midst
of her wrath, mimic her to her face with such irresistible drollery as to cause the torrent of reproof to end in a dissonant
laugh, accompanied by a submissive cry for quarter.

"I declare, Tina Percival," she said to her one day, "you 're
saucy enough to physic a horn-bug! I never did see the beater
of you! If Miss Mehitable don't keep you in better order, I
don't see what 's to become of any of us!"

"Why, what did become of you before I came?" was the
undismayed reply. "You know, Polly, you and Aunty both
were just as lonesome as you could be till I came here, and
you never had such pleasant times in your life as you 've had
since I 've been here. You 're a couple of old beauties, both of
you, and know just how to get along with me. But come,
boys, let 's take our raisins and go up in the garret and play
Thanksgiving."

In the corner of the great kitchen, during all these days, the
jolly old oven roared and crackled in great volcanic billows of
flame, snapping and gurgling as if the old fellow entered with
joyful sympathy into the frolic of the hour; and then, his
great heart being once warmed up, he brooded over successive generations of pies and cakes, which went in raw and
came out cooked, till butteries and dressers and shelves and
pantries were literally crowded with a jostling abundance.

A great cold northern chamber, where the sun never shone,
and where in winter the snow sifted in at the window-cracks,
and ice and frost reigned with undisputed sway, was fitted up
to be the storehouse of these surplus treasures. There, frozen
solid, and thus well preserved in their icy fetters, they formed
a great repository for all the winter months; and the pies
baked at Thanksgiving often came out fresh and good with
the violets of April.

During this eventful preparation week, all the female part
of my grandmother's household, as I have before remarked,
were at a height above any ordinary state of mind,—they
moved about the house rapt in a species of prophetic frenzy.
It seemed to be considered a necessary feature of such festivals, that everybody should be in a hurry, and everything in
the house should be turned bottom upwards with enthusi-

asm,—so at least we children understood it, and we certainly did our part to keep the ball rolling.

At this period the constitutional activity of Uncle Fliakim increased to a degree that might fairly be called preternatural. Thanksgiving time was the time for errands of mercy and beneficence through the country; and Uncle Fliakim's immortal old rubber horse and rattling wagon were on the full jump, in tours of investigation into everybody's affairs in the region around. On returning, he would fly through our kitchen like the wind, leaving open the doors, upsetting whatever came in his way,—now a pan of milk, and now a basin of mince,—talking rapidly, and forgetting only the point in every case that gave it significance, or enabled any one to put it to any sort of use. When Aunt Lois checked his benevolent effusions by putting the test questions of practical efficiency, Uncle Fliakim always remembered that he'd "forgotten to inquire about that," and skipping through the kitchen, and springing into his old wagon, would rattle off again on a full tilt to correct and amend his investigations.

Moreover, my grandmother's kitchen at this time began to be haunted by those occasional hangers-on and retainers, of uncertain fortunes, whom a full experience of her bountiful habits led to expect something at her hand at this time of the year. All the poor, loafing tribes, Indian and half-Indian, who at other times wandered, selling baskets and other light wares, were sure to come back to Oldtown a little before Thanksgiving time, and report themselves in my grandmother's kitchen.

The great hogshead of cider in the cellar, which my grandfather called the Indian Hogshead, was on tap at all hours of the day; and many a mugful did I draw and dispense to the tribes that basked in the sunshine at our door.

Aunt Lois never had a hearty conviction of the propriety of these arrangements; but my grandmother, who had a prodigious verbal memory, bore down upon her with such strings of quotations from the Old Testament that she was utterly routed.

"Now," says my Aunt Lois, "I s'pose we've got to have Betty Poganut and Sally Wonsamug, and old Obscue and his wife, and the whole tribe down, roosting around our doors, till we give 'em something. That 's just mother's way; she always keeps a whole generation at her heels."

"How many times must I tell you, Lois, to read your Bible?" was my grandmother's rejoinder; and loud over the sound of pounding and chopping in the kitchen could be heard the voice of her quotations: "If there be among you a poor man in any of the gates of the land which the Lord thy God giveth thee, thou shalt not harden thy heart, nor shut thy hand, from thy poor brother. Thou shalt surely give him; and thy heart shall not be grieved when thou givest to him, because that for this thing the Lord thy God shall bless thee in all thy works; for the poor shall never cease from out of the land."

These words seemed to resound like a sort of heraldic proclamation to call around us all that softly shiftless class, who, for some reason or other, are never to be found with anything in hand at the moment that it is wanted.

"There, to be sure," said Aunt Lois, one day when our preparations were in full blast,—"there comes Sam Lawson down the hill, limpsy as ever; now he 'll have his doleful story to tell, and mother 'll give him one of the turkeys."

And so, of course, it fell out.

Sam came in with his usual air of plaintive assurance, and seated himself a contemplative spectator in the chimney-corner, regardless of the looks and signs of unwelcome on the part of Aunt Lois.

"Lordy massy, how prosperous everything does seem here!" he said, in musing tones, over his inevitable mug of cider; "so different from what 't is t' our house. There 's Hepsy, she 's all in a stew, an' I 've just been an' got her thirty-seven cents' wuth o' nutmegs, yet she says she 's sure she don't see how she 's to keep Thanksgiving, an' she 's down on me about it, just as ef 't was my fault. Yeh see, last winter our old gobbler got froze. You know, Mis' Badger, that 'ere cold night we hed last winter. Wal, I was off with Jake Marshall that night; ye see, Jake, he hed to take old General Dearborn's corpse into Boston, to the family vault, and Jake, he kind o' hated to go alone; 't was a drefful cold time, and he ses to me, 'Sam, you jes' go 'long with me'; so I was sort o' sorry for him, and I kind o' thought I 'd go 'long.

Wal, come 'long to Josh Bissel's tahvern, there at the Half-way House, you know, 't was so swinging cold we stopped to take a little suthin' warmin', an' we sort o' sot an' sot over the fire, till, fust we knew, we kind o' got asleep; an' when we woke up we found we 'd left the old General hitched up t' th' post pretty much all night. Wal, did n't hurt him none, poor man; 't was allers a favorite spot o' his'n. But, takin' one thing with another, I did n't get home till about noon next day, an', I tell you, Hepsy she was right down on me. She said the baby was sick, and there had n't been no wood split, nor the barn fastened up, nor nothin'. Lordy massy, I did n't mean no harm; I thought there was wood enough, and I thought likely Hepsy 'd git out an' fasten up the barn. But Hepsy, she was in one o' her contrary streaks, an' she would n't do a thing; an', when I went out to look, why, sure 'nuff, there was our old tom-turkey froze as stiff as a stake,— his claws jist a stickin' right straight up like this." Here Sam struck an expressive attitude, and looked so much like a fro-zen turkey as to give a pathetic reality to the picture.

"Well now, Sam, why need you be off on things that 's none of your business?" said my grandmother. "I 've talked to you plainly about that a great many times, Sam," she contin-ued, in tones of severe admonition. "Hepsy is a hard-working woman, but she can't be expected to see to everything, and you oughter 'ave been at home that night to fasten up your own barn and look after your own creeturs."

Sam took the rebuke all the more meekly as he perceived the stiff black legs of a turkey poking out from under my grandmother's apron while she was delivering it. To be ex-horted and told of his shortcomings, and then furnished with a turkey at Thanksgiving, was a yearly part of his family pro-gramme. In time he departed, not only with the turkey, but with us boys in procession after him, bearing a mince and a pumpkin pie for Hepsy's children.

"Poor things!" my grandmother remarked; "they ought to have something good to eat Thanksgiving day; 't ain't their fault that they 've got a shiftless father."

Sam, in his turn, moralized to us children, as we walked beside him: "A body 'd think that Hepsy 'd learn to trust in Providence," he said, "but she don't. She allers has a Thanksgiving dinner pervided; but that 'ere woman ain't grateful for it, by no manner o' means. Now she 'll be jest as cross as she can be, 'cause this 'ere ain't *our* turkey, and these 'ere ain't our pies. Folks doos lose so much, that hes sech dispositions."

A multitude of similar dispensations during the course of the week materially reduced the great pile of chickens and turkeys which black Cæsar's efforts in slaughtering, picking, and dressing kept daily supplied.

Besides these offerings to the poor, the handsomest turkey of the flock was sent, dressed in first-rate style, with Deacon Badger's dutiful compliments, to the minister; and we children, who were happy to accompany black Cæsar on this errand, generally received a seed-cake and a word of acknowledgment from the minister's lady.

Well, at last, when all the chopping and pounding and baking and brewing, preparatory to the festival, were gone through with, the eventful day dawned. All the tribes of the Badger family were to come back home to the old house, with all the relations of every degree, to eat the Thanksgiving dinner. And it was understood that in the evening the minister and his lady would look in upon us, together with some of the select aristocracy of Oldtown.

Great as the preparations were for the dinner, everything was so contrived that not a soul in the house should be kept from the morning service of Thanksgiving in the church, and from listening to the Thanksgiving sermon, in which the minister was expected to express his views freely concerning the politics of the country, and the state of things in society generally, in a somewhat more secular vein of thought than was deemed exactly appropriate to the Lord's day. But it is to be confessed, that, when the good man got carried away by the enthusiasm of his subject to extend these exercises beyond a certain length, anxious glances, exchanged between good wives, sometimes indicated a weakness of the flesh, having a tender reference to the turkeys and chickens and chicken pies, which might possibly be overdoing in the ovens at home. But your old brick oven was a true Puritan institution, and backed up the devotional habits of good housewives, by the capital care which he took of whatever was committed to his capacious bosom. A truly well-bred oven would have been ashamed of himself all his days, and blushed redder than his own fires, if a God-fearing house-matron, away at the temple of the Lord, should come home and find her pie-crust either burned or underdone by his over or under zeal; so the old fellow generally managed to bring things out exactly right.

When sermons and prayers were all over, we children rushed home to see the great feast of the year spread.

What chitterings and chatterings there were all over the house, as all the aunties and uncles and cousins came pouring in, taking off their things, looking at one another's bonnets and dresses, and mingling their comments on the morning sermon with various opinions on the new millinery outfits, and with bits of home news, and kindly neighborhood gossip.

Uncle Bill, whom the Cambridge college authorities released, as they did all the other youngsters of the land, for Thanksgiving day, made a breezy stir among them all, especially with the young cousins of the feminine gender.

The best room on this occasion was thrown wide open, and its habitual coldness had been warmed by the burning down of a great stack of hickory logs, which had been heaped up unsparingly since morning. It takes some hours to get a room warm, where a family never sits, and which therefore has not in its walls one particle of the genial vitality which comes from the in-dwelling of human beings. But on Thanksgiving day, at least, every year, this marvel was effected in our best room.

Although all servile labor and vain recreation on this day were by law forbidden, according to the terms of the proclamation, it was not held to be a violation of the precept, that all the nice old aunties should bring their knitting-work and sit gently trotting their needles around the fire; nor that Uncle Bill should start a full-fledged romp among the girls and children, while the dinner was being set on the long table in the neighboring kitchen. Certain of the good elderly female relatives, of serious and discreet demeanor, assisted at this operation.

But who shall do justice to the dinner, and describe the turkey, and chickens, and chicken pies, with all that endless variety of vegetables which the American soil and climate have contributed to the table, and which, without regard to the French doctrine of courses, were all piled together in jovial abundance upon the smoking board? There was much carving and laughing and talking and eating, and all showed that cheerful ability to despatch the provisions which was the ruling spirit of the hour. After the meat came the plum-puddings, and then the endless array of pies, till human nature was actually bewildered and overpowered by the tempting variety; and even we children turned from the profusion offered to us, and wondered what was the matter that we could eat no more.

When all was over, my grandfather rose at the head of the table, and a fine venerable picture he made as he stood there, his silver hair flowing in curls down each side of his clear, calm face, while, in conformity to the old Puritan custom, he called their attention to a recital of the mercies of God in his dealings with their family.

It was a sort of family history, going over and touching upon the various events which had happened. He spoke of my father's death, and gave a tribute to his memory; and closed all with the application of a time-honored text, expressing the hope that as years passed by we might "so number our days as to apply our hearts unto wisdom"; and then he gave out that psalm which in those days might be called the national hymn of the Puritans.

> "Let children hear the mighty deeds
>   Which God performed of old,
> Which in our younger years we saw,
>   And which our fathers told.
>
> "He bids us make his glories known,
>   His works of power and grace.
> And we 'll convey his wonders down
>   Through every rising race.
>
> "Our lips shall tell them to our sons,
>   And they again to theirs;
> That generations yet unborn
>   May teach them to their heirs.

"Thus shall they learn in God alone
    Their hope securely stands;
That they may ne'er forget his works,
    But practise his commands."

This we all united in singing to the venerable tune of St.
Martin's, an air which, the reader will perceive, by its multiplicity of quavers and inflections gave the greatest possible
scope to the cracked and trembling voices of the ancients,
who united in it with even more zeal than the younger part
of the community.

Uncle Fliakim Sheril, furbished up in a new crisp black suit,
and with his spindle-shanks trimly incased in the smoothest
of black silk stockings, looking for all the world just like an
alert and spirited black cricket, outdid himself on this occasion in singing *counter*, in that high, weird voice that he must
have learned from the wintry winds that usually piped around
the corners of the old house. But any one who looked at him,
as he sat with his eyes closed, beating time with head and
hand, and, in short, with every limb of his body, must have
perceived the exquisite satisfaction which he derived from this
mode of expressing himself. I much regret to be obliged to
state that my graceless Uncle Bill, taking advantage of the fact
that the eyes of all his elders were devotionally closed, station-
ing himself a little in the rear of my Uncle Fliakim, performed
an exact imitation of his *counter*, with such a killing facility
that all the younger part of the audience were nearly dead
with suppressed laughter. Aunt Lois, who never shut her eyes
a moment on any occasion, discerned this from a distant part
of the room, and in vain endeavored to stop it by vigorously
shaking her head at the offender. She might as well have
shaken it at a bobolink tilting on a clover-top. In fact, Uncle
Bill was Aunt Lois's weak point, and the corners of her own
mouth were observed to twitch in such a suspicious manner
that the whole moral force of her admonition was destroyed.

And now, the dinner being cleared away, we youngsters,
already excited to a tumult of laughter, tumbled into the best
room, under the supervision of Uncle Bill, to relieve ourselves
with a game of "blind-man's-buff," while the elderly women
washed up the dishes and got the house in order, and the

men-folks went out to the barn to look at the cattle, and walked over the farm and talked of the crops.

In the evening the house was all open and lighted with the best of tallow candles, which Aunt Lois herself had made with especial care for this illumination. It was understood that we were to have a dance, and black Cæsar, full of turkey and pumpkin pie, and giggling in the very jollity of his heart, had that afternoon rosined his bow, and tuned his fiddle, and practised jigs and Virginia reels, in a way that made us children think him a perfect Orpheus.

As soon as the candles were lighted came in Miss Mehitable with her brother Jonathan, and Tina, like a gay little tassel, hanging on her withered arm.

Mr. Jonathan Rossiter was a tall, well-made man, with a clear-cut, aquiline profile, and high round forehead, from which his powdered hair was brushed smoothly back and hung down behind in a long cue. His eyes were of a piercing dark gray, with that peculiar expression of depth and intensity which marks a melancholy temperament. He had a large mouth, which he kept shut with an air of firmness that suggested something even hard and dictatorial in his nature. He was quick and alert in all his movements, and his eyes had a searching quickness of observation, which seemed to lose nothing of what took place around him. There was an air of breeding and self-command about him; and in all his involuntary ways he bore the appearance of a man more interested to make up a judgment of others than concerned as to what their judgment might be about himself.

Miss Mehitable hung upon his arm with an evident admiration and pride, which showed that when he came he made summer at least for her.

After them soon arrived the minister and his lady,—she in a grand brocade satin dress, open in front to display a petticoat brocaded with silver flowers. With her well-formed hands shining out of a shimmer of costly lace, and her feet propped on high-heeled shoes, Lady Lothrop justified the prestige of good society which always hung about her. Her lord and master, in the spotless whiteness of his ruffles on wrist and bosom, and in the immaculate keeping and neatness of all his clerical black, and the perfect *pose* of his grand full-bottomed clerical wig, did honor to her conjugal cares. They moved through the room like a royal prince and princess, with an appropriate, gracious, well-considered word for each and every one. They even returned, with punctilious civility, the awe-struck obeisance of black Cæsar, who giggled over straightway with joy and exultation at the honor.

But conceive of my Aunt Lois's pride of heart, when, following in the train of these august persons, actually came Ellery Davenport, bringing upon his arm Miss Deborah Kittery. Here was a situation! Had the whole island of Great Britain waded across the Atlantic Ocean to call on Bunker Hill, the circumstance could scarcely have seemed to her more critical.

"Mercy on us!" she thought to herself, "all these Episcopalians coming! I do hope mother 'll be careful; I hope she won't feel it necessary to give them a piece of her mind, as she 's always doing."

Miss Deborah Kittery, however, knew her soundings, and was too genuine an Englishwoman not to know that "every man's house is his castle," and that one must respect one's neighbor's opinions on his own ground.

As to my grandmother, her broad and buxom heart on this evening was so full of motherliness, that she could have patted the very King of England on the head, if he had been there, and comforted his soul with the assurance that she supposed he meant well, though he did n't exactly know how to manage; so, although she had a full consciousness that Miss Deborah Kittery had turned all America over to uncovenanted mercies, she nevertheless shook her warmly by the hand, and told her she hoped she 'd make herself at home. And I think she would have done exactly the same by the Pope of Rome himself, if that poor heathen sinner had presented himself on Thanksgiving evening. So vast and billowy was the ocean of her loving-kindness, and so firmly were her feet planted on the rock of the Cambridge Platform, that on it she could stand breathing prayers for all Jews, Turks, Infidels, Tories, Episcopalians, and even Roman Catholics. The very man that burnt Mr. John Rogers might have had a mug of cider in the kitchen on this evening, with an exhortation to go and sin no more.

You may imagine the astounding wassail among the young people, when two such spirits as Ellery Davenport and my Uncle Bill were pushing each other on, in one house. My Uncle Bill related the story of "the Wry-mouth Family," with such twists and contortions and killing extremes of the ludicrous as perfectly overcame even the minister; and he was to be seen, at one period of the evening, with a face purple with laughter, and the tears actually rolling down over his well-formed cheeks, while some of the more excitable young people almost fell in trances, and rolled on the floor in the extreme of their merriment. In fact, the assemblage was becoming so tumultuous, that the scrape of Cæsar's violin, and the forming of sets for a dance, seemed necessary to restore the peace.

Whenever or wherever it was that the idea of the sinfulness of dancing arose in New England, I know not; it is a certain fact that at Oldtown, at this time, the presence of the minister and his lady was held not to be in the slightest degree incompatible with this amusement. I appeal to many of my readers, if they or their parents could not recall a time in New England when in all the large towns dancing assemblies used to be statedly held, at which the minister and his lady, though never uniting in the dance, always gave an approving attendance, and where all the decorous, respectable old church-members brought their children, and stayed to watch an amusement in which they no longer actively partook. No one looked on with a more placid and patronizing smile than Dr. Lothrop and his lady, as one after another began joining the exercise, which, commencing first with the children and young people, crept gradually upwards among the elders.

Uncle Bill would insist on leading out Aunt Lois, and the bright color rising to her thin cheeks brought back a fluttering image of what might have been beauty in some fresh, early day. Ellery Davenport insisted upon leading forth Miss Deborah Kittery, notwithstanding her oft-repeated refusals and earnest protestations to the contrary. As to Uncle Fliakim, he jumped and frisked and gyrated among the single sisters and maiden aunts, whirling them into the dance as if he had been the little black gentleman himself. With that true spirit of Christian charity which marked all his actions, he invariably chose out the homeliest and most neglected, and thus worthy Aunt Keziah, dear old soul, was for a time made quite prominent by his attentions.

Of course the dances in those days were of a strictly moral nature. The very thought of one of the round dances of modern times would have sent Lady Lothrop behind her big fan in helpless confusion, and exploded my grandmother like a full-charged arsenal of indignation. As it was, she stood, her broad, pleased face radiant with satisfaction, as the wave of joyousness crept up higher and higher round her, till the elders, who stood keeping time with their heads and feet, began to tell one another how they had danced with their sweethearts in good old days gone by, and the elder women began to blush and bridle, and boast of steps that they could take in their youth, till the music finally subdued them, and into the dance they went.

"Well, well!" quoth my grandmother; "they 're all at it so hearty, I don't see why I should n't try it myself." And into the Virginia reel she went, amid screams of laughter from all the younger members of the company.

But I assure you my grandmother was not a woman to be laughed at; for whatever she once set on foot, she "put through" with a sturdy energy befitting a daughter of the Puritans.

"Why should n't I dance?" she said, when she arrived red and resplendent at the bottom of the set. "Did n't Mr. Despondency and Miss Muchafraid and Mr. Readytohalt all dance together in the Pilgrim's Progress?"—and the minister in his ample flowing wig, and my lady in her stiff brocade, gave to my grandmother a solemn twinkle of approbation.

As nine o'clock struck, the whole scene dissolved and melted; for what well-regulated village would think of carrying festivities beyond that hour?

And so ended our Thanksgiving at Oldtown.

XXVIII.

The Raid on Oldtown, and Uncle Fliakim's Bravery

THE next morning after Thanksgiving, life resumed its usual hard, laborious course, with a sharp and imperative reaction, such as ensues when a strong spring, which has been for some time held back, is suddenly let fly again.

Certainly Aunt Lois appeared to be astir fully an hour earlier than usual, and dispelled all our golden visions of chicken pies and dancings and merry-makings, by the flat, hard summons of every-day life. We had no time to become demoralized and softened.

Breakfast this next morning was half an hour in advance of the usual time, because Aunt Lois was under some vague impression of infinite disturbances in the house, owing to the latitude of the last two weeks, and of great furbishings and repairs to be done in the best room, before it could be again shut up and condemned to silence.

While we were eating our breakfast, Sam Lawson came in, with an air of great trepidation.

"Lordy massy, Mis' Badger! what *do* you s'pose has happened?" he exclaimed, holding up his hands. "Wal! if I ever— no, I never did!"—and, before an explanation could be drawn out of him, in fluttered Uncle Fliakim, and began dancing an indignant rigadoon round the kitchen.

"Perfectly abominable! the selectmen ought to take it up!" he exclaimed,—"ought to make a State affair of it, and send to the Governor."

"Do for mercy's sake, Fliakim, sit down, and tell us what the matter is," said my grandmother.

"I can't! I can't!! I can't!!! I 've just got to hitch right up and go on after 'em; and mebbe I 'll catch 'em before they get over the State line. I just wanted to borrow your breech-band, cause ours is broke. Where is it? Is it out in the barn, or where?"

By this time we had all arisen from table, and stood looking at one another, while Uncle Fliakim had shot out of the back door toward the barn. Of course our information must now be got out of Sam Lawson.

"Wal, you see, Deacon, who ever would ha' thought of it? They 've took every child on 'em, every one!"

"Who 's taken? what children?" said my grandmother. "Do pray begin at the right end of your story, and not come in here scaring a body to death."

"Wal, it 's Aunt Nancy Prime's children. Last night the kidnappers come to her house an' took her an' every single one of the child'en, an' goin' to carry 'em off to York State for slaves. Jake Marshall, he was round to our house this mornin', an' told me 'bout it. Jake, he 'd ben over to keep Thanksgivin', over t' Aunt Sally Proddy's; an' way over by the tenmile tahvern he met the waggin, an' Aunt Nancy, she called out to him, an' he heerd one of the fellers swear at her. The' was two fellers in the waggin, an' they was a drivin' like mad, an' I jest come runnin' down to Mr. Sheril's, 'cause I know his horse never gits out of a canter, an' 's pretty much used to bein' twitched up sudden. But, Lordy massy, s'posin' he could ketch up with 'em, what could he do? He couldn't much more 'n fly at 'em like an old hen; so I don't see what 's to be done."

"Well," said my grandfather, rising up, "if that 's the case, it 's time we should all be on the move; and I 'll go right over to Israel Scran's, and he and his two sons and I 'll go over, and I guess there 'll be enough of us to teach them reason. These kidnappers always make for the New York State line. Boys, you go out and tackle the old mare, and have our wagon round to the house; and, if Fliakim's wagon will hold together, the two will just carry the party."

"Lordy massy! I should like to go 'long too," said Sam Lawson. "I hain't got no special business to-day but what could be put off as well as not."

"You never do have," said Aunt Lois. "That 's the trouble with you."

"Wal, I was a thinkin'," said Sam, "that Jake and me hes been over them roads so often, and we kind o' know all the ups an' downs an' cross-roads. Then we 's pretty intimate with some o' them Injun fellers, an' ye git them sot out on a trail arter a body, they 's like a huntin' dog."

"Well, father," said Aunt Lois, "I think it 's quite likely that Sam may be right here. He certainly knows more about such things than any decent, industrious man ought to, and it 's a pity you should n't put him to some use when you can."

"Jes' so!" said Sam. "Now, there 's reason in that 'ere; an' I 'll jes' go over to Israel's store with the Deacon. Yeh see ye can't take both the boys, 'cause one on 'em 'll have to stay and tend the store; but I tell you what 't is, I ain't no bad of a hand a hittin' a lick at kidnappers. I could pound on 'em as willingly as ever I pounded a horseshoe; an' a woman 's a woman, an' child'en 's child'en, ef they be black; that 's jes' my 'pinion."

"Sam, you 're a good fellow," said my grandmother, approvingly. "But come, go right along."

Here, now, was something to prevent the wave of yesterday's excitement from flatting down into entire insipidity.

Harry and I ran over instantly to tell Tina; and Tina with all her eloquence set it forth to Miss Mehitable and Polly, and we gave vent to our emotions by an immediate rush to the garret and a dramatic representation of the whole scene of the rescue, conducted with four or five of Tina's rag-dolls and a little old box wagon, with which we cantered and re-cantered across the garret floor in a way that would have been intolerable to any less patient and indulgent person than Miss Mehitable.

The fact is, however, that she shared in the universal excitement to such a degree, that she put on her bonnet immediately, and rushed over to the minister's to give vent to her feelings, while Polly, coming up garret, shouldered one of the guns lovingly, and declared she 'd "like nothing better than to fire it off at one o' them fellers"; and then she told us how, in her young days, where she was brought up in Maine, the painters (panthers) used to come round their log cabin at night, and howl and growl; and how they always had to keep the guns loaded; and how once her mother, during her father's absence, had treed a painter, and kept him up in his perch for hours by threatening him whenever he offered to come down, until her husband came home and shot him.

Pretty stanch, reliant blood, about those times, flowed in the bosoms of the women of New England, and Polly relieved the excitement of her mind this morning by relating to us story after story of the wild forest life of her early days.

While Polly was thus giving vent to her emotions at home, Miss Mehitable had produced a corresponding excitement in the minister's family. Ellery Davenport declared his prompt intention of going up and joining the pursuing party, as he was young and strong, with all his wits about him; and, with the prestige of rank in the late Revolutionary war, such an accession to the party was of the greatest possible importance. As to Miss Deborah Kittery, she gave it as her opinion that such uprisings against law and order were just what was to be expected in a democracy. "The lower classes, my dear, you know, need to be kept down with a strong hand," she said with an instructive nod of the head; "and I think we shall find that there 's no security in the way things are going on now."

Miss Mehitable and the minister listened with grave amusement while the worthy lady thus delivered herself; and, as they did not reply, she had the comfort of feeling that she had given them something to think of.

All the village, that day, was in a ferment of expectation; for Aunt Nancy was a general favorite in all the families round, and was sent for in case of elections or weddings or other high merry-makings, so that meddling with her was in fact taking away part of the vested property of Oldtown. The loafers who tilted, with their heels uppermost, on the railings of the tavern veranda, talked stringently of State rights, and some were of opinion that President Washington ought to be apprised of the fact without loss of time. My grandmother went about house in a state of indignation all day, declaring it was a pretty state of things, to be sure, and that, next they should know, they should wake up some morning and find that Cæsar had been gobbled up in the night and run off with. But Harry and I calmed the fears which this seemed to excite in his breast, by a vivid description of the two guns over in Miss Mehitable's garret, and of the use that we should certainly make of them in case of an attack on Cæsar.

The chase, however, was conducted with such fire and ardor that before moonrise on the same night the captives were brought back in triumph to Oldtown village, and lodged for safe-keeping in my grandmother's house, who spared nothing in their entertainment.

A happy man was Sam Lawson that evening, as he sat in the chimney-corner and sipped his mug of cider, and re-counted his adventures.

"Lordy massy! well, 't was providential we took Colonel Devenport 'long with us, I tell you; he talked to them fellers in a way that made 'em shake in their shoes. Why, Lordy massy, when we fust came in sight on 'em, Mr. Sheril an' me, we wus in the foremost waggin, an' we saw 'em before us just as we got to the top of a long, windin' hill, an' I tell you if they did n't whip up an' go lickity-split down that 'ere hill,— I tell you, they rattled them child'en as ef they 'd ben so many punkins, an' I tell you one of 'em darned old young-uns flew right over the side of the waggin, an' jest picked itself up as lively as a cricket, an' never cried. We did n't stop to take it up, but jes' kep' right along arter; an' Mr. Sheril, he hollers out, 'Whoa! whoa! stop! stop thief!' as loud as he could yell; but they jes' laughed at him; but Colonel Devenport, he come ridin' by on horseback, like thunder, an' driv' right by 'em, an' then turned round an' charged down on their horses so it driv' 'em right out the road, an' the waggin was upsot, an' the fellers, they were pitched out, an' in a minute Colonel Devenport had one on 'em by the collar an' his pistol right out to the head o' t'other. 'Now,' ses he, 'if you stir you 're a dead man!'

"Wal, Mr. Sheril, he made arter the other one,— he always means mighty well, Mr. Sheril does,— he gin a long jump, he did, an' he lit right in the middle of a tuft of blackberry-bushes, an' tore his breeches as ef the heavens an' 'arth was a goin' asunder. Yeh see, they never 'd a got 'em ef 't had n't ben for Colonel Devenport. He kep' the other feller under range of his pistol, an' told him he 'd shoot him ef he stirred; an' the feller, he was scart to death, an' he roared an' begged for mercy in a way 't would ha' done your heart good to hear.

"Wal, wal! the upshot on 't all was, when Israel Scran come down with his boy (they was in the back waggin), they got out the ropes an' tied 'em up snug, an' have ben a fetchin' on

'em along to jail, where I guess they 'll have one spell o' considerin' their ways. But, Lordy massy, yeh never see such a
sight as your uncle's breeches wus. Mis' Sheril, she says she
never see the beater of him for allus goin' off in his best
clothes, 'cause, you see, he heard the news early, an' he jes'
whips on his Thanksgivin' clothes an' went off in 'em just as
he was. His intentions is allus so good. It 's a pity, though,
he don't take more time to consider. Now I think folks ought
to take things more moderate. Yeh see, these folks that hurries allus, they gits into scrapes, is just what I 'm allus a tellin'
Hepsy."

"Who were the fellows, do you know?" said my grandmother.

"Wal, one on 'em was one of them Hessians that come
over in the war times,—he is a stupid crittur; but the other
is Widdah Huldy Miller's son, down to Black Brook there."

"Do tell," said my grandmother, with the liveliest concern;
"has Eph Miller come to that?"

"Yes, yes!" said Sam, "it 's Eph, sure enough. He was exalted to heaven in p'int o' privilege, but he took to drink and
onstiddy ways in the army, and now here he is in jail. I tell
you, I tried to set it home to Eph, when I was a bringin' on
him home in the waggin, but, Lordy massy, we don't none
of us like to have our sins set in order afore us. There was
David, now, he was crank as could be when he thought Nathan was a talkin' about other people's sins. Says David, 'The
man that did that shall surely die'; but come to set it home,
and say, 'Thou art the man,' David caved right in. 'Lordy
massy bless your soul and body, Nathan,' says he, 'I don't
want to die.'"

It will be seen by these edifying moralizings how eminently
Scriptural was the course of Sam's mind. In fact, his turn for
long-winded, pious reflection was not the least among his
many miscellaneous accomplishments.

As to my grandmother, she busied herself in comforting
the hearts of Aunt Nancy and the children with more than
they could eat of the relics of the Thanksgiving feast, and
bidding them not to be down-hearted nor afeard of anything,
for the neighbors would all stand up for them, confirming her
words with well-known quotations from the Old Testament,

to the effect that "the triumphing of the wicked is short," and that "evil-doers shall soon be cut off from the earth."

This incident gave Ellery Davenport a wide-spread popularity in the circles of Oldtown. My grandmother was predisposed to look on him with complacency as a grandson of President Edwards, although he took, apparently, a freakish delight in shocking the respectable prejudices, and disappointing the reasonable expectations, of people in this regard, by assuming in every conversation precisely the sentiments that could have been least expected of him in view of such a paternity.

In fact, Ellery Davenport was one of those talkers who delight to maintain the contrary of every proposition started, and who enjoy the bustle and confusion which they thus make in every circle.

In good, earnest, intense New England, where every idea was taken up and sifted with serious solemnity, and investigated with a view to an immediate practical action upon it as true or false, this glittering, fanciful system of fencing which he kept up on all subjects, maintaining with equal brilliancy and ingenuity this to-day and that to-morrow, might possibly have drawn down upon a man a certain horror, as a professed scoffer and a bitter enemy of all that is good; but Ellery Davenport, with all his apparent carelessness, understood himself and the world he moved in perfectly. He never lost sight of the effect he was producing on any mind, and had an intuitive judgment, in every situation, of exactly how far he might go without going too far.

The position of such young men as Ellery Davenport, in the theocratic state of society in New England at this time, can be understood only by considering the theologic movements of their period.

The colonists who founded Massachusetts were men whose doctrine of a Christian church in regard to the position of its children was essentially the same as that of the Church of England. Thus we find in Doctor Cotton Mather this statement: —

"They did all agree with their brethren at Plymouth in this point: that the children of the faithful were church-members with their parents; and that their baptism was a seal of their being so; only, before their admission to fellowship in any particular church, it was judged necessary that, being free from scandal in life, they should be examined by the elders of the church, upon whose approbation of their fitness they should publicly and personally own the covenant, and so be received unto the table of the Lord. And accordingly the eldest son of Mr. Higginson, being about fifteen years of age, and laudably answering all the characters expected in a communicant, was then so received."

The colony under Governor Winthrop and Thomas Dudley was, in fact, composed of men in all but political opinion warmly attached to the Church of England; and they published, on their departure, a tract called "The Humble Request of His Majesty's Loyal Subjects, the Governor and Company lately gone for New England, for the Obtaining of their Prayers, and the Removal of Suspicions and Misconstruction of their Intentions"; and in this address they called the Church of England their dear mother, acknowledging that such hope and part as they had attained in the common salvation, they had sucked from her breasts; and entreating their many reverend fathers and brethren to recommend them unto the mercies of God, in their constant prayers, as a church now springing out of their own bowels. Originally, therefore, the first young people who grew up in New England were taught in their earliest childhood to regard themselves as already members of the church, as under obligations to comport themselves accordingly, and at a very early age it was expected of them that they would come forward by their own act and confirm the action of their parents in their baptism, in a manner much the same in general effect as confirmation in England. The immediate result of this was much sympathy on the part of the children and young people with the religious views of their parents, and a sort of growing up into them from generation to generation. But, as the world is always tending to become unspiritual and mechanical in its views and sentiments, the defect of the species of religion thus engendered was a want of that vitality and warmth of emotion which attend the convert whose mind has come out of darkness into marvellous light,—who has passed through interior conflicts which have agitated his soul to the very depths. So there was always a party in New England who maintained that only those who could relate a change so marked as to be characterized as supernatural should hope that they were the true elect of God, or be received in churches and acknowledged as true Christians.

Many pages of Cotton Mather record the earnest attention which not only the ministers, but the governors and magistrates, of New England, in her early days, gave to the question, "What is the true position of the baptized children of the Church?" and Cotton Mather, who was warmly in favor of the Church of England platform in this respect, says: "It was the study of those prudent men who might be called our seers, that the children of the faithful should be kept, as far as may be, under a church watch, in expectation that they might be in a fairer way to receive the grace of God; so that the prosperous condition of religion in our churches might not be a matter of one age alone."

Old Cotton waxes warm in arguing this subject, as follows:—

"The Scriptures tell us that men's denying the children of the Church to have any part in the Lord hath a strong tendency in it to make them cease from fearing the Lord, and harden their hearts from his fear. But the awful obligations of covenant interest have a great tendency to soften the heart and break it, and draw it home to God. Hence, when the Lord would powerfully win men to obedience, he often begins with this: that he *is* their God. The way of the Anabaptists, to admit none unto membership and baptism but adult professors, is the straitest way. One would think it should be a way of great purity, but experience hath shown that it has been an inlet unto great corruption, and a troublesome, dangerous underminer of reformation."

And then old Cotton adds these words, certainly as explicit as even the modern Puseyite could desire:—

"If we do not keep in the way of a converting, grace-giving *covenant*, and keep persons *under those church dispensations wherein grace is given*, the Church will die of a lingering, though not a violent death. The Lord hath not set up churches, only that a few old Christians may keep one another warm while they live and then carry away the Church into the cold grave with them when they die. No; but that they might with all care and with all the obligations and advantages to that care that may be, nurse up another generation of subjects to our Lord, that may stand up in his kingdom when they are gone."

It was for some time doubtful whether the New England Church would organize itself and seek its own perpetuation on the educational basis which has been the foundation of the majority of the Christian Church elsewhere; and the question was decided, as such society questions often are, by the vigor and power of one man. Jonathan Edwards, a man who united in himself the natures of both a poet and a metaphysician, all whose experiences and feelings were as much more intense than those of common men as Dante's or Milton's, fell into the error of making his own constitutional religious experience the measure and standard of all others, and revolutionizing by it the institutions of the Pilgrim Fathers.

Regeneration, as he taught it in his "Treatise on the Affections," was the implantation by Divine power of a new spiritual sense in the soul, as diverse from all the other senses as seeing is from hearing, or tasting from smelling. No one that had not received this new, divine, supernatural sense, could properly belong to the Church of Christ, and all men, until they did receive it, were naturally and constitutionally enemies of God to such a degree, that, as he says in a sermon to that effect, "If they had God in their power, they would kill him."

It was his power and his influence which succeeded in completely upsetting New England from the basis on which the Reformers and the Puritan Fathers had placed her, and casting out of the Church the children of the very saints and martyrs who had come to this country for no other reason than to found a church.

It is remarkable that, in all the discussions of depravity inherited from Adam, it never seemed to occur to any theologian that there might also be a counter-working of the great law of descent, by which the feelings and habits of thought wrought in the human mind by Jesus Christ might descend through generations of Christians, so that, in course of time, many might be born predisposed to good, rather than to evil.

Cotton Mather fearlessly says that *"the seed of the Church are born holy,"*—not, of course, meaning it in a strictly theological sense, but certainly indicating that, in his day, a mild and genial spirit of hope breathed over the cradle of infancy and childhood.

Those very persons whom President Edwards addresses in such merciless terms of denunciation in his sermons, telling them that it is a wonder the sun does not refuse to shine upon them,—that the earth daily groans to open under them,—and that the wind and the sun and the waters are all weary of them and longing to break forth and execute the wrath of God upon them,—were the children for uncounted generations back of fathers and mothers nursed in the bosom of the Church, trained in habits of daily prayer, brought up to patience and self-sacrifice and self-denial as the very bread of their daily being, and lacking only this supernatural sixth sense, the want of which brought upon them a guilt so tremendous. The consequence was, that, immediately after the time of President Edwards, there grew up in the very bosom of the New England Church a set of young people who were not merely indifferent to religion, but who hated it with the whole energy of their being.

Ellery Davenport's feeling toward the Church and religion had all the bitterness of the disinherited son, who likes nothing better than to point out the faults in those favored children who enjoy the privileges of which he is deprived. All the consequences that good, motherly Cotton Mather had foreseen as likely to result from the proposed system of arranging the Church were strikingly verified in his case. He had not been able entirely to rid himself of a belief in what he hated. The danger of all such violent recoils from the religion of one's childhood consists in this fact,—that the person is always secretly uncertain that he may not be opposing truth and virtue itself; he struggles confusedly with the faith of his mother, the prayers of his father, with whatever there may be holy and noble in the profession of that faith from which he has broken away; and few escape a very serious shock to conscience and their moral nature in doing it.

Ellery Davenport was at war with himself, at war with the

traditions of his ancestry, and had the feeling that he was regarded in the Puritan community as an apostate; but he took
a perverse pleasure in making his position good by a brilliancy of wit and grace of manner which few could resist; and,
truth to say, his success, even with the more rigid, justified
his self-confidence. As during these days there were very few
young persons who made any profession of religion at all, the
latitude of expression which he allowed himself on these subjects was looked upon as a sort of spiritual sowing of wild
oats. Heads would be gravely shaken over him. One and another would say, "Ah! that Edwards blood is smart; it runs
pretty wild in youth, but the Lord's time may come by and
by"; and I doubt not that my grandmother that very night,
before she slept, wrestled with God in prayer for his soul with
all the enthusiasm of a Monica for a St. Augustine.

Meantime, with that easy facility which enabled him to
please everybody, he became, during the course of a somewhat extended visit which he made at the minister's, rather a
hero in Oldtown. What Colonel Davenport said, and what
Colonel Davenport did, were spoken of from mouth to
mouth. Even his wicked wit was repeated by the gravest and
most pious,—of course with some expressions of disclaimer,
but, after all, with that genuine pleasure which a Yankee
never fails to feel in anything smartly and neatly hit off in
language.

He cultivated a great friendship with Miss Mehitable,—
talking with her of books and literature and foreign countries,
and advising her in regard to the education of Tina, with
great unction and gravity. With that little princess there was
always a sort of half whimsical flirtation, as she demurely insisted on being treated by him as a woman, rather than as a
child,—a caprice which amused him greatly.

Miss Mehitable felt herself irresistibly drawn, in his society,
as almost everybody else was, to make a confidant of him. He
was so winning, so obliging, so gentle, and knew so well just
where and how to turn the conversation to avoid anything
that he did n't like to hear, and to hear anything that he did.
So gently did his fingers run over the gamut of everybody's
nature, that nobody dreamed of being played on.

Such men are not, of course, villains; but, if they ever should happen to wish to become so, their nature gives them every facility.

Before she knew what she was about, Miss Mehitable found herself talking with Ellery Davenport on the strange, mysterious sorrow which imbittered her life, and she found a most sympathetic and respectful listener.

Ellery Davenport was already versed in diplomatic life, and had held for a year or two a situation of importance at the court of France; was soon to return thither, and also to be employed on diplomatic service in England. Could he, would he, find any traces of the lost one there? On this subject there were long, and, on the part of Miss Mehitable, agitating interviews, which much excited Miss Tina's curiosity.

XXIX.

My Grandmother's Blue Book

READER, this is to be a serious chapter, and I advise all those people who want to go through the world without giving five minutes' consecutive thought to any subject to skip it. They will not find it entertaining, and it may perhaps lead them to think on puzzling subjects, even for so long a time as half an hour; and who knows what may happen to their brains, from so unusual an exercise?

My grandmother, as I have shown, was a character in her way, full of contradictions and inconsistencies, brave, generous, energetic, large-hearted, and impulsive. Theoretically she was an ardent disciple of the sharpest and severest Calvinsim, and used to repeat Michael Wigglesworth's "Day of Doom" to us in the chimney-corner, of an evening, with a reverent acquiescence in all its hard sayings, while practically she was the most pitiful, easy-to-be-entreated old mortal on earth, and was ever falling a prey to any lazy vagabond who chose to make an appeal to her abounding charity. She could not refuse a beggar that asked in a piteous tone; she could not send a child to bed that wanted to sit up; she could not eat a meal in peace when there were hungry eyes watching her; she could not, in cool, deliberate moments, even inflict transient and necessary pain for the greater good of a child, and resolutely shut her eyes to the necessity of such infliction. But there lay at the bottom of all this apparent inconsistency a deep cause that made it consistent, and that cause was the theologic stratum in which her mind, and the mind of all New England, was embedded.

Never, in the most intensely religious ages of the world, did the insoluble problem of the WHENCE, the WHY, and the WHITHER of mankind receive such earnest attention. New England was founded by a colony who turned their backs on the civilization of the Old World, on purpose that they might have nothing else to think of. Their object was to form a community that should think of nothing else.

Working on a hard soil, battling with a harsh, ungenial climate, everywhere being treated by Nature with the most rigorous severity, they asked no indulgence, they got none, and they gave none. They shut out from their religious worship every poetic drapery, every physical accessory that they feared would interfere with the abstract contemplation of hard, naked truth, and set themselves grimly and determinately to study the severest problems of the unknowable and the insoluble. Just as resolutely as they made their farms by blasting rocks and clearing land of ledges of stone, and founded thrifty cities and thriving money-getting communities in places which one would think might more properly have been left to the white bears, so resolutely they pursued their investigations amid the grim mysteries of human existence, determined to see and touch and handle everything for themselves, and to get at the absolute truth if absolute truth could be got at.

They never expected to find truth agreeable. Nothing in their experience of life had ever prepared them to think it would be so. Their investigations were made with the courage of the man who hopes little, but determines to know the worst of his affairs. They wanted no smoke of incense to blind them, and no soft opiates of pictures and music to lull them; for what they were after was *truth*, and not happiness, and they valued *duty* far higher than enjoyment.

The underlying foundation of life, therefore, in New England, was one of profound, unutterable, and therefore unuttered, melancholy, which regarded human existence itself as a ghastly risk, and, in the case of the vast majority of human beings, an inconceivable misfortune.

My grandmother believed in statements which made the fortunate number who escaped the great catastrophe of mortal life as few and far between as the shivering, half-drowned mariners, who crawl up on to the shores of some desert island, when all else on board have perished. In this view she regarded the birth of an infant with a suppressed groan, and the death of one almost with satisfaction. That more than half the human race die in infancy,—that infanticide is the general custom in so many heathen lands,—was to her a comforting consideration, for so many were held to escape at once the awful ordeal, and to be gathered into the numbers of the elect.

As I have said, she was a great reader. On the round table that stood in her bedroom, next to the kitchen, there was an ample supply of books. Rollin's Ancient History, Hume's History of England, and President Edwards's Sermons, were among these.

She was not one of those systematic, skilful housewives who contrive with few steps and great method to do much in little time; she took everything the hardest end first, and attacked difficulties by sheer inconsiderate strength. For example, instead of putting on the great family pot, filling it with water, and afterwards putting therein the beef, pork, and vegetables of our daily meal, she would load up the receptacle at the sink in the back room, and then, with strong arm and cap-border erect, would fly across the kitchen with it and swing it over the fire by main strength. Thus inconsiderately she rushed at the daily battle of existence. But there was one point of system in which she never failed. There was, every day, a period, sacred and inviolable, which she gave to reading. The noon meal came exactly at twelve o'clock; and immediately after, when the dishes were washed and wiped, and the kitchen reduced to order, my grandmother changed her gown, and retired to the sanctuary of her bedroom to read. In this way she accomplished an amount which a modern housekeeper, with four servants, would pronounce to be wholly incredible.

The books on her table came in time to be my reading as well as hers; for, as I have said, reading was with me a passion, a hunger, and I read all that came in my way.

Her favorite books had different-colored covers, thriftily put on to preserve them from the wear of handling; and it was by these covers they were generally designated in the family. Hume's History of England was known as "the brown book"; Rollin's History was "the green book"; but there was one volume which she pondered oftener and with more intense earnestness than any other, which received the designation of "the blue book." This was a volume by the Rev. Dr. Bellamy of Connecticut, called "True Religion delineated, and distinguished from all Counterfeits." It was originally published by subscription, and sent out into New England with a letter of introduction and recommendation from the Rev. Jonathan Edwards, who earnestly set it forth as being a condensed summary, in popular language, of what it is vital and important for human beings to know for their spiritual progress. It was written in a strong, nervous, condensed, popular style, such as is fallen into by a practical man speaking to a practical people, by a man thoroughly in earnest to men as deeply in earnest, and lastly, by a man who believed without the shadow of a doubt, and without even the comprehension of the possibility of a doubt.

I cannot give a better idea of the unflinching manner in which the deepest mysteries of religion were propounded to the common people than by giving a specimen of some of the headings of this book.

Page 288 considers, "Were we by the Fall brought into a State of Being worse than Not to Be?"

The answer to this comprehensive question is sufficiently explicit.

"Mankind were by their fall brought into a state of being worse than not to be. The damned in hell, no doubt, are in such a state, else their punishment would not be infinite, as justice requires it should be. But mankind, by the fall, were brought into a state, *for substance*, as bad as that which the damned are in."

The next inquiry to this is, "How could God, consistent with his perfections, put us into a state of being worse than not to be? And how can we ever thank God for such a being?"

The answer to this, as it was read by thousands of reflecting minds like mine, certainly shows that these hardy and courageous investigators often raised spirits that they could not lay. As, for instance, this solution of the question, which never struck me as satisfactory.

"Inasmuch as God did virtually give being to all mankind, when he blessed our first parents and said, 'Be fruitful and multiply'; and inasmuch as *Being*, under the circumstances that man was *then* put in by God, was very desirable: we ought, therefore, to thank God for our being, considered in this light, and justify God for all the evil that has come upon us by apostasy."

On this subject the author goes on to moralize thus:—

"Mankind, by the fall, were brought into a state of being infinitely worse than not to be; and were they but so far awake as to be sensible of it, they would, no doubt, all over the earth, murmur and blaspheme the God of Heaven. But what then? there would be no just ground for such conduct. We have no reason to think hard of God,—to blame him or esteem him e'er the less. What he has done was fit and right. His conduct was beautiful, and he is worthy to be esteemed for it. For that constitution was holy, just, and good, as has been proved. And, therefore, a fallen world ought to ascribe to themselves all the evil, and to justify God and say: 'God gave us being under a constitution holy, just, and good, and it was a mercy. We should have accounted it a great mercy in case Adam had never fallen; but God is not to blame for this, nor, therefore, is he the less worthy of thanks.'"

After this comes another and quite practical inquiry, which is stated as follows:—

"But if mankind are thus by nature children of wrath, in a state of being worse than not to be, how can men have the heart to propagate their kind?"

The answer to this inquiry it is not necessary to give at length; I merely state it to show how unblinking was the gaze which men in those days fixed upon the problems of life.

The objector is still further represented as saying,—

"It cannot be thought a blessing to have children, if most of them are thought to be likely to perish."

The answer to this is as follows:—

"The most of Abraham's posterity for these three thousand years, no doubt, have been wicked and perished. And God knew beforehand how it would be, and yet he promised such a numerous posterity under the notion of a great blessing. For, considering children as to this life, they may be a great blessing and comfort to their parents; and we are certain that God will do them no wrong in the life to come. All men's murmuring thoughts about this matter arise from their not liking God's way of governing the world."

I will quote but one more passage, as showing the hardy

vigor of assertion on the darkest of subjects,—the origin of evil. The author says:—

"When God first designed the world, and laid out his scheme of government, it was easy for him to have determined that neither angels nor men should ever sin, and that misery should never be heard of in all his dominions; for he could easily have prevented both sin and misery. Why did not he? Surely not for want of goodness in his nature, for that is infinite; not from anything like cruelty, for there is no such thing in him; not for want of a suitable regard to the happiness of his creatures, for that he always has: but because in his infinite wisdom he did not think it best on the whole.

"But why was it not best? What could he have in view, preferable to the happiness of his creatures? And, if their happiness was to him above all things most dear, how could he bear the thoughts of their ever any of them being miserable?

"It is certain that he had in view something else than merely the happiness of his creatures. It was something of greater importance. But what was that thing that was of greater worth and importance, and to which he had the greatest regard, making all other things give way to this? What was his great end in creating and governing the world? Why, look what end he is at last likely to obtain, when the whole scheme is finished, and the Day of Judgment passed, and heaven and hell filled with all their proper inhabitants. What will be the final result? What will he get by all? Why, this: that he will exert and display every one of his perfections to the life, and so by all will exhibit a most perfect and exact image of himself.

"Now it is evident that the fall of angels and of man, together with all those things which have and will come to pass in consequence thereof, from the beginning of the world to the Day of Judgment and throughout eternity, will serve to give a much more lively and perfect representation of God than could possibly have been given had there been no sin or misery."

This book also led the inquirer through all the mazes of mental philosophy, and discussed all the problems of mystical religion, such as,—

"Can a man, merely from self-love, love God more than himself?"

"Is our impotency only moral?"

"What is the most fundamental difference between Arminians and Calvinists?"

"How the love to our neighbor which is commanded by God is a thing different from natural compassion, from natural affection, from party-spirited love, from any love whatever that arises merely from self-love, and from the love which enthusiasts and heretics have for one another."

I give these specimens, that the reader may reflect what kind of population there was likely to be where such were the daily studies of a plain country farmer's wife, and such the common topics discussed at every kitchen fireside.

My grandmother's blue book was published and recommended to the attention of New England, August 4, 1750, just twenty-six years before the Declaration of Independence. How popular it was, and how widely read in New England, appears from the list of subscribers which stands at the end of the old copy which my grandmother actually used. Almost every good old Massachusetts or Connecticut family name is there represented. We have the Emersons, the Adamses, the Brattles of Brattle Street, the Bromfields of Bromfield Street, the Brinsmaids of Connecticut, the Butlers, the Campbells, the Chapmans, the Cottons, the Daggetts, the Hawleys, the Hookers, with many more names of families yet continuing to hold influence in New England. How they regarded this book may be inferred from the fact that some subscribed for six books, some for twelve, some for thirty-six, and some for fifty. Its dissemination was deemed an act of religious ministry, and there is not the slightest doubt that it was heedfully and earnestly read in every good family of New England; and its propositions were discussed everywhere and by everybody. This is one undoubted fact; the other is, that it was this generation who fought through the Revolutionary war. They were a set of men and women brought up to *think*,—to think not merely on agreeable subjects, but to wrestle and tug at the very severest problems. Utter self-renunciation, a sort of grand contempt for personal happiness when weighed with things greater and more valuable, was the fundamental principle of life in those days. They who could calmly look in the face, and settle themselves down to, the idea of being resigned and thankful for an existence which was not so good as non-existence,—who were willing to be loyal subjects of a splendid and powerful government which was conducted on quite other issues than a regard for their happiness,—were possessed of a courage and a fortitude which no mere earthly mischance could shake. They who had faced eternal ruin with an unflinching gaze were not likely to shrink before the comparatively trivial losses and gains of any mere earthly conflict. Being accustomed to combats with the Devil, it was rather a recreation to fight only British officers.

If any should ever be so curious as to read this old treatise, as well as most of the writings of Jonathan Edwards, they will perceive with singular plainness how inevitably monarchical and aristocratic institutions influence theology.

That "the king can do no wrong,"—that the subject owes everything to the king, and the king nothing to the subject,—that it is the king's first duty to take care of himself, and keep up state, splendor, majesty, and royalty, and that it is the people's duty to give themselves up, body and soul, without a murmuring thought, to keep up this state, splendor, and royalty,—were ideas for ages so wrought into the human mind, and transmitted by ordinary generation,—they so reflected themselves in literature and poetry and art, and all the great customs of society,—that it was inevitable that systematic theology should be permeated by them.

The idea of God in which theologians delighted, and which the popular mind accepted, was not that of the Good Shepherd that giveth his life for the sheep,—of him that made himself of no reputation, and took unto himself the form of a servant,—of him who on his knees washed the feet of his disciples, and said that in the kingdom of heaven the greatest was he who served most humbly,—this aspect of a Divine Being had not yet been wrought into their systematic theology; because, while the Bible comes from God, theology is the outgrowth of the human mind, and therefore must spring from the movement of society.

When the Puritans arrived at a perception of the political rights of men in the state, and began to enunciate and act upon the doctrine that a king's right to reign was founded upon his power to promote the greatest happiness of his subjects, and when, in pursuance of this theory, they tried, condemned, and executed a king who had been false to the people, they took a long step forward in human progress. Why did not immediate anarchy follow, as when the French took such a step in regard to their king? It was because the Puritans transferred to God all those rights and immunities, all that unquestioning homage and worship and loyalty, which hitherto they had given to an earthly king.

The human mind cannot bear to relinquish more than a certain portion of its cherished past ideas in one century. Society falls into anarchy in too entire a change of base.

The Puritans had still a King. The French Revolutionists had nothing; therefore, the Puritan Revolution went on stronger and stronger. The French passed through anarchy back under despotism.

The doctrine of Divine sovereignty was the great rest to the human mind in those days, when the foundations of many generations were broken up. It is always painful to honest and loyal minds to break away from that which they have reverenced,—to put down that which they have respected. And the Puritans were by nature the most reverential and most loyal portion of the community. Their passionate attachment to the doctrine of Divine sovereignty, at this period, was the pleading and yearning within them of a faculty robbed of its appropriate object, and longing for support and expression.

There is something most affecting in the submissive devotion of these old Puritans to their God. Nothing shows more completely the indestructible nature of the filial tie which binds man to God, of the filial yearning which throbs in the heart of a great child of so great a Father, than the manner in which these men loved and worshipped and trusted God as the ALL LOVELY, even in the face of monstrous assertions of theology ascribing to him deeds which no father could imitate without being cast out of human society, and no governor without being handed down to all ages as a monster.

These theologies were not formed by the Puritans; they were their legacy from past monarchical and mediæval ages;

and the principles of true Christian democracy upon which they founded their new state began, from the time of the American Revolution, to act upon them with a constantly ameliorating power; so that whosoever should read my grandmother's blue book now would be astonished to find how completely New England theology has changed its base.

The artist, in reproducing pictures of New England life during this period, is often obliged to hold his hand. He could not faithfully report the familiar conversations of the common people, because they often allude to and discuss the most awful and tremendous subjects. This, however, was the inevitable result of the honest, fearless manner in which the New England ministry of this second era discussed the Divine administration. They argued for it with the common people in very much the tone and with much the language in which they defended the Continental Congress and the ruling President; and every human being was addressed as a competent judge.

The result of such a mode of proceeding, in the long run, changed the theology of New England, from what it was when Jonathan Edwards recommended my grandmother's blue book, into what it is at this present writing. But, during the process of this investigation, every child born in New England found himself beaten backwards and forwards, like a shuttlecock, between the battledoors of discussion. Our kitchen used to be shaken constantly by what my grandfather significantly called "the battle of the Infinites," especially when my Uncle Bill came home from Cambridge on his vacations, fully charged with syllogisms, which he hurled like catapults back on the syllogisms which my grandmother had drawn from the armory of her blue book.

My grandmother would say, for example: "Whatever sin is committed against an infinite being is an infinite evil. Every infinite evil deserves infinite punishment; therefore every sin of man deserves an infinite punishment."

Then Uncle Bill, on the other side, would say: "No act of a finite being can be infinite. Man is a finite being; therefore no sin of man can be infinite. No finite evil deserves infinite punishment. Man's sins are finite evils; therefore man's sins do not deserve infinite punishment." When the combatants had got thus far, they generally looked at each other in silence.

As a result, my grandmother being earnest and prayerful, and my uncle careless and worldly, the thing generally ended in her believing that he was wrong, though she could not answer him; and in his believing that she, after all, might be right, though he *could* answer her; for it is noticeable, in every battle of opinion, that honest, sincere, moral earnestness has a certain advantage over mere intellectual cleverness.

It was inevitable that a people who had just carried through a national revolution and declared national independence on the principle that "governments owe their just power to the consent of the governed," and who recognized it as an axiom that the greatest good to the greatest number was the object to be held in view in all just governments, should very soon come into painful collision with forms of theological statement, in regard to God's government, which appeared to contravene all these principles, and which could be supported only by referring to the old notion of the divine right and prerogative of the King Eternal.

President Edwards had constructed a marvellous piece of logic to show that, while true virtue in man consisted in supreme devotion to the general good of all, true virtue in God consisted in supreme regard for himself. This "Treatise on True Virtue" was one of the strongest attempts to back up by reasoning the old monarchical and aristocratic ideas of the supreme right of the king and upper classes. The whole of it falls to dust before the one simple declaration of Jesus Christ, that, in the eyes of Heaven, one lost sheep is more prized than all the ninety and nine that went not astray, and before the parable in which the father runs, forgetful of parental prerogative and dignity, to cast himself on the neck of the far-off prodigal.

Theology being human and a reflection of human infirmities, nothing is more common than for it to come up point-blank in opposition to the simplest declarations of Christ.

I must beg my readers' pardon for all this, but it is a fact that the true tragedy of New England life, its deep, unutterable pathos, its endurances and its sufferings, all depended

upon, and were woven into, this constant wrestling of
thought with infinite problems which could not be avoided,
and which saddened the days of almost every one who grew
up under it.

Was this entire freedom of thought and discussion a bad
thing, then? Do we not see that strength of mind and
strength of will, and the courage and fortitude and endurance
which founded this great American government, grew up out
of characters formed thus to think and struggle and suffer? It
seems to be the law of this present existence, that all the
changes by which the world is made better are brought about
by the struggle and suffering, and sometimes the utter shipwreck, of individual human beings.

In regard to our own family, the deepest tragedy in it, and
the one which for a time brought the most suffering and sorrow on us all, cannot be explained unless we take into consideration this peculiar state of society.

In the neighboring town of Adams there lived one of the
most remarkable clergymen that New England has ever produced. His career influenced the thinking of Massachusetts,
both in regard to those who adopted his opinions, and in the
violent reaction from those opinions which was the result of
his extreme manner of pushing them.

Dr. Moses Stern's figure is well remembered by me as I saw
it in my boyhood. Everybody knew him, and when he appeared in the pulpit everybody trembled before him. He
moved among men, but seemed not of men. An austere, inflexible, grand indifference to all things earthly seemed to give
him the prestige and dignity of a supernatural being. His Calvinism was of so severe and ultra a type, and his statements
were so little qualified either by pity of human infirmity, or
fear of human censure, or desire of human approbation, that
he reminded one of some ancient prophet, freighted with a
mission of woe and wrath, which he must always speak,
whether people would hear or whether they would forbear.

The Revolutionary war had introduced into the country a
great deal of scepticism, of a type of which Paine's "Age of
Reason" was an exponent; and, to meet this, the ministry of
New England was not slow or unskilful.

Dr. Stern's mode of meeting this attitude of the popular

mind was by an unflinching, authoritative, vehement reiteration of all the most unpopular and unpleasant points of Calvinsim. Now as Nature is, in many of her obvious aspects, notoriously uncompromising, harsh, and severe, the Calvinist who begins to talk to common-sense people has this advantage on his side,—that the things which he represents the Author of Nature as doing and being ready to do, are not very different from what the common-sense man sees that the Author of Nature is already in the habit of doing.

The farmer who struggles with the hard soil, and with drouth and frost and caterpillars and fifty other insect plagues,—who finds his most persistent and well-calculated efforts constantly thwarted by laws whose workings he never can fully anticipate, and which never manifest either care for his good intentions or sympathy for his losses, is very apt to believe that the God who created nature may be a generally benevolent, but a severe and unsympathetic being, governing the world for some great, unknown purpose of his own, of which man's private improvement and happiness may or may not form a part.

Dr. Stern, with characteristic independence and fearlessness, on his own simple authority cut loose from and repudiated the whole traditional idea of the fall in Adam as having anything to do with the existence of human depravity; and made up his own theory of the universe, and began preaching it to the farmers of Adams. It was simply this: that the Divine Being is the efficient cause of all things, not only in matter but in mind,—that every good and every evil volition of any being in the universe is immediately caused by Him and tends equally well in its way to carry on his great designs. But, in order that this might not interfere with the doctrines of human responsibility, he taught that all was accomplished by Omniscient skill and knowledge in such a way as not in the slightest degree to interfere with human free agency; so that the whole responsibility of every human being's actions must rest upon himself.

Thus was this system calculated, like a skilful engine of torture, to produce all the mental anguish of the most perfect sense of helplessness with the most torturing sense of responsibility. Alternately he worked these two great levers with an almost supernatural power,—on one Sunday demonstrating with the most logical clearness, and by appeals to human consciousness, the perfect freedom of man, and, on the next, demonstrating with no less precision and logic the perfect power which an Omniscient Being possessed and exercised of controlling all his thoughts and volitions and actions.

Individually, Dr. Stern, like many other teachers of severe, uncompromising theories, was an artless, simple-hearted, gentle-mannered man. He was a close student, and wore two holes in the floor opposite his table in the spot where year after year his feet were placed in study. He refused to have the smallest thing to do with any temporal affair of this life. Like the other clergymen, he lived on a small salary, and the support of his family depended largely on the proceeds of a farm. But it is recorded of him, that once, when his whole summer's crop of hay was threatened with the bursting of a thunder-shower, and, farmhands being short, he was importuned to lend a hand to save it, he resolutely declined, saying, that, if he once began to allow himself to be called on in any emergency for temporal affairs, he should become forgetful of his great mission.

The same inflexible, unbending perseverance he showed in preaching, on the basis of his own terrible theory, the most fearful doctrines of Calvinism. His sermons on Judas, on Jeroboam, and on Pharaoh, as practical examples of the doctrine of reprobation, were pieces of literature so startling and astounding, that, even in those days of interrupted travel, when there were neither railroads nor good roads of any kind, and almost none of our modern communicative system of magazines and newspapers, they were heard of all over New England. So great was the revulsion which his doctrines excited, that, when he exchanged with his brother ministers, his appearance in the pulpit was the signal for some of the most independent of the congregation to get up and leave the meeting-house. But, as it was one of his maxims that the minister who does not excite the opposition of the natural heart fails to do his work, he regarded such demonstrations as evident signs of a faithful ministry.

The science of Biblical criticism in his day was in its infancy; the Bible was mostly read by ministers, and proof-texts quoted from it as if it had been a treatise written in the English language by New-Englanders, and in which every word must bear the exact sense of a New England metaphysical treatise. And thus interpreting the whole wide labyrinth of poetry and history, and Oriental allegory and hyperbole, by literal rules, Dr. Stern found no difficulty in making it clear to those who heard him that there was no choice between believing his hard doctrines and giving up the Bible altogether. And it shows the deep and rooted attachment which the human heart has for that motherly book, that even in this dreadful dilemma the majority of his hearers did not revolt from the Bible.

As it was, in the town where he lived his preaching formed the strongest, most controlling of all forces. No human being could hear his sermons unmoved. He would not preach to an inattentive audience, and on one occasion, observing a large number of his congregation asleep, he abruptly descended from the pulpit and calmly walked off home, leaving the astonished congregation to their own reflections; nor would he resume public services until messages of contrition and assurances of better conduct had been sent him.

Dr. Stern was in his position irresistible, simply because he cared nothing at all for the things which men ordinarily care for, and which therefore could be used as motives to restrain the declarations and actions of a clergyman. He cared nothing about worldly prosperity; he was totally indifferent to money; he utterly despised fame and reputation; and therefore from none of these sources could he be in the slightest degree influenced. Such a man is generally the king of his neighborhood,—the one whom all look up to, and all fear, and whose word in time becomes law.

Dr. Stern never sought to put himself forward otherwise than by the steady preaching of his system to the farming population of Adams. And yet, so great were his influence and his fame, that in time it became customary for young theological students to come and settle themselves down there as his students. This was done at first without his desire, and contrary to his remonstrance.

"I can't engage to teach you," he said; but still, when scholars came and continued to come, he found himself, without
seeking it, actually at the head of a school of theology.

Let justice be done to all; it is due to truth to state that the
theological scholars of Dr. Stern, wherever they went in the
United States, were always marked men,—marked for an unflinching adherence to principle, and especially for a great
power in supporting unpopular truths.

The Doctor himself lived to an extreme old age, always retaining and reiterating with unflinching constancy his opinions. He was the last of the New England ministers who preserved the old clerical dress of the theocracy. Long after the
cocked hat and small-clothes, silk stockings and shoe-buckles,
had ceased to appear in modern life, his venerable figure, thus
apparelled, walked the ways of modern men, seeming like one
of the primitive Puritans risen from the dead.

He was the last, also, of the New England ministers to
claim for himself that peculiar position, as God's ambassador,
which was such a reality in the minds of the whole early Puritan community. To extreme old age, his word was law in
his parish, and he calmly and positively felt that it should be
so. In time, his gray hairs, his fine, antique figure and quaint
costume came to be regarded with the sort of appreciative
veneration that every one gives to the monuments of the past.
When he was near his ninetieth year, he was invited to New
York to give the prestige of his venerable presence to the religious anniversaries which then were in the flush of newly
organized enthusiasm, and which gladly laid hold of this
striking accessory to the religious picturesque.

Dr. Stern was invited and fêted in the most select upper
circles of New York, and treated with attentions which would
have been flattering had he not been too entirely simple-
minded and careless of such matters even to perceive what
they meant.

But at this same time the Abolitionists, who were regarded
as most improper people to be recognized in the religious
circles of good society, came to New York, resolving to have
their anniversary also; and, knowing that Dr. Stern had always professed to be an antislavery man, they invited him to
sit on the stage with them; and Dr. Stern went. Shocking to

relate, and dreadful to behold, this very cocked hat and these picturesque gray hairs, that had been brought to New York on purpose to ornament religious anniversaries which were all agreed in excluding and ignoring the Abolitionists, had gone right over into the camp of the enemy! and he was so entirely ignorant and uninstructible on the subject, and came back, after having committed this abomination, with a face of such innocent and serene gravity, that nobody dared to say a word to him on the subject.

He was at this time the accepted guest in a family whose very religion consisted in a gracious carefulness and tenderness lest they should wake up the feelings of their Southern brethren on the delicate subject of slavery. But then Dr. Stern was a man that it did no good to talk to, since it was well known that, wherever there was an unpopular truth to be defended, his cocked hat was sure to be in the front ranks.

Let us do one more justice to Dr. Stern, and say that his utter inflexibility toward human infirmity and human feeling spared himself as little as it spared any other. In his early life he records, in a most affecting autobiography, the stroke which deprived him, within a very short space, of a beloved wife and two charming children. In the struggle of that hour he says, with affecting simplicity, "I felt that I should die if I did not submit; and I did submit then, once for all." Thenceforward the beginning and middle and end of his whole preaching was *submission,* — utter, absolute, and unconditional.

In extreme old age, trembling on the verge of the grave, and looking back over sixty years of intense labor, he said, "After all, it is quite possible that *I* may not be saved"; but he considered himself as but one drop in the ocean, and his personal salvation as of but secondary account. His devotion to the King Eternal had no reference to a matter so slight. In all this, if there is something terrible and painful, there is something also which is grand, and in which we can take pride, as the fruit of our human nature. Peace to his ashes! he has learned better things ere now.

If my readers would properly understand the real depth of sorrowful perplexity in which our friend Miss Mehitable Ros-

siter was struggling, they must go back with us some years
before, to the time when little Emily Rossiter was given up
to the guardianship and entire control of her Aunt Farnsworth.

Zedekiah Farnsworth was one of those men who embody
qualities which the world could not afford to be without, and
which yet are far from being the most agreeable. Uncompromising firmness, intense self-reliance, with great vigor in that
part of the animal nature which fits man to resist and to subdue and to hold in subjection the forces of nature, were his
prominent characteristics. His was a bold and granite formation,—most necessary for the stability of the earth, but without a flower.

His wife was a woman who had once been gay and beautiful, but who, coming under the dominion of a stronger nature, was perfectly magnetized by it, so as to assimilate and
become a modified reproduction of the same traits. A calm,
intense, severe conscientiousness, which judged alike herself
and others with unflinching severity, was her leading characteristic.

Let us now imagine a child inheriting from the mother a
sensitive, nervous organization, and from the father a predis-
position to morbid action, with a mind as sensitive to external
influence as a daguerreotype-plate, brought suddenly from
the warmth of a too-indulgent household to the arctic regularity and frozen stillness of the Farnsworth mansion. It will
be seen that the consequences must have been many conflicts,
and many struggles of nature with nature, and that a character
growing up thus must of course grow up into unnatural and
unhealthy development.

The problem of education is seriously complicated by the
peculiarities of womanhood. If we suppose two souls, exactly
alike, sent into bodies, the one of man, the other of woman,
that mere fact alone alters the whole mental and moral history
of the two.

In addition to all the other sources of peril which beset the
little Emily, she early developed a beauty so remarkable as to
draw upon her constant attention, and, as she grew older,
brought to her all the trials and the dangers which extraordinary beauty brings to woman. It was a part of her Aunt Farns-

worth's system to pretend to be ignorant of this great fact, with a view, as she supposed, of checking any disposition to pride or vanity which might naturally arise therefrom. The consequence was that the child, hearing this agreeable news from every one else who surrounded her, soon learned the transparent nature of the hoax, and with it acquired a certain doubt of her aunt's sincerity.

Emily had a warm, social nature, and had always on hand during her school days a list of enthusiastic friends whose admiration of her supplied the light and warmth which were entirely wanting from every other source.

Mrs. Farnsworth was not insensible to the charms of her niece. She was, in fact, quite proud of them, but was pursuing conscientiously the course in regard to them which she felt that duty required of her. She loved the child, too, devotedly, but her own nature had been so thoroughly frozen by maxims of self-restraint, that this love seldom or never came into outward forms of expression.

It is sad to be compelled to trace the ill effects produced by the overaction and misapplication of the very noblest faculties of the human mind.

The Farnsworth family was one in which there was the fullest sympathy with the severest preaching of Dr. Stern. As Emily grew older, it was exacted of her, as one of her Sabbath duties, to take notes of his discourses at church, which were afterwards to be read over on Sunday evening by her aunt and uncle, and preserved in an extract-book.

The effect of such kinds of religious teaching on most of the children and young people in the town of Adams was to make them consider religion, and everything connected with it, as the most disagreeable of all subjects, and to seek practically to have as little to do with it as possible; so that there was among the young people a great deal of youthful gayety and of young enjoyment in life, notwithstanding the preaching from Sunday to Sunday of assertions enough to freeze every heart with fear. Many formed the habit of thinking of something else during the sermon-time, and many heard without really attaching any very definite meaning to what they heard.

The severest utterances, if constantly reiterated, lose their power and come to be considered as nothing. But Emily Rossiter had been gifted with a mind of far more than ordinary vigor, and with even a Greek passion for ideas, and with capabilities for logical thought which rendered it impossible for her to listen to discourses so intellectual without taking in their drift and responding to their stimulus by a corresponding intellectual activity.

Dr. Stern set the example of a perfectly bold and independent manner of differing from the popular theology of his day in certain important respects; and, where he did differ, it was with a hardihood of self-assertion, and an utter disregard of popular opinion, and a perfect reliance on his own powers of discovering truth, which were very apt to magnetize these same qualities in other minds. People who thus set the example of free and independent thinking in one or two respects, and yet hope to constrain their disciples to think exactly as they do on all other subjects, generally reckon without their host; and there is no other region in Massachusetts where all sorts of hardy free-thinking are so rife at the present day as in the region formerly controlled by Dr. Stern.

Before Emily was fourteen years old she had passed through two or three of those seasons of convulsed and agonized feeling which are caused by the revolt of a strong sense of justice and humanity against teachings which seem to accuse the great Father of all of the most frightful cruelty and injustice. The teachings were backed up by literal quotations from the Bible, which in those days no common person possessed the means, or the habits of thought, for understanding, and thus were accepted by her at first as Divine declarations.

When these agonized conflicts occurred, they were treated by her aunt and uncle only as active developments of the natural opposition of the human heart to God. Some such period of active contest with the Divine nature was on record in the lives of some of the most eminent New England saints. President Edwards recorded the same; and therefore they looked upon them hopefully, just as the medical faculty of those same uninstructed times looked upon the writhings and agonies which their administration of poison produced in the human body.

The last and most fearful of these mental struggles came

after the death of her favorite brother Theodore; who, being supposed to die in an unregenerate state, was forthwith judged and sentenced, and his final condition spoken of with a grim and solemn certainty, by her aunt and uncle.

How far the preaching of Dr. Stern did violence to the most cherished feelings of human nature on this subject will appear by an extract from a sermon preached about this time.

The text was from Rev. xix, 3. "And again they said Alleluia. And her smoke rose up for ever and ever."

The subject is thus announced: —

"The heavenly hosts will praise God for punishing the finally impenitent forever."

In the *improvement* or practical application of this text, is the following passage: —

"Will the heavenly hosts praise God for all the displays of his vindictive justice in the punishment of the damned? then we may learn that there is an essential difference between saints and sinners. Sinners often disbelieve and deny this distinction; and it is very difficult to make them see and believe it. . . . . They sometimes freely say that they do not think that heaven is such a place as has been described; or that the inhabitants of it say 'Amen, Alleluia,' while they see the smoke of the torments of the damned ascend up for ever and ever. They desire and hope to go to heaven, without ever being willing to speak such a language, or to express such feelings in the view of the damned. And is not this saying that their hearts are essentially different from those who feel such a spirit, and are willing to adopt the language of heaven? Good men do adopt the language of heaven before they arrive there. And all who are conscious that they cannot say 'Amen, Alleluia,' may know that they are yet sinners, and essentially different from saints, and altogether unprepared to go with them to heaven and join with them in praising God for the vindictive justice he displays in dooming all unholy creatures to a never-ending torment."

It was this sermon that finally broke those cords which years of pious descent had made so near and tender between the heart of Emily and her father's Bible.

No young person ever takes a deliberate and final leave of the faith of the fathers without a pang; and Emily suffered so

much in the struggle, that her aunt became alarmed for her
health. She was sent to Boston to spend a winter under the
care of another sister of her mother's, who was simply a
good-natured woman of the world, who was proud of her
niece's beauty and talents, and resolved to make the most of
them in a purely worldly way.

At this time she formed the acquaintance of a very interesting French family of high rank, who for certain family reasons
were just then exiled to America. She became fascinated with
their society, and plunged into the study of the French language and literature with all the enthusiasm of a voyager who
finds himself among enchanted islands. And French literature
at this time was full of the life of a new era,—the era which
produced both the American and the French Revolution.

The writings of Voltaire were too cold and cynical for her
enthusiastic nature; but Rousseau was to her like a sudden
translation from the ice and snow of Massachusetts to the
tropical flowers of a February in Florida. In "La Nouvelle
Héloïse," she found, not merely a passionate love story, but
the consideration, on the author's side, of just such problems
as had been raised by her theological education.

When she returned from this visit she was apparently quiet
and at peace. Her peace was the peace of a river which has
found an underground passage, and therefore chafes and frets
no more. Her philosophy was the philosophy of Émile, her
faith the faith of the Savoyard vicar, and she imitated Dr.
Stern only in utter self-reliance and fearlessness of consequences in pursuit of what she believed true.

Had her aunt and uncle been able to read the French language, they would have found her note-book of sermons
sometimes interspersed by quotations from her favorite author, which certainly were quite in point; as, for instance, at
the foot of a severe sermon on the doctrine of reprobation
was written:—

"Quand cette dure et décourageante doctrine se déduit de
l'Écriture elle-même, mon premier devoir n'est-il pas
d'honorer Dieu? Quelque respect que je doive au texte sacré,
j'en dois plus encore à son Auteur; et *j'aimerais mieux croire la
Bible falsifée ou inintelligible, que Dieu injuste ou malfaisant.* St.
Paul ne veut pas que le vase dise au potier, Pourquoi m'as-tu

fait ainsi? Cela est fort bien si le potier n'exige du vase que des services qu'il l'a mis en état de lui rendre; mais s'il s'en prenait au vase de n' être pas propre à un usage pour lequel il ne l'aurait pas fait, le vase aurait-il tort de lui dire, Pourquoi m'as-tu fait ainsi?"*

After a period of deceitful quiet and calm, in which Emily read and wrote and studied alone in her room, and moved about in her daily circle like one whose heart is afar off, she suddenly disappeared from them all. She left ostensibly to go on a visit to Boston to her aunt, and all that was ever heard from her after that was a letter of final farewell to Miss Mehitable, in which she told her briefly, that, unable any longer to endure the life she had been leading, and to seem to believe what she could not believe, and being importuned to practise what she never intended to do, she had chosen her lot for herself, and requested her neither to seek her out nor to inquire after her, as all such inquiries would be absolutely vain.

All that could be ascertained on the subject was, that about this time the Marquis de Conté and his lady were found to have sailed for France.

This was the sad story which Miss Mehitable poured into the sympathetic ear of Ellery Davenport.

*"When this harsh, discouraging doctrine is deduced from the Scriptures themselves, is not my first duty to honor God? Whatever respect I owe to the sacred text, I owe still more to its Author, *and I should prefer to believe the Bible falsified or unintelligible to believing God unjust or cruel*. St. Paul would not that the vase should say to the potter, Why hast thou made me thus? That is all very well if the potter exacts of the vase only such services as he has fitted it to render; but if he should require of it a usage for which he has not fitted it, would the vase be in the wrong for saying, Why hast thou made me thus?"

XXX.

We Begin to Be Grown-up People

W E begin to be grown-up people. We cannot always remain in the pleasant valley of childhood. I myself, good reader, have dwelt on its scenes longer, because, looking back on it from the extreme end of life, it seems to my weary eyes so fresh and beautiful; the dew of the morning-land lies on it,—that dew which no coming day will restore.

Our childhood, as the reader has seen, must be confessed to have been reasonably enjoyable. Its influences were all homely, innocent, and pure. There was no seductive vice, no open or covert immorality. Our worst form of roaring dissipation consisted in being too fond of huckleberry parties, or in the immoderate pursuit of chestnuts and walnuts. Even the vagrant associates of uncertain social standing who abounded in Oldtown were characterized by a kind of woodland innocence, and were not much more harmful than woodchucks and squirrels.

Sam Lawson, for instance, though he dearly loved lazy lounging, and was devoted to idle tramps, was yet a most edifying vagrant. A profane word was an abomination in his sight; his speculations on doctrines were all orthodox, and his expositions of Scripture as original and abundant as those of some of the dreamy old fathers. As a general thing he was a devout Sunday keeper and a pillar of the sanctuary, playing his bass-viol to the most mournful tunes with evident relish.

I remember being once left at home alone on Sunday, with an incipient sore-throat, when Sam volunteered himself as my nurse. In the course of the forenoon stillness, a wandering Indian came in, who, by the joint influence of a large mug of cider and the weariness of his tramp, fell into a heavy sleep on our kitchen floor, and somehow Sam was beguiled to amuse himself by tickling his nose with a broom-straw, and laughing, until the tears rolled down his cheeks, at the sleepy snorts and struggles and odd contortions of visage which were the results. Yet so tender was Sam's conscience, that he had frequent searchings of heart, afterward, on account of this profanation of sacred hours, and indulged in floods of long-winded penitence.

Though Sam abhorred all profanity, yet for seasons of extreme provocation he was well provided with that gentler Yankee litany which affords to the irritated mind the comfort of swearing, without the commission of the sin. Under great pressure of provocation Sam Lawson freely said, "Darn it!" The word "darn," in fact, was to the conscientious New England mind a comfortable resting-place, a refreshment to the exacerbated spirit, that shrunk from that too similar word with an *m* in it.

In my boyhood I sometimes pondered that other hard word, and vaguely decided to speak it, with that awful curiosity which gives to an unknown sin a hold upon the imagination. What would happen if I should say "damn"? I dwelt on that subject with a restless curiosity which my grandmother certainly would have told me was a temptation of the Devil. The horrible desire so grew on me, that once, in the sanctity of my own private apartment, with all the doors shut and locked, I thought I would boldly try the experiment of saying "damn" out loud, and seeing what would happen. I did it, and looked up apprehensively to see if the walls were going to fall on me, but they did n't, and I covered up my head in the bedclothes and felt degraded. I had committed the sin, and got not even the excitement of a catastrophe. The Lord apparently did not think me worth his notice.

In regard to the awful questions of my grandmother's blue book, our triad grew up with varying influences. Harry, as I have said, was one of those quiet human beings, of great force in native individuality, who silently draw from all scenes and things just those elements which their own being craves, and resolutely and calmly think their own thoughts, and live their own life, amid the most discordant influences; just as the fluid, sparkling waters of a mountain brook dart this way and that amid stones and rubbish, and hum to themselves their own quiet, hidden tune.

A saintly woman, whose heart was burning itself away in the torturing fires of a slow martyrdom, had been for the first ten years of his life his only companion and teacher, and, dying, had sealed him with a seal given from a visibly opened heaven; and thenceforward no theologies, and no human authority, had the power and weight with him that had the remembrance of those dying eyes, and the sanctity of those last counsels.

By native descent Harry was a gentleman of the peculiarly English stock. He had the shy reserve, the silent, self-respecting pride and delicacy, which led him to keep his own soul as a castle, and that interested, because it left a sense of something veiled and unexpressed.

We were now eighteen years old, and yet, during all these years that he had lived side by side with me in closest intimacy, he had never spoken to me freely and frankly of that which I afterwards learned was always the intensest and bitterest mortification of his life, namely, his father's desertion of his mother and himself. Once only do I remember ever to have seen him carried away by anger, and that was when a coarse and cruel bully among the school-boys applied to him a name which reflected on his mother's honor. The anger of such quiet people is often a perfect convulsion, and it was so in this case. He seemed to blaze with it,—to flame up and redden with a delirious passion; and he knocked down and stamped upon the boy with a blind fury which it was really frightful to see, and which was in singular contrast with his usual unprovokable good-humor.

Ellery Davenport had made good his promise of looking for the pocket-book which Harry's father had left in his country-seat, and the marriage certificate of his mother had been found in it, and carefully lodged in the hands of Lady Lothrop; but nothing had been said to us children about it; it was merely held quietly, as a document that might be of use in time in bringing some property to the children. And even at the time of this fight with the school-boy, Harry said so little afterward, that the real depth of his feeling on this subject was not suspected.

I have reason to believe, also, that Ellery Davenport did succeed in making the father of Harry and Tina aware of the existence of two such promising children, and of the respectability of the families into which they had been adopted. Captain Percival, now Sir Harry Percival, had married again in England, so Ellery Davenport had informed Miss Mehitable in a letter, and had a son by this marriage, and so had no desire to bring to view his former connection. It was understood, I believe, that a sum of money was to be transmitted yearly to the hands of the guardians of the children, for their benefit, and that they were to be left undisturbed in the possession of those who had adopted them.

Miss Mehitable had suffered so extremely herself by the conflict of her own earnest, melancholy nature with the theologic ideas of her time, that she shrunk with dread from imposing them on the gay and joyous little being whose education she had undertaken. Yet she was impressed by that awful sense of responsibility which is one of the most imperative characteristics of the New England mind; and she applied to her brother earnestly to know what she should teach Tina with regard to her own spiritual position. The reply of her brother was characteristic, and we shall give it here:—

"MY DEAR SISTER:—I am a Puritan,—the son, the grandson, the great-grandson of Puritans,—and I say to you, Plant the footsteps of your child on the ground of the old Cambridge Platform, and teach her as Winthrop and Dudley and the Mathers taught their children,—that she 'is already a member in the Church of Christ,—that she is in covenant with God, and hath the seal thereof upon her, to wit, baptism; and so, if not regenerate, is yet in a more hopeful way of attaining regeneration and all spiritual blessings, both of the covenant and seal.'* By teaching the child this, you will place her mind in natural and healthful relations with God and religion. She will feel in her Father's house, and under her Father's care, and the long and weary years of a sense of disinheritance with which you struggled will be spared to her.

"I hold Jonathan Edwards to have been the greatest man, since St. Augustine, that Christianity has turned out. But when a great man, instead of making himself a great ladder for feeble folks to climb on, strikes away the ladder and bids them come to where he stands at a step, his greatness and his

*Cambridge Platform. Mather's Magnalia, page 227, article 7.

goodness both may prove unfortunate for those who come
after him. I go for the good old Puritan platform.

                              "*Your affectionate brother,*
                                    "JONATHAN ROSSITER."

The consequence of all this was, that Tina adopted in her
glad and joyous nature the simple, helpful faith of her
brother,—the faith in an ever good, ever present, ever kind
Father, whose child she was and in whose household she had
grown up. She had a most unbounded faith in prayer, and in
the indulgence and tenderness of the Heavenly Power. All
things to her eyes were seen through the halo of a cheerful,
sanguine, confiding nature. Life had for her no cloud or darkness or mystery.

As to myself, I had been taught in the contrary doctrines,—
that I was a disinherited child of wrath. It is true that this
doctrine was contradicted by the whole influence of the minister, who, as I have said before, belonged to the Arminian
wing of the Church, and bore very mildly on all these great
topics. My grandmother sometimes endeavored to stir him up
to more decisive orthodoxy, and especially to a more vigorous
presentation of the doctrine of native human depravity. I remember once, in her zeal, her quoting to him as a proof-text
the quatrain of Dr. Watts:—

>   "Conceived in sin, O woful state!
>   Before we draw our breath,
>   The first young pulse begins to beat
>   Iniquity and death."

"That, madam," said Dr. Lothrop, who never forgot to be
the grand gentleman under any circumstances,—"that, madam,
is not the New Testament, but Dr. Isaac Watts, allow me to
remind you."

"Well," said my grandmother, "Dr. Watts got it from the
Bible."

"Yes, madam, a *very long way* from the Bible, allow me to
say."

And yet, after all, though I did not like my grandmother's
Calvinistic doctrines, I must confess that she, and all such as

thought like her, always impressed me as being more earnestly religious than those that held the milder and more moderate belief.

Once in a while old Dr. Stern would preach in our neighborhood, and I used to go to hear him. Everybody went to hear him. A sermon on reprobation from Dr. Stern would stir up a whole community in those days, just as a presidential election stirs one up now. And I remember that he used to impress me as being more like a messenger from the other world than most ministers. Dr. Lothrop's sermons, by the side of his, were like Pope's Pastorals beside the Tragedies of Æschylus. Dr. Lothrop's discourses were smooth, they were sensible, they were well worded, and everybody went to sleep under them; but Dr. Stern shook and swayed his audience like a field of grain under a high wind. There was no possibility of not listening to him, or of hearing him with indifference, for he dealt in assertions that would have made the very dead turn in their graves. One of his sermons was talked of for months afterward, with a sort of suppressed breath of supernatural awe, such as men would use in discussing the reappearance of a soul from the other world.

But meanwhile I believed neither my grandmother, nor Dr. Stern, nor the minister. The eternal questions seethed and boiled and burned in my mind without answer. It was not my own personal destiny that lay with weight on my mind; it was the incessant, restless desire to know the real truth from some unanswerable authority. I longed for a visible, tangible communion with God, I longed to see the eternal beauty, to hear a friendly voice from the eternal silence. Among all the differences with regard to doctrinal opinion, I could see clearly that there were two classes of people in the world,— those who had found God and felt him as a living power upon their spirits, and those who had not; and that unknown experience was what I sought.

Such, then, were we three children when Harry and I were in our eighteenth year and Tina in her fifteenth. And just at this moment there was among the high consulting powers that regulated our destiny a movement as to what further was to be done with the three that had hitherto grown up together.

Now, if the reader has attentively read ancient and modern history, he will observe that there is a class of women to be found in this lower world, who, wherever they are, are sure to be in some way the first or the last cause of everything that is going on. Everybody knows, for instance, that Helen was the great instigator of the Trojan war, and if it had not been for her we should have had no Homer. In France, Madame Récamier was, for the time being, reason enough for almost anything that any man in France did; and yet one cannot find out that Madame Récamier had any uncommon genius of her own, except the sovereign one of charming every human being that came in her way, so that all became her humble and subservient subjects. The instance is a marked one, because it operated in a wide sphere, on very celebrated men, in an interesting historic period. But it individualizes a kind of faculty which, generally speaking, is peculiar to women, though it is in some instances exercised by men,—a faculty of charming and controlling every person with whom one has to do.

Tina was now verging toward maturity; she was in just that delicious period in which the girl has all the privileges and graces of childhood, its freedom of movement and action, brightened with a sort of mysterious aurora by the coming dawn of womanhood; and everything indicated that she was to be one of this powerful class of womankind. Can one analyze the charm which such women possess? I have a theory that, in all cases, there is a certain amount of genius with it,—genius which does not declare itself in literature, but in social life, and which devotes itself to pleasing, as other artists devote themselves to painting or to poetry.

Tina had no inconsiderable share of self-will; she was very pronounced in her tastes, and fond of her own way; but she had received from nature this passion for entertaining, and been endowed with varied talents in this line which made her always, from early childhood, the coveted and desired person in every circle. Not a visage in Oldtown was so set in grimness of care, that it did not relax its lines when it saw Tina coming down the street; for Tina could mimic and sing and dance, and fling back joke for joke in a perfect meteoric shower. So long as she entertained, she was perfectly indifferent who the party was. She would display her accomplishments to a set of strolling Indians, or for Sam Lawson and Jake Marshall, as readily as for any one else. She would run up and catch the minister by the elbow as he solemnly and decorously moved down street, and his face always broke into a laugh at the sight of her.

The minister's lady, and Aunt Lois, and Miss Deborah Kittery, while they used to mourn in secret places over her want of decorum in thus displaying her talents before the lower classes, would afterward laugh till the tears rolled down their cheeks and their ancient whalebone stays creaked, when she would do the same thing over in a select circle for them.

We have seen how completely she had conquered Polly, and what difficulty Miss Mehitable found in applying the precepts of Mrs. Chapone and Miss Hannah More to her case. The pattern young lady of the period, in the eyes of all respectable females, was expressed by Lucilla Stanley, in "Cœlebs in Search of a Wife." But when Miss Mehitable, after delighting herself with the Johnsonian balance of the rhythmical sentences which described this paragon as "not so much perfectly beautiful as perfectly elegant,"—this model of consistency, who always blushed at the right moment, spoke at the right moment, and stopped at the right moment, and was, in short, a woman made to order, precisely to suit a bachelor who had traversed the whole earth, "not expecting perfection, but looking for consistency,"—when, after all these charming visions, she looked at Tina, she was perfectly dismayed at contemplating her scholar. She felt the power by which Tina continually charmed and beguiled her, and the empire which she exercised over her; and, with wonderful good sense, she formally laid down the weapons of authority when she found she had no heart to use them.

"My child," she said to her one day, when that young lady was about eleven years of age, "you are a great deal stronger than I. I am weak because I love you, and because I have been broken by sorrow, and because, being a poor old woman, I don't trust myself. And you are young and strong and fearless; but remember, dear, the life you have to live is yours and not mine. I have not the heart to force you to take my way instead of your own, but I shall warn you that it will be better you should do so, and then leave you free. If you don't take my way, I shall do the very best for you that I can in your way, and you must take the responsibility in the end."

This was the only kind of system which Miss Mehitable was capable of carrying out. She was wise, shrewd, and loving, and she gradually controlled her little charge more and more by simple influence, but she had to meet in her education the opposition force of that universal petting and spoiling which everybody in society gives to an entertaining child.

Life is such a monotonous, dull affair, that anybody who has the gift of making it pass off gayly is in great demand. Tina was sent for to the parsonage, and the minister took her on his knee and encouraged her to chatter all sorts of egregious nonsense to him. And Miss Deborah Kittery insisted on having her sent for to visit them in Boston, and old Madam Kittery overwhelmed her with indulgence and caresses. Now Tina loved praises and caresses; incense was the very breath of her nostrils; and she enjoyed being fêted and petted as much as a cat enjoys being stroked.

It will not be surprising to one who considers the career of this kind of girl to hear that she was not much of a student. What she learned was by impulses and fits and starts, and all of it immediately used for some specific purpose of entertainment, so that among simple people she had the reputation of being a prodigy of information, on a very small capital of actual knowledge. Miss Mehitable sighed after thorough knowledge and discipline of mind for her charge, but she invariably found all Tina's teachers becoming accomplices in her superficial practices by praising and caressing her when she had been least faithful, always apologizing for her deficiencies, and speaking in the most flattering terms of her talents. During the last year the schoolmaster had been observed always to walk home with her and bring her books, with a humble, trembling subserviency and prostrate humility which she rewarded with great apparent contempt; and finally she announced to Miss Mehitable that she "did n't intend to go to school any more, because the master acted so silly."

Now Miss Mehitable, during all her experience of life, had always associated with the men of her acquaintance without ever being reminded in any particular manner of the difference of sex, and it was a subject which, therefore, was about the last to enter into her calculations with regard to her little charge. So she said, "My dear, you should n't speak in that way about your teacher; he knows a great deal more than you do."

"He may know more than I do about arithmetic, but he does n't know how to behave. What right has he to put his old hand under my chin? and I won't have him putting his arm round me when he sets my copies! and I told him to-day he should n't carry my books home any more,—so there!"

Miss Mehitable was struck dumb. She went that afternoon and visited the minister's lady.

"Depend upon it, my dear," said Lady Lothrop, "it's time to try a course of home reading."

A bright idea now struck Miss Mehitable. Her cousin, Mr. Mordecai Rossiter, had recently been appointed a colleague with the venerable Dr. Lothrop. He was a young man, finely read, and of great solidity and piety, and Miss Mehitable resolved to invite him to take up his abode with them for the purpose of assisting her educational efforts. Mr. Mordecai Rossiter accordingly took up his abode in the family, used to conduct family worship, and was expected now and then to drop words of good advice and wholesome counsel to form the mind of Miss Tina. A daily hour was appointed during which he was to superintend her progress in arithmetic.

Mr. Mordecai Rossiter was one of the most simple-minded, honest, sincere human beings that ever wore a black coat. He accepted his charge in sacred simplicity, and took a prayerful view of his young catechumen, whom he was in hopes to make realize, by degrees, the native depravity of her own heart, and to lead through a gradual process to the best of all results.

Miss Tina also took a view of her instructor, and without any evil intentions, simply following her strongest instinct, which was to entertain and please, she very soon made herself an exceedingly delightful pupil. Since religion was evidently the engrossing subject in his mind, Tina also turned her attention to it, and instructed and edified him with flights of devout eloquence which were to him perfectly astonishing. Tina would discourse on the goodness of God, and ornament her remarks with so many flowers, and stars, and poetical fire-works, and be so rapt and carried away with her subject, that he would sit and listen to her as if she was an inspired being, and wholly forget the analysis which he meant to propose to her, as to whether her emotions of love to God proceeded from self-love or from disinterested benevolence.

As I have said, Tina had a genius for poetry, and had employed the dull hours which children of her age usually spend in church in reading the psalm-book and committing to memory all the most vividly emotional psalms and hymns. And these she was fond of repeating with great fervor and enthusiasm to her admiring listener.

Miss Mehitable considered that the schoolmaster had been an ill-taught, presumptuous man, who had ventured to take improper liberties with a mere child; but, when she established this connection between this same child and a solemn young minister, it never occurred to her to imagine that there would be any embarrassing consequences from the relation. She considered Tina as a mere infant, — as not yet having approached the age when the idea of anything like love or marriage could possibly be suggested to her.

In course of time, however, she could not help remarking that her cousin was in some respects quite an altered man. He reformed many little negligences in regard to his toilet which Miss Tina had pointed out to him with the nonchalant freedom of a young empress. And he would run and spring and fetch and carry in her service with a zeal and alertness quite wonderful to behold. He expressed privately to Miss Mehitable the utmost astonishment at her mental powers, and spoke of the wonderful work of divine grace which appeared to have made such progress in her heart. Never had he been so instructed and delighted before by the exercises of any young person. And he went so far as to assure Miss Mehitable that in many things he should be only too happy to sit at her feet and learn of her.

"Good gracious me!" said Miss Mehitable to herself, with a sort of half start of awakening, though not yet fully come to consciousness; "what does ail everybody that gets hold of Tina?"

What got hold of her cousin in this case she had an opportunity of learning, not long after, by overhearing him tell her young charge that she was an angel, and that he asked nothing more of Heaven than to be allowed to follow her lead through life. Now Miss Tina accepted this, as she did all other incense, with great satisfaction. Not that she had the slightest idea of taking this clumsy-footed theological follower round the world with her; but having the highest possible respect for him, knowing that Miss Mehitable and the minister and his wife thought him a person of consideration, she had felt it her duty to *please* him,—had taxed her powers of pleasing to the utmost, in his own line, and had met with this gratifying evidence of success.

Miss Mehitable was for once really angry. She sent for her cousin to a private interview, and thus addressed him:—

"Cousin Mordecai, I thought you were a man of sense when I put this child under your care! My great trouble in bringing her up is, that everybody flatters her and defers to her; but I thought that in you I had got a man that could be depended on!"

"I do *not* flatter her, cousin," replied the young minister, earnestly.

"You pretend you don't flatter her? did n't I hear you calling her an angel?"

"Well, I don't care if I did; she *is* an angel," said Mr. Mordecai Rossiter, with tears in his eyes; "she is the most perfectly heavenly being I ever saw!"

"Ah! bah!" said Miss Mehitable, with intense disgust; "what fools you men are!"

Miss Mehitable now, much as she disliked it, felt bound to have some cautionary conversation with Miss Tina.

"My dear," she said; "you must be very careful in your treatment of Cousin Mordecai. I overheard some things he said to you this morning which I do not approve of."

"O yes, Aunty, he does talk in a silly way sometimes. Men always begin to talk that way to me. Why, you 've no idea the things they will say. Well, of course I don't believe them; it 's only a foolish way they have, but they all talk just alike."

"But I thought my cousin would have had his mind on better things," said Miss Mehitable. "The idea of his making love to you!"

"I know it; only think of it, Aunty! how very funny it is! and there, I have n't done a single thing to make him. I 've been just as religious as I could be, and said hymns to him, and everything, and given him good advice,—ever so much,—because, you see, he did n't know about a great many things till I told him."

"But, my dear, all this is going to make him too fond of you; you know you ought not to be thinking of such things now."

"What things, Aunty?" said the catechumen, innocently.

"Why, love and marriage; that 's what such feelings will come to, if you encourage them."

"Marriage! O dear me, what nonsense!" and Tina laughed till the room rang again. "Why, dear Aunty, what absurd ideas have got into your head! Of course you can't think that he 's thinking of any such thing; he 's only getting very fond of me, and I 'm trying to make him have a good time,— that 's all."

But Miss Tina found that was not all, and was provoked beyond endurance at the question proposed to her in plain terms, whether she would not look upon her teacher as one destined in a year or two to become her husband. Thereupon at once the whole gay fabric dissolved like a dream. Tina was as vexed at the proposition as a young unbroken colt is at the sight of a halter. She cried, and said she did n't like him, she could n't bear him, and she never wanted to see him again,— that he was silly and ridiculous to talk so to a little girl. And Miss Mehitable sat down to write a long letter to her brother, to inquire what she should do next.

XXXI.

What Shall We Do with Tina?

"M Y DEAR BROTHER:—I am in a complete *embarras* what to do with Tina. She is the very light of my eyes,—the sweetest, gayest, brightest, and best-meaning little mortal that ever was made; but somehow or other I fear I am not the one that ought to have undertaken to bring her up.

"She has a good deal of self-will; so much that I have long felt it would be quite impossible for me to control her merely by authority. In fact I laid down my sceptre long ago, such as it was. I never did have much of a gift in that way. But Tina's self-will runs in the channel of a most charming persuasiveness. She has all sorts of pretty phrases, and would talk a bird off from a bush, or a trout out of a brook, by dint of sheer persistent eloquence; and she is always so delightfully certain that her way is the right one and the best for me and all concerned. Then she has no end of those peculiar gifts of entertainment which are rather dangerous things for a young woman. She is a born mimic, she is a natural actress, and she has always a repartee or a smart saying quite *apropos* at the tip of her tongue. All this makes her an immense favorite with people who have no responsibility about her,—who merely want to be amused with her drolleries, and then shake their heads wisely when she is gone, and say that Miss Mehitable Rossiter ought to keep a close hand on that girl.

"It seems to be the common understanding that everybody but me is to spoil her; for there is n't anybody, not even Dr. Lothrop and his wife, that won't connive at her mimicking and fripperies, and then talk gravely with me afterward about the danger of these things, as if I were the only person to say anything disagreeable to her. But then, I can see very plainly that the little chit is in danger on all sides of becoming trivial and superficial,—of mistaking wit for wisdom, and thinking she has answered an argument when she has said a smart thing and raised a laugh.

"Of late, trouble of another kind has been added. Tina is a little turned of fifteen; she is going to be very beautiful; she is very pretty now; and, in addition to all my other perplexities, the men are beginning to talk that atrocious kind of nonsense to her which they seem to think they must talk to young girls. I have had to take her away from the school on account of the schoolmaster, and when I put her under the care of Cousin Mordecai Rossiter, whom I thought old enough, and discreet enough, to make a useful teacher to her, he has acted like a natural fool. I have no kind of patience with him. I would not have believed a man could be so devoid of common sense. I shall have to send Tina somewhere,—though I can't bear to part with her, and it seems like taking the very sunshine out of the house; so I remember what you told me about sending her up to you.

"Lady Lothrop and Lois Badger and I have been talking together, and we think the boys might as well go up too to your academy, as our present schoolmaster is not very competent, and you will give them a thorough fitting for college."

To this came the following reply:—

"SISTER MEHITABLE:—The thing has happened that I have foreseen. Send her up here; she shall board in the minister's family; and his daughter Esther, who is wisest, virtuousest, discreetest, best, shall help keep her in order.

"Send the boys along, too; they are bright fellows, as I remember, and I would like to have a hand at them. One of them might live with us and do the out-door chores and help hoe in the garden, and the other might do the same for the minister. So send them along.

"Your affectionate brother,
"JONATHAN ROSSITER."

This was an era in our lives. Harry and I from this time felt ourselves to be *men*, and thereafter adopted the habit of speaking of ourselves familiarly as "a man of my character," "a man of my age," and "a man in my circumstances." The comfort and dignity which this imparted to us were wonderful. We also discussed Tina in a very paternal way, and gravely considered what was best for her. We were, of course, properly shocked at the behavior of the schoolmaster, and greatly applauded her spirit in defending herself against his presumption.

Then Tina had told Harry and me all about her trouble with the minister, and I remember at this time how extremely aged and venerable I felt, and what quantities of good advice I gave to Tina, which was all based on the supposition of her dangerously powerful charms and attractions. This is the edifying kind of counsel with which young gentlemen of my age instruct their lady friends, and it will be seen at once that advice and admonition which rest on the theory of superhuman excellence and attractions in the advised party are far more agreeable than the rough, common admonitions, generally addressed to boys at this time of life, which are unseasoned by any such pleasing hallucination.

There is now a general plea in society that women shall be educated more as men are, and we hear much talk as if the difference between them and our sex is merely one of difference in education. But how could it be helped that Tina should be educated and formed wholly unlike Harry and myself, when every address made to her from her childhood was of necessity wholly different from what would be made to a boy in the same circumstances? and particularly when she carried with her always that dizzying, blinding charm which turned the head of every boy and man that undertook to talk reason to her?

In my own mind I had formed my plan of life. I was to go to college, and therefrom soar to an unmeasured height of literary distinction, and when I had won trophies and laurels and renown, I was to come back and lay all at Tina's feet. This was what Harry and I agreed on, in many a conversation, as the destined result of our friendship.

Harry and I had sworn friendship by all the solemn oaths and forms known in ancient or modern history. We changed names with each other, and in our private notes and letters addressed each by the name of the other, and felt as if this was some sacred and wonderful peculiarity. Tina called us both brothers, and this we agreed was the best means of preserving her artless mind unalarmed and undisturbed until the future hour of the great declaration. As for Tina, she absolutely could not keep anything to herself if she tried. Whatever agitated her mind or interested it had to be told to us. She did not seem able to rest satisfied with herself till she had proved to us that she was exactly right, or made us share her triumphs in her achievements, or her perplexity in her failures.

At this crisis Miss Mehitable talked very seriously and sensibly with her little charge. She pointed out to her the danger of living a trivial and superficial life,—of becoming vain, and living merely for admiration. She showed her how deficient she had been in those attainments which require perseverance and steadiness of mind, and earnestly recommended her now to devote herself to serious studies.

Nobody was a better subject to preach such a sermon to than Tina. She would even take up the discourse and enlarge upon it, and suggest new and fanciful illustrations; she entered into the project of Miss Mehitable with enthusiasm; she confessed all her faults, and resolved hereafter to become a pattern of the contrary virtues. And then she came and related the whole conversation to us, and entered into the project of devoting herself to study with such a glow of enthusiasm, that we formed at once the most brilliant expectations.

The town of Cloudland, whither we were going, was a two days' journey up into the mountains; and, as travelling facilities then were, it was viewed as such an undertaking to send us there, that the whole family conclave talked gravely of it and discussed it in every point of view, for a fortnight before we started. Our Uncle Jacob, the good, meek, quiet farmer of whom I have spoken, had a little business in regard to some property that had been left by a relative of his wife in that place, and suggested the possibility of going up with us himself. So weighty a move was at first thrown out as a mere proposal to be talked of in the family circle. Grandmother and Aunt Lois and Aunt Keziah and my mother picked over and discussed this proposition for days, as a lot of hens will pick over an ear of corn, turning it from side to side, and looking at it from every possible point of view. Uncle Fliakim had serious thoughts of offering his well-worn equipage, but it was universally admitted that his constant charities had kept it in such a condition of frailty that the mountain roads would finish it, and thus deprive multitudes of the female population of Oldtown of an establishment which was about as much their own as if they had the care and keeping of it.

I don't know anybody who could have been taken from Oldtown whose loss would have been more universally felt and deplored than little Miss Tina's. In the first place, Oldtown had come into the way of regarding her as a sort of Child of the Regiment, and then Tina was one of those sociable, acquaintance-making bodies that have visited everybody, penetrated everybody's affairs, and given a friendly lift now and then in almost everybody's troubles.

"Why, lordy massy!" said Sam Lawson, "I don't know nothin' what we 're any on us goin' to do when Tiny 's gone. Why, there ain't a dog goes into the meetin'-house but wags his tail when he sees her a comin'. I expect she knows about every yellow-bird's nest an' blue jay's an' bobolink's an' meadow-lark's that there 's ben round here these five years, an' how they 's goin' to set an' hatch without her 's best known to 'emselves, I s'pose. Lordy massy! that child can sing so like a skunk blackbird that you can't tell which is which. Wal, I 'll say one thing for her; she draws the fire out o' Hepsy, an' she 's 'bout the only livin' critter that can; but some nights when she 's ben inter our house a playin' checkers or fox an' geese with the child'en, she 'd railly git Hepsy slicked down so that 't was kind o' comfortable bein' with her. I 'm sorry she 's goin', for my part, an' all the child'en 'll be sorry."

As for Polly, she worked night and day on Tina's outfit, and scolded and hectored herself for certain tears that now and then dropped on the white aprons that she was ironing. On the night before Tina was to depart, Polly came into her room and insisted upon endowing her with her string of gold beads, the only relic of earthly vanity in which that severe female had ever been known to indulge. Tina was quite melted, and fell upon her neck.

"Why, Polly! No, no; you dear old creature, you, you 've been a thousand times too good for me, and I 've nearly plagued the life out of you, and you sha' n't give me your poor, dear, old gold beads, but keep them yourself, for you 're as good as gold any day, and so it 's a great deal better that you should wear them."

"O Tina, child, you don't know my heart," said Polly, shaking her head solemnly; "if you could see the depths of depravity that there are there!"

"I don't believe a word of it, Polly."

"Ah! but, you see, the Lord seeth not as man sees, Tina."

"I know he don't," said Tina; "he 's a thousand times kinder, and makes a thousand more excuses for us than we ever do for ourselves or each other. You know the Bible says, 'He knoweth our frame, he remembereth that we are dust.' "

"O Tina, Tina, you always was a wonderful child to talk," said Polly, shaking her head doubtfully; "but then you know the heart is so deceitful, and then you see there 's the danger that we should mistake natural emotions for grace."

"O, I dare say there are all sorts of dangers," said Tina; "of course there are. I know I 'm nothing but just a poor little silly bird; but He knows it too, and he 's taken care of ever so many such little silly people as I am, so that I 'm not afraid. He won't let me deceive myself. You know, when that bird got shut in the house the other day, how much time you and I and Miss Mehitable all spent in trying to keep it from breaking its foolish head against the glass, and flying into the fire, and all that, and how glad we were when we got it safe out into the air. I 'm sure we are not half as good as God is, and, if we take so much care about a poor little bird that we did n't make and had nothing to do with, he must care a good deal more about us when we are his children. And God is all the Father I have or ever knew."

This certainly looked to Polly like very specious reasoning, but, after all, the faithful creature groaned in spirit. Might not this all be mere natural religion and not the supernatural grace? So she said trembling: "O Tina, did you always feel so towards God? wa' n't there a time when your heart rose in opposition to him?"

"O, certainly," said Tina, "when Miss Asphyxia used to talk to me about it, I thought I never wanted to hear of him, and I never said my prayers; but as soon as I came to Aunty, she was so loving and kind that I began to see what God must be like,—because I know he is kinder than she can be, or you, or anybody can be. That 's so, is n't it? You know the Bible says his loving-kindness is infinite."

The thing in this speech which gave Polly such peculiar satisfaction was the admission that there had been a definite point of time in which the feelings of her little friend had undergone a distinct change. Henceforth she was better satisfied,—never reflecting how much she was trusting to a mere state of mind in the child, instead of resting her faith on the Almighty Friend who so evidently had held her in charge during the whole of her short history.

As for me, the eve of my departure was to me one of triumph. When I had seen all my father's Latin books fairly stowed away in my trunk, with the very simple wardrobe which belonged to Harry and me, and the trunk had been shut and locked and corded, and we were to start at sunrise the next morning, I felt as if my father's unfulfilled life-desire was at last going to be accomplished in me.

It was a bright, clear, starlight night in June, and we were warned to go to bed early, that we might be ready in season the next morning. As usual, Harry fell fast asleep, and I was too nervous and excited to close my eyes. I began to think of the old phantasmagoria of my childish days, which now so seldom appeared to me. I felt stealing over me that peculiar thrill and vibration of the great central nerves which used to indicate the approach of those phenomena, and, looking up, I saw distinctly my father, exactly as I used to see him, standing between the door and the bed. It seemed to me that he entered by passing through the door, but there he was, every line and lineament of his face, every curl of his hair, exactly as I remembered it. His eyes were fixed on mine with a tender human radiance. There was something soft and compassionate about the look he gave me, and I felt it vibrating on my nerves with that peculiar electric thrill of which I have spoken. I learned by such interviews as these how spirits can communicate with one another without human language.

The appearance of my father was vivid and real even to the clothing that he used to wear, which was earthly and home-like, precisely as I remembered it. Yet I felt no disposition to address him, and no need of words. Gradually the image faded; it grew thinner and fainter, and I saw the door through it as if it had been a veil, and then it passed away entirely.

What are these apparitions? I know that this will be read by many who have seen them quite as plainly as I have, who, like me, have hushed back the memory of them into the most secret and silent chamber of their hearts.

I know, with regard to myself, that the sight of my father was accompanied by such a vivid conviction of the reality of his presence, such an assurance radiated from his serene eyes that he had at last found the secret of eternal peace, such an intense conviction of continued watchful affection and of sympathy in the course that I was now beginning, that I could not have doubted if I would. And when we remember that, from the beginning of the world, some such possible communication between departed love and the beloved on earth has been among the most cherished legends of humanity, why must we always meet such phenomena with a resolute determination to account for them by every or any supposition but that which the human heart most craves? Is not the great mystery of life and death made more cruel and inexorable by this rigid incredulity? One would fancy, to hear some moderns talk, that there was no possibility that the departed, even when most tender and most earnest, could, if they would, recall themselves to their earthly friends.

For my part, it was through some such experiences as these that I learned that there are truths of the spiritual life which are intuitive, and above logic, which a man must believe because he cannot help it,—just as he believes the facts of his daily experience in the world of matter, though most ingenious and unanswerable treatises have been written to show that there is no proof of its existence.

XXXII.

The Journey to Cloudland

THE next morning Aunt Lois rapped at our door, when there was the very faintest red streak in the east, and the birds were just in the midst of that vociferous singing which nobody knows anything about who is n't awake at this precise hour. We were forward enough to be up and dressed, and, before our breakfast was through, Uncle Jacob came to the door.

The agricultural population of Massachusetts, at this time, were a far more steady set as regards locomotion than they are in these days of railroads. At this time, a journey from Boston to New York took a fortnight, — a longer time than it now takes to go to Europe, — and my Uncle Jacob had never been even to Boston. In fact, the seven-mile tavern in the neighborhood had been the extent of his wanderings, and it was evident that he regarded the two days' journey as quite a solemn event in his life. He had given a fortnight's thought to it; he had arranged all his worldly affairs, and given charges and messages to his wife and children, in case, as he said, "anything should happen to him." And he informed Aunt Lois that he had been awake the biggest part of the night thinking it over. But when he had taken Tina and her little trunk on board, and we had finished all our hand-shakings, and Polly had told us over for the fourth or fifth time exactly where she had put the cold chicken and the biscuits and the cakes and pie, and Miss Mehitable had cautioned Tina again and again to put on her shawl in case a shower should come up, and my grandmother and Aunt Lois had put in their share of parting admonitions, we at last rolled off as cheery and merry a set of youngsters as the sun ever looked upon in a dewy June morning.

Our road lay first along the beautiful brown river, with its sweeping bends, and its prattling curves of water dashing and chattering over mossy rocks. Towards noon we began to find

ourselves winding up and up amid hemlock forests, whose
solemn shadows were all radiant and aglow with clouds of
blossoming laurel. We had long hills to wind up, when we
got out and walked, and gathered flowers, and scampered,
and chased the brook up stream from one little dashing water-
fall to another, and then, suddenly darting out upon the road
again, we would meet the wagon at the top of the hill.

Can there be anything on earth so beautiful as these mountain rides in New England? At any rate we were full in the
faith that there could not. When we were riding in the wagon, Tina's powers of entertainment were brought into full
play. The great success of the morning was her exact imitation
of a squirrel eating a nut, which she was requested to perform
many times, and which she did, with variations, until at last
Uncle Jacob remarked, with a grin, that "if he should meet
her and a squirrel sitting on a stone fence together, he believed he should n't know which was which."

Besides this, we acted various impromptu plays, assuming
characters and supporting them as we had been accustomed to
do in our theatrical rehearsals in the garret, till Uncle Jacob declared that he never did see such a musical set as we were. About
nightfall we came to Uncle Sim Geary's tavern, which had been
fixed upon for our stopping-place. This was neither more nor
less than a mountain farm-house, where the few travellers who
ever passed that way could find accommodation.

Uncle Jacob, after seeing to his horses, and partaking of a
plentiful supper, went immediately to bed, as was his innocent custom every evening, as speedily as possible. To bed,
but not to sleep, for when, an hour or two afterward, I had
occasion to go into his room, I found him lying on his bed
with his clothes on, his shoes merely slipped off, and his hat
held securely over the pit of his stomach.

"Why, Uncle Jacob," said I, "are n't you going to bed?"

"Well, I guess I 'll just lie down as I be; no knowin' what
may happen when you 're travelling. It 's a very nice house,
and a very respectable family, but it 's best always to be prepared for anything that may happen. So I think you children
had better all go to bed and keep quiet."

What roars of laughter there were among us when I described this scene and communicated the message of Uncle Jacob! It seemed as if Tina could not be got to sleep that night, and we could hear her giggling, through the board partition that separated our room from hers, every hour of the night.

Happy are the days when one can go to sleep and wake up laughing. The next morning, however, Uncle Jacob reaped the reward of his vigilance by finding himself ready dressed at six o'clock, when I came in and found him sleeping profoundly. The fact was, that, having kept awake till near morning, he was sounder asleep at this point of time than any of us, and was snoring away like a grist-mill. He remarked that he shouldn't wonder if he had dropped asleep, and added, in a solemn tone, "We've got through the night wonderfully, all things considered."

The next day's ride was the same thing over, only the hills were longer; and by and by we came into great vistas of mountains, whose cloudy purple heads seemed to stretch and veer around our path like the phantasmagoria of a dream. Sometimes the road seemed to come straight up against an impenetrable wall, and we would wonder what we were to do with it; but lo! as we approached, the old mountain seemed gracefully to slide aside, and open to us a passage round it. Tina found ever so many moralities and poetical images in these mountains. It was like life, she said. Your way would seem all shut up before you, but, if you only had faith and went on, the mountains would move aside for you and let you through.

Towards night we began to pull in earnest up a series of ascents toward the little village of Cloudland. Hill after hill, hill after hill, how long they seemed! but how beautiful it was when the sun went down over the distant valleys! and there was such a pomp and glory of golden clouds and rosy vapors wreathing around the old mountain-tops as one must go to Cloudland to know anything about.

At last we came to a little terrace of land, where were a white meeting-house, and a store, and two or three houses, and to the door of one of these our wagon drove. There stood Mr. Jonathan Rossiter and the minister and Esther.

You do not know Esther, do you? neither at this minute did we. We saw a tall, straight, graceful girl, who looked at us out of a pair of keen, clear, hazel eyes, with a sort of inquisitive yet not unkindly glance, but as if she meant to make up her mind about us; and when she looked at Tina I could see that her mind was made up in a moment.

LETTER FROM TINA TO MISS MEHITABLE.

"CLOUDLAND, June 6.

"Here we are, dear Aunty, up in the skies, in the most beautiful place that you can possibly conceive of. We had such a good time coming! you 've no idea of the fun we had. You know I am going to be very sober, but I didn't think it was necessary to begin while we were travelling, and we kept Uncle Jacob laughing so that I really think he must have been tired.

"Do you know, Aunty, I have got so that I can look exactly like a squirrel? We saw ever so many on the way, and I got a great many new hints on the subject, and now I can do squirrel in four or five different attitudes, and the boys almost killed themselves laughing.

"Harry is an old sly-boots. Do you know, he is just as much of a mimic as I am, for all he looks so sober; but when we get him a going he is perfectly killing. He and I and Horace acted all sorts of plays on the way. We agreed with each other that we 'd give a set of Oldtown representations, and see if Uncle Jacob would know who they were, and so Harry was Sam Lawson and I was Hepsy, and I made an unexceptionable baby out of our two shawls, and Horace was Uncle Fliakim come in to give us moral exhortations. I do wish you could hear how we did it. Uncle Jacob is n't the brightest of all mortals, and not very easily roused, but we made him laugh till he said his sides were sore; and to pay for it he made us laugh when we got to the tavern where we stopped all night. Do you believe, Aunty, Uncle Jacob really was frightened, or care-worn, or something, so that he hardly slept any all night? It was just the quietest place that ever you saw, and there was a good motherly woman, who got us the nicest kind of supper, and a peaceable, slow, dull old man, just like Uncle Jacob. There was n't the least thing that looked as if we had fallen into a cave of banditti, or a castle in the Apennines, such as Mrs. Radcliffe tells about in the Mysteries of Udolpho; but, for all that, Uncle Jacob's mind was so oppressed with care that he went to bed with all his clothes on, and lay broad awake with his hat in his hand all night. I did n't think before that Uncle Jacob had such a brilliant imagination. Poor man! I should have thought he would have lain down and slept as peaceably as one of his own oxen.

"We got up into Cloudland about half past six o'clock in the afternoon, the second day; and such a sunset! I thought of a good subject for a little poem, and wrote two or three verses, which I 'll send you some time; but I must tell you now about the people here.

"I don't doubt I shall become very good, for just think what a place I am in,—living at the minister's! and then I room with Esther! You ought to see Esther. She 's a beautiful girl; she 's tall, and straight, and graceful, with smooth black hair, and piercing dark eyes that look as if they could read your very soul. Her face has the features of a statue, at least such as I think some of the beautiful statues that I 've read about might have; and what makes it more statuesque is, that she 's so very pale; she is perfectly healthy, but there does n't seem to be any red blood in her cheeks; and, dear Aunty, she is alarmingly good. She knows so much, and does so much, that it is really discouraging to me to think of it. Why, do you know, she has read through Virgil, and is reading a Greek tragedy now with Mr. Rossiter; and she teaches a class in mathematics in school, besides being her father's only housekeeper, and taking care of her younger brothers.

"I should be frightened to death at so much goodness, if it were not that she seems to have taken the greatest possible fancy to me. As I told you, we room together; and such a nice room as it is! everything is just like wax; and she gave me half of everything,—half the drawers and half the closet, and put all my things so nicely in their places, and then in the morning she gets up at unheard-of hours, and she was beginning to pet me and tell me that I need n't get up. Now you know, Aunty, that 's just the way people are always doing with me, and the way poor dear old Polly would spoil me; but I told Esther all about my new resolutions and exactly how good I intended to be, and that I thought I could n't do better than to do everything that she did, and so when she gets up I get up; and really, Aunty, you 've no idea what a sight the sunrise is here in the mountains; it really is worth getting up for.

"We have breakfast at six o'clock, and then there are about three hours before school, and I help Esther wash up the breakfast things, and we make our bed and sweep our room, and put everything up nice, and then I have ever so long to study, while Esther is seeing to all her family cares and directing black Dinah about the dinner, and settling any little cases that may arise among her three younger brothers. They are great, strong, nice boys, with bright red cheeks, and a good capacity for making a noise, but she manages them nicely. Dear Aunty, I hope some of her virtues will rub off onto me by contact; don't you?

"I don't think your brother likes me much. He hardly noticed me at all when I was first presented to him, and seemed to have forgotten that he had ever seen me. I tried to talk to him, but he cut me quite short, and turned round and went to talking to Mr. Avery, the minister, you know. I think that these people that know so much might be civil to us little folks, but then I dare say it 's all right enough; but sometimes it does seem as if he wanted to snub me. Well, perhaps it 's good for me to be snubbed; I have such good times generally that I ought to have something that is n't quite so pleasant.

"Life is to me such a beautiful story! and every morning when I open my eyes and see things looking so charming as they do here, I thank God that I am alive.

"Mr. Rossiter has been examining the boys in their studies. He is n't a man that ever praises anybody, I suppose, but I can see that he is pretty well pleased with them. We have a lady principal, Miss Titcomb. She is about forty years old, I should think, and very pleasant and affable. I shall tell you more about these things by and by.

"Give my love to dear old Polly, and to grandma and Aunt Lois, and all the nice folks in Oldtown.

"Dear Aunty, sometimes I used to think that you were depressed, and had troubles that you did not tell me; and something you said once about your life being so wintry made me quite sad. Do let me be your little Spring, and think always how dearly I love you, and how good I am going to try to be for your sake.

"*Your own affectionate little*

"TINA."

XXXIII.

School-Life in Cloudland

THE academy in Cloudland was one of those pure wells from which the hidden strength of New England is drawn, as her broad rivers are made from hidden mountain brooks. The first object of every colony in New England, after building the church, was to establish a school-house; and a class of the most superior men of New England, in those days of simple living, were perfectly satisfied to make it the business of their lives to teach in the small country academies with which the nooks and hollows of New England were filled.

Could materials be got as profuse as Boswell's Life of Johnson to illustrate the daily life and table-talk of some of the academy schoolmasters of this period, it would be an acquisition for the world.

For that simple, pastoral germ-state of society is a thing forever gone. Never again shall we see that union of perfect repose in regard to outward surroundings and outward life with that intense activity of the inward and intellectual world, that made New England, at this time, the vigorous, germinating seed-bed for all that has since been developed of politics, laws, letters, and theology, through New England to America, and through America to the world. The hurry of railroads, and the rush and roar of business that now fill it, would have prevented that germinating process. It was necessary that there should be a period like that we describe, when villages were each a separate little democracy, shut off by rough roads and forests from the rest of the world, organized round the church and school as a common centre, and formed by the minister and the schoolmaster.

The academy of Cloudland had become celebrated in the neighborhood for the skill and ability with which it was conducted, and pupils had been drawn, even from as far as Boston, to come and sojourn in our mountain town to partake of these advantages. They were mostly young girls, who were boarded at very simple rates in the various families of the place. In all, the pupils of the academy numbered about a hundred, equally divided between the two sexes. There was a class of about fifteen young men who were preparing for college, and a greater number of boys who were studying with the same ultimate hope.

As a general rule, the country academies of Massachusetts have been equally open to both sexes. Andover and Exeter, so far as I know, formed the only exceptions to this rule, being by their charters confined rigorously to the use of the dominant sex. But, in the generality of country academies, the girls and boys studied side by side, without any other restriction as to the character of their studies than personal preference. As a general thing, the classics and the higher mathematics were more pursued by the boys than the girls. But if there were a daughter of Eve who wished, like her mother, to put forth her hand to the tree of knowledge, there was neither cherubim nor flaming sword to drive her away.

Mr. Rossiter was always stimulating the female part of his subjects to such undertakings, and the consequence was that in his school an unusual number devoted themselves to these pursuits, and the leading scholar in Greek and the higher mathematics was our new acquaintance, Esther Avery.

The female principal, Miss Titcomb, was a thorough-bred, old-fashioned lady, whose views of education were formed by Miss Hannah More, and whose style, like Miss Hannah More's, was profoundly Johnsonian. This lady had composed a set of rules for the conduct of the school, in the most ornate and resounding periods. The rules, briefly epitomized, required of us *only* absolute moral perfection, but they were run into details which caused the reading of them to take up about a quarter of an hour every Saturday morning. I would that I could remember some of the sentences. It was required of us all, for one thing, that we should be perfectly polite. "Persons truly polite," it was added, "invariably treat their superiors with reverence, their equals with exact consideration, and their inferiors with condescension." Again, under the head of manners, we were warned, "not to consider romping as indicative of sprightliness, or loud laughter a mark of wit."

The scene every Saturday morning, when these rules were

read to a set of young people on whom the mountain air acted like champagne, and among whom both romping and loud laughter were fearfully prevalent, was sufficiently edifying.

There was also a system of marks, quite complicated, by which our departure from any of these virtuous proprieties was indicated. After a while, however, the reciting of these rules, like the reading of the Ten Commandments in churches, and a great deal of other good substantial reading, came to be looked upon only as a Saturday morning decorum, and the Johnsonian periods, which we all knew by heart, were principally useful in pointing a joke. Nevertheless, we were not a badly behaved set of young people.

Miss Titcomb exercised a general supervision over the manners, morals, and health of the young ladies connected with the institution, taught history and geography, and also gave special attention to female accomplishments. These, so far as I could observe, consisted largely in embroidering mourning pieces, with a family monument in the centre, a green ground worked in chenille and floss silk, with an exuberant willow-tree, and a number of weeping mourners, whose faces were often concealed by flowing pocket-handkerchiefs.

Pastoral pieces were also in great favor, representing fair young shepherdesses sitting on green chenille banks, with crooks in their hands, and tending some animals of an uncertain description, which were to be received by faith as sheep. The sweet, confiding innocence which regarded the making of objects like these as more suited to the tender female character than the pursuit of Latin and mathematics, was characteristic of the ancient *régime*. Did not Penelope embroider, and all sorts of princesses, ancient and modern? and was not embroidery a true feminine grace? Even Esther Avery, though she found no time for works of this kind, looked upon it with respect, as an accomplishment for which nature unfortunately had not given her a taste.

Mr. Rossiter, although he of course would not infringe on the kingdom of his female associate, treated these accomplishments with a scarce concealed contempt. It was, perhaps, the frosty atmosphere of scepticism which he breathed about him touching those works of art, that prevented his favorite scholars from going far in the direction of such accomplishments. The fact is, that Mr. Rossiter, during the sailor period of his life, had been to the Mediterranean, had seen the churches of Spain and Italy, and knew what Murillos and Titians were like, which may account somewhat for the glances of civil amusement which he sometimes cast over into Miss Titcomb's department, when the adjuncts and accessories of a family tombstone were being eagerly discussed.

Mr. Jonathan Rossiter held us all by the sheer force of his personal character and will, just as the ancient mariner held the wedding guest with his glittering eye. He so utterly scorned and contemned a lazy scholar, that trifling and inefficiency in study were scorched and withered by the very breath of his nostrils. We were so awfully afraid of his opinion, we so hoped for his good word and so dreaded his contempt, and we so verily believed that no such man ever walked this earth, that he had only to shake his ambrosial locks and give the nod, to settle us all as to any matter whatever.

In an age when in England schools were managed by the grossest and most brutal exercise of corporal punishment, the schoolmasters of New England, to a great extent, had entirely dropped all resort to such barbarous measures, and carried on their schools as republics, by the sheer force of moral and intellectual influences. Mr. Jonathan Rossiter would have been ashamed of himself at even the suggestion of caning a boy,—as if he were incapable of any higher style of government. And yet never was a man more feared and his will had in more awful regard. Mr. Rossiter was sparing of praise, but his praise bore a value in proportion to its scarcity. It was like diamonds and rubies,—few could have it, but the whole of his little commonwealth were working for it.

He scorned all conventional rules in teaching, and he would not tolerate a mechanical lesson, and took delight in puzzling his pupils and breaking up all routine business by startling and unexpected questions and assertions. He compelled everyone to think, and to think for himself. "Your heads may not be the best in the world," was one of his sharp, off-hand sayings, "but they are the best God has given you, and you must use them for yourselves."

To tell the truth, he used his teaching somewhat as a mental gratification for himself. If there was a subject he wanted to investigate, or an old Greek or Latin author that he wanted to dig out, he would put a class on it, without the least regard to whether it was in the course of college preparation or not, and if a word was said by any poor mechanical body, he would blast out upon him with a sort of despotic scorn.

"Learn to read Greek perfectly," he said, "and it 's no matter what you read"; or, "Learn to use your own heads, and you can learn anything."

There was little idling and no shirking in his school, but a slow, dull, industrious fellow, if he showed a disposition to work steadily, got more notice from him than even a bright one.

Mr. Rossiter kept house by himself in a small cottage adjoining that of the minister. His housekeeper, Miss Minerva Randall, generally known to the village as "Miss Nervy Randall," was one of those preternaturally well-informed old mermaids who, so far as I know, are a peculiar product of the State of Maine. Study and work had been the two passions of her life, and in neither could she be excelled by man or woman. Single-handed, and without a servant, she performed all the labors of Mr. Jonathan Rossiter's little establishment. She washed for him, ironed for him, plaited his ruffled shirts in neatest folds, brushed his clothes, cooked his food, occasionally hoed in the garden, trained flowers around the house, and found, also, time to read Greek and Latin authors, and to work out problems in mathematics and surveying and navigation, and to take charge of boys in reading Virgil.

Miss Minerva Randall was one of those female persons who are of Sojourner Truth's opinion, — that if women want any rights they had better take them, and say nothing about it. Her *sex* had never occurred to her as a reason for doing or not doing anything which her hand found to do. In the earlier part of her life, for the mere love of roving and improving her mind by seeing foreign countries, she had gone on a Mediterranean voyage with her brother Zachariah Randall, who was wont to say of her that she was a better mate than any man he could find. And true enough, when he was confined to his berth with a fever, Miss Minerva not only nursed him, but navigated the ship home in the most matter-of-fact way in the world. She had no fol-de-rol about woman's rights, but she was always wide-awake to perceive when a thing was to be done, and to do it. Nor did she ever after in her life talk of this exploit as a thing to be boasted of, seeming to regard it as a matter too simple, and entirely in the natural course of things, to be mentioned. Miss Minerva, however, had not enough of the external illusive charms of her sex, to suggest to a casual spectator any doubt on that score of the propriety of her doing or not doing anything. Although she had not precisely the air of a man, she had very little of what usually suggests the associations of femininity. There was a sort of fishy quaintness about her that awakened grim ideas of some unknown ocean product,—a wild and withered appearance, like a wind-blown juniper on a sea promontory,—unsightly and stunted, yet not, after all, commonplace or vulgar. She was short, square, and broad, and the circumference of her waist was if anything greater where that of other females decreases. What the color of her hair might have been in days of youthful bloom was not apparent; but she had, when we knew her, thin tresses of a pepper-and-salt mixture of tint, combed tightly, and twisted in a very small nut on the back of her head, and fastened with a reddish-yellowish horn comb. Her small black eyes were overhung by a grizzled thicket of the same mixed color as her hair. For the graces of the toilet, Miss Nervy had no particular esteem. Her clothing and her person, as well as her housekeeping and belongings, were of a scrupulous and wholesome neatness; but the idea of any other beauty than that of utility had never suggested itself to her mind. She wore always a stuff petticoat of her own spinning, with a striped linen short gown, and probably in all her life never expended twenty dollars a year for clothing; and yet Miss Nervy was about the happiest female person whose acquaintance it has ever been my fortune to make. She had just as much as she wanted of exactly the two things she liked best in the world,—books and work, and when her work was done, there were the books, and life could give no more. Miss Nervy had no sentiment,—not a particle of romance,—she was the most perfectly contented mortal that could possibly be imagined. As to station and position, she

was as well known and highly respected in Cloudland as the
schoolmaster himself; she was one of the fixed facts of the
town, as much as the meeting-house. Days came and went,
and spring flowers and autumn leaves succeeded each other,
and boys and girls, like the spring flowers and autumn leaves,
came and went in Cloudland Academy, but there was always
Miss Nervy Randall, not a bit older, not a bit changed, doing
her spinning and her herb-drying, working over her butter
and plaiting Mr. Jonathan's ruffled shirts and teaching her
Virgil class. What gave a piquancy to Miss Nervy's discourse
was, that she always clung persistently to the racy Yankee dialect of her childhood, and when she was discoursing of Latin
and the classics the idioms made a droll mixture. She was the
most invariably good-natured of mortals, and helpful to the
last degree; and she would always stop her kitchen work, take
her hands out of the bread, or turn away from her yeast in a
critical moment, to show a puzzled boy the way through a
hard Latin sentence.

"Why, don't you know what that 'ere is?" she would say.
"That 'ere is part of the gerund in *dum*; you 've got to decline
it, and then you 'll find it. Look here!" she 'd say; "run that
'ere through the moods an' tenses, and ye 'll git it in the sub-
junctive"; or, "Massy, child! that 'ere is one o' the deponent
verbs. 'T ain't got any active form; them deponent verbs allus
does trouble boys till they git used to 'em."

Now these provincialisms might have excited the risibles of
so keen a set of grammarians as we were, only that Miss Randall was a dead shot in any case of difficulty presented by the
learned languages. No matter how her English phrased it, she
had taught so many boys that she knew every hard rub and
difficult stepping-stone and tight place in the Latin grammar
by heart, and had relief at her tongue's end for any distressed
beginner.

In the cottage over which Miss Randall presided, Harry
and I had our room, and we were boarded at the master's
table; and so far we were fortunate. Our apartment, which
was a roof-room of a gambrel-roofed cottage, was, to be sure,
unplastered and carpetless; but it looked out through the
boughs of a great apple-tree, up a most bewildering blue vista
of mountains, whence the sight of a sunset was something

forever to be remembered. All our physical appointments, though rustically plain, were kept by Miss Nervy in the utmost perfection of neatness. She had as great a passion for soap and sand as she had for Greek roots, and probably for the same reason. These wild sea-coast countries seemed to produce a sort of superfluity of energy which longed to wreak itself on something, and delighted in digging and delving mentally as well as physically.

Our table had a pastoral perfection in the articles of bread and butter, with honey furnished by Miss Minerva's bees, and game and fish brought in by the united woodcraft of the minister and Mr. Rossiter.

Mr. Rossiter pursued all the natural sciences with an industry and enthusiasm only possible to a man who lives in so lonely and retired a place as Cloudland, and who has, therefore, none of the thousand dissipations of time resulting from our modern system of intercommunication, which is fast producing a state of shallow and superficial knowledge. He had a ponderous herbarium, of some forty or fifty folios, of his own collection and arrangement, over which he gloated with affectionate pride. He had a fine mineralogical cabinet; and there was scarcely a ledge of rocks within a circuit of twelve miles that had not resounded to the tap of his stone hammer and furnished specimens for his collection; and he had an entomologic collection, where luckless bugs impaled on steel pins stuck in thin sheets of cork struggled away a melancholy existence, martyrs to the taste for science. The tender-hearted among us sometimes ventured a remonstrance in favor of these hapless beetles, but were silenced by the authoritative dictum of Mr. Rossiter. "Insects," he declared, "are unsusceptible of pain, the structure of their nervous organization forbidding the idea, and their spasmodic action being simply nervous contraction." As nobody has ever been inside of a beetle to certify to the contrary, and as the race have no mode of communication, we all found it comfortable to put implicit faith in Mr. Rossiter's statements till better advised.

It was among the awe-inspiring legends that were current of Mr. Rossiter in the school, that he corresponded with learned men in Norway and Sweden, Switzerland and France, to whom he sent specimens of American plants and minerals

and insects, receiving in return those of other countries. Even
in that remote day, little New England had her eyes and her
thoughts and her hands everywhere where ship could sail.

Mr. Rossiter dearly loved to talk and to teach, and out of
school-hours it was his delight to sit surrounded by his disciples, to answer their questions, and show them his herbarium
and his cabinet, to organize woodland tramps, and to start us
on researches similar to his own. It was fashionable in his
school to have private herbariums and cabinets, and before a
month was passed our garret-room began to look quite like a
grotto. In short, Mr. Rossiter's system resembled that of
those gardeners who, instead of bending all their energies toward making a handsome head to a young tree, encourage it
to burst out in suckers clear down to the root, bringing every
part of it into vigorous life and circulation.

I still remember the blessed old fellow, as he used to sit
among us on the steps of his house, in some of those resplendent moonlight nights which used to light up Cloudland like
a fairy dream. There he still sits, in memory, with his court
around him,—Esther, with the thoughtful shadows in her
eyes and the pensive Psyche profile, and Tina, ever restless,
changing, enthusiastic, Harry with his sly, reticent humor and
silent enjoyment, and he, our master, talking of everything
under the sun, past, present, and to come,—of the cathedrals
and pictures of Europe, describing those he had not seen apparently with as minute a knowledge as those he had,—of
plants and animals,—of the ancients and the moderns,—of
theology, metaphysics, grammar, rhetoric, or whatever came
uppermost,—always full and suggestive, startling us with par-
adoxes, provoking us to arguments, setting us out to run eager tilts of discussion with him, yet in all holding us in a state
of unmeasured admiration. Was he conscious, our great man
and master, of that weakness of his nature which made an
audience, and an admiring one, always a necessity to him? Of
a soul naturally self-distrustful and melancholy, he needed to
be constantly reinforced and built up in his own esteem by
the suffrage of others. What seemed the most trenchant self-
assertion in him was, after all, only the desperate struggles of
a drowning man to keep his head above water; and, though
he seemed at times to despise us all, our good opinion, our

worship and reverence, were the raft that kept him from sinking in despair.

The first few weeks that Tina was in school, it was evident that Mr. Rossiter considered her as a spoiled child of fortune, whom the world had conspired to injure by over-much petting. He appeared resolved at once to change the atmosphere and the diet. For some time in school it seemed as if she could do nothing to please him. He seemed determined to put her through a sort of Spartan drill, with hard work and small praise.

Tina had received from nature and womanhood that inspiration in dress and toilet attraction which led her always and instinctively to some little form of personal adornment. Every wild spray or fluttering vine in our woodland rambles seemed to suggest to her some caprice of ornamentation. Each day she had some new thing in her hair,—now a feathery fern-leaf, and anon some wild red berry, whose presence just where she placed it was as picturesque as a French lithograph; and we boys were in the habit of looking each day to see what she would wear next. One morning she came into school, fair as Ariadne, with her viny golden curls rippling over and around a crown of laurel-blossoms. She seemed to us like a little woodland poem. We all looked at her, and complimented her, and she received our compliments, as she always did coin of that sort, with the most undisguised and radiant satisfaction. Mr. Rossiter was in one of his most savage humors this morning, and eyed the pretty toilet grimly. "If you had only an equal talent for ornamenting the *inside* of your head," he said to her, "there might be some hopes of you."

Tears of mortification came into Tina's eyes, as she dashed the offending laurel-blossoms out of the window, and bent resolutely over her book. At recess-time she strolled out with me into the pine woods back of the school-house, and we sat down on a mossy log together, and I comforted her and took her part.

"I don't care, Horace," she said,—"I don't care!" and she dashed the tears out of her eyes. "I 'll *make* that man like me yet,—you see if I don't. He shall like me before I 'm done with him, so there! I don't care how much he scolds. I 'll give

in to him, and do exactly as he tells me, but I'll conquer
him,—you see if I don't."

And true enough Miss Tina from this time brushed her
curly hair straight as such rebellious curls possibly could be
brushed, and dressed herself as plainly as Esther, and went at
study as if her life depended on it. She took all Mr. Rossiter's
snubs and despiteful sayings with the most prostrate humility,
and now we began to learn, to our astonishment, what a
mind the little creature had. In all my experience of human
beings, I never saw one who learned so easily as she. It was
but a week or two after she began the Latin grammar before,
jumping over all the intermediate books, she alighted in a
class in Virgil among scholars who had been studying for a
year, and kept up with them, and in some respects stood
clearly as the first scholar. The *vim* with which the little puss
went at it, the zeal with which she turned over the big dictionary and whirled the leaves of the grammar, the almost inspiration which she showed in seizing the poetical shading of
words over which her more prosaic companions blundered,
were matters of never-ending astonishment and admiration to
Harry and myself. At the end of the first week she gravely
announced to us that she intended to render Virgil into English verse; and we had not the smallest doubt that she would
do it, and were so immensely wrought up about it that we
talked of it after we went to bed that night. Tina, in fact, had
produced quite a clever translation of the first ten lines of
"Arma virumque," &c. and we wondered what Mr. Rossiter
would say to it. One of us stepped in and laid it on his writing-desk.

"Which of you boys did this?" he said the next morning, in
not a disapproving tone.

There was a pause, and he slowly read the lines aloud.

"Pretty fair!" he said,—"pretty fair! I should n't be surprised if that boy should be able to write English one of these
days."

"If you please, sir," said I, "it 's Miss Tina Percival that
wrote that."

Tina's cheeks were red enough as he handed her back her
poetry.

"Not bad," he said,—"not bad; keep on as you 've begun, and you may come to something yet."

This scanty measure of approbation was interpreted as high praise, and we complimented Tina on her success. The project of making a poetical translation of Virgil, however, was not carried out, though every now and then she gave us little jets and spurts, which kept up our courage.

Bless me, how we did study everything in that school! English grammar, for instance. The whole school was divided into a certain number of classes, each under a leader, and at the close of every term came on a great examination, which was like a tournament or passage at arms in matters of the English language. To beat in this great contest of knowledge was what excited all our energies. Mr. Rossiter searched out the most difficult specimens of English literature for us to parse, and we were given to understand that he was laying up all the most abstruse problems of grammar to propound to us. All that might be raked out from the coarse print and the fine print of grammar was to be brought to bear on us; and the division that knew the most—the division that could not be puzzled by any subtlety, that had anticipated every possible question, and was prepared with an answer—would be the victorious division, and would be crowned with laurels as glorious in our eyes as those of the old Olympic games. For a week we talked, spoke, and dreamed of nothing but English grammar. Each division sat in solemn, mysterious conclave, afraid lest one of its mighty secrets of wisdom should possibly take wing and be plundered by some of the outlying scouts of another division.

We had for a subject Satan's address to the sun, in Milton, which in our private counsels we tore limb from limb with as little remorse as the anatomist dissects a once lovely human body.

The town doctor was a noted linguist and grammarian, and his son was contended for by all the divisions, as supposed to have access to the fountain of his father's wisdom on these subjects; and we were so happy in the balloting as to secure him for our side. Esther was our leader, and we were all in the same division, and our excitement was indescribable. We had also to manage a quotation from Otway, which I remember contained the clause, "Were the world on fire." To parse "on fire" was a problem which kept the eyes of the whole school waking. Each division had its theory, of which it spoke mysteriously in the presence of outsiders; but we had George Norton, and George had been in solemn consultation with Dr. Norton. Never shall I forget the excitement as he came rushing up to our house at nine o'clock at night with the last results of his father's analysis. We shut the doors and shut the windows,— for who knew what of the enemy might be listening?— and gathered breathlessly around him, while in a low, mysterious voice he unfolded to us how to parse "on fire." At that moment George Norton enjoyed the full pleasure of being a distinguished individual, if he never did before or after.

Mr. Rossiter all this while was like the Egyptian Sphinx, perfectly unfathomable, and severely resolved to sift and test us to the utmost.

Ah, well! to think of the glories of the day when our division beat!—for we did beat. We ran along neck and neck with Ben Baldwin's division, for Ben was an accomplished grammarian, and had picked up one or two recondite pieces of information wherewith he threatened for a time to turn our flank, but the fortunes of the field were reversed when it came to the phrase "on fire," and our success was complete and glorious. It was well to have this conflict over, for I don't believe that Tina slept one night that week without dreams of particles and prepositions,—Tina, who was as full of the enthusiasm of everything that was going on as a flossy evening cloud is of light, and to whose health I really do believe a defeat might have caused a serious injury.

Never shall I forget Esther, radiant, grave, and resolved, as she sat in the midst of her division through all the fluctuations of the contest. A little bright spot had come in each of her usually pale cheeks, and her eyes glowed with a fervor which showed that she had it in her to have defended a fortress, or served a cannon, like the Maid of Saragossa. We could not have felt more if our division had been our country and she had led us in triumph through a battle.

Besides grammar, we gave great attention to rhetoric. We

studied Dr. Blair with the same kind of thoroughness with which we studied the English grammar. Every week a division of the school was appointed to write compositions; but there was, besides, a call for volunteers, and Mr. Rossiter had a smile of approbation for those who volunteered to write every week; and so we were always among that number.

It was remarkable that the very best writers, as a general thing, were among the female part of the school. There were several young men, of nineteen and twenty years of age, whose education had been retarded by the necessity of earning for themselves the money which was to support them while preparing for college. They were not boys, they were men, and, generally speaking, men of fine minds and fine characters. Some of them have since risen to distinction, and acted leading parts at Washington. But, for all that, the best writers of the school, as I have before said, were the girls. Nor was the standard of writing low: Mr. Rossiter had the most withering scorn for ordinary sentimental nonsense and school-girl platitudes. If a bit of weakly poetry got running among the scholars, he was sure to come down upon it with such an absurd parody that nobody could ever recall it again without a laugh.

We wrote on such subjects as "The Difference between the Natural and Moral Sublime," "The Comparative Merits of Milton and Shakespeare," "The Comparative Merits of the Athenian and Lacedæmonian Systems of Education." Sometimes, also, we wrote criticisms. If, perchance, the master picked up some verbose Fourth of July oration, or some sophomorical newspaper declamation, he delivered it over to our tender mercies with as little remorse as a huntsman feels in throwing a dead fox to the dogs. Hard was the fate of any such composition thrown out to us. With what infinite zeal we attacked it! how we riddled and shook it! how we scoffed, and sneered, and jeered at it! how we exposed its limping metaphors, and hung up in triumph its deficient grammar! Such a sharp set of critics we became that our compositions, read to each other, went through something of an ordeal.

Tina, Harry, Esther, and I were a private composition club. Many an hour have we sat in the old school-room long after all the other scholars had gone, talking to one another of our literary schemes. We planned poems and tragedies; we planned romances that would have taken many volumes to write out; we planned arguments and discussions; we gravely criticised each other's style, and read morsels of projected compositions to one another.

It was characteristic of the simple, earnest fearlessness of those times in regard to all matters of opinion, that the hardest theological problems were sometimes given out as composition subjects, and we four children not unfrequently sat perched on the old high benches of the school-room during the fading twilight hours, and, like Milton's fallen angels,—

> "Reasoned high
> Of providence, foreknowledge, will, and fate;
> Fixed fate, free will, foreknowledge absolute, ...
> Of happiness and final misery."

Esther, Harry, and I were reading the "Prometheus Bound" with Mr. Rossiter. It was one of his literary diversions, into which he carried us; and the Calvinism of the old Greek tragedian mingling with the Calvinism of the pulpit and of modern New England life, formed a curious admixture in our thoughts.

Tina insisted on reading this with us, just as of old she insisted on being carried in a lady chair over to our woodland study in the island. She had begun Greek with great zeal under Mr. Rossiter, but of course was in no situation to venture upon any such heights; but she insisted upon always being with us when we were digging out our lesson, and in fact, when we were talking over doubtfully the meaning of a passage, would irradiate it with such a flood of happy conjecture as ought to have softened the stern facts of moods and tenses, and *made* itself the meaning. She rendered some parts of it into verse much better than any of us could have done it, and her versifications, laid on Mr. Rossiter's desk, called out a commendation that was no small triumph to her.

"My forte lies in picking knowledge out of other folks and using it," said Tina, joyously. "Out of the least bit of ore that you dig up, I can make no end of gold-leaf!" O Tina, Tina, you never spoke a truer word, and while you were with us you made everything glitter with your "no end of gold-leaf."

It may seem to some impossible that, at so early an age as ours, our minds should have striven with subjects such as have been indicated here; but let it be remembered that these problems are to every human individual a part of an unknown tragedy in which he is to play the role either of the conqueror or the victim. A ritualistic church, which places all souls under the guardianship of a priesthood, of course shuts all these doors of discussion so far as the individual is concerned. "The Church" is a great ship, where you have only to buy your ticket and pay for it, and the rest is none of your concern. But the New England system, as taught at this time, put on every human being the necessity of crossing the shoreless ocean alone on his own raft; and many a New England child of ten or twelve years of age, or even younger, has trembled at the possibilities of final election or reprobation.

I remember well that at one time the composition subject given out at school was, "Can the Benevolence of the Deity be proved by the Light of Nature?" Mr. Rossiter generally gave out the subject, and discussed it with the school in an animated conversation, stirring up all the thinking matter that there was among us by vigorous questions, and by arguing before us first on one side and then on the other, until our minds were strongly excited about it; and, when he had wrought up the whole school to an intense interest, he called for volunteers to write on either side. Many of these compositions were full of vigor and thought; two of those on the above-mentioned subject were very striking. Harry took the affirmative ground, and gave a statement of the argument, so lucid, and in language so beautiful, that it has remained fixed in my mind like a gem ever since. It was the statement of a nature harmonious and confiding, naturally prone to faith in goodness, harmonizing and presenting all those evidences of tenderness, mercy, and thoughtful care which are furnished in the workings of natural laws. The other composition was by Esther; it was on the other and darker side of the subject, and as perfect a match for it as the "Penseroso" to the "Allegro." It was condensed and logical, fearfully vigorous in conception and expression, and altogether a very melancholy piece of literature to have been conceived and written by a girl of her age. It spoke of that fearful law of existence by which the sins of parents who often themselves escape punishment are visited on the heads of innocent children, as a law which seems made specifically to protect and continue the existence of vice and disorder from generation to generation. It spoke of the apparent injustice of an arrangement by which human beings, in the very outset of their career in life, often inherit almost uncontrollable propensities to evil. The sorrows, the perplexities, the unregarded wants and aspirations, over which the unsympathetic laws of nature cut their way regardless of quivering nerve or muscle, were all bitterly dwelt upon. The sufferings of dumb animals, and of helpless infant children, apparently so useless and so needless, and certainly so undeserved, were also energetically mentioned. There was a bitter intensity in the style that was most painful. In short, the two compositions were two perfect pictures of the world and life as they appear to two classes of minds. I remember looking at Esther while her composition was read, and being struck with the expression of her face,—so pale, so calm, so almost hopeless,—its expression was very like despair. I remember that Harry noticed it as well as I, and when school was over he took a long and lonely ramble with her, and from that time a nearer intimacy arose between them.

Esther was one of those intense, silent, repressed women that have been a frequent outgrowth of New England society. Moral traits, like physical ones, often intensify themselves in course of descent, so that the child of a long line of pious ancestry may sometimes suffer from too fine a moral fibre, and become a victim to a species of morbid *spiritual ideality*.

Esther looked to me, from the first, less like a warm, breathing, impulsive woman, less like ordinary flesh and blood, than some half-spiritual organization, every particle of which was a thought.

Old Dr. Donne says of such a woman, "One might almost say her body thought"; and it often came in my mind when I watched the movements of intense yet repressed intellect and emotion in Esther's face.

With many New England women at this particular period,

when life was so retired and so cut off from outward sources of excitement, *thinking* grew to be a disease. The great subject of thought was, of course, theology; and woman's nature has never been consulted in theology. Theologic systems, as to the expression of their great body of ideas, have, as yet, been the work of man alone. They have had their origin, as in St. Augustine, with men who were utterly ignorant of moral and intellectual companionship with woman, looking on her only in her animal nature as a temptation and a snare. Consequently, when, as in this period of New England, the theology of Augustine began to be freely discussed by every individual in society, it was the women who found it hardest to tolerate or to assimilate it, and many a delicate and sensitive nature was utterly wrecked in the struggle.

Plato says somewhere that the only perfect human thinker and philosopher who will ever arise will be the MAN-WOMAN, or a human being who unites perfectly the nature of the two sexes. It was Esther's misfortune to have, to a certain degree, this very conformation. From a long line of reasoning, thinking, intellectual ancestry she had inherited all the strong logical faculties, and the tastes and inclinations for purely intellectual modes of viewing things, which are supposed to be more particularly the characteristic of man. From a line of saintly and tender women, half refined to angel in their nature, she had inherited exquisite moral perceptions, and all that flattering host of tremulous, half-spiritual, half-sensuous intuitions that lie in the borderland between the pure intellect and the animal nature. The consequence of all this was the internal strife of a divided nature. Her heart was always rebelling against the conclusions of her head. She was constantly being forced by one half of her nature to movements, inquiries, and reasonings which brought only torture to the other half.

Esther had no capacity for illusions; and in this respect her constitution was an unfortunate one.

Tina, for example, was one of those happily organized human beings in whom an intellectual proposition, fully assented to, might lie all her life dormant as the wheat-seed which remained thousands of years ungerminate in the wrappings of a mummy. She thought only of what she liked to think of; and a disagreeable or painful truth in her mind dropped at once out of sight,—it sank into the ground and roses grew over it.

Esther never could have made one of those clinging, submissive, parasitical wives who form the delight of song and story, and are supposed to be the peculiar gems of womanhood. It was her nature always to be obliged to see her friends clearly through the understanding, and to judge them by a refined and exquisite conscientiousness. A spot or stain on the honor of the most beloved could never have become invisible to her. She had none of that soft, blinding, social aura,—that blending, blue haze, such as softens the sharp outlines of an Italian landscape, and in life changes the hardness of reality into illusive and charming possibilities. Her clear, piercing hazel eyes seemed to pass over everything with a determination to know only and exactly the truth, hard and cold and unwelcome though it might be.

Yet there is no doubt that the warm, sunny, showery, rainbow nature of Tina acted as a constant and favorable alterative upon her. It was a daily living poem acting on the unused poetical and imaginative part of her own nature; for Esther had a suppressed vigor of imagination, and a passionate capability of emotion, stronger and more intense than that of Tina herself.

I remarked this to Harry, as we were talking about them one day. "Both have poetical natures," I said; "both are intense; but how different they are!"

"Yes," said Harry, "Tina's is electricity, and that snaps and sparkles and flashes; Esther's is galvanism, that comes in long, intense waves, and shakes and convulses; she both thinks and feels too much on all subjects."

"That was a very strange composition," I said.

"It is an unwholesome course of thought," said Harry, after thinking for a few moments with his head on his hands; "none but bitter berries grow on those bushes."

"But the reasoning was very striking," said I.

"Reasoning!" said Harry, impatiently; "we must trust the intuition of our hearts above reason. That is what I am trying to persuade Esther to do. To me it is an absolute demonstration, that God never could make a creature who would be *better* than himself. We must look at the noblest, best human beings. We must see what generosity, what tenderness, what magnanimity can be in man and woman, and believe all that and more in God. All that there is in the best fathers and best mothers *must* be in him."

"But the world's history does not look like this, as Mr. Rossiter was saying."

"We have not seen the world's history yet," said Harry. "What does this green aphide, crawling over this leaf, know of the universe?"

XXXIV.

Our Minister in Cloudland

THE picture of our life in Cloudland, and of the developing forces which were there brought to bear upon us, would be incomplete without the portrait of the minister.

Even during the course of my youth, the principles of democratic equality introduced and maintained in the American Revolution were greatly changing the social position and standing of the clergy. Ministers like Dr. Lothrop, noble men of the theocracy, men of the cocked hat, were beginning to pass away, or to appear among men only as venerable antiquities, and the present order of American citizen clergy was coming in.

Mr. Avery was a cheerful, busy, manly man, who posed himself among men as a companion and fellow-citizen, whose word on any subject was to go only so far as its own weight and momentum should carry it. His preaching was a striking contrast to the elegant Addisonian essays of Parson Lothrop. It was a vehement address to our intelligent and reasoning powers,—an address made telling by a back force of burning enthusiasm. Mr. Avery preached a vigorous system of mental philosophy in theology, which made our Sundays, on the whole, about as intense an intellectual drill as any of our week-days. If I could describe its character by any one word, I should call it *manly* preaching.

Every person has a key-note to his mind which determines all its various harmonies. The key-note of Mr. Avery's mind was "the free agency of man." Free agency was with him the universal solvent, the philosopher's stone in theology; every line of his sermons said to every human being, "You are free, and you are able." And the great object was to intensify to its highest point, in every human being, the sense of individual, personal responsibility.

Of course, as a Calvinist, he found food for abundant discourse in reconciling this absolute freedom of man with those declarations in the standards of the Church which assert the absolute government of God over all his creatures and all their actions. But the cheerfulness and vigor with which he drove and interpreted and hammered in the most contradictory statements, when they came in the way of his favorite ideas, was really quite inspiring.

During the year we had a whole course of systematic theology, beginning with the history of the introduction of moral evil, the fall of the angels, and the consequent fall of man and the work of redemption resulting therefrom. In the treatment of all these subjects, the theology and imagery of Milton figured so largely that one might receive the impression that Paradise Lost was part of the sacred canon.

Mr. Avery not only preached these things in the pulpit, but talked them out in his daily life. His system of theology was to him the vital breath of his being. His mind was always running upon it, and all nature was, in his sight, giving daily tributary illustrations to it. In his farming, gardening, hunting, or fishing, he was constantly finding new and graphic forms of presenting his favorite truths. The most abstract subject ceased to be abstract in his treatment of it, but became clothed upon with the homely, every-day similes of common life.

I have the image of the dear good man now, as I have seen him, seated on a hay-cart, mending a hoe-handle, and at the same moment vehemently explaining to an inquiring brother minister the exact way that Satan first came to fall, as illustrating how a perfectly holy mind can be tempted to sin. The familiarity that he showed with the celestial arcana,—the zeal with which he vindicated his Maker,—the perfect knowledge that he seemed to have of the strategic plans of the evil powers in the first great insurrection,—are traits strongly impressed on my memory. They seemed as vivid and as much a matter of course to his mind as if he had read them out of a weekly newspaper.

Mr. Avery indulged the fond supposition that he had solved the great problem of the origin of evil in a perfectly satisfactory manner. He was fond of the Socratic method, and would clench his reasoning in a series of questions, thus:—

"Has not God power to make any kind of thing he pleases?"

"Yes."

"Then he can make a kind of being incapable of being governed except by motive?"

"Yes."

"Then, when he has made that kind of being, he cannot govern them except by motive, can he?"

"No."

"Now if there is no motive in existence strong enough to govern them by, he cannot keep them from falling, can he?"

"No."

"You see then the necessity of moral evil: there must be experience of evil to work out motive."

The Calvinism of Mr. Avery, though sharp and well defined, was not dull, as abstractions often are, nor gloomy and fateful like that of Dr. Stern. It was permeated through and through by cheerfulness and hope.

Mr. Avery was one of the kind of men who have a passion for saving souls. If there is such a thing as apostolic succession, this passion is what it ought to consist in. It is what ought to come with the laying on of hands, if the laying on of hands is what it is sometimes claimed to be.

Mr. Avery was a firm believer in hell, but he believed also that nobody need go there, and he was determined, so far as he was concerned, that nobody should go there if he could help it. Such a tragedy as the loss of any one soul in his parish he could not and would not contemplate for a moment; and he had such a firm belief in the truths he preached, that he verily expected with them to save anybody that would listen to him.

Goethe says, "Blessed is the man who believes that he has an idea by which he may help his fellow-creatures." Mr. Avery was exactly that man. He had such faith in what he preached that he would have gone with it to Satan himself, could he have secured a dispassionate and unemployed hour, with a hope of bringing him round.

Generous and ardent in his social sympathies, Mr. Avery never could be brought to believe that any particular human being had finally perished. At every funeral he attended he contrived to see a ground for hope that the departed had found mercy. Even the slightest hints of repentance were magnified in his warm and hopeful mode of presentation. He has been known to suggest to a distracted mother, whose thoughtless boy had been suddenly killed by a fall from a horse, the possibilities of the merciful old couplet,—

> "Between the saddle and the ground,
>   Mercy was sought, and mercy found."

Like most of the New England ministers, Mr. Avery was a warm believer in the millennium. This millennium was the favorite recreation ground, solace, and pasture land, where the New England ministry fed their hopes and courage. Men of large hearts and warm benevolence, their theology would have filled them with gloom, were it not for this overplus of joy and peace to which human society on earth was in their view tending. Thousands of years, when the poor old earth should produce only a saintly race of perfected human beings, were to them some compensation for the darkness and losses of the great struggle.

Mr. Avery believed, not only that the millennium was coming, but that it was coming fast, and, in fact, was at the door. Every political and social change announced it. Our Revolution was a long step towards it, and the French Revolution, now in progress, was a part of that distress of nations which heralded it; and every month, when the Columbia Magazine brought in the news from Europe, Mr. Avery rushed over to Mr. Rossiter, and called him to come and hear how the thing was going.

Mr. Rossiter took upon himself that right which every free-born Yankee holds sacred,—the right of contravening his minister. Though, if he caught one of his boys swelling or ruffling with any opposing doctrine, he would scath and scorch the youngster with contemptuous irony, and teach him to comport himself modestly in talking of his betters, yet it was the employment of a great many of his leisure hours to run argumentative tilts against Mr. Avery. Sometimes, when we were sitting in our little garret window digging out the Greek lessons, such a war of voices and clangor of assertion

and contradiction would come up from among the tassels of
the corn, where the two were hoeing together in the garden,
as would have alarmed people less accustomed to the vigorous manners of both the friends.

"Now, Rossiter, that will never do. Your system would upset moral government entirely. Not an angel could be kept in
his place upon your supposition."

"It is not my supposition. I have n't got any supposition,
and I don't want any; but I was telling you that, if you must
have a theory of the universe, Origen's was a better one than
yours."

"And I say that Origen's system would upset everything,
and you ought to let it alone."

"I sha' n't let it alone!"

"Why, Rossiter, you will destroy responsibility, and annihilate all the motives of God's government."

"That 's just what you theologians always say. You think
the universe will go to pieces if we upset your pine-shingle
theology."

"Rossiter, you must be careful how you spread your ideas."

"I don't want to spread my ideas; I don't want to interfere
with your system. It 's the best thing you can make your people take, but you ought to know that no system is anything
more than human theory."

"It 's eternal truth."

"There 's truth in it, but it is n't eternal truth."

"It 's Bible."

"Part, and part Milton and Edwards, and part Mr. Avery."

Harry and I were like adopted sons in both families, and
the two expressed their minds about each other freely before
us. Mr. Avery would say: "The root of the matter is in Rossiter. I don't doubt that he 's a really regenerate man, but he
has a head that works strangely. We must wait for him, he 'll
come along by and by."

And Mr. Rossiter would say of Mr. Avery: "That 's a growing man, boys; he has n't made his terminal buds yet. Some
men make them quick, like lilac-bushes. They only grow a
little way and stop. And some grow all the season through,
like locust-trees. Avery is one of that sort: he 'll never be done
thinking and growing, particularly if he has me to fight him

on all hands. He'll grow into different opinions on a good many subjects, before he dies."

It was this implied liberty of growth—the liberty to think and to judge freely upon all subjects—that formed the great distinctive educational force of New England life, particularly in this period of my youth. Monarchy, aristocracy, and theocracy, with their peculiar trains of ideas, were passing away, and we were coming within the sweep of pure republican influences, in which the *individual* is *everything*. Mr. Avery's enthusiastic preaching of free agency and personal responsibility was more than an *individual impulse*. It was the voice of a man whose ideas were the reflection of a period in American history. While New England theology was made by loyal monarchists, it reflected monarchical ideas. The rights and immunities of divine sovereignty were its favorite topics. When, as now, the government was becoming settled in the hands of the common people, the freedom of the individual, his absolute power of choice, and the consequent reasonableness of the duties he owed to the Great Sovereign Authority, began to be the favorite subjects of the pulpit.

Mr. Avery's preaching was immensely popular. There were in Cloudland only about half a dozen families of any prestige as to ancestral standing or previous wealth and cultivation. The old aristocratic idea was represented only in the one street that went over Cloudland Hill, where was a series of wide, cool, roomy, elm-shadowed houses, set back in deep door-yards, and flanked with stately, well-tended gardens. The doctor, the lawyer, the sheriff of the county, the schoolmaster, and the minister, formed here a sort of nucleus; but outlying in all the hills and valleys round were the mountain and valley farmers. Their houses sat on high hills or sunk in deep valleys, and their flaming windows at morning and evening looked through the encircling belts of forest solitudes as if to say, "We are here, and we are a power." These hard-working farmers formed the body of Mr. Avery's congregation. Sunday morning, when the little bell pealed out its note of invitation loud and long over the forest-feathered hills, it seemed to evoke a caravan of thrifty, well-filled farm-wagons, which, punctual as the village-clock itself, came streaming from the east and west, the north and south. Past the parsonage they streamed, with the bright cheeks and fluttering ribbons of the girls, and the cheery, rubicund faces of children, and with the inevitable yellow dog of the family faithfully pattering in the rear. The audience that filled the rude old meeting-house every Sunday would have astonished the men who only rode through the village of a week-day. For this set of shrewd, toil-hardened, vigorous, full-blooded republicans I can think of no preaching more admirably adapted than Mr. Avery's. It was preaching that was on the move, as their minds were, and which was slowly shaping out and elaborating those new forms of doctrinal statement that inevitably grow out of new forms of society. Living, as these men did, a lonely, thoughtful, secluded life, without any of the thousand stimulants which railroads and magazine and newspaper literature cast into our existence, their two Sunday sermons were the great intellectual stimulus which kept their minds bright, and they were listened to with an intense interest of which the scattered and diversified state of modern society gives few examples. They felt the compliment of being talked to as if they were capable of understanding the very highest of subjects, and they liked it. Each hard, heroic nature flashed like a flint at the grand thought of a free agency with which not even their Maker would interfere. Their God himself asked to reign over them, not by force, but by the free, voluntary choice of their own hearts. "*Choose* you this day whom ye will serve. If the Lord be God, serve him, and if Baal be God, serve him," was a grand appeal, fit for freemen.

The reasoning on moral government, on the history of man,—the theories of the universe past, present, and to come,—opened to these men a grand Miltonic poem, in which their own otherwise commonplace lives shone with a solemn splendor. Without churches or cathedrals or physical accessories to quicken their poetic nature, their lives were redeemed only by this poetry of ideas.

Calvinism is much berated in our days, but let us look at the political, social, and materialistic progress of Calvinistic countries, and ask if the world is yet far enough along to dispense with it altogether. Look at Spain at this hour, and look back at New England at the time of which I write,—both having just finished a revolution, both feeling their way along the path of national independence,—and compare the Spanish peasantry with the yeomen of New England, such as made up Mr. Avery's congregation;—the one set made by reasoning, active-minded Calvinism, the other by pictures, statues, incense, architecture, and all the sentimental paraphernalia of ritualism.

If Spain had had not a single cathedral, if her Murillos had been all sunk in the sea, and if she had had, for a hundred years past, a set of schoolmasters and ministers working together as I have described Mr. Avery and Mr. Rossiter as working, would not Spain be infinitely better off for this life at least, whether there is any life to come or not? This is a point that I humbly present to the consideration of society.

Harry and I were often taken by Mr. Avery on his preaching tours to the distant farm parishes. There was a brown school-house in this valley, and a red school-house in that, and another on the hill, and so on for miles around, and Mr. Avery kept a constant stream of preaching going in one or other of these every evening. We liked these expeditions with him, because they were often excursions amid the wildest and most romantic of the mountain scenery, and we liked them furthermore because Mr. Avery was a man that made himself, for the time being, companionable to every creature of human shape that was with him.

With boys he was a boy,—a boy in the vigor of his animal life, his keen delight in riding, hunting, fishing. With farmers he was a farmer. Brought up on a farm, familiar during all his early days with its wholesome toils, he still had a farmer's eye and a farmer's estimates, and the working-people felt him bone of their bone, and flesh of their flesh. It used to be a saying among them, that, when Mr. Avery hoed more than usual in his potato-field, the Sunday sermon was sure to be better.

But the best sport of all was when some of Mr. Avery's preaching tours would lead up the course of a fine mountain trout-brook in the vicinity. Then sometimes Mr. Rossiter, Mr. Avery, Harry, and I would put our supper in our pockets, and start with the sun an hour or two high, designing to bring up at the red school-house, as the weekly notice phrased it, at "early candle-lighting."

A person who should accidentally meet Mr. Avery on one
of these tours, never having seen him before, might imagine
him to be a man who had never thought or dreamed of anything but catching trout all his days, he went into it with such
abandon. Eye, voice, hand, thought, feeling, all were concentrated on trout. He seemed to have the quick perception, the
rapid hand, and the noiseless foot of an Indian, and the fish
came to his hook as if drawn there by magic. So perfectly
absorbed was he that we would be obliged to jog his memory, and, in fact, often to drag him away by main force, when
the hour for the evening lecture arrived. Then our spoils
would be hid away among the bushes, and with wet feet he
would hurry in; but, once in, he was as completely absorbed
in his work of saving sinners as he had before been in his
temporal fishery. He argued, illustrated, stated, guarded, answered objections, looking the while from one hard, keen,
shrewd face to another, to see if he was being understood.
The phase of Calvinism shown in my grandmother's blue
book had naturally enough sowed through the minds of a
thoughtful community hosts of doubts and queries. A great
part of Mr. Avery's work was to remove these doubts by substituting more rational statements. It was essential that he
should feel that he had made a hit somewhere, said something
that answered a purpose in the minds of his hearers, and
helped them at least a step or two on their way.

After services were over, I think of him and Mr. Rossiter
cheerily arguing with and contradicting each other a little beyond us in the road, while Harry and I compared our own
notes behind. Arrived at the parsonage, there would be Tina
and Esther coming along the street to meet us. Tina full of
careless, open, gay enthusiasm, Esther with a shy and wistful
welcome, that said far less, and perhaps meant more. Then
our treasures were displayed and exulted over; the supper-
table was laid, and Mr. Avery, Mr. Rossiter, and we boys
applied ourselves to dressing our fish; and then Mr. Avery,
disdaining Dinah, and, in fact, all female supervision, presided himself over the frying-pan, and brought our woodland
captives on the table in a state worthy of a trout brook. It
should have comforted the very soul of a trout taken in our
snares to think how much was made of him, and how per-

fectly Mr. Avery respected his dignity, and did him justice
in his cookery.

We two boys were in fact domesticated as sons in the family. Although our boarding-place was with the master, we
were almost as much with the minister as if we had been of
his household. We worked in his garden, we came over and
sat with Esther and Tina. Our windows faced their windows,
so that in study hours we could call to one another backward
and forward, and tell where the lesson began, and what the
root of the verb was, or any other message that came into our
heads. Sometimes, of a still summer morning, while we were
gravely digging at our lessons, we would hear Esther in tones
of expostulation at some madcap impulse of Tina, and, looking across, would see her bursting out in some freak of droll
pantomimic performance, and then an immediate whirlwind
of gayety would seize us all. We would drop our dictionaries
and grammars, rush together, and have a general outbreak of
jollity.

In general, Tina was a most praiseworthy and zealous student, and these wild, sudden whisks of gayety seemed only
the escape-valves by which her suppressed spirits vented
themselves; but, when they came, they were perfectly irresistible. She devoted herself to Esther with that sympathetic adaptation which seemed to give her power over every nature.
She was interested in her housekeeping, in all its departments,
as if it had been her own glory and pride; and Tina was one
that took glory and pride in everything of her friends, as if it
had been her own. Esther had been left by the death of her
mother only the year before the mistress of the parsonage.
The great unspoken sorrow of this loss lay like a dark chasm
between her and her father, each striving to hide from the
other its depth and coldness by a brave cheerfulness.

Esther, strong as was her intellectual life, had that intense
sense of the worth of a well-ordered household, and of the
dignity of house-economies, which is characteristic of New
England women. Her conscientiousness pervaded every nook
and corner of her domestic duties with a beautiful perfection;
nor did she ever feel tempted to think that her fine mental
powers were a reason why these homely details should be
considered a slavery. Household cares are a drudgery only

when unpervaded by sentiment. When they are an offering of love, a ministry of care and devotion to the beloved, every detail has its interest.

There were certain grand festivals of a minister's family which fill a housekeeper's heart and hands, and in which all of us made common interest with her. The Association was a reunion when all the ministers of the county met together and spent a social day with the minister, dining together, and passing their time in brotherly converse, such as reading essays, comparing sermons, taking counsel with each other in all the varied ups and downs of their pastoral life. The Consociation was another meeting of the clergy, but embracing also with each minister a lay delegate, and thus uniting, not only the ministry, but the laymen of the county, in a general fraternal religious conference.

The first Association that Esther had to manage quite alone as sole mistress of the parsonage occurred while we were with her. Like most solemn festivals of New England, these seasons were announced under the domestic roof by great preparatory poundings and choppings, by manufacture, on a large scale, of cakes, pies, and provisions for the outer man; and at this time Harry, Tina, and I devoted all our energies, and made ourselves everywhere serviceable. We ran to the store on errands, we chopped mince for pies with a most virtuous pertinacity, we cut citron and stoned raisins, we helped put up curtains and set up bedsteads. We were all of us as resolved as Esther that the housekeeping of the little parsonage should be found without speck or flaw, and should reflect glory upon her youthful sovereignty.

Some power or other gilded and glorified these happy days,— for happy enough they were. What was it that made everything that we four did together so harmonious and so charming? "Friendship, only friendship," sang Tina, with silver tongue. "Such a *perfect* friendship," she remarked, "was *never* known except just in our particular case"; it exceeded all the classical records, all the annals, ancient and modern.

But what instinct or affinity in friendship made it a fact that when we four sat at table together, with our lessons before us, Harry somehow was always found on Esther's side? I used to notice it because his golden-brown mat of curls was such a contrast to the smooth, shining black satin bands of her hair as they bent together over the dictionary, and looked up innocently into each other's eyes, talking of verbs and adjectives and terminations, innocently conjugating "amo, amare" to each other. Was it friendship that made Esther's dark, clear eyes, instinctively look towards Harry for his opinion, when we were reading our compositions to one another? Was it friendship, that starry brightness that began to come in Harry's eyes, and made them seem darker and bluer and deeper, with a sort of mysterious meaning, when he looked at Esther? Was it friendship that seemed to make him feel taller, stronger, more manly, when he thought of her, and that always placed him at her hand when there was some household task that required a manly height or handiness? It was Harry and Esther together who put up the white curtains all through the parsonage that spring, that made it look so trim and comely for the ministers' meeting. Last year, Esther said, innocently, she had no one to help her, and the work tired her so. How happy, how busy, how bright they were as they measured and altered, and Harry, in boundless complacency, went up and down at her orders, and changed and altered and arranged, till her fastidious eye was satisfied, and every fold hung aright! It was Harry who took down and cleansed the family portraits, and hung them again, and balanced them so nicely; it was Harry who papered over a room where the walls had been disfigured by an accident, and it was Esther by him who cut the paper and trimmed the bordering and executed all her little sovereignties of taste and disposal by his obedient hands. And Tina and I at this time gathered green boughs and ground-pine for the vases, and made floral decorations without end, till the bare little parsonage looked like a woodland bower.

I have pleasant recollections of those ministers' meetings. Calvinistic doctrines, in their dry, abstract form, are, I confess, rather hard; but Calvinistic ministers, so far as I have ever had an opportunity to observe, are invariably a jolly set of fellows. In those early days the ministry had not yet felt the need of that generous decision which led them afterwards to forego all dangerous stimulants, as an example to their flock. A long green wooden case, full of tobacco-pipes and a quantity of papers of tobacco, used to be part of the hospitable stock prepared for the reception of the brethren. No less was there a quantity of spirituous liquor laid in. In those days its dispensation was regarded as one of the inevitable duties of hospitality. The New England ministry of this period were men full of interest. Each one was the intellectual centre of his own district, and supplied around him the stimulus which is now brought to bear through a thousand other sources. It was the minister who overlooked the school, who put parents upon the idea of giving their sons liberal educations. In poor districts the minister often practised medicine, and drew wills and deeds, thus supplying the place of both lawyer and doctor. Apart from their doctrinal theology, which was a constant source of intellectual activity to them, their secluded life led them to many forms of literary labor.

As a specimen of these, it is recorded of the Rev. Mr. Taylor of Westfield, that he took such delight in the writings of Origen, that, being unable to purchase them, he copied them in four quarto volumes, that he might have them for his own study. These are still in the possession of his descendants. Other instances of literary perseverance and devotion, equally curious, might be cited.

The lives that these men led were simple and tranquil. Almost all of them were practical farmers, preserving about them the fresh sympathies and interests of the soil, and laboring enough with their hands to keep their muscles in good order, and prevent indigestion. Mingling very little with the world, each one a sort of autocrat in his way, in his own district, and with an idea of stability and perpetuity in his office, which, in these days, does not belong to the position of a minister anywhere, these men developed many originalities and peculiarities of character, to which the simple state of society then allowed full scope. They were humorists,—like the mossy old apple-trees which each of them had in his orchard, bending this way and turning that, and throwing out their limbs with quaint twists and jerks, yet none the less acceptable, so long as the fruit they bore was sound and wholesome.

We have read of "Handkerchief Moody," who for some years persisted in always appearing among men with his face covered with a handkerchief,—an incident which Hawthorne has worked up in his weird manner into the story of "The Minister with the Black Veil."

Father Mills, of Torringford, was a gigantic man who used to appear in the pulpit in a full-bottomed white horse-hair wig. On the loss of a beloved wife, he laid aside his wig for a year, and appeared in the pulpit with his head tied up in a black handkerchief, representing to the good housewives of his parish that, as he always dressed in black, he could in no other way testify to his respect for his dear wife's memory; and this tribute was accepted by his parish with the same innocent simplicity with which it was rendered.

On the whole, the days which brought all the brother ministers to the parsonage were days of enlivenment to all us young people. They seemed to have such a hearty joy in their meeting, and to deliver themselves up to mirth and good-fellowship with such a free and hearty *abandon*, and the jokes and stories which they brought with them were chorused by such roars of merriment, as made us think a ministers' meeting the most joyous thing on earth.

I know that some say this jocund mirthfulness indicated a want of faith in the doctrines they taught. But do not you and I, honest friends, often profess our belief in things which it would take away our appetite and wither our strength to realize, but notwithstanding which we eat and drink and sleep joyously? You read in your morning paper that the city of so-and-so has been half submerged by an earthquake, and that after the earthquake came a fire and burnt the crushed inhabitants alive in the ruins of their dwellings. Nay, if you are an American, you may believe some such catastrophe to have happened on the Erie Railroad a day or two before, and that men, women, and children have been cooped up and burnt, in lingering agonies, in your own vicinity. And yet, though you believe these things, you laugh and talk and are gay, and plan for a party in the evening and a ride on the same road the next week.

No; man was mercifully made with the power of ignoring what he believes. It is all that makes existence in a life like this tolerable. And our ministers, conscious of doing the very best they can to keep the world straight, must be allowed

their laugh and joke, sin and Satan to the contrary notwithstanding.

There was only one brother, in the whole confraternity that
used to meet at Mr. Avery's, who was not a married man;
and he, in spite of all the snares and temptations which must
beset a minister who guides a female flock of parishioners,
had come to the afternoon of life in the state of bachelorhood. But O the jokes and witticisms which always set the
room in a roar at his expense! It was a subject that never
wearied or grew old. To clap Brother Boardman on the back
and inquire for Mrs. Boardman,—to joke him about some
suitable widow, or bright-eyed young lamb of his flock, at
each ministers' meeting,—was a provocative of mirth ever
fresh and ever young. But the undaunted old bachelor was
always a match for these attacks, and had his rejoinder ready
to fling back into the camp of the married men. He was a
model of gallant devotion to womanhood in the abstract, and
seemed loath to give up to one what was meant for womankind. So, the last that I ever heard of him, he was still
unmarried,—a most unheard-of thing for a New England
parson.

Mr. Avery was a leader among the clergy of his State. His
zeal, enthusiasm, eloquence, and doctrinal vigor, added to a
capacity for forming an indefinite number of personal friendships, made him a sort of chief among them.

What joyous hours they spent together in the ins and the
outs, the highways and by-ways, of metaphysics and theology! Harry and Esther and Tina and I learned them all. We
knew all about the Arminians and Pelagians and the Tasters
and the Exercisers, and made a deal of fun with each other
over it in our private hours. We knew precisely every shade
of difference between tweedle-dum and tweedle-dee which
the different metaphysicians had invented, and tossed our
knowledge joyously back and forward at one another in our
gayer hours, just as the old ministers did, when they smoked
and argued in the great parsonage dining-room. Everything
is joyful that is learned by two young men in company
with two young women with whom they are secretly in
love. Mathematics, metaphysics, or no matter what of dry

and desolate, buds and blossoms as the rose under such circumstances.

Did you ever go out in the misty gray of morning dawn, when the stars had not yet shut their eyes, and still there were rosy bands lying across the east? And then have you watched a trellis of morning-glories, with all the buds asleep, but ready in one hour to waken? The first kiss of sunlight and they will be open! That was just where we were.

XXXV.

The Revival of Religion

N o New England boy or girl comes to maturity without a full understanding of what is meant by the term at the head of this chapter.

Religion was, perhaps, never so much the governing idea in any Commonwealth before. Nowhere has there been a people, the mass of whom acted more uniformly on considerations drawn from the unseen and future life; yet nowhere a people who paid a more earnest attention to the life that is seen and temporal.

The New England colonies were, in the first instance, the outgrowth of a religious enthusiasm. Right alongside of them, at the same period of time, other colonies were founded from a religious enthusiasm quite as intense and sincere. The French missionary settlers in Canada had a grandeur of self-sacrifice, an intensity of religious devotion, which would almost throw in the shade that of the Pilgrim Fathers; and the sole reason why one set of colonists proved the seed of a great nation, and the other attained so very limited success, is the difference between the religions taught by the two.

The one was the religion of asceticism, in view of which contempt of the body and of material good was taught as a virtue, and its teachers were men and women to whom marriage and its earthly relations were forbidden. The other was the spirit of the Old Testament, in which material prosperity is always spoken of as the lawful reward of piety, in which marriage is an honor, and a numerous posterity a thing to be desired. Our forefathers were, in many essential respects, Jews in their thoughts and feelings with regard to this life, but they superadded to this broad physical basis the intense spiritualism of the New Testament. Hence came a peculiar race of men, uniting the utmost extremes of the material and the spiritual.

Dr. Franklin represents that outgrowth of the New England mind which moves in the material alone, and scarcely ever rises to the spiritual. President Edwards represents the mind so risen to the spiritual as scarcely to touch the material. Put these two together, and you have the average New England character,—that land in which every *ism* of social or religious life has had its origin,—that land whose hills and valleys are one blaze and buzz of material and manufacturing production.

A revival of religion in New England meant a time when that deep spiritual undercurrent of thought and emotion with regard to the future life, which was always flowing quietly under its intense material industries, exhaled and steamed up into an atmosphere which pervaded all things, and made itself for a few weeks the only thought of every person in some town or village or city. It was the always-existing spiritual becoming visible and tangible.

Such periods would come in the labors of ministers like Mr. Avery. When a man of powerful mind and shrewd tact and great natural eloquence lives among a people already thoughtfully predisposed, for no other purpose than to stir them up to the care of their souls, it is evident that there will come times when the results of all his care and seeking, his public ministrations, his private conversations with individuals, will come out in some marked social form; and such a period in New England is called a revival of religion.

There were three or four weeks in the autumn of the first year that we spent in Cloudland, in which there was pervading the town a sort of subdued hush of emotions,—a quiet sense of something like a spiritual presence brooding through the mild autumn air. This was accompanied by a general inclination to attend religious services, and to converse on religious subjects. It pervaded the school; it was to be heard at the store. Every kind of individual talked on and about religion in his own characteristic way, and in a small mountain town like Cloudland everybody's characteristic way is known to every one else.

Ezekiel Scranton, the atheist of the parish, haunted the store where the farmers tied up their wagons when they brought their produce, and held, after his way, excited theological arguments with Deacon Phineas Simons, who kept the store,—arguments to which the academy boys sometimes listened, and of which they brought astounding reports to the school-room.

Tina, who was so intensely sympathetic with all social influences that she scarcely seemed to have an individuality of her own, was now glowing like a luminous cloud with religious zeal.

"I could convert that man," she said; "I know I could! I wonder Mr. Avery has n't converted him long ago!"

At this time, Mr. Avery, who had always kept a watchful eye upon us, had a special conversation with Harry and myself, the object of which was to place us right in our great foundation relations. Mr. Avery stood upon the basis that most good New England men, since Jonathan Edwards, have adopted, and regarded all young people, as a matter of course, out of the fold of the Church, and devoid of anything truly acceptable to God, until they had passed through a mental process designated, in well-known language, as conviction and conversion.

He began to address Harry, therefore, upon this supposition. I well remember the conversation.

"My son," he said, "is it not time for you to think seriously of giving your heart to God?"

"I have given my heart to God," replied Harry, calmly.

"Indeed!" said Mr. Avery, with surprise; "when did that take place?"

"I have always done it."

Mr. Avery looked at him with a gentle surprise.

"Do you mean to say, my son, that you have always loved God?"

"Yes, sir," said Harry, quietly.

Mr. Avery felt entirely incredulous, and supposed that this must be one of those specious forms of natural piety spoken of depreciatingly by Jonathan Edwards, who relates in his own memoirs similar exercises of early devotion as the mere fruits of the ungrafted natural heart. Mr. Avery, therefore, proceeded to put many theological questions to Harry on the nature of sin and holiness, on the difference between manly, natural affections and emotions, and those excited by the supernatural movement of a divine power on the soul,—the good man begging him to remember the danger of self-deception, saying that nothing was more common than for young people to mistake the transient movements of mere natural emotions for real religion.

I observed that Harry, after a few moments, became violently agitated. Two large blue veins upon his forehead swelled out, his eyes had that peculiar flash and fire that they had at rare intervals, when some thought penetrated through the usual gentle quietude of his surface life to its deepest internal recesses. He rose and walked up and down the room, and finally spoke in a thick, husky voice, as one who pants with emotion. He was one of the most reserved human beings I have ever known. There was a region of emotion deep within him, which it was almost like death to him to express. There is something piteous and even fearful in the convulsions by which such natures disclose what is nearest to their hearts.

"Mr. Avery," he said, "I have heard your preaching ever since I have been here, and thought of it all. It has done me good, because it has made me think deeply. It is right and proper that our minds should be forced to think on all these subjects; but I have not thought, and cannot think, exactly like you, nor exactly like any one that I know of. I must make up my opinions for myself. I suppose I am peculiar, but I have been brought up peculiarly. My lot in life has been very different from that of ordinary boys. The first ten years of my life, all that I can remember is the constant fear and pain and distress and mortification and want through which my mother and I passed together,—she a stranger in this strange land,—her husband and my father worse than nothing to us, oftentimes our greatest terror. We should both of us have died, if it had not been for one thing: she believed that her Saviour loved her, and loved us all. She told me that these sorrows were from him,—that he permitted them because he loved us,—that they would be for good in the end. She died at last alone and utterly forsaken by everybody but her Saviour, and yet her death was blessed. I saw it in her eyes, and she left it as her last message to me, whatever happened to me, *never to doubt God's love*,—in all my life to trust him, to seek his counsel in all things, and to believe that all that hap-

pened to me was ordered by him. This was and is my religion; and, after all that I have heard, I can have no other. I
do love God because he is good, and because he has been
good to me. I believe that Jesus Christ is God, and I worship
God always through him, and I leave everything for myself,
for life and death are in his hands. I know that I am not very
good. I know, as you say, I am liable to make mistakes, and
to deceive myself in a thousand ways; but *He* knows all
things, and he can and will teach me; he will not let me lose
myself, I feel sure."

"My son," said Mr. Avery, "you are blessed. I thank God
with all my heart for you. Go on, and God be with you!"

It is to be seen that Mr. Avery was a man who always corrected theory by common sense. When he perceived that a
child could be trained up a Christian, and grow into the love
of a Heavenly Father as he grows into the love of an earthly
one, by a daily and hourly experience of goodness, he yielded
to the perceptions of his mind in that particular case.

Of course our little circle of four had, at this time, deep
communings. Tina was buoyant and joyous, full of poetic images, delighted with the news of every conversion, and taking
such an interest in Mr. Avery's preaching that she several
times suggested to him capital subjects for sermons. She
walked up to Ezekiel Scranton's, one afternoon, for no other
object than to convert him from his atheism, and succeeded
so far as to exact a promise from him that he would attend all
Mr. Avery's meetings for a fortnight. Ezekiel was one of the
converts of that revival, and Harry and I, of course, ascribed
it largely to Tina's influence.

A rough old New England farmer, living on the windy side
of a high hill, subsisting largely on codfish and hard cider,
does not often win the flattering attention of any little specimen of humanity like Tina; and therefore it was not to be
wondered at that the results of her missionary zeal appeared
to his mind something like that recorded in the New Testament, where "an angel went down at a certain season and
troubled the waters."

But, while Tina was thus buoyant and joyous, Esther
seemed to sink into the very depths of despondency. Hers, as
I have already intimated, was one of those delicate and sensi-

tive natures, on which the moral excitements of New England acted all the while with too much power. The work and care of a faithful pastor are always complicated by the fact that those truths, and modes of presenting truths, which are only just sufficient to arouse the attention of certain classes of hearers, and to prevent their sinking into apathetic materialism, are altogether too stimulating and exciting for others of a more delicate structure.

Esther Avery was one of those persons for whom the peculiar theory of religious training which prevailed in New England at this period, however invigorating to the intellect of the masses, might be considered as a personal misfortune. Had she been educated in the tender and paternal manner recommended by the Cambridge platform, and practised among the earlier Puritans, recognized from infancy as a member of Christ's Church, and in tender covenant relations with him, her whole being would have responded to such an appeal; her strongest leading faculties would have engaged her to fulfil, in the most perfect manner, the sacred duties growing out of that relation, and her course into the full communion of the Church would have been gentle and insensible as a flowing river.

"'T is a tyranny," says old Dr. Cotton Mather, "to impose upon every man a record of the precise time and way of their conversion to God. Few that have been restrained by a religious education can give such an one."

Esther, however, had been trained to expect a marked and decided period of conversion,—a change that could be described in the same language in which Paul described the conversion of the heathen at dissolute Corinth and Ephesus. She was told, as early as she was capable of understanding language, that she was by nature in a state of alienation from God, in which every thought of her heart and action of her life was evil, and evil only; and continually that she was entirely destitute of holiness, and exposed momently to the wrath of God; and that it was her immediate duty to escape from this state by an act of penitence for sin and supreme love to God.

The effort to bring about in her heart that state of emotion was during all her youth a failure. She was by constitution delicately, intensely self-analytic, and her analysis was guided by the most exacting moral ideality. Every hopeful emotion of her higher nature, as it rose, was dissolved in this keen analysis, as diamond and pearls disappeared in the smelting furnaces of the old alchemists. We all know that self-scrutiny is the death of emotion, and that the analytic, self-inspective habit is its sure preventive. Had Esther applied to her feelings for her own beloved father the same tests by which she tried every rising emotion of love to the Divine Being, the result would have been precisely the same.

Esther was now nineteen years of age; she was the idol of her father's heart; she was the staff and stay of her family; she was, in all the duties of life, inspired by a most faultless conscientiousness. Her love of the absolute right was almost painful in its excess of minuteness, and yet, in her own view, in the view of the Church, in the view even of her admiring and loving father, she was no Christian. Perfectly faultless in every relation so far as human beings could observe, reverent to God, submissive to his will, careful in all outward religious observances, yet wanting in a certain emotional experience, she judged herself to be, and was judged to be by the theology which her father taught, utterly devoid of virtue or moral excellence of any kind in the sight of God. The theology of the times also taught her that the act of grace which should put an end to this state, and place her in the relation of a forgiven child with her Heavenly Father, was a voluntary one, momently in her power, and that nothing but her own persistent refusal prevented her performing it; yet taught at the same time that, so desperate was the obstinacy of the human heart, no child of Adam ever would, or ever could, perform it without a special interposition of God,—an interposition which might or might not come. Thus all the responsibility and the guilt rested upon her. Now, when a nature intensely conscientious is constantly oppressed by a sense of unperformed duty, that sense becomes a gnawing worm at the very root of life. Esther had in vain striven to bring herself into the required state of emotion. Often for weeks and months she offered daily, and many times a day, prayers which brought no brightness and no relief, and read conscientiously that Bible, all whose tender words and comforting promises were like the distant vision of Eden to the fallen exiles, guarded by a flaming sword which turned every way. Mute and mournful she looked into the paradise of peace possessed by the favored ones whom God had chosen to help through the mysterious passage, and asked herself, would that helping hand ever open the gate to her?

Esther had passed through two or three periods of revival of religion, and seen others far less consistent gathered into the fold of the Church, while she only sunk at each period into a state of hopeless gloom and despondency which threatened her health. Latterly, her mind, wounded and bruised, had begun to turn in bitter reactions. From such experiences as hers come floods of distracting intellectual questions. Scepticism and doubt are the direct children of unhappiness. If she had been, as her standards stated, born "utterly indisposed, disabled, and made opposite to all good, and wholly inclined to all evil," was not this an excuse for sin? Was it *her* fault that she was born so? and, if her Creator had brought her into being in this state, was it not an act of simple justice to restore her mind to a normal condition?

When she addressed these questions to her father, he was alarmed, and warned her against speculation. Mr. Avery did not consider that the Assembly's catechism and the Cambridge platform and a great part of his own preaching were, after all, but human speculation,—the uninspired *inferences* of men from the Bible, and not the Bible itself,—and that minds once set going in this direction often cannot help a third question after a second, any more than they can help breathing; and that third question may be one for which neither God nor nature has an answer. Such inquiries as Esther's never arose from reading the parables of Christ, the Sermon on the Mount: they are the legitimate children of mere human attempts at systematic theology.

How to deliver a soul that has come from excessive harassments, introspections, self-analysis, into that morbid state of half-sceptical despondency, was a problem over which Mr. Avery sighed in vain. His cheerful hopefulness, his sympathetic vitality, had drawn many others through darkness into light, and settled them in cheerful hope. But with his own daughter he felt no power,—his heart trembled,—his hand was weak as the surgeon's who cannot operate when it is the life of his best beloved that lies under his hands.

Esther's deliverance came through that greatest and holiest of all the natural sacraments and means of grace,—LOVE.

An ancient gem has upon it a figure of a Psyche sitting with bound wings and blindfolded and weeping, whose bonds are being sundered by Love. It is an emblem of what often occurs in woman's life.

It has sometimes been thrown out as a sneer on periods of religious excitement, that they kindle the enthusiasm of man and woman towards each other into earthly attachments; but the sneer should wither as something satanic before the purity of love as it comes to noble natures. The man who has learned to think meanly of *that*, to associate it with vulgar thoughts and low desires,—the man who has not been lifted by love to aspire after unworldly excellence, to sigh for unworldly purity, to reverence unworldly good,—has lost his one great chance of regeneration.

Harry and Esther had moved side by side for months, drawn daily to each other,—showing each other their compositions, studying out of the same book, arguing together in constant friendly differences,—and yet neither of them exactly conscious whither they were tending. A great social, religious excitement has often this result, that it throws open between friends the doors of the inner nature. How long, how long we may live in the same house, sit at the same table, hold daily converse, with friends to whom and by whom these inner doors are closed! We cannot even tell whether we should love them more or less if they were open,—they are a mystery. But a great, pure, pervading, social excitement breaks like some early spring day around us; the sun shines, the birds sing; and forthwith open fly all the doors and windows, and let in the sunshine and the breeze and the bird-song!

In such an hour Esther saw that she was beloved!—beloved by a poet soul,—one of that rare order to whom the love of woman is a religion!—a baptism!—a consecration!

Her life, hitherto so chill and colorless, so imprisoned and bound in the chains of mere and cold intellect, awoke with a sudden thrill of consciousness to a new and passionate life. She was as changed as the poor and silent Jungfrau of the

Swiss mountains, when the gray and ghostly cold of the night bursts into rosy light, as the morning sunbeams rise upon it. The most auspicious and beautiful of all phenomena that ever diversify this weary life is that wonderful moment in which two souls, who hitherto have not known each other, suddenly, by the lifting of a veil or the falling of a barrier, become in one moment and forever after one. Henceforth each soul has in itself the double riches of the other. Each weakness is made strong by some corresponding strength in the other; for the truest union is where each soul has precisely the faculty which the other needs.

Harry was by nature and habit exactly the reverse of Esther. His conclusions were all intuitions. His religion was an emanation from the heart, a child of personal experience, and not a formula of the head. In him was seen the beginning of that great *reaction* which took place largely in the young mind of New England against the tyranny of mere logical methods as applied to the ascertaining of moral truths.

The hour of full heart union that made them one placed her mind under the control of his. His simple faith in God's love was an antidote to her despondent fears. His mind bore hers along on its current. His imagination awakened hers. She was like one carried away by a winged spirit, lifted up and borne heavenward by his faith and love. She was a transfigured being. An atmosphere of joy brightened and breathed around her; her eyes had a mysterious depth, her cheeks a fluttering color. The winter was over and past for her, and the time of the singing of birds had come.

Mr. Avery was in raptures. The long agony was past. He had gained a daughter and a son, and he was too joyful, too willing to believe, to be analytic or critical. Long had he secretly hoped that such faultless consistency, such strict attention to duty, might perhaps indicate a secret work of divine grace, which would spring into joy if only recognized and believed in. But now, when the dove that had long wandered actually bent her white wings at the window of the ark, he stretched forth his hand and drew her in with a trembling eagerness.

XXXVI.

After the Revival

B UT the revival could not always last. The briefness of
these periods, and the inevitable gravitation of everybody back to the things of earth, has sometimes been mentioned with a sneer.

"Where's your revival now?"

The deacon whose face was so radiant as he talked of the
love of Christ now sits with the same face drawn into knots
and puckers over his account-book; and he thinks the money
for the mortgage is due, and the avails for the little country
store are small; and somehow a great family of boys and girls
eat up and wear out; and the love of Christ seems a great way
off, and the trouble about the mortgage very close at hand;
and so the deacon is cross, and the world has its ready sneer
for the poor man. "He can talk about the love of Christ, but
he's a terrible screw at a bargain," they say. Ah, brother, have
mercy! the world screws us, and then we are tempted to screw
the world. The soil is hard, the climate cold, labor incessant,
little to come of it, and can you sneer that a poor soul has,
for a brief season, forgotten all this and risen out of his body
and above his cares, and been for a little while a glorified
deacon instead of a poor, haggling, country store-keeper?

Plato says that we all once had wings, and that they still
tend to grow out in us, and that our burnings and aspirations
for higher things are like the teething pangs of children. We
are trying to cut our wings. Let us not despise these teething
seasons. Though the wings do not become apparent, they
may be starting under many a rough coat, and on many a
clumsy pair of shoulders.

But in our little town of Cloudland, after the heavenly
breeze had blown over, there were to be found here and there
immortal flowers and leaves from the tree of life, which had
blown into many a dwelling.

Poor old drunken Culver, who lived under the hill, and was

said to beat his wife, had become a changed man, and used to come out to weekly prayer-meetings. Some tough old family quarrels, such as follow the settlement of wills in a poor country, had at least been brought to an end, and brother had shaken hands with brother: the long root of bitterness had been pulled up and burned on the altar of love. It is true that nobody had become an angel. Poor sharp-tongued Miss Krissy Pike still went on reporting the wasteful excesses she had seen in the minister's swill-barrel. And some that were crabbed and cross-grained before were so still, and some, perhaps, were a little more snarly than usual, on account of the late over-excitement.

A revival of religion merely makes manifest for a time what religion there is in a community, but it does not exalt men above their nature or above their times. It is neither revelation nor inspiration; it is impulse. It gives no new faculties, and it goes at last into that general average of influences which go to make up the progress of a generation.

One terrestrial result of the revival in our academy was that about half a dozen of the boys fell desperately in love with Tina. I have always fancied Tina to be one of that species of womankind that used to be sought out for priestesses to the Delphic oracle. She had a flame-like, impulsive, ethereal temperament, a capacity for sudden inspirations, in which she was carried out of herself, and spoke winged words that made one wonder whence they came. Her religious zeal had impelled her to be the adviser of every one who came near her, and her sayings were quoted, and some of our shaggy, rough-coated mountain boys thought that they had never had an idea of the beauty of holiness before. Poor boys! they were so sacredly simple about it. And Tina came to me with wide brown eyes that sparkled like a cairngorm-stone, and told me that she believed she had found what her peculiar calling was: it was to influence young men in religion! She cited, with enthusiasm, the wonderful results she had been able to produce, the sceptical doubts she had removed, the conceptions of heavenly things that she had been able to pour into their souls.

The divine priestess and I had a grand quarrel one day, because I insisted upon it that these religious ministrations on the part of a beautiful young girl to those of the opposite sex would assuredly end in declarations of love and hopes of marriage.

Girls like Tina are often censured as flirts,—most unjustly so, too. Their unawakened nature gives them no power of perceiving what must be the full extent of their influence over the opposite sex. Tina was warmly social; she was enthusiastic and self-confident, and had precisely that spirit which should fit a woman to be priestess or prophetess, to inspire and to lead. She had a magnetic fervor of nature, an attractive force that warmed in her cheeks and sparkled in her eyes, and seemed to make summer around her. She excited the higher faculties,—poetry, ideality, blissful dreams seemed to be her atmosphere,—and she had a power of quick sympathy, of genuine, spontaneous outburst, that gave to her looks and words almost the value of a caress, so that she was an unconscious deceiver, and seemed always to say more for the individual than she really meant. All men are lovers of sunshine and spring gales, but they are no one's in particular; and he who seeks to hold them to one heart finds his mistake. Like all others who have a given faculty, Tina loved its exercise,— she loved to influence, loved to feel her power, alike, over man and woman. But who does not know that the power of the sibyl is doubled by the opposition of sex? That which is only acquiescence in a woman friend becomes devotion in a man. That which is admiration from a woman becomes adoration in a man. And of all kinds of power which can be possessed by man or woman, there is none which I think so absolutely intoxicating as this of personal fascination. You may as well blame a bird for wanting to soar and sing as blame such women for the instinctive pleasure they feel in their peculiar kind of empire. Yet, in simple good faith, Tina did not want her friends of the other sex to become lovers. She was willing enough that they should devote themselves, under all sorts of illusive names of brother and friend and what-not, but when they proceeded to ask her for herself there was an instant revulsion, as when some person has unguardedly touched a strong electric circle. The first breath of passion repelled her; the friend that had been so agreeable the hour before was unendurable. Over and over again have I seen her go the same illusive round, always sure that in this instance it was understood that it was to be friendship, and only friendship, or brotherly or Christian love, till the hour came for the electric revulsion, and the friend was lost.

Tina had not learned the modern way of girls, who count their lovers and offers as an Indian does his scalps, and parade the number of their victims before their acquaintances. Every incident of this kind struck her as a catastrophe; and, as Esther, Harry, and I were always warning her, she would come to us like a guilty child, and seek to extenuate her offence. I think the girl was sincere in the wish she often uttered, that she could be a boy, and be loved as a comrade and friend only. "Why must, why would, they always persist in falling into this tiresome result?" "O Horace!" she would say to me, "if I were only Tom Percival, I should be perfectly happy! but it is so stupid to be a girl!"

In my own secret soul I had no kind of wish that she should be Tom Percival, but I did not tell her so. No, I was too wise for that. I knew that my only chance of keeping my position as father-confessor to this elastic young penitent consisted in a judicious suppression of all peculiar claims or hopes on my part, and I was often praised and encouraged for this exemplary conduct, and the question pathetically put to me, "Why could n't the others do as I did?" O Tina, Tina! did your brown eyes see, and your quick senses divine, that there was something in me which you dreaded to awaken, and feared to meet?

There are some men who have a faculty of making themselves the confidants of women. Perhaps because they have a certain amount of the feminine element in their own composition. They seem to be able to sympathize with them on their feminine side, and are capable of running far in a friendship without running fatally into love.

I think I had this power, and on it I founded my hopes in this regard. I enjoyed, in my way, almost as much celebrity in our little circle for advising and guiding my friends of the other sex as Tina did, and I took care to have on hand such a list of intimates as would prevent my name from being coupled with hers in the school gossip.

In these modern times, when man's fair sister is asking ad-

mission at the doors of classic halls, where man has hitherto
reigned in monastic solitude, the query is often raised by our
modern sociologists, Can man and woman, with propriety,
pursue their studies together? Does the great mystery of sex,
with its wide laws of attraction, and its strange, blinding, dazzling influences, furnish a sufficient reason why the two halves
of creation, made for each other, should be kept during the
whole course of education rigorously apart? This question,
like a great many others, was solved without discussion by
the good sense of our Puritan ancestors, in throwing the
country academies, where young men were fitted for college,
open alike to both sexes, and in making the work of education of such dignity in the eyes of the community, that first-
rate men were willing to adopt it for life. The consequences
were, that, in some lonely mountain town, under some brilliant schoolmaster, young men and women actually were
studying together the branches usually pursued in college.

"But," says the modern objector, "bring young men and
young women together in these relations, and there will be
flirtations and love affairs."

Even so, my friend, there will be. But flirtations and love
affairs among a nice set of girls and boys, in a pure and simple
state of community, where love is never thought of, except as
leading to lawful marriage, are certainly not the worst things
that can be thought of,—not half so bad as the grossness and
coarseness and roughness and rudeness of those wholly male
schools in which boys fight their way on alone, with no humanizing influences from the other sex.

There was, to be sure, a great crop of love affairs, always
green and vigorous, in our academy, and vows of eternal constancy interchanged between boys and girls who afterwards
forgot and outgrew them, without breaking their hearts on
either side; but, for my own part, I think love-making over
one's Latin and Greek much better than the fisting and cuff-
ing and fagging of English schools, or than many another
thing to which poor, blindly fermenting boyhood runs when
separated from home, mother, and sister, and confined to an
atmosphere and surroundings sharply and purely male. It is
certain that the companionship of the girl improves the boy,
but more doubt has been expressed whether the delicacy of

womanhood is not impaired by an early experience of the flatteries and gallantries of the other sex. But, after all, it is no worse for a girl to coquette and flirt in her Latin and mathematical class than to do it in the German or the polka. The studies and drill of the school have a certain repressive influence, wholly wanting in the ball-room and under the gas-light of fashionable parties. In a good school, the standard of attraction is, to some extent, intellectual. The girl is valued for something besides her person; her disposition and character are thoroughly tested, the powers of her mind go for something, and, what is more, she is known in her every-day clothes. On the whole, I do not think a better way can be found to bring the two sexes together, without that false glamour which obscures their knowledge of each other, than to put them side by side in the daily drill of a good literary institution.

Certainly, of all the days that I look back upon, this academy life in Cloudland was the most perfectly happy. It was happier than college life, because of the constant intertwining and companionship with woman, which gave a domestic and family charm to it. It was happy because we were in the first flush of belief in ourselves, and in life.

O that first belief! those incredible first visions! when all things look possible, and one believes in the pot of gold at the end of the rainbow, and sees enchanted palaces in the sunset clouds!

What faith we had in one another, and how wonderful we were in one another's eyes! Our little clique of four was a sort of holy of holies in our view. We believed that we had secrets of happiness and progress known only to ourselves. We had full faith in one another's destiny; we were all remarkable people, and destined to do great things.

At the close of the revival, we four, with many others, joined Mr. Avery's church,—a step which in New England, at this time, meant a conviction of some spiritual experience gained, of some familiar communion with the Great Invisible. Had I found it then? Had I laid hold of that invisible hand, and felt its warmth and reality? Had I heard the beatings of a warm heart under the cold exterior of the regular laws of nature, and found a living God? I thought so. That hand and heart were the hand and heart of Jesus,—the brother, the friend, and the interpreting God for poor, blind, and helpless man.

As we stood together before the pulpit, with about fifty others, on that Sunday most joyful to Mr. Avery's heart, we made our religious profession with ardent sincerity. The dear man found in that day the reward of all his sorrows, and the fruit of all his labors. He rejoiced in us as first fruits of the millennium, which, having already dawned in his good honest heart, he thought could not be far off from the earth.

Ah! those days of young religion were vaguely and ignorantly beautiful, like all the rest of our outlook on life. We were sincere, and meant to be very good and true and pure, and we knew so little of the world we were living in! The village of Cloudland, without a pauper, with scarcely an ignorant person in it, with no temptation, no dissipation, no vice,—what could we know there of the appalling questions of real life? We were hid there together, as in the hollow of God's hand; and a very sweet and lovely hiding-place it was.

Harry had already chosen his profession; he was to be a clergyman, and study with Mr. Avery when his college course was finished. In those days the young aspirants for the pulpit were not gathered into seminaries, but distributed through the country, studying, writing, and learning the pastoral work by sharing the labors of older pastors. Life looked, therefore, very bright to Harry, for life was, at that age, to live with Esther. Worldly care there was none. Mr. Avery was rich on two hundred and fifty dollars, and there were other places in the mountains where birds sung and flowers grew, where Esther could manage another parsonage, as now her father's. She lived in the world of taste and intellect and thought. Her love of the beautiful was fed by the cheap delights of nature, and there was no onerous burden of care in looking forward to marriage, such as now besets a young man when he meditates taking to himself some costly piece of modern luxury,— some exotic bird, who must be fed on incense and odors, and for whom any number of gilded cages and costly surroundings may be necessary. Marriage, in the days of which I speak, was a very simple and natural affair, and Harry and Esther enjoyed the full pleasure of talking over and arranging what their future home should be; and Tina, quite as interested as they, drew wonderful pictures of it, and tinted them with every hue of the rainbow.

Mr. Avery talked with me many times to induce me to choose the same profession. He was an enthusiast for it; it was to him a calling that eclipsed all others, and he could wish the man he loved no greater blessedness than to make him a minister.

But I felt within myself a shrinking doubt of my own ability to be the moral guide of others, and my life-long habit of half-sceptical contemplation made it so impossible to believe the New England theology with the perfect, undoubting faith that Mr. Avery had, that I dared not undertake. I did not disbelieve. I would not for the world controvert; but I could not believe with his undoubting enthusiasm. His sword and spear, so effective in his hands, would tremble in mine. I knew that Harry would do something. He had a natural call, a divine impulse, that led him from childhood to sacred ministries; and though he did not more than I accept the system of new-school theology as complete truth, yet I could see that it would furnish to his own devotional nature a stock from which vigorous grafts would shoot forth.

Shall I say, also, that my future was swayed unconsciously by a sort of instinctive perception of what yet might be desired by Tina? Something a little more of this world I seemed to want to lay at her feet. I felt, somehow, that there was in her an aptitude for the perfume and brightness and gayeties of this lower world. And as there must be, not only clergymen, but lawyers, and as men will pay more for getting their own will than for saving their souls, I dreamed of myself, in the future, as a lawyer,—of course a rising one; of course I should win laurels at the bar, and win them by honorable means. I *would* do it; and Tina should be mistress of a fine, antique house in Boston, like the Kitterys', with fair, large gardens and pleasant prospects, and she should glitter and burn and twinkle like a gem, in the very front ranks of society. Yes, I was ambitious, but it was for her.

One thing troubled me: every once in a while, in the letters from Miss Mehitable, came one from Ellery Davenport, written in a free, gay, dashing, cavalier style, and addressing Tina

with a kind of patronizing freedom that made me ineffably
angry. I wanted to shoot him. Such are the risings of the
ancient Adam in us, even after we have joined the Church.
Tina always laughed at me because I scolded and frowned at
these letters, and, I thought, seemed to take rather a perverse
pleasure in them. I have often speculated on that trait wherein
lovely woman slightly resembles a cat; she cannot, for the life
of her, resist the temptation to play with her mouse a little,
and rouse it with gentle pats of her velvet paw, just to see
what it will do.

I was, of course, understood to be under solemn bond and
promise to love Tina only as a brother; but was it not a
brother's duty to watch over his sister? With what satisfaction
did I remember all Miss Debby Kittery's philippics against
Ellery Davenport! Did I not believe every word of them heartily? I hated the French language with all my soul, and Ellery
Davenport's proficiency in it; and Tina could not make me
more angry than by speaking with admiration of his graceful
fluency in French, and expressing rather wilful determinations
that, when she got away from Mr. Rossiter's dictation, she
would study it. Mr. Davenport had said that, when he came
back to America, he would give her French lessons. He was
always kind and polite, and she did n't doubt that he 'd give
me lessons, too, if I 'd take them. "French is the language of
modern civilization," said Tina, with the decision of a professor. But she made me promise that I would n't say a word to
her about it before Mr. Rossiter.

"Now, Horace dear, you know," she said, "that French to
him is just like a red rag to a bull; he 'd begin to roar and
lash his sides the minute you said the words, and Mr. Rossiter
and I are capital friends now. You 've no idea, Horace, how
good he is to me. He takes such an interest in the development of my mind. He writes me a letter or note almost every
week about it, and I take his advice, you know, and I
would n't want to hurt his feelings about French, or anything
else. What do you suppose he hates the French so for? I
should think he was a genuine Englishman, that had been
kept awake nights during all the French wars."

"Well, Tina," I said, "you know there is a great deal of
corrupt and dangerous literature in the French language."

"What nonsense, Horace! just as if there was n't in the English language, too, and I none the worse for it. And I 'm sure there are no ends of bad things in the classical dictionary, and in the mythology. He 'd better talk about the French language! No, you may depend upon it, Horace, I shall learn French as soon as I leave school."

It will be inferred from this that my young lady had a considerable share of that quality which Milton represents to have been the ruin of our first mother; namely, a determination to go her own way and see for herself, and have little confidential interviews with the serpent, notwithstanding all that could be urged to the contrary by sober old Adam.

"Of course, Adam," said Eve, "I can take care of myself, and don't want you always lumbering after me with your advice. You think the serpent will injure me, do you? That just shows how little you know about me. The serpent, Adam, is a very agreeable fellow, and helps one to pass away one's time; but he don't take me in. O no! there 's no danger of his ever getting around *me*! So, my dear Adam, go your own way in the garden, and let me manage for myself."

Whether in the celestial regions there will be saints and angels who develop this particular form of self-will, I know not; but in this world of what Mr. Avery called "imperfect sanctification," religion does n't prevent the fair angels of the other sex from developing this quality in pretty energetic forms. In fact, I found that, if I was going to guide my Ariadne at all, I must let out my line fast, and let her feel free and unwatched.

XXXVII.

The Minister's Wood-Spell

IT was in the winter of this next year that the minister's "wood-spell" was announced.

"What is a wood-spell?" you say. Well, the pastor was settled on the understanding of receiving two hundred dollars a year and his wood; and there was a certain day set apart in the winter, generally in the time of the best sleighing, when every parishioner brought the minister a sled-load of wood; and thus, in the course of time, built him up a mighty wood-pile.

It was one of the great seasons of preparation in the minister's family, and Tina, Harry, and I had been busy for two or three days beforehand, in helping Esther create the wood-spell cake, which was to be made in quantities large enough to give ample slices to every parishioner. Two days beforehand, the fire was besieged with a row of earthen pots, in which the spicy compound was rising to the necessary lightness, and Harry and I split incredible amounts of oven-wood, and in the evening we sat together stoning raisins round the great kitchen fire, with Mr. Avery in the midst of us, telling us stories and arguing with us, and entering into the hilarity of the thing like a boy. He was so happy in Esther, and delighted to draw the shy color into her cheeks, by some sly joke or allusion, when Harry's head of golden curls came into close proximity with her smooth black satin tresses.

The cake came out victorious, and we all claimed the merit of it; and a mighty cheese was bought, and every shelf of the closet, and all the dressers of the kitchen, were crowded with the abundance.

We had a jewel of a morning,—one of those sharp, clear, sunny winter days, when the sleds squeak over the flinty snow, and the little icicles tingle along on the glittering crust as they fall from the trees, and the breath of the slow-pacing oxen steams up like a rosy cloud in the morning sun, and then falls back condensed in little icicles on every hair.

We were all astir early, full of life and vigor. There was a holiday in the academy. Mr. Rossiter had been invited over to the minister's to chat and tell stories with the farmers, and give them high entertainment. Miss Nervy Randall, more withered and wild in her attire than usual, but eminently serviceable, stood prepared to cut cake and cheese without end, and dispense it with wholesome nods and messages of comfort. The minister himself heated two little old andirons red-hot in the fire, and therewith from time to time stirred up a mighty bowl of flip, which was to flow in abundance to every comer. Not then had the temperance reformation dawned on America, though ten years later Mr. Avery would as soon have been caught in a gambling-saloon as stirring and dispensing a bowl of flip to his parishioners.

Mr. Avery had recently preached a highly popular sermon on agriculture, in which he set forth the dignity of the farmer's life, from the text, "For the king himself is served of the field"; and there had been a rustle of professional enthusiasm in all the mountain farms around, and it was resolved, by a sort of general consent, that the minister's wood-pile this year should be of the best: none of your old make-shifts,— loads made out with crooked sticks and snapping chestnut logs, most noisy, and destructive to good wives' aprons. Good straight shagbark-hickory was voted none too good for the minister. Also the axe was lifted up on many a proud oak and beech and maple. What destruction of glory and beauty there was in those mountain regions! How ruthlessly man destroys in a few hours that which centuries cannot bring again!

What an idea of riches in those glorious woodland regions! We read legends of millionnaires who fed their fires with cinnamon and rolled up thousand-dollar bills into lamp-lighters, in the very wantonness of profusion. But what was that compared to the prodigality which fed our great roaring winter fires on the thousand-leafed oaks, whose conception had been ages ago,— who were children of the light and of the day,— every fragment and fibre of them made of most celestial influences, of sunshine and rain-drops, and night-dews and clouds, slowly working for centuries until they had wrought the wondrous shape into a gigantic miracle of beauty? And then snuffling old Heber Atwood, with his two hard-fisted boys, cut one down in a forenoon and made logs of it for the minister's wood-pile. If this is n't making light of serious things, we don't know what is. But think of your wealth, O ye farmers!—think what beauty and glory every year perish to serve your cooking-stoves and chimney-corners.

To tell the truth, very little of such sentiment was in Mr. Avery's mind or in any of ours. We lived in a woodland region, and we were *blasé* with the glory of trees. We did admire the splendid elms that hung their cathedral arches over the one central street of Cloudland Village, and on this particular morning they were all aflame like Aladdin's palace, hanging with emeralds and rubies and crystals, flashing and glittering and dancing in the sunlight. And when the first sled came squeaking up the village street, we did not look upon it as the funereal hearse bearing the honored corpse of a hundred summers, but we boys clapped our hands and shouted, "Hurrah for old Heber!" as his load of magnificent oak, well-bearded with gray moss, came scrunching into the yard. Mr. Avery hastened to draw the hot flip-iron from the fire and stir the foaming bowl. Esther began cutting the first loaf of cake, and Mr. Rossiter walked out and cracked a joke on Heber's shoulder, whereat all the cast-iron lineaments of his hard features relaxed. Heber had not the remotest idea at this moment that he was to be branded as a tree-murderer. On the contrary, if there was anything for which he valued himself, and with which his heart was at this moment swelling with victorious pride, it was his power of cutting down trees. Man he regarded in a physical point of view as principally made to cut down trees, and trees as the natural enemies of man. When he stood under a magnificent oak, and heard the airy rustle of its thousand leaves, to his ear it was always a rustle of defiance, as if the old oak had challenged him to single combat; and Heber would feel of his axe and say, "Next winter, old boy, we 'll see,—we 'll see!" And at this moment he and his two tall, slab-sided, big-handed boys came into the kitchen with an uplifted air, in which triumph was but just repressed by suitable modesty. They came prepared to be complimented, and they were complimented accordingly.

"Well, Mr. Atwood," said the minister, "you must have had pretty hard work on that load; that's no ordinary oak; it took strong hands to roll those logs, and yet I don't see but two of your boys. Where are they all now?"

"Scattered, scattered!" said Heber, as he sat with a great block of cake in one hand, and sipped his mug of flip, looking, with his grizzly beard and shaggy hair and his iron features, like a cross between a polar bear and a man,—a very shrewd, thoughtful, reflective polar bear, however, quite up to any sort of argument with a man.

"Yes, they're scattered," he said. "We're putty lonesome now 't our house. Nobody there but Pars, Dass, Dill, Noah, and 'Liakim. I ses to Noah and 'Liakim this mornin', 'Ef we had all our boys to hum, we sh'd haf to take up two loads to the minister, sartin, to make it fair on the wood-spell cake.'"

"Where are your boys now?" said Mr. Avery. "I have n't seen them at meeting now for a good while."

"Wal, Sol and Tim's gone up to Umbagog, lumberin'; and Tite, he's sailed to Archangel; and Jeduth, he's gone to th' West Injies for molasses; and Pete, he's gone to the West. Folks begins to talk now 'bout that 'ere Western kentry, and so Pete, he must go to Buffalo, and see the great West. He's writ back about Niagry Falls. His letters is most amazin'. The old woman, she can't feel easy 'bout him no way. She insists 'pon it them Injuns 'll scalp him. The old woman is just as choice of her boys as ef she had n't got just es many es she has."

"How many sons have you?" said Harry, with a countenance of innocent wonder.

"Wal," said Heber, "I've seen the time when I had fourteen good, straight boys,—all on 'em a turnin' over a log together."

"Dear me!" said Tina. "Had n't you any daughters?"

"Gals?" said Heber, reflectively. "Bless you, yis. There's been a gal or two 'long, in between, here an' there,—don't jest remember where they come; but, any way, there's plenty of women-folks 't our house."

"Why!" said Tina, with a toss of her pretty head, "you don't seem to think much of women."

"Good in their way," said Heber, shaking his head; "but

Adam was fust formed, and then Eve, you know." Looking more attentively at Tina as she stood bridling and dimpling before him, like a bird just ready to fly, Heber conceived an indistinct idea that he must say something gallant, so he added, "Give all honor to the women, as weaker vessels, ye know; that 's sound doctrine, I s'pose."

Heber having now warmed and refreshed himself, and endowed his minister with what he conceived to be a tip-top, irreproachable load of wood, proceeded, also, to give him the benefit of a little good advice, prefaced by gracious words of encouragement. " I wus tellin' my old woman this mornin' that I did n't grudge a cent of my subscription, 'cause your preachin' lasts well and pays well. Ses I, 'Mr. Avery ain't the kind of man that strikes twelve the fust time. He 's a man that 'll wear.' That 's what I said fust, and I 've followed y' up putty close in yer preachin'; but then I 've jest got one word to say to ye. Ain't free agency a gettin' a leetle too top-heavy in yer preachin'? Ain't it kind o' overgrowin' sovereignty? Now, ye see, divine sovereignty hes got to be took care of as well as free agency. That 's all, that 's all. I thought I 'd jest drop the thought, ye know, and leave you to think on 't. This 'ere last revival you run along considerable on 'Whosoever will may come,' an' all that. Now, p'r'aps, ef you 'd jest tighten up the ropes a leetle t'other side, and give 'em sovereignty, the hull load would sled easier."

"Well," said Mr. Avery, "I 'm much obliged to you for your suggestions."

"Now there 's my wife's brother, Josh Baldwin," said Heber; "he was delegate to the last Consociation, and he heerd your openin' sermon, and ses he to me, ses he, 'Your minister sartin does slant a leetle towards th' Arminians; he don't quite walk the crack,' Josh says, ses he. Ses I, 'Josh, we ain't none on us perfect; but,' ses I, 'Mr. Avery ain't no Arminian, I can tell you. Yeh can't judge Mr. Avery by one sermon,' ses I. 'You hear him preach the year round, and ye 'll find that all the doctrines gits their place.' Ye see I stood up for ye, Mr. Avery, but I thought 't would n't do no harm to kind o' let ye know what folks is sayin'."

Here the theological discussion was abruptly cut short by Deacon Zachary Chipman's load, which entered the yard amid the huzzahs of the boys. Heber and his boys were at the door in a minute. "Wal, railly, ef the deacon hain't come down with his shagbark! Wal, wal, the revival has operated on him some, I guess. Last year the deacon sent a load that I'd ha' been ashamed to had in my back yard, an' I took the liberty o' tellin' on him so. Good, straight-grained shagbark. Wal, wal! I'll go out an' help him onload it. Ef that 'ere holds out to the bottom, the deacon's done putty wal, an' I shall think grace *has* made some progress."

The deacon, a mournful, dry, shivery-looking man, with a little round bald head, looking wistfully out of a great red comforter, all furry and white with the sharp frosts of the morning, and, with his small red eyes weeping tears through the sharpness of the air, looked as if he had come as chief mourner at the hearse of his beloved hickory-trees. He had cut down the very darlings of his soul, and come up with his precious load, impelled by a divine impulse like that which made the lowing kine, in the Old Testament story, come slowly bearing the ark of God, while their brute hearts were turning toward the calves that they had left at home. Certainly, if virtue is in proportion to sacrifice, Deacon Chipman's load of hickory had more of self-sacrifice in it than a dozen loads from old Heber; for Heber was a forest prince in his way of doing things, and, with all his shrewd calculations of money's worth, had an open-handed generosity of nature that made him take a pride in liberal giving.

The little man shrank mournfully into a corner, and sipped his tumbler of flip and ate his cake and cheese as if he had been at a funeral.

"How are you all at home, deacon?" said Mr. Avery, heartily.

"Just crawlin', thank you,—just crawlin'. My old woman don't git out much; her rheumatiz gits a dreadful strong hold on her; and, Mr. Avery, she hopes you'll be round to visit her 'fore long. Since the revival she's kind o' fell into darkness, and don't see no cheerin' views. She ses sometimes the universe ain't nothin' but blackness and darkness to her."

"Has she a good appetite?" said Mr. Avery.

"Wal, no. She don't enjoy her vittles much. Some say she's got the jaunders. I try to cosset her up, and git her to take relishin' things. I tell her ef she 'd eat a good sassage for breakfast of a cold mornin', with a good hearty bit o' mince-pie, and a cup o' strong coffee, 't would kind o' set her up for the day; but, somehow, she don't git no nourishment from her food."

"There, Rossiter," we heard Mr. Avery whisper aside, "you see what a country minister has to do,—give cheering views to a dyspeptic that breakfasts on sausages and mince-pies."

And now the loads began coming thick and fast. Sometimes two and three, and sometimes four and five, came stringing along, one after another, in unbroken procession. For every one Mr. Avery had an appreciative word. Its especial points were noticed and commended, and the farmers themselves, shrewdest observers, looked at every load and gave it their verdict. By and by the kitchen was full of a merry, chatting circle, and Mr. Rossiter and Mr. Avery were telling their best stories, and roars of laughter came from the house.

Tina glanced in and out among the old farmers, like a bright tropical bird, carrying the cake and cheese to each one, laughing and telling stories, dispensing smiles to the younger ones,—treacherous smiles, which meant nothing, but made the hearts beat faster under their shaggy coats; and if she saw a red-fisted fellow in a corner, who seemed to be having a bad time, she would go and sit down by him, and be so gracious and warming and winning that his tongue would be loosened, and he would tell her all about his steers and his calves and his last crop of corn, and his load of wood, and then wonder all the way home whether he should ever have, in a house of his own, a pretty little woman like that.

By afternoon the minister's wood-pile was enormous. It stretched beyond anything before seen in Cloudland; it exceeded all the legends of neighboring wood-piles and wood-spells related by deacons and lay delegates in the late Consociation. And truly, among things picturesque and graceful, among childish remembrances, dear and cheerful, there is nothing that more speaks to my memory than the dear, good old mossy wood-pile. Harry, Tina, Esther, and I ran up and down and in and about the piles of wood that evening with a joyous satisfaction. How fresh and spicy and woodsy it smelt! I can smell now the fragrance of the hickory, whose clear, oily bark in burning cast forth perfume quite equal to cinnamon. Then there was the fragrant black birch, sought and prized by us all for the high-flavored bark on the smaller limbs, which was a favorite species of confectionery to us. There were also the logs of white birch, gleaming up in their purity, from which we made sheets of woodland parchment.

It is recorded of one man who stands in a high position at Washington, that all his earlier writing-lessons were performed upon leaves of the white birch bark, the only paper used in the family.

Then there were massive trunks of oak, veritable worlds of mossy vegetation in themselves, with tufts of green velvet nestled away in their bark, and sheets of greenness carpeting their sides, and little white, hoary trees of moss, with little white, hoary apples upon them, like miniature orchards.

One of our most interesting amusements was forming landscapes in the snow, in which we had mountains and hills and valleys, and represented streams of water by means of glass, and clothed the sides of our hills with orchards of apple-trees made of this gray moss. It was an incipient practice at landscape-gardening, for which we found rich material in the wood-pile. Esther and Tina had been filling their aprons with these mossy treasures, for which we had all been searching together, and now we all sat chatting in the evening light. The sun was going down. The sleds had ceased to come, the riches of our woodland treasures were all in, the whole air was full of the trembling, rose-colored light that turned all the snow-covered landscape to brightness. All around us not a fence to be seen,—nothing but waving hollows of spotless snow, glowing with the rosy radiance, and fading away in purple and lilac shadows; and the evening stars began to twinkle, one after another, keen and clear through the frosty air, as we all sat together in triumph on the highest perch of the wood-pile. And Harry said to Esther, "One of these days they 'll be bringing in our wood," and Esther's cheeks reflected the pink of the sky.

"Yes, indeed!" said Tina. "And then I am coming to live

with you. I'm going to be an old maid, you know, and I shall help Esther as I do now. I never shall want to be married."

Just at this moment the ring of sleigh-bells was heard coming up the street. Who and what now? A little one-horse sleigh drove swiftly up to the door, the driver sprang out with a lively alacrity, hitched his horse, and came toward the house. In the same moment Tina and I recognized Ellery Davenport!

XXXVIII.

Ellery Davenport

TINA immediately turned and ran into the house, laughing, and up stairs into her chamber, leaving Esther to go seriously forward,—Esther always tranquil and always ready. For myself, I felt such a vindictive hatred at the moment as really alarmed me. What had this good-natured man done, with his frank, merry face and his easy, high-bred air, that I should hate him so? What sort of Christian was I, to feel in this way? Certainly it was a temptation of the Devil, and I would put it down, and act like a reasonable being. So I went forward with Harry, and he shook hands with us.

"Hulloa, fellows!" he said, "you 've made the great leap since I saw you, and changed from boys into men."

"Good evening, Miss Avery," he said, as we presented him to her. "May I trench on your hospitality a little? I am a traveller in these arctic regions, and Miss Mehitable charged me to call and see after the health and happiness of our young friends here. I see," he said, looking at us, "that there need be no inquiries after health; your looks speak for themselves."

"Why, Percival!" he said, turning to Harry, "what a pair of shoulders you are getting! Genuine Saxon blood runs in your veins plainly enough, and one of these days, when you get to be Sir Harry Percival, you 'll do honor to the name."

The proud, reserved blood flushed into Harry's face, and his blue eyes, usually so bright and clear, sparkled with displeasure. I was pleased to see that Ellery Davenport had made him angry. Yes, I said to myself, "What want of tact for him to dare to touch on a subject that Harry's most intimate friends never speak of!"

Esther looked fixedly at him with those clear, piercing hazel eyes, as if she were mentally studying him. I hoped she would not like him; yet why should I hope so?

He saw in a moment that he had made a mistake, and glided off quickly to another subject.

"Where 's my fair little enemy, Miss Tina?" he said.

His "fair little enemy" was at this moment attentively studying him through a crack in the window-curtain. Shall I say, too, that the first thing she did, on rushing up to her room, was to look at her hair, and study herself in the glass, wondering how she would look to him now. Well, she had not seen herself for some hours, and self-knowledge is a virtue, we all know. And then our scamper over the wood-pile, in the fresh, evening air, must have deranged something, for Tina had one of those rebellious heads of curls that every breeze takes liberties with, and that have to be looked after and watched and restrained. Esther's satin bands of hair could pass through a whirlwind, and not lose their gloss. It is curious how character runs even to the minutest thing,—the very hairs of our heads are numbered by it,—Esther, always in everything self-poised, thoughtful, reflective; Tina, the child of every wandering influence, tremulously alive to every new excitement, a wind-harp for every air of heaven to breathe upon.

It would be hard to say what mysterious impulse for good or ill made her turn and run when she saw Ellery Davenport. That turning and running in girls means something; it means that the electric chain has been struck in some way; but how?

Mr. Davenport came into the house, and was received with frank cordiality by Mr. Avery. He was a grandson of Jonathan Edwards, and the good man regarded him as, in some sort, a son of the Church, and had, no doubt, instantaneous promptings for his conversion. Mr. Avery, though he believed stringently in the doctrine of total depravity, was very innocent in his application of it to individuals. That Ellery Davenport was a sceptic was well known in New England, wherever the reputation of his brilliant talents and person had circulated, and Mr. Avery had often longed for an opportunity to convert him. The dear, good man had no possible idea that anybody could go wrong from anything but mistaken views, and he was sure, in the case of Ellery Davenport, that his mind must have been perplexed about free agency and decrees, and thus he hailed with delight the Providence which had sent him to his abode. He plunged into an immediate conversation with him about the state of France, whence he had just returned.

Esther, meanwhile, went up stairs to notify Tina of his arrival.

"Mr. Ellery Davenport is below, and has inquired for you."

Nobody could be more profoundly indifferent to any piece of news.

"Was that Mr. Ellery Davenport? How stupid of him to come here when we are all so tired! I don't think I can go down; I am too tired."

Esther, straightforward Esther, took the thing as stated. Tina, to be sure, had exhibited no symptoms of fatigue up to that moment; but Esther now saw that she had been allowing her to over-exert herself.

"My darling," she said, "I have been letting you do too much altogether. You are quite right; you should lie down here quietly, and I 'll bring you up your tea. Perhaps by and by, in the evening, you might come down and see Mr. Davenport, when you are rested."

"O nonsense about Mr. Davenport! he does n't come to see me. He wants to talk with your father, I suppose."

"But he has inquired for you two or three times," said Esther, "and he really seems to be a very entertaining, well-informed man; so by and by, if you feel rested, I should think you had better come down."

Now I, for my part, wondered then and wonder now, and always shall, what all this was for. Tina certainly was not a coquette; she had not learned the art of trading in herself, and using her powers and fascinations as women do who have been in the world, and learnt the precise value of everything that they say and do. She was, at least now, a simple child of nature, yet she acted exactly as an artful coquette might have done.

Ellery Davenport constantly glanced at the door as he talked with Mr. Avery, and shifted uneasily on his chair; evidently he expected her to enter, and when Esther returned without her he was secretly vexed and annoyed. I was glad of it, too, like a fool as I was. It would have been a thousand times better for my hopes had she walked straight out to meet him, cool and friendly, like Esther. There was one comfort; he was a married man; but then that crazy wife of his might die, or might be dead now. Who knew? To be sure, Ellery

Davenport never had the air of a married man,—that steady, collected, sensible, restrained air which belongs to the male individual, conscious, wherever he moves, of a home tribunal, to which he is responsible. He had gone loose in society, pitied and petted and caressed by ladies, and everybody said, if his wife should die, Ellery Davenport might marry whom he pleased. Esther knew nothing about him, except a faint general outline of his history. She had no prepossessions for or against, and he laid himself out to please her in conversation, with that easy grace and quick perception of character which were habitual with him. Ellery Davenport had been a thriving young Jacobin, and Mr. Avery and Mr. Rossiter were fierce Federalists.

Mr. Rossiter came in to tea, and both of them bore down exultingly on Ellery Davenport in regard to the disturbances in France.

"Just what I always said!" said Mr. Rossiter. "French democracy is straight from the Devil. It's the child of misrule, and leads to anarchy. See what their revolution is coming to. Well, I may not be orthodox entirely on the question of total depravity, but I always admitted the total depravity of the whole French nation."

"O, the French are men of like passions with us!" said Ellery Davenport. "They have been ground down and debased and imbruted till human nature can bear no longer, and now there is a sudden outbreak of the lower classes,—the turning of the worm."

"Not a worm," said Mr. Rossiter, "a serpent, and a strong one."

"Davenport," said Mr. Avery, "don't you see that all this is because this revolution is in the hands of atheists?"

"Certainly I do, sir. These fellows have destroyed the faith of the common people, and given them nothing in its place."

"I am glad to see you recognize that," said Mr. Avery.

"Recognize, my dear sir! Nobody knows the worth of religion as a political force better than I do. Those French people are just like children,—full of sentiment, full of feeling, full of fire, but without the cold, judging, logical power that is frozen into men here by your New England theology. If I have got to manage a republic, give me Calvinists."

"You admit, then," said Mr. Avery, delightedly, "the worth of Calvinism."

"As a political agent, certainly I do," said Ellery Davenport. "Men must have strong, positive religious beliefs to give them vigorous self-government; and republics are founded on the self-governing power of the individual."

"Davenport," said Mr. Avery, affectionately laying his hand on his shoulder, "I should like to have said that thing myself, I could n't have put it better."

"But do you suppose," said Esther, trembling with eagerness, "that they will behead the Queen?"

"Certainly I do," said Ellery Davenport, with that air of cheerful composure with which the retailer of the last horror delights to shock a listener. "O certainly! I would n't give a pin for her chance. You read the account of the trial, I suppose; you saw that it was a foregone conclusion?"

"I did, indeed," said Esther. "But, O Mr. Davenport! can nothing be done? There is Lafayette; can he do nothing?"

"Lafayette may think himself happy if he keeps his own head on his shoulders," said Davenport. "The fact is, that there is a wild beast in every human being. In our race it is the lion. In the French race it is the tiger,—hotter, more tropical, more blindly intense in rage and wrath. Religion, government, education, are principally useful in keeping the human dominant over the beast; but when the beast gets above the human in the community, woe be to it."

"Davenport, you talk like an apostle," said Mr. Avery.

"You know the devils believe and tremble," said Ellery.

"Well, I take it," said Mr. Rossiter, "you 've come home from France disposed to be a good Federalist."

"Yes, I have," said Ellery Davenport. "We must all live and learn, you know."

And so in one evening Ellery witched himself into the good graces of every one in the simple parsonage; and when Tina at last appeared she found him reigning king of the circle. Mr. Rossiter, having drawn from him the avowal that he was a Federalist, now looked complacently upon him as a hopeful young neophyte. Mr. Avery saw evident marks of grace in his declarations in favor of Calvinism, while yet there was a spicy flavor of the prodigal son about him,—enough to engage him for his conversion. Your wild, wicked, witty prodigal son is to a spiritual huntsman an attractive mark, like some rare kind of eagle, whose ways must be studied, and whose nest must be marked, and in whose free, savage gambols in the blue air and on the mountain-tops he has a kind of hidden sympathy.

When Tina entered, it was with an air unusually shy and quiet. She took all his compliments on her growth and change of appearance with a negligent, matter-of-course air, seated herself in the most distant part of the room, and remained obstinately still and silent. Nevertheless, it was to be observed that she lost not a word that he said, or a motion that he made. Was she in that stage of attraction which begins with repulsion? or did she feel stirring within her that intense antagonism which woman sometimes feels toward man, when she instinctively divines that he may be the one who shall one day send a herald and call on her to surrender. Women are so intense, they have such prophetic, fore-reaching, nervous systems, that sometimes they appear to be endowed with a gift of prophecy. Tina certainly was an innocent child at this time, uncalculating, and acting by instinct alone, and she looked upon Ellery Davenport as a married man, who was and ought to be and would be nothing to her; and yet, for the life of her, she could not treat him as she treated other men.

If there was in him something which powerfully attracted, there was also something of the reverse pole of the magnet, that repelled, and inspired a feeling not amounting to fear, but having an undefined savor of dread, as if some invisible spirit about him gave mysterious warning. There was a sense of such hidden, subtile power under his suavities, the grasp of the iron hand was so plain through the velvet glove, that delicate and impressible natures felt it. Ellery Davenport was prompt and energetic and heroic; he had a great deal of impulsive good-nature, as his history in all our affairs shows. He was always willing to reach out the helping hand, and helped to some purpose when he did so; and yet I felt, rather than could prove, in his presence, that he could be very remorseless and persistently cruel.

Ellery Davenport inherited the whole Edwards nature, without its religious discipline,—a nature strong both in intellect and passion. He was an unbelieving Jonathan Edwards.

It was this whole nature that I felt in him, and I looked upon the gradual interest which I saw growing in Tina toward him, in the turning of her thoughts on him, in her flights from him and attractions to him, as one looks on the struggles of a fascinated bird, who flees and returns, and flees and returns, each time drawn nearer and nearer to the diamond eyes.

These impressions which come to certain kinds of natures are so dim and cloudy, it is so much the habit of the counter-current of life to disregard them, and to feel that an impression of which you have no physical, external proof is of necessity an absurdity and a weakness, that they are seldom acted on,—seldom, at least, in New England, where the habit of logic is so formed from childhood in the mind, and the believing of nothing which you cannot prove is so constant a portion of the life education. Yet with regard to myself, as I have stated before, there was always a sphere of impression surrounding individuals, for which often I could give no reasonable account. It was as if there had been an emanation from the mind, like that from the body. From some it was an emanation of moral health and purity and soundness; from others, the sickly effluvium of moral decay, sometimes penetrating through all sorts of outward graces and accomplishments, like the smell of death through the tube-roses and lilies on the coffin.

I could not prove that Ellery Davenport was a wicked man; but I had an instinctive abhorrence of him, for which I reproached myself constantly, deeming it only the madness of an unreasonable jealousy.

His stay with us at this time was only for a few hours. The next morning he took Harry alone and communicated to him some intelligence quite important to his future.

"I have been to visit your father," he said, "and have made him aware what treasures he possesses in his children."

"His children have no desire that he should be made aware of it," said Harry, coldly. "He has broken all ties between them and him."

"Well, well!" said Ellery Davenport, "the fact is Sir Harry has gone into the virtuous stage of an Englishman's life, where a man is busy taking care of his gouty feet, looking after his tenants, and repenting at his leisure of the sins of his youth. But you will find, when you come to enter college next year, that there will be a handsome allowance at your disposal; and, between you and me, I'll just say to you that young Sir Harry is about as puny and feeble a little bit of mortality as I ever saw. To my thinking, they'll never raise him; and his life is all that stands between you and the estate. You know that I got your mother's marriage certificate, and it is safe in Parson Lothrop's hands. So you see there may be a brilliant future before you and your sister. It is well enough for you to know it early, and keep yourself and her free from entanglements. School friendships and flirtations and all that sort of thing are pretty little spring flowers,—very charming in their way and time; but it is n't advisable to let them lead us into compromising ourselves for life. If your future home is to be England, of course you will want your marriage to strengthen your position there."

"My future home will never be England," said Harry, briefly. "America has nursed me and educated me, and I shall always be, heart and soul, an American. My life must be acted in this country."

The other suggestion contained in Ellery Davenport's advice was passed over without a word. Harry was not one that could discuss his private relations with a stranger. He could not but feel obliged to Ellery Davenport for the interest that he had manifested in him, and yet there was something about this easy, patronizing manner of giving advice that galled him. He was not yet old enough not to feel vexed at being reminded that he was young.

It seemed but a few hours, and Ellery Davenport was gone again; and yet how he had changed everything! The hour that he drove up, how perfectly innocently happy and united we all were! Our thoughts needed not to go beyond the present moment: the moss that we had gathered from the wood-pile, and the landscapes that we were going to make with it, were greater treasures than all those of that unknown world of brightness and cleverness and wealth and station, out of which Ellery Davenport had shot like a comet, to astonish us, and then go back and leave us in obscurity.

Harry communicated the intelligence given him by Ellery

Davenport, first to me, then to Tina and Esther and Mr. Avery, but begged that it might not be spoken of beyond our little circle. It could and it should make no change, he said. But can expectations of such magnitude be awakened in young minds without a change?

On the whole, Ellery Davenport left a trail of brightness behind him, notwithstanding my sinister suspicions. "How open-handed and friendly it was of him," said Esther, "to come up here, when he has so much on his hands! He told father that he should have to be in Washington next week, to talk with them there about French affairs."

"And I hope he may do Tom Jefferson some good!" said Mr. Avery, indignantly,—"teach him what he is doing in encouraging this hideous, atheistical French revolution! Why, it will bring discredit on republics, and put back the cause of liberty in Europe a century! Davenport sees into that as plainly as I do."

"He 's a shrewd fellow," said Mr. Rossiter. "I heard him talk three or four years ago, when he was over here, and he was about as glib-tongued a Jacobin as you 'd wish to see; but now my young man has come round handsomely. I told him he ought to tell Jefferson just how the thing is working. I go for government by the respectable classes of society."

"Davenport evidently is not a regenerated man," said Mr. Avery, thoughtfully; "but as far as speculative knowledge goes, he is as good a theologian as his grandfather. I had a pretty thorough talk with him, before we went to bed last night, and he laid down the distinctions with a clearness and a precision that were astonishing. He sees right through that point of the difference between natural and moral inability, and he put it into a sentence that was as neat and compact and clear as a quartz crystal. I think there was a little rub in his mind on the consistency of the freedom of the will with the divine decrees, and I just touched him off with an illustration or two there, and I could see, by the flash of his eye, how quickly he took it. 'Davenport,' said I to him, 'you are made for the pulpit; you ought to be in it.'

" 'I know it,' he said, 'Mr. Avery; but the trouble is, I am not good enough. I think,' he said, 'sometimes I should like to have been as good a man as my grandfather; but then, you see, there's the world, the flesh, and the Devil, who all have something to say to that.'

" 'Well,' says I, 'Davenport, the world and the flesh last only a little while—'

" 'But the Devil and I last forever, I suppose you mean to say,' said he, getting up with a sort of careless swing; and then he said he must go to bed; but before he went he reached out his hand and smiled on me, and said, 'Good night, and thank you, Mr. Avery.' That man has a beautiful smile. It 's like a spirit in his face."

Had Ellery Davenport been acting the hypocrite with Mr. Avery? Supposing a man is made like an organ, with two or three banks of keys, and ever so many stops, so that he can play all sorts of tunes on himself; is it being a hypocrite with each person to play precisely the tune, and draw out exactly the stop, which he knows will make himself agreeable and further his purposes? Ellery Davenport did understand the New England theology as thoroughly as Mr. Avery. He knew it from turret to foundation-stone. He knew all the evidences of natural and revealed religion, and, when he chose to do so, could make most conclusive arguments upon them. He had a perfect appreciation of devotional religion, and knew precisely what it would do for individuals. He saw into politics with unerring precision, and knew what was in men, and whither things were tending. His unbelief was purely and simply what has been called in New England the natural opposition of the heart to God. He loved his own will, and he hated control, and he determined, *per fas aut nefas*, to carry his own plans in this world, and attend to the other when he got into it. To have his own way, and to carry his own points, and to do as he pleased, were the ruling purposes of his life.

XXXIX.

Last Days in Cloudland

THE day was coming now that the idyl of Cloudland must end, and our last term wound up with a grand dramatic entertainment.

It was a time-honored custom in New England academies to act a play once a year as the closing exercise, and we resolved that our performance should surpass all others in scenic effect.

The theme of the play was to be the story of Jephthah's daughter, from the Old Testament. It had been suggested at first to take Miss Hannah More's sacred drama upon this subject; but Tina insisted upon it that it would be a great deal better to write an original drama ourselves, each one taking a character, and composing one's own part.

Tina was to be Jephthah's daughter, and Esther her mother; and a long opening scene between them was gotten up by the two in a private session at their desks in the schoolroom one night, and, when perfected, was read to Harry and me for our critical judgment. The conversation was conducted in blank verse, with the usual appropriate trimmings and flourishes of that species of literature, and, on the whole, even at this time, I do not see but that it was quite as good as Miss Hannah More's.

There was some skirmishing between Harry and myself about our parts, Harry being, as I thought, rather too golden-haired and blue-eyed for the grim resolve and fierce agonies of Jephthah. Moreover, the other part was to be that of Tina's lover, and he was to act very desperate verses indeed, and I represented to Harry privately that here, for obvious reasons, I was calculated to succeed. But Tina overruled me with that easy fluency of good reasons which the young lady always had at command. "Harry would make altogether the best lover," she said; "he was just cut out for a lover. Then, besides, what does Horace know about it? Harry has been practising for six months, and Horace has n't even begun to think of such things yet."

This was one of those stringent declarations that my young lady was always making with regard to me, giving me to understand that her whole confidence in me was built entirely on my discretion. Well, I was happy enough to let it go so, for Ellery Davenport had gone like an evening meteor, and we had ceased talking and thinking about him. He was out of our horizon entirely. So we spouted blank verse at each other, morning, noon, and night, with the most cheerful courage. Tina and Harry had, both of them, a considerable share of artistic talent, and made themselves very busy in drawing and painting scenery,—a work in which the lady principal, Miss Titcomb, gave every assistance; although, as Tina said, her views of scenery were mostly confined to what was proper for tombstones. "But then," she added, "let her have the whole planning of my grave, with a great weeping willow over it,— that 'll be superb! I believe the weeping willows will be out by that time, and we can have real branches. Won't that be splendid!"

Then there was the necessity of making our drama popular, by getting in the greatest possible number of our intimate friends and acquaintances. So Jephthah had to marshal an army on the stage, and there was no end of paper helmets to be made. In fact, every girl in school who could turn her hand to anything was making a paper helmet.

There was to be a procession of Judæan maidens across the stage, bearing the body of Jephthah's daughter on a bier, after the sacrifice. This took in every leading girl in the school; and as they were all to be dressed in white, with blue ribbons, one may fancy the preparation going on in all the houses far and near. There was also to be a procession of youths, bearing the body of the faithful lover, who, of course, was to die, to keep the departed company in the shades.

We had rehearsals every night for a fortnight, and Harry, Tina, and I officiated as stage-managers. It is incredible the trouble we had. Esther acted the part of Judæan matron to perfection,—her long black hair being let down and dressed after a picture in the Biblical Dictionary, which Tina insisted upon must be authentic. Esther, however, rebelled at the

nose-jewels. There was no making her understand the Oriental taste of the thing; she absolutely declined the embellish-
ment, and finally it was agreed among us that the nose-jewels
should be left to the imagination.

Harry looked magnificent, with the help of a dark mustache, which Tina very adroitly compounded of black ravelled
yarn, arranging it with such delicacy that it had quite the effect of hair. The difficulty was that in impassioned moments
the mustache was apt to get awry; and once or twice, while
on his knees before Tina in tragical attitudes, this occurrence
set her off into hysterical giggles, which spoiled the effect of
the rehearsal. But at last we contrived a plaster which the
most desperate plunges of agony could not possibly disar-
range.

As my eyes and hair were black, when I had mounted a
towering helmet overshadowed by a crest of bear-skin, fresh
from an authentic bear that Heber Atwood had killed only
two weeks before, I made a most fateful and portentous Jephthah, and flattered myself secretly on the tragical and
gloomy emotions excited in the breasts of divers of my female
friends.

I composed for myself a most towering and lofty entrance
scene, when I came in glory at the head of my troops. I could
not help plagiarizing Miss Hannah More's first line:—

"On Jordan's banks proud Ammon's banners wave."

Any writer of poems will pity me, when he remembers his
own position, if he has ever tried to make a verse on some
subject and been stuck and pierced through by some line of
another poet, which so sticks in his head and his memory that
there is no possibility of his saying the thing any other way.
I tried beginning,—

"On Salem's plains the summer sun is bright";

but when I looked at my troop of helmets and the very startling banner which we were to display, and reflected that Josh
Billings was to give an inspiring blast on a bugle behind the

scenes, I perfectly longed to do the glorious and magnificent, and this resounding line stood right in my way.

"Well, dear me, Horace," said Tina, "take it, and branch off from it,—make a text of it."

And so I did. How martial and Miltonic I was! I really made myself feel quite serious and solemn with the pomp and glory of my own language; but I contrived to introduce into my resounding verses a most touching description of my daughter, in which I exhausted Oriental images and similes on her charms. Esther and I were to have rather a tender scene, on parting, as she was to be my wife; but then we minded it not a jot. The adroitness with which both these young girls avoided getting into relations that might savor of reality was an eminent instance of feminine tact. And while Harry was playing the impassioned lover at Tina's feet, Esther looked at him slyly, with just the slightest shade of consciousness,—something as slight as the quivering of an eyelash, or a tremulous flush on her fair cheek. There was fire under that rose-colored snow after all, and that was what gave the subtle charm to the whole thing.

We had an earnest discussion among us four as to what was proper to be done with the lover. Harry insisted upon it, that, after tearing his hair and executing all the other proprieties of despair, he should end by falling on his sword; and he gave us two or three extemporaneous representations of the manner in which he intended to bring out this last scene. How we screamed with laughter over these discussions, as Harry, whose mat of curls was somewhat prodigious, ran up and down the room, howling distractedly, running his fingers through his hair until each separate curl stood on end, and his head was about the size of a half-bushel! We nearly killed ourselves laughing over our tragedy, but still the language thereof was none the less broken-hearted and impassioned.

Tina was vindictive and bloodthirsty in her determination that the tragedy should be of the deepest dye. She exhibited the ferocity of a little pirate in her utter insensibility to the details of blood and murder, and would not hear of any concealment, or half-measures, to spare anybody's feelings. She insisted upon being stabbed on the stage, and she had rigged up a kitchen carving-knife with a handle of gilt paper, orna-

mented with various breastpins of the girls, which was celebrated in florid terms in her part of the drama as a Tyrian
dagger.

"Why Tyrian," objected Harry, "when it is the Jews that
are fighting the Ammonites?"

"O nonsense, Harry! Tyrian sounds a great deal better, and
the Ammonites, I don't doubt, had Tyrian daggers," said
Tina, who displayed a feminine facility in the manufacture of
facts. "Tyre, you know," she added, "was the country where
all sorts of things were made: Tyrian purple and Tyrian man-
tles,—why, of course they must have made daggers, and the
Jews must have got them,—of course they must! I 'm going
to have it, not only a Tyrian dagger, but a sacred dagger,
taken away from a heathen temple and consecrated to the service of the Lord. And only see what a sheath I have made for
it! Why, at this distance it could n't be told from gold! And
how do you suppose that embossed work is made? Why, it 's
different-colored grains of rice and gilt paper rolled up!"

It must be confessed that nobody enjoyed Tina's successes
more heartily than she did herself. I never knew anybody who
had a more perfect delight in the work of her own hands.

It was finally concluded, in full concert, that the sacrifice
was to be performed at an altar, and here came an opportunity for Miss Titcomb's proficiency in tombstones to exercise
itself. Our altar was to be like the lower part of a monument,
so we decided, and Miss Titcomb had numerous patterns of
this kind, subject to our approval. It was to be made life-size,
of large sheets of pasteboard, and wreathed with sacrificial
garlands.

Tina was to come in at the head of a chorus of wailing
maidens, who were to sing a most pathetic lamentation over
her. I was to stand grim and resolved, with my eyes rolled up
into my helmet, and the sacrificial Tyrian dagger in my hands,
when she was to kneel down before the altar, which was to
have real flame upon it. The top of the altar was made to
conceal a large bowl of alcohol, and before the entering of
the procession the lights were all to be extinguished, and the
last scene was to be witnessed by the lurid glare of the burning light on the altar. Any one who has ever tried the ghostly,
spectral, supernatural appearance which his very dearest

friend may be made to have by this simple contrivance, can appreciate how very sanguine our hopes must have been of the tragical power of this *dénouement*.

All came about quite as we could have hoped. The academy hall was packed and crammed to the ceiling, and our acting was immensely helped by the loudly expressed sympathy of the audience, who entered into the play with the most undisguised conviction of its reality. When the lights were extinguished, and the lurid flame flickered up on the altar, and Tina entered dressed in white with her long hair streaming around her, and with an inspired look of pathetic resignation in her large, earnest eyes, a sort of mournful shudder of reality came over me, and the words I had said so many times concerning the sacrifice of the victim became suddenly intensely real; it was a sort of stage illusion, an overpowering belief in the present.

The effect of the ghastly light on Tina's face, on Esther's and Harry's, as they grouped themselves around in the preconcerted attitudes, was really overwhelming.

It had been arranged that, at the very moment when my hand was raised, Harry, as the lover, should rush forward with a shriek, and receive the dagger in his own bosom. This was the last modification of our play, after many successive rehearsals, and the success was prodigious. I stabbed Harry to the heart, Tina gave a piercing shriek and fell dead at his side, and then I plunged the dagger into my own heart, and the curtain fell, amid real weeping and wailing from many unsophisticated, soft-hearted old women.

Then came the last scene,—the procession of youths and maidens across the stage, bearing the bodies of the two lovers,—the whole ending in an admirably constructed monument, over which a large willow was seen waving. This last gave to Miss Titcomb, as she said, more complete gratification than any scene that had been exhibited. The whole was a most triumphant success.

Heber Atwood's "old woman" declared that she caught her breath, and thought she "should ha' fainted clean away when she see that gal come in." And as there was scarcely a house in which there was not a youth or a maiden who had borne part in the chorus, all Cloudland shared in the triumph.

By way of dissipating the melancholy feelings consequent upon the tragedy, we had a farce called "Our Folks," which was acted extemporaneously by Harry, Tina, and myself, consisting principally in scenes between Harry as Sam Lawson, Tina as Hepsie, and myself as Uncle Fliakim, come in to make a pastoral visit, and exhort them how to get along and manage their affairs more prosperously. There had been just enough strain upon our nerves, enough reality of tragic exultation, to excite that hysterical quickness of humor which comes when the nervous system is well up. I let off my extra steam in Uncle Fliakim with a good will, as I danced in in my black silk tights, knocking down the spinning-wheel, upsetting the cradle, setting the babies to crying, and starting Hepsie's tongue, which lost nothing of force or fluency in Tina's reproduction. How the little elf could have transformed herself in a few moments into such a peaked, sharp, wiry-featured, virulent-tongued virago, was matter of astonishment to us all; while Harry, with a suit of fluttering old clothes, with every joint dissolving in looseness, and with his bushy hair in a sort of dismayed tangle, with his cheeks sucked in and his eyes protruding, gave an inimitable Sam Lawson.

The house was convulsed; the screams and shrieks of laughter quite equalled the moans of distress in our tragedy.

And so the curtain fell on our last exhibition in Cloudland. The next day was all packing of trunks and taking of leave, and last words from Mr. Rossiter and Mr. Avery to the school, and settling of board-bills and school-bills, and sending back all the breastpins from the Tyrian dagger, and a confused kicking about of helmets, together with interchanges between various Johns and Joans of vows of eternal constancy, assurances from some fair ones that, "though they could not *love*, they should always regard as a brother," and from some of our sex to the same purport toward gentle-hearted Aramintas,—very pleasant to look upon and charming to dwell upon,—who were not, after all, our chosen Aramintas; and there was no end of three and four-paged notes written, in which Susan Ann told Susan Jane that "never, never shall we forget the happy hours we 've spent together on Cloudland hill,—never shall the hand of friendship grow cold, or the heart of friendship cease to beat with emotion."

Poor dear souls all of us! We meant every word that we said.

It was only the other day that I called in a house on Beacon Street to see a fair sister, to whom on this occasion I addressed a most pathetic note, and who sent me a very pretty curl of golden-brown hair. Now she is Mrs. Boggs, and the sylph that was is concealed under a most enormous matron; the room trembles when she sets her foot down. But I found her heart in the centre of the ponderous mass, and, as I am somewhat inclining to be a stout old gentleman, we shook the room with our merriment. Such is life!

The next day Tina was terribly out of spirits, and had two or three hours of long and bitter crying, the cause of which none of our trio could get out of her.

The morning that we were to leave she went around bidding good by to everybody and everything, for there was not a creature in Cloudland that did not claim some part in her, and for whom she had not a parting word. And, finally, I proposed that we should go in to the schoolmaster together and have a last good time with him, and then, with one of her sudden impulsive starts, she turned her back on me.

"No, no, Horace! I don't want to see him any more!"

I was in blank amazement for a moment, and then I remembered the correspondence on the improvement of her mind.

"Tina, you don't tell me," said I, "that Mr. Rossiter has—"

She turned quickly round and faced on the defensive.

"Now, Horace, you need not talk to me, for it is *not my fault! Could* I dream of such a thing, now? *Could* I? Mr. Rossiter, of all the men on earth! Why, Horace, I do love him dearly. I never had any father—that cared for me, at least," she said, with a quiver in her voice; "and he was beginning to seem so like a father to me. I loved him, I respected him, I reverenced him,—and now was I wrong to express it?"

"Why, but, Tina," said I, in amazement, "Mr. Rossiter cannot—he could not mean to marry you!"

"No, no. He says that he would not. He asked nothing. It all seemed to come out before he thought what he was saying,—that he has been thinking altogether too much of me, and that when I go it will seem as if *all* was gone that he cares for. I can't tell you how he spoke, Horace; there was something fearful in it, and he trembled. O Horace, he loves me nobly, disinterestedly, truly; but I felt guilty for it. I felt that such a power of feeling never ought to rest on such a bit of thistle-down as I am. Oh! why would n't he stay on the height where I had put him, and let me reverence and admire him, and have him to love as my father?"

"But Tina, you cannot, you must not now—"

"I know it, Horace. I have lost him for a friend and father and guide because he will love me too well."

And so ends Mr. Jonathan Rossiter's Spartan training.

My good friends of the American Republic, if ever we come to have mingled among the senators of the United States specimens of womankind like Tina Percival, we men remaining such as we by nature are and must be, will not the general hue of politics take a decidedly new and interesting turn?

Mr. Avery parted from us with some last words of counsel.

"You are going into college life, boys, and you must take care of your bodies. Many a boy breaks down because he keeps his country appetite and loses his country exercise. You must balance study and brain-work by exercise and muscle-work, or you 'll be down with dyspepsia, and won't know what ails you. People have wondered where the seat of original sin is; I think it 's in the stomach. A man eats too much and neglects exercise, and the Devil has him all his own way, and the little imps, with their long black fingers, play on his nerves like a piano. Never overwork either body or mind, boys. All the work that a man can do that can be *rested by one night's sleep is good for him*, but fatigue that goes into the next day is always bad. Never get discouraged at difficulties. I give you both this piece of advice. When you get into a tight place, and everything goes against you till it seems as if you could n't hold on a minute longer, *never give up then*, for that 's just the place and time that the tide 'll turn. Never trust to prayer without using every means in your power, and never use the means without trusting in prayer. Get your evidences of grace by pressing forward to the mark, and not by groping with a lantern after the boundary-lines,—and so, boys, go, and God bless you!"

XL.

We Enter College

HARRY and I entered Cambridge with honor. It was a matter of pride with Mr. Rossiter that his boys should go more than ready,—that an open and abundant entrance should be administered unto them in the classic halls; and so it was with us. We were fully prepared on the conditions of the sophomore year, and thus, by Mr. Rossiter's drill, had saved the extra expenses of one year of college life.

We had our room in common, and Harry's improved means enabled him to fit it up and embellish it in an attractive manner. Tina came over and presided at the inauguration, and helped us hang our engravings, and fitted up various little trifles of shell and moss work,—memorials of Cloudland.

Tina was now visiting at the Kitterys', in Boston, dispensing smiles and sunbeams, inquired after and run after by every son of Adam who happened to come in her way, all to no purpose, so far as her heart was concerned.

> "Favors to none, to all she smiles extends;
> Oft she rejects, but never once offends."

Tina's education was now, in the common understanding of society, looked upon as finished. Harry's and mine were commencing; we were sophomores in college. She was a young lady in society; yet she was younger than either of us, and had, I must say, quite as good a mind, and was fully as capable of going through our college course with us as of having walked thus far.

However, with her the next question was, Whom will she marry?—a question that my young lady seemed not in the slightest hurry to answer. I flattered myself on her want of susceptibility that pointed in the direction of marriage. She could feel so much friendship,—such true affection,—and yet was apparently so perfectly devoid of passion.

She was so brilliant, and so fitted to adorn society, that one would have thought she would have been *ennuyée* in the old Rossiter house, with only the society of Miss Mehitable and Polly; but Tina was one of those whose own mind and nature are sufficient excitement to keep them always burning. She loved her old friend with all her little heart, and gave to her all her charms and graces, and wound round her in a wild-rose garland, like the eglantine that she was named after.

She had cultivated her literary tastes and powers. She wrote and sketched and painted for Miss Mehitable, and Miss Mehitable was most appreciative. Her strong, shrewd, well-cultivated mind felt and appreciated the worth and force of everything there was in Tina, and Tina seemed perfectly happy and satisfied with one devoted admirer. However, she had two, for Polly still survived, being of the dry immortal species, and seemed, as Tina told her, quite as good as new. And Tina once more had uproarious evenings with Miss Mehitable and Polly, delighting herself with the tumults of laughter which she awakened.

She visited and patronized Sam Lawson's children, gave them candy and told them stories, and now and then brought home Hepsie's baby for a half-day, and would busy herself dressing it up in something new of her own invention and construction. Poor Hepsie was one of those women fated always to have a baby in which she seemed to have no more maternal pleasure than an old fowling-piece. But Tina looked at her on the good-natured and pitiful side, although, to be sure, she did study her with a view to dramatic representation, and made no end of capital of her in this way in the bosom of her own family.

Tina's mimicry and mockery had not the slightest tinge of contempt or ill-feeling in it; it was pure merriment, and seemed to be just as natural to her as the freakish instincts of the mocking-bird, who sits in the blossoming boughs above your head, and sends back every sound that you hear with a wild and airy gladness.

Tina's letters to us were full of this mirthful, effervescent sparkle, to which everything in Oldtown afforded matter of amusement; and the margins of them were scrawled with droll and lifelike caricatures, in which we recognized Sam

Lawson, and Hepsie, and Uncle Fliakim, and, in fact, all the Oldtown worthies,—not even excepting Miss Mehitable and Polly, the minister and his lady, my grandmother, Aunt Lois, and Aunt Keziah. What harm was there in all this, when Tina assured us that aunty read the letters before they went, and laughed until she cried over them?

"But, after all," I said to Harry one day, "it 's rather a steep thing for girls that have kept step with us in study up to this point, and had their minds braced just as ours have been, with all the drill of regular hours and regular lessons, to be suddenly let down, with nothing in particular to do."

"Except to wait the coming man," said Harry, "who is to teach her what to do."

"Well," said I, "in the interval, while this man is coming, what has Tina to do but to make a frolic of life?—to live like a bobolink on a clover-head, to sparkle like a dewdrop in a thorn-bush, to whirl like a bubble on a stream? Why could n't she as well find the coming man while she is doing something as while she is doing nothing? Esther and you found each other while you were *working* side by side, your minds lively and braced, toiling at the same great ideas, knowing each other in the very noblest part of your natures; and you are true companions; it is a mating of *souls* and not merely of bodies."

"I know that," said Harry, "I know, too, that in these very things that I set my heart on in the college course Esther is by far my superior. You know, Horace, that she was ahead of us in both Greek and mathematics; and why should she not go through the whole course with us as well as the first part? The fact is, a man never sees a subject thoroughly until he sees what a woman will think of it, for there is a woman's view of every subject, which has a different shade from a man's view, and that is what you and I have insensibly been absorbing in all our course hitherto. How splendidly Esther lighted up some of those passages of the Greek tragedy! and what a sparkle and glitter there were in some of Tina's suggestions! All I know, Horace, is that it is confoundedly dull being without them; these fellows are well enough, but they are cloddish and lumpish."

"Well," said I, "that is n't the worst of it. When such a gay creature of the elements as Tina is has nothing earthly to do to steady her mind and task her faculties, and her life becomes a mere glitter, and her only business to amuse the passing hour, it throws her open to all sorts of temptations from that coming man, whoever he may be. Can we wonder that girls love to flirt, and try their power on lovers? And then they are fair game for men who want to try their powers on them, and some man who has a vacation in his life purpose, and wants something to amuse him, makes an episode by getting up some little romance, which is an amusement to him, but all in all to her. Is that fair?"

"True," said Harry, "and there 's everything about Tina to tempt one; she is so dazzling and bewildering and exciting that a man might intoxicate himself with her for the mere pleasure of the thing, as one takes opium or champagne; and that sort of bewilderment and intoxication girls often mistake for love! I would to Heaven, Horace, that I were as sure that Tina loves you as I am that Esther loves me."

"She does love me with her *heart*," said I, "but not with her imagination. The trouble with Tina, Harry, is this: she is a woman that can really and truly love a man as a sister, or as a friend, or as a daughter, and she is a woman that no man can love in that way long. She feels nothing but affection, and she always creates passion. I have not the slightest doubt that she loves me dearly, but I have a sort of vision that between her and me will come some one who will kindle her imagination; and all the more so that she has nothing serious to do, nothing to keep her mind braced, and her intellectual and judging faculties in the ascendant, but is fairly set adrift, just like a little flowery boat, without steersman or oars, on a bright, swift-rushing river. Did you ever notice, Harry, what a singular effect Ellery Davenport seems to have on her?"

"No," said Harry, starting and looking surprised. "Why, Horace, Ellery Davenport is a good deal older than she is, and a married man too."

"Well, Harry, did n't you ever hear of married men that liked to try experiments with girls? and in our American society they can do it all the more safely, because here, thank Heaven! nobody ever dreams but what marriage is a perfect regulator and safeguard."

"But," said Harry, rubbing his eyes like a person just waking up, "Horace, it must be the mere madness of jealousy that
would put such a thing into your head. Why, there has n't
been the slightest foundation for it."

"That is to say, Harry, you 've been in love with Esther,
and your eyes and ears and senses have all run one way. But
I have lived in Tina, and I believe I have a sort of divining
power, so that I can almost see into her heart. I *feel in myself*
how things affect her, and I *know*, by feeling and sensation,
that from her childhood Ellery Davenport has had a peculiar
magnetic effect upon her."

"But, Horace, he is a married man," persisted Harry.

"A fascinating married man, victimized by a crazy wife, and
ready to throw himself on the sympathies of womanhood in
this affliction. The fair sex are such Good Samaritans that
some fellows make capital of their wounds and bruises."

"Well, but," said Harry, "there 's not the slightest thing
that leads me to think that he ever cared particularly about
Tina."

"That 's because you are Tina's brother, and not her lover,"
said I. "I remember as long ago as when we were children,
spending Easter at Madam Kittery's, how Ellery Davenport's
eyes used to follow her,—how she used constantly to seem
to excite and interest him; and all this zeal about your affairs,
and his coming up to Oldtown, and cultivating Miss Mehitable's acquaintance so zealously, and making himself so necessary to her; and then he has always been writing letters or
sending messages to Tina, and then, when he was up in
Cloudland, did n't you see how constantly his eyes followed
her? He came there for nothing but to see her,—I 'm perfectly sure of it."

"Well, Horace, you are about as absurd as a lover need
be!" said Harry. "Mr. Davenport is rather a conceited man of
the world; I think he patronized me somewhat extensively;
but all this about Tina is a romance of your own spinning,
you may be sure of it."

This conversation occurred one Saturday morning, while
we were dressing and arraying ourselves to go into Boston,
where we had engaged to dine at Madam Kittery's.

From the first of our coming to Cambridge, we had remembered our old-time friendship for the Kitterys, and it was an arranged thing that we were to dine with them every Saturday. The old Kittery mansion we had found the same still, charming, quaint, inviting place that it seemed to us in our childhood. The years that had passed over the silvery head of dear old Madam Kittery had passed lightly and reverently, each one leaving only a benediction.

She was still to be found, when we called, seated, as in days long ago, on her little old sofa in the sunny window, and with her table of books before her, reading her Bible and Dr. Johnson, and speaking on "Peace and good-will to men."

As to Miss Debby, she was as up and down, as high-stepping and outspoken and pleasantly sub-acid as ever. The French Revolution had put her in a state of good-humor hardly to be conceived of. It was so delightful to have all her theories of the bad effects of republics on lower classes illustrated and confirmed in such a striking manner, that even her indignation at the destruction of such vast numbers of the aristocracy was but a slight feature in comparison with it.

She kept the newspapers and magazines at hand which contained all the accounts of the massacres, mobbings, and outrages, and read them, in a high tone of voice, to her serving-women, butler, and footman after family prayers. She catechized more energetically than ever, and bore more stringently on ordering one's self lowly and reverently to one's betters, enforcing her remarks by the blood-and-thunder stories of the guillotine in France.

We were hardly seated in the house, and had gone over the usual track of inquiries which fill up the intervals, when she burst forth on us, triumphant.

"Well, my English papers have come in. Have you seen the last news from France? They're at it yet, hotter than ever. One would think that murdering the king and queen might have satisfied them, but it don't a bit. Everybody is at it now, cutting everybody's else throat, and there really does seem to be a prospect that the whole French nation will become extinct."

"Indeed," said Harry, with an air of amusement. "Well, Miss Debby, I suppose you think that would be the best way of settling things."

"Don't know but it would," said Miss Debby, putting on her spectacles in a manner which pushed her cap-border up into a bristling, helmet-like outline, and whirling over her file of papers, seemingly with a view to edifying us with the most startling morsels of French history for the six months past.

"Here's the account of how they worshipped 'the Goddess of Reason'!" she cried, eying us fiercely, as if we had been part and party in the transaction. "Here's all about how their philosophers and poets, and what not, put up a drab, and worshipped her as their 'Goddess of Reason'! And then they annulled the Sabbath, and proclaimed that 'Death is an Eternal Sleep'! Now, that is just what Tom Jefferson likes; it's what suits him. I read it to Ellery Davenport yesterday, to show him what his principles come to."

Harry immediately hastened to assure Miss Debby that we were staunch Federalists, and not in the least responsible for any of the acts or policy of Thomas Jefferson.

"Don't know anything about that; you see it's the Democrats that have got the country, and are running as hard as they can after France. Ah, here it is," Miss Debby added, still turning over her files of papers. "Here are the particulars of the execution of the queen. You can see,—they had her on a common cart, hands tied behind her, rattling and jolting, with all the vile fishwomen and dirty drabs of Paris leering and jeering at her, and they even had the cruelty," she added, coming indignantly at us as if we were responsible for it, "to stop the cart in front of her palace, so that she might be agonized at seeing her former home, and they might taunt her in her agonies! Anybody that can read that, and not say the French are devils, I'd like to know what they are made of!"

"Well," said Harry, undismayed by the denunciations; "the French are an exceedingly sensitive and excitable people, who had been miseducated and mismanaged, and taught brutality and cruelty by the examples of the clergy and nobility."

"Excitable fiddlesticks!" said Miss Debby, who, like my grandmother, had this peculiar way of summing up an argument. "I don't believe in softening sin and iniquity by such sayings as that."

"But you must think," said Harry, "that the French are human beings, and only act as any human beings would under their circumstances."

"Don't believe a word of it!" said she, shortly. "I agree with the man who said, 'God made two kinds of nature,—human nature and French nature.' Voltaire, was n't it, himself, that said the French were a compound of the tiger and the monkey? I wonder what Tom Jefferson thinks of his beautiful, darling French Republic now! I presume he likes it. I don't doubt it is just such a state of things as he is trying to bring to pass here in America."

"O," said I, "the Federalists will head him at the next election."

"I don't know anything about your Democrats and your Federalists," said she. "I thank Heaven I wash my hands of this government."

"And does King George still reign here?" said Harry.

"Certainly he does, young gentleman! Whatever happens to *this* government, *I* have no part in it."

Miss Debby, upon this, ushered us to the dinner-table, and said grace in a resounding and belligerent voice, and, sitting down, began to administer the soup to us with great determination.

Old Madam Kittery, who had listened with a patient smile to all the preceding conversation, now began in a gentle aside to me.

"I really don't think it is good for Debby to read those bloody-bone stories morning, noon, and night, as she does," she said. "She really almost takes away my appetite some days, and it does seem as if she would n't talk about anything else. Now, Horace," she said to me, appealingly, "the Bible says 'Charity rejoiceth not in iniquity,' and I can't help feeling that Debby talks as if she were really glad to see those poor French making such a mess of things. I can't feel so. If they are French, they 're our brothers, you know, and Debby really seems to go against the Bible,—not that she means to, dear," she added, earnestly, laying her hand on mine; "Debby is an excellent woman; but, between you and me, I think she is a little excitable."

"What's that mother's saying?" said Miss Debby, who kept a strict survey over all the sentiments expressed in her household. "What was mother saying?"

"I was saying, Debby, that I did n't think it did any good for you to keep reading over and over those dreadful things."

"And who does keep reading them over?" said Miss Debby, "I should like to know. I 'm sure I don't; except when it is absolutely necessary to instruct the servants and put them on their guard. I 'm sure I am as averse to such details as anybody can be."

Miss Debby said this with that innocent air with which good sort of people very generally maintain that they never do things which most of their acquaintances consider them particular nuisances for doing.

"By the by, Horace," said Miss Debby, by way of changing the subject, "have you seen Ellery Davenport since he came home?"

"No," said I, with a sudden feeling as if my heart was sinking down into my boots. "Has he come home to stay?"

"O yes," said Miss Debby; "his dear, sweet, model, Republican France grew too hot to hold him. He had to flee to England, and now he has concluded to come home and make what mischief he can here, with his democratic principles and his Rousseau and all the rest of them."

"Debby is n't as set against Ellery as she seems to be," said the old lady, in an explanatory aside to me. "You know, dear, he 's her cousin."

"And you really think he intends to live in this country for the future?" said I.

"Well, I suppose so," said Miss Debby. "You know that poor, miserable, crazy wife of his is dead, and my lord is turned loose on society as a widower at large, and all the talk here in good circles is, Who is the blessed woman that shall be Mrs. Ellery Davenport the second? The girls are all pulling caps for him, of course."

It was perfectly ridiculous and absurd, but I suddenly lost all appetite for my dinner, and sat back in my chair playing with my knife and fork, until the old lady said to me compassionately:—

"Why, dear, you don't seem to be eating anything! Debby,

put an oyster-*paté* on Horace's plate; he don't seem to relish his chicken."

I had to submit to the oyster-*paté*, and sit up and eat it like a man, to avoid the affectionate importunity of my dear old friend. In despair, I plunged into the subject least agreeable to me, and remarked:—

"Mr. Davenport is a very brilliant man, and I suppose in very good circumstances; is he not?"

"Yes, enormously rich," said Miss Debby. "He still passes for young, with that face of his that never will grow old, I believe. And then he has a tongue that could wheedle a bird out of a tree; so I don't know what is to hinder him from having as many wives as Solomon, if he feels so disposed. I don't imagine there is anybody would say 'No' to him."

"Well, I hope he will marry a good girl," said the old lady, "poor dear boy. I always loved Ellery; and he would make any woman happy, I am sure."

"That depends," said Miss Debby, "on what the woman wants. If she wants laces and cashmere shawls, and horses and carriages, and a fine establishment, Ellery Davenport will give her those. But if she wants a man to love her all her life, that's what Ellery Davenport can't do for any woman. He is a man that never cares for anything he has got. It's always the thing that he has n't got that he's after. It's the 'pot of money at the end of the rainbow,' or the 'philosopher's stone,' or any other thing that keeps a man all his life on a canter, and never getting anywhere. And no woman will ever be anything to him but a temporary diversion. He can amuse himself in too many ways to want *her*."

"Yes," said the old lady, "but when a man marries he promises to cherish her."

"My dear mother, that is in the Church Service, and I assure you Ellery Davenport has got beyond that. He's altogether too fine and wise and enlightened to think that a man should spend his days in cherishing a woman merely because he went through the form of marriage with her in church. Much cherishing his crazy wife got of him! but he used his affliction to get half a dozen girls in love with him, so that he might be cherished himself. I tell you what,—Ellery Davenport lays out to marry a real angel. He's to swear and she's to pray! He is to wander where he likes, and she is always to meet him with a smile and ask no questions. That is the part for Mrs. Ellery Davenport to act."

"I don't believe a word of it, Debby," said the old lady. "You 'll see now,—you 'll see."

XLI.

Night Talks

WE walked home that night by starlight, over the long bridge between Boston and Cambridge, and watched the image of the great round yellow moon just above the horizon, breaking and shimmering in the water into a thousand crystal fragments, like an orb of golden glass. We stopped midway in the calm obscurity, with our arms around each other, and had one of those long talks that friends, even the most confidential, can have only in the darkness. Cheek to cheek under the soft dim mantle of the starlight, the night flowers of the innermost soul open.

We talked of our loves, our hopes, of the past, the present, and the great hereafter, in which we hoped forever to mingle. And then Harry spoke to me of his mother, and told in burning words of that life of bitterness and humiliation and sorrow through which he had passed with her.

"O Harry," said I, "did it not try your faith, that God should have left her to suffer all that?"

"No, Horace, no, because in all that suffering she conquered,—she was more than conqueror. O, I have seen such divine peace in her eyes, at the very time when everything earthly was failing her! Can I ever doubt? I who saw into heaven when she entered? No, I have seen her crowned, glorified, in my soul as plainly as if it had been a vision."

At that moment I felt in myself that magnetic vibration of the great central nerves which always prefaced my spiritual visions, and looking up I saw that the beautiful woman I had seen once before was standing by Harry, but now more glowing and phosphorescent than I saw her last; there was a divine, sweet, awful radiance in her eyes, as she raised her hands above his head, he, meanwhile, stooping down and looking intently into the water.

"Harry," said I, after a few moments of silence, "do you believe your mother sees and knows what you do in this world, and watches over you?"

"That has always been one of those things that I have believed without reasoning," said Harry, musingly. "I never could help believing it; and there have been times in my life when I felt so certain that she must be near me, that it seemed as though, if I spoke, she must answer,—if I reached out my hand, it would touch hers. It is one of my instinctive certainties. It is curious," he added, "that the difference between Esther and myself is just the reverse kind of that which generally subsists between man and woman. She has been all her life so drilled in what logicians call reasoning, that, although she has a glorious semi-spiritual nature, and splendid moral instincts, she never trusts them. She is like an eagle that should insist upon climbing a mountain by beak and claw instead of using wings. She must always see the syllogism before she will believe."

"For my part," said I, "I have always felt the tyranny of the hard New England logic, and it has kept me from really knowing what to believe about many phenomena of my own mind that are vividly real to me." Here I faltered and hesitated, and the image that seemed to stand by us slowly faded. I could not and did not say to Harry how often I had seen it.

"After all I have heard and thought on this subject," said Harry, "my religious faith is what it always was,—a deep, instinctive certainty, an embrace by the soul of *something* which it could not exist without. My early recollections are stronger than anything else of perfect and utter helplessness, of troubles entirely beyond all human aid. My father—" He stopped and shuddered. "Horace, he was one of those whom intemperance makes mad. For a great part of his time he was a madman, with all the cunning, all the ingenuity, the devilishness of insanity, and I have had to stand between him and my mother, and to hide Tina out of his way." He seemed to shudder as one convulsed. "One does not get over such a childhood," he said. "It has made all my religious views, my religious faith, rest on two ideas,—man's helplessness, and God's helpfulness. We are sent into this world in the midst of a blind, confused jangle of natural laws, which we cannot by any possibility understand, and which cut their way through and over and around us. They tell us nothing; they have no sympathy; they hear no prayer; they spare neither vice nor virtue. And if we have no friend above to guide us through the labyrinth, if there is no Father's heart, no helping hand, of what use is life? I would throw myself into this river, and have it over with at once."

"I always noticed your faith in prayer," said I. "But how can it consist with this known inflexibility of natural laws?"

"And what if natural laws were meant as servants of man's moral life? What if Jesus Christ and his redeeming, consoling work were the *first* thing, and all things made by him for this end? Inflexible physical laws are necessary; their very inflexibility is divine order; but 'what law cannot do, in that it is weak through the flesh, God did by sending his Son in the likeness of sinful flesh.' Christ delivers us from slavery to natural law; he comes to embody and make visible the paternal idea; and if you and I, with our small knowledge of physical laws, can so turn and arrange them that their inflexible course shall help, and not hinder, much more can their Maker."

"You always speak of Christ as God."

"I have never thought of God in any other way," he answered. "Christ is the God of sufferers; and those who learn religion by sorrow always turn to him. No other than a suffering God could have helped my mother in her anguish."

"And do you think," said I, "that prayer is a clew strong enough to hold amid the rugged realities of life?"

"I do," said Harry. "At any rate, there is my great venture; that is my life-experiment. My mother left me that as her only legacy."

"It certainly seems to have worked well for you so far, Harry," said I, "and for me too, for God has guided us to what we scarcely could have hoped for, two poor boys as we were, and so utterly helpless. But then, Harry, there must be a great many prayers that are never answered."

"Of course," said Harry, "I do not suppose that God has put the key of all the universe into the hand of every child; but it is a comfort to have a Father to ask of, even though he refuse five times out of six, and it makes all the difference between having a father and being an orphan. Yes," he added, after a few moments of thought, "my poor mother's prayers seemed often to be denied, for she prayed that my father might reform. She often prayed from day to day that we might be spared miseries that he still brought upon us. But I feel sure that she has seen by this time that her Father heard the prayers that he seemed to deny, and her faith in him never failed. What is that music?" he said.

At this moment there came softly over the gleaming water, from the direction of the sea, the faintest possible vibration of a sound, like the dying of an organ tone. It might be from some ship, hidden away far off in the mist, but the effect was soft and dreamy as if it came from some spirit-land.

"I often think," said Harry, listening for a moment, "that no one can pronounce on what this life has been to him until he has passed entirely through it, and turns around and surveys it from the other world. I think then we shall see everything in its true proportions; but till then we must walk by faith and not by sight,—faith that God loves us, faith that our Saviour is always near us, and that all things are working together for good."

"Harry," said I, "do you ever think of your father now?"

"Horace, there is where I wish I could be a more perfect Christian than I am. I have a bitter feeling toward him, that I fear is not healthful, and that I pray God to take away. Tonight, since we have been standing here, I have had a strange, remorseful feeling about him, as if some good spirit were interceding for him with me, and trying to draw me to love and forgive him. I shall never see him, probably, until I meet him in the great Hereafter, and then, perhaps, I shall find that her prayers have prevailed for him."

It was past twelve o'clock when we got to our room that night, and Harry found lying on his table a great sealed package from England. He opened it and found in it, first, a letter from his father, Sir Harry Percival. The letter was as follows:—

"HOLME HOUSE.

"MY SON HARRY:—

"I have had a dozen minds to write to you before now, having had good accounts of you from Mr. Davenport; but, to say truth, have been ashamed to write. I did not do right by your mother, nor by you and your sister, as I am now free to acknowledge. She was not of a family equal to ours, but she was too good for me. I left her in America, like a brute as I was, and God has judged me for it.

"I married the woman my father picked out for me, when I came home, and resolved to pull up and live soberly like a decent man. But nothing went well with me. My children died one after another; my boy lived to be seven years old, but he was feeble, and now he is dead too, and you are the heir. I am thinking that I am an old sinner, and in a bad way. Have had two turns of gout in the stomach that went hard with me, and the doctor don't think I shall stand many such. I have made my will with a provision for the girl, and you will have the estate in course. I do wish you would come over and see a poor old sinner before he dies. It is n't in the least jolly being here, and I am dev'lish cross, they say. I suppose I am, but if you were minded to come I 'd try and behave myself, and so make amends for what 's past beyond recall.

"*Your father,*
"HARRY PERCIVAL."

Accompanying this letter was a letter from the family lawyer, stating that on the 18th day of the month past Sir Harry Percival had died of an attack of gout. The letter went on to give various particulars about the state of the property, and the steps which had been taken in relation to it, and expressing the hope that the arrangements made would meet with his approbation.

It may well be imagined that it was almost morning before we closed our eyes, after so very startling a turn in our affairs. We lay long discussing it in every possible light, and now first I found courage to tell Harry of my own peculiar experiences, and of what I had seen that very evening. "It seems to me," said Harry, when I had told him all, "as if I *felt* what you saw. I had a consciousness of a sympathetic presence, something breathing over me like wind upon harp-strings, something particularly predisposing me to think kindly of my father. My feeling towards him has been the weak spot of my inner life always, and I had a morbid horror of him. Now I feel at peace with him. Perhaps her prayers have prevailed to save him from utter ruin."

XLII.

Spring Vacation at Oldtown

IT was the spring vacation, and Harry and I were coming again to Oldtown; and ten miles back, where we changed horses, we had left the crawling old Boston stage and took a foot-path through a patch of land known as the Spring Pasture. Our road lay pleasantly along the brown, sparkling river, which was now just waked up, after its winter nap, as fussy and busy and chattering as a housekeeper that has overslept herself. There were downy catkins on the willows, and the water-maples were throwing out their crimson tassels. The sweet-flag was just showing its green blades above the water, and here and there, in nooks, there were yellow cowslips reflecting their bright gold faces in the dark water.

Harry and I had walked this way that we might search under the banks and among the dried leaves for the white waxen buds and flowers of the trailing arbutus. We were down on our knees, scraping the leaves away, when a well-known voice came from behind the bushes.

"Wal, lordy massy, boys! Here ye be! Why, I ben up to Siah's tahvern, an' looked inter the stage, an' did n't see yer. I jest thought I 'd like to come an' kind o' meet yer. Lordy massy, they 's all a lookin' out for yer 't all the winders; 'n' Aunt Lois, she 's ben bilin' up no end o' doughnuts, an' tearin' round 'nough to drive the house out o' the winders, to git everything ready for ye. Why, it beats the Prodigal Son all holler, the way they 're killin' the fatted calves for yer; an' everybody in Oldtown 's a wantin' to see Sir Harry."

"O nonsense, Sam!" said Harry, coloring. "Hush about that! We don't have titles over here in America."

"Lordy massy, that 's just what I wus a tellin' on 'em up to store. It 's a pity, ses I, this yere happened arter peace was signed, 'cause we might ha' had a real live Sir Harry round among us. An' I think Lady Lothrop, she kind o' thinks so too."

"O nonsense!" said Harry. "Sam, are the folks all well?"

"O lordy massy, yes! Chirk and chipper as can be. An' there 's Tiny, they say she 's a goin' to be an heiress nowadays, an' there 's no end of her beaux. There 's Ellery Devenport ben down here these two weeks, a puttin' up at the tahvern, with a landau an' a span o' crack horses, a takin' on her out to ride every day, and Miss Mehitable, she 's so sot up, she 's really got a bran-new bonnet, an' left off that 'ere old un o' hern that she 's had trimmed over spring an' fall goin' on these 'ere ten years. I thought that 'ere bonnet 's going to last out my time, but I see it hain't. An' she 's got a new Injy shawl, that Mr. Devenport gin her. Yeh see, he understan's courtin', all round."

This intelligence, of course, was not the most agreeable to me. I hope, my good friends, that you have never known one of those quiet hours of life, when, while you are sitting talking and smiling, and to all appearance quite unmoved, you hear a remark or learn a fact that seems to operate on you as if somebody had quietly turned a faucet that was letting out your very life. Down, down, down, everything seems sinking, the strength passing away from you as the blood passes when an artery is cut. It was with somewhat this sensation that I listened to Sam's chatter, while I still mechanically poked away the leaves and drew out the long waxy garlands that I had been gathering for *her!*

Sam seated himself on the bank, and, drawing his knees up to his chin and clasping his hands upon them, began moralizing in his usual strain.

"Lordy massy, lordy massy, what a changin' world this 'ere is! It 's jest see-saw, teeter-tawter, up an' down. To-day it 's I 'm up an' you 're down, an' to-morrow it 's you 're up and I 'm down! An' then, by an' by, death comes an' takes us all. I 've ben kind o' dwellin' on some varses to-day,—

> 'Death, like a devourin' delūge,
>   Sweeps all away.
> The young, the old, the middle-aged,
>   To him become a prey.'

That 'ere is what Betty Poganut repeated to me the night

we sot up by Statiry's corpse. Yeh 'member Statiry Poganut? Well, she 's dead at last. Yeh see, we all gits called in our turn. We hain't here no continuin' city."

"But, Sam," said I, "how does business get along? Have n't you anything to do but tramp the pastures and moralize?"

"Wal," said Sam, "I 've hed some pretty consid'able spells of blacksmithin' lately. There 's Mr. Devenport, he 's sech a pleasant-spoken man, he told me he brought his team all the way up from Bostin a purpose so that I might 'tend to their huffs. I 've ben a shoein' on 'em fresh all round, an' the off horse, he 'd kind o' got a crack in his huff, an' I 've been a doctorin' on 't; an' Mr. Devenport, he said he had n't found nobody that knew how to doctor a horse's huffs ekal to me. Very pleasant-spoken man Mr. Devenport is; he 's got a good word for everybody. They say there ain't no end to his fortin, an' he goes a flingin' on 't round, right an' left, like a prince. Why, when I 'd done shoein' his horses, he jest put his hand inter his pocket an' handed me out ten dollars! ripped it out, he did, jest as easy as water runs! But there was Tiny a standin' by; I think she kind o' sot him on. O lordy massy, it 's plain to be seen that *she* rules him. It 's all cap in hand to her, an' 'What you will, madam,' an' 'Will ye have the end o' the rainbow, or a slice out o' the moon, or what is it?' It 's all ekal to him, so as Miss Tiny wants it. Lordy massy," he said, lowering his voice confidentially to Harry, "course these 'ere things is all temporal, an' our hearts ought n't to be too much sot on 'em; still he 's got about the most amazin' fortin there is round Bostin. Why, if you b'lieve me, 'tween you an' me, it 's him as owns the Dench Place, where you and Tiny put up when you wus children! Don't ye 'member when I found ye? Ye little guessed whose house ye wus a puttin' up at then; did yer? Lordy massy, lordy massy, who 'd ha' thought it? The wonderful ways of Providence! 'He setteth the poor on high, an' letteth the runagates continoo in scarceness.' Wal, wal, it 's a kind o' instructive world."

"Do you suppose," said Harry to me, in a low voice, "that this creature knows anything of what he is saying?"

"I 'm afraid he does," said I. "Sam seems to have but one talent, and that is picking up news; and generally his guesses turn out to be about true."

"Sam," said I, by way of getting him to talk of something else, rather than on what I dreaded to hear, "you have n't said a word about Hepsy and the children. How are they all?"

"Wal, the young uns hes all got the whoopin' cough," said Sam, "an' I 'm e'en a'most beat out with 'em. For fust it 's one barks, an' then another, an' then all together. An' then Hepsy, she gets riled, an' she scolds; an', take it all together, a feller's head gits kind o' turned. When ye hes a lot o' young uns, there 's allus suthin' a goin' on among 'em; ef 't ain't whoopin' cough, it 's measles; an' ef 't ain't measles, it 's chicken-pox, or else it's mumps, or scarlet-fever, or suthin'. They 's all got to be gone through, fust an' last. It 's enough to wean a body from this world. Lordy massy, yest'day art-ernoon I see yer Aunt Keziah an' yer Aunt Lois out a cuttin' cowslip greens t'other side o' th' river, an' the sun it shone so bright, an' the turtles an' frogs they kind o' peeped so pleas-ant, an' yer aunts they sot on the bank so kind o' easy an' free, an' I stood there a lookin' on 'em, an' I could n't help a thinkin', 'Lordy massy, I wish t' I wus an old maid.' Folks 'scapes a great deal that don't hev no young uns a hangin' onter 'em."

"Well, Sam," said Harry, "is n't there any news stirring round in the neighborhood?"

"S'pose ye hain't heerd about the great church-quarrel over to Needmore?" he said.

"Quarrel? Why, no," said Harry. "What is it about?"

"Wal, ye see, there 's a kind o' quarrel ris 'tween Parson Perry and Deacon Bangs. I can't jest git the right on 't, but it 's got the hull town afire. I b'lieve it cum up in a kind o' dispute how to spell Saviour. The Deacon he 's on the school-committee, an' Parson Perry he 's on 't; an' the Deacon he spells it *iour*, an' Parson Perry he spells it *ior*, an' they would n't neither on 'em give up. Wal, ye know Deacon Bangs,—I *s'pose* he 's a Christian,—but, lordy massy, he 's one o' yer dreadful ugly kind o' Christians, that, when they gits their backs up, will do worse things than sinners will. I reelly think they kind o' take advantage o' their position, an' think, es they 're goin' to be saved by grace, grace shell hev enough on 't. Now, to my mind, ef either on 'em wus to give way, the Deacon oughter give up to the Parson; but the Dea-

con he don't think so. Between you and me," said Sam, "it 's
my opinion that ef Ma'am Perry hed n't died jest when she
did, this 'ere thing would never ha' growed to where 't is. But
ye see Ma'am Perry she died, an' that left Parson Perry a widower, an' folks did talk about him an' Mahaley Bangs, an' fact
was, 'long about last spring, Deacon Bangs an' Mis' Bangs an'
Mahaley wus jest as thick with the Parson as they could be.
Why, Granny Watkins told me about their havin' on him to
tea two an' three times a week, an' Mahaley 'd make two
kinds o' cake, an' they 'd have preserved watermelon rinds an'
peaches an' cranberry saace, an' then 't was all sugar an' all
sweet, an' the Deacon he talked 'bout raisin' Parson Perry's
salary. Wal, then, ye see, Parson Perry he went over to Oldtown an' married Jerushy Peabody. Now, Jerushy's a nice,
pious gal, an' it 's a free country, an' parsons hes a right to
suit 'emselves as well 's other men. But Jake Marshall, he ses
to me, when he heerd o' that, ses he, 'They 'll be findin' fault
with Parson Perry's doctrines now afore two months is up;
ye see if they don't.' Wal, sure enuff, this 'ere quarrel 'bout
spellin' Saviour come on fust, an' Deacon Bangs he fit the
Parson like a bulldog. An' next town-meetin' day he told Parson Perry right out before everybody thet he was wuss then
'n Armenian,—thet he was a rank Pelagian; 'n' he said there
was folks thet hed taken notes o' his sermons for two years
back, 'n' they could show thet he hed n't preached the real
doctrine of total depravity, nor 'riginal sin, an' thet he 'd got
the plan o' salvation out o' j'int intirely; he was all kind o'
flattin' out onter morality. An' Parson Perry he sed he 'd
preached jest 's he allers hed. 'Tween you 'n' me, we know he
must ha' done that, 'cause these 'ere ministers thet hev to go
preachin' round 'n' round like a hoss in a cider-mill,—wal,
course they *must* preach the same sermons over. I s'pose they
kind o' trim 'em up with new collars 'n' wris'bands. But we
used to say thet Parson Lothrop hed a bar'l o' sermons, 'n'
when he got through the year he turned his bar'l t'other side
up, and begun at t'other end. Lordy massy, who 's to know
it, when half on em 's asleep? And I guess the preachin 's full
as good as the pay anyhow! Wal, the upshot on 't all is, they
got a gret counsel there, an' they 're a tryin' Mr. Perry for
heresy an' what not. Wal, I don't b'lieve there 's a yaller dog

goes inter the Needmore meetin'-house now that ain't got his mind made up one way or t'other about it. Yer don't hear nothin' over there now 'xcept about Armenians an' Pelagians an' Unitarians an' total depravity. Lordy massy! wal, they lives up to that doctrine any way. What do ye think of old Sphyxy Smith's bein' called in as one o' the witnesses in council? She don' know no more 'bout religion than an' old hetchel, but she 's ferce as can be on Deacon Bangs's side, an' Old Crab Smith he hes to hev' his say 'bout it."

"Do tell," said Harry, wonderingly, "if that old creature is alive yet!"

"'Live? Why, yis, ye may say so," said Sam. "Much alive as ever he was. Ye see he kind o' pickles himself in hard cider, an' I dunno but he may live to hector his wife till he 's ninety. But he 's gret on the trial now, an' very much interested 'bout the doctrine. He ses thet he hain't heard a sermon on sovereignty, or 'lection, or reprobation, sence he can remember. Wal, t'other side, they say they don't see what business Old Crab an' Miss Sphyxy hev to be meddlin' so much, when they ain't church-members. Why, I was over to Needmore townmeetin' day jest to hear 'em fight over it; they talked a darned sight more 'bout that than 'bout the turnpikes or town business. Why, I heard Deacon Brown (he 's on the parson's side) tellin' Old Crab he did n't see what business *he* had to *boss* the doctrines, when he warn't a church-member, and Old Crab said it *was* his bisness about the doctrines, 'cause he *paid* to hev 'em. 'Ef I *pay* for good strong doctrine, why, I want to *hev* good strong doctrine,' says Old Crab, says he. 'Ef I pays for hell-fire, I want to hev hell-fire, and hev it hot too. I don't want none o' your prophesyin' smooth things. Why,' says he, 'look at Dr. Stern. His folks hes the very hair took off their heads 'most every Sunday, and he don't get no more 'n we pay Parson Perry. I tell yew,' says Old Crab, 'he 's a lettin' on us all go to sleep, and it 's no wonder I ain't in the church.' Ye see, Old Crab and Sphyxy, they seem to be kind o' settin' it down to poor old Parson Perry's door that he hain't converted 'em, an' made saints on 'em long ago, when they 've paid up their part o' the salary reg'lar, every year. Jes' so onreasonable folks will be; they give a man two hundred dollars a year an' his wood, an' spect him to git all on em' inter the kingdom o' heaven, whether they will or no, jest as the angels got Lot's wife and daughters out o' Sodom."

"That poor little old woman!" said Harry. "Do tell if she is living yet!"

"O yis, she's all right," said Sam; "she's one o' these 'ere little thin, dry old women that keep a good while. But ain't ye heerd? their son Obid 's come home an' bought a farm, an' married a nice gal, and he insists on it his mother shall live with him. An' so Old Crab and Miss Sphyxy, they fight it out together. So the old woman is delivered from him most o' the time. Sometimes he walks over there an' stays a week, an' takes a spell o' aggravatin' on 'er, that kind o' sets him up, but he 's so busy now 'bout the quarrel 't I b'lieve he lets her alone."

By this time we had reached the last rail-fence which separated us from the grassy street of Oldtown, and here Sam took his leave of us.

"I promised Hepsy when I went out," he said, "thet I 'd go to the store and git her some corn meal, but I 'll be round agin in th' evening. Look 'ere," he added, "I wus out this mornin', an' I dug some sweet-flag root for yer. I know ye used ter like sweet-flag root. 'T ain't time for young wintergreen yit, but here 's a bunch I picked yer, with the berries an' old leaves. Do take 'em, boys, jest for sake o' old times!"

We thanked him, of course; there was a sort of aroma of boyhood about these things, that spoke of spring days and melting snows, and long Saturday afternoon rambles that we had had with Sam years before. And we saw his lean form go striding off with something of an affectionate complacency.

"Horace," said Harry, the minute we were alone, "you must n't mind too much about Sam's gossip."

"It is just what I have been expecting," said I; "but in a few moments we shall know the truth."

We went on until the square white front of the old Rossiter house rose upon our view. We stopped before it, and down the walk from the front door to the gate, amid the sweet budding lilacs, came gleaming and glancing the airy form of Tina. So airy she looked, so bright, so full of life and joy, and threw herself into Harry's arms, laughing and crying.

"O Harry, Harry! God has been good to us! And you, dear

brother Horace," she said, turning to me and giving me both her hands, with one of those frank, loving looks that said as much as another might say by throwing herself into your arms. "We are all so happy!" she said.

I determined to have it over at once, and I said, "Am I then to congratulate you, Tina, on your engagement?"

She laughed and blushed, and held up her hand, on which glittered a great diamond, and hid her face for a moment on Harry's shoulder.

"I could n't write to you about it, boys,—I could n't! But I meant to tell you myself, and tell you the first thing too. I wanted to tell you about him, because I think you none of you know him, or half how noble and good he is! Come, come in," she said, taking us each by the hand and drawing us along with her. "Come in and see Aunty; she 'll be so glad to see you!"

If there was any one thing for which I was glad at this moment, it was that I had never really made love to Tina. It was a comfort to me to think that she did not and could not possibly know the pain she was giving me. All I know is that, at the moment, I was seized with a wild, extravagant gayety, and rattled and talked and laughed with a reckless *abandon* that quite astonished Harry. It seemed to me as if every ludicrous story and every droll remark that I had ever heard came thronging into my head together. And I believe that Tina really thought that I was sincere in rejoicing with her. Miss Mehitable talked with us gravely about it while Tina was out of the room. It was most sudden and unexpected, she said, to her; she always had supposed that Ellery Davenport had admired Tina, but never that he had thought of her in this way. In a worldly point of view, the match was a more brilliant one than could ever have been expected. He was of the best old families in the country,—of the Edwards and the Davenport stock,—his talents were splendid, and his wealth would furnish everything that wealth could furnish. "There is only one thing," she continued gravely; "I am not satisfied about his religious principles. But Tina is an enthusiast, and has perfect faith that he will come all right in this respect. He seems to be completely dazzled and under her influence now," said Miss Mehitable, taking a leisurely pinch of snuff, "but then, you see, that's a common phenomenon, about this time in a man's life. But," she added, "where there is such a strong attachment on both sides, all we can do is to wish both sides well, and speed them on their way. Mr. Davenport has interested himself in the very kindest manner in regard to both Tina and Harry, and I suppose it is greatly owing to this that affairs have turned out as prosperously as they have. As you know, Sir Harry made a handsome provision for Tina in his will. I confess I am glad of that," she said, with a sort of pride. "I would n't want my little Tina to have passed into his arms altogether penniless. When first love is over, men sometimes remember those things."

"If my father had not done justice to Tina in his will," said Harry, "I should have done it. My sister should not have gone to any man a beggar."

"I know that, my dear," said Miss Mehitable, "but still it is a pleasure to think that your father did it. It was a justice to your mother's memory that I am glad he rendered."

"And when is this marriage to take place?" said I.

"Mr. Davenport wants to carry her away in June," said Miss Mehitable. "That leaves but little time; but he says he must go to join the English Embassy, certainly by midsummer, and as there seems to be a good reason for his haste, I suppose I must not put my feelings in the way. It seems now as if I had had her only a few days, and she has been so very sweet and lovely to me. Well," said she, after a moment, "I suppose the old sweetbrier-bushes feel lonesome when we cut their blossoms and carry them off, but the old thorny things must n't have blossoms if they don't expect to have them taken. That 's all we scraggly old people are good for."

XLIII.

What Our Folks Thought about It

At home, that evening, before the great open fire, still the same subject was discussed. Tina's engagement to Ellery Davenport was spoken of as the next most brilliant stroke of luck to Harry's accession to the English property. Aunt Lois was all smiles and suavity, poor dear old soul! How all the wrinkles and crinkles of her face smoothed out under the influence of prosperity! and how providential everything appeared to her!

"Providence gets some pay-days," said an old divine. Generally speaking, his account is suffered to run on with very lax attention. But when a young couple make a fortunate engagement, or our worldly prospects take a sudden turn to go as we would, the account of Providence is gladly balanced; praise and thanksgiving come in over-measure.

For my part, I could n't see the Providence at all in it, and found this looking into happiness through other people's eyes a very fatiguing operation.

My grandfather and grandmother, as they sat pictured out by the light of a magnificent hickory fire, seemed scarcely a year older; but their faces this evening were beaming complacently; and my mother, in her very quiet way, could scarcely help triumphing over Aunt Lois. I was a sophomore in Cambridge, and Harry a landed proprietor, and Tina an heiress to property in her own right, instead of our being three poor orphan children without any money, and with the up-hill of life to climb.

In the course of the evening, Miss Mehitable came in with Ellery Davenport and Tina. Now, much as a man will dislike the person who steps between him and the lady of his love, I could not help, this evening, myself feeling the power of that fascination by which Ellery Davenport won the suffrages of all hearts.

Aunt Lois, as usual, was nervous and fidgety with the

thought that the call of the splendid Mr. Davenport had surprised them all at the great kitchen-fire, when there was the best room cold as Nova Zembla. She looked almost reproachfully at Tina, and said apologetically to Mr. Davenport, "We are rough working folks, and you catch us just as we are. If we'd known you were coming, we'd have had a fire in the parlor."

"Then, Miss Badger, you would have been very cruel, and deprived us of a rare enjoyment," said he. "What other land but our own America can give this great, joyous, abundant home-fire? The great kitchen-fire of New England," he added, seating himself admiringly in front of it, "gives you all the freshness and simplicity of forest life, with a sense of shelter and protection. It's like a camp-fire in the woods, only that you have a house over you, and a good bed to sleep in at hand; and there is nothing that draws out the heart like it. People never can talk to each other as they do by these great open fires. For my part," he said, "I am almost a Fire-worshipper. I believe in the divine properties of flame. It purifies the heart and warms the affections, and when people sit and look into the coals together, they feel a sort of glow of charity coming over them that they never feel anywhere else."

"Now, I should think," said Aunt Lois, "Mr. Davenport, that you must have seen so much pomp and splendor and luxury abroad, that our rough life here would seem really disagreeable to you."

"Quite the contrary," said Ellery Davenport. "We go abroad to appreciate our home. Nature is our mother, and the life that is lived nearest to nature is, after all, the one that is the pleasantest. I met Brant at court last winter. You know he was a wild Indian to begin with, and he has seen both extremes, for now he is Colonel Brant, and has been moving in fashionable society in London. So I thought he must be a competent person to decide on the great question between savage and civilized life, and he gave his vote for the savage."

"I wonder at him," said my grandmother.

"Well, I remember," said Tina, "we had one day and night of savage life—don't you remember, Harry?—that was very pleasant. It was when we stayed with the old Indian woman,—do you remember? It was all very well, so long as the sun shone; but then when the rain fell, and the wind blew, and the drunken Indian came home, it was not so pleasant."

"That was the time, young lady," said Ellery Davenport, looking at her with a flash in his blue eyes, "that you established yourself as housekeeper on my premises! If I had only known it, I might have picked you up then, as a waif on my grounds."

"It's well you did not," said Tina, laughing; "you would have found me troublesome to keep. I don't believe you would have been as patient as dear old Aunty, here," she added, laying her head on Miss Mehitable's shoulder. "I was a perfect brier-rose,—small leaves and a great many prickles."

"By the by," said Harry, "Sam Lawson has been telling us, this morning, about our old friends Miss Asphyxia Smith and Old Crab."

"Is it possible," said Tina, laughing, "that those creatures are living yet? Why, I look back on them as some awful pre-Adamite monsters."

"Who was Miss Asphyxia?" said Ellery Davenport. "I have n't heard of her."

"O, 't was a great threshing-machine of a woman that caught me between its teeth some years ago," said Tina. "What do you suppose would ever have become of me, Aunty, if she had kept me? Do you think she ever could have made me a great stramming, threshing, scrubbing, floor-cleaning machine, like herself? She warned Miss Mehitable," continued Tina, looking at Ellery and laughing shyly, "that I never should grow up to be good for anything; and she spoke a fatal truth, for, since she gave me up, every mortal creature has tried to pet and spoil me. Dear old Aunty and Mr. Rossiter have made some feeble attempts to make me good for something, but they have n't done much at it."

"Thank Heaven!" said Ellery Davenport. "Who would think of training a wild rose? I sometimes look at the way a sweetbrier grows over one of our rough stone walls, and think what a beautiful defiance it is to gardeners."

"That is all very pretty to say," said Tina, "when you happen to be where there are none but wild roses; but when you were among marchionesses and duchesses, how was it then?"

For answer, Ellery Davenport bent over her, and said something which I could not hear. He had the art, without seeming to whisper, of throwing a sentence from him so that it should reach but one ear; and Tina laughed and blushed and dimpled, and looked as if a thousand little graces were shaking their wings around her.

It was one of Tina's great charms that she was never for a moment at rest. In this she was like a bird, or a brook, or a young tree, in which there is always a little glancing shimmer of movement. And when anything pleased her, her face sparkled as a river does when something falls into it. I noticed Ellery Davenport's eyes followed all these little motions as if he had been enchanted. O, there was no doubt that the great illusion, the delicious magic, was in full development between them. And Tina looked so gladly satisfied, and glanced about the circle and at him with such a quiet triumph of possession, and such satisfaction in her power over him, that it really half reconciled me to see that she was so happy. And, after all, I thought to myself as I looked at the airy and *spirituel* style of her beauty,—a beauty that conveyed the impression of fragility and brilliancy united to the highest point,—such a creature as that is made for luxury, made for perfume and flowers and jewelry and pomp of living and obsequious tending, for old aristocratic lands and court circles, where she would glitter as a star. And what had I to offer,—I, a poor sophomore in Harvard, owing that position to the loving charity of my dear old friend? My love to her seemed a madness and a selfishness,—as if I had wished to take the evening star out of the heavens and burn it for a household lamp. "How fortunate, how fortunate," I thought to myself, "that I have never told her! For now I shall keep the love of her heart. We are friends, and she shall be the lady of my heart forever,—the lady of my dreams."

I knew, too, that I had a certain hold upon her; and even at this moment I saw her eye often, as from old habit, looking across to me, a little timidly and anxiously, to see what I thought of her prize. She was Tina still,—the same old Tina, that always needed to be approved and loved and sympathized with, and have all her friends go with her, heart and hand, in all her ways. So I determined to like him.

At this moment Sam Lawson came in. I was a little curious to know how he had managed it with his conscience to leave his domestic circle under their trying circumstances, but I was very soon satisfied as to this point.

Sam, who had watched the light flaring out from the windows, and flattened his nose against the window-pane while he announced to Hepsy that "Mr. Devenport and Miss Mehitable and Tiny were all a goin' into the Deacon's to spend th' evenin'," could not resist the inexpressible yearning to have a peep himself at what was going on there.

He came in with a most prostrate air of dejection. Aunt Lois frowned with stern annoyance, and looked at my grandmother, as much as to say, "To think *he* should come in when Mr. Davenport is making a call here!"

Ellery Davenport, however, received him with a patronizing cheerfulness, — "Why, hulloa, Sam, how are you?" It was Ellery Davenport's delight to start Sam's loquacity and develop his conversational powers, and he made a welcoming movement toward the block of wood in the chimney-corner. "Sit down," he said, — "sit down, and tell us how Hepsy and the children are."

Tina and he looked at each other with eyes dancing with merriment.

"Wal, wal," said Sam, sinking into the seat and raising his lank hands to the fire, while his elbows rested on his knees, "the children's middlin', — Doctor Merrill ses he thinks they 've got past the wust on 't, — but Hepsy, she 's clean tuckered out, and kind o' discouraged. An' I thought I 'd come over an' jest ask Mis' Badger ef she would n't kind o' jest mix 'er up a little milk punch to kind o' set 'er up agin."

"What a considerate husband!" said Ellery Davenport, glancing around the circle with infinite amusement.

My grandmother, always prompt at any call on her charity, was already half across the floor toward her buttery, whence she soon returned with a saucepan of milk.

"I 'll watch that 'ere, Mis' Badger," said Sam. "Jest rake out the coals this way, an' when it begins ter simmer I 'll put in the sperits, ef ye 'll gin 'em to me. 'Give strong drink ter him as is ready to perish,' the Scriptur' says. Hepsy 's got an amazin' sight o' grit in 'er, but I 'clare for 't, she 's ben up an' down nights so much lately with them young uns thet she 's a'most clean wore out. An' I should be too, ef I did n't take a tramp now 'n' then to kind o' keep me up. Wal, ye see, the head o' the family, he *hes* to take car' o' himself, 'cause ye see, ef *he* goes down, all goes down. 'The man is the head o' the woman,' ye know," said Sam, as he shook his skillet of milk.

I could see Tina's eyes dancing with mirthfulness as Ellery Davenport answered, "I 'm glad to see, Sam, that you have a proper care of your health. You are such an important member of the community, that I don't know what Oldtown would be without you!"

"Wal, now, Mr. Devenport, ye flatter me; but then everybody don't seem to think so. I don't think folks like me, as does for this one an' does for that one, an' kind o' spreads out permiskus, is appreciated allers. There 's Hepsy, she 's allers at me, a sayin' I don't do nothin' for her, an' yet there las' night I wus up in my shirt, a shiverin' an' a goin' round, fust ter one and then ter 'nuther, a hevin' on 'em up an' a thumpin' on their backs, an' clarin' the phlegm out o' their thruts, till I wus e'en a'most fruz; and Hepsy, she lay there abed scoldin' 'cause I hed n't sawed no wood thet afternoon to keep up the fire. Lordy massy, I jest went out ter dig a leetle sweet-flag root ter gin ter the boys, 'cause I wus so kind o' wore out. I don't think these 'ere women ever 'flects on *men's* trials. They railly don't keep count o' what we do for 'em."

"What a picture of conjugal life!" said Ellery Davenport, glancing at Tina. "Yes, Sam, it is to be confessed that the female sex are pretty exorbitant creditors. They make us pay dear for serving them."

"Jes' so! jes' so!" said Sam. "They don't know nothin' what we undergo. I don't think Hepsy keeps no sort o' count o' the nights an' nights I 've walked the floor with the baby, whishin' an' shooin' on 't, and singin' to 't till my thrut wus sore, an' then hed to git up afore daylight to split oven-wood, an' then right to my blacksmithin', jest to git a little money to git the meat an' meal an' suthin' comfort'ble fur dinner! An' then, ye see, there don't nothin' *last*, when there 's so many mouths to eat it up; an' there 't is, it 's jest roun' an' roun'. Ye git a good piece o' beef Tuesday an' pay for 't, an' by Thursday it 's all gone, an' ye hev to go to work agin!

Lordy massy, this 'ere life don't seem hardly wuth hevin'. I s'pose, Mr. Devenport, you 've been among the gret folks o' th' earth, over there in King George's court? Why, they say here that you've ben an' tuk tea with the king, with his crown on 's head! I s'pose they all goes roun' with their crowns on over there; don't they?"

"Well, no, not precisely," said Ellery Davenport. "I think they rather mitigate their splendors when they have to do with us poor republicans, so as not to bear us down altogether."

"Jes' so," said Sam, "like Moses, that put a veil over 's face 'cause th' Israelites could n't bear the glory."

"Well," said Ellery Davenport, "I 've not been struck with any particular resemblance between King George and Moses."

"The folks here 'n Oldtown, Mr. Devenport, 's amazin' curus to hear the partic'lars 'bout them grand things 't you must ha' seen; I 's a tellin' on 'em up to store how you 'd ben with lords 'n' ladies 'n' dukes 'n' duchesses, 'n' seen all the kingdoms o' the world, an' the glory on 'em. I told 'em I did n't doubt you 'd et off 'm plates o' solid gold, an' ben in houses where the walls was all a crust o' gold 'n' diamonds 'n' precious stones, 'n' yit ye did n't seem ter be one bit lifted up nor proud, so't yer could n't talk ter common folks. I s'pose them gret fam'lies they hes as much's fifty ur a hundred servants, don't they?"

"Well, sometimes," said Ellery Davenport.

"Wal, now," said Sam, "I sh'd think a man 'd feel kind o' curus,—sort o' 's ef he was keepin' a hotel, an' boardin' all the lower classes."

"It is something that way, Sam," said Ellery Davenport. "That 's one way of providing for the lower classes."

"Jest what th' Lord told th' Israelites when they would hev a king," said Sam. "Ses he, 'He 'll take yer daughters to be confectioners 'n' cooks 'n' bakers, an' he 'll take the best o' yer fields 'n' yer vineyards 'n' olive-yards, an' give 'em to his sarvints, an' he 'll take a tenth o' yer seed 'n' give 'em ter his officers, an' he 'll take yer men-sarvints 'n' yer maid-sarvints, 'n' yer goodliest young asses, an' put 'em ter his works.'"

"Striking picture of monarchical institutions, Sam," said Ellery Davenport.

"Wal, now, I tell ye what," said Sam, slowly shaking his shimmering skillet of milk, "I should n't want ter git inter that ere' pie, unless I could be some o' the top crust. It 's jest like a pile o' sheepskins,—'s only the top un lies light. I guess th' undermost one 's squeezed putty flat."

"I 'll bet it is, Sam," said Ellery Davenport, laughing.

"Wal," said Sam, "I go for republics, but yit it 's human natur' ter kind o' like ter hold onter titles. Now over here a man likes ter be a deacon 'n' a cap'n 'n' a colonel in the milishy 'n' a sheriff 'n' a judge, 'n' all thet. Lordy massy, I don't wonder them grand English folks sticks to their grand titles, an' the people all kind o' bows down to 'em, as they did to Nebuchadnezzar 's golden image."

"Why, Sam," said Ellery Davenport, "your speculations on politics are really profound."

"Wal," said Sam, "Mr. Devenport, there 's one pint I want ter consult ye 'bout, an' thet is, what the king o' England's name is. There 's Jake Marshall 'n' me, we 's argood that pint these many times. Jake ses his name is George Rix,— R-i-x,— an' thet ef he 'd come over here, he 'd be called Mr. Rix. I ses to him, 'Why, Jake, 't ain't *Rix*, it 's Rex, an' 't ain't his name, it 's his title,' ses I,—'cause the boys told me thet Rex was Latin 'n' meant king; but Jake 's one o' them fellers thet allers thinks he knows. Now, Mr. Devenport, I 'd like to put it down from you ter him, 'cause you 've just come from the court o' England, an' you 'd know."

"Well, you may tell your friend Jake that you are quite in the right," said Ellery Davenport. "Give him my regards, and tell him he 's been mistaken."

"But you don't call the king Rex when ye speak to 'im, do yer?" said Sam.

"Not precisely," said Ellery Davenport.

"Mis' Badger," said Sam, gravely, "this 'ere milk 's come to the bile, 'n' ef you 'll be so kind 's to hand me the sperits 'n' the sugar, I 'll fix this 'ere. Hepsy likes her milk punch putty hot."

"Well, Sam," said my grandmother, as she handed him the bottle, "take an old woman's advice, and don't go stramming off another afternoon. If you 'd been steady at your blacksmithin', you might have earned enough money to buy all these things yourself, and Hepsy 'd like it a great deal better."

"I suppose it 's about the two hundred and forty-ninth time mother has told him that," said Aunt Lois, with an air of weary endurance.

"Wal, Mis' Badger," said Sam, " 'all work an' no play makes Jack a dull boy,' ye know. I *hes* to recreate, else I gits quite wore out. Why, lordy massy, even a saw-mill hes ter stop sometimes ter be greased. 'T ain't everybody thet 's like Sphyxy Smith, but she grits and screeches all the time, jest 'cause she keeps to work without bein' 'iled. Why, she could work on, day 'n' night, these twenty years, 'n' never feel it. But, lordy massy, I gits so 'xhausted, an' hes sech a sinking 't my stomach, 'n' then I goes out 'n' kind o' *Injunin'* round, an' git flag-root 'n' wintergreen 'n' spruce boughs 'n' gensing root 'n' sarsafrass 'n' sich fur Hepsy to brew up a beer. I ain't a wastin' my time ef I be enjoyin' myself. I say it 's a part o' what we 's made for."

"You are a true philosopher, Sam," said Ellery Davenport.

"Wal," said Sam, "I look at it this 'ere way,—ef I keep on a grindin' and a grindin' day 'n' night, I never shell hev nothin', but ef I takes now 'n' then an arternoon to lie roun' in the sun, *I gits suthin' 's I go 'long.* Lordy massy, it 's jest all the comfort I hes, kind o' watchin' the clouds 'n' the birds, 'n' kind o' forgettin' all 'bout Hepsy 'n' the children 'n' the black-smithin'."

"Well," said Aunt Lois, smartly, "I think you are forgetting all about Hepsy and the children now, and I advise you to get that milk punch home as quick as you can, if it 's going to do her any good. Come, here 's a tin pail to put it into. Cover it up, and do let the poor woman have some comfort as well as you!"

Sam received his portion in silence, and, with reluctant glances at the warm circle, went out into the night.

"I don't see how you all can bear to listen to that man's maundering!" said Aunt Lois. "He puts me out of all sort of patience. 'Head of the woman' to be sure! when Hepsy earns the most of what that family uses, except what we give 'em. And I know exactly how she feels; the poor woman is mad with shame and humiliation half the time at the charities he will accept from us."

"O come, Miss Lois," said Ellery Davenport, "you must take an æsthetic view of him. Sam's a genuine poet in his nature, and poets are always practically useless. And now Sam's about the only person in Oldtown, that I have seen, that has the least idea that life is meant, in any way, for enjoyment. Everybody else seems to be sword in hand, fighting against the possibility of future suffering, toiling and depriving themselves of all present pleasure, so that they may not come to want by and by. Now I've been in countries where the whole peasantry are like Sam Lawson."

"Good gracious!" said Aunt Lois, "what a time they must have of it!"

"Well, to say the truth, there's not much progress in such communities, but there is a great deal of clear, sheer animal enjoyment. And when trouble comes, it comes on them as it does on animals, unfeared and unforeseen, and therefore unprovided for."

"Well," said my grandmother, "you don't think that is the way for rational and immortal creatures to live?"

"Well," said Ellery Davenport, "taking into account the rational and immortal, perhaps not; but I think if we could mix the two races together it would be better. The Yankee lives almost entirely for the future, the Italian enjoys the present."

"Well, but do you think it is *right* to live merely to enjoy the present?" persisted Aunt Lois.

"The eternal question!" said Ellery. "After all, who knows anything about it? What *is* right, and what *is* wrong? Mere geographical accidents! What is right for the Greenlander is wrong for me; what is right for me is wrong for the Hindoo. Take the greatest saint on earth to Greenland, and feed him on train oil and candles, and you make one thing of him; put him under the equator, with the thermometer at one hundred in the shade, and you make another."

"But right is right and wrong is wrong," said Aunt Lois, persistently, "after all."

"I sometimes think," said Ellery Davenport, "that right and wrong are just like color, mere accidental properties. There is no color where there's no light, and a thing is all sorts of colors according to the position you stand in and the hour of the day. There's your rocking-chair in the setting sun becomes a fine crimson, and in the morning comes out dingy gray. So it is with human actions. There's nothing so bad that you cannot see a good side to it, nothing so good that you cannot see a bad side to it. Now we think it's shocking for our Indian tribes, some of them, to slay their old people; but I'm not sure, if the Indian could set forth his side of the case, with all the advantages of our rhetoric, but that he would have the best of it. He does it as an act of filial devotion, you see. He loves and honors his father too much to let him go through all that horrid process of draining out life drop by drop that we think the thing to protract in our high civilization. For my part, if I were an Indian chief, I should prefer, when I came to be seventy, to be respectfully knocked on the head by my oldest son, rather than to shiver and drivel and muddle and cough my life out a dozen years more."

"But God has given his commandments to teach us what is right," said Aunt Lois. " 'Honor thy father and mother.' "

"Precisely," said Ellery; "and my friends the Sioux would tell you that they *do* honor their fathers and mothers by respectfully putting them out of the way when there is no more pleasure in living. They send them to enjoy eternal youth in the hunting-grounds of the fathers, you know."

"Positively, Ellery," said Tina, "I sha' n't have this sort of heathen stuff talked any longer. Why, you put one's head all in a whirl! and you know you don't believe a word of it yourself. What's the use of making everybody think you 're worse than you are?"

"My dear," said Ellery, "there 's nothing like hearing all that can be said on both sides of subjects. Now there 's my good grandfather made an argument on the will, that is, and forever will remain, unanswerable, because he proves both sides of a flat contradiction perfectly; that method makes a logic-trap out of which no mortal can get his foot."

"Well," said my grandmother, "Mr. Davenport, if you 'll take an old woman's advice, you 'll take up with your grandfather's *good resolutions*, and not be wasting your strength in such talk."

"I believe there were about seventy-five—or eighty, was it?—of those resolutions," said Ellery.

"And you would n't be the worse for this world or the next if you 'd make them yourself," said my grandmother.

"Thank you, madam," said Ellery, bowing, "I 'll think of it."

"Well, come," said Tina, rising, "it's time for us to go; and," she said, shaking her finger warningly at Ellery Davenport, "I have a private lecture for you."

"I don't doubt it," he said, with a shrug of mock apprehension; "the preaching capacities of the fair sex are something terrific. I see all that is before me."

They bade adieu, the fire was raked up in the great fireplace, all the members of the family went their several ways to bed, but Harry and I sat up in the glimmer and gloom of the old kitchen, lighted, now and then, by a sputtering jet of flame, which burst from the sticks. All round the large dark hearth the crickets were chirping as if life were the very merriest thing possible.

"Well, Harry," I said, "you see the fates have ordered it just as I feared."

"It is almost as much of a disappointment to me as it can be to you," said Harry. "And it is the more so because I cannot quite trust this man."

"I never trusted him," said I. "I always had an instinctive doubt of him."

"My doubts are not instinct," said Harry, "they are founded on things I have heard him say myself. It seems to me that he has formed the habit of trifling with all truth, and that nothing is sacred in his eyes."

"And yet Tina loves him," said I. "I can see that she has gone to him heart and soul, and she believes in him with all her heart, and so we can only pray that he may be true to her. As for me, I can never love another. It only remains to live worthily of my love."

XLIV.

Marriage Preparations

Aᴺᴰ now for a time there was nothing thought of or talked of but marriage preparations and arrangements. Letters of congratulation came pouring in to Miss Mehitable from her Boston friends and acquaintances.

When Harry and I returned to college, we spent one day with our friends the Kitterys, and found it the one engrossing subject there, as everywhere.

Dear old Madam Kittery was dissolved in tenderness, and whenever the subject was mentioned reiterated all her good opinions of Ellery, and her delight in the engagement, and her sanguine hopes of its good influence on his spiritual prospects.

Miss Debby took the subject up energetically. Ellery Davenport was a near family connection, and it became the Kitterys to make all suitable and proper advances. She insisted upon addressing Harry by his title, notwithstanding his blushes and disclaimers.

"My dear sir," she said to him, "it appears that you are an Englishman and a subject of his Majesty; and I should not be surprised, at some future day, to hear of you in the House of Commons; and it becomes you to reflect upon your position, and what is proper in relation to yourself; and, at least under this roof, you must allow me to observe these proprieties, however much they may be disregarded elsewhere. I have already informed the servants that they are always to address you as Sir Harry, and I hope that you will not interfere with my instructions."

"O certainly not," said Harry. "It will make very little difference with me."

"Now, in regard to this marriage," said Miss Debby, "as there is no *church* in Oldtown, and no clergyman, I have felt that it would be proper in me, as a near kinswoman to Mr. Davenport, to place the Kittery mansion at Miss Mehitable Rossiter's disposal, for the wedding."

"Well, I confess," said Harry, blushing, "I never thought but that the ceremony would be performed at home, by Parson Lothrop."

"My dear Sir Harry!" said Miss Debby, laying her hand on his arm with solemnity, "consider that your excellent parents, Sir Harry and Lady Percival, were both members of the Established Church of England, the only true Apostolic Protestant Church,—and can you imagine that their spirits, looking down from heaven, would be pleased and satisfied that their daughter should consummate the most solemn union of her life out of the Church? and in fact at the hands of a man who has never received ordination?"

It was with great difficulty that Harry kept his countenance during this solemn address. His blue eyes actually laughed, though he exercised a rigid control over the muscles of his face.

"I really had not thought about it at all, Miss Debby," he said. "I think you are exceedingly kind."

"And I 'm sure," said she, "that you must see the propriety of it now that it is suggested to you. Of course, a marriage performed by Mr. Lothrop would be a legal one, so far as the civil law is concerned; but I confess I always have regarded marriage as a religious ordinance, and it would be a disagreeable thing to me to have any connections of mine united merely by a *civil* tie. These Congregational marriages," said Miss Debby, in a contemptuous voice, "I should think would lead to immorality. How can people feel as if they were married that don't utter any vows themselves, and don't have any wedding-ring put on their finger? In my view, it 's not respectable; and, as Mrs. Ellery Davenport will probably be presented in the first circles of England, I desire that she should appear there with her wedding-ring on, like an honest woman. I have therefore despatched an invitation to Miss Mehitable to bring your sister and spend the month preceding the wedding with us in Boston. It will be desirable for other reasons, as all the shopping and dressmaking and millinery work must be done in Boston. Oldtown is a highly respectable little village, but, of course, affords no advantages for the outfit of a person of quality, such as your sister is and is to be. I have had a letter from Lady Widgery this morning.

She is much delighted, and sends congratulations. She always, she said, believed that you had distinguished blood in your veins when she first saw you at our house."

There was something in Miss Debby's satisfied, confiding faith in everything English and aristocratic that was vastly amusing to us. The perfect confidence she seemed to have that Sir Harry Percival, after all the sins of his youth, had entered heaven *ex officio* as a repentant and glorified baronet, a member of the only True Church, was really *naïve* and affecting. What would a church be good for that allowed people of quality to go to hell, like the commonalty? Sir Harry, of course, repented, and made his will in a proper manner, doubtless received the sacrament and absolution, and left all human infirmities, with his gouty toes, under the family monument, ·where his body reposed in sure and certain hope of a blessed and glorious resurrection. The finding of his children under such fortunate circumstances was another evidence of the good Providence who watches over the fortunes of the better classes, and does not suffer the steps of good Churchmen to slide beyond recovery.

There were so many reasons of convenience for accepting Madam Kittery's hospitable invitation, it was urged with such warmth and affectionate zeal by Madam Kittery and Miss Debby, and seconded so energetically by Ellery Davenport, to whom this arrangement would secure easy access to Tina's society during the intervening time, that it was accepted.

Harry and I were glad of it, as we should thus have more frequent opportunities of seeing her. Ellery Davenport was refurbishing and refurnishing the old country house, where Harry and Tina had spent those days of their childhood which it was now an amusement to recall, and Tina was as gladly, joyously beautiful as young womanhood can be in which, as in a transparent vase, the light of pure love and young hope has been lighted.

"You like him, Horace, don't you?" she had said to me, coaxingly, the first opportunity after the evening we had spent together. What was I to do? I did not like him, that was certain; but have you never, dear reader, been over-persuaded to think and say you liked where you did not? Have you not scolded and hushed down your own instinctive dis-

trusts and heart-risings, blamed and schooled yourself for
them, and taken yourself sharply to task, and made yourself
acquiesce in somebody that was dear and necessary to some
friend? So did I. I called myself selfish, unreasonable, foolish.
I determined to be generous to my successful rival, and to
like him. I took his frankly offered friendship, and I forced
myself to be even enthusiastic in his praise. It was a sure way
of making Tina's cheeks glow and her eyes look kindly on me,
and she told me so often that there was no person in the
world whose good opinion she had such a value for, and she
was *so* glad I liked him. Would it not be perfectly abominable
after this to let sneaking suspicions harbor in my breast?

Besides, if a man cannot have love, shall he therefore throw
away friendship? and may I not love with the love of chiv-
alry,—the love that knights dedicated to queens and princesses, the love that Tasso gave to Leonora D'Este, the love
that Dante gave to Beatrice, love that hopes little and asks
nothing?

I was frequently in at the Kittery house in leisure hours,
and when, as often happened, Tina was closeted with Ellery
Davenport, I took sweet counsel with Miss Mehitable.

"We all stand outside now, Horace," she said. "I remember
when *I* had the hearing of all these thousand pretty little important secrets of the hour that now must all be told in another direction. Such is life. What we want always comes to
us with some pain. I wanted Tina to be well married. I would
not for the world she should marry without just this sort of
love; but of course it leaves me out in the cold. I would n't
say this to her for the world,—poor little thing, it would
break her heart."

One morning, however, I went down and found Miss Mehitable in a very excited state. She complained of a bad head-
ache, but she had all the appearance of a person who is constantly struggling with something which she is doubtful of
the expediency of uttering.

At last, just as I was going, she called me into the library.
"Come here, Horace," she said; "I want to speak to you."

I went in, and she made a turn or two across the room in
an agitated way, then sat down at a table, and motioned me
to sit down. "Horace, my dear boy," she said, "I have never

spoken to you of the deepest sorrow of my life, and yet it often seems to me as if you knew it."

"My dear Aunty," said I, for we had from childhood called her thus, "I think I do know it,—somewhat vaguely. I know about your sister."

"You know how strangely, how unaccountably she left us, and that nothing satisfactory has ever been heard from her. I told Mr. Davenport all about her, and he promised to try to learn something of her in Europe. He was so successful in relation to Tina and Harry, I hoped he might learn something as to her; but he never seemed to. Two or three times within the last four or five years I have received letters from her, but without date, or any mark by which her position could be identified. They told me, in the vaguest and most general way, that she was well, and still loved me, but begged me to make no inquiries. They were always postmarked at Havre; but the utmost research gives no clew to her residence there."

"Well?" said I.

"Well," said Miss Mehitable, trembling in every limb, "yesterday, when Mr. Davenport and Tina had been sitting together in this room for a long time, they went out to ride. They had been playing at verse-making, or something of the kind, and there were some scattered papers on the floor, and I thought I would remove them, as they were rather untidy, and among them I found—" she stopped, and panted for breath—"I found THIS!"

She handed me an envelope that had evidently been around a package of papers. It was postmarked Geneva, Switzerland, and directed to Ellery Davenport.

"Horace," said Miss Mehitable, "*that is Emily Rossiter's handwriting*; and look, the date is only two months back! What shall we do?"

There are moments when whole trains of thought go through the brain like lightning. My first emotion was, I confess, a perfectly fierce feeling of joy. Here was a clew! My suspicions had not then been unjust; the man was what Miss Debby had said,—deep, artful, and to be unmasked. In a moment I sternly rebuked myself, and thought what a wretch I was for my suspicions. The very selfish stake that

I held in any such discovery imposed upon me, in my view, a double obligation to defend the character of my rival. I so dreaded that I should be carried away that I pleaded strongly and resolutely with myself for him. Besides, what would Tina think of me if I impugned Ellery Davenport's honor for what might be, after all, an accidental resemblance in handwriting.

All these things came in one blinding flash of thought as I held the paper in my hands. Miss Mehitable sat, white and trembling, looking at me piteously.

"My dear Aunty," I said, "in a case like this we cannot take one single step without being perfectly sure. This handwriting may accidentally resemble your sister's. Are you perfectly sure that it is hers? It is a very small scrap of paper to determine by."

"Well, I can't really say," said Miss Mehitable, hesitating. "It may be that I have dwelt on this subject until I have grown nervous and my very senses deceive me. I really cannot say, Horace; that was the reason I came to you to ask what I should do."

"Let us look the matter over calmly, Aunty."

"Now," she said, nervously drawing from her pocket two or three letters and opening them before me, "here are those letters, and your head is cool and steady. I wish you would compare the writing, and tell me what to think of it."

Now the letters and the directions were in that sharp, decided English hand which so many well-educated women write, and in which personal peculiarities are lost, to a great degree, in a general style. I could not help seeing that there was a resemblance which might strike a person,—especially a person so deeply interested, and dwelling with such intentness upon a subject, as Miss Mehitable evidently was.

"My dear Aunty," said I, "I see a resemblance; but have you not known a great many ladies who wrote hands like this?"

"Yes, I must say I have," said Miss Mehitable, still hesitating,—"only, somehow, this impressed me very strongly."

"Well," said I, "supposing that your sister has written to Ellery Davenport, may she not have intrusted him with communications under his promise of secrecy, which he was bound in honor not to reveal?"

"That may be possible," said Miss Mehitable, sighing deeply; "but O, why should she not make a confidante of me?"

"It may be, Aunty," said I, hesitatingly, "that she is living in relations that she feels could not be justified to you."

"O Horace!" said Miss Mehitable.

"You know," I went on, "that there has been a very great shaking of old established opinions in Europe. A great many things are looked upon there as open questions, in regard to morality, which we here in New England never think of discussing. Ellery Davenport is a man of the European world, and I can easily see that there may be circumstances in which your sister would more readily resort to the friendship of such a man than to yours."

"May God help me!" said Miss Mehitable.

"My dear Aunty, suppose you find that your sister has adopted a false theory of life, sincerely and conscientiously, and under the influence of it gone astray from what we in New England think to be right. Should we not make a discrimination between errors that come from a wrong belief and the mere weakness that blindly yields to passion? Your sister's letters show great decision and strength of mind. It appears to me that she is exactly the woman to be misled by those dazzling, unsettling theories with regard to social life which now bear such sway, and are especially propagated by French literature. She may really and courageously deem herself doing right in a course that she knows she cannot defend to you and Mr. Rossiter."

"Horace, you speak out and make plain what has been the secret and dreadful fear of my life. I never have believed that Emily could have gone from us all, and stayed away so long, without the support of some attachment. And while you have been talking I have become perfectly certain that it is so; but the thought is like death to me."

"My dear Aunty," I said, "our Father above, who sees all the history of our minds, and how they work, must have a toleration and a patience that we have not with each other.

He says that he will bring the blind by a way they knew not, and 'make darkness light before them, and crooked things straight'; and he adds, 'These things will I do unto them, and will not forsake them.' That has always seemed to me the most godlike passage in the Bible."

Miss Mehitable sat for a long time, leaning her head upon her hand.

"Then, Horace, you would n't advise me," she said, after a pause, "to say anything to Ellery Davenport about it?"

"Supposing," said I, "that there are communications that he is bound in honor not to reveal, of what use could be your inquiries? It can only create unpleasantness; it may make Tina feel unhappy, who is so very happy now, and probably, at best, you cannot learn anything that would satisfy you."

"Probably not," said she, sighing.

"I can hand this envelope to him," I said after a moment's thought, "this evening, if you think best, and you can see how he looks on receiving it."

"I don't know as it will be of any use," said Miss Mehitable, "but you may do it."

Accordingly, that evening, as we were all gathered in a circle around the open fire, and Tina and Ellery, seated side by side, were carrying on that sort of bantering warfare of wit in which they delighted, I drew this envelope from my pocket and said, carelessly, "Mr. Davenport, here is a letter of yours that you dropped in the library this morning."

He was at that moment playing with a silk tassel which fluttered from Tina's wrist. He let it go, and took the envelope and looked at it carelessly.

"A letter!" said Tina, snatching it out of his hand with saucy freedom,—"dated at Geneva, and a lady's handwriting! I think I have a right to open it!"

"Do so by all means," said Ellery.

"O pshaw! there 's nothing in it," said Tina.

"Not an uncommon circumstance in a lady's letter," said Ellery.

"You saucy fellow!" said Tina.

"Why," said Ellery, "is it not the very province and privilege of the fair sex to make nothing more valuable and more agreeable than something? that's the true secret of witch-craft."

"But I sha'n't like it," said Tina, half pouting, "if you call my letters nothing."

"Your letters, I doubt not, will be an exception to those of all the sex," said Ellery. "I really tremble, when I think how profound they will be!"

"You are making fun of me!" said she, coloring.

"I making fun of you? And what have you been doing with all your hapless lovers up to this time? Behold Nemesis arrayed in my form."

"But seriously, Ellery, I want to know whom this letter was from?"

"Why don't you look at the signature?" said he.

"Well, of course you know there is no signature, but I mean what came in this paper?"

"What came in the paper," said Ellery, carelessly, "was a neat little collection of Alpine flowers, that, if you are interested in botany, I shall have the honor of showing you one of these days."

"But you have n't told me who sent them," said Tina.

"Ah, ha! we are jealous!" said he, shaking the letter at her. "What would you give to know, now? Will you be *very* good if I will tell you? Will you promise me for the future not to order me to do more than forty things at one time, for example?"

"I sha'n't make any promises," said Tina; "you ought to tell me!"

"What an oppressive mistress you are!" said Ellery Davenport. "I begin to sympathize with Sam Lawson,—lordy massy, you dunno nothin' what I undergo!"

"You don't get off that way," said Tina.

"Well," said Ellery Davenport, "if you must know, it's Mrs. Breck."

"And who is she?" said Tina.

"Well, my dear, she was my boarding-house keeper at Geneva, and a very pretty, nice Englishwoman,—one that I should recommend as an example to her sex."

"Oh!" said Tina, "I don't care anything about it now."

"Of course," said Ellery. "Modest, unpretending virtue

never excites any interest. I have labored under that disadvantage all my days."

The by-play between the two had brought the whole circle around the fire into a careless, laughing state. I looked across to Miss Mehitable; she was laughing with the rest. As we started to go out, Miss Mehitable followed me into the passage-way. "My dear Horace," she said, "I was very absurd; it comes of being nervous and thinking of one thing too much."

XLV.

Wedding Bells

THE fourteenth of June was as bright a morning as if it had been made on purpose for a wedding-day, and of all the five thousand inauspicious possibilities which usually encumber weddings, not one fell to our share.

Tina's dress, for example, was all done two days beforehand, and fitted to a hair; and all the invited guests had come, and were lodged in the spacious Kittery mansion.

Esther Avery was to stand as bridesmaid, with me as groomsman, and Harry, as nearest relative, was to give the bride away. The day before, I had been in and seen both ladies dressed up in the marriage finery, and we had rehearsed the situation before Harry, as clergyman, Miss Debby being present, in one of her most commanding frames of mind, to see that everything was done according to the Rubric. She surveyed Esther, while she took an approving pinch of snuff, and remarked to me, aside, "That young person, for a Congregational parson's daughter, has a surprisingly distinguished air."

Lady Widgery and Lady Lothrop, who were also in at the inspection, honored Esther with their decided approbation.

"She will be quite presentable at court," Lady Widgery remarked. "Of course Sir Harry will wish her presented."

All this *empressement* in regard to Harry's rank and title, among these venerable sisters, afforded great amusement to our quartette, and we held it a capital joke among ourselves to make Esther blush by calling her Lady Percival, and to inquire of Harry about his future parliamentary prospects, his rent-rolls and tenants. In fact, when together, we were four children, and played with life much as we used to in the dear old days.

Esther, under the influence of hope and love, had bloomed out into a beautiful woman. Instead of looking like a pale image of abstract thought, she seemed like warm flesh and blood, and Ellery Davenport remarked, "What a splendid contrast her black hair and eyes will make to the golden beauty of Tina!"

All Oldtown respectability had exerted itself to be at the wedding. All, however humble, who had befriended Tina and Harry during the days of their poverty, were bidden. Polly had been long sojourning in the house, in the capacity of Miss Mehitable's maid, and assisting assiduously in the endless sewing and fine laundry work which precedes a wedding.

On this auspicious morning she came gloriously forth, rustling in a stiff changeable lutestring, her very Sunday best, and with her mind made up to enter an Episcopal church for the first time in her life. There had, in fact, occurred some slight theological skirmishes between Polly and the High Church domestics of Miss Debby's establishment, and Miss Mehitable was obliged to make stringent representations to Polly concerning the duty of sometimes repressing her testimony for truth under particular circumstances.

Polly had attended one catechising, but the shock produced upon her mind by hearing doctrines which seemed to her to have such papistical tendencies was so great that Miss Mehitable begged Miss Debby to allow her to be excused in future. Miss Debby felt that the obligations of politeness owed by a woman of quality to an invited guest in her own house might take precedence even of theological considerations. In this point of view, she regarded Congregationalists with a well-bred, compassionate tolerance, and very willingly acceded to whatever Miss Mehitable suggested.

Harry and I had passed the night before the wedding-day at the Kittery mansion, that we might be there at the very earliest hour in the morning, to attend to all those thousand and one things that always turn up for attention at such a time.

Madam Kittery's garden commanded a distant view of the sea, and I walked among the stately alleys looking at that splendid distant view of Boston harbor, which seemed so bright and sunny, and which swooned away into the horizon with such an ineffable softness, as an image of eternal peace.

As I stood there looking, I heard a light footstep behind

me, and Tina came up suddenly and spattered my cheek with a dewy rose that she had just been gathering.

"You look as mournful as if it were you that is going to be married!" she said.

"Tina!" I said, "you out so early too?"

"Yes, for a wonder. The fact was, I had a bad dream, and could not sleep. I got up and looked out of my window, and saw you here, Horace, so I dressed me quickly and ran down. I feel a little bit uncanny,—and eerie, as the Scotch say,— and a little bit sad, too, about the dear old days, Horace. We have had such good times together,—first we three, and then we took Esther in, and that made four; and now, Horace, you must open the ranks a little wider and take in Ellery."

"But five is an uneven number," said I; "it leaves one out in the cold."

"O Horace! I hope you will find one worthy of you," she said. "I shall have a place in my heart all ready for her. She shall be my sister. You will write to me, won't you? Do write. I shall so want to hear of the dear old things. Every stick and stone, every sweetbrier-bush and huckleberry patch in Old-town, will always be dear to me. And dear old precious Aunty, what ever set it into her good heart to think of taking poor little me to be her child? and it 's too bad that I should leave her so. You know, Horace, I have a small income all my own, and that I mean to give to Aunty."

Now there were many points in this little valedictory of Tina to which I had no mind to respond, and she looked, as she was speaking, with tears coming in her great soft eyes, altogether too loving and lovely to be a safe companion to one forbidden to hold her in his arms and kiss her, and I felt such a desperate temptation in that direction that I turned suddenly from her. "Does Mr. Davenport approve such a disposition of your income?" said I, in a constrained voice.

"Mr. Davenport! Mr. High and Mighty," she said, mimicking my constrained tone, "what makes you so sulky to me this morning?"

"I am not sulky, Tina, only sad," I said.

"Come, come, Horace, don't be sad," she said, coaxingly, and putting her hand through my arm. "Now just be a good boy, and walk up and down with me here a few moments, and let me tell you about things."

I submitted and let her lead me off passively. "You see, Horace," she said, "I feel for poor old Aunty. Hers seems to me such a dry, desolate life; and I can't help feeling a sort of self-reproach when I think of it. Why should I have health and youth and strength and Ellery, and be going to see all the beauty and glory of Europe, while she sits alone at home, old and poor, and hears the rain drip off from those old lilac-bushes? Oldtown is a nice place, to be sure, but it does rain a great deal there, and she and Polly will be so lonesome without me to make fun for them. Now, Horace, you must promise me to go there as much as you can. You must culti-vate Aunty for my sake; and her friendship is worth cultivat-ing for its own sake."

"I know it," said I; "I am fully aware of the value of her mind and character."

"You and Harry ought both to visit her," said Tina, "and write to her, and take her advice. Nothing improves a young man faster than such female friendship; it 's worth that of dozens of us girls."

Tina always had a slight proclivity for sermonizing, but a chapter in Ecclesiastes, coming from little preachers with lips and eyes like hers, is generally acceptable.

"You know," said Tina, "that Aunty has some sort of a trouble on her mind."

"I know all about it," said I.

"Did she tell you?"

"Yes," said I, "after I had divined it."

"I made her tell me," said Tina. "When I came home from school, I determined I would not be treated like a child by her any longer,—that she should tell me her troubles, and let me bear them with her. I am young and full of hope, and ought to have troubles to bear. And she is worn out and weary with thinking over and over the same sad story. What a strange thing it is that that sister treats her so! I have been thinking so much about her lately, Horace; and, do you know? I had the strangest dream about her last night. I dreamed that Ellery and I were standing at the al-tar being married, and, all of a sudden, that lady that we saw in the closet and in the garret rose up like a ghost between us."

"Come, come," said I, "Tina, you are getting nervous. One shouldn't tell of one's bad dreams, and then one forgets them easier."

"Well," said Tina, "it made me sad to think that she was a young girl like me, full of hope and joy. They did n't treat her rightly over in that Farnsworth family,—Miss Mehitable told me all about it. O, it was a dreadful story! they perfectly froze her heart with their dreary talk about religion. Horace, I think the most irreligious thing in the world is that way of talking, which takes away our Heavenly Father, and gives only a dreadful Judge. I should not be so happy and so safe as I am now, if I did not believe in a loving God."

"Tina," said I, "are you satisfied with the religious principles of Mr. Davenport?"

"I 'm glad you asked me that, Horace, because Mr. Davenport is a man that is very apt to be misunderstood. Nobody really does understand him but me. He has seen so much of cant, and hypocrisy, and pretence of religion, and is so afraid of pretensions that do not mean anything, that I think he goes to the other extreme. Indeed, I have told him so. But he says he is always delighted to hear me talk on religion, and he likes to have me repeat hymns to him; and he told me the other day that he thought the Bible contained finer strains of poetry and eloquence than could be got from all other books put together. Then he has such a wonderful mind, you know. Mr. Avery said that he never saw a person that appreciated all the distinctions of the doctrines more completely than he did. He does n't quite agree with Mr. Avery, nor with anybody; but I think he is very far from being an irreligious man. I believe he thinks very seriously on all these subjects, indeed."

"I am glad of it," said I, half convinced by her fervor, more than half by the magic of her presence, and the touch of the golden curls that the wind blew against my cheek,—true Venetian curls, brown in the shade and gold in the sun. Certainly, such things as these, if not argument, incline man to be convinced of whatever a fair preacher says; and I thought it not unlikely that Ellery Davenport liked to hear her talk about religion. The conversation was interrupted by the breakfast-bell, which rung us in to an early meal, where we found Miss Debby, brisk and crisp with business and authority, apologizing to Lady Widgery for the unusually early hour, "but, really, so much always to be done in cases like these."

Breakfast was hurried over, for I was to dress myself, and go to Mr. Davenport's house, and accompany him, as groomsman, to meet Tina and Harry at the church door.

I remember admiring Ellery Davenport, as I met him this morning, with his easy, high-bred, cordial air, and with that overflow of general benevolence which seems to fill the hearts of happy bridegrooms on the way to the altar. Jealous as I was of the love that ought to be given to the idol of my knight-errantry, I could not but own to myself that Ellery Davenport was most loyally in love.

Then I have a vision of the old North Church, with its chimes playing, and the pews around the broad aisle filled with expectant guests. The wedding had excited a great deal of attention in the upper circles of Boston. Ellery Davenport was widely known, having been a sort of fashionable meteor, appearing at intervals in the select circles of the city, with all the prestige of foreign travel and diplomatic reputation. Then the little romance of the children had got about, and had proved as sweet a morsel under the tongues of good Bostonians as such spices in the dulness of real life usually do. There was talk everywhere of the little story, and, as usual, nothing was lost in the telling; the beauty and cleverness of the children had been reported from mouth to mouth, until everybody was on tiptoe to see them.

The Oldtown people, who were used to rising at daybreak, found no difficulty in getting to Boston in season. Uncle Fliakim's almost exhausted wagon had been diligently revamped, and his harness assiduously mended, for days beforehand, during which process the good man might have been seen flying like a meteor in an unceasing round, between the store, the blacksmith's shop, my grandfather's, and his own dwelling; and in consequence of these arduous labors, not only his wife, but Aunt Keziah and Hepsy Lawson were secured a free passage to the entertainment.

Lady Lothrop considerately offered a seat to my grand-mother and Aunt Lois in her coach; but my grandmother declined the honor in favor of my mother.

"It 's all very well," said my grandmother, "and I send my blessing on 'em with all my heart; but my old husband and I are too far along to be rattling our old bones to weddings in Boston. I should n't know how to behave in their grand Epis-copal church."

Aunt Lois, who, like many other good women, had an in-nocent love of the pomps and vanities, and my mother, to whom the scene was an unheard-of recreation, were, on the whole, not displeased that her mind had taken this turn. As to Sam Lawson, he arose before Aurora had unbarred the gates of dawn, and strode off vigorously on foot, in his best Sunday clothes, and arrived there in time to welcome Uncle Fliakim's wagon, and to tell him that "he 'd ben a lookin' out for 'em these two hours."

So then for as much as half an hour before the wedding coaches arrived at the church door there was a goodly assem-blage in the church, and, while the chimes were solemnly pealing the tune of old Wells, there were bibbing and bob-bing of fashionable bonnets, and fluttering of fans, and rus-tling of silks, and subdued creakings of whalebone stays, and a gentle undertone of gossiping conversation in the expectant audience. Sam Lawson had mounted the organ loft, directly opposite the altar, which commanded a most distinct view of every possible transaction below, and also gave a prominent image of himself, with his lanky jaws, protruding eyes, and shackling figure, posed over all as the inspecting genius of the scene. And every once in a while he conveyed to Jake Mar-shall pieces of intelligence with regard to the amount of prop-erty or private history—the horses, carriages, servants, and most secret internal belongings—of the innocent Bostonians, who were disporting themselves below, in utter ignorance of how much was known about them. But when a man gives himself seriously, for years, to the task of collecting informa-tion, thinking nothing of long tramps of twenty miles in the acquisition, never hesitating to put a question and never for-getting an answer, it is astonishing what an amount of infor-

mation he may pick up. In Sam, a valuable reporter of the
press has been lost forever. He was born a generation too
soon, and the civilization of his time had not yet made a place
for him. But not the less did he at this moment feel in himself
all the responsibilities of a special reporter for Oldtown.

"Lordy massy," he said to Jake, when the chimes began to
play, "how solemn that 'ere does sound!

> 'Life *is* the time to sarve the Lord,
>   The time *to* insure the gret reward.'

I ben up in the belfry askin' the ringer what Mr. Devenport's goin' to give him for ringin' them 'ere chimes; and how
much de ye think 't was? Wal, 't was jest fifty dollars, for jest
this 'ere one time! an' the weddin' fee 's a goin' t' be a
hunderd guineas in a gold puss. I tell yer, Colonel Devenport 's a man as chops his mince putty fine. There 's Parson
Lothrop down there; he 's got a spick span new coat an' a
new wig! That 's Mis' Lothrop's scarlet Injy shawl; that 'ere
cost a hunderd guineas in Injy,—her first husband gin 'er
that. Lordy massy, ain't it a providence that Parson Lothrop 's married her? 'cause sence the war that 'ere s'ciety fur
sendin' the Gospil to furrin parts don't send nothin' to 'em,
an' the Oldtown people they don't pay nothin'. All they can
raise they gin to Mr. Mordecai Rossiter, 'cause they say ef
they hev to s'port a colleague it 's all they can do, 'specially
sence he 's married. Yeh see, Mordecai, he wanted to git Tiny,
but he could n't come it, and so he 's tuk up with Delily Bar-
ker. The folks, some on 'em, kind o' hinted to old Parson Lothrop thet his sermons was n't so interestin' 's they might be, 'n'
the parson, ses he, 'Wal, I b'lieve the sermons 's about 's good 's
the pay; ain't they?' He hed 'em there. I like Parson Lothrop,—
he 's a fine old figger-head, and keeps up stiff for th' honor o'
the ministry. Why, folks 's gittin' so nowadays thet ministers
won't be no more 'n common folks, 'n' everybody 'll hev their
say to 'em jest 's they do to anybody else. Lordy massy, there 's
the orgin,—goin' to hev all the glories, orgins 'n' bells 'n'
everythin'; guess the procession must ha' started. Mr.
Devenport's got another spick an' span new landau, 't he or-

dered over from England, special, for this 'casion, an' two prancin' white hosses! Yeh see I got inter Bostin 'bout daybreak, an' I 's around ter his stables a lookin' at 'em a polishin' up their huffs a little, 'n' givin' on 'em a wipe down, 'n' I asked Jenkins what he thought he gin for 'em, an' he sed he reely should n't durst to tell me. I tell ye, he 's like Solomon,—he 's a goin' to make gold as the stones o' the street."

And while Sam's monologue was going on, in came the bridal procession,—first, Harry, with his golden head and blue eyes, and, leaning on his arm, a cloud of ethereal gauzes and laces, out of which looked a face, pale now as a lily, with wandering curls of golden hair like little gleams of sunlight on white clouds; then the tall, splendid figure of Ellery Davenport, his haughty blue eyes glancing all around with a triumphant assurance. Miss Mehitable hung upon his arm, pale with excitement and emotion. Then came Esther and I. As we passed up the aisle, I heard a confused murmur of whisperings and a subdued drawing in of breath, and the rest all seemed to me to be done in a dream. I heard the words, "Who giveth this woman to be married to this man?" and saw Harry step forth, bold, and bright, and handsome, amid the whisperings that pointed him out as the hero of a little romance. And he gave her away forever,—our darling, our heart of hearts. And then those holy, tender words, those vows so awful, those supporting prayers, all mingled as in a dream, until it was all over, and ladies, laughing and crying, were crowding around Tina, and there were kissing and congratulating and shaking of hands, and then we swept out of the church, and into the carriages, and were whirled back to the Kittery mansion, which was thrown wide open, from garret to cellar, in the very profuseness of old English hospitality.

There was a splendid lunch laid out in the parlor, with all the old silver in muster, and with all the delicacies that Boston confectioners and caterers could furnish.

Ellery Davenport had indeed tendered the services of his French cook, but Miss Debby had respectfully declined the offer.

"He may be a very good cook, Ellery; I say nothing against him. I am extremely obliged to you for your polite offer, but

good English cooking is good enough for me, and I trust that
whatever guests I invite will always think it good enough for
them."

On that day, Aunt Lois and Aunt Keziah and my mother
and Uncle Fliakim sat down in proximity to some of the very
selectest families of Boston, comporting themselves, like good
republican Yankees, as if they had been accustomed to that
sort of thing all their lives, though secretly embarrassed by
many little points of etiquette.

Tina and Ellery sat at the head of the table, and dispensed
hospitalities around them with a gay and gracious freedom;
and Harry, in whom the bridal dress of Esther had evidently
excited distracting visions of future probabilities, was making
his seat by her at dinner an opportunity, in the general clatter
of conversation, to enjoy a nice little *tête-à-tête*.

Besides the brilliant company in the parlor, a long table
was laid out upon the greensward at the back of the house,
in the garden, where beer and ale flowed freely, and ham and
bread and cheese and cake and eatables of a solid and sustaining description were dispensed to whomsoever would. The
humble friends of lower degree—the particular friends of the
servants, and all the numerous tribe of dependants and hangers-on, who wished to have some small share in the prosperity
of the prosperous—here found ample entertainment. Here
Sam Lawson might be seen, seated beside Hepsy, on a gar-
den-seat near the festive board, gallantly pressing upon her
the good things of the hour.

"Eat all ye want ter, Hepsy,—it comes free 's water; ye can
hev 'wine an' milk without money 'n' without price,' as
't were Lordy massy, 's jest what I wanted. I hed sech a stram
this mornin', 'n' hain't hed nothin' but a two-cent roll, 't I
bought 't the baker's. Thought I should ha' caved in 'fore
they got through with the weddin'. These 'ere 'Piscopal weddin's is putty long. What d' ye think on 'em, Polly?"

"I think I like our own way the best," said Polly, stanchly,
"none o' your folderol, 'n' kneelin', 'n' puttin' on o' rings."

"Well," said Hepsy, with the spice of a pepper-box in her
eyes, "I liked the part that said, 'With all my worldly goods,
I thee endow.' "

"Thet 's putty well, when a man hes any worldly goods," said Sam; "but how about when he hes n't?"

"Then he 's no business to git married!" said Hepsy, definitely.

"So *I* think," said Polly; "but, for my part, I don't want no man's worldly goods, ef I 've got to take him with 'em. I 'd rather work hard as I have done, and hev 'em all to myself, to do just what I please with."

"Wal, Polly," said Sam, "I dare say the men 's jest o' your mind,—none on 'em won't try very hard to git ye' out on 't."

"There 's bin those thet hes, though!" said Polly; "but 't ain't wuth talkin' about, any way."

And so conversation below stairs and above proceeded gayly and briskly, until at last the parting hour came.

"Now jest all on ye step round ter the front door, an' see 'em go off in their glory. Them two white hosses is imported fresh from England, 'n' they could n't ha' cost less 'n' a thousan' dollars apiece, ef they cost a cent."

"A thousand!" said Jenkins, the groom, who stood in his best clothes amid the festive throng. "Who told you that?"

"Wal!" said Sam, "I thought I 'd put the figger low enough, sence ye would n't tell me perticklers. I like to be accurate 'bout these 'ere things. There they be! they 're comin' out the door now. She 's tuk off her white dress now, an' got on her travellin' dress, don't ye see? Lordy massy, what a kissin' an' a cryin'! How women allers does go on 'bout these 'ere things! There, he 's got 'er at last. See 'em goin' down the steps! ain't they a han'some couple! There, he 's handin' on 'er in. The kerrige 's lined with blue satin, 'n' never was sot in afore this mornin'. Good luck go with 'em! There they go."

And we all of us stood on the steps of the Kittery mansion, kissing hands and waving handkerchiefs, until the beloved one, the darling of our hearts, was out of sight.

XLVI.

Wedding After-Talks at Oldtown

WEDDING joys are commonly supposed to pertain especially to the two principal personages, and to be of a kind with which the world doth not intermeddle; but a wedding in such a quiet and monotonous state of existence as that of Oldtown is like a glorious sunset, which leaves a long after-glow, in which trees and rocks, farm-houses, and all the dull, commonplace landscape of real life have, for a while, a roseate hue of brightness. And then the long after-talks, the deliberate turnings and revampings, and the re-enjoying, bit by bit, of every incident!

Sam Lawson was a man who knew how to make the most of this, and for a week or two he reigned triumphant in Oldtown on the strength of it. Others could relate the bare, simple facts, but Sam Lawson could give the wedding, with variations, with marginal references, and explanatory notes, and enlightening comments, that ran deep into the history of everybody present. So that even those who had been at the wedding did not know half what they had seen until Sam told them.

It was now the second evening after that auspicious event. Aunt Lois and my mother had been pressed to prolong their stay over one night after the wedding, to share the hospitalities of the Kittery mansion, and had been taken around in the Kittery carriage to see the wonders of Boston town. But prompt, on their return, Sam came in to assist them in dishing up information by the evening fireside.

"Wal, Mis' Badger," said he, "'t was gin'ally agreed, on all hands, there had n't ben no weddin' like it seen in Boston sence the time them court folks and nobility used to be there. Old Luke there, that rings the chimes, he told me he hed n't seen no sech couple go up the broad aisle o' that church. Luke, says he to me, 'I tell yew, the grander o' Boston is here to-day,' and ye 'd better b'lieve every one on 'em had on their

Sunday best. There was the Boylstons, an' the Bowdoins, an' the Brattles, an' the Winthrops, an' the Bradfords, an' the Penhallows up from Portsmouth, an' the Quinceys, an' the Sewells. Wal, I tell yer, there was real grit there!—folks that come in their grand kerridges I tell you!—there was such a pawin' and a stampin' o' horses and kerridges round the church as if all the army of the Assyrians was there!"

"Well, now, I 'm glad I did n't go," said my grandmother. "I 'm too old to go into any such grandeur."

"Wal, I don't see why folks hes so much 'bjections to these here 'Piscopal weddin's, neither," said Sam. "I tell yer, it 's a kind o' putty sight now; ye see I was up in the organ loft, where I could look down on the heads of all the people. Massy to us! the bunnets, an' the feathers, an' the Injy shawls, an' the purple an' fine linen, was all out on the 'casion. An' when our Harry come in with Tiny on his arm, tha' was a gineral kind o' buzz, an' folks a risin' up all over the house to look at 'em. Her dress was yer real Injy satin, thick an' yaller, kind o' like cream. An' she had on the Pierpont pearls an' diamonds—"

"How did you know what she had on?" said Aunt Lois.

"O, I hes ways o' findin' out!" said Sam. "Yeh know old Gineral Pierpont, his gret-gret-grandfather, was a gineral in the British army in Injy, an' he racketed round 'mong them nabobs out there, an' got no end o' gold an' precious stones, an' these 'ere pearls an' diamonds that she wore on her neck and in her ears hes come down in the Devenport family. Mis' Delily, Miss Deborah Kittery's maid, she told me all the partic'lars 'bout it, an' she ses there ain't no family so rich in silver and jewels, and sich, as Ellery Devenport's is, an' hes ben for generations back. His house is jest chock-full of all sorts o' graven images and queer things from Chiny an' Japan, 'cause, ye see, his ancestors they traded to Injy, an' they seem to hev got the abundance o' the Gentiles flowin' to 'em."

"I noticed those pearls on her neck," said Aunt Lois; "I never saw such pearls."

"Wal," said Sam, "Mis' Delily, she ses she 's tried 'em 'long-side of a good-sized pea, an' they 're full as big. An' the ear-rings 's them pear-shaped pearls, ye know, with diamond nubs atop on 'em. Then there was a great pearl cross, an' the biggest kind of a diamond right in the middle on 't. Wal, Mis' Delily she told me a story 'bout them 'ere pearls," said Sam. "For my part, ef it hed ben a daughter o' mine, I 'd ruther she 'd 'a' worn suthin' on her neck that was spic an' span new. I tell yew, these 'ere old family jewels, I think sometimes they gits kind o' struck through an' through with moth an' rust, so to speak."

"I 'm sure I don't know what you mean, Sam," said Aunt Lois, literally, "since we know gold can't rust, and pearls and diamonds don't hurt with any amount of keeping."

"Wal, ye see, they do say that 'ere old Gineral Pierpont was a putty hard customer; he got them 'ere pearls an' diamonds away from an Injun princess; I s'pose she thought she 'd as much right to 'em 's he hed; an' they say 't was about all she hed was her jewels, an' so nat'rally enough she cussed him for taking on 'em. Wal, dunno 's the Lord minds the cusses o' these poor old heathen critturs; but 's ben a fact, Mis' Delily says, thet them jewels hain't never brought good luck. Gineral Pierpont, he gin 'em to his fust wife, an' she did n't live but two months arter she was married. He gin 'em to his second wife, 'n' she tuck to drink and le'd him sech a life 't he would n't ha' cared ef she had died too; 'n' then they come down to Ellery Devenport's first wife, 'n' she went ravin' crazy the fust year arter she was married. Now all that 'ere does look a little like a cuss; don't it?"

"O nonsense, Sam!" said Aunt Lois, "I don't believe there 's a word of truth in any of it! You can hatch more stories in one day than a hen can eggs in a month."

"Wal, any way," said Sam, "I like the 'Piscopal sarvice, all 'ceppin' the minister's wearin' his shirt outside; that I don't like."

"'T is n't a shirt!" said Aunt Lois, indignantly.

"O lordy massy!" said Sam, "I know what they calls it. I know it 's a surplice, but it looks for all the world like a man in his shirt-sleeves; but the words is real solemn. I wondered when he asked 'em all whether they hed any objections to 't, an' told 'em to speak up ef they hed, what would happen ef anybody should speak up jest there."

"Why, of course 't would stop the wedding," said Aunt Lois, "until the thing was inquired into."

"Wal, Jake Marshall, he said thet he 'd heerd a story when he was a boy, about a weddin' in a church at Portsmouth, that was stopped jest there, 'cause, ye see, the man he hed another wife livin'. He said 't was old Colonel Penhallow. 'Mazin' rich the old Colonel was, and these 'ere rich old cocks sometimes does seem to strut round and cut up pretty much as if they hed n't heard o' no God in their parts. The Colonel he got his wife shet up in a lunatic asylum, an' then spread the word that she was dead, an' courted a gal, and come jest as near as that to marryin' of her."

"As near as what?" said Aunt Lois.

"Why, when they got to that 'ere part of the service, there was his wife, good as new. She 'd got out o' the 'sylum, and stood up there 'fore 'em all. So you see that 'ere does some good."

"I 'd rather stay in an asylum all my life than go back to that man," said Aunt Lois.

"Wal, you see she did n't," said Sam; "her friends they made him make a settlement on her, poor woman, and he cleared out t' England."

"Good riddance to bad rubbish," said my grandmother.

"Wal, how handsome that 'ere gal is that Harry 's going to marry!" continued Sam. "She did n't have on nothin' but white muslin', an' not a snip of a jewel; but she looked like a queen. Ses I to Jake, ses I, there goes the woman 't 'll be Lady Percival one o' these days, over in England, an' I bet ye, he 'll find lots o' family jewels for her, over there. Mis' Delily she said she did n't doubt there would be."

"I hope," said my grandmother, "that she will have more enduring riches than that; it 's small matter about earthly jewels."

"Lordy massy, yes, Mis' Badger," said Sam, "jes' so, jes' so; now that 'ere was bein' impressed on my mind all the time. Folks oughtenter lay up their treasures on airth; I could n't help thinkin' on 't, when I see Tiny a wearin' them jewels, jest how vain an' transitory everythin' is, an' how the women 't has worn 'em afore is all turned to dust, an' lyin' in their

graves. Lordy massy, these 'ere things make us realize what a
transitory world we 's a livin' in. I was tellin' Hepsy 'bout
it,—she 's so kind o' worldly, Hepsy is,—seemed to make her
feel so kind o' gritty to see so much wealth 'n' splendor, when
we hed n't none. Ses I, 'Hepsy, there ain't no use o' wantin'
worldly riches, 'cause our lives all passes away like a dream,
an' a hundred years hence 't won't make no sort o' diffurnce
what we 've hed, an' what we heve n't hed.' But wal, Miss
Lois, *did* ye see the kerridge?" said Sam, returning to temporal things with renewed animation.

"I just got a glimpse of it," said Aunt Lois, "as it drove to
the door."

"Lordy massy," said Sam, "I was all over that 'ere kerridge
that mornin' by daylight. 'T ain't the one he had up here,—
that was jest common doin's,—this 'ere is imported spic an'
span new from England for the 'casion, an' all made jest 's
they make 'em for the nobility. Why, 't was all quilted an'
lined with blue satin, ever so grand, an' Turkey carpet under
their feet, an' the springs was easy 's a rockin'-chair. That 's
what they 've gone off in. Wal, lordy massy! I don't grudge
Tina nothin'! She 's the chipperest, light-heartedest, darlin'est
little creetur that ever did live, an' I hope she 'll hev good luck
in all things."

A rap was heard at the kitchen door, and Polly entered. It
was evident from her appearance that she was in a state of
considerable agitation. She looked pale and excited, and her
hands shook.

"Mis' Badger," she said to my grandmother, "Miss Rossiter
wants to know 'f you won't come an' set up with her to-
night."

"Why, is she sick?" said grandmother. "What 's the matter
with her?"

"She ain't very well," said Polly, evasively; "she wanted
Mis' Badger to spend the night with her."

"Perhaps, mother, I 'd better go over," said Aunt Lois.

"No, Miss Lois," said Polly, eagerly, "Miss Rossiter don't
wanter see anybody but yer mother."

"Wal, now I wanter know!" said Sam Lawson.

"Well, you can't know everything," said Aunt Lois, "so you
may want!"

"Tell Miss Rossiter, ef I can do anythin' for 'er, I hope she 'll call on me," said Sam.

My grandmother and Polly went out together. Aunt Lois bustled about the hearth, swept it up, and then looked out into the darkness after them. What could it be?

The old clock ticked drowsily in the kitchen corner, and her knitting-needles rattled.

"What do you think it is?" said my mother, timidly, to Aunt Lois.

"How should I know?" said Aunt Lois, sharply.

In a few moments Polly returned again.

"Miss Mehitable says she would like to see Sam Lawson."

"O, wal, wal, would she? Wal, I 'll come!" said Sam, rising with joyful alertness. "I 'm allers ready at a minute's warnin'!"

And they went out into the darkness together.

XLVII.

Behind the Curtain

IN the creed of most story-tellers marriage is equal to translation. The mortal pair whose fortunes are traced to the
foot of the altar forthwith ascend, and a cloud receives them
out of our sight as the curtain falls. Faith supposes them rapt
away to some unseen paradise, and every-day toil girds up its
loins and with a sigh prepares to return to its delving and
grubbing.

But our story must follow the fortunes of our heroine beyond the prescribed limits.

It had been arranged that the wedding pair, after a sunny
afternoon's drive through some of the most picturesque scenery in the neighborhood of Boston, should return at eventide
to their country home, where they were to spend a short time
preparatory to sailing for Europe. Even in those early days
the rocky glories of Nahant and its dashing waves were
known and resorted to by Bostonians, and the first part of
the drive was thitherward, and Tina climbed round among
the rocks, exulting like a sea-bird with Ellery Davenport ever
at her side, laughing, admiring, but holding back her bold,
excited footsteps, lest she should plunge over by some unguarded movement, and become a vanished dream.

So near lies the ever possible tragedy at the hour of our
greatest exultation; it is but a false step, an inadvertent movement, and all that was joy can become a cruel mockery! We
all know this to be so. We sometimes start and shriek when
we see it to be so in the case of others, but who is the less
triumphant in his hour of possession for this gloomy shadow
of possibility that forever dogs his steps?

Ellery Davenport was now in the high tide of victory. The
pursuit of the hour was a success; he had captured the butterfly. In his eagerness he had trodden down and disregarded
many teachings and impulses of his better nature that should
have made him hesitate; but now he felt that he *had* her; she
was his,—his alone and forever.

But already dark thoughts from the past were beginning to flutter out like ill-omened bats, and dip down on gloomy wing between him and the innocent, bright, confiding face. Tina he could see had idealized him entirely. She had invested him with all her conceptions of knighthood, honor, purity, religion, and made a creation of her own of him; and sometimes he smiled to himself, half amused and half annoyed at the very young and innocent simplicity of the matter. Nobody knew better than himself that what she dreamed he was he neither was nor meant to be,—that in fact there could not be a bitterer satire on his real self than her conceptions; but just now, with her brilliant beauty, her piquant earnestness, her perfect freshness, there was an indescribable charm about her that bewitched him.

Would it all pass away and get down to the jog-trot dustiness of ordinary married life, he wondered, and then, ought he not to have been a little more fair with her in exchange for the perfect transparence with which she threw open the whole of her past life to him? Had he not played with her as some villain might with a little child, and got away a priceless diamond for a bit of painted glass? He did not allow himself to think in that direction.

"Come, my little sea-gull," he said to her, after they had wandered and rambled over the rocks for a while, "you must come down from that perch, and we must drive on, if we mean to be at home before midnight."

"O Ellery, how glorious it is!"

"Yes, but we cannot build here three tabernacles, and so we must say, *Au revoir.* I will bring you here again";—and Ellery half led, half carried her in his arms back to the carriage.

"How beautiful it is!" said Tina, as they were glancing along a turfy road through the woods. The white pines were just putting out their long fingers, the new leaves of the silvery birches were twinkling in the light, the road was fringed on both sides with great patches of the blue violet, and sweet-fern, and bayberry, and growing green tips of young spruce and fir were exhaling a spicy perfume. "It seems as if we two alone were flying through fairy-land." His arm was around her, tightening its clasp of possession as he looked down on her.

"Yes," he said, "we two are alone in our world now; none can enter it; none can see into it; none can come between us."

Suddenly the words recalled to Tina her bad dream of the night before. She was on the point of speaking of it, but hesitated to introduce it; she felt a strange shyness in mentioning that subject.

Ellery Davenport turned the conversation upon things in foreign lands, which he would soon show her. He pictured to her the bay of Naples, the rocks of Sorrento, where the blue Mediterranean is overhung with groves of oranges, where they should have a villa some day, and live in a dream of beauty. All things fair and bright and beautiful in foreign lands were evoked, and made to come as a sort of airy pageant around them while they wound through the still, spicy pine-woods.

It was past sunset, and the moon was looking white and sober through the flush of the evening sky, when they entered the grounds of their own future home.

"How different everything looks here from what it did when I was here years ago!" said Tina,—"the paths are all cleared, and then it was one wild, dripping tangle. I remember how long we knocked at the door, and couldn't make any one hear, and the old black knocker frightened me,—it was a black serpent with his tail in his mouth. I wonder if it is there yet."

"O, to be sure it is," said Ellery; "that is quite a fine bit of old bronze, after something in Herculaneum, I think; you know serpents were quite in vogue among the ancients."

"I should think that symbol meant eternal evil," said Tina,—"a circle is eternity, and a serpent is evil."

"You are evidently prejudiced against serpents, my love," said Ellery. "The ancients thought better of them; they were emblems of wisdom, and the ladies very appropriately wore them for bracelets and necklaces."

"I would n't have one for the world," said Tina. "I always hated them, they are so bright, and still, and sly."

"Mere prejudice," said Ellery, laughing. "I must cure it by giving you, one of these days, an emerald-green serpent for a bracelet, with ruby crest and diamond eyes; you've no idea what pretty fellows they are. But here, you see, we are coming to the house; you can smell the roses."

"How lovely and how changed!" said Tina. "O, what a world of white roses over that portico,—roses everywhere, and white lilacs. It is a perfect paradise!"

"May you find it so, my little Eve," said Ellery Davenport, as the carriage stopped at the door. Ellery sprang out lightly, and, turning, took Tina in his arms and set her down in the porch.

They stood there a moment in the moonlight, and listened to the fainter patter of the horses' feet as they went down the drive.

"Come in, my little wife," said Ellery, opening the door, "and may the black serpent bring you good luck."

The house was brilliantly lighted by wax candles in massive silver candlesticks.

"O, how strangely altered!" said Tina, running about, and looking into the rooms with the delight of a child. "How beautiful everything is!"

The housekeeper, a respectable female, now appeared and offered her services to conduct her young mistress to her rooms. Ellery went with her, almost carrying her up the staircase on his arm. Above, as below, all was light and bright. "This room is ours," said Ellery, drawing her into that chamber which Tina remembered years before as so weirdly desolate. Now it was all radiant with hangings and furniture of blue and silver; the open windows let in branches of climbing white roses, the vases were full of lilies. The housekeeper paused a moment at the door.

"There is a lady in the little parlor below that has been waiting more than an hour to see you and madam," she said.

"A lady!" said both Tina and Ellery, in tones of surprise. "Did she give her name?" said Ellery.

"She gave no name; but she said that you, sir, would know her."

"I can't imagine who it should be," said Ellery. "Perhaps, Tina, I had better go down and see while you are dressing," said Ellery.

"Indeed, that would be a pretty way to do! No, sir, I allow no private interviews," said Tina, with authority,—"no, I am all ready and quite dressed enough to go down."

"Well, then, little positive," said Ellery, "be it as you will; let 's go together."

"Well, I must confess," said Tina, "I did n't look for wedding callers out here to-night; but never mind, it 's a nice little mystery to see what she wants."

They went down the staircase together, passed across the hall, and entered the little boudoir, where Tina and Harry had spent their first night together. The door of the writing cabinet stood open, and a lady all in black, in a bonnet and cloak, stood in the doorway.

As she came forward, Tina exclaimed, "O Ellery, it is she,— the lady in the closet!" and sank down pale and half fainting.

Ellery Davenport turned pale too; his cheeks, his very lips were blanched like marble; he looked utterly thunderstruck and appalled.

"Emily!" he said. "Great God!"

"Yes, Emily!" she said, coming forward slowly and with dignity. "You did not expect to meet ME here and now, Ellery Davenport!"

There was for a moment a silence that was perfectly awful. Tina looked on without power to speak, as in a dreadful dream. The ticking of the little French mantel clock seemed like a voice of doom to her.

The lady walked close up to Ellery Davenport, drew forth a letter, and spoke in that fearfully calm way that comes from the very white-heat of passion.

"Ellery," she said, "here is your letter. You did not *know* me—you could not know me—if you thought, after *that letter*, I would accept anything from you! *I* live on your bounty! I would sooner work as a servant!"

"Ellery, Ellery!" said Tina, springing up and clasping his arm, "O, tell me who she is! What is she to you? Is she—is she—"

"Be quiet, my poor child," said the woman, turning to her with an air of authority. "I have no claims; I come to make none. Such as this man is, *he is your husband*, not mine. You believe in him; so did I,—love him; so did I. I gave up all for him,—country, home, friends, name, reputation,—for I thought him such a man that a woman might well sacrifice her whole life to him! He is the father of my child! But fear not. The world, of course, will approve *him* and condemn *me*. They will say he did well to give up his mistress and take a wife; it's the world's morality. What woman will think the less of him, or smile the less on him, when she hears it? What woman will not feel herself too good even to touch my hand?"

"Emily," said Ellery Davenport, bitterly, "if you thought I deserved this, you might, at least, have spared this poor child."

"*The truth* is the best foundation in married life, Ellery," she said, "and the truth you have small faculty for speaking. I do her a favor in telling it. Let her start fair from the commencement, and then there will be no more to be told. Besides," she added, "I shall not trouble you long. *There*," she said, putting down a jewel-case,—"there are your gifts to me,—there are your letters." Then she threw on the table a miniature set in diamonds, "There is your picture. And now God help me! Farewell."

She turned and glided swiftly from the room.

Readers who remember the former part of this narrative will see at once that it was, after all, Ellery Davenport with whom, years before, Emily Rossiter had fled to France. They had resided there, and subsequently in Switzerland, and she had devoted herself to him, and to his interests, with all the single-hearted fervor of a true wife.

On her part, there was a full and conscientious belief that the choice of the individuals alone constituted a true marriage, and that the laws of human society upon this subject were an oppression which needed to be protested against.

On his part, however, the affair was a simple gratification of passion, and the principles, such as they were, were used by him as he used all principles,—simply as convenient machinery for carrying out his own purposes. Ellery Davenport spoke his own convictions when he said that there was no subject which had not its right and its wrong side, each of

them capable of being unanswerably sustained. He had played
with his own mind in this manner until he had entirely oblit-
erated conscience. He could at any time dazzle and confound
his own moral sense with his own reasonings; and it was
sometimes amusing, but, in the long run, tedious and vexatious to him, to find that what he maintained merely for convenience and for theory should be regarded by Emily so seriously, and with such an earnest eye to logical consequences.
In short, the two came, in the course of their intimacy, precisely to the spot to which many people come who are united
by an indissoluble legal tie. Slowly, and through an experience of many incidents, they had come to perceive an entire
and irrepressible conflict of natures between them.

Notwithstanding that Emily had taken a course diametri-
cally opposed to the principles of her country and her fathers,
she retained largely the Puritan nature. Instances have often
been seen in New England of men and women who had renounced every particle of the Puritan theology, and yet retained in their fibre and composition all the moral traits of
the Puritans—their uncompromising conscientiousness, their
inflexible truthfulness, and their severe logic in following the
convictions of their understandings. And the fact was, that
while Emily had sacrificed for Ellery Davenport her position
in society,—while she had exposed herself to the very coarsest misconstructions of the commonest minds, and made
herself liable to be ranked by her friends in New England
among abandoned outcasts,—she was really a woman standing on too high a moral plane for Ellery Davenport to con-
sort with her in comfort. He was ambitious, intriguing, unscrupulous, and it was an annoyance to him to be obliged to
give an account of himself to her. He was tired of playing the
moral hero, the part that he assumed and acted with great
success during the time of their early attachment. It annoyed
him to be held to any consistency in principles. The very devotion to him which she felt, regarding him, as she always
did, in his higher and nobler nature, vexed and annoyed him.

Of late years he had taken long vacations from her society,
in excursions to England and America. When the prospect of
being ambassador to England dawned upon him, he began
seriously to consider the inconvenience of being connected

with a woman unpresentable in society. He dared not risk introducing her into those high circles as his wife. Moreover, he knew that it was a falsehood to which he never should gain her consent; and running along in the line of his thoughts came his recollections of Tina. When he returned to America, with the fact in his mind that she would be the acknowledged daughter of a respectable old English family, all her charms and fascinations had a double power over him. He delivered himself up to them without scruple.

He wrote immediately to a confidential friend in Switzerland, enclosing money, with authority to settle upon Emily a villa near Geneva, and a suitable income. He trusted to her pride for the rest.

Never had the thought come into his head that she would return to her native country, and brave all the reproach and humiliation of such a step, rather than accept this settlement at his hands.

XLVIII.

Tina's Solution

HARRY and I had gone back to our college room after the wedding. There we received an earnest letter from Miss Mehitable, begging us to come to her at once. It was brought by Sam Lawson, who told us that he had got up at three o'clock in the morning to start away with it.

"There 's trouble of some sort or other in that 'ere house," said Sam. "Last night I was in ter the Deacon's, and we was a talkin' over the weddin', when Polly came in all sort o' flustered, and said Miss Rossiter wanted to see Mis' Badger; and your granny she went over, and did n't come home all night. She sot up with somebody, and I 'm certain 't wa'n't Miss Rossiter, 'cause I see her up tol'able spry in the mornin'; but, lordy massy, somethin' or other 's ben a usin' on her up, for she was all wore out, and looked sort o' limpsy, as if there wa' n't no starch left in her. She sent for me last night. 'Sam,' says she, 'I want to send a note to the boys just as quick as I can, and I don't want to wait for the mail; can't you carry it?' 'Lordy massy, yes,' says I. 'I hope there ain't nothin' happened,' says I; and ye see she didn't answer me; and puttin' that with Mis' Badger's settin' there all night, it 'peared to me there was suthin', I can't make out quite what."

Harry and I lost no time in going to the stage-house, and found ourselves by noon at Miss Mehitable's door.

When we went in, we found Miss Mehitable seated in close counsel with Mr. Jonathan Rossiter. His face looked sharp, and grave, and hard; his large gray eyes had in them a fiery, excited gleam. Spread out on the table before them were files of letters, in the handwriting of which I had before had a glimpse. The brother and sister had evidently been engaged in reading them, as some of them lay open under their hands.

When we came into the room, both looked up. Miss Mehitable rose, and offered her hands to us in an eager, excited way, as if she were asking something of us. The color flashed into Mr. Rossiter's cheeks, and he suddenly leaned forward over the papers and covered his face with his hands. It was a gesture of shame and humiliation infinitely touching to me.

"Horace," said Miss Mehitable, "the thing we feared has come upon us. O Horace, Horace! why could we not have known it in time?"

I divined at once. My memory, like an electric chain, flashed back over sayings and incidents of years.

"The villain!" I said.

Mr. Rossiter ground his foot on the floor with a hard, impatient movement, as if he were crushing some poisonous reptile.

"It 's well for him that *I* 'm not God," he said through his closed teeth.

Harry looked from one to the other of us in dazed and inquiring surprise. He had known in a vague way of Emily's disappearance, and of Miss Mehitable's anxieties, but it never had occurred to his mind to connect the two. In fact, our whole education had been in such a wholesome and innocent state of society, that neither of us had the foundation, in our experience or habits of thought, for the conception of anything like villany. We were far enough from any comprehension of the melodramatic possibilities suggested in our days by that heaving and tumbling modern literature, whose waters cast up mire and dirt.

Never shall I forget the shocked, incredulous expression on Harry's face as he listened to my explanations, nor the indignation to which it gave place.

"I would sooner have seen Tina in her grave than married to such a man," he said huskily.

"O Harry!" said Miss Mehitable.

"I would!" he said, rising excitedly. "There are things that men can do that still leave hope of them; but a thing like this is *final*,—it is decisive."

"That is my opinion, Harry," said Mr. Rossiter. "It is a sin that leaves no place for repentance."

"We have been reading these letters," said Miss Mehitable; "they were sent to us by Tina, and they do but confirm what I always said,—that Emily fell by her higher nature. She learned, under Dr. Stern, to think and to reason boldly, even when differing from received opinion; and this hardihood of mind and opinion she soon turned upon the doctrines he taught. Then she abandoned the Bible, and felt herself free to construct her own system of morals. Then came an intimate friendship with a fascinating married man, whose domestic misfortunes made a constant demand on her sympathy; and these charming French friends of hers—who were, as far as I see, disciples of the new style of philosophy, and had come to America to live in a union with each other which was not recognized by the laws of France—all united to make her feel that she was acting heroically and virtuously in sacrificing her whole life to her lover, and disregarding what they called the tyranny of human law. In Emily's eyes, her connection had all the sacredness of marriage."

"Yes," said Mr. Rossiter, "but see now how all these infernal, fine-spun, and high-flown notions always turn out to the disadvantage of the weaker party! It is *man* who always takes advantage of woman in relations like these; it is she that *gives* all, and he that *takes* all; it is she risks everything, and he risks nothing. Hard as marriage bonds bear in individual cases, it is for woman's interest that they should be as stringently maintained as the Lord himself has left them. When once they begin to be lessened, it is always the weaker party that goes to the wall!"

"But," said I, "suppose a case of confirmed and hopeless insanity on either side."

He made an impatient gesture. "Did you ever think," he said, "if men had the laws of nature in their hands, what a mess they would make of them? What treatises we should have against the cruelty of fire in *always* burning, and of water in *always* drowning! What saints and innocents has the fire tortured, and what just men made perfect has water drowned, making *no* exceptions! But who doubts that this inflexibility in natural law is, after all, the best thing? The laws of morals are in our hands, and so reversible, and, therefore, we are always clamoring for exceptions. I think they should cut their way like those of nature, *inflexibly* and *eternally*!"

Here the sound of wheels startled us. I went to the window, and, looking through the purple spikes of the tall old lilacs, which came up in a bower around the open window, I saw Tina alighting from a carriage.

"O Aunty," I said involuntarily, "it is she. *She* is coming, poor child."

We heard a light fluttering motion and a footfall on the stairs, and the door opened, and in a moment Tina stood among us.

She was very pale, and there was an expression such as I never saw in her face before. There had been a shock which had driven her soul inward, from the earthly upon the spiritual and the immortal. Something deep and pathetic spoke in her eyes, as she looked around on each of us for a moment without speaking. As she met Miss Mehitable's haggard, care-worn face, her lip quivered. She ran to her, threw her arms round her, and hid her face on her shoulder, and sobbed out, "O Aunty, Aunty! I did n't think I should live to make you this trouble."

"You, darling!" said Miss Mehitable. "It is not *you* who have made it."

"I am the cause," she said. "I know that he has done dreadfully wrong. I cannot defend him, but oh! I love him still. I cannot help loving him; it is my duty to," she added. "I promised, you know, before God, 'for better, for worse'; and what I promised I must keep. I am his wife; there is no going back from that."

"I know it, darling," said Miss Mehitable, stroking her head. "You are right, and my love for *you* will never change."

"I am come," she said, "to see what can be done."

"NOTHING *can be done*!" spoke out the deep voice of Jonathan Rossiter. "She is lost and we disgraced beyond remedy!"

"You must not say that," Tina said, raising her head, her eyes sparkling through her tears with some of her old vivacity. "Your sister is a noble, injured woman. We must shield her and save her; there is every excuse for her."

"There is NEVER any excuse for such conduct," said Mr. Rossiter, harshly.

Tina started up in her headlong, energetic fashion. "What right have you to talk so, if you call yourself a Christian?" she said. "Think a minute. WHO was it said, 'Neither do I con-

demn thee'? and *whom* did he say it to? Christ was not afraid
or ashamed to say *that* to a poor friendless woman, though
he knew his words would never pass away."

"God bless you, darling,—God bless you!" said Miss Mehitable, clasping her in her arms.

"I have read those letters," continued Tina, impetuously.
"He did not like me to do it, but I claimed it as my right,
and I *would* do it, and I can see in all a noble woman, gone
astray from noble motives. I can see that she was grand and
unselfish in her love, that she was perfectly self-sacrificing, and
I believe it was because Jesus understood these things in the
hearts of women that he uttered those blessed words. The law
was against that poor woman, the doctors, the Scribes and
Pharisees, all respectable people, were against her, and Christ
stepped between all and her; he sent them away abashed and
humbled, and spoke those lovely words to her. O, I shall forever adore him for it! He is my Lord and my God!"

There was a pause for a few moments, and then Tina spoke
again.

"Now, Aunty, hear my plan. You, perhaps, do not believe
any good of *him*, and so I will not try to make you; only I
will say that he is anxious to do all he can. He has left everything in my hands. This must go no farther than us few who
now know it. Your sister refused the property he tried to settle on her. It was noble to do it. I should have felt just as she
did. But, dear Aunty, *my* fortune I always meant to settle on
you, and it will be enough for you both. It will make you
easy as to money, and you can live together."

"Yes, my dear," said Miss Mehitable; "but how can this be
kept secret when there is the child?"

"I have thought of that, Aunty. I will take the poor little
one abroad with me,—children always love me. I can make
her so happy; and O, it will be such a motive to make amends
to her for all this wrong. Let me see your sister, Aunty, and
tell her about it."

"Dear child," said Miss Mehitable, "you can do nothing
with her. All last night I thought she was dying. Since then
she seems to have recovered her strength; but she neither
speaks nor moves. She lies with her eyes open, but notices
nothing you say to her."

"Poor darling!" said Tina. "But, Aunty, let me go to her. I am so sure that God will help me,—that God sends me to her. I *must* see her!"

Tina's strong impulses seemed to carry us all with her. Miss Mehitable arose, and, taking her by the hand, opened the door of a chamber on the opposite side of the hall. I looked in, and saw that it was darkened. Tina went boldly in, and closed the door. We all sat silent together. We heard her voice, at times soft and pleading; then it seemed to grow more urgent and impetuous as she spoke continuously and in tones of piercing earnestness.

After a while, there were pauses of silence, and then a voice in reply.

"There," said Miss Mehitable, "Emily has begun to answer her, thank God! Anything is better than this oppressive silence. It is frightful!"

And now the sound of an earnest conversation was heard, waxing on both sides more and more ardent and passionate. Tina's voice sometimes could be distinguished in tones of the most pleading entreaty; sometimes it seemed almost like sobbing. After a while, there came a great silence, broken by now and then an indistinct word; and then Tina came out, softly closing the door. Her cheeks were flushed, her hair partially dishevelled, but she smiled brightly,—one of her old triumphant smiles when she had carried a point.

"I 've conquered at last! I 've won!" she said, almost breathless. "O, I prayed so that I might, and I did. She gives all up to me; she loves me. We love each other dearly. And now I 'm going to take the little one with me, and by and by I will bring her back to her, and I will make her so happy. You must give me the darling at once, and I will take her away with us; for we are going to sail next week. We sail sooner than I thought," she said; "but this makes it best to go at once."

Miss Mehitable rose and went out, but soon reappeared, leading in a lovely little girl with great round, violet blue eyes, and curls of golden hair. The likeness of Ellery Davenport was plainly impressed on her infant features.

Tina ran towards her, and stretched out her arms. "Darling," she said, "come to me."

The little one, after a moment's survey, followed that law of attraction which always drew children to Tina. She came up confidingly, and nestled her head on her shoulder.

Tina gave her her watch to play with, and the child shook it about, well pleased.

"Emily want to go ride?" said Tina, carrying her to the window and showing her the horses.

The child laughed, and stretched out her hand.

"Bring me her things, Aunty," she said. "Let there not be a moment for change of mind. I take her with me this moment."

A few moments after, Tina went lightly tripping down the stairs, and Harry and I with her, carrying the child and its little basket of clothing.

"There, put them in," she said. "And now, boys," she said, turning and offering both her hands, "good by. I love you both dearly, and always shall."

She kissed us both, and was gone from our eyes before I awoke from the dream into which she had thrown me.

———

"Well," said Miss Mehitable, when the sound of wheels died away, "could I have believed that anything could have made my heart so much lighter as this visit?"

"She was inspired," said Mr. Rossiter.

"Tina's great characteristic," said I. "What makes her differ from others is this capacity of inspiration. She seems sometimes to rise, in a moment, to a level above her ordinary self, and to carry all up with her!"

"And to think that such a woman has thrown herself away on such a man!" said Harry.

"I foresee a dangerous future for her," said Mr. Rossiter. "With her brilliancy, her power of attraction, with the temptations of a new and fascinating social life before her, and with only that worthless fellow for a guide, I am afraid she will not continue *our* Tina."

"Suppose we trust in *Him* who has guided her hitherto," said Harry.

"People usually consider that sort of trust a desperate resort," said Mr. Rossiter. " 'May the Lord help her,' means, 'It 's all up with her.' "

"We see," said I, "that the greatest possible mortification and sorrow that could meet a young wife has only raised her into a higher plane. So let us hope for her future."

XLIX.

What Came of It

THE next week Mr. and Mrs. Ellery Davenport sailed for
England.

I am warned by the increased quantity of manuscript which
lies before me that, if I go on recounting scenes and incidents
with equal minuteness, my story will transcend the limits of
modern patience. Richardson might be allowed to trail off
into seven volumes, and to trace all the histories of all his
characters, even unto the third and fourth generations; but
Richardson did not live in the days of railroad and steam, and
mankind then had more leisure than now.

I am warned, too, that the departure of the principal character from the scene is a signal for general weariness through
the audience,—for looking up of gloves, and putting on of
shawls, and getting ready to call one's carriage.

In fact, when Harry and I had been down to see Tina off,
and had stood on the shore, watching and waving our handkerchiefs, until the ship became a speck in the blue airy distance, I turned back to the world with very much the feeling
that there was nothing left in it. What I had always dreamed
of, hoped for, planned for, and made the object of all my
endeavors, so far as this world was concerned, was gone,—
gone, so far as I could see, hopelessly and irredeemably; and
there came over me that utter languor and want of interest in
every mortal thing, which is one of the worst diseases of the
mind.

But I knew that it would never do to give way to this lethargy. I needed an alterative; and so I set myself, with all my
might and soul, to learning a new language. There was an old
German emigrant in Cambridge, with whom I became a pupil, and I plunged into German as into a new existence. I
recommend everybody who wishes to try the waters of Lethe
to study a new language, and learn to think in new forms; it
is like going out of one sphere of existence into another.

Some may wonder that I do not recommend devotion for this grand alterative; but it is a fact, that, when one has to combat with the terrible lassitude produced by the sudden withdrawal of an absorbing object of affection, devotional exercises sometimes hinder more than they help. There is much in devotional religion of the same strain of softness and fervor which is akin to earthly attachments, and the one is almost sure to recall the other. What the soul wants is to be distracted for a while,—to be taken out of its old grooves of thought, and run upon entirely new ones. Religion must be sought in these moods, in its active and preceptive form,— what we may call its business character,—rather than in its sentimental and devotional one.

It had been concluded among us all that it would be expedient for Miss Mehitable to remove from Oldtown and take a residence in Boston.

It was desirable, for restoring the health of Emily, that she should have more change and variety, and less minute personal attention fixed upon her, than could be the case in the little village of Oldtown. Harry and I did a great deal of house-hunting for them, and at last succeeded in securing a neat little cottage on an eminence overlooking the harbor in the outskirts of Boston.

Preparing this house for them, and helping to establish them in it, furnished employment for a good many of our leisure hours. In fact, we found that this home so near would be quite an accession to our pleasures. Miss Mehitable had always been one of that most pleasant and desirable kind of acquaintances that a young man can have; to wit, a cultivated, intelligent, literary female friend, competent to advise and guide one in one's scholarly career. We became greatly interested in the society of her sister. The strength and dignity of character shown by this unfortunate lady in recovering her position commanded our respect. She was never aware, and was never made aware by anything in our manner, that we were acquainted with her past history.

The advice of Tina on this subject had been faithfully followed. No one in our circle, or in Boston, except my grandmother, had any knowledge of how the case really stood. In fact, Miss Mehitable had always said that her sister had gone abroad to study in France, and her reappearance again was only noticed among the few that inquired into it at all, as her return. Harry and I used to study French with her, both on our own account, and as a means of giving her some kind of employment. On the whole, the fireside circle at the little cottage became a cheerful and pleasant retreat. Miss Mehitable had gained what she had for years been sighing for,—the opportunity to devote herself wholly to this sister. She was a person with an enthusiastic power of affection, and the friendship that arose between the two was very beautiful.

The experiences of the French Revolution, many of whose terrors she had witnessed, had had a powerful influence on the mind of Emily, in making her feel how mistaken had been those views of human progress which come from the mere unassisted reason, when it rejects the guidance of revealed religion. She was in a mood to return to the faith of her fathers, receiving it again under milder and more liberal forms. I think the friendship of Harry was of great use to her in enabling her to attain to a settled religious faith. They were peculiarly congenial to each other, and his simplicity of religious trust was a constant corrective to the habits of thought formed by the sharp and pitiless logic of her early training.

A residence in Boston was also favorable to Emily's recovery, in giving to her what no person who has passed through such experiences can afford to be without,—an opportunity to help those poorer and more afflicted. Emily very naturally shrank from society; except the Kitterys, I think there was no family which she visited. I think she always had the feeling that she would not accept the acquaintance of any who would repudiate her were all the circumstances of her life known to them. But with the poor, the sick, and the afflicted, she felt · herself at home. In their houses she was a Sister of Mercy, and the success of these sacred ministrations caused her, after a while, to be looked upon with a sort of reverence by all who knew her.

Tina proved a lively and most indefatigable correspondent. Harry and I heard from her constantly, in minute descriptions of the great gay world of London society, into which she was thrown as wife of the American minister. Her letters were like her old self, full of genius, of wit, and of humor, sparkling with descriptions and anecdotes of character, and sometimes scrawled on the edges with vivid sketches of places, or scenes, or buildings that hit her fancy. She was improving, she told us, taking lessons in drawing and music, and Ellery was making a capital French scholar of her. We could see through all her letters an evident effort to set forth everything relating to him to the best advantage; every good-natured or kindly action, and all the favorable things that were said of him, were put in the foreground, with even an anxious care.

To Miss Mehitable and Emily came other letters, filled with the sayings and doings of the little Emily, recording minutely all the particulars of her growth, and the incidents of the nursery, and showing that Tina, with all her going out, found time strictly to fulfil her promises in relation to her.

"I have got the very best kind of a maid for her," she wrote,—"just as good and true as Polly is, only she is formed by the Church Catechism instead of the Cambridge Platform. But she is faithfulness itself, and Emily loves her dearly."

In this record, also, minute notice was taken of all the presents made to the child by her father,—of all his smiles and caressing words. Without ever saying a word formally in her husband's defence, Tina thus contrived, through all her letters, to produce the most favorable impression of him. He was evidently, according to her showing, proud of her beauty and her talents, and proud of the admiration which she excited in society.

For a year or two there seemed to be a real vein of happiness running through all these letters of Tina's. I spoke to Harry about it one day.

"Tina," said I, "has just that fortunate kind of constitution, buoyant as cork, that will rise to the top of the stormiest waters."

"Yes," said Harry. "With some women it would have been an entire impossibility to live happily with a man after such a disclosure,—with Esther, for example. I have never told Esther a word about it; but I know that it would give her a horror of the man that she never could recover from."

"It is not," said I, "that Tina has not strong moral perceptions; but she has this buoyant hopefulness; she believes in herself, and she believes in others. She always feels adequate to manage the most difficult circumstances. I could not help smiling that dreadful day, when she came over and found us all so distressed and discouraged, to see what a perfect confidence she had in herself and in her own power to arrange the affair,—to make Emily consent, to make the child love her; in short, to carry out everything according to her own sweet will, just as she has always done with us all ever since we knew her."

"I always wondered," said Harry, "that, with all her pride, and all her anger, Emily did consent to let the child go."

"Why," said I, "she was languid and weak, and she was overborne by simple force of will. Tina was so positive and determined, so perfectly assured, and so warming and melting, that she carried all before her. There was n't even the physical power to resist her."

"And do you think," said Harry, "that she will hold her power over a man like Ellery Davenport?"

"Longer, perhaps, than any other kind of woman," said I, "because she has such an infinite variety about her. But, after all, you remember what Miss Debby said about him,—that he never cared long for anything that he was sure of. Restlessness and pursuit are his nature, and therefore the time may come when she will share the fate of other idols."

"I regard it," said Harry, "as the most dreadful trial to a woman's character that can possibly be, to love, as Tina loves, a man whose moral standard is so far below hers. It is bad enough to be obliged to *talk* down always to those who are below us in intellect and comprehension; but to be obliged to *live down*, all the while, to a man without conscience or moral sense, is worse. I think often, 'What communion hath light with darkness?' and the only hope I can have is that she will fully find him out at last."

"And that," said I, "is a hope full of pain to her; but it seems to me likely to be realized. A man who has acted as he has done to one woman certainly never will be true to another."

Harry and I were now thrown more and more exclusively upon each other for society.

He had received his accession of fortune with as little exterior change as possible. Many in his situation would have rushed immediately over to England, and taken delight in coming openly into possession of the estate. Harry's fastidious reticence, however, hung about him even in this. It annoyed him to be an object of attention and gossip, and he felt no inclination to go alone into what seemed to him a strange country, into the midst of social manners and customs entirely different from those among which he had been brought up. He preferred to remain and pursue his course quietly, as he had begun, in the college with me; and he had taken no steps in relation to the property except to consult a lawyer in Boston.

Immediately on leaving college, it was his design to be married, and go with Esther to see what could be done in England. But I think his heart was set upon a home in America. The freedom and simplicity of life in this country were peculiarly suited to his character, and he felt a real vocation for the sacred ministry, not in the slightest degree lessened by the good fortune which had rendered him independent of it.

Two years of our college life passed away pleasantly enough in hard study, interspersed with social relaxations among the few friends nearest to us. Immediately after our graduation came Harry's marriage,—a peaceful little idyllic performance, which took us back to the mountains, and to all the traditions of our old innocent woodland life there.

After the wholesome fashion of New England clergymen, Mr. Avery had found a new mistress for the parsonage, so that Esther felt the more resigned to leaving him. When I had seen them off, however, I felt really quite alone in the world. The silent, receptive, sympathetic friend and brother of my youth was gone. But immediately came the effort to establish myself in Boston. And, through the friendly offices of the Kitterys, I was placed in connection with some very influential lawyers, who gave me that helping hand which takes a young man up the first steps of the profession. Harry had been most generous and liberal in regard to all our family, and insisted upon it that I should share his improved fortunes. There are friends so near to us that we can take from them as from ourselves. And Harry always insisted that he could in no way so repay the kindness and care that had watched over his early years as by this assistance to me.

I received constant letters from him, and from their drift it became increasingly evident that the claims of duty upon him would lead him to make England his future home. In one of these he said: "I have always, as you know, looked forward to the ministry, and to such a kind of ministry as you have in America, where a man, for the most part, speaks to cultivated, instructed people, living in a healthy state of society, where a competence is the rule, and where there is a practical equality.

"I had no conception of life, such as I see it to be here, where there are whole races who appear born to poverty and subjection; where there are woes, and dangers, and miseries pressing on whole classes of men, which no one individual can do much to avert or alleviate. But it is to this very state of society that I feel a call to minister. I shall take orders in the Church of England, and endeavor to carry out among the poor and the suffering that simple Gospel which my mother taught me, and which, after all these years of experience, after all these theological discussions to which I have listened, remains in its perfect simplicity in my mind; namely, that every human soul on this earth has One Friend, and that Friend is Jesus Christ its Lord and Saviour.

"There is a redeeming power in being beloved, but there are many human beings who have never known what it is to be beloved. And my theology is, once penetrate any human soul with the full belief that *God loves him*, and you save him. Such is to be my life's object and end; and, in this ministry, Esther will go with me hand in hand. Her noble beauty and gracious manners make her the darling of all our people, and she is above measure happy in the power of doing good which is thus put into her hands.

"As to England, mortal heart cannot conceive more beauty than there is here. It is lovely beyond all poets' dreams. Near to our place are some charming old ruins, and I cannot tell you the delightful hours that Esther and I have spent there. Truly, the lines have fallen to us in pleasant places.

"I have not yet seen Tina,—she is abroad travelling on the Continent. She writes to us often; but, Horace, her letters begin to have the undertone of pain in them,—her skies are certainly beginning to fade. From some sources upon which I place reliance, I hear Ellery Davenport spoken of as a daring, plausible, but unscrupulous man. He is an *intrigant* in politics, and has no domestic life in him; while Tina, however much she loves and appreciates admiration, has a perfect woman's heart. Admiration without love would never satisfy her. I can see, through all the excuses of her letters, that he is going very much one way and she another, that he has his engagements, and she hers, and that they see, really, very little of each other, and that all this makes her sad and unhappy. The fact is, I suppose, he has played with his butterfly until there is no more down on its wings, and he is on the chase after new ones. Such is my reading of poor Tina's lot."

When I took this letter to Miss Mehitable, she told me that a similar impression had long since been produced on her mind by passages which she had read in hers. Tina often spoke of the little girl as very lovely, and as her greatest earthly comfort. A little one of her own, born in England, had died early, and her affections seemed thus to concentrate more entirely upon the child of her adoption. She described her with enthusiasm, as a child of rare beauty and talent, with capabilities of enthusiastic affection.

"Let us hope," said I, "that she does take her heart from her mother. Ellery Davenport is just one of those men that women are always wrecking themselves on,—men that have strong capabilities of passion, and very little capability of affection,—men that have no end of sentiment, and scarcely the beginning of real feeling. They make bewitching lovers, but terrible husbands."

One of the greatest solaces of my life during this period was my friendship with dear old Madam Kittery. Ever since the time when I had first opened to her my boyish heart, she had seemed to regard me with an especial tenderness, and to connect me in some manner with the image of her lost son. The assistance that she gave me in my educational career was viewed by her as a species of adoption. Her eye always brightened, and a lovely smile broke out upon her face, when I came to pass an hour with her. Time had treated her kindly; she still retained the gentle shrewdness, the love of literature, and the warm kindness which had been always charms in her. Some of my happiest hours were passed in reading to her. Chapter after chapter in her well-worn Bible needed no better commentary than the sweet brightness of her dear old face, and her occasional fervent responses. Many Sabbaths, when her increasing infirmities detained her from church, I spent in a tender, holy rest by her side. Then I would read from her prayer-book the morning service, not omitting the prayer that she loved, for the King and the royal family, and then, sitting hand in hand, we talked together of sacred things, and I often wondered to see what *strength* and discrimination there were in the wisdom of love, and how unerring were the decisions that she often made in practical questions. In fact, I felt myself drawn to Madam Kittery by a closer, tenderer tie than even to my own grandmother. I had my secret remorse for this, and tried to quiet myself by saying that it was because, living in Boston, I saw Madam Kittery oftener. But, after all, is it not true that, as we grow older, the relationship of souls will make itself felt? I revered and loved my grandmother, but I never idealized her; but my attachment to Madam Kittery was a species of poetic devotion. There was a slight flavor of romance in it, such as comes with the attachments of our maturer life oftener than with those of our childhood.

Miss Debby looked on me with eyes of favor. In her own way she really was quite as much my friend as her mother. She fell into the habit of consulting me upon her business affairs, and asking my advice in a general way about the arrangements of life.

"I don't see," I said to Madam Kittery, one day, "why Miss Deborah always asks my advice; she never takes it."

"My dear," said she, with the quiet smile with which she often looked on her daughter's proceedings, "Debby wants somebody to *ask* advice of. When she gets it, she is settled at once as to what she *don't* want to do; and that's something."

Miss Debby once came to me with a face of great perplexity.

"I don't know what to do, Horace. Our Thomas is a very valuable man, and he has always been in the family. I don't know anything how we should get along without him, but he is getting into bad ways."

"Ah," said I, "what?"

"Well, you see it all comes of this modern talk about the rights of the people. I've instructed Thomas as faithfully as ever a woman could; but—do you believe me?—he goes to the primary meetings. I have positive, reliable information that he does."

"My dear Miss Kittery, I suppose it 's his right as a citizen."

"O, fiddlestick and humbug!" said Miss Debby; "and it may be my right to turn him out of my service."

"And would not that, after all, be more harm to you than to him?" suggested I.

Miss Debby swept up the hearth briskly, tapped on her snuff-box, and finally said she had forgotten her handkerchief, and left the room.

Old Madam Kittery laughed a quiet laugh. "Poor Debby," she said, "she 'll have to come to it; the world will go on."

Thomas kept his situation for some years longer, till, having bought a snug place, and made some favorable investments, he at last announced to Miss Debby that, having been appointed constable, with a commission from the governor, his official duties would not allow of his continuance in her service.

L.

The Last Chapter

It was eight years after Tina left us on the wharf in Boston when I met her again. Ellery Davenport had returned to this country, and taken a house in Boston. I was then a lawyer established there in successful business.

Ellery Davenport met me with open-handed cordiality, and Tina with warm sisterly affection; and their house became one of my most frequent visiting-places. Knowing Tina by a species of divination, as I always had, it was easy for me to see through all those sacred little hypocrisies by which good women instinctively plead and intercede for husbands whom they themselves have found out. Michelet says, somewhere, that "in marriage the maternal feeling becomes always the strongest in woman, and in time it is the motherly feeling with which she regards her husband." She cares for him, watches over him, with the indefatigable tenderness which a mother gives to a son.

It was easy to see that Tina's affection for her husband was no longer a blind, triumphant adoration for an idealized hero, nor the confiding dependence of a happy wife, but the care-worn anxiety of one who constantly seeks to guide and to restrain. And I was not long in seeing the cause of this anxiety.

Ellery Davenport was smitten with that direst curse, which, like the madness inflicted on the heroes of some of the Greek tragedies, might seem to be the vengeance of some incensed divinity. He was going down that dark and slippery road, up which so few return. We were all fully aware that at many times our Tina had all the ghastly horrors of dealing with a madman. Even when he was himself again, and sought, by vows, promises, and illusive good resolutions, to efface the memory of the past, and give security for the future, there was no rest for Tina. In her dear eyes I could read always that sense of overhanging dread, that helpless watchfulness, which one may see in the eyes of so many poor women in our modern life, whose days are haunted by a fear they dare not express, and who must smile, and look gay, and seem confiding, when their very souls are failing them for fear. Still these seasons of madness did not seem for a while to impair the vigor of Ellery Davenport's mind, nor the feverish intensity of his ambition. He was absorbed in political life, in a wild, daring, unprincipled way, and made frequent occasions to leave Tina alone in Boston, while he travelled around the country, pursuing his intrigues. In one of these absences, it was his fate at last to fall in a political duel.

Ten years after the gay and brilliant scene in Christ Church, some of those who were present as wedding guests were again convened to tender the last offices to the brilliant and popular Ellery Davenport. Among the mourners at the grave, two women who had loved him truly stood arm in arm.

After his death, it seemed, by the general consent of all, the kindest thing that could be done for him, to suffer the veil of silence to fall over his memory.

Two years after that, one calm, lovely October morning, a quiet circle of friends stood around the altar of the old church, when Tina and I were married. Our wedding journey was a visit to Harry and Esther in England. Since then, the years have come and gone softly.

Ellery Davenport now seems to us as a distant dream of another life, recalled chiefly by the beauty of his daughter, whose growing loveliness is the principal ornament of our home.

Miss Mehitable and Emily form one circle with us. Nor does the youthful Emily know why she is so very dear to the saintly woman whose prayers and teachings are such a benediction in our family.

Not long since we spent a summer vacation at Oldtown, to explore once more the old scenes, and to show to young Master Harry and Miss Tina the places that their parents had told them of. Many changes have taken place in the old homestead. The serene old head of my grandfather has been laid beneath the green sod of the burying-ground; and my mother, shortly after, was laid by him.

Old Parson Lothrop continued for some years, with his antique dress and his antique manners, respected in Oldtown as the shadowy minister of the past; while his colleague, Mr. Mordecai Rossiter, edified his congregation with the sharpest and most stringent new school Calvinism. To the last, Dr. Lothrop remained faithful to his Arminian views, and regarded the spread of the contrary doctrines, as a decaying old minister is apt to, as a personal reflection upon himself. In his last illness, which was very distressing, he was visited by a zealous Calvinistic brother from a neighboring town, who, on the strength of being a family connection, thought it his duty to go over and make one last effort to revive the orthodoxy of his venerable friend. Dr. Lothrop received him politely, and with his usual gentlemanly decorum remained for a long time in silence listening to his somewhat protracted arguments and statements. As he gave no reply, his friend at last said to him, "Dr. Lothrop, perhaps you are weak, and this conversation disturbs you?"

"I should be weak indeed, if I allowed such things as you have been saying to disturb me," replied the stanch old doctor.

"He died like a philosopher, my dear," said Lady Lothrop to me, "just as he always lived."

My grandmother, during the last part of her life, was totally blind. One would have thought that a person of her extreme activity would have been restless and wretched under this deprivation; but in her case blindness appeared to be indeed what Milton expressed it as being, "an overshadowing of the wings of the Almighty." Every earthly care was hushed, and her mind turned inward, in constant meditation upon those great religious truths which had fed her life for so many years.

Aunt Lois we found really quite lovely. There is a class of women who are like winter apples,—all their youth they are crabbed and hard, but at the further end of life they are full

of softness and refreshment. The wrinkles had really almost
smoothed themselves out in Aunt Lois's face, and our children found in her the most indulgent and painstaking of
aunties, ready to run, and wait, and tend, and fetch, and
carry, and willing to put everything in the house at their disposal. In fact, the young gentleman and lady found the old
homestead such very free and easy ground that they announced to us that they preferred altogether staying there to
being in Boston, especially as they had the barn to romp in.

One Saturday afternoon, Tina and I drove over to Needmore with a view to having one more gossip with Sam Lawson. Hepsy, it appears, had departed this life, and Sam had
gone over to live with a son of his in Needmore. We found
him roosting placidly in the porch on the sunny side of the
house.

"Why, lordy massy, bless your soul an' body, ef that ain't
Horace Holyoke!" he said, when he recognized who I was.

"An' this 'ere 's your wife, is it? Wal, wal, how this 'ere
world does turn round! Wal, now, who would ha' thought
it? Here you be, and Tiny with you. Wal, wal!"

"Yes," said I, "here we are."

"Wal, now, jest sit down," said Sam, motioning us to a seat
in the porch. "I was jest kind o' 'flectin' out here in the sun;
ben a readin' in the Missionary Herald; they 've ben a sendin'
missionaries to Otawhity, an' they say that there ain't no winter there, an' the bread jest grows on the trees, so 't they don't
hev to make none, an' there ain't no wood-piles nor splittin'
wood, nor nothin' o' that sort goin' on, an' folks don't need
no clothes to speak on. Now, I 's jest thinkin' that 'ere 's jest
the country to suit me. I wonder, now, ef they could n't find
suthin' for me to do out there. I could shoe the hosses, ef
they hed any, and I could teach the natives their catechize,
and kind o' help round gin'ally. These 'ere winters gits so cold
here I 'm e'en a'most crooked up with the rheumatiz—"

"Why, Sam," said Tina, "where is Hepsy?"

"Law, now, hain't ye heerd? Why, Hepsy, she 's been dead,
wal, let me see, 't was three year the fourteenth o' last May
when Hepsy died, but she was clear wore out afore she died.
Wal, jest half on her was clear paralyzed, poor crittur; she
could n't speak a word; that 'ere was a gret trial to her. I

don't think she was resigned under it. Hepsy hed an awful
sight o' grit. I used to talk to Hepsy, an' talk, an' try to set
things afore her in the best way I could, so 's to git 'er into a
better state o' mind. D' you b'lieve, one day when I 'd ben a
talkin' to her, she kind o' made a motion to me with her eye,
an' when I went up to 'er, what d' you think? why, she jest
tuk and BIT me! she did so!"

"Sam," said Tina, "I sympathize with Hepsy. I believe if I
had to be talked to an hour, and could n't answer, I should
bite."

"Jes' so, jes' so," said Sam. "I 'spex 't is so. You see, women
must talk, there 's where 't is. Wal, now, don't ye remember
that Miss Bell,—Miss Miry Bell? She was of a good family in
Boston. They used to board her out to Oldtown, 'cause she
was 's crazy 's a loon. They jest let 'er go 'bout, 'cause she
did n't hurt nobody, but massy, her tongue used ter run 's ef
't was hung in the middle and run both ends. Ye really
could n't hear yourself think when she was round. Wal, she
was a visitin' Parson Lothrop, an' ses he, 'Miss Bell, do pray
see ef you can't be still a minute.' 'Lord bless ye, Dr. Lothrop,
I can't stop talking!' ses she. 'Wal,' ses he, 'you jest take a
mouthful o' water an' hold in your mouth, an' then mebee ye
ken stop.' Wal, she took the water, an' she sot still a minute
or two, an' it kind o' worked on 'er so 't she jumped up an'
twitched off Dr. Lothrop's wig an' spun it right acrost the
room inter the fireplace. 'Bless me! Miss Bell,' ses he, 'spit out
yer water an' talk, ef ye must!' I 've offun thought on 't," said
Sam. "I s'pose Hepsy 's felt a good 'eal so. Wal, poor soul,
she 's gone to 'er rest. We 're all on us goin', one arter another. Yer grandther 's gone, an' yer mother, an' Parson Lothrop, he 's gone, an' Lady Lothrop, she 's kind o' solitary. I
went over to see 'er last week, an' ses she to me, 'Sam, I
dunno nothin' what I shell do with my hosses. I feed 'em
well, an' they ain't worked hardly any, an' yet they act so 't
I 'm 'most afeard to drive out with 'em.' I 'm thinkin' 't would
be a good thing ef she 'd give up that 'ere place o' hern, an'
go an' live in Boston with her sister."

"Well, Sam," said Tina, "what has become of Old Crab
Smith? Is he alive yet?"

"Law, yis, he 's creepin' round here yit; but the old woman,

she 's dead," said Sam. "I tell you she 's a hevin' her turn o' hectorin' *him* now, 'cause she keeps appearin' to him, an' scares the old critter 'most to death."

"Appears to him?" said I. "Why, what do you mean, Sam?"

"Wal, jest as true 's you live an' breathe, she does 'pear to him," said Sam. "Why, 't was only last week my son Luke an' I, we was a settin' by the fire here, an' I was a holdin' a skein o' yarn for Malviny to wind (Malviny, she 's Luke's wife), when who should come in but Old Crab, head first, lookin' so scart an' white about the gills thet Luke, ses he, 'Why, Mistur Smith! what ails ye?' ses he. Wal, the critter was so scared 't he could n't speak, he jest set down in the chair, an' he shuk so 't he shuk the chair, an' his teeth, they chattered, an' 't was a long time 'fore they could git it out on him. But come to, he told us, 't was a bright moonlight night, an' he was comin' 'long down by the Stone pastur, when all of a suddin he looks up an' there was his wife walkin right 'long-side on him,—he ses he never see nothin' plainer in his life than he see the old woman, jest in her short gown an' petticut 't she allers wore, with her gold beads round her neck, an' a cap on with a black ribbon round it, an' there she kep' a walkin' right 'long-side of 'im, her elbow a touchin' hisn, all 'long the road, an' when he walked faster, she walked faster, an' when he walked slower, she walked slower, an' her eyes was sot, an' fixed on him, but she did n't speak no word, an' he did n't darse to speak to her. Finally, he ses he gin a dread-ful yell an' run with all his might, an' our house was the very fust place he tumbled inter. Lordy massy, wal, I could n't help thinkin' 't sarved him right. I told Sol 'bout it, last town-meetin' day, an' Sol, I thought he 'd ha' split his sides. Sol said he did n't know 's the old woman had so much sperit. 'Lordy massy,' ses he, 'ef she don't do nothin' more 'n take a walk 'long-side on him now an' then, why, I say, let 'er rip,— sarves him right.'"

"Well," said Tina, "I 'm glad to hear about Old Sol; how is he?"

"O, Sol? Wal, he 's doin' fustrate. He married Deacon 'Bi-jah Smith's darter, an' he 's got a good farm of his own, an' boys bigger 'n you be, considerable."

"Well," said Tina, "how is Miss Asphyxia?"

"Wal, Sol told me 't she 'd got a cancer or suthin' or other the matter with 'er; but the old gal, she jest sets her teeth hard, an' goes on a workin'. She won't have no doctor, nor nothin' done for 'er, an' I expect bimeby she 'll die, a standin' up in the harness."

"Poor old creature! I wonder, Horace, if it would do any good for me to go and see her. Has she a soul, I wonder, or is she nothing but a 'working machine'?"

"Wal, I dunno," said Sam. "This 'ere world is cur'us. When we git to thinkin' about it, we think ef we 'd ha' had the makin' on 't, things would ha' ben made someways diffurnt from what they be. But then things *is* just *as* they is, an' we can't help it. Sometimes I think" said Sam, embracing his knee profoundly, "an' then agin I dunno.——There 's all sorts o' folks hes to be in this 'ere world, an' I s'pose the Lord knows what he wants 'em fur; but I 'm sure I don't. I kind o' hope the Lord 'll fetch everybody out 'bout right some o' these 'ere times. He ain't got nothin' else to do, an' it 's his lookout, an' not ourn, what comes of 'em all.——But I *should* like to go to Otawhity, an' ef you see any o' these missionary folks, Horace, I wish you 'd speak to 'em about it."

THE END.

Chronology

1811   Harriet Elizabeth Beecher is born June 14 in Litchfield,
        Connecticut, the seventh child and fourth daughter of Ly-
        man and Roxana Foote Beecher. The son of a blacksmith,
        Lyman Beecher had become one of New England's lead-
        ing Evangelical clergymen; Roxana had been raised in the
        home of an uncle who served as a general in Washington's
        army during the Revolution.

1813   Henry Ward Beecher, her brother and the closest compan-
        ion of her childhood and youth, is born and she is
        weaned.

1816   Roxana Beecher dies after a short illness, having given
        birth to nine children in fifteen years.

1818   Lyman Beecher marries Harriet Porter, a stepmother
        with whom Harriet Beecher feels neither comfortable nor
        intimate.

1819–24 Attends Miss Sarah Pierce's School in Litchfield.

1824–27 Attends Hartford Female Seminary, founded by her older
         sister Catharine, which offers one of the most advanced
         courses of study available to young women in the United
         States.

1825   Experiences religious rebirth or conversion while visiting
        at home in Litchfield and hearing one of her father's
        sermons.

1827   Begins to teach at Hartford Female Seminary. Supports
        herself during the next nine years before her marriage by
        teaching.

1832   Moves to the frontier and border city of Cincinnati with
        the rest of the Beecher family, where Lyman Beecher be-
        comes president of Lane Theological Seminary and pastor
        of the Second Presbyterian Church. Teaches in the West-
        ern Female Institute, also founded by Catharine Beecher.

1833   Visits the home of a student in nearby Kentucky, where she makes her only firsthand observations of slavery. Co-authors with Catharine Beecher a *Primary Geography for Children*.

1834   Begins to write short stories, four of which are published in Cincinnati's *Western Monthly Magazine*.

1836   Marries Calvin Stowe, Professor of Biblical Literature at Lane. He had been the husband of Harriet Beecher's best friend, Eliza Tyler Stowe, until her death in 1835. Later, Harriet Beecher Stowe gives birth to twin girls, Harriet and Eliza. Never marrying, these daughters assist their mother in multiple ways, including copying her writings for publication. Observes the three days of riots in Cincinnati led by men of property and social standing against James G. Birney's abolitionist newspaper.

1837   Negro servant in the Stowe household who said she was free admits to being a fugitive slave whose master is searching for her. Harriet and Calvin help her escape via the underground railroad.

1838   Henry Ellis Stowe is born.

1839   Begins to publish stories in national periodicals, especially *Godey's Lady's Book*, for which she receives $1.50 to $2.00 per page. Buys household furnishings with her earnings, Calvin Stowe's income being very small.

1840   Frederick William Stowe is born and Harriet Beecher Stowe is very ill for six months afterwards.

1843   Georgiana May Stowe is born and both mother and daughter are ill for almost a year. Catharine Beecher organizes the publication of a collection of Harriet Beecher Stowe's stories, *The Mayflower; or, Sketches of Scenes and Characters among the Descendants of the Pilgrims*.

1845   Writes "Immediate Emancipation" for the *Evangelist*, a Congregational paper with abolitionist sympathies to which Harriet Beecher Stowe has been a frequent contributor of domestic stories. This essay marks a turning point in her attitude toward slavery, departing from the more conservative views of her father and sister and adopting the more radical views of her brothers.

1846   Spends fifteen months at a water-cure spa in Brattleboro, Vermont, where her health, weakened after bearing five children in ten years, is restored.

1848   Calvin Stowe spends fifteen months at the Brattleboro water cure.

1849   Samuel Charles Stowe is born and dies during a cholera epidemic. This death deeply affects Harriet Beecher Stowe. Calvin Stowe accepts a position as Professor of Natural and Revealed Religion at Bowdoin College, his alma mater, in Brunswick, Maine, and the family moves there in 1850.

1850   The Fugitive Slave Act is passed, making it possible for slaves to be hunted throughout the United States and containing inadequate protection for free blacks. Harriet Beecher Stowe vows to write about the evils of slavery. Begins to publish stories in the *National Era*, an abolitionist paper in Washington, D.C. Reads the novels of Sir Walter Scott and Charles Dickens aloud to her children. Charles Edward Stowe is born.

1851   *Uncle Tom's Cabin; or, Life among the Lowly*, her first novel, is published in installments in the *National Era*.

1852   *Uncle Tom's Cabin* appears as a book, published by J.P. Jewett in Boston, selling an unprecedented 3,000 copies the first day and 300,000 copies the first year. Receiving a royalty of 10 percent, Harriet Beecher Stowe earns $10,000 in the first four months of the novel's publication, although she lost a fortune by declining to enter a joint venture that would have split the costs and profits with the publisher. Stowe family moves to Andover, Massachusetts, where Calvin becomes Professor of Sacred Literature at Andover Theological Seminary.

1852–60   *Uncle Tom's Cabin* is reprinted in twenty-two different languages ranging from Armenian to Welsh, becoming the world's second most popular book, second only to the Bible.

1853   *A Key to Uncle Tom's Cabin*, seeking to verify the facts of the novel and relying particularly heavily on Theodore Weld's *American Slavery as It Is* (1839), is published. Travels to Europe, where she is celebrated by nobility and commoner alike.

1854   Publishes *Sunny Memories of Foreign Lands*, describing her travels.

1856   *Dred: A Tale of the Great Dismal Swamp* is published by Phillips, Sampson in Boston. Based on the Nat Turner rebellion of the 1830s, its sales are disappointing to Harriet Beecher Stowe and her publisher. Second trip abroad.

1857   Death of oldest son, Henry, a student at Dartmouth College, while swimming in the Connecticut River.

1859   *The Minister's Wooing*, published by Derby and Jackson in New York, the first of her novels about New England, explores the theological and personal conflicts generated by Henry's death and the fact that he died before he had experienced religious conversion. Third European trip.

1862   *The Pearl of Orr's Island* and *Agnes of Sorrento* are published by Ticknor and Fields in Boston. Meets with President Lincoln in the White House, who calls her "the little woman who started this great war."

1863   Stowe family moves to Hartford and Calvin retires from teaching. Harriet Beecher Stowe builds a large and impractical villa, which is sold at a loss in 1870. *A Reply to the Women of England in Behalf of the Women of America* is published. It was written to celebrate the Emancipation Proclamation. Lyman Beecher dies after nearly a decade of senility. Harriet Beecher Stowe shifts allegiance to the Episcopal Church.

1865   *House and Home Papers* appears, written under the pseudonym of Christopher Crowfield.

1868   Purchases a new home in Mandarin, Florida, where she and Calvin Stowe spend winters. Builds smaller new home in Hartford.

1869   *Oldtown Folks* is published by Fields, Osgood in Boston. Coauthors *The American Woman's Home* with Catharine Beecher.

1870   In *Lady Byron Vindicated*, she defends the late wife of the poet against aspersions on her character.

1871   *My Wife and I* (New York: J.B. Ford) and *Pink and White Tyranny* (Boston: Robert Bros.) are published. These two domestic novels were designed to bring in money to support Calvin Stowe, their twin daughters, alcoholic son Fred, and married son Charles, all of whom were dependent on her earnings.

1872   *Oldtown Fireside Stories* is published by J.R. Osgood in Boston.

1873   *Palmetto-Leaves* and *Women in Sacred History* are published.

1875   *We and Our Neighbors* published by Fords, Howard, & Hulbert in New York. Lends emotional support to Henry Ward Beecher when he is accused of adultery with a member of his Plymouth Church congregation in Brooklyn.

1878   *Poganuc People* (New York: Fords, Howard, & Hulbert) is published.

1882   Celebrates her seventieth birthday at a reception given by her publishers, Houghton, Mifflin and Company of Boston, which is attended by two hundred distinguished literary men and women.

1884   *Our Famous Women* is published.

1886   Calvin Stowe dies.

1896   Dies on July 1 from a stroke.

Note on the Texts

This edition of Harriet Beecher Stowe's three most important novels uses the texts of the first American book edition of each. Two of these first appeared in serial publications— *Uncle Tom's Cabin* in *National Era*, June 1851–April 1852, and *The Minister's Wooing* in *Atlantic Monthly*, December 1858– December 1859. Both the periodical and book publications contain extensive punctuation changes from Stowe's original manuscript, for she relied primarily on dashes, and as she wrote in 1868, "My printers always inform me that I know nothing of punctuation, and I give thanks that I have no responsibility for any of its absurdities!" Since Stowe did some proofreading and correcting for the book publication, based on the periodical publication, the book edition represents Stowe's intentions more completely.

The first edition of *Uncle Tom's Cabin* (Boston: J.P. Jewett, 1852) appeared in two volumes and contained some minor revisions. Stowe changed the name of Senator Burr to Senator Bird and corrected portions of the text. In addition, she wrote a preface for the book. Stowe's identification, in a footnote, of Rev. Dr. Joel Parker of Philadelphia as the author of the view that the evils of slavery were linked with evils "inseparable from any other relations in social and domestic life" led to an extended controversy with Parker, although the footnote was removed in later printings. Stowe's decreasing correction of Negro dialect in the novel indicates her increasing confidence in her use of black colloquial language.

The Minister's Wooing was written in monthly installments in 1858 and published in book form in 1859 by Derby and Jackson of New York. Stowe's letters reveal that she proofread the novel by reading aloud to friends the periodical version when the proofs arrived from the *Atlantic Monthly*. Presumably she made corrections in the book version at that time, since there are numerous differences between the periodical and book versions of the text.

Oldtown Folks (Boston: Fields, Osgood, 1869) is the only one of Harriet Beecher Stowe's major novels that was not originally published in periodical form. The sale of some of her previous works had disappointed her, and she hoped that by bringing out *Oldtown Folks* directly in book form it would do better. The plates for the original Fields, Osgood edition were used for many subsequent reprintings by Houghton, Mifflin and Company.

The standards for American English continue to fluctuate and in some ways were conspicuously different in earlier periods from what they are now. In nineteenth-century writings, for example, a word might be spelled in more than one way, even in the same work, and such variations might be carried into print. Commas were sometimes used expressively to suggest the movements of voice, and capitals were sometimes meant to give significances to a word beyond those it might have in its uncapitalized form. Since modernization would remove these effects, this volume has preserved the spelling, punctuation, capitalization, and wording of the first editions, which, of the available texts, appear most faithful to Stowe's intentions.

The present edition is concerned only with representing the texts of these editions; it does not attempt to reproduce features of the typographic design—such as the display capitalization of chapter openings. Footnotes within the text are by Stowe. Open contractions are retained as they appeared in the original texts. However some changes have been made. A Table of Contents has been added to *The Minister's Wooing* corresponding to the chapter titles in the original edition. Typographical errors have also been corrected. The following is a list of those errors, cited by page and line numbers: 37.37, parlor?; 65.15, swet; 81.1, [title omitted]; 137.26, peacably; 144.2, chewing; 252.13, knees; 257.3, Ohpelia's; 349.40, down.; 381.9, shope; 395.5, in in; 409.30, grad; 537.8, candes; 542.13, lowers; 564.39–40, Armenian; 572.14, Marvyn he; 600.13, gods and; 611.39, Chatechism; 633.3, "Candace, said; 683.36, as not.; 684.10, instrument, it; 701.30, he; 746.24, affection"; 749.5, money,; 758.9, is'n't; 759.13, love?; 849.39, know.; 909.36, wrong"; 950.35–36, Rosseter; 955.24,—*We*; 1012.37, 'There 's; 1068.17, "There . . . it!"; 1083.20, it?; 1161.17, lips,'; 1194.23, lady; 1258.19, Héloise,'; 1348.35, You; 1408.8, and,'; 1433.6, livin.'; 1440.3, down.; 1447.16, 'O Aunty; 1448.34, aunty. Errors corrected June 1982: 7.4, see; 815.36, stocial.

Notes

In the notes below, the reference numbers denote page and line of the present volume (the line count includes chapter headings).

UNCLE TOM'S CABIN

18.40–19.4   The general . . . one;]   Economic and social historians have shown that this regional difference was largely based on different work processes involved in the production of tobacco in border states such as Kentucky and Virginia and the production of cotton, rice, and sugar in the more southern states of South Carolina, Alabama, Louisiana, Georgia, and Texas. Since the U.S. Constitution ended the legal importation of slaves from Africa in 1808, the latter states relied on the former to supply their labor needs.

80.9   constitutional relations]   Reference here is made to the Fugitive Slave Act of 1850, which was part of the Missouri Compromise, allowing fugitive slaves in the free states to be hunted, captured, and returned to their owners.

129.32–39   "Ran . . . killed."]   Much of Harriet Beecher Stowe's knowledge of slavery came from such newspaper advertisements, which were featured in Theodore Weld's *American Slavery as It Is* (1839).

162.2   The Quaker Settlement.]   Quakers formed the backbone of the anti-slavery movement from 1830 to 1850.

232.34–35   Hungarian fugitives]   Refers to immigrants after the Hungarian revolution of 1848, especially as represented by Louis Kossuth.

THE MINISTER'S WOOING

540.34–37   The system . . . institutions.]   Refers to Dr. Samuel Hopkins (1721–1803), minister of the First Congregational Church of Providence, Rhode Island. One of the most creative and important disciples of Jonathan Edwards, he argued that the redeemed were limited to those who had experienced religious conversion and he attempted to limit church membership to those who could testify about their religious rebirth. Hopkins's condemnation of slavery made him unpopular with many of his parishioners.

656.7–9   Sprung . . . this]   Aaron Burr's maternal grandfather was Jonathan Edwards. Edwards's influence on New England religious life extended far beyond his own lifetime (1703–1758) because he combined vivid hell-fire preaching with a theology that reconciled Lockean empiricism and Calvinist beliefs in predestination.

718.21   I . . . know.]   James Marvyn's death was prefigured in Harriet

Beecher Stowe's experience not only by the death of her son Henry, in 1857, before he had experienced religious conversion, but also by the death in 1822 of Catharine Beecher's fiance, Alexander M. Fisher, Professor of Natural Philosophy at Yale College, in a similar spiritual state. A vigorous discussion of this issue can be found in the correspondence of Catharine and Lyman Beecher at this time (Schlesinger Library, Radcliffe College).

OLDTOWN FOLKS

924.40   lay figure]   A manikin used by artists as a means of displaying drapery.

LIBRARY OF CONGRESS CATALOGING IN PUBLICATION DATA

Stowe, Harriet Beecher, 1811–1896.
  Three novels: Uncle Tom's cabin; The minister's wooing; Oldtown folks.

  (The Library of America)
  Contents: Uncle Tom's cabin, or, Life among the lowly—The Minister's wooing—Oldtown folks.
  I. Sklar, Kathryn Kish. II. Title. III. Uncle Tom's cabin. 1982.
IV. The minister's wooing. 1982. V. Oldtown folks. 1982. VI. Series: The Library of America.
PS2951.5.S5   1982   813'.3   81-18629
ISBN 0–940450–01–1   AACR2

This book is set in 10 point Linotron Galliard, a face designed for photocomposition by Matthew Carter and based on the sixteenth-century face Granjon. The paper is Olin Nyalite and conforms to guidelines adopted by the Committee on Book Longevity of the Council on Library Resources. The binding material is Brillianta, a 100% rayon cloth made by Van Heek-Scholco Textielfabrieken, Holland. Composition by Haddon Craftsmen, Inc. and The Clarinda Company. Printing and binding by R. R. Donnelley & Sons Company. Designed by Bruce Campbell.

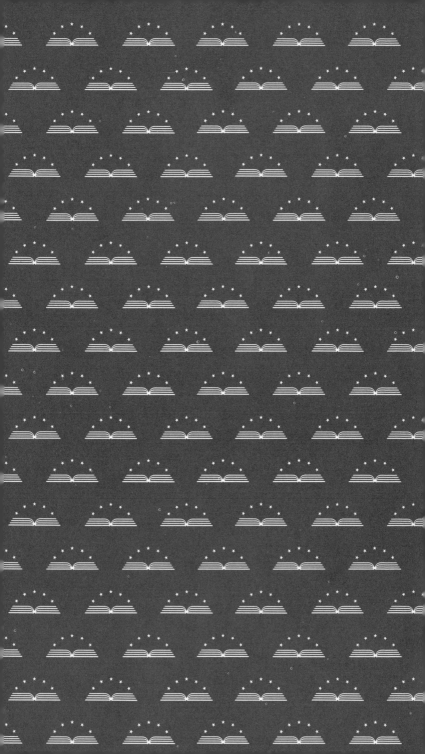